GLASTONBURY

THE NOVEL OF CHRISTIAN ENGLAND

DONNA FLETCHER CROW

CROSSWAY BOOKS • WHEATON, ILLINOIS
A DIVISION OF GOOD NEWS PUBLISHERS

Glastonbury.

Published by Crossway Books, a division of
Good News Publishers, 1300 Crescent St., Wheaton, Illinois 60187.

Cover illustration: Chuck Gillies
Cover title lettering: Dennis Hill

First printing, 1992

Printed in the United States of America

Library of Congress Cataloging-in-Publication Data
Crow, Donna Fletcher.
Glastonbury : the novel of Christian England
p. cm.
1. Glastonbury (England)—Church history—Fiction.
2. Arthurian romances—Adaptations. I. Title.
PS3553.R5872G58 1992 813'.54—dc20 91-42958
ISBN 1-58134-162-8

15 14 13 12 11 10 09 08 07 06 05 04 03 02 01 00
15 14 13 12 11 10 9 8 7 6 5 4 3 2 1

GLASTONBURY—
the holiest earth in England.
These are the legends,
this is the history
that have made it so.

Jerusalem
The Glastonbury Hymn

And did those feet in ancient time
  Walk upon England's mountains green?
And was the holy Lamb of God
  On England's pleasant pastures seen?
And did the Countenance Divine
  Shine forth upon our clouded hills?
And was Jerusalem builded here
Among these dark Satanic mills?

Bring me my bow of burning gold!
  Bring me my arrows of desire!
Bring me my spear: O clouds, unfold!
  Bring me my chariot of fire!
I will not cease from mental fight,
  Nor shall my sword sleep in my hand,
Till we have built Jerusalem
In England's green and pleasant land.

William Blake (1757–1827)

CONTENTS

TIME LINE

Birth of Christ	4 B.C.
Stoning of Stephen	A.D. 31 or 32
Conversion of Paul	41
Roman Conquest of Britain	43
Building of Hadrian's Wall	117-138
King Lucius Declares Britain Christian	156
St. George Martyred by Diocletian	303
End of Roman Rule in Britain	410
St. Patrick Is First Abbot of Glastonbury	c. 455
Arthur Defeats Saxons	c. 530
Pope Gregory Sends Augustine to Britain	597
King Ine Reigns in Wessex	688-725
Bede Writes *History of the Kings of England*	731
First Viking Raid in Britain	787
Alfred the Great Rules	871-899
St. Dunstan Becomes Abbot of Glastonbury	943
Norman Conquest	1066
Fire Destroys Glastonbury Abbey	1184
Monks Find Arthur's Tomb	1190
Richard Coeur de Lion Leads Third Crusade	1190-1192
Magna Carta	1215
Main Structure of Abbey Rebuilt	1250
First Attack of Bubonic Plague	1348
Caxton Prints First Book in English	1477
Malory Writes *Morte D'Arthur*	1485
Dissolution of Glastonbury Abbey	1539

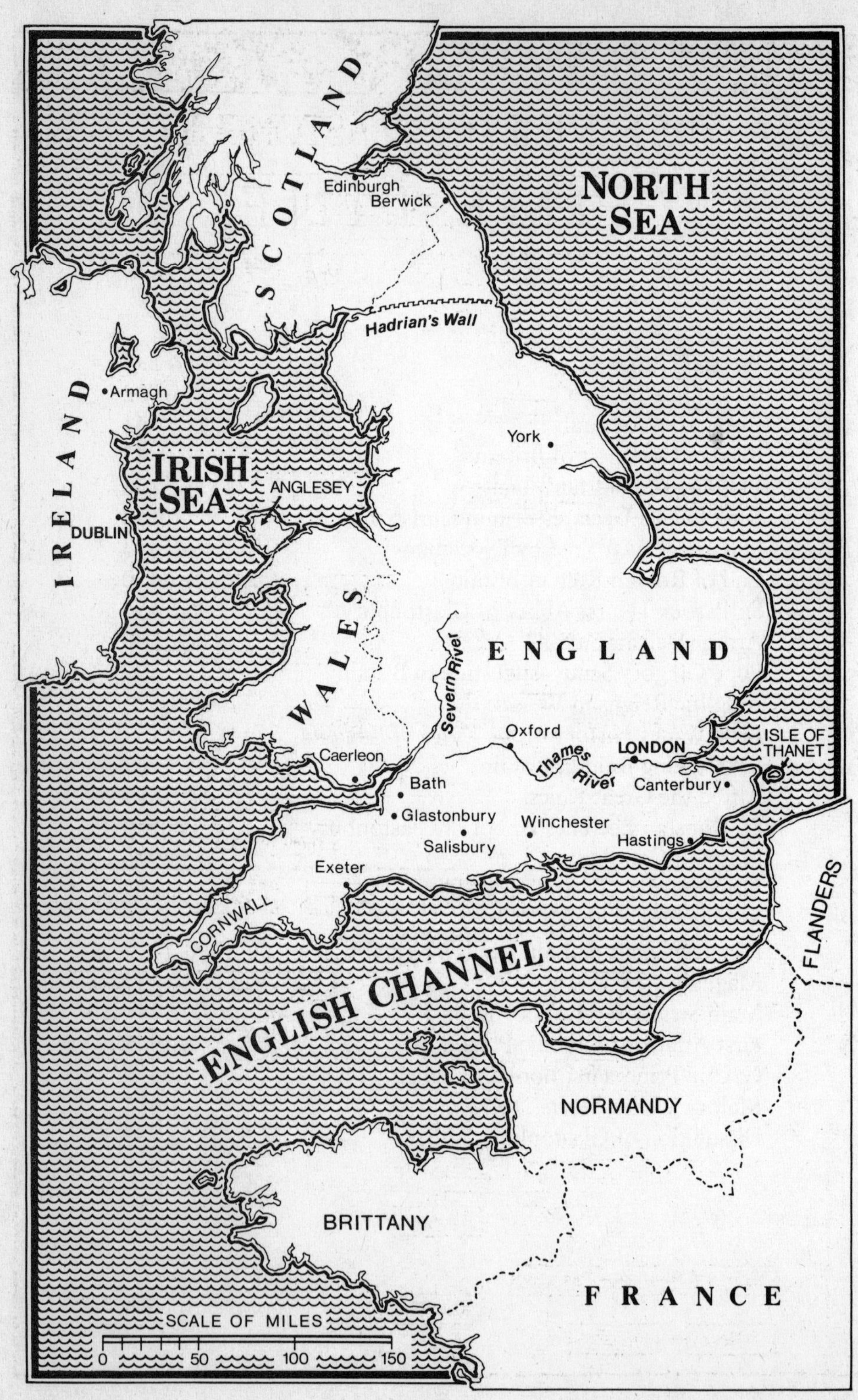
SCOTLAND
Edinburgh
Berwick
NORTH SEA
Hadrian's Wall
IRELAND
Armagh
IRISH SEA
ANGLESEY
DUBLIN
York
WALES
Severn River
ENGLAND
Oxford
Thames River
LONDON
ISLE OF THANET
Caerleon
Bath
Canterbury
Glastonbury
Salisbury
Winchester
Hastings
Exeter
CORNWALL
FLANDERS
ENGLISH CHANNEL
NORMANDY
BRITTANY
FRANCE
SCALE OF MILES
0 50 100 150

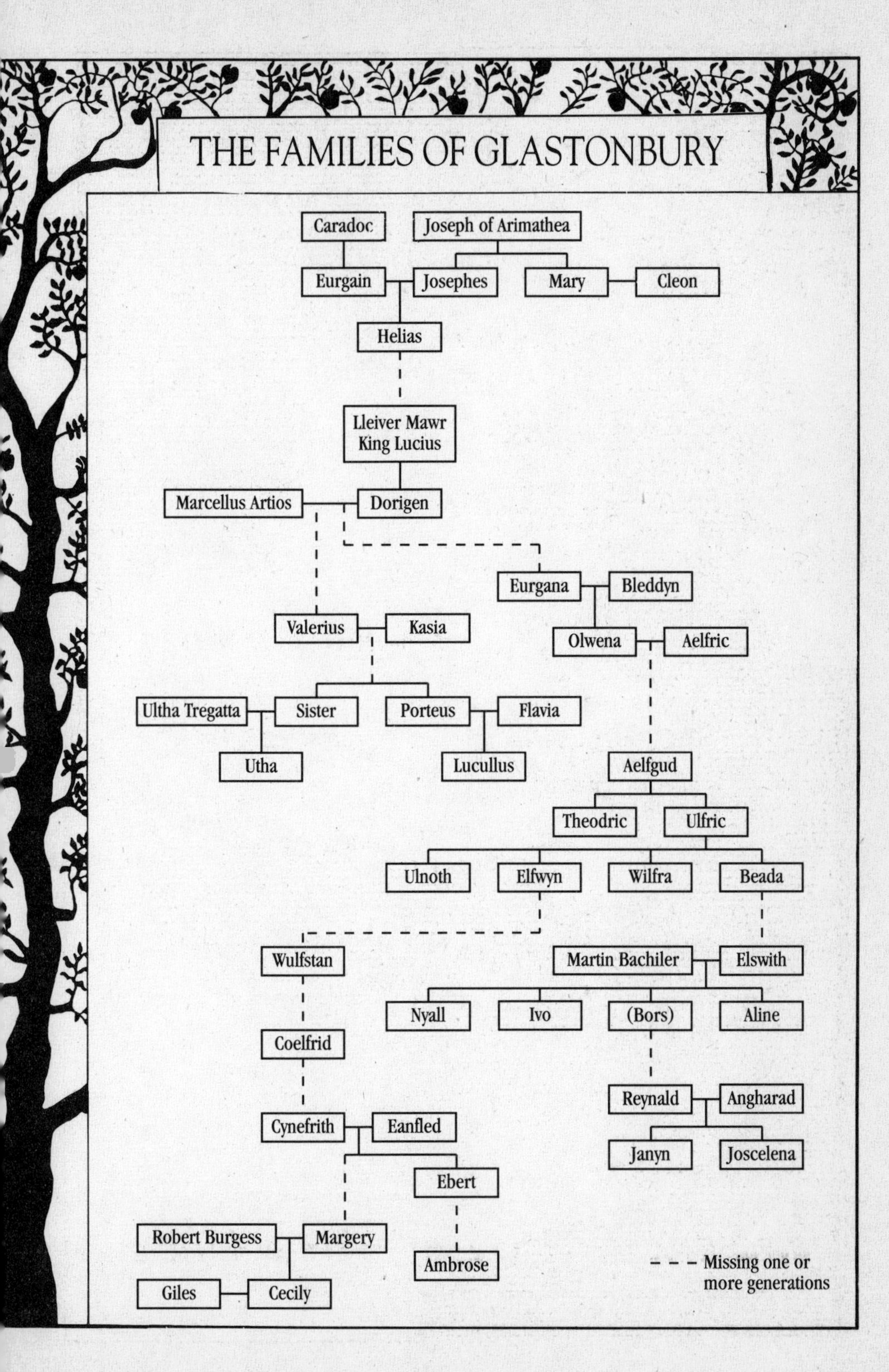
THE FAMILIES OF GLASTONBURY
Caradoc
Joseph of Arimathea
Eurgain
Josephes
Mary
Cleon
Helias
Lleiver Mawr
King Lucius
Marcellus Artios
Dorigen
Eurgana
Bleddyn
Valerius
Kasia
Olwena
Aelfric
Ultha Tregatta
Sister
Porteus
Flavia
Utha
Lucullus
Aelfgud
Theodric
Ulfric
Ulnoth
Elfwyn
Wilfra
Beada
Wulfstan
Martin Bachiler
Elswith
Nyall
Ivo
(Bors)
Aline
Coelfrid
Reynald
Angharad
Janyn
Joscelena
Cynefrith
Eanfled
Ebert
Robert Burgess
Margery
Ambrose
Giles
Cecily
Missing one or more generations

PROLOGUE

he star flamed in the sky. Even as they watched from atop their high green pinnacle, it flared brighter yet. Balan, the newly elected druid Deon in his long white robe, consulted his charts and checked his peeled-willow divining sticks. "For three phases of the moon past it is increasing steadily in brightness, and in that time it has moved across the sky twenty-seven degrees to the westward. It is seeming there can be no mistake. And yet it does not coincide with any other calculations ever made."

His four assistants moved forward into the circle atop the Tor to inspect Balan's astronomical charts by the light of their flaring torches.

"Nothing like it have we seen before—it is a message from the gods."

"A sign of such wonder can be coming only from the high god Lugh."

"But what is its meaning? Does it portend good or evil?"

"There is nothing in our wisdom to deal with this. But surely the gods would use a heavenly body of such magnitude only to announce a marvelous event—the birthing of a king of great power."

"But are you knowing it is a birth, Master? If a flaming star portends death, as we know, couldn't this be meaning a momentous death?"

Balan had studied at the great druid college at Mon for twenty years, learning especially the divining of heavenly bodies. And for nearly a year he had been chief of the druid center above the lake village on the Glass Isle, judging in local disputes, pronouncing the proper time for planting and harvesting and the mating of cattle, and leading worship of the deities. But nothing in all his learning could answer these questions about the great star.

For more than thirty years he had no answers. Then stranger events occurred. On an early spring day Balan was meditating at his favorite seat atop the Tor, when suddenly a heavy, deep darkness descended. He rose and began to grope his way down the hill, but then the earth trembled beneath his feet. He fell to his knees, feeling the same inexplicable excitement that had come with the mysterious star so many years before—and the same longing to know what it meant gripped his heart.

Now he was an old man, wise in the ways of the oak, with many young students hanging on his every word. He must not fail them; he must not let them see his confusion; he must find the answers.

At last the earth stilled, and the darkness lifted as if at dawn. Balan made his way slowly down the Tor to the sacred oak grove where his pupils awaited him with their endless questions.

"If the telling of such an event is not in our wisdom, then we must read the entrails—perhaps of a night creature since the shaking came with darkness," suggested Atadoc, the most promising of the young druids.

"No!" Tarana, an excitable lad with fiery red hair, almost shouted. "It must be a human sacrifice. The gods are angry because it has been many, many years since an oblation of human blood was made. This was a warning. If we are not giving them what they demand, the next shaking will bring the Tor down on our heads."

Murmurs of agreement spread through the nine long-robed students.

"Lugh, the all-father, is angry."

"Only by the shedding of blood may we assuage him—the shedding of human blood."

"Renew the old ways!" Tarana cried.

Balan stood, light glinting from the three rays of the gold tiara he wore. He grasped the ceremonial bronze sword on the altar, holding it by its point to symbolize his willingness to suffer for the truth. The murmurs quieted. "Three things are required of man—to worship the gods, to do no evil, and to maintain manly behavior. Such fear as I hear in your voices is betraying a lack of the valor that lives at the heart of our wisdom."

Now all was silent in the grove. "There are three things the all-god alone can do—endure the eternities of infinity, participate in all being without changing, renew everything without annihilating it. Lugh of the Long Hand may shake the earth without bringing annihilation or requiring the shedding of human blood."

The druids turned from outcries to consideration. Indeed, it had been many years since human blood had been shed in the sacred grove to placate the high god. Among many druid cors, the custom now was to execute only criminals. But would not the all-power be more pleased with a pure sacrifice? The debate at Ynis Witrin reflected the larger controversy stirring the great cors on the Isle of Mon and other places, but today Balan spoke words from the oldest of druid wisdom: "Someday there will be one sacrifice that will be satisfying the gods for all times, and there will be no more human sacrifice."

A stunned silence met his words. Atadoc was the first to speak. "How is it possible that one life could be worth so much?"

Balan shook his gray head. "I am not knowing. It must be that he will be a great king."

"Sacrifice a king?" Tarana shouted. "Unthinkable!"

BOOK I

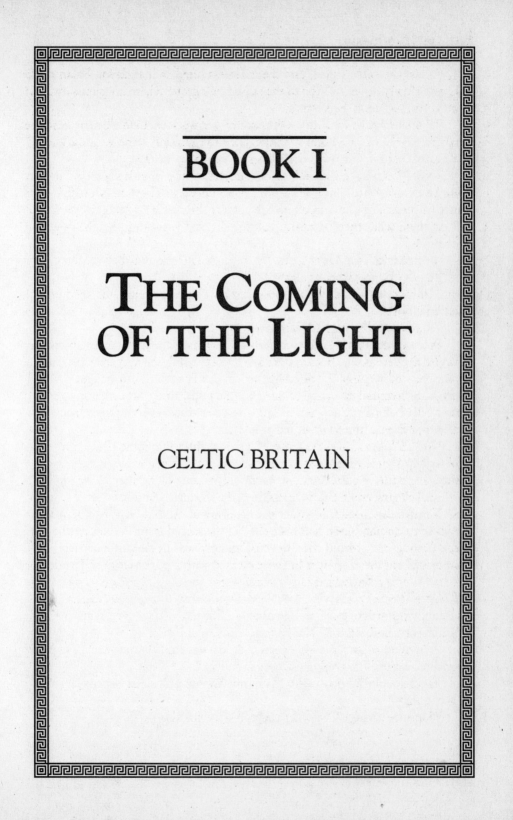

THE COMING OF THE LIGHT

CELTIC BRITAIN

My candle gutters. The light flickers and grows dim, just as my eyes dim with age. But as my outward sight dims, my inner vision brightens. The knowledge from my years of study glows with the radiance of certainty. Much that was told me many years ago when I came to Glastonbury as a young novitiate now takes on a significance I could little appreciate then. And now that the books are gone, all that I have read lies illuminated in my memory.

Now I understand Father Whiting's wisdom when my guilt became unbearable and I confessed my sin. It wasn't the reading itself that I feared had become a sin, but my ardor. I read with a voracious hunger that I knew I must confess because such enthusiasm violated my vows of temperance. But, ah, what reading in the great library of Glastonbury that generations of holy men had worked to restore to the glory it had achieved before the fire—but I run ahead of my story. I was telling of my reading: The chronicles of William of Malmesbury, that great scholar who came to Glastonbury to study and wrote an account of our abbey; and the writings of our own John of Glastonbury, the greatest scholar of our house; the wisdom of the ages collected in manuscripts from every corner of Christendom. And then what wonderful freedom I experienced when I made my painful confession, and Father Whiting in his gentle way gave me absolution and bade me return to my reading in the grace and peace of God our Father and His Son Jesus Christ.

"Zeal for knowledge of our Lord and of His work is no sin, my son; it is a gift of God. Nurture it in the light of His grace." I can still feel the radiance those words spread on my soul.

Even in those early days, Father Whiting declared my mission would be a special one. But he had no idea that my destiny would be the saddest of all—that I, Austin Ringwode, last of the Glastonbury monks, would record the end of the greatness that was Glastonbury.

Yet perhaps in setting it all down, I can make sense of the senselessness—discover our Lord's hand in all the seemingly pointless destruction.

And perhaps in this journey—this act of searching it all out and setting it down for later generations—I can solve the greatest of Glastonbury's mysteries. Perhaps I can discover at last that most blessed of all objects. Perhaps it will be given to this humble servant to find the holy grail. This is my prayer. This, my quest.

Perhaps now, in Glastonbury's darkest hour, that marvelous vessel from which our Lord drank at His Last Supper, that has inspired His true servants in this island for more than fifteen hundred years, will be revealed to me at the end.

And yet, perhaps it is not the end, but a beginning. My heart swells with the hope that perhaps there will be a new life for Glastonbury, just as there was new life for all after the crucifixion of our Lord.

1

he dark shape of the Tor rose behind him, a brooding presence commanding all his attention and then drawing his eyes upward toward the vast adumbral sky, far and far above the wind-rustled boughs of the mysterious oak grove at the mountain's base. He saw pale moonlight shimmering on the inky surface of Meare Pool, silhouetting the circle of wattle huts inside the palisade standing on pilings in the lake. And on every side of him mists rose from the river and marshland that separated this small piece of land with its cluster of hills from the rest of the world. The inhabitants called it Ynis Witrin, the Glass Isle, but to this newcomer's eye, with only the silvery moon for a lamp, the shrouded waters resembled not crystal, but obsidian. A shift in the breeze bore a wisp of fog to him. He shivered.

Joseph looked down on the thatched roofs of the lake village where his eleven companions slept in guest quarters. The strangeness of the hill's greendarkness, of its windswept isolation, of its apartness from the rest of the world, chilled him. An almost deafening chorus of crickets and frogs assailed him, and a few drops of dew fell on his cheek as he surveyed this foreign landscape illumined by a cold moon.

What had he done in bringing his little band of believers, many of them women and youths, to this alien land? What awaited them tomorrow? Would the druid leader welcome missionaries of a new faith? Would he listen to the good news of the way of peace and love? Or would he institute one of the sacrifices Caesar had pictured after his visit to Britannia almost a hundred years ago—stuffing a giant wicker figure with human beings and setting it ablaze? Joseph shuddered.

How much had his brief contacts with Britannic tin traders taught him about life in this wild land where he planned to make his new home? Julius Caesar had invaded the eastern shores briefly, and tales of his visit were known to every Roman schoolboy and to those who, like Joseph, had been educated with the sons of Roman officials in Jerusalem.

Joseph thought of the picture Caesar had drawn of exuberant warriors who painted their bodies blue with woad and stiffened their flowing hair with lime. The Romans sneered at these people's childlike love of display, but Joseph thought it rather appealing. And he thought also of the darker things he had read—of strange, mystical rituals conducted by the druids, often ending in human sacrifice. Joseph had no way of knowing how much of this was true. Certainly, he himself had seen a rustic way of life here, but not barbarism.

A sharp gust of wind made Joseph shiver again and draw his light Judean cloak tighter. Did the deep shadows to his left move? Surely this place wasn't inhabited by wild beasts as well as by wild people? But why not? Did the fact that the tin traders had been friendly and courteous and fair in their dealings insure that the other inhabitants would be as well? Wouldn't he and his companions have been better off to have stayed in Jerusalem and taken their chances with those who persecuted the Followers of the Way?

A vision of Stephen's broken body, the white skin streaked with mud and congealing blood, made Joseph shudder. No. He couldn't let his own son and daughter live in a world where being a disciple of Christ could mean such an end.

"Stone him!"

"Fanatic!"

"Worshiper of the blasphemer!"

The shouts of the angry mob rang in Joseph's ears until he clapped his hands over them. But the memories would not be silenced. Again he saw Saul of Tarsus dragging believers to prison, beating them, putting them to death. Joseph saw lifelong friends, fellow believers, fleeing Jerusalem for their lives. It seemed it took the persecutions of a madman to prod believers into following Jesus' instructions to carry His word into all the world.

And still Joseph did not feel personally in danger. Even though he had clearly aligned himself with the new sect when he asked for Jesus' body to bury in his own tomb, Joseph had not been stripped of his civic position as Nobilis Decurio. Many who wished to continue their friendship or business relations with him excused his eccentric behavior as simply carrying out his duty as next of kin to the prophet (and didn't every family have a radical youngster somewhere whose activities were a bit embarrassing?). So Joseph's business continued to flourish, and life in his comfortable home near the Mount of Olives was good.

And indeed, for a time it seemed miraculously as if all would be peaceful. The believers in Jerusalem heard with amazed joy that a bright light from heaven struck Saul of Tarsus on his way to carry out further persecution. Saul heard the voice of Jesus Christ. His heart wondrously changed, Saul embraced the new faith and received a new name—Paul. For some time he stayed in Damascus preaching the word of the Christ he had formerly hoped to destroy. And all the Followers of the Way prayed and rejoiced.

But then, just when the ferocity of the Jewish persecution lessened, peril came from another source. Within a few weeks of Saul's conversion, the new

Roman Emperor Tiberius Claudius sentenced followers of this new faith to death by the sword, the torture chamber, or the lions in the Colosseum.

To Joseph's horror, his son Josephes chose that moment to preach on the Temple porch. The young man openly declared the truth of Jesus' preaching and His resurrection. It was a miracle he was not stoned on the spot. But Joseph knew his son might not be so fortunate another time. It seemed that every day Josephes was becoming an ever more outspoken advocate of the Way. Josephes took after his deceased mother in this fierce determination to speak his own mind. The martyred Stephen might look to heaven with his blood-streaked face shining and say, "Father, lay not this action to their account." But Joseph knew he could not be so forgiving if an angry mob stoned his son—or even Cleon, the son of his oldest friend.

Even after Joseph reached his carefully thought-out decision, it took months to complete arrangements with his partner in the trading company and to gather the little band, urging them, "Did not our Lord bid us to do this very thing? You were there on the hillside, Lazarus Bar Esas." He looked at his oldest friend, an uncle of the Lazarus of Bethany whom Jesus had raised from the dead. Then he turned to his son's friend. "Eutropius, I saw you in the crowd that afternoon—just ahead of me with Josephes and Stephen—" His voice caught on the name of their martyred friend.

"And Joanna . . ." Joseph turned to the woman who had raised his children since his wife died giving birth to their daughter. "I saw your face when He said, 'Go ye into all the world.' Wasn't it as if He spoke directly to you? I know His eyes pierced mine, and my heart leapt in response, and I thought, 'Yes, Lord, send me!' Did you not feel so called?"

Joseph's words persuaded his friends and family. And at that moment he believed them with all his heart—he was ready to stake everything—ready to die to carry out the command of his risen Master. And so he had vowed to the Apostle Philip when he had knelt before him. And Philip had laid his hands on Joseph's head and commissioned him, Joseph of Arimathea, Apostle to Britain.

In his mind he lived it all again—the warmth and energy that flowed from Philip's hands into his very soul, the assurance he felt that he was doing the right thing, the love and support showered on all the band by the believers in that room. The room was the same upper story of his home where Jesus and His disciples had met for their Last Supper and later where so many followers had waited for the promised Comforter to come. And then Joseph and his companions took their last supper there also, with Joseph even directing Joanna and his daughter Mary to use the same cups and serving vessels Christ and His disciples had used. Had He not commanded them to repeat that ceremony in His memory? And Joseph himself, with an overwhelming sense of humility, drank the wine of the new covenant from the very olivewood cup, slightly larger than the others, from which his Lord had drunk.

Then Joseph packed it carefully among the few possessions he would take with him on his journey and awaited word from his steward that the ship was ready. That same night they slipped silently to the wharf and sailed with the morning tide.

Salome, young second wife of his friend Lazarus, was heavy with her first child. The tossing ship added to her discomfort, and she became ill many times on the journey. But the other women nursed her carefully, and many long weeks later when the weary voyagers sailed into port at Icthas, all were in good health.

Joseph immediately called on his old friend Cyfner at the trading post where they had struck so many profitable deals in the past. But this time the business was of an entirely different nature.

Cyfner's face went blank when he heard that Joseph's ship carried little of the precious olive oil, Gaulish wine, and red-glazed pottery his wealthier customers desired. He was even more surprised at Joseph's request. "You are wishing me to escort you to the court of King Arviragus? You, my old friend, and your eleven companions are wishing to make your homes in Silure?"

"That is so. We would have your king's permission to occupy land here." Joseph's voice carried more assurance than he felt.

Cyfner nodded and the finely-wrought gold brooch clasping his cloak glinted in the sun. "Yes, a farmstead in the land of the Silures is a fine thing. But it is in my mind, Joseph of the Swift Ships, that you know little of growing crops."

Joseph smiled and admitted that he knew nothing of farming and had little desire to learn.

"So then—why—?" The Briton's gold armbands shone as he pulled at his flowing red-gold mustache.

"I will explain as we journey, if you will agree to accompany me and offer an introduction to your king. Besides permission to settle on land here, I would tell Arviragus of great events in our country."

Cyfner threw back his head and gave a hearty laugh as he slapped Joseph's shoulder. "Glad we are for the hearing of distant news. I am more than willing to be guiding you to the royal dun, but I am unknown to King Arviragus. My introduction would be doing you little good—"

"Surely, the word of one of his tribesmen who can attest to having known me for years—" Joseph protested.

"Yes, yes, it would be better than nothing. But I know one who will better serve—a druid Deon who attends at court part of each year. We will be going to him first."

Joseph approved Cyfner's plan. Though Salome's eyes grew tense over lengthening the journey, the trip up the River Briw in Cyfner's light, serviceable coracles was peaceful. Joseph's confidence strengthened as the sturdy little oval boats made of sewn skins stretched over willow limbs skimmed up the river.

Tufted reeds and willows on the banks trailed their boughs in the gentle current. At times only the experience of their boatmen could distinguish between river channel and the watery marshland around it. But the oarsmen's paddles dipped and splashed with confidence, and the deep quiet, broken only by the occasional call of a heron or willow wren, settled into Joseph's soul. After all those years in the midst of the bustling financial and political life of Jerusalem, this was a peace he had never hoped to find—and yet had always longed for without knowing it.

By the time they arrived at Ynis Witrin, surrounded by lakes and marshes, covered with apple trees heavy with unripe fruit, and watched over by the high green Tor in the center, Joseph had no doubts as to the rightness of their mission. The lake villagers were cautious, but not hostile at the sight of these strangely-robed visitors. When Cyfner explained in their native tongue that these visitors from a distant land had come seeking the aid of the druid Deon to gain an introduction to their king, the village chief instantly agreed to provide food and shelter for the night. "And may you have sound sleeping in the guest huts of our village."

All had gone well so far, but now, with the dark green wind howling on a dark green hill and dark green shadows menacing, Joseph felt compelled to look deeper into his soul. Now there were no encouraging disciples making plans to carry out their Lord's commission, no joyous women repeating the Master's words, no fellow believers singing hymns. Now there was only his little band asleep in the village on the lake below him, sleeping peacefully in the faith that Joseph, their leader, knew what he was doing and that Jehovah held their future securely in His hand, leading them according to His plan.

As he recalled the stealth of their late-night trek through the streets of Jerusalem at the beginning of their journey and his insistence on secrecy surrounding all they did to get ready, he had to ask himself: Was this a bold striking out for the sake of his family? Was it a noble missionary venture to carry the teachings of Christ to those who had never heard? Or was this yet another of his cowardly escapes from confrontation and ridicule? Had he only made this journey for the sake of his family and the little band of believers? Or could he claim the noble purpose he had urged on his fellow travelers?

Even in the cold air his cheeks grew warm as he recalled his fear that night when he had come to Jesus seeking advice. Jesus—his own nephew, the little boy he had once held on his lap—had by then become a popular but dangerously controversial teacher.

That was always it, wasn't it? The controversy. Joseph knew he would far rather face the physical dangers of life in a wild new country than live with the daily conflict and ridicule of being a follower of Christ in his old Jewish/Roman world.

He felt a sense of shame that he had not come here solely to carry out the Lord's commission. His motives had been partly selfish.

Overcome with his inadequacies and a sense of helplessness apart from Jehovah God, Joseph raised his hands to Heaven. "God of our fathers and Jesus Christ His Son, hear my prayer in this strange land. Forgive my selfish motives. Help our journey to further Your kingdom. Help us to bring Your light to those who live in darkness. Guide us that You who are the Light of the World will shine forth on this island . . ."

He stopped as a sense of the holy engulfed him. He could form no more words. A vision of a bright beam of light filled his mind—light that seemed to come straight from Heaven and then swirl around him in a warm sense of assurance and love. His anxieties faded, the substance of the world withdrew, and he was alone with the God of love and light.

God's words to Abraham came to him. "For the Lord your God is bringing you into a good land, a land of brooks and water, of fountains and springs, flowing forth in valley and hills . . . a land in which you will eat bread without scarcity, in which you will lack nothing, a land whose stones are iron, and out of whose hills you can dig copper. And you shall eat and be full, and you shall bless the Lord your God for the good land He has given you."

Yes, he was sure. God had called him to a new promised land, to build a new Jerusalem. Right here in Ynis Witrin, here on the Tor, he would found a city set on a hill that would be a light to the whole world.

He had no idea how long that radiant moment lasted, but when, at length, the intensity of the glow faded, he was left with a deep peace. The air no longer chilled him.

He lowered his hands and opened his eyes, knowing he had acted rightly in coming to Britannia. And he must trust that it was equally right for the eleven others for whom he was responsible.

The breezes stirred with greater urgency, lapping the waters of Meare Pool against the shore and shifting the mists to reveal a bright path of moonlight on the water.

The words came to Joseph anew, "Go into all the world—Go—"

"Lord, I have gone. Now what?"

"Lo, I am with you always—even to the end of the world."

2

oseph awoke the next morning to the scent of warm oat cakes and a chorus of birdsong above the chatter of women's voices. In spite of the language barrier, the Judean women and the lake village women were having little trouble communicating as they prepared breakfast. Some stirred pots over the central hearth of their own huts; others baked cakes in the clay broch behind the chief's lodge.

Joseph stretched and rubbed his eyes. And then, as on every day's awakening, his thoughts turned to his God, Father, and King in Heaven. There was no water available in the hut, so he washed his hands by rubbing them with the fresh herbs beside his pallet of piled skins and put on his little round cap. "I offer thanks to You, living and eternal King, for You have mercifully restored my soul within me; Your faithfulness is great . . ." And he continued on through the Morning Blessings.

Now ready for his day, he looked around him. He had no idea what the hour was when he had left his vigil on the hillside and made his way across Ynis Witrin to the ten-reed-long, yellow clay causeway. However, when he called out to the sleepy sentry to lower the drawbridge to the artificial island, the guard welcomed the visitor. Joseph had slept well on his pile of skins near his son's pallet on the clay floor.

"Come and eat, Father," his daughter called as he emerged from the sleeping lodge. Mary walked across the compound carrying a tray of the fragrant oat cakes. He followed her into the chief's dining hall where the men of the village and their male guests were being served by the women. At a long wooden table Joseph took his seat beside Cyfner and Mawr, the village chief. Joseph gladly accepted a bowl of stirabout from Joanna and nodded as Mawr clapped his hands to signal a fair village girl in a green tunic that their guest's cup should be filled with home-brewed barley beer. The guest glanced hungrily at the plates filled with oat cakes, sour cheese curds, and dried fruit.

Mawr, as most of this island race, was tall with creamy skin, flowing reddish-gold hair, and blue eyes. From his previous visits, Joseph was familiar with the male custom of wearing plaid trousers under short, belted tunics, but from the sidelong glances and blushes he noticed among the women of his group, he could tell that the style was startling to them. When all the men had been served, the women took their places at tables on the women's side of the hall for their breakfast. Joseph noticed Joanna was late joining them. *She probably slipped out to water the precious basket of roots and seedlings she's been mothering all through the journey,* he thought.

Then Joseph smiled to himself as he caught the few Cymric words he knew and realized that Cyfner, true to his calling as a trader, was striking a bargain with Mawr for an order of terra cotta bowls like those they were eating their porridge from. Lake village potters shaped the clay without use of a potter's wheel and ornamented the bowls with flowing lines in a particularly graceful, satisfying pattern. Cyfner was sure he could develop a brisk market for them.

Joseph examined the jug on the trestle table before him. The design could only have come from an artist whose heart was in tune with his world. The pitcher's lines flowed into one another as naturally and joyfully as the sea embraced the land and the land embraced the sky—interlocking, swirling, and intertwining with the natural rhythms of sea, of seasons, of branches in the wind and flowers in the field. It was an everyday jug for carrying water or serving the crude barley beer it held this morning. Yet, as Joseph reached out for it, he felt as if he held a sacred vessel that spoke of the God of creation. He drank the freshly poured, bitter beer as the bargaining continued beside him.

"And Cyfner of the Skillful Barter, would you be adding a lathe for my carpenters for the making of looms and cartwheels along with your supply of bronze and iron for the smithing of tools?"

Cyfner's laughter reached to the rooftrees of the hall. "It is my friend Mawr that should bear the title of Skillful Barterer. It is in my mind that I could be supplying a lathe and metals for your craftsmen if you would be adding twenty each of your fine carved-antler loom combs and knife handles."

As they talked, Joseph's attention followed Anna moving gracefully across the rush-strewn clay floor with a basket of small russet apples. Joseph smiled at the picture—Anna, pretty and shy, with large brown eyes that seldom met one's own for long but that would follow Josephes unblinkingly whenever his back was turned. Joseph considered it an acceptable match—whenever his son was ready. At twenty-five Josephes was still backward in the matter of choosing a wife. Since he had no need to make his own fortune before marrying, Joseph couldn't understand why his son hadn't chosen from among the many eligible women believers in Jerusalem.

But he hadn't, and now the field of eligible women was narrowed to Anna. Joseph considered. Perhaps that was what Josephes had had in mind all along. Was not his son the one who had urged Anna to join their group rather than the mission to Gaul?

But if so, why was the usually impulsive Josephes now so slow to speak or to show the young woman any favor? Josephes was always polite, but Joseph could detect nothing beyond courtesy in his manner to Anna.

When this worrying matter of where they were to live was settled, Joseph would have to speak to his son, unless nature and propinquity took their course. He watched as Anna in her light green gown offered the fruit to Josephes. It was obvious Anna would concur with Joseph's line of thought.

The trading completed, the chief turned to Joseph and asked, through Cyfner, "And did our far-traveled guest sleep well last night?"

"Very well, indeed," Joseph replied. "But I fear I was a nuisance to your sentry. I trust my ramblings disturbed no one else." And he told them of his late return over the causeway after a time meditating on the Tor.

Mawr's thick eyebrows, a darker red than his long hair, rose when he understood that Joseph had been alone on the Tor at midnight.

"And you saw or heard nothing alarming?" Cyfner translated. "No howling or yapping of the hunt pack?"

Joseph was mystified. He started to explain that for some time he had been interested in developing a trade in the excellent British hunting dogs so popular with Roman nobility, but now all such decisions would be in the hands of his partner in Jerusalem. He quickly saw by Mawr's reactions, however, that this was not what his host was talking about.

Without waiting for Mawr to reply, Cyfner took over the conversation. "The chief is amazed and distressed that you spent the dark hours on the Tor. It is from long generations the burial place for the dead of this village and the neighboring village at the end of the lake. But it is more also; the Tor is the abode of Avallach, lord of the Otherworld."

Joseph paused in chewing his oat cake. He had indeed met God on the Tor, but not the deity to whom his host referred. He hugged the warm, intensely personal memory to himself. His open expression encouraged Cyfner to continue.

"The Tor is the earthly gate where the Wild Hunt rides, whisking the souls of the dead out of their bodies and into Anwn."

Joseph nodded. "And Anwn is . . . ?"

If Cyfner was surprised that one so well-educated as Joseph would not know this, he was too polite to show it. "Anwn is the Otherworld. The Tor is Avallach's abode on earth. It is Avalon—the rendezvous of the dead, where they pass into the Otherworld."

Joseph nodded and drank from his cup, appreciating the ancient awe and reverence that surrounded the hill where he had contemplated bringing the light of Christ to this place. "Tell Mawr I had nothing to fear. My soul is in safekeeping from the Wild Hunt."

The chief's expressive face clearly said he had no idea what his guest meant, but such strangeness was to be expected of one from a distant land. Then shifting to a more mundane topic, Mawr offered to escort his guests around the village. Joseph and Josephes, Lazarus and his son Cleon, and the three other male newcomers followed the expansive Mawr around the artificial island, which

Joseph judged to be about three furlongs in each direction. Through Cyfner's translation, their guide explained how his ancestors had built the irregular polygon on massive logs cemented with clay, covered with peat, and held in place by long piles driven into the deep lakebed.

Joseph surveyed the formidable oak and wattle-work palisade that surrounded the sixty-some wattle buildings. He had no difficulty picturing the village defense Cyfner described as he told how enemies approaching in boats were showered with red-hot terra cotta pellets. But on this peaceful morning, it was much easier to imagine the red clay pellets being used to shoot waterfowl from the hollowed-out oak canoes gliding around the lagoon. Joseph watched village men fishing with nets weighted with small lead sinkers. A heron skimmed over the water and dived for a fish. Pelicans stood on the stockade, waiting for fish to jump at the flies skimming just above the lake. It all seemed so familiar that Joseph had to blink to assure himself that he wasn't watching fishermen on the shores of the River Jordan.

And Mawr's words reflected Joseph's turn of thought. "The people of the lake are not warriors; we are hunters and craftsmen. We are prepared to defend ourselves should any attack, but the Isle of Avalon has always been a place of peace—a holy place where many would fear to attack lest the souls of their fathers have not completed the journey to the Otherworld and be yet on the Tor. One would not be wishing to make his father's spirit restless with battle."

Cyfner added his own, less mystical explanation. "Besides, only one raised in this swampland could possibly make his way through it. In the warm seasons of Beltine and early Lugnasad, it is possible to approach the island in a chariot if one is knowing the way and is willing to risk losing a wheel in the bog. But in the days of Samain and Imbolc, the seas rise and the Glass Isle is an island indeed. And at any time it requires the luck of Lugh not to get caught in the mists that swirl around this place like steam from a cookpot."

Mawr led them from the fishermen to the livestock pens. Sheep, horses, pigs, cows, and goats were fed on the grain villagers grew on Ynis Witrin, hauled over the causeway, and then pounded to powder in rotary stone querns. Joseph admired all he saw, especially the fine workmanship of the artisans—bronze mirrors, bowls, and brooches in intricate designs—all as expressive as the jug he had admired earlier. Surely Caesar had overstated the case when he labeled these people barbarian. Of course their life had none of the refinements of the Roman Court, but it didn't seem so different from the village life Joseph had seen elsewhere in the Empire. And when he remembered the peace that surrounded him last night on the Tor, Joseph thought perhaps his new home would offer a graciousness he had found nowhere else.

If their mission succeeded. On the morning's tour, Joseph had put out of his mind the interview he must face with the druid Deon. He knew something of the power and influence this priest/judge/poet class held. If the druids refused his mission, there would be little hope of persuading the king to accept their presence. Already this crystal island surrounded by thickets, woods, and marshes had a hold on him. He did not want to be turned away by a jealous priest.

This first encounter was crucial.

Before leaving with Cyfner, Joseph asked Josephes to gather the others of their band and pray—pray for success, that he who, from fear of ridicule, had gone to Christ by night could find again the kind of courage that later led him to ask Pilate for the body of Jesus. How ironic it was. He and Nicodemus, the two Sanhedrin members who had approached Jesus secretly, were the two followers to openly take Him down from the cross, wrap Him in linen winding sheets befitting a king, and bury Him in Joseph's own tomb. But surely that had all been part of God's plan—that His Son should not be buried in a criminal's grave, but in a nobleman's tomb. And only he, Joseph of Arimathea, could have performed that high office, for only the supreme regard given by both Roman and Jewish law to the right of the next of kin to perform burial rites could have taken precedence over the rule of burying one who had been crucified in the common grave of thieves and murderers.

Joseph straightened his shoulders and sat up in the coracle behind Cyfner. The fact that Jehovah God had chosen him and prepared him to perform that function for the Christ surely meant that He would be with him now. *As I have been, so will I be.* The words formed in Joseph's mind, and he looked toward the Tor with new confidence.

As they drew ashore at the foot of a gentle rise Cyfner called Blawan Hill, the boatman explained, "The cors is in the hollow between Blawan and the Tor."

Joseph looked up. Strange, he knew the Tor must be there, but he could not see it. Cyfner continued, "This is but a small center for the druid learning, but it is highly respected, as Balan, the Chief Druid, has taught here for forty burnings of the Samain fires and is holding the title of Pencerdd, he of the highest druid learning."

"Does he teach alone?"

Cyfner extended his hand to help the older man around a pool formed by a small stream bubbling joyfully through the green field. "Balan has three or four assistants, some who have been here almost as long as he. One, Tarana, holds the office of Deon when Balan is at court." Cyfner smiled. "I have heard tales calling him Tarana of the Hot Head, and the community is always happy when Balan returns. Tarana's wife is a druidess also, and many say her chief use of wisdom is in the calming of her husband."

"Is it usual for a Chief Druid to spend part of his time at court?" Joseph eagerly sought information to help him prepare for the coming encounter.

Cyfner shrugged. "I am not knowing how it's done among other tribes. It is in my mind that it is not unusual. But Balan's record of service is long and long, from the days when Guiderius, Arviragus's father, was king and Balan journeyed to the royal dun to report on strange happenings in the eastern world."

Joseph caught his breath. What could he mean? Surely the eastern world he referred to was merely Gaul, but was it possible that word of events beyond the Tyrrhenian had reached this island on the edge of the world? He tried to sound casual. "What events?"

"I was young at the time, learning the trading business from my father as he had the learning from his, but that is how I first met Balan. Ever since he had the charting of a strange star in the sky, Balan sought word of an eastern king." He paused and frowned. "Did I never make mention of it to you when you called in Icthas in former times? Traders told me tales of a miracle-working prophet, and Balan was anxious to hear more, thinking this might be the one whose natal star he saw."

Joseph's conscience stabbed him. Surely he of all people should have been the one to bear such news. If only he had been bolder. And then an old memory, long buried, surfaced. The child Jesus—He couldn't have been more than ten years old—dancing with excitement when Uncle Joseph took him to visit the great wharves at Joppa. He could see again the wonder in the child's large brown eyes and hear the longing in the young voice as He pleaded, "The next time you go on a journey to the tin islands, could I go with you, Uncle Joseph? Please take me."

Joseph had put off the childish request with vague words and didn't even think of it when he made his next journey. But now he wondered what would have happened if he had taken the request seriously.

Yet who could blame him for not recognizing his own nephew as the long-awaited Messiah? Mary had always been a bit fanciful—not that he had ever known her to lie—but a person who might mistake a dream for a vision. So he was never absolutely sure, even when he heard from Mary's own lips, of miraculous events surrounding the boy's birth.

But then Joseph accompanied Mary and her husband as they took Jesus to the Temple for His twelfth birthday. When Joseph heard Him talking to the leaders, he realized that certainly the boy was special.

But it had been another twenty years, twenty years taken up with business and political success, before he knew the truth about Mary's son. In Jerusalem for Passover, Jesus healed a crippled man by the Pool of Bethesda. Joseph was among the Jewish leaders when the Pharisees came complaining that Jesus defied the Law and worked on the Sabbath. And Joseph was there when Jesus replied, "In truth, the Son can do nothing by himself; He does only what He sees the Father doing. My Father has never yet ceased His work, and I am working too." That had made Joseph think. Jesus could not be referring to Mary's husband, Joseph the carpenter. Jesus was claiming with His own mouth to be the Son of God, as many had claimed for Him. Joseph was shocked and yet intrigued. Could it be that his niece's claims of angelic visitation were not just a young girl's fancy?

And then Jesus looked right at him in the center of the crowd and spoke the words Joseph would never forget, "I say to you, anyone who gives heed to what I say and puts his trust in Him who sent me has hold of eternal life, and does not come up for judgment, but has already passed from death to life. In truth, in very truth I tell you, as the Father has life-giving power in Himself, so has the Son, by the Father's gift."

And Joseph believed.

Cyfner's cry jerked Joseph back to the present. "Ah, now there's a fine view of the Tor. It is strange seeming, isn't it, how one can't be seeing such a great high thing until one is almost upon it. It is in my mind that this is what gave rise to the many stories of its magical appearings and disappearings—that and the comings and goings of the mists that so often hide it." Joseph's gaze followed his guide's pointing arm. "Some say it's man-made—or put here by the gods of the ancients after the formation of the earth. At any rate, it was here long before the first druids came. And its spiral terracing is belonging to the mysteries of the ancients—the little dark people who were here when the first of our people came—" He interrupted himself with a chuckle. "Be that as it may, I haven't much time to be worrying about tales of gods of the Otherworld; I have my hands full with this world, all that is for the caring of the druids—that's what they're good for." Cyfner's unreserved laughter echoed off the side of the Tor. "Ah, and here comes one of the priestkind now. Balan himself, it is. I saw to the sending of a messenger from the village before the fastbreaking."

The druid approached from the circle of wattle buildings sheltered by the Tor. His beard was long and silvery gray. The sun gleamed on the crescent-shaped tonsure extending from ear to ear, then glistened more brightly from the finely wrought, twisted gold torque around his neck and bracelets on his wrists. His robe gleamed with six bright colors, proclaiming him higher than the village chief who wore only four colors in his tunic.

Cyfner made brief introductions. Then Balan led them to a bench shaded by apple trees near the cors. A druid with bright red hair brought a guest cup of intricately wrought bronze over green glass, and they all drank deeply of the rich Gallic wine. "This is Tarana, my assistant," Balan said. "I have asked him to join us. Your messenger said you are coming with a request, Cyfner of the Favorable Barter."

Cyfner laughed as he noted Balan had omitted saying for whom his barters were favorable. Then he explained, as briefly as his expansive speech allowed, his years of association with Joseph and his friend's need of an introduction to King Arviragus.

Balan's blue eyes examined Joseph. "And why are you and your companions wishing to live among us?"

Joseph knew his answer now was crucial. He cleared his throat.

"I have come for many reasons, all of which I will be glad to explain to you, but let me tell you first what has happened in the land I left." Balan nodded, and Joseph continued. "I am told that many years ago you saw the star that heralded the birth of a great lord."

Balan turned and pointed to the top of the Tor almost directly above their heads, now shining in its smooth green covering and shorn of its ominous threats of the night before. "Night after night I had the charting of the star from atop this very hill. I have heard many stories of its meaning, but I have never been sure."

Joseph began telling of the holy birth, but before he had gone far, Tarana interrupted. "Fah! We have had the hearing of such tales—a king born in a stable! Do you mean to be wearying us with that again?" Joseph was shocked by the cold fury in the assistant Deon's voice.

But Balan held up his hand. "Tarana Redbeard, I would be reminding you that there are three things that maintain one in life: truth in the heart, strength in the arms, and fulfillment in the tongue. We will grant our visitor fulfillment in the tongue of all he would say, that we may increase the truth in our hearts."

Redbeard scowled, but was silent.

Joseph searched his mind for a common ground where he could meet these men in a way they would understand. Then he recalled Caesar's words, "The druids make immortality of the soul the basis of all their teaching, holding it to be the principal incentive and reason for a virtuous life." He knew what to say.

"I hope not to weary you, but rather to declare unto you One who taught the way to life everlasting." Balan nodded and Joseph continued, telling of Jesus' life and ministry and again returning to Caesar to explain the crucifixion. "I am told that you teach that only by the ransoming of man by the life of a man is reconciliation with the divine justice of the Immortal possible."

"Yes, that is true. But for long and long such practices have been disregarded! I have warned repeatedly of the dangers of abandoning our duty—" A look from Balan silenced Tarana's outburst.

"That is what I have come to tell you." Joseph's voice was quiet. A breeze stirred the apple boughs above their heads, and spots of sunshine danced on the grass. "It is no longer necessary for man to offer sacrifices. The ransom has been paid. The supreme reconciliation has been made for us."

Tarana made a scoffing noise, but Balan was thoughtful. "It is the tradition of the druids that all are descended from Dis, a common father, and that there are many gods and goddesses, but one threefold power over all. It is in my mind that the unnamed three-in-one power could be this Jehovah of Father,

Son, and Spirit you declare. The matter will be needing much consideration. Yesu as a god-name is not unknown to us."

"Yesu is a god-word, of a truth, but that is no reason to be forsaking the others. Our druid wisdom has no need of such alien tales!" Tarana jumped to his feet and faced Balan. "Will you listen to these foreign-born tales? These are no more the ways of our people than are the ways of the Romans. With every full moon we sacrifice that Lugh of the Shining Spear may send strength and valor to the Pendragon—that he may protect us from Roman invading; but who will protect us from this invading of foreign ideas? It strikes me that such false tales may bring more harm to the ways of our people than would a Roman spear."

The sun gleamed in three rays from Balan's headdress as he rose and turned to his assistant. "But *are* they foreign tales, Tarana Thunderer? Much in our wisdom seems to lie alongside the words this Joseph brings us. I have today had the hearing of many things that seem to me answers to questions I have pondered long and long. Our druid wisdom is great and has understood many of the hidden ways of gods and men for hundreds and hundreds of years. But there are mysteries I would have answered. There are hidden paths to truths I have not found. There are ways of the High God I would know more of."

Tarana raised his hand in a rebellious gesture as if to defy Balan, the Tor, and Lugh the High God himself if necessary to protect the ways of his people. "You, Balan of the Oak, would betray your people and the beliefs of your fathers and their fathers for the ways of foreigners!"

Balan's voice was quiet, but filled with an intensity that made the trees over them seem to tremble. "I will never betray my people. I will never betray them by turning my back on old truths or by cringing before new truths. Each would be equally a betrayal. And now I must think. Would the betrayal be in the acceptance or in the rejection of what we have heard from the lips of Joseph Far-Traveler?"

Tarana whirled to stride away from the group, but the voice of his Deon stopped him.

"Wait, Tarana. You will have the hearing of my decree." Balan took a step forward. "I would have you recall that our very title of druid is coming from the word *druthin*—servant of truth. We cannot be serving the truth, Tarana, unless we are seeking it. And when we find it, we will be true to the motto of all druids to defend that truth against all the world." Tarana dropped his gaze, but his mouth was set in an impervious line.

Balan turned from his assistant to Joseph. "Much of what I have heard today fits the pattern of our knowledge, but one must take care, for the lord of the underworld speaks with great cunning, disguising his words in honey and light that many may be enticed to his kingdom. I will think on it. But such a decision is not for me alone to make. King Arviragus will hear you, and I will take counsel with his Archdruid Bran."

As they left the side of the Tor, Joseph's heart rejoiced over Balan's open mind. Surely, he could have hoped for no more . . . unless that Balan should not be influenced by his thundering assistant. With a worried frown that slowed his steps, Joseph asked Cyfner, "Why does Balan keep so headstrong an assistant?"

Cyfner laughed. "It is not of his choosing—Tarana Thundercloud is elected by the druid council—as are they all. But it is in my mind that the Thunderer is not such a bad choice as he is seeming. He is headstrong for what he believes to be the best for our people. He does not always speak from cool reason, but he speaks with a heart of passion for our people and their ways. And he is carrying in his head a full store of druid wisdom—a valuable possession—for the priestkind write nothing down. The knowledge of all ages must be carried in the head of the priest."

Joseph forced aside the confusion Tarana seemed to rouse in him and sought comfort in Cyfner's words. Yes, truly, God was with him as He had promised, even here at the end of the world. In spite of the bubbling in his heart, however, Joseph's steps lagged. He realized now how much he had steeled himself for that interview, and the relief was enormous. The strain, after only a few hours of sleep the night before, had left him incredibly weary.

As they again crossed the little stream at the foot of Blawan and faced the long green ridge that was the third of Ynis Witrin's hills, Joseph suddenly saw with a glad recognition that the cluster of people he had first supposed to be villagers watching their cattle was actually his band of companions. Leaning heavily on his olivewood staff, he turned from the path to climb the small hill where they waited.

"I see your friends await you," Cyfner said. "It is in my mind that you will be wanting to tell them of your good hearing from Balan. I will be going on to the village. You can walk back at any time as the causeway will be open."

Joseph clasped his friend warmly on the shoulder. "I cannot thank you enough. I—"

Cyfner gave a wide grin that made his teeth look startling white. "It is happy I am to have the helping of an old friend. The druids have one of their triads about helping the stranger to our shores—but then they are having a triad for everything." Laughing, he sat in his coracle, dipped his paddle, and pushed off from shore in one smooth motion.

Mary ran down the hill. "Father! Oh, Jehovah be praised! You met with success." She grabbed Joseph's hand and pulled him toward the group.

Before Joseph had a chance to say a word, he was engulfed by all eleven of them, clapping him on the back and rejoicing. At last he disentangled himself and held up a hand. "Wait! You're right, we do have cause to rejoice, but how did you know?"

"It's so obvious, Father!" Mary's round, dark eyes danced.

The others agreed, but Joseph looked puzzled. Josephes embraced his father, and then stood back at arms' length. "It's your face, Father. Like Moses when he had been on Mount Sinai—he returned with his face shining, and he knew it not."

Joseph smiled broadly and then sat on the lush grass with a sigh. "Ah, so, I understand. The Tor is not Sinai, and I can hardly say I met God face to face, yet I am very certain He was with me. Indeed we should rejoice, but I am so very weary."

The others were weary too, especially Salome, who seemed to grow larger each day. Lazarus Ben Esas clasped his wife's hand. "It has been a *long journey*, but hitherto has the Lord led us."

"That phrase rings in my mind also." Joseph nodded and motioned for the others to sit with him. He described his interview with Balan. "And now, my friends, we have an even greater task before us. We must look to the future, but never forget the past. Evidences of God's past mercies will give us strength to go on."

Joseph paused. All during the time he had been talking, an idea was growing in his mind. "We must never forget this first major sign of God's presence with us in Britannia. I believe we should build an altar. Just as Samuel and our forefathers built at Mizpah to declare that Jehovah had led them, so shall we raise our Ebenezer."

"Shall we gather stones?" Mary asked, looking ready to spring to her feet.

"Will you offer a sacrifice as our forefathers did?" Marcella asked.

Joseph smiled kindly, but his heart sank at her lack of understanding. He shook his head. "You have forgotten—the old ways ended when the Promised One came. He was God's perfect lamb, and we no longer need to make atonement. No, Mary, sit still, my child. We will not have an altar of stone as our fathers of old."

Joseph paused and looked at the green world around him, bright with promise in the light of the new day. And he looked at the basket of green shoots Joanna had brought with her even here, never allowing her great treasure to leave her side. "Not an altar of stone, but a living Ebenezer, a symbol of the growing life on this island and of the sacrifice of our Lord. We shall plant a tree."

Joanna gave a small gasp, and her hand flew protectively to the basket, as a mother's to a child. Joseph turned his slow, kind smile on the woman who had been like a mother to his children for seventeen years. He knew how much these plants meant to her—a living tie to her homeland and to the garden she cherished there. "Joanna, we know how you love your little garden. But could you spare one for our new Mizpah?"

She put the tray on her lap and caressed the tender green leaves as she might have the cheek of the baby she had never borne. "See how they've grown? I selected only the tiniest shoots, but they must be planted soon, or they will wither for lack of space."

Her hand paused over the tiny thorn sprig she had nurtured the most anxiously of all. All the specimens came from her own cherished garden—except this one. "The night our Lord was crucified I was hiding in the grove when the soldiers came to this tree. 'He says he's a king—he should have a crown.' They laughed and jeered. 'A crown of a special design.' I heard the branches snap." Joanna looked up. Her face was wet.

"Later I saw what they had done . . ." She choked. "When we decided on this journey and I knew I must bring my garden with me, I felt as if bringing a shoot of that thorn tree would somehow . . ." Her voice failed.

"Help you remember His sacrifice?" Joseph suggested.

Joanna shook her head. "No, help me remember His love." She closed her eyes. "I saw Him with the thorns piercing His brow—the blood—His blood—but He looked right at me, and I saw the love behind His pain." She wiped her cheeks with the backs of her hands and then pushed the tray toward Joseph.

"Here, take them all. Plant a grove in our Mizpah."

Joseph looked at her. He knew how much this offer cost her. "That won't be necessary, but if you will give your thorn tree?"

"Oh, yes, yes. Please. It shall be our Ebenezer—our living reminder of His love."

Just beyond them the hill paused in its gentle slope to offer a small level shelf. Joseph started to walk toward it and then threw up his hands. "In my enthusiasm, I forgot. Our tools are all in the village."

As always, Mary darted forward first. "You rest here, Father. I'll go get them." Her stole slipped from her head revealing her thick black hair. She didn't even bother to replace it.

Watching her race down the hill, so lightly her feet barely seemed to touch the surface, Joseph remembered his weariness. He looked at Salome who leaned against her husband for support. She was rubbing her lower back with both hands. "I don't know what our hosts call this hill, but I believe we should name it Wearyall Hill."

"It seems to fit," agreed Salome.

Leaning on his staff, Joseph felt the late afternoon sun warm on his head, reminding him again of Philip's benediction. Sounds of sheep and cattle carried to him from the other side of the hill. He thought of the cattle on Judean hillsides and remembered Jesus' words, "My Father owns the cattle on a thousand hills." Joseph had had no idea back then that any of those hills could be this far away from Jerusalem. He closed his eyes.

"Here, Father. All that we need." It didn't seem possible Mary could have returned so soon.

He took the spade and dug a small hole. Joanna lovingly placed the tender seedling in and pushed soil around its roots. "It needs water." She looked around for a stream.

"I thought of that." Mary was proud of herself. "I brought your cup, Father." She held it out.

"But you didn't think to bring water in it, did you?" her brother chided her.

Joseph took the cup. "There is a stream; we crossed it this morning."

"I'll go." Mary seemed to be perennially poised for flight.

"My turn, I think." Josephes reached for the vessel.

"Thank you, but I'll go. I remember where the stream is, and I'm feeling refreshed." Staff and cup in hand, Joseph walked down the hill and across a little vale toward the Tor. Just as he remembered, the stream tumbled from the slope of the Blawan. He started to kneel to fill his cup and then paused to look up the hill toward its source.

There on the side of the hill, water bubbled freely from an ever-flowing spring. Joseph caught his breath, then blinked to be sure of what he was seeing. Was it a vision of the Lord's bleeding side? On the second look he realized he was viewing a perfectly natural phenomenon—the water was crystal clear, but some mineral in it had turned the stones over which it flowed blood red. However, he knew this well would always stay in his memory as a symbol of the living water Christ promised the thirsting believer.

This hillside held a quality of peace and beauty quite distinct from the other hills of Ynis Witrin he had visited. Although no hand had arranged the landscape, it was as if Joseph were in a secluded garden. Apple trees and yew stood side by side in a pleasing pattern of lacy light greens and solid dark green. Wild flowers grew in clumps of blue, yellow, and white over the mossy green grass, and a natural outcropping of rock formed an inviting bench where Joseph would have liked to sit. But the others were waiting. He knelt and dipped the olivewood cup into the water. He blinked. Had the rays of the westering sun played a trick, or had the iron properties of the water affected the cup? For a moment the cup seemed filled with blood. On second look, however, it was again crystal.

When Joseph returned, all were waiting patiently in a ring around the thorn. They stood as Joseph approached. He knelt to pour the water on the plant so that none of it would be lost in splashing. Then he stood and spoke. "May the living water in this cup nourish the tree as the springs of water in the desert nourished Moses and our ancestors when they were led of God in the wilderness. And may we say with them, 'Hitherto hath the Lord led us.' And may it be, as our forefathers prayed," he raised his hands, palms upward, "that we, Your people, may be all righteous; may we inherit forever the land to which You have brought us; and may we, like this thorn shoot, be the branch of Your planting."

3

he next morning Joseph wakened to the sound of the cockcrow above the call of heron, geese, and crane. As he had been taught from childhood, he began his day by reciting the Morning Blessings. "Blessed are You, Lord our God, King of the universe, who has sanctified us with Your commandments . . .

"Blessed are You, Lord our God, King of the universe, who has formed man in wisdom . . .

"Blessed are You, Lord our God, King of the universe, who spoke to Moses, saying, 'May the Lord bless you and guard you. May the Lord make His countenance to shine upon you and be gracious to you. May the Lord turn His countenance toward you and grant you peace.'"

No sooner had Joseph completed the Blessings than he realized what day it was—the Sabbath. Now that the Followers of the Way knew that salvation came through faith in Jesus and not in keeping the Law, Joseph's head told him that Sabbath laws, as other laws, could be relaxed. Still the devotions of a lifetime were not to be forsaken. There were not ten adult Jewish males in their company, so they could not have a formal service, but he would gather their band for informal prayers. He paused to think where. Then he knew. At their Mizpah—the thorn tree on Wearyall Hill would witness their first Sabbath service in this new land.

According to custom, the twelve washed their hands carefully after the fast-breaking. Then excusing themselves from their hosts, they walked across the causeway to the green hill as the golden rays of sunshine drove away the clinging night mists. Their sandals and the hems of their garments were soaked with dew by the time they reached the level spot on the hill. Facing east with the rising sun shining on their faces, the group recited the Eighteen Blessings silently.

When Joseph judged each had had time to complete his own prayers, he chanted the Blessings out loud, should any have failed to complete them by memory. "My Lord, open my lips, and my mouth shall declare Your praise. Blessed are You, Lord our God and God of our fathers, God of Abraham, God of Isaac and God of Jacob, the great, mighty, and awesome God, exalted God, who bestows bountiful kindness, who creates all things, who remembers the piety of the patriarchs, and who, in love, brings a redeemer to their children's children, for the sake of His name."

Joseph continued, his chanted words wafting on the breeze and surely reaching to the top of the Tor before ascending to Heaven as the sweet smell of incense before the throne of God. This was Joseph's favorite part of the service, for his heart rejoiced in praising his King.

And then came the Adoration, a prayer that strangely troubled Joseph's soul today. "It is incumbent upon us to praise the Master of all things, to exalt the Creator of all existence, that He has not made us like the nations of the world, nor caused us to be like the families of the earth; . . . for they bow to vanity and nothingness. But we bend the knee, bow down, and offer praise before the supreme King of kings, the Holy One, blessed be He . . ."

As the worshipers prayed, bending their knees, bowing down, and putting their faces to the ground, Joseph thought of their commission to lead these island people, who were accustomed to bowing "to vanity and nothingness," to worship the true God.

Suddenly, Joseph's mind, following his own thoughts rather than the voice of Lazarus Ben Esas reading the seven Psalms, entertained a vision. He saw a Logres, a Land of the Logos—the Word of God—a true B'rith ain—a covenant land—where those not born of the inheritance of Israel would be born of the light of the Son.

The service ended. With a new sense of mission, Joseph gave praise that Jesus had by example lifted the restriction against Sabbath travel. Though Joseph would have preferred to spend the day quietly with his family, singing psalms and thinking on spiritual things, it was time to continue their journey.

Now under the guidance of Balan, the party sailed across Mor Hafren and up the River Usk toward the Silurian court. The lake village boatman explained that the Usk was a tidal river and that the journey must be timed just right for easy landing. If they arrived before the river reached full tide, they would have a steep, muddy bank to climb; if they came after the tide turned, paddling against it would be difficult, if not impossible. But he assured them of his long experience in mastering the dangerous river.

Joseph allowed himself to relax to the motion of the boat. It moved even more swiftly than the current, which was carrying bits of brushwood upstream with them. These they rapidly overtook and passed due to the boatman's steady paddling. Joseph was amazed anew at the greenness of the land. He had thought no spot on earth could be more verdant than the apple-groved Ynis Witrin, but this land to the west was an even deeper, thicker green. It sometimes seemed they were traveling through tunnels hewn out of tree branches. Was it possible that the royal dun of Caer Leo would be even more peaceful than Ynis Witrin?

They left their coracles on the river bank and walked toward the hilltop fort of Caer Leo. Joseph discovered with a jolt how wrong his notion of serenity could be. *Peaceful* was the last word he would use to describe Arviragus's court. On a broad green field at the foot of the fort, the Silurian warriors were practicing charioteer skills. The light wattle and hide chariots, pulled by pairs of brown ponies, flew in every direction. The drivers turned them so sharply they fairly spun. Warriors brandished their spears, shrieked war cries at one another, and even leaped from the chariots to stand on the wooden yokes between the horses. The sun glistened on the warriors' bodies, which were naked to the waist, and on their bronze helmets, colorful shields, and golden armlets. Their lime-stiffened hair stood out wildly, and their long, flowing mustaches added a fearsome touch. Some had even painted elaborate blue designs on their bodies, as if going into actual battle.

Though the viewers were dazzled by the unrestrained energy, skill, and flamboyance, they drew back. The women averted their eyes in modesty from the half-naked bodies, and Joseph recoiled at the sight of the war paint. The Torah said that the body was sacred to God; desecrating it with paint was an abomination to the Lord.

Yet Joseph had been sent to these people. Jesus had taught that it was what was inside a man—hate, envy—that defiled him. This was to be Joseph's message here. But first, Joseph must understand it and follow it himself. He stepped forward to stand by Balan and watch the display.

Mary gasped in fear as two chariots barely missed colliding right in front of them. Joseph's thoughts came back to his companions. It had been a long day of traveling for Salome although she never complained. At a word from Joseph, Balan led them around the practice field and up a long, steep incline. They passed three layers of deep, v-shaped ditches that would discourage the most determined enemy from storming the palisaded fortress on top. Halfway up, they all turned to view the scene behind them. Mary exclaimed with delight, "Oh, Father, who would have thought even Jehovah could have made anything so beautiful!"

Although the hillside had been scrupulously cleared of brush that could provide cover for an attacking army, bluebells, buttercups, and daisies grew in wild profusion among the long grasses. Beyond the broad, flat garth where the warriors continued in boisterous tumult, the Usk curved in a silver streak. Already, Joseph noted, the tide was ebbing, and the bracken they had passed a short time before was making its repeat journey to Mor Hafren. As they turned to continue their ascent, a chorus of birdsong from chaffinch, blackcaps, and blue tits welcomed them. If only the royal welcome would be as congenial.

The heavy, timbered gates stood open. Guards posted beside the massive carved gateposts greeted Balan with respect. From the cluster of wattle buildings inside rose a large, rectangular timbered hall, its steeply pitched roof reaching even above the highest point of the palisade. Women in bright tunics and older children went about their work grinding flour, baking bread, and caring for animals, while small children tumbled with puppies nearby. From the workshops came the clang of the blacksmith's anvil, and in the flagged court before the king's hall, warriors sharpened swords and spears at a tall black stone. All paused in their work to greet Balan with an open-handed salute.

The king's personal guards at the gateposts gave Balan immediate entrance to the royal presence. King Arviragus of the Silurians stood before them, a tall, broad-shouldered man in breeks of checkered fabric, tunic of fine saffron wool, rawhide boots, and with a bronze-sheathed dagger at his belt. Everywhere about him—the torque at his neck, the bands at his wrists and high on his arms, shot through the fabric of his seven-colored cloak, and in the twisted wires that bound back his long fair hair—was the rich glint of gold.

Arviragus received Balan with courtesy, but surprise. "I was not thinking to see the Deon of Ynis Witrin until Lugnasad. What is bringing you and such a large company here even before the first full moon in Beltine?"

Balan presented Joseph and his request for an audience.

Arviragus spoke the Greek taught to all druids and knew a little Latin as well. "Ah, we welcome visitors to our company—especially those who bring goods from the East. We shall talk more of your matter later. Tonight we will have double gladness for our feasting."

An expansive wave of the king's arm brought the newcomers' attention to the others in the room. Bran, the king's archdruid, stood near the high seat, his long gray beard flowing over the gold breastplate he wore atop his colorful robe. Lubrin, the king's bard, wore an equally colorful robe, but his red-gold hair was cut just below his ears, and his face was clean-shaven.

Two men now approached from the side of the hall where they had been playing a board game with a carved bone shaker and rectangular dice. The king presented the visitors to his son Coillus, whose slim gold collar marked him as heir to the throne. Then Arviragus turned a broad smile on the brawny man at his side. "My cousin Caradoc, Pendragon of the Trinovantes, son of Cymbeline and brother to King Togomundus of the Trinovantes."

All the company made appropriate replies, but it required Balan's explanation for the newcomers to appreciate fully the importance of the man before them. "King Cymbeline was a mighty man like an oak who had the ruling of all of southeast Britain. His brother Guiderius had the fathering of Arviragus. Cymbeline has now been succeeded by his son Togomundus, and to Caradoc has fallen the election of Pendragon—the war leader of his people." In a quieter voice he added, "It is in my mind to fear that the coming of the Pendragon means rumblings of war."

There was much Joseph would have liked to say, but a tug from Mary's hand and her tipped head toward Salome reminded him of the needs of his people. "I thank you for your gracious reception, Your Majesty, but our women are weary—"

He hadn't even finished his sentence before Arviragus clapped his hands for a messenger. "Bring the Princess Gladyl." The king sank back on the pile of thick fur rugs covering the high seat and indicated that all should be seated. In a few moments the servant returned with three from the royal women's place—a child, a girl approaching womanhood, and a woman—each bearing a gold guest cup. They walked among the visitors, passing the cups as Arviragus introduced them. He presented the elder of the three as his sister, Gladyl.

"Drink and be welcome." She held the cup out to Joseph. Joseph thought she was the most beautiful woman he had ever seen. Her unbound hair fell over her gold-shot gown in a copper waterfall to well below her hips. She greeted them in fluent Greek, then asked just as fluently if they would prefer Latin.

"Greek will do well," Joseph replied. "We are delighted to meet so accomplished and beautiful a lady."

"My sister is also a fine poet," Arviragus said with obvious pride. "She will read a poem for you at tonight's feasting."

Gladyl smiled in reply, without the shyness required of a Judean woman.

The two girls were Caradoc's daughters—Eurgain, the elder, darker, and more serious of the two, and Gladys who, although still a child, showed promise of becoming a beauty like her aunt. The three led the female guests from the hall to the women's quarters. Prince Coillus offered to join Balan in showing the men around the compound. His voice called Josephes's gaze back from following the British princesses. His face bore a sheepish look, but once outside, his eyes swept the courtyard for another glimpse of the Celtic princesses.

The royal dun was considerably larger than the lake village. By the time they had seen the cow-byres, barns, and bothies beyond the chariot court, and had the lodgings for household warriors, harpers, priests, and royal craftsmen pointed out to them, they were more than happy to go to the guest lodge to prepare for the feast. On first entering the compound, they had smelled the roasting meats, and their appetites had been growing steadily ever since.

Joseph and the others had no more than finished washing from the ewers of water brought to them by slaves and had donned clean robes by the light of seal oil lamps, when the air was filled with a long, low wail. It seemed to start just outside the guest lodge door and swelled in intensity until it echoed from hill to hill and beyond even the sweep of the eye from atop the royal fortress.

Josephes sprang to the door ahead of his father. Then both stopped just outside. Bran and five lesser druid priests stood in two rows outside the great hall, blowing ox horns. As they blew, warriors coming late from the practice field careened through the gate and into the chariot court, pulling their horses to a rearing halt. Craftsmen left their forges and pottery kilns; and from across the valley, in all the scattered steadings, those of the Silurian truath answered the call to the great feast in the king's hall. Laying aside their work and quickly donning their brightest cloaks, they made their way on foot, by cart, or on horseback toward the steep entrance to Caer Leo. And as the first of the guests arrived, the Judean visitors joined them.

The king sat at the high seat in a scarlet and gold tunic worn over tartan breeks. Beside him was Caradoc in a plaid tunic and purple mantle held with a massive round brooch. The priests Balan and Bran were also seated at the high table, adorned in abundant gold and bronze. The Judean men in their more somber robes and cloaks of muted stripes were shown to the guest place just below the high table, but Joseph was escorted to a seat between Arviragus and Bran.

The hall filled quickly as all within hearing of the ox horns answered their call. The scent of rosemary from the rush-strewn floor mingled with smoke from the central fire pit and from pine-knot torches in iron sconces mounted on the massive timbers supporting the roof. Joseph's gaze followed the wavering torch light to the heavy, smoke-blackened roof trees where red- and ochre-daubed skulls of ancient enemies hung as trophies of past battles. Slaves, mostly taken from the little dark people of the north, entered with heavy wooden trenchers of roast boar, honey-baked badger, and stacks of warm, sweet honey cakes.

Joseph looked at the boar meat on his platter, its edges a crisp brown, the inside rich and juicy. Around it flowed a sauce thickened with barley meal, a golden brown gravy of meat juices and fat. And Joseph's stomach recoiled. The age-old restriction against eating animals with cloven hooves had been lifted from the Followers of the Way, as had the requirements to follow all the old laws. Christ was the fulfillment of the Law and the prophets. But for fifty-three years of his life, pork had never touched Joseph's lips. His God might not be offended if he ate, but Joseph knew his stomach would be. A tray of fowl followed, and Joseph gratefully took a large cut.

The women entered, led by Gladyl and the Trinovante princesses clad in flowing tunics embroidered with gold around the neck and sleeves. They served wine from long-necked bronze jars brought to Britain in ships like Joseph's—perhaps even in one of Joseph's ships. The pleasures of feast-making were denied to no one in the truath. Even the children and hunting dogs sat among the reeds under the tables, tumbling like young cubs and eating the scraps the feasters threw down.

To honor their guests, Gladyl had donned an ivory gown enriched with her own gold embroidery and had braided her hair into a coronet around her head with a small golden bell woven into each plait. The younger princesses wore their hair gathered into an embroidered net. After serving the fine Roman wine, the royal ladies took seats on the women's side to the right of the high table, and Arviragus signaled a servant who produced several trays covered with sleek marten skins. The king called his guests forward and presented them with the gifts on the trays—jewel-studded brooches for the men, and for the women amber necklaces similar to those worn by the princesses Gladys and Eurgain. Joseph was especially pleased for the women. Although they followed the rabbinical admonition to wear makeup and jewelry as beautiful daughters of God, they seemed drab in this dazzling company.

In return, Joseph produced the gifts he had brought for such an occasion—a pouch of softest camel leather filled with carved ivory ornaments; packets of saffron, cardamom, mace, and other spices from the East; and lengths of the famous Phoenician fabric dyed purple from their rare mollusks.

These gifts pleased Arviragus who shouted for more wine. The feasting continued with slaves bearing ever more platters of cakes dripping with honey and meat swimming in rich gravy. When Joseph felt he could hold no more—indeed, his last serving had gone to the red hound lying at his feet—Arviragus turned to Lubrin who was sitting on a stool by the stone-flagged central hearth strumming his harp. "Harper, we will hear your harpsong. What have you for our hearing tonight?"

The bard ran his long white fingers over the strings in an undulating glissando that seemed to make the flames of the fire dance to its rhythm. Then he silenced the strings with the palm of his hand and held the pale gold ashwood harp from him. "A fine tale of high adventure, my lord, whenever you are commanding it. But perhaps you would be wishing to hear the Lady Gladyl first?"

Arviragus agreed to this, and Lubrin slipped from his seat with a sweeping bow to his princess. Gladyl took her place before the hearth, the light of the flames dancing on the gold thread in her gown and the tiny bells in her hair tinkling whenever she moved her head. Lubrin, sitting cross-legged in the rushes at her feet, strummed his harp lightly as she spoke.

"Today I walked by the River Usk; I had the hearing of a blackbird and the watching of a bee . . ." She continued her introduction in the Cymric of her audience, and Balan translated for the foreign guests. But when she began to read the poem, Joseph shook his head at the priest. The Cymric language was the most lyrical he had ever heard, and the natural rhythm of the words in the speaker's soft voice was music not requiring the literal understanding of words.

When she had finished, however, Gladyl turned to the Judean party and made her own translation into Greek.

The little bird, he blows his whistle
With a trilling from the point of his bright yellow beak,

(Lubrin's harp sang as cheerily as ever bird warbled.)

Sending forth a singing into the world—
A blackbird on a branch in the well-wooded plain.

The poem continued, and Joseph was enthralled by this woman's gift to observe and love nature in its tiniest expressions. The poem presented no sustained story, but rather a succession of images that the poet called up with light and skillful touches. Joseph could see the buttercups waving and hear the bees buzzing as clearly as he could see the shimmer of firelight on Gladyl's amber necklace and hear the tinkle of bells from her headdress.

Nimble flies the yellow bee from cup to cup,
With brave adventuring under the sun;
Flitting with boldness afar in the field,
Then safely rejoining his brethren at honey-hive.

The harp followed the bumblebee's flight, and the feasters pounded their long wooden tables and shouted in appreciation of the performance. But most of the child cubs and dogs under the tables had fallen asleep and merely stirred and whimpered at the banging over their heads. Those on the women's side now withdrew before Lubrin began his tale, for it was sure to be a long listening, lasting far into the night and accompanied by heavier drinking. Joseph noticed Josephes watching the departing women. His brow furrowed when he realized that his handsome son's dark eyes followed not their Anna, but the princesses.

With the women gone, the dark, heady wine went round again, and Lubrin struck a louder tune on the harp strings to introduce his song-making. The story he had chosen for the feast was an ancient one, taught him by a Hibernian bard, now familiar to all the truath and therefore greeted by cheers as they never tired of hearing their favorites.

The harp sang first, the voice of its strings calling forth images of days long past, of heroes since fallen, of glories lived, now to be relived in the soul-songs of the people.

And then Lubrin's voice joined the harp's and painted the pictures in fuller color: Warriors gather in festive feasting around the high-blazing fire, taking still-sizzling joints off the flaming spits. But before the meat is cool enough to eat, the air is rent by the sound of approaching battle horns.

The harp sang high in increasing intensity as the war cries approached the hall. Then the bardic words joined the harpsong: Cuchulain, battle champion to King Ulster, leads his men from the hall, ready at once to answer the call of his king for honor and pride. The message-bringer is brief. Queen Maeve of the Connaughts is invading their cantref. She would have a fine brown bull with gleaming white horns which once she forfeited to King Ulster and now would break honor by tearing the prize from its pastured seclusion.

The torches flared and flickered, illuming the faces of all who were swept with the story of the harpsinger: And the torches of Cuchulain flare as he leads his warriors forward to battle the spear host of the enemy-invader, the honor of the truath resting in his sword. But before they reach the forces of Queen Maeve, she works her evil magic. With a gasp of darkness, Cuchulain's warriors fall ill, and all his druid's power cannot relieve the cess.

His valor never wavering, Cuchulain grasps Druatha, his sword of truth, and fights alone. Sun-shafts strike through the leaves and glint off Druatha defending the Ulster honor. A faint mist rises with the sunset, but Druatha slashes deeper. Moonlight pierces through the tree boughs, but Druatha is unstilled, bright in the darkness. Yet when morning dawns, silence hangs like the mist among the trees. Druatha is still. Cuchulain lies wounded. Queen Maeve drives off the splendid bull in jeering triumph at the victory of her evil sorcery.

Lubrin's harp-skill never sang more mournfully as the fallen hero lay before the mind's eye of all in the hall. But then with a higher note, the bardsong brought hope to the listeners as the mists of the song and the smoke of the room mingled in the firelight: For in the warrior's fallen weakness, the High God Lugh of the Shining Spear comes to Cuchulain bringing a sleep of healing. For three days the red-gold torchlight dances in Cuchulain's sleep chamber, keeping the Wild Hunt from his soul, preserving him from Avallach, for his time is not yet. And then Cuchulain rises from his pallet, grasps Druatha, and vows to right the wrongs inflicted on his people.

But Queen Maeve is ready for him. Cuchulain must face the dark queen's champion—none other than Fer Diad—Cuchulain's foster brother.

The air quivers as the storm-darkness gathers over the brothers' sword-clashing. The day is long while the ringing of metal sounds over the green valley. And still the brothers fight.

But by evening neither is champion, and Cuchulain sends healing herbs for the wounds of Fer Diad. The sun rises on the second day of battle, and the sword-clashing continues. The curlew calls from the marshes, and the heron gathers her young. And still the brothers fight.

That night Fer Diad sends Cuchulain a share of his warrior-meat. And the day is the third, and the sword-clash continues. The whitethorn fades, and the bluebell droops. And still the brothers fight.

At nightfall valor-messages fly from one champion fireside to the other. And the brothers sleep. But on the morning of the fourth day, Cuchulain takes not Druatha to battle, but a weapon of greater power and mystery. The Gae Bolga has never failed to bring victor-glory to the Ulster champion. It does not fail him now. Fer Diad is slain. And the brothers fight no more.

The vanquisher returns, leading the battle-prize to Ulster. But there is no victory as Cuchulain kneels before his king. The valiant brother-heart breaks, and the champion dies.

As the women of the truath keen for their departed champion, journey-rituals are prepared for his soul. Death fires blaze, and Cuchulain the champion is laid in the Royal House of Sleep.

The harpsong ended with a final strum, and all those awake in the hall cheered the harper, rousing most of the others asleep on their benches. The warriors and other revelers would sleep in the hall tonight, but those at the high table and Joseph's company retired to their lodges.

Joseph's head ached from the rich wine and heavy smoke. He had been much stirred by the rugged pageantry and exuberant hospitality of this strange court, so unlike anything he had ever experienced before. In spite of his polite, receptive hearing from Balan, would Arviragus and his court receive Joseph's message—so unlike the bardsong? And yet, perhaps there were similarities, some links he could draw on as bridges to understanding. With the god's help the hero had slept for three days for his wounds to heal. And the hero had died to achieve a victory for his people . . . Joseph shook his head. The analogy seemed weak and strained.

With a groan Joseph threw himself on his bearskin pallet separated by a partition from Josephes and the others. But as he was drifting off to sleep, the words he had heard so clearly two nights ago on the Tor came to him again, "I am with you—even to the end of the world."

It was near midday before Joseph awakened. He sat up and shook his head, unsure of what had roused him. It was not the song of the harp in his dreams, not the summons of the ox horns—only a vivid memory now, and not the shouts of the warriors racing their chariots across the court outside. The sound had been much closer. Then it came again—a knocking on the door post and his daughter's voice calling with a note of desperation. "Father, come quickly! It's Salome. Please hurry, Father!"

I have set the Lord before me at all times; His glory fills the whole earth. An abbreviated blessing would have to do. Joseph slipped his feet into his sandals and pushed out into the bright sunlight. "Is it her time?"

"Yes. The pains started hours ago, but Joanna says it's not like any birth she has attended before. She thinks the babe is backward. We must pray."

Mary led him to the porch of the birthing hut where all the Judean company was gathered. Joanna confirmed Mary's words. "This baby doesn't want to be born."

Lazarus was white around the mouth, and his eyes looked desperate as Joseph clasped his arm. "We will ask our Lord to undertake," Joseph said and led the little band in prayer.

When they looked up, Gladyl and Balan were approaching across the courtyard with a small, bent, gray-haired woman in a plain brown tunic. "This is Cetil," Gladyl said. "She has helped as many cubblings enter the world as there are days from Beltine to Lugnasad."

"And I have prepared a draught that many women are needing when their time is upon them." Balan held out a small cup.

Everyone looked at Joseph. Should they accept the help of these people with unknown ways? What would Cetil do? What was in Balan's potion? And yet what choice did they have? Salome's cry from inside the hut rent the air, and Joanna and Mary darted in to join Anna and Marcella at her side. If something was not done, surely Salome and the babe would both die. These offers of help had come swiftly on the heels of their prayer. Surely they could accept them as from God. Lazarus gave a slight nod. Joseph turned to Gladyl and the druid. "Thank you. Please do what you can. And God bless you."

Balan handed his cup to Cetil who went into the hut with Gladyl. When the women were gone, he said to Joseph, "The king and archdruid are ready to hear your speaking."

Joseph looked at the leather flap closed tightly over the doorway of the birthing hut, then turned toward his oldest friend and saw Lazarus fully supported by the men of the band. There was nothing more he could do here. He nodded to Balan.

As they crossed the courtyard, Joseph silenced his momentary fear by recalling Philip's words, "Our God will preserve you from this people to whom I am sending you. I send you to open their eyes and turn them from darkness to light."

Smoke from the night before still hung in the rafters, but the floor of the hall had been swept clean and fresh rushes strewn on it. Arviragus sat again on the high seat, and Bran stood behind him. Lubrin, who never seemed to leave the king's side, sat at his feet. Joseph was offered a seat near the king, and they greeted one another while a dark, silent boy passed cups of wine. Arviragus shifted his heavy red cloak and said, "And why have you come to us, Joseph of Arimathea? I am thinking it is not for tin and lead alone you have to come to Silure."

Before Joseph could answer, Prince Coillus entered with a message from his Uncle Caradoc who was directing the warriors in their practice. This gave Joseph time to consider. Perhaps it would have been better had there been no pause, because the old fears gnawed again. Certainly it was not court splendor that caused apprehension, for this crude hall would look primitive next to even a provincial governor's hall. But there was something else here—an energy, a feeling of raw power—that made Joseph hesitate to speak out, made him fear to take a strong stand on a subject so likely to offend Arviragus and his archdruid.

Joseph hated the conflict that often followed a proclamation of the faith. He placed such a high value on living at peace with those around him that his failure to speak out often came close to cowardice. Then he thought of Jesus, of His quiet courage to do the right thing, no matter what the consequence. He thought of Jesus returning to Bethany and raising Lazarus (the nephew of his companion) from the dead, over the protests of all His disciples who knew the chief priests were lying in wait to seize Him.

Coillus concluded his discussion with his father and left the hall. Joseph took a deep breath. "We bring good news which we would share with your people, Your Majesty."

Arviragus nodded, and Joseph found the words he had prayed would come to him. "On my earlier voyages here I have learned something of your beliefs. I know you believe in a supreme god who is chief over all and has many manifestations. And I am told you believe there is one who is yet to come. I declare unto you, He has come."

Bran the archdruid inhaled sharply and leaned forward. "The gods sometimes appear in human shape to be making their will known to us. Could it be that you are such a one?"

The question gave Joseph a perfect opening. "No, not I. I am a man just as you see here, but I bring you word of Jehovah God who became man."

"And you are His messenger?" Bran asked.

"I am His messenger." Joseph bowed his head, then continued. "The fulfillment of the prophecy of your triads, the Three-in-One has come as your priests foretold. The true Son of God—God Himself—dwelt among us. He taught us the true way of peace and happiness—the way to life eternal."

Joseph was now in complete control as his voice rang confidently to the farthest reaches of the great hall and echoed off the ancient painted skulls hanging in the rooftrees. "And then our God gave Himself as a sacrifice that no more sacrifices need be made to justify man to God. It is now only necessary to accept His love in faith and worship Him." Joseph felt that was the heart of the matter, so he stopped.

"And you are wishing permission to live among us and tell our people of your Jehovah God and His Son?" Arviragus asked.

"That is so, most noble Arviragus."

Arviragus leaned back on his thick pile of pelts and waved his hand for Bran to speak. "It is in my mind that the reality of a physical afterlife is the heart of our wisdom, and we are favorable to the learning of a God who prepares the way for His people. But we would not have our teachings contradicted or our people confused by foreign beliefs . . ."

The archdruid continued questioning Joseph. As he asked about Christ's sacrifice, Joseph felt yet again a niggling of the old fears. Though Christ's final sacrifice might have satisfied Jehovah, if the druid priests declared Joseph's words untrue, Lugh of the Long Hand might well be deemed to require another life—his. Again he thought of Caesar's writings—would the twelve of them be stuffed inside a giant wicker cage and set ablaze to satisfy the lust of a Celtic god?

The *Pax Romana* did not exist here. That meant more freedom, to be sure, but also less order—a lack of order that could doubtless crumble into anarchy should these unrestrained Celts choose to steal another tribe's horses or decide to follow an avenging druid pledged to defend the old gods.

But whatever the consequences, Joseph had no choice. The Jews had always taken their God with them wherever they went—into foreign captivity, into war, into the Promised Land, and into heathen lands. Joseph could do no less.

Arviragus looked at his priest. The druid's face was inscrutable. "What will you be saying, Bran of the Golden Sickle?"

"The voyager's words are worthy of consideration. We will withdraw to the sacred grove and consult our wisdom."

Arviragus nodded his approval. "Consult the auguries." Then he turned to Joseph. "And you pray to your Jehovah and His Son. There is much to be decided." Arviragus rose as a signal that the council was ended.

Bran and Balan left the hall, but before Joseph could thank the king for his hearing, Gladyl came in, escorting Mary to her father. "She is delivered, Father. Both are very weak—we fear . . ."

Gladyl explained the situation to the king. He immediately declared that the visitors must remain at court as his guests until Salome was well enough to travel. The message that he would then decide their fate was left unspoken.

4

he baby was the tiniest, reddest creature Joseph had ever seen. Although the Law forbade men to enter the birthing room for seven days, Joseph's hesitation had been brief. They could dispense with tradition in these strange surroundings with this urgent need. The little child, snugly wrapped in swaddling skins of leather as soft as fabric, lay so still Joseph was afraid she was already dead. Then she stirred and made a small mewing sound. Salome, on the pallet beside her, was as white as her daughter was red. At the sound from the baby, the mother turned her head and made a weak effort to reach her, but it was obvious she would be unable to nurse the infant. Lazarus gripped his wife's hand and looked at Joseph with desperation. Cleon, standing behind his father, spoke to Mary. "Is there nothing more we can do for her?"

Mary shook her head.

"I know you've done so much—all that you could—" Cleon looked as if he would grasp Mary's hand as his father held his stepmother's.

"We must name the babe," Joseph said. "Have you chosen what you will call her?"

Lazarus shook his head.

"Perhaps Elisabeth after our Lord's cousin?" Joseph suggested. "Elisabeth Britannia for the first of our people to be born in this land? You consider, and I'll be right back."

Joseph hurried to his lodge, washed his hands, and gathered what he needed for the simple ceremony. Gladyl and Caradoc's two daughters met him outside the birthing hut. Eurgain was the first to speak in her soft, lilting voice. She carried a handful of blue and yellow flowers, and even in the stress of the moment, Joseph noted how they matched her azure eyes and golden gown. "How fares the cubbling and its mother? I gathered flowers for them."

"Should we be making a sacrifice to Matres for you?" Gladys asked, her blue eyes as concerned as her older sister's. "The Mother Goddess loves all mothers."

Joseph smiled at her kindly. "I appreciate your concern, but our God requires no sacrifices, only our love. Come and see. I am going to name the babe before the Most Holy One in faith that she may live for His honor."

The hut was crowded, and Joseph asked that they leave the door open for more light and air. He took the tiny bundle in his arms and looked at Lazarus who said, "She shall be Elisabeth Britannia, as you suggest."

But before the Naming, it was proper for Lazarus Ben Esas to recite the Thanksgiving on Deliverance from Danger for his wife and child that had so far come safely through childbirth. "Blessed are You, Lord our God, King of the universe, who bestows beneficences upon the culpable, for He has bestowed goodness upon me."

And the Judean band responded, "May He who has bestowed beneficence upon you always bestow every beneficence upon you."

For the enlightenment of their guests, as well as for the comfort of his companions, Joseph recounted how Jesus loved children and rebuked the disciples who would keep them away from Him. "'For of such is the Kingdom of Heaven,' our Lord said. And of such is Elisabeth Britannia."

Then Joseph, who in his hurry had left his cap behind, put his prayer shawl over his head and prayed, "O God, heal the ailments of the fruit of the vine which is stricken. Awaken Your compassion, answer those who call upon You, hear the plea of those who cry to You. You who hear the needy, have mercy on Your children as a father has mercy on his children."

Although it was awkward in the crowded hut, the Judeans shifted so that they faced eastward, as they had been accustomed to pray since earliest childhood. Joseph continued, "Our Lord—who fulfilled the promise of old, who came as a light of revelation to the heathen and a glory to Your people Israel—who is like You, O God? Who is like You in tenderness of heart, You who have delivered Your creatures from evil and given us life, who has conquered death! We present to You and to Your lovingkindness this new daughter of Yours and name her before You Elisabeth Britannia, that she may live for Your glory."

And the tiny congregation said, "Glory to You."

Joseph looked around the room, then raised his face even higher with his eyes open as if he could see through the thatch of the roof to God's clear sky. "Mighty Lord, hope of the weak and confidence of the poor . . ."

Then he lowered his face and placed his right hand on Salome's forehead, still cradling the babe in his left arm. "Our Lord and our God, You know future events and accomplish them through us, You, O Lord, are the planter of the good tree, by Your hands are all good works brought forth. You are Lord; . . . You dwell in all Your works and are manifest in all their workings. O Jesus Christ, Son of Mercy, Perfect Healing Savior, Christ, Son of the Living God, Undaunted Power, who has overthrown the enemy, I call to You, Lord Jesus, for Your healing touch on our sister Salome."

And Salome added her weak whisper to the voices of the others, "Glory to You."

The eyes of the British princesses were open wide in amazement at the sense of power and fervency in these simple prayers unaccompanied by the ritual dancing, charmed herbs, or the sacrifices required by the druids. Joseph saw Eurgain move a step closer as a shimmer of tears spilled from her blue eyes.

Elisabeth cried—so weakly that only those standing next to her could hear it. Joseph despaired for her life and wondered what sort of witness her death would be to the strength of their God. Surely these people who prized valor so highly would accept only a god of demonstrated power. But he had done all he could do—he had presented her to God—all was in His hands.

A shadow from the open doorway made him look up. It was Cetil with a young woman from the nearest farmstead. "The fever had the taking of Bryn's cub. I am bringing her to suckle the new babe."

No one had a better plan, so at a nod from Joseph the girl stepped to the bedplace and picked up the baby Joseph had returned to her mother's arms. A look of deep content came over Bryn's face as she opened the front of her tunic and snuggled the infant to her breast. But in a moment she looked up with a worried frown and said something in Cymric to Cetil. "The cubbling is too weak to be sucking," Gladyl translated.

But Cetil seemed to know what to do. Shooing everyone else from the bedside, she began to instruct Bryn.

In the following days life at court appeared to take on a routine for the far-traveled visitors, but Eurgain found her world had turned upside down. At first she blamed her unrest on her father's preoccupation with the warriors and thought that if she and Gladys could return to Camulodunum, all would be well. But for some reason she didn't understand, the thought of leaving Caer Leo left her feeling desolate.

She tried to explain this strange mood to Prince Coillus when he came in from the practice field a few evenings later. Her cousin shrugged with impatience, yet he agreed on one thing. "There's too much talk about war-making. For too long we have abandoned our hunting-runs. It is not good." Shaking his head, he walked on to sharpen his throw-spear.

Eurgain seethed inwardly. It was not the hunting-runs that upset her. She wasn't sure what it was, but she supposed it was Coillus. She had been brought to her uncle's dun with the clear, if unspoken, understanding that she was to be marrying the Silurian prince. "He took Valor at the Warrior Feast five Beltains past and must be soon doing his duty to the tribe," was all her Pendragon father said, but it was enough. Coillus was a valiant warrior, she had no doubt, but she also had no doubt that he had as little interest in her as she had in him.

And that spark could have no chance to ignite with him spending every minute at weapons practice. Even now as she stood in the courtyard, Eurgain could hear the ring of hammer on anvil from the smithies and armorers as fresh iron tires were fitted to chariot wheels, old shields refurbished, and the store of swords and throw-spears increased. And she knew that in every rath and steading across the green hills of Silure the horse breakers and chariot builders were at work at the Pendragon's orders. She picked up a small pebble and flung it at the weapon-stone. Coillus, examining his spear point, didn't even look up.

Wishing she had a handful of rocks to fling at her cousin, Eurgain hitched her tunic skirt into her wide bronze belt so that her stride would be unhampered and stalked out of the compound. Of their own volition, her feet took her to her favorite walk along the banks of the Usk. But before she had reached its smooth, flowing waters, she heard her name on the wind.

"Eurgain! Eurgain!" She turned and saw Josephes coming toward her, his dark, curly hair clinging to his forehead, the sun sparking highlights in his short, neat beard, and his deep eyes shining with something more than a love of sword-skill, which was all she found in the young men of the truath. She stopped for him.

"I have called you five times. You must be deep in reverie. Do you mind if I join you?"

"I am not sure I will be making good company. I am so sick of swords and spears and war-chariots. It seems we are forever fighting these Romans who have not been here since the time of our grandfathers' grandfathers. I am sick of hearing of wars."

Josephes fell into step beside her and found that this one who was usually as gentle as a dove could nearly outstride him in her agitation. "Yes, it is true, there will always be wars and rumors of wars. The important thing is to have peace inside oneself—for one is not likely to have it outside in this life."

When they reached the river bank, Eurgain let her skirt down and slowed her step. "Was it like this in your own country? It is in my mind that it must be a great undertaking to travel from lands beyond the Great Water."

Josephes broke off a bough from one of the ash trees lining the bank and dangled it in the water that was rapidly ebbing even as their pace slowed. "Always in the history of our people there have been wars. Seldom—perhaps never—have we known the freedom you have here. And in our last generations, living under the yoke of Rome, while they are supposed to keep the peace with their famous *Pax Romana*, there is little enough of it. When Yesu was on earth, He said men would cry, 'Peace, peace,' but there would be no peace—except what He gives us in our hearts."

Now their steps completely stopped, and they sat in the long, lush grass above the muddy banks. Swirling eddies made patterns in the wide river, and the sun hanging low in the sky behind them lay a silver path on the brown water. As they sat in silence, an enormous white swan flew low across the river, its feet dragging in the water, and glided to the river's edge below them. It began feeding on the tender green shoots of water plants that were exposed only a short time each day. The evening was filled with gentle swirling sounds of the water and the chirping of birds in the ash trees behind them. And as the fires of agitation stilled within Eurgain, her wide eyes once more smiled with sweetness. "I would hear more of the ways of your people—sometime. But it is in my mind now to wonder how you found me on my walk."

Josephes gave a jerky, half-embarrassed laugh and ran his fingers across his closely-trimmed beard, as if hoping she would not find so foreign a style repellent. "Have you not noticed my eyes on you since first I saw you in the King's Hall?"

"So you hunted me like something on the trail?" She got to her feet, not in anger, but as a signal that the conversation was at an end.

"Not as a quarry, but as something of great value that deserves guarding."

Eurgain laughed—a high, nervous tinkling. "A princess of the Trinovantes has no need of guarding. My sister and I were taught our sword-skill with our brothers as soon as we could hold a weapon."

Josephes stared in amazement. "What? Women—girls—are taught to fight?"

"And why not? I could often best my brothers in the practice field. I did not especially enjoy it, as some of our women do, but I am very good—should I ever need to be calling on my skill."

"But you wouldn't go into battle?" Josephes was horrified.

Eurgain shrugged. "It is unlikely. Many tribes, the Iceni of the Horse Goddess and the Brigantes of the Blue War Shield, are led in battle by their queens through whom the life of the tribe flows. That is not our way, although many women of the truath choose to battle beside their marriage lords."

As they talked, the sun sank lower and the silver path turned golden; the tide turned and the water began rising. When it reached the feeding swan, she settled smoothly into it and glided off, her paddling feet leaving the slimmest of wakes. Likewise, Eurgain turned and led Josephes in the opposite direction through a thicket of beech and alder trees, their path carpeted with ivy and fallen leaves. For some reason she had taken a perverse delight in shocking him, as if wounding Josephes were somehow settling her own score with the men who frustrated her. And yet, making him unhappy seemed to deepen her own frustration. She increased the length of her stride.

For some time the only sound in the woods was that of their feet rustling the underbrush and the birdsong overhead, but suddenly a sharp, chirping cry and beating of wings made Eurgain dart forward. A wren was caught in a fine mesh net cunningly hung between two branches in such a way that no bird would see it until it was too late. The little brown ball of feathers struggled against its snare, only to become more deeply enmeshed. "Oh, it's one of those wicked nets the priestkind set to trap their sacrifices. I hate them! It is in my mind that if Beli the creator god saw fit to make such creatures, not even an archdruid should be destroying them. Bran says the sacrifice returns the creature to its creator. But it is not seeming right to me."

Josephes took a striding leap and grasped the bottom limb of the tree. As he struggled to pull himself up, he longed for a pair of Celtic breeks rather than his hampering Judean robe. But still, he managed to scramble his way to the next higher limb and stretch out along it to free the bird. The little wren did not fly away, but lay stunned in his hand, so he was forced to climb down one-handed.

When he jumped to the ground, he placed the soft ball of feathers in Eurgain's hands. "Perhaps he will recover." The words came out in a strangled sound as he momentarily held her hand.

But Eurgain, apparently immune to his touch, gave him a long, level look, then hitched up her skirt, and turned to stride rapidly back to the dun.

As Anna left the birthing hut after her turn at sitting with Salome, she saw Josephes and Eurgain enter together. She knew that the pain in her throat was as much for the look of distress on Josephes's face as for her own ache at seeing him with the Celtic princess. But a heartbeat later Joanna stepped from the hut to ask her to fetch fresh water, and Anna turned to her duties with a forced brightness.

Through the next few days Anna and the other women continued their turns at the birthing hut. Gladyl and Gladys were always available as well, bringing flowers, cool drinks, and tender morsels of meat for the invalid who refused to die, but seemed to gain little strength. But Eurgain held herself strangely apart from their guests, although at times when the Judean women were dozing, she often slipped into the hut and sat in awed silence while Bryn nursed the tiny babe. It seemed to her not much larger than the wren she was nursing in the royal women's lodge. Indeed, it seemed to be sucking no more milk at each feeding than the few drops of water that Eurgain coaxed down her little bird's beak.

Balan returned to the cors on Ynis Witrin. But before he left, he brought a dark red elixir which Cetil, who directed the nursing of mother and child with the same iron-fisted authority Caradoc exerted on the weapons field, spoon-fed to Salome three times a day. And Joseph met almost daily with Bran and his priests, answering their questions, telling them more of Christ's teachings and His fulfillment of the ancient Law. But always there were unanswered questions and assertions of the old ways, and Joseph left the priest grove beyond the hill-fort with slower steps each day.

But days at Caer Leo were not all war-worry and nursing and talk of the gods. No one could live among the unreserved Celts without absorbing some of their effervescence. On rainy days, and there were many of them, the young people sat in the Great Hall before the blazing central hearth with the sharp resin tang of pitch torches in the air and talked and played branfad to the accompaniment of harpsong.

But when the mists were gentle, or the sun shone cleanly on the green hills and meadows, and the curlew in the wood gave his questioning weee? weee? call from his long, slender, down-curved bill, they took rambling walks across the countryside, or fished for roach, shad, and perch in side-slips of the Usk, or laughed together as the visitors attempted the Celtic skill of horseback riding. And for this, even Eurgain was coaxed out of her reserve by her younger sister. Mary and Anna drew back with maidenly blushes when Eurgain and Gladys lifted their tunics and sat astride the horses. But when the stately Gladyl encouraged the Judean women by mounting herself, they agreed to try. With shrieks of frightened laughter, Mary clung to her mount's flowing mane as a slave led her horse around the forecourt. When Josephes and Cleon suggested they go for a ride beyond the palisade, however, she declined and dismounted. But Eurgain and Gladys were delighted with the suggestion. They led the way through the gate and down the guarded path at a daring speed, followed by the Judean men. Mary and Anna watched the departing figures in solemn silence. Then they walked slowly back to the women's lodge where they helped Joanna tend her little garden, now transplanted to three baskets to give it more room.

As the riders raced across the valley, skirting the wide field where the war-chariots raced at throw-spear practice, Eurgain's horse slackened pace, and she pulled it slightly up-valley away from the others. Josephes, who was seldom unaware of her doings, allowed his mount to fall behind the others and pulled aside to follow her. On the far side of a little hill they found themselves in a green hollow that seemed shut off from the rest of the world.

The opposite slope was heavily wooded, but on their side they rode through thick meadow grass to a small stream that ran down the valley to join distant tributaries before tumbling at last into Mor Hafren. Josephes drew aside of Eurgain, who had allowed her horse to slow to a walk. "How is your little wren, Princess Eurgain?"

She gave him a level look before she answered. "His wing was broken from struggling in the net, but it mends. He will fly with his cloud-fellows again. But it is to my thinking that you did not follow me all this way to inquire after the bird."

"I would rather inquire after you if you would not think me too forward. I would know why you have flown from me as your bird would have flown from its snare."

At first her voice was so low he could hardly hear her. "You have your answer in the question." Then she flung at him with a note of defiance, "I would not be a sacrifice to your God."

At first her words were senseless to him. "But I have told you, Jehovah requires no sacrifice. His Son Yesu—"

"Fa! I have heard and heard all that. The priestkind talk of nothing else. They have been so busy talking they have not even noticed their net was destroyed. And I must wonder how many birds and small animals languish in their sacrifice snares. It would be far better to have the taking of their life with the golden sickle than a slow strangling. But that is not what I talk of. The peace you talk of is more frightening to me than the war of the Romans. At least our people understand war. We do not understand your ways." Abruptly she dropped her eyes and her voice. "And I do not understand you."

The horses had stopped, unnoticed by their riders, and now they stood side by side in the knee-deep grass. Josephes slipped to the ground and held out his hand to Eurgain. To his delighted surprise, she followed him. Without a thought for the fact that in Jerusalem he would not have spoken to the one he hoped to wed before their betrothal, much less ride off alone with her to an isolated spot, Josephes walked slowly across the meadow, savoring her nearness and relishing the silence between their comments as much as the sound of her voice.

He longed to reach out and touch the dark hair with red-gold lights falling around her shoulders and, shocked by his own impropriety, he realized that his arms ached to hold her slender form, his lips to kiss her white brow, her smooth cheek, her soft lips. But it would not do—not until she was his before God.

Even as he told himself that such could not be, his arm went around her.

For a moment she leaned toward him, then pulled away, breaking his hold as easily as she would have a spider web.

"Do you understand that?" he asked.

"It is the understanding that frightens me." She turned to her horse, and Josephes bent to help her, but she vaulted to her mount as lightly as any trained warrior. She dug her heels into her horse's flanks and was halfway across the valley before Josephes was on his horse.

A few days later a messenger arrived from Ynis Witrin bearing gifts from Balan—baskets of small, tart, freshly ripened green and russet apples. Mary seized one in each hand with delight and raced to the birthing hut. Surely their fresh, tangy juiciness would tempt Salome's appetite. Anna was sitting with Salome, and together the girls cut the apples and held tiny slices for Salome to nibble. "Oh, they are so good," she said, and gave the strongest smile she had since the birth. From that time on, Salome seemed to gain strength. Although her progress was slow, fears for her death lessened.

But Mary had something new to worry about. As they cut the apples together that afternoon, Anna said to her in a soft voice, "I think your brother is much taken with the princess."

Mary blinked in surprise. "Which one? Oh, you mean Eurgain? Oh, he amuses himself playing that silly branfad game with her, but it doesn't . . ." She stopped suddenly. She had been about to say it didn't mean a thing, but what if it did? Had Anna seen something none of them had noticed? Or had Mary been too busy watching Cleon to see the obvious? Surely Josephes couldn't be seriously interested in a pagan, no matter how beautiful she was.

That night in the Great Hall Mary watched both young men closely as Lubrin sang his harpsong. Tonight the tale was not one of heroism and valor in battle, but, since the women stayed to listen also, a gentle story of a quest for love. In the wavering glow of the torchlight, Lubrin's voice and harp painted a picture of king's men searching for a maiden to be their queen. They came upon a young woman sitting beside a well. The harper strummed, and Mary's mind filled with the scene. Already she had learned quite a bit of Cymric, and Gladyl beside her translated the rest. "The maiden's cloak was of richest purple, spun by her own hand from finest fleece and clasped to her bosom by a gold-chased silver brooch. Her smock was green, more emerald than the grass, and rich with delicate gold work. The sun fell upon her, shone upon her, brightened all around her, so that the men saw all in a gleam of gold, a radiant aureole against a field of green.

"And the maiden, ready to wash her hair in the crystal waters of the well, unbound her deep red-gold hair, and it fell in a cascade through all the shafts of the sun. And her arms, reaching out from beneath her cloak, were white and soft as the snows of night with the kiss of Epona upon them. And her gentle cheeks were soft and smooth, red as the blush of a mountain flower . . ."

The harper sang and the pine-knot torches flared in their iron brackets around the room. Mary looked at her brother, and she gasped. There was no mistaking his look at Eurgain, whose beauty the song could well be describing.

Should she speak to her father? Or to her brother? What could she say to Anna? Was Cleon perhaps looking in an equally besotted manner at some other girl? No, she wouldn't think of her own happiness, but of her friend's. Would Anna be comforted with the thought that there were other unattached men in their party? Eutropius, Trophimus, and Sidonius were all somewhat older, but unwed, and not unattractive. But she knew the answer to that question. After all, she hardly found the thought comforting that there were others in the group, should she lose Cleon. Perhaps she could find an opportunity to talk to Eurgain herself, although Mary had no idea what she would say to her on so delicate a topic.

Her opportunity came sooner than she thought, however, for the next morning Mary was with Joanna tending the plants in the garden spot behind the women's lodge when Gladyl and Eurgain joined them. The two had been working together to compose a new poem and were walking in the garden for inspiration. They paused by Joanna's baskets and asked questions about each plant she showed them. "But you must come to Ynis Witrin to see my most precious," Joanna said.

The royal ladies seated themselves on the green grass and listened intently as Joanna told about her thorn tree and went on from there to tell of Jesus' crucifixion and resurrection. Gladyl listened intently, but it was Eurgain who asked the most probing questions. "And your God taught that we should be loving our enemies as well as our own people—and strangers also?"

Mary answered, "He taught that love is the highest value of all, and we should love everyone. But that's only possible if we have God's love in our hearts to give to others."

Eurgain was silent for a long time before she spoke. "Yes, I would need the help of a god to open my heart so."

Joanna clipped a yellow leaf off a six-inch olive seedling that was not flourishing, then turned to Eurgain. "And our Yesu also taught that perfect love—His love—casts out fear. If you will forgive me, it has seemed to me that your people carry around a great fear of displeasing their many gods. But when we have Jehovah God's love in our hearts and follow it, there is no need to fear displeasing Him."

Gladyl looked thoughtful, but Eurgain went further. "It is in my mind that your God is the unnamed three-faced god Bran has told us of. How does one get Yesu from the mind into the heart?"

"Eurgain, that's wonderful!" Mary sprang up to embrace her. Then she explained, "You open your whole heart to Him, holding nothing back. You turn away from choosing your own ways and walk in His ways. He sends His Spirit into your heart to stay there always and help you do that. And He becomes your most intimate, loving Friend."

Gladyl stopped them with a question. "What will your father say, Eurgain?"

Mary quailed before the thought of the powerful Pendragon. Joseph had explained the Way to Arviragus and the priests, but Caradoc, spending all his time with the war host, had heard little of the discussion. Would he accept his daughter's faith, or be furious and demand she renounce it? The choice of which gods the tribe was to follow was a prerogative of the king—would these leaders allow their people to make an individual choice for the now-named Three-in-One?

But Eurgain wasn't the least intimidated. "Oh, I doubt Father will take notice of me. All he can be thinking of is rumors of the Romans."

Then Mary, who had listened many times to her father talking to the druids, knew what to say. "I heard my father tell Bran yesterday that the druid wisdom has always understood some of the principles of our faith. You are not asked to renounce the *truths* your faith teaches, but to accept the complete and more perfect revelation through Jesus Christ. That is what we have done with our Judaism. We are still the children of Israel, and we serve the God of Israel, but in following His Messiah, we have found the perfect fulfillment to our faith." Mary paused. She hoped she had quoted her father accurately.

"What do I do?" Eurgain asked, her clear blue eyes showing her determination to follow this new light.

Mary clasped her hand. "We will pray, and Father will baptize you." So Mary prayed that the Celtic princess would know the joy of the Lord and the assurance of salvation. Then she prayed the prayer of the heart opening to its Creator.

Eurgain's prayer was little more than, "Yes, Yesu, that is my desiring." But it was enough. Mary joyfully embraced the new believer—the first in Britannia.

Still holding hands, the girls raced toward the Great Hall where Mary hoped to find her father. Joseph, indeed, was in the hall, but was conferring again with the king and his priests with such concentration that Mary felt she could not interrupt, even for such momentous news as she bore.

In a few moments, however, an interruption came from another source as Balan arrived at the hall. Arviragus sprang forward to greet the Deon. "Ah, welcome, Balan of the Oak. Is it time for the Lammas fires already? I have spent too long with all this talking when I should be in the field with Caradoc and my warriors." A servant hurried in with the ritual cup, and Balan took the guest seat, but the king paced the floor with pent-up energy. "This talk of gods is all very well for the priestkind, but I've had enough and enough of it." He turned to a servant. "Bring my chariot. Bran, you decide this matter, and Balan shall be seeing to the festival of Lugh. It is," he paused, "three nights to Lugnasad?"

The priests agreed his calculations were correct, and the king strode from the room. The women moved forward to greet the newcomer, and Mary had only a moment to inform her father of Eurgain's decision. Joseph embraced Eurgain as was customary among believers, but had no time to discuss the matter, as the druids required his attention.

And Joseph had not yet had time to speak further to either Eurgain or Mary later that day when Josephes came to him in the lodge where he had retired to wash before the evening meal. Josephes wasted no words, but went straight to the heart of his business. "Father, I want to take a wife—if she will have me or even listen to my suit."

Joseph threw out his arms and turned to embrace his son. "At last! I have long hoped to hear these words, my son. Have you spoken to Anna? Of course it is proper that I should speak to Lazarus Ben Esas first as he stands in place of her father."

Josephes gaped at his father. "Anna? I want to marry Eurgain, Father. Will you speak to Caradoc for me?"

Now it was Joseph's turn to stare open-mouthed. His hands fell from Josephes's shoulders and hung limp at his sides. "Eurgain? Caradoc's daughter? You wish to *marry* a Celtic woman?"

"Yes, I do. Anna is a sweet girl and a dear friend, but I have no wish to make her my wife."

Joseph sat on his pallet and leaned against the wattle wall of the lodge. "This comes as too much of a shock for me to discuss it now. Leave me."

Joseph watched his son's back as he left the building. It had never occurred to Joseph that his son would consider marrying any but a Hebrew woman. Joseph had even concluded that if Josephes did not choose to take Anna for a wife, he would send his son back to Jerusalem on some matter of business in hopes he would find a wife there. Certainly Josephes must marry—but one of his own race.

Joseph sat long, considering. Jesus had healed the daughter of a Syrophenician woman, a Gentile who had asked only for crumbs left over from the table of the rightful Jewish heirs. And He had told the story of the Good Samaritan—pointing out that the one who showed love was the true neighbor, rather than one of blood kindred. Yet . . . Joseph stood and began pacing the length of the lodge.

It was clear that God intended full acceptance into the faith for Gentiles. But still, *marriage?* His own son and a native Briton? Even though Eurgain was a princess and had become a believer, many of the ways of these people were foreign and often uncultured, if not actually barbaric.

Joseph looked around the guest lodge he had been staying in these many weeks. How would they adjust if they took permanent residence here? Was he to live for the rest of his life in a wattle and daub hut—a house of woven reeds, plastered with mud—when he had been accustomed to one of the best homes in Jerusalem—filled with soft carpets, carved ivory, and bronze lamps—the finest he could find from the trading ports of the world? He looked at the rush-strewn floor and thought of the luxurious red carpet woven with a rich blue and gold pattern that lay over the tiles of the main hall in the house he had left behind. But then a movement of his foot stirred the fresh herbs strewn among the reeds, and the air was filled with a clean, sweet scent quite unlike any he had encountered in the East.

Back to the problem at hand—if their families were to intermarry, Arviragus could then hardly refuse to grant their company permission to remain there. But such concerns, although regularly used by royal families for treaty-making, did not seem to Joseph, who had married for love all those many years ago, to be a solid basis for marriage. Not the marriage he wanted for his son.

Yet, what of the brotherhood Jesus had proclaimed? Did Joseph really believe that all believers were one? An hour ago he would have vowed that he did. But taking a Celt for an actual daughter-in-law was different from embracing her as a daughter in the faith.

And what of Anna? Her feelings for Josephes had been obvious. What would happen to their mission if there were hurt feelings and strife among the twelve?

Joseph determined to say nothing for the moment. He would pray and meditate on the question. If only God would give him a vision as He had Peter. He wouldn't even need to have it repeated three times as Peter did.

At the feast that night Joseph frowned at his food. Here was the same heavy menu of roast and boiled meats, relieved only by more of Balan's apples. Joseph toyed with a thick slice of stringy roast ox, then tossed it to the hound under the table; soon an over-baked oat cake followed. What he wouldn't give for succulent dates, fresh figs, ruby-red pomegranates, and a certain flaky honey pastry he always bought from Simeon's stall in the market near his house.

He turned to accept an apple from the red pottery bowl a server held out to him. Then he saw it was Eurgain. She was holding the bowl toward him, but her eyes were on Josephes. And Josephes returned her look. In that moment, Joseph knew he didn't need a voice from heaven.

He turned to Josephes. "You have my blessing. I will speak to Caradoc." The apple he bit into was the sweetest he had ever tasted.

5

hat night, under a wide, star-flung sky, with the sounds of cattle calling softly from the hills and night birds singing in the trees, Josephes knew the sweetness of hearing the two things he most desired in all the world.

When several of the women's side left before the harpsong, Josephes hurried out after Eurgain, fearing that she would run from him yet again. He was determined to press his question. But Eurgain responded without a demur to his suggestion that they go for a walk. "The gates are secured for the night, but it will be quiet beyond the smith-place."

However, once they were there, in spite of Eurgain's apparent compliance and the gentle breeze that seemingly bade him speak, Josephes found himself tongue-tied.

"It is in my mind that you would speak of your Yesu of the great love again—it is seeming you people speak of little else."

Her voice had a gentle humor and a confidence Josephes dearly wished for himself at that moment. "A true love is never far from one's mind, Eurgain. But it is my love for you I would speak of, if you would let me." And his voice took on a throaty richness as he added in the Cymric he had been struggling to learn, "Eurgain, heart-of-my-heart."

Her smile was as soft as the call of the wood wren in the distance. "Since the sun was high in the sky today, I have known Yesu's love in my heart. Now I would be knowing yours—and have you know mine, Josephes, heart-of-my-heart."

With a happiness so sharp it was painful, Josephes could think of no reply but to take her into his arms again as he had in their secluded green valley. This time she did not leap onto her horse and gallop away.

As Eurgain had predicted, her father gave an off-handed consent to her baptism into the new faith and to her marriage to the foreigner, although he could not promise to attend the bride-making. Word had come from a trader that Roman troops were massing in Gaul, and Caradoc's every thought was given to integrating the strategies of his Trinovante war host with the Silurian men. Although it was unlikely the Romans would sail across the Great Water so late in the season, the Pendragon must soon join the men of his own truath.

But Joseph's announcement of the forthcoming wedding had remarkable results with other hearers. The next morning several of Arviragus's household and all the Judean band, except Salome who was still too weak and Marcella who stayed with her mistress, gathered for Eurgain's baptism on the green banks of a slipstream which filled to its banks when the Usk was in high tide. Joseph was explaining the symbolism of the ceremony he was about to perform when Bran, wearing the white robe druids reserved for religious ceremonies, stepped forward. "Joseph of Arimathea, by consenting to marriage between our people, you have shown that you have accepted us. We likewise accept you. We will be one people with one God, for I believe that what you have told us is true. I shall also have this baptism of your Three-in-One God."

Joseph's heart swelled with joy. Indeed, he had heard the voice of Jehovah. He was overcome with a great humility that he should be the one to lead the conversion of this land. He held his hand out and rested it on Bran's shoulder in a gesture of welcome and brotherhood. "May the joy and peace of God rest on you. From now on you shall be known as Bran the Blessed."

And then Balan came. Although a knot of the older ones held back, many of the younger druid priests came forward to join their archdruid in accepting the revelation of faith Joseph had presented.

Joseph's cup was full, but it had not yet run over, for there was more to come. Gladyl likewise removed her scarlet and purple plaid cloak and stepped to the river bank. "I, too, believe."

Eurgain, the first to believe, was the first to be baptized. She stepped to the edge of the water and slipped out of her tunic, letting it fall onto the sandy bank, in accordance with Joseph's earlier instructions that nothing must come between her and the washing of the Living Water which was an aspect of God Himself. The men turned their backs, but Joseph, the official witness, held out his hand to guide her into the water.

The water was cold, but fresh as it rippled past them on its way to Mor Hafren, and flecks of golden sun danced around them on the surface. When they were waist deep, Joseph stopped and, supporting her firmly around the shoulders, immersed Eurgain three times, dipping her fully so that the water closed over her head each time. "In the name of God, the Father and Lord of all, and of our Savior, Jesus Christ, and of the Holy Ghost, receive the washing with water. For our Lord Jesus Christ said, 'Unless you be born again, you shall not enter into the Kingdom of Heaven.'" Eurgain emerged dripping and radiant.

When the others had been baptized and again fully robed, they stood facing their spiritual brothers and sisters, and Joseph, standing between the two groups, spoke. "We will entreat the Creator of the universe, that He may keep His people in the world through His beloved Son, Jesus Christ. Through Him

He called us from darkness to light, from ignorance to the knowledge of His glorious name."

Then facing east, he raised his hands in prayer and the newly baptized believers followed the Judean band in raising their hands to heaven as Joseph prayed, "On Your name, O Lord, You have called us to hope. You opened the eyes of our hearts to know You, to know the Highest on High. All nations shall know that You alone are God, and Jesus Christ is Your servant. We are Your people and the sheep of Your pasture. Grant harmony and peace to us and to all the inhabitants of the earth. Grant it to us so that we shall be obedient to Your almighty and glorious name."

And the members of Joseph's band replied, "Glory to You, Father. Glory to You, Word. Glory to You, Grace. Glory to You, Spirit. Glory to You, Holy One, Glory to Your glory. We praise You, Father. We thank You, O Light in whom there is no darkness."

At the end of the prayer all was silent for the space of several heartbeats. Then as one person, the newcomers to the land moved forward to greet the newcomers to the faith with the kiss of peace.

They walked back over the fields, but Joseph felt he was barely touching ground. The light glimmering on the water had seemed to him to be a promise from the One who had said, "I am the light of the world."

Joseph recalled the darkness that had covered the land at Christ's crucifixion—surely that had been the darkest moment in the history of the earth. But the light had triumphed so soon—so much sooner than anyone had dared to hope.

Resurrection morning had dawned—with the joy of the women, the unfolding of the flowers, the brightness of the dawn in a joyous shout of universal triumph echoing His words on the cross—now ringing with victory: "It is finished. It is finished. It is finished." The power of the dark is broken. Light for all ages to come. Light that would forever triumph over the dark wherever men would let it shine—open their hearts and minds and let the light shine in. Let the light shine—the people that walked in darkness have seen a great light.

These new converts had opened their hearts, and now Joseph was confident that the light would spread throughout the island.

Across the valley beyond the royal dun, however, another kind of light was occupying the people. In two nights it would be Lugnasad, and on every hilltop people were building great pyres of sticks to be set ablaze for the Lammas fires. Both Balan and Bran had told him how the fires on every hill would invoke Lugh the Sun God to shed his light and blessing on the crops that there might be an abundant harvest. Following the example of the ripening cornstalks, the men and maidens of the tribe would lay beyond the blaze of the fires and whisper to the Earth Mother that through them many strong warriors might grow up in the tribe. Joseph considered this. Should he tell Bran to forbid the fires?

Would the people understand? Or would they rebel at such an order? Or could he somehow turn the festival from its pagan purposes to teach the new Way?

As he entered the compound, the smell of roasting boar made him think again of Peter's vision and how God had put His own seal of approval on the uncircumcised Cornelius to be a member of His church. Surely this was a guide for Joseph.

Joseph, Balan, and Bran had already decided to meet at the grove to discuss the wedding of Josephes and Eurgain, which was also to take place at Lugnasad. Joseph decided to broach the matter of the fires first. "If we are to teach the people the way of Christ, they must learn that all blessings come from Jehovah God. Invoking one of the old gods for their harvest is not right."

The druids frowned, uncertain of what was to come next.

Joseph considered. Always there was this dilemma—how to blend old traditions with new beliefs. Traditions were valuable, even precious to a people—their heritage of ties to their forefathers. And yet, one must not accommodate to the point of denying the Truth one confessed. Anything obviously pagan or immoral could not be countenanced, but surely the more innocent aspects of the practices could be adapted to new ways—as the Followers of the Way had now substituted the Lord's Supper for the Passover sacrifice, and yet kept the feast day.

"We need not forbid a festival, but can you explain to the people that the true God will bless them because He loves them as His children and asks only that they return His love? Lugh has no power to bless their fires, but God will hear and answer their prayers." He took a deep breath and forged ahead. "And tell them that it is the will of the Three-in-One that all babes be born in wedlock, not as the cattle of the field."

Bran nodded. Joseph smiled. "Truly, you are Bran the Blessed."

For two days rain fell on the valley, until Joseph wondered if there had been any need for him to worry about the Lammas fires. Perhaps this was God's answer to the problem, for this year at least. But by afternoon of the second day, the rain turned to mist, and by late afternoon a weak sun sent golden rays between the clouds, shining on all who answered the call of the ox horns to the wedding feast.

In the men's place, Cleon and Eutropius helped Josephes clasp his cloak with a gold and silver circular brooch set with amber, a gift from Arviragus. Then, with a slap of encouragement on each shoulder, they sent him out. The forecourt was already alive with guests and growing more so every moment as others arrived from far and near. Here was an even larger gathering than for the welcoming of the Pendragon, for runners had been sent to beckon those beyond the voice of the ox horns. Many would feast in the courtyard, filling their mead horns from the large, double-handed vats set out there for those whom the King's Hall could not hold.

A murmur went through the gathering as Josephes drew closer. "The marriage lord comes. The marriage lord comes! Who comes with the marriage lord?"

And from the deepening shadows behind Josephes, Cleon and Coillus led others of their companions in answering, "We come with him!" Coillus, in his relief that he need not be bothered with the role of marriage lord, shouted just louder than the others. And at their words, a way parted in the gathered throng, and Josephes, his head high, his eyes searching for his beloved, entered the Great Hall of the King of the Silures for his marriage feast.

Eurgain had entered earlier from the women's side with Gladys and Gladyl, Mary, and a determinedly smiling Anna. The bride stood now at the High Place, her purple and scarlet gown so heavily embroidered with gold work that in the shimmering torchlight she seemed to be dressed all in gold. When she stepped forward to meet Josephes, the bronze discs hanging about the hem of her skirt clanged softly as a greeting song to him.

Eurgain and Josephes sat on piled skins and pillows at the high table to the right of Arviragus, who was to take the place of Eurgain's father, with Joseph to the king's left. The warriorkind were all in their finest cloaks of saffron, blue, and crimson. The bronze and gold glint of brooches and torques gleamed in the torchlight. And on the women's side, gowns of richly woven colors and gold, bronze, and amber adorned those from even the smallest steadings. The scent of fresh herbs strewn on the floor mingled with that of the vervain blossoms braided into the women's hair. Carcasses of whole bullocks and sheep were brought in from the cooking-pits, and all ate their fill to the accompaniment of Lubrin's harp and the flare of the pine-knot torches.

After the feasting, those of the women's side gathered around the hearth and, to their own accompaniment of reed-pipes and harps, raised their voices in a bridesong that was at once plaintive and joyous. The chant began low, then swelled as the waves of the sea, with the call of one lone seabird soaring above all the others—the song of a maiden searching for her soul-mate. The chanting swelled in a sound of rich gold as the sun washing the waves, and the voice of the lone singer was joined by the deep, strong throat of the longest harp string representing the bridegroom that would seek her and bring her heart fulfillment.

The singers began moving around the fire, weaving an intricate dance pattern of swaying and hesitating steps. At each pause in the dance they threw into the fire small bunches of flowers and herbs they carried in their bronze-and-amber studded belts. The flames crackled and leapt at the maidens' offerings, filling the hall and even the courtyard with a sweet, spicy scent—at once soothing and exciting.

The chant died slowly as a fading dream, the last chords of the harp following the scented smoke through the roof hole in the center of the hall. The singers came and stood in two lines before the High Place. Gladyl reached into the basket beside her stool, and as the bridal couple stood, she approached Eurgain with the royal wedding diadem worn by all the brides of their family for time out of mind. She wound two leather thongs through Eurgain's thick auburn hair until the tall swirls of silver and gold, each ending with a little bell, sat firmly on the bride's head, and the bridal couple, followed by their attendants, began the procession from the hall accompanied by the muted sound of ox horns in the forecourt.

With Celtic marriage fires burning on either side of them and the truath gathered around as far as Caer Leo would hold, Josephes and Eurgain took their place under the Hebrew marriage canopy, emblem of the home they would be building and symbol of God's love. The staves of each corner were held by Cleon, Eutropius, Trophimus, and Sidonius. And the presence of this ancient tradition of Josephes's people represented not only God's blessing on this union of two individuals, but also the union of two cultures in this wedding that was a blending of the most ancient rites of both people.

Bran spoke first. "There are three things a man must give for his bride—his hearth for her warmth, his skill for her food, his shield for all that threatens her."

"I bring them." Turning to his bride, Josephes looked into her deep blue eyes reflecting the firelights all around them. "My hearth for your warmth." He placed his palm over his heart. "My skill for your food." He placed his palm to his forehead. "And my shield for all that threatens you." He placed the palm of his right hand over his left forearm—his shield arm.

Then, the firelight dancing on the rays of his sun-crown as he held a golden sickle, symbol of druid power, aloft in his right hand and a sprig of mistletoe, symbol of fortune and healing, in his left, Bran walked three times, sun-wise around the outside of the canopy.

Joseph was next, with the blessing of his people. "Blessed are You, Lord our God, King of the universe, who has sanctified us with Your commandments and commanded us concerning marriages." He held out a cup of wine—the most elaborate gold and silver, amber-studded guest cup from the king's own kist. The groom drank, then the bride.

Then Josephes slipped a ring on Eurgain's slim, white index finger. "With this ring, you are consecrated to me according to the Law of Moses and Israel."

And then Joseph, in a chanting voice that needed only Lubrin's harp accompaniment to make it sound like a Celtic ode, pronounced the blessings:

"Blessed are You, Lord our God, King of the universe, who has created all things for Your glory.

"Blessed are You, Lord our God, King of the universe, creator of man . . .

"Grant abundant joy to these loving friends, as You bestowed gladness upon Your created beings in the Garden of Eden of old. Blessed are you, Lord, who gladdens the groom and bride.

"Blessed are You, Lord our God, King of the universe, who created joy and happiness, bride and groom, gladness, jubilation, cheer and delight, love, friendship, harmony and fellowship . . . Blessed are You, Lord, who gladdens the groom with the bride." Taking Eurgain's hand, Joseph led her seven times around her husband under the canopy, then gave her hand back into his.

King Arviragus was the next to approach the bridal couple, adding his blessing, the blessing of all the Silures, and in the name of Caradoc Pendragon, the blessing of the Trinovantes as well, for they would be one people in wishing the blessing of the gods on the royal bride and her bridegroom.

Then it was Josephes's turn. To the accompaniment of Lubrin's harp, he chanted in a style that was part Jewish, part Celtic, as his life would always be from that day forward:

As the breath of wind sweeps through the harp
And the chords sing,
So the breath of the Lord's Spirit
Sweeps through my members,
And I sing in His love.

His look of love went deep in the next stanza, as he praised Jehovah for breaking down the walls his beloved would have built against him:

For He destroys what is false
And all that is hostile.
Thus it has been from the beginning
And shall be to the end:
Nothing shall stand against Him,
And nothing shall resist Him.
Thus we give praise to His Name.
And our spirits sing praises
To His Holy Spirit.

And then the harp swelled to a higher pitch, and the voice of a single reed pipe joined in, followed shortly by the voice of the bride:

A little stream sprang up
And became a river mighty and broad.
It swept away everything and broke it up
And tore down the strong place.
No bulwarks or structures could check it,
Nor dams built by the art of man.

It streamed over the face of the whole earth
And filled everything;
All the thirsty on earth drank therefrom,
And their thirst was quenched and slaked,
For the drink was the gifting of the Most High.

And the groom's voice finished strongly:

And He gave light to their eyes,
For they knew one another in the Lord
And were redeemed by the eternal water of immortality.
Hallelujah!

As the final "Hallelujah!" was repeated by all the Judean band, the ox horns, harps, and reed pipes all burst forth in a joyous song, and the bridal couple received a shower of herbs from the hands of their well-wishing guests. Beyond the dun, stars peeped around the cloud-strewn sky, and on every hillside a blazing bonfire added to the exultation. Joseph turned to repeat his blessing to the bride and groom and hurry them on their way to the piled skins of the bedplace.

But the words never left his mouth.

The shouting of excited voices, the thunder of pounding hooves, and the heaving of winded horses shattered the joy of the celebration.

Iron chariot tires ground on the broad courtyard stones, spraying sparks in all directions. The rider jumped from the chariot before his driver had brought the team to a plunging halt just inside the massive gateposts. "The Pendragon sends word. The Romans have landed!"

6

With his mud-spattered cloak flowing behind him, the wild-haired messenger placed his palm to his forehead in a salute to Arviragus and held out a leather pouch. The king grabbed the pouch and, after a moment's glance, read the message aloud, "Romans landed. Surprise attack. Skirmish lost. Battle waiting. Gather war host at Dun Camulus."

Arviragus waited until the excited murmur moving through the crowd quieted, then shouted his orders. "Sharpen your spears! We ride at dawn!"

Immediately the entire compound was thrown into a flurry of activity. It seemed impossible that the time they had so long prepared against was now come. Caradoc had assured them the invasion would not be until the wild geese flew north in the spring, especially since the Roman soldiers' dislike, even fear, of water was well-known, and the rising of quick storms in the Great Water was common in leaf-falling times from Lugnasad to Samain. But it had happened. The enemy was here, and now they must put their training to use and defend their land against the red-crested tyrants.

The night sounds changed from the rejoicing of ox horns and reed pipes to the ominous, tearing tones of long boar-headed bronze war-horns and the thrum of wolfskin drums. The wedding fires died. In their place, torches flared around the weapon stone, and sparks flew as spears, knives, and swords were honed razor-sharp. Slaves and drivers rushed to and fro preparing chariots, horses, and harness. And the women's side was also astir preparing food and supplies for their men and polishing their shield bosses. Many women packed bundles for themselves as well—those who were warrior-trained and would fight beside their men in battle, sometimes as spear-mates, fighting back-to-back, and then sleeping rolled in their cloaks with the same shield as pillow.

In the royal quarters, the princesses threw themselves into the preparations more vigorously than any. Josephes watched his bride preparing a ration pouch for her cousin Coillus, then turned to his father with a light in his eyes. "I shall go, too. These are my people now."

Joseph hesitated. They had come to Britannia to declare a way of peace and love. He had come to find a quiet life free from conflict. Had they left the persecution of the Jews and Romans to make a new home in a land that was now to bow under the subjugation of Rome? Under the yoke of an emperor who, as one of his first official acts, had declared that acceptance of the new faith was an offense punishable by death?

Joseph had noted Bran directing his priests and preparing his own things, for, although druids never bore arms, the priest always went into battle with his king. Joseph thought of how the priests of his people accompanied the Hebrew nation to battle, carrying the Ark of the Covenant before them. Although Joseph did not see himself in the tradition of Joshua at the Battle of Jericho, he did feel his place was with Bran. He shrank from the tumult of war, the horror of killing, but he would put his courage to the test and do what he believed to be right.

"My son, I would ask you to remain here as leader of our band in my absence." He clapped his hand on Josephes's shoulder.

"Your absence?" Josephes's eyebrows rose in surprise.

"I shall go with the king and Bran. It is my place."

Josephes started to argue his youth, his greater strength, his desire to ride with Coillus, but Joseph held up his hand. Josephes would obey his father. Joseph turned to make his own preparations. "Mary, I have need of your help. Bring a serving trencher and poker from the cooking place kist." And he instructed her in his plans.

Two other things Joseph must do. First, he carefully put his scrolls of sacred Scripture in their leather carrying pouches. He would leave them all in Josephes's care except the Torah. That he would take with him. The Torah, the Law given to his people as a personal covenant from God, the Law that set them apart from all the other peoples of the world and established them as God's holy children. The Torah, doubly sacred to him now that the Law had been fulfilled in the sacrifice of the blessed Lamb of God, opening the door to those who would live with God in the new covenant.

Joseph hastily washed his hands and donned cap and prayer shawl. Just as in his own life Joseph had blended the old and new ways of his people, so in bringing the faith to Britain, he must apply its new ways to the life of the people here. Crossing the thronging courtyard, Joseph found Bran inside a circle of low-burning pitch torches, directing which of his priests should accompany the war band and which remain at the dun. When there was a break in the activity, Joseph asked Bran to join him in reciting the Prayer for Travelers that God's mercy might accompany their host. Bran and two of the priests who had been baptized stepped with him outside the palisade where the eastern sky was just beginning to streak red and gold. They walked to a quiet spot beyond the guarded entrance where they turned toward the slim golden eastern streaks.

Joseph prayed, "May it be Your will, Lord our God and God of our fathers, to lead us in peace and direct our steps in peace, to guide us in peace, to support us in peace, and to bring us to our destination in life with joy and peace."

Even as he chanted, Joseph was aware of the irony of this prayer for peaceful travel in a land erupting in war. But still he prayed for the harmony of the Prince of Peace to reign in every heart.

"Deliver us from the hands of every enemy and lurking foe. . . . Grant grace, kindness, and mercy in Your eyes and in the eyes of all who behold us, and bestow bountiful kindness upon us. Hear the voice of our prayer, for You hear everyone's prayer. Blessed are You Lord, who hears prayer."

And the priestkind, as they had been instructed by Joseph, replied, "Amen."

But before the last syllable faded on the morning breeze, a sharp war cry rang out along with the clashing of spears on bronze and wooden shields.

The warriors were assembled, and the wagons rolled forward, loaded with weapons, food, fur rugs, and all that the war host would need for its trek across Britain to the gathering of the forces. Long rays of the sun were breaking golden over the hills as the king's third chariot pulled up for Joseph. Its wicker sides had been painted a blazing red, and as streams of sunlight struck it, Joseph felt as if he were stepping into a chariot of fire. The woven leather floor swayed as the driver jumped the horses forward, and Joseph clutched the sides for support. It was a finely balanced chariot, far lighter than the Roman ones Joseph was accustomed to. Entirely latched together with thongs of tightly stretched leather, the agile structure felt almost alive, giving to every rut and dip. As they careened past the gateposts and down the steep path from the fort, Joseph grasped the chariot sides tighter yet. With a clatter of iron wheels, the chariots poured forth from Caer Leo, the sound of the priests' horns following them long past the last barley garth and carrying them forward on the wind of their going.

There had been no time for leave-taking. Joseph had not even seen some of his band in the confusion of the past hours. A hurried farewell to Mary and Josephes and a quick clasp of Lazarus's hand had been all there was time for. But as the host drove northward toward the ford across Mor Hafren, Joseph had time to reflect. Such a rash decision and hurried action was so unlike him, it was now frightening to wonder what he'd done. His chariot bounced across the miles and his hands grew numb from gripping the sides as they lurched at yet another furze root or washout in the track. He could form no clear thoughts, but as always, the promise was there: "Lo, I am with you always—always."

Although the supply wagons, foot warriors, and women fell behind, the charioteers traveled swiftly, stopping only during the darkest hours to sleep and let the horses rest, and keeping always spare chariot horses at their side to replace any in danger of foundering. As they traveled through the lands of the Coritani and Catuvellauni, Joseph thought it a shame that their warriors, too, were not joining the hosting, but the Pendragon had had no time to form a union of the tribes. By the end of the week, they arrived at the Trinovante capital. But Caradoc and his warriors were not there. The Pendragon had left one of his cryptic messages for them: "Father of Rivers, gathering place."

By nightfall the Silurian king and the first of his war host arrived at the Trinovante camp. Joseph couldn't help wondering if it had been wise to leave the heavy fortifications Caradoc's father Cymbeline had built at Dun Camulus to meet the enemy in the open. But then he knew nothing of battle strategy. Arviragus, however, gave voice to his complaint when he saw how carelessly the warriors were camped. Caradoc assured them that the Romans could not cross the water without a bridge, so there was no worry. Even the portable bridges of the Romans, which traders had talked of, took time to put in place, and there was no sign of such yet—undoubtedly these were merely figments of boastful imagination.

They all felt more confident as Caradoc showed them his strategy. He had selected a position for battle in which advance and retreat alike would be difficult for the Romans and their war machines, but would be comparatively easy for the Britons with their light, mobile chariots. The days his warriors had been there had been spent in piling stone ramparts atop the hills that sloped up from the river, forming in effect a strong hillfort into which a chariot-born war host could retreat and regroup should the Red Crests be too troublesome. The Pendragon was confident his defenses were secure.

It stormed during the night, but the war host slept secure in their horsehide tents, and on the morrow the dark, low-hanging clouds dispersed with break of day. Before they had finished their morning bowls of barley meal stirabout, the bulk of the Silurian supplies arrived, and the warriors took their places.

"Let you have good hunting."

"Good hunting, my brother."

The warriors wished one another well in the coming battle. Across the river the Romans massed, looking like a red and gold sea as the morning sun struck their bronze helmets.

Now was the moment for which Joseph had prepared. From the bottom of his pouch he brought the wooden standard on which Mary had worked most of the night before they left Caer Leo. Holding out the smooth plank with the simple shape of a fish burned in it, he approached Arviragus. "Your majesty, as a symbol of the new faith that has come to your people, I have an ensign that identifies Followers of the Way. May the Lord be with you today in battle."

Arviragus nodded with brief courtesy and, somewhat absently, directed his driver to lash the standard to a pole at the back of his chariot before turning to weightier matters.

The war host waited, chariot horses stamping in their traces—heron, plover, and eagle feathers riffling around the collars of the burnished throw-spear each warrior carried. As Caradoc had predicted, the legionnaires apparently refused to go into the water. But from their hillside position behind the stone ramparts, the Britons could see that there was activity among the enemy. The situation could change at any moment. It would not do for Caradoc to let his troops relax. Arviragus turned to his warriors and shouted, "Courage, men of Silure! Hold to your bold spirit! There shall be none fearing among us today. None shall ever say that the Silurians quailed in battle!"

At each shout from their king, the warriors shouted an answering reply and beat their shields with their swords and spears in an outburst that must have rung in the ears of the Romans across the water. Arviragus went from rank to rank of his men, kindling their spirit.

And Caradoc was everywhere in the field, the sun glowing like fire on his huge, dragon-shaped, red-enameled war brooch, and glinting from the horns of his bronze helmet. He flew from one side of the field to the other, shouting, "This day and this battle shall be the securing of our freedom or our everlasting bondage!"

The warriors brandished their spears and held their shields high so that the new-risen sun glinted off them fiercely as the men shouted, "Freedom!"

"Remember your forefathers and my ancestor Tasciovanus, whose valor won the driving back of the dictator Caesar!"

"Freedom!" came the answering shout.

"Remember your forefathers, by whose valor we have known living free from Roman axe and Roman tribute!"

"Freedom!"

"Remember your forefathers whose valor served for preserving the persons of our wives and our children!"

"Freedom!"

"Men, I call upon your valor for shrinking from neither weapons nor wounds!"

And again the affirmation. "Freedom!"

Across the river, the Roman general seemed confounded by such enthusiasm from the masses of fighting men with the frowning hilltops at their backs and the rushing river at their feet. A movement of red and gold made it appear that the Romans would turn back, perhaps to await the building of a bridge, as Caradoc had predicted.

But then the cheers died in the waiting Britons' throats as a surge from the rear brought an auxiliary of warriors in crude, brown leather armor to the front. Without a pause they approached the riverbank and continued their advance. The Britons watched in amazement as these armor-clad warriors from Germania dove into the turbulent water and swam across, holding swords and axes above their heads, looking as though the very rocks were swimming.

It was now not the sacred ox horn that blew across the valleys of Britain, but the sharper, more alarming cry of the long-tubed, bronze battle trumpets, calling forth the splendid ferocity of the Celtic heroes. They shrieked in one long, sharp blast that tore equally at the deep-clinging roots and the top-most branches of the trees and sent the birds fluttering for cover.

Caradoc shouted orders to his men in the face of the unexpected. As the Germans swarmed up the steep bank, they were met by a barrage of spears and missiles, driving them back. A shout went up from the Pendragon's forces as the front-line warriors prepared for another spear attack. At first the casualties were heavy among the auxiliaries, but then they formed the testudo taught them by their Roman commanders and the square of overlapping shields provided protection for the advance of the Roman eagle. They drove forward up the hill, over the bodies of their fallen comrades.

"*Y Gwir erbyn y Byd!*" Bran, his three-rayed headband glinting in the sun, led the Britons in their traditional battle cry, "The Truth against the World!" Others of the priestkind took up the chant. "*Y Gwir erbyn y Byd!*"

And another shower of spears hailed down on the attackers.

In the melee, Joseph could not tell who was winning, but whenever he glimpsed the sturdy standard with its boldly forged fish standing strong in

Arviragus's chariot, his faith was renewed and fears put to rest. Until the next assault came from the enemy.

When darkness fell, the matter was still undecided. The Britons withdrew behind their ramparts to bind their wounds, the healer-priests doing their work with pots of herbal salve. And below the hill, the death fires burned for the Red Crests and their kind that would be needing no healing salves. And on both sides of the riverbank the men of the eagles camped for the night.

But the next morning, matters took a perilous turn. While the Pendragon's men were still at their cookpots, the Roman general Vespasian located a ford higher up the river. Now the entire legion surged red and gold toward the hill-fort. The testudo was unstoppable. Now the stone ramparts fell as wave after wave of Roman soldiers swarmed the hill.

Abandoning the fortifications, the Britons took to the field for their favorite style of chariot warfare. While the first of the Romans to arrive were held at bay by mounted cavalry, the Celtic warriors, their nearly naked bodies painted blue with woad, raced breakneck over the field, passing each other within inches, shouting ferociously, and beating their spears on their shields.

These were men used to fighting as a game or as sport intended to defend their valor and the valor of the tribe. Rather than a killing machine, war was a show to frighten other tribes from their hunting-runs and discourage horse stealing. But suddenly, the nature of the game had taken a deadly turn. The Roman eagles were not here for sport, and they would not be frightened. Now the chariot line of the Pendragon must defeat the foreign invader or live forever as his slaves. This knowledge added a fire to their driving, a ferocity to their war cries, and a power to the thrust of their weapons. And Coillus, fierce at the front of the battle line, was most intensely aware of the urgency of the outcome.

At a signal from the Pendragon, the chariots spun as one and raced toward their own cavalry. At the last moment, the line of horsemen parted with a growling shout, and the chariots charged headlong into the sea of Red Crests. Coillus flung his first spear as soon as the enemy came into range. The Red Crest went down, leaving a momentary gap in the Roman square, but before a second spear could make its way, the gap was closed with another Red Crest and the bronze-shielded square moved forward like a huge armored animal.

The two fighting hosts came full together with a great shouting of men, a ringing crash of weapons, and a screaming chaos of horses. As soon as his throw-spears were depleted, Coillus leaped from his chariot, his sword slashing with the ferocity of a wildcat. His driver, Edlo, withdrew to the sidelines, as others did when their warriors leaped into the fray, but he never took his eyes from the surge where his master fought. He was ready to dart in at any moment Coillus needed to retreat. Coillus pushed forward, and on every side of him woad-painted foot-fighters swarmed, their daggers reddened to the hilt.

But with every fall of a Red Crest, it seemed as if two sprang up to take his place, as the orderly Romans pushed against the furious frenzy of the Pendragon's war host. Coillus felt his eyes burn with the strain of seeking a chink in the wall of Roman shields. The instant he spotted one, he plunged in his sword, then dragged it out again, dripping red, before the foe crumpled.

At last the Roman host within the square had spent the last of their pilums, as Coillus and his fellows had long since their throw-spears, and the square broke for hand-to-hand sword fighting. This was a battle the war host understood. Most had been skilled swordsmen since before they even entered the Boy's House for their warrior training. The Celts fought back-to-back, covering their front sides with their bronze shields and slashing ever forward with their double-whetted blades until the hills shook with the clang of metal. And Coillus, as many of the others, made an equally ferocious weapon of his shield, jabbing with the heavy pointed bronze boss in the center.

And as always, for each one Coillus knocked down, two sprang up to take his place. Coillus felt his sword arm tire and knew his blade thrust had slowed ever so slightly. If he were not alert, that minute edge would be enough for the enemy. Then the warrior fighting at Coillus's back took a sword in the chest, and with the cry of a wounded animal, crumpled at Coillus's feet, leaving his back exposed.

Coillus whirled to meet the attack of the Red Crest who had felled his companion. In the whirl, he knocked the Roman's sword aside with his shield, and a quick sword thrust avenged his fallen companion, leaving the Roman to die with a surprised look on his face.

But Coillus was not quick enough in his return whirl to meet the enemy at his now-exposed back. He felt the blade cut on his shoulder like a searing iron, but numbness did not come until he had made a return thrust that dispatched the Red Crest.

And then Edlo was there, pulling him onto his chariot and racing from the field, the chariot wheels lurching over red-crested and blue-painted bodies alike and coming up red on each turn.

At the edge of the field, Bran, his robe of many colors mottled a reddish brown with blood, turned from the warrior he had just bandaged to examine his king's son. "It is deep, but a clean cut. If the wound-fever is not setting in, you shall fight many more such battles."

Coillus grimaced as the herbs in Bran's black salve fueled the fire in the cut to blaze anew. "It is not another battle I am needed for, but this one," he ground out through clenched teeth and struggled to rise.

Bran pushed him back down. "Your spear-companions continue. And the mountain shadows fall. Already the sun no longer gleams on the cursed eagle standards. I am thinking Roman war bellies grow as empty as British for their stewpots." He completed the bandaging with a final tug at the knot. "Now get you to the camp, and see that you go easily. Enough blood has been spilled today without you jarring more out of yourself."

Coillus smiled weakly and accepted Edlo's help.

The host that gathered around the cook fires that night was far smaller than the one that had eaten stirabout together that morning. Their only consolation was that the Red Crest loss had been even heavier. But the thing that would not bear speaking of was the knowledge that, while their own host could be numbered, the Red Crest flood was limitless.

On the third day it was clear that the Romans could have easily defeated the remnant of the Britannic war host and declared victory for the emperor. But to everyone's amazement, they did not strike. The Romans bore their dead from the field on their shields, and the Britons did likewise, with the death fires burning on both sides of the broken chariots and fallen horses that lay amongst the bracken of the field. Bran and Joseph oversaw the work and together shared the task of saying the Prayer for the Deceased over each pyre. "O God, full of compassion, who dwells on high, grant true rest . . . May the All-Merciful One shelter him with the cover of His wings forever, and bind his soul in the bond of life. The Lord be his heritage; may he rest in his resting-place in peace; and let us say, amen."

And although for all of his life Joseph had shunned the touching of dead bodies as an unclean act that would defile him before God and require ritual purification, he now fought his instincts with the knowledge that the new covenant of Christ had changed all that. So now to demonstrate the love of God whose messenger he was, he endeavored to tend the dead bodies with the same love with which he had attended the body of his Lord.

All day the British guards kept watch for the least sign of movement in the Roman camp, but there was none. "They are seeming to wait for something," a guard reported to Caradoc. But it was hard to see what they could be waiting for. Although the British warriors had given casualty for casualty, perhaps better, their spies reported that the battle had taken little toll of the nearly twenty thousand men in the four legions under Aulus Plautius's command. It was likewise obvious from the well-ordered camp across the field that the Romans lacked nothing in supplies. Why then the delay? And yet they waited.

Two days later the answer came with a messenger who had been keeping watch above the white chalk cliffs by the Great Water. "Three galleys from Gaul. It is said the Emperor Claudius himself is bringing reinforcements, but I did not stay to see."

That night Arviragus and the Pendragon went among their warriors, encouraging them by making light of their fears, kindling their hopes, and inspiring them to the heroic valor they so prized. And later, in the king's tent, Lubrin, who had never left Arviragus's side during the battle—for a bard must be with his king so he can compose harpsongs to honor the courage of the people and their leader after the battle—sang a ballad of daring fortitude that stiffened the determination of all who heard it.

But later, leaving the king's tent in search of the solitude he so needed but found in short supply in a war camp, Joseph came upon a sight that pierced his heart as deeply as if a Roman pilum had found its mark. In a grove of trees to the side of the camp, three of the old priests who had chosen not to be baptized into the new Way with their archdruid sat around an improvised stone altar. Joseph watched as, to the accompaniment of a low, mesmeric chant, the first priest slit his own thumb with the point of a dagger and mixed his blood with the barley meal on the altar, then handed the dagger to the next. And the ritual continued around the circle in a sun pattern.

The oldest among them spoke in a high, singsong chant that a short distance away could have been mistaken for the crying of the wind.

O Lugh of the Long Hand,
O Lugh of the Shining Spear,
We call the Sun God Lugh,
We call the High God Lugh,
We call the War God Lugh,
God of our people from time unto time,
Accept our offering
Bring enemy blood to our warriors' spears.

The blood-drawing complete, the priests stood and moved sun-wise around the altar, their arms swaying over their heads while the old one repeated his invocation.

Joseph turned away with a sick heart to seek Bran, whom he found just leaving the king's tent. Joseph described the scene he had witnessed. At first he thought Bran's displeasure was with the old priests and offered to go with him to cleanse the grove, thinking of how his Lord had chased the moneychangers from the temple. But then he realized Bran was angry with him.

"It is forbidden for any to watch the druid at his sacred rites. None may even read of them. For this protection the priestkind studies many years and carries his wisdom in his head that none of it need be written down and will remain inviolate."

"But that is of the past. You, Bran the Blessed, have found the new Way, the way of peace and joy of Jehovah. You know there is no power in sacrificing to false gods."

Bran placed a hand on Joseph's shoulder and walked him toward the sleeping place. "Forgive my heated speaking, Joseph, brother. You speak truth. I have found the new Way. But many among us have not. Our king has not declared for the Three-in-One God—so the tribe did not change. Many among them are thinking that their archdruid has taken a strange notion into his head, but that one so exalted can be forgiven his strangeness. It will be long and long before such change is complete, and the old ways are left behind, Joseph of the Loving Word."

That night when Joseph rolled into his bearskin rug, he knew that the Romans were not the only ones engaged in a battle for this land, and he knew that his would be the longer in the waging.

At the next dawning, before the morning oat cakes were eaten, it was clear to the Pendragon's host that the messenger had been accurate. The emperor's arrival was announced by the magnificent pavilion raised for him across the field with his personal standard flying above. And before the Roman camp, it looked more as if the legionnaires had been called to parade for military inspection than to prepare for battle, as trumpets blared and the troops marched in rows beneath their eagles. To those watching across the distance of the battlefield, it appeared that the commander for the day was not Aulus Plautius, whose rugged form had become familiar, but rather a large man with a shocking white thatch of hair who limped when he walked. The rumor went around that—hard as it was to believe—this was the emperor.

Surveying the host assembling before them, Joseph sought for courage and found it in the thought of the many times the Lord God had led Israel to victory over a much more powerful enemy—of Barak defeating Sisera with his nine hundred iron chariots, of Joshua winning the battle of Jericho, of David slaying the Philistines. With renewed hope he prayed in the words of King David:

Rise up, Lord; save us, O my God.
Strike our foes across the face
And break the teeth of the wicked.
Yours is the victory, O Lord,
And may Your blessing rest upon Your people.
I will praise You, O Lord, with all my heart,
I will rejoice and exult in You,
I will praise Your name in psalms, O Most High,
when my enemies turn back,
When they fall headlong and perish at Your appearing;
So may the Lord be a tower of strength for the oppressed,
A tower of strength in time of need.
That those who acknowledge Your name may trust in You;
For You, Lord, do not forsake those who seek You.

But Joseph realized that few of these people did seek the Lord God. The old priest's cry to the host was a blow to his ears and heart alike, "Lugh of the Shining Spear grant a good war trail to you!"

Caradoc ordered his warriors to mount in readiness. This was clearly to be the decisive battle—today would bring freedom or bondage. Arviragus chose a battle chariot armed with hooks and scythes, and Bran invited Joseph to join him in the king's flame-red chariot still bearing its engraved fish standard as firmly as any legionnaire carried his eagle.

"*Y Gwir erbyn y Byd!*"

"The Truth against the World!"

"Freedom!"

The warriors shouted in response to the druid's call to each rank. If Plautius hoped to wage a battle of nerves by his strange tactics across the field, it was clear that the maneuver would not break the Britons' courage.

At last the Romans started forward in squares. With a shout that showed the warriors' pent-up excitement, the host of charioteers raced forward. Before the testudo could break into its fighting position, the war band hurled their throw-spears into the center of the squares, so that the Romans were forced to hold their shields over their heads, thereby leaving their bodies open to attack from foot soldiers' sword thrusts.

The ferocity of the Celtic attack drove the Romans backward, and a great cheer went up from the British ranks, who then pushed forward with greater momentum. It seemed to Joseph, watching from a nearby hillock with Bran, that their warriors would soon overrun the emperor's pavilion. After two near defeats, the final victory seemed within their reach.

The Roman squares parted as if they would retreat, and another victory shout rang from the Celtic side. Then, without warning and for no apparent reason, mass confusion broke out among the British charioteers. Joseph first saw a warrior running along the traces of his team's yoke to gain an advantage of height thrown to the ground when his horses reared and swerved unexpectedly. Then all across the field, chariot horses and cavalry bolted in like frenzy.

In a moment, the chariot field lost all pattern and broke into a swirling mass of confusion. The chariots careened and circled, wheel locked in wheel, while drivers fought for control and off-balance warriors strove to find space to aim throw-spears at Red Crests. Cavalry horses likewise went berserk, throwing their warriors and running riderless among the chariots, causing added confusion and death among the Pendragon's host. The foot-fighters hung on the fringes of the battle, driving in a valiant thrust wherever a space opened up, brandishing swords and daggers red to the hilt. But with their horses running rampant, the war host could make no progress against the enemy.

And then Joseph, on his hillock, saw the reason. From behind the Roman camp, six enormous gray elephants lumbered toward the battlefield. These were the reinforcements Claudius had brought to Britannia, these the cause of the pandemonium. It was not the strange sight of these giant creatures with their flapping ears and swaying trunks that terrified the superbly trained British war horses—but the scent.

The odor reached the horses in waves as the elephants trudged inexorably forward. When the smell hit them, the horses tossed their heads in the air, nostrils flaring. They stamped and shook their heads, and at the second scent, went out of control. The final moment came when the largest elephant, near the center of the field, stopped, raised his trunk, and bellowed a trumpeting noise that shook the hills, followed by a volley of Roman pilums thrown into the center of the tumult.

The Pendragon's host poured from the field in disarray through the gaps in their foot-fighters—chariots with only one man in them, chariots with driver and warrior both slumped on their leather floors, chariots dragged askew by one wild-eyed horse whose yoke-mate had fallen and been cut free.

Claudius's elephants had conquered Britannia.

To elude capture, the Britons melted into the forested hills, following sunken drove roads, tunnelled forest tracks, and winding fen waterways back to their homes. That night Joseph camped with Arviragus and several Silurian warriors some miles west of the scene of their humiliation. For hours they had traveled under the cover of night as swiftly and quietly as possible, knowing that the final ignominy would be neither defeat nor death, but capture as a Roman slave.

Finally stopped by exhaustion and rolled in a bearskin beneath a thickly boughed tree which hid the cloudy sky, Joseph relived the events of the past days. What would Arviragus say now? Would he blame the lost battle on the new faith Joseph had brought to his people? Would the king say he would have done better had he carried a sacred oak leaf into battle rather than the fish of the new Way? Would Joseph and his band now be told to leave Britain and all they had accomplished be lost?

Now, at the low point in the life of these people and perhaps of his own, Joseph knew that, more than ever before, he wanted to stay in this land. Even in the face of Roman tyranny, he wanted to carry forth his mission to spread the light of faith here. And more than ever, after witnessing the chaos of battle, Joseph yearned for the peace he had so long sought and thought he had found at last. More than anything, he longed to be back on Ynis Witrin, drinking from its crystal well, tending their Ebenezer thorn tree, and teaching the way of light and peace. Now when it was lost, he realized the value of what he had so nearly possessed.

Even Heaven seemed silent to his prayers. He listened long into the night for the voice within that promised, "I am with you." But tonight the voice of promise was silent. He could only grope for his faith in a God who had promised, "As I have been, so shall I be."

Many days on end the rain came down, and the mists rose so thickly they could see the path only one footfall ahead. At night they rolled in their fur rugs, those with shields remaining to them putting them on top for cover rather than under their heads for a pillow.

And without fail, every morning on this journey of retreat and defeat, just as he had on every morning of the outward journey of advance and hope, Joseph prayed the Prayer of Travelers: "May it be Your will, Lord our God and God of our fathers, to lead us in peace and direct our steps in peace . . ." If only God was hearing him.

With the exhaustion of battle and the need to avoid the main routes where Romans might already be posted to take captives, they were many days following the ancient, secret ways back to Caer Leo. And across the garth, ripe unto harvest but now with far fewer young men of the truath to aid in the ingathering, and from along the wooded riverbank, now red and gold in the fall-of-the-leaf, the mourning keen of the women was borne to the sick, the wounded, and the dispirited as they made their dragging way to the royal dun. And when they arrived within the compound, the mood of their welcome told them even more loudly than the mourning wail that defeat had overwhelmed the dun.

Arviragus, battle-scarred, face lined with weariness and the grime of travel, gave a grim greeting to Coillus who had arrived before him with Bran and Lubrin. The king ordered an assembly in the Great Hall. Mary threw her arms around her father in welcome and greeted him with the good news that Salome seemed fully recovered and Elisabeth Britannia grew every day. And Joseph saw by the light in the newlyweds' eyes that all had gone well in the marriage hut. But everywhere else, the sad faces and hollow eyes of these normally jubilant people spoke of loss. Word had spread that Caradoc's brother, Togomundus, King of the Trinovantes, had been killed. No one knew if Caradoc remained free, and his daughters' quiet, tense dignity was perhaps the hardest of all to bear.

But when Arviragus had washed and drunk deeply of the sourly refreshing barley beer and joined his family and priests assembled in the hall, it was not of war that he wished to talk. The king looked first at Bran and his druids, then at Joseph and the Judean band. "Joseph of the Stout Heart, valor is the quality most prized by our people, and you have shared this in the going to war and the encouraging of our warriors side by side with our archdruid and priests. In this sharing, as in the marriage of our families, our people are one. Your Jehovah did not choose to give us victory, but neither did Lugh of the Shining Spear. So be the ways of the gods.

"Now we must look to the future. There are three things a king must have in a well-peopled land—men of war, men of work, and men of prayer. You have come to us as a man of prayer.

"We welcome you to stay among us and teach more of your ways to those who are wishing to hear. And since there are three persons who have a right of public maintenance—the old, the babe, and the foreigner who cannot speak the Brythonic tongue, we will grant you a charter of land. You are coming to us a band of twelve, so you will have the granting of twelve hides of land. As a hide is reckoned the amount of land needed to support a person, you may be living in comfort." He turned to Balan. "Balan has suggested that this land be located on Ynis Witrin. It is to be of our most ancient holy ground—the Avalon which was sacred to the little dark people when the world was new before our people came here."

Joseph tried to speak, but his heart was so full no words came out. He bowed his head in gratitude—gratitude to the King of the Silures for his generosity and gratitude to the King of Heaven who had been faithful as He had promised. To the Holy One of Israel—His Friend and Father who, in this deep hour of defeat, had granted victory.

"May the sun and the moon shine on your path, Joseph Light-bringer. And may your God grant you a living free of the grasping hand of Rome," Arviragus concluded with weariness in his voice.

7

All the band felt a heart-singing gladness to be back on Ynis Witrin. They had been gone for a number of months, but so much had happened it seemed like years. None was happier to be back than Joanna, who dropped her bundles at the guest lodge in the lake village and fairly ran the rest of the way up Wearyall Hill to her thorn tree. And Joseph wasn't far behind her. The shoot, which hadn't been above the span of a man's hand when they planted it, was now triple that.

"Every day I prayed for gentle rains and warm sunshine for it," Joanna said. "The Lord has been gracious."

And indeed all through the leaf-falling time and the months of darkening days and sleeping earth, the little band on the Glass Isle became ever more conscious of how gracious God was. On this quiet, sheltered island, all was at peace. It seemed to Joseph, with his love of beauty and silence, that he had found here an answering call from some inherited memory of pre-Fall Eden. At times, especially when the spring-of-the-bud came with a waking earth and he was sitting in the garden by the well, walking the terraced slopes of the Tor, or surveying his group's twelve hides of land, it was as if he could catch a glimmer of what it must have been like before sin entered the world—and an ephemeral glimpse of Heaven to come. The impression was always as fleeting as a butterfly flitting across the landscape, but it left Joseph with an unspeakable sense of longing for something he couldn't express.

And across the twelve hides, the little band began to build their homes. Before they built, Joseph thought long and carefully about the style in which they should live. In the king's compound at Caer Leo, the unmarried men and women slept in separate lodges on their own sides of the compound, with families occupying smaller round huts. Members of the royal family had larger versions with such amenities as wooden doors rather than leather aprons over the doorplace. In the lake village all but the chief lived in small wattle and daub huts, circular structures with a central hearth, the smoke exiting through holes in the thatched roofs. Every part of family life was carried on in that one room around the fire where the cookpot simmered while the wife worked at her upright loom, the husband polished his shield and furbished his hunting spear, and the children played on the floor. After the family ate their evening stew and oat cake, the children would nod, and their parents would lay them on their fur pallets on one side of the hut before retiring to their own bedplace on the other. It was warm and cozy, woven into the natural rhythm of life as lived by these people for hundreds and hundreds of years.

But it was entirely contrary to the formal, highly regulated life of a proper Jewish family with their carefully scrubbed and whitewashed rooms. Although Followers of the Way no longer believed their salvation depended on the ritual washings demanded by the Law of Moses, they still liked to live with the same thorough cleanliness. Could they ever adjust to living in a hut of woven sticks plastered with mud?

It was not a decision for Joseph to make alone—it must be decided by the group because each one would be affected. In the end, it was Joanna who spoke for them all. After Joseph had put the question to them as they sat by the bubbling waters of the well watching the sun sink gently into a pink western sky, this woman who had always put the needs and wishes of others before her own said, "Did not Bran accept the faith in part because we accepted his people and their ways? How can we minister to the people of the lake and others who come to us if we live in a manner that says their ways are not good enough for us?"

Mary nodded and added, "And I'd like to have some gowns of heavier British fabric. The things I brought with me are far too cool for this climate." The other women agreed.

"Yes." Lazarus spoke for his family. "The round hut is really a very practical design for this northern climate—there are no cold dark corners or rooms left unheated as there would be if we built Judean-style homes."

Mary gave a soft chuckle. "I can't imagine what one would do here with a sun roof such as we enjoyed at home on hot evenings. Perhaps use it for bathing in the rain, but certainly not for sleeping, if the weather continues as it has."

"Judging from the thickness of the vegetation, I'd guess we can expect more rain, rather than less," Cleon said.

Salome looked up from the sleeping baby in her arms. "But might we have real doors with hewn lintels like in Arviragus's hall, rather than deerskin door-flaps? It would be much snugger for the little one."

Lazarus looked at his wife and child with softly smiling eyes, and Joseph nodded.

And so it was decided. The Judean band began building sturdy round homes of the wattle and daub design. The lake village people taught them how to drive the support poles deep into the earth, then to weave the framework of supple reeds from the river in and out over the poles, so tightly fit together that it almost seemed the over-plastering of clay from the lake bed would be unnecessary. Then the houses were snugly roofed with thick, cone-shaped thatch, leaving only a hole in the center for smoke from the fireplace to escape.

But only on Ynis Witrin did such domestic tranquility reign, for throughout the larger island beyond the Glass Isle, the fighting went on. For long spells of quiet the throw-spears and chariots would be calm, like the long grass of the grazing garth when the breeze had stilled, and then it would flare up in some new place or in many places at once as the people of the Pendragon drove thrust after thrust against the red and bronze invader that would rule their land. And as word of the frenzy of war and tumult in the world around them reached the Judeans' isolated garden, it seemed even more of a paradise, a place set apart.

After the Pendragon's stunning defeat, Claudius himself had led the twentieth legion into Dun Camulus which had formerly been the capitol of Caradoc's brother Togomundus. The Romans put the members of the royal family there under house arrest, occupied the slain king's fort, and renamed it Camulodunum with the planting of the Roman eagle. Claudius and his elephants then sailed back to Rome where he received a Triumph and a new title—Britannicus. But Caradoc, in hiding in the western hills, waited.

And the war continued. The ninth legion swept northward to the land of the blue war shields, the Brigantes. There King Venitius and his Queen Cartimandua signed a treaty with the Red Crests. And Caradoc waited.

The second legion, the Augusta, rolled southward over the land of the Atrebates, then turned westward, but stopped before they engaged the Dumnoni. Still Caradoc waited.

Then the fourteenth, Legio Gemina, marched, seemingly straight toward Ynis Witrin. Daily messengers would gallop near the island and send a runner from some nearby farmstead to the island with news while the messenger sped on to Caer Leo with his report of the Roman advance. Caradoc waited.

But Joseph did more than wait. Every day he prayed. Gathering his band of believers, now including some from the village, and Balan and those from the cors who had accepted the new faith, Joseph led in prayers for God's protection on this land and His will for the people. And always he ended, as Jesus had taught His followers, "For Yours is the Kingdom and the power, and the glory, forever. Amen."

At the same time, Tarana and a faction of priests who remained with the old ways scoffed at the idea of relying on prayers to only one God. Nightly, by the light of Epona moon goddess when she shone in the fullness of her white glory, or in midday when Lugh the Sun God sent his shining spears flying to earth from his long hand, the priests gathered in the sacred grove for the rituals and incantations of the ancients. Tarana spoke always of love for his people as he gathered his followers, and yet his insistence that he be obeyed unquestioningly made the love appear to be more for his own self-centered way.

One day, after the second burning of the Beltine fires since the coming of the Red Crests, Joseph was making his way toward the well when the sound of chanting stopped him. Watching from a distance, he saw Tarana and his fellows wearing the white robes of a religious service coming in a procession through the dark green yew trees that lined the approach to the well. Joseph had from the first noted the pleasing symmetry of their planting, but had not considered that his favorite spot for praying to Jehovah might also have been a place used by the old ones to invoke their gods, even though he had learned that natural springs were considered places of deep magic long before the coming of the Celts.

When they reached the spot where the water bubbled up crystal-clear from the green hillside to flow downward over its red-stained rockway, the priests formed a circle around the pool, each druid holding a sacred object. The two nearest Tarana, which Joseph recognized as the Redbeard's sons Myfyr and Morganwg, waved sprigs of mistletoe and branches of oak leaves over their heads in a rhythm with the continuing chant. The two behind them carried sacrifices, one a small animal with its entrails removed—undoubtedly on the altar back in the oak grove—and the other a tray of barley meal mixed with blood. The last in the line was Tarana's druidess wife, bearing the golden sickle in both hands.

But the object Tarana held in his hands, raising it up and down, inward and outward in an intricate weaving motion, was something Joseph had not seen before. It appeared to be a small, round, pock-marked apple.

The scene brought pain to Joseph's heart. That so much energy and faith should go into a false worship when the true God had been proclaimed to them, that they should shut their hearts and turn their backs on the truth—they who were sworn to defend the truth against the world, that they would be leading others to turn from God Almighty and take their guidance from the entrails of slain animals rather than His Word.

But Joseph knew an even greater sorrow—that no matter how much he hurt, his pain could never match the agony Christ suffered on the cross for the souls of these people who were rejecting Him.

Joseph tried to pray, but his very prayers seemed to be blocked by the spirits Tarana and his priests were summoning. With a heart so heavy he could hardly bear it, Joseph turned to go, to find a place of clean air where he could breathe and feel the Holy Spirit breathing in him. But as he turned, he heard Tarana's voice calling his name. Then he realized what in his agony of spirit he had not noticed earlier. The druid chant had ended, and the priests were leaving as they had come. Tarana alone remained behind.

"There is no need for you to go, Joseph of the One God. The processional rites are not forbidden to observers—although I am doubting that such would matter to one who despises our ways." The druid was coldly regal.

Joseph moved uphill along the stream toward Tarana. "You are wrong, Tarana. I do not despise your ways. As I have told you many times, I bring you fulfillment, not rejection. My own people have changed their ways in accepting God's new covenant; so may you, as Balan and others have. A change for the better, an adoption of new truth, is not an abandonment. Christ Himself declared that He came to fulfill the Law, not to destroy it."

Tarana's voice was icily controlled. "And yet you would have us abandon the ways of our fathers, no matter what you call it. I have pledged to work without ceasing to pass our wisdom on to my sons that they may do so to their sons as well. It must not be lost—it is a great wealth of learning we possess—the heritage of our people. It must not be lost!" His voice rose to a frenzied pitch, abandoning its earlier control. Joseph felt that such agitation bespoke hidden motives, but he knew this was not the time to confront Tarana.

"The object you carry—it is of long tradition?" Joseph asked.

Tarana's voice calmed a little. "This is the Anguinum—the druid egg of strong magic. It will bring success and favor to our people."

"Is it truly an egg?"

Again the druid's voice rose in pitch. "Of greater and greater power than any mere egg, the Anguinum is formed of the spittle of angry snakes. And it will bring us not only power over the Romans, Joseph Tradition-breaker, it will bring us power over you. I will be fighting you, you and your kind, as the Pendragon will be fighting the Red Crests. Our ways will not be lost! Lugh will be supreme over your Three-in-One. There is a reason the god of three faces was unnamed—he was not worth naming, and Yesu was ever a minor godling—so shall he stay."

Now Tarana was screaming, his face as red as his beard. "The old ways will not die! They will not die!" For a moment the frenzied druid made Joseph think of a writhing snake—the pit of hissing snakes whose spittle had formed the egg Tarana held above his head. But then the image vanished, leaving in its stead a feeling of immense weight. Tarana spun on his heel and, brandishing the egg like a weapon, raced up the hill.

Joseph stood until the wild figure disappeared beyond the yew trees. His own heavy, rapid breathing showed the turmoil in his spirit. Could the true light he bore penetrate this darkness? Joseph believed with all his heart that God's love was the most powerful force in the universe, and yet it could be resisted. The priest could choose for himself, but what of the others he would lead into the darkness? Would Logres, the true, the spiritual B'rith ain, be forced to live in the shadow land of half-truths? He thought of the three-rod druid symbol of God in the priest's headdress, which Bran had explained to him represented the true Logos. Surely, if Jehovah had so prepared these people through the symbols of their ancient ways to receive His new Way, there would be victory.

As those on Ynis Witrin were using this threshold time in their own way, so Caradoc in the green hills to the west was also doing more than waiting. He trained his warriors in a new style of fighting as they forged and sharpened fresh spear heads, cut strong white alderwood branches to fashion the straightest of spear handles, and hunted heron in the marshes to furbish their war spears with the long, slender feather collars that insured true flight.

The Ordovice warriors joined the Silurians and the remnant of Trinovantes. They hid out in forests, marshes, and deep-creviced valleys, striking at the Roman garrisons at will, wreaking havoc among the emperor's orderly troops, then fading again into the hills.

"He is hoping to wear out the invaders, so that, as in the days of our forefathers, they will sail back, leaving us at peace within our borders," Arviragus explained to Joseph on one of the latter's frequent visits to Caer Leo.

"My fierce cousin has gained his title among these would-be enslavers. They are calling him 'The Scourge of the Romans.'"

And for a while it seemed that Caradoc's tactics might be successful. The Romans moved a garrison of the fourteenth as far west as Mor Hafren, but there they stopped. No land was taken by the Romans without a battle. The Roman Senate appointed Aulus Plautius Governor of Britain, but still he had to subdue the land he would rule.

On a warm day in high summer, Joseph accompanied Josephes and Eurgain to the royal dun where Eurgain was delighted to be with her sister Gladys again.

At first the girls chatted and giggled in the Woman's Place as they had when children. Eurgain teased her sister, who was fast leaving childhood behind her, because she spent all her time writing poetry with their aunt and none with the young men. "When our father returns from his wars and finds none asking you to share his houseplace, he will not be pleased."

"Perhaps if our father hadn't taken all the young men to war with him, I might be finding one to please me," Gladys returned. Then, after a pause, with her eyes sparkling like sunshine on the River Usk, Gladys asked, "What is it like to kiss a man with hair on his chin?"

And although Eurgain intended her reply to be light, it came out with a sharpness that brought a cloud over the sunshine. "What are you about—thinking of kissing men—hair on the chin or no, my little sister?"

With the dimming of their laughter, both girls thought of another disappointment that would await their father. Eurgain put her hand on her still-flat stomach with a worried look. This coming Lugnasad would be the third since her marriage fires burned, and still there was no child.

Gladys dropped her voice. "Let you listen to me. There is a wise woman in the hills. Cetil has told me of her. She knows many charms."

"No." Eurgain was adamant. "Josephes says it is in God's hands. He will bless us in His time. We must be submitting to His will."

Gladys shrugged. "So. But it is in my mind that we could at least ask one of the priests to cast an augur. Not all of them have abandoned the old ways as Bran has. Some nights I slip down to the sacred grove, so I know. There is an old priest who is very fond of my poems. He would read the entrails, and then you would be knowing how long you must wait for your Jehovah's pleasure."

Eurgain shook her head. "I know you are meaning to help, my sister. But Josephes says we are to learn patience. I think that is not a virtue that comes easily to our people—certainly not to the line of Caradoc—but I will wait."

There was no knowing how long they must wait to hear from Jehovah, but an arrival at the Great Hall made it seem that the girls might not have to wait long to hear from their father.

At first a great alarm had gone through the dun at the announcement that a contingent of Romans approached. The few warriors left to guard the compound flew to their chariots, and old men went to the weapons kist for swords in need of sharpening. But before the battle horns could be sounded, the farthest guard saw that, in the way of Celts seeking peace, the Red Crests bore a green willow bough, and sent word back to the dun, "They come in peace." And the hillfort gates were opened to them.

Arviragus was away conferring with the king of the Ordovices about a reported treachery of the Cornovi tribe that bordered both their lands, so it fell to the king's archdruid, assisted by Joseph, to escort the Roman leader into the Great Hall. He announced himself as Aulus Plautius, Governor of Brittanica.

Gladyl, as the highest royal person present, received the Roman with a guest cup full of the finest wine from his homeland and offered him a seat.

Plautius, as most Romans, was shorter than the Celtic men, but heavily built. His close-cropped black hair curled around his tanned forehead, and his dark eyes snapped above his aquiline nose. "I seek your 'king.' We have had enough of this senseless killing. If he will sign a treaty with Rome as Venutius of the Brigantes and Verica of the Atrebates have done, the emperor will be generous. Arviragus will be allowed to keep his title and his home as the others have."

Joseph thought it more likely that the governor was there to try to ferret out Caradoc's whereabouts than to sign a peace treaty, but there was no danger of betrayal. No one knew where Caradoc was.

Gladyl answered Plautius, and it was a great amusement to the onlookers to see the amazement in his face when she spoke to him fluently in his own tongue. Plautius was obviously having trouble coming to terms with the fact that the people he had conquered were not savages cowering at the edge of the world. "I know nothing of political affairs, sir. But you may remain at Caer Leo as my guest until my brother returns in a while and a while. I fear you must be making do with my company." Gladyl refilled Plautius's cup and saw to it that his men were served and offered water for washing.

Out of desperation for some way to fill the time, Gladyl turned the conversation to the only common ground she could hope to find between them. "I know little of Rome or Roman ways, but I know of your poets."

Again the Roman general-made-governor choked in surprise. "Yes?" He coughed. "Yes, indeed, we have many. Have you, er—" It was obvious he was searching for a tactful way to put his question. "Er, have you had opportunity to read any of them?"

"Very little, I fear. Roman manuscripts are not a likely commodity for a trading merchant to carry. There is a manuscript of Virgil's *Aeneid* at the cors at Mon, however, and I have had the reading of some of it."

"Ah, my favorite as a boy!" Plautius smiled in honest pleasure.

"And do you also remember *The Messiah?*" she asked. Plautius nodded. "That is my favorite," she continued. "It has been long and long since I read it, but perhaps I can recall a little: 'A golden progeny from heaven descends . . .' oh, I have forgotten—something about the child's birth—but the lines I loved are: 'The jarring nations he in peace shall bind, and with paternal virtues rule mankind.'" She was silent, hoping he might take her subtle reproof of his "jarring nation," but the guest made no reply. She could think of nothing further to say, but to offer to read him some of her own poetry.

As the sun grew high in the sky and then began its descent, Gladyl began to despair of her ability to entertain their visitor. In case his talk of peace was a sham, she felt it best to keep him within the confines of the Great Hall, rather than let him wander around the dun where he could see their meager defenses. So it was with a sigh of relief that she at last heard the arrival of horses' hooves in the forecourt, accompanied by a shout that she recognized as her brother's.

To everyone's surprise, the leaders did agree on a truce, and Joseph was able to return once again to Ynis Witrin with renewed hope that the people of his adopted land would have external peace to match the internal peace he had come to proclaim.

Through Lugnasad and Samain the truce held, and there was no word of fighting in the land.

And on the twelve hides the building of homes, begun so long ago but continually interrupted by hunting and harvesting as well as by the alarms of war and the greater duty of telling the good news they had come to share, progressed slowly. Eutropius and Sidonius each moved from the guest quarters in the lake village to his own houseplace. Then all building ceased again while everyone, including the newcomers to the community, helped in planting the early wheat that had so amazed the invaders. They reported back to Rome that Britannia reaped two harvests of spelt and emmu wheat each year. But before the green shoots showed in the fields or the white blossoms appeared in the apple garth, the truce with Rome ended as Caradoc, The Scourge of Rome, led a new uprising in the lands to the northwest and defeated a Roman garrison.

Perhaps Rome felt a harsher hand was required to subdue these unruly people, for Governor Aulus Plautius was recalled and replaced by Ostorius Scapula. Plautius received an Ovation in Rome, but Scapula was given no triumphal parade in Britain.

And yet peace remained on Ynis Witrin. At last all the homes were finished. Joseph, who had noted with some interest that the family of Ben Esas had seemingly built one more house than required for their needs, finally found fulfillment of one of his fondest hopes.

Joseph was sitting in the garden near the well by which he had chosen to build his house—as much for the beauty of the spot as for the practical consideration of having flowing water handy—when his daughter ran to him.

"Father, it is Lazarus and Cleon. They would speak with you." Her joy, which always seemed to bubble just below the surface, now flowed over.

Joseph had no need for the soul-searching he had had to do before granting his blessing to his son's marriage. "Cleon, son of my oldest friend, I gladly give my daughter to you."

The young man, who had repeatedly in the past months shown himself a stalwart spokesman for the faith as he helped with the teaching, now showed himself a careful suitor. He explained that he had long wished to ask for Mary's hand, but shrank from doing so until he had a home to offer her. Now that he had as fine a one as any on Ynis Witrin, although not what he would have had in Jerusalem, he hoped she would share it with him.

"Have you brought the betrothal ring?" Joseph asked.

Cleon held out a beautifully fashioned gold and silver band. "I bespoke it of a craftsman in the lake village. My heart was hopeful I would not be refused." He and Mary exchanged smiles of shy delight.

Joseph went into his hut and returned in a moment with a cup of wine. Holding it in both hands, he chanted, "Blessed are You, Lord our God, King of the universe, who has sanctified us with Your commandments and commanded us concerning the betrothal. Blessed are You, Lord, who sanctifies Your people."

He held the cup to Cleon, who drank first—then to Mary. Cleon slipped the ring on Mary's finger as she trembled with joy, and he said, "With this ring, you are consecrated to me."

"I think I have always been consecrated to you, Cleon." Mary could hardly speak for happiness. "Jehovah made me for you; I have always known it. But I thought perhaps He forgot to tell you."

Joseph laughed. "Well, at least He told Lazarus and me. We had this settled years ago." And their joyous laughter mingled with the bubbling of the stream by which they stood.

As none of the new buildings was large enough to accommodate all the Judean band along with their friends from the lake village and from the cors, the marriage procession, attended by singers, players of harps and bells, and rejoicing friends, wound from the banks of Meare Pool, across Wearyall Hill by the flourishing thorn tree and stopped at the yew-lined garden beside the well for the marriage ceremony and the feast following. Then Cleon bore his bride across the green valley to the home he had so lovingly built for her.

No one in the company marched with more joy or feasted with more contentment than Mary's friend Anna, who had earlier that day been invited to view the newly completed home of the kind and stalwart Eutropius.

Among the guests at the wedding were also some newcomers, druid priests and students from the great cors on Mon. They had come at Balan's invitation so that Joseph could instruct them in the new Way. Most of the Ynis Witrin druids as well had joined their Deon in learning from Joseph and then teaching the new Way to others. Those who listened with open hearts to Joseph and the teachers found a living Truth, and their faith grew.

But Tarana scoffed unbendingly at the faith and continued sacrifices to Lugh and the old gods and read the entrails of slain animals and the portents from the divining rods in the sacred grove. Mary prayed for the druid, but only the outspoken Josephes would challenge Tarana openly. Whenever the assistant Deon announced an augur or claimed the power of an old god, Josephes was the one to confront him. "Your gods have no more power than the stones on which you make sacrifices to them. Jehovah God said, 'You shall have no other gods before me, and you shall not worship graven images.' Repent, Tarana, or you will be punished for your evil practices."

On one of the few occasions when an augur came true, Josephes faced him before a large group of visiting druids. "That was nothing more than a lucky guess, Tarana. At least we should hope so, because if there is any supernatural power to your fortunetelling, it is the power of the Evil One, sent to lead you to destruction." And again, Josephes called on the druid and his family to repent.

Like John the Baptist crying in the wilderness, Joseph thought. But he saw the look of open hatred Tarana cast at Josephes and chilled with fear.

"You will be regretting your opposition to the power I serve," Tarana bellowed.

Joseph, standing just behind his son, felt the active presence of hatred bombard them in all its destructive force.

8

oanna's growing garden brought continual joy. Each new year tiny sprouts she had mothered so tenderly grew and blossomed. They reminded all of the homeland left behind and symbolized all the intangible things brought with them as well. At times Joseph felt almost guilty over the beauty and peace on their twelve hides when the rest of the world was in turmoil. He didn't know why he had been chosen for such contentment—he who had twice failed his Lord. But he did understand that such contentment was a gift of the grace of God, a fulfillment of Christ's promise to give His followers a more abundant life—a foretaste of Heaven on earth. And he understood that since it came by grace, there was no way he could ever repay so great a blessing. He could only say thank you. And indeed he did so daily—hourly—in his prayers. But he longed to do something more.

And baby Elisabeth grew. Indeed, she had long since ceased to be a baby, as her toddling footsteps steadied and her infant babbling turned to words. She ran singing all over the twelve hides with far more energy than her mother or any of her adopted aunts could keep up with.

And then, before the next burning of the Beltine fires, Mary told her father that Elisabeth Britannia would soon have a playmate. In all the rejoicing that greeted the announcement, there was only one whose smiles never reached her eyes and whose face was drawn and tight when no one was looking.

Eurgain and Josephes had passed eight turnings of the new year since their wedding celebration at Caer Leo and never once had she missed her courses. Yet every day she prayed to the God whose way she had accepted and in whom her husband believed with all his heart. But what good was a God who couldn't give one a baby? Surely, that must be one of the easiest things a supplicant could ask.

As her unhappiness mounted, doubts also took root. Perhaps she should have married Coillus as had been planned for her. Did she offend the old gods in choosing a foreign husband—in breaking the ancient pattern? Always she had had an unusually religious turn of mind and had borne patiently much chiding from her brothers at Dun Camulus who told her she should study to become a druidess. Foremost in her mind and nearest her heart was the wish to please the gods. That was why she had so readily accepted the Three-in-One. Her heart was prepared to believe, and she had opened it.

But now she had to wonder if she had acted rightly. In choosing the One God, had she offended the others? Josephes said there were no others. But what if he were wrong? Jehovah-Yesu-Great Spirit was right for Josephes and his people—but what of herself and her people? Confusion overwhelmed her.

With her melancholy heavy upon her, Eurgain found herself gravitating back to the sacred oak grove of her old gods. And there she often found Tarana instructing his sons in the old ways. One day, about a month after Mary's announcement, when Eurgain's courses had come again, she thought, as she so often did now, of her sister urging her to seek the ancient wisdom. She made a decision.

This time her steps toward the grove were not rambling, but a firm stride. Jehovah-Yesu-Spirit might well be the Three-in-One God her people had always known existed, but all six of His ears were deaf to her petitions. If Matres, the mother goddess, would not help her, at least Dagda, the Lord of Perfect Knowledge, could give her understanding to make her barrenness more supportable.

Tarana, his white robes streaked with blood, stepped from the grove to meet her. His eyes glistened when he heard her petition. "Ah, daughter of Caradoc, welcome back to the ancient way of your people. This caprice that has affected even such learned druids as Balan and Bran will soon be revealing itself for the falsehood it is. It may be well for weakling foreigners, but it will not do for our ancient, valorous people. A god who allows himself to be hung on a tree—Tcha!—I spit on him. And did this god and his sacred fish bring victory against the Romans? It is no wonder he has not answered your prayers for a child—he is as helpless to aid his followers as he was helpless to save his own life."

Eurgain shrank from the ferocity of Tarana's words. It always seemed impossible to think clearly in the redbeard's presence. A spirit of confusion seemed to surround him, and yet he showed no indecision himself. Indeed, his very immutability added to her confusion. She made no effort to explain the joy and peace—the sense of cleanness—she had experienced from following this new God. Even now, when she shifted her mind from her desperation, she could recall the feelings. But Tarana's voice rang louder.

"Think, Eurgain, you were married at the great festival of Lugh when all our cattle should have been driven between the Lammas fires to insure their fertility. But that Joseph," he spat out the name, "bewitched Bran into declaring that the ancient practice of our people would displease the new god. So, oh, yes—we burned our fires, but we didn't worship Lugh! And what is the result? Rome conquers our warriors and our princess is barren."

Tarana turned his back on her and disappeared into the sacred grove. In a moment he returned, bearing a sprig of mistletoe. "Now go to your bedplace. Sleep with this under your cushions. If your courses come again, return to me for a fresh sprig. When Epona is full in the sky, I will sacrifice a female stoat on the sacred altar. When I find one whose womb is in flower, we will be knowing that the gods have honored our supplications."

Clutching her sprig of mistletoe, Eurgain raced home. As she slipped it beneath the wool and bearskin cushions of the pallet she shared with Josephes, she felt a tangle of emotions—sadness and despair over deceiving her husband and abandoning her new faith, yet elation at having taken matters into her own hands. And besides, she salved her conscience, Josephes wanted a child as much as she.

Several days later the peace of Ynis Witrin, which Joseph had come to think of as indestructible, was shattered. For some time he had suspected that all was not well at the home of Josephes bar Joseph, but he had not wanted to intrude. Now, however, Josephes stood before him holding the shriveled mistletoe branch he had found after a sleepless night of tossing and pulling at the fur skins.

The inevitable had happened. Joseph knew that the clash between the old ways and the new would eventually come, especially as Tarana grew more bold in his defiance of Balan's teaching and Josephes answered him in equally fiery speeches. But unlike Elijah confronting the prophets of Baal, Joseph's contest would not set fire to any altar atop the Tor. The way of love conquered softly.

"Go home, my son. Do as you think best about letting your wife know you have found this, but above all, do not berate her. Treat her with love and tender kindness. And pray. Morning, noon, and night of each day I shall seek our Lord's mercy for you."

That the outspoken Josephes followed his father's advice attested to Christ's power in him. But as the months dragged on, each time he found a fresh sprig under their bed, Josephes found the going more difficult. Joseph saw the strain around his son's mouth, the tightness in his eyes, and the father prayed harder.

But if Josephes showed loving restraint toward his wife, he redoubled his clashes with Tarana. Joseph knew something must soon be done. When the sacrificial fires of a great bull billowed beyond the oak grove and filled the air over the twelve hides with stinking black smoke, held there by mists from the marshes, Joseph knew the time for confrontation had come.

"Tarana's ways are certainly old—as old as evil itself. Our Lord never shrank from confronting evil with authority, and we can do no less, in His name. Love is stronger than hate, and it must not be shown as weakness." Joseph strode ahead of Josephes.

Below the grove, Tarana and his sons faced Joseph and his son. The druids formed a stiff, unblinking wall.

"This, the sacrifice of rams and bulls, was the old way of my people also, and it pleased Jehovah," Joseph began. "An offering of blood was required for the remission of sins. But that way is past for your people as for ours, as God is the God of all people. His statutes are the same for all. God has no need of bloody sacrifices, libations, and incense. We honor Him by prayer and by thanksgiving and by praising His name. The only homage truly worthy of Him is not to consume by fire the things He created for our nourishment, but rather to thank Him for our own creation, for everything which gives life and health, for the bounties of nature, including those creatures of His you would slay on your altars, and thereby make a mockery of the sacrifice of His own Son."

Joseph paused, breathless. In his fervor his discourse had almost become a tirade, something he was determined to avoid. But he looked into the cold, hard eyes of the druid and knew his words had fallen on stony ground. Tarana was totally unsubordinated to anything higher than himself. Joseph took his son's arm and turned away with slow steps. He had done all he could.

On the fifth day in Beltine, a great joy arrived, pushing these troubles aside. Mary Penardin bar Cleon, Joseph's first grandchild, burst into the world with a lusty squall to give emphasis to her red face and unruly mop of black hair. Joseph, who had feared that his daughter's confinement might be as difficult as Salome's, thought the babe in his smiling daughter's arms was the most beautiful creature God had ever made.

First thing in the morning, when the babe was eight days old, just as Jesus had been presented in the temple for dedication, Joseph presented his granddaughter for her Naming. She opened her eyes and gave her grandfather what he would ever afterward claim to be her first smile, crooked and wobbly, but indescribably precious. "Mary Penardin bar Cleon, you bear a name of the Hebrew people from which you come and a name of the Celtic people to which you have come. May your life be a blessing to both peoples, but more, may you live to the glory of God, your Heavenly Father, and His Son, Jesus Christ." He closed the benediction with a kiss on the velvety brow. And together those in the hut chanted: "To You be glory, who lovest compassion! To You be glory, name of the Messiah! To You be glory, O power that dwellest in Christ!"

He handed the precious bundle back to his daughter who pushed her gown aside and snuggled her babe to her breast. With a heart full of gratitude for God's goodness, Joseph left Cleon's home. Not even the sight of Eurgain slipping furtively toward the druid grove upset Joseph's sense of the presence of God as he made his way to the well. He dipped the olivewood cup into its depths.

"My Lord, I have no wine such as You admonished we should drink in memory of You, but this well You brought me to has ever reminded me of the sacred blood which poured from Your side in sacrifice for my sins. Help me to be worthy of Your great blessings." Still on his knees by the flowing waters, Joseph drank the memorial cup.

Then, with head bowed, he walked slowly to the mossy boulder where he so often sat for meditation. After a time, he looked up, and his eyes swept the green valley between the hills where his band had built their homes. He thought of the Temple in Jerusalem where the Christ Child had been presented. Suddenly, Joseph knew what he wanted to do to thank God for His goodness.

Joseph would build a church.

God had allowed Solomon the special privilege of first building His house—the house of worship David had longed to build. But God had refused David because of the sins in his life. Joseph prayed that his past failures would not be held against him in performing this task.

Israel had gone for four hundred years with only a tent as God's dwelling place among them; this band of believers had been eight years in Britain without a place of worship. They had built homes for their families. Now they would build a home for their God. Joseph thought of the grand scale of the Temple in Jerusalem, massive stones and cedar beams overlaid with precious metals—the richness of gold and silver and ivory.

He had no such materials. But Christ had referred to His body as the temple—which would be destroyed and rebuilt in three days (as indeed it was at the crucifixion and resurrection). So perhaps a simpler structure, where the worshipers would focus only on the sacrifice and love of their Lord, would be acceptable. This would be the first house built solely for worshiping Christ.

The idea fired his imagination. Maybe he should not look to the Temple for inspiration, but to the Tabernacle, God's first dwelling place on earth. He would build his church to the same dimensions—sixty cubits long, twenty cubits broad, thirty cubits high.

Joseph sat long, imagining his task. All the band were now expert in working with the local building materials, having practiced on their own homes. They would build the house of worship with carefully woven wattle and firmly packed daub, and their work would be as conscientious and loving as that of Miriam and her mother building a much smaller vessel out of similar materials for the baby Moses. Then when the roof was thickly thatched to keep out the heaviest rain, what would he put inside? Joseph thought of the contents of the Tabernacle in times long gone—the Ark of the Covenant, made of acacia wood and overlaid with pure gold, topped with the Mercy Seat and two golden cherubim; the golden, branched candlestick, as tall as a woman; the table of shewbread, holding twelve loaves of bread as a symbol of gratitude to God for daily bread; the great brass laver where priests washed their hands before ministering at the altar; the golden altar for the burning of incense . . .

No, those were all used to worship God under the old covenant. The new covenant declared by Christ did not require those symbols of priestly sacrifice. The new church would contain symbols of Christ's fulfillment of that Law. What would he use as a centerpiece, as an emblem of God's presence with them?

Then he knew. The cross. The symbol used throughout the Empire to persecute and to mock Christians. He would place it in the front of his church, pointing the way to victory. He would carve this symbol of the triumph of love from branches of the strongest oak tree he could find. And he would build an altar, not for sacrifices, but as a place for believers to kneel in prayer, instead of standing to pray as Hebrews had always done—kneel as Christ had in the garden before going to the cross. And on the altar . . . what would he place on the altar? He thought of the wooden standard engraved with a fish which King Arviragus had borne in battle. He wished that standard of faith had been preserved from the melee of war that he might now place it here before God, but it was long gone, splintered beneath the foot of a Roman horse or used as kindling for a Roman funeral pyre. Joseph would like something less destructible to stand as a symbol of indestructible faith.

Then he thought of Christ in the wilderness being tempted of Satan to turn stones into bread, but finding the strength to resist the temptation. *May future worshipers who come to this sacred spot find such strength* . . . Joseph would choose a stone to place on his altar—but not just a rough stone that could be misunderstood in its meaning. He would work with a craftsman from the lake village in shaping a stone into the symbol of the Way such as he had carved into Arviragus's standard. Joseph smiled with satisfaction at the rightness he felt about his decisions.

And there was one more item he would place on the altar. The cup of the Last Supper.

Secure in his plans, Joseph walked beyond the hill and climbed the Tor to survey the twelve hides. Where should he build his church? If he had not built his own house near the well, he might have chosen that site. But the church should be more centrally located. The Tor was farther to the side yet and was too steep. Neither did Wearyall Hill seem to be the right place. Then Joseph looked at the green hollow between the hill of the well and the hill where the thorn tree now flourished. Entering a house of worship there would truly be like entering the hollow of His hand. That was where Joseph would build the church.

Joseph had no idea how long he had been planning and praying, but suddenly he realized that the sun had disappeared, and the blue sky had now turned the color of a bruise.

It was even darker on the other side of Ynis Witrin where Eurgain had gone to escape the rejoicing over Mary's babe. Heaviness of heart bade her, with the instincts of a wounded animal, to seek solitude. She found a quiet place at the base of the Tor near the oak grove. Curled up in her misery, she must have slept, for when she awoke, it was not the sun that greeted her, but the moon.

She struggled stiffly to her feet. Josephes would want his evening meal, and her slave was forever letting the stewpot boil dry or failing to put enough honey in the barley cakes that he so enjoyed. If she couldn't be a mother, she still strove to be a good wife.

In the confusion of waking in the dark, Eurgain walked toward the grove rather than away from it. Too late she realized it was occupied. She started to turn away. Then she froze at the sight before her. The priest dropped his ceremonial robe and stood naked under the moon save for his white loincloth and golden torque and armbands that glinted coldly in Epona's pale light. His skin was whiter than the robe that lay at his feet and took on an eerie luminescence in the moonlight.

He began to sway and dance, his arms extended as if he would pull the shafts of moonlight from the sky. With small steps he rhythmically circled the flagged floor of the oak grove, keeping away from the shadows of the branches that grew in a great circle, keeping to the moonlight as if he were washing in it.

Then he began reaching even higher and pulling handfuls of the goddess's light down on him, rubbing his hands over his arms and torso after each clawing grasp. Each movement was accompanied by a low chant of strange words that sounded to Eurgain as if they came from a language more ancient than that of the Cymri—something from the old ones who lived there before the tribes came.

The druid's small, strange steps continued round and round in mesmerizing rhythm. Gradually his voice gained strength until the chant reached above his head, above the circling oak boughs, up, it seemed, to the moon mother herself.

Then he stopped. All was quiet in the grove. Not a leaf rustled. Even the druid's breathing seemed stilled. He stood rigid before the altar where the moonlight fell coldly on the etched bronze of the ritual sword of truth. Extending his arms in a jerking motion, he grasped the sword. Then with stiff arms he held it up to the goddess as if for an offering.

Slowly he lowered it, making a low sound that was more a crooning cry than chanted words. And with the sound he began swaying again and turning around the sacred floor, not in the wide circle as before, but whirling in place.

At first Eurgain thought the sword was merely casting shadows on the priest's white skin as he held it against his body, but then she realized the shadows remained after the sword moved.

Tarana slashed his body again and again, and the long dark cuts dripped blood onto the floor of the sacred oak circle in an invocation to the mother goddess.

Horrified, Eurgain clapped her hands over her eyes and backed away.

"Halt! Who dares to disturb Tarana Thunderer in the sacred grove?" The sword fell to the ground with a clatter of bronze on stone. The chill wind returned to the trees as if it had been held off by enchantment.

Eurgain would have run, but her legs would not.

The moonlight fell full on the priest's face, and she looked into his eyes—the bright blue eyes that she had so often seen squint against the sun or flash with cold rage or cloud in contemplation of a vision only he could see. But now they were not the druid's eyes at all. They were turbulent cauldrons like the storms of Samain when the dead walked. Strange and terrible things seemed to lurk just beneath the surface, and it was as if these demons would leap out at her at any moment. She tried to pull away, and yet she was held against her will. She felt a fear she had never known in her life, yet beneath it, a strange excitement.

"So, Princess of Brython, you would spy on that which is forbidden to any uninitiated to see." His words were honey-covered still. "The Great Mother, whom I worship in your behalf, has two faces as a coin has two faces and yet are the same coin. The Great Mother gives all things and takes all things back in death. Which will it be for the child you would bear?"

She hesitated.

"The Great Mother is patient with you, Eurgain, as a mother with a wayward child, but she will not forever hold her hand. Choose you whom you will serve—Lugh of the Long Hand and the Great Mother and all the gods who have served these islands so well, or the new god of foreign ways who demands you renounce the ways our people have followed for hundreds beyond hundreds of years."

"It's not a renunciation; it's a fulfillment—" she started to protest, but the words died, half-spoken.

"Oh, yes, that is what the smooth-voiced foreigner will tell you. It is a trick to turn our people away from the truth. But are you fulfilled, Eurgain?"

She laid her hand on her flat abdomen, and tears stung her eyes. The druid held out a blood-streaked hand and drew her into the circle. But even as her pulse quickened in excitement, she knew that the emptiness she felt was not only in her womb.

The druid advanced and grasped her wrist so tightly Eurgain cried out, but his fingers bit more deeply as he said, "I have made my last supplication for you, my Princess. Now you shall go to your destiny for your people."

No one heard her cry.

Joseph had not yet finished his Morning Blessings when his son's frantic voice called him from his hut.

"Father! Father! A messenger has come from Caer Leo." Josephes gulped air before he continued. "Caradoc lost a battle three days ago. He went to Venutius, the Brigante king, to beg reinforcements, and that traitorous wife of Venutius turned Caradoc over to the Romans."

"What? Caradoc has been taken captive?"

Josephes nodded curtly and continued in a bitter voice. "Cartimandua handed him over in chains. It seems that she's the real power in the Brigante kingdom, and she has chosen to 'honor' her clientship with Rome. Honor, my eye. Her land marches with the land under Roman control, and she thinks by this cowardly act to avoid trouble for herself. Betraying one of her own people! It's inconceivable."

"Perhaps she didn't look on someone from another tribe as one of her own people," Joseph suggested, but Josephes ignored him.

"Wait. You haven't heard it all yet." Josephes's face was set in a hard line. "They have taken Caradoc's family as well. His sons were with him, and the Red Crests overpowered Caer Leo and took Gladys and Gladyl."

Silence fell between them.

Joseph broke it. "And Eurgain?"

Josephes shook his head. "No one has seen her since the babe's Naming. She did not come to our bed last night. I have searched everywhere. Every house. The lake village. The cors." Again he shook his head. "And that treacherous Tarana Redbeard is missing, too."

Joseph called all their band to gather and pray at the spot where his church was to stand. Then Joseph, Josephes, and all on Ynis Witrin began searching. But it was not until the middle of the next morning that they learned what had happened.

Balan came first to Joseph. Then they went together to Josephes. Balan looked as haggard as the other two. "Tarana has returned—with a purse of

Roman gold. I questioned him and learned the truth." Balan paused and looked uneasy. "He couched his answers in terms of 'wise diplomacy' and 'keeping peace for our people,' but I can see it only as a betrayal." The druid looked at Josephes. "Tarana has given Eurgain to the Romans. She is to be sent to Rome with her father."

"Judas!" Josephes's cry of agony and anger rang all over the twelve hides.

Joseph jumped up to restrain his son who looked as if he would next rush from the room to tear Tarana limb from limb. "Let God have the vengeance, my son. We must rescue Eurgain. I will go to Ostorius Scapula. When the governor hears that she is married to a Roman citizen, the son of a former Nobilis Decurio, he will free her."

At his father's words Josephes's reason returned. "You are right, Father. But *I* will go. If he won't release her, I'll go to Rome."

"Josephes, let me—"

"No! Thank you, Father. But this is my job. Philip appointed you apostle to the Britons; your place is here."

Joseph saw that further argument was useless. "Go in the grace and peace of God our Father and His Son, Jesus Christ, my son."

9

The military cavalcade drew to a halt on the plains before the Praetorian camp just outside Rome. In spite of the magnificence of the scene and the furious activity on all sides, Josephes couldn't take his mind off the question his wife voiced. "What will happen to us now?"

The best answer he could give was to clasp her to him and vow, "Whatever happens, I won't leave you, my heart!"

Although the British captives had proved better sailors than the Romans on the long voyage across the Oceanus Atlanticus, around Hispania, and across the Mare Tyrrhenum to the port of Ostia, the strain of the journey showed on every captive face. The prisoners had not been ill-treated. The Romans did not forget that their captives were royal and, under Roman law, not to be punished until sentence was pronounced by the emperor himself. Therefore, their quarters, though more crowded, were as carefully tended as those of Ostorius Scapula who was personally escorting his prisoners back to the Imperial City to receive the honor due him. And their meals were as regularly served, although the salted fish and dried millet cake called polenta, staple diet of the legionnaire, left much to be desired.

"It's so ugly here. No wonder the Romans were wanting our Brython," Eurgain said with contempt, her apprehension conquered for the moment. "It's all brown."

Josephes looked around in surprise. To him the countryside looked refreshingly like his native land with its warm, dry air and golden-brown soil accented by scattered clumps of dark green cypress and umbrella pines. A patchwork of carefully tended flower and vegetable market gardens filled the valleys beyond. But he had no time to comment, for Ostorius had finished changing his dusty travel clothes for the purple cloak and gold-banded toga appropriate to a conquering hero. The procession was forming.

Mounted legionnaires rode up and down the field shouting orders as they arranged everyone in proper order. First came the aquifilers, or standard-bearers, holding aloft the eagles of the four legions who had won this great victory. Then a statue of a reclining Jupiter was borne at shoulder height by priests from the Temple of Jupiter on Capitoline Hill. Behind the recumbent god followed wagons laden high with the spoils of war—bronze shields and helmets glinting under the bright Italian sun beside golden torques, ladies' hand mirrors, and delicately carved ivory. Next marched a group of pipers in graceful white togas, each playing a jubilant tune on a double-headed pipe. After the pipers plodded four pure white sacrificial bulls, led by axe-carrying priests.

A soldier galloped up in a cloud of dust and checked his horse just short of charging into the prisoners. "Next! Behind the bulls!"

With a flash of humor, Josephes smiled at his wife. "I'm sure they mean it as an honor, but it might have been cleaner walking farther back."

Eurgain's eyes met his, and she returned a glimmer of a wry smile. "I hope our placement isn't meaning we're bound for the same sacrificial altar as the bulls."

Although they had enjoyed the freedom of the ship on their voyage, the prisoners were now bound with chains for the procession—Caradoc's warrior sons, Cyllinus and Cynon, first, then Gladyl, Gladys, and Eurgain. Josephes, who refused to leave his wife's side, presented a problem. His Roman citizenship proclaimed by the toga he wore, he could hardly be marched into the city in chains as one conquered. At last the harried legionnaire grunted that he could walk behind his wife.

Behind the prisoners and their guards marched the horn players—one row with long bronze horns that encircled the players' bodies and curved high into the air, then a row of long-tubed trumpets that resembled Celtic battle horns. Josephes wasn't sure which was worse—the blasting horns behind him or the droppings from the bulls in front.

They all grew sweaty under the remorseless sun, and each time a horse galloped by, they were engulfed in a cloud of dust until all their faces were streaked with mud. Josephes moved forward and wiped his wife's lined face with his unchained hands, rubbing his palms on his tunic. "Courage, my little one," he whispered, "this, too, shall pass. Remember, I will be praying for you every step of the way."

She lowered her eyes, but Josephes was warmed by the softness in her look. In all the weary days of the voyage to Rome, he had treated her with the tenderness his father had advised. But she had not opened her heart to him regarding her faith. Of course, a husband could simply *tell* his wife she was to worship his God, and that would be that. And many of his friends in Jerusalem who had chosen the Way had done just that—but Josephes had never been convinced that that was good for the wife, for the marriage, or even good in the eyes of God. Christ had invited men and women equally to follow Him of their own choice, and Josephes prayed that she would renew her commitment from her own heart. If the Romans let them live long enough.

Caratacus, as Caradoc was called by his captors, was shouted into place behind the musicians, and he was followed by more bearers displaying captured Celtic war weapons. He was wearing a long tunic over his breeks, as trousers were forbidden by law on Roman streets, although breeches were acceptable for members of the cavalry—and apparently for captured foreign kings. The procession began to move, and Josephes stepped out of line for just a moment to look backward. Behind the wagons of piled spears and swords, a cluster of the fasces-bearing lictors, who always accompanied Roman magistrates in public appearances, announced the coming of the honored general. The triumphant Ostorius Scapula rode in a chariot drawn by four horses. Behind him marched senators in their long white togas, followed by a line of soldiers flowing back as far as Josephes could see.

They marched around the wall and entered Imperial Rome along the poplar-lined Flaminian Way. The moment the procession entered the city, it seemed the marchers would be knocked down by the sheer force of the cheers and cries of the crowds. The name "Caratacus!" was on every lip. The fame of the warrior who had defied the might of Rome for nine long years had spread throughout Italy, across Gaul, and into all the provinces. And Rome, a city of one million people, was today host to at least a million more who had come to witness the grand spectacle of this vanquished hero.

Josephes realized it had been ridiculous to worry about the noise of the trumpets behind him, as all were drowned out in the cacophony. He had been to Rome twice before with his father, and above the heads of the crowd, he could glimpse a few familiar landmarks. The great city of brick and marble shone like the queen she claimed to be. Every temple and shrine was decked with flower garlands and burning incense, that any god or goddess who had aided in the victory might not be slighted.

As far as he could see on every side, houses, great palaces, public buildings, temples, monuments, and shrines covered the rolling hills with an incomparable magnificence. It was all the more startling to Josephes because he had seen it before and thought himself prepared—could Rome, continuously enriched by the spoils of war and by tribute, have changed that much in the fifteen years since he'd been there? Or had the change been in himself, now accustomed to a gentler, simpler way of life?

He looked at his wife and her family in front of him. They were obviously overcome by the heat and the noise and the strain. They walked, heads down, their chained hands hanging limply before them. Guilt smote him. He had forgotten his vow to pray for Eurgain.

He couldn't even think which way was east, disoriented as he was by heat and noise, and the sun straight overhead gave no clue. He would have to ignore the tradition of facing east, and of covering his head, for, in the Roman fashion, he was bareheaded. But the words of the prayer for deliverance from danger were time-honored.

"Blessed are You, Lord our God, King of the universe, who brings deliverance from danger. May You bestow beneficence on the one You have given me to wife and on her family. Blessed be the name of the Lord."

And then he added, "And our Savior Jesus Christ."

With renewed hope, Josephes darted to the side before a guard could shove him back in line and looked quickly behind. Unlike the other captives, Caradoc/Caratacus was not overcome. Every powerful ripple of his bronze muscles, every proud lift of his head, every bold stride he took shouted back to the crowd that he might be in chains, but he was not conquered. And the crowd loved it. Here, indeed, was a foe worthy of mighty Rome. It was no disgrace that such a warrior had held four legions at bay for nine years in over forty campaigns. The cheers rang louder yet. Ostorius would receive the Triumph, but Caratacus was the hero of the hour.

At last the procession reached the Forum at the foot of Palatine Hill. The large, open colonnaded area in the narrow valley between two hills was the heart of the city. Here Romans had traditionally gathered for politics, news, gossip, and shopping since Rome was a mere village of mud huts. But the Forum was more than the center of the city—it was also the center of the Empire. Here was the Rostrum from which all of Rome's great men had spoken and where many had lain in state when they could speak no more. Here Cicero had delivered his great orations and Julius Caesar had been mourned after his murder by Mark Antony. On ahead, above Augustus's colonnaded arches, rose the Capitoline Hill, the ancient seat of Roman power, and at its foot lay the golden milestone from which all the roads in the Empire were measured.

The sun glistened on the white marble of the Corinthian columns topped by statues of *Winged Victory* looming over the British captives. And the walls of Augustus's Forum, with each arch framing a statue of a god, reflected back the blinding light. Here the procession disbanded.

Ostorius Scapula was escorted to an inner chamber to be honored by the Senate while the bulls, lumbering behind the statue of Jupiter, were driven up Capitoline Hill to be sacrificed to the father-god of Rome. Spared a similar fate, the relieved prisoners were marched away by their guards to the Mamertine Prison on Virnival Hill to await Claudius Caesar's pleasure at their trial.

"Not you." A burly guard stuck his arm out to bar Josephes's entrance to the prison. "I have no orders to house you here." Josephes started to protest, but there was no time. He had a fleeting glance of his wife being borne into the recesses of the prison. Then the iron gate slammed in his face.

The stricken look on Eurgain's face cut Josephes as if one of the guards had pierced him with his sword. Only a few hours before he had vowed not to leave her. But what could he do? Would she understand?

"Please, let me send my wife a message," he begged the guard.

The man only shrugged.

Slowly Josephes turned and walked down the hill. He was desolate. After the turmoil of the morning, he was alone. And not just alone, but useless. All those weeks on board ship he had been constantly on call, supporting Eurgain, trying to prepare his friends for what to expect in Rome, acting as a go-between for prisoners and guards. Suddenly it was over. The unanswered questions remained, but the action was in Caesar's hands. There was nothing he could do for Eurgain; there was nothing he could do for his British family; there was nothing he could do for the Way. There was simply nothing he could do.

Aimlessly, he followed the throng. Everyone seemed to be moving in the same direction. When the crowd of men, women, and children began to funnel toward entrances to a colossal, oval brick building, Josephes realized he was at the Circus Maximus. Lacking anything better to do, he filed inside one of its arched passages. Since he was wearing a toga, he was admitted freely, although the man behind him, clad only in a tunic, was turned away.

The sun beat down on him as he found a narrow seat on a wooden bench on one of the higher tiers among the rabble. He looked down on the front rows far below him where senators, magistrates, and vestal virgins filled the more spacious stone seats. In the center of the arena and around the great length of its raceway stretched row upon row of the gilded, marble statues that adorned every public building. Josephes shifted his heavy toga which lay like a blanket over his left shoulder and wiped the sweat trickling into his beard.

The sound of an approaching band heralded the chariot-borne entrance of the presiding consul, followed by his retinue of lictors, legionnaires, and cavalry. The applause was polite for the officials, but ringing cheers met the performers. Two- and four-horse teams, driven by charioteers in red, green, white, or blue tunics with their horses' reins strapped around their waists, circled the raceway. The passionate welcome for each color given from various sections of the stadium displayed the spectators' fierce loyalties to their teams. And undoubtedly more than loyalty, since race-cards and placards advertising the horses and their drivers for betting circulated widely.

The performers were followed by singers, priests, and incense-bearers carrying gold and silver censers. The priests pulled wheeled images of gods and goddesses. As priests and deities completed the circuit, the procession was over. The consul, in his box across the arena from Josephes, stood to a fanfare of trumpets and dropped a white handkerchief onto the sanded track. The races began.

The first four teams, with a driver of each color, rushed out in the first missus of the day. It seemed to Josephes that on each turn the drivers whipped their teams harder and leaned farther forward in the light, two-wheeled racing chariots. At one time their skill would have impressed him, but he had seen equal or greater expertise among the Celtic warriors. The cheers increased in volume and frenzy, reverberating off the surrounding walls and inside Josephes's head. He thought he had heard all the shrieking throngs in the world that morning, but the vitality of Rome's mob seemed endless.

The horses had just entered the fifth lap, coming around the curve to Josephes's left, when a horse in the red team stumbled. The crowd's roar increased as the chariot overturned and the driver, with the reins around his body, was unable to cut himself free before being dragged to his death.

The sight of the bloody pulp that a few minutes before had been a man did not sicken Josephes nearly so much as the blood-lusty cries of the mob. At first he had thought they were shouting for the other drivers to do something for their fallen member, but then he realized they were shouting for more speed, more action, more blood.

Dizzy with heat and noise, Josephes stumbled to his feet. Had the Imperial City, the Queen of the Empire, always been like this? It had seemed glamorous and exciting when he visited it as a boy, but now he would give all the gold in his purse for a cool, quiet, green spot.

If only he could remember the names of his father's friends here. When they had last come to Rome, Joseph had made some important contacts for his trading company in one of the commercial houses. But the home where they had been entertained had not belonged to any business associates. Their host had been a tent-maker, as Josephes recalled, a devout member of the synagogue known for hospitality. Of course, the family might not even still be here after so long a time.

Not even bothering to notice which team won, Josephes forced his way through the cheering mob and stood at last with the Circus behind him. He took a deep breath. Well, in spite of all its unpleasantness, Rome offered one amenity unsurpassed in all the world. The blood-lust of the jostling, sweating crowd had left him feeling as dirty on the inside as the dust of the Flaminian Way had left him on the outside. Josephes wanted a bath.

He asked directions to the Thermal Agrippa, the newest and most lavish addition to what had once been mere public washhouses, but was now a splendid recreation center of gold and marble, offering fully equipped gymnasia, garden, and library. As he paid the doorkeeper the admission price of one quadrans, the smallest Roman coin, his only thought was how wonderful it would feel to soak clean in the warm water of the tepidarium and then plunge into the cold water of the frigidarium.

Josephes left his tunic and toga with the cloakroom attendant and, since he had no slave of his own to perform the service, hired an attendant to carry his towels and to scrape his body down with the long, curved-bladed, wooden strigilis after the steamy water drew out the impurities.

The caressing of the water and the stroking of the strigilis were soothing, but Josephes did not find his quiet retreat. Romans, it seemed, could make quite as much noise at their baths as at the Circus Maximus. The high walls, painted with scenes of cloud-borne gods and goddesses and supported by marble pillars, rang with singing, whistling, and shouted conversations.

Josephes did not need warmth, nor did he need to induce any more perspiration, but he made his way to the hot, steamy calidarium in hopes that it would be less crowded.

With a sigh of relief, he sat on a wooden bench in the blessedly quieter room and took a deep breath of the warm, moist air. A few other men were using the steam room, talking together in clusters, and noise from the more raucous crowds in other rooms carried through the walls, but this was better. Josephes closed his eyes and leaned back.

"I beg your pardon, I wonder if I might share your bench?"

Josephes sat up and looked at a man about his own age. It was obvious why the stranger had chosen Josephes; their beards proclaimed them to be the only Jews in the calidarium. "Please do. I would be happy for your company." Josephes moved to make more room on the bench, and suddenly he realized how much he really did welcome the young man's company—cut off as he was from his family.

Josephes explained that this was his first trip to Rome in many years and that his father had a trading company in Jerusalem. In turn he learned that Patrobas was a native Roman who lived in the Jewish sector across the Tiber. He had lived for a time in Athens with his family after Claudius had expelled the Jews from Rome.

Josephes was dismayed. Now he would never find his father's friends—they could be scattered anywhere in the Empire. "I'm sorry—I had not heard—I have been, er, traveling in Britannia. Why did Claudius do such a thing?"

Patrobas was quiet for a moment; then he spoke in a low voice. "There was trouble in the synagogue. We were quarreling over matters of faith . . ." His voice trailed off, and at first Josephes thought the memory was too painful for him to continue. Then he saw the question in Patrobas's eyes and noticed a slight movement of his right hand on the moist bench beside them. With the smallest gesture, Patrobas had drawn a curved line on the steam-covered surface.

Josephes blinked. What had he heard from a gossiping trader in Caer Leo—something about this new sect of Jews being afraid to declare themselves openly? Then the memory slipped into place—that was what had started the conversation—they had been eating fish at the time. With an equally economical gesture, Josephes topped Patrobas's curve with an inverted one of his own, crossing the lines at one end to form a fish. It looked much like the one his father had carved for Arviragus on the night that had changed their world.

Patrobas broke into a wide smile and clasped Josephes's hand. "Brother! We are meeting tonight. You must come with me."

And so it was that a short time later, the two young men made their way down the Via Ostia toward the Aventine Hill where the Tiber formed the bottom of its S-curve in the southwest corner of the city.

As it was long past the hour for cena, the main Roman meal of the day, they stopped in a cookshop for a bowl of wheat meal porridge flavored with vegetables and fish. When the steaming food was set before him, Josephes realized how hungry he was and fell on it with vigor after murmuring the briefest of blessings.

When they continued on their way, it seemed again to Josephes that he was seeing Rome through new eyes. They walked along ever narrower, more winding streets. Josephes was appalled. The splendid villas of the rich left behind them, they now walked past block after block of tenements, each forming its own island of apartments built above shops where families lived in rooms stacked on top of each other. As they neared the Tiber, the evening air carried the stench of the sewage and garbage swept into the river.

But Patrobas seemed oblivious to the odor as he strode along, talking in rhythm with his steps. "Now that the synagogue is closed to us, we meet regularly at the home of Priscilla and Aquila. They—"

Josephes grabbed Patrobas's arm and spun him around. "That's it! I've been trying to remember all day! That's who we stayed with years ago! And they are still here after all?"

"Newly returned. They went first to Corinth and then to Ephesus where they worked with the Apostle Paul—worked both as fellow tent-makers and as teachers of the Way. Many of the Jews are filtering back quietly, very quietly."

"I especially remember Priscilla—how could I ever have forgotten her name? She was unusually outspoken for a woman. I had the feeling my father was often shocked, and yet he seemed to enjoy her logical mind."

Patrobas laughed. "Yes, you've described her just right. We used to wonder how Aquila felt about having such an unconventional wife, but now I believe he's proud of her."

Their conversation had brought them to Aquila's small home on a street near the river. While not lavish, this area was far better than the insulas of tenement buildings they had passed earlier. They entered a brick archway leading directly into the shop. Shuttered windows on both sides provided access for cool breezes in the summer and sunshine in the winter. But tonight they were shut tightly to ensure secrecy.

Patrobas led the way through the shop and into the small atrium, a partially roofed courtyard with an open center where smoke could escape when a fire burned on the hearth, although on this warm evening there was no need for one.

Patrobas introduced his visitor to Aquila, and suddenly Josephes found himself surrounded by friends. The son of Joseph of Arimathea, who had buried their crucified Lord in his own tomb, was welcomed warmly. Aquila went around the room making introductions. "This is Tryphaena and Tryphosa, diligent workers for our Lord." Two women smiled at him. "And our beloved Persis." A gray-haired man, bent with age, stood to greet Josephes with a kiss. "Asyncritus, Phlegon . . ." Josephes returned each kiss of greeting. "And this is Hermas, who is dividing the Word of Truth for us tonight." Hermas set aside his scroll to greet the newcomer.

Then Aquila beckoned to an aristocratic-looking couple on the far side of the atrium. "This is Rufus, an outstanding follower of the Lord from the Pudenti, one of the first families of Rome." The handsome young man in a toga welcomed Josephes and then turned to the woman beside him with her long lavender palla pushed back from her elegantly coifed graying hair. "And Rufus's mother, Olympa, but we all call her Mother."

The introductions completed, Josephes was offered a drink and water to wash, but he insisted that be postponed, as he had obviously interrupted their lesson. He begged Hermas to continue.

He and Patrobas took seats on cushions, as all the stools were occupied. Hermas spoke. "Daily there are those who become disciples of our Christ and forsake the way of error. Enlightened by His Spirit, they receive gifts according to their merits. One receives the spirit of understanding, the other of counsel, this one the spirit of fortitude, that one of healing, the one the spirit of prophecy, the other of teaching, and yet another the spirit of the fear of God . . ."

The sermon was followed by a question-and-answer period. Then Aquila passed a basket of bread around the circle, and each person tore off a piece in memory of the Lord.

After all had eaten and drunk, Hermas stood in their midst and raised his hand to the star-speckled sky above the atrium.

We will praise the Lord, all His children,
And proclaim the truth of His faith.
By Him His sons are known,
Therefore we sing in His love.

Then all in the room rose and replied in a cross between a song and a chant:

We rejoice in the Lord through His grace
And receive life through His Christ.
For He caused a great day to shine upon us,
A wonderful day, because He gave us of His glory.
Our faces shall shine in His light,
And our hearts shall meditate in His love.
By day and by night let us exult
In jubilation about the Lord.
The Savior is come,
The Son of the Most High,
He is come in the perfection of His Father.
And light has arisen from the Logos,
Light that was in Him from the beginning.
Hallelujah!

At the conclusion of the ode, all resumed their seats and relaxed into conversation. Josephes told briefly of his father's work, and others talked of events in Rome, but mostly the conversation centered on their spreading faith. "Paul has gone on another missionary journey into Galatia," Aquila said.

"And Silas with him," Priscilla continued. "I don't suppose you know Silas, Josephes, but he was a leader in the Judean church."

"Oh, forgive me, Josephes. I forget you have been gone for so many years. Did you know about the conversion of Saul of Tarsus who was responsible for Stephen's death?" Aquila asked.

Josephes nodded. His throat still tightened when he thought of the death of his friend. "Yes, that was shortly before we left Judea, and we have received some news since. Britain may be at the end of the world, but it is not beyond it. But what of more recent events? All the traders have talked of lately is Roman politics."

Hermas spoke up. "The news is heartening, indeed. Thousands have responded to Paul's preaching in Antioch. And here, in spite of the emperor's edict against *Christiani*, many are added to our number weekly."

Josephes's eyebrows rose questioningly. "Christiani?"

Priscilla, in her graceful way, gave a light laugh. "Yes, is it not a good name for us? The new believers at Antioch were called that, and the name has stuck."

"Christiani—those who are of Christ." Josephes tried it out slowly. "Yes, it is indeed a good name."

Then the group questioned Josephes in more detail about everything happening in Britain, the work of his father, and how he came to be in Rome. His hearers hung on every word, hungry for news from so remote a corner of the Empire. When he told of his wife's imprisonment, their faces showed concern.

Again Priscilla spoke first. "We must pray for their release, just as the Christiani at Jerusalem did when Herod imprisoned Peter."

"What?" Josephes asked. "We did not hear of that."

"Did you know that James, the brother of John, was beheaded by the Tetrarch?"

"I don't understand; we had heard that Herod died." Josephes frowned in confusion.

"Yes, this is Herod Agrippa, son of the Tetrarch that mocked Christ—and just as cruel," Patrobas explained. "But the night before he was to kill Peter, all the believers in Jerusalem gathered to pray. In the middle of the night an angel entered Peter's cell and led him out, right past the sleeping guards."

Priscilla laughed. "Yes, and when Peter turned up at the home of the praying Christiani, they didn't believe it was he."

Hermas, smiling too, shook his head. "Oh, ye of little faith."

"But we shall pray for the release of Eurgain and her family," Priscilla said with determination. "And when they are freed, we will not be unbelieving, but rejoicing."

They all agreed. Hermas slipped his shawl over his head to begin the intercession, and others followed, sometimes individually, sometimes several praying at once. Some prayed kneeling, some sitting with bowed heads, some standing with face and arms reaching heavenward. When all had finished, members of the group began leaving quietly in separate directions. Before she left, Olympa Pudens clasped Josephes's arm. "We will go with you tomorrow to the prison to visit your wife. There should be no problem with your visiting freely, but Rufus will know how to deal with it, should any difficulty arise."

The next day, in spite of the treatment Josephes had received the day before, they met no resistance at the Mamertine. Josephes felt a pang as he surveyed his proud-spirited family, used to the freedom of forested hills and green valleys, confined in walls of stone with iron gates and fierce-looking guards.

"Are they mistreating you?" Josephes asked Eurgain anxiously.

"Not really. We have adequate for eating—their wheat meal porridge is not unlike our stirabout—and the sleeping pallets are not uncomfortable. But I am thinking life is not of much use to be always in a cage. I feel like one of those poor birds caught in the priest's snare."

Josephes held her tightly. "Do not despair, my heart. There will soon be an end to this."

Then the guard banged on the bars of Eurgain's cell, and Josephes had to go.

Throughout the following days, as the prisoners waited to learn their fate at Caratacus's trial, Rufus visited them every day with Josephes. After a time, Josephes protested that he could go alone, as Rufus must have pressing business affairs. But the twinkle in Rufus's eyes told Josephes more than the young man's actual words. "Oh, no, but I insist. It's a pleasure to go with you to the prison."

On their next visit, after Josephes spent a short time with Eurgain, Gladyl came to him, her normally smooth brow furrowed in perplexity. "A most strange thing has happened. Aulus Plautius has been to see me."

"What? The conqueror of Britain? Came to lord it over you, did he?"

"No. Not at all. That perhaps might not have been so perplexing. No, he has asked me to agree to changing my imprisonment to house arrest at his home. His wife has been very depressed of late, and he thinks I would be a cheering companion for her."

Josephes was amazed. "You would make an excellent companion for anyone. But how could he possibly know?"

"I don't remember whether you were at Caer Leo when Plautius came there—to negotiate a truce with Arviragus?"

"Oh, yes. I recall; you read him some of your poetry."

Gladyl filled in a few of the details of that meeting.

"So, what's the problem? Do you think his offer dishonorable?"

"Oh, no. Not in the way you mean. I'm sure it is his wife's happiness he is thinking of. Their only son died in a difficult childbirth last summer, and she hasn't recovered yet—still dresses in mourning clothes, lives completely retired.

"It's a very generous offer, but that's the problem. I feel a traitor to my own people if I go off to live in a fine villa leaving them here in prison. I have been helping Father prepare the speech he will deliver before Caesar, and he might be needing me for other things." She paused. "And it is in my mind that I might not like living in a pagan household. I might be expected to worship their household gods."

Josephes thought for a moment. "Yes, but on the other side of the coin, perhaps it is God's will for you to carry the light to this Roman family in this way."

"As you and your group brought it to my people?" She was quiet for several moments.

"If that is your call, you must not turn your back on it. But only you can decide if this is an opportunity for service rather than a temptation. If you decide God is leading you, you can be sure that He will help you, but the way may not be without heartaches and trials."

The next time he went to the prison, Josephes learned that Gladyl had indeed gone to the house of the Plautii. And Caradoc's trial was set for the next week, two days before the Ides of July. Eurgain's nervousness showed in the way she clung to her husband's hand.

To comfort her, he repeated the story of Peter's miraculous release from prison. He emphasized the humorous element. "The angel said, 'Put your sandals on and wrap your cloak around you and follow me.' Peter obeyed, but he thought he was dreaming until he was outside the prison in the street. Can you imagine his surprise?"

Eurgain smiled weakly.

"But the part of the story I love most is when Peter went to John Mark's house where he knew they were praying for him. He knocked on the door, and a maid answered it. When she recognized Peter's voice, she was so excited that instead of opening the door, she ran in and announced that Peter was standing outside." Josephes smiled broadly. "Can't you just see poor Peter standing there in the dark banging away and nobody coming to unlock the door? But then the best part is that everybody told the maid she was crazy. They thought it must be Peter's guardian angel. Here they'd been praying all night for God to rescue Peter, and when He did, they didn't believe it." This time Eurgain's smile broadened. "But good old Peter just kept knocking on the door, and they finally let him in and saw that it was true."

Josephes paused and looked at his wife. "My little one, we must believe. God will answer. We will continue to knock on the doors of Heaven, just as Peter knocked on John Mark's door."

On the day of the trial, Aquila, Hermas, and Rufus accompanied Josephes to the Forum. Inside the council chamber, with its walls composed of rows of columns, the sun glared on the white marble of the curved benches—benches rapidly filling with toga-clad senators and magistrates. The observers took seats in the back of the room.

At the approach of the prisoners, a minor controversy arose. A guard challenged Gladys who was clutching her father's hand with both her chained hands. "Women do not enter the Senate chamber."

Gladys drew herself up tall and looked straight at the guard. "Is mighty Caesar afraid of a woman? My future is on trial today, too. I will not be leaving my father."

The guard looked as amazed as if one of the marble statues by the doorway had spoken. He looked around for someone to advise him and saw Aulus Plautius approaching with a group of senators. The guard explained the situation to him. Plautius waved his hand. "I understand Agrippina is to attend today as well. Let them pass."

When the room was full to bursting, there was a flourish of trumpets, and the emperor entered with his slow, limping gait, his head held awkwardly to one side. But even from where Josephes sat in the back, there was no mistaking the intelligence in the piercing blue eyes under the shock of white hair. Claudius was accompanied by Narcissus, his favorite slave, and Agrippina—was she his third or fourth wife?—a beautiful woman, twenty years his junior.

When the trumpets silenced, an official stepped forward to proclaim Claudius's titles in a ringing voice that echoed from the marble columns. "The Emperor Tiberius Claudius, son of Drusus, Caesar Augustus Germanicus, Pontifex Maximus, Britannicus, with the tribunician power for the eleventh time, Consul for the fifth time, saluted as Imperator twenty-two times, Censor, Father of his country, recipient of the formal submission of eleven British kings, the first to bring barbarian tribesmen across the ocean under the sway of the Roman people—All Hail!"

Caratacus jerked his head up defiantly at the word *barbarian,* but the room reverberated with the cry, "Hail, Caesar!" "Hail, Caesar!" "Hail, Caesar!" Then another blast of the trumpets echoed from the columns as Claudius sat down and Agrippina took a seat of honor, elevated only slightly less than Caesar's, on the other side of the chamber.

A magistrate briefly addressed Caesar, then turned to Caratacus in a condescending manner, and announced, "Caesar will hear you."

Caratacus took his place before the Senate. His heavy torque, fashioned with bulls' heads facing each other, gleamed, as did his golden bracelets. He wore plaid breeks under his tunic. A brief murmur went through the crowd, but then quieted instantly as the foreign king began to speak in fluent Latin.

"Mighty Caesar, thank you for hearing me." The prisoner's voice rang with the courageous conviction of a man born free.

"Had my moderation in prosperity been equal to my noble birth and fortune, I should have entered this city as your friend rather than as your captive; and you would not have disdained to receive, under a treaty of peace, a king descended from illustrious ancestors and ruling many nations."

The senators leaned forward on their benches, not wanting to miss a word of what was obviously going to be a memorable speech. Two scribes seated at a table below Caesar scribbled every word, writing with styli on papyrus scrolls.

"My present lot is as glorious to you as it is degrading to myself. I had men and horses, arms and wealth. What wonder if I parted with them reluctantly? If you Romans choose to lord it over the world, does it follow that the world is to accept slavery?"

Josephes caught his breath. Surely such plain speaking would offend Caesar and make their position worse than ever. He looked fearfully at Claudius, but the emperor, famed for his quirky sense of humor, seemed to be amused. Caratacus continued.

"Had I been at once delivered up as a prisoner, neither my fall nor your triumph would have become famous."

Josephes blinked. Did Claudius nod? Surely, it was just his much-mocked tic.

Caratacus paused to give emphasis to his conclusion. "I am now in your power. If you are determined to take revenge, my fate will soon be forgotten, and you will derive no honor from the transaction. Bid me live. I shall survive forever in history as one example of Roman clemency."

The room erupted in a spontaneous thunder of applause. Then, seemingly, the spectators realized they were applauding an enemy of Rome before the emperor. The clapping subsided.

Caratacus stood tall before Caesar. Waiting.

Caesar stood, and the room fell silent. "I grant cl-clemency."

Again, cheering erupted. A Praetorian Guard came forward to remove the chains from all the British prisoners. When order was restored, the terms of Claudius's clemency were spelled out. Caratacus and his family would have their possessions returned to them, and they were free to live at liberty in Rome. Caratacus was to agree never to bear arms against Rome, and his sons would be allowed to return to Britain where Cyllinus, the elder, would rule the Trinovantes as regent in place of his father to whom the title had passed on the death of Togomundus.

All the prisoners approached Caesar, bowed to show their acceptance of the terms, and each made a gracious speech, thanking Claudius for his mercy. Then they turned and likewise paid homage to Agrippina. She waved a bejeweled hand imperiously. "You do well to praise me, for I am a partner in the Empire which my ancestors have won. It pleases me to see that you are conscious of the favor you have received from the emperor. And you are doubly favored to be allowed to live in Rome, the Queen of Cities. Do not forget this boon has come from Caesar." Then, apparently bored with the situation, she strolled from the chamber on the arm of her son Nero.

Across the room, Gladys was in conversation with Claudius who was obviously taken with the girl's sparkling fresh beauty, in contrast to the Roman women who wore heavy make-up over their darker complexions. As soon as they began to talk, however, it was more than her beauty that arrested his attention. "Your Majesty, I understand that you are possessing a great library of manuscripts and that you, yourself, are a scholar and author. Is there any possibility that the great generosity you have shown today might be extended to permitting me to be reading in your library?"

Claudius, who, like most Romans, still labored under Julius Caesar's depiction of the British as savages, was much taken back at this request. "D—do you mean to s-say you read?"

"Oh, yes, Your Majesty. I have been educated in both Greek and Latin." She did not go on to say that her education had been at a druid cors, for she had heard rumors that Claudius intended to outlaw druidism as he had Christianity.

"Well, then, my d-dear. My manuscripts would be honored to have s-so charming a reader." He looked around. "Ah, there's young P-Pudens." A wave of the imperial arm brought Rufus to his emperor's side. "P-Pudens, I want you to es-es—er, bring this young lady to my palace tomorrow afternoon. We shall read together."

Rufus's face showed that he was pleased by more than the notice from his emperor. "It will be a pleasure, Caesar."

The trumpets blew and Caesar, accompanied by his slave, limped from the Forum.

The next day Caratacus would begin his search for a home, since Caesar had decreed that Rome was to be his permanent residence. But for that night they all went back to the home of Aquila and Priscilla. Even such a modest home was a new world to these Britons who, though royal, had never seen a residence finer than Cymbeline's Great Hall at Dun Camulus on which Arviragus had modeled his. The greatest wonder, however, was not the marble columns supporting the atrium roof which, while more elegantly carved, were not so unlike the oak beams supporting Arviragus's Great Hall. It was not the silken cushions which, while lighter and brighter, were no softer than the fur pillows used at Caer Leo. But the absolute miracle of Roman engineering was the running water brought right into the house through lead pipes attached to the city aqueduct. "Ours flows very meagerly," Priscilla explained to her guests, to whose eyes it was a veritable waterfall. "The charge is made according to the size of the pipe, so our pipes are small."

The oil in the terra cotta lamps had been flickering and smoking, in about equal parts, for some time before the guests were settled in their assigned rooms. Josephes and Eurgain had their first chance for a truly private conversation since they had been carried off from Britain. Josephes opened his arms and Eurgain, a bit hesitantly, but with a great sigh of relief, went into them. After a time of holding each other, they moved to sit on a couch in one corner of the atrium.

She reached out to touch him. His beard was rough and crisp against her fingers, and when he turned his head, she felt his lips first on her hand, then on her brow, eyes, and finally on her lips.

"Josephes, my marriage-lord, can you forgive me? I see so clearly now how wrong I've been. That silly statue in the procession and those poor bulls going to the temple to be sacrificed—everywhere you look in this city there's a shrine or a temple to some god or goddess. It's just like Tarana and his sacrifices of birds and stoats to his old gods. And the true God isn't at all powerless as I thought—look what He did for us today—the first time in history Rome has spared the life of a defeated enemy. It is a miracle like for your Peter."

Josephes held her closer, but did not interrupt.

"I knew before this—in my heart—I knew the God of the Way was true, but I—I—Oh, I don't know—Josephes, I was so confused. Everything Tarana said made sense when I was with him—and then when I was alone, I was not hearing the true God. It is in my mind that I was screaming so loud on the inside that I couldn't hear Him."

In most tender Cymric Josephes murmured, "Little-one-of-my-heart," with his lips close to her ear. Then he moved back to continue in Greek. "He's always there—the Comforter He promised never leaves us—but we have to listen for His still, small voice. That's hard sometimes—I know—it was for me when I couldn't find you on Ynis Witrin." He pulled her to him and held her fiercely as the memory of his desperation washed over him.

"I see the difference now—the truth of your love and the lies of Tarana. Always he lied—about how much he was loving me and our people. Oh, Josephes, can you forgive me?"

"Of course I forgive you, my love." And again he held her long. "But you must also ask God to forgive you."

They bowed their heads. All was quiet except for an occasional soft sniff from Eurgain. When they looked up, her face was radiant. "My heart is glad. I won't go back on Him again. The darkness of the old way blinded me—but now I am seeing. The freedom of this way is so precious. He is so precious! Tarana and the unbelieving druids with all their bloody entrails and mistletoe magic—I see them now for the evil they are.

"It was a terrible thing—being taken prisoner by Rome, but maybe I needed to get away from it all to see that I had been captured by a darker force.

"This has been an awful time, Josephes—I am thinking perhaps it was worse for you than for me. But I'll be a better—what's the new word? *Christiani?*—now that I truly see the difference—not just adding Yesu to the old gods, but really turning my back on darkness and living in light. Mary once said something to me about laying down the old way for a fuller revelation. I accepted the second part without truly laying down the first."

Again they sat in silence for several minutes, rejoicing in the presence of their God. Then Eurgain spoke. "Oh, Josephes, I wish we could go back. I want to tell others now that I truly understand. I don't know—start my own cors, or something. Not one where deceivers like Tarana serve alongside good priests like Balan, but a place dedicated just to Yesu." Then she stopped, and her words caught in her throat. "But I guess it's too late. For all that Caesar gave us the freedom of the city, we're still prisoners."

10

The British, living in their strange state of captive freedom, did their best to adjust to Roman ways. They learned to count their days from kalends to ides of each of the twelve Roman months. They shopped in the imperial square built by Augustus where goods from every corner of the Empire were displayed in sumptuous and confusing profusion. And slowly, usually being carried about in litters, they learned their way about the winding, congested streets of the city that sprawled over seven hills.

It was all bewildering and stimulating, but it was also overwhelmingly confining. No more the pleasant strolls by the green, unspoiled banks of the Usk with no sounds but that of the lark in the ash tree. The Tiber was polluted with garbage and choked with barge traffic bearing goods from every corner of the Empire. No more a wild, free race in a chariot across miles of green-carpeted valley between rugged mountains that made Rome's seven hills look like ant mounds. No more the clean, fresh breezes that blew in from the sea and tossed the wild flowers in the meadow, the barley in the field, and the blossoms in the apple garth. Roman air was confined within the Servian Wall, just as their life was, and it smelled stale and polluted.

Yet there were good things, too. With the income of his British estates which the Claudian tribunal had decreed he could keep, Caratacus bought a villa on Esquiline Hill, not far from that of Aulus Plautius, where Gladyl was still living. The British royal family moved into the Palatium Britannicum—the British Palace—as it soon came to be known.

The women retained many of the same duties they had performed in Britain, directing slaves in preparing food, washing and cleaning, and assisting in serving guests. It was easier for them to adjust to this new way of life than for Caradoc, who stalked the marble floors of his palatium like a caged animal. "There can be little difference in being Caesar's guest or his prisoner—all of Rome is a prison." And he stalked from the atrium, the villa's reception room, to the peristylum, behind which was an elegant column-surrounded courtyard enclosing a garden with a tinkling fountain. The family bedrooms, kitchen, dining room, and offices all opened off this. It was spacious in the finest Roman fashion, but the hard, cold surfaces of the house, the straight lines of walls and floors, the sparse, stiff furniture—all seemed unfriendly and forbidding to a Celt who had always sought softness and warmth in surroundings and flowing lines in decor. The arrangement was sensible for the hot climate, however, and necessary for one who, for honor's sake—his own and the honor of the people he represented—must live like royalty, no matter how foreign and uncomfortable he found it.

And one great source of comfort—even survival—for Caradoc was that their self-appointed family friend, Rufus Pudens, offered him free use of his stables, although it was a far cry from the exhilaration of riding break-neck across his native lands with his warrior host at his heels. Caradoc grudgingly settled into life as a Roman, cheering his favorite red team at the Circus, plunging into the frigidarium—he never adjusted to the steamy atmosphere of the calidarium—at the baths, and giving and attending dinner parties at other villas as stark as his.

Roman society, always looking for a new amusement, took the British with their "refreshing, if barbarian" ways to their hearts. And the British, who found sitting on Roman stools perfectly comfortable and adjusted quickly to sleeping on couches, but never learned to enjoy eating and drinking lying down, accepted and returned invitations for several dinners a week in spite of the discomfort. The company they enjoyed the most was that of Rufus and Olympa Pudens, and the most surprising friendship that developed was with the household of Aulus Plautius, their former enemy.

When the family of Caradoc had lived in Rome for almost a year, the uncle of Rufus Pudens, head of the family Pudenti, came to Caradoc to request the marriage of his nephew to Gladys. Caradoc sighed. Both of his daughters would then be wed to foreigners. But they were fine men in spite of their different ways. Caradoc, who always frowned when anyone called him by his Roman name Caratacus, consented, as his daughter had months ago in her heart, although she and Rufus could not speak of it until their families agreed. That left one more consent to be obtained—that of Claudius Caesar.

Gladys had made frequent use of Claudius's invitation to read in his private library. The emperor, who was laughed at as much for his scholarly pursuits as for his physical disabilities, and the uprooted foreign princess found a companionship of the mind in a society alien to many of the natural instincts of both of them.

Claudius claimed Gladys as his "adopted" daughter and asked her to assume the name Claudia. "For after all, my name is Br-Britannicus, too," Claudius had told her in a grandfatherly manner one afternoon when she was reading in the garden off his library. She wrote a charming poem in Latin dedicated to her new "father" and then translated it into her native Cymric to amuse the emperor. In return, Claudius gave his blessing to the marriage and sent a magnificent bronze lamp as a betrothal gift. And Caratacus deeded the Palatium Britannicum to his future son-in-law as Gladys's dowry.

Even Aulus Platius's wife, Pomponia Graecina, brightened somewhat in the excitement over the approaching marriage and declared that the wedding feast must be held at their villa.

On the wedding day, slaves arrived at the British palace at first light bearing baskets of flowers from the market. And Gladyl, instructed by Pomponia in Roman wedding customs, prepared her niece for the ceremony. With Eurgain's help, they divided Gladys's long golden hair into six sections with a spear-shaped comb used only for brides and bound each loop of hair with a scarlet ribbon.

Her wedding dress was a white tunic, woven all in one piece of the finest wool. The tunico recta fell straight from her shoulders to her feet. Gladyl, following Pomponia's instructions, bound a woolen sash around the bride's waist in a knot of Hercules.

Patting her finished job, Gladyl said, "There now, no one can untie that except your husband tonight."

Gladys blushed almost as red as the scarlet bridal veil Eurgain draped over her head. Josephes knocked on the bedroom door. "Are you ready? The witnesses have been waiting in the atrium for hours, and the groom's family will be here any moment."

The door opened, and a radiant Gladys came out followed closely by Gladyl. They crossed the peristylum quickly, but Eurgain walked more slowly, holding her husband's arm.

The groom and his family arrived, and before the witnesses from the Christiani congregation—Aquila and Priscilla, Patrobas, and Hermas—Gladys gave her husband the three copper coins called asses. Rufus kept one as a symbolic dowry, and the other two, which in a pagan household would have been sacrificed to the household gods, were given instead to Hermas to be used for charity.

Then with everyone carrying an armful of flowers, which they waved before the bridal couple and tossed on the ground for them to walk on, the procession wound around Esquiline Hill to the villa of Aulus Plautius for the wedding feast.

Pomponia nervously awaited her guests. She desperately wanted to please her husband. Aulus had been very patient with her in her deep unhappiness since the death of their son and the Greek physician's pronouncement that she would bear no more children. Aulus had so wanted a son to follow him to greatness— they both wanted it. But she could not give him that prize—he who had been given an Ovation as a conqueror of nations could not have the title he most longer for—that of father. Most men would have divorced her. Many put their wives away for far less cause—indeed, it had almost become fashionable in society to change wives yearly. But Aulus bore her true love, and she was grateful to him. And she was happy he had brought the lovely Gladyl to her. At first she had been fearful he was bringing the beautiful woman with golden hair home as her replacement, rather than her companion, but Aulus was a man of honor.

Her friendship with Gladyl grew, and at the British princess's urging, she returned to writing the poetry for which she had in happier times been granted the honorary title Graecina. Her world had widened and her sorrow eased—ever so slightly.

She had insisted on having the wedding feast at her home as an expression of appreciation to her British friends and as a sign to her husband that his patience would be rewarded. If he was not to have a son, at least he would have the hostess-wife due a Roman senator. And for that reason everything must be perfect. She had planned every detail of the menu and the serving and entertainment with her chief steward. It had been three years since she had attempted such an undertaking, and she felt out of practice and insecure. How she would have loved to retreat to her chamber with a cold compress on her forehead. But she would not surrender.

Clasping her hands together to stop their shaking, she forced a smile at Aulus. "They will be here soon, my lord. I trust you will find all to your liking. I have ordered several of your favorite dishes to be prepared."

"The room is arranged perfectly." He looked at the urns of flowers, garland-bedecked statues, and low-burning lamps. "You have done well, my dear. This shall be the first of many such successes for you."

At his words, Pomponia felt an icy grip of fear. In these times of political unrest it was hard enough to give a successful dinner party even among Romans of the same class. There were so few safe topics of conversation, and spies were everywhere. When conversation lagged among guests, and it often did, the hostess would be expected to fill in with witty gossip or a salacious story. Pomponia knew no such brittle chatter, and in this strangely mixed crowd, any gossip would be meaningless anyway. Not only were many of the guests British, held in Rome against their will, but many others were Jewish. Although Claudius's interdict against Jews had been softened, it was still not popular to be a Jew in Rome. What would any of them care about talk of love affairs, divorces, and domestic scandals in Roman society? And then, Gladyl had dropped hints that led Pomponia to wonder if some of her guests might be members of the despised Christiani sect. She felt completely helpless to direct hours of safe, amusing conversation under these circumstances. Yet, if she failed to do so, if she failed to be a hostess as she had failed to be a mother, could even Aulus's love sustain that?

However, there was no more time for fretting. The sound of singing and laughter announced the arrival of the marriage procession. Pomponia and Aulus moved forward to greet their guests and direct them to their tables.

In groups of nine each, the wedding party reclined around three low tables, reaching across their wide sofas for the food so tastefully served by well-trained, attractive slaves. Pomponia Graecina might be depressed, as her white mourning robe proclaimed, but it was evident she had a firm hand on her household. The first course, or gustatio, of radishes, mushrooms, eggs, and oysters, was accompanied by lively chatter as the guests recounted scenes along the procession for their host and hostess, and the radiant bride and groom accepted gentle teasing. Any momentary lulls were filled gracefully by the musicians performing on harps and pipes in one corner of the room. Pomponia began to relax.

At her signal, the first course was removed, and the muslum served. As the glasses were filled with the heavy, honey-sweetened wine, several of the guests offered toasts to the newlyweds. "Blessings and long life to the bride and groom in the name of One who sanctified marriage by turning water into wine at a wedding feast." Josephes held his glass high in salute and then drank.

Patrobas was next. "Blessed may you be, in the name of Him who created all things for His glory."

Pomponia, alert to any undercurrents in the room, caught her breath. Surely these salutes didn't apply to the father-god Jupiter—she had heard no such claims for him before. It must be true then that there were members of the Christiani sect here. What would Aulus say? She stole a sidelong glance at her husband reclining at the next table, but he seemed unperturbed. His mind appeared to be elsewhere—probably on the political machinations that always surrounded his life.

Her speculation was confirmed a few moments later, before Aquila's toast could be offered, when a slave entered bearing a sealed message for Aulus. He excused himself from his guests. With the senator gone, the speakers seemed to feel more free. Or was it the effect of the rich wine loosening their tongues? Pomponia's anxiety increased. Even slaves could be spies.

Aquila spoke boldly, holding his freshly refilled glass high. "We ask abundant joy for these loving friends from One who bestowed gladness upon His created beings in the Garden of Eden of old. Blessed is the Lord, who gladdens the groom and bride."

And to Pomponia's horror, the guests replied, "Blessed are you, Lord our God, King of the universe." She could only hope Aulus's errand had taken him beyond earshot of the dining room. Only one toast remained. Perhaps it would be over before her husband returned and she could signal the musicians to play loudly.

All looked to Hermas. "May the barren one rejoice and be happy at the ingathering of her children to her midst in joy. Blessed are You, Lord."

The words dazed Pomponia. Instinctively she sensed that the blessing was one of ancient tradition, and yet it struck her with personal freshness. She found herself wanting to respond with the others in a blessing to their God. Whoever He might be, He had enlivened her heart.

But then everyone's attention turned to eating as Aulus returned and serving began with a seemingly endless procession of courses—mackerel, eels, prawns, boar, venison, wild goat, ostrich, partridge, peacock . . . Again Pomponia held her breath. Her nerves had allowed her to eat almost nothing, but now even her bravely kept-up smile wavered. She had purposely not ordered suckling pig, knowing of many of her guests' Jewish background, but prawns and boar were special favorites of Aulus, so she had included them. Had she acted foolishly? What if someone said something awkward or took offense and left the banquet? What could she do? If it hadn't been too late, she would have signaled her waiters to return to the kitchen.

A slave knelt to offer a platter of shellfish to Aquila beside her. To her surprise and relief, he took several of the curved, pink shrimp and began deftly peeling them. He dipped one in the rich tomato sauce accompanying it. "Excellent," he said to his hostess. "A most sumptuous banquet."

"Oh, I'm so glad . . . I, er—wasn't sure—about the prawns."

Aquila removed the shell from another, while Priscilla on the other side of him said softly so no one but Pomponia could hear, "We do not believe it is what goes into a person that defiles him, but what comes out."

Pomponia frowned, not understanding.

Priscilla smiled. "Perhaps I should say, it is not what is in the stomach that is important, but what is in the heart. Life does not come from following rules, but from loving."

Pomponia gave her first real smile of the day—and of many, many days before that.

But the dinner was not over yet. Aulus, who had fully enjoyed the many excellent dishes, rose and approached the shrine in the corner of the room where he made the traditional offering of wheat, salt, and wine to the household gods. In telling her about the bride-buying, Gladyl had mentioned to Pomponia that the two-ass brideprice had been given to the poor rather than to the gods, so she could imagine how some of her guests might feel about her husband's action. *Don't let anyone say anything awkward,* Pomponia prayed to all the gods in the Pantheon.

And some god must have heard her, because the most awkward thing that happened was the small swarm of flies that followed the platters of honey-sweetened cakes and fruit served next. This minor complication was solved by a flick of the hostess's wrist as she summoned slaves waving peacock-feather fans to chase away the offending insects.

It was only later, when the wine goblets had again been refilled by silent slaves and the hired entertainers were regaling the company with songs and poetry in the bridal pair's honor, that the fear returned—and then it was as fleeting and nameless as a shadow.

In the time they had been together, Gladyl had often mentioned that she was praying for her mistress to find joy in her life. Gladyl's poetry, though full of longing for her homeland, was also full of references to the love and peace she found in Yesu. Now, after an evening with these people, Pomponia had seen some of what Gladyl was talking about. Certainly these people—both the British and the native Romans—were unlike any company she had ever met at a dinner party. The talk was pleasant, the humor gentle, and the whole atmosphere of their relationships seemed to be loving.

On an impulse Pomponia turned to Priscilla. "I feel you understand much that I have often questioned. I would like to know more. Would you visit me again?"

It was only after Priscilla agreed to come the next day that Pomponia noticed the slave standing behind her, frowning silently.

But the next day Priscilla's sweet smile chased the vague shadows away. And no one could give better answers to Pomponia's questions than Priscilla. She told Pomponia of her own sorrow at the death of a child, although she thanked the Lord that she also had two healthy ones. "I don't really understand the bad things in life—oh, I know we live in an imperfect world because of sin, but that doesn't explain specific things like the death of a baby. But I do understand the good things—they are gifts of God who loves His children and delights in blessing them. And I believe that someday the bad things will be made right, too—or at least we'll understand."

Pomponia nodded and squeezed Priscilla's hand before calling a slave to bring them refreshments. If the slave appeared a moment too quickly, Pomponia forgot about it in the excitement of the moment. When she decided to accept Priscilla's invitation to attend one of their meetings, she was careful to make sure Aulus knew that she and Gladyl were going to visit friends, and she watched to see that their litter was not followed.

Ever since Claudius's decree had given them the freedom of Rome, Josephes and Eurgain, Gladys and Rufus, and others from the British palace frequently crossed Rome to the home of Aquila and Priscilla, where they studied and worshiped. They were delighted as gradually, first in sporadic visits, then, drawn by their love, with increasing regularity, a new member was added to their group. Pomponia Graecina, still in her mourning clothes and with bowed head, accompanied Gladyl to the meetings of the Christiani.

In the late spring of the year A.D. 53, an important event took place. A woman named Phoebe from Cenchreae, a suburb of Corinth, arrived with a letter from Paul addressed to all believers in Rome. Suddenly the weekly meetings became nightly meetings and lasted into the early hours of the morning. Everyone was anxious to hear every word the apostle had written and Hermas's comments on the letter. Night after night, Pomponia, whose face now showed moments of animation in place of its former sorrow, was among the first to arrive and last to leave. She listened intently to each word and then asked insightful questions about the meaning of Paul's letter and the beliefs of the Christiani.

One night, after the second week of such meetings, Hermas read from Paul's letter: "'For all who are moved by the Spirit of God are sons of God. The Spirit you have received is not a spirit of slavery leading you back into a life of fear, but a Spirit that makes us sons, enabling us to cry, "Abba! Father!" In that cry the Spirit of God joins with our spirit in testifying that we are God's children; and if children, then heirs. We are God's heirs and Christ's fellow-heirs, if we share His sufferings now in order to share His splendor hereafter.'"

Suddenly a radiant smile broke across Pomponia's face. "Oh, now I see why you Christiani are so happy. Truly you live without fear. This must explain it."

"Yes, and our freedom comes through salvation based on no law or anything we do, but totally upon Christ's mercy," Hermas responded. "Christ, out of the goodness of His heart, forgives people's sins. Their standing before God depends not on what they have done, but on what Christ has done for them. And that is why Christ is entitled to our absolute allegiance and whole-hearted devotion—no matter what."

Pomponia nodded her head. "Yes, I have heard of the bravery of those who have died for their faith. I did not understand such devotion until now. And then one hears such horrible stories—that you eat the flesh of babies and drink warm blood . . ." She stopped with a shudder. "Of course, I have seen how false all the charges of immorality are, but that wasn't enough. Now I truly understand. Now I believe."

From that moment, her perpetual strained, haunted look began to give place to a gentle glow. It was a subtle change, but those who knew her well saw it and rejoiced. That night Pomponia Graecina was welcomed into the fellowship of believers.

But only a few nights later their joy was shattered. Gladyl arrived at the meeting without Pomponia. Every eye turned to the tall British princess as she announced, "A charge was brought in the Senate. Pomponia Graecina has been accused of following a 'foreign superstition.' She is to be tried at their home, with her husband as judge."

Shock appeared on the faces of those in the atrium, and they voiced their fearful questions. "What will they do to you, Gladyl?" "Will she deny the faith?" "Why is she to be tried at home by her husband?"

Gladyl tried to give sensible answers to a situation that seemed senseless. "It is an ancient custom—a right of aristocratic families to try their own members when family honor is at stake. To the Romans, being a Christiani is synonymous with practicing immorality."

"How could they believe that—with all their immoral ways?"

Hermas answered, "Is not that the way of the Deceiver? To strike at one's strongest point and twist it. Remember, he is the father of lies."

"But what of Pomponia? Will she be put to death?"

"We must pray for her—it's all we can do."

"What of us? Are we in danger? If she's been observed coming here, perhaps we should begin meeting again in the catacumbus."

Gladyl answered, "I don't believe we are in danger. Plautius believes this to be the work of his political enemies."

But it was Priscilla's calm voice that quieted them. "Our Lord has not given us a spirit of fear, but of strength and love. What did Paul say about that, Brother Hermas?"

Hermas picked up the scroll beside him and read, as he had on the night Pomponia announced her faith, "'The Spirit you have received is not a spirit of slavery leading you back into a life of fear, but a Spirit that makes us sons, enabling us to cry, "Abba! Father!"'"

The fear in the room vanished as they turned to prayer. "Lord our God, King of the universe, we pray for the strengthening of Your daughter Pomponia and that we may speedily behold the splendor of Your might to perfect the world under the sovereignty of the Almighty. All mankind shall invoke Your name. Then all the inhabitants of the world will recognize and know that every knee should bend to You. Before You, Lord, our God, they will give honor to the glory of Your name. May You soon reign over them forever and ever, for kingship is Yours, and to all eternity You will reign in glory."

A week later, when all the Plautii were assembled in the great column-encircled peristyle of Aulus's home, Gladyl was the only member of the Roman Christian community present to support Pomponia, but the prayers of the entire congregation surrounded them.

Aulus Plautius sat at the front of the chamber, looking severe in his best toga with narrow purple bands. The strain of the past days clearly showed on his face. It was well known that he loved his wife and did not seek an excuse to put her away. And yet, his honor was equally well known. If the charge were proven true, that Pomponia posed a danger to the state, Aulus Plautius would banish his wife.

Pomponia sat before him, her stark mourning dress particularly well-suited to the occasion. As this was a family tribunal, a member of the Plautii, Aulus's nephew Setonius, who was studying the law, would lead her defense. Castulus Quinta, the senator who had brought the charge, would lead the prosecution.

He had become Aulus's strongest political enemy when Aulus made it clear that he would not support Agrippina's son Nero to succeed the aging Claudius.

Aulus Plautius declared the tribunal open in the name of Claudius Caesar, and the hum of gossip in the room immediately ceased. Castulus, a short, bald man with showy wide bands on his toga, stalked to the front of the room. "If it please the court—or not, as the case may be," he added with a sneer, almost under his breath. "In the name of the same Claudius Caesar in which you opened this court, I shall prove that one Pomponia Graecina has regularly visited the home of Jews indulging the lewd practices of the cult of Christiani which the emperor declared illegal and, therefore, must be punished under the law."

He whirled dramatically to face Pomponia who sat with her hands calmly resting in her lap, her face composed. "Pomponia Graecina, have you entered into lewd and adulterous practices with this Christiani sect?"

Her voice was clear. "I have not."

"Do you deny participating in 'love feasts' where men and women freely kiss one another outside the marriage vows and eat the flesh of little children and drink their blood?"

"I deny it."

The prosecutor began to sweat. He wiped his high, bald forehead. Gladyl looked at her serene friend and thought of their Christ who made no attempt to defend Himself before His accusers. *Help her, Lord,* she prayed. *Give her Your peace, that Your light may shine forth in her life as the sun in the sky speaks of Your love.*

Castulus stepped aside to refer to the parchment roll of charges on the table by his stool, then took a position only a few inches from Pomponia's face. "Have you participated in the indecent ritual of public nude bathing with mixed sexes which I understand is the membership rite of this disgusting faction?"

Pomponia looked him straight in the eye; her voice echoed to the second story balcony above. "Certainly not."

A look of relief began to play across Plautius's face.

Castulus took a step backwards, paused, and thrust with his fatal question. "Ah, Pomponia Graecina, you deny all that, but do you deny belief in this Christ these people worship?"

Gladyl felt her face blanch as white as the marble columns around her. With everyone in the room she held her breath. Would Pomponia give up her new-found internal peace for external peace?

Pomponia was the only one who seemed unperturbed as she raised her head to speak. "I believe Jesus Christ is the Son of the one true God."

Castulus took his seat with a smug look on his face. His case was won.

Setonius stood before the judge. "Your Honor, the defendant freely admits that she has participated with Christiani in study and worship. Such activities, however, in no way involve any of the immoral practices suggested by the prosecution, and we wish to show to this court that her actions have never at any time broken a duly constituted law of Rome."

All in the room, hoping for the release of their kinswoman, leaned forward.

"Although she has not undergone the formal membership ritual known as baptism, Pomponia Graecina has stated she agrees with the beliefs of the Christiani. But what harm is that? Is not Pomponia Graecina a Roman? Is not a Roman free?" A murmur of agreement met his words. "May not a Roman *think?*" The murmur increased. "May not a Roman *believe?*"

Now the murmur rose in volume. "Of course we may." "What harm in that?" "He's right."

Then the defense took another tack. "Pomponia Graecina, along with every other free-born Roman citizen, has the right to act and think freely as long as she breaks no duly constituted law." Here the judge nodded. "And I declare that she has broken no law." Several eyebrows went up at this, for all knew of Claudius's proclamation against this sect. Setonius answered their looks. "Indeed, in spite of the fact that Rome has always recognized the right of the Jews to worship their God, Claudius decreed the cult of Christ illegal—but the Senate did not. And let me remind you, it is the Senate that makes the laws in Rome. Until such a time as the Senate takes such action, I contend that the Christiani sect of Judaism is a *religio licita*—a legally accepted religion."

As counsel for the defense took his seat, the face of Aulus Plautius clearly showed his gratitude for his nephew's fine legal mind. He took only a few moments to look back through his notes on the proceedings before motioning his wife to stand before him. Their eyes met; then he looked beyond her to the rest of the room. "I find no fault in the defendant and declare Pomponia Graecina not guilty."

A general tumult of approval filled the courtyard. Castulus paused only once in his angry stride from the room to warn a member of the Plautii standing near Gladyl, "You cheer today. You may all be Christiani, for all I know. But just you wait. When we bring Nero to the throne . . ."

Some weeks later Josephes realized that though God's hand was on his family and the believers in blessing, and though his heart was often filled with praise, the gnawing homesickness never completely disappeared. One evening he expressed the ache he carried inside by singing to Eurgain one of the ancient songs of his people:

By the rivers of Babylon, there we sat down,
Yea, we wept when we remembered Zion.
We hanged our harps upon the willows in the midst there.
For they that carried us away captive required of us a song;

And they that wasted us required of us mirth,
Saying, "Sing us one of the songs of Zion."
How should be sing the Lord's song in a new land?

Eurgain rubbed her fingers lightly against his beard. "It is beautiful, my heart, but is it longing for Jerusalem or for Britain you sing of?"

Josephes took her hand and looked at the slim, white fingers. "I do not know. They somehow seem the same in my mind—they are both home, both the place of my heart. But Rome can never have a place in my heart even if I must live here for the rest of my life."

At that Eurgain burst into tears, and Josephes was long in consoling her. This outburst puzzled and concerned him. When he looked more closely, he realized that she looked paler and thinner than usual, yet there was a new brightness in her eyes. What could it be?

In the coming days, Josephes thought much over his wife's passionate reaction. Certainly she complained as loudly as the rest of their company about being jostled by the throng in the market, about the stench from the Tiber, and about the rumble of noises that went on all night—the only time heavy traffic was allowed on Rome's narrow streets—with the curses of the drivers clanging louder than the iron wheels of their carts. And certainly she shared the fears all Romans had—of being hit by slop thrown from an upper window when one passed an insula, of being struck by falling brick from the notoriously ill-constructed buildings, and greatest of all—the constant terrifying danger of fire. But none of these fears seemed really to explain Eurgain's soul-wrenching sobs.

At last he spoke to her. "Eurgain, my dove, what is it? I fear for your health."

Her answer gave him little consolation. "I am not sure—yet."

His hand tightened on her arm. "Then you must make sure, my heart. The Greek physician who attends Gladys—you must consult him."

She did not answer. It was as if fear held her back. What terrible thing was she afraid of? Josephes's heart lurched. "Promise me. You must promise. You will see Dr. Kronos."

"I will." Her voice was barely above a whisper.

In turmoil of spirit, Josephes wrote a long letter to his father on three sheets of precious parchment. As lucidly as possible, he recounted the sorrows and blessings of their lives. Then, in a highly personal note, he confided one further blessing. Gladys and Rufus Pudens were soon to become parents. Although, as Josephes assured his father, Eurgain seemed to be genuinely happy for her sister, Josephes couldn't help but worry that his wife might plunge into another deep depression. Was Eurgain's problem not physical, but something deeper?

Josephes sat long, chewing the end of his stylus before he concluded his letter with a greeting to all his family and friends in Britain.

It was two o'clock in the morning, according to one Greek slave who looked outside and calculated by the stars, on kalends June when the Palatium Britannicum was aroused by the arrival of its newest member. Rufus proudly announced the birth of his son Timotheus, immediately dispatched a messenger to his mother Olympa at her villa outside Rome, and allowed no one to go back to bed for the rest of the night.

Later the next morning, Josephes found his wife alone in their quarters after her visit to her sister and the babe. The look of longing on her face stabbed him. Josephes put his arm around his wife. "It's the babe, isn't it?"

Eurgain looked surprised at his question, but agreed. "Yes. Yes, it's the babe. I've been longing so to return home. And now we must be finding a way, Josephes."

He held his wife closer. "I understand, my love. But we can't run away. Little Timotheus—"

"Run away? Whatever are you meaning? I'm not suggesting we sneak off. I've just been talking to Gladys about it, and she says she's sure Claudius would grant her petition to allow us to leave—now that there's the baby to consider."

"Eurgain, I would be as thrilled as you to return to Britain, and I suppose it's worth a try for Gladys to speak to Claudius, but I fail to see why Caesar would let us go just because his adopted daughter has a baby. He's more likely to say we should stay here now as his 'grandchild' will need aunts and uncles."

Eurgain turned around in Josephes's arm to face him. "Stupid man! Haven't you been understanding one thing I've said? It's not Timotheus I'm talking about. It's our babe."

Josephes was speechless. "Our . . . you mean . . . Oh, Eurgain! Is that what was wrong? Is Dr. Kronos sure?"

Eurgain laughed and threw her arms around him. "Very sure. At last. But I would not speak sooner until he was certain. There was no need of our both being disappointed. But Jehovah be praised. He has granted us this greatest of blessings!"

"Praise God! Praise God!" exulted Josephes.

"Still we must pray. Gladys received a message from the Capitoline—Claudius is coming to see her tomorrow. She says he'll deny her nothing; but, oh, Josephes, I'm so worried—we must get back to Britain. Our babe must be born at home."

And the next day, Caesar agreed. "Daughter of Ca-Caratacus, see that my Britannia is ruled well and that your s-s-sons and daughters are good Roman citizens."

Eurgain knew that her sister would have felt free to embrace noble Caesar, but she merely bowed her head in gratitude as her eyes filled with tears of joy.

11

fter the tumult of Rome, the peace of Ynis Witrin was overwhelming. A sturdy three-year-old bounded across the thick grass to greet Josephes. He grabbed the child and swung him up in the air. "Ah, John Marcus! So this is the nephew I never met." He turned the child around. "And this is your Aunt Eurgain. She will soon produce a playmate for you—although it doesn't look as though you lack for many here." Joseph watched a cluster of laughing Celtic and Jewish children, including Anna's little Dorcas, racing across the valley.

Then the adults who had come to greet Josephes's boat caught up with them, and for a time Ynis Witrin seemed as tumultuous as Rome. Josephes was shocked that his father had aged so much, but on second look he saw that the white hair and wrinkled skin were only outward signs. Joseph's clear, shining eyes told his son that the inner man was stronger than ever.

"Come," Joseph said. "Your home is ready for you. Mary cleaned it every week while you were gone as an act of faith that you would return. And Joanna has planted flowers all around it."

When Josephes stepped back inside his wattle and daub home, so meager compared to their Roman villa and yet so much more beloved, he felt as if he had never been away. But a few minutes later when eleven-year-old Elisabeth Britannia greeted him, it seemed as if a great chunk of time must have melted and simply run out under his feet.

That night they had a feast at the cors. Balan, whose white beard now reached past his waist and who had become hard of hearing, insisted that Josephes and Eurgain repeat all that had happened at least three times before he was satisfied. And Caradoc's speech he wanted to hear *five* times. But his face darkened at the recalling of how Tarana, under the guise of taking her to a wise druid, had sold Eurgain to Ostorius.

"Tarana Redbeard violated all that a druid believes in. There are three duties of man—to reverence the deity, to abstain from evil, to behave valiantly. He did none of these. Above all, a druid seeks wisdom, and the three primary ornaments of wisdom are love, truth, courage. Tarana behaved with none of those qualities. At the Gorsedd that year, it was my sad duty to report his betrayal, and the national assembly of druids voted him out of our number."

"Where is he now?" Josephes asked.

Balan shrugged. "Probably in the pay of some Roman. We have not been seeing his red beard around here for these two years or more, although there are rumors of his equally treacherous sons appearing on Ynis Witrin occasionally. Seeming about the time cattle is reported missing in the lake village. But let us not be talking of such grim matters. Tell me again, what did Caradoc say to the tribunal?"

There was a soft groan from down the table, and Josephes caught the eye of Cynon, Caradoc's son. He had been allowed to return to Britain with his older brother and was now studying at the cors. The slim gold collar which marked him as a king's son gleamed in the torchlight.

"Ah," Balan said, "this lad is proud enough to be wearing his royal collar, but he wearies of his royal father's words."

Josephes was certain Cynon was not the only one in the company weary of the speech, but he obediently repeated it yet again for Balan, who nodded at every word.

The next morning Joseph took his son alone to view his proudest work—the wattle church Joseph had been contemplating building the very day their lives had been torn apart by the Roman capture. "Father, you can't imagine how blessed we are here to have such a building. In Rome the temples stand practically on top of each other, and yet the Christiani must worship secretly in homes at night. And when the emperor decides to hunt them out and stop them, they are forced to meet outside the city in the catacumbus." He shivered. "But this is beautiful, Father. So simple, yet so sacred. I think it would be impossible to enter here without praying." And he raised his hands in blessing.

In the coming days, Josephes found himself going every morning to the church for prayer, especially asking God's help for believers in parts of the Empire less blessed than this. But the days barely had time to settle into routine before the long-awaited child arrived. His parents named him Josepheus Helias—Helias meaning the sense of kindness God requires His children to show all men. Above all else, they wanted their son to show the love and mercy of God in his life.

But Joseph, with a special fondness in his eyes, always called the child Nepos, "Little One." As much as Joseph loved his other grandchildren, Nepos was his special joy. This was the child of promise, the special evidence of God's blessing on the house of Joseph of Arimathea, the child through whom the inheritance of the family would pass.

Joseph, sitting beside his well, thought long on Nepos's dedication service. What, of all his years of teaching, did he most want to leave with his people after he was gone? He knew this service would remain vivid in the minds and hearts of all who attended and that it would be recounted to Nepos as part of his spiritual heritage. This service would be Nepos's birthright, just as Isaac had passed his portion to Jacob. The line of Joseph and the message his house stood for would be secured in this child.

When the day came for the service, Joseph was more thankful than ever that God had allowed him to build His church. As the company came into the building and stood quietly, Joseph turned to face the front of the room and surveyed the symbol he had placed there—an ever-present reminder of Christ's great gift of love. As he looked at the shadows behind the white alderwood cross, Joseph remembered the darkness at the crucifixion—the darkness of a world without Christ. And then, almost as soon as the memory filled his mind, a beam of light came in through the east window, driving all thought of darkness away—just as the light Joseph had brought to this land would continue to drive all darkness before it.

Joseph turned and placed a scroll on the reading table. This Psalm of David had become ever more precious to Joseph through the years at Ynis Witrin. He chanted:

Oh come, let us sing unto the Lord,
let us heartily rejoice in the strength of our salvation.
Let us come before His presence with thanksgiving
and show ourselves glad in Him with psalms.
For the Lord is a great God, and a great King above all gods.

The faces of the congregation glowed with the joy of the words, and Joseph's heart sang as he continued:

In His hands are all the corners of the earth;
and the strength of the hills is His also.
The sea is His, and He made it;
and His hands prepared the dry land.
Oh come, let us worship and fall down,
and kneel before the Lord our Maker.
For He is the Lord our God;
and we are the people of His pasture,
and the sheep of His hand.

And all responded, "Selah."

Then Balan, in his white ceremonial robes and golden crown with three rays of light, stepped forward to pronounce his blessing. "There are three men that ought to look on with affection—he that with affection looks on the face of the earth; he that is delighted with ordered works of art; and he that looks lovingly on little infants." Commanding no less respect from his people because his voice shook with the weight of his years, Balan smiled at little Helias in his father's arms and continued, "We look lovingly on this child and know that God does likewise. He is now the third generation of his line to live on Ynis Witrin, and this is but the beginning. Our people will live together in the peace and joy of the Lord which you have taught us, Joseph of the Light."

And then Eurgain sang to her own harp accompaniment a hymn of praise she had written on the birth of her son, as she reveled in the graciousness of God:

My heart is magnifying the Lord,
The God of Heaven, the King of the universe,
For He has blessed me.
And with the mother of our Yesu
I am praising Him who regards the lowly estate of this
handmaiden.
For He has blessed me.
I was a stranger in a strange land, and He blessed me.
I longed for a returning to my home and my people, and He
blessed me.
I cried unto the Lord for a son, and He blessed me.
I praise Him who has blessed me.

At the conclusion of the hymn, Joseph stepped to Josephes to take the babe in his own arms, and he prayed, "Blessed are You, Lord our God, King of the universe, who has taught the hearts of Your faithful people by sending them the light of Your Holy Spirit, grant this child by the same Spirit to have a right judgment in all things, that we might evermore rejoice at Your working in his life. Through the merits of the only worthy One, Jesus Christ our Savior, who lives and reigns with You, in the unity of the same Spirit, one God, world without end."

And they all said, "Amen."

Joseph handed Nepos, who had slept peacefully throughout the whole time, back to his father and took the olivewood cup in his hands. The cup felt warm, as if he held the hand of a living person, and Joseph remembered Christ's promise that had become so personal to him, "Lo, I am with you always." Joseph looked at the rich, red contents of the cup and was reminded of the blood of Christ. Then he spoke, "Blessed are You, Lord our God, King of the universe, who created the fruit of the vine. Especially today, this is the cup of blessing. I say with King David, 'My cup runs over.'"

Joseph drank, then passed the cup around the room. "And as we partake of this cup, feel the nearness of the One who promised never to leave us or forsake us." Joseph smiled at his own words, recalling how often that promise had sustained him.

But Joseph was not satisfied. He had said and done all he had planned, and yet he had an unfinished feeling. The cup completed its circle of the company, and Joseph took it from the hands of Joanna who had been the last to drink. As he turned to place it on the altar, it caught a shaft of sunlight from the window and glowed as if wrought from gold. Suddenly Joseph knew the final legacy he wanted to leave his people.

"This very cup from which our Lord drank on His last night on earth," he said holding it out in both hands, "is in very truth the cup of the New Testament, the cup of His love poured out for us. Just as the stone tablets of the Law were the centerpiece of worship under the old covenant, so let this cup of Christ's love be your centerpiece of the new.

"And let this be a sign unto you—to you and to all true believers in B'rithain, that God has vouchsafed this cup of His covenant to Logres, to the land of His word."

The sun shimmered on the few drops of wine left in the cup, and the light and its reflection seemed to grow until for a few minutes the whole church was filled with a shimmering red radiance. The light vibrated like harp strings, sending out further shafts of red-gold. Red for blood, red for royal jewels, red for fire. And Joseph knew that all those elements would play a part in the life of the cup of Logres.

The vision faded slowly, leaving behind more a sense of a song than of a sight, and the worshipers departed silently. Only Joseph remained, still holding the precious grail.

His hand trembled, and he stood dazed, as a second vision came upon him. This one—not glowing and luminous, filling the church with radiance as the first, but a pale, misty picture, dim with distance—of this cup covered not in light, but in darkness, not a high holy emblem for all people, but hidden from sight . . . The mists shifted, and Joseph shook his head to clear his sight, but the vision did not return. He was left with the strangest sense of journeying, of seeking, of searching for the very object he held in his hands. And the words in his head made even less sense to him: *And darkness was upon the face of the deep . . . and God saw that it was good . . .*

He turned slowly and with still trembling hands placed the cup on the altar, confused, yet with an assurance that whatever was to befall the cup and the people to whom he had dedicated it, God would see that it was good. Then Joseph stepped out into the sunshine and crossed the green expanse to Wearyall Hill.

This time he felt anything but weary as he sat under the now mature thorn tree that blossomed every spring and again in midwinter at the time of Jesus' birth. Joseph looked out across the twelves hides where his transplanted people also prospered. The warmth of the sun made the tree's patch of shade a welcome haven. He had planted well. The tree had grown and flourished, just as the small flame of faith that he and his band had planted had increased.

Joseph was an old man now. The nurturing of the light would soon pass to the hands of younger, stronger disciples, but Joseph knew he had done well in bringing his flickering torch to this green land.

A large white seabird flew by, swooping toward the fish that populated the marshes and waterways beyond Ynis Witrin. Its call awakened a memory Joseph had long suppressed. He was again on the wharf at Joppa, his nephew at his side, clapping his sun-bronzed hands. "Oh, take me with you, Uncle!" The child danced with delight. "I want to see it all—take me with you on your next voyage!" With the memory, the ache returned. The grief of having failed this holy child who was so anxious to see through human eyes the wonders of the world He had created as God—the world He would all too soon die for.

A sob tore from the depths of Joseph's being. But as quickly as it was uttered, the familiar words were there, "Lo, I am with you always."

And at last, Joseph understood. He had not failed his Lord. He had brought Jesus to Britain. In the truest sense of all, Joseph *had* brought the Christ here, and now His feet did walk on these green and pleasant hills as He lived in the hearts of all who walked in the light of His faith.

BOOK II

THE UNFURLING OF THE BANNER

ROMAN BRITAIN

Today I walked again on the abbey grounds. The ancient hallowed nave, now roofless, was bare and cold, and my sandals slapped hollowly on the stones, scaring the mice that have come in from the field and the birds that nest in the great pillars. I saw it all—the doors broken, the windows smashed, the sacred furniture splintered, and—my heart breaks to think of it—our holy relics gone. All gone.

And yet God is not gone. Nor has His worship ceased, for I am here, and even the humblest of servants may offer praise.

Among those silent stones, I thought again of my poor story I have been toiling over. Caradoc died in Rome, and it was said by many that his spirit entered into Boudicca, Queen of the Iceni, who led a courageous, but ill-fated rebellion against the Romans the next year. After that, Britain settled down to four hundred years of Roman rule.

With the passage of the years, the lake village ceased to be occupied, its fortifications no longer necessary under the Pax Romana, *and it sank into the Meare. The homes built by Joseph and his companions were occupied by a few holy hermits and then fell into disrepair. Weeds grew beside the thorn tree, and animals crept around the wattle church, sheltering against its walls in times of storm. A few ragged druids clung to the old ways on the far side of the Tor. Joseph of Arimathea's light quivered dimly.*

Has such near extinction of the faith come to Glastonbury again?

Pondering this in great sadness, I walked to the site of the Old Church and the burial place of Joseph of Arimathea. There I vowed that the light shall not be quenched. I shall renew my search for the grail. Even in our isolation here, word has reached us of King Henry's continued persecutions. If ever there was a time when our country needed the grail, surely it is now. We are a people hungry for a vision, for a renewal of faith, for a new torch of light.

It is clear to me now that Joseph indeed brought the cup to England. But then what happened? As I stood near what must have been Joseph's grave, I wondered if the sacred vessel had been buried with him. And I wondered briefly—God and His saints forgive me, for I know all doubting is of the devil—if it had ever existed at all. If Henry's vandals couldn't find it, had it ever been here? But then I recalled all I had learned of Joseph, and I knew it had existed. So in the fifteen hundred years since Joseph's time, what has become of this holiest of objects?

Suddenly a new thought seized my mind. Why is this object—of all that Christ touched—so revered? Why is the grail sought with even more devotion than pieces of the true cross or our Lord's robe? And then—my hand shakes with excitement as I write—I saw with a strange certainty that the grail is more than the sacred cup we have always longed for.

It is not just the grail itself, as an object, that I must find. I must find its meaning. When England finds the true meaning of the grail, there will be peace in this broken land.

Joseph, by the grace of God, brought spiritual light to this land as surely as he brought the grail. Is the grail then spiritual light? I must think on it.

My heart pounds, my mind swells with excitement. I pray God to lead His most humble of servants in this journey to discover the truth sought with such longing.

PART ONE

1

Marcellus surveyed the great stone and earthwork wall rising twelve feet above his head. The world called it Hadrian's Wall, but Marcellus thought of it as his wall. For three years now he had been chief engineer at Vercovicium, in charge of the continual refortifications and repairs necessitated by this foul wet climate and the even more foul, more vicious Picti and their eternal raiding parties. But this morning, it was neither the elements nor the savage Picti that worried Marcellus. It was Prefect Festus, engineer-in-charge from Coristopinum, the one person in the entire eighty Roman miles of the wall to whom Marcellus was answerable in matters of wall construction. All others answered to Marcellus.

Certainly no one could fault Festus on his engineering skills nor on his diligence in the line of duty. His ability to build bridges of stone was faultless. Since Marcellus prided himself on possessing equal skills, applied with equal attention to detail and duty, and since in his five years of following the eagle he had tended to neglect any people-reaching skills he might possess, the relationship between the two men had never been comfortable. Indeed, their exchanges often stung as much as the quicklime which held the massive stones of the wall in place.

But in all his years of suffering under Festus's bouts of nitpicking inspection, Marcellus had never had to bear such an outrage. The courier had arrived a few moments after cockcrow sounded and accosted Marcellus in his barracks with a salute that was sloppy if not insolent. Marcellus could still feel the parchment crinkle in his hand as he crushed the message in anger. "No reply. Dismissed." He turned on his heel even before the messenger could retreat.

With an icy stoicism that matched the early March climate, Marcellus grabbed his sponge and strode to the latrine at the far corner of the fort. Then he returned to his barracks to don the mail shirt and ornamented greaves that clearly marked him as a centurion. He clapped his transverse-crested helmet over his curly brown, close-cropped hair. Gripping his vinewood staff that served both as badge of office and instrument of discipline should any slack in their duty, he called his men to attention and marched them to the section of wall to be repaired today.

For two hours, while his men worked in response to his barked orders, he paced the wall—his wall—the wall to whose care he had devoted three years of his life. How could that officious ignoramus find fault with his work? Had he ever failed an inspection in all his years here? Had his wall ever once crumbled unexpectedly from frost, rain, or enemy battering? Had any of his men suffered accidents from sloppy, unsupervised work?

The words of the message went round and round in his mind like a spinning chariot wheel:

> Centurion Gaius Marcellus Artios:
>
> Greetings in the name of Emperor Antonius Pius. Word has come to my attention of improper procedures in use at Vercovicium. I shall arrive midday today for a full inspection and explanation.
>
> Prefect V. Festus Martinus
> Engineer-in-charge, Augusta

Marcellus ground his teeth. He supposed he should be grateful for the warning. Festus would claim it was intended as a courtesy—as if Festus ever did anything as a courtesy. And the very fact that his superior warned him was evidence that he knew Marcellus had nothing to cover up. Marcellus saw to it that his men built for time beyond time. It was with great pride that his centurial working party marked on a facing stone as each section of repairs was finished so that the standard of the work could be assessed. "Century of G. Marcellus Artios, Legio II Augusta, restituit" marked quality work.

"Pack that rubble down good and firm," he directed the men pouring fill between the two sides of the stone wall. "We are to be honored with a visit from the engineer-in-charge today, and by Jove, I do not want to be found lacking."

He turned to two legionnaires approaching with wooden buckets of lime from the mixing pits overseen by his senior optio. "Be careful with that stuff. I don't want to have to report any men in sick bay with lime burns when Jupiter II arrives."

The men replied, "Aye, sir," with barely repressed smiles at his sarcasm. They moved on, the metal plates of their armor grating against each other. Marcellus gave a final inspection to yesterday's work. The mortar was still warm from its final water-slaking, having, as it were, cooked itself into solid stone. Marcellus nodded in satisfaction. All was ready for his Lord-High-and-Mighty's inspection. He had built well.

With a shake of his head, Marcellus put the coming inspection out of his mind and walked on westward, ostensibly inspecting the ramparts, but in fact allowing his gaze to wander far. To the north the land dropped sharply behind the wall, and beyond the scrub and furze that clung intrepidly to the ground, a great forest of primeval oak stretched as far as the eye could see. For all he knew the forest covered all of the seventy-some miles northward to where the Emperor Antonius was having his own wall built—a turf barrier to hold the Picti farther back and mark out more land for the Empire. Marcellus was glad his century had not been among the four from Vercovicium ordered north to work on the new wall, even if the serious understaffing meant more work for those left behind.

To the south the land rolled away, covered with thorn and scrub that supported a few lean cows and sheep herded by the natives living in the vicus outside the fort. As he stood there now, the sound of rooks cawing in a clump of trees reached him, mingled with the gentler sounds of cows from the farmstead in the draw to the east. Deserted, windswept, cold. There was no reason Marcellus should feel any fondness for this outpost, and yet . . .

He felt he'd been on the wall forever. The routine of the work and the loneliness of the place, the square-built fort that was like every other fort in the Empire and made them all blend into one in a person's mind . . . It was easy enough to forget time while engineering the road-building along the Thenus in Germania—not that there had been anything memorable about those two years anyway—and it was almost easy to forget his old life in Rome . . . at times.

But at moments like this, when the wind blew from the west bringing with it the scent of newly green grass and ruffling the tiny daisies in the turf that grew right up to the great vallum that protected the wall . . . Checking to make sure he was out of sight of his men, Marcellus sat on a rise in the rampart and gazed at the unbroken northern horizon through narrowed eyes. Somewhere out there where that other contingent was building another wall, was another chief engineer sitting on his ramparts, gazing southward and thinking long thoughts?

Marcellus was twenty-seven now. This was the year 909 since the founding of Rome, the eighteenth year of the reign of the Emperor Antonius Pius. Marcellus had been twenty-two when he surprised everyone, himself most of all, and distressed his family by joining the legion. For four years before that, he had studied engineering under his Uncle Titus, all the time his head filled with visions of building great marble baths, constructing aqueducts to carry water to elegant villas and palaces, and designing hypocaust systems to heat fine libraries and public buildings. The thought of engineering a road from Rome to a new part of the Empire had fired his imagination, but never in his wildest imaginings had he seen himself immured on a stone and earthwork wall at the literal edge of the world, fending off savage little raiders who wanted to steal their neighbors' cattle, or keeping the peace among the equally troublesome Brigantes to the south.

Yes, he was twenty-seven now, but he had been only twenty when he met

Julia, and she just seventeen. He seldom allowed himself to indulge in thoughts of Julia, of recalling their eager visions of the fine villa he would one day build for them with the very latest and best in heating and water systems, of future children splashing in the fountain he would place in the center of their peristylum . . .

The musty-sweet scent of a small, white wild flower that grew in profusion along the ditch bank reached him, and his mouth tightened in pain. Just so had the lilies at Festa's funeral smelled. The pain of loss shared with Julia and her family as his betrothed's twin sister was decked with flowers and laid in the Mausoleum of the Virgins. And then the sharper, more personal pain of hearing that very night that Julia had been chosen by the Pontifix Maximum to replace her twin in the service of the Goddess Vestal. Festa had been chosen—a great honor to her family—at age ten. She should have continued for another twenty years, tending the perpetual fire in the Temple of Vesta, preparing ritual food, and presiding at the Vestalia worship had not a putrid fever changed everything in less than twenty-four hours. And then two days later, Julia, who should have been robed in bridal scarlet and showered with marriage blossoms, was led in virgin white up the Sacred Way to the first rise in the Capitoline Hill above the Forum to the Temple of Vesta. The flowers she carried and wore wreathed around her head were the same variety of musky lily that had decked her sister's body.

The next day Marcellus joined the legion, the Second Augusta. At least he came from a family of position and could go to the rank of centurion without having to spend years working his way up as most did.

The shout of a sentry, a call of the trumpet, and a clatter of horse's hooves in the fort below told Marcellus that Festus had arrived. Marcellus grimaced. He would undoubtedly be reprimanded like a schoolboy for not being there to welcome his superior officer. But then, if he had been there, he would have been shouted off for not attending to duty on the wall.

By the time Marcellus arrived at the praetorium in the center of the fort, Festus was seated on a stool in the commander's office, drinking a cup of the sour army-ration wine that could clear the dustiest journey from one's throat in a single gulp.

Commander Caius Valens returned Marcellus's open-palmed salute. "Prefect Festus has received a disturbing report of work on the wall, Centurion." He gestured for Marcellus to take a seat on the other stool near the table the commander used for a desk, but Marcellus preferred to remain standing.

"Am I to understand we are harboring spies in our midst, sir?"

Festus gave his cold smile that always seemed to Marcellus to be more of a smirk. "I prefer to think that we have men in the legion with exceptional devotion to duty."

"I believe I have never been found wanting in attention to duty," Marcellus replied with equal ice.

The commander rose. "Well, I'm sure a simple inspection will clear the matter up. Would the prefect care for another cup of wine?"

Festus tipped his cup up for a final mouthful. "That will be sufficient, thank you. Shall we go, Centurion?"

Festus strode ahead, his gladius clanking at his side and his hobnailed caligae clanging on the cobbled Via Principalis as they went out the west gate. "You, you, and you," he shouted at the first three men he met on the wall, "fetch buckets of water, and be quick about it!"

The men saluted hastily and scurried off toward the troughs of rain water. When they reached yesterday's working, Festus grabbed a crowbar and began gouging a hole in the partially set mortar. He paused at the first pieces of rubble he uncovered. "Rather large, aren't they? Don't you instruct your men to break up the rubble so it will pack more tightly between layers of mortar?"

Marcellus stood at stiff attention. "It will hold, sir."

"Will it indeed? We shall see." Festus's visage was even more hawklike than usual.

"You! Optio! Licinus! I want three men with crowbars. Dig this out."

Marcellus was amazed when the men appeared as if by magic. The men under his command were never slovenly in following his orders, but this lightning speed was not usual. By the time the others arrived with the sloshing buckets of water a gaping, ragged cavity defaced Marcellus's wall.

"All right. One at a time." Festus pointed at the buckets. "And don't slosh it about. I want it all in this hole!"

By now the entire contingent had ceased their work and gathered around the hole. Marcellus held his breath as each load of water filled the well. He had overseen this work personally, leaving little to his senior optio. He was always scrupulous that the rubble be tamped down thoroughly before a load of mortar was poured over it, and he had seen that the lime was thoroughly slaked and mixed evenly with sand, mortar, and their special hardening ingredient to prevent crumbling. He had no reason to be nervous. And yet the beads of sweat stood out on his forehead in spite of the fresh breeze blowing across the wall.

The last bucket was emptied. Marcellus thought he could hear a common intake of breath among all the cohort. The water held. Only a ripple on the surface from the wind.

But Festus wasn't so easily satisfied. He lifted his heavily shod foot and stomped it down. "All right, men, let's see if this would hold up to a Pictish battering."

Marcellus knew it would be fruitless to point out that battering rams were Roman weapons and that the Picts were far more likely to attempt sneaking through the gate in broad daylight disguised as traders and shepherds. With his head held defiantly high, he added the stamping of his own mailed sandals.

The water held. The men, like a crowd at the arena cheering for a favorite gladiator, threw their arms in the air with a shout and stamped harder.

And then, with an awful sucking sound, the breeze-rippled surface swirled into a whirlpool and drained from sight. A stunned silence fell over all.

"As I suspected. Air pockets. I want this entire working dug out by sundown." Festus raised his gaze and shouted, "Do you hear me, men? If any of this section is still standing by nightfall, you'll spend a week in the guardhouse! All of you!" As the men scrambled for their tools, Festus turned back to Marcellus. "I shall report this to the commander. Then I shall oversee the rebuilding myself." He glared at Marcellus. "Personally. If you will follow me to the praetorium."

"Carry on," Marcellus ordered Optio Licinus in an attempt to keep his dignity before his men.

"I am giving the orders now. You will follow me," Festus barked.

Marcellus had thought that nothing in his life could equal the bitterness of losing Julia and leaving home, family, and country. But in the following days as he sat kicking his heels in his small, bare barracks room, only slightly less confining than the guardhouse, he plumbed new depths of outrage. His job had never been a replacement for all he had lost, had never fulfilled his dreams. But it had been a life. It provided moments of satisfaction. It gave him something to do, something he could take pride in.

The ordered life of a Roman fort gave structure to his life: trumpets sounding cockcrow, trumpets sounding mealtimes, trumpets sounding lights out. And now even that shred of a second-best replacement had been snatched from him. What did the fates have against him? Marcellus vaguely believed that the gods directed everything in the life of the state and in the lives of individuals, as he had been taught. Although never personally devout, and certainly less so since Julia had been snatched from him to be sacrificed to the state religion, he had not bothered to turn his back on his childhood training. Simply ignoring it was sufficient.

And his father was always scrupulous in leading his family in daily reverence at the shrine where the *Lar familiaris,* the guardian spirit of the home, was worshiped. Marcellus gave a sardonic smile. In his mind he could see his mother and two sisters in anxious prayer before the family shrine, asking the guiding spirits to smile on their son and brother who even now was serving the Empire to protect *Lares et Penates*—hearth and home. And then in reverence to Vesta they would tend the family hearth.

Well, somehow all the prayers offered for him had gone sadly awry. But as a man of action, Marcellus doubted that his ill fortune could all be laid at the door of the gods. There was something wrong here, and he intended to find out what it was. His fate at Vercovicium seemed pretty well sealed, for even if he could prove that the fault in the work was not his own, his loss of face before his men would necessitate moving to a new post. The best he could hope for was to lessen the ignominy of his next assignment.

He heard the clatter of a returning patrol, shouted orders, and the new clatter of a fresh patrol leaving, then a moment of relative quiet before the trumpet signaled the midday meal. No one would be surprised if he didn't show his face in officers' mess, and this hour while the men would be off the wall at their bowls of stew would be an ideal time to look around.

But the freshly redone workings on the wall offered no explanation of what had happened. To all appearances, the repair had been redone in precisely the same manner he had directed his men to build it in the first place. He walked over every inch of the past three days' workings, but could find nothing amiss. Not that he had expected to find sloppy work occurring under Festus's eagle-eye—much as it might have delighted him to do so.

With a sigh he turned from the workings, descended the wall, and, with a salute to the sentry on duty, walked through the north gate and down the earthen ramp. He had no idea what he hoped to find. He certainly had no suspicions of Picti activity undermining his work, and the unusually mild weather they'd had lately could hardly be expected to provide any clues. It was simply his thorough nature, demanding he see a problem from every angle, that sent him to the northern side of the wall.

After his second time pacing the entire length of the reworked section, he found a smooth spot beside a clump of gorse and sat down to try once more to make sense of what had happened. He hoped he would be out of view of the men returned to work on the wall above him. The unanswered questions ran in circles through his mind. Was it the malice of the fates or of a human hand? If the fates, why? If human, how? Was it simple bad luck, or had he been careless? Had someone mixed the mortar with too much sand or omitted the hardening ingredient? Could one of his own men have been that careless or that disloyal? And why? Who had reported him to Festus? And why, why, why?

He had thought his men faithful to the century and to the legion even if he had made no effort to bind them to himself with personal loyalty. He had spent no time reveling in the native-run wine shops in the vicus outside the walls of the fort, nor did he choose to accompany the men when they visited the huts at the end of the street that offered another pleasure. He had tried that once or twice in an effort to forget Julia, but found the cheap version only increased his sense of loss. He had on occasion joined hunting parties and enjoyed exploring the British countryside, so unlike his native Italy. But he found killing for sport distasteful, and so preferred solitary rambles. All these things, he knew, did not make him a personal favorite with his men. Yet he had always believed they respected him for his fairness in command and the quality of work he demanded.

He picked up a clod of dirt and hurled it at a rabbit peeking from behind a gorse bush. That was the most bitter irony of all. His one pleasure, his one satisfaction, had been pride in his work. The wall had come to replace the fine villas and waterways he had hoped to engineer in Rome. And now he had been disgraced for slovenly work on his wall. It was as if he had been accused of being unfaithful to the woman he loved.

He picked up another clod, but his arm halted mid-thrust. For the first time he focused on the hole the rabbit had fled into. That was no mere rabbit hole hidden under the bushes. With his heart pounding in his throat, Marcellus approached the carefully concealed excavation and dropped to his hands and knees. He stuck his arm into the hole as far as it would reach and felt around. No doubt about it, the channel went up, not down, as a rabbit burrow would, and it had been carefully lined with stone inside to prevent a cave-in.

He sat back on his heels and gazed up at the wall. The place of his humiliation was directly over his head. He had no doubt that a few quickly turned shovelfuls of sod would reveal a drainage shaft cut all the way down from his workings. That explained the mechanics, but left him in a deeper puzzle over the motive. Digging the shaft had been an enormous job requiring careful planning and execution. And the skill in timing, to coordinate the placement of the tunnel with that particular day's workings and Festus's arrival—even though the perpetrator had obviously sent a message to Festus, he couldn't know for certain when Festus would arrive. Not unless it was a coordinated effort. But why? If Festus wanted to get rid of him, he could simply request Marcellus's transfer. Such an elaborate scheme was unnecessary.

In the full light of day, not caring who saw him or what they thought, he marched through the north gate, along the main street, and into the praetorium, barely bothering to return the sentry's salute. He did not pause until he stood in the commandant's doorway.

"By your leave, sir, I would like to show you something on the wall."

"Centurion Marcellus, were you not confined to quarters at Prefect Festus's order?"

"Sir, if you will come with me, I believe you will agree my information more than makes up for any breach of conduct." At least Marcellus hoped so. Had he been too rash? Could there be a simple, logical explanation for what he had found? Could someone have been ordered to implement a perfectly harmless drainage system without the knowledge of the chief engineer? Unlikely. He squared his shoulders. "If you please, sir. You won't be disappointed."

With a sigh the commander dropped the stylus with which he had been making out the endless reports required of a fort commander and rose to accompany Marcellus.

They were nearly to the gate when, to Marcellus's intense frustration, their progress was halted by Optio Licinus. Until two days ago Licinus was Marcellus's chief assistant; now he was slated to step into the centurion's position. The commander quickly dealt with the message Licinus carried from Festus, and they continued through the gate, but Marcellus felt Licinus's eyes following them until they were out of sight.

He paused before the man-made rabbit hole and pointed. Wordlessly the commander knelt and, much as Marcellus had before, explored it the length of his arm. After several minutes he stood up, brushing the dirt from his arm. "The digging appears to be fresh."

"Since our last rain five days ago, I would say, sir," Marcellus replied.

Commander Caius's eyes traced a line up the wall, as Marcellus had earlier, and one could almost see him coming to the same conclusion.

"It's my theory—" Marcellus began.

"Centurion Gaius Marcellus Artios, it is not your place to speculate."

"No, sir, but—"

"You are no longer attached to Vercovicium, Centurion. Your new posting arrived this morning."

Marcellus stared. So soon? He had known it would come, but how could a messenger possibly cover the ground from Isca that quickly, let alone leave time for the turning of the military machinery at the fortress of the Legio Augusta in southwestern Britain? "It seems that our couriers ride with the speed of Mercury." He made no attempt to disguise the suspicion in his voice.

"Even so. And I believe it will be advisable for us to obey them with equal speed."

"And my orders are?" Marcellus held his breath. Anywhere in the Empire would do—but he didn't want to be posted to Rome and have to live daily with old memories.

"You are to be attached to the fort at Glevum, with engineering responsibilities for the lead and tin mining nearby. Report before the Ides of May. Optio Licinus has already assumed your duties here, and Prefect Festus will stay on until this section of repairs is completed to his satisfaction. So you may leave at once."

"By your leave, I shall go pack, sir."

Commander Caius gave a salute of dismissal.

Marcellus slapped his palm to his forehead in return and spun on his heel, barely aware that the commander remained behind, digging in the turf with his gladius. But he had a burning awareness of Festus's hawklike visage glaring at him from the stairway beside the gatehouse.

2

art of the great genius of the Roman military mind was the fact that every fort, from one end of the Empire to the other, was laid out as nearly as possible in the same four-square pattern with the same four gates in the wall, the same Via Praetoria and Via Principalis crossing in the center with the headquarters and commandant's house at the crossroads. It sometimes seemed to Marcellus that all Rome was a series of squares with every legionnaire in the Empire sleeping in the same order every night. And the beauty of it was that the newest arrival, within a few hours of entering a fresh posting, could be completely at home.

But for Marcellus, it didn't work. It had been three days since his chariot-borne arrival at Glevum, and he still felt lost. His assignment to lead a century engaged in lead and tin mining, while not a reduction in rank, was clearly a slap in the face. Living in Glevum, however, was anything but a come-down in circumstances. As one of Rome's four self-governing colonies in Britain where aging legionnaires were literally put out to pasture with grants of land to farm and a thousand active-duty legionnaires were stationed, it boasted all the amenities. Arcaded shops, a theater, civic forum, and gladiatorial amphitheater lined metaled streets that were complete with drainage gullies. Rows of terrace houses replaced the similarly planned barrack blocks in the old fortress. And—most important of all—there was a public bath house.

Just as the layout of the fort was the same from one end of the Empire to the other, so was the life of the legionnaire: up at cockcrow to the summons of the trumpet, a hurried jentaculum of bread dipped in wine and a handful of dates or olives—if one ate at all, and the call to order to march to the day's labor.

Marcellus could no longer feel stationed on the edge of the world, even if he was on the border of the rugged, green mountainous country to the west that was inhabited by tribes subdued by Rome in name only. He still remembered the stories that had fired his boyhood imagination—of the wild, savage Caratacus who had ruled this part of the country a hundred years ago and harried Roman troops for nine years before being subdued by the eagles and led in chains through Rome. He remembered prancing up and down his tutor's garden with his schoolfellows, brandishing a wooden gladius and capturing this fierce foe of the glorious Empire in bloody battle. But never in his wildest imaginings had he thought he would one day be living practically on the legendary Caratacus's doorstep.

Perhaps those childhood memories made him feel a little more settled in Glevum, as if the place had a tie with his home. But still he missed the wall; he missed the empty sweep of windy landscape; he missed the clear bleat of the sheep floating up to him on the sharp air from the valley far below.

However, Marcellus had no time to become accustomed to life at Glevum. On his sixth day there he received orders to take the century newly under his command to the mines in the hills southwest of Glevum. The native miners were much in need of firm Roman organization to increase their productivity as they were falling behind in supplying ore to the smelter works on the coast.

It should have been a two-day march from Glevum to the mines, but the incessant rains that had suddenly begun to fall after a dry spring slowed even these hardy legionnaires.

By the time they had pitched their rectangular deerskin tents—eight men to a tent—in straight lines, with a larger tent for Marcellus and his staff at the end, dug latrine pits, and enclosed the entire camp inside a rectangular ditch, they were a full day behind schedule. Marcellus, worrying that a bad report had followed him from Vercovicium and anxious to make up time and fulfill production quotas, urged his men to greater vigor.

But again and again the mud defeated them.

In spite of Marcellus's best efforts at building drains, the mine pits filled with water, and the men worked up to their knees in mud. The wooden ramps leading out of the pits were slippery wet, treacherous for men bearing leather stretchers of ore, especially when the soles of their boots clogged with clay. Iron shovels, pickaxes, and hammers rusted, decreasing their efficiency. The tempers of Roman and native workers alike grew shorter and shorter.

In an effort to avoid the danger of the wooden ramps, Marcellus directed the men to erect three great tripod derricks on the edge of the pit. Then, with a pulley arrangement of ropes, the ore could be brought to the surface in baskets. One advantage his new posting had over the bleak sweep of country around the wall was that the verdant, wooded western lands offered giant trees from which sturdy poles could be cut for his derricks.

Marcellus also issued an unusual order. Dressed, as always, in full armor with sword and dagger at his side and his heavy woolen cloak flowing around his shoulders, he stood before his men in an intermittent drizzle. "Century, attention! Official dress for the day is tunics and breeches. Armor may be removed."

Marcellus, who had never once issued an order with any consideration as to whether or not it would be popular, found a strange pleasure in the cheers his order brought.

In a short time the men were at work with renewed vigor, dragging the freshly felled fifty-foot poles to the edge of the mine pit. Marcellus realized with surprise that when his men worked without armor, except for their darker hair and shorter stature, it was difficult to tell them from the natives who worked beside them. By the time the trumpet signaled the midday meal at two-thirty, the poles had been bound with ropes, the pulleys affixed, and two of the three machines levered into upright position, ready to begin hauling ore up to fill the waiting carts.

Cena over, the men returned to work with their bacon and wheat rations warming their stomachs. The rain had stopped, and they attacked their work with renewed vigor. A native who had arrived with his ore cart during the meal break joined the work and introduced himself as Elfan. "Ah, and a fine way this will be to load the wagons, with dumping from above. It is in my mind that not all Roman ways are to be resisted." He accompanied his words with a broad smile and a powerful tug at the ropes.

The newcomer's native clothing and flowing mustache marked him as one who clung fiercely to the British ways, rather than adopting a Romanized lifestyle as so many of the natives had. He was obviously one of the drivers who carried the raw ore to waiting barges on the nearby River Axe to take it on to the smelts. But unlike the other drivers, he chose to lend his muscles to the task of bringing up the ore rather than engaging in a game of dice in the shelter of a cart. Marcellus welcomed him, as every pair of strong arms would help in making up his quotas.

"Hold that rope tight!" Marcellus shouted at the newcomer as the tripod threatened to slip back down the steep bank they had just drawn it up.

"Medwy, my son," the Celt shouted to a young man remaining in his cart, "be lending your strength to your father."

Medwy clambered off the cart and gripped the rope near his father. The completed contingent of workers maneuvered the derrick to the top. "Now," Marcellus barked, "pull on these poles and push with that one. We'll raise it here."

Groaning with the intense effort, the men raised the tripod to three-quarters of its height. "Harder! Pull harder!" Marcellus shouted.

The poles rose a few feet, then swayed. "By Jove! Are you men? Are you Romans? For the honor of the regiment—pull!" The tripod rose to its full, upright position on the edge of the precipice. "Halt!" Marcellus barked.

At that moment the soggy mud on the edge of the mine crumbled under the weight of the men and poles. Medwy, who was holding the end of the rope nearest the pit, slipped over the edge. He fell with a high-pitched cry. Silence followed the thud of his body.

Marcellus was the first down the ramp. He knelt by the still, twisted body and felt for a heartbeat. At first he found none. Then he shouted up to the boy's father, "There's life in him!" Marcellus interpreted the answering shout from above as one of joy, but did not look up as he began checking Medwy's limbs for broken bones.

A heartbeat later, the shout reached him again. This time definitely not a shout of joy. Marcellus looked up. As if in slow motion, he saw the mud crumble further and the great logs of the tripod topple over the edge toward him.

Without time to think, he threw himself over the body of the boy. He took the weight of the impact across his shoulders, then knew nothing more.

A strange white light stung Marcellus's eyes, making his headache sharper yet. Dim shapes moved in the distance. He closed his eyes with a groan. A cool, efficient hand placed a vinegar-soaked cloth on his forehead, and a voice he didn't recognize said, "It's all right, Centurion. Concussion, broken collarbone, bruises, but you'll recover."

Marcellus struggled to sit up, but was pushed back down on his cot by the orderly. "What is this?" he asked in a raspy voice that didn't sound like his own.

"Hospital at Aqua Sulis, sir. Native boatman brought you in yesterday with his son. Apparently you saved the boy's life."

Marcellus nodded, then wished he hadn't, as the motion made his head swim painfully. "I remember, edge of the pit crumbled. How's Medwy?"

"Four broken ribs. Even more bruises than you. He'll recover though. Medical officer advises a good spell in the baths for both of you."

Marcellus sank back on his cot and drifted off to a sleep repeatedly troubled by dreams of trees and walls falling on him. For the next several days he drifted in and out of consciousness. At times he was aware of Elfan visiting his room, one time telling him of the coracle trip from the mine to the nearest hospital of Aqua Sulis, another time telling him Medwy was out of the hospital and bathing regularly to speed his recovery. Another time he regained consciousness fully enough for the orderly to read a dispatch from Marcellus's optio at the mines informing him that the derricks were working and they were well on their way to making up for lost time. Then he slept again, but this time in more peace.

Midway through his second week the doctor declared Marcellus well enough to move to the guest house and begin therapeutic bathing in the curative mineral waters that flowed from the sacred spring into the great bath of Aqua Sulis. Marcellus was happy indeed to move into the well-appointed mansio that offered every convenience to the traveler. But he found even this simple task left him weak and shivering after so long in the hospital. And his left shoulder, tightly strapped in immobility, ached abominably. He flung himself on his cot and pulled a woolen blanket under his chin. He should follow the doctor's orders and go to the baths, but the effort seemed too great.

He didn't know how long he had slept before he wakened to the rich smell of stewed venison. "And I'm bringing you a fine fat oat cake with a pot of the sweetest honey in Aqua Sulis," Elfan said when Marcellus opened his eyes. When the stewpot was empty and the oat cake reduced to crumbs, Elfan insisted on driving Marcellus to the baths in a chariot he had rented. Marcellus tried to protest that he was capable of taking care of himself, but Elfan wouldn't hear of it. "I am to be thanking you for the life of my son. A pot of stew and a chariot ride are small matters indeed."

Marcellus saw that it was useless to argue. "And how is Medwy?"

"As hardy as ever he was. Except that he must be holding his side when he laughs. But then, he never was such a laugher as his father." And with that Elfan tossed his head back and demonstrated his hearty chortle that urged their horses to greater speed down the metaled street of the elegant spa town that had surrounded the sacred waters since ancient times. The chariot wheels clattered across the paving of the temple district where the Celtic god Sulis and the Roman goddess Minerva were melded in worship at the classical temple of Sulis Minerva. Roman men in white togas, women in graceful stolas, and natives in colorful tunics crowded the courtyard around the altar, exchanging the gossip of the day. In the southeast corner of the temple precinct rose the great domed structures of the bathing complex. The first dome covered the sacred spring, attended only by the priests and votaries who threw their offerings to the gods through arched enclosures into the steamy waters. The succeeding series of domes covered the circular bath, the great bath, and a maze of steam rooms, cold plunges, and gaming rooms.

At the bathing complex Marcellus gave his clothes to a slave in the changing room and sank into the steamy water of the tepidarium. It was glorious. "Ahh, I thought I'd never be warm again. How do you manage to put up with this climate? Do you have any idea what it's like in Rome now?" Marcellus lay back in the water, letting the heat penetrate to his bones, and smiled at Elfan.

"I was one time delivering a shipload of tin and copper to Ostia and took it into my head to travel up to the great city just to see what all the fuss was about. It was—" Elfan stopped.

"It was what time of the year?" Marcellus asked.

"August."

"Ah, the golden month of Augustus—and the sun shone every day, and the sky was clearest, unbroken blue."

Heads turned from every part of the pool at Elfan's sudden outburst of laughter. "And who would ever think a Roman eagle could be speaking more poetically than a bard-descended Celt? It was in my mind to say that it was hot and dusty."

Marcellus joined in the laughter and suddenly found himself wondering how long it had been since such sounds had issued from his mouth. "Well, if you dislike the heat, perhaps you'll find the frigidarium more to your liking. It's certainly more what you're used to." He climbed from the hot pool, Elfan following, to plunge into the cold water.

Marcellus surfaced with a shout that seemed to get his momentarily arrested circulation functioning again. As they emerged from the pool, Elfan suggested that when they had completed their ablutions by being oiled and scraped by slaves, Marcellus join him in meeting his son at the wine shop by the theater. Perhaps it was the shock of the icy water that led him to do anything so uncharacteristic, but Marcellus accepted.

Physically, Medwy was a younger version of his tall, blond father, his shoulders slightly broader, his teeth slightly whiter, and his hair considerably longer. But Marcellus soon saw that the similarity ended there. Medwy was the quietest Briton Marcellus had encountered—not that he had spent much time fraternizing with the natives, but his work had brought him into frequent contact with stonemasons, traders, and shopkeepers of every description. Some showed restraint when dealing with Roman officialdom, but none appeared to be so contemplative even after his second cup of wine.

After the shopkeeper's daughter had served their third round of cups, Medwy finally spoke what was on his mind. "And have you been hearing of the trouble in the north, Father?"

Elfan shook his head. "Be telling us about it, my son."

"I was speaking today to a pottery trader from Ebercanum, and he said the Brigantes are wielding their blue war shields again. It seems their rebel queen had a plot with the Picti to attack the Red Crests from both sides."

Even when reporting news of such moment, Medwy maddeningly understated it. "And what was the outcome, man? What has happened? Where did they attack?" Marcellus barked at him as he would at a subordinate who slopped mortar or carelessly threw ore.

But Medwy merely shook his head. "I was thinking mayhap the centurion would have word."

Marcellus slammed his fist on the table, jarring his shoulder with a sharp pain that made him wince. "By Jove, I've been out of circulation too long. I've heard nothing. But I mean to learn more. If they struck at Vercovicium, our men wouldn't have had much of a chance. It's mostly just a repair crew and a few sentries. All the real fighting forces are stationed on the Antonine Wall. Any surprise attack would have done its job long before word could even reach them that help was needed." Marcellus knew his men had always suspected him of caring more for smooth mortar and well-quarried stone than for people, but at heart, that wasn't the case. The stone and mortar were important because they protected people. The faces of his men swam before him. Were they even now lying among the gorse of the wind-swept moor with a Brigante spear or a Picti arrow in them?

But the next day Marcellus learned that the information he sought was not to be found. Indeed, there were rumors running everywhere, undoubtedly spread by the traders who lined Aqua Sulis's market district with their wares. And the wine shops buzzed with tales of a flattened wall and massive slaughter—although whether the slaughter was of Romans or of Brigantes depended upon who was telling the tale. Since Aqua Sulis was merely a spa built around its wonderful water, there was no official posting to which Marcellus could apply for news.

As the days passed and his body healed, Marcellus became increasingly concerned for the fate of his fellows in the north. No matter what he thought of Caius Valens's abrupt dismissal of himself, the commander deserved a better end than a Pictish arrow. Licinus had ever been an alert optio, and Festus—well, the prefect's manner aside, he was a superb builder. And the men of his century, the rank and file legionnaires drawn together from all parts of the Empire to serve, even briefly, under his command: Lucius Vitellius from Hispania, Tancinus from Germania, Julius Severus from Dacia . . .

Three days after the Greek doctor had removed the harness from his shoulder and pronounced him well enough to return to duty, a messenger arrived at the mansio with orders for Marcellus to report to legion headquarters at Isca.

Marcellus frowned at the curt message. "Did they say why I'm summoned?"

"I have told you all I know, Centurion. The legate requests that you go today if you are well enough to travel."

"I am."

"Good. Will it take you long to prepare to leave?"

"An hour, little more." Marcellus's kit was still in his tent at the mines, and he had acquired little more than a woolen blanket and latrine sponge to pack here.

"Very good. Shall I requisition a chariot for you?"

Marcellus thought. He wasn't even sure where Isca was. The commander unrolled a map on his table and pointed. "There. Eighteen miles to the Sabrina." He sketched a line straight west to a wide river flowing into the Oceanus Atlanticus. "Then across to the fortress beside this river."

Marcellus opened his mouth to agree to the chariot, then paused. "I think I'll go by boat. I'll arrange it with a native."

With the typical Roman dislike of sailing, the messenger frowned. "As you wish, Centurion."

Marcellus returned the messenger's salute and watched his departing back. The summons was as abrupt as any in Marcellus's career—even more so than his hasty orders to remove to Glevum. Was he to be dismissed after less than a month at his new posting? Had the legion commander heard of his conflict with Festus and somehow blamed him for a part in the uprising? Was he to be blamed for shoddy work that made the wall more easily breached by invading Picti?

Marcellus shook his fist in the general direction of the temple of Sulis Minerva that dominated the city. The fates were plaguing him again. There was nothing for it, however, but to follow orders. He knew Elfan would be only too happy to take him to Isca. The thought of the company of the cheerful Briton on the journey was Marcellus's only comfort.

The trip in the small, wood-framed, hide-covered coracle Elfan provided was far pleasanter than Marcellus could have imagined. The River Ebona, which took them almost as straight west from Aqua Sulis as a Roman road, flowed gently through lush countryside. Alders lined the river on both banks, and willows dipped their graceful boughs into the water. Songbirds, filling the arching branches, sang the travelers on their way. For once the sky was clear, and flecks of sun danced on the water as Elfan and Medwy rhythmically broke the surface with their short paddles, shattering the soft green reflections.

They crossed the ten-mile span of the Sabrina at sunset while native coracles carried fishermen all around them, and several Roman barges and trading vessels made for port farther north. The sunset was slow and gentle with a trail of gold in the water changing slowly to silver as the sun slipped below the horizon.

"Ah, we're in luck! The tide is with us!" Elfan shouted as they completed their crossing of the Sabrina and sailed into the mouth of a rapidly flowing, muddy river that swept them westward so rapidly Elfan and Medwy had no need to paddle. "This is the Isca your people have named the fortress for. But for time out of mind my people have called it the Usk. She's a fine river, but like a high-spirited woman she is."

Marcellus looked questioningly at Elfan.

"Ah, you must be knowing her ways, her ups and downs, and there's no fighting her, just go with her tides; that's the only way." And he gave his characteristic laugh.

They arrived at the fortress of Isca, which Elfan called by the name of the old hillfort Caer-Silurum. It was late dusk, and Marcellus knew the praetorium would have been left in the hands of the propraetorian legate for the night, so he needn't report until morning.

"Would you be going to the mansio then, or prefer you to join us at the home of a friend?" Elfan asked. "It is a piece of a chariot ride to the north. Or perhaps you are feeling ready for your bed; you are not long yet from leaving the hospital."

Marcellus hesitated, looking at the high-arching roof of the baths inside the fortress palisade. The delights of the steamy water, followed by an oil massage from a skillful slave, and then the smooth, clean feeling of having his body scraped with a gently curved strigilis . . . the pleasure sang its siren song. But then he thought of spending the night alone at another mansio worrying about whatever unpleasant news or reprimand the legate had to deliver on the morrow.

"This friend of yours, does he keep a good supply of wine?"

Elfan laughed, "Would I be taking the centurion to a house that could not provide the hospitality of the Silurians? I assure you a choice of native drink and the finest imported from your land. Enough to slake even a Celtic thirst."

"Let us make haste to find a chariot then."

"That will be taking little effort. My own is here. This is a journey I make often."

And it was obvious that Elfan knew his way well as he skillfully guided the ponies along the road in the deepening shadows, although any stranger could have easily found his way down the fine Roman road running between Isca and Venta Silurum. When they arrived at the major market town of the Silures, Elfan shouted in Cymric to the guard at the gate and was admitted. "The eagles were so confident of their power over the Silures they first built this town without defenses." Elfan waved his chariot whip in salute to the guard as they passed through the gate. "But we've ever been a stubborn warrior people. So they finally dug this earthen rampart about twenty years ago. It is in my mind they might as well have built their forum and temples inside the walls of the hillfort, but that is not the Roman way."

As the chariot clattered down the night-quiet metaled street, Marcellus recognized all the requisite buildings of a Roman town—a forum enclosed on three sides by colonnaded shops, a basilica with its administrative offices, a Romano-Celtic temple, a bath complex, and a mansio. They passed the common strip houses, where the owners lived behind their shops, and went on to a section of impressive quadrangular houses built around a courtyard of the Italian pattern familiar to Marcellus.

Elfan stopped at one of these houses and was immediately admitted by a slave who took the chariot around to the stables at the side.

"Who is this friend of yours?" Marcellus asked. "Are you sure he won't mind our coming in on him at this hour?"

"Exacting sure, I am. Did I not tell you? This is the home of King Lleiver Mawr of the Silurians and Atrebates. I expect you'd be calling him Lucius in your tongue. His Silurian hall, this is—the royal dun of the Atrebates is in their land to the east." He gestured vaguely.

"King, you say?"

"By courtesy of Emperor Antonius, that is. You Romans do all the real ruling, but when the Red Crests moved our people from their ancient hillforts to live in square-cornered Roman-built towns, we were allowed a tribal senate. King Lleiver Mawr is the head of the '*Respublica Civitatis Silurum*.'" Elfan pronounced the title in as clipped a Latin tone as his Celtic tongue was capable of producing.

When he considered how traumatic the Roman disruption of the deeply-rooted Celtic ways must have been to these people, Marcellus was amazed at the openness and lack of bitterness in Elfan, although it was impossible to judge how the silent Medwy felt. They paused midway across the grassy courtyard before entering the colonnaded verandah.

"King Lleiver bears respect among our people, descended as he is from two of our greatest leaders."

"Yes?" Marcellus responded absently.

"King Arviragus of the Silurians and Caradoc, Pendragon at the time of the coming of the Red Crests."

Now he had Marcellus's attention. "Caradoc? The one we call Caratacus? Man, why didn't you tell me we were going to meet a celebrity?" He began rubbing the brass fittings on his uniform.

Elfan gave a laugh that must have wakened any infants sleeping in the upper story of the house. "You needn't be worrying. The king will be looking on the inside of yourself, not at your brass trappings."

"Well, I just hope he isn't planning to rise against Rome like the Brigante queen. That would cook my goose with the commander if he heard I spent the night in the hall of an enemy."

"Ah, you'll not need to be worrying about that. King Lleiver is that greatest of rarities—especially in a Silurian. He is a king that would rather think than fight. It's a great pity the druid cors have all been—" He looked at his companion's Roman uniform. "—er, closed. He is such a one as would have spent his life in study. That's why we were becoming fast friends on one of my first trading trips here—he is much like Medwy. Though it breaks my heart to say it, my son would have made a better druid than a trader."

Marcellus wondered how the unphilosophical Elfan fit into this friendship, but the question was soon answered.

"Ah, but they are both fine fisherman. An excellent activity for those who like to think, they're telling me. Me, I just like to catch fish." Again he disturbed the quiet of the night with his laugh. "Only thing better than the catching is the eating." And then the aromas from the cookplace behind the royal hall reached them. "And I hope His Majesty's cooks have stewed up something good for tonight. My belly won't be easily satisfied with a cold oat cake."

Elfan led the way along the raised mosaic floor of the verandah. But for all the Roman appearance of the building's exterior, when they entered the main hall and were saluted by honor guards wearing scarlet cloaks and plaid breeks, Marcellus felt as if he had stepped back a hundred years to the days before Rome came and imposed her square-cornered law and order on these exuberant people.

A bard seated by the central brazier was chanting something in the native tongue to the accompaniment of a six-stringed harp. The king, on a raised dais at the front of the room, and his court and family at tables around the bard lounged in typical Roman fashion on low couches. Yet the flowing mustaches and colorful clothing of the men and the gold-embroidered tunics of the women were defiantly native.

Even in the incongruous Roman setting, it all seemed far removed from anything Roman, and yet so vital. There was an energy here in their very clinging to ancient custom, an energy that grew from the land and its history that had nothing to do with square lines and trumpet calls and duty to Empire and emperor.

Was this all that a hundred years of Roman rule had amounted to—a thin veneer of administrative efficiency, with everything going on as if the eagles didn't exist? Had they moved the people from their hillforts into modern towns in body only while their spirits remained in the halls of their ancestors?

The bard's song ended, and the sentry led them to the high table where the king welcomed his old friend and the young Roman and bade them take the guest place to his right. The king was clad in a gold-embroidered scarlet tunic and a saffron cape held at his shoulder by a heavy bronze circular brooch inlaid with red enamel. The light played on the twisted gold torque at his neck and the gold circlet around his head. As he greeted the newcomers, the king smiled beneath his flowing flaxen mustache, but Marcellus noticed that his eyes, although kind, never matched the sparkle of his words. He seemed to be a man carrying a great weight and gave the impression of immense age, although his voice was that of a man not yet past his prime. Marcellus hoped that his burden of care did not spring from a plot against the Romans.

But the king showed no hesitation in welcoming an armor-clad centurion into his midst, nor did he seem at all awed by Marcellus's position. Any who asked hospitality at his hearth and table were welcome, whether British or Roman.

He clapped his hands for a slave to bring the guest cups. "And shall we fish tomorrow, my friend?" the king asked Elfan. Marcellus did not hear the reply, for at that moment several from the women's side rose to refill the empty cups resting on the long tables before the feasters, and a vision captured Marcellus's attention. In the strangeness of the setting, after a day of travel, he hardly trusted his senses to tell him that what he saw was real. She was tall, fair, and graceful in a sky blue tunic belted with cords of twisted gold thread. Her hair was braided with similar golden cords, but the blueness of her eyes and the sweetness of her smile far outshone the glimmer of gold adornment.

Elfan, having finished making his fishing plans with the king, noted the direction of his friend's gaze. "Ah, noticing you are Princess Dorigen, King Lleiver's daughter. Shall I be introducing you?"

He didn't wait for an answer. As soon as the king's cup had been refilled and the girl turned to offer more wine to the newly arrived guests, Elfan spoke. "Princess Dorigen, I must be making you known to my friend Marcellus Artios. Tomorrow he goes to the Red Crest fortress, but tonight he will see the Britain of our forefathers and their fathers before them since the world was new."

"Welcome be you to the hall of my father, Lleiver Mawr, Marcellus of the Red Crests. Would you be liking more wine?"

Since his cup was still full to the brim, Marcellus could hardly accept. And words simply would not come to him. "No. Er, thank you, Princess," was the best he could manage.

Servants offered the newcomers platters of roasted meats and boiled vegetables while the bard sang another harp-accompanied song. Later, his stomach full of rich meat and warm wine, his senses reeling from the lights, the smoke, the music—and most of all the radiant vision of Princess Dorigen that had surely been conjured up by the strange magic of the night—Marcellus was hardly aware of Elfan leading him through the crisp air and cold moonlight across the courtyard to a guest room and bidding him to sleep well.

3

arcellus woke the next morning without the aid of a trumpet signaling cockcrow, evidence of how thoroughly accustomed his system was to Roman fort life. But his bed didn't feel like anything he had experienced in a Roman fort, or anywhere else. He sat up, rubbing the sleep from his eyes, and then looked around the room. It was a typical Roman bedroom with stools for sitting, shelves to hold his belongings, a table for the washing-bowl, a narrow, stiff sofa for a bed . . . then he looked down at where he had slept. The hard, straight sleeping-sofa was piled high with soft, thick animal skins and cushions. He had not slept so deeply and warmly since he was an infant. Marcellus was still running his hand over the thick bearskin in amazement when a slave entered with a bowl of water and a stack of hand-loomed flaxen towels.

As he made his way across the courtyard a short time later and entered the dining room, Marcellus looked for Princess Dorigen among the women. But she did not appear to break fast with her father in the hall. Marcellus was not surprised. Hadn't he known she was a vision, drawn forth by some of the ancient druid magic that must still belong to these people? And morning light had brought Marcellus back to reality. Last night had been of the imagination; today he must face the cold light of reality and Legate Dominitus Potentinus's decree of his fate—whatever that might be.

After only a few mouthfuls of stirabout and a few gulps of barley beer, Marcellus strode from the hall, head up, shoulders back, caligae sounding on the mosaic floor, looking every inch the emissary of Imperial Rome and keeper of the peace that he was.

Following a swift chariot ride, Marcellus strode into the praetorium in his martial manner. The legate, informed by a duty officer of the centurion's arrival, was seated on the raised tribunal platform from which judgments were issued and official proclamations made. "Centurion Gaius Marcellus Artios, reporting for duty as ordered, sir." He gave his sharpest salute.

The legate returned his salute. "Well come, Centurion. Take a seat."

Surprised at the cordiality of the greeting, Marcellus pulled a stool forward and sat. Surely if he were to be read out of the ranks, the commander would not have asked him to sit.

"You have heard of the uprising in the north?" Dominitus began.

"Just rumors, sir. I believe the trouble started shortly after I left." A clerk seated below the dais noted his words on a block of wax.

The commander rose and began pacing the floor, hands behind his back. "Yes, that is what I was given to understand. And yet my information is inadequate. Even though three cohorts from our legion were stationed on the wall, no recent messengers have been sent to me—or if sent, none have come through. I am determined to learn precisely what happened. Tell me all you know of the situation when you left, Centurion. You were at Vercovicium?" Marcellus nodded. "I understand that was where the wall was breached and the heaviest damage done before the northern troops arrived."

Marcellus drove all thoughts of the fate of his men from his mind and searched for any information that would be of use. For the moment he wouldn't allow even feelings of relief at his own reprieve.

"I believe you had been in charge of repair on the wall?"

"Yes. There had been considerable frost damage from the winter, and there were always rumors of trouble with the Picts. But the repairs were in good order, sir. No matter what charges might have come to your ears," he added with a note of defiance.

"I understand there was some disagreement over that, Centurion."

Were the commander's level voice and mild manner a deception calculated to lead him into telling something he wouldn't have willingly revealed? Marcellus bristled. He wanted no misunderstanding about this. "By your leave, sir, I will tell you precisely what happened."

"That is why I ordered you here, Centurion Marcellus."

With the precision and attention to detail becoming a Roman engineer, Marcellus recounted exactly the events of his last days on the wall.

"And the fort commander saw this newly dug shaft and examined it himself?"

"As clearly as I did, sir."

Dominitus turned to his clerk diligently scratching every word onto his wax tablets. "Did you note that, Julius?"

"Yes, sir." The scribe nodded his head without looking up or stopping the motion of his stylus.

"And how would you evaluate the commander's abilities, Centurion? A candid answer, if you please."

Marcellus had no difficulty being candid. He had the highest regard for Caius Valens, no matter what he thought of his own unfair treatment.

"And Prefect Festus? His skills?"

"His engineering knowledge was superb and his attention to detail flawless, sir." Even if Marcellus had tried to keep the stiffness out of his voice, he wouldn't have been successful.

The legate paused to assess the situation before asking his next question. "And I believe Commander Valens was a chief centurion, therefore outranked by the engineer-in-command?" Dominitus turned to check this on a sheet of papyrus, but Marcellus assured him that was correct. "Yes, I see. A most interesting situation. That sort of thing occurs frequently in the tangle of political and military promotions one finds in the legions. Still—it's a most effective body.

"Now, Centurion Marcellus, I want you to think carefully before you answer and then speak candidly. How would you assess Prefect Festus's loyalties?"

Marcellus had no need to think. He had done little else since his dismissal. "Until I found that shaft, I had no reason to doubt him in the slightest."

"And now?"

Marcellus shook his head. "Someone with great engineering ability planned that drainage shaft. But if Festus planned it for some treasonous reason to undermine the wall, why would he make such public display of the wall's weakness?"

"It seems to me, Centurion, it was not the wall that was undermined, but yourself."

That was how it seemed to Marcellus, too, but it made no sense. "Have you had any report on casualties, sir? Do you know if Festus or Commander Caius—?"

For the first time Dominitus displayed anger. He struck the table in front of him. "I have had no report on anything. What am I to do? The legion commander with no information to act on. I've sent couriers to Ebercanum; still I hear nothing definite."

He began pacing again. "And your senior optio? What of him? I must get a picture of the situation."

Marcellus told him all he knew, repeating many parts in detail, until at last both he and the commander seemed satisfied that he had no more to tell.

"Should you receive any private word from acquaintances, you will notify me at once."

"It is extremely unlikely, sir. I had no close ties at Vercovicium."

"Nevertheless, I may call on you again for an evaluation. In the meantime, you may return to your duties at Glevum when your sick leave is up."

Marcellus saluted and left, feeling that Legio II Augusta was in capable hands. The interview concluded hours—if not days—earlier than he had expected, Marcellus felt like a schoolboy let out for the Feast of Saturnalia. He walked down to the riverbank, wondering if Elfan would already have set off for the day. At the quay he picked out his friend and the tall, thin form of Lleiver Mawr, or Lucius, as he preferred to call him. Many others in boats were setting off for a day of hunting or fishing as the tide turned the waters of the Isca toward the Sabrina. Every coracle held golden-haired Britons armed with fishing nets or hunting spears. Several seemed to be father and son pairs, as the ways of the tribe were handed from generation to generation. But the tense looks on every face showed that this was more than tradition or sport—this was survival, for failure today, after the past weeks of unremitting rainfall, would mean empty cookpots tonight. The winter wheat crop that should by this time be safely stored away in underground clay pots had rotted in the sodden garths that now defied spring planting.

This was an ironically bitter blow following the disastrous drought of the summer before. Marcellus, living in the cool air far north and eating regularly from the annona, the levy of grain that supplied the army, had paid scant attention when messengers from Isca recounted the unusual dryness. Then the tales held a nervous undertone as later travelers brought reports of August lightning storms setting dry grain garths afire. They were told the guard had been doubled on the granaries at Isca as native unrest brought worries that the storehouses might be stormed. Seeing it all at first-hand sharpened Marcellus's memory.

Elfan waved to Marcellus and paddled his boat back to the shore from which he had just set out. "Ah, and would you be joining us for our fishing?" He looked at the heavy, leaden sky. "If the rains will be coming, we must be getting our catch before the muds clog the water."

"Gladly. I've no intention of returning to those mine pits any sooner than required." Marcellus waded through the wet sand and climbed aboard. "Will those birds leave anything for us?" He looked at a flock of waterfowl skimming just above the silvery morning surface of the water, rhythmically dipping their long beaks to come up with wriggling fish that quickly disappeared. Occasionally a lucky fowl would have its breakfast come to it, as it caught in midair a fish jumping for a fly.

Elfan laughed. "Have no fear. My friend Lleiver knows all the secret spots of the ancients. For that it is, I believe, they call him Mawr, which means 'great one,' rather than for all his royal blood."

The king laughed grimly in reply. "In these times, it is undoubtedly more practical to be a fisherman than to be a king."

Marcellus noted that the proud Celts were reluctant to admit to a Roman outsider that their need was nearly desperate. Last night they had freely shared the produce of the hunting trail—and Marcellus, in the way of one who has always known plenty, had eaten ravenously without considering he might be denying another. That, of course, was how they wanted it, and no one had spoken of the need.

"And so you've combined the best of both by being a fisherking," Marcellus suggested.

At the Sabrina, which Elfan called Mor Hafren, they quickly left behind their fellows who made straight for favored spots in the main channel. Marcellus, although less than an expert fisherman, could imagine that the shady, willow-lined banks would indeed harvest rich crops for the evening stewpots—a bounty that would last for a while yet—until flooding streams brought too much silt into the channel, choking the fish and destroying the egg-filled nests of the waterfowl. But rather than seeking such a sanctuary of their own, Elfan expertly steered their small craft into a river on the eastern shore.

Shortly after leaving the waters of Mor Hafren behind, Marcellus felt he was entering another world. The morning light that glittered on the water behind them softened and paled. The landscape to the west, so rugged and aggressively green, flattened and blurred. Marcellus, who moments before had been thinking himself too warmly dressed, shivered and pulled his cape closer around his shoulders. Mists clung to the reedy, blue-green water grasses growing over the marshy land. Birds called from clumps of bushes and trees, and fish jumped with an almost constant rippling of the water, attesting to the riches Lucius had promised.

The coracle rocked gently, and Marcellus wondered how long it had been since he had felt so at peace. Lucius handed him a weighted net, and Marcellus let it drag over the side as Elfan propelled them upstream, his paddle barely rippling the water. In a few minutes, a drag on his net told Marcellus he had a fish. With a grunt of excited pleasure, he jerked his arm upward to swing the net aboard. A flash of wriggling silver broke the surface of the water, and Marcellus grabbed for it. But before his arm could reach out, the net tore and the silver trout swam free.

Lucius's smile was sympathetic. "The first thing fishing teaches one is patience, my friend. A hurried fish will be a lost fish. You Romans think it is only necessary to give commands, and the world obeys. But our fish have not been Romanized; they must be treated as gently as the wheat shoots that will not be hurried in the garth. Would you be expecting to yank a spring sprout to maturity by pulling it up with your hand?"

Shoving the guilty thought that his haste might mean a hungry belly to one of Lucius's people, Marcellus smiled. "I see why fishing is the sport of philosophers. I will guide my next catch aboard more gently."

For some time they moved silently through the silvery world, wisps of mist wrapping around them, then floating free as the small craft slipped on. Lucius netted a large striped bass, played it for some time in the net, then, so gradually the fish couldn't have known what was happening, he moved it ever closer to the craft. At last he reached over the side and scooped the shining creature into the coracle. Confident that he would land his next catch the same way, Marcellus threw out his net and felt an almost immediate answering drag. He turned to tell Lucius, but at the sight before him all thoughts of fish left his mind. Through the mist rose a great green mountain, so surrounded by fog at its base that it seemed to be suspended over the marshy land. Its smooth green sides rose steeply to a leveled top. Marcellus noticed terraced rings circling upward, as if man-made. "What is it?" he whispered.

Lucius answered, "That is Avalon, the Isle of the Blest, our forefathers' abode of the dead, and our holy place."

Elfan added, "It is also called Ynis Witrin, the Glass Isle. What you see there is the Tor."

"My ancestors worshiped here since time out of mind," Lucius said. "But now—"

"Now?" asked Marcellus.

Lucius shook his head. "I am not knowing. I search my mind and my heart for the right way to lead my people, but the world is so changed since last our people used the altars they built here. Our druid cors have been destroyed and much of the ancient wisdom lost. You Romans have brought many new gods whose ways seem strange to us, and travelers such as Elfan bring back tales of the worship of a god Christus who promises love and peace." He shook his head. "You Red Crests will be telling us that with the *Pax Romana* we have no need of a god to bring peace, but I fear there is hunger ahead for my people if the rains are not ceasing so the seeds can cling to their earth mother for nourishment to grow. Even mighty Rome cannot bid the rains to stop. That is in the hands of the gods, and I must know which god to be praying to. Before the cors at Mon was destroyed and all the priests slain, such things were known."

A tug on the king's net brought him back to the present. "Ah, but for today the rain's gentle, and we may fish."

Marcellus was quiet for several moments, watching Lucius work his net but still mindless of his own. Then he said, "I'd not say that Roman eagles have replaced gods in keeping the peace—our trouble in the north is proof enough of that—but I've bothered little with the gods. That is work for women and priests."

Lucius sighed. "Yes, and a king should be something of a priest, but I fear I've failed my people." He pulled the fish in.

The mist wafted across the prow of the coracle and Elfan, unable to judge the shoreline, brought them to land with a thud that snapped Marcellus's net from his hand and jerked the forgotten fish free. Marcellus stepped out on the thick green grass, half expecting it to sink under his feet and prove to be as insubstantial as all the marshland they had just journeyed through. But the turf held. As they walked toward the high green sentinel his guides called the Tor, Elfan pointed to the north where another body of water washed the island. "The small lake we call Meare Pool. There was a village on the lake when our grandfather's fathers knew the Glass Isle. See, some of the pilings are still there."

Marcellus stopped and looked, wondering where all the people had gone. Where were the houses those pilings had supported, where the belongings that once filled the houses? "Is Ynis Witrin inhabited now?"

"A few priests of the old ways on the far side of the Tor. For a time there was a famous cors here—tribes from all over Britain sent their princes and priests to study."

They had been moving slowly uphill as they talked, but now Marcellus stopped in amazement. The Tor had disappeared. He looked around. Had he lost his sense of direction? Had a sudden fog arisen to cover it?

Elfan laughed. "You are looking for our high hill of mystery? It will be reappearing on the other side of this ridge they once called Wearyall, now Wirral." He led the way along the crest of the long low hill until Marcellus stopped at an unusual little tree.

"That's interesting—at home we call that the Jerusalem thorn. I didn't know they grew in Britain."

Elfan looked at the short, dark green tree with its frosting of white Maytime blossoms. "I don't know of another like that; it blooms every spring and in late Samain as well."

Marcellus considered. "Kalends of January? Seems an odd time for blooming in this climate."

But Lucius was hurrying forward with his long stride, making for a thickly wooded hollow below them. Little furry animals rustled into the underbrush as they walked through the flowering apple trees. Marcellus had no trouble understanding why this spot was venerated above all others. It had an unreal, ethereal beauty as green grass, scented blossoms, gentle mists, and weak lemon-colored sunbeams mingled bewilderingly around him.

Lucius stopped before a small wattle building, its door hanging from one rusted iron hinge. Like backward smoke, mist fell downward through a great hole in the side of its thatched roof. A family of birds sang from a nest in the ragged thatch. But even in its broken condition, Marcellus could sense that this was a place of importance, a place that in the past had been cared for with love. "This was the home of someone much respected?" he asked.

"An ancestor of mine who came from a distant land more than a hundred years ago built it as a place of worship. His name was Joseph Arimathean, and he was a very holy man."

"I understood you were descended from Caratacus—er, Caradoc." Marcellus was disappointed.

"That is the way of it—Caradoc on one branch of the tree and Joseph on the other. That is one learning that has not been lost with the closing of the cors—we carry our families with us." Their entry into the building set off a scurrying of tiny furry paws and swishing of little tails. Against the eastern wall lay the remains of a carved wooden cross in the shape of the Greek letter *T*, now decayed with wet and mold. Lucius traced the pattern with his finger. "I come here whenever I visit the island. I have often wondered what this means."

Marcellus also stroked the wood. In spots it retained its original satiny texture. "I have seen such things in Rome." He gave an ironic smile. "Oh, I've seen many of them used for their actual purpose to execute criminals. But I've sometimes seen them used as some sort of symbol as well. It seems a strange thing to me—unless it is meant to warn criminals to mend their ways lest they wind up on one."

Lucius turned from the cross. "My grandfather said my ancestor Joseph's grave is near here, but I've not seen it."

He sighed and sat on a stump that had probably been dragged in for just that purpose. "Perhaps it is my advancing age, but I seem to be spending more time here as the years pass, as if the spirits of my ancestors draw me. The druids teach that our souls never die, so perhaps my people are still here unseen in the abode of Avallach."

A little gray mouse scurried across the floor, and Marcellus watched the creature until the last of its tiny pink tail disappeared under the pile of broken thatch in the corner. Then his eye caught something sticking out from beneath the rubble. He walked over and picked up a pale golden carved stone. It was about the length of his hand from fingertip to wrist and nestled perfectly in the hollow of his hand.

"A fish." He ran his finger over the satiny polished surface and was surprised that it felt warm. He held it out to Lucius. "This must be yours, Your Majesty Fisherking."

Lucius took the little carving. "Strange, I've never seen it before. It must be of the old ones living here in Joseph's day, for the druids never come here. Infested with foreign spirits, they say of it."

Marcellus had not taken his eyes off the object since he found it. The stylized shape of the fish, as if it had been drawn by only two cupped lines that intersected to form the tail—that meant something. It wasn't just any fish.

"I will take it to Dorigen. It will please her," Lucius said.

The mention of Dorigen made Marcellus think of his dark-haired Julia at the same time the image of the golden princess formed in his mind. Then Marcellus knew where he had seen such a fish before. Julia of the heartache. With a stab of pain, Marcellus remembered the day a friend had come to comfort him and had enigmatically drawn such a figure in the cooled ashes of the family hearth. Marcellus had thought it a strange thing to do, and his friend had blown it away with one quick puff of breath.

He laughed as he puffed the crude fish away. "I did not expect a response, my friend, and yet it is best to be certain of one's standing. It is rumored that Antonius Pius rather favors the Christiani personally, but he feels he must uphold the law, so martyrdoms for the faith continue."

Marcellus was more confused than ever. "But what has that to do with a fish?"

"Our Lord bade us to be fishers of men. We use the symbol as a mark of identity with other believers when it is unsafe to speak openly. But, my friend, I will put my life in your hands and speak to you. Remember that symbol of the fish, Marcellus, for it can lead you to healing for your heart."

Marcellus snorted. No mystic symbol or anything else could bring him peace of heart. He had been sure that day, and he was still sure now. Five years and thousands of miles later, and he had found no peace. Although perhaps there had been something to what Eleutherius said. Certainly he had known a moment of peace while fishing today. Had that been what his friend meant? Marcellus thought not, for he had continued, "Let me take you to my Uncle Eleutherius—yes, I was named for my father's brother. He can tell you far better than I about our Christus, a man of sorrows Himself, who can heal your sorrows."

They had been interrupted then by servants bringing in wine and cakes, and the two never returned to the conversation. He never saw Eleutherius again, for the next day Marcellus joined the eagles. He had thought on his friend's words a few times, but soon gave up trying to make sense of them. Others had referred to this Christus as a god, but Eleutherius called him a man; Eleutherius spoke of him as if he were alive, yet he had died more than a hundred and fifty years ago on a cross, so the story went.

"Oh, that's it!" He spoke so suddenly his companions in the silent room jumped. "I know why that cross is here—at least I know what it means, although I can't see why your ancestor would have chosen to put one up for a decoration." And he told them the little he remembered about the cross and the fish and his friend's words.

Lucius was silent for some time, stroking the stone fish in his hand. "You have called me the fisherking, a title that seems most fitting, and it seems as if this carving of my ancestors' is bringing me a special message. Do you suppose this Eleutherius is still in Rome—either your friend or his uncle?"

Marcellus shrugged. "I don't see why not. They're a well-connected family. My friend's father was in trading." He turned to Elfan. "You may have seen some of his ships in port and not known it."

Elfan nodded. "Likely. Very likely. What is the family name? I shall look out for them on my next journey."

"Esurbius. The father, who is head of the family, is Felix Esurbius."

Lucius jumped to his feet with more lightness than Marcellus had seen in him since they met. "My friend Elfan of the sea journey, will you do more than make casual inquiries? For the sake of your king and your people, will you go seeking out this one Eleutherius and ask for knowledge of this Christus, God of the cross who heals heartaches? Perhaps He can also heal an aching land as well. My people are hungry, and my heart is hungry for knowledge. I am a king without a throne, a chief without a tribe. I will not be a man without a god."

"Gladly will I do that for my king and my people. If Marcellus's miners can pull enough ore from the mud, I will set out before the next moon of Beltine. Before the second moon of Lugnasad, you should have your answer."

Lucius gripped his arm. "May the sun and the moon smile on your going; may the wind and the waves bring you swiftness; may the gods honor the goodness of your heart." Suddenly, with a great sigh of relief, he said, "Thirsty I am. Let us drink from Joseph's Well before we return to our fishing."

They walked through the grass, which even in midday held enough dew to wet through Marcellus's caligae, to a small hill beyond the wattle building. Marcellus heard the bubbling of water above the birdsong even before he noted the circle of yew trees Lucius was leading them toward. The sound made him thirsty too. But when he saw the water, he stopped and pulled back in horror. He couldn't drink that. Then he smiled at his mistake and moved toward the well. At his first glance, the iron-stained rock around the spring did make it appear as if blood, not water, flowed from the pierced hillside.

He knelt and drank the tangy mineral water, finding it unusually refreshing. He stood and they had turned to go when the sound of hurrying footsteps and angry murmuring on the stone path above the well made them turn back.

Four long-bearded men and a woman with streaming red hair, all wearing tattered robes that had once been white, rushed toward them down the yew-lined path. "Hail, King Lleiver Mawr of the Silures and Atrebates," the woman cried and raised a bronze sword above her head with both hands. Then she stopped and looked in some confusion from the king to Marcellus in his Roman uniform and back again to the king.

"And why is this one of the foreign ways drinking at our holy well, my king? Have not our gods enough displeasure in the abandonment of the old ways without our incurring further anger?"

Lucius spoke calmly. "Marcellus Artios is my friend. He and *I,*" said the king, putting a slight emphasis on the latter pronoun, "meant no disrespect to the gods by quenching our thirst at the well they provide from their bounty for all men."

"And is their provision for our people bountiful, my king?" The four priests stood in a semicircle behind their priestess, demonstrating united strength as she spoke. "Were the gods bountiful when they withheld the rains last Lugnasad, drying the lands, then playing with the thunderbolts of Lugh of the Long Hand until lightning fell to earth and caused fires to rip through the unharvested grain? Were the gods bountiful this springtime when they opened the floodgates, and rain washed the seedlings from the earth and the baby lambs from their mothers' sheltering?" She turned to Marcellus with a hard stare. "Were the gods bountiful when the Red Crests," she stopped just short of spitting at the word, "demanded their payment in tax even from those who serve the sacred grove and took young men from garth and village to train in their foreign ways and serve in their foreign wars? Are the gods bountiful, King Lleiver Mawr?"

Lucius opened his mouth to answer, but the priestess tossed her red mane flowing from the three-horned golden crown she wore and continued in a voice barely below a shout. "The gods are not bountiful, I tell you. But the fault is not with the gods. The fault is with us. We abandoned the gods before they abandoned us. We withheld much from the gods before they withheld from us. And we must satisfy the gods with sacrificial gold and bronze before they will satisfy us with crop-producing weather; we must honor the gods with the sacrifice of birds and animals before they will honor us with bountiful hunting trails; and we must appease the gods with the blood of humans before they will purge our land of the plague of Red Crests."

Her voice took on a chanting quality, echoed by the priests as they moved sun-wise around the well, seemingly forgetful of the presence of the king and his companions.

Lugh, the Father God over all,
Matres, Mother Goddess,
Epona, Moon Goddess,
Beli, creator,
Dogda, the good,
Manawgdan, God of the sea,

Gofannon, God of the metals—
O bring to us your mercy, bring to us your power,
Bring to us your bounty, let our people prosper.
Let our land flower forth,
Wheat in the garth, fish in the sea, calves in the pen, deer in the hunting-runs.
God of the sun,
Goddess of the moon,
Creator of all,
Mother of all,
God of the sea,
God of the metals,
Turn not away.

When the ritual ceased, the priestess once more elevated the sword toward a darkening sky, then stood quietly.

Lucius spoke. "Cunedag, I am as aware as you of the needs of my people—both their physical and their spiritual needs. I have been just now entreating my friend Elfan ap Goddyn to journey for word of a powerful new god who promises healing."

Cunedag's eyes flashed, and she seemed to grow taller before their eyes. "There is no need for the word of foreign priests and their tales of foreign gods. We are priests. We have our gods. They must be satisfied. King Lleiver Mawr, you bring foreign gods to our land at great peril—the peril of our people and the peril of yourself."

Lucius walked a few steps up the hillside until he stood on level ground with the priestess, looking down into her eyes. "Cunedag of the sacred grove, I am your king and the king of all Silures and Atrebates. I will meet the needs of my people and of the gods as well. When I have found what I seek, I will return to Ynis Witrin. I will not countenance waste in the making of unneedful, unavailing sacrifices. I will find the right god to heal our land, and then I will return."

He turned and walked down the hill at a regal pace, followed by Elfan and Marcellus.

But before they reached Elfan's coracle, the rain started far heavier than before, driving waterfowl to cover and fish deep into the water. There would be no more hunting or fishing that day. The king could only hope enough had been caught that morning to fill the cookpots of his people for that night.

4

n the trip back to Glevum the next day, Elfan and Marcellus were as waterlogged as if the coracle had sprung a leak and they had simply swum back up Mor Hafren. It was clear from his unusual silence and the faraway look in his eyes that Elfan's mind was on his next journey and his commission from Lucius. Marcellus, likewise, was wrapped in his thoughts of the new world he had found in Lucius's royal dun and on Ynis Witrin.

The next day he reported to his commander at Glevum and then returned to the mud-choked mines. By the end of the week they had extracted enough ore for Elfan and Medwy to set out in their trading ship *The Curlew* with a load for the smelting works at Icthas. There they would exchange it for a cargo of tin, copper, and lead ingots, all stamped with the name of the legion, and continue on around Hispania on the long journey to Ostia. Before they left, they received word that Lucius had removed to Dun Atrebates, and Marcellus felt a strange void at the thought that Dorigen was now several days' journey farther away.

The days returned to the routine of cockcrow and lights out, of cutting channels in the earth for a new vein of lead, and of turning the waterwheels ever faster to keep the water from rising more quickly than the men could work—for the rain let up only rarely. All was the same. And yet in some way everything had changed for Marcellus.

Often when his mind should have been on the best placement of a drainage channel or the arrangement of a pulley system, he would find a picture of Dorigen filling his mind. It couldn't, by any stretch of the imagination, be said she looked like Julia. Dorigen's tall stature and long golden hair couldn't have been more different from Julia. It was the strangest thing that knowing Dorigen made him recall Julia and yet forget her at the same time. More and more he found himself thinking of Julia as if she were dead. Dorigen almost seemed to fulfill all his sweet memories and longings for Julia while blotting out her image. And now, when his mind strayed briefly to the Temple of Vesta above the Forum in Rome, he was jerked out of the daydream by the shock of realizing he had invested one of the virgin priestesses with flowing yellow hair.

Then he berated himself. He had seen the Celtic princess only once and had spoken fewer than five sentences to her. There was nothing in that to build a vision on, even if Elfan, grinning broadly, had assured him that Princess Dorigen was not promised to another.

At times he would allow his mind to wander farther into the future. What if he were to seek that title in her life? Would a Celtic king of ancient lineage consider allowing his family's royal blood to be mixed with Roman? Apparently Dorigen was her father's only heir, although Marcellus hadn't thought to ask. Were the fates playing him for a fool again by offering him forbidden fruit?

Summer wore on. The seeds replanted in a burst of optimism during a few dry days rotted in the field and were washed into the swollen rivers. Still the rains came. Waterfowl and field birds laid their eggs in sodden nests and sheltered them with their bodies, but either the eggs didn't hatch or the young, unable to fluff their feathers, died almost immediately. And still the rains came. The wild deer in the woods and the cattle in the garth stood in mud until their hooves rotted and their stomachs rejected the moldy fodder and they sickened and died. And still the rains came. When the rising water in the mine defied even Roman engineering skill, Marcellus ordered his mining detachment back to Glevum.

He had been back in the fort two days when Marcellus heard the news he had been waiting for ever since his time in Isca Silurum. Licinus Natalis, his senior optio from Vercovicium, arrived in Glevum en route to legion headquarters to make his report on the northern uprising.

"We've heard you had a bit of excitement up there, but couldn't get any straight news on it," said Marcellus. He refilled Licinus's cup as they sat at a little table in the back of the wine shop. The rain-induced shortages were affecting even officers' mess these days, and Marcellus found he more and more frequently visited the local shops to supplement an unsatisfying meal—even if they had raised their prices to the point of extortion.

Licinus shifted his cup to get a firm grip on it with his left hand. His right arm was still in a sling from his battle wounds. He shook his head and blew out a long breath. "You had a lucky escape over that mortar business. A native uprising isn't a pretty thing. Those savage little Picti paint snakes and dragons all over their vile bodies and fight totally naked." He shook his head again and continued in a harsh voice. "What they can do to men and horses with those long knives of theirs you wouldn't want to know. And they can move through that blasted moorgrass as silently as the wind and then rain a whole battery of arrows on a cohort before you have time to form a testudo."

He paused to take a gulp of the sour local wine and wiped his mouth on the back of his hand. "And those Brigantes with their blue war shields. They paint their bodies too—all blue, but at least they wear breeks and some bits of bronze armor—the men at least. Their women fight like the furies—shrieking as if to raise the dead and hair streaming out like Medusae—but it's easy enough to forget they're women and do what you've been trained to do." His smile made Marcellus recoil.

"Yes, I'm sure it was Tartarus itself, but what really happened? What caused it all? Does anyone know?"

"As far as the commander can figure—and that's what I'm on my way to report—besides whatever he's written in these sealed papers I carry," he said as he patted the long, thin leather pouch hung around his neck, "is that that fiendish Brigante queen plotted with the Picti on the other side of the wall and somehow managed to sneak in and kill our guards. Jove knows, it wouldn't have been hard to do with no more men than we had at Vercovicium. Those little savages flooded in and attacked. Must have snuck some inside the fort before the gates were locked, too, because the stores and armory were burned from the inside. Anyway, they made quick enough work of us and moved on to Thirwall before we had a chance to get a message through to the poor devils there."

Again he paused for a drink, but continued before Marcellus could ask a question. "They'd have taken the whole wall, I'm sure of it, if troops from the Antonine hadn't reached us before the fiends could finish their work. Only Jove knows how the northern troops managed to get there so fast—should have been a four days' march."

"What about our century?" Marcellus's voice was strained and low.

Licinus thought for a moment. "Well, I'm here. Last I saw, Julius and Severus were still on their feet. I took a Brigante spear in my wrist and fainted from loss of blood. They took me for dead and drove their chariots right over me. How I survived, I don't know—much of me as did—that is." For the first time, Marcellus saw that Licinus's hand and about half his forearm were missing inside the sling. Licinus shrugged. "Won't be building any more walls, but I guess they figure I'm good enough for carrying messages. Where was I?"

"Left for dead."

"Oh, right. Well, when I came to, the battle had moved on, and the fort was a smoking ruin, so I found a native woman to nurse me and then made my way down to Ebercanum. Caius Valens eventually returned there and sent me off on his errand—and here I am."

"And the uprising is settled?"

"Oh, we settled 'em, all right. What Picti survived we herded back to the other side of the wall and shut the gate on 'em tight. There'll be a piece of repair work to do there now, I can tell you. Seems everything we did all spring crumbled as if we'd used flour for mortar."

"What!" Marcellus slammed the table with a doubled fist. "By Jove, there was nothing wrong with our work. I checked every bit of it. The rubble was packed, the stones were square, the mortar was stirred. We built it right."

Licinus held up his hand and gave an ingratiating smile. "Easy, I wasn't making any accusations. I told the commander maybe they sent an inferior batch of hardening ingredient. Anyway, our fellows caught the rebel queen and executed her. Her husband's all right, though; he signed a treaty with Rome. It'll be different up there now, I'll wager. I can't think the eagles will march back to the northern wall for a long time, if ever. We need every man to keep the peace on the frontier Hadrian established."

Licinus talked on about the horrors of the battle, his own toll on the enemy before the spear brought him down, and the importance of his current errand. It was clear he intended to make his way up in the eagles even if he only had one hand left to claw with.

The next morning Licinus was on his way to Isca with two cavalry guards and a driver in a chariot that was constantly stopped by mud-choked wheels. Hard on his departure arrived an order for Marcellus to return to the mines. More mine rubble was needed by the road-building detachments working from Londinium to Sorviodunum to Deva. Every crew needed more fill for roadbeds sinking in the mire. But in the following days as Marcellus executed new plans for more efficient mine procedures and shouted orders to his men, he considered Licinus's words. How could the Brigantes have managed to open the gate for the Picti? How could spies have been secreted inside the fort to set it afire? And, most galling of all, how could the wall, *his work,* have crumbled? None of it made any sense, and yet it had happened. Would he be summoned to Isca now to face the charges he thought he had escaped?

"Move to the right! Watch where you pile that rubble!" he shouted at the nearest legionnaire. If he was going to be dragged off to headquarters to be charged with incompetence, at least he would leave a smooth-running mine behind him for his successor to take credit for. He smiled sardonically and, with every step making a sucking sound, walked over to take a sighting on the groma to direct his men in laying out a straight trench.

That night after he had finished the bowl of wheat-meal porridge that was eaten at the end of a day's work from one end of the Empire to the other, Marcellus left the camp and walked out into the countryside, still thinking of Licinus's account of the uprising. He strolled for some time in the growing dark, listening to the evening call of the thrush and thanking Jove it wasn't raining. Suddenly he stopped in horror.

On a small hillock in front of him, a bonfire sprang to life. No sooner had the first sparks flared than another answered to his left. Then two on the right, simultaneously. He turned in a circle and realized that on every hilltop around him for as far as he could see, the camp was surrounded by bonfires sending who knew what signal to distant tribes.

As he turned and sped back to his men at a full run, it seemed that far into the distance he could see the twinkle of firelight, as if the stars in the sky had come down to Britain's hilltops. When he reached the gate, the sentry thudded his pilum into the ground in salute.

"Don't just stand there, man! Don't you see the signal fires? Sound the alarm—it's an uprising!"

Marcellus was appalled by the young man's broad grin. What was the matter with the imbecile?

"You must be new, sir, if you'll pardon my saying so. But this here's one of their native festivals—drive the cattle between the fires to make 'em fertile or something." He gave a leering grin. "Do the same with their women, I understand—then a quick roll in the grass to see if it worked."

Marcellus was glad it was dark enough to hide his embarrassment over his mistake. If the northern tribes had participated in the ritual, Vercovicium was too isolated for him to have observed it. "Thank you for your information, soldier. Carry on."

The legionnaire grounded his pilum again, and Marcellus passed through the gate. Now he remembered, this was Lugnasad—the festival of Lugh. He'd heard of it, but hadn't paid much attention. Kalends August, it was to the Empire. And Elfan had said he would return before the second moon of Lugnasad—before September then. It would be good to have his friend back and get news from the rest of the world—if he hadn't been carted off to Rome under guard by then.

As it happened, Marcellus was still at his labors when Elfan beat his own prediction by two weeks. Early morning, the day after the Ides of August, Elfan and his son showed up at the mine workings, much to Marcellus's surprise.

Elfan gave his open-throated laugh. "Fair winds we had—it is not raining in the entire Empire, you know."

"And how was Rome, my family—did you see them, deliver my letter?" Marcellus's mind filled with images of white marble glistening under a warm sun, of his mother and sisters in their long stolae preparing cool drinks to be sipped by family and friends sitting around the splashing fountain in the peristylum, and of his father showing no emotion at his son's letter except the warmth creeping into his eyes.

Elfan slapped him on the back. "Rome was hot, dusty, crowded, and smelly—as ever. But, yes, your family is fine, your sisters beautiful—they are preparing for Octavia's wedding, did you know?" He held up a hand to thwart Marcellus's next impatient question. "Whoa, I am carrying their letters to you—you would do better to have their reading than to hear my prattle."

Holding the rolls of parchment with the familiar seals was like holding his mother's hand when he was a child. But Marcellus could postpone the pleasure of the reading. He thrust them into his tunic. "And what of Lucius's commission—did you find Eleutherius?"

Again Elfan laughed. "Indeed I did—the uncle that is. Seems your friend joined the eagles like yourself and is off in some other part of the Empire. I would never have been knowing there were so many fishmongers in Rome if all those kindhearted but misguided people hadn't thought I wanted to be buying fish every time I made that little squiggle you showed me.

"Finally I had learning of the family by asking at the barges down by that stinking river of yours. Anyway, Eleutherius asked to be remembered to you—he says his nephew spoke of you often—and he sent two fellows along to be telling the king some good news, as he put it. Seeming it is he's an important fellow—they call him a bishop—something like an archdruid, I'm thinking. Anyway, the chaps he sent are pleasant enough, not afraid to be helping out on the boat, and not seasick above five days on the whole journey. Good record that is for a Roman." This time his laugh was enough to make the miners turn their heads. Many waved, as the trader was a familiar figure around the workings.

Marcellus smiled at his friend's account, but didn't say anything, as he knew Elfan would need no prompting to continue.

"I'll be delivering these chaps to Lucius tomorrow—assuming he's back at Isca by now. Why don't you beg a few days leave and go with me? Might even be getting in some more fishing."

Marcellus started to refuse. Thoughts of Isca brought only the dread of official censure. Then he allowed memories of his last visit to return—the peace of fishing, the pleasure of Lucius's company, the strange beauty of Ynis Witrin . . . and the haunting vision of Dorigen. No, he wouldn't refuse. "Perhaps. Not tomorrow, couldn't arrange leave that quickly. Perhaps in a week or two. Take greetings to Lucius and—ah, his court for me."

Elfan's broad grin showed he had not missed the significance of Marcellus's earlier attention to Dorigen.

"So be it, Marcellus of the muddy mines. You will come to the Glass Island when it is suiting, and I will be greeting Lleiver Mawr in your name. In the meantime, I leave *The Curlew* here for you to fill her empty belly with ore that I may make another profitable trip when the moon and tides are willing."

That evening Marcellus's foursquare tent furnished with cot, stool, and table seemed emptier than ever as Elfan's laughter lingered like an echo of sunlight in the shadows and his family's letters sounded voices from the distant past. There was no mention of Julia—but then, why should there be? Octavia was ecstatic over her coming marriage to the son of a family friend that Marcellus remembered as a young puppy—how could those two possibly be old enough to wed? He could remember the youth chasing his giggling sister around the garden, treading on some of his mother's prized flowers. Marcellus shook his head and smiled over the memory, then reread the letters. His mother sounded sad over the prospect of losing her eldest daughter to another household, and he couldn't help thinking that if he had wed, Julia would be a daughter in the Artios household, and there would be grandchildren to comfort his mother.

The routine days of work droned on, and Marcellus began to regret not having asked for leave to go with Elfan. His desire to make the trip grew until he began to think he would welcome even the dreaded summons to Isca.

But when it came five days later, the anxiety it caused made him change his mind. Desired or dreaded, however, the summons could not be avoided. The more dreaded the situation, the more need to face it quickly. Although his orders did not require him to report for four days yet, Marcellus left that evening with his escort and stopped for only a few hours' rest, camped around their wolf-repelling fire.

They arrived at Isca Silurum before lights out the next day, and Marcellus sent his escort to the fortress with word that Centurion Marcellus would report as required in two days' time to answer all inquiries. In the meantime, he would be with friends. He turned toward Venta without fully returning the legionnaire's salute.

A short time later, Lucius's sentry, who easily recognized the king's Roman friend, led him into the hall. As before, stepping into the Celtic court with its smoke and firelight dancing to the strains of the harpist, Marcellus felt himself entering another world. Lucius greeted him with a warm kindness that went far to cover the king's persistent look of worry and begged Marcellus to eat with them.

Aware of their shortages, however, Marcellus had taken care to eat his fill from his own rations before coming to the dun. "My stomach is full, my friend. Let me feast in the pleasure of your company." As happy as Marcellus was to see the kindly Lucius, he could not keep his eyes from straying to the women's side in search of Dorigen.

"You seek your other friends also?" Lucius noted his searching glance. "They are on the holy isle. I came back only to be with my people, and I return to Ynis Witrin tomorrow. The teachings of the Christiani brothers Fagan and Dyfan are most instructive. I will hear more and more. You will be going with me?"

Marcellus replied that indeed he would.

The next morning, following a coracle bearing Urych, Lucius's bard, and another servant, Lucius and Marcellus were paddled across the Sabrina and up the River Briw, which was now almost indistinguishable from the rest of the flood-soaked marshland. Marcellus found himself watching ever more intently for his first glimpse of the Tor. Today was less misty than on his trip last spring, so its green steepness should appear more quickly.

The call of a curlew took his attention for a moment; then he turned back. There it was, rising magically from the marsh. It was not as high as it had grown in his memory, and yet it was somehow more mysterious and compelling. "It's strange," he said to Lucius, "nothing could be less like Rome, and yet I have a sense of coming home." Lucius, who had just pulled in his third silver trout, smiled and nodded with a look he sometimes held in his eyes that bespoke a wisdom of many ages, as if he understood far more than he gave word to, and perhaps far more than he even knew he understood.

Medwy and the newcomers from Rome met them at the shoreline, and the young man introduced Marcellus to the tall, commanding Faganus and the shorter, heavier, and older Durvianus. "Welcome, fellow Roman, to the Isle of the Blest. My brother Dyfan and I have been here only a short time, and already we truly believe it is so."

Marcellus commented on the variation in the form of their names. "Yes," Faganus replied. "Of course, if you're more comfortable calling us by our Roman names, that's quite all right. But we thought it best to use the Cymric forms, since we've been sent to live among these people. And for us the Cymric is easy. Our ancestors came from Gaul, so we share the Celtic blood—but that is unimportant since in Christus all men are brothers."

Marcellus stared in confusion, but Medwy stepped forward. "My father will be sorry to be missing you, but he has returned to business matters." He gave a shy smile. "I think he was glad to leave me here. He always said I should be one of the priestkind—although I don't believe he meant it for a compliment. Come, see what we have done."

Medwy led the way to the old wattle building where they first had the idea of sending to Rome for one to tell them about the God of the cross. Once back on the island, it seemed to Marcellus he had never been away. It was impossible to believe a whole season had slipped by, and yet when he looked at the building, he could see that, indeed, time had been spent on it. The thatched roof had been repaired, although it was a miracle to have found decent thatch in this harvestless summer; the interior had been cleared and cleaned; a new cross had been fashioned and placed on the eastern wall with a small altar in front of it.

"This is truly a holy place," Fagan said with his face shining. "Elfan and Medwy brought us here, but we believe God was guiding us to this church built by the hands of our Lord's apostles."

For the first time Dyfan spoke in his soft voice. "Finding here a house of prayer filled us with ineffable joy. In Rome we worship in homes and sometimes even in the catacumbus to escape the long arm of the Praetorian Guard, but here we can—" He stopped suddenly, and his round cheeks flooded with red as he stared at Marcellus's centurion uniform.

"Here you may worship freely," Marcellus finished for him. "I take no interest in the gods, nor will I report you to anyone who does." He walked toward the altar and picked up the sole item on it—the little stone fish. "I thought you were going to give this to Dorigen." He held it toward Lucius.

"He did," a rich, musical voice said from the doorway. "But I thought it more fitting here than in a box in my bedplace."

Marcellus hoped no one could see his heart leap to his throat as Dorigen entered in a rust and gold tunic that matched the lights in her unbound hair. "I did not know we were honored with a visitor, or I would have brought a guest cup." Her smile went to Marcellus's head like the strongest wine, but he could only assure her in a voice he hoped sounded normal that he was not thirsty. She turned to her father. "Rhodric sends me to know if you bring fish for the stew-pot, Father. These have been too busy about their prayers to catch anything." She pointed at the missionaries, but the twinkle in her eyes softened her words.

"You are unfair, Princess. We tried both the river and the lake, but the fish do not come to our nets as they do for your fisherking father."

Lucius smiled at Marcellus. "You see, the name you gave me has stuck. And I have lived up to it, my daughter. We shall take the catch to Rhodric for her hungry pot."

The day they had gone to the well to drink, Marcellus had noted the circle of posts still standing from a building that once might have been a house. To his surprise it had now been rebuilt as a home for the missionaries, and a little distance away stood another for Lucius and his daughter, with huts for the servants beyond that.

Marcellus admired the speed and sturdiness of their work. "Yes," replied Fagan, "it has been satisfying work. We must also have dwellings for those who will come here to learn and to pray. But of late there has been trouble."

"Trouble?" Marcellus and Lucius asked together.

"Yes, for three nights now the work we do in the day is destroyed by morning. Last night the thatch on our own roof would have burned had not a sudden rain shower extinguished it."

"And our supplies stolen," Dyfan added. "The host and wine from the very altar of the church, but I praise God I had more under my pallet, so our worship continues."

In a short time, savory scents were coming from Rhodric's cookpot near Lucius's hut, and Dorigen bade them come eat the tasty fish stew. Marcellus had a few dry corn cakes left in his pack, which he added to the meal, and the company sat down to feast. But before Marcellus could get the first spoonful to his mouth, indeed, while it was in midair, Fagan stood and raised his hands. "Lord Jesus Christ and our Father God, who by the Spirit didst create everything and dost provide everything for Your creatures, we give You praise and pray that You will make us truly thankful. In the name of the Father and the Son and the Holy Spirit, world without end. Amen."

Dyfan and Medwy joined him on the final amen, and then all began eating accompanied by the strains of Urych's harp. When the first of their hunger had been appeased, Lucius called for Rhodric to refill their cups, then turned to Fagan. "I am ready for hearing more of your Creator God of good and light."

Fagan washed down the last morsel of his corn cake with wine. "You speak true, my king, when you say Creator God, for all things were made by Him, and, as it is written, without Him was not anything made. And God the Creator will make all who believe in Him a new creation."

Dyfan added, "And the Apostle John goes on to say that in Him was life, and that life was the light of men."

"Which is meaning—?" Lucius asked.

Fagan answered, "The writer means that man doesn't have inward light of his own apart from the Christus. The light of Jesus will bring us into all truth. Before God sent His son Jesu Christus to earth to bring us from darkness to light, He sent one John to bear witness of the coming of the Light. We also are come to you to witness concerning the light of truth and salvation."

Marcellus was just thinking that all their words sounded very poetic and pretty, a perfect bardsong for Urych's music, but not of much practical use, when a sharp wind whipped at the fire under the cookpot, nearly extinguishing it. Dorigen shivered in her light tunic. "The wind bears the cutting edge of rain. Let us go into my houseplace for shelter." Lucius picked up his half-full wine cup but left his stew bowl for the servant to clear away. Dorigen hesitated. "Join us, daughter. I would have you hear the words of the new God."

"Will not Lugh be angry, Father, if he is replaced with another all-god?"

"There cannot be more than one All-God. An All-God must be the God of all knowledge and cannot be angered by His creatures desiring more knowledge of Him."

Dorigen looked uncertain, but she followed her father inside the hut where Medwy was kindling a fire on the central hearth. A thin line of smoke meandered upward to the smoke-hole in the center of the roof.

Marcellus felt he could no longer be silent. "All this talk of creation and knowledge is fine, but Lucius and these people need a god to do something about this weather. If I thought sacrificing to Jupiter would do any good, I'd build an altar with my own hands—although where we'd find a fat bull to sacrifice in this hungry land, I can't imagine."

"Our Christus died on the cross to make such slaughter unnecessary," Fagan said. "Faith and healing come not from sacrifices, but from asking of God's grace."

And in his quiet way, Dyfan added, "And then He will calm the storm."

"You mean it? This God of yours will stop the rain if we ask Him?" Out of politeness, Marcellus tried to keep the skepticism out of his voice.

"Those who have written accounts of His sacred life tell us that once the Christus and His disciples were out in a boat at night. A great storm arose, and the disciples, many of whom were fishermen well acquainted with storms at sea, feared for their lives. The disciples woke their sleeping master and cried out in fear. He spoke words of peace to the wind. And it was still."

All was silent in the wattle hut save for the crackling of the fire, but outside the wind whistled and tore at the roof thatch as if it would fling it from the building. Instinctively, all drew closer to the hearth. In a moment of calm after the blast, Dyfan said, "And the sacred writings say that if God's people, who are called by His name, will turn from their wicked ways and call on Him, He will hear from heaven and heal their land."

Lucius did not reply to this, but his eyes shone brightly in the firelight, until a draft of wind whipped down the smoke hole and filled the hut with smoke so that no one could see anything.

Later that night in a half-waking state, rolled in a bearskin by the still-smoking fire, Marcellus thought of the words of the Christiani. They were pretty stories, indeed—a God who sacrificed Himself for His people and calmed their storms. But like all the gods in the pantheon, one must ask for His favor. Marcellus could use some help, divine or otherwise, to withstand the blast of his coming trial, but once one asked, surely this God would be as greedy as Vesta and all the others.

Marcellus turned away from the fire. He would ask no favors of any god.

The next morning, despite whatever truth there might have been to Fagan's story of his God calming storms, the weather had not cleared on Ynis Witrin. The wind had dropped, it is true, but it left behind it a thicker fog than any Marcellus had seen before, even in this mist-shrouded land. There would be no return to Isca Silurum until this cleared, for even one as well acquainted with the waterways as Lucius's boatman would lose his way in this. Marcellus fumed. Was he then to be late to his own trial and add this misdemeanor to his already black list? The fact that he could do nothing to remedy the situation would carry little weight in Isca Silurum, especially since he had made the side trip on his own responsibility.

But Medwy and the others were not deterred from their work by the dampness. After the morning stew, a watered-down version of the leftovers from the night before, the men set out across the green meadowland, that now was more a shallow pond, to the site of another ancient hut they were rebuilding. Although plastering with daub would be impossible in weather almost as wet as the plaster, the upright poles pounded easily deep into the damp soil, and the willow rods, in no danger of drying out and becoming brittle, wove with supple flexibility to make the basis for a solid wall.

If he had had any doubts before, Marcellus was quickly convinced of the rightness of Eleutherius's choice in sending Faganus and Durvianus to Britain to tell their story. These two could talk with enthusiasm of their God in any conditions, without missing a spot in their careful weaving of the wattle.

At first Marcellus tried not to listen. He was an engineer, a builder, and even if he were only building a wattle and daub hut, he would give the best of his skills to make it straight and sturdy—just as he had given his best for the wall. But eventually the gentle words penetrated his consciousness, and he had to admit they sounded more pleasant than his own thoughts. Besides, these men had traveled long at the bidding of the friend whom *he* had recommended.

". . . and so the Christus was the Logos—the Word of God made flesh. And He came to earth and dwelt among us. As the Apostle John wrote, 'We beheld His glory, the glory of the only begotten Son of the Father.'"

Fagan would have ended there, but Dyfan added, almost as a prayer, "'Full of grace and truth, and we have received grace upon grace.'"

Again, the words made little sense to Marcellus in a logical manner, yet he was gripped by their beauty. It was clear, though, that Lucius was held by more than poetry.

"And what must one do that this Logos God will speak His word? I would hear Him speak to me, as He seems to through your words." The king still sat, as he had throughout the morning, on his skin-covered stool in the center of the work. Yet the excitement in his voice was as if he had risen and spoken from the high place in his Great Hall.

Now Fagan, too, lay down his handful of willow branches and turned to the king. "Everyone who turns from his sins, from walking in his own way rather than the way of Jesu, and who believes that Jesu is the Christus—the true, one and only Son of God—is born of God and becomes His child. One has only to ask for His presence, for His grace, for His Logos."

Lucius was quiet for several moments. Then he asked, "Is that all? That is seeming to be too simple."

Fagan smiled. "God asks of His children other things in holy living. But we do them out of love for our Father, not in order to earn our place in His family. And He gives us His Holy Spirit to make us holy. It is not something we can do or be in ourselves."

Again it was quiet in the half-built hut. At last Lucius smiled and opened his mouth to speak. But the words never left his lips. Out of the thick, swirling fog, a clutch of ominous figures suddenly appeared, brandishing clubs and rocks. Cunedag of the wild hair and fierce tongue strode into the wattle structure as into a sacred druid ring, holding the bronze ceremonial sword aloft over her head. "Lugh will be avenged. He will not permit foreign gods on his sacred island, and we of his priestkind will not permit foreign priests to desecrate this holy land."

Fagan faced the sword-brandishing priestess empty-handed. "Indeed, this land is holy, for it was created by the holy God, maker of heaven and earth. And it is right that the Creator be worshiped here as in all the earth."

Cunedag brought her sword down with a great slash that missed Fagan by less than an inch. Marcellus was impressed. Even where he stood several feet behind the missionary, he could feel the swish of air as the sword cut through everything in its path, and yet Faganus had not flinched.

But his valor only further enraged the druidess. "You will die here! Why don't you leave?" The long-robed priests behind her moved forward, menacing with their crude weapons.

"No." Fagan's voice was clear, and yet he spoke so low that all within the circle of waist-high wattle leaned forward to hear. "No, it is not we who are in danger, but you. Our souls are in safekeeping, but *you* are dying."

The half-circle of druids waved their sticks and stones, but did not attempt to stop his speaking. "We have brought you the word of life. Christus our Lord lived among us as the light of the world that we might walk in His light, and not in the darkness of death. You will die if we leave. Our Lord said, 'I have come that they might have life.' We are come to share that life with you."

Cunedag held her ground, but a few of her priests lowered their weapons.

Fagan put his hand inside his tunic and brought out a leather pouch hanging there from a thong around his neck. "When we were restoring the sacred house of worship built by the ancestor of your king," Fagan said pointing with a commanding gesture that made all heads turn toward the wattle church, "I found this under the altar sealed in a clay pot. This charter is from the hand of King Arviragus, another ancestor of your King Lleiver Mawr. In this, the king granted twelve hides of land to Joseph of Arimathea, the first apostle to bring the word of life and light to these shores. And your good King Lleiver has renewed this charter of land."

Again Cunedag punctuated her words with slashes of her sword. "Fah! Your paper means nothing. The holy Avalon is not for any man to give. It is the abode of the gods—our gods, the ancient gods of this land and of this island. The gods of the Tor will not tolerate a new god in a wattle hut. The signing of a paper does not change the gods."

Still Fagan held out the paper. "But it is not only King Lleiver's ancestors who made this grant. It is your spiritual ancestors as well. Look you. Here is the signature of Bran the Blessed—archdruid of the court of Arviragus. You and your priests are of the order of Bran the Blessed, and the One-God of love and light was his God, too, as He is rightly your God."

Cunedag jerked her sword high over her head with both hands, spun on her heel, and leapt outside the wattle barrier. "I will hear no more blasphemy against the gods. They will be avenged."

She disappeared into the mists as suddenly as she had appeared. And her priests followed her. All but two. Brach and Corfil stayed behind to examine the document Fagan held out to them. "We would hear more. We will return tonight," they said. Then they, too, disappeared into the fog.

All in the circle let their breath out together. Then Fagan fell to his knees beside the already kneeling Dyfan. "Lord, have mercy. Father, have mercy. Spirit, have mercy. Father of love, source of all strength, help us to hold to Your promises and to lead the way to You. Help us to pass from our old life of sin to the new life of grace."

Fagan paused and Dyfan said, "Lord, have mercy."

Fagan concluded, "We ask this through Your Son, our Lord Jesu Christus, who lives and reigns with You and the Holy Spirit, one God, for ever and ever."

And to Marcellus's own surprise, he joined the others in saying, "Amen."

But when he looked up, he lost all thought of gods and priestesses—whether serving on the Tor or on the Capitoline. For Dorigen entered the hut. She appeared through the mist as suddenly as Cunedag had, but her fresh radiance made her a sharp contrast to the wild-eyed priestess. Dorigen came with a soft glow that warmed the fog. At that moment, as she stood before him like a ray of sunlight in a gray world, Marcellus knew that he loved the British princess. It was fine for Faganus and Durvianus to talk of a God of love and light, but he had found these qualities in quite another source.

As the realization filled him, he looked from the daughter to the father and knew that just as he resisted asking God for His favors of mercy, so he wrestled against the thought of asking Lucius for his daughter. The British king was unlikely to welcome a Roman son-in-law, and Marcellus would not beg. For too long he had been independent of any man, for too long unwilling to ask for anything that might be denied him, for too long self-sufficient to break the pattern now for man or god. Or for woman.

5

origen turned to address her father. "Will you come for midday stewpot, Father? It is the last of the fish, but Rhodric has found some fresh herbs, and the gods have gloriously provided a few apples that escaped rotting on the branch."

Marcellus now noticed the basket of small red and green apples she carried under her left arm. In a normal year such small, uneven specimens would be thrown to the birds, but now they did, indeed, appear to be food of the gods.

"If the fog lifts, you must fish again this afternoon, Father." Dorigen took his arm to lead the way to the cookfire.

Marcellus, close behind them, said, "Yes, and you'll have two fewer mouths to feed, for the boatman and I will be gone when the way is clear."

Dorigen turned back to him, and he hoped the fading of her smile was for his going. Certainly he found no pleasure in the leave-taking a few hours later when the mists lifted with a light breeze and he and the boatman climbed into the coracle.

At Isca Silurum a guard met Marcellus at the main gate of the fortress and ushered him directly up the Via Praetoria into the cross hall of the principia where Legate Dominitus sat on his tribunal. The first thing Marcellus saw was a clerk writing furiously at a small table to the left of the raised dais and to the commander's right, Caius Valens, Marcellus's former commander from Vercovicium, regarding the late-arrived Marcellus with a severe frown.

Marcellus gave a smart palm-to-forehead salute and stood at stiff attention.

"Centurion Marcellus Artios," Dominitus said. "Be seated. Your evidence will be taken next."

Marcellus turned to a narrow bench along the far wall and for the first time became aware of the two men sitting there—Festus Martinus and Licinus Natalis. Were his old rival and the grasping optio here to give evidence against him? Was he not to be allowed to call anyone in his own defense? But who would he call? The work had been done under his orders, and it had crumbled. What help would it be for fellow legionnaires to stand before the commander and declare that he was a fine fellow—if any could be found to do so? His work had crumbled. His wall had testified against him.

He sat on the darkest end of the bench, and Dominitus continued his questioning of Optio Licinus. "And I understand that the mixing of the mortar was your responsibility."

"I saw that it was mixed according to his orders." He inclined his head toward Marcellus.

"And those orders were?"

"One part cement, three parts lime, five parts sand, one part hardening agent." He barked out the formula and then added quickly, "Well-cooled lime and not over-much water."

"Those were your orders?" Caius Valens looked at Marcellus.

"Of course, sir. That is the proper mixture for the strongest mortar. It should have held a thousand years—two thousand."

"And you as the commander saw to it that those orders were carried out precisely?"

"I did."

The questioning continued in a similar vein, and it gradually dawned on Marcellus that something was wrong here. He had heard no formal charges read. The trial had begun before he was present; he had been asked only a few casual questions. This was not the manner in which a Roman citizen was tried, even in a military inquiry.

Then he wondered if his summons had been to give evidence, not to stand trial. Was it possible that it was not Marcellus Artios who was on trial, but one of these men who sat before the legion commander? Feeling foolishly disoriented, he followed the questioning even more carefully. If he hadn't been delayed by the fog, he would have been here when the proceedings began and would know where he stood. Not that it made any difference as to how he answered the occasional question directed to him. He gave simple, straightforward answers to the commander's questions regarding his work, the work of his men, and his finding of the channel undercutting the wall on the day of his dismissal.

"And so, Licinus Natalis." Commander Dominitus paused and looked the optio hard in the eye. "If you carried out the orders of your chief engineer to the letter, how do you explain the fact that Caius Valens's examination of the crumbled wall revealed a mortar that must have been only two parts lime to six parts sand with very little hardening agent?" The silent room rang as the question repeated itself in each person's mind. "Licinus Natalis, did you purposely use the wrong mixture, or were you negligent in your supervision?"

Again the room was silent. Licinus's face grew red, and sweat broke out on his forehead. His dark eyes darted from one face to another, and he looked less like a man than like a cornered rat.

Suddenly he sprang to his feet. "It was *his* order! He said after the revolt, he'd be procurator, and I'd be commander of Vercovicium." He jerked the stub of his right arm at Marcellus.

All the blood drained from Marcellus's face, and he felt dizzy. Could such an outrageous lie stick? Was the former accusation of incompetence to be turned into a charge of treason? He jumped to his feet to protest, but the quick movement increased his light-headedness, and he staggered against the wall.

In that moment he saw his mistake. Licinus was not pointing at him, but at Festus. He was accusing the engineer-in-charge of betraying the Empire. Marcellus lowered himself slowly to the bench.

Festus remained stonily silent except for one sentence. "As a Roman citizen, I demand my right to trial before Emperor Antonius Pius."

But with the crumbling of Licinus, the pieces fell into place around Festus, and the picture of treachery became clear. By collaborating with the Brigante queen and the Picti and playing upon their readily roused passions for revolt, Festus had sought to overthrow those in charge and, as the only Roman with tribal support, gain procuratorship of all of northern Britain. All he needed was a collaborator inside the fort to undermine the wall and to get rid of the one person in a position to block improper building procedures, a person who could then be blamed. By position and by personal inclination, Licinus had been the perfect choice of co-conspirator—except that he was not one who would stand firm if anything went wrong. And it had gone wrong indeed, thanks to Marcellus's diligent investigation of the wall and Caius Valens's follow-up—both in inspecting the mortar and in calling for the troops from the Antonine Wall at the first suspicious sign.

Now that their glorious scheme lay in ruins, Licinus turned on Festus in a rage. "I gave my right arm for your grand plot. Going to be Lord High Procurator, you were—and who could say if not Governor next? And what's it come to?" He shook his left hand under Festus's nose. But Festus ignored him.

Dominitus clapped his hands. The guard outside his door entered smartly and dragged a still-shouting Licinus off to the guardhouse. "And this one, too." The commander waved the remaining guard to the silent Festus. "He has appealed to the emperor. It shall, of course, be granted. But he will await his summons to Rome in the guardhouse."

When the room had been cleared, Marcellus shook his head and stood up. "Sir, that all happened so fast. I—I thank you, Commander Caius—I had no idea you took my findings seriously. I—"

Caius smiled and waved Marcellus back to his seat. "At ease, Centurion. A commander must take any irregularity seriously. The defense of the Empire often depends on something so small as a rat hole in a wall. Festus needed control of the Vercovicium for his plot to work. He knew the commander's position was invulnerable, but the engineer could be, er, engineered out. I suspected that something like this was afoot. The evidence you provided was all I needed to send for reinforcements. If we had had more warning, we could have stopped the uprising altogether. As it is—we won at a great price."

"But why did you not let me stay and prove myself?"

"I was certain that your life was in danger. What would someone determined enough to undermine the wall care for the life of one centurion? And I thought, since it seemed obvious you were the target of the plot, that with you out of the way, they could more freely show their hand and trap themselves." He paused. "I can only trust in the wisdom of Jupiter that I was right—the desolation of burned fields and rotting corpses . . ." He shook his head.

Dominitus stood to his feet. "You were quite right, Commander Caius. Without your clear thinking and quick action, the entire north might have been lost. I will make that clear in my report to Governor Verus and to Rome. I am certain the Senate will wish to reward you." Both men saluted dismissal to Marcellus.

Still feeling dazed, he walked from the fortress and made his way to the over-full banks of the Isca, not even noticing the gentle rain falling. He had been vindicated. His work had been vindicated. Only now that the enormous weight was lifted did he realize the burden he had been carrying all these months. And now what would he do? Now perhaps he could return to his wall. Yes, surely he could—there would be great resources assigned to the rebuilding, and they would need his skills. He would go back and apply to Dominitus now.

A fish jumped in the river, making him think of his new life here in the west country. Did he want to leave it? Elfan and Lucius were the first friends he had made in his years in Britain—practically the only friends he had in the world. He looked at the lush beauty of the land, so different from the stark isolation of the country to the north. He thought of his work at Glevum and the pride he took in using his engineering skills to keep the mines running in the face of fierce obstacles. He thought of the peace of Ynis Witrin that even now tugged at his heart. He had been gone only a few hours, and he had been witness to a bitter altercation while there, and yet the Tor and its island drew him with a heart-longing akin to homesickness.

And he thought of Dorigen, her gentle blue eyes, her shining golden hair, her clear, soft voice—the attractive features that he knew mirrored the inner woman. And yet, the appeal of Dorigen herself perhaps was reason to leave, as no Roman soldier could be lawfully married. His twenty remaining years of service stretched before him like eternity.

Well, he needn't decide now whether or not to request transfer. His leave from Glevum was indefinite; he could now return to Ynis Witrin.

Immediately after cockcrow the next morning, Marcellus packed all the corn cakes and wheat-meal he could talk the commissioner out of and went to the river to hire a boat. In a few hours Marcellus was back on Ynis Witrin. It had seemed to him that with each dip of the paddle he had felt himself relax, and with his first sight of the Tor, he felt a quiet happiness seep into him, replacing the tension. At the island he paid the boatman, then turned toward the Tor. Marcellus went first to the church, but found no one there; nor were they at work on the wattle hut. The sound of a soft singing made him turn. Had he truly heard something, or was it his heightened imagination in this mystical place? Now he heard nothing. Then it came to him again, a gentle melody seeming to call him. Perhaps the birds singing, since the rain had let up for the moment? But the third time the song came to him, he knew it was human singing and that it was coming from the ridge below the Tor, perhaps in the area of the well.

He turned and walked that direction, his steps quickening as the sound of singing became clearer. He reached the group just as the song ended. Lucius and Dorigen stood to one side of the well, Medwy to the other. They wore only their linen undergarments. In front of them, above the spring, were Faganus and Durvianus wearing their best white togas. Standing almost hidden by a yew tree were the two druids who had remained behind after Cunedag's confrontation.

Faganus clasped his hands and extended them over the flowing water. "Our Father in Heaven, You give us Your grace through this act that tells of the wonders of Your power. In this service of baptism we use Your gift of water which

You made at the dawn of creation, breathing on the waters with Your Spirit, making them the wellspring of holiness. In the waters of the great flood, You made a sign of the waters of baptism, as a sign of an end of sin and a new beginning of goodness.

"In the waters of the Jordan, Your Son, our Savior, was baptized and anointed with the Spirit. Water and blood flowed from the side of our Savior as He hung upon the cross bearing our sins. And after His resurrection, He told His disciples to go and teach all nations, baptizing them in the name of the Father, and of the Son, and of the Holy Spirit." He unclasped his hands and raised them heavenward.

"Father, look now upon us with Your love, and by the power of Your Spirit, give grace to the water of this well which You have provided for us out of Your abundance. You created man in Your image; cleanse him from sin with a new birth in You by water and by the Spirit. We ask, Father, with Your Son, to send the Holy Spirit upon the waters of this spring."

Marcellus spotted Elfan standing a little apart from the others and walked quietly to him. "What's going on?"

Elfan whispered, "The king and those are wanting to be made Christiani. This is how they go about it. Baptism, they call it."

Fagan dipped a cup into the well and held it before Lucius. "As in the pouring of water at baptism, our Lord pours Himself into His children. King Lleiver Mawr of the Silurians and Atrebates, is it your will to be so filled with our Christus?"

Lucius took a step toward Fagan. "That is my will."

"Then, King Lleiver, I baptize you in the name of the Father." Fagan poured the water over the king's head, then stooped to refill the cup. "And of the Son." Again he poured and refilled. "And of the Holy Spirit." As he poured the contents of the cup over the head of the king a third time, the company joined him in saying, "Amen."

Dyfan handed the king a linen towel to dry his head on, and the ceremony was repeated for Dorigen and Medwy. Marcellus had never thought it possible that his radiant one, as he had come to think of Dorigen, could glow with more inner shining. But as she looked at him with the merest hint of a smile while the waters of the third cup were still falling from her hair, he knew that the glow now came from deeper within her than ever before.

Elfan's reaction to his son's baptism seemed to be one of mingled skepticism and pride. "He never was of much use in the trading business. It is seeming that following this new God has settled him a bit."

Then their attention turned back to the group around the well as Fagan's clear voice declared, "As streams in a dry land, those who are sowing in tears will sing as they reap."

In spite of the seriousness of the moment, Elfan's infectious laughter rang out, mingling with the raindrops. "Surely you could be making a better metaphor. By no imagination could this be called a dry land."

Dyfan turned to him. "Ah, my brother, that is exactly what it is. Even as the land is drowning in floods, it is parching spiritually. This land will be brought to flower not with drops of rain, nor with floods of human tears, but with the healing tears of Jesu the Christus."

Those who had received baptism knelt by the pool. Lucius prayed first. "Claim me as Your own, Lord God of Heaven and earth. Be sending, I ask, Your mercy on me, Your servant." Each of the new converts repeated his words in turn.

Fagan placed both hands on the king's head and, with his face turned toward heaven, said, "Let us give thanks to God the Father most high for having made you worthy through the blood of His Son to share the lot of the saints in light. The Lord has rescued us from the power of darkness and brought us into the Kingdom of His beloved Son. Through Him we have redemption, the forgiveness of our sins, and the healing of our land. Now may you be able to grasp fully the breadth and length and height and depth of the love of our Lord Jesu Christus. And may you experience this love which surpasses all human knowledge so that you may attain to the fullness of God Himself and so lead your people. To Him be glory in the church and in Jesu the Christus through all generations, world without end. Amen."

The worshipers rose, and Dyfan began speaking to them, but his gentle voice was drowned by a demanding Cymric chant from the other side of the hill. Looking up the yew-lined path, Marcellus saw four long-haired, long-robed druid priests approaching behind their sword-wielding priestess.

"I have warned you, King Lleiver Mawr. You go too far in desecrating our sacred well with your god. And now you presume to perform your heretical rites before two priests of the sacred oak."

Spitting fire in her gaze and her words, Cunedag advanced on King Lleiver. "Lugh of the Shining Spear, I call upon you to guide the vengeance of your priestess."

The ancient bronze sword slashed through the air at the king.

King Lleiver took one step back and found himself against the trunk of a tree. He looked at the enraged druidess flailing the bronze sword inches from him. He could feel the rush of air with every slash of the sword. But now all his own anger and fear drained away. Beneath all the swagger and thrust of the druid, the king could see a frightened, confused woman groping in the dark.

Lucius flung out his arms as if he would embrace her. And in that moment, as he stood against the tree in a gesture of love and submission, the ancient ritual sword lunged forward and pierced his side. "Father, forgive . . ." he said, then lost consciousness.

Dorigen's cry was the only sound as Lleiver Mawr crumpled to the ground, a red stain soaking the side of his baptismal linen and washing into the waters of the spring over which he had fallen.

Cunedag flung both arms upward and shouted to the top of the Tor, "O Great Lugh, smile on your avenging servant! By your strength I have accomplished the vanquishing of your enemy!" The priests began to chant and, swaying to the rhythm of their words, moved sun-wise around the pool of water and blood where their fallen king lay. Then they followed Cunedag back up the path.

The spell of horror broke, and all rushed to the king. "Father, Father," Dorigen sobbed and cradled his head in her lap, the skirt of her own shift falling into the water.

Fagan knelt to examine the wound. "The medical supplies," he shouted to Dyfan, who set off toward their hut at a run.

Marcellus fell to his knees and grasped the royal hand. He had had no idea the king was so frail. In his tunic, cape, and gold jewelry, Lucius always looked every inch the representative of the ancient royal line of his people. Marcellus felt the bony wrist for a pulse. Nothing. Dorigen's choked sobs beside him increased his desperation. Trying not to be rushed by panic, Marcellus moved his finger to another spot, hoping he was wrong. The three blue veins were so easy to see under the transparent white skin—it would be hard to mistake his reading.

He gently replaced the lifeless hand on the green earth and lay his ear on the king's chest. Again he could sense no life. With his ear still against Lucius's skin, he started to shake his head. The motion brought his pressed ear more firmly over the king's heart. He stopped. Holding his own breath, he listened again. Yes. He let his breath out in a long sigh. "Yes. It is unbelievably weak, but there is life."

Dorigen's sob was one of joy as she reached out her hand to him. "Oh, thank you. Thank you."

Marcellus was not sure whether she was thanking him or her new God for the news, but he took her hand.

Fagan finished examining the wound, which he washed repeatedly with water from the spring. "It is deep and jagged. But perhaps—if we can staunch the flow of blood—perhaps . . ."

Dyfan returned with a satchel of ointments and bandages. The two friendly druids approached. "We know of healing herbs . . ."

Dorigen spoke. "Oh, yes—please. We must do all we can. All of us. He must recover. He must." She gripped Marcellus's hand fiercely as she stifled her sob.

The next hours blurred in Marcellus's mind as the fog that so often shrouded Ynis Witrin itself, but certain images remained clear: the gentleness with which Fagan and Dyfan bound the king's wounded side and bore him on a litter back to his bedplace; the care with which the druids prepared their paste of herbs, cooking the essence from some, grinding others to use fresh; and the firm courage with which Dorigen sat by her father, placing drops of water on his blue lips and rubbing his cold hands. After her first outburst of sobbing, she remained dry-eyed and silent, obviously forcing herself to think of her father's needs and not her own fear and sorrow.

At long last, the bandages and compresses ceased to soak through with blood. The first skirmish had been won—if they weren't too late. Again Marcellus listened for the fluttering pulse, thought it had gone, and then found it at last, faint as a sleeping baby's breath.

Dorigen looked at the pile of soaked red rags in the corner of the hut. "He must have red meat. If not . . ."

With the joy of being given something useful to do, Marcellus seized Lucius's hunting spear. "Badger? Squirrel? Will a small animal do?" It would be hard enough to provide that. He didn't want to raise her hopes by suggesting deer.

"Yes. Anything." She turned to him, unshed tears brimming her eyes. "Thank you. God go with you."

Elfan joined him at the door. "My spear is in Medwy's hut."

Elfan rowed them to the southeast across the flooded marshland until they came to a deserted hillfort on the edge of the great forest. "It is long and long since our people lived in Caer-Cam. If there is game to be found, it will be in the hunting-runs of the forest."

By nightfall the hunters had only two rabbits for the stewpot. Elfan shook his head. "Their tender white meat will not be providing the strength King Lleiver is needing, although Dorigen can make a strengthening pudding of their blood stirred with wheat-meal."

Climbing the eroded entryway of the ancient hillfort, they found a sheltered spot in a corner of the broken ramparts and curled up for the night in their bearskins. In the morning they breakfasted on dried oat cake dipped in barley beer and a piece of goat cheese Marcellus had begged from the commissioner at Isca. Then they resumed their hunt.

By midmorning they had added only three small birds to their bag. Marcellus's desperation was mounting when the sound of snapping twigs in the forest ahead brought him to a standstill. It had to be a large animal moving through the brush. His hand went to his pilum, and he saw Elfan, who had also heard the sounds, balance his throw-spear.

The stag appeared, moving sedately through the trees, fifty yards ahead of them. Marcellus threw first, but his aim was hurried. The pilum grazed the deer's neck, causing him to bolt sideways. Cursing himself and every god whose name he could recall, Marcellus reached for the dagger at his waist.

But there was no need. As if he had foreseen what would happen, Elfan aimed at where the quarry would be. His throw-spear sank deep in the animal's throat, bringing it to its knees.

"The gods be praised!" Marcellus gasped. "That's the finest hunting I've ever seen."

Elfan knelt by the stag, turned it on its back, and quickly slit it open. The heart, which had just ceased to pump, gave a flutter and was still. Elfan removed the heart and liver, slipping them into his wolfskin game bag. "My coracle cannot be carrying two men and a stag. We shall hang the carcass high in a tree where it will be safe from wolves, and I shall return for it tomorrow. This will be the best medicine our friend can be taking."

Marcellus, suppressing the wish that it could have been his spear that felled the animal, raced to keep up with Elfan's pace back to the coracle. "Lleiver Mawr will remain in the land of the living with such as this in his belly," Elfan almost shouted as he plied his oar across the swamp.

When they arrived at Ynis Witrin in the late afternoon, Marcellus could see by Dorigen's eyes that her father yet lived, but was no better. She brightened immediately, though, when she saw what their bags held. "Rhodric, Rhodric, quick! Cut the liver into little pieces while I cook a healing broth. Oh, Marcellus, how can I be thanking you for the life of my father. This will make him well."

Marcellus grimaced. "I did nothing. It was Elfan's spear, not mine, that felled the deer." And as he spoke, he felt a deeper guilt than that of merely missing his aim. As a representative of Emperor Antonius, he was here to keep the peace. Somehow he should have prevented the dreadful incident at the well instead of merely standing by. And worse yet, perhaps his own presence as a member of the Roman military that had slaughtered so many druids and smashed their cors had added to the priestess's rage. Far from being the one Dorigen had to thank, she should rather blame him.

"No, no." Dorigen laid her hand lightly on his arm as if she read his mind. "It matters not whose spear did the piercing. The hunting was successful."

And before he could protest, she sped away to the cookplace.

By the next morning the stews and herbs had done their work, and Lucius could speak in a weak whisper. Marcellus knelt beside the royal bedplace. "Your Majesty, I praise Jupiter that you live. With your leave, I shall go now and arrest the one who did this to you. She shall stand trial at Isca, and all shall know that Roman justice does not allow such outrage."

Lucius shook his head slowly. "No, Medwy has already gone to the civitas council at Venta. We have our tribal justice which is older than your Roman system. The druidess will be dealt with in our own way."

Marcellus started to protest. Surely there was something he could do. He had ever been a man of action, accustomed to dealing with his own problems and those of the people in his charge. This impotence was something outside his experience.

The deerskin flap on the door fluttered, and Fagan and Dyfan entered. Shaking his head, Fagan said, "This is the hour when darkness reigns. This is the testing of your faith. We must trust."

Marcellus wanted to cry out, *faith, trust?* How could these priests babble so? Someone must *do* something.

Dyfan spoke. "The psalmist also suffered greatly. Would Your Majesty find it comforting to hear his words?"

Lucius nodded and sank back on his cushions, his eyes closed to listen the more carefully. Dyfan took a scroll from a leather tube, unrolled it, and began to read.

Lord, my God, I call for help by day;
I cry at night before You.
Let my prayer come into Your presence.
Oh, turn Your ear to my cry.

My soul is filled with shadows;
my life is on the brink of the grave.
I am reckoned as one in the tomb:
I have reached the end of my strength.

I call to You, Lord, all the day long;
to You I stretch out my hands.
Lord, I call to You for help;
in the morning my prayer comes before You.

Dyfan rolled up the parchment, and Lucius spoke softly, his eyes still closed. "It is right. We must be calling to Him the All-High."

Fagan led in prayer. "You are in our midst, O Lord, Your name we bear; do not forsake us, O Lord, our God!"

Marcellus moved quietly from the hut. He had heard enough. Old men and priests might choose to sit around praying and reading poetry while the king's life fluttered on the edge of the grave, but that was not his way. He would take action. Why had he been so slow to think of it? Surely it was the sense of Ynis Witrin being a world apart. But now he would go to Isca for help. The fortress maintained the best hospital in all this part of Britain. If only Lucius weren't so weak, he would insist on taking him there, but since the trip would clearly be too much for him, they must make do with second best. He would fetch the head doctor for the king.

For hours Marcellus paced around the island, awaiting Elfan's return with the carcass of the deer. As soon as he arrived, Marcellus impatiently helped him lug the stag to the cookplace. Then without an explanation to anyone but Elfan, he insisted they set out immediately for the fortress.

Marcellus thought he would explode with frustration when they missed the flood tide of the Isca and so were forced to spend the night on the banks of the Mor Hafren with a group of fishermen, likewise awaiting the return tide in the early morning. Marcellus slept little from sheer impatience and irritation. If the wound began bleeding again or became infected while they kicked their heels around a campfire, it would be all his fault. He had convinced himself that he bore the full responsibility for Lucius's life, and he must act.

By the time they reached the hospital, there was a line of soldiers by the herb garden in the courtyard seeking treatment for various minor ailments. Two or three were holding their jaws with obvious dental problems; another was shivering with fever; several awaited treatment for the painful pinkeye that afflicted so many, especially when their diets lacked fresh vegetables. Marcellus, by virtue of his rank, strode to the head of the line and on into the surgery theater where Andronicos, the Greek doctor, was extracting a tooth with pliers while two orderlies held the man down. The operation took only a matter of minutes, and the man was administered a cup of wine to ease his pain.

Marcellus explained the situation briefly. Andronicos gave him no argument, but began immediately issuing orders to his assistants to fill his bag with instruments and salves. If the doctor had argued, Marcellus would have simply ordered the man to his duty, but it was pleasant not to have to argue. While he waited, Marcellus stepped out into the long corridor that ran by the sick rooms. Two youths from the vicus were sweeping and scrubbing the floor. The hospital was quiet and fresh-smelling, but Marcellus could not relax in its peaceful atmosphere. He turned to order the doctor to hurry and almost bumped into him. "I am ready," the gentle Greek voice said.

This time the tide of the river was with them, and their journey was speedy, even though it seemed endless to the impatient Marcellus. Elfan conversed with the doctor almost the entire way, but Marcellus sat in stiff silence, urging the coracle to move faster and yet faster until they arrived at last.

"Ah, you have kept the wound clean." Andronicos nodded his gray head at Dorigen. "That is good."

Dorigen, Marcellus, and Elfan held their breath while Andronicos continued his examination of the wound and then smelled and tasted the pot of herb-paste salve they had used. "Hypericum and millefolium I recognize. There is also something with which I am unfamiliar." He sniffed the dark green mixture again and rubbed some on his own hand. "It seems to have served well, but I will leave you a pot of my own ointment. Many a legionnaire owes his life to its application after a battle."

Then he talked quietly with his patient. The king was so weak others in the small room were barely able to hear his replies. Andronicos made another examination of the wound, applied his ointment thickly, and bound it all in clean linen. Then he sat for several moments, running his fingers through his curly gray beard. At last he stood to make his pronouncement. "You will live, Your Majesty. Your care has been excellent, and I see no sign of infection. I fear, however, that I cannot promise a full recovery. The sword was dull and dirty. Bronze makes a cruel weapon; it tears more than cuts, and this slash was deep and ragged. I think it likely that the wound will continue to bleed. Strong broth will build your strength to a point, but you must accustom yourself to staying close to your cot and bearing pain."

Dorigen sobbed in protest. "But is there nothing more we can do?"

Andronicos considered. "I could sew the wound closed, but if I am correct that it will continue to seep body fluids, it would be better to keep it bound with fresh linen. It is my observation that linen dipped in boiling water and dried in the sun makes the most effective wound-wrap."

"He shall have the best care," Dorigen vowed.

"I am confident of that." Andronicos looked back at the king, lying on his pallet with his eyes closed. The doctor shook his head and left the hut.

6

"I must be seeing to my business," Elfan said. "I shall return the doctor to the fortress and continue on to Glevum. Will you be joining me, Marcellus?"

Marcellus was torn. He had never in his life slacked his duty. But where did his duty lie? Mining operations were important to the Empire. And if he didn't report back soon, he would find himself doing time in the guardhouse. Yet he felt a greater weight of responsibility for the king. None of his actions had been effective, but still he felt responsible to do something.

"If you can wait, I will write a letter to the commander telling him I have been delayed. Let him make of that what he will." He caught sight of the missionaries coming up the path from the church. "Brother Fagan, can you loan me writing materials?"

A short time later Elfan and Andronicos left with the letter. Marcellus had gained a few more days on the island, perhaps at the displeasure of his commander. Now what was he to do with his time?

"Will you join us for evening prayer?" Dyfan asked.

Marcellus nodded and followed him into the king's hut where Dorigen sat by her father while Urych played a gentle harpsong.

It was not the strains of the harp, however, but the sound of the spongy earth squashing under their feet as they had walked to the hut that remained in Marcellus's ears while Fagan read from his scroll by the smoking seal oil lamp. Why did he feel responsible even for the rains? What could he do? As he wrestled in his mind, Fagan's words penetrated his consciousness. "'Ask and it shall be given you, seek and you shall find, knock and it shall be opened to you.'"

Ask and it shall be given you. Ask and it shall be given you . . . But what should he ask?

As if in answer to his own thoughts, Fagan's voice came again. "Our Heavenly Father waits to give all good gifts to His children through His grace. His hand will withhold nothing from them, but they must ask. Ask first for His salvation. Then ask for His fullest blessing. Ask for the privilege of serving Him, and ask for the greatest privilege of all—to worship Him. Asking is the key that unlocks His grace."

If this had not been a sacred moment for the others, Marcellus would have scoffed openly. Asking was not the Roman way. Romans took. Romans commanded. Romans built their own world. Romans did not ask.

Dorigen rose quietly to place a square of peat on the fire as the rain beat harder on the thatch. When she had returned to her place, Dyfan clasped his hands and prayed: "O God, our mighty Heavenly Father, enthroned on high and yet in our very hearts, at the close of day we come to You, weary, yet knowing that in You we will find rest. As the darkness falls around us, You are the light that never fades. Shine in the darkness of our night, we pray. Forgive our sins and our failings and draw us ever closer to Your light. We ask this through our Lord Jesu Christus, Your Son, who lives and reigns with You and the Holy Spirit, one God, for ever and ever."

The king's voice, weak but unwavering, concluded, "Amen."

Marcellus went out into the night to his lonely bedplace. He did not even bother to light his fire as he flung himself on his pallet.

In the morning he still had found no answers. Perhaps he was wrong to remain here where he was constantly tormented by his powerlessness. But even if he decided to return, the coracles were all on the other side of the Sabrina. He would have to wait. He stood on the riverbank watching the raindrops make concentric circles in the gray water.

You have not because you ask not.

"What?" Marcellus spoke out loud before he realized the voice he heard had been internal only. Where had the words come from? From his own memory, surely, yet he had no idea when he might have heard them. Perhaps something Fagan had said when he wasn't really listening.

But what did they mean? What was it he didn't have? What was he supposed to ask? And of whom?

For a whole day Marcellus resisted the growing feeling that Fagan and Dyfan or the king held the answers. How would it look if a Roman centurion turned to representatives of the forbidden religion for help? Technically, he had been remiss in his duty to Rome by not reporting their presence on the island long ago. But no matter what arguments he gave himself, he knew that underneath it all, his reluctance lay in the fact that he had for so long lived closed inside himself. Asking left one vulnerable, open, exposed.

The coracles did not return. Marcellus wrestled the questions through another endless night. By morning he was determined. Although it made no sense to think that asking a few simple questions could succeed where all his activity had failed, he would ask.

Inside the royal hut the king lay in pain on his cushions. As Andronicos had predicted, he did not die and neither did he get better. He lingered in a half-lighted world between the kingdom of life and the kingdom of death. And still the rains came.

Fagan and Dyfan nodded silently to Marcellus as he entered and quietly sat beside the smoking hearth. Marcellus was startled when Lucius's voice came from the pallet. "You may speak. I am not asleep."

"Your Majesty, I would not weary you, but I have come to ask—" He had come this far; could he go on?

"Yes. What would you ask?" Lucius prodded.

He hesitated. It was his final chance to pull back. Again the voice spoke in his head, *You have not because you ask not.*

"What is grace?" The question hung in the air.

Lucius nodded and raised a hand for Fagan to answer.

"It is God reaching down to man," the missionary said.

Marcellus blinked as he thought. A God who reached to man—rather than man striving to reach God? Marcellus knew little of religions, but he realized this was unique. "Where do I find it?"

"In your heart when you believe on the Lord Jesu Christus."

Marcellus sat there, turning his mind to his own inward being and to the God who asked to reside there. He realized that in asking he had opened himself up to this new, undemanding God who was in truth the oldest and most demanding of all because He required not a simple sacrifice, but one's whole heart.

He had his answers. What would he do with them? It was quiet in the room as he looked at his soul. Did he want to open it to this God of grace? Did he want the gifts of any God? As he had refused to give to the gods, so had he refused to accept anything from them. What of this God who made the sacrifices Himself, offered His love freely, and yet asked more than any other god had dared to ask?

"Allow the All-God to love you and love Him in return," Fagan urged. Nothing Marcellus had ever heard in his life sounded so easy, or so hard. He looked at those around him. Suddenly he knew the light in their eyes was more than friendship. He saw shining far brighter than the hearthfire the light of *filios* love. And he realized he returned it. Now he was ready for the *agape* love of the All-God. He slipped to his knees.

Dyfan moved quietly to stand behind Marcellus and put his hands on the Roman's head. "O God, our Father, who knows the hearts of Your creatures better than we know our own, You alone know the depth of the struggle that comes to our hearts before peace. You know that such is the pattern of all things. You know that so struggled Your Son, our Lord, in the garden before He gave himself as sacrifice for all creation. So, Father of mercy, we ask You to hear the prayers of your repentant, struggling child who calls on You in love. Enlighten his mind. Sanctify his heart. Bring peace to his struggles. We ask this through our Lord Jesu Christus, Your Son, who lives and reigns with You and the Holy Spirit, one God, for ever and ever."

As his heart followed Dyfan's prayer, Marcellus felt a lightness of his spirit and a lightness in the atmosphere of the hut. He had the sense of a storm passing.

Lucius sat up on his cot, the lines of pain in his face eased. He held out his right hand over the room like a benediction. "Lord, now is Your servant finding peace. Your word has come to fulfillment. With my own eyes I have seen the salvation You have prepared for all people, a light to be the revealing of yourself to the nation and to be the glory of Your people."

Not until he had left the hut and stood blinking in the sunlight did Marcellus realize that the rains had ceased.

Then he saw, coming toward him across the green valley below, the vision that never failed to bring his heart to his throat. As he watched Dorigen in her green and gold tunic with the sunlight falling on her golden hair, he knew that there was another question he longed to ask. And yet, that seemed just as impossible as the asking he had just done. It would be twenty long years before he received his discharge and the usual reward of a plat of land for faithful service. Until then he would have nothing in Britain to offer a wife. She was a king's daughter with duties to her people. And she was a true Celt, born to ways of freedom that would never be comfortable in his restricted Roman world. Yet if he committed to stay here, was he prepared never to go home again? After he lost Julia, he thought he never wanted to see Rome again. Now he must be very certain.

Dorigen's steps came near. "Oh, Marcellus! Is it not wonderful! It is seeming the sun never shone so. How have you done such a miracle?"

Her words flabbergasted him. "I? What makes you say that I have done anything?"

Her laughter was as golden as the sunshine that turned the drops still falling from the trees into jewels. "I do not know. But I feel it in my heart. Somehow you have brought great goodness to our land. Come." She grabbed his hand. "Let us climb the Tor. There will be a rainbow."

Her light steps sped ahead of him up the steep mountain until they reached the top, breathless and laughing together. Then they turned to the southeast, and there was the rainbow, arcing its many colors from their own Avalon across the silvery-green marsh to Caer-Cam. "Look, it is a bridge!" Dorigen flung out her arms in delight, and Marcellus caught them and pulled her to himself. Her lips were on his for only a moment of time, and yet their kiss would last through all eternity.

"Oh, my radiant one. You are my sunshine, and yet you are far brighter than all the burning chariots Apollo ever drove across the sky. You are mine." In the perfect rightness of the moment there was no need to ask; there was no need to quell any former doubts. Dorigen was his, whatever he would do about his army obligation.

"Of course, my bear. I am yours." She laughed at his puzzled look. "You are surprised I use your name so. But is not that the meaning of Artios?"

"Yes, yes, it is so. And you shall be Dorigen Artios—the radiant bear."

"Come, we must ask my father's blessing."

They found Lucius leaning against a pile of cushions in his bedplace. He was weak, but the deep lines of pain that had gouged his face in past days were eased, and healthy color replaced his former death-pallor. Some of the new color drained from his face, however, at Dorigen and Marcellus's request. His brows knit in thought. "So." In the long pause Marcellus clenched his fists so tightly his nails bit into the flesh of his palms.

"So. Is my grandson and heir to be half-Roman and half-British as is my country?"

"Our ancestor Joseph Arimathea was not British, Father," Dorigen reminded him softly.

"And so is our ancient blood to be diluted more yet?" Lleiver Mawr spoke slowly, sadly. He did not argue; he did not refuse. But neither did he grant their request. The couple waited.

"The passing of old ways is never without pain. Sometimes I long for the days of our ancestors when the life of the tribe was all in all. But such is not the time we live in, nor the times our children's children will live in. Perhaps it is best to be ruled by both Roman and British, to draw strength and wisdom from both our ways. Perhaps it is best. But it is not easy. And much in me does not accept it easily. I must be sure."

He turned to Marcellus. "From the time Dorigen's mother, my beloved

Teleri, died in giving birth to the man-child who died with her, I have reared my daughter to be a queen and have asked the gods to give her a fine marriage lord to stand beside her. It may be that you are the one to so stand, Marcellus. And yet there are fine men of pure blood from the tribe. I must be sure."

Through the open doorway they saw two long-robed figures approach. "Ah, Brach and Corfil have followed their king in accepting the faith and have now accepted my invitation to feast. Help me to the table, my daughter."

They sat long at table, feasting on the last of Elfan's venison and watching the long streaks of sunlight slip beyond Wirral Hill. For a moment the rays focused on the thorn tree standing a sturdy sentinel on the hillside.

Then the evening shadows lengthened, and the golden glow of an autumn sunset spread over the island. Fagan struck a spark of flint and lighted the logs in a circle of stones near the banquet table. Urych slipped from his seat near the king and placed his stool by the fire. At first he fingered the strings of his harp almost idly, letting the music come as it would, rather than from any direction of his own will. An evening thrush sang, and the harpsong answered it. The flames danced, and the melody swayed with them. Autumn leaves rustled in the trees, and harp notes chased them.

Then, as if the poet-musician had made a decision, he struck a chord, and the harp was silent. The bard spoke. "Those who have come among us bearing new God-words have told me of a kingly bard of their land by the name of David." Urych's fingers gave the lightest flutter, and the harp sang a trill. "I shall sing one of the bard David's songs and then one of my own composing." Trill followed trill, leading the listeners into the song. Urych closed his eyes and sang:

Praise the name of the Lord,
Praise Him, servants of the Lord.
We are His servants who stand in the house of the Lord.
In the courts of the house of our God are we.
Praise the Lord, for the Lord is good.
Sing a psalm to His name, for He is loving.
For I know the Lord is great,
that our Lord is high above all gods.
The Lord does whatever He wills,
in heaven, on earth, and in the seas.
He summons clouds from the ends of the earth;
He makes lightning produce the rain;
from his treasuries He sends for the wind.

The harp produced the sounds of wind and rain, and those gathered around the fire on the darkening island drew their cloaks closer as the song continued. "Even so did the rains descend upon our land. Day upon day and night upon night the waters descended and would not be stopped. And the land groaned under its burden. But the gods of old could not heal the land of its curse. And the rains came.

"And the earth suffered as under a mighty blow. Even so did our king suffer from a dolorous blow, and the healing came not. Day upon day and night upon night, the king suffered upon his pallet. And the herbs failed, and the droughts failed, and the salves failed. And still the blood and water flowed from the royal side, and the royal strength lessened.

"And then came one of the Romankind, an equus-knight and bold. He tried his might for the royal healing, but it was not enough. He tried his skill for the royal healing, but it was not enough. He tried his strength for the royal healing, but it was not enough. And the rains fell, and the king groaned. And a great sadness was upon the land.

"And then the equus-knight and bold of the Romankind, on bended knee before all Heaven, asked his questions two of the All-God—asked of His grace and where to find it. And healing benediction poured forth in the radiance and goodness of the All-God. And the land rejoiced. And the king was healed, and the people rejoiced."

The harpsong swelled to a note of triumph. "Let all the people sing; let all the people dance; let the land sing and dance, for the Lord, the God-Among-Us is come, and mighty is His name. He has brought us out of darkness and into the light of His making."

When the last joyous chord had soared beyond the Tor and out of their hearing, the company still sat in awe of the beauty of the song, but more in the wonder of the miracle it had recounted. And then Marcellus felt a new warmth, and his eyes sought Dorigen. Her own eyes met his in a look of deep love that he returned.

The look held between them for a glorious space. Then she turned to her father. "You should be in your bed, my father."

"Aye, daughter. And tonight I shall sleep a sleep of rest." All rose when the king stood. "Good night, my daughter. Good night, Marcellus."

Marcellus lay long in his bedplace that night wondering if ever Lucius would call him by a closer name. After the great joys of the day and the quantity of wine at the feast, however, Marcellus could wrestle with no problems that night.

It was midday on the morrow when Marcellus realized how far his problems were from over. Indeed, he had greater ones yet to face as the long arm of the Empire reached out to grasp him. At first they thought the coracle that slipped up the Briw with its native oarsman was Elfan and Medwy returned to them sooner than expected. Marcellus, Dorigen, Fagan, and Dyfan all hurried toward the riverbank to meet them, leaving King Lleiver, no longer in pain, but far from full strength, resting on a pile of skins in the sunshine near his hut.

Marcellus was the first to see who had come. He pulled himself smartly to attention and raised his hand in a flat-palmed salute, wishing he had taken time to don his uniform that morning. "Legate Dominitus."

Dominitus returned his salute as soon as he was firmly on dry ground. "At ease, Centurion. We shall speak in a moment. You may present your companions."

"Princess Dorigen, daughter of King Lleiver, and Faganus and Durvianus from Rome."

Dominitus nodded his head and took note of the togas the two men wore. "I see you are citizens. What has brought you so far to this lonely island?"

And with that question, the true horror of the situation dawned upon Marcellus. Not only had the commander of the whole legion come to Ynis Witrin to drag him back in disgrace for deserting his post of duty, but now he had exposed his Christiani friends to the severity of Roman punishment. Perhaps even the king himself would be deposed by Rome for following this forbidden religion. Why had he stayed so long? Why had he ever come here in the first place? He had brought nothing but disaster upon these people.

"We are teachers, sir. We have been teaching the king on this island where his people have studied from times long past."

The wisdom of Fagan's answer made Marcellus let his breath out in a rush. Perhaps his friends would be spared and only he punished for his misdemeanors.

"Would you like to meet my father, sir?" Dorigen stepped forward.

Dominitus smiled at her. "Indeed I would be happy to meet Rome's client king who rules the local affairs with such efficiency." Dorigen led the way, and Marcellus strode firmly in line behind his commander.

The king rose slowly, but unaided, to greet his important visitor, and Dorigen slipped into the royal hut to prepare the guest cup. "Will you accept the hospitality of the Silurians and Atrebates, Legate Dominitus?" Lucius asked.

Dominitus sat on the stool offered him by the king's side. "Only briefly, King Lleiver. I have a commission of some importance to execute. I chose to do it myself rather than to send a messenger for Centurion Marcellus, as I welcome an opportunity to see more of the land I hold for Emperor Antonius." He smiled at Dorigen as he accepted the guest cup. When he had drained it, he rose and drew a leather pouch from beneath his elegant bronze scale mail shirt. "Centurion Gaius Marcellus Artios."

Marcellus stepped forward. This was it. He was to be placed under arrest before his friends, humiliated before the woman he loved and her father, the king. It was as well their union had not been blessed, for Lucius would have had to withdraw it now.

"Centurion Gaius Marcellus Artios," Dominitus repeated, and Marcellus, standing at attention, wished the legate would get on with it. "On behalf of

Emperor Antonius Pius, the Roman Senate, and Governor Julius Verus, it is my privilege to award you with this citation of honor for services rendered in extraordinary attention to detail which aided the Empire to quell the recent unpleasantness in the north. In return for this service you are to be awarded your plat of land at this early time, and this silver bracelet is to bear witness of the fact."

Not at all sure he had heard rightly, certainly not understanding the full meaning of the legate's words, Marcellus held out his left wrist, and the commander snapped a wide silver bracelet bearing the Capricorn insignia of Legio II onto his wrist. "Thank you, sir. I thank the emperor, the Senate, and Governor Verus. All I did was in the line of duty. I expected no reward."

Dominitus smiled broadly, "Ah, but what it pleases the gods to bestow, it is for man to enjoy. Well done, Centurion."

It was not until Commander Dominitus had exchanged a few more words with King Lucius and taken leave of the group that the impact of what had happened hit Marcellus. He had been granted his parcel of land. Twenty years ahead of schedule his service had been rewarded. He could now leave the legion as a man of property. He would now be free to marry. If the king would accept him. His right hand went to his left wrist, and he rubbed his bracelet. When had anyone been so honored for simple honesty and steadfastness? "I did nothing to earn this." His voice reflected his amazement.

Dyfan smiled. "Our Lord's gifts of grace are not necessarily spiritual only. It pleases Him to give good gifts to His children."

"And where is your steading to be?" Dorigen asked quietly at his side.

For the first time Marcellus thought to look at his deed. But now he was afraid to. What if it were in Syria, or Hispania, or even Gaul? It could be anyplace in the Empire. In the early days of his service he had always imagined his land would be in Italy, that in his advancing years he would return to the land of his birth and farm from a villa built under the warm southern sunshine. And more recently he had taken it for granted that his land would be in Britain. For now Britain was his land. He could live nowhere else in true contentment. He picked up the leather pouch as if it were a snake. Had the fates at this late hour played another cruel trick on him? Seeming to grant wishes beyond his fondest dreams and then twisting them cruelly?

The parchment slipped out of the pouch. He blinked at the words there. "Praise be to the All-God! It is in Britain!"

"But, of course. Where else would it be?"

He threw back his head and laughed as he had thought only Elfan could laugh. "Oh, my dear one, you have no idea. But this is wonderful—stupendous—it is in the land of King Lucius, between Glevum and Aqua Sulis. A fine, fertile tract it should be. And I will build there the finest villa . . ." For us, he longed to say, but could not until the king decreed him that right. Suddenly the old dreams he had buried with the loss of Julia came rushing back. The villa with columns and mosaics, a hypocaust, and a bath. It would be the best his engineering skill could produce . . . if he were allowed to build it for Dorigen. Without her it would have no meaning.

The next morning the coracle that arrived at their island was indeed the expected Elfan and Medwy. Dorigen ran ahead of Marcellus, so was the first to break the wonderful news of the king's improvement and Marcellus's reward. Questions, answers, and exclamations fell over each other in a tangle as the four made their way to the king's house. But there they had to restrain themselves, for although King Lucius greeted his friends with a warm smile and raised hand, it was clear he was intent on Fagan's reading. "Join us, my friends. My teachers are reading to me from the writings of one Paulinus. It is in my mind that he was a man of great wisdom and that I would learn much from his words."

The newcomers sat in a circle around the king, and Fagan continued. "This is a letter our beloved brother wrote to those in Ephesus whom he loved as children, just as God loves us." He unrolled the scroll.

"'Praised be the God and Father of our Lord Jesu Christus, who has bestowed on us in His Son every spiritual blessing in the heavens. God chose us in Him before the world began, to be holy and blameless in His sight. Such was His will and pleasure, so that all might praise the glorious favor He had bestowed on us in His Beloved. In Him and through His blood, we have been redeemed, and our sins forgiven, so immeasurably generous is God's favor to us. God has given us the wisdom to understand fully the mystery, the plan He was pleased to decree in His Son. A plan to be carried out in the Christus, in the fullness of time, to bring all things into one in Him, in the heavens and on earth.'"

Lucius leaned forward, but still showed signs of weakness. Dorigen slipped to her father's side to support him. "It is all right, my daughter. These words are brightening my mind with thoughts I have never had before. I am seeing new things from this teacher who has come to us. But, Fagan, I would know who is this 'us' the writer says God has called to know His favor. Is that only for those Ephesians your Paulinus was writing to and others you choose to tell?"

"It is for all believers, as God is the same in all times and all places and to all people."

"So He speaks to all nations? I am asking that you be very clear on this, my teacher."

"It is for all people as individuals, and it is for all nations. Dyfan and I, as do all Christiani, pray daily for Rome and for our emperor, that he might come to know the true God and that mighty Rome might be turned from wicked ways in worshiping false gods. For Rome shall be judged, as shall her people."

Lucius sat up higher yet. "And Britain shall be judged?"

Fagan laid his scroll aside and approached Lucius's seat. "The holy Scripture teaches us that, just as there is a judgment for all souls, so is there a judgment of the nations. The life of Christus is to be lived out by the individual, and it is to be lived out by the nation. For a nation to live true to God, their Heavenly Father, that nation must be just and compassionate, holy and steadfast. And with the nation, as with the individual, to whom much is given, much will be required."

Lucius nodded. "We have been much blessed with great riches. Of us much will be required." He sank back on his cushions. "You may be leaving me now. I have matters of weight to think on."

Fagan paused at the edge of the circle. "I would not weary you, King Lucius, but allow me to leave with you a parting blessing in the words Paulinus wrote to other friends of his, the Colossians."

Lucius raised his hand in assent.

"'May you attain full knowledge of God's will through perfect wisdom and spiritual insight. Then you will lead a life worthy of the Lord and pleasing to Him in every way. You will multiply good works of every sort and grow in the knowledge of God. By the might of His glory you will be endowed with the strength needed to stand fast, even to endure joyfully whatever may come, giving thanks to the Father for having made you worthy to share the lot of the saints in light. He rescued us from the power of darkness and brought us into the kingdom of his beloved Son. Amen.'" Fagan made the sign of the cross over the king and led the others from the king's presence.

Lucius did not appear at the feast table that night, and the trencher Dorigen carried to her father returned with little eaten. "He does not eat, nor would he let me attend to his wound-wrappings. He requests Fagan and Dyfan to attend him." A worried frown creased her brow.

A short time later concerns for the king increased as Urych joined the group with dragging step. "The king has sent his bard away from his presence. Never does a bard leave his king. It is the job of the bard to serve the king and keep his knowledge for the people of the tribe yet to come." He shook his head. "It is not right that Urych should be sent away."

Dorigen laid her hand on his drooping shoulder. "You may serve the daughter of the king. Our hearts, too, are heavy with worry for the strange behavior of my royal father. Will you give us a harpsong to lighten our fears?"

"Oh, my princess. Forgive me." Urych looked more distressed than ever. "There is no song in my heart. A song cannot come from the mouth and the fingers. A song must be born of the soul. My soul is silent."

Dorigen nodded. "Yes, Urych. As is mine. But do not fret. We shall have a song in the morning."

On the morrow, however, the king's strange behavior continued. He emerged from his hut to eat morning stirabout with the company, but he spoke to no one as his mind was deep in thought. Before all bowls were empty he rose. "I have been long in meditation. Now I have that of importance I would say to all my people within hearing. Bid those who will come from the druid side to meet us in the Old Church before the sun is above the Tor."

At the royal signal, Fagan and Dyfan followed the king into his hut, and the women hurried to rub the porridge bowls with sand and wash them clean. Marcellus and Elfan appointed themselves messengers to the druid compound. By midmorning all were assembled in their best garments, seated on benches in the little church. Fagan and Dyfan, in gleaming white togas, stood at each end of the altar. In the center, splendid in his scarlet tunic and gold torque and circlet, stood the king. The full brightness of the morning sun fell across his face from the eastern window, and the cross behind him took on its own radiance. The king raised his hand although there was no need to silence his waiting audience.

"My beloved children and subjects, it is in my mind that in spite of the *Pax Romana* there is much darkness in this land. I, Lleiver Mawr, which means 'great light,' wish to declare this light which I have found in the one God for all our people.

"A great vision has come upon my mind. A vision of a Britain uncorrupted with darkness. Blessed as we are with such resources, such beauty, such people, should not we of all the people of the Empire of which we are a part set the standard that will make of all Rome—all the world—a land of blessing, a land living in harmony with the Word of God?

"Here we can light the fire. Here we can become a city set on a hill to be a light to all nations. Here we can live above the natural inclination to bend to the dark. We must live in the light. We must hold it high to shine out to others."

He turned toward Fagan who handed him the scroll he had been holding at his side. The king unrolled the scroll and read his proclamation. "I, Lleiver Mawr, Son of Coel, son of Cyllinus, son of Caratacus, son of Branfor, son of Llyr; King of the tribes of the Atrebates and the Silures, with rights validated by Imperial Rome, do declare that only the All-God Christus shall be head of this portion of the land of Britain over which I rule and that all herein who are my loyal subjects shall worship Him only as the one true God—Father, Son, and Holy Spirit, blessed be He."

He let the scroll roll closed. "So may we live true to this declaration forever, and so may Britain become the kingdom of the Logres, the land of Christus, the Word of God." He dropped to his knees with bowed head.

Fagan began to recite the ancient and beautiful words of the Eucharist that seemed to draw down from highest Heaven the very presence of the Most High God into their midst. Fagan picked up the bread from the altar, elevated it, then broke off a small piece and dipped it in the cup of wine. "May the mingling of the body and blood of our Lord Jesu Christus bring eternal life to us who receive Him."

Fagan and Dyfan partook of the elements. Then Fagan turned to the kneeling king and placed a morsel on his tongue. As the missionaries had taught him, Lucius murmured, "May the body of the Christus bring me to everlasting life. May the blood of the Christus bring me to everlasting life."

When the Eucharist was ended the king rose. "Marcellus, I would have you stand before me."

Marcellus's heart leapt to his throat. He was to receive the answer his heart had awaited these three days. He stood before the king with bowed head to hear his fate. "To Marcellus and to all my people I say, we are not British, we are not Roman. We are Christian. And as such shall all be accepted. Marcellus, accept my blessings as my son-to-be." Lucius looked at Dorigen. "Daughter, stand before me with your marriage lord and receive my blessings and the blessings of the All-God." Dorigen took her place before Lucius and slipped her hand into Marcellus's.

Urych stepped forward. "Now is my heart making a song for my harp. Words of the bard David spring to my mind and my harp would sing them, if it please my lord."

"Indeed, it would please me greatly." Lucius sat on a stool beneath the cross, and his bard stood beside the couple at the altar as the song of praise and prophecy sprang from his heart:

Sing to the Lord a new song,
Let His praise ring from the end of the earth.
Let the sea and all that fills it resound,
Let the coastlands and those who dwell in them sound His praise.
Let the inhabitants of the land exult and shout from
the top of the mountains.
Let them sing glory to the Lord and utter His praise
in the coastlands.
The Lord God will lay His hand on the mountains and hills and
all the fields will bring forth crops.
He will turn the floods into rivers and the marshes into dry land.
By paths unknown will He guide His people.
He will turn darkness into light before them
and make crooked ways straight.

In the silence at the end of the song Fagan turned to the king. "Your Majesty, this is an occasion that must live for all time and all ages. We must build a great monument of stone that it will not be forgotten."

"An oratory, a place of prayer," Dyfan added.

"Yes." Lucius stood. "That is to my mind a most excellent idea. We shall set my city on a hill atop the Tor. It shall be a beacon of prayer."

Marcellus spoke quietly. "I am not without building skills, Your Majesty. My engineering knowledge is at your service."

Suddenly it seemed as if everyone were speaking at once, adding their ideas and offering what they could contribute. Brach and Corfil announced that now that Cunedag and the priests who had supported her had been borne away by representatives from the tribal senate, they would establish a new teaching at the cors based on the Scripture-scrolls of Fagan and Dyfan.

Medwy turned first to this father, then to the druids and asked permission to join them. His proposal was gladly accepted.

And last of all, the urging that had been growing in Marcellus's heart found words. "And I shall be baptized before I undertake the building of a house of prayer."

As the rust-red leaves fell from the trees at the base of the Tor, blocks of the dark-colored whinstone that formed the core of the mountain rose on its top. Marcellus sent Elfan to Glevum to purchase lime and hardening agent for their mortar. Far more quickly than anyone could have thought possible, the four-sided arch rose to completion.

On a day of golden late-autumn splendor, the company met inside the small temple and looked out through the rounded arches, down the green slopes of the Tor dotted with purple low-growing flowers, and across the marshy waterways that surrounded their sacred Avalon. Dorigen, standing next to Marcellus, pointed across the mists to Caer-Cam, her eyes alight with smiling memory of the first time they stood together and looked at that rainbow-arched scene.

Then Fagan called them to the dedicatory prayer. Standing before the arch that faced Wirral Hill and the thorn tree planted by an earlier missionary to those shores, he raised his hands and prayed, "Lord, You are the one true and only King of all the ages. Your ways are perfect and true. Unto You, our Lord and King, we dedicate this place of worship. May it be as a city set on a hill that none can hide, as a beacon that points to You, a beacon to lead the hearts of all who herein worship to the one true God and King, our Lord and Father, maker of heaven and earth. For Yours is the kingdom and the power and the glory forever. Amen."

Then Urych called forth a harp glissando that floated to the vaulted roof of the oratory and on to the heavens beyond. "Let us sing to the Lord, glorious in His triumph," he said, and the harp sprang into a song which the bard's voice followed:

Mighty and wonderful are Your works which we praise,
Lord God Almighty!

Righteous and true are Your ways which we follow,
O King of the nations!
Mighty and wonderful, righteous and true are You,
the God of our land!
Who would dare refuse You honor or the glory due Your name,
O Lord, the All-God?
Because you alone are holy,
all nations shall come and worship in Your presence.
Your mighty deeds are seen of all men;
Let us praise them.

As the quiet, devout brother Dyfan looked at Marcellus and Dorigen, standing strong and radiant in the golden archway that led to Caer-Cam, words not formed of his own will sprang to his lips, and he held up his hand in blessing. "The Lord will bless your union and the fruit of your body. If you keep His covenant in truth, your sons shall rule on this throne from age to age. For the Lord has chosen this land. He has desired it for His dwelling. He will greatly bless her produce and fill her poor with bread. He will clothe her priests with salvation, and her faithful shall ring out their joy. He will prepare a lamp of His anointed, and on Him shall the crown of the Lord shine. We praise the Lord God Almighty, who is and was and ever shall be, world without end, amen."

And the worshipers descended the hill in peace.

PART TWO

7

uintus Valerius Artios, shoulders rigid, his face in a deep frown, strode across the intricately designed ochre and terra-cotta mosaic floor of their family villa to his father's chamber. How much easier it would be if he could simply mount Vixatrix and ride off to Isca to join his calvary ala without this final encounter with his family. He was barely through the door before Lavinia, his nine-year-old sister flung herself into his arms. "Oh, Val, must you leave today? When will I see you again? Can't you wait just a little longer? Why did you have to join the army anyway? There's plenty of work on the villa. Will you come home for Christmas?" She clung to him, sobbing.

"Don't be so wet, Vini," chided fifteen-year-old Gaius. He offered a stoic, "Good-bye, Val," to his brother.

Valerius firmly disengaged himself from his sister's arms before their father could reprimand them both for an untoward show of emotion. "I do not expect to return for *Saturnalia*, Vini." He emphasized the name of the Roman holiday that came at the same time as the Christian celebration.

Aquila stepped forward and grasped his elder son's arm. "My son, I won't prolong this with unwanted speeches. I wish you great success in your chosen career. May you find that which you seek in the army of the Caesars." He paused and rubbed the silver bracelet on his left wrist with the broad fingers of his right hand. Valerius forbade his eyes to follow the gesture. At twenty-three he was long past the age when the family Capricorn bracelet should have been passed to the oldest son. And yet Aquila desisted in parting with it. Would the patriarch of the Artoii perform the ceremony this morning as part of Valerius's leave-taking?

Aquila withdrew his hand, leaving the bracelet still on his wrist. "Valerius, as you go to take your place in the world, it would be of great comfort to me to send you forth wearing the emblem of all that your family has stood for during the past one hundred and fifty years since your ancestor Marcellus was awarded this bracelet and built this villa on the land granted to him."

Valerius held his breath. It would please him, too, to wear the heirloom as a badge of his place in the family, a place no one seemed to think him worthy of.

"Sadly, I cannot give this to you, my son. It would not be right to give the bracelet of Marcellus to one who has turned his back on the God of his forefathers, the God Marcellus lived for and dedicated this villa to." His gaze swept across the mosaic floor patterned with cross, fish, and chi-rho, then returned to his son's eyes. He shook his head. "I am sorry, Valerius, but it would desecrate all the Artoii have stood for for one hundred and fifty years were our family emblem to be worn in the service and worship of Mithra."

Lavinia stifled a sob and turned for comfort to her mother who was sitting quietly on her couch in the corner. Lucia gave her daughter a pat and then rose to face the stepson she had raised from his early childhood. "Godspeed, Valerius. See you come home whenever you have time off. Vixatrix is the swiftest mare in our stables; she will return you to us whenever you give her her head."

Valerius returned her gentle embrace. That was so like Lucia. She had ever covered any uncomfortable situation with soft words.

But Aquila, who would speak for the right as he saw it no matter what, was not yet finished. "Even though I feel that in honor I must withhold the bracelet, I would bless your going, whether or not you would wish me to." He placed a hand on Valerius's shoulder. "May the grace and peace of God, the Father, and of his Son, our Lord Jesus Christ, rest and abide on you now and forever more. Amen."

With a final kiss from Lavinia and Lucia and a last arm-clasp from Gaius and his father, Valerius vaulted into the saddle and clattered across the cobbled stable yard. Let his family think his impatience was to reach his regiment with the Second Augusta in Isca. There was no need for them to know that for weeks he had been planning this journey to coincide with his first-level initiation into the mysteries of Mithra at the Mithraeum just outside the fortress walls.

As Vixatrix's hooves beat a steady rhythm on the frost-crusted metaled road running west of the Sabrina, Valerius blew a puff of white breath on the crisp November air. It seemed he had been holding his breath for days, if not weeks, ever since he had announced his decision to join the cavalry unit attached to the second legion. None of their family had followed the eagles since Marcellus, who had established their line in Britain. And since that time they had worked for the good of the Empire and of Britain as civic leaders and villa operators. And as servants of Jesus Christ.

Valerius's dark eyes hardened. But he would find his own way and his own god. He had no doubt what the means to his goals would be. He had known since his first conversation three years ago with Thaleus in the tepidarium of the baths at Glevum. The grizzled retired decurio who preached the glories of the cavalry and the glories of Mithras with equal fervor had inflamed an excitement in Valerius.

Anxious as he was to arrive at Isca, however, Valerius was unwilling to sweat Vixatrix, so it was late that night when the walls and watchtowers of the fortress came into sight. But not too late to find worshipers at the temple. Mostly clad in tunics and breeches, but some still in their workaday armor, legionnaires and officers alike sat on the raised platforms on each side of the wide center aisle, attending to the two white-robed priests officiating at the front. Like all Mithraic temples, the room was dark, suggesting the cave where Mithra slew the bull.

Valerius entered between statues of two torch-bearers, one with his torch pointing up, the other pointing down. Although not yet initiated, Valerius knew the torch-bearers who always attended Mithra symbolized day and night, summer and winter, heat and cold, life and death.

He took a seat on the dais to the right, near a burly legionary leaning against the wall. The priests stood beside three stone altars, each bearing an inscription to Mithra. Behind them was the great stone bas relief depicting the central mystery of the faith—Mithra slaying the cosmic bull from whose body all beneficial plants and animals sprang to fill the earth. The priest was speaking of this mystery as Valerius focused on his words. "The light of our sun god dissipates darkness and restores happiness and life on earth." The priest waved his arm at the left-hand altar bearing a carving of Mithra wearing the sun crown. The rays of the crown were pierced so that a light placed behind the stone shone through them. In the cavelike temple they indeed radiated like the sun.

"Mithra is the lord of wide pastures, the one that renders them fertile. Mithra's Sol gives increase, he gives abundance, he gives cattle, he gives progeny and life." As the one priest spoke, the other attended a fire at the altar on which the body of a small bird was being offered. The acrid smell of burning feathers filled the temple.

"On them that honor him, Mithra bestows health of body, abundance of riches, and talented posterity. His it is to dispense material blessings and spiritual advantages on those that worship him. And ever strength of arms and victory in battle to those who sacrifice to him. Praise be to Mithra."

All those initiated into the mysteries turned now to place a handful of incense in the bronze bowls standing on the small altars lining the central aisle. The priest carried fire from the sacrificed bird to ignite the offerings of Mithra's votaries as they sang a hymn. Then the service was over.

The soldier next to Valerius introduced himself, "Plotius, from Germania originally. First Ala, Sixth Turma is home now. Augusta, of course."

Valerius took the extended arm. "Ah, you're cavalry then. So am I, but I don't know which regiment or unit yet. I just arrived. Valerius is the name."

"Well, Val, plenty of time to find a bunk. Come along to the wine shop."

"Thanks, I'd like to, but I want to speak to the priest first—to arrange for my initiation."

Plotius slapped him on the back with his thick, hairy arm. "Fine, fine. First level, are you? I'm *Miles*." He proudly displayed the mark that had been burned into his forehead with a red-hot iron when he had attained soldier rank. "Fine, the magus will be happy to receive you. Ask anyone directions to the Serpent's Tongue when you're ready for a cup of the sourest wine in Britain."

The wine was indeed sour, but it was fortunate that Valerius drank enough of it to make sleep possible on the wooden slab of a barrack's bunk with only a borrowed woolen blanket. The next morning at cockcrow he carefully rubbed the stubble of a heavy beard from his chin with a pumice stone and repeatedly ran his best ivory comb through his black curly hair. Plotius returned from the latrine to catch him checking his reflection in a sheet of polished tin. "Ah, getting pretty for the legate, are you? They say Candidus has an eye for the women, but I hadn't heard that it extended to more exotic tastes."

Valerius picked up his sponge, still dripping with vinegar, and flung it at the German, who blocked it neatly and flung it back, catching him in the neck. Plotius let out a bellow of a laugh. "And let that be a lesson to you not to take on one of Caesar's finest before you've had so much as a day in the training field."

Valerius didn't dare check his appearance a second time, so he could only hope he would make a good impression at the principia.

Apparently he did, because his assignment pleased him thoroughly—First Ala, Sixth Turma. The spare bunk he had shivered in the night before would be his to shiver in permanently.

Plotius gave him another hearty slap on the back. "Well, that's fine. Just fine. Until last month I'd have congratulated you on being assigned to the best unit in the whole legion. Now . . ."

"Now what?" Valerius stowed his newly issued shield, spurs, and spatha on the shelves in the storage room in front of their sleeping cubicle.

"It started at the Ludi Romani last month. We had our own games right here in the amphitheater—smaller, but just as stirring as any you'd see in Rome. You should have seen our turma drill—fastest, closest formations ever done in that arena, I'll wager. Jupiter should have been honored, I can tell you."

He stopped to rub the stubble he had not bothered removing from his chin for several days. "Maybe the games were too enthralling because someone stole from the granaries while everyone was distracted. Can't think why any special suspicion should have fallen on the Sixth, but the whole barracks block is rife with rumors, and Primus, our decurion, barks louder every day. Personally, I suspect the Third. Their captain is a greasy little Gaul named Julius, and his optio, Aaron, is from Palestine." He spit on the floor. "Can't trust those sneaky little Jews, always moaning to that god of theirs. Now if they had a religion with some teeth in it like ours—"

Valerius interrupted the speech that was quickly turning into a tirade. "But why should anyone steal from the stores? There's no shortage of food, surely."

Plotius shrugged. "Sell it to the natives to augment their pay, I suppose. Mithra knows we could all use more bronze. Anyway, point is, no matter who did it, the whole thing's bad for morale—rumors, counterrumors tearing the place apart. Especially bad for drill. You have to trust fellows when you spur your horse full tilt for a space that's timed to open when you get there and not a horsehair before. Now Primus is pushing us to take it faster than ever." He grabbed his spurs and a wooden practice spatha off the top shelf. "And there'll be Tartarus to pay if we're late on the drill field."

Hours later, after endless runs of repeating the same dozen drill patterns that snaked and jumbled in an impossible maze in Valerius's head while Primus shouted at him harshly, Valerius pulled off his helmet and barely resisted the temptation to fling it to the ground. Who would have thought it possible to sweat like this in November? Would he ever end up in the right place at the right time?

"Welcome to the Sixth." A voice made him turn to his left. He had noticed the owner of the voice on the drill field. More than once in that crazy pattern Valerius was supposed to whisk like lightning two inches in front of this man's huge white mount. And every time, had it not been for the man's quick action, a Gordian knot of men and mounts would have resulted, with Primus sending them all out to double sentry duty, if not the whipping post.

Valerius grimaced. "Surprised you say welcome after the muddle I made of it out there."

The white horse's rider grinned. "First day is awful, isn't it? Whole first week will be pretty bad; then it just all sorts itself out in your mind. One suggestion to make it easier—"

Valerius nodded.

"Pick a post or stone or something on the other side of the field and ride straight for it. Keep your eye on the goal, not on side distractions. It takes a bit of faith, but it works every time."

Valerius started to thank the man, but at a barked order from their decurion, the turma was dismissed to the amphitheater for spatha practice. After another lifetime spent thrusting and hacking his long-bladed cavalry sword at a wooden practice post while wielding a forty-pound shield, Valerius's arms ached and his vision blurred. Plotius's back slap almost knocked him off his feet. "Time to make for the baths, soldier. This is Marius." He indicated a lanky soldier who looked tall and thin standing next to the broad Plotius. "We'll meet you in the tepidarium."

After storing his kit, Valerius passed through the high masonry wall around the tile-roofed bathing complex. He crossed the open courtyard with its long narrow swimming pool where even in the chill, late November afternoon many legionnaires were swimming laps. Not Valerius, though. He would take his cold plunge in the frigidarium with its controlled climate under a high-vaulted ceiling. After a refreshing plunge that left his skin tingling, he anointed his body with oils from the green and blue glass bath flasks supplied by slaves. He donned a pair of wooden sandals to protect his feet from the hot tiled floors of the heated rooms and purchased a pork pasty before settling down to relax in the tepidarium.

"Care for an olive to go with that?" The rider of the white horse lounged next to him on the steps of the warm pool.

"Thanks." Valerius took a small black olive from the bag extended to him, savored its oily brininess, and spit the seed into the pool. A Roman drain system could handle anything.

"Georgus Nestor Anastasius of Lydda," his new friend introduced himself with a warm grin.

Valerius was delighted. Lydda was the capitol city of Cappadocia, the birthplace of Mithraism, which had grown from a small Persian cult to the strongest religion in the Roman Empire. Very likely the man had been nurtured in the faith from the cradle. Valerius longed to ask him about it, but felt this noisy public pool was not the place to discuss the mysteries. When they finished their snack, Georgus suggested they return to the frigidarium for a shower and then move on to the basilica for a wrestling workout. Valerius surveyed his friend's broad, well-muscled shoulders and then shrugged. Why not? Perhaps he could overbalance Georgus with the quickness the Artoii had inherited with their Celtic blood, a heritage his own dark hair and eyes belied.

As the two stood at the central drain of the frigidarium while slaves dumped buckets of water over their heads, they were joined by Plotius and Marius. Valerius noted that Georgus greeted his turma mates with the same relaxed friendliness with which he seemed to approach everything and also with the same touch of reserve he maintained while observing everything with his keen blue eyes—the blue eyes that stood out so surprisingly in his olive skin under the disheveled dark brown hair with its golden lights.

Each man took a turn standing at the floral-designed drain in the center of the tile floor as slaves brought in more buckets of water. When the slave approached with a bucket of cold water to pour over Marius, however, he stepped back from the drain. "Ah, I think I'll forego the pleasure today." As he turned, Valerius noted the fresh welts on Marius's shoulders. Apparently their decurion had been living up to his reputation as a harsh disciplinarian.

Ablutions completed, the four of them moved on to the enormous recreation hall that extended beyond the northwest wall of the baths. The long central nave had a high ceiling supported on each side by rows of Corinthian columns, and its vast open spaces were filled with legionnaires engaged in wrestling, weight-lifting, and various body-building calisthenics. Georgus and

Valerius left Plotius and his lanky friend to their exercises and took an empty space in the center of the vast nave. For a few moments they circled, hunched forward, sizing each other up. Then Valerius lunged as Galba, his tutor, had taught him to do to get the upper hand. For a second his quick attack to his opponent's left leg held Georgus off balance. Then the Cappadocian twisted and hauled his opponent over his foot in a move Galba had neglected to teach Valerius, and he found himself pinned to the floor. The match could have ended there, but Georgus loosened his hold, allowed Val to spring to his feet, and the contest continued.

The next fall went to Valerius with a bowstring, the next two to Georgus. At the end they grasped arms, and Valerius noted that his opponent was barely breathing hard after what he considered to be an intense workout. "Hate to think what you could do if you were in shape," Val said with a grin.

"Little more practice with the regiment, and you'll make a top contender." Georgus clasped his shoulders. "Want me to show you how to follow through with that first hold you used?" He locked his hands behind Val's knee. "See, lock your hand rather than grasping the sides of my knee. Now lift and keep moving forward." Valerius fell with a thud, and almost as quickly Georgus pulled him to his feet again. "There, next time you'll have me with that one. You're quick."

Valerius took a towel from a slave and wiped the sweat off his face. Plotius approached. "The winner want a real match now? What do you say to two asses on it?"

Georgus faced his challenger, his face a study of concentration, but still with the faintest smile in his eyes. The first fall went to Plotius with a shoulder lock and backward roll that left Georgus pinned under Plotius's brute weight. The second went to Georgus after he dropped Plotius with the simple lock and thrust he had just taught Val. The third fall was harder fought. Plotius held Georgus in a pin just long enough for a look of triumph to register on the broad face, and then Georgus arched and slipped out. Seconds later Georgus rolled over and caught the German in the same hold, then sucked him into a viselike grip from which the challenger could not break free. The determination in Plotius's face suddenly changed to a flush of rage. The observers could see that the contest was now more than simple exercise.

The next fall would determine the match.

The opponents circled in an armlock, then broke with a grunt from Plotius. With a quicksilver movement Georgus feinted to the left, darted right in a side twist, grasped his opponent around the waist and brought Plotius backward over his own knee. Only Valerius saw the deftly administered hit on the side of Georgus's neck with which Plotius reversed the situation and claimed victory.

Georgus sat up rubbing his neck. The humor was gone from his face, but he only said, "My purse is in the changing room. I'll pay you there."

Later when they sat over their cups in the bath wine shop, Valerius asked, "Why didn't you accuse Plotius of cheating?"

Georgus took a sip of wine and shrugged. "If he needed to win that much, it doesn't hurt me to let him. Well, that's not quite true—that Scythian hit did rather hurt."

Valerius shook his head. "I can't believe you, Georg. You're cheated out of winning a match, not to mention two asses, and you sound amused."

Even in the dim wine shop the sparkle showed in Georgus's eyes. "That's my problem. I've always been able to detach myself from a situation—as if I were standing aside and watching it. When you do that, you see the humor."

"Is that a problem? It sounds like a great ability to gain perspective."

"Well, it can be. But sometimes I'm amused when I shouldn't be—like when the decurion is reading me out for untidy barracks or something. I can keep my mouth straight, but I can't keep my eyes serious. Then I really get yelled at. 'Think that's funny, do you, Anastasius?' I try to assure him I don't, but I've walked miles of sentry duty on account of my blasted sense of humor."

They laughed, and Valerius called for a refill for their wine cups. Georgus doodled a curved line in the dust of the table with his forefinger. "I do take my job seriously, whatever the decurion may think, but it's not all there is to life."

Ah, here was the opening Valerius had been waiting for. "I believe that, too," he said eagerly. "I've been hoping to get a chance to talk to you about your religion. You see, my first-level initiation is scheduled for tomorrow, and I'm excited about getting deeper into the mysteries. Of course, I could talk to Plotius; he's *Miles*, but you must be much higher."

Georgus erased the curve with barely a flick of his hand, but the movement brought it into focus in Valerius's mind. He gaped open-mouthed. "Oh, blood of bulls! Not in the legion!" He hit the table with his fist. "I left home to get away from that love-your-brother nonsense. But you'd best be careful. Not many in the legion will know what you're about—if I hadn't grown up in a home of Christians, I wouldn't have—and with Constantius Chlorus Caesar of the West there's not much persecution in Britain. Some even say his wife's one of them—but everyone says Diocletian is going to crack down on Christ worshipers. You go around drawing fish on the wrong tables, and you'll lose your head, my friend. You won't be able to keep your detachment from that . . ." Valerius frowned. How could he have made a pun about that? Georgus's sense of humor must be contagious.

But Georgus did not find persecution a laughing matter. He nodded. "What you say is true. You have been greatly blessed with your freedom here in Britain. It is far less in most of the Empire. But since you now know the worst about me, let us speak freely. My head is in your hands." He took a sip of wine. "And you have chosen to follow the Persian sun god. I wonder why?"

Valerius drank deeply before answering. "As far as I can see the doctrines of the two, it's like choosing wheat or oats. Lord Mithra brought all good things to the earth by slaying the great white bull. Herbs, plants, corn, bread—all plenty sprang from its body. The sacred drink of the mysteries flowed out in his blood—just as you drink the blood of the Christus. The Evil One sent his demons to poison the life-giving source; the serpent strove in vain to suck out the sacred blood—but all were powerless against the great miracle. See the parallels?"

Georgus leaned closer across the table. "And you really find this easier to believe than the Christian account of Christ's sacrifice on the cross?"

Valerius shrugged. "Christ or Mithra, you can take your choice as far as I can see, but I'm a man of action and Mithraism exalts in action. Strength is higher than gentleness; courage is better than leniency. It's no accident that Mithraism is the most popular religion in the army. Mithra extols the military virtues above all others, and just look at all the times he's helped us triumph over barbarous enemies."

Georgus sat for several moments regarding Valerius with an expression of deep sadness. "Valerius, my friend, I wish I could answer you. I know you are wrong, but I've never been much of a theology student, and I'm certainly no debater. I guess that's a disadvantage of growing up in the faith—it came so early and so easily I never had to work through such doubts on my own. I don't know what to say to you, and yet I believe with all my heart that the Lord Jesus alone is worthy of worship and that you are making a grave error."

Suddenly the sparkle returned to his eyes. "I'm afraid I've done it again. But with no pun intended, I tell you that faith in Jesus as the Christ is the only belief that counts beyond the grave—the only way to eternal life."

"But Mithra assures his followers salvation both in this world and the next. We believe in the conscious survival of the soul and in punishments and rewards beyond the tomb."

Georg was serious again. "I wish I could answer you. I can see that I need to study more."

"Well then, study both sides. Come with me tomorrow night to my initiation."

"Will they allow one who isn't an initiate to attend?"

Val shrugged. "You're my friend. They won't question you. Besides, Plotius will be there. It wouldn't hurt you to curry a bit of favor in that direction."

"I wouldn't do it for that reason."

Valerius regarded his friend's strong cheekbones and firm chin. "No, I can see you're not one to play games for personal gain."

Sundown came early in November. Valerius, Georgus, Plotius, and Marius met at the dexter gate the next evening and went together to the Mithraeum. The temple seemed darker and more cavelike than ever as Valerius walked sedately down the aisle and knelt before the priest at the altar. The priest chanted a prayer while a bundle of sacred twigs burned on the altar. When the flames were reduced to ashes, the priest poured an oblation of milk, oil, and honey on top of the offering, staying well back from the altar as he did so, lest his breath contaminate the divine flame that consumed the drops of oil.

Then the priest spoke. "Quintus Valerius Artios, you have come tonight before the Lord Mithra, maker and sustainer of heaven and earth, to receive initiation as a raven in the faith. Remember that it was the raven who carried the message from the Over-god to Mithra telling him that he must slay the bull. As such, may you be a faithful messenger of Mithra.

"Mithra is a god of help, whom the faithful never invoke in vain. He is an unfailing haven, the anchor of salvation for mortals in all their trials, the dauntless champion who sustains his followers through all the tribulations of life. He is the defender of truth and justice, the protector of holiness, and the intrepid antagonist of the powers of darkness. May you always so oppose evil in his name."

Then the congregation rose and, following the priest who was carrying a tray of sacred objects, passed in somber procession from the temple to the hills behind Isca. Plotius, bearing a torch pointed upright, lighted their way. Marius, bearing his torch downward, brought up the rear. "As you go deeper into the mysteries, Valerius Artios," the priest said, "you will undertake a new ablution at each stage to wash away your guilty stains. For the *Corax*-raven degree you will be bound hand and eye and will leap over this stream of rushing water as a symbol of purification."

Valerius extended his arms, wrists together. The priest bandaged his eyes and then bound his wrists with the entrails of a chicken brought from the temple altar. Blood of the chicken was sprinkled over his head. With an easy leap he crossed the stream. The priest chanted a final prayer. Plotius dipped a ritual sword given him by the priest in more of the chicken's blood, and with an arcing slash, severed the bonds holding Valerius's wrists.

Quintus Valerius Artios, descendant of the first Roman Christian in Britain and of King Lucius who a century and a half before had declared Britain a Christian nation, was now a fully initiated servant of the sun god Mithra.

"Well, what did you think, Georg?" he asked later when their other companions had retired to the Serpent's Tongue for a game of dice.

Georgus thought before he answered. "It was very impressive, very mysterious. But it's all external. Are you any different inside? I believe in external washing—in baptism—but only as a sign of inward cleansing. Are you clean inside?"

Valerius didn't answer.

8

or the next several days Valerius spent increased time in the congenial, free-spending company of Plotius and Marius and their circle of dice-throwing friends at the Serpent's Tongue. He had no desire to wrestle with questions he couldn't answer.

On the morning beginning his second week at Isca, however, the comradery shattered. Valerius awoke to find the barracks block humming with rumors: "More thefts. The whole granary emptied." "No, no, only ten bags missing, but that's enough." "The decurion arrested." "No, no. Not our decurion, decurion of the Third. Ah, knew they were a pack of thieves—whole turma probably in on it." "No, not the decurion, his optio." "Ah, that's that Jew-fellow, isn't it? What, not him? Our optio? Impossible." "No, no, not an officer, but one of our men . . ."

Valerius looked around for Plotius. He always knew the latest gossip. But he didn't see Plotius, and Marius didn't know where he was either. "Just been to the latrine; didn't see him there. Maybe he's out at his cookpot." Marius picked up his own bag of wheat meal to go to his cookpot along the back wall.

Valerius learned no more that morning, and the questions increased by midmorning when, at the appearance of a messenger from the principia, Primus called a halt in drill practice and ordered Georgus to the headquarters building. It wasn't until the end of a long afternoon of weapons practice that Valerius got his answers.

Georgus was waiting for him at his barracks. "What would you think of a break from drill practice?"

Valerius flung his helmet on the shelf and pulled off his mail shirt. "What? Who could possibly tear himself away from the practice field?" He dropped down on his bunk. "Where have you been all day?"

"Principia mostly. Our friend Plotius is accused of these storehouse thefts. Seems someone thinks they saw him in the area of the granaries at the time of the changing of the guard, which the commandant figures would be the most likely time for the theft to occur. Plotius asked I be called for a character witness."

Valerius gave a gasp of laughter. "You! He cheats you at wrestling, then expects you to testify to his character?"

Georgus shrugged. "I expect he's forgotten about cheating. He called me to witness his devotion to Mithra. Seems everyone knows devout sun worshipers are required to be honest—at least outside the wrestling ring, I guess." Georgus paused and frowned. "Then he accused Julius and Aaron from the Third. Seems he has information that Aaron's brother is a merchant working in the area, so would be an obvious contact for selling stolen goods. The upshot of it is that the commandant locked them all in the guardhouse and appointed me junior optio to investigate this mess of rumor and counterrumor."

Valerius sat up, barely missing cracking his head on the bunk above his. "You? Why you?"

Georgus grinned. "Well, he needed someone, and I was handy. Also the accused parties all seemed to have faith in me."

Valerius frowned. "All? What do those fellows from the Third know of you?"

Georgus didn't answer, but his eyes sparkled. "We've uh, met—at wine shops and such . . . the baths, you know."

Valerius groaned and flung himself back on the bunk. "Blood of bulls! More of you! Is the legion riddled with Christ worshipers?"

"I have no idea. It's not widely discussed. For health reasons, you know. But the more immediate question is—do you want a change of pace? I've asked the commandant for your assistance in this investigation."

This time Valerius did crack his head on the upper bunk when he sprang up. "Absolutely."

"Good. Pack your kit. We leave at first tide in the morning. Just after cockcrow, the boatman said."

"Leave? But the crime happened here. Where are we going?"

"We need to question that merchant brother of Aaron's. Seems when he's not traveling, he stays on some island on the other side of the Sabrina."

Georgus expressed mounting excitement as the boat carried them toward Ynis Witrin the next morning. Aaron had told him some time ago of his brother's studying there with a group of holy hermits. When he had first heard of it, Georgus had been intrigued, maybe even slightly amused. He had always been very matter-of-fact about his faith, and anything so mystical as withdrawing to an island for nothing but study and prayer seemed to be rather overdoing it. Now, however, knowing Val had shown him that simple belief wasn't enough. He wanted to be able to express his faith. He needed to know more.

As the small boat slipped through the swirling mists, Georgus and Valerius pulled their cloaks tighter around them in the chill air. The native boatman Georgus had hired for the trip pointed at a steep shape rising through the fog. "There she is. That's Ynis Witrin."

"Ghost of Caesar, what a sight!" Georgus caught his breath.

"The Isle of Avalon, my father called it," Valerius said. "Seems my ancestors spent a lot of time here. We're descended from some ancient Celtic royalty through the wife of the legionnaire who founded our family here, Marcellus, according to my father's stories. I've never seen this place before. It's impressive, isn't it? No wonder the old ones thought it was a magical place. I can imagine a thoroughly level-headed Roman mistaking it for Olympus. Looks like there's even some sort of temple on top."

The coracle bumped the shore gently, and the boatman jumped out to hold it steady for his passengers. "The hermitage is just beyond this long ridge and across a little valley at the foot of the Tor," explained the boatman. "I've taken visitors to the brothers there before. People say they come to study, but I don't know what one could be learning from a bunch of hermits who never leave the island. Will you be wanting me to lead you up there?"

"Thank you, no. We'll find our own way." Georgus handed him two bronze quadrantes bearing the image of Emperor Diocletian.

The boatman departed, and the legionnaires turned toward the Tor. Tall brown grass rose almost to their knees. Along the side of the hill, they walked beneath gnarled apple trees, branches now bare and black in the November fog. They went without talking through the gray and silver world, the only sound the rustle of their caligae in the grass and an occasional snap of a twig beneath their feet.

"What do you want?" The harsh question, coming disembodied from the fog, made both men start.

"We are looking for the hermitage. We have questions of one who studies here."

"No one studying here now. Just the twelve brothers and me to serve them. Too cold for studying." A stocky form emerged from behind the mist-shrouded, nearby tree. "I'm Tellean. I'll take you to Brother Cadfrawl." The servant eyed the newcomers suspiciously. "We don't get many Romans here. You won't be comfortable in our guest huts."

"We won't bother you long. We just need some information," Georgus said. The red-haired native shrugged and turned toward the Tor. Soon a circle of wattle and daub huts surrounding a small rectangular building came into view.

Brother Cadfrawl, in long brown tunic, greeted them kindly with no show of surprise at their sudden appearance and offered them a guest hut where they put their small packs. "We are just beginning our evening prayers. Will you join us? We can talk of your matters afterwards."

Georgus accepted with enthusiasm, and they followed the holy brother to the rectangular building, which turned out to be a church. Eleven other brothers were on their knees inside. Georgus slipped to his knees beside a robed figure near the door. Not knowing what else to do, Valerius joined him.

Cadfrawl, standing before the cross at the front of the room, lifted his hands and prayed, "Lord, from the rising of the sun to its going down, Your name is worthy of all praise. Let our prayers rise before You like sweet-smelling incense. May the lifting up of our hands be as an evening sacrifice acceptable to You, O Lord, our maker and our God. You are our refuge, Lord; You are all that we desire in life. We humbly ask for Your goodness, Lord. Help us to hope only in You, and give us a share with Your chosen ones in the eternal land of the living. Amen."

The brothers moved quietly from their knees to sit on the wooden benches lining the room, and another hermit rose to read from a scroll. He drew near to the single candle burning on the altar as the gray light from the small window grew dimmer yet. "'Though He was in the form of God, our Lord Jesus did not deem equality with God something to be grasped at. Rather, He emptied Himself and took the form of a servant, being born in the likeness of man. He came in human form; thus He humbled Himself, obediently accepting death, even the death of a cross.'" The candle flickered, making shadows dance on the cross behind the reader. "'Because of this, God highly exalted Him and bestowed on Him the name above every other name, so that at Jesus' name every knee must bend in the heavens and on earth. There is no other name by which men may be saved. Let every tongue proclaim to the glory of God the Father that Jesus Christ is Lord.'"

Valerius glanced at Georgus's face. He saw a peace there that he had never seen before. For a moment his fellow cavalryman had the look of the holy hermit that stood before them.

Prayers continued, but Valerius slipped out the door. This was the sort of thing he had joined the legion to get away from. If Georg wanted to sit in there and pray with a bunch of hermits, he could do it without Valerius.

Valerius wandered around the foot of the Tor, but in the fog and deep dusk he did not dare wander far. Soon he returned to the hermitage and joined Georgus, Cadfrawl, and three other brothers who sat around the central fire in Cadfrawl's hut. Georg smiled and made room for another stool by the hearth. "It seems that our information was correct. Aaron's brother Bartholomew does spend a great deal of time here. Unfortunately, he is on a trip to Londinium at the moment. But as he is expected back in a day or two, we may as well wait. You won't mind missing a few extra days of Primus's field drill will you, Val?"

"Hardly." Val grinned and accepted the cup of imported wine Tellean offered him.

"As long as we're here, we might as well take advantage of the brothers' knowledge to increase our own. Cadfrawl was just showing me his impressive library." Georgus motioned to a triple row of sturdy shelves that circled around a quarter of the hut. The shelves held leather cylinders and terra-cotta vessels, all containing scrolls.

"I have just obtained a copy of the biography of our Lord written by the physician Lucas. It is of great value because it was written after our Lord's death and based on careful interviews and evidence-gathering by one who came late to the faith." Cadfrawl pointed to another shelf. "And I have a nearly complete collection of the known letters of the Apostle Paulinus. But many of our others are mere fragments. Bartholomew searches for us on his trading trips. And we have commissioned a copy of the letters of Peter from the great library in Nicomedia. But it will be some time yet before the weather is fit for his sailing so far."

"May we be permitted to read while we're here?" Georgus asked.

"But of course. That is what they are for. We have many who come from afar to read our sacred scrolls. Although you are the first of Caesar's eagles to do so."

Georgus grinned at Valerius. "I have recently encountered many questions about the faith which I cannot answer. Now I regret not taking advantage of my grandfather's library when I was at home. It seems life never holds enough time for all one would choose to do."

"And you also have questions, Valerius?" Brother Cadfrawl looked at Val with his gentle brown eyes.

Valerius shifted on his stool. "My father also had a considerable library which I neglected. It seems Georgus and I have backgrounds which are much the same, but lately my, ah, studies have been in a different direction—" His unfinished sentence hung in the smoky air.

"Have no hesitancy to ask what you will, my friend. We welcome here all who search for the Way."

Well, why not, Valerius thought. *If I'm really seeking truth, this is the place to ask.* "I am a student of Mithras." He hadn't meant for the words to sound so defiant, but Cadfrawl merely nodded and waited for him to continue.

"Lord Mithra is the defender of truth. He stands for obedience to divine law, for justice and rectitude—besides providing abundance. And he lives for eternity, protecting the souls of the just against the demons that seek to drag them to Hell. So what's so different about your religion?"

"As you express it, there seems to be little difference." Cadfrawl spoke so quietly his listeners had to lean toward him to hear above the crackling fire. "What's different about Christianity is grace—God reaching out to His creation in love without the need for the blood of bulls."

Valerius warmed to his topic. "But Mithraism is older than Christianity. It was already ancient in the time of Alexander. Wouldn't the older religion be the true one?"

"I am sure you will correct me if I am wrong, but did not much of the theology and the ethical system of Mithra come from Babylonia?"

"Yes, it did."

"And are you not aware that the children of Israel spent many generations in captivity in Babylonia? There our Judaic forefathers held true to their doctrines of truth and justice. Their captors learned from them and adopted their ways."

Valerius was beginning to wonder if it had been a good idea to enter into discussion with this learned man. "But my point is that there is nothing unique in your religion. For example, the Mithraic sacred writing tells of a great flood that covered the earth and one man who was secretly advised by the gods to construct a great boat and save his family and his cattle."

Cadfrawl smiled and nodded. "All the old mythologies contain a flood story—that shows it really happened. Christianity is unique in that God became a man and, as such, died for the sins of all men, and then rose from the dead."

"But Mithra offers his followers a communion feast, he promises a second coming, and he assures us of a final judgment when all humanity will unite in one grand assembly. As the god of truth he will separate the good from the evil and take the good to paradise. These doctrines are the same."

"Yes, the holy Scriptures describe our enemy as a roaring lion walking around seeking whom he may devour. But he far oftener goes in innocence in sheep's clothing or slithering silently as a serpent. He has indeed done a fine job in this attempt to lead man astray. This counterfeit of the true faith is indeed an excellent copy."

"But how do you know which is the fake and which true?"

"By the fruit borne inside the faithful of the true Way. That the enemy cannot counterfeit. The follower of the true God will be loving and steadfast unto the death, even as was our Lord, because the true faith is not a matter of external sacrifices and washings, but of God's love shed abroad in our hearts."

A log snapped on the fire, and all pulled back. Cadfrawl turned to the company. "My children, we should be in our beds. We have morning prayers just before sunrise. You are welcome to join us if you choose."

When Valerius roused himself long after sunrise the next morning, he was still disturbed by the quiet assurance of the hermit's words. He wished he could be that sure of the way he had chosen. Perhaps it would come with deeper levels of initiation. Although he didn't express it so eloquently, Georg did seem to have that sureness of his faith.

But when he finally found his friend, Georgus's brow was knit in perplexity and his mind full of questions. It had taken Valerius some time to find him. He wasn't at Cadfrawl's hut as Valerius had expected. "After morning prayers I loaned him one of my scrolls. Perhaps he took it to the church to read."

But the church was empty, save for two brothers kneeling in prayer.

Crossing the compound, Valerius almost tripped over Tellean who had a disturbing habit of springing up from bushes. At Valerius's query, the perpetually scowling servant pointed almost straight up. Valerius's gaze followed the gesture to the dark stone tower on the top of the steep hill. Leave it to Georg to pick the most difficult spot around to get to. Valerius was breathing heavily by the time he reached the summit.

Georgus sat with the scroll in its pouch at his feet, rubbing his forehead in concentration. His stiff brown hair, which always sprang at awkward angles rather than lying in obedient curls as fashion dictated, seemed to have more of a mind of its own than ever. "Thought I'd find you reading," Valerius said.

Georgus looked up slowly. "Morning, Val. I was. John's biography of Christ. It's great. But I'm having trouble concentrating. This robbery has me stumped. Nothing seems to make sense."

Valerius sat on the stone bench against the opposite side of the small tower. "Such as?"

"I can't believe we have the right people at all, and yet it must be someone from the legion. No native could get in to steal. It's too well guarded. And as much as I hate to admit it, the Third and the Sixth Turmae are the most likely because our barracks are right against the granary that's been robbed. Of course there must be a native collaborator, too. You couldn't hide sacks of stolen grain in the fortress . . ." His voice wandered off in thought.

"What I don't understand," Valerius said after a moment, "is why you're defending Plotius. He cares little enough for you, and if you let him take the blame, that leaves your friends Julius and Aaron free."

"But I have to defend Plotius; I'm sure he's innocent. I may not be eloquent, but I can say yes or no for the right."

"Sometimes that's the most eloquent thing a person can say. But what makes you so sure he's innocent?"

"If we're at all correct about when the robberies occurred, he was with me both times."

"So why didn't you tell the commandant?"

"I did. He seemed impressed, but Primus said that since we didn't know exactly the time of the robberies, we needed more evidence. So here we are—on a wild boar hunt in the fog."

At least Georgus had his studying to keep him occupied while they awaited Bartholomew's return. Valerius had nothing to do but wander idly around the island. It seemed every spot recalled something his father or grandfather had told him of their family legends—the thorn tree that had sprung into marvelous flower when their ancestor planted it, the well that turned to blood when he dipped in some magical cup—or maybe the water was blood and the cup purified it—no, that was Moses in Egypt. For the first time Val began to wish he had paid more attention to those stories.

Valerius idly threw a pebble into the spring and watched it tumble down the hill with the water. Just looking at that crystal water made him thirsty, but he wanted something stronger. Tellean could get him a cup of that excellent Roman wine he had served at their evening meal last night. He walked toward the servant's hut. He was almost to the door when the little servant burst out through the leather flap, his red hair looking wilder than ever as his face flushed. "What do you want?" He closed the flap carefully behind him.

"I was hoping for a cup of wine, if it isn't too much trouble?"

"Wine, eh? Well, you'll not be finding any here. The brothers don't trust me with their precious imported amphora. They keep that at Cadfrawl's."

"Why do you stay here if you aren't of the faith?" Valerius had wondered about this ever since they met the strange servant who seemed so out of tune with the serenity of the island.

He scowled and hunched his shoulders. "I've always been here. Why should I go? Anyway, they give me food and lodging, and I have plenty of time to catch fish and sell them for the market at Venta."

"Ah, you have a boat? I was wondering how we'd get off this island if that trader fellow doesn't show up pretty soon."

"I'll take you anytime." It was the first time the servant had shown enthusiasm in offering a service.

But the next day Bartholomew returned as promised, and they could get on with their work. The short, gray-bearded merchant regarded the soldiers with bright, dark eyes. "Yes, yes, I'm frequently approached about buying wheat for export. It's a major part of my business. No, I haven't purchased any since Ludi Romani. Not because I had any idea it might be illegal grain I was offered, but simply because it's bad sailing weather, and the wheat would likely rot before I got it south. Bad business, very bad."

"Can you recall who has approached you since the games?"

He stroked his long, full beard. "Other than my usual suppliers?" He thought for a moment longer. "A legionary the last time I was in Isca visiting my brother. If he mentioned his name, I've forgotten it. Must have been cavalry, though, because he carried one of those long swords you fellows use, not the short, broad kind you see on most of the soldiers."

Georgus leaned forward attentively. "Wasn't that unusual to find a legionary wanting to sell wheat?"

"I suppose it was. But I deal with all kinds. He said he had a native friend from a villa up the river. He offered me a good price."

"But you refused?" Bartholomew nodded, and Georgus continued. "What did he look like?"

Bartholomew shook his head. "You fellows all look alike in uniform. He was thinner than most, though, I did notice that."

"And this undernourished cavalryman is the only unusual person who's offered to sell you wheat since September?"

"That's all I can think of. Besides Tellean."

"Tellean?"

"He took some in exchange for his fish for market. I didn't buy it, but I did take it up to Londinium for him. I had extra room in my cart. Seemed the least I could do for him. After all, he serves me my meals when I'm here—not in very good grace, but he does it."

That seemed to be all they could accomplish on Ynis Witrin, so they decided to go back to Isca in the morning. "I'll go find Tellean and see if he'll take us in his coracle," Val said, taking leave of Georgus and Bartholomew. He had a feeling those two who enjoyed studying with hermits would like some time to talk privately.

The evening fog turned to rain as Valerius crossed the valley to the servant's hut. It was raining hard by the time he arrived. There was no answer to his repeated knocks, so he decided to go inside to wait. The fire had died to a single glowing ember, and it was black inside the small circular room. Valerius found an oil lamp and lit it with a spark. Nothing to do but sit on the pile of skins in the corner and wait. But after a few minutes the chill in the hut made him draw the wolfskin around his shoulders for warmth.

It was several minutes before it registered with him what was under the skin. Sacks. Empty sacks that had recently held grain.

He moved the lamp closer to inspect them. Some with the stamp of Legio II, some with a mark he didn't recognize.

He was standing there holding the sacks when Tellean burst through the door and flung himself at Val with a small dagger. Valerius was completely unprepared for the attack, but he deflected the first thrust with a fling of the sacks.

The scuffle was short, but the Celt kicked, bit, and jabbed with his dagger like a cornered animal. Valerius was bleeding from several slashes when he led his captive to Georgus.

They arrived back at Isca the next day, ferried there by Bartholomew, who was as anxious to see his brother as the other two were to present their evidence—incomplete as it was. But the minute they entered the dexter gate, they could tell something was wrong. A Roman fortress was never that quiet at midday. Those they saw on the Via Praetoria walked straight ahead with their heads down, as if they didn't want to encounter anyone else. No sounds of drill came from the field or amphitheater.

But if it was strangely quiet outside, the principia was a hub of tension. Georgus and Valerius were thoroughly inspected by the guards before they were allowed to enter, and Tellean and Bartholomew were ushered in at spear point.

Plotius, Julius, and Aaron sat with faces ghostly white, their heads bowed, on a bench before the tribunal. "What? Are they trying them already? Wait, we have evidence." Georgus started forward, but was stopped by the guard.

"Not trying them. They're the only men in the legion who couldn't have done it. They were locked up. Just an inquiry. It'll take a lot of evidence to prepare a murder trial."

"Murder?" Georgus stared at the guard. "Who was killed?"

"Some Marius fellow from the cavalry. Sixth Turma."

In a state of shock the newcomers were taken to a small room behind the cross hall where the body of Marius lay on a table, a dagger wound black with dried blood showed startlingly against his thin white chest.

"What happened?" Georgus asked, but before the guard could answer, Bartholomew gasped.

"He's the one who wanted to sell me that wheat."

"You're sure?"

Bartholomew was sure. Then Georgus realized Tellean hadn't moved since they stepped inside the room. He stood there now, barely breathing, his pale blue eyes hugely round. "You knew him, too?"

The defiant posture the servant had held ever since attacking Valerius in his hut suddenly crumpled. "The Roman wheat sacks. They were from him. I met him at the market. We got to talking; he asked if I knew any merchants . . ." The defiance returned. "Lugh knows I needed the money. Those hermits pay me nothing, and the little I get for the wheat—" He stopped abruptly.

"For the wheat you manage to steal from them?" Valerius finished for him. "I suspected that must be what those other sacks were, but Cadfrawl said something about not wanting to cast the first stone. So you put everything in unmarked bags, and Bartholomew was an innocent carrier for you?"

For a moment a light flashed in Tellean's eyes. He looked Bartholomew up and down, then shrugged. Apparently he decided he had nothing to gain by making false accusations. "That's right."

They moved back into the cross hall and found space on the benches to hear Plotius's interview while they waited to give their own evidence. "I have my suspicions." The big German spoke in a hushed whisper.

In the silence the commandant's barked order for him to stand up and state his case made everyone in the room jump.

Plotius stood, but he didn't speak. He regarded his decurion sitting on the front bench for a full thirty seconds. When he did speak, it was with belligerent determination. "All right. I knew Marius was tied up with that wheat stealing. That's why I tried to divert suspicion to the Third by accusing these fellows." He waved toward Julius and Aaron. "I also knew he was taking orders from someone else."

"Who?" Candidus barked.

"I don't know for sure. But I know who he owed a lot of money to. He was always losing dice games in the Serpent's Tongue. But one person he lost to more regularly than any other. He told me he was beginning to suspect the dice were loaded." He made the last statement looking straight at Decurion Primus.

The cavalry officer sprang to his feet. "That's a lie! You have no evidence at all. I'll see you in Tartarus for this!" The words came out with a cold intensity far more threatening than if he'd yelled.

From his back bench Tellean rose and walked to the dais, much to the consternation of the guard who was keeping him under pilum point. "It is in my mind that I have the evidence he lacks. If I could be having the commander's assurance that he would not be charging me . . ."

Georgus stepped forward and informed Commandant Candidus of what he had learned on Ynis Witrin and in the room beyond the cross hall. "Produce your evidence. We'll see." Tellean reached inside his tunic and drew out a scarlet feather on a leather thong.

"What's that?" Primus scoffed. "Every decurion and centurion in the Empire wears a row of those on his helmet."

"Yes, but not many of them wind up stuck to sacks of stolen grain where I found this." Tellean twirled the feather on the thong.

"Nor do many decurions wear helmets with a broken feather in their crests, Primus." Georgus picked up the transverse crested helmet from under Primus's bench and carried it to Tellean. The feather fit exactly into the broken quill in the left rear of Primus's crest.

The trial would come later, but the evidence was sufficient to arrest Primus and release Plotius, Julius, and Aaron. With a sigh of relief, the legion returned to normal.

After three days on a fog-bound island, being slashed by a sharp dagger, and coming back to such drama, Valerius thought that no bath had ever felt as good as the one he had that evening. "Go easy on that arm, man!" he directed the slave scraping him with a strigilis.

After a thorough massage with a variety of oils, he joined Georgus in the caldarium. "Funny—this steam looks just like the fog on Ynis Witrin, but it sure feels different." He settled back to soak in the warmth of the moist air.

"Ironic, isn't it, that Primus killed Marius to keep his theft hidden, and that's the very thing that brought it to light."

Georgus was quiet, so Valerius continued. "Did you hear the gossip in the tepidarium? They say Plotius is taking credit for solving the case. Seems he thinks he'll be made the new decurion now."

Georgus's answer was laconic. "Mmm, I heard."

"What's the matter with you? Something on your mind?"

"I was thinking about my family."

Val nodded. "Ynis Witrin made me think a lot about mine. Many old family legends are tied up with that place." He wiped a trickle of sweat off his face with a linen towel. "Tell me about your family."

Georg was quiet again before he spoke. "Guess the thing that got me going was the other gossip I heard in the tepidarium. Foolish to listen to it, but they say Galerius Caesar has finished his campaigns in the east and moved into the palace at Nicomedia with Diocletian. His announced goal is to persuade the Augusta to move ahead with stamping out what he calls the atheistic Christian cult."

"Probably true," Valerius said. "Sounds consistent with what I've heard of Galerius. But he's only a Caesar—not half the power Diocletian Augusta holds. Diocletian has been moderate in that direction."

"I'm not so sure. After all, Galerius is married to Diocletian's daughter, and the Augusta will do anything he believes is necessary to strengthen the Empire. So far you've got to admit he's done pretty well, too."

"So why does all this political maneuvering make you think of your family?"

"They'll be in great danger if the guards go out arresting Christians. My father was an army officer, but he died when I was only ten. My mother and sisters live with her parents. Grandpapa is the Count of Lydda; they've been Christians since the Apostle Peter visited there and 'converted all who dwelt at Lydda and Sharon'—I read that in one of the scrolls Cadfrawl had. Anyway, a purge is likely to start at the top, and they would be the most obvious targets in the whole plain of Sharon."

"Sisters, you say?" Val made an obvious attempt to change Georgus's gloomy mood.

"Wipe that grin off your face. Since you've already told me your sister is nine years old, there's no quid pro quo in this. Kasia and Matterona they are. Matterona is betrothed to an old friend of mine, Quintillian—he's with the eagles in Gaul. But our lovely, dark-eyed Kasia prefers reading with Grandpapa to the company of young men she considers frivolous."

Valerius looked at the ceiling, grinning. "Maybe she wouldn't consider me frivolous."

"But you'll never know. Cappadocia is a long way from here." Georg's teasing tone changed. "And tonight it seems farther than usual."

The men got out of the warm water and started toward the frigidarium for a final cold rinse. "What you need is a diversion, Georgus. Come with me to the Mithraeum tonight."

Georg shook his head.

"Oh, come on. No one will think you're going soft on the truth. It's only fair after I talked to those priests on Ynis Witrin." Val really wanted Georgus's company. He used his strongest argument. "Besides, how can you convince me I'm wrong if you don't know what I believe?"

Georg gave his amused half-grin. "Persuasive, aren't you? You should have a seat in the Senate someday."

It was now the middle of December, and the sixteenth of each month was sacred to Mithra, so the service was an especially elaborate one with sacrifices burning on all three altars. This month the celebrations would increase in fervor until the twenty-fifth when the new birth of the sun would be celebrated by sacred festivals. Tonight blood from the sacrificial animals on the altars was collected in a trench and poured out as libations to the sun and the sacred planets. All the while the priests chanted long psalms and hymns:

O Mithra, the bull-slayer, O Mithra, the sun god,
O Mithra, provider and keeper and helper,
We sing to you, mighty god of light, in the heaven you rule;
Protector of truth, defender of faith,
Assailant of falsehood, corrector of error;
Mediate between us and the unapproachable, unknowable god
that reigns in the ethereal spheres . . .

Those initiated in the faith then approached the altars. At his turn, Valerius came before the sculpture of Mithra slaying the bull, dipped his cupped hands in the trench of blood, and poured the warm, sticky substance over his head to the accompaniment of pipes and priests' chants.

As they walked back to the fortress through the frosty night, Valerius's elation shone like a torch. "Now do you see why I choose Mithra? He offers everything your Christ does—grace, truth, eternal life—but more. Mithras is more active. I'm not at the mercy of a god I must take on faith as you are."

Characteristically, Georg was silent awhile before he answered. "I can see you're excited by your religion. But, Val, do you have joy and peace?"

Valerius laughed. "Joy and peace? Georg, I do believe you're getting more eloquent!"

Valerius lay long in his bunk, with the smell of bull's blood still on his head. He had never known anything as captivating to his imagination or as stimulating to his sense as the mysteries of Mithra. And yet far in the background of his mind Cadfrawl's words faintly whispered. Was it possible that anything so thrilling could be a mere counterfeit? Well, if there was anything false in the way he had chosen, he supposed it would become clear as he worked his way up the levels. For now he was satisfied.

The next morning, with his hair freshly washed, Valerius strode into Georgus's room. "Ah, the air's fresh this morning. So good to have that robbery business cleared up. Trouble's all over."

Georgus's voice was heavy. "No. It's just started."

Now Val really looked at his friend. He had never seen him look so ghastly, his face white and drawn, dark circles under dull eyes. "Georg! What is it? You look like you've spent the night in Tartarus."

"I have."

"Well, come on—what's started?"

"The persecution of Christians. We knew it would come, but not like this."

"Like what? Tell me what happened, Georg!"

"The Theban Legion serving in Gaul—Maximian ordered a general sacrifice—the whole army was to burn incense to Caesar before wiping out Christianity in Gaul." Georg rubbed his hand over his eyes. "Val, the whole legion was Christian—every man of them. Not a single one would perform the sacrifice or swear the oath." His voice dropped. "So Maximian ordered the legion decimated."

"Literally, you mean?"

Georg nodded. "A literal decimation. Every tenth man put to the sword. Had to call in a special auxiliary to do it. Then he ordered the sacrifice again."

"And?"

"Not a one. Not a single man gave in. So Maximian ordered a second decimation." Georg got to his feet and paced the tiny room, his hand shading his eyes as if to blot out the visions this news brought. "The remaining soldiers persevered in their faith. They drew up a petition to Diocletian, swore their allegiance to Empire and emperor, but asserted their privilege as Roman citizens to worship their God."

"And?" Valerius prodded.

"Caesar refused. He put them to the sword, Val. The whole regiment. More than six thousand loyal, well-trained fighting men. He had them slaughtered."

Valerius caught a sense of horror more from Georgus's voice than from his words. "There must be a mistake. You know how rumors grow."

Georg shook his head. "This is no rumor. A letter was waiting for me when I came in last night. It was from Quintillian, my sister's betrothed. He was one of those who drew up the petition to Diocletian. He wanted me to know what happened in case the petition failed. I've just returned from the principia. Candidus told me the end of the story. His report came with the same messenger that brought my letter. Quintillian was probably the finest man I've ever known." Georg stopped pacing and dropped to his stool, his head in his hands.

Valerius tried to find something comforting to say. "I am sorry about your friend."

Georg looked at him from hollow eyes. "It's happening here too."

"Here?" Val took a step toward his friend. "Georg—you, too?"

"No, but it should be." Georg ran his fingers through his already disheveled hair. "Last night while I was at the Mithraeum with you, they came through the barracks with a censor. Only two refused to burn incense to Caesar. Julius and Aaron are in the guardhouse again—this time on a charge they have no desire to be cleared of. I feel like a traitor. I should be in there with them, and yet—"

Before Valerius could answer, they heard a pounding at the barracks door. Two guards entered and grounded their pilums in salute. "Legionary Georgus Nestor Anastasius, you're wanted in the principia."

Georg rose, squared his shoulders, and walked out between the guards.

9

ongratulations!" Valerius dropped Vixatrix's brush and sprang across the stable to clasp Georgus's arm. "Here I was, thinking they'd taken you to lop your head off, and they made you decurion instead!"

Georg grinned. "All the way up the Via Praetoria I kept thinking what a great world this is and how I'd hate to leave it. I prayed I'd be able to stand strong. I wasn't sure I could." He shook his head. "Glad I didn't have to find out."

Valerius gave him a long, level look. "You'd have stood. No doubt about it."

"I hope so. That walk made me take a real quick look at what is really important to me. I started with the usual things: I'd like to go home again; I want to make my family proud of me; I'd like to get married. Then I realized that I may die without doing all those other things, but I must not die without having done something worthwhile with my life, something for God.

"Oh, but I didn't tell you the rest of the news—we're leaving Britain."

Valerius's brush stopped halfway down his horse's long, dark mane. "Leaving Britain?"

"Whole turma ordered to Nicomedia. Leave with the tide in three days."

Valerius whistled. "Talk about putting your head into the lion's mouth. You'll have to watch your step there, or you will lose that head of yours yet."

Georgus's eyes twinkled. "You could be right. It's not just any old assignment in Nicomedia even. Palace guard."

Valerius shook his head. "Like I said—lion's mouth. Well, at least you're a quiet sort. That should help."

Georg raised one of the heavy dark eyebrows that framed his humorous eyes. "That's something I'll have to get over. I visited Julius and Aaron in the guardhouse. I promised to present their case to the Augusta personally."

Valerius groaned. "And what makes you think you'll fare any better than Quintillian and the Theban Legion?"

"I expect Diocletian may be having regrets about the barbaric action he allowed Galerius to talk him into. Anyway, I don't have to be rash about it, just present a letter from a fellow officer in my ala. I won't ask to celebrate Eucharist in the palace or anything.

"If anything happens to me, it'll be a step up for you," Georgus added.

"Me?"

"I've asked that you be appointed my optio. Based my case on your efficiency in finding those bags in Tellean's hut."

"That was just pure dumb luck, but I'd be honored to be your optio if the legate agrees. What about Plotius though? He wanted the decurion job. Shouldn't you choose him optio?"

"That's precisely why I can't trust him as optio. I know he's out for my job. I need someone whose loyalty I can count on."

Georgus turned to a legionary on messenger duty and handed him a parchment roll. "Take this to the principia for me." The messenger saluted and left. Georgus smiled. "Ah, first reward of my new position—sending a letter to my family in the official letter pouch. And the result of it should be my second reward. I've asked Mother to send my personal servant Pasicrates to me at Nicomedia. When one can tear him away from his constant stylus-scratching, that man gives the best massages in the Empire."

Georg picked up a brush and began grooming Bayard, his white charger. "I borrowed a scroll from Cadfrawl. Now I'll have to return it not half-read. Want to go back to the island with me?"

Valerius gave a final tug to the cinch and swung into his saddle. "Sure, when?"

"Tomorrow's tide." Georgus touched his spurs to Bayard's side and led off to the drill field where he would command the turma in their last practice in Britain. "Next month we do this before Caesar," he shouted to the unit assembled on the field, "so get it right, men!"

Not until the next afternoon, as the boat glided through the chilly, fog-shrouded marshes, did Georg find time for quiet reflection. Ynis Witrin had held the key to his robbery investigation. Would it also hold the key to his need for spiritual growth? It was such a mystical place—filled with the sense of the infinite, unseen God of love and power. Surely if he were to find the strength to be more forceful for the faith, it would be here. For all his lighthearted approach, he knew he needed spiritual armor to face the testing of his faith likely to come in this new assignment.

Cadfrawl welcomed his visitors with open arms. "Ah, my friends. You are most welcome. And just in time for the evening meal. You will notice a vast improvement in the hospitality of our table. Not only have we taken a servant who is a fellow believer and will not steal from us, but he brings his daughter who is exceedingly skilled with the cookpot and baking oven."

Cadfrawl introduced his cousin's son Caafan, who replaced the surly Tellean, and Caafan's sixteen-year-old daughter Maelgwn. Georgus's eyes sparkled when the golden-haired Maelgwn gracefully acknowledged the introduction. "And I have just taken a fresh tray of honey cakes from the oven, if you would care to eat," she said with a smile.

Maelgwn's honey cakes were the sweetest Georg had ever tasted, and her hair the most golden he had ever seen as she served the brothers and their guests by the light of the fire and wavering torches. Later when the company repaired to the church for evening prayers, he found it hard to keep his mind on holy things as the candlelight made an aureole around Maelgwn's bowed head. With a physical wrenching, Georg turned his mind to Cadfrawl's words: "Lord, be with us through this night which You have provided for our rest. When day comes, may we rise from sleep to rejoice in the resurrection of Your Christ who lives and reigns forever and ever.

"Lord, we beg You to visit us here in this hermitage dedicated to Your holy name. Banish from it all the deadly power of the enemy. May Your holy angels dwell here to keep us in peace, and may Your blessings be upon us always. . . . In the name of the Father, Son, and Holy Spirit."

The company crossed themselves and departed to their pallets.

The next morning Cadfrawl hurried Georg into his hut as soon as they had finished their bowls of Maelgwn's wheat-meal stirabout topped with milk and honey. "A brother from Londinium arrived shortly after you left with Tellean. He brought us a most precious prize." Cadfrawl removed the lid from a terracotta pot and carefully drew out a rolled parchment. "It is a most amazing writing, most poetic and imaginative, and yet with the power of truth. A fragment of the Revelation of St. John the Divine." He tenderly unrolled the scroll and held it near his lamp. "Ah, that we had more of it—this is such a small part. I hope it is not greed in me to hunger for more when the Lord has bestowed such riches on us. I tell myself I must never forget to be grateful for His gifts. Here, take it and read. Let the fire of this vision engulf your heart." He thrust the scroll into Georgus's hands.

Georgus moved toward the lamp and began to read, "We praise You, O Lord God Almighty, who is and was and ever shall be. You have assumed Your great power; You have begun Your mighty reign upon the earth." Georg thought of Quintillian and the Theban Legion. It was hard to believe that God was reigning on the earth. He thought of Valerius and the thousands upon thousands of worshipers of the bull-slayer who filled the ranks of the legions and the populace of the Empire. It was hard to believe in God's mighty power.

Smoke from the lamp burned his eyes. With a nod to Cadfrawl, he lay the scroll aside. "I will read more later." Without giving thought to his direction, Georg walked around the foot of the Tor toward the Meare, although in the midwinter dampness it was hard to tell which was swamp and which lake.

A movement among the rushes growing at the edge of the lake caught his eye and he smiled. *Ah, there would be fish stew for the midday meal.* Maelgwn was fishing from a small coracle not far from the shore. She returned Georgus's wave, then returned her attention to her fishing. With a small grin, Georg sat on a boulder. The girl's blue tunic was far brighter than the gray-blue water and sky around her, and her golden hair outshone the sun's weak attempts to burn through the mist. A flash of silver gleamed by the coracle as Maelgwn brought a wriggling bass aboard in her net. A curlew called from the reeds beyond. Yes, with such islands of peace in the world it was possible to believe that God reigned.

But suddenly the peace was shattered as Maelgwn screamed, backed toward the side of the boat, lost her balance, and plunged into the water.

"Maelgwn!" Georgus jumped to his feet with a shout.

At the same moment, he saw a giant water snake, hideous head erect, moving toward the struggling girl. He lunged into the water and waded toward her. Fighting the water, which slowed all his actions, he unsheathed his spatha and slashed at the undulating creature.

Maelgwn cried out a second time as the serpent rose up to strike. Clasping her around the waist with one arm, Georg hacked and slashed at the beast with his long-bladed sword.

"Oh, praise be, he's gone!" Maelgwn cried as the snake slithered into a thicket of rushes. Georg backed up to a firmer footing and set Maelgwn on the shore.

But a second later, the snake coiled for a spring and lashed at Georg with all the fury of a beast whose lair has been disturbed. Its forked tongue flicked out like a dagger.

Georg thrust his sword below the evil-looking head.

The creature flung backward, a flow of red blood staining the water. But in the force of its recoil, Georgus's spatha was wrenched from his hand and slipped into the murky lake.

Georg waded forward and grasped the limp body of his opponent, dragging it to shore. Maelgwn's cries brought those in the hermitage running, headed by Caafan, her father, who clutched his trembling daughter in his arms. Valerius and two of the brothers plunged into the lake to retrieve the overturned coracle, but could not find Georgus's sword in the mud-topped peat that lined the lake bed.

Shaking his head, Cadfrawl surveyed the slain serpent sprawled on the shore. "Never have I seen such a creature on this island. Water snakes we have, but nothing like this leviathan. Caafan, you will take his meat to the tribe that they may eat of it. In the winter season of sparse hunting, they will be glad for its nourishment."

Valerius observed the creature thoughtfully. His gaze moved across the scene to Maelgwn, then back to Georgus, standing with the serpent dead at his feet. "All this creature needs is a pair of wings to make this a perfect illustration for Perseus rescuing Andromeda from the sea dragon." He slapped his friend on his back. "But if we don't all get into some dry clothes, this story may not have the happy ending the ode-makers give it."

Some time later when they had all dried themselves by well-fed fires and drunk their fill of hot wine, Cadfrawl led his company up the Tor to King Lucius's oratory for a service of praise. The mists were rising, and the mountaintop with its small cluster of worshipers inside the stone tower seemed an island alone in the world as white clouds filled all the valley for as far as they could see on every side.

"Georgus Anastasius of Lydda, surely the psalmist of old was thinking of just such a one as you when he said, 'You shall tread upon the asp and the cobra, the snake and dragon shall you trample under your foot. For my God is King of old, working salvation in the midst of the earth. He divided the sea by His strength, and He broke the heads of the dragons in the waters. He broke the heads of leviathan in pieces and gave him to be meat to the people inhabiting the wilderness.'"

Cadfrawl turned to the brother standing beside him and held out his hand. The brother drew an ornate broad sword from beneath his tunic and handed it to Cadfrawl. Georgus recognized the sharp iron sword with its ornate bronze handle as the type carried by elite officers of the guard three centuries before. "This is Meribah, one of the most prized possessions of our hermitage. It is the sword that Peter, that redoubtable servant of our Lord, snatched from a soldier and used to cut off the ear of one in the party arresting our Lord in the Garden of Gethsemane. As an example to all those who follow the Prince of Peace, our Lord restored the severed ear and would do no violence to those who came against Him. So may we follow in His footsteps.

"Georgus of Lydda, may you take Meribah with you as you go forward to fight in the name of the Lord. May you slay the great dragon of iniquity as you have here today slain an evil serpent.

"This sword was brought to our shores by Joseph the Arimathean. It is right that as you travel back toward the land of our Lord's birth with one descended from Joseph, you should bear his sword with you."

Georg held out his hands and received the sword. Had this very sword once been in the hand of Peter, or Joseph of Arimathea, perhaps of the Lord Himself? He looked at the fine etching on the hilt and the deep red enamel insets.

Cadfrawl followed his gaze. "Let the red of the enamel remind you ever of the blood our Lord shed for your salvation—shed as truly and as freely for you as if you had been the only person in the world in need of His sacrifice."

With bowed head Georg said quietly, "I am unworthy."

"We are all unworthy," Cadfrawl replied. "We stand in the worth of our great Savior and gratefully serve Him in love."

"So let me serve." Georgus held the sword before him, his face shining.

10

othing could have contrasted more sharply with the gray and green fog-bound shores of western Britain than the eastern Roman capital of Nicomedia. Vineyard-covered slopes rolled down to the sparkling waters of the Gulf of Nicomedia, that narrow body of water connecting the Mare Aegaeum to the Pontus Euxinus. The ship had stopped briefly at Byzantium to deposit a contingent of Thracian archers, delighted to be returning to duty so near to home, and then it sailed proudly up the isthmus to the power center of the world.

Villa after villa lined the shores of the gulf, each with its own serene garden circled by rustling bamboo trees, pale green bays, and darker junipers inside white walls. A few larger villas had private piers running into the water where canopied pleasure barges rode at anchor.

Standing on the deck beside Georg, Valerius swept his arm at the scene before them. "After the three days we spent in that stinking, crowded Rome, it's easy to see why Diocletian chose to make this place his capital."

Georg grinned. "They say it's strategy. Diocletian can have his troops deployed and his orders carried out while that pompous debating club of senators in Rome is still haggling to define the terms of his proclamation."

In the center of the city, on a rolling hillside far above the bustle of the quay, stood the imperial palace, its white marble bulk commanding the view just as the dominating presence of the man who lived there commanded the lives of his subjects.

When the boat finally docked and their mounts were unloaded from the hold, Georgus and Valerius rode through the busy streets. Temples to the most popular Roman gods lined the way here as solidly as they had in Rome. The stadium, amphitheater, and baths stood in eloquent testimony to the city's prosperity. Everywhere merchants and craftsmen bustled about their business while members of the aristocracy rode in slave-borne litters.

At the palace walls they were about to turn right toward the stables when Valerius pointed to an unusually beautiful building with a wood-domed roof just across a narrow valley from the palace. "That appears to be a temple of some sort, but there are no statues."

Georg smiled; then the twinkle in his eyes disappeared in a look of worry. "Who but Christians would dare build a church so near the lion's mouth, as you once put it? Remember Cadfrawl telling us he had commissioned a manuscript from the library in Nicomedia? There it is—probably the finest in the world. I'll have to call in there and see how his scroll is progressing. Maybe I can send it to him in the imperial pouch."

Valerius gasped. "You wouldn't dare!"

Georg shrugged. "Why not? Who would think of searching the emperor's dispatch bag for Christian writings?"

Valerius shook his head. "I'd best watch carefully how you do your job—it looks like I'll be saddled with it any day now."

As soon as they had settled their horses in the well-appointed stables of the palace cavalry guard, the men went on to the barracks. The guard grounded his pilum in salute. "There is someone waiting for you in the decurion's quarters, sir. I hope I did the right thing to let them in."

"Waiting for me? We've been in the city less than two hours. Who could possibly know we're here?"

They passed the tribune's headquarters and turned into the colonnaded veranda lining the barracks, but before they entered the decurion's quarters, a small dark figure in a lime green stola flew across the walkway and into Georgus's arms. "Oh, Georg! Georg! I've been longing so to see you! I thought you'd never get here!"

Georg pushed the delicate creature back to observe her at arms' length, then pulled her to him again. "Kasia! More beautiful than ever. What in all the Empire are you doing here?"

"We got your letter. Mother prepared to send Pasicrates off immediately, and I begged and pleaded and was ready to cry and refuse to eat until she let me come, but she gave in at my argument that I could take them all firsthand word of you. Of course, I had to bring about half the household servants with me for protection—although what there was to protect me from I'm sure I couldn't say."

Georg threw back his head and laughed. "Oh, Kasia, what a breath of joy you are! I had no idea how I'd missed you all. Have you found a comfortable mansio?"

"Oh, yes, just down the street. Behind the church. We've been here three days, and I went to a wonderful service at the church with Pastor Eusebius. Oh, but you mustn't go." Suddenly all the bubbling joy died. "You've heard about Quintillian?"

Georg nodded. "I heard."

"Harrumph." Valerius cleared his throat sharply from just behind Georgus's left shoulder.

Georg grinned at his friend. "All right, all right. This pushy fellow is Quintus Valerius Artios. My baby sister Kasia. He's from a good enough family, Kasia, but I advise you not to have anything to do with him . . ." Georg stopped his bantering as it became obvious that neither Kasia nor Val were listening to him. Both stood where they were, simply staring at each other.

How long that ridiculous state of affairs might have gone on they would never know, for just then Pasicrates entered from the inner room. His bronzed, Grecian features split in a wide grin. "Ah, Mar Georg, it is good to be in your service again. Where is your kit? I'll see to it."

Georgus took his servant's arm and then embraced him in a hug. "Pasicrates, I can't tell you how good it is to have you with me. Forget the pack; let's go to the baths. I've been longing for one of your massages."

For the next two days the newcomers to Nicomedia spent every off-duty hour getting acquainted with the beautiful, bustling city. Kasia never tired of exploring the busy marketplace where members of every class rubbed shoulders, the wealthy in their embroidered silken tunics and high leather boots and the craftsmen in short, rough tunics and wooden sandals. The three went from shop to shop, up and down a seemingly endless maze of streets with Valerius making Kasia a present of every pretty trinket that caught her eye. There seemed to be no rhyme or reason to the arrangement of the shops as veterinary surgeons, seamstresses, fruit sellers, sheep shearers, attendants for the bath, importers of fine silk, barbers, scribes, and jewelers all displayed their wares and skills in a tumbling confusion along streets choked with ox-carts, chariots, litters, and equestrians.

After a filling meal at the best cookshop in the district on their second day of exuberant sightseeing, the men were returning Kasia to her mansio when they rounded a corner onto the Via Nerva. Kasia was the first to see the black smoke billowing from the back of the mansio. "Fire!" she cried and darted forward. "No! No! My new scroll!"

Valerius ran ahead of her to help rescue the scroll of the histories of Josephus he had bought for her the day before. But when they arrived, gasping for breath, they saw that their efforts had been unnecessary. It was not the mansio that was burning, but a large bonfire attended by the Imperial Guard.

On second look Kasia's relief turned to dismay, and she ran to her brother. "Georg! It's the library! They're burning everything from the church!"

Georgus stared in unbelieving horror as guard after guard emerged from the church, arms laden with scrolls, sacred relics, vessels, and furniture, piling it all on the devouring flames. The finest collection of sacred writings in all the Empire was turning to ashes in front of his eyes.

Before his companions could protest, he darted forward. His cavalry uniform blended with those of the Imperial Guard, and in the confusion of smoke and crackling flames no one noticed another soldier. He darted to the left where the smoke was the thickest and one guard's enthusiastic fling had sent an arm load of scrolls just beyond the blaze. Thankful for the concealing folds of his cloak, Georg gathered the scrolls and stuffed them up the back of his tunic.

Smoke stung his eyes, and flying sparks singed the feathers cresting his helmet. Within a few minutes the bronze of his helmet was glowing hot, burning his head through its leather lining. Sweat dripped from his body. He stepped back for a breath of air. "Move it, soldier! Bring another load!" a centurion barked at him.

In response to the order Georg dashed into the church. Why hadn't he thought of this sooner? He filled his arms with a bundle of scrolls. When no one was looking, he dashed out the back door. He looked about desperately for a place to hide his precious loot. This time of year the gardens were far too sparse to provide cover.

"Georg, here! I'll take them!" Kasia pulled her long palla from her head to wrap around the bundle.

Georg started to protest that it was too dangerous when another voice interrupted. "I'll take care of her." Valerius pulled the scrolls from his arms.

On his second foray, Georg wasn't so lucky. The centurion who had ordered him into the church was in the nearly empty library, and Georgus was ordered to carry his load to the crackling flames. Again he chose a smoke-shrouded spot and made his aim as bad as possible, but rescuing the lot was impossible. He started to turn away when just beyond the place his load had landed, a piece of parchment snapped in the flames and rolled open. Georgus saw the large block letters of the signature: PAUL. The flames covered it.

Without thinking, Georg dashed to the burning pile and grabbed at the scroll from which the signature had broken. It was high in the blazing pyramid, just beyond his reach. He grabbed a piece of flaming wood and struck at the scroll to dislodge it. Standing almost in the fire itself, he grabbed the treasure and thrust it under his cloak.

A heavy hand clasped his shoulder and dragged him backward. "Our orders are to burn scrolls, not soldiers." It was the commanding centurion. "What do you think you're doing? You're not in my detachment."

"No, sir. I was just returning to quarters when I saw—"

"Your enthusiasm to stamp out this evil cult is laudable, decurion, but not your inefficient methods." His gaze went to Georgus's hands. "You may find handling your reins rather painful for the next few days. Better go have those seen to."

Georg looked at his hands. The flesh was red and scorched. Already blisters were forming. He'd had no idea he'd done that. But now the pain seared.

The centurion turned at the approach of his optio. "Shall we fire the church, sir?" the junior officer asked.

"No. Galerius wanted to. But Diocletian countermanded the order. Said it was too close to the palace; flames might spread."

"That's all then, sir. Church is empty."

"Very good. That should teach them a lesson. Can't defy Caesar and get away with it." He turned to disperse the crowd pushing ever closer to the flames. Georgus melted into the rabble with his treasured spoils.

In spite of the pain that now extended up his arms and made him sick to his stomach, Georg turned not to the hospital, but toward the mansio to hide his scrolls in Kasia's room. He would send them off tomorrow with his mother's servants. And Kasia, too. It was far too dangerous for her in Nicomedia. Someone could easily have spotted her worshiping at the church while she awaited his arrival. If he could just make it to the mansio. His head swam, and his knees wobbled.

When he was across the street, he leaned against a wall to regain his equilibrium. *Don't let me pass out now,* he prayed.

The scrolls would be burned yet if they were discovered under his cloak. He took a step forward, but the movement had been too soon. The pavement lurched beneath his feet. He fell forward on his knees and blistered hands. *Get up,* he commanded himself. But the pain and inhaled smoke were too much for him. He felt his shoulder hit the street before everything went black.

"Mar Georg! Mar Georg!" He opened his eyes slowly and looked into Pasicrates's worried eyes. "You are better now, Mar Georg?"

Georg looked around, then closed his eyes with a groan. Kasia's gentle fingers stroked his cheek. "Val and Pasicrates found you. Pasi bandaged your hands. He swears his salve is better than anything they'll have at the army hospital." She held his head, and he managed to swallow a few gulps of the strong wine she held to his lips.

In a few minutes his head cleared, but he lay still with his eyes closed, thinking. Their holiday was over. They had had two glorious days of sightseeing. Now he must get his sister to safety and get on with what he had come for. His stomach lurched with a sickness that had nothing to do with smoke inhalation. What if Julius and Aaron had been executed while he had been attending chariot races at the arena with his companions or lounging at the baths with his unit? He had been wasting time when there was far too little of it to begin with.

He sat up. He must not let on what he was about, or the arguments would go on all night, and he did hope for sleep before morning. "Kasia, the scrolls we have rescued are not safe anywhere in Nicomedia. You must take them home to Lydda tomorrow."

"Oh . . ." Kasia's large dark eyes misted over, and she looked at Val with a trembling chin. But Georg knew her love of the sacred word would win over her attachment for their friend. "I will go," she said.

"Optio," he said to Valerius.

Val saluted, palm to forehead. "Yes, sir."

"You lead the turma in guard duty tomorrow. I'll sleep here tonight." Valerius didn't argue. The bandages were excuse enough. Val didn't know that Georg could easily have controlled Bayard with pressure from his knees and done a full duty drill without touching his reins, as the North African Light Horsemen did. But Georg had a higher duty to attend to in the morning.

Kasia saw Valerius to the door of her apartment and returned to her brother with her eyes shining softly. Georg would have liked to hold her hands for what he must say to her next. When they were young and she brought her problems to him, he had always held her hands. The harder she squeezed, the harder she was trying not to cry. She seldom cried, but she often squeezed hard enough to leave nail cuts in his hand.

"Kassi, my dear. Sit by me." She, too, started to hold out her hands, then drew back when she saw his bandages. "It's all right. I'll hold them in my heart," he said.

She sat beside him, and he continued. "Kassi, Valerius is one of the finest men I know. But you must not give your heart to him. He's not a believer."

The shadow over her eyes told him that he was giving words to a battle she was already fighting. "But he helped me save the scrolls tonight."

"Yes. And I believe he would have done the same even if it were not for his love for you. But if you do not marry one of the faith, you will not be able to share the most important thing in your life with your husband. I was only ten when our father died, and you were far too young to remember, but I know how much it meant to our parents to share their faith. Do not marry without it, my dear one."

Kasia looked away from him. When she spoke, there was a note of bitterness in her voice. "I don't know. I've been thinking maybe I should marry an unbeliever. Look at the grief being betrothed to a Christian has brought Matterona."

"The holy Scripture warns again unequal marriages. Eventually your happiness would wither away."

Kasia stood and began pacing the floor. "All right, I've listened to your advice, brother. Now you must listen to me. It was a very brave and very, very foolish thing you did tonight. Have you thought of the grief it will bring to our family if you are to share Quintillian's fate?" She turned back to him and gently placed her hands over his bandaged ones. "Oh, Georg. Please be careful. Promise me! Please!"

He smiled at her, his eyes crinkling at the corners. "Don't worry, Kasia. I won't do anything foolish. I have far too much to live for. There are so many things I want to do yet."

Kasia looked unconvinced. "Oh, yes, you say that. But when did you ever give in because it was expedient? You think I'm too young to remember, but I still recall our nurse's despair when she could neither bribe you with fig cakes nor force you with threatened punishments. Mosia always said it was fortunate you chose to do right, for if you had determined on evil, no one could have turned you from it."

"And now would you turn me from the right for a handful of fig cakes?" He grinned. "Well, I *am* rather hungry at the moment."

But Kasia wouldn't be deterred. "No, Georg, don't joke. I'm not asking you to abandon the faith. All I'm saying is, if you have a choice—if it doesn't really matter—"

"The right always matters, Kasia." His voice was almost a whisper.

"But how do you know what's right? How do you know what has the highest value? If Quintillian could have escaped the martyrdom, perhaps he could have lived to accomplish a much higher work—how do you know?"

"Do you really believe that, Kassi?"

She turned away from him, her eyes bright with unshed tears. And when it was time for her to leave in the morning, it was obvious she was still worried, but she didn't reopen the argument.

"See that you take good care of those scrolls. When I get leave, I want to come home and read them. If you can find time to do some copying, see if you can send a copy of that one I singed my hands over to Cadfrawl on Ynis Witrin. Any trader sailing to Isca could carry it for you."

When Kasia and her corps of servants had left, Georg and Pasicrates turned toward the barracks. It took Pasicrates two hours of hard scrubbing on Georgus's mail, greaves, and helmet before he pronounced his master suitable to appear in the imperial palace. Georg had not told him what his errand really was, simply that he had a letter to deliver.

Other than his bandaged hands Georgus looked as impressive as any member of the Imperial Guard when he returned the salute of the sentry at the palace gate and strode down the mosaic hallway to the audience room. Despite its imposing facade, the palace was furnished as sparsely as any fashionable villa where good taste demanded empty spaces of marble and mosaic broken only by occasional pieces of furniture of superb quality. Georgus gave the password to the sentry and was admitted to the antechamber of Diocletian's throne room. He sat on a straight-legged cypress wood stool and looked at the elegantly carved cedar and ivory table beside him. That single table undoubtedly cost more than his yearly pay. Rich oriental draperies, thicker than the woolen blanket on his bunk, hung at the window. Two unoccupied stools completed the room's furnishings.

The door across from Georg burst open, and, as the guards snapped to attention, a red-faced, toga-clad magistrate stormed from the room. Georgus repeated the day's password to the guard and was admitted to the presence of the Augusta. Diocletian, surrounded by aides and clerks, was sitting on a stool beside a writing table. His graying hair curled tightly across his forehead, and deep grooves ran from each side of his nose past a firm mouth to a square jaw.

Georgus dropped to one knee. "Imperator." He extended the sealed parchment he had borne from Isca.

Diocletian rubbed a hand over his brow and signaled Georg to rise. "What is this?" He waved a hand at the scroll.

"A letter from a fellow decurion in Isca. I promised to deliver it personally, Imperator. I can attest to the man's loyalty to the legion and to the Empire."

Scowling, Diocletian took the letter and leaned toward a tall bronze lamp stand in the center of the table. Each of its four hanging lamps burned brightly, casting shadows on the emperor's face as he read. Suddenly he jerked his head up, let the scroll roll shut with a snap, and hit the table with it. "Decurion, do you know what this letter contains?"

"I have not read it, sir. But I believe it is an appeal for the lives of two loyal soldiers."

"Loyal! How can you say they're loyal when they refuse to burn incense to me?"

"They are well-trained, hard-fighting soldiers. They would lay down their lives in duty to the Empire, sir."

"But they are atheists. They reject all our traditional gods. I cannot build a stable empire without religious unity. Such seditionaries must be rubbed out—especially in the army. If the army is riddled with atheists, we cannot hope to hold the Empire together among the civilians."

He rose and handed the letter to the nearest clerk. "They shall certainly be executed as an example to any others in Britain considering such disloyalty. I thought putting that Alban fellow in Verulamium to the sword would be a lesson, but those Britons have ever been a stubborn lot. See to the order," he barked at his clerk.

Georg felt desperate. He wanted to cry out, to protest, to argue. But he could think of nothing more to say. Diocletian turned back to him and for the first time noticed his hands. "How did you do that, decurion?"

"The bonfire last night, Imperator."

"Got too close to the flames, eh? Let that be a warning to you. Seems to be a needed lesson to someone who would present me with a letter from sworn enemies."

Georg knew the case was hopeless, yet he could not let it go. "Decurion Julius is not—"

Diocletian slammed his fist against the table. "All Christians are enemies of the state and of its Augusta. And it's clear to me you need some time in the guardhouse to consider that fact. Guard!"

As he walked out between the guards, Georgus's slumped shoulders were not for his own predicament, but for the failure of his mission. By presenting their case to Diocletian, he had sealed the doom of his friends as surely as if he had intentionally given evidence against them.

11

uardhouse gloom was the same from one end of the Empire to the other, and it made no difference that this jail was attached to the imperial palace. From sheer boredom, Georg rose and stood on the narrow wooden bed so he could see out the small window of his cell. Well, that was one advantage this guardhouse had over others less auspiciously located. The window looked out on the palace gardens. Even in February the rough oaks and olive trees showed a hint of green leaves between the pines bordering the garden wall, and small clumps of white windflowers and purple crocus bloomed in the sunnier corners. Then Georg smiled. Ah, this prison had a decided advantage. The garden was not deserted.

A young woman, not more than twenty years of age, he judged, strolled along the far wall attended by a servant and a small brown lap dog. The maiden's fair hair was arranged in an elegant coiffure, and the graceful folds of her yellow silken stola indicated that she was of the nobility. Strange that he thought of her as a maiden since she was clearly past marriageable age. Then he looked again. No, she was wearing none of the heavy make-up fashionable matrons painted on their faces. She must be younger than her serious expression had led him to believe. She tossed a small ball, and the dog bounded after it. Georg wished she would walk to his side of the garden, but he was not to be so lucky. The small party exited through the gate in the far wall.

"Mar Georg, Mar Georg." His servant's welcome voice summoned Georg to the heavy door of his cell with its small barred window.

"Pasi! How did you get in here?"

The servant smiled. "Mar Valerius is duty officer for the guardhouse today. I have only ten minutes, but he let me in without searching me." His dark eyes gleamed. "I have brought you something to read, but do not let the guard find you with it. I would not be guilty of bringing punishment on you." He slipped a scroll through the bars, and Georg took it awkwardly with his bandaged hands. "I bought this from a Jewish rabbi. Since it is of their sacred writings and not just Christian, if you are caught with it, perhaps they will think you are of the Jewish faith and let you go."

Georg laughed. "Oh, Pasicrates, what would I do without you?" He looked at the label on the cylinder, "The Prophet Jeremiah." "I have never read him. This will indeed help the hours pass. By the way, Pasi, do you hear the servants' gossip? Do you know the names of any of the young noblewomen living in the palace?"

"I hear everything, Mar Georg." Pasicrates seemed affronted that his master could doubt it. "The Lady Valeria, Diocletian's daughter, is here with her mother, the Empress Prisca."

"The Lady Valeria, what does she look like?"

"I have never seen her, Mar Georg, but they say she is short and dark, ripely plump like a plum."

"No, that is not the one I saw. Who else have you heard of?"

"Galerius's daughter, the Lady Alexandra. She was betrothed to Maximian's nephew, but Galerius and Maximian have quarreled, and they say the betrothal has been broken off."

"What a treasure house you are, Pasi. Do you continue with your writing?"

"Yes, Mar Georg. Always. But I am almost out of papyrus leaves."

"Well, if I'm not out of this cell in time to help you, ask Valerius to buy you some. Tell him I'll pay him back when I get out."

The guard rattled the door at the end of the hall as a signal that Pasicrates's time was up.

Georg heard the door clang shut. He was alone again. Strange. He had thought he was growing accustomed to the solitude, but even such a small taste of fellowship showed him how much he missed his friends and his active life. He longed to leap astride Bayard and gallop over the rolling hills that he could just glimpse through his barred window. He paced his cell for a time, three strides to one wall, about-face, three strides back. How he would like an invigorating plunge in the baths and a good workout in the exercise yard.

At last he flung himself on his bunk and picked up the scroll Pasi had brought him. He had to unroll it against his left arm and hold it open with his right elbow to keep from hurting his hands, but he soon got used to it. But the light was too dim. He climbed up on his bunk and stood by the open window to read. After a few sentences he shook his head and started over. He couldn't concentrate on the words, even though they had been styled by an exceedingly neat copyist. He started again.

The words swam before his eyes like fish in the household carp pond. The scroll could have been written in a barbaric language for all the sense it was making to him. He started to fling it aside; then the sound of a bird outside his window made him realize that part of the trouble was the absolute silence of his cell. He was the only prisoner in the guardhouse at the moment, and the guards were standing duty outside the hall door. Well, it could do no harm to attempt reading out loud. There was only the small brown bird to hear him. Besides, as Pasi had pointed out, if anyone heard him in passing they would think him Jewish.

Moving closer to the window for better light, Georg read, "'Blessed is the man who trusts in the Lord, whose hope is the Lord.'" At first the sound of his own voice startled him. Even his hushed tones reverberated off the jail walls. But in a moment the beauty of the words gripped him, and he read louder.

"'He is like a tree planted beside the waters that stretches out its roots to the stream. It fears not the heat when it comes; its leaves stay green. In the year of drought it shows no distress, but still bears fruit.'"

He read on until the light of God's presence filled his soul, and he lowered the scroll and lifted his voice to Heaven. "'O God who cares for the needs of all who follow You, hear me now. Lord God of hosts, happy is the man who trusts in You, even in the time of drought as we now endure. Send Your spirit of love to make us faithful witnesses to You in the sight of all mankind—'" He paused for breath. "'—no matter what the cost. You desire to bring all nations to salvation. Let all Your servant does bring praise to You and carry out Your loving plan.'" He dropped his voice to a whisper. "Grant this through Christ our Lord, amen."

There was a small rustle outside his window. The bird flew away. Another reading had been copied after the words of the prophet, but the light was growing dim, so Georg replaced the scroll in its cylinder and tucked it under his blanket before the guard brought in his evening bowl of wheat gruel. Tonight the coarse soldiers' soup contained chunks of goat meat and boiled lentils with a slab of hard bread beside it. It made a filling, even tasty meal.

The next morning he was wakened by a trill from his little brown friend on the olive branch outside his window. Jentaculum consisted of a hunk of panis siccus, the ubiquitous army bread made of soaked spelt grits mixed with raisin juice and baked hard in earthenware pots. He dipped it in his cup of wine to soften it, then chewed each bite thoroughly to make it more filling. Odd how he could normally do a full morning of drill on such fare and never think of hunger, but here where there was nothing to do but think, he was ever hungry.

He turned again to his scroll. *Bless Pasi for smuggling it in.* Again Georg stood on his bunk to catch the light. The copyist had taken this reading from the Psalms, and it soon became apparent to Georg that the only way to experience fully the beauty of the words was to read aloud. "'I will give You glory, O God my King; I will bless Your name forever. Day after day, for so long as I live, I will praise Your name. Age to age shall proclaim Your works and declare Your mighty deeds. They shall speak of Your splendor and glory and tell of Your wonderful works. The kingdom of our Lord is an everlasting kingdom. His rule endures from age to age.'"

The last he read as the true prayer of his heart. "'To You, O Lord, my God, I lift up my soul. It is in Your hands. I trust in You. Do not let your enemies triumph over the faith. Those who hope in You shall not be disappointed, but those who break faith shall reap desolation.'"

In the quiet that followed his reading Georg heard again the gentle rustle outside his window. But this time he realized that the bird was still on its branch.

It was midday before the quiet of the cell was broken again, this time by the tramp of heavy caligae on stone floors and the clank of a massive door. "Decurion Anastasius, you're to go. Caesar says the service'll do you good. Although what one of the faith is doing in the guardhouse is beyond me." He flung the cell door back with a clank and motioned forward with his pilum. Georg barely had time to snatch up his blanket with the scroll inside. "By the blood of the sun, you'll give us all a bad name if you don't behave."

Georgus was too confused by the man's speech even to ask questions as he was marched from the jail. Val was waiting for him outside. "What is going on?" Georg asked his friend as soon as they were out of the guard's hearing. "That guard was rambling on about the blood of the Son."

Valerius laughed. "*S-u-n* that was. See, confusion of the religions can be a handy thing. And, my friend, it's the light of Mithras that's shining on your head today."

"What are you talking about?"

"I appealed to Galerius for your release—said you were in there for delivering a letter from a fellow officer who happened to be a Christian. But you needed to be out in time for a Mithra initiation this evening."

Georg groaned. "First Pasi wants me to go around masquerading as a Jew. Now you're trying to turn me into a bull-worshiper. Why don't I just give up and burn incense to Jupiter?" He did a sharp about-face in the street. "On second thought, I preferred life in the guardhouse."

Valerius grabbed his arm and spun him around again. "Not your initiation—mine. Of course, I omitted that detail in my discussion with Galerius." An eager glitter suddenly filled Valerius's eyes. "I'm to become *Perses* tonight, Georg. I can't tell you what it means to me. I want you there. Do you realize I have only two more levels to go until I can enter the pit and be baptized with the blood of a sacrificed bull!"

Georg shook his head. How foreign this was from the peace he had known a few hours ago in his cell reading from the sacred writings.

At deep dusk that night Valerius donned the white tunic and Phrygian cap of an initiate and led the way to the sacred grotto in the hills beyond Nicomedia. The magus and several of the faith who had attained high levels were gathered at the mouth of the cave. Each was robed in a garment of his rank—a raven with black feathers and a beak, a soldier in armor, a lion in a magnificent lion skin, a Persian in Phrygian cap, a runner of the sun in a golden radiate headdress. Georgus observed the last figure for several minutes before he recognized him as Plotius. With a start he realized that even though the man was under his command, he had hardly thought of him since they came to Nicomedia. He wondered if the German still wanted his job.

The priest recited a prayer. Then all the worshipers chanted a hymn. Only Georgus stood apart from the ceremony. Valerius approached the priest who took an amber flask and poured honey over the hands of the initiate and onto his tongue. "This sweet substance, produced under the influence of the moon, contains marvelous preservative powers. This was the food of the blessed ones of old, and by its absorption you become a peer of the gods," the magus said.

When Valerius had eaten the honey, he chanted the charmed invocation, "*Nama, Nama Sebesio. Nama, Nama Sebesio.*" The procession moved into the cave beyond Georgus's view. When they returned some time later, chanting another hymn, they stopped at the mouth of the cave and knelt. The priest passed down the row of worshipers with a loaf of bread and cup of wine from which each partook. Then the service was over.

Valerius talked in an excited, high-pitched voice all the way back to the barracks. "Georgus, if only I could tell you what it felt like—the solitude of the sacred grotto—the mystical sensations. The whole universe sang—shining stars, whispering wind, babbling brook—even the very earth under my feet was divine."

Georg ushered the effusive Val into the decurion's cubicula. "Just two more levels and I shall attain perfect wisdom and purity!"

Pasicrates entered from the back room. "Some cold water for our friend to wash his face in, I think, Pasi."

After a few cold splashes Valerius was calm enough to sit on the stool Georg offered him. "How can you attend such an event and not be moved to fear for the infinite forces that sway the universe?"

"Because the Infinite Force that sways the universe is my friend. Those called of God have no need to fear because He accepts them in love. There is no fear that I haven't worked my way up to a high enough level."

At last Valerius's voice was steady. "And you have been called by your God—you have been chosen?"

"Certainly. We are all God's creation. He calls all, and all who answer His call are chosen."

Valerius shook his head and turned to his own cubicula.

As February ran toward March and the rolling green hillsides above the bay blossomed forth with wild flowers, life in the Palace Guard seemed in harmony with nature. Guard duty followed its routine—everyone rode to precision in drill practice; uniforms and armor shone with amazing polish at inspection. There were no new rumors of Christian persecutions, and the world seemed at peace.

In Georgus's room one evening after drill, peace expanded into joy for Valerius when he discovered in the weekly mail packet two letters for him. Perusing the first, a slow smile spread over his face. "Ah, your sister is eloquent with her stylus."

Georg looked up from his own letter from his family. "Yes, it sounds as though everything is well at the Villa Anastasii. Sometimes I long to be back there. Do you ever regret joining the legion, Val?"

"Not me. I have no desire to return to the family villa until I am deemed worthy of my position in the family—which probably means never—so the legion is the place for me. You want to go back?"

Georg nodded slowly, a faraway look in his eye. "I was just thinking—if anything ever happened, I'd want to be buried there."

Val laughed. "Such gloomy thoughts are unlike you. You're sure to die an old, old man with twenty grandchildren around your knobby knees pulling on your long gray beard. Especially now that Caesar seems to have backed off a bit."

They both returned to their letters. Suddenly Valerius broke the silence. "Blood of bulls! What did I just say about easing up? Letter from my father. He reports they put Julius and Aaron to the sword. There was another general sacrifice in the legion just after we left. Julius and Aaron refused to recant or burn incense, so Candidus ordered their execution. Father says many feared they would be thrown to wild animals in the amphitheater on Lupercalia, but as they were Roman citizens, they were spared that indignity and beheaded quietly."

Georg shook his head, then dropped it into his almost healed hands. "At least they weren't tortured. A quick death is a merciful gateway to paradise. But torture—" He shuddered. "Wait. Did you say Lupercalia? The Ides of February? Ah, then my bumbling appeal to Diocletian didn't have anything to do with it. The deed had been done a week before."

Valerius placed his hand gently on his friend's back. "I'm sorry about your friends . . . but at least we have peace here now. That's the way these emperors are—burn a few scrolls, lop off a head here and there; then we can all get back to normal. Just be sure to duck when the Imperator's in a sword-swinging mood."

Val went off to bed, but Georg could not sleep. *Burn a few scrolls?* The greatest library of sacred writings in the world? *Lop off a head here and there?* The Theban Legion, Quintillian, Julius, Aaron. How many hundreds—thousands—of fellow Christians had been tortured and had died for the faith in the three hundred years since Christ was on earth?

But the thought of Christ calmed him. Nothing any follower of Christ could possibly be asked to bear could be as great as the anguish He bore when He took the sins of the world upon His shoulders on the cross. No matter how much one wanted to cry out and rage against the torments inflicted by evil, in the end it had to be a glory to be chosen to share even a small part of His Lord's suffering.

The quiet during which Georg rolled into his blanket and drifted off to sleep lasted until two hours before cockcrow. The clanging of an alarm bell brought him upright in his bunk. Pasicrates rushed in with his tunic and sandals. "Fire, Mar Georg! The church, I think. I see flames just beyond the wall." He gestured wildly as Georg dressed hastily. Although Nicomedia had a Cohortes Vigilum to provide police and fire protection like the one Augusta had organized in Rome, any alarm in the palace district was the business of the Guard. Georg grabbed his helmet and strode to the stable to order his turma into formation. They would be lucky if they could control the crowd that would already be gathering.

Riding up the Via Nerva, Georg saw that Pasicrates had been wrong. It was not the church that was aflame, but the imperial palace itself. He ordered the cavalry to cordon the palace and push back the excited onlookers who would have gladly swarmed over the walls and looted their emperor. The foot guard was forming a fire brigade—armed with buckets, axes, some inefficient leather hoses, and hand pumps.

It was amazing that a marble and mosaic building could burn. Yet, as the second leather hose burst, sending more water over the cavalry guards than over the palace, the flames seemed to burn brighter than ever. Suddenly Georg became aware of a pool of calm efficiency in the sea of confusion. A tall legate in an Imperial Guard uniform shouted firm commands to his cohort. As if his commands had been to the hoses themselves, water began to flow onto the blaze.

In a shorter time than Georgus could have thought possible, the orange flames turned to black smoke. The legate's orders changed to commands for cleaning out the smoke-damaged rooms and checking for anyone injured inside the wrecked rooms. Soldiers pulled still-smoking couches into the garden and piled half-burned oriental rugs beneath the veranda at his direction. The onlookers began to drift away as sunrise called them to jentaculum and the day's work. Georgus dismissed half his men, then ordered the remaining half to continue street patrol. "Who is that legate?" he asked Valerius who rode up to receive fresh orders.

"Constantine. Son of Constantius Chlorus. Rumor is that when the Caesar of the West threatened to become too powerful after his victories in Britain and Gaul, Diocletian ordered Chlorus's son to be sent to court as a sort of hostage. Of course that's just rumor, but he doesn't seem very happy here.

Before Georg could reply, a carnyx sounded orders. Officers were to assemble. Georgus gathered his reins and rode toward the front of the palace. Diocletian addressed his officers from the top of the palace steps with a triumphant-looking Galerius standing behind him. "Men, I thank you for your quick work tonight that has saved my palace. The ladies' chambers have been much damaged, but no lives lost. Repairs shall begin before sundown." A cheer greeted the Augusta's speech.

He held up his hand for quiet. "Further, the cause of the fire has been uncovered by noble Galerius. The evil, atheistic cult followers who live among us and call themselves Christians set this fire in retaliation for my orders that their temple be purged of blasphemous writings. We will not tolerate such insurrection. Lawlessness will not go unpunished in my Empire. Jupiter and the gods will be avenged!"

Now the cheers were jubilant. "Hail Caesar!" "Hail Augusta!" "Hail Imperator!" As the shouts rose in pitch, Georg noticed that the tall legate standing a little apart from the others was the only other officer who remained silent.

Georg rode slowly back to the barracks with Bayard on a loose rein, wondering what form this new extermination order would take. It seemed there was little the emperor could do that hadn't been attempted already. Perhaps now it would get bad enough that the Lord would return to take His own home. Perhaps this was to be the great persecution of the end times. Surely three hundred years of waiting and enduring was enough. Georg smiled at the thought of the awe, then fear that would replace Galerius's smirk when the Lord returned.

No matter how he argued to himself that Galerius was God's creation, he could find no love in his heart for this man who seemed to radiate evil. Christianity had grown and flourished under a policy of toleration during the first twenty years of Diocletian's reign. But as soon as Galerius returned from his Persian wars, the Christians had been blamed and punished for everything that went wrong in the Empire. Even the sheer political force of the vast numbers of Christians in every class of society was no deterrent to this man's fanaticism. Georg thought of Meribah standing in the corner of his barracks room. With a sudden anger, Georg could fully sympathize with the rage that had led the Apostle Peter to cut off a man's ear.

In Georgus's imagination Galerius took on the form of the great serpent he had slain on Ynis Witrin. And Georg attacked with the bronze sword of Peter, driving the blade deep into the throat of the dragon of iniquity until he lay still at Bayard's feet.

Georg clenched his fists on his reins. At that moment he felt he could gladly take on all the forces of evil in single combat and conquer them in the name of the Lord Jesus Christ.

But in fact he could do nothing. He turned Bayard toward the drill field to begin a day of routine duty.

12

he quiet of routine was shattered, however, when they returned from drill duty two days later to see a large crowd gathered around the high wooden front door of the church. A white parchment square gleamed in the sun in the center of the door. Georg and Valerius drew their horses to a halt at the back of the crowd. Eusebius stood on the top step before the church he had pastored faithfully for so many years. The church that had once stood as a sentinel of the faith and a treasure house of its writings was an empty shell, but the pastor continued his shepherding duties.

Eusebius turned to read the document posted there by the Imperial Guards who now retreated up the street. He shook his head, then read again, as if the words would change at another reading. Finally he turned to the assembled crowd and read aloud to them:

> By the imperial decree of Augusta Gaius Aurelius Valerius Diocletian, be it known that the seditious activities of the cult of those who call themselves Christians and refuse to do rightful honor and worship to the gods of the Empire shall forthwith cease. If those calling themselves Christians continue in their betrayal of the Empire and its gods, their property shall be seized and their lives forfeit.
>
> By my hand,
> Caesar Galerius

Consternation swept through the crowd. Their property? Their lives? Did the Augusta have any idea how many Christians there were in the Empire? Even just here in Nicomedia? Many of the emperor's own servants and higher palace staff members—his loyal minister of finance who was said to be such a genius at balancing the budget. Rumor even said Diocletian's own wife and daughter had espoused the faith. Could such an edict be enforced?

From the back of the crowd a voice rang out above their confused murmurings. "No! That is an instrument of evil. It should not hang on the door of this sacred building." The anger of Georgus's imaginary battle with the serpent/Galerius, with evil itself, returned to fill his mind. The moment he had waited for all his life had come.

"Georg, be careful." Valerius reached out to restrain his friend, but already Georg was moving forward on his mount, the crowd parting to make room. The sun gleamed golden on Georgus's bronze helmet and on Bayard's milk-white coat, rippling down the flowing mane and tail like a waterfall. At the foot of the stairs Georg dismounted.

The crowd quieted, and the tread of each mailed sandal reverberated on the stone steps as Georg ascended. Eusebius stepped forward to meet him at the top step holding out his arms like a prophet of old. "And Rome shall be like mighty Babylon. Her end shall be like that foreseen by the prophet Isaiah: The glory of the kingdom shall be no more. And the wild beasts shall cry in their desolate houses and the dragons in their pleasant places. Her time draws near, and her days have not long to run. And it shall be a habitation of dragons."

Eusebius stepped back, and Georg drew his sword. That morning he had chosen to wear Meribah rather than his regulation sword. Now he knew why. Stepping forward, Georg held aloft the sword of Saint Peter, thrust it behind the heavy parchment document, and rent the edict from top to bottom.

The crowd half-cheered, half-gasped in fear. Many stood in frozen shock, many cried, many prayed. Georg alone showed no emotion. He stood before them, the sun shining on his strong, tanned features, his eyes steady as he watched the approach of the guards up the Via Venta. His only movement was to hand Meribah to Valerius, who had moved forward to hold Bayard. Val would care for his two most prized possessions.

Eusebius, just behind him, spoke again in his rich voice. "'And there was war in heaven; Michael and his angels fought against the dragon; and the dragon fought and his angels. And the great dragon was cast out, that old serpent, called the Devil, and Satan, which deceiveth the whole world. He was cast out into the earth and his angels were cast out with him. And I heard a loud voice saying in heaven, "Now is come salvation, and strength, and the kingdom of our God, and the power of His Christ."'"

The guards reached the bottom of the steps and leveled their pilums. Georg didn't make them come up for him, but stepped down, taking his place between the spear points.

As they marched through the crowd, Eusebius's voice followed them.

"'And they overcame the evil one by the blood of the Lamb and by the word of their testimony, and they loved not their lives unto the death.'"

Claiming the right of a Roman citizen, Georgus appealed to Diocletian, but the appeal was denied. Caesar Galerius would hear his case. The great basilica of the seat of Roman power was crowded with spectators as Galerius and the sixty-nine nobles who were to sit in judgment took their places on the curving marble benches under the great arched ceiling.

All through the night Georg had prayed for strength for this trial. He had always been an intensely private person. He had stood for what he believed, but only on individual terms, not as a spokesman for the faith. He had sought the ability to be more eloquent as he studied with Cadfrawl, but no moving speeches or fluent prayers came to his mind. During the night he had thought only of Christ in the garden and had prayed with Him, "If it is Your will, let this cup pass from me." Now he looked out on those who had come to view the trial, mostly strangers, but a few faces he recognized—a broadly grinning Plotius, Valerius looking distressed, Pasicrates weeping openly, and Constantine, whom he had not seen since the palace fire, watching with a look of open questioning. The only prayer his mind would form ran over and over, *Lord, let me stand. Let me honor You.*

"Georgus Nestor Anastasius, Decurion of the Sixth Turma, First Ala, Legio II Augusta, you are charged with willfully and publicly destroying imperial property in tearing down the emperor's edict against the evil Christian cult. You are furthermore charged with being a member of the aforesaid cult in opposition to the wishes and decrees of the emperor. The penalty is death. How do you plead?"

Here was Georgus's chance to make an eloquent, brilliantly reasoned speech that would convince his jury of the rightness of his stand and turn the hearts of his listeners to Christ. As he sought for those words, however, the only image that came to him was of Christ standing silent before His accusers.

"What does the prisoner have to say for himself?" the prosecutor roared.

"I am a Christian. I believe on the Lord Jesus Christ."

The room was silent. Georg stood straight, his head up as his words seemed to echo and reecho off the marble walls. The sixty-nine nobles turned their thumbs down. Georgus was found guilty as charged.

Galerius, in his elegantly draped toga with purple bands, spoke from an elevated stool in the center of the nobles. "Come now, it would be apparent from your face and bearing, even if I did not know your distinguished lineage, that you are noble. In the three years that I have sat in this seat of judgment, I have never heard a voice that rang like yours with the statement, 'I am a Christian.'

"But we cannot forgive your blasphemy simply because you are noble and speak with conviction. For it is not us alone whom you have blasphemed, but also our gods. You have denied their divinity.

"From this very moment if you will abandon such speech, repent, and bow down and worship the gods, all the Caesars will welcome you. You shall receive from us and from our gods great honors and royal rank. You shall be governor over ten of the greatest cities of the world, with their provinces and their peoples."

And the devil took him up into a high mountain and showed Him all the kingdoms of the world and the glory of them; "All these things will I give you, if you will fall down and worship me." As the image filled Georgus's mind, the devil bore Galerius's face. Small webbed wings grew on his scaly back, and a barbed tail flicked beneath his robe.

Georg heard himself answer, "'It is written, you shall worship the Lord your God, and Him only shall you serve.'"

Galerius's face contorted with anger. Then, as he overcame his rage with a visible effort, a sly gleam shone from his eyes. "I will not be the executioner of the grandson of the Count of Lydda. Georgus Anastasius, you are to come to the palace as my guest where we shall all pray to Jupiter and the gods that you may be redeemed from the error of your ways."

Confusion filled the basilica at Galerius's announcement. As Georg walked out behind Caesar and the other nobles, the auditorium rang with both cheers and angry comments. Plotius was among the angry. Pasicrates wept passionately—but this time for joy. Valerius looked relieved, and Constantine, with no change in his watching attitude, joined the procession up the hill to the palace.

Georg looked around his elegantly appointed room in the palace in amazement. This morning he had thought his head would be off his shoulders by sundown. Instead he had been given one of the finest guest rooms. He stepped out onto his second-story veranda and looked across the garden. At first he thought he was looking at the same garden he had seen from his guardhouse cell, but then he remembered he had seen the women's garden from there, so this would be different. The palace was so sprawling, it was impossible to keep one's bearings.

Still with a sense of unreality, he stepped back into the room just as a knock sounded at his door. Expecting a slave with his evening linen, Georg called out, "Come in."

He was surprised that a serving girl should be so finely dressed. With an appreciative smile he watched the gold and scarlet silk-clad figure cross his room. Then she pushed her palla back from her head, and Georgus recognized the lady he had observed walking in the garden. "The Lady Alexandra, I believe." He made a deep bow. "I am honored, my lady."

She had come without her maid, but her little brown dog scampered from beneath the folds of her stola. As she stood there in the center of the room, she seemed suddenly shy, as if only now did she realize what a brazen thing she was doing in visiting a man in his room—a prisoner even, although this luxurious house arrest hardly seemed like an imprisonment.

"You have come with a message from your father, Galerius?" Georg prompted her.

"Yes. I—that is, no—" She looked at her hands, then sought to locate her dog. "Here, Leto." The little brown bundle scampered to her mistress.

"Leto? The gentlest and kindest of all the Olympian wives."

Alexandra scooped up her pet and held her in her arms. "Yes, actually she's a squirmy nuisance, but I thought if I gave her a gentle name, it might have a calming effect."

"And has it worked?"

Leto wriggled in her mistress's arms. "Alas, no."

Georg crossed the room and gently stroked the dog on her chest. She calmed instantly and lay her head on Georgus's red-scarred hand. Alexandra gasped. "Why, I've never seen her do that! How did you know what to do?"

Georg smiled. "I had a dog very much like this when I was a boy. . . . Won't you sit down, my lady? I am surprised Galerius would send his daughter into the lions' den." Then his eyes twinkled. "Ah, but then, it's only Christians who need fear being thrown to the lions, isn't it?"

"Don't!" She held out a hand in protest, and her eyes filled with concern.

"I'm sorry if my small joke distresses you, my lady. What is the message your father would have you deliver?"

Alexandra perched on the edge of the stool Georg offered her. "I—I am to persuade you of the error of your ways." She looked at the floor. "By any means possible." The last came out in a whisper.

Georg stared in amazement. Surely not even Galerius . . . "You have nothing to fear from me, my lady."

She looked up with a shy, but bright smile. "Oh, I know that. That is why I consented to the errand. But in truth I have come to learn more of your God. I would have you read more to me."

"Read—more—?"

"When you were in the guardhouse. It was you, wasn't it, who read by the open window? I was certain it was when I heard your voice again."

Georg frowned, trying to recall what she was talking about. "Yes, I read aloud in my cell, but—Ah, I do remember—the tiny rustle I thought was a bird. You were listening?"

Alexandra nodded. "This silly scamp," she said looking at the dog who now snuggled calmly in her arms, "carried her ball to that side of the garden, and I chased her. I have never heard such words. I would hear more."

"My lady—"

"Please." She looked at him from under her long eyelashes. "My friends call me Sabra."

"Sabra. That is lovely." Georg felt a weight on his chest as if he were wearing mail instead of his loose tunic. The room seemed short on air.

"Will you read more to me?"

"Gladly." He jumped to his feet. But what would he read? Surely his scrolls hadn't been brought with his kit from the barracks. He turned to the pack on the floor by his couch. Amazingly, they were there. "It is a miracle. I can't think who would have risked his neck to bring these into the royal palace." He unrolled a scroll and read the first thing he came to.

If he had searched all the scrolls of Cadfrawl's library, however, he couldn't have found one that better expressed his feelings at the moment. "'Praise ye the Lord. Praise the Lord, O my soul. While I live, I will praise the Lord. I will sing praises to my God while I have any being. Put not your trust in princes nor in the son of any man. Man's breath goes forth, and he returns to earth. But happy is he that has the God of Jacob for his help, whose help is in the Lord his God which made heaven and earth, the sea and all that is. He keeps truth forever. The Lord preserves the righteous, but the way of the wicked He turns upside down. The Lord shall reign forever, even your God, to all generations. Praise be to the Lord.'"

Sabra sat long after the words ended. "That is even more beautiful than I remembered. And you read it with such conviction. Every word rings with truth. Tell me about the Christ that makes you so happy even in the face of a death sentence."

Georgus's words tumbled over themselves as he told her of the Son of God who came to earth as a baby, lived and taught among men, and died for their sins. He told her how one could come to know God personally and have His peace in his heart through faith. And when he was done, he looked at her in amazement. "That is the longest speech I've ever made in my life. I can't believe it. Oh, I mean, I believe every word I said, I just find it hard to believe I said it all." Sabra joined his laughter.

"It was wonderful! Thank you. I shall tell my father we talked and talked of nothing but religion, but that you are not yet fully convinced of the error of your ways, and that I should return—to the lions' den."

Georg walked her to the door, his eyes sparkling. "Please, do not suggest lions to your father."

At the door she turned, serious once more, but all she said was a whispered, "Good night."

Georgus's meals were brought to his room by a team of slaves, dishes as rich and as graciously served as any that could have appeared before Caesar. He was shown to the palace baths and urged to make full use of the exercise rooms, gardens, and library as well. Never could a convicted enemy of the state have had a more sumptuous arrest.

But Georg fully understood the message. Bow to Caesar, and all this shall be yours. Well, he had no intention of bowing, but he could see no harm in enjoying a bath.

Late that evening, after a slave had left with the remains of cena, Georg heard the knock he had been anticipating all day. But when he flung the door open, he stopped in surprise. "Well, I must say, you don't look very pleased to see your best friend." Valerius dismissed the servant who had accompanied him and entered the room.

"Of course I'm pleased to see you, just surprised."

"Oh, there was no trouble getting in. I've been made the new decurion, and Plotius finally got his optio position. I would have come sooner, but we've had duty all day—while you've been living the life of the Caesars up here at the palace." He plucked a pomegranate from a brass bowl and tore open its russet skin. He sucked several of the shimmery, ruby seed clusters before he spoke. "Georg, Pasi misses you, Bayard misses you, I miss you. Drill was a mess today without you there. And think of your family. Think of Kassi." He said her name with a special tenderness. "It's a great world out there, and you've just got a good start on things. Don't give it all up for an idea."

Georg looked at him sadly. "I think I've just got a start on something you don't even know about."

Encouraged, Val continued. "Right! Now look, you don't have to say you believe in Jupiter. Hardly anyone does anyway—he's just a symbol of the Empire, or something. I'm not really sure what all that pantheon business is. But now, you've seen how similar Mithra is to Christianity. It shouldn't be difficult to change religions; the moral code is exactly the same."

"Yes. The morals are the same. But you don't have Christ, and any moral code is meaningless without a Savior."

"We have Mithra. And he offers eternity, too. So why get your head lopped off when you can't be sure which religion is right anyway?"

"But I am sure. You once told me you chose Mithra because it's active. You could earn your way up the steps. I'm sure because I don't have to rely on my own actions. If I had to earn my way, I could never be sure I was good enough. But I don't have to be good enough because Christ is, and He's given me His righteousness."

"And you're sure enough to bet your life on it?"

"I'm betting something a lot more important than my life on it—a few years one way or another aren't that important—I'm betting eternity on it."

Shaking his head, Valerius put the half-eaten pomegranate back in its bowl and left the room. *What kind of God could inspire a man to give up everything, even life itself?* he wondered. *Would I die for Mithra?* He knew the answer.

Sabra did not come for two more days. Georg was thoroughly bored with rich food, luxurious baths, and walks in the garden. If Galerius's object had been to teach the emptiness of such material things, his plan would have been a great success.

On the third day, Georgus opened his door to a light knock and beheld a tear-streaked Sabra. He had barely closed the door before she flung herself into his arms. "Oh, Georg, I could not come back to you until I was sure. This afternoon I prayed as you told me how, and I found Him—I am sure."

He held her to him. "Sabra, that's wonderful! But why are you crying?"

"Because I am so happy. And so frightened."

"You needn't be frightened. Even Galerius—er, your father won't punish you for your belief."

"Oh, no." She pushed back and smiled at him through glistening eyes. "I'm not frightened for that. I'm frightened because knowing Him is so wonderful. I never knew such exquisite happiness existed. But I'm afraid it cannot last . . . and I fear for your life." Her eyes seemed to say more than her lips, and he read in them the pain of hopes that dared not spring to life, of dreams still-born.

He pulled her to him again, and his own pain welled up and threatened to consume him. He held her in silence for few moments. Then he put his lips on hers. It was a kiss as full of the promise of joy as of its fulfillment, of tender sweetness and awakened desire.

Heavy footsteps stopped outside the room, and the sound of metal crashing on the door made them jump apart. Georg turned to open the door, but before he could, it was flung open and four palace guards marched in. "Caesar demands to know if this is the way you repay his hospitality!" The first guard stood six inches in front of Georg, shouting at him while the other three ransacked the room.

Georg moved to shield Sabra, but then he realized the soldiers had no interest in her. "I could save your men some time if you'd tell me what they're looking for."

"We have received a report that you have had the audacity to bring your filthy pornography into the palace where you stay as a guest of Caesar Galerius."

"Oh." A great deal suddenly became clear to Georg. "A report from the new optio of the Sixth—who undoubtedly packed my kit bag to send it over here. Well, tell Plotius I wish him well. You'll find the scroll under my couch. It rolled there when I finished reading this afternoon."

The guard crashed his pilum to the floor hard enough to chip a mosaic. "So, you admit it!"

It was not the dark, dampness, and discomfort of the dungeon that bothered Georg half so much as his memory of Leto's pitiful whimper and the look of desolation in Sabra's eyes as he had been marched from the room.

Georgus had no idea how many days—or nights he had languished there. Since it was always dark, it was impossible to know. At first he kept count of the number of times he was served barley gruel, but the exercise seemed pointless. He calculated that it must be getting on into spring, but no warmth penetrated the thick stone walls, and the only flowers or birdsong were in his memory. He saw the jailer twice a day when he brought the gruel and emptied Georgus's slop pail. Other than that his only companions were the rats.

He feared he might be left there literally to rot. But then, without warning, he was roused from a fitful sleep. With a clang of iron locks and stamp of mailed caligae on stone floors, two legionnaires pulled him to his feet and shoved him along a corridor. If he had hoped for an improvement in circumstances, his hopes were dashed when he saw the room they now entered. Even the dim light made him blink. In one corner lay a stack of clubs, some bearing dark brown stains from use in carrying out a sentence of fastuarium—beating to death—the usual punishment meted out on deserters. At the far end of the room Georgus saw a large spiked wheel. In brackets on the left wall hung a collection of francisia, the most efficient execution tools known.

If Georg could choose his instrument of torture, he wanted the quick, clean battle-axe. But he was not given a choice. From another bracket the guard took down a scourging whip of many tails, about half of its long, narrow leather thongs tipped with small iron balls. It was favored by a tormentor who wished to appear lenient because it could turn the deeper layers of a victim's flesh into a pulp without breaking the skin. Many a prisoner had been crippled for life with a few skillfully applied cracks of the whip and yet bore not a cut or bruise on the skin.

The soldier shook out the tails in the whip, flexed his wrist, and then took a practice swing that made every thong snap. As if on cue, a clerk entered and sat at a small table, a block of wax and stylus in his hand. "Georgus N. Anastasius?"

"Yes."

"Do you repent of your declaration of belief in the false religion known as Christianity?"

"I do not."

"Do you renounce your belief in the divinity of an executed criminal known as Jesus Christ?"

"I do not."

The clerk nodded to the guard.

Georg prayed for strength as the first blow fell across his bare back. The pain in his shoulder shot clear through his body, but he remained on his feet.

The second blow was aimed lower and he heard his ribs crack. As the blows fell with increased fury, Georg felt waves of pain engulf him. *Lord, help me. Lord . . .* his mind cried out with each blow of the iron balls.

Just when he thought he would slip into merciful oblivion, the blows ceased.

"Do you recant your faith in Jesus Christ?"

"No."

"Do you repent of your dealings with the treasonous cult of Christians?"

"No."

The blows came again, harder and faster than before, but now he was so numb he could hardly feel the iron balls crashing into his broken body with dull thuds. He fell to his knees.

Georg was bracing against the rhythm of the thuds with such concentration that it took a second for him to realize that the torture had stopped.

"Repent."

"No."

The clerk shrugged and left the room. Georg had no idea if he could walk—indeed if he would ever walk again—as many of the blows had fallen on his thighs, breaking deep into the heavy muscles. But for the moment it didn't matter, as his torturers simply dragged him back to his cell and threw him on the dirty straw covering the floor. He landed on his broken rib and passed out.

He was a child again, home in Lydda, running free across a green field, his face to the wind. He laughed and shook his head like a horse, savoring the exquisite wonder of life. A butterfly flew just ahead of him, and the sun was warm on his head, the grass sweet beneath his feet. Ah, life! The beauty of life as God had created it to be in His world, unspoiled, uncorrupted. The butterfly flew into the sun, and as Georg watched it, the world spun, and he fell into the grass laughing. But he must have landed on a rock because his side hurt.

A flicker of consciousness returned, and Georg willed himself to sink into oblivion again. He couldn't face the pain. But this time the dream was more painful than the reality. *Sabra was before him. Beautiful, gentle Sabra, holding out her hands to him, telling him she loved him. Never had the world seemed a more beautiful place than now that he knew it contained Sabra. She was in the world and in his heart, and wonder of wonders, he was in hers. He did not want to leave the world that held Sabra. He reached out his arms to her, and she came into them, sweet and warm and alive.*

But this time when he awoke, he could not will himself back to oblivion. He must face the pain, the dark, the stench. He shifted to put more weight on his less damaged side and scooped a little straw under his shoulder to protect it from the hard stone. Even awake his dream was with him. He could close his eyes and feel her gentle touch on his cheek. And he knew that it need not be only a dream. He could recant. Burn a chunk of incense, bow before a marble statue, and live the rest of his life with Sabra. He needn't even sacrifice eternity. God would forgive him. He could repent and be taken back into the Savior's arms. He could. It was possible.

The beauty of the world, the challenge of the eagles, the sweetness of Sabra—they could still all be his. Then, as clearly as if spoken by human voice, the question came to him: *Do you love these more than Me?*

Another image filled his mind—not a dream this time. He saw his dying Lord on the cross, pouring out His life's blood for him, for Georg. He looked into the Savior's pain-filled eyes, and he saw love there—incredible love—love that had given him being in the first place and now held nothing back—love that melted his heart and warmed his entire being. Georg felt himself drawn into the depths within those eyes until he felt a oneness with his suffering Savior, a wholeness, aliveness, indescribable intimacy, and a sense of destiny—for this moment he had been created.

"Oh, my God . . . my God . . ." he wept. He could find no more words.

For three more days he lay in his cell. He forced himself to drink a little of the barley gruel the jailer brought twice a day. He wanted to have the physical strength to face the end. He forgot the darkness of the cell, for his mind was filled with bright pictures whether he was dreaming or awake—relaxing at home with his family, riding Bayard over the green fields near Isca, studying with Cadfrawl on Ynis Witrin, joking with Valerius, sharing brief moments with Sabra . . . but mostly he talked with his Lord. Soon they would be together face to face. The thought made Him more real to Georg. As each memory sprang to mind, he prayed for the person—his grandfather, his mother, Matterona, Kasia, Pasicrates, Sabra. It was harder to pray for Valerius, but he asked God to open Val's eyes to His truth. And it was harder yet to pray for Plotius. He knew he should say, "Father, forgive him." For a time his prayers were blocked. And then he thought of Meribah, of Jesus healing His captor at His arrest, and he found he *could* pray, "Father, forgive."

And he prayed for others in the legion. As he prayed, one face recurrently came to him—the intelligent, thoughtful face of one he had only seen from a distance, but even then had sensed a bond with. Not knowing why, he prayed for Constantine. And he prayed for Galerius and Diocletian and their successors, whoever they might be. For three hundred years since the time of Christ on earth, Christians had been persecuted. Thousands had been tortured far worse than anything he had endured. It must stop. Sometime, somehow, it must stop. There was a way to achieve that. There must be a Christian emperor. It seemed too much to hope for, too much to ask for. Yet he asked.

Finally, he prayed for himself. "My God, I would not choose to leave this life unless for Your glory. Lord, come to my aid. I am here, and I call, knowing You hear me. Turn Your ear to me, hear my words. I ask that You show Your great love, You whose right hand saves Your friends. Hide me in the shadow of Your wings from the violent attack of the wicked. Rescue Your servant if it is Your will.

"But if it is Your will that I should die for You as so many others have, help me to stand firm to the end. Please stay beside me all the way. And I especially ask that You will stay close to those who remain here to struggle on. Receive me into Your glory, my Lord and my Father. Amen."

On the morning of the fourth day, guards marched into Georgus's cell and yanked him to his feet. He prayed for the strength to stand unaided. He could stand, but his damaged muscles could not move his legs, so he was dragged from his cell. "Caesar says we're to clean you up. Seems he wants a pretty sacrifice." One of the guards laughed as he poured a bucket of water over Georgus's head and scrubbed at him with a sponge.

The other guard dragged a coarse bone comb through Georgus's hair, pulling chunks of hair out with the straw. Then they pulled a white tunic over his head and hauled him forward. At the door of the prison he was shoved into a litter and carried to the front of the palace. Galerius sat on the highest step, surrounded by top officers from the Guard. A large crowd had gathered in the street below. This execution was intended as a warning to all who would defy Caesar, so people had been rounded up from every corner of the city. It was not as great a spectacle as a wild beast show in the arena, but a Roman citizen had a right to death by beheading.

As Georgus was lifted from the litter, he saw the world with a new clarity, as if by the light of a brightly burning fire that had purified the air of any smoke or dust. *Lord, grant me this last favor,* he prayed. *Let me not suffer the ignominy of being dragged to the post.* He felt the strength flow into his legs. Pushing his guards firmly to the side, he stepped unaided to the execution post. He made the six steps in triumph. He grasped the stake in front of him and lifted his face to the warmth of the sun. A special golden light surrounded him, light not of this world, but the glory of the world to come.

In the first row of observers, Valerius saw the aureole surrounding Georgus. Suddenly it was as if a light turned on in his own mind. He saw clearly now the answers to the questions he had been asking himself for all these months. He knew the truth. Jesus was truly the light of the world. The sun god Mithra was the counterfeit. Jesus was a God worth dying for. Jesus was the God Val would live for. Joy surged through his heart as he bowed his head. *Lord, I believe. I believe.*

Then Valerius's attention was caught by a low, but firm voice speaking from somewhere behind him. It was Eusebius. He spoke out with great courage, given fire by the man who stood before them with the light of heaven radiating from his face. "'And the dragon was wroth and went to make war with the saints which keep the commandments of God and have the testimony of Jesus Christ. . . . And all that dwell upon the earth shall worship Him—all those whose names are not written in the book of life of the Lamb who was slain from the foundation of the world. But it shall be given to those who believe on the only begotten Son of God to trample upon serpents. If any man have an ear, let him hear.'"

In the moment of silence that followed, Georg cried out, "Fear not, my friends. If the spirit of Him who raised Jesus from the dead dwells in you, then He who raised Christ from the dead will bring your mortal bodies to life also through His Spirit dwelling in you."

Galerius jumped to his feet in anger and signaled to the executioner. The man started forward, sun glinting off the sharpened edge of his francisia. But Georg didn't falter. "It matters nothing whether life is on earth or in heaven. Christ died for our sins to make for us an offering to God. Rejoice in that offering of yourselves to Him, whether for service here or above."

The executioner was in place, and the axe was swinging as Georgus looked up to heaven and cried, "My Lord Christ, by Your death on the cross You opened the gates of heaven. Admit into Your kingdom one who hopes in You."

The flow of red blood made a stripe down the front of Georgus's white tunic, and the rush of air following the return swing of the axe blew a red line across the first, forming a cross.

The gloating look left Galerius's face as Constantine rose from his bench just below Caesar. The tall legate knelt beside the fallen body and gently pulled off the blood-stained tunic. Holding aloft the pristine white banner bearing the red cross of Georgus's blood, Constantine spoke so quietly that only Sabra, Valerius, and those standing closest heard. "This shall be my banner, and someday I will raise it over the Empire."

PART THREE

13

ucullus heard the hounds barking and the trilling of a panpipe before he heard his friend calling from the courtyard. He reluctantly laid his oat cake smothered in soft fresh cheese back on his plate and started to rise.

"Finish your jentaculum while it's warm." His mother Flavia was already halfway to the dining room door. "Succat Patricius can wait for you. Boys need a good meal in their stomachs before they go fishing."

Lucullus noted his fourteen-year-old sister's eyes light up at the mention of his friend's name. Julia slipped quietly from the room.

Carrying his pipe, Patricius came into the room with Flavia. His blond curly hair looked windblown, and his blue eyes shone from the sprint across the fields to the Villa Artoii. "Still stuffing yourself, Lucul? I thought you were the one who liked to be out to see the sunrise." The newcomer flung himself on a couch at the foot of the table near Marcellus, the elder Artios son.

"Father, are you sure it's safe to let these cubs go fishing in the Sabrina?" asked Marcellus. "I've heard reports of Hibernian raiders in Dumnoni."

Porteus shrugged. "Those savages should have enough to keep them busy in Dumnoni. Although I do worry about my sister there. Why she had to marry someone so far away, I don't know, even if he does claim descent from the old royal line."

Flavia smiled at her husband. "He's a second cousin to King Constantus, and besides, Ultha Tregatta is a very handsome man."

"Without a brain behind his handsome face," scoffed Porteus. "I received a letter from him last week addressed to Porteus *Artorius*—can't even spell his wife's family name."

"He is a brave soldier," Lucullus managed to inject around a mouthful of his third oat cake.

"Precisely my objection," Porteus said. "He leaves my sister alone to direct the villa while he goes off with that ragtag army Constantus has gathered up. It wouldn't be so bad if it were a proper legion like we had when I was young."

"But what are we to do, Father?" Marcellus set his wine cup down with a bang. "Since Honorius called all his soldiers back to defend Rome against the Visigoths, we must raise our own army. Fine thing for an emperor to do—leaving half his Empire defenseless. If he hadn't been such a weakling in the first place . . ."

Julia slipped back into the dining room and set a tray of cakes and cheese in front of Patricius with a shy smile that was entirely wasted on the sixteen-year-old boy.

"Oh, I know, I know. 'Look to your own defense,' he said. And so we must. But it should be done in proper Roman fashion. Britain should build a proper legion. These ragtag war bands forming around 'kings' are no better than the barbarians they try to protect us against." Porteus looked at the silver band on his arm, worn so thin with time that the jeweler had put a new backing on it several years ago. "The bracelet of Marcellus—for whom you were named, my son—is not meant for a cohort of brigands."

In an effort to calm the conversation, Flavia turned to Patricius. "I understand your father has been ordained a deacon. That is a fine thing for your family."

He grimaced. "Well, at least it'll free us from the tax burden of his being on the city council."

Lucullus laughed. "Cynical Succat—as usual. Let's be off."

The boys were almost to the door when Marcellus asked, "And what of Senn? Will he join the army?"

Succat laughed. "It's unlikely. My mother says the nephew of so holy a man as Martin of Tours must not take up the sword. That's why she insists on both of her sons being called Patricius—so we won't forget we're patrician even if barbarians are overrunning the world. But I think the real reason they want to keep him home is to run the villa—they know I'd be hopeless."

"You could do anything you put your mind to, Patricius." But Julia spoke so softly no one heard her.

Patricius's long-legged red hound bounded toward his master as the boys stepped onto the veranda and jumped at him with tongue-wagging enthusiasm. He stepped backward, and the weight of boy and dog fell against one of the columns supporting the tile roof. A piece of rainspout crashed to the stone walk on the courtyard. "Oh, I am sorry!" Patricius scrambled to help his friend pick up the pieces, Rufus bouncing after him.

Lucullus held a piece of the preformed tile spout in his hand and shook his head. "Well, the rain will just have to go its own way. There's not much chance of getting more of these from Rome nowadays."

Patricius laughed as he picked up the last pieces. "Oh, who knows, maybe Honorius will teach the Visigoths how to make tiles."

The boys tossed the pieces into a barrel and bounded across the field of spelt and down the long slope to the Sabrina. They pulled their small coracles from a cave, piled in their fishing nets, and pushed off into the channel. Rufus barked and leaped about on the shore. "Sorry, Rufus, you'd sink us all, besides scaring all the fish away with your infernal yapping. Go on home and play with Senn's dogs."

Rufus sat down on the sand with a whimper and, with dark, sad eyes, watched the fishermen depart. "Go home, Rufus!" Patricius repeated his order.

"How cruel. Don't you care that you're breaking his heart?"

"No, I'm not. He's a good actor, the big baby. What a gift for a tutor to give."

Lucullus dipped his oar into the water and pushed to keep abreast of his friend's boat so they could talk. They wouldn't start fishing until they were farther down the channel in the clearer, silt-free waters where the Sabrina was deep and swift-moving. "Well, what could Justin do? He knew better than to give you a Latin scroll."

It's as well the boys weren't fishing yet, for Patricius's burst of laughter would certainly have scared the fish away. "Praises be, I've done with Latin scrolls forever."

"But you can't spend all your time at playing the pipes and dice games, Patri. What will you do?"

"For starters, I won't be a Latin scholar, and I'll continue to soak in the baths at Glevum as long as the civitas can manage to keep them open—but my father says that may not be much longer. Hmmm, I don't know . . . maybe I'll become a merchant—I'd like to see the world. I want to see things—and learn things, but not Latin. What about you? What do you want to do, Lucul?"

Lucullus was quiet for a long time. Patricius started to repeat his question when Lucullus shook his head. "I guess what I want is to make up my mind. I'm not sure."

The coracles drifted apart. Lucullus's rowing slowed as he pondered the question. No one was pushing him yet. He'd just finished his lessons, and he needn't make a decision until he reached his seventeenth birthday in November, but it was frustrating not knowing. He had always liked to set a goal, work for it, and then enjoy the sense of satisfaction when he achieved it. Now suddenly he had no goal.

Marcellus would inherit the villa, so there was no point in choosing farming for a career. And unlike Patricius, he did not find the life of a merchant appealing. He loved to sit by the hearth and eat his mother's oat cakes while sharing news of the day's events with his family. The rootless life of an itinerant would never suit him.

The church offered careers for those who enjoyed a settled life. The bishops at Londinium and Ebercanum maintained schools for the priesthood, and his family was devout—they would be happy to have a son enter the service of the church. And, as Patri never let him forget, he was good at Latin—although that had come about more from a dislike of being in trouble with his tutor than from any burning desire to be a Latin scholar.

And, of course, there was the army. Ragtag though it was, someone had to defend Britain from the Hibernian raiders to the east and the Picts and Scoti to the north. And one shuddered to think what would happen if the vandals who were rampaging in Gaul should look across the Fretum Gallicum.

"Ho, Lucullus! Did you come to fish or to daydream?" Patri's sharp call from some distance downstream made him jump. Lucullus plied his oar and was soon beside Patricius, who already had his net in the water.

But this was not the day for fishing. Even though Lucul often said Patri's piping could charm the fish into nets, today it, too, failed. They moved downstream, fishing new pools for several hours and weighting their nets with additional lead sinkers to plumb greater depths, but their nets continued to return empty. At last Patri pulled in his net and dropped it in the bottom of the coracle. "Useless. I don't think there's a fish in the whole of the Sabrina. Let's do something else." As always in a quiet moment, he pulled his panpipe out of his tunic and played a trill.

Lucullus pulled in his net. "Like what? Say, let's go to the island."

"What could be more boring than a clutch of old hermits?"

Lucullus shrugged. "I don't think they're boring. They have interesting ideas. They think a lot."

Patricius laughed. "I'll bet they do! What else is there to do sitting under a mountain on an island but think?"

Lucullus looked up at the dark storm clouds forming above them. "Boring or not, we had better go. It looks like we're going to get wet, and there is no closer shelter."

Patri tucked his pipe into his tunic, and the boys paddled their coracles up the river. Soon large rain drops fell around them. The wind seemed sometimes to be driving them forward, sometimes pushing them back.

Through streaking wet and gathering dark, Lucullus could just make out the looming shape of the Tor ahead. Fortunately he had been there before and, when the coracles were beached, he remembered his way well enough to lead his friend along the low ridge of Wirral Hill toward the cluster of tattered huts where the hermits lived. Thick-leaved apple trees provided some shelter, but the boys were chilled when they knocked on the door of the nearest cone-shaped, wattle hut. Water ran in rivulets off its thatched roof.

A wide smile erased Lucullus's worried frown when he recognized the anchorite who opened to his knock. "Brother Bremwal, isn't it? I'm Lucullus Artios. You may remember when I was here with my brother last summer. This is Succat Patricius; his brother Senn Patricius was here also."

"Ah, friend Lucullus, how could I be forgetting a descendant of Lleiver Mawr, and it is said, even of Joseph of Arimathea. Come you in."

But as the stragglers stepped across the threshold into the welcome warmth, angry voices rose from the other side of the fire in the open, central hearth. Bremwal interrupted the argument to present their visitors to Hyn and Wellias.

The two acknowledged the introduction and made room for the boys by the fire, but returned immediately to their debate as if no one else were there.

"I say the world is crumbling. Rome has failed. It is time to return to the ways that ruled in this land from the beginning of time." Hyn's face was flushed nearly as angry a red as his wild hair that tumbled onto the shoulders of a tattered rust tunic.

"You would turn from Jesus Christ, Hyn?"

"I would turn from no man and from no God. I would worship Jesus and acknowledge Lugh. I would remain an anchorite here, but I would bring a wife to me—as the druids of old did. I would deny nothing. God is loving and benevolent. He wants His children to partake of all."

The ancient, stooped brother Wellias, whose white hair and skin looked almost ghostly in contrast to Hyn, crossed himself before he answered. "Hyn, my heart fears your words echo those of the serpent in the garden. You cannot celebrate the Eucharist of our Lord with another god in your heart."

Hyn jumped to his feet, "So, the pious brother Wellias would deny me the communion cup for speaking my mind?"

"I would deny no one who truly loves our Lord. Do you love Him, Hyn?"

It was silent in the hut until Bremwal spoke. "That indeed is the question we all must answer one day—'Do you love Me?'"

Hyn flung a heavy green cloak around his shoulders as he stomped from the room. The question hung on the air with the eye-stinging smoke from the fire.

Bremwal shook his head as he offered his guests cups of strong sour wine from a basin heating by the fire. "I am fearing our brother is not one in spirit with us."

Wellias also took a cup of wine. "The trouble is that he is one in spirit with several of our number. He is quite right that the old world—the Roman world—is crumbling under our feet, and no one has anything else to offer. So there are many who would return to even older ways."

Bremwal agreed. "It is to my thinking that since the time of Constantine the Great, Christianity and Roman government have been synonymous. Now we must find a way to cling to the one when we no longer have the other." He took a slow sip of wine as a damp log snapped and sputtered on the hearth.

"I believe a life of prayer and devotion is the way," Wellias said.

A blast of smoke sent Lucullus into a coughing fit as the door burst open and two more brothers, introduced as Brumban and Swelwes, entered. Swelwes, who couldn't have been much older than Patri and Lucullus, with snapping bright eyes, spoke first. "We could hear Hyn's voice above the wind.

He is gathering Hiregaan, Banttomeweng, and Hinloernus to persuade them to his side."

"Not that they need much persuading," Brumban added as he folded his cloak to sit on it across the fire from Lucullus.

"And you two," Bremwal asked in his slow, soft voice. "Are Swelwes and Brumban needing persuading to find the truth?"

After a moment Swelwes spoke. "I need no persuading to know the love of God. Its place in my heart is its own persuasion. But as to the rules of our community . . ."

Brumban laughed. "What our brother would say is—as he has found the love of God so radiant in his heart, he would like to share it with others—especially with the lovely Catha."

"Our cenobite ways are not for all, Swelwes. St. Paul said it is better to marry than to burn." Bremwal spoke quietly. "If you yearn for Catha—"

"No. It is not for Hyn's 'niece' who helps with the cookpots . . ." A blast of wind shook the hut. Swelwes pulled his cape from under him, wrapped it around himself, and withdrew into it.

Bremwal turned to his guests. "Happy I am that you have sheltered here from the storm, but I am fearing you have not found a place of perfect calm. As it is a time of change and upheaval across the Empire, so it is on Ynis Witrin."

"Er, how many of you are there here?" asked Patricius to steer the conversation another direction.

"We are twelve, as has always been the number to worship in the Old Church, honoring our Lord's choosing of twelve disciples."

"Yes, but even he had a Judas." Wellias's remark produced silence in the hut.

"It is time we were on our pallets, my brothers." Bremwal opened the door for the agitated brothers to leave. He shook his head as he returned to his guests and handed them each a thick blanket.

The next morning the storm had gentled, and Patricius and Lucullus went to the stream to wash before breaking fast. In the rain-washed greenness, by apple trees hung thickly with small green balls just taking on a blush of red, it was hard to think that arguments could disturb the serenity here. Surely, the birdsong that wreathed about their heads bespoke a harmony of all nature on the island.

Patricius sloshed water vigorously over his own face and then playfully splashed at his friend. "What do you think? It sounds to me like we've come to an interesting place after all—I can't wait to see this Catha. If she's got all these doddering old hermits in a buzz to get married, she must be something."

"Ahh, and what of the blue-eyed Lucia who waits for you and your pipes with such fidelity outside the baths at Glevum?"

Patricius laughed and led the way toward the scents of the cookpot near the Old Church. The building was in even worse repair than the ramshackle huts huddled around it, its mangy thatch resembling a lean gray wolf with spots of its winter coat rubbed off. The daub had cracked and broken out of much of the wattle, and apparently no attempt had been made to repair the damage of many a winter's storm.

But the young woman bending over the cookpot looked anything but drab. Her red-gold hair fell loose to her shoulders, just brushed behind her ears and held with a bronze comb. Her green eyes lit with pleasure at their approach, and her smile showed perfect white teeth. "Ah, I had been told we had pilgrims. Make you welcome to the hospitality of Ynis Witrin." She held a bowl of porridge out to each.

Lucullus took a bite, then almost choked. He hated barley—slimy stuff—and this was relieved with neither meat nor vegetables. But Patricius was swallowing large spoonfuls without tasting them as he bantered playfully with the cook. When his bowl was empty, he took Lucullus aside. "Look here, our parents will know we've taken shelter for the night. They won't worry if we delay our return a little. We can tell them we stopped to pray with the hermits or something."

Lucullus started to protest, but Patri would hear no argument. "What's a couple of hours, Lucul? She's an opportunity that doesn't come every day."

"But—"

"Say, I think you're jealous. But I spoke for her first—after all, you're the scholarly, religious one. What do you care for girls?"

The argument ended abruptly when they saw the object of their conversation approaching, her green-gold tunic blowing gently against her slim body as she crossed the wet summer's grass. "Succat Patricius, my Uncle Hyn has heard of your family—he says they yield much influence in the church and the government both here and in Gaul."

Patri gave a self-satisfied smile, "Well, that's a bit of an overstatement. But we do have a few connections, it's true."

Her green eyes smiled at him. "I was sure it was true. My uncle would speak with you. His hut is the third one beyond the Old Church." She pointed with a delicate white arm.

Patricius did not move. "But I would much rather speak with his niece."

"Oh, no. Uncle says it is most urgent. And while you are about your business, I will entertain your friend, so you need have no hurry." She turned to Lucullus. "Would you care to climb to the small temple on the top of the Tor?"

Lucullus made a gallant bow and offered the lady his arm. But the laughter he felt inside was dampened by the glare he got from Patricius.

Two hours later when the boys set out for home, Patricius's wounded pride was stirring his emotions more violently than the wind was tossing the rapidly gathering dark clouds over their heads. Under the guise of doing some fishing, and in spite of Lucullus's urging that they should hurry before another storm caught them, Patricius let Lucullus go on ahead. He was too angry to talk. That Lucullus had done nothing to rouse this resentment simply increased the wound to Patricius's pride. If it had been an open contest over Catha, Patricius could have covered his pique with bravado. But Lucullus had made no effort to win the girl's attention and had undoubtedly done nothing with the opportunity once he had her alone. Patri could not bear the sight of Lucullus's self-righteous face.

Never before had Patricius felt such jealousy—this spirit-squeezing, wall-building constriction between him and Lucullus, blocking years of friendship. He had certainly never been jealous of Lucullus's certainty of faith—Patricius placed little value on that. But that the flame-haired girl should choose Lucullus over him—and that Lucullus was so slow as to ignore an opportunity that Patricius would have made the most of . . .

Swamped with his emotions, Patricius hardly noticed the lowering storm. Finally a sharp clap of thunder brought him to. Lucullus was out of sight, but where Lucullus's small coracle should have been, a large, dark hulk loomed on the wind-chopped waters of the Sabrina. The heavy keel of the wooden boat sat deep in the water, and a row of stout oars on each side moved it forward rapidly. Patricius blinked in surprise, trying to think what sort of merchant would run such a vessel. Then he saw that the boat was not alone. Four or five more hulks made dark streaks on the Sabrina in the near distance. Not merchant vessels, but war boats.

Now he knew who the seamen were. Hibernian raiders. They should never have been this far up the channel, but they were. Patricius put all his energy into a frenzy of rowing. If he could just reach shore, he could outrun these barbarians. He was young and swift. He knew the land, and they didn't.

At first he made great speed, and his spirits soared. But then a gust of wind blew him backwards, almost into the path of the plunderers. Patricius fought valiantly, but for every rod he rowed forward, the wind blew him back two. He felt the raiding boat's closeness as if it were an animal breathing down his neck. And then he felt more than heard the clunk of an oar holding his craft. His coracle was secured like a market basket clutched firmly to a kitchen maid's side.

Rough hands dragged him on board the Eirran galley, and harsh Gaelic voices floated around his head. From where he lay dazed on the bottom of the boat, the whole world seemed plunged into senseless chaos.

He struggled to right himself. A burly man with a fiery beard bound Patricius's wrists together with a leather thong that cut into his flesh. The man barked an order at him, but Patricius did not understand. The man grabbed him under one arm and flung him against the side of the boat. He landed in a more-or-less upright position. In a desperate attempt to make sensible contact with these barbarians, Patricius cried out in the best Latin he could muster, "Does anyone speak Latin?"

The crew laughed at the strange sounds he made. He tried again, this time in Cymric, "Does anyone speak Celtic?"

From the prow of the boat a stocky figure moved forward. "My mother was of the British kind. I have some speaking."

"Who are you?" Patricius demanded.

"Claith I am. We ride the sea god's white-maned horses for Niall, High King of Tara. Best be getting used to that name, for I'm thinking he'll be your king now too." Suddenly his captor's eye was caught by the fineness of Patricius's woolen tunic. He picked up a corner of it and rubbed it slowly between his freckled fingers. Then his eyes caught the slim glimmer of gold at Patricius's throat that proclaimed him the son of a decurio.

Claith turned to his fellow raiders in excitement, and Patricius was overwhelmed with a babble of Gaelic. Then Claith pulled him to his feet, and still clutching his tunic, demanded, "Where is your home, son of a gold-wearing Briton?"

Patricius considered. Perhaps they meant to hold him for ransom. But perhaps they only wanted to raid a prosperous holding. Playing for time, Patricius pretended to look around as if finding his bearings in order to answer them. He looked at his little coracle bobbing free in the water and thought of Lucullus rowing on ahead. Then he knew what to say. A slow smile of revenge for his wounded pride spread over his face. He gave his captors precise directions to the Villa Artoii.

Claith gave a bellow of laughter and flung the prisoner against the side of the boat. Patricius felt his head crash against the crossbeam far louder than the lowering thunder. Then everything went black.

As the storm drew closer, Lucullus dared not wait for his friend. He gave all his attention to rowing, ducking his head to avoid the spray that blew into his face. When he rounded the last bend in the Sabrina, he raised his face to the wind, hoping to catch a glimpse of a light in the villa window. Lucullus gasped and blinked in disbelief. There was no golden square of light to greet him. Instead an angry orange blaze seared the blackness. One of the outbuildings must be on fire.

Lucullus rowed the last furlong in a frenzy and leaped to the shore, barely bothering to beach his coracle. If it were the stables, his father and Marcellus would need every hand to get the horses out. "Castellores!" He shouted the name of his dove-gray horse as he ran forward.

But long before his stumbling rush brought him to the villa, Lucullus could see that more than one building was ablaze. The whole villa was in flames. Yet as he approached, he could see no moving figures rescuing animals or throwing water on the fire. Lucullus yelled the names of his family and their servants. His only answer was the crackle of the flames. The roof of a byre behind him fell in with a crash, leaving the timbers smoldering. Where was his family?

His hand over his eyes to shade them from the heat and smoke, he moved forward and almost tripped over the small mound. He knelt to examine it. Julia. Her throat slit, her red blood congealed black on her pale yellow tunic. With a sob of anguish Lucullus clutched her cold, stiff body to him. And as he did so, his eyes fell on the larger mound that had been his mother. Gentle Flavia, seeing to all her family's needs with quiet love, an encouraging smile, a reassuring caress, a platter of warm oat cakes with fresh cheese . . .

Dazed with grief, Lucullus stumbled on. By the door of the courtyard he found his answer—the bodies of three Eirran raiders. Marcellus and his father had fought well. Thank God the raiders had killed his mother and sister rather than carrying them into slavery.

The body of another raider lay near the stable. As Lucullus shoved it aside with his foot, he found another tragic answer. Marcellus lay beneath his slain enemy—the Eirran short sword still in his chest where the savage had plunged it.

Only his father left now. Lucullus couldn't make room in his mind to think about the servants, some as close as family members. He didn't want to find his father. Yet he couldn't stop. "Father!" he cried without hope of answer. Yet somehow the sound of his own voice, sob-choked as it was, gave him courage to go on, and he cried out again. "Father! Father!" Was that a groan from beyond the cattle pen?

Lucullus plunged into the darkness where the flames had burnt themselves out. Yes, he heard a groan. Not stopping to think that it might be the voice of a foe, Lucullus ran toward the dark figure on the ground.

"Lucullus." Porteus's voice came out in a raspy whisper, his face a ghostly white in the dim light. Lucullus knelt and cradled his father's head in his lap.

With his right hand Porteus made a weak gesture toward his left wrist. At first Lucullus could see nothing but the dark streaks of blood down his father's arm, but a second spasmodic gesture focused his gaze on the family bracelet. He touched the cold silver. "You want me to have it, Father?"

Porteus nodded and closed his eyes.

Lucullus pulled the sides of the band open and snapped it onto his own wrist. His finger traced the faint pattern of the engraved horned goat—the Capricorn insignia under which his ancestor had served almost three hundred years ago. That Artoii had fought to keep the land free, to keep the barbarians out. So would Lucullus fight. There would now be no room in Lucullus's life for the church or the farm. He would give all to the life of a soldier. Laying his father's lifeless head on the grass, Lucullus stumbled back to the body of his brother. Sweating with the intensity of the effort, he pried the rigid fingers off the hilt of his sword and curled his own fingers in the place of his brother's. With the bracelet of that long-ago Marcellus and the sword of this generation's Marcellus, Lucullus was now the last of his line. But he would avenge his family. He would avenge all who had fallen to ravaging barbarians.

14

atricius sat on the gentle green mound his captors called the Hill of Skerry and stared dazedly at the flock of sheep grazing below him. The straight white fleece and black legs and faces of the horned sheep were as strange to Patri as everything else in his new surroundings. It seemed impossible that his entire life could have changed so dramatically in just a few days. He rubbed the still-sore, but less-swollen lump on the back of his head. He didn't know how long he had been unconscious, but when he had opened his eyes, it had been daylight and the war boat was sailing into a harbor backed by rocky, mist-shrouded, green hills. The event swam in his mind, a confusion of barking dogs, shrieking children, and unrelenting orders which he couldn't understand through the pain in his head.

From long habit he reached inside his tunic for his pipe, then drew his hand out empty. The pipe had been lost on that same night he had been torn from everything he knew in life. He dropped his hand. It was as well it was gone. There was no song in his heart anyway.

He remembered being hauled ashore by Claith and shoved into line with what seemed like a thousand other prisoners as each boat disgorged its booty. They had followed a track over the mountains that apparently ringed the entire coast of Eire (which seemed to be their word for Hibernia). Then they marched into a green bowl-shaped basin broken by occasional hill-rises that stretched as far as he could see until the land was swallowed in mist. They passed scattered farmsteads, all built in the same round pattern—a rock wall ringing a circular stone house with thatched roof. Although the living conditions appeared unspeakably primitive to Patricius, he could see the practicality of the design where cattle could be driven into the grassy yard for the night and the single entrance sealed with a thorn bush against marauders—animal or human.

Patricius looked around at a world untouched by Rome. True, the influence of the Caesars was fading and crumbling in his own world, but this was like Britain must have been four hundred years ago—no straight roads, only muddy tracks meandering off in the directions chosen by cattle; no organized civitas or villas, only occasional stone or turf steadings; no square-built forts with guarded palisades and extensive baths, only circular raths enclosed by stone walls atop flat, green hills.

Claith, standing nearby, pointed to three such flat-topped hills standing in a row. "Ach, and those are the hills of Meath, leveled when Fergus MacRoy in his battle fury slashed them with his two-edged sword that left an arc of light like the rainbow."

Patricius looked at the man beside him, his captor and yet the nearest he had to a friend in this strange land. His hair was the color of iron rust, and freckles as thick as pollen dotted his face and arms. It was impossible to say what had drawn them together beyond Claith's halting ability in Cymric, and yet, as Claith recounted the legends of the Eirran, he sensed pipesong behind the prisoner's wall of resistance.

"And beyond is Slemon Midi—the Hill of the Slain—where Cuchulain and the warriors of Ulster defeated all the war hosts of Eire massed under Queen Maeve who would keep for herself the brown bull of Ulster."

Patricius nodded and smiled for the first time in many a day. Claith should have been a bard for his love of hero-songs.

"But now none may ascend the hill save high druid priests. It is the habitation of poisonous snakes and stinging serpents, and only the druid magic gives protection." But a clap of thunder interrupted his story. Patricius ducked and pulled the cowl of his tunic over his head. The bright, slanting sunlight that had shone on them moments ago was now covered with dark clouds rolling in from the west. Only two days in this land and already Patricius had learned to recognize the approach of one of their frequent rain showers.

The Eirran captors were expert charioteers, and their little mountain ponies, urged on by bronze-tipped goads, made excellent time over mud-choked, rutted roads. But the captives, stumbling along rebelliously on foot, slowed the procession. Several of those around Patricius came under the lash of the whip, but for Patricius the cracking noise was warning enough. He increased his stride in spite of the sharp rocks beneath his soft leather boots.

By the time the rain slackened and a rainbow arched in the sky, they were at the foot of a hill topped with a magnificent complex of circular raths and a rectangular hall that must rival the forum of Augustus. "*Teamhair na Riogh*," Claith said, the freckles standing out on his nose and cheeks as his heart swelled with emotion. "Tara of the Kings. When Cormac MacArt, High King, ruled at Tara, Finn MacCool was captain of the Fianna—"

Patricius smiled at the coming of another hero story, but a charioteer, whip snapping in the air over their heads, reprimanded Claith for talking too much. The procession hurried forward. Claith turned to his duties of keeping the captives in order, and the triumphant raiders surged forward to present their booty to Niall of the Nine Hostages, High King of Tara.

A week later, after many more miles of goaded marching, Patricius now sat on a mist-sodden, heather-covered hill, recalling his rebellion at being herded into the Hall of the High King like one of his father's own sheep. After years of watching slaves being auctioned in the forum at Glevum, Patricius still couldn't believe his fate. He—Magonus Succatus Patricius, son of Calpurnius, decurio and deacon, and grandson of Potitius, decurio and priest—a slave. He shook a defiant fist heavenward. To his amazement, his gesture met with an answer. In his mind the quiet voice of his mother came to him. *My brother, the Bishop of Tours, always said the greatest sin was pride. He taught that people should live like angels, but that our pride was the greatest stumbling block to such a holy life.*

Patricius lowered his fist. He had no desire to live like an angel, but his pride did get him into trouble. To survive in his new life as a slave in the household of the chieftain/druid Michlu Maccu Boin who had bought him, he would indeed have to learn humility. No matter how it galled him.

As the most powerful man in this area of Ulster, Michlu's steading was a mighty ring-fort. Patricius could see it now from where he watched the sheep on the hill. The hill of the rath was circled by a wooden palisade since trees were plentiful from the nearby Wood of Voclut. On the broad green between wall and houseplace, farmers, warriors, and craftsmen who served the chieftain had their small round huts of turf and stone. Upon their arrival, Patricius, with the other new slaves, had been prodded in like cattle with a bronze goad to do homage to their new master who sat between his sons in the high place in a carved seat covered with skins. Above, a thatched roof was supported by ornately carved wooden beams decorated with silver and gold. The central, curbed hearth warmed the rush-covered paved floor onto which the slaves were prodded to their knees beside the huge hounds crouched at the hearthplace gnawing on bones.

Michlu Maccu Boin was a figure to impose fear on the heart of any slave. Tall and heavy-boned, he and his sons wore their silver-fair hair shoulder-length and their beards full. Unlike the darker tunics and cloaks Patricius had seen on Niall's warriors, Michlu and his family wore garments dyed bright red, blue, and purple and displayed their wealth of gold and bronze jewelry set with bright blue glass bought from northern traders.

After doing obeisance to Michlu as chieftain, the slaves were ordered to follow him to the Wood of Voclut where as druid he would lead in the worship of Dagada.

Patricius had sorely missed the garrulous Claith, left behind at Tara, to explain the proceedings to him. He shuddered as he recalled the strange chanting above the cries of the sacrificed animals as they died by the bronze sword on the stone altar, and their blood slowly drained away into a bronze cauldron filled with meal. The overseer, who spoke a substandard Latin, attempted a narration for the newcomers. "Dagada, the great he, the Father-god, is the eternal holder of the great cauldron of plenty. The chief druid priest makes offering of blood-porridge to Dagada so that the harvest will be plentiful."

When the porridge was prepared, the bard stood beside the priest and chanted a story which the overseer translated. The slaves stood in numb awe, but the true worshipers swayed to the rhythm of the harp strings and even joined the singer in familiar passages of the story which told of the time before time when evil Fomori stole Eire from the gods. But the gods could not rest without this, the fairest of their jewels, so they massed for a great battle. None but the gods should rule in the Emerald Isle. On the eve of battle the Fomori flouted the power of Dagada by stealing his cauldron and preparing a stupendous porridge in it. The evil ones then taunted Dagada and challenged him to eat the porridge or face death.

A battle-challenge could not go unanswered. So Dagada swallowed all he could scrape from the cauldron with a ladle, then scraped the bowl with his fingers. Only for Dagada would the cauldron of plenty be empty, that he might defeat the Fomori. But the great cauldron of plenty, now that the evil ones had been defeated, would never be empty for Eire. The worshipers praised Dagada of the club, Dagada of the harp, Dagada of the cauldron.

At the memory, Patricius's nose again stung with the acrid smoke and the heavy, sweet smell of blood-soaked wheat meal. Then his stomach lurched as he saw again Michlu dipping a long-handled bronze spoon into the pot and swallowing a scoop of the red-brown mass.

The bark of a wolfhound bounding toward Patricius interrupted his thoughts. "Hello, Rufus." He had no idea what this Eirran hound's name was, but he had christened him Rufus in memory of the dog he would likely never see again. His throat tightened as he reached out to pet the animal.

In spite of his loneliness, however, he turned away from the gray-bearded old shepherd, who approached with his noon meal. Unperturbed, Ossian sat beside him and drew the cheese and barley bread out of his pouch. "Aye. Slavery's a bitter herb to be swallowing. But ye'll be getting used to it. Michlu's none such a bad master—so long as you keep the wolves away from his sheep, you'll never go hungry." As if making an object lesson, he took a bite of a thick slab of pale yellow sheep-milk cheese. Then he untied skins holding hazelnuts and sweet, blue bilberries.

Patricius bit off a crust of bread, but did not answer. He had heard Ossian's story two days ago when the new batch of slaves arrived in Slemish and were shown to their straw pallets in a building Patricius's father would not have housed his cattle in. Ossian had shepherded the flocks of Michlu Maccu Boin for twenty years. He had been in one of the first boat loads of Britons brought back by Eirran raiders—even before the legions had withdrawn and left their farthest outpost of the Empire defenseless. Now Ossian was chief shepherd, answerable only to Michlu and his sons. To Patricius it didn't matter that Ossian was once a captive like himself. In his own mind, the old shepherd was one of the enemy.

Patricius bit fiercely at his hunk of dark brown bread. He didn't need anyone. He would survive on his own. He turned his back more completely on Ossian, but of its own volition, his hand sought the soft hollow at the base of Rufus's warm neck. Ossian picked up the empty pouch and, leaning heavily on his staff, walked up the hill.

Several weeks later Patricius left the slaves' sleeping-shed one morning to find the world glistening with frost. He shivered and yanked his cowl over his head. Ossian pulled the blanket from Patricius's straw pallet and handed it to him. "Ye'll be needing this a' mornin', lad. It's bitter cold on the hillside when the frosts come."

Patricius took the blanket with muttered thanks and flung it around his shoulders. Ossian, undeterred by the young slave's sullenness, continued to walk beside him. "Now our job becomes hard. The cold will bring the wolves in from the mountains. We'll have to be increasing the night watch. You come back at midday and sleep. Ye'll take the first dark watch with Gussacht and Dhu."

Patricius nodded his assent to the orders and trudged on up the hill, Rufus at his heels. The other slave shepherds walked together in a group below him, their voices ringing on the crisp air. Patricius's scowl deepened as he heard laughter. How could they be cheerful? It was a personal insult to his own bitterness.

When they reached the flock, Gussacht, Dhu, and the others greeted the shivering shepherds going off duty, but Patricius walked stoically on to his favorite distant post at the farthest section of the flock. He walked once around the band to make certain all was well. Then he scratched the frost off a flat-topped rock and sat down to—to what? To hate his circumstances. Was that all his life had come to? Was that all it was to be? Certainly it was all it had been in—what? A month? Two months? He'd made no effort to keep track.

At first his hatred had helped get him through the days. But what if the months became years as they had for Ossian? How long could one go on hating all the people around him, hating himself, hating God? Then, as once before when he had flung his anger out on the universe, his mother's voice came to him. *Remember, my son, St. Paul learned in whatever circumstances he found himself to be content. You are one who would change all circumstances to suit yourself, but sometimes one must suit himself to circumstances.*

How could he be content with these miserable circumstances? And yet it was pleasant to recall his mother's voice. His hand went to the empty spot in his tunic where his pipe had always lain. It was gone like all the happiness in life.

The distant cry of a wolf sent a tingle up the base of his skull, and all thoughts of his former life fled his mind. He cared nothing for Michlu and his sheep. He would be happy to have the whole pack carried off by wolves—it would serve the druid right. But Patricius had seen the overseers' whips coiled on the wall of the sleepshed. He had no desire to come into closer contact with them.

"Come, Rufus!" It was time to walk around the band and check for strays. Moving would help warm him anyway.

A few hours later, after following Ossian's orders for a midday rest, Patricius and the obedient Rufus were trudging the same path along the hillside; only now it was dark, several degrees colder, and the wolf howls sounded closer and more chilling.

Patricius noted nervous sheep milling about in the farthest downhill section. A clutch of silly ewes were walking in circles, bleating for no apparent reason. Patricius spoke irritably to them and prodded with his staff to move them back into the flock. He was just going to prod a large ewe who still had her last-spring's lamb by her side, when a low growl broke from Rufus's throat.

"What's the matter, boy?" Patri turned to the dog.

At that moment a large gray wolf sprang from behind a granite boulder and leaped at the lamb. It bleated a startled cry, and Rufus threw himself at the wolf's throat. The big gray animal released the lamb. Patricius pulled the sheep back with his staff while the dog kept the attacker at bay.

The wolf was taller and many pounds heavier than the hound, but the hound had greater speed. The two creatures circled, growling at one another from deep in their throats. Rufus was the first to spring, sinking his teeth into the wolf's neck.

The animals rolled on the ground. First Rufus on top, then the wolf. And always the slashing claws and ripping teeth drew blood until in the dark it was hard to tell which animal was which.

As Patricius stood helpless to defend his one friend—the one creature he cared about in all of Eire—he realized how much the animal's companionship meant to him. He had thought his life could be no worse. But now he knew that without Rufus it would be unbearable. For the first time in many years he turned his heart-cry to God. "Help, O Lord God, help!"

The opponents pulled apart and circled again in halting limps that left drops of dark blood on the frost-white grass. The wolf snapped and growled, but seemed unwilling to move in. With a burst of courageous speed, Rufus flung himself at the wolf, rolled the beast over, and sank his teeth into the base of his throat. The hound hung on in spite of the deep gashes the dying wolf's claws tore in the dog's soft underbelly.

At last the gray creature lay limp and still. With a final shake of his head, Rufus released his jaws and crawled whimpering to Patricius. Patri fell to his knees and cradled the dog's head in his arms.

"Aye, and I've never seen a more valiant creature." Ossian approached from the far side of the flock and knelt beside the dog who lay unmoving except for the heaving of his sides. Ossian opened the leather pouch he wore around his neck and took out a small pot of ointment. "It's seeming we can do little good, but we must try our best for one so noble-hearted." He smoothed ointment on the long wounds, and Rufus seemed to find the old shepherd's touch comforting.

The two sat on the frozen ground beside the dog until Patricius felt his own limbs becoming as stiff and cold as the world around him. It was several minutes longer before he realized that Rufus had made no movement for some time. "Ossian?" he said.

The shepherd lay his hand on the dog's still chest, then bent to press his ear to the animal's heart. At last he sat up. "Aye, lad. And that I'm sorry. I know he was your friend. A hound fine enough for a Fian chief—fine enough for Finn MacCool himself."

Patricius's first impulse was to shake his fist in the face of God and rage against the universe. But it all seemed too futile. "He gave his life for a worthless sheep who's too dumb even to know it."

Ossian was silent for a long time. At last he said quietly, as if to himself, "Aye. As did our Lord."

Patricius gasped in amazement. He couldn't have heard right. Not in this barbarian land. "Do you mean to say you're a Christian?"

"Aye, that I am. There are many of us scattered across the whole of Eire. The Eirran have been raiding Britain for twenty years and more. They care not whether they capture Christian or pagan—either can serve as slave so long as he has a strong back."

"But there are no churches—no priests—no mass—"

"Aye. Ye speak sadly true. We have no leader. I pray daily that God will send us such a leader. Ah, but he would need to be a brave man indeed—the druids of Dagada would fight him with all their dark powers." He put his arm around Patricius's shoulder and urged him to his feet. "Come, lad, we must be seeing to the sheep. We'll bury your friend in the morning."

And in the weeks of increasing cold that followed, Patricius found the warmth of Ossian's friendship to be all that sustained his frozen heart. Another fine red wolfhound was assigned to him, but Patri didn't bother to learn the pronunciation of his complicated Gaelic name. Instead he merely called him Hound. But Patri clung to the memory of Ossian's understanding and gentleness as he had buried Rufus. That had sealed the friendship between the young and old shepherds. With that small melting of his heart, Patricius found it in him to gather reeds from the shore of the lough at the foot of the Hill of Skerry and make a new panpipe.

Many a night through the long, rain-washed winter when daylight lasted for only a few hours, they kept the cold and dark at bay sitting around the watch fire with Patricius playing his pipe and Ossian talking of their native land. It sometimes seemed that even though he had been gone from it for so long, Ossian knew the hearts of its people better than Patricius who had just left it.

"I remember when I was a wee lad, my old grandda' said the evil one had once tried to kill the truth by subtlety with a false copy of Christianity. Had it not been for Constantine the Great raising the banner of the cross, the serpent might have won. At least, that's what my grandda' said—but of course, that was before his time, too.

"Trouble is, we won only a battle; the end of the struggle is not yet, my boy. Who's to say if it will come in your time? But having failed to win by subtlety, the enemy now seeks to win by cruelty. And it is my fear that we have seen only the first of it, you and me."

Patricius stirred the coals at the edge of the fire with a stick, and Ossian paused in his midnight philosophizing to listen. The steady rhythm of the sheep breathing, a few scattered stampings on the frozen ground, and the cry of a night bird said all was well. Ossian nodded, and Patri continued his pipesong while Ossian talked. "We must be strong, my boy. Strong enough inside to withstand the fiery blasts of the enemy on the outside. The attack of a wolf on a sheep is nothing compared to the attack of the barbarian on the land. And that is yet as nothing compared to the attack of the ancient foe on the soul."

Ossian struggled to his feet, his limbs stiffer than usual from the cold. Patricius likewise rose. It was time to walk around the band again, each going in opposite directions. They would meet at the bottom of the flock, nod to each other, then continue back up to the top as they had done for so many nights now that Patricius was beginning to feel as if there had been no other way of life.

Yet often his failures of the old days haunted him. Where was he to find this strength Ossian spoke of? Surely, if the smiles of a pretty girl could cause him to fall into blind jealousy and betrayal, his soul must be as straw before the wind. Surely his soul could be as easily taken by the enemy as his body had been captured by the Eirran.

His mind went back to his last night of peace in his old life—himself and Lucullus in the hut of the hermit Bremwal on Ynis Witrin. It seemed like peace now, but at the time the night had been torn with strife as the hermits argued. Memory of the strife increased Patricius's despair. Surely, if one could not find peace in that green secluded spot, it was not possible to find it on earth.

He recalled the words of Christ which Brother Bremwal had posed to the irate Hyn, "Do you love Me?"

Like Hyn on that long ago night, Patricius had no answer.

Nor had Lucullus found the fulfillment he sought in joining the thrown-together army of the aged Duke of Britannia Prima. In the secluded mountains of the west, the duke was struggling to maintain his feeble grasp on the civilized Roman world. Lucullus had tried as much as possible to blot the events of that blood-gorged night so many months ago out of his mind. He took what comfort he could from finding his beloved Castellores when he returned to the smoking ruins of the Villa Artoii the next morning with Calpurnius and Senn, with whom he had taken refuge in the wee hours of the morning. The horse had somehow managed to escape from his burning byre.

He reached down now and patted the dappled gray neck as the horse snorted and blew a cloud of steam in the frosty air. Silly thing to be keeping guard when the mountain passes were frozen shut. There would be no raiders before spring. But military order of some sort must be maintained. And there was always the chance of a bear or wolf coming into the camp. If only one would, he could spear it for the camp cookpots. Their hunters had had little success, and the portions of roast venison were smaller every night.

For one whose chief delights in life had included sleeping in on rainy mornings, early walks to enjoy the sunrise, and eating warm, cheese-covered cakes by the hearth with his family, no change could have been more radical. He seemed a different person from the young man who had lived in that other world—that former life. He thought for a moment about the land his father had loved. Had Calpurnius been able to take care of it for him, as he had offered? Lucullus didn't really care. He doubted he would ever return. What difference would it make if one more burned-out, abandoned villa were added to the ravaged landscape? It was best to be serving with the duke's army. At least he could try to prevent other villas and their inhabitants from suffering similar fates.

Lucullus gave a palm-to-forehead salute as he met his friend Ulpius who shared his guard duty. Then he turned back to repeat his route along the eastern edge of the ancient hillfort they were refortifying under the direction of Aurelius Peregrinus, who at least in title remained the Dux Britannia Prima. When the wooden ramparts were finished, such nighttime patrols could be abandoned to the watchfulness of the guards at the entrance, but felling trees was laborious in knee-deep snow, and the walls progressed slowly, as did all their work.

Lucullus blew impatiently on his hands to warm them. He had not joined the army to be a woodcutter or a carpenter. He had wanted to avenge the deaths of his family by killing barbarians. He was frustrated. He could only hope it would get better in the spring. But he was not convinced that life would ever be satisfying again.

It seemed to Lucullus on his night patrol as if the legions had taken the sun with them when they withdrew their protection, leaving only a pale glimmer in the sky that neither warmed the earth fully nor lighted it adequately.

The land needed a new light, a new warmth—a protection against barbarism on the outside and despair on the inside. The world was slipping toward a great void. Even if it weren't pushed into it by raiding Hibernians from the west, marauding Scoti and Picts from the north, or plundering Vandals and Visigoths from the east, it would surely fall into the dark of its own accord.

A few months earlier, such a mental soliloquy would have led Lucullus to pray, "God, give us light." But now Lucullus was neither sure that there was a God, nor that there was any light to be had.

Castellores tossed his head. At least Lucullus was fortunate to be in the cavalry. He was one of the youngest members of their band. Only Ulpius had not yet reached his seventeenth year as Lucullus had last month, and Marcus was barely eighteen. But even if Lucullus had not presented himself with a badly needed horse, he would not have been turned away. They needed every hand, untrained as most of them were, whether green youth or doddery old man.

And they needed every spear, sword, or bow they could gather. Since Rome had discouraged, if not outright forbidden, the keeping of weapons by natives and the eagles had taken their own weapons with them, anything heavier than hunting spears and knives was in pitiful supply. Lucullus smiled to think how their band would be derided by the proud, orderly eagles in their straight rows of gleaming armor and regulation gear. A few of Britannia Prima's band indeed possessed full Roman armor with bronze helmets, plated body mail, and warm officers' cloaks—the best in all the Empire had been made in Britain for four hundred years. But most of them, like Lucullus and his young friends, wore only the rough belted and cowled homespun tunics with the thong-wrapped leggings of the native farmers. Those without woolen cloaks, or with cloaks frayed threadbare, wore the skins of wolves and bears over their shoulders. Some fashioned their own leather armor, similar to that worn by the German auxiliaries, from the prizes of hunting forays. And all who could fastened tanned skins over their light wooden shields, to better repel enemy sword slashes. Lucullus gave an ironic smile. He could hear his father's voice: *Ragtag army . . . wouldn't be so bad if it were a proper legion.*

Lucullus doubted that the world would ever see a proper legion again. He shifted his own leather-covered shield higher on his shoulder. It had not been tested against enemy arms, but Lucullus knew them well. The short sword of the Eirran raider was a particularly deadly instrument, weighted for maximum accuracy. And the sword arms of the raiders were legendary for their untiring power. But Lucullus did not fear the foe. He had seen the color of blood in the firelight of his burning villa, and he knew the Eirran could bleed like any man. Lucullus put his hand to the sword he had taken from the slain body of his brother. Come spring, as soon as the Eirran had their crops in, they would be sailing across their narrow sea, and Lucullus would get his chance.

His chance, however, came far sooner. Two weeks later a scout stationed along the eastern shore of the Sabrina rode up the snow-packed slope of the hillfort entrance shouting that Hibernian raiding ships had been spotted in the channel. Gathering all they had managed to amass of spears, swords, and shields, the army of Britannia prepared for battle. The guards weren't sure, because evening had been falling when they spotted the ships, but there were at least five of the large, heavy war-galleys heading up the Sabrina. That could mean as many as a hundred warriors. For months the men had drilled, planned, and talked of war. Some, like the duke himself, were seasoned legionnaires and had served under the eagles. But most were little more than boys for whom a hunting-run had been the closest they had ever come to a battlefield. Now they were to be tested.

The cavalry went first, Lucullus's friends Ulpius and Marcus following single file behind him down the narrow entryway from the hillfort. A long slow note from the carnyx hung on the frosty air as the cavalry rode toward the Sabrina with the infantry marching double time behind them. This must be a particularly daring band of raiders to challenge the storms of the Hibernian Sea.

A hard, glinting elation sustained Lucullus against cold or fear, even when they reached the Sabrina and could find no raiding party. "We need a navy," Marcus said. "Just because the Romans never built a very strong naval fleet, that doesn't mean we can't. After all, we're defending an island—how better to do it than in boats?"

Ulpius agreed. "Especially since our enemies come from the sea. That way we could attack them before they land."

Lucullus listened to his friends, but he was glad to be in the cavalry. That night, rolled in a bear skin on the frozen ground, his head was full of visions of riding Castellores full-tilt at a band of raiders, brandishing his sword until it dripped red.

The next morning a scout returned shortly before first light. He had located the landing site of the Eirran. Lucullus was among the first to wash down his cold corn cake with a flask of barley beer and spring into his saddle. As his muscles were stiff from sleeping on the cold ground, he gave an appreciative thought to the innovation the duke had added to his cavalry's saddles—stirrups—an idea adapted from the invaders sweeping the continent from the north. Although a proper Roman cavalry would have spurned the idea, it certainly made riding in the mountains more comfortable and made horses easier to control in battle.

A two hours' ride brought them within sight of the enemy. Or to be more precise, within sight of the burning buildings the raiders had just put to the torch. The twenty-some cavalrymen thundered behind their duke, horses' hooves striking hard on the frozen ground. They would sweep upon the booty-flushed raiders, and although the Britons would be outnumbered, they would have the advantage of surprise. And the infantry would follow to finish off any the horsemen had missed.

Lucullus lost all sight of the frozen countryside and hardly glanced at the flaming village they swept by. A doctor marched with the infantry; he could see to any who had not met speedy deaths by the barbarians' swords. To Lucullus there was only the goal. They rode to the crest of a small rise that ran down to the channel. There it lay before them, as in all his dreams of the past months. A raiding party, the winter sun glinting on their bronze war helmets. They were slow in their movements from the load of spoils they carried in baskets and hand-drawn carts, from the bewildered animals they drove before them, and from the captives who stumbled, wrists bound, across fields their families had farmed as free men for hundreds of years.

The raiders were mere black figures against the frost-whitened ground, but to Lucullus each one's features were as clear as if they stood face-to-face. Each one had the staring green eyes, blood-caked red beard, and teeth-bared snarl of the raider who had killed Marcellus.

At a signal from the duke, the cavalry charged. It was nothing like the orderly, well-drilled ranks of a Roman charge. It bore far more heritage from the early Celtic tribes whose blood ran in some measure in all their veins. With a wild cry Lucullus spurred Castellores forward. He would be in the apex of the charge. His would be the first sword to draw blood.

The Eirran warriors made no attempt to stand at battle position. Instead, they focused everything on reaching their boats before the main thrust of the battle engaged. Lucullus aimed his mount straight toward a raider on the outside of a group herding a straggling cow. The plunderer turned at the sound of Castellores's hoofbeats. His hand went to the sword at his side. But the gesture was too late. As Lucullus felt the satisfying drag on his sword, and his victim turned, his one emotion was surprise. The boy was younger than himself.

For the next hour Lucullus moved in a frenzied red world as the flowing red hair of the raiders, the confusion of the red cattle, and the red of blood all mingled with the red rage of his own temper. He spurred and slashed, whirled and stabbed. This was what he had dreamed of doing for months. This was the revenge his life had focused on. This would fill the void in his heart. The clash of metal on metal rang in the air. He barely bothered to parry blows with his shield. It was quicker to slash at his attacker's sword arm from his superior height on his mount.

When the carnyx sounded the end of the battle, Lucullus found himself still slashing and flailing at an already-fallen foe. The ground was littered with the bodies of three-fourths of the raiding party. The others had escaped to their boats with their wounds and a handful of booty. Their would-be captives stood in huddled clumps, some silent with shock, others crying, but most praising their deliverers.

The duke rode among his troops, giving words of commendation, assessing wounds, and counting his own dead. Noting the path of his progress, Lucullus saw with a sudden ache in his throat that Marcus was among those who would battle no more.

They made camp that night near the burned-out village, and the mead and ale flowed freely among troops that were now seasoned, now welded together in a true brotherhood by having been tried in battle—literally blood brothers.

But in spite of Ulpius's repeated urgings that he join the band around the campfires, Lucullus sat apart. The blood of the enemy was still on his sword—the blood he had coveted for so long. And all he could think was, *Is this all there is to it?* A thrill of excitement as the sword thrust goes home—then nothing. He had reached his goal, and now he had less than before. He had gained the mountaintop, and it didn't satisfy. Now he didn't even have his goal to sustain him.

Yet, what else was possible in this world but to kill barbarians? Kill or be killed. He thought of Marcus, fallen in the field today. Now Lucullus had another death to avenge. Could vengeance keep one going forever? He thought of those whose deaths he had avenged today—his father and mother, Julia and Marcellus. His sword had accounted for more than four barbarians today. And Patricius. Had he killed one for his friend, too?

As so often in the past months, he wondered whether Patricius truly was dead as his family thought him. They had searched all the countryside between their villa and the Sabrina and the coastline up and down the channel. His empty coracle, washed ashore three days after the raid, told them nothing. At least there was no blood in it, so one could hope—if the life of a slave in Hibernia was a hopeful prospect. And Rufus. Lucullus determined that at the next battle he would also avenge the fine hound who had refused to eat when his master failed to return and had died of a broken heart.

Seeing the group of captives that had been bound for slavery today brought Patricius more sharply to Lucullus's mind than he had been for months. Was Patri a slave in Hibernia? Somehow he did not believe his friend was dead. Lucullus sat long into the night staring into the flames.

15

he wood snapped, sending a shower of sparks into the black sky, like stars come close to earth on the clear, cold, late winter night. Patricius stared at the flames, but didn't bother raising his eyes to the stars. For almost six years he had sat thus, staring into flames that looked the same, listening to sheep that sounded the same, and thinking thoughts that ran in the same vein. Six years of sitting and staring, six years of doing nothing, being nothing. Six years that might well be the rest of his life. He played a sad air on his pipes; even their light, hollow sound reflected the emptiness of his life.

Ossian's words and friendship had been his only lifeline, his only source of nurturance. And now Ossian was dead. During the last icy snowfall a month ago, he had taken a cold on his chest. As head shepherd he could easily have refused night duty, assigned it to the younger slaves, but he chose to sit on that frozen white hillside with Patricius and talk of his God in a loving way that Patricius, the nephew of a bishop, the grandson of a priest, and the son of a deacon, had never heard. But now even that comfort had been taken away from him, and his captivity closed in on him.

Like the children of Israel captive by the waters of Babylon, Patricius poured out his desolation. "Oh, Lord, my soul cries to You like the lonely seabirds cry. Why do You not answer me? I am a captive on the brink of the world, my life hovers on the brink of the pit. I see nothing but sheep from day to day and week to week, like one alone among the dead."

The Children of Israel had sung aloud, accompanying themselves on harps. Patricius formed the words in his mind and heart, the only sound coming from the pipes at his lips. And yet the cry of his soul was louder than any voiced words could have been. "Have You forgotten me? Am I entirely cut off from You? You have taken away my friends. I am imprisoned. I cannot escape. I call to You for help, but You reject me. You hide Your face. Family, friends, and neighbors You have taken away. Loneliness and darkness are my only companions."

Patricius was no happier after this outburst, but perhaps the fire felt a little warmer. It was time to walk around the herd. He called to Hound, who obediently padded along at his side. From far below to his right he could hear Dhu and Gussacht singing as they tended their part of the flock. Patricius did not sing.

From that night on, however, Patricius formed the habit of praying to the accompaniment of his pipes. Although his complaining, grumbling prayers were unlike the simple praises Ossian had voiced, the act began to fill the void his friend's death had left.

At last spring came and with it the end of the snows. The wolves moved higher into the hills, and shepherding became a less rigorous ordeal. As a slave with six years' experience, Patricius was now allowed to take only day duty and leave the night herding to those captured in recent raiding trips. Patricius occasionally heard talk of raids that had been entirely routed or at least reduced by a thrown-together British army. He was glad his people were resisting, but thought bitterly that such efforts had come too late to help him.

Gradually, however, as the world softened with springtime, Patricius's bitterness began to soften. His prayers occasionally included a few words of praise and worship recalled from church services at home or from Ossian's simple prayers.

At last, a morning came when Patricius, who had once sneered at Lucullus's delight in a sunrise, now sat on Skerry's slope and gloried in a golden morning sky. A lark sang, and Patricius reminded himself, as Ossian had so often in the past, that this was God's world. And it followed that if this was God's world, all in it must be God's creatures. Including himself. And if he was God's, he was not truly alone.

As the warming glow of the sun spread over the hillside, Patricius felt a thaw in his heart that had been frozen for six years of perpetual winter. He opened his morning food pouch—a small loaf of bread and a skin of wine was all he had to see him through the long hours. He took the loaf in both hands and pulled it apart.

As he did so, he was no longer on a green hill in Eire surrounded by bleating sheep; he was at church in Glevum, surrounded by his family and friends of long ago. It was not his hands that broke the morning meal loaf, but the hands of a priest breaking the Eucharistic loaf. And then not mere bread, but the body of Christ.

"But I am no priest!" Patricius was so horrified he almost dropped the bread. There was no priest in all Eire, no one who could celebrate the sacrament. Christ's body and blood were not present in this heathen land. And yet, Ossian had said others still believed, still worshiped. Surely, Christ was here in their hearts. But not in Patricius's. *I am a sinner—the worst of sinners who betrayed a friend through pride and jealousy. I am Judas.*

"My God, forgive me," he cried aloud. "By Your mercy make me worthy to eat this bread."

But his heart did not lighten. What was he to do? He stared at the broken host in his hands. He could not put the body of Christ back in the pouch, and he was not fit to eat it.

He could only pray. "Lord God, reach down from heaven and take hold of Your servant. I empty myself. I prostrate myself. I bow before Your presence in the universe. Let all that happens to me, all that I achieve, be what You desire. Not my will, but Yours."

A great energy entered his body, a torrent capable of sweeping him along and taking all before it. Such energy was terror and ecstasy.

He looked again at the bread in his hands. "This is Your body, Your sacrifice for me, Your great gift. In it is the destiny You have chosen for me. I eat now this bread of the new covenant as a submission to Your will. I surrender myself to be torn away from myself and my will, to take on danger and strife, burdens and separations for Your sake."

He ate of the bread. "My Lord, I am willing to be made a new creature in You, to be possessed by You. Let my former desires pass away that I may climb new heights in You. Free me from my fears, fill me with power to experience Your presence, help me, O God, to live in Your presence."

He took the wineskin and held it up to heaven. *This is My blood of the new covenant which was shed for you.* As Patricius held the bag, golden rays of the morning sun struck it, and the simple wineskin took on a holy aura. For a moment Patricius held in his hand the cup Christ had held when he drank of the new covenant with His disciples four hundred years before. *Drink ye all of this.*

Patricius drank.

From that time on, Patricius was filled with a new sense that all would be well. At the same time, he felt a new restlessness that he was not where he should be. Earlier, his restlessness had come from rebellion, from hating his surroundings and fighting his circumstances. Now he accepted them, but felt a strange urgency to leave them, not from any desire of his own, but from the growing sense that God would have him elsewhere.

Patricius became a better slave, more diligent in his attention to the sheep, more helpful to the other slaves, more obedient in spirit as well as in action to Michlu and his overseers. In the days following his epiphany experience, Patricius prayed upon rising, prayed with every meal, and prayed at bedtime. But soon he found this was not enough to satisfy his soul. He longed for constant communion with God. He began rising earlier to spend more time in prayer before he went to the fields, seeking a quiet spot in the Wood of Voclut beyond the sleeping bothie where he could pray without interruption. He learned to pray constantly throughout the day, and between his own words, staying silent to listen for God's reply to his soul. Even his pipe playing became a prayer—a means of winging his words heavenward.

But the restlessness remained. He did not understand what he was to do.

He now felt completely yielded to God, a oneness with Him. But God had something for him to do, and he could not understand what it was.

In his fervor, Patricius added fasting to his devotional life and ate only the Eucharistic meal each morning at daybreak. But he still found no answers.

His unrest produced sleeplessness, and he began spending the entire night in the woods in prayer. The guard of the sleeping place was used to his odd ways and aware of his faultless record. The Eirran did not object. Michlu's property was well guarded by ban-hounds who would bark and attack if a slave attempted to run away. And so, in a green thicket in the wood where the shamrocks grew, Patricius kept watch.

On the third night of his vigil, however, human weariness overcame spiritual fervor, and Patricius fell asleep, wrapped in his woolen cloak.

"Patricius." He jerked awake. Was the guard coming to check on him?

"Here I am. What do you want?" But there was no answer. An owl hooted in the distance, and leaves rustled over his head. Patricius drew his cloak more closely around himself and drifted back to sleep.

"Patricius." He stumbled to his feet in a sleep-dazed state and walked around the thicket. Had Dhu and Gussacht followed him? Were they now teasing him? Again his only answer was the hooting of an owl. He lay down to sleep a third time.

"Patricius."

He at last recognized the voice of his Summoner. He was not sure whether he was asleep or awake as he said, "Speak, Lord, for Your servant hears."

"It is well that you fast. Soon you will go to your own country." The words were sensible, and yet they were not. He seemed to sleep on, and again the voice came to him. "See, your ship is ready." In his dream Patricius saw a ship, far larger than the raiders' war ships. Wind billowed its great white sails, and gulls flew around its masts. The harbor was not one Patricius recognized. Certainly from the steepness of the rock formations, it was nowhere along the Slemish coast.

Long after he awoke and sat puzzling over the meaning of his strange dream, the words echoed in his mind, *Go to your own country . . . your ship is ready . . . your own country . . . ship is ready . . . go . . . go . . . go . . .*

For the next several days, Patricius continued to celebrate Eucharist, but he no longer refused his other meals. Bread, cheese, and oat cakes he wrapped in his cloak which he kept rolled beside the straw of his pallet. Stirabout and stew which could not be stored, he ate to give his body added strength. And every night he continued his vigil in the woods, praying and sleeping, as the Spirit moved him. But he had no more strange dreams. There was no need. The meaning of the first one had been clear.

On the fifth night after his dream, he wound his cloak around his arm so that the food would not fall out, nodded to the guard, and walked to the woods.

Here he paused to pray, but then, instead of lying down to sleep, he rose and walked. He gave no thought to the direction he walked, he simply walked. At the edge of the woods he saw a figure moving ahead of him in the moonlight. He started to pull back, then realized that if he was ever to leave Michlu's land, he must pass the ban-hounds.

Speaking softly, so that his approach wouldn't startle the animals, he walked forward. At the sound of Patricius's voice, the large creature he had spotted earlier stopped in his nighttime prowling and gave a low rumble from deep in his throat. Patricius took two steps forward. The hound sprang at him.

Patricius fell backwards into the brush, the wolfhound on top of him. He struggled to push the beast off. "Stop it, Hound! You great awkward thing, get off me." After washing Patricius's face with three slobbery licks, Hound moved aside, and Patricius regained his feet. "I don't have enough food for both of us, but if you can catch your own rabbits, you can go with me." He patted the smooth head. Together man and dog left the service of Michlu Maccu Boin, druid of Dagada.

Many times on the ten days' walk, Patricius was glad for Hound's company. After five days Patricius's food ran out, and Hound snared rabbits and small birds which Patricius dressed and roasted over open fires built in secluded spots out of the sight of farmers and other travelers. But never once on his journey was Patricius stopped or questioned about his affairs. His aristocratic bearing, drilled into him by his mother and a succession of tutors, and the Gaelic, which he now spoke like a native, kept anyone from thinking that the fine-looking young man traveling toward the south with the well-bred wolfhound might be a runaway slave.

On the morning of the tenth day, the travelers crested a small hill, and there before them lay the sparkling waters of the Hibernian Sea. It had been many days since Patricius had had bread and wine to celebrate Eucharist, but his heart leaped in a great *gloria* at reaching the end of his journey.

Or rather the beginning. For there in the harbor was the ship precisely as she had appeared in his dream, the wind ruffling her two white sails, the sun shining on her deck. Patricius's impulse was to dash down the hill right into the harbor and shout for the captain to take him aboard. But it occurred to him that perhaps the captain had not had the same dream.

The morning sun warmed Patricius's head like the *benedictus*, giving him courage to take on this last challenge to his leaving Eire. Squaring his shoulders, he walked down the path. His heart soared when he saw a man on the dock, who must surely be the captain, shouting orders to everyone in sight. Small rowboats laden with barrels of food and water for the crew and cargo for the merchant trade set off from the dock. Some of the boats carried bales of fine wool from the spring shearing, and some were laden with wheels of the yellow sheep's cheese Patricius had eaten almost every day for six years. But by far the greatest part of the cargo was beautiful red, gray, and brindled Eirran wolfhounds, so popular throughout the Empire as hunting dogs.

The dock swarmed with sharp-toothed beasts, barking and howling at the tops of their lungs and straining at their leashes. As he got closer, Patricius could see this might not be the best time to approach the captain. His temper seemed to rise with every increase in volume from the dogs. Hound started to add his voice to the cacophony, but Patricius lay a hand on his head. "Now don't you start, too, boy. You be quiet and show them how to behave." Hound was obedient as dog and master lounged on the waterfront, waiting for an opportunity to approach the captain.

At last the final growling hound was shoved onto a rowboat, his breeder paid, and the captain, mopping his brow, set off for the wineshop at the top of the muddy lane that ran from the wharf. "Nasty-tempered beasts. We'll be lucky if they don't tear us all limb from limb in our sleep. Gallicus, I want that hold locked tight the whole journey. Understand?"

"Aye, Captain," the first mate replied, following his captain up the dirt track.

Patricius fell into step beside them. "They aren't really such bad beasts." He spoke haltingly; he hadn't used his Latin for six years. He had no idea he'd forgotten so much. "The boats frighten them. They'll settle down."

The captain gave Patricius a scowl and all but growled at Hound. As the men reached the wineshop, he stamped his feet on the cobbled step and led the way into the small, gray stone building. Three long planked tables stood on the straw-covered floor with stools around them. The central hearth was cold, and fresh air blew in through the open shutters. The captain took a seat at the table nearest the window, and his first mate and Patricius followed him. Hound made himself comfortable under the table.

Patri waited. The landlord, a ruddy man in a coarse brown tunic, served them all mugs of the local ale, and the captain had drunk two good mouthfuls before Patricius broached his subject. He gave the captain his full name and said, "I would like to take passage on your ship. I haven't a screpall to my name. But I could pay for my fare with my hound. I saw what you put on board—he'll fetch a higher price than any animal in your hold."

The captain took a third long pull on his mug, then wiped his mouth on the back of his hand. He shook his head. "I've got all the hounds I want—about 100 percent more than I want, to be exact."

Patricius opened his mouth to argue, but he saw it was no use. What was he to do now? This was the very ship he had seen in his dream. He had followed the Lord's guidance, walking two hundred miles across Eire, and now the captain said no. Was it possible that God's plan could be thwarted by a heathen sea captain?

"Come on, Hound." Patricius rose from his wooden stool and walked out the door. He had seen a small hut about a mile back up the road; it looked like the home of a sheepherder. Perhaps he could take shelter there or even find work until another ship came into the harbor. Perhaps this wasn't the ship he saw in his dream—no matter how identical it looked.

"Succat Patricius!" He had just reached the hill above the village when he heard the first mate calling his name.

"Captain changed his mind. He says he doesn't want your hound as cargo, but if you'll agree to tend the beasts in the hold, he'll take the two of you free of charge. You're what we need if you can make those creatures obey as well as you do that one of yours."

With his broadest smile in six years, Patricius spun around in the middle of the road and clapped Gallicus on the back. "Aye, that should be no trouble at all. Just give them sufficient food and water; they'll sleep all the way to Britain."

"Britain?" Gallicus said. "This ship sails to Gaul."

Patricius stared. Gaul. Had he heard right? The voice in his dream had said, *You will go to your own country.*

And yet this was the ship. He had to trust his vision. He put his hand on the comforting warm head of Hound.

"I will go," he said.

Hound gave a throaty rumble of satisfaction as Patricius, stretched on a couch before the hearth in the Villa Patricii, scratched his ears. "Of all my time in captivity, it was my most harrowing six months," Patricius said to his family who was gathered around, hanging on his every word.

They could not get over their amazement at how he had changed. The sixteen-year-old boy they had known and mourned for dead had returned to them a man of twenty-three, tall, broad-shouldered, with a golden beard to match the curly blond hair they remembered.

And they had all changed, too. Patricius could not accustom himself to seeing streaks of gray in his mother's beautiful, gold hair and new lines on her face, nor his father, though still vigorous, moving more slowly and balding. And Senn Patricius at twenty-seven was a hard-muscled man who did the work of two or three slaves in the field.

Patricius smiled fondly at them all.

"And then your return trip. Tell us of it," his mother urged.

"You can imagine my consternation when I learned the ship was going to Gaul—that was farther from home than Eire—er, Hibernia was. But I tried to accept it all as being in the will of God. They laughed at me for my daily prayers, but it gave me an opportunity to tell them of Christ, and they did like my piping for them. We had smooth sailing, so the captain said he was pleased with whatever god anyone wished to invoke, and it took us only three days to reach our port in Gaul. But it was an entirely different matter when we reached port. The captain had expected to take on food and water and exchange most of the hounds for wine before sailing on to Italy. And I had hoped to find a ship sailing back to Britain. Instead, we found nothing."

"What do you mean nothing?" Calpurnius asked.

"The city was a heap of rubble and ashes. The Vandals had been there only days or weeks before, and they left not one building standing nor one person or animal alive. We found a stream of fresh water, but there was no food for miles. The fields had been burned as far as one could see in any direction."

Conchessa's dark eyes grew large with horror. "Oh, Patricius, how awful. What did you do?"

"We could not sail on without supplies, so the captain left a few men to guard the ship, and the rest of us set out walking. We took the hounds with us in hopes they could forage enough to keep themselves alive. For eighteen days we traveled through desolate, ravaged country. Three of our party perished from hunger and thirst, and we all expected to meet that fate.

"The morning after the third man died—it was Gallicus, the first mate—the captain came to me. He said, 'Tell me, Christian, you say that your God is great and all-powerful. Why then do you not pray for us?' I blush to tell you, Mother, I had not thought to do so. It took the words of a heathen sea captain to remind me of my Christian privileges.

"So I said to them all, 'Be truly converted with all your heart to the Lord God. Nothing is impossible for Him. This very day He may send us food, for He has abundance everywhere.' And the captain and the entire crew knelt down in the dust of the road and confessed their sins and prayed to God."

Patricius paused in his narrative to sip his wine, but his family urged him on.

"And then a herd of pigs—undoubtedly the only such herd in southern Gaul to have escaped the Vandals—came wandering down the road before us. They were as near exhaustion as we, so it was no work for the men and hounds to round up the whole herd and slaughter them. And an equally great miracle was that some of our men found a grove where the Vandals' fire had been doused—perhaps by a rain shower—before all the wood was consumed, so we were able to roast the pork. We stayed there for three days, resting and feasting until men and hounds were fully restored. And I led in prayers before every meal.

"I'm not sure how thoroughly they understood the Christian teachings, though, because on the day before we left that spot, one of the men found some wild honey. The men started to eat it, but the captain stopped them. 'This we offer in sacrifice,' he said. I tried to explain that our God requires no sacrifice, only our love." Patri shook his head sadly. "But I don't think my explanation was adequate. How often now I wish I had paid more attention to old Justin and my other tutors." He paused for another sip of wine. "Well, anyway, ten days later our food ran out. I prayed again, and that night we met a band of people—the first we had encountered alive in almost a month. We had great rejoicing and sharing of adventures. Our new friends knew where the captain could get supplies for his men and where I could get a ship to Britain." He spread his arms out to embrace the room. "And here I am!"

"And now let us show you over the place," Senn said jumping to his feet. "While you've been off seeing the world, little brother, the rest of us have been scrambling here to keep our tiny spot of the Empire from crumbling like the rest of it."

"It appears you've been doing a good job of that." Patri looked around him with a smile. After six years in Eire he thought the Villa Patricii looked sumptuous indeed. The chips in the mosaics and the threadbare spots in the wall hangings were imperceptible to him.

Patricius and Hound strode enthusiastically beside Senn and Calpurnius. He admired the cattle in the byre, even though the wooden barn was more dilapidated than the stone buildings where Michlu's cattle lived. He felt a tug toward the band of sheep on the far hill, although they were smaller than the Eirran breed. He waded into the middle of them to pat them on their woolly heads—he who had spent six years hoping never to see a sheep again. And the brothers and father wandered over the green fields of spelt and emu, knee-high and promising a good harvest.

A sharper contrast couldn't be found to the ravaged, burned-out country he had just traveled through. "Do you have any idea how exceedingly blessed we are here—how protected by the grace of God? Certainly we have been raided—no one knows that better than I—but if you saw what it's like elsewhere . . ." He turned away and feasted his eyes on the rich, verdant rolling fields dotted with flocks of cattle and thick green woods.

Yet oddly, Patricius felt a strange sort of homesickness for Eire—its green slopes broken with sudden, dramatic cliffs of dark lava rock—so different from the rolling green gentleness of his western Britain; its air heavy with moisture, yet fresh with sea breeze, seemingly possessed of a special, more invigorating quality than his own gentler clime. Even the harsh speech of its people, untutored heathen though they were, still rang in his heart, with their heroic tales of Cuchulain and Finn MacCool. He found himself throwing Gaelic words into the mixture of Latin and Cymric his family normally spoke.

When it was time for cena, the three turned their steps back toward the villa. There was one question Succat Patricius had longed to ask all day, but guilt and fear held him back. No one had spoken of Lucullus or of the family Artoii all day. The weight of this silence grew on him. Patricius felt certain that no one spoke of his old friend because they did not want to blight his homecoming with the news of another death—a death he had caused, although they could not know that.

When they arrived back at the villa, a slave was just leaving the arched gate in the stone wall that fronted the courtyard. He led a large gray horse around to the stables at the side. Patri watched the horse in frowning concentration, unable to believe what his memory told him. "Isn't that Castellores?" he asked at last. If Lucullus's favorite horse were here, perhaps . . .

Senn slapped him on the back. "So you haven't forgotten your old friend. We wondered why you did not ask, but we had determined to surprise you if we could."

Calpurnius broke in. "This is indeed a day of homecomings. We received a message two days ago that Lucullus would be visiting." He flung an arm around his younger son's shoulder. "It will be like old times again. Come, let us go greet him."

Lucullus was seated by the fish pond in the courtyard. Although it had contained no goldfish for many years, Conchessa still kept it clean of algae and grew small yellow and purple flowers along its bank. Lucullus, with his rough soldier's beard and coarse army tunic, looked oddly out of place in so refined a setting. The two old friends had thought each other likely dead for six years, but as soon as they greeted one another, the differences and the years fell away.

A smiling Conchessa kept the servants scurrying between kitchen and courtyard with trays of cheese, fruit, and honey cakes while the young men shared their adventures.

"And what will you do now?" Patricius asked. "Are you finished soldiering?"

"Finished? No! We have barely made a beginning. I'll not be done while there is a raider left to kill. I have come only to see how my lands fare, and then I am off east to Maxima Caesariensis. There is a new war leader there, raising an army at Venta Belgarium. They call him Vortigern the Fox. Some whisper that he poisoned Constantus to gain the kingship, but many believe he will be as great as Maximus."

"But why are you leaving the Dux Britannia?" Senn asked.

Lucullus returned his half-eaten honey cake to his platter and leaned forward, his elbows on his knees. "Many are going with me. We go with the old duke's blessing. If Britain is to be strong, we must have a powerful army—not scattered bands of brigands little better than the raiders they oppose.

"Vortigern commands all the troops to the south and east of us. This is our opportunity to make Britain safe once more. Why don't you join us, Patricius? Senn? Nothing is more important than driving the barbarians out of our lands." His eyes took on a hard glitter quite unlike anything Patricius remembered in his old friend who had loved sunrises and walks in the rain.

"I don't know . . ." Patri began slowly. "I have come to know a new kind of power. I am not sure what I will do . . ."

Senn shook his head. "Father needs me here."

Silence fell, broken then by the entrance of Conchessa. "If you have finished your gustatio, come into the triniculum for primae mensae."

It had been six years since either Patricius or Lucullus had lounged around a proper Roman table to eat such a meal—Parthicus chicken flavored with fish sauce, accompanied by minced-meat rissoles, mushrooms, asparagus, sausages, and boiled ham. Patricius doused his rissoles generously with liquamen. Then, holding up the cruet of fermented fish sauce, he gave a sigh of satisfaction. "Do you realize how long it's been since I've even *seen* this? I used to smell it in my dreams in Hibernia." He scooped up a large portion of the salty chopped meat with his fingertips, gobbled it down, smacked his lips at the almost-forgotten flavor, then wiped his fingers on his sponge before he reached for a pig's liver sausage, likewise flavored with liquamen.

At last Conchessa clapped her hands for the kitchen slaves to serve the mensae secundae, a final sweet course. Tonight she had prepared three sweets—tyropatina cheese cake; a panis dulcis of milk-soaked bread, fried and covered with honey; and Patricius's favorite sweet, dates stuffed with nuts and cooked in honey. Patri popped one last date into his mouth, washed his hands on his sponge, and rolled back on his couch with a groan.

"Oh, Mother. There is no food like that in the highest courts in Eire."

Senn laughed. "There is probably no such food as this in the highest courts in Rome anymore. It is said Valentinian tends pigs on his villa and leaves the running of the Empire—such as it is—to his general Aetius."

But no one was inclined to talk politics on a full stomach. "Lucullus, I couldn't have had a better homecoming than to have you here for my welcome dinner." Patricius looked across the table and smiled at his old friend. "But we mustn't be selfish. Your family must be eagerly awaiting your arrival. You seem to have been gone from home almost as much as I have been."

The uncomfortable silence in the room was louder than if everyone had shouted at once.

At last Lucullus spoke. "Has no one told you?"

"Told me what?"

"My family was all murdered and our villa burned by raiders on the night you were captured." The lack of emotion in Lucullus's voice cut like a cold iron sword. "Your family has kept up my lands the best they can, for which I am grateful . . ."

Lucullus spoke on in his hard, flat voice, but Patricius could not take in the words. So this was the result of his terrible sin of jealousy and betrayal. When he saw Lucullus alive and well, he had thought himself absolved, that somehow his crime had not brought the unspeakable results he had feared. But it had been far worse. The whole family—brave Marcellus, sweet, smiling Julia . . . the weight of their lives on his conscience was more than he could bear. Blindly he stumbled from the room and groped his way to his old couch upstairs.

He could not pray. The weight of this sin was too great. He could not ask God to forgive so much—he did not want it forgiven. He wanted to carry the full burden. It could be the only possible penance. He would somehow dedicate his life to carrying this burden and working to expiate his crime. But what could one do in a single lifetime to earn forgiveness for so many lives? He stared at the silent, dark walls of his room, but no answer came. There was no answer. There could be no expiation.

At last he drifted into an uneasy slumber, filled with visions of sword-slashed bodies and flame-ravaged buildings. Toward morning he woke to a half-conscious state, just enough to be aware of his pain and the reason for it. Still he could not pray, but he must do something. So he did all he was capable of: *Jesus, Jesus, Jesus* . . . he repeated the holy name over and over.

This time his sleep was free of the dreadful images. Now he was met in his sleep by one wearing the tunic of a household slave of Michlu. "I am Victoricus," the vision announced. Victoricus came to him bearing a huge leather pouch full of letters. He dumped the letters, and it seemed they flooded the room, flowing under his couch. Others didn't fall, but flew, took wings as birds and flew around his room and out the window. No, those weren't letters, but the seabirds he used to watch sitting on the Hill of Skerry.

Victoricus held out one of the letters. Patricius took it in a hand that was his and yet not his. He unrolled it and read printed there the words: *The voice of the Eirran.* And as he read the letter, he was no longer reading it, but hearing the words spoken beyond the trees where he was standing. He realized he was back in the Wood of Voclut. All around him, as if from behind every tree, voices called out, "Come and walk among us once more." "Come and walk among us." "Come."

Patricius began to cry in his dream and woke to find the tears were real. His sofa was wet. Now he knew what he could do. He could never bring the family Artoii back to life. But he could save others. The way to end the raids was not by killing the raiders, trading bloody corpse for bloody corpse as Lucullus was attempting. The way was to convert the raiders—to teach them the way of peace and love. Only then would the world be freed of rape and plunder.

He would teach them that God's goodness, freely given, was far greater than any response Dagada's cauldron could provide in exchange for their sacrifice. He would teach them to follow a way of love and peace through faith in the blood of Christ in the chalice of the Eucharist—not the blood meal porridge of a druid cauldron.

The family was gathered around the jentaculum table when Patricius came down that morning, still rubbing his eyes and trying to make sense out of what he had seen. At first he thought he would keep the vision in his heart until he saw his way more clearly, but his wheat-meal porridge would not go down for the fullness of his heart, and he had to speak. He lay his bowl down with a clatter that was like calling them to attention. While everyone stared at him, he cleared his throat. "I, er, I had a dream last night. Well, really, it was more like a vision." There was no gentle way to break it to them. "I'm to go back to Hibernia."

Conchessa was the first to speak. "Back to Hibernia? Patricius, no! It's unthinkable."

Calpurnius shook his head. "They'll kill you, my son. Or thrust you back into slavery. Is this what you want?"

Senn spoke only one word. "Why?"

"I will take them the gospel. There are many Christians scattered throughout the country there, but they are leaderless. But it is not just missionary work among the heathen or strengthening the faithful; it is for Britain, too."

Their silence told him they had no idea what he meant.

"Don't you see? Without Rome we can never be strong enough to defend against the barbarians. Only when the raiders are no longer barbaric will they cease to raid our shores. I will teach them God's love and peace, and they will become our brothers in Christ."

Lucullus, who had not spoken the entire time, slammed his fist on the table, making the wine cups jiggle. "No! They were born heathen. They have lived as heathen. They should die heathen. Let them go to the Hell that has been prepared for heathen."

"Hell was prepared for the devil and his angels." Calpurnius's soft rebuke went unheard.

"They should be punished eternally for what they have done," Lucullus continued. "If there is a Heaven, I do not want to share it with my enemies!"

"But if they have the love of God in their hearts, they won't be your enemies. They'll be your brothers."

"Never." Lucullus strode from the room.

Calpurnius broke the uncomfortable silence. "If you are to do this, my son, you must be prepared. Your Latin was always deplorable, and it is worse now after six years of disuse. You do not know enough of the Word of God to preach it to others or to explain the faith."

"You're right about that, Father. The Bishop of Londinium ordained you deacon. Perhaps I could study with him."

Conchessa wiped her eyes with the back of her hand. "I do not like it, but if it is to be, perhaps you should study in Gaul at one of the great centers—if the Vandals haven't overrun them all. If only my brother Martin were still alive, you could study with him at Tours . . ." Then tears choked her brave words and she was silent.

Patricius went out to the stable. A ride over the countryside would calm him and give his family time to adjust to this surprise he had sprung on them less than forty-eight hours after returning. He noticed that Castellores was not in his stall—apparently Lucullus had gone for a ride also. Patricius knew that before he left, he would have to face riding to the ruins of the Villa Artoii and confronting the results of his own villainy. But not today. Today he would ride along the Sabrina.

It was inexpressibly good to be out on Pertinax. The fine bay stallion had always been one of the best in Calpurnius's stable. The air this morning held just a nip of the coming autumn, and the topmost leaves of some trees bore a fringe of red and gold. As a boy, he had loved this time of the year. He remembered watching squirrels in the woods while all the world was swathed in liquid gold. He remembered how Lucullus, always the more poetic one, used to speculate on whether the leaves were gilded from the golden air, or whether the air took its special autumn color as a reflection of the leaves.

But those formerly happy thoughts turned the knife in his stomach. Almost worse than the death of the Artoii family was the change in Lucullus. This bitter man bore little resemblance to the mellow, humorous companion he had known, whose faith in God had seemed to spring so naturally from his inner depths.

Patricius prayed for his friend, but the burden and the guilt did not lift.

Patri had chosen to ride toward the Sabrina, thinking to follow her pleasant waters. But a hubbub at the wharf caught his attention. With trade so sharply reduced in the Empire these days, merchant vessels in port were rare, so a large crowd had gathered on shore. Excited voices carried through the clear air. But Patricius could not believe his ears at the words he was hearing. Or, to be precise, the word he was hearing. "*Alleluia!*" Over and over, the single word was repeated, first randomly with a note of surprise, then as more people joined the throng, it became an intense chant. "*Alleluia! Alleluia! Alleluia!*"

Patricius dug his heels into Pertinax's flanks and cantered down the slope. At closer range, he could distinguish an undercurrent of excited conversation: Saxons and Picts invading—had he heard correctly, Saxons and Picts, not Eirran? Yes. "Saxons and Picts, and some added Angles attacking Verulamium to the east, a great horde of them—plundering heathen as far as the eye could see . . ." "A small band of British soldiers and one holy man . . ." The babble continued in confusion against the backdrop of "Alleluia! Alleluia!"

Patricius jumped off Pertinax, flung his reins over a convenient post, and waded into the crowd. He spotted a young man about his own age with dark, intelligent eyes, speaking fluent Latin. He grabbed the fellow by the shoulder and pulled him to the side. "Tell me, what has happened?" he demanded.

The young man flung an arm toward a large, bearded man standing on a piling by the wharf. "That there's the merchant captain—said he's just sailed all the way around from Londinium—seems we're the last in all of Britain to hear the news. A huge barbarian army was sweeping down on Verulamium—Picts, Saxons, Angles, whatever. There was a holy man—a bishop or something—there from Gaul. Sent over by the Pope to see if he could stamp out some false belief in the church there.

"Anyway, all they had to protect them was a ragtag band of farmers and merchants with pitchforks and clubs, and the bishops and whatnot at the council who refused to take up arms of any kind." Patricius's informer paused and looked around. "I'm thirsty, aren't you? There's a wine shop just up the road. Shall we go there?"

Patricius, who had been hanging on every word, struggled to hide his annoyance. "Finish your story, man. Then I'll buy you the largest mugful in the best house in the district."

"Well, it seems this bishop, Germanus of Auxerre, they call him, said they would protect the city the same way Joshua in the Bible destroyed one. Everyone in the city—men, women, children—everyone followed him and the priests in a great procession outside the city walls, around and around. And every time this Germanus fellow raised the cross he was carrying, everyone shouted 'Alleluia!' at the top of their lungs."

The storyteller stopped.

"Well?" Patricius could have shook him with impatience. "What happened?"

The young man shrugged. "Nothing happened. The enemy ran off."

Patricius was thunderstruck. "Nothing! You call that nothing? The greatest miracle since Jericho?" He thrust a bronze coin into the fellow's hand. "Here, buy your own ale. I must tell my family."

He arrived back at the Villa Patricii, handed the sweating Pertinax over to a slave to be cooled down, and bounded into the courtyard shouting, "Alleluia!"

He had to tell the story three times to make his parents understand what had happened. Then Senn returned from the fields, and he repeated it again. Finally Lucullus returned from his solitary ride, and Patricius recounted it for the fifth time. Each time he told it, the miracle overwhelmed him anew. The great God of Old Testament power was at work intervening in today's world.

This Germanus of Auxerre must be a man of dynamic faith. His eyes shining, Patricius leaned toward Lucullus. "See, there lies the true strength of Britain. We are a tiny corner of the Empire. We can never be strong enough militarily to withstand the hordes of barbarians that batter at our shores. Think—even mighty Rome has been overrun at her very heart. Military strength is not the answer. Faith in God is the way to overcome the heathen. I will seek out this Germanus of Auxerre and learn from him. Join me, Lucullus."

"You've been listening to the tales of drunken sailors." Lucullus snorted. "There is only one thing barbarians understand—a stronger, swifter sword than their own. And I intend to wield it. For the sake of old friendship, though, let us travel our first day's journey together. I leave tomorrow."

"And I." Patricius clasped his friend's arm.

"Tomorrow?" Conchessa's lips trembled at the thought of her son leaving so soon, but she did not protest.

By common, unspoken consent the next morning, the two companions turned their pack-laden mounts to the south. Aqua Sulis, the former thriving market town and elegant spa, had fallen into disrepair, and stones from the great bath were being used as a quarry by local farmers trying to shore up old byres. The travelers took the Fosse Way. Lucullus, whose hand seldom left his sword hilt, was ever on the lookout. "I've heard it said that in the old days of the Empire a woman could travel alone—the eagles kept it that safe."

Patricius laughed. "From robbers maybe, but who would protect her from the eagles?" Then he sobered. "But it's true, barbarians from the outside aren't all we have to fear."

After another silence broken only by the sound of their horses' hooves, Patricius said, "I have often looked back on our night on Ynis Witrin. Have you thought of the brothers there?"

Lucullus's voice was cold and flat. "No. I have tried to forget everything about that night."

Patri nodded. "I, too. I have even prayed to forget." Now he should confess his sin and beg his friend's forgiveness. He tried to find the words, but they would not come. At last he said, "Shall we shelter with the brothers there tonight? Perhaps our visit would be happier this time."

"It could be no worse."

In this dry time of the year before the autumn rains began, it was possible to approach the island on foot. Leaving the Fosse, they picked their way carefully so as not to ride their mounts into a bog. Birds sang from bushes, and leaves, newly red and gold from a sudden drop in the temperature during the past nights, made a colorful world. They arrived at Ynis Witrin just as the setting sun crowned the Tor, illuminating the dilapidated chapel on top like a diadem.

In spite of the warm welcome and the beauty of the place, it was easy for them to see that the hermitage was getting along no better. In fact, the visitors realized, as they sat around the evening stewpot with the brothers, that the situation had deteriorated.

When all had eaten their fill of stew and barley cakes, Catha appeared. Her former startling freshness of beauty had ripened to a less showy, but even more appealing serenity. Her hair now braided and wrapped around her head in a coronet, her deep green tunic falling in soft folds, she greeted them with the bearing of a queen.

When she had returned to her hut, Patricius turned to Bremwal. "I'm surprised to see that Catha is still here; I would have thought her gone to her marriage lord long before now."

"Sadly, she is." The aging hermit spoke in a low voice. "Swelwes is her husband. Even when we learned the truth, which many of us had long suspected—that she is Hyn's illegitimate daughter—Swelwes would not be deterred."

"And they live here still?"

Wellias, who had been listening to the quiet conversation, answered, "What are we to do? In many ways Swelwes is the most devout of all. And his hut is his hut."

Bremwal nodded. "We are needing rules to make us a community, but we cannot agree on them. Many of our number will not even listen to the words of the church fathers."

Wellias's voice grew heavy with sadness. "We have no schedule of prayers, no singing of hymns, no order of mass." He shook his head slowly. "We can no longer be called Holy Avalon."

After fast-breaking the next morning, Patricius invited Lucullus to climb the Tor with him before they parted. All night it had been in the back of his mind that perhaps in the ancient chapel on the hill he could confess his great sin. He knew Lucullus would be wearing his sword—it never left his side—and he knew that Lucullus might be capable of avenging his family's death on the spot. But Patricius felt he could no longer bear the weight of his burden.

For each one step up the hill, the weight of the sin Patricius carried would have pulled him backward two, and yet he struggled onward to the top. When they arrived at the chapel, Patricius allowed himself to look at his friend. He was afraid his guilt was writ so large across his face that Lucullus would know instantly.

Instead, Lucullus smiled and swept the green and golden landscape below them with his arm. "This is wonderful. I slept the best last night I have in six years. I had forgotten about the strange, drawing peace of this place. I don't see how the brothers who live here can be at odds with each other. Don't you feel it? The peace—you can almost reach out and touch it."

And Patricius could not speak. He could not destroy the first peace his friend had found since he himself had destroyed Lucullus's whole world. Patricius then saw what his penance was to be. Bearing his own guilt, carrying the weight of his sin without his friend's forgiveness.

Silently they descended the steep slope and mounted their horses to go their separate ways. Lucullus, turning his back on the peace of the island, would seek another kind of peace through war, and Patricius, bearing a burden of guilt, would seek peace through love.

A grove of old giant oak trees stood at the base of the Tor, an ancient druid holy place, some said. At that point the ways through the swampland separated east and south. The friends clasped hands. "I wonder if we'll meet again," Lucullus said.

Patricius shook his head. "Only God knows. May He go with you."

16

atricius had never been a scholar, and now, approaching middle age, it was a grinding experience to tackle deep study of the Scriptures—both Jewish and Christian—and the writings of the church fathers. Many a time in the past five years Patricius had left his reading table in the monastery at Auxerre with burning eyes, splitting head, and aching back, but with little or no new understanding of the message he dreamed of carrying to the Eirran.

He knew what skillful debaters the druids could be, how superstitious the people were, and how tenaciously their leaders clung to the traditions of their forefathers. Patricius must be steeped in the Word of God and able to explain it forcefully, but at the moment he couldn't have explained anything to a British schoolboy. He had been too tired and discouraged even to play his pipes for weeks.

Rubbing his eyes, he closed the codex-style book on the wooden reading table in front of him, and, nodding to Brother Jude in charge of the book room, left his studies for the day. It was an hour yet before the brothers would meet in the oratory for prayers before the evening meal. He walked out into the warm, dry air of the late summer's afternoon—so different from any he had experienced in Eire. It hadn't rained here for weeks, and the fields beyond the monastery, miraculously spared the Vandals' plunder, were turning brown and gold ready for harvest. In the space between refectory, oratory, and dorter, orange and gold flowers bloomed in bright corners. The warmth, order, and quiet of the place spoke peace to his troubled soul, and yet he could not be at peace. Why would God place this call on his heart—even send a vision—if he would never be worthy to fulfill it?

In his despair he wondered whether he was being punished for the great sin he had committed. Would he ever be free of that guilt? Surely, since one of his prime reasons for wanting to take the gospel to Hibernia was to reduce the number of raids, such as the one that had killed Lucullus's family, there was no more adequate penance he could do. So why did God not open the way for him to return? Why must he continue slaving over books when he would be winning souls?

"I'm sorry, I didn't quite catch that."

Patricius jumped at the sound of another's voice. He had been so deep in his soul-searching he had not realized he had spoken aloud. Nor had he seen Brother Deisignatus tending the flowers at the side of a low stone wall. Patricius sighed and sat on a bench near the flower bed. "I fear I was reciting my sins. They are heavy on my heart at the moment."

Deisignatus brushed the sandy soil from his brown tunic and sat down beside him. "Would it help to confess it to another?"

The idea was a welcome one. Patricius had found no relief in carrying his guilt alone all these years. Even in his moments of joyful worship in Hibernia, remorse for his pride and jealously had been with him, and then when he had returned home and learned the result of his betrayal . . . five years of study, first at Lerins, and more recently here at Auxerre under the saintly Bishop Germanus himself, had not brought freedom to his spirit.

He turned to the kindly-seeming Deisignatus. "When I was a lad of sixteen I sinned grievously . . ."

The clanging of the bronze hand bell for evening prayers had long since faded with the sunset when Patricius finished his narrative. Deisignatus listened quietly and at the end merely said, "I will pray for you, my brother."

The confession did not bring the relief he sought, but it had been good to talk to another. Patricius, however, chose to skip the evening meal and go directly to his cell when Deisignatus turned toward the refectory. He was determined to wait as long as the Lord required, but he could not help asking, "How long will it yet be, Lord?"

The answer, it appeared, came quickly. On a September morning when the first rays of sunlight after morning prayers announced the coming of autumn by highlighting the golden leaves, Patricius was summoned to Germanus's study. As soon as Patricius sat down on a stool before the table piled high with books, scrolls, and documents that filled most of the small room, the bishop rose and clapped Patricius on the shoulder. "My son, I know how hard you have studied and how ardently you have longed to return to the land of your captivity with the message of freedom. I want you to know that the time draws nigh."

Patricius was too overcome to speak. Germanus continued. "The Christians in Hibernia have sent a formal request to the bishops of Britain to supply their land with a bishop. The selection, of course, will be at the will of a British synod, but I wish to place your name before them."

"Most Reverend Father." Patricius lowered his head.

"Palladius, Deisignatus, and I leave for Londinium next week." Patricius jerked his head up in surprise. "No, my son, you are not to go with us at this time. You will remain here and continue your study. And you will, I know, be much in prayer about the matter."

Patricius bowed his head in consent.

But during the following weeks that grew into months, Patricius found it difficult to wait submissively. Ever the man of action, he longed to take ship. Already he knew the brothers he would invite to accompany him on his mission—Auxilius, Isernius, Secundinus . . . the items he would take with him—censors, crosses, chalices . . . and his itinerary. First he would go to the High King of Tara. If he could gain permission from Niall of the Nine Hostages to preach in the land, none would refuse to listen to him. Then he would go to Slemish to face his old master Michlu, then to the druids of Crom Cruach who persisted in their vile practice of human sacrifice . . .

He forced his attention back to the scroll before him, *Papias's Explanation of the Lord's Discourses.*

It was not surprising that no messages arrived from the delegation to Britain that winter. The weather was unusually violent, and crossings of the Fretum Gallicum would have been nearly impossible. But finally in late February a messenger arrived at Auxerre.

Patricius, listening with the other brothers to the reading of the letter from their bishop, tried not to show his impatience. Finally the reader came to the last portion of the letter. "'And at the last meeting of the synod, a bishop was elected to serve our fellow believers in the land to the west. Palladius is to be so ordained by Pope Celestine and will go to Hibernia next year.'

"So ends the reading of our most Reverend Father's letter." The monk rolled up the parchment sheets and placed them back in their leather pouch. "Oh, and he encloses a private communication for Brother Patricius."

Disappointment, outrage, shock surged through Patricius in waves, but he took the small scroll with an outward calm and carried it to his cell. What could have happened? The position was as much as promised to him. Palladius? How could that be? What did Palladius know of the Eirran? Had he spent six years in that rough, mystical land learning their customs and beliefs? Did he know the homes and titles of the rulers? Could he face a druid and argue with him from a knowledge of the Gael's own religion—and in the Gael's own tongue?

At last he broke the wax wafer and read, "My son, I know of the disappointment this letter brings you, and my heart aches. I did my best, but it seems that our Lord in His wisdom knows that the time is not yet right for you to go to Hibernia. Your name was much debated and your qualifications of knowing the country urged forcefully, but many in the synod felt your position as deacon and your educational qualifications are not high enough for so great a responsibility. Deisignatus at first argued hotly for your appointment, but was finally persuaded by the arguments in favor of choosing one with greater academic qualifications. In the end he confided to us with great heaviness of heart, the story of your early sin . . ."

There was more, but Patricius could read no further. Was he to be forever haunted by what he had done in his boyhood in one day, no—in one hour—because he was not then strong in the faith? He fell to his knees on the hard stone floor of his cell. But his agony of spirit was too great to pray. His mind would form no words to express the darkness in his soul. He could only kneel there in the cold and the dark.

An hour before sunrise the youngest of the brothers knocked at the door of his cell to call him to lauds. Patricius's legs were too stiff and numb to move. At first Benegius thought he had opened the door on a corpse and drew back in alarm. Then he saw Patricius's eyes move and knew he was alive.

"Help me to my cot, boy. I must wait." Benegius put his arms around Patricius's chest and lifted him toward the hard wooden pallet. "I must wait and study, and wait and pray, and wait. Blessed be the name of the Lord."

Lucullus, with the army of Vortigern, was also waiting. He sat at the foot of the long trestle table in the smoky timber-built hall which replaced the old Roman forum in Venta Belgarum. The forum had been destroyed three years ago by Picti and Scoti raiders. At the high table Vortigern, with his thin face and pointed red beard that had given him his nickname "The Fox," argued hotly with his sons and generals. But Lucullus could feel only a weary indifference to the outcome.

The results of their day's patrol had been good enough. They had not beaten the enemy, but they had surprised a band of raiders at a villa near Noviomagus and chased them back to the sea. The Picts had been forced to leave all their captives and much of their booty behind in their flight. But, of course, they would be back tomorrow or the next day, perhaps to strike a villa or civitas where no army patrolled. And so it went.

As they so often did in quiet moments, Lucullus's fingertips sought the engraved Capricorn on his bracelet. That long ago Marcellus had built Hadrian's Wall to keep the Picts out. Now they came by sea. The low, flat boats glided over the waves, and the raiders then swarmed inexorably over the land plundering villas and markets.

Sometimes the army scored a real victory. Vortigern's son Vortemir led the cavalry, and their swift strikes were extremely effective against the Picts who could move only slowly on foot. But the cavalry was pitifully small—even smaller than the infantry Vortigern had been able to raise. And their victories were too few and too far apart to produce lasting security.

Or lasting satisfaction. Even after a decisive victory, not just a draw as today's encounter had been, but when they had soundly defeated the enemy, Lucullus still felt himself overcome by this lassitude. He looked at his bracelet. Had Marcellus felt this unrest at the end of a day? What had his ancestor done to find contentment, he wondered. Or had he found it?

Lucullus turned to the man beside him, a relative only by marriage, but family to one who had so long been alone in the world. Lucullus's one pleasure in serving Vortigern had been the company of his Uncle Tregatta. Even had they not been related, it would have been a joy to serve with this man. Taller by a head than any man in the room, with hair more golden than even the king's crown, Ultha Tregatta was also the bravest and strongest of the warriors, evidencing the royal blood that ran in his veins. Lucullus looked at the man now and thought that, in spite of his father's long ago misgivings, his aunt had married well. "And how are things in Dumnoni, Uncle?"

Ultha tossed back his great golden head and raised his drinking cup high to catch the firelight. "My time at home last harvest season was not ill-spent. I received word only today that my wife, your aunt, has given me a fine healthy son after these many years of marriage. We shall call him Utha, and he shall be a fine warrior. When he is of age, I shall see to his training myself."

Lucullus congratulated his uncle warmly. In spite of all the ravages of barbarian and raider, the line of Artios had not been extinguished.

But suddenly heads turned as the argument at the high table grew more heated. A general wearing a heavy bronze torque above his wine-colored tunic slammed his fist against the table to emphasize his words. "We'll fight on as we are! We must. It is the only way. Other chieftains will join us with their men when they see our victories."

"Na, na! We should consolidate with the Roman party. No one knows the threat of the Picti like Britannia Secunda. The Bishop of Ebercanum—" Vortemir jerked back on his stool as his father's heavy, ringed hand shot toward him.

"Enough! No son of mine will defy me by sniveling to those who serve the Pope. If General Aetius can bring peace to Rome by subduing Attila, we may look to him for help, but we will not align with those who follow the church like faithful hounds every time the Pope sends that Germanus fellow over here to tell us what to think."

Vortemir gave a guffaw of laughter, followed by a deep drink from his cup of barley beer. "I did not know you cared so much for your religion, my father."

Vortigern's face turned almost as red as his wispy beard. "I will not be laughed at by my son—especially by a son who would align true Britons with lackeys of Rome. I care not for any god or his priests, and I will snivel to none for my power."

The king's eyes took on a sharp glint that made even Lucullus at the end of the room shiver. "I will make my own alliances." Vortigern rose and flung his dark blue cloak back from his shoulders. His heavy gold and amber necklace glowed in the firelight, and the royal circlet around his head emphasized the sharpness of his features. He rapped on the table with the hilt of his dagger to command the attention of every warrior in the hall. "We shall soon have allies. Two days ago I sent my envoys to Hengist of the Saxons."

Stunned silence met the announcement. A general in a dark green tunic jumped to his feet and leaned across the table until his face was only inches from his king's. "You have made a treaty with the *Saxons?* The very enemy we have defended these shores against for two hundred years?"

Vortemir now jumped to his feet, forcing himself between the king and general. "It is unthinkable, Father! You have delivered us into the hands of our enemies. Better to be overrun by Picts and Scots from our own island than by invaders from across the northern sea!"

With an angry gesture Vortigern shoved both his opponents down on their stools. "It was the policy of Rome for four hundred years in this land to defend the Empire with auxiliary troops from barbarian lands. You, my son, who so favor Roman ways, should be pleased that your father has chosen to follow a Roman policy."

"The policy worked only because Rome was strong enough to keep the foreigners in line. We are not so strong, my father."

Vortigern gave a high-pitched chortle surprising from a warrior-king. "We are not so strong, so we must be smarter. I will give the Saxons lands for their families. Then it will be their own homes they are defending—we will not have to force them to fight for us."

Vortemir picked up the dagger with which he had eaten his hunk of roast meat and slammed it against the table. "It will not work. You have betrayed Britain, thrown open the door to her oldest enemies."

Vortigern seized the dagger and held it aloft, firelight glinting off its iron point, aimed straight at his own son. Vortemir did not flinch, but held his father in a hard stare. Vortigern brought the dagger down in a great slashing arc, inches in front of Vortemir. The blade sank deep into the table. "I will not be called a traitor to my own land!" His gaze locked with his son's for a full minute before he pulled back with his strange, spine-tingling laugh. Suddenly his anger seemed to drain from him. He flung his arm out to the room. "More beer! Fill the cups! Harper, play!" The king held his cup aloft. "We will await the results of my treaty."

The day at Auxerre had begun like any other—with the clanging of the dissonant quadrangular hand bell before sunrise signaling lauds. For two years Patricius had been true to his vow to wait. God had called him. He had answered, "Here am I, Lord, send me." He had done all that was required of him. Now he waited.

After his morning portion of ale and bread, taken in silence in the refectory before he would return to his cell to continue his study, Patricius's schedule was interrupted by the arrival of a messenger. Without any sense that his entire life was about to change, Patricius filled the cup of the haggard-looking monk who sat across the table from him in a tattered, hooded tunic.

The brother drank deeply before telling his story. Even after it was complete, Patricius sat long, going over every detail in his mind. Palladius was dead. After less than a year in Hibernia, he had fallen ill with a virulent fever that left him weak and wasted. Hearing of the hermitage on Ynis Witrin, he had been carried there by two of his companions in hopes of finding restoration for both body and spirit. But he arrived more dead than alive. Now his body rested in Avalon, but his spirit had gone on to Paradise.

Patricius was amazed that his second chance had come so soon and so suddenly, but also he was astounded that Palladius, the first Bishop of Hibernia, lay at rest on that lovely green island Patricius himself held so dear. He had spent only a few hours in Palladius's company, yet it seemed that their destinies were strangely intertwined.

Germanus was waiting for Patricius when he knocked at the door of the bishop's cell. "There should be no debate this time, my son. I have already sent a dispatch to His Holiness. In the briefest time possible I expect to receive word from Pope Celestine that he has appointed you bishop to Hibernia."

17

atricius looked at the rainbow in the intensely blue sky and smiled. This was Eire. And Eire at the best time of all when the white bloom was on the thorn and newborn lambs tumbled from their mothers. He gestured toward the radiant sky and called to his companions. "Enjoy it, my friends. In a few minutes this glistening beauty will be engulfed by dark clouds from the west, and you'll be seeking shelter from the rain."

Auxilius, Isernius, and Secundinus looked at Patricius doubtfully as they beheld the sparkling, cloudless sky before them. Surely he exaggerated.

"You doubt my words, my sons? See." He pointed to the west. "I see a cloud no bigger than a man's hand, but it may bring rains as large as those that fell for Elijah." Patricius became more serious. "And the battles we face may be much like those Elijah fought with the prophets of Baal. You have come on this mission with me for the glory of God, but the cost may be high."

The brothers helped the boatmen load their equipment on the boats Patricius had engaged to take them up the river Boyne to Tara while Patricius stood aloof, seeking, as he had learned to do, God's help for the mission that lay ahead of him. After so many years of preparation, he must not fail now. At last he had learned that only by leaning constantly on God's help and presence could he hope to succeed.

He was still lithe and quick, a man made for action. His hair was now gray as a gull's breast, but it retained its curl-spring, even as his step retained its bounce. And the light burned even more intensely in his blue eyes as the fire kindled brighter within him.

When all was loaded in the slim river coracles so suited to the smooth, rapidly flowing Eirran waters, Patricius took his place in the first boat. They were no more than a few yards down the river when, as Patricius had predicted, the first drops of rain began to fall. After his years in the warm, dry climate of central Gaul, Patricius shivered under his cloak, yet he welcomed the invigorating freshness. No sooner had he made the contrast between Eire and Gaul, however, than he focused inward on the contrast in himself from the first time he had seen this moist, green land, so soft and yet so sharply rocky.

The shallow soil, the rocky cliffs, the often-sullen weather were like the sixteen-year-old boy Niall's raiders had brought here—headstrong, rebellious, always rushing into things without thought. But he had returned a new man—calm inside, relying on God's direction, and willing to wait when he must. One thing, however, had not changed. He put his hand inside his tunic and drew out his pipes. The boatmen broke into broad smiles as the notes fell more silver than the raindrops on the water.

The brief rain shower passed on, and long, golden sunbeams slanted through gaps in the massed gray clouds over their heads. Patricius thought of the people to whom he had come with the Word of God. How would they receive it? The crucial question was how would the kings and chieftains receive it, for if they accepted him, there would be little trouble with the people. He had long ago determined that he would focus on converting the kings—especially the High King of Tara.

Patricius knew though that the real contest for the hearts of the people would not be between himself and the kings—not even the High King—but between himself and the druids, who ruled the kings. The thought would have been terrifying if he had not experienced the power of God in his own life and knew how much greater his God was than Dagada, Lugh, Crom Cruach, or any of the lesser gods.

The April countryside was a patchwork of every imaginable shade of green, from the forest black of ancient hill junipers to the tinted yellow of newborn shoots of spring wheat. And around every rath and on every hillside, baby lambs bleated, tottering after their mothers. Rocks, trees, and clouds shaded the land with blue, purple, and gray shadows, and Patricius thanked God that they should have arrived at this wonderful season of the renewing of life—on the very eve of Jesus' victory over death. Tomorrow would be Easter.

Tonight he and his companions would camp near a hill where they could light their Paschal fire. In the morning they would celebrate the most joyful, most holy Mass of the year to inaugurate their mission.

Patricius turned to his bandy-legged little boatman who sat paddling with sure strokes in the back of the boat. "Do you know if King Niall is in residence at Tara just now?"

Righ, the boatman, shook his head. "Niall sleeps with his fathers these three years and past. Leoghaire, son of Niall, is now king in Tara."

Patricius closed his eyes at the news. He had not thought of the changes that would have occurred in his absence. Leoghaire. Patricius remembered him—taller, broader, louder than his father. And he remembered the tales he had heard of his cruelty. Leoghaire did not take hostages as his father had; he killed all his enemies in the most painful manner he could devise.

"And who are his chief druids?" Patricius asked.

"Lochru and Lucetmal, as served his father." Righ dipped his paddle into the water and slipped it skillfully through the smooth water.

Patricius nodded. He remembered their names. Men of great power. If he could reach these men, he could then preach anywhere in Eire. He looked across the garden patchwork of the countryside. Ahead and to their left, as on his first time here, Patricius saw the Hill of Tara crowned with ancient buildings: the banqueting hall of the kings, the oval Rath na Riogh—Well of Kings—surrounding the tall round Lia Fail, the coronation stone, and behind that the Rath Leoghaire where the king lived. Just a little farther on was another hill, slightly smaller, but open to view on every side. There could be no better spot to light their Paschal fire. Claith had told him about it—the Hill of the Slain where the mighty Cuchulain had slaughtered his foes. The bards of Eire still sang of the deeds before the feast-fires. Yes, here Patricius would also light a victory fire that would burn forever throughout the land.

He pointed. "We will camp there tonight. This is the eve of our greatest holy day. Tonight we will burn a fire on that hill in honor of the resurrection of our Lord, whose truth burns in our hearts."

The boatman's eyes grew large with fear, and his patchy beard seemed to bristle. At first, Patricius, who had gone five years without speaking Gaelic, thought he had said something wrong, but then he realized Righ had understood perfectly. "On the Hill of the Slain? You build a fire? Tonight?"

Patricius nodded calmly. "I don't understand your alarm. Fires on hilltops are common here—I remember well seeing them in the distance when I watched over the sheep in Slemish."

"Ah, but not on that hill. It is forbidden. Only druids may go onto the Hill of the Slain. Only they are safe from the snakes."

Patricius frowned. Where had he heard that before? Ah, yes, he remembered. So Claith had told him. The druids kept all from the hill by calling it the habitation of snakes.

Righ nodded with such energy he broke the rhythm of his rowing, as he urged his point. "The druids go there at the dark of the moon to make kill-offerings to Dagada that his cauldron of plenty will not fail our land. Only then the snakes will not harm them."

Patricius shook his head. "Our God is stronger than Dagada. We are not afraid."

The boatman persisted. "But not tonight. You must not light your fire tonight. There are no fires in all of Tara on this one night of the year."

"And why is that?"

"Tomorrow is Leoghaire's birthday. All fires save the king's feast-fire are to be cold in Tara tonight until the High King himself lights the first one in the morning. Then all will light their fires in honor of the day that gave our king birth."

"No. We will light our fire first in honor of the day that God gave the new birth to man."

The boatman leaned forward and gripped Patricius's arm. "But it is a dying matter to disobey the king in this."

Patricius had not expected such a violent confrontation to come so soon. But this solved one problem that had been puzzling him for days—how was he to gain admittance to the High King? Now if he were to be brought before Leoghaire for judgment, he would have an opportunity to speak. Even if the death sentence followed, he would speak first. Leoghaire would hear God's message.

A few hours later the the sun streaked the evening sky red, pink, and yellow as the companions made their camp. Auxilius cleared away their evening meal, and Isernius unfolded the leather tents under which they would sleep, while Patricius and Secundinus scoured the countryside for dry thorn bushes to make their bonfire. Through the evening mist they could look across the valley between their camp and the rath of King Leoghaire atop Tara Hill. Even a small fire would glare in the eyes of the king. But Patricius was determined that theirs should not be a small fire.

Patricius had especially chosen Secundinus for his love of music which would match well with the lyrical Eirran. Brother Secundinus, the youngest and smallest of their party, looked around nervously as they carried their first arm loads of firewood up the hill. "What of the snakes?"

Patricius's voice was calm. "I have seen no snakes. I suspect the snakes are the druids themselves. Remember Scripture, my son—'Wicked men from birth have taken to devious ways; liars, no sooner born than they go astray, venomous with the venom of serpents.'"

Three more loads and Patricius judged they had enough fuel for the fire that was to burn to the glory of God. They waited another hour until the land was thoroughly shrouded in black. "I believe it is time now." Patricius filled a small pot with glowing embers from their dying cookfire and led the small procession up the hill. Isernius followed holding a small bronze cross in both hands. Then came Auxilius with the other vessels Patricius had prepared for their first service in Eire. Secundinus brought up the rear, singing a hymn of his own composition.

They stood in a semicircle around the pile of wood while Patricius knelt and shoveled scoops of glowing coals in three piles around the base. He stood back and watched the thorn twigs crackle and and the fire catch onto the larger branches. When the fire was burning freely, he raised his hand in a blessing to his companions and said, "'You are the light of the world. A light on a hill cannot be hidden. When a lamp is lit, it is not put under a meal tub, but on a lamp stand, where it gives light to all.' And you, my friends, like the lamp, and like this, our Paschal fire, must shed light among all those in this, our new land, so that they may come to know and glorify our Father in heaven."

Then he took a small loaf of bread from the basket Auxilius carried. He blessed it, broke it in half, and held it up to be illuminated by the leaping flames. "*Corpus Christi*—the body of Christ. Our Lord said, 'This is My body.' We also are His body—as a group we are drawn together, and we go out to do His work as His hands and His feet—members of His body. So may we serve Him."

Patricius placed a small piece of the sacred bread on Auxilius's tongue. "*Corpus Christi.*" He turned to Isernius. "*Corpus Christi.*" And to Secundinus. "*Corpus Christi.*"

Then he took the cup and filled it with water and wine from cruets he had prepared earlier. The firelight played on the bronze chalice, and Patricius, as he held the cup high, thought of all the Eucharists he had celebrated in the past and of all Christians now gathered around the table of the Lord on this Paschal Eve. From one end of the Empire to the other, Christians were celebrating their Lord's death and resurrection.

"We are all Your children around Your table, Lord." And as he said the words, he knew he was not alone in an alien land surrounded by priests of a diabolical religion. He was at home at God's table—with his family in Britain, with the brothers he left behind in Gaul, with the faithful in Rome—all over the Empire believers celebrated this great sacrament and received His grace as one body. With such a great cloud of witnesses around him, Patricius knew he could succeed in his mission. He drank deeply from the cup, as in so doing he shared in Christ's sacrifice.

"'Drink all of this in remembrance of Me.'" He offered the grail to Auxilius. "The blood of Christ."

The celebration was barely over when they heard angry shouts. The flatha, Leoghaire's warriors, stormed up the hill with drawn swords. A whirlwind chariot ride brought them to Tara, and, as if the years between had not existed, Patricius stood once again, hands bound with iron chains, in the Tech Midchuarta, the Great Hall of Tara. Some six hundred fifty feet long and one hundred feet wide, the hall was the largest structure Patricius had ever seen. The age-darkened timbers held many and many a head of defeated enemies, but the gray stone walls were richly covered with embroidered hangings. Crimson and gold magical beasts and birds intertwined with leaves and trailing branches. And within the hall colorfully-clad warriors, peasants, and nobles had gathered to celebrate their king's birthday.

As Caelchon, the flatha captain, led the missionaries into the hall at swordpoint, vast quantities of food and drink were being served up and down the long tables while jugglers, clowns, magicians, bards, drummers, pipers, harpers performed to the honor of King Leoghaire. Patricius thought that surely Caelchon would not interrupt the celebration. But as his captor approached the royal couple sitting at the high table, Patricius realized that he and his companions were to be part of the entertainment.

A silence fell over the top of the hall and gradually made its way down the cavernous length. Every head turned toward the high table. Revelers left their heather-honey mead cups and moved forward. Many stood on the tables to see better. These foreign-looking men in their somber brown, hooded robes, with the front of their heads shaved from ear to ear, had actually defied the High King by lighting a fire on his birthday eve? And on the Hill of the Slain? They had gone up the hill of snakes and returned alive? These strange men must worship powerful gods.

Leoghaire rose. Even in the vastness of his poorly-lit hall, he was a commanding sight. His crimson, purple, and gold cloak billowed over his emerald tunic. Gold and amber glinted on his brow, neck, and arms, but were all outshone by the exquisite Brooch of Tara on his shoulder. Although small, its very power was in its delicacy, as the animals, reptiles, and humans fashioned from filigree wire all winked and sparkled at one another in the firelight, and the contrasting colors of the gilt surface and molded dark glass reflected varying lights. Leoghaire's shoulder-length hair, the color of age-darkened amber, flowed to the folds of his cape, adding to the fierce appearance of his bearded, mustachioed face.

"Why have you dared to desecrate my birthday celebration by the lighting of your own hill-fire?" he bellowed.

Patricius stepped forward. "Bid your captain to unchain me, and I will gladly answer."

Leoghaire hesitated.

"We are unarmed. We come as men of peace. You have no need to fear us unbound."

Leoghaire made an impatient gesture toward Caelchon, and Patricius and his companions were unchained.

"I mean no disrespect to Your Majesty." Patricius spoke loudly, constantly aware that the real power was wielded by the druids behind the power-seat. "I wish you the happiest of natal celebrations. But there is One higher even than the High King of Tara whose holy day must also be celebrated."

From the indrawn breath behind him, Patricius knew he was reaching his audience. "I have come to Eire—rather, returned to the land where I served many years of slavery as a youth, brought here by your father Niall of the Nine Hostages. King Leoghaire, I have come back to tell you of the High God who offers all men what no other god can offer—love and peace and salvation. I have come to you, King Leoghaire, to seek your permission to tell the people of Eire of this God."

"No!" Before even the king could answer, Lochru and Lucetmal strode forward. "There can be no other high god in Tara or in all Eire but Dagada. Those who defy Dagada must be sacrificed to him. Tomorrow you shall be given to Dagada on the very hill where you lit your blasphemous fire."

Only a short time ago Patricius had drunk of the communion cup on that hill. On the night He was crucified, Christ had asked His disciples if they could drink of the cup that He would drink. Would Patricius's communion cup be to the death as that of his Lord's was?

Patricius turned to the people in the guise of speaking to the druids. "Yes. I lit the fire to my God on the very hill that you have kept your people from with fearful tales of poisonous snakes. Our God does not keep His followers away with fear, but bids them come to Him with love. The love of our God gives His followers power. He promises His followers that they may step on asp and cobra; they may tread safely on snake and serpent. That is the power of our God and His Son our Lord Jesus Christ whom we bring to you." A gentle murmur behind Patricius told him his message was getting through.

"No! Such a God is not for the High King, not for Tara, not for Eire . . ." Both druids raised their hands and, swaying slightly in their multicolored robes, sacred gold moon-shaped lunula about their necks, chanted:

Dagada with his harp of three tunes gives the Eirran feeling.
Dagada plays on his harp of three strings:
With one pluck he grants the people sleep,
with another stroke he gives the Eirran mirth,
with yet another touch he brings mourning.
Dagada wields his club of great power:
With one slash he grants the people strength,
with another blow he gives the Eirran victory,
with yet another hit he brings mighty triumph.
Dagada holds his unquenchable cauldron of plenty.
With one bestowal he gives the people abundance,
with another favor he grants the Eirran riches,
With yet another outpouring flows life and health.
May Dagada the high god of all Eire ever be worshiped by his faithful people.
Dagada the harper,
Dagada the strong,
Dagada the abundant.
Dagada, Dagada, Dagada.

As the swaying and chanting mingled with the smoke and firelight and many behind Patricius took up the chant, he realized that the contest was not one of fires or snakes or priests. It was a contest between the cauldron of Dagada's plenty and the cup of the Lord's Supper. Somehow he must make them see that the power of Christ's sacrifice was greater than Dagada's club.

But combating the mystical emotion generated by the druids seemed impossible. And then the intensity of the chant increased as up and down the great length of the hall, the drummers and pipers took up the rhythm of the chant. Lochru waited for the perfect moment. When the chant had reached its peak, he signaled with an upraised hand to the harpers to join. The voice of the instrument most beloved by all of Eire and sacred to Dagada soared above all other voices to the blackened rafters where the heads of defeated enemies hung by their own hair.

At the sound of the harpvoice, Patricius knew what to do. When at last the music softened and the chanting faded, he turned to Leoghaire, who had remained aloof from the frenzy. The bishop bowed deeply before the king. "O High One, I beg you to forgive any offense I have caused you by lighting a fire to honor my God. In respect for your own great occasion, may I sing you a harptale of our God that you may know of His love and power and better judge my act?"

The offer of a harpsong was irresistible. Leoghaire signaled for everyone to be seated. Lochru and Lucetmal scowled, but they had no option but to obey their king.

At a signal from Leoghaire a bard stepped forward to offer his harp. Patricius recognized the freckles first, for the hound-red hair had turned barley-pale with the years. "My old friend Claith, the first of the Eirran to speak a kind word to me. I always thought you were more harpsinger than warrior at heart."

Claith made no reply, but held out his harp. Patricius signaled Secundinus.

The monk came forward, took the black bogwood harp of seven strings, and seated himself before the high table. He nestled the instrument against one bent knee and leaned the top in the hollow of his left shoulder. After a few brilliant, flowing glissandos, he gentled the strings to a soft background and Patricius's pipe music joined the harp. When all in the hall were leaning forward, Patricius lowered his pipes and called out in a chanting voice that reached to the very end of the room, "And in the beginning, in the time before time, the Lord God created a garden."

The joy of the story was upon Patricius, and his eyes lit with the fire within him. With a bold stroke, Patricius abandoned all that Germanus had taught him of the land of the Jewish Scriptures and described for his listeners their own land, for after all, had not the Lord God created Eire as truly as He created the Garden of Eden?

"A garden of emerald green hills covered by intense blue skies billowing with white clouds. And He gave rain and slanting sunlight and rainbows to declare His glory. He made joyous waterfalls to tumble from the hills and little lakes to fill every hollow of the ground. He surrounded the land by a blue sea with mighty waves that crashed against black cliffs. And set startling white seabirds to fly against the blue sky and nest in the dark rocks. And lambs and cattle and ponies and great, red wolfhounds—the Lord God created them all. And in the midst of this land of beauty and plenty and abundance, He set a man and a woman. And God told the man and the woman to be happy and to enjoy the bounty of His land."

At a look from Patricius, Secundinus struck a low, ominous note on the harp and held it until its warning of doom had faded. "But there was a serpent in the garden. And the serpent worshiped not the Lord God, nor loved the man and the woman. The wily, subtle serpent led the man and the woman from the worship of the true God by tempting them to taste of evil."

Again the death-sounding notes. When they had faded, Patricius smiled, and Secundinus changed to a joyous flight of strings, joined briefly by the pipe before Patricius continued. "But our God would not leave His people to evil. He came to earth even as a man to live and teach and offer Himself as a sacrifice that none may ever need follow the way of the snake. This is the night of His sacrifice, of His entombment, of His victory over evil. For in the morning

He rose from the grave and offers Himself now to all who will believe on Him, as He offered His own body to His believers for an abundance of life. Oh come, taste and see that the Lord is good; blessed is the man that trusts in Him."

Patricius paused for a celebration of harpsong, then continued. "Come to the banquet table of our Lord, drink of His cup of the new life. Turn away from the cauldron of Dagada that the wily serpent in the garden would offer you."

Patricius was exhausted. He let the harp finish his story.

He and his companions spent the rest of the night in chains on a pile of animal skins in a locked room—perhaps one of the rooms where Niall's nine hostages had been kept, and not unlike the room where Patricius spent his first night in Eire. Patricius knew he should be praying and leading the brothers in devotions, but he was too weary. He could neither pray nor sleep. He could only be grateful that, whatever the outcome, he had been allowed to preach the gospel in Eire.

In the hall of Vortigern in Venta Belgarum, the harping had not yet ceased for the night. Had Lucullus thought of praying, he would also have found himself too tired—and too drunk. A yellow-haired Saxon girl in a yellow-green kirtle bent close to Lucullus to refill his mead horn.

At first he had been angry when Vortigern's court had adopted the barbaric practice of drinking their Saxon-brewed mead from vulgar ox horns—he who had been raised with the best wine in the finest Roman goblets. But, like most of Vortigern's army, he had accepted the practice—in honor of their allies, Vortigern insisted. Few dared to whisper that, in truth, it was simply one more submission to their former enemies who had become their conquerors under the name of ally.

True, Vortigern's policy succeeded for several years. Hengist and his stocky, yellow-haired brother Horsa brought first their large families, then whole villages to the Island of Tanatus where the River Thamesis flowed into the Fretum Gallicum. They built wooden, thatched-roofed huts, tilled the fertile soil, and raised families.

And in return for this rich land, the Saxons drove the Picts and Scoti back to the north beyond the old Roman wall so that the Britons in the southeast could also till their soil and raise their families.

But then more Saxons came to join their families and friends in the rich lands of Hengist and Horsa, and then the Island of Tanatus was not sufficient. Vortigern still sat in the high place. But his yellow-haired Saxon wife sat beside him, plaiting her golden braids with jewels from the British treasury, and robing herself in finest scarlet from the British looms. Rowena, the bewitchingly beautiful daughter of Hengist, had seduced the British king from his British wife and the mother of his children.

Now Hengist and Horsa held all of the lands west of Tanatus from Londinium to Venta Belgarum. And more of their countrymen from the north poured in in their dragon-headed long ships every month. How long would they be happy with this increase in their grant? How long until the Saxons gobbled up all of Britain?

Lucullus had heard whisperings, the merest rippling on the breeze, of strange tidings to the west—perhaps as far west as Segontium where the Hibernian Sea lapped the farthest mountains of the Cymri, or was it to the south of there in the land of the Dumnoni? The rustlings in the grass were never definite, but somewhere beyond the reach of Vortigern and Hengist, the Roman party was not dead. True, the Duke of Britannia Prima, whom Lucullus had followed in his youth, was long gone, as was the whole Roman idea of a Britannia Prima. Yet there was a leader who believed in laws and order and drank wine from a cup like a civilized man, a son of the murdered Constantus, some said . . . Lucullus looked at the plank table in front of him where his sloshed mead lay in a pale yellow pool by his hand.

One could not put much faith in the rustlings of the grass and the stirrings of the breezes, and yet the name Ambrosius wafted like the smoke from the cookfire where an ox carcass sizzled over the coals. And when Vortemir, the king's son, ceased to fill his place at the high table, the whisperings said he had gone to join this Ambrosius. But Lucullus had ceased to trust in the strength of arms and war leaders. Neither had brought peace to his land or to his heart.

The serving girl leaned closer to refill his spilled horn. He smelled the sweet womanliness of her. Why not? Mead had ceased to bring oblivion; he would seek it elsewhere. Lucullus put his arms around the girl.

But even as they sank onto the floor-rushes beneath the table, his mind caught at a pale glimmer of memory. There had been another girl once in a pale green tunic. A girl he had not lain with in the rushes, but had climbed with to the top of a tall green mountain. It had not been acrid brown smoke that had whirled around him with that long-ago maiden, but light, fresh mist, touched with the morning sunlight. And she had taken him up the mountain to visit a place of prayer.

Patricius sat in the morning sunlight, playing a pipe-tune as light as the sea air and watching the rolling waves below him smash against the lava cliffs, white foam spewing, then ebbing with every in-sweep of the waves. A gannet with its six-foot wingspan soared above him, flying up until it was only a tiny speck against the blue sky. Then, as Patricius held his breath at the spectacular feat, the bird plunged straight down into the water. It hit the surf at a tremendous speed, only to resurface a few heartbeats later with a fish in its beak.

Patricius felt he would like to sit on that jagged cliff edge overlooking the sea and watch the dancing water-light for the rest of the day.

But now there was work to do—the Lord's work—for which Patricius had been born. It was now many weeks since the Easter morning Claith had come to him in his locked stone room bearing a truce-branch of green willow from King Leoghaire. "The High King will remain true to the gods of his people, but to no bard will he refuse the right to sing harpsong to his people."

The heavy-timbered door stood open to Patricius, and all Eire was open to the Word of God. But he did not move. "And you, my old friend? Would you drink the cup of life our Lord offers?"

Claith bowed his head. "My heart has already so drunk. I would hear more of Him that I may make harpsongs to the people of Tara."

So Claith was baptized and traveled with the brothers for many days to learn from them. They made their way from Tara to the northernmost tip of the country, even taking boats to some of the outlying islands to teach the Word. Everywhere they met tiny bands of believers—three, five, seven Christians who came joyously to celebrate the Eucharist, then brought their friends to hear Patricius preach and to be baptized. Eventually Claith returned to Tara, and Auxilius and Isernius established a headquarters at Armagh. Auxilius directed builders in erecting a church and houses, and Isernius longed to start a school. But Patricius could not stay in one place. There was too much to do, too many who needed to hear the Word.

It was now high summer, and day meant long hours of sun hanging low in the sky, shining in one's eyes. Today he would reach a long-held goal. Not far ahead of him was the Wood of Voclut. And beyond that the rath from which he had escaped so many years ago that he had now lost count. He had inquired at the steading of Christians where he had ministered last night. Yes, Michlu Maccu Boin was still druid at Slemish. An old, old man, his sons did the chieftain's duties, but Michlu never slacked in his sacrifices. He had just returned from the yearly sacrifice gathering to Crom Cruach at the standing stones in Domach—the most powerful idol in the land.

Today Patricius would face his former owner. It was his heart prayer that he could bring to his old master freedom from the slavery of sin. He walked toward the wood where he had asked Secundinus to wait for him while he meditated. It did not take him long to find his companion, for he heard the gentle monk's singing long before he saw the dark-robed figure sitting in a green glade.

Secundinus smiled as Patricius approached. "I was thinking on writing a new hymn, but no words came to me." He looked at the bouquet in his hand. "So I spent my time gathering flowers for you instead. The little yellow flower reminds me of the sunshine, the white one of the clouds, the round green leaves of this land's gentle green hills, but I haven't found a blue flower for her skies. And even then, no song would come. I wish to celebrate the Eirran love of nature that can be transformed into a worship experience. I would have them learn to see Christ reflected in all created things. But the song will not sing."

He started to throw the flowers away, but Patricius reached out for them. He fingered the three-leafed green shamrock. "It is a beautiful thought you have, my son. Continue to think on it—the Spirit will give you words."

They walked through the woods where Patricius had spent so many hours praying for God to find him and use him. Now he smiled at the desperation of his own prayers. God was there all the time. All Patricius had needed was to reach out and take His hand. Beyond the wood they crossed a green field pasturing a band of sheep. A young boy sat watching them with a brindled wolfhound at his feet. Patricius felt as if he could be seeing himself. He only wished old Ossian, the first Christian he had met in Eire, could be here now.

On the hill above the field was the gray stone circle of Michlu's rath. At midday the gates were open and all of the household busy at their labors. Patricius started to cross the open green to the central hall, then stopped suddenly as the sound of a keening wail filled the air. He held out his hand to stop his companion, and they both stood silent. "Ockone. Ockone." The high-pitched mournful wail rose and fell like water tumbling over rocks. Suddenly the green was full. From every byre and outbuilding carpenters, blacksmiths, weavers left their tasks and ran to see what had happened in the hall of their master.

The howl of hounds added to the wail, and suddenly the door of the houseplace was flung open from inside. Those who had started to rush forward fell back at the face of Seschen Maccu Michlu, Michlu's eldest son. His normally ruddy face was drained of all color, making his blue eyes black as the night sky. Deep lines furrowed his brow as his eyes swept the silent crowd. At last he stopped. "You. You have killed my father." He pointed straight at Patricius.

"This morning he received word of your coming. At the assembly of all high druids in the land, the idol of Crom Cruach cracked and fell to the ground. For thousands of years Crom Cruach has stood on Domach. Now he has fallen. Your God is stronger than Crom Cruach. But my father would not face you. It was more honor that he should take his own life than to die at the hands of your God."

Two red spots of color appeared in Sechen's curd-white face as he addressed the people of his rath assembled before him. "The red life-blood of Michlu Maccu Boin flowed from him with the plunging of the bronze druid sword by his own hand. Let none say that he was afraid to meet his own gods." Inside the keening wail of the women rose and fell.

Patricius stepped forward. "Seschen Maccu Michlu, sorrowful I am that your father is dead. Even more grievous it is that he killed himself in fear of the Lord God. My God is a God of love. He is not to be feared except by those who defy Him. I came to tell your druid-father that my God offers life."

Through the open door behind Seschen, Patricius could see the women with their cloaks drawn across their heads keening and laying the body of Michlu Maccu Boin on a scarlet and heather plaid robe on the central table. Carefully they placed his best jewels and prized possessions of gold, silver, and age-darkened amber around the body, preparing him to go to the next life.

"May I tell you of my God that none need fear life or death in His hands?" Patricius asked.

Seschen shook his head. "In two days my father will be with his fathers." He pointed to the burial mounds beyond the rath. "You may come back then."

Patricius and Secundinus spent two days preaching and baptizing in the steadings of Ulster. On the morning of the third day they turned again toward Rath Michlu. As he walked toward his former home, Patricius pondered. How would he explain his God of Father, Son, and Holy Spirit to the household of a druid of Dagada? How could he make these people understand the mystery of the Trinity?

They crossed through Voclut Wood and passed the glade where Secundinus had picked wild flowers and shamrocks. As Patricius looked at the carpet of three-petaled leaves before him, the lovely green plant that grew so abundantly on this rain-soaked island, he knew the answer to his question. He would present his God to them through the plant they were most familiar with—a symbol made by the very Three-in-One God Himself.

True to his word, Seschen had gathered the entire household of family, servants, and slaves in Michlu's hall. The first two faces Patricius recognized were Dhu and Gussacht, his former fellow-sheepherders. They had grown older and stockier and become head shepherds, but nothing in their lives had really changed. Not until Patricius presented Jesus Christ to them and they believed. Then all things became morning-new, just as life was becoming new all over Eire, because people were new on the inside.

At the end of the service Patricius led the believers down to the river to be baptized. A young household servant, whom Patricius had not noticed in the hall, stepped forward. "I am Victoricus. I was a Christian before the raiders brought me here. For many years I prayed someone would come to tell these people of the true God."

Patricius was speechless. He clasped the young man on the shoulder and saw again, as if he had dreamed it only the night before, this very same face in his dream and this man, of the name Victoricus, coming from Eire with countless letters. And he heard again the voice of the Eirran crying to him, "We ask you, boy, come and walk among us once more."

18

he time had come for Lucullus to make a decision. Soldiering was a young man's job, and he was no longer young. But more than that—to belong now to the British army was to belong to the army of her enemies. Even Vortigern had at last admitted that his "allies" held a stranglehold on Britain and had written to Rome, begging for help from General Aetius—which, to no one's surprise, was refused.

The Saxon foederati had now pushed their holdings fifty miles northwest of Londinium to control all of the land nearly to the Fosse Way. Lands that were not given to them by treaty, they took by force, burning the villas and markets and establishing their own reed-thatched steadings and muddy-streeted burgs in the place of the once-fine Roman buildings. Trade with other nations had almost ceased, and soon Britain would be hungry, isolated, and enslaved by her own "protectors." Lucullus had followed the way of strength for thirty years, and he saw now that it had led to weakness.

The rumors persisted of a new Roman-style leader in the mountains to the west. At times Lucullus thought of seeking out this Ambrosius and offering him his sword arm. Tregatta had long ago left the court of Vortigern and even now was training his Utha for the service of the new leader. But these were only thoughts. In his heart Lucullus knew he had had enough of wars and treaties and intrigues. They did not satisfy.

And as his dissatisfaction with his chosen way of life grew, so did his longing grow for the one place that held meaning in his memory. If he had a home he would return to it, but the Villa Artoii was no longer even a memory, blotted out as it had been by pain and fire. Ynis Witrin, where he had spent his last night before horror entered his life and tore it apart, stood in the place of home in his mind. If only it had not been overrun by the foederati, as had everything civilized in the area of Venta Belgarum—overrun and pillaged and burned by their allies while the army of Vortigern sat by helpless.

From old habit his fingers sought the bracelet of the Artoii and traced the symbol of the long-departed legion. It was a soldier's bracelet. He would send it to Tregatta that Utha might wear it in the service of Ambrosius. *If there is any strength of our ancestors left to the line of Artoii, may it pass to Utha to use in the service of Britain.*

It was a mark of the lack of order in Vortigern's court that it was necessary for Lucullus neither to request leave nor to resign his position. He simply left.

Patricius also felt he must make a decision. Every cold rain brought aches in his arms and legs, and he could no longer spend his days striding along the roads of his beloved Eire preaching the gospel, baptizing new Christians, and serving the Eucharist as he had when he was younger. Nor was it necessary that he do so. Eire was Christian. From one end of the island to the other, churches, monasteries, and schools stood as monuments to the power of God. Many of the churches were built of native gray stone by a method his monks developed—overlapping stones without mortar so the walls slanted upward and inward until they met in a ridged roof. Tall stone crosses with circles around their cross shafts marked the buildings and the land as Christian.

The druids, no longer sacrificing to idols, were becoming a class of poets, judges, and scholars. Many monks joined Patricius and his companions, including Brother Benegius who had been the youngest novitiate at Auxerre in Patricius's days there.

Patricius could rest. Those around him told him he should rest. But his heart was not at rest. In spite of all he had done, he still felt remorse for his one great sin. He never doubted God's forgiveness. But he knew he could never forgive himself until he had made confession and begged Lucullus's forgiveness for his betrayal.

Patricius sat in his small cell in his monastery at Armagh. Next to baptizing new Christians and celebrating the Eucharist, his greatest joy came in establishing monasteries. He liked to think that these small centers of faith and learning would someday grow to be great hubs of Christianity like Tours, Lérins, and Auxerre. He never wearied of the organizing and administrating required. But now he turned from his account books.

For many months he had been working at odd hours on his *Confessio,* the story of how God had guided his life. This time, however, as he looked back over his life, searching for the events he should record, he was overcome with a great wave of homesickness. He now felt he was more Gael than Briton, and yet, how he would love to see his own country, his own family—how he would love to go to Gaul and visit his brethren. And he found his stylus moving across the parchment, recording his thoughts as if of its own accord. "God knows that I much desire to go. But I am bound by the Spirit, who gives evidence against me if I do this, telling me that I shall be guilty, and I am afraid of losing the labor which I have begun—nay, not I, but Christ the Lord who bade me come here and stay with them for the rest of my life.

"This I presume I ought to do, but I do not trust myself, for strong is he who daily strives to turn me away from the faith and the purity of true religion to which I have devoted myself to the end of my life. Yet I know that in part I did not lead a perfect life as did the other faithful . . ."

His writing slowed, and his mind wandered. Even as he wrote of the impossibility of returning to his native land, his heart ached to do so. "Oh, God, give me perseverance. Help me be a faithful witness to You to the end of my life," he prayed. "My God, allow me to shed my blood as an exile and a captive for Your sake—even if I should be denied a grave."

He dropped his bearded chin to his chest and sat for some moments lost in meditation. A rap at his door jerked him back to the present. Brother Benegius stood before him with a letter. At first he could not believe the signature. He went back to the beginning, reading slowly to take it all in. Surely the Lord worked in mysterious ways.

My old friend Patricius,

I hope I may call you so still. I have left the service of Vortigern and his life of the sword for the service of our Lord and the life of His Word. On a visit to the Villa Patricii (which remains one of the few villas in Britain where all is well), Senn Patricius told me they are no longer bothered with Eirran raiders, for you have turned their hearts to the way of peace. You were right, my friend, your way is strongest.

I have found a haven on the island of Ynis Witrin. But all is not peaceful here. I would spend my days in contemplation of God's Word as I sometimes did in my youth, but the controversies we encountered on our first visit here—do you remember so long ago, my old friend?—still continue. The worthy Bremwal and Wellias and hot-tempered Hyn have gone to their rewards, but many remain: Swelwes, Wencreth, Brumban, Hiregaan, and others. But we are leaderless.

Your works in Hibernia are well-known—how you organize monasteries and how your foundations flourish. We long to shine here as a light in a land quickly being overcome by the dark, but the wind of confusion threatens to extinguish our feeble flames. Will you come help us?

Lucullus Artios

Had he misunderstood God's intention for his life? Was not this as clear a call as his long ago vision of Victoricus bringing letters from the Eirran begging him to walk among them? Had his growing homesickness then been a leading of God rather than a temptation of the devil? Was he at last to have an opportunity to make his peace with Lucullus?

He found Benegius scrubbing the stone floors in a room just down the hall from his own and sent him to find Isernius. Isernius and Auxilius, his faithful companions from the first, could care for things at Armagh in his absence. He did not plan to be gone long, and yet one could not be sure.

All the way up the River Briw Patricius's mind kept going back over that night from his youth when he and Lucullus had paddled so furiously through the storm to take shelter on the island. He had not recalled the scene for years, and yet it was as fresh as if it had been last week: the ever-growing dark as rain-heavy clouds massed overhead in the evening sky, then the winds blowing slanting rain in their faces and pushing them backward even as they strained to row their coracles forward. It now seemed as if the struggles of that night could be a metaphor for much of his life, always pushing through the dark and storm to reach peaceful shelter.

Brothers Amulf and Ogmar, who had come with him from Armagh, took turns rowing. Were it not for the boat's greater size, Patricius might have thought this the very osier-framed, hide-covered coracle in which he had rowed to the island that first time.

He opened his eyes and was surprised to find himself in a gentle gray and green world as a thin mist clung to reeds and water grasses in the swampy land. The memory of the storm had been so strong he had expected to find it in reality. Through the gray evening he made out the dark shape of the Tor and caught his breath at the sharp sense of homecoming. Across the marshes birds called and fish jumped, as if to welcome him. Even from the riverbank he could see the apples hanging thickly red and gold on the trees beneath Wirral Hill.

Great was his welcome at the little circle of huts around the ever-springing chalybeate well when he and his two companions arrived a short time later. Wencreth, who had assumed a loose leadership after the death of Bremwal, brought out the guest cup and insisted upon giving the hospitality of his hearth to Amulf and Ogmar. Patricius would share Lucullus's bedplace after the evening meal.

Patricius, though glad to be among his old friends again, was shocked at the deterioration of the hermitage, and even more shocked when the brothers ate without washing their hands or giving thanks and later retired for the night without evening prayers. The beautiful Catha had died in childbirth, solving for the time the hotly debated question of celibacy. But Swelwes's daughter was as lovely as her mother had been and was now at the age when most girls drank the bride-cup. It was easy to predict that such a debate would soon arise again among the younger brothers.

Patricius, sitting between Lucullus and Wencreth at the evening hearth, shook his head. "I see why you asked for my help. I shall do my best. You must look on yourselves as a true monastery, a place of worship, learning, and daily labor to the glory of God. You see yourselves as a cluster of individual hermits whose cells happen to be close to each other. But that is not right. God has called you together in His name. Your spirit of love must shine against the evil of the world; your sense of order must fight against the chaos around us. You are to be the outshining of the glory of Jesus Christ to a world that lives in darkness.

"You must offer such light to the world that others will find in your revelation of truth that which will banish their darkness. Light cannot shine in chaos. The winds of confusion will extinguish it. You must dwell in a peace and order that reflects the order of God's universe. God desires a world of order and beauty—as He created it—but it can only exist as it exists in His followers. Only as it exists in you."

Wencreth and Lucullus leaned forward, their eyes bright in the firelight. Wencreth spoke. "Yes, yes. That is what I want, what we want, for Ynis Witrin. But how do we so shine?"

Patricius sighed. He had promised to return soon to his beloved Eire, but here was work that must be done. "I will teach you. We must have an order of prayers and duties. We must teach the Scriptures first to our brethren and then to others who will come here seeking the light. We must rebuild our buildings—starting with the Old Church and the oratory on the hill. We must trim our wicks and fill our lamps with oil that we will not be found wanting when the Bridegroom comes. We must seek the face of God in prayer. I shall send to my brother Senn Patricius for building materials. He will help us. We can accomplish much with two Patrici on Ynis Witrin." As he spoke, the weariness of the journey fell away from Patricius. His work was not yet finished. The Lord had here another calling for him that the flame of truth should burn ever stronger and brighter.

They talked long around the chill-chasing fire, making plans and creating visions of all that Ynis Witrin could do and be. Ynis Witrin was to become once more the true Avalon, the Isle of the Blest. It was to serve as a haven and a sanctuary for those seeking the way of peace. There was to be an end to the squabbles, and in their place should rise the sweet incense of prayer.

At last the conversation flagged. Amulf and Ogmar, wrapped in their cloaks, nodded on the far side of the hearth in the firelight. Patricius rose. "Lucullus and I shall go to our own bedplace. Before the first light of dawn I will call the brothers to prayer that we may begin."

Wencreth agreed and bade them good night. But Patricius did not go straight to Lucullus's hut. He had a vigil to keep first. "I understand Bishop Palladius is buried here. Show me his grave."

A few moments later, Patricius knelt beside a small mound near the old church. The dim light of the lantern, which Lucullus insisted that he keep by him to ward off stray animals, flickered. When his friend's footsteps disappeared into the mist, he turned to Palladius as if the bishop were there in person. "I have come to beg your forgiveness and the forgiveness of God. I was once jealous of you, as I had been jealous of Lucullus. That jealousy of my friend led me to a great sin. The revelation of that sin kept me from the appointment to Eire which you undertook. Your appointment led you to your death. Only God knows best. We must trust in His mercy and providence, but I must ask your forgiveness in any way that I might have wronged you. The weight of many years is upon me. I do not wish to face my Creator with my sins on my hands."

He knelt there long in the cold, dark and damp until at last a sense of release came to him. Perhaps Palladius had heard and forgiven him; perhaps God was reminding him that all was covered by the blood of Jesus Christ. Whatever the peace meant, it came. Patricius rose, his knees creaking with stiffness, and walked in the wavering light of the lantern to Lucullus's hut. He had one more absolution to ask—the hardest of his life.

Lucullus had piled the fire with dry thorn brush and rolled out an extra pallet, so all was ready for Patricius when he entered. But Patricius did not go to his bed. Instead, he fell on his knees before Lucullus. "I have come to beg your forgiveness, to seek an indulgence. I am not worthy, yet I ask it. Lucullus, my oldest friend, I have sinned against you and against God. God has forgiven me. May you find it in your heart to do so also . . ."

Lucullus sat silently beside his friend as Patricius's heart unburdened itself of the great weight it had carried for forty years and more. His shame over his jealousy, his contrition over his betrayal, his remorse for the devastation he had caused. At last his story was ended, and there was silence in the hut.

Throughout the narrative Lucullus's face had registered unbelief and confusion. Now he looked at his friend with compassion and reached out to clasp his arm in both hands. "But, Patricius, friend and brother, don't you see? You couldn't have caused the raid on my family. The fires were burning down, the bodies stiff when I arrived. The raiders had been there many hours before they captured you."

The relief was too great. Tears filled Patricius's eyes and overflowed. He made no attempt to check them, but they would not have stopped if he had. It was a cleansing flood, washing away the grief and contrition of years. Suddenly a great truth dawned in Patricius's heart—the voice of the Spirit speaking. *I did not ask you to do penance for your sin. You can do nothing to pay for sin. I carried all—every last one of your sins to My cross and took your guilt.* Patricius was overwhelmed. He needn't have carried that burden for all those years. He could have gone to Eire in love and freedom. For two-thirds of his life he had lived beneath his privileges as a forgiven child of God.

Lucullus went to a small wicker kist and took out a tray of oat cakes and a pot of fresh cheese. Without speaking he warmed the cakes by the fire and spread them thickly with cheese. When all was ready, he invited his friend and brother to share his table. "Let us come together as we once did in our boyhood days for bread-breaking. And let us thank the Father in whose name we are gathered, for He has done all things well."

They ate the warm oat cakes in big, hungry bites, as they had done when they were sixteen. Then Lucullus poured cups of tangy buttermilk and held one out to Patricius. Together they drank the cup of reconciliation. Here was the true fulfillment of the divine covenant of redemption, of deliverance from bondage, from sin, from fear. Patricius looked at Lucullus. There was now no barrier between them. "Surely, God has remembered His people," he said.

Patricius drew out his pipes and played long and thoughtful notes, as tunes not of his own making sang from his heart. At length he lowered the reeds and gave voice to the words that filled him to overflowing. "The people who do not speak according to the Word of God have no light of dawn. . . . Those who look only to the earth see only distress and darkness and fearful gloom. But there will be no more gloom for those who wait in faith. The people walking in darkness have seen a great light; on those living in the land of the Logres falls now the shadow of death. But a light is dawning. A leader will come. The Lord God of hosts shall enlarge the nation and increase joy. His people will rejoice before all Heaven as those who rejoice at the harvest.

"In the day of the enemies' defeat, our Lord will shatter the yoke of burden and the rod of the oppressor. . . . For unto us a child is born, unto us a Son is given, and the government will be upon His shoulder. Of the increase of His kingdom there will be no end. He will reign over His Kingdom, establishing and upholding it with justice and righteousness from that time on. The zeal of the Lord Almighty will accomplish this."

Then all was quiet on Ynis Witrin.

BOOK III

THE ANOINTING OF THE KING

ARTHURIAN BRITAIN

My quest grows long, but am I any nearer an answer? I am not even sure of the question. I am coming to understand that the grail and the quest are not the same thing. The quest is active; the grail symbolic—intangible. The quest is national; the grail personal. And yet, in having said that, have I said anything? The answers dart through my mind like the shadows in my room—always elusive—always beyond my grasp.

But the grail is not only symbol. I have seen that in looking at the life of our beloved Saint Patrick. Every communion cup is the holy grail. Every celebration of the Eucharist makes all things holy, all things gracious. All who so celebrate are seekers of the grail.

Today I came again in my journey through my memory upon the history William of Malmesbury wrote while studying at the great library of Glastonbury shortly before fire destroyed it in the twelfth century. But forgive me, I fear that, as our sainted Abbot Whiting so often warned me, I am too previous. Still the words of this great historian, writing about our house, are so very dear to me that I cannot but dwell on them. And I praise the Father Almighty that it was given to me to commit them to memory before all was destroyed a second time.

"After the Romans departed," our brother wrote, "the strength of the Britons decayed, their diminished hopes went backwards; and straightway they would have come to ruin, had not Ambrosius, the sole survivor of the Romans, who was monarch of the realm after Vortigern, repressed the overweening barbarians through the distinguished achievement of the warlike Arthur. This is that Arthur of whom the trifling of the Britons talks so much nonsense even today; a man clearly worthy not to be dreamed of in fallacious fables, but to be proclaimed in veracious histories, as one who long sustained his tottering country, and gave the shattered minds of his fellow citizens an edge for war. Finally, at the siege of

Mount Badon, relying upon the image of the mother of the Lord which he had sewn upon his armor, he made head single-handed against nine hundred of the enemy and routed them with incredible slaughter."

The body of Austin Ringwode is the feeble body of an old man bowed with age, but I praise God in His glory that my mind remains useful. I dwell on the brilliance of Brother William's words, "Arthur deserved not to be dreamed of in fallacious fables, but to be proclaimed in veracious histories." And yet I ask myself as I think upon those times, what is history and what is fable? What is truth?

Ah, my mind is useful, but it runs in circles, and I am again at the questions that plague me even in my sleep—what of the grail? Last night I awoke from a dream with a flash of certainty that the grail is godliness. But as sleep receded and reason increased, I looked at my writings of the past days and asked myself—if the grail is godly living, should not good King Lucius, or St. George, or St. Patrick have achieved it? If not them, then who?

The answer remains hidden, but I search on.

1

*he king is dead. Long live the king!*

The king was dead. King Ambrosius Aurelianus had kept the Angli and the Saxons and the Jutes at bay, preventing the entire overwhelming of the land. But now a Saxon seax had slipped in under his black bull-hide buckler at the place of a badly mended link in his chain mail shirt and let out the royal blood. The king was dead.

Long live the king! But who should the king be? King Ambrosius, grandson of that Ambrosius who defeated Vortigern the Fox at Dinas Emrys, died without an heir and without naming his successor. The scourge of sea wolves he had nearly driven from the land returned as nobles and lesser kings fought over who should be High King. So now it fell to the council to settle the question, and most speedily, while there was yet a land for the High King to rule over. More specifically, the responsibility fell to Merlinus Ambrosius Dubricius—himself named after the first High King—Archbishop of Caerleon and president of the council. It would not be an easy task. Many of the chieftains and kinglets supported Cador of Cornwall, last in the direct line of Constantine the Great through Magnus Maxima. And Cador was a good man. But therein lay the trouble. A good man, but not a great man. Britain could do with no less than greatness at this hour. The man chosen must be the greatest Britain had ever seen, or Britain would see no more.

Long live the king. Not that Dubricius had any doubt about who should wear the mantle, but getting the support of the council would be another matter. Arthurius, whom many called Artos the bear—as much for his size, strength, and thick pelt of hair as for the derivation of his name—carried the blood of the Caesars in his veins. And he had been carefully schooled in war skills as a lieutenant to Ambrosius and schooled in statecraft by Merlinus Dubricius himself.

But the line of descent had many bendings and twistings, and some said they were the inventions of the bards, although nothing could make Ulfius, Dubricius's bard, more angry than this accusation. Then Ulfius would launch into a long account, not only of the Roman lineage of Arthurius's royal Roman blood, but also of his royal Celtic descent on his mother's side from the godly King Lleiver Mawr who had first declared Britain Christian while the fine purple-wearing Romans were still burning incense to Jupiter. Did not even the red and gold lights in Arthurius's dark curling hair bespeak his Romano-Celtic lineage? Did not the gold shine so brightly sometimes in the sun that it sometimes looked as if he wore already a wreath of copper beech leaves in the Roman fashion or a slim golden circlet as the son of a Celtic king? But for all his careful study of law and history, Ulfius was prone to lose himself in the poetic, and such arguments would weigh little with the council. Long live the king.

Dubricius slipped an embroidered surplice over his white robe and turned to prepare for the evening. First would come the Christ Mass. Nobles had been gathering all week to Caerleon, called Isca in Roman days, to celebrate this high holy season in the church dedicated to the martyrs Julius and Aaron. Then the council would convene. On the morrow they would all have much need of the prayers of the mass to guide them.

The archbishop gathered his robes about him for the brief walk across the former courtyard of the old Roman baths. Their fallen stones now formed the houses of Dubricius and those who served him and the church. He prayed that God's light would shine in the hearts of those who came tonight—as the birth of Christ heralded the dawn of God's light shining on mankind. Dubricius shivered as an icy wind whipped up the loosely fallen snow and flung it against his thin frame. He could see ahead the soft glow of candlelight from the two stories of arched windows of the basilica, some shuttered but others glazed against the wind with thin sheets of parchment. They shone like rows of hopeful beacons—dim, but steady—as he made his careful way across patches of ice to the midnight vigil.

The great Roman basilica, the last building erected in the bath complex and used by legionnaires of the Second Augusta as a recreation hall, had long stood empty save for the owls who nested in the cross-beamed rafters and the small, scurrying creatures who hid in dark corners. But when the Synod of Brefi established the three British bishoprics at Londinium, Ebercanum, and Caerleon-upon-Usk, the crumbling stones had been repaired as well as might be and the long central nave, lined on each side with fluted marble columns, was fitted with a high altar at the east. Wooden benches were provided for worshipers. Their own small brotherhood of monks and priests saw to the daily needs of the altar and the chanting of prayers and psalms. On special occasions they were assisted by brothers from the ancient hermitage at Ynis Witrin, which some said was founded by Bishop Patrick, and others said was founded by St. Joseph of Arimathea, apostle to Britain, and yet others said was founded by the Lord Himself in honor of His Holy Mother.

As Dubricius entered the basilica by the west door, he was glad to see that a company of the holy brotherhood filled the front quire benches, as well as several holy sisters from their house established by St. Bridget on another hill of the holy island some called Avalon. The brothers had begun the pre-mass vigil, chanting their prayers in undisturbed adoration while repeated openings of the door brought blasts of snowy wind lashing down the nave, accompanied by the stamping of heavy boots and muttered comments as each noble arrived with his entourage. The chanting of the psalms continued and the basilica filled, much to the chagrin of latecomers, including Maelgwyn who ruled in Arfon of the Cymri and The Ancelot from Berwick on the edge of the Caledon forest. Each of these highborn men swore, not entirely under his breath, when he saw that the nave was filled and he and his company would have to sit on the side isles beyond the marble pillars, obscured from the view of other worshipers.

When the rush of arrivals subsided, Dubricius raised his staff, the badge of his high holy office and signaled Ulfius. The bard walked before him with the censor that in earlier days might have been used to seal the doom of Christians, but was now used as a symbol of their prayers rising upwards to the throne of God. Leaving behind a trail of the sweet scent of blessings, they made their stately way up the long nave to the accompaniment of the brothers and sisters chanting from the Psalms, "'O praise the Lord, Jerusalem. Zion, praise your God . . .'"

The archbishop was aware of the stillness in the congregation at his passing. With the death of the High King, Dubricius, as the eldest of the three archbishops in the land, now held the highest power in Britain, held it temporarily to pass on to another whom he should anoint. Whether or not men agreed with him, they respected the power residing in his frail personage.

The God most high has strengthened the bars of your gates,
He established peace on your borders,
He feeds you with finest wheat . . .

Dubricius reached the altar and took his place on the high seat behind the table of the sacraments. When the psalm ended, the archbishop rose to lead the congregation in the response: "He comes in splendor, the King who is our peace."

Silently Dubricius prayed, *Lord, even so, let Him come to us now on an earthly throne.*

A priest stood before the assembly in a somber homespun robe, the candlelight shining on his tonsured forehead, and read the lesson from the Scriptures. As the archbishop repeated the responsory, "Today will you know the coming of the King, today will you know the coming . . . ," he could not keep his mind on the coming of the King of Heaven, but found his thoughts straying to the young man on the first bench. Even seated, he was head and shoulders above all others, and his chestnut hair gave off glints of red-gold as bright as the candlelight reflected in it. The golden torque around his neck, which had passed to him when his father Uther fell leading a cavalry charge against Picti in the north four campaigning seasons ago, proclaimed his important birth but no more. Would it be enough? Dubricius's long fingers fumbled with the edge of his surplice.

Dubricius wondered how many of the tribal chieftains and their captains crowded into the church understood the Latin words they were mouthing with the priest, or how many would proclaim them as a personal faith if they did understand. "Our God of endless ages, Father of all goodness, we keep vigil for the dawn of salvation and the birth of Your Son . . ."

Another priest rose to read from the heavy volume of the book of Isaiah that rested on a high table to the left of the altar. "'For Jerusalem's sake I will not rest until the vindication of this nation shines forth like the dawn. Your victory shall burn like a torch. All nations shall behold it. You shall be a glorious crown in the hand of the Lord, a royal diadem held by your God. No more shall men call you Forsaken or your land Desolate.'"

Then followed a reading of the lineage of Jesus Christ. As it continued through its droning list of names, Dubricius knew that he would have to deal with this issue tomorrow. He took comfort from the fact that priests of Jesus' day also had had to argue the matter of pedigree.

The reading of the birth of Christ concluded just as the youngest brother, who had been intently watching the last grains of sand drain through the glass in the back of the basilica, slipped out the door and began tolling the hour on the large brass bell that hung between two tall posts in the courtyard. When twelve solemn tolls had been struck, the archbishop rose and went to the sacred table before the altar. He removed the veil from the golden chalice there and poured wine and water into it, symbolizing the blood and water which flowed from the side of the Lord.

He elevated the grail for all to see. From his seat on the front row Arthurius was the first in line to be served the sacred cup. Dubricius elevated it even higher for his prayer. "Through the night hours of the darkened earth, we Your people await the coming of Your promised Son. As we wait, give us, we ask, a foretaste of the joy that will be ours when the fullness of His glory has filled the earth, who lives and reigns with You forever and ever. Amen."

Arthurius's bowed head caught the reflected candlelight from the grail, and for an instant it shone as if he had already been crowned.

But the next day when the council of kings and chiefs met in the archbishop's hall, Merlinus Ambrosius Dubricius, Archbishop of Caerleon, knew that no matter what religious symbolism *he* had found in the Christ Mass, many of those ranged on skin-covered benches before him would not be swayed by such arguments. And he knew that it would challenge even his skills of statecraft to get the chiefs of tribes from Caledonia to Dumnonia, from Arfon of the Cymri to the very borders of the East Angles and the South Saxons to unite behind any one man—let alone behind one of debatable blood lines—even though the man had already proven the valor of that blood often enough in battle.

Dubricius had done all he could do in preparation, however, to remind the lords of their duty. From the small shrine room off the main hall where the legions in earlier times had kept their sacred eagle and the standards of each cohort and century, the archbishop had brought the symbols of Britain in his keeping. Before the assembly, on a low table just off the dais, he had placed the High King's scepter, bearing in regal splendor the great amethyst that men said had once been set in Maximus's sword hilt. And elevated on the tribunal, on a stone pillar evolved from the Red Crest practice of hanging their swords and shields on trees as a war memorial, he had hung Clarent, the Sword of Britain.

But the verbal battle raged in the hall without regard to any of his careful preparations.

"I say look to the record!" Ectorius, who held the rich corn-growing lands around Sorviodunum, slammed his fist on the table, making the currency bracelets on his arm clang. "The Bear Cub has led eleven successful battles against the Angli and Saxon. It is in my mind to ask how many men in this room who are twice his age can claim such a record? Can Cador of the Dumnoni?" He shook his fist in the air for emphasis. Then with a fierce shifting of the heavy deer-hide cloak held at his shoulder by the most massive bronze ring of any in the room, Ectorius took his seat by Caius his son who was attending his first council as preparation for someday taking his gray-haired father's place.

The room was quiet, as if each man were counting his own battles on his fingers and trying to recall Duke Cador's record. And as each man searched for an answer, for the first time all realized what Dubricius had long ago noted. Cador of Dumnonia was not among the council. Nor had he been at the mass last night. Dubricius's forehead wrinkled in a frown. What was Cador planning? Always he had known the Dumnonian to be a straightforward, if rough, man. Not one to be feared for his deviousness, nor to be admired for his brilliance. One who would neither shirk nor scheme at such a moment as this.

Black-haired Maelgwyn, who ruled in Arfon of the Cymri and kept his high seat in an ancient hillfort at the base of the Mountain of the Snows, spoke next—although it was more a thundering than a speaking. "Aye, the Bear Cub has battle honors enough. None could deny him that. Although it should be none too surprising that even a small army well-mounted from the horse-runs of the Cymri should be victorious against a rabble horde on foot. But is sword-skill the only test for the kingship? What of blood? Are we to be led by one no higher born than any of us in this hall?"

Baudwin of the ancient lands of the Silures, who had served as battle captain in nine of Arthurius's eleven victorious battles, rose in his graceful way that was more like an unfolding. "And have none of you in this high council chamber heard the harpsongs recounting the lineage of Artos the Bear?" Baudwin was known as something of a harper himself—at least an admirer of those who could develop the art without interruption from the press of battle. "Those of you who have not been privileged with the hearing around the campfire at night have missed a rare treat for refreshing your memories of the great events and great people of our land—for of such is his lineage—including that of Constantine himself, such as Cador claims descent from."

"Claims? Does my Lord Baudwin mean to imply that Cador's royal lineage is in doubt?" Maelgwyn growled out his question and shook a leather-gloved fist in Baudwin's direction.

Baudwin bowed toward his fellow Cymric chief. "It was in my mind to make no such implication. None of us here disputes Lord Cador's lineage. It is only that we claim Arthurius's equal on that score—and the Bear's superiority on the field of battle."

Teliau, who had been driven from his Iceni lands by Octa, son of Hengist, but still wore the golden horse-head torque of his people with pride, argued that indeed Maelgwyn's position had validity—Arthurius was a man of greatness with horse and battle sword. But what did they know of him with the scepter of state that Ambrosius had wielded with such skill?"

"Aye, and it was the Bear's skill with horse and battle sword and leading men in the field that gave Ambrosius the freedom to occupy himself with border disputes, the claims of petty kings, and foreign treaties," Ectorius's son Caius shouted from his seat—an audacious thing to do for someone in the role of observer.

The mention of Ambrosius's name unleashed a round of new arguments—some merely shouted from the seats, others accented by their speakers' charging to their feet and banging the table. "Aye, and why did not Ambrosius name Arthurius his successor if he was so well acquainted with his skill?"

"Death took him unawares; he had no time."

"Death takes no man unawares—all men know it comes soon or late. Ambrosius would not name his successor because he would not alienate the captain he so needed on the field of battle, but did not choose for the high seat of the Council of Kings."

"You lie! No man in this room can seriously doubt that Ambrosius would have the choice fall on Arthurius."

Baudwin tried again, although a note of weariness in his voice betrayed his lack of confidence in winning the mind of the council by logic. "Ambrosius believed the choice of Arthurius so obvious he felt no rush to make the naming. Cador, Lord of Dumnonia, has done a fine job holding his western lands for Britain; none can doubt that. But what has he done to show that he is capable on a larger scale as Arthurius has? And if Cador would be so set on the high kingship of Britain, where is he now?" Baudwin gave a meaningful look at Arthurius listening without show of emotion to the arguments raging around him. Then Baudwin let his glance linger on the empty seat to the left of the archbishop.

As if in reply, a muffled clatter of horse hooves on the broken flags of the courtyard outside, a jangling of bronze-studded harness, and a shouting to servants rang through the hall. The heavy double doors on the side of the room flung open, and Cador of Dumnonia strode into the room, flinging snowflakes from his long dark hair and furred cloak. "My lords, I beg your forgiveness!" He strode to the raised tribunal where the archbishop sat, where generations of commandants had presided before him dispensing justice to the farthest outpost of the Empire. "My Lord Archbishop, I arrive late." He dropped briefly to one knee, then stood to announce, "But I do not arrive without good tidings." Flinging his arms out as if he would embrace all in the room, he cried, "My wife has borne me a fine, healthy son. We have named him Constantine, and so shall he be christened, after his great, great-grandsire who ruled in these lands before Vortigern the Fox let in the floodtide of Saxons!" The announcement was met with much table thumping of fists and dagger hilts and shouts of congratulations as if the newborn Constantine himself had been proclaimed High King.

Cador bowed his thanks to the thunderous reception and strode to his seat beside the archbishop. Arthurius rose to congratulate his kinsman, and Dubricius gave outward sign of congratulation. But inside he was sick. All the hopes he had placed in the symbolism of the mass—the coming king who would bring a new age of peace—now any who had listened sufficiently (and there were few enough of those) to take his hidden meanings would apply them to the newborn son of Cador. Surely now Cador, who could offer an unbroken succession, would be proclaimed.

Maelgwyn and three other chieftains who had spoken fiercely for Cador jumped to their feet. But before they could speak, every eye in the room was drawn to Arthurius who had risen to his full looming height. Such was his power of command that even standing silent he took the attention of all. "My lords, you know me well as a man of war and a leader of combat. It is now in my mind to tell you what I see when I gaze into the campfire on the night before a battle, that seeing what I see, you might better judge the Britain I would build when there is an end to the fighting—as there must be an end. You who say that warskill is not enough to make a king, speak truth. The warskill must come first, but also there must be a vision for what will come after.

"The warskill is necessary because we face an enemy whose mind and heart is possessed by evil ideas—evil that would destroy—trample the windflower underfoot, burn the willow wren from her nest, and take the heart from the young deer. Evil that would destroy the heritage our people have held in this land from time beyond time. I would use my sword-skill for Britain that I may preserve the heritage the wolves from the sea would destroy. The tearers, the destroyers, the bringers of the dark—they must be held off. If you choose me as your leader, I pledge my sword-skill to you and to Britain for this end."

The table-thumping and hilt-clanging ruffled the heavy leather hangings that served to keep the cold from seeping further through the walls and fluttered the tallow candles in their iron brackets. Dubricius smiled within himself. No bard could have spun better word pictures, no harp sung more sweetly than the Bear's own voice. The lines in the archbishop's long thin face relaxed. Their cause was not lost.

Yet. The council argued on. Every petty thought or deed that had been passed from father to son from the time of Vortigern and beyond was argued. It seemed that they must listen to every old grievance from before the coming of the Caesars—and no one could be certain whether the debts were to be charged against Cador or against Arthurius.

At last Dubricius judged that it was time and past time for him to exercise his power of office. He rose before them on the high tribunal, his long gray robe hanging full from his thin shoulders. He grasped the staff of office in his right hand and raised both arms over the assembly, his bony wrists extending beyond the full sleeves of his tunic. "My lords, we have heard your arguments, we have heard your grievances, you have spoken your desires, and you have spoken your loyalties. Now our business is before us. Choose you this day whom you will serve. For God and for Britain let every man look into his own heart and choose whom he will have for leader."

Yet in the end, after repeated poll-taking with thumbs up and thumbs down, as was the old style when voting for the life or death of a gladiator in the arena—appropriate enough for that day on which they voted for the life of Britain—they did not choose a High King. God be praised, they chose the right man, Arthurius, but they would not proclaim one of clouded birth lines as king over them. Arthurius received the title *Comes Britanniae*—Count of the Britains. The title was an honorable one. It had been established by Stilicho himself, one of Rome's greatest generals, after he led British troops in their last victory as a Roman province. From that time the defense of Britain had often rested in the hands of such Comes directing small mobile strike forces that could ride swiftly to wherever the defenses were weakest and the threat most severe. Just such a role had the Bear fulfilled these past years spent winning battles for Ambrosius while winning the respect of all men for himself.

Well, most men. Dubricius sighed as he looked at the scepter of Ambrosius which he had hoped to bestow upon Arthurius that very day. Such must wait. The high kingship was not yet. But there was another badge of office he could bestow.

Merlinus Dubricius looked from the marten-skin-covered table where the scepter lay to the stone pillar on the other side of the tribunal where the Sword of Britain hung. "My lords, at last we have raised our own Count of Britain, just as our father's fathers appealed to Aetius fifty years ago." He made his voice ring to the highest rafters of the hall that all men present would see this decision as a great moment in British history and would carry the memory in their hearts as a great victory. Dubricius would not let this moment slip away as the half-defeat Arthurius's enemies would have it be.

"Arthurius, *Comes Britanniae,* draw the Sword of Britain from its resting place and kneel before me." With a gesture worthy of the long ago performers in Rome's great amphitheater, Dubricius pointed the full length of his long arm at the pillar stone so that none might miss the sight of Comes Arthurius drawing the sword of Britain from the stone for his own. And as if he had been similarly schooled by a master of the Roman stage, Arthurius rose with all the dignity won of repeated victories on the battlefield and strode the length of the tribunal.

Arthurius stood before Clarent, the Sword of Britain, and, as if on cue from some ghostly Roman stage director, the sun broke through its midwinter cloud cover and streamed through the row of windows high in the long wall. The gold of the sword hilt and the gold streaks in Arthurius's hair struck light together. Arthurius drew the sword from its stony bracket, held it aloft, and then knelt before the archbishop with Clarent resting on his knees.

This was not the coronation Dubricius had hoped for, but he would not be robbed of the speech he would make. "Comes Arthurius, you kneel before me with the badge of your office, Clarent, the Sword of Britain. This is not a battle sword, but a sword of peace. You have drawn it from the rock as from Christ the rock of our salvation, the Prince of Peace.

"It will be your task to fight—as fight must we all who would follow the way of right. But the sword of peace will remind you that even as a war leader, peace is the better way. Take now Clarent, the sword of right and truth and peace, and use it in the name of Him who is the source of all truth and peace. And let this sword also remind you that danger surrounds power as dark surrounds the light. Vigilance must also be the name of the Sword of Britain.

"The battle before us is twofold—physical and spiritual. You, Arthurius of Britain, are to lead the physical battle with force and might of arms to achieve the right—to make room for truth and justice under the law, to make room for the blessings of peace upon this land. And I, my friend and my count, pledge to you to fight by your side as a brother of a different sword. By the God of all power, I pledge to lead the spiritual battle to fight back the principalities and powers of darkness that would overcome the soul of this land.

"Together by the grace of God, we will let the light shine forth—the light of Logres—the true brightness at the heart of Britain. That is our task, the twofold burden and privilege that has been given to us. The all-wise God has called us to the great undertaking of rescuing the body and soul of Britain for His glory."

The archbishop rested his hand for an instant on Arthurius's head in a blessing. Then he lifted it in a signal that he should rise and stand beside him. "Now let all who would join us this day in the glorious task that lies before us come forward and swear his fealty."

Cador of Dumnonia, who all this while had sat a silent observer of the proceedings, rose to his feet. Every eye in the council chamber followed him as he walked from the tribunal dais. The great silence in the room bespoke the pivotal point of this moment. If Cador strode from the room, Teliau of the Iceni, and many of the lords of the north, perhaps including The Ancelot of Caledonia, would follow him and the battle for Britain would be engaged, not Briton against Saxon, but Briton against Briton.

Cador paused at the foot of the tribunal, Arthurius on his right, the doorway on his left. The space of a heartbeat passed. Then the Dumnonian chief turned right and knelt to pledge his fealty to the newly proclaimed Count of the Britains.

Arthurius grasped Clarent in both hands and held the blade out at chest level. "As the old order of Comes has been reestablished in me today, so will I reestablish an old order in my followers. Those of you who today renew your loyalty to the peace and safety of Britain, or for the first time choose to take up this badge of office and follow me, I will declare *Eques Britanniae,* Knight of Britain." He lowered Clarent to tap Cador lightly on each shoulder with the blade that had never seen battle. "Rise, Cador of Dumnonia, first Knight of Britain."

Baudwin, lord of the high seat of the Silures, lieutenant of Artos the Bear, and sometimes harper, was next to kneel and receive his knighthood. Then followed gray-bearded Ectorius and his rambunctious son, who were both rumored to have on occasion worn togas in their crumbling Roman-style villa in Sorviodunum, but who could fight like battle-frenzied Celts of old when faced with a pack of sea wolves.

Gwalchmai ap Gwyar, Arthurius's cousin from the old Brigante lands of the north, then Olwin, Teliau, Eleden, Doldavius followed in quick succession, and on until each man in the room had lain his sword at the feet of the Count of the Britains and sworn his loyalty. All that is, except The Ancelot, who sat unmoving in the back of the room, his eyes level under his bushy blond eyebrows, a slight scowl on his forehead under his flowing mane of yellow hair.

The scowl seemed to bespeak deep thought rather than disapproval and proclaimed that The Ancelot had never been rushed in his decision-making, and he would not be rushed now. Caledonia beyond the Roman wall had ever made its own way, and it would make its own way now. The laird would confer with his own council and decide this matter on the grounds of what was best for Caledonia, not what was best for Britain. The scowl had deepened to a frown only once during the proceedings—when King Maelgwyn of Arfon stormed from the room shortly after the thumbs up had finally gone to Arthurius. Apparently The Ancelot had been the only one in the room to note Maelgwyn's leaving and to wonder how many rebel lords not of this council chamber would follow him.

2

ut I am a war leader, Myrddin Emrys." When Arthurius was very agitated, he gave his old mentor his Cymric name. "Even before you managed to bestow this old Roman title upon me, it was true, but all the more so now. I must be about my father's business—to use your words—and every day I delay, the sea wolves howl nearer. If prayer is needful—and I'm not doubting that it was ever more so—let you go to Ynis Witrin and pray with the brothers in their perpetual quire. And let me be the avenging angel, if you will have it so, that carries out God's judgment on the Saxon. But it must be done before they sweep over us."

Outside, evening had fallen on the snows of Isca Caerleon, which more and more men called simply Caerleon. The council members, both the satisfied and the disgruntled, had long departed from the archbishop's hall to prepare to depart in the morning; and yet Dubricius and Arthurius sat long over the brazier in the center of the room, scented applewood crackling on top of the slower-burning charcoal.

Dubricius, who knew full well the impact his Old Testament prophet stance could have even on one who knew him as well as Artos did, rose from his cross-legged stool, strode to the high seat where his staff of office lay, and seized it. Holding the rod at arm's length, he shook his head so as to give full justice to his ample gray beard and flowing hair. "Tomorrow the brothers and sisters who gathered for the Christ Mass return with the tide to their holy houses on the island. You and I will sail with them. Your new-made Cambrogi of Eques of Britain can ride forth each to gather his war band. As you well know, it will take weeks and longer to assemble the hosting. And it is in my mind, as in yours, that the Saxons are no fonder of a winter battle than are your men."

Arthurius threw up his arms, let them fall in a particularly bearlike gesture, then threw back his great head and gave a shout of laughter that made the otherwise empty hall ring. "It is to my thinking that it is as well the council did not make me king, but that it would have made little difference. You would have commanded me just the same. Have you any idea, my Lord Archbishop, how much there is to be done before the battling season you so rightly foresee?

"There is a hillfort unused since Roman times just beyond your Glass Isle. It is to my mind the strongest position for defending all of the lands to the west of us and from there advancing northward and eastward to push the wolves ahead of us. But the fortifications are broken, there are no supplies, the blacksmiths and armorers must have forges . . . it has been how many months since Ambrosius's death? Yet all that time has been lost in squabbles when we could have been preparing. We dare delay no more."

Dubricius sighed and returned to his stool. "Always your mind is practical—preparing the war band, counting the horses, drawing the maps. And you are right. That is your gift. I ask only three days. By the time the companions who go directly with you have ridden the distance, boatmen from the island will have you at Caer Cam—Sa, sa, I know the ancient hill to which you refer with the crooked stream running at its feet, *Comes Britanniae.*"

And so the next morning, inwardly seething to be astride Magnus leading the closest of his Cambrogi forward to begin the refortification of Caer Cam, Arthurius instead left careful instructions with Baudwin and resignedly settled himself in one of the coracles making for Ynis Witrin. Although he allowed his body to be borne to the island to fulfill the archbishop's spiritual agenda, his mind was his own. He found the dip and splash of the boatman's oar as conducive to making battle plans as the rhythm of Magnus's hoofbeats. If each Eques could fulfill his promise to raise no fewer than one hundred fully armed men—and several had vowed many times that—and each provided the ten cart loads of grain and supplies he had asked—or more like demanded—and if the Saxon, Angli, Picti, Anacotti, or any others who might band with them, would hold off their hosting until the spring thaws, the thing would be possible. Best of all would be if those who marched under the Pendragon banner could be first in the field to prevent the coming together of the wolf packs. But that all depended on the cooperation of his men, his own skills of organization, and that great imponderable—the weather. A list indeed worthy of Dubricius's prayers.

The sharp cry of a winter-nested seabird cut across the gray sky, and a thin mixture of snow and rain fell on them, making the brown-robed brothers in nearby coracles pull their cowls over their tonsured foreheads and the sisters from the holy house of Our Lady of the Lake wrap themselves deeper in their homespun woolen cloaks. Arthurius shook the wetness off his heavy hair, as would the bearkind he was called after, but did not bother to shelter under his elk-hide cloak. He liked the feel of the cold rain, and he breathed deeply of the fresh air. The heavy, stagnant air of overheated, smoky rooms he could not abide.

Armorers—if they could keep three at work full time, with assistants to fetch and carry and help from the blacksmiths and wheelwrights for some of the heavier work, all of the mail shirts stripped from fallen Saxon chiefs in last summer's victories could be in working order, plus bull-hide breast shields made for most of their horses.

Much of Artos's success as a cavalry leader had come from his insistence on armor for horses as well as for men. It not only protected the horses which, especially in the early days of their campaigning, had been almost as valuable as the lives of the men, but also the added weight of the armor gave increased force to a cavalry charge. The distance gained into the enemy lines had given a winning edge to many a battle.

Well-balanced spears after the model of Roman pilums—every warrior must have no fewer than three. He had requested The Ancelot to bring the specially-skilled Caledonian fletchers to put the feathers on their arrows for perfect aim and balance in flight, but the laird of Berwick had answered him with an unreadable look and a dipped head. Which way that one would jump was as uncertain as a bounding stag in his own wild Caledon forest.

And special hot forges for the crafting of swords . . . In his mind Arthurius saw the glowing red iron bars pulled from the coals with long tongs and heard the ring of hammer on anvil as the bars were twisted together, hammered out to produce a patterned blade, then given their cutting edges with additional bars. His armorers would produce long, sleek double-edged blades unlike the fierce little single-edged seax of the Saxons. The hilt of the long sword would be perfectly formed for the hand of its owner.

Unconsciously his right hand went to the wolfskin sheath hanging at his left side and gripped the hilt of the sword resting there. Not Clarent, which remained in the archbishop's hall to be used for ceremonial occasions, but his own battle sword. And yet not his own. The sword he had carried into ten victorious battles had broken in the first encounter of the eleventh. In the heat of the fray he had seized the weapon from a fallen sword-brother, and it had carried them to victory. It was a good sword, made of well-tempered steel, straight and balanced. It had served him well. Yet he was not completely satisfied. The valiant fighter from whom he had seized it, was a smaller man than himself. Therefore the hilt was just a fraction smaller than he needed. The balance of the blade was exquisite, but Arthurius would be happier with a sword of greater heft.

As they left the wide Sabrina and their boatmen began paddling single file up the narrower Briw, the snowy rain which had slackened for a while began again with vigor. Dubricius reached into the leather pouch he carried slung over his shoulder and handed Artos a slab of cold meat from last night's feast. Arthurius chewed it slowly as he continued his thoughts, and Dubricius did not interrupt. He had won his point the day before.

By the time the coracles reached Ynis Witrin, the thickening snow mingled with the early winter darkness to screen even the majestic Tor from view. But the boats had no sooner touched shore than a cluster of brown-robed monks hurried down the path from the hermitage to meet them, and from St. Bridget's nunnery came sisters in unbleached woolen tunics that blended into the snowy background. Even in the snow they knelt to their archbishop and then again to the Count of Britain. The sisters turned like a small flock of sheep to their house on Wirral Hill, led by their prioress Nimue. Her staff bearing the bell of St. Bridget tinkled softly as their muffled steps disappeared up the gentle slope.

At Caerleon Arthurius had met Brother Indract, abbot of the hermitage, continuing in the tradition established by Patricius who had laid down rules of holy living and schedules for prayers three generations before. But now Indract presented the brothers who had not made the journey to Caerleon to the newly proclaimed war leader of their land: Bremwal, Wencreth, Loyor, Breden, Benegius . . . Brother Indract explained that his own name had been taken from the sainted Eirran pilgrim who, returning from a pilgrimage to Rome, had turned aside to visit St. Patricius's tomb, but was then tragically murdered by bandits before he could reach his homeland. And the brothers, a majority of them from Eire themselves, some even trained at Patricius's own monastery at Armagh, had taken names of former brothers of Ynis Witrin.

Arthurius's leather-booted feet were getting colder by the moment. Fearing for the frostbite the sandal-shod monks must be enduring, he caught Dubricius's eye with a gleam of amusement, and the archbishop called his charges to their duties. "Surely, Brother Indract, it is time for evening prayer." With that, the procession of hooded monks bearing torches against the darkness that cast long, wavering shadows across the snow, led the Pendragon and archbishop to the tiny ancient church at the foot of the Tor.

They were just ready to enter when a scowling, brown-robed figure appeared through the dark silhouettes of the bare apple trees. At first Arthurius thought the stooped monk with the lined face must be the oldest of the brotherhood, but when he raised his head and his cowl fell back, letting the light of a torch shine on his piercing, dark intelligent eyes, Arthurius could have gasped. He was no more than a boy. "This is the newest member of our community, Brother Gildas. He is in charge of our scriptorium." Indract laid his hand on the youngster's shoulder. "And how is your headache, Brother Gildas?"

"The headache is strong and healthy; it is the rest of me that suffers."

Arthurius was unsure whether to laugh or sympathize. Was the youth complaining or making a joke at his own expense? But either way, a sharp edge of pain was in his voice. Dubricius stepped forward, and Gildas bowed his head before his archbishop. "My son, it was good of you to come meet us when you are unwell."

Gildas's scowl increased as if to ask how an archbishop could so misjudge a situation. "I leave my work to answer the summons to prayer. It is required."

Blinking in surprise at the curt reply, Dubricius led the way into the little church. Indract shook his head and said to Arthurius, "I despair of making an obedient child of the church of that one. But he has been with us only a short time. He was preparing for a sea voyage with his brothers when a spar fell on his head. They brought him here for nursing. More dead than alive, he was. Brother Benegius is gifted in the healing arts and saved his life, even if his herbcraft is not sufficient to cure the headaches. And we praise God that while Gildas was convalescing, he also began a spiritual life in Christ. He now refers to this as the year of his birth."

Indract shook his head. "But he remains a mystery. We suspect the sea voyage he was preparing for may have been more of a raiding trip, but that only deepens the mystery."

"How so?" Arthurius asked. "Are there not many who pillage and steal? As if the sea wolves are not enough, it seems we must always be looking over our shoulders for those of our own kind from the back."

"So, it is true. But that is not the mystery. The mystery is how one who would enter such a life could be so well-schooled in Latin. He writes a perfect hand, and when he has finished copying St. Patricius's *Confessio* to send to our brothers at Malmesbury, he wants to begin writing his own history of Britain."

Arthurius laughed. "A fine ambition indeed for a cub. We shall have to give him something worthy of writing about."

The next day Arthurius heard in detail the history of the Island of Avalon. Although the brothers disagreed as to whether the Old Church was built by Joseph of Arimathea or by Christ Himself, none doubted that the oratorio atop the Tor had been erected by King Lucius who first declared Britain to be Christian.

Arthurius strained to be polite. He could not see why Dubricius had insisted on his coming at this time to hear stories, most of which he had already heard, and all of which he could hear with greater pleasure when his mind was at rest. Dubricius himself seemed as intent on the brothers' tales as if he were hearing them for the first time, although Artos noted a frequent lifting of the gray head and a listening look on the wise, thin face as if the archbishop were waiting for something.

At last the tinkle of a tiny bell brought a smile to his face. "Ah, thank you, brothers, I hear the approach of the Abbess Nimue. And now the count will go with Our Lady of the Lake that she may bestow the blessing of her house upon him."

Still feeling a strange bewilderment, as if he were dreaming the whole thing, Arthurius followed Merlinus Dubricius and went out to meet the prioress. She carried her badge of office, a staff with the bell of St. Bridget, which she used regularly to call her house to prayer. She wore a gray mantle over her belted tunic of unbleached homespun. A close-fitting, knitted gray cap with a wide band under the chin framed a small white face with enormous dark eyes. She bowed her head to the archbishop, then turned. "Will you come with me, my Lord Arthurius?"

This was apparently what Dubricius had been waiting for. Arthurius suspected he was to be shown the holy thorn which had burst into miraculous flower when Joseph of Arimathea in a Moses-like gesture threw his staff before a gathering of pagan druids, thereby converting them with the sight of the miracle. The bush should be in full flower now for the Christ Mass, as it would be again in the springtime. Arthurius ground his teeth and clenched his fists. It would not do to explode at the archbishop on his holy isle. The lady walked serenely on in front of him, her tiny bell signaling the way when patches of mist obscured her temporarily.

The mist thickened for a moment, hiding the apple orchard and the walls of the nunnery chapel which they approached. The sound of the bell stopped, and so did Arthurius. In a few moments the breeze pushed the mist on, and he could see that the lady now stood a little distance downhill of him. In the newly cleared air he saw the waters of the Meare lapping gently against their snow-covered banks. But the astonishing thing about the scene was what the lady held in her hands—not the staff of St. Bridget, but instead a gleaming sword which she had apparently retrieved from the nunnery chapel in the space of time it took the fog to drift by. A pale sun broke through the clouds, and shafts more silver than gold shone on the sword, the lady, and the lake before him. Dubricius at his shoulder gave him a little shove. "Go to her. Take it. It is yours."

Slowly Arthurius walked forward until he stood only an arm's length from the sword. The Lady of the Lake held it out to him. "It is said that once a great knight rescued a maiden by the slaying of a dragon on this island. And that the dragon in its death throes pulled the sword from the knight's hand. Although not in living memory have there been dragons in the land—save those of your own Pendragon banner—there must be some truth to the bardtale. The first prioress of our house found this while bathing in the Meare. It was well preserved by the peat, but it has been polished to newness by the swordsmith who comes to our island every year to see to our cutlery.

"It has long been the greatest treasure of our house. We held it though, not for ourselves, but in trust for one who would come that would use it for the saving of Britain. It is called Caliburnus, the Sword of Logres."

With both arms extended she elevated the sword above her head as an archbishop might a crown at a coronation or a priest might a grail at a mass. Arthurius felt as if he should kneel, but instead he extended his hands to receive the sword. "Arthurius of Britain, take Caliburnus, the Sword of Logres. Use it for the service of this land and the service of God to keep the light burning bright, to serve the cause of truth and justice, to fight only for the right."

Slowly she lowered her arms and placed the sword in Arthurius's hands. It was a fine, long-bladed sword designed for fighting on horseback or on foot, its iron blade heat-tempered to a great strength so as to neither shatter nor rust, its hilt finely engraved gold. He grasped the hilt. It felt almost warm to his touch. It fit into his hand as if molded for him. It was a sword worthy of the task that lay before it.

He looked at the prioress to express his gratitude, but she shook her head. "It is a gift of our Lady. Use it always in her service." Then a new cloud of mist engulfed them. When it blew past, the lady was gone, as if she had melted with the fog.

Arthurius turned to Dubricius and smiled. "And now I may go about my work?"

"Now you may go. A boatman will be ready to take you across the marshland waterways at first light tomorrow."

Arthurius would have gone then, on foot if needs be, for it was possible to cross the marshes on foot before the spring thaw if one knew the way—but at Caerleon he had bowed to Dubricius's request for three days. He would not renege now.

The unmelodious, yet somehow pleasant clanging of an old bronze bell reached them from the other side of the island. "I suggest we give the brothers the pleasure of our company at their prayers now," the archbishop said. "It is part of the wickedness of evil men that they do not give thanks for the goodness of God. May we never be guilty of that sin."

Dubricius turned his kind, smiling eyes with the crinkles at the corners on Artos. "My Bear, I have done all I can do to equip you. You and your work are now in the hands of the great God. You have told me of all the preparations you have to make, and I, too, have my work for Britain. Did I not say the fight was twofold and that I would do mine?"

"Yes, Emrys, you be the prophet of reconciliation who brings about the miracle of cooperation between these British warlords, and I'll be the Old Testament warrior who leads his people into battle to destroy God's enemies." The Pendragon brandished Caliburnus over his head like a small boy playing warrior and threw his head back with a shout of laughter that rang off Wirral Hill behind them. It was ever one of Arthurius's greatest charms that he never took himself too seriously.

The sound of the ringing bell mingled with Arthurius's laughter, and they turned their steps toward the old wattle church. An hour later, when the prayers ended and the last lingering echo of ". . . one God forever and ever, world without end, amen" had ascended off the top of the Tor, Arthurius turned to bid Dubricius farewell.

"Let us take our leave now, my old friend, for I shall depart at first light in the morning." He clasped Dubricius's thin shoulders in his powerful hands.

"May the sun and moon shine on the path of your going, and may the wind be always at your back, and may God make His countenance to shine upon you." Dubricius gave Arthurius blessings from the two worlds they both represented and made the sign of the cross over him. But already Arthurius could see by the archbishop's eyes that the old man was well on his way on his own journey, away inside himself—and beyond—to the shining regions to dwell in a crystal cave that could be reached only in his mind. The archbishop came often to the Glass Isle for such withdrawal from the physical world—a retreat that taught him much about the nature of good and evil, of heaven and earth, of physical and spiritual. It was on many such sojourns into the mind of God that he had learned the wisdom that he then shared with Arthurius.

With a final embrace, Arthurius turned and climbed the Tor. He did not have the ability to go away inside himself for long periods of time as did Dubricius, but moments to sit and think were every bit as needful for the man of war as for the man of peace, if only because they were so rare.

Arthurius sat long with his face to the west, Caliburnus of the cut steel across his knees, taking into his being the peace that seemed to rise with the mists from the reed beds below. The copper splendor of the winter sunset flared beyond the Sabrina, burnishing the water marshes and snow-coated islands with radiant color. But even as the warm red-gold colors flared before him, Arthurius shivered. For the splendor of the sunset heralded the darkness to follow.

3

he spring thaws came late that year, giving Arthurius and his Cambrogi time to carry out his careful plans for the reception of the sea wolves. They felled strong trees and dragged them across the snow like sledges and up the steep hillsides of Caer Cam for their fort. God granted them a gentle winter with frequent thaws which allowed the workers to dig the three rings of ditches around the hillside deep into the rock. The dug-out material they carted in rush baskets and on leather slings up to the fort where it was tamped into place to build a flat-topped turf wall. The timber palisade grew on top of the turf while the iron hammer and saw sang in the wintry air, as sweet to Arthurius's ears as any bardsong. Inside they rebuilt the circular timber hall of a pre-Roman Silurian chieftain and hung its single entrance with a leather apron. When peace would allow for more elegant building, the daubed walls would be smoothed and lime-washed and a proper wooden door fitted in the frame. But for now, this would serve.

However, no effort was spared on the gate that barricaded the top of Caer Cam's double-turned entryway beside a stone guardhouse. Its single, heavy gate was hung with iron pivot-rods set in stone sockets for easy, if noisy, turning should the need arise to close them quickly against the enemy. There would be no simple thorn-work barricade for the strongplace of the *Comes Britanniae*.

Daily inside the palisade, now that the passes were open, chieftains and kings who had sworn fealty to the Pendragon answered the hosting-call. Baudwin, Bors, Ectorius, Caius, Gwalchmai ap Gwyar—those of the inner circle had been with him throughout the winter, as they had for many winters before, directing the building, the preparing, and the storing that must always precede a campaigning season.

Cador of Dumnonia was the first to arrive with three hundred men and glowing reports of his infant son Constantine. Teliau came with less welcome reports of the actions of the Saxon Southfolk and Northfolk, but no less welcome well-armed and armored warriors. Eleden, Doldavius, and the others came, as well as the war bands of the Cambrogi who had gone home to their own steadings to pass the winter months at their own hearths with their own hounds, eating the honey cakes of their wives' making and hopefully begetting their own cubs to greet them with healthy squalls when they returned to their hearths with the autumn winds.

But The Ancelot did not come. He had honored Arthurius's request by sending a contingent of arrowsmiths and fletchers—the best in the world came from Caledonia—and two wagons heaped high with coppice poles from the Caledon forest for the making of spears and arrows. But the laird did not come, nor did they receive word of his warriors.

They did, however, receive word from the spies Arthurius had sent out weeks before to learn the movements of the barbarians. The picture that emerged from the combined reports was grim. "And yet," Artos told the Cambrogi gathered around the central hearth in his rebuilt hall, the deer-hide apron hung over the door to keep the piercing spring winds outside, "it is in my mind that it is better this way, for then we shall make an end of it all at once."

In reply to their questioning looks for the newest reports, he replied, "Aelle of the South Seax they have chosen for their war king. It would seem that Osric, son of Octa, son of Hengist, is to be his lieutenant. Ingil comes with his East Angles in black war boats up the Thamesis for as far as the Father of Rivers may take them."

"Fa!" Caius spat into the fire. "It is to my mind a wonder that the Father of Rivers does not swallow them whole rather than be defiled with their filth."

Arthurius went on, "Cissa of the Jutes leads no fewer than a thousand men—mostly archers. And my kinsman," he spoke the word with curled lip, "Cheldric, flying the red fox tail of his grandfather Vortigern, commands some say two thousand, some say four."

"And is there news from the laird of Berwick in Caledonia, Artos?" Baudwin asked.

"No word. And I can wait no longer. The ground is now firm enough for cavalry to travel and spring grass green enough for the horses to forage. From my scouts' reports, it is seeming that the sea wolf hosting will be—" He unrolled a parchment map, and those on the other side of the fire came around to his side. "Here." He placed his finger on the map on a spot that, using the old Roman calculation of twenty miles to a days' march, was two and a half days to the northeast of Caer Cam. "If our war host can gather first, we will take the old hillfort of Caer Lidding for our base. If the wolves are first to the lair, then the forest around Coate Water must give us cover and the slopes of Mount Badonicus serve for our strongplace."

The Cambrogi agreed with their leader's conclusions as he traced lines on the map, recounting each scout's report. "We can wait no longer if we are to have any hope of getting in the first strike. We must move now without The Ancelot—no matter how great our need may be for his men."

"Fa, and after the great victory you made for him two seasons ago against the sons of Caw and that rebel Urien of Lothian at Cat Coit Caledon! He sends us two wagon loads of sticks and stays snug in his lands." Caius spit again into the brazier. "We should have let the wolves have him for fodder. Then they would be less hungry for our western lands."

"I have sent him a message. He may yet reply." Arthurius tapped the map with a charcoal stick to focus their attention. "Baudwin, I would have you lead your squadron at first light to cut off Ingil when they leave their war ships in the Thamesis—about here. They will still be a day's march from the hosting if you can reach them in time."

"So. If it may be done, it will be done."

Arthurius turned to his oldest companion. "Ectorius, I would have you lead your men straight to the east to make Colgrim of the Canti lands late for the hosting."

"Aye. That would be a pleasure."

"I will bring the rest of our troops, but the baggage wagons will be with us, so we shall arrive two days' travel behind you."

Ectorius slapped his leather-clad thigh. "Time and enough for us to have prevented the full gathering of the wolf pack."

"Let us hope so, my brothers, for the sea wolves outnumber our cavalry as the wolves of the forest outnumber the horses of our runs."

"And yet a well-trained war horse may slay two wolves as one with the slashing of his feet."

"Let us hope so, my brothers. Let us pray so."

Even before the first streaks of sunlight the next morning the iron pivots grated in their stone sockets, swinging the gates of Caer Cam open as the aurochs' horns sounded, trumpeting Baudwin and his squadron, which equaled a full Roman equitata of five hundred cavalry, past the rock-cut guard chamber and down the steep, in-turned entrance. They traveled fast, stopping only as necessary to rest the horses and allow the men a few hours of sleep in the darkest of the night. Their advance scouts sent back no word of Anglish wolves in the woods, so spirits held high that they would be in time.

On the evening of the third day a scout returned to Baudwin just as the men were finishing their evening stirabout around the cookfires. "The Angli have left their black currachs in the Father of Rivers. They make camp in the woods three hours' ride from here."

Baudwin nodded. The course was clear. Cavalry was at a disadvantage in the woods, but the advantage of a surprise attack at night was not to be sacrificed. He gave his orders swiftly. Olwin, his second in command, was to take half the squadron and go with the scout, circling around the Angli camp to cut them off from retreat to the river. Baudwin would bring his own men on through the woods. He questioned the scout closely as to landmarks, trails, and the disposition of the Angli guard-pickets. Then he went over the details of the attack carefully with the leader of each unit.

They smothered their fires and moved as quickly and quietly as possible. It was unlikely Angli scouts would be this far yet, but surprise was essential to the success of the plan. Total darkness had fallen by the time the troops were in position. A spy, recruited from the small, dark people of the north, who made the best lookouts, reported that the Angli camp was quiet, the pickets posted at wide-spaced intervals. All well so far. But the initial estimates that the enemy was at least twice their own number were confirmed before the informant melted into the forest as quietly as an animal. Baudwin could only hope for the advantage of surprise to carry them through.

He signaled for his men to move forward silently, praying that no horse would give them away by whinnying. When they were in position, at the darkest, quietest hour of the night, his trumpeter blew a mighty, night-tearing blast on the aurochs' horn. Those in the foreguard struck light to their torches, sweeping forward with piercing battle cries like the tribesmen of old. Crashing through the woods, they overran the picket lines before the guards could anymore than turn from their posts, and swept on into the camp, slashing through the black of night with streaks of fiery light. They hacked the Angli tent ropes and fired their cloth covers.

Meanwhile, Olwin's contingent cut loose the currachs moored three-deep, set them ablaze, and pushed them to float free—cutting off a water retreat. Then they turned to engage those who had made their way to the riverbank.

As soon as the torches had done their work, Baudwin signaled another blast from his trumpeter, and the third group of his men swarmed into action. Those of the Angli who, sleep-fuddled and light-blinded, had escaped the burning of their camp and the confused clashing of their own comrade's swords made to escape into the forest, and Baudwin's men gave chase.

It was not possible to pursue them far into the darkness, but that night far more Angli blood ran into the forest floor than did Cambrogi. It was clear when Baudwin gave orders for the camp to be searched at dawn that although Ingil appeared to have escaped, he would arrive at the hosting with less than half the men Aelle Bretwalda expected.

Meanwhile Ectorius led his equitata to the southeast, hoping to cut off Colgrim's contingent of Jutes and Saxons from the old Canti lands south of the Thamesis where first Vortigern granted British lands to the barbarian. For two days they rode at a rapid, but not uncomfortable speed through spring green birch and hazel woods with little white and yellow flowers bowing before their horses' hooves. Caius, riding ahead with the scouts, reported nothing to slow their progress. But that was what worried Ectorius. They were not out for a pleasure ride. Were their scouts mistaken? Were Colgrim's men ahead of them, or behind? They had seen no signs of troops passing that way, and certainly several hundred armed barbarians could not travel through an area without leaving signs aplenty. But if they had taken an entirely different route or were hosting at a different place . . .

By the morning of the third day Ectorius decided that if they found nothing that day, they would abandon their wolf-hunt and rejoin Arthurius. He dare not miss the main hosting.

But by the time the sun was high overhead, Caius returned with a report of sighted enemy—at least a small advance party. Surely this was not the bulk of Colgrim's force, for the Jute war prince would command far more than two hundred men. Ectorius questioned his son for all the details of the land and the men and was satisfied that Caius had done well on his first scouting assignment. "So. Listen carefully, my cub. We will attack thus, and it is you who must serve as bait to lure the wolves . . ."

Caius watched carefully, nodding at each new line his father drew in the soft spring turf. It was a daring plan, and if it worked, could rid the Count of the Britains of an entire wolf pack. Well worth a day's troubling. "Sa, sa Father. It is as good as done."

Returning to his small scouting band, Caius explained the plan. Bucklers behind their shoulders and swords sheathed, they strode forward. Open, unprotected, as if doing no more than inspecting the apple trees of their own garths. But for all his careless-seeming, each man's eyes and ears were hound-alert. Caius carefully calculated where the enemy should be now from the place they had spotted him, and turned his men in a straight line toward the horned war helmets.

A flock of tiny, gray-brown sparrows scattered to the treetops, chirping wildly, no more than two spear throws ahead of them. With heart hammering beneath his mail shirt, Caius increased his stride.

Suddenly the woods took on an unnatural waiting silence. Caius knew they had arrived. One, two, three, four—he counted his strides. Then, hoping he had timed his move for the most effect and not a spear throw too soon or too late, he jumped and shrieked as if an iron barb had pierced his breast, thrashed mightily in the woods, and at the first gleam of sun on a crested helmet, led his men in wild retreat with Colgrim, his white horsetail standard now in full view, pursuing them.

Crashing, yelling, and jumping, Caius's twenty men fled from Colgrim with the noise of two hundred, keeping always a tantalizing spear throw ahead. Ectorius and his men, hidden well back in the woods, heard every crash and shout and could judge to the precise moment exactly where the troops were in the woods. Caius was making straight for the small clearing his father had indicated earlier. With superb timing the Jute band rushed into the meadow, and Ectorius's men closed the circle.

The wolves turned with angry howls, enraged even more by the trap than by the attackers' spears. In the spring-green meadow that normally rang with song of robin and willow wren, the clash of swords, tramping of horses, and surprised shrieks of dying men blotted out all else.

It was over as suddenly as it had begun, leaving a stench of blood and sweat and red-stained grass that could be washed clean only by many rains. Although Colgrim in his boar-crested helmet could not be found among the battle dead, it was a great victory for the Cambrogi, one that would make good hearing for the *Comes Britanniae*. Except for one thing—one loss that overbore all the victory. Ectorius of the gray beard, Arthurius's oldest friend on the practice ground and in the battlefield, lay with a throwing axe piercing his helmet.

Caius, to whom the command of the equitata fell, ordered that the enemy dead be piled and burned and their own dead be buried. Except Ectorius. He would be placed across his horse and borne to Arthurius that the brave old warrior's leader might say the prayers for his soul. Already the Cambrogi had lost the first of the season's new-made eques.

When Caius and his men met at the hosting, the sight of Ectorius's slain body was the sharpest of Arthurius's woes, added to an already long and growing list. The successful advance forays had, as it were, caught only two buckets of raindrops in a deluge. Arthurius was too late to prevent the gathering of the wolf pack. The Bretwalda had arrived with his white horsetail standards and full band of troops at least a day ahead of the Britons, and now the Saxons commanded Caer Lidding, leaving the less desirable Mons Badonicus to their opponents. With each day Arthurius's hope of The Ancelot arriving to add even a small balance-weight to their numbers grew fainter.

He placed his huge hand on Caius's shoulder and gripped it. "This is a sorry sight, my friend. Ectorius shall be missed by all, but by none more than myself. He taught us both most of our sword-skill, and there was no better teacher. Now we must use that skill to avenge his death. You will command his equitata, Caius." He turned to others of his companions. "Gwalchmai, Bors! See to the preparations. I would have my captain buried in the manner of the chiefs of our forefathers, but there is no time for the hollowing out of a log—" He paused and looked around for an acceptable substitute.

Small, dark Gwalchmai, whose people at some time surely must have mingled their blood with that of the little hill people, stepped forward in his silent way. "There is no need for the hollowing, Lord Artos. When we were making camp this afternoon, I saw two such logs by the stream that runs to Coate Water. It is in my mind that they are used for fishing by those of nearby steadings, but they would be honored to have their logs so used for the burial of a captain of the Pendragon."

"It is good. Bring them."

When a shallow grave had been dug and the body placed in one log with the other beside it to use for a cover before the mother earth blanketed all, Arthurius bade his trumpeter signal the call for captains on the ox horn. Those who had fought together for so many seasons gathered to bid their friend farewell. "As we are without a priest among our number, let each man say what prayers he will and give whatever herb or green branch he will to our friend to wish him a peaceful journey."

"No priest among you? Will not I do?"

Arthurius turned with a jerk at the sound of the familiar voice. "Merlinus Dubricius! I thought not to see you until we could offer the prayers of thanksgiving for a successful battle." He embraced his friend. "But, oh, the sight of you gladdens my heart more than I had hoped anything could."

So Ectorius of the Cambrogi was buried with the prayers of an archbishop to speed his soul on its way. But before the completion of ". . . and yea, though I walk through the valley of the shadow of death . . ." a scout arrived and stood waiting at the edge of the torchlight, for night was now upon them.

Arthurius stepped aside to hear the report. It was heavy hearing. "So. And that confirms all I had suspected. See if there is any stew left in the cookpots,

Eu of the Green Plover, and a cup of heather beer; we shall all have need of hearty stomachs in the morning."

The prayers were ended, and the time for council was come. Arthurius ordered his armorbearer to bring the great round cloth from his tent and spread it on the ground inside a circle of his captains. As their leader spoke, he began to draw a map with a charred stick.

"By the latest report we are outnumbered at least three to one. But we have met odds as great and greater before and emerged victorious. The horses themselves come close to evening the numbers. The challenge is the greatest we have faced, but so will be the victory. Our scouts report that all the sea wolf captains have answered Aelle Bretwalda's hosting call. This gives them the great numbers, but two things it gives us—for the first time we can defeat them all at once and finish this endless campaigning that is little better than putting out wildfires in the corn; and the greater their numbers under different leaders, the more we can hope for barbarian disorder to work for us."

He paused to let the men in the flame-brightened circle comment and ask questions. Dubricius sat a silent observer behind his right shoulder. "Yes, Colgrim of the Canti lands escaped as Caius feared. And as we suspected, the band Ectorius's men defeated was only one section of his host. Ingil of the East Angles has but a small number left after Baudwin's brave victory, but they have licked their wounds and arrived at Caer Lidding."

Even as he spoke, Arthurius and his men looked across the narrow valley and saw the enemy campfires flickering behind the battlements of the old fort and spilling on down the side of the hill as numerous as if the stars of the heavens rested there. "Osric serves under the Bretwalda, and Cissa leading the South Seax, Balduf with his wolf pack, and," as always, Arthurius ground out the name, "Cheldric." That he should have a kinsmen among the enemy leaders galled the Count of Britain almost beyond speaking.

He drew the little stream that ran through the valley to mark the battle line, then a sweeping curve to indicate Mount Badonicus. "Cador, you will lead the foot archers first to do what may be done to even the numbers from a distance. Then Gwalchmai will bring in the testudo. Bors, your equitata will hold the left flank, Baudwin, the right." He drew curving lines on each side of Badonicus. "And when the charge is sounded, you will sweep so . . ." More wide-arcing lines appeared on the white cloth and one firm, straight line in the center. That line was Arthurius's squadron. "Caius, you will remain hidden in the woods for a surprise attack. We have little enough to hold in reserve, but your men are brave. They must serve."

"They will serve."

"As will we all." Baudwin's voice was firm with resolution.

"Aye. All will stand for Britain and for her Count," Gwalchmai added.

The charcoal lines of the map stood out sharply in the torchlight, making an indelible impression on those who the next day must lead their men through the plan amidst the confusion of battle. The one disadvantage to the cloth field table was that it made little noise when the men pounded it with their dagger hilts. Most of the company departed to get what sleep they might before dawn's light brought armor-donning time. But Baudwin, Caius, and Gwalchmai drew close to Arthurius and Dubricius, sitting still in the torchlight after Arthurius had rolled up the cloth and sent it to his tent with Peredur. After the battle, washing the cloth would be one of the armorbearer's duties.

"And when The Ancelot arrives, where will you put him on the map?" Caius asked, taking one of the cups of beer being handed around.

Artos gave a short, harsh shout of laughter. "I guess that depends on which side he chooses to fight for."

With one of his swift mood changes that could be so refreshing, Arthurius raised his cup. "No more lines on the battle map tonight. Baudwin, give us a harpsong."

Baudwin had already taken his pale alderwood harp from the embroidered doeskin bag slung over his shoulder—in the manner of the old druid bards from which he was descended. His fingers found a pleasing flight of notes. "When the victory is ours, my Lord Artos, I will make you a new song. For tonight, a lament for the pain this land has felt from sea wolf raids for a hundred years and a hundred before that." Again his fingers glided over the strings and the very flames of the torches wavered in their rhythm. "Tonight, the 'Deathsong of the Peaceful Vale,' that after tomorrow's battle fires, no more laments need be sung." His fingers fluttered a glissando, and the words followed:

Take a harp,
wander through the ruins,
O men of valor.
Take a harp,
and weep for the beauty vanished;
cry for the peace that is banished.

Pluck the strings skillfully.
Sing a song of the past,
  of the time before the destruction,
  of the time before the foederati.

Here green grew the corn,
here happy played the babes,
here secure stood the hearth.
The tree flowered,

the robin sang,
the cattle grazed.

Then came the sea wolf,
bloody of sword.
Then cried the cubbling,
Then fell the hearthstone,
Then died the warrior
defending his vale.
And the sword of the foederati ran red.

Pluck the harp,
Sing and weep
that men may remember.

The strings of the harp silenced under the singer's fingers, and all sat silent, listening to the hiss of the torch flames above them and the quiet, night-grazing noises of the horse herd in the field below them. At last Arthurius spoke quietly to Dubricius. "Our part is so small, so pitifully small."

"And yet, it is part of the whole, my bear cub."

"The whole?"

"The whole fabric of the light. Without that part—as without any part wherever men fight for the light—without that part there would be a hole in the weaving."

From where he sat, Arthurius could see his own tent with the woven door-flap pulled back, awaiting his arrival. "Sa, sa. A mighty, ragged hole that would indeed let the cold wind blow through."

4

he camp was astir before first light, each man going as steadily about his preparations as if this day he were to plant the corn in his garth. Armorbearers in every section of the camp helped their chieftains pull the chain-link mail shirt over their undersark or, if they had the more comfortable side-opening kind, did the buckles or thongs at the side. A few of the newcomers still wore boiled-leather armor, but in four seasons of campaigning and after eleven victories, few seasoned warriors had not stripped a mail shirt and iron battle helmet from a fallen foe. The archers' quivers were full of fine, straight, Caledonian arrows, and every sword and dagger hung brightly burnished and razor-sharp inside its sheath.

Arthurius finished his bannock and hunk of hard yellow cheese with a swallow of sour beer. He gave the conscientious Peredur one last chance to see that every buckle was firm, and then strapped on his leather-lined, bowl-shaped iron helm and raised the hinged visor.

"Are you ready, my valiant bearer?"

"Ready, my Lord Comes." Peredur saluted gravely, open-palmed in the old Roman manner, and followed his leader from the tent. Peredur, who would serve as standard-bearer in the field, seized the tall dragon-blazed pennant from its place outside the tent and strode after Arthurius.

According to each captain's orders, the troops stood assembled at the foot of the western slope of the mountain, out of view of the enemy, but within a few minutes' ride to their assigned positions. Arthurius rode uphill of the army, the first rays of the sun streaking over the hill behind him and gleaming on the bronze fittings of the bull-hide shield on his shoulder and the red dragon banner fluttering over his head. Always before battle he reviewed his troops and wished them good hunting, but he was happy to leave the speeches to the archbishop who stood above him on the hillside, the breeze rippling his long robes, the sun sparking from his thick gray hair. For all of his age and thin frame, Merlinus Ambrosius Dubricius yet had a voice that could echo from any mountainside to the farthest men in the valley, and this morning it boomed with vigor. He threw his arms out to full length. "Men of Britain, men who fight for Logres, the Kingdom of God within Britain, remember today your fellow men, remember today your country, remember today your God. And pray today for the strengthening of the light." He lowered his arms, but not his voice. "Remember today your countrymen who have died before you under barbarian sword and axe. Let you press heartily forward to avenge their deaths and to make the land free from any more such bloodletting.

"Fight you therefore for your country. And if you live, live proudly in a war-free land. And if you die, do it willingly for your country's sake. For death itself is victory and a healing to the soul, inasmuch as he that shall have died for his brethren offers himself a living sacrifice to God and thereby does he follow in the footsteps of Christ who laid down His own life for His brethren.

"Whoever, therefore, among you that shall live, shall live gloriously, and whoever that shall die this day, to him shall be the absolution of all his sins, if he now receive it willingly through the cross of our Lord Jesus Christ." The archbishop extended his arms in blessing and made the sign of the cross over the troops. Then he turned to Arthurius, sitting downhill of him on Magnus, and with his crucifix-tipped staff tapped the count's shoulder three times. "In the name of the Father, and of the Son, and of the Holy Spirit, amen."

In the flush of the blessing and the rising sun, Arthurius drew Caliburnus, flung out his sword arm, and shouted, "My brothers, we have known a dark age, an age without law, without order—an age when the strong have preyed upon the weak, when the sea wolves have preyed upon the lambs of our steadings. Now we go forth to rid our hunting-runs of wolves! A good hunting and a clean kill, my sword brothers!" And with the aurochs' horn sounding the call, he led them forward.

Across the valley the booming of the long Saxon war horns shook the hillside as the flood of warriors spilled forward, filling the valley, here and there a white horsetail standard marking a horn-crested captain among his men. Arthurius had no advantage of surprise, of numbers, or of position. He could only rely on skillful execution of their battle plans by men and horses—and on the prayers of Merlinus Dubricius, who had taken his position on the hilltop above them.

And on speed. The wolf pack was still milling in confusion when Cador led his archers to within an arrow-flight of the enemy across the rushing stream. Arthurius thrilled at their precision as the front row knelt, as if one man, and notched their arrows, while at the same time the row behind them took aim over their heads. The first barrage fell before the Saxons could do more than raise their round wooden shields. Cador's first lines fell back to renotch their arrows and their positions were filled by the next ranks. For an instant the sky was black as if with the flighting of birds, and a sharp singing noise filled the air. Already hampered by the bodies of fallen men, the wolves struggled forward to return a ragged fire. Some of their arrows found their marks on the British side, but far more arrows bearing well-clipped Caledonian feathers bloodied their iron tips in Saxon and Anglish blood.

Soon the British arrow supply ran low, and the Saxon line pushed forward in places. Cador sounded the signal for his men to pull back, and Gwalchmai moved his footmen forward, locked in tight squares, shield to shield as the Roman testudo. Suddenly, from his elevated view of the field, Arthurius saw his mistake. Against such a vast wall of warriors, the individual turtles would make little headway, unable to penetrate holes in the lines to make way for the cavalry charge to follow. They would lose precious time in changing the plan, but they were still out of range of enemy fire. It could be done. Spurring Magnus forward and signaling his trumpeter at the same time, he saw from the side of the field Teliau's horse archers close in in response to the aurochs' blast. They would provide a firing wall behind which Gwalchmai and he could rearrange the testudo. If they had enough men. And if they could move rapidly enough. It was a desperate measure to change plans this early in battle and thereby risk confusing his men as well as giving up the reserve attack of a whole squadron of horse archers.

The horse archers held. By the time the foederati had scrambled over the bodies of their fallen companions and pressed forward, the horsemen could withdraw. The newly assembled war machine of the *Comes Britanniae* was ready. Instead of a field of individual squares, the squadrons of the white horse-tails now faced one giant V which swept the width of the central field with its point bearing straight at them. Rather than filled solidly with men, however, the V was only three men deep, so they could afford few losses. To protect the advance of his machine, Arthurius signaled the foot and horse archers to continue fire from the sides, giving as much cover as possible.

At first the advance was rapid. Only a few of the Pendragon's men fell from Jute and Anglish arrows, and as one man fell, his place was filled from behind, keeping the wall solid. But when they got within range of the Saxons' fierce throwing axes, the losses became greater. The V wavered, then closed in, smaller than before, but solid and still driving its sharp point forward. Arthurius held his breath. A few feet further and they would be across the stream, driving their wedge into the heart of the Saxon ranks. Then he could send in the cavalry. *Let them make it. Dear God, let them make it.* A few feet more, an opening big enough for the space of two or three horses would do. He had once attacked with space enough for only one horse, and they had cut the enemy line.

The first man of the V was across the stream, his fellows on both sides of him wet to the ankles, each man pushing ahead, using the boss of his shield as a weapon while the men behind him aimed spear throws over his head. The break in the lines had to come now, for when the V moved uphill, such a method would not work. For a moment the Saxon line sagged, and Arthurius raised his hand to signal the charge. Then it happened.

Knowing that Arthurius would try to get his men across the stream and into Saxon ranks, Aelle had dammed the water upstream leaving little more than a ditch to wade. But at his own signal horn, the dike was broken, and a wall of water rushed through the valley washing a great hole in the V.

In the space of a few sword-slashes, the torrent passed, leaving a somewhat larger, but not unfordable stream. But the damage was done. Arthurius's V was broken. The point had pierced enemy ranks, but not so deeply as hoped for, and now the wolves were closing over the heads of those who had made it across. Nothing to do but sound the main cavalry charge.

The ox horn blew clear and strong from the slopes of Mount Badonicus, echoing off the Saxon-covered side of Caer Lidding, calling Britain's finest troops to battle. With a pounding of hooves and the wind of their going rippling spear pennants, they struck the Saxon wall at the stream, the ancient Cymric war cry "Yr Widdfa!" meeting the savage, blood-chilling war cry of the Jutes and the wolf howl of the Saxon.

The sheer force of the speed and weight of armored horses drove the Saxons back upon themselves, trampling over the bodies of those already slain and often catching underfoot those not yet hit. Arthurius thrust and slashed on every side of him with his spear, its handle growing red and slippery with enemy blood as he pressed Magnus forward, controlling him with his knees so as to keep both hands for fighting with shield and sword. And Magnus took his number as he had been trained to do, striking out with his sharp, iron-shod front hooves.

All around Arthurius the Cambrogi fought their way forward in the face of savage counterattack. The height of the horses was an advantage, and each man killed more than the three-to-one which he must. Yet British blood enough and more than enough flowed with Anglish and Saxon, making the stream run red and clogging the ground with bodies.

When Arthurius sensed the Saxon line was beginning to close behind them, which would bring the defeat of his valiant squadron, he signaled the trumpeter. The ox horn rang the Pendragon's message to Baudwin and Bors waiting with their equitatae behind the crested slopes of Mount Badonicus.

The two cavalry flanks flew forward at the sides of the enemy line, sweeping it before them, then suddenly curving inward, and drove the wolf pack in on itself. The foederati were so tightly packed together they hit their own men when they raised their seax to thrust at the Britons. Now their numbers worked against them as the line straightened. Then the ends curved backward, giving ground before the British who drove them back toward their own fort.

With a shout of triumph, Arthurius spotted Aelle battling just ahead of him and spurred Magnus to engage the Saxon war king. Aelle raised his shield to deflect Arthurius's spear thrust, and the weapon broke in the Pendragon's hand. Flinging it away, Arthurius drew Caliburnus and fought forward against thrusts of Aelle's seax. Osric saw his Bretwalda engaged, and he flung at Magnus. Arthurius spun his horse. The glinting hooves felled the wolf captain. But Aelle escaped.

Then Peredur, bravely bearing the Pendragon standard at his leader's side, received a thrust likely meant for Arthurius, for even barbarians seldom attacked unarmed bearers. Peredur fell, taking with him the standard of Britain. It was only a few sword-slashes until Teliau saw what had happened, seized the standard, and raised it again, but it was enough. Caius, waiting hidden in the woods, in the stress of his first command, saw the pennant fall and thought the Pendragon himself had fallen. Without waiting for the aurochs' signal, he threw his troops in, arriving with the last of Arthurius's precious reserves at a place on the left flank which Bors was holding very well with his own men.

Arthurius, who had fought his way to a position high enough up Caer Lidding to see what had happened, cursed at his unseasoned captain's rashness, but there was nothing to be done now but to battle on. Abandoning strategy, for it had all been played out, his battle-fury came upon him and translated itself to his men. They slashed to right and left and on every side. When a horse was slain, its rider grabbed the mount of a fallen comrade and battled on. When a sword broke in a warrior's hand, he grabbed one from a death-stilled hand, be it British or Saxon, and battled on. A red mist of battle fury and blood-splattered weapons rose before their eyes, and the slopes of the hill and the green valley ran red with blood.

For a space the Saxons fell back and back. But then Arthurius heard an ugly war boom from a Saxon horn and looked upon the broken ramparts of Caer Lidding. There he saw a sight he had thought not to see. Not the white horsetail standards of Saxon, but the white battle shields of the Scoti, who since Vortigern's day had kept their lime-washed bucklers busy behind the wall fighting their former allies, the Picti, and the Cymric chieftains of the north.

To Arthurius's surprise, their leader was not Scoti, but rebel Briton—Urien of Lothian. Arthurius had defeated him two seasons ago at Cat Coit Caledon and had not thought to fight him again, for Urien had given his daughter Morgana as lady in waiting to The Ancelot's court. So was that why The Ancelot was not there—had there been an uprising in his own lands? But if so, why had he not sent a message? Was the heather ablaze in Caledonia—burning a fire that would leap the wall and engulf them all with new numbers added to the foederati?

The reinforcements now drove the white horsetails forward, breaking the British cavalry into little V's as Gwalchmai's foot-warrior charge had done to the enemy earlier.

Now Arthurius longed for the reserves brash Caius had flung in too soon. They gave ground at great cost. Now he must fall back and try to regroup his men, a nearly impossible task in the melee, but their only hope. He signaled for the aurochs to sound the fall-back and heard the answering thunder of horses' hooves.

But surely the pounding of hooves was too great for the pitifully small numbers left him. For a moment he thought he had become confused in the press of battle. It seemed the men were moving the wrong direction. The Saxon were retreating. He shook his head and turned in the saddle for a clearer view of the field.

A gladder sight had never met his eyes. With red and saffron plaid pennants flying, The Ancelot galloped into battle with more than three hundred well-armed fresh troops. Their long, wild hair flying, the sun glinting off the fiercely sharp little dirks they held between their teeth, The Ancelot's men threw themselves into battle with a fury.

Now the British pushed forward with renewed life, and the press of battle brought Arthurius once more to Aelle. Arthurius thrust his shield away from him, as it hampered his turning Magnus in such tight fighting, but then at a flash of the Bretwalda's throwing axe, the valiant war horse fell, red running from the milk white neck and matting the long mane. Arthurius jumped free and sprang at Aelle, using both hands on Caliburnus. The Saxon was a strong man and a mighty fighter with his sharp seax, but Arthurius rained blow after blow on the mailed head and shoulders, until at last Aelle staggered and dropped his seax.

One sword thrust, and it would all be over. Arthurius held Caliburnus at the war king's throat, open above his mail shirt. "Aelle Bretwalda, will you swear by Thor and all your gods to withdraw your wolves and meet me at the treaty table if I hold my hand?"

Aelle snarled like a cornered beast, but Arthurius saw him looking across the field, calculating the loss of his own men, seeing the fresh Caledonian warriors pushing forward at every sword thrust. Again he snarled, then broke into an open growl. Arthurius jerked Caliburnus for the kill. "I yield." Aelle howled like a wounded wolf.

Arthurius knew he would be true to his word. Aelle signaled his horn blower to sound the retreat. As a great cry of pain from a dying animal, the signal boomed down the valley. Bors rode to his leader. "Take him." Arthurius pushed Aelle forward with the point of Caliburnus. "Guard him well. We will talk when the death fires have burned out."

And then he saw Cador. "Pursue them—push them to the east. Let no wolves get among our lambs behind Ambrosius's dyke."

Stepping carefully on the blood-slick hillside, Arthurius made his way to where he had last seen Gwalchmai. He found him nearby, already directing his men in the sorting of the field—the British dead to be buried beneath Mount Badonicus and the foederati fed to death fires on their own hill. Already across the vast hillside, warriors were searching the bodies of the fallen for the spoils of war. Arthurius looked on silently for a moment, then shrugged. "Leave them at it; they are paid little enough in currency rings. They have earned the day's wage. Bring me word when you know how the wolf captains fared. I dealt with Osric, and Aelle is captured. But I could not get within a spear thrust of Cheldric's fox tail all day."

Next the war leader heard a report from his newest captain. Caius's blustering showed how much he felt the weight of his earlier mistake.

"It nearly cost us the battle, Caius. Let not you disobey my orders again."

"I thought you fallen, my lord."

"All the more reason to hold to my plan!" Yet Arthurius could not long hold his anger against Caius's rough enthusiasm. "It was a good hunting, sa?"

"Excellent hunting, Lord Artos. My father is avenged. Colgrim's blood ran red on my sword."

Before Arthurius could hear the rest of Caius's report, The Ancelot strode forward, his flowing blond beard flicked with enemy blood and his red and saffron plaid cloak shredded from seax slashes. However, a brilliant gleam of victory lighted his pale blue eyes. "Well and well. Artos, my bear, we showed the wolves the valor of Britain today. It is in my mind they will think long before they choose to come hunting in our runs again." He clasped the Pendragon around both shoulders with his powerful arms.

"And it is in my mind to assure they keep to their own runs. But, my Caledonian friend, you almost missed the quarry. I thought you had chosen to stay behind your wall."

"What! And would The Ancelot miss the greatest wolf hunt Britain has ever seen? We were delayed three days by a wall of lime-white Scoti shields thrown up by that foul Urien to keep us from the hunt, else we would have been here before ye."

Before Arthurius could reply, The Ancelot dropped to one knee. "And now it is in my mind to finish what was left undone at the Christ Mass. Arthurius, Count of Britain, The Ancelot of Caledonia is your man."

"It is my thinking that you have already proved that far beyond words or sword-dubbing today." Arthurius smiled as he drew Caliburnus, dark in spots with dried blood, and tapped the laird on each shoulder. "Welcome to the Cambrogi of Eques."

The newest of Arthurius's knights stood before him on the blood-hardened field. Arthurius's heart lifted. But not for long. He suddenly realized he had not seen Baudwin since his captain first flew with his men into battle at the sounding of the charge. Even the making of this valiant new eques would mean little to him if Baudwin's blood mingled with that of the battle-slain.

With fear-slowed step the Pendragon turned toward the green garth at the foot of Mons Badonicus where the wounded were being cared for. The field was a heavy place, filled with the weary living ministering to the half living. The reek of scorched flesh from the death fires mingled with the smell of live flesh being cauterized by hot irons. Men who would never cry out from enemy strikes did so now as the iron seared their flesh with a sharp sizzling crackle. But it was their best weapon against the wound sickness. And occasionally the air was freshened with the clean, pungent scent of fresh, healing herbs being ground into a life-saving unguent. All went forward under the direction of Merlinus Dubricius, most gifted of all men in herb-craft, which he had learned from his mother and grandmother in the distant Cymri mountains. Yet his skill was more than knowledge. To many he seemed gifted with special power to fight the dark forces of unlife.

Everywhere around him Arthurius saw destruction. But in spite of the men lying with ragged, evil wounds on a blood-slick field, a prayer of thanksgiving rose within him—thanksgiving that this might be the last of such scenes for a space of time, for as long as he could hold the peace by God's grace.

Then the prayer died in his heart. Just ahead he saw Dubricius kneeling over a still form lying on a blood-soaked cloak. The archbishop was signing the cross as for the departing of the soul, and there on the ground was an embroidered doeskin harp bag.

"My sword brother!" Artos flung himself to the ground beside them with a sob.

Baudwin turned his head with a slow smile. "It was good hunting, my brother."

"Baudwin—" He could say no more.

"Na, na. The thing is over. May a one-handed brother not serve his Pendragon? And my harpskill will be affected not at all."

"One-handed?" Then Arthurius saw with a flood of relief that Baudwin's left arm ended in an abrupt bandage, but that the blackening blood that covered him was not from death-wounds—at least not his own.

"Aye." Baudwin's voice was weak. "Those double-barbed Jute spears were forged in hell. But if one must take one, the wrist is the best place—especially if one has the herb skill and the prayers of our Myrddin Emrys to speed the healing." It had been a long speech for a wounded man, and Baudwin gasped for breath.

At the sound of Dubricius's familiar name, Artos recalled that Baudwin and the archbishop were from the same region of the southern Cymri. It had always made a special bond between them. He laughed in relief. "And here I was thinking you were receiving your last rites. Sa. Recover quickly, my harper. We shall have gentler uses for this hand of yours in the days to come." He grasped Baudwin's healthy right hand in his enormous bear claw and held it for three heartbeats. Then he released it. "Sleep now, my brother, and dream of that new harpsong you promised me. I shall hear it when we come again to Caer Cam."

One more piece of good news waited. Teliau of the Iceni horse people who had lost none of their age-old wisdom came to the Pendragon covered in foul-smelling black unguent to his elbows, but with a smile of triumph on his face.

"It is well, my lord. Magnus the ever-valiant shall live."

At Teliau's words Arthurius felt a dam-burst of joy. Magnus's recovery seemed an omen for the recovery of all war-ravaged Britain. He clasped his eques's arm in a tight grip, but could not speak for the fullness in his heart that threatened to trickle from his eyes.

Long evening shadows were stretching over the slopes of Mount Badonicus as Arthurius and Dubricius walked slowly to the top of the hill. Beyond the red-soaked bandages of the wounded, beyond the new-turned burial mounds, beyond the ashes of the death fires, the waters of the Coate ran clear and glistening into the green fastness of a spring-fresh forest where birds sang their evening prayers, and beyond that the westering sun painted the sky red and gold with the promise of a new day.

"The bards will sing of this day's victory for time beyond time, my Comes," Dubricius said.

"Sa, sa. It is so. And that is good. But I fear the winning of the peace was the easy part. Now must come the keeping of it."

5

ith the stench of the death fires still fouling the spring air the next morning, Aelle, true to the words he spoke at sword point, sent out message bearers to those who would represent his fallen chieftains at the council. Some were scattered with their men beyond the pursuit of Cador, and some were barricaded in the confusion that was Caer Lidding, but Aelle Bretwalda's call would be obeyed even in defeat.

So it was that three days later in a drizzling spring rain buffeted by gusting winds, Arthurius and his Cambrogi rode through the broken, weed-clogged streets of the formerly bustling civitas of Cunetio. Though not much remained of the old Roman town, it was a convenient meeting place—a three-hour ride south of Badonicus, away from the stench of battle, on ground not fought over, and offering buildings which, although in disrepair, could provide some comfort.

A few thatched hovels had been thrown up against the walls of the city by those native Britons and descendants of the eagles who had chosen to remain there. Surprised, curious, and alarmed, the inhabitants came out to stare at the mail- and leather-clad men whose horses clattered through the usually silent street. When word ran through the crowd that this was the Count of Britain, victorious from a battle with the sea wolves, the crowd broke into cheers. One little girl in a homespun tunic stepped forward and held a handful of yellow flowers up to Arthurius. He took them with a shout of joyous laughter that called forth an answering cheer from the watchers as he stuck the bright clump in the ring brooch at his shoulder.

Leaving Magnus with Blaise, who had replaced the much-mourned Peredur as armorbearer, Arthurius led his councilors into the long-abandoned forum hall in the center of Cunetio. Rain beat against the broken shutters and dripped through holes in the roof. There had been no time to cover broken tiles with thatch or to make preparations for the meeting other than sending three men ahead to light a fire, sweep up broken masonry, and set up stools. A short time later Aelle arrived, unbound but guarded by Teliau and Doldavius. Those who had answered the Bretwalda's call followed. The uneasy council of foes, now in the roles of victor and vanquished, could begin.

On the raised dais where the civitas council had sat in old times, Arthurius, with Dubricius behind him, faced Aelle, backed by Cheldric seated on skin-covered cross-legged stools. There were not enough unbroken stools or benches left for the others, so the remaining councilors simply sat on piled skins around a central fire built right on the broken terrazzo floor, as no braziers remained. Arthurius looked at his half circle of men sitting just below him and was glad of their presence

He also thought of those who were not there. The Ancelot, in his usual enigmatic manner, had ridden north with a small band of his best men. He vowed to deal with Urien, his treaty-breaking neighbor, and then said, "Arthurius, Count of Britain, I shall return. And I shall see you made High King."

And Arthurius sorely missed the gray head of Ectorius, whose seat was filled by the brash Caius, yet many years from learning his father's wisdom. But perhaps this council would make a beginning for him. Also the absence of Baudwin left a great void. He, of all the Cambrogi, was the one whose mind was most attuned to Arthurius's own. But it would be many days and more before the Cymri captain could travel without danger of being overtaken by the wound-fever.

On the other side of the smoking, sputtering fire, for all that could be found was rain-soaked wood, sat the foederati: Balduf, replacing Colgrim on the Canti lands, his oat-white hair tied with a leather thong at his neck; Eosa of the Southfolk and Eldad of the Northfolk, scowling in an attempt to cover their extreme youth, which told of the battle loss of the older men . . . And on around the half crescent, past many faces Arthurius did not recognize to one that he did recognize with a start. He had not seen the man-child before, but it was such a mirror image of Cheldric's thin face, snapping dark eyes, and fox-red hair that this twelve-year-old could only be Cheldric's son, Vortigern's great grandson, and Arthurius's own nephew.

But why would Cheldric bring a child to the council fires?

With an effort Arthurius pushed his thoughts and doubts aside. It was time to begin. In order to make the most of his powerful size and victorious position, Arthurius rose and stood before the council, hands on hips, heavy, fur-lined leather cloak held out by each arm, firelight gleaming on his gold torque, brooch, and armlets in the dim room. "Aelle Bretwalda of the Saxons, when I held you at sword point three days ago after the great clashing of our war hosts, you swore to meet me in council that we might seek a way to end such slaughter of our peoples. You have come. That is good.

"But it is in my mind and in the minds of my companions to ask why we should deal so with you. We have shown ourselves strong—stronger than you. But we believe not only in strength. We believe in the rule of law. In the rule of right over might. In justice for all our people, not just for the strong. Your kind has not shown that you seek to live by such laws, so it is in our minds to ask why we should bargain with you. How can our peoples live side by side?"

Arthurius Pendragon remained standing, but he paused for the Saxon chief to speak. Aelle was beaten, but not cowed. He too rose to speak, in a thickly accented dialect of the Cymric tongue with frequent Saxon words thrown in.

His wheat-colored hair flowing over his rough, brown woolen cloak that was held at his shoulder by a massive disc brooch, he stood with his legs wide-planted in leather-gaitered leggings under a dark tunic, and wolfskin cape over all. "Aye, it is known that you are a people of laws, Arthurius Pendragon. But we also have our laws. My people are not only as you see on the battlefield. We are farmers before we are warriors. We come to this land from the thin soil and harsh weather of the north with few possessions saving the clothes we stand up in and our grandfathers' brooches. My people would ask for nothing but to work the land in peace and feed our cubs as you do."

"If this is your wish, why do you gather at the battle-hosting season after season instead of minding the wheat garth and cattle field, Aelle Bretwalda?"

"And it is in my mind to ask you, Arthurius Pendragon, if you are a people of laws, why do you not honor the laws of the one who ruled before you and let us keep our treaty lands?"

Arthurius took a step forward to silence the growl of approval from the Saxon side of the fire. "We can have no council meeting if you will not speak truth, Aelle Bretwalda. It has been long and long since there was a battle in your treaty lands. It is you who will not honor the laws of your predecessor and live within your lands." Now the murmur of approval came from the British side.

Aelle was silent. A new gust of wind splattered the rain against the forum hall and sent it splashing through the broken roof. The fire sputtered and smoked, making several on both sides of the council cough. At last Aelle spoke. "Hear this, Arthurius Pendragon, and believe what you will. Our first choice is not to massacre and annihilate, but rather to eat the fruits of civilization from which the Romankind always walled us out—confining our people to lands of thin soil and short growing seasons. Our women and children are hungry. Do you wonder that we fight for your rich lands?"

Arthurius stepped to within an arm's length of the Saxon. "But it is not only the farm lands you fight over. It is our towns and steadings you burn. It is our walls, built for safety against your kind, that you batter and break. What has that to do with farming and husbandry, Aelle Bretwalda?"

Perhaps it was only the wavering smoke that made it appear as if the Bretwalda took a step backward. "I have no quarrel with walls. We will not attack the British towns now standing within our treaty lands."

Arthurius was fully aware of the price it cost the Saxon war king to make this promise. And Arthurius was sure the Bretwalda meant his own words at that moment. But Arthurius also knew it would require steadfast vigilance to keep him in mind of them. "So. I hear your words, Aelle Bretwalda. And my chieftains hear your words. We will talk among ourselves."

With a wave of his arm Arthurius drew his Cambrogi into a side room for privacy. Claiming his seniority in age, if not in rank, Cador of Dumnonia spoke first. "Fa! Treaty! These barbarians have never known the rule of law. How can they abide, even if they intend to—which I doubt—in good faith?"

"It will be our part of the bargain to teach them as a wild horse may be broken to the bit or a wolf cub trained as a hound to lie at the hearth."

"Sa, sa." Bors pulled his cloak closer around his shoulders in the unheated room. "And what hearth fires would you have them lie by, my Lord Artos?"

"I would have them abide in their south and east coastal strips."

Cador flung himself forward with a force that would have knocked to the floor any who stood in his way. "You would give some of the richest lands in Britain, those of the ancient Iceni and Canti, to the barbarian king?"

"Give? It is not I who do the giving, but our kinsman Vortigern the Fox who long before my time and my father's time did the giving—after, men say, the Fox poisoned Constantus for his golden torque. Be that as it may, the treaty was struck, and the sea wolves fulfilled their part—they did drive the Picti and Scoti north beyond the wall where they remain. The thing is done. Today Saxon bairns live on the land where they were bred. We should be the wolves—very foolish wolves at that—if we attempted to push them from it."

"No! Let us push!" Caius thrust forward and stood by Arthurius. "My father's blood is on their swords—I would make them wash them in the sea!" Some nodded in agreement.

"And how many more of our men would you have die on Saxon swords to do such pushing and to keep them pushed? There are more of the Saxon and Anglish kind than there are of the Celtic kind. We cannot keep them forever in the sea. There are not enough of us to build a shield wall around our island, and if there were, there would be none left for husbandry in the field or at the garth."

"For years beyond years the wolves have burned our steadings and stolen our lands. How can there now be peace?" Eleden spoke from the back of the room.

"I am not sure I can tell you how. But I can tell you that it must be," Arthurius answered. "I believe Aelle speaks true when he says not all of the Saxonkind are as we see on the battlefield. I have heard tell of Southfolk villages where Saxon and Celtic share the same burial ground. If they can lie nearby in death, cannot we work nearby in life?"

"It cannot be. Our losses have been too great."

"Our losses have been great. But theirs have been greater. It is to stop such great losses that we must make treaty."

"Fa. If I could but redden my sword with the blood of that Cheldric, the others might live their dog lives." Caius's hand went to his empty scabbard, as none came armed to the council.

Arthurius shook his head and tried reason once more.

"It is in my mind that Saxon farmers are none so bad at their husbandry. It is to the benefit of all to firm the lines back to their treaty lands and have them beat their spears into plowshares."

In frustration at having no table to beat upon, Cador pounded a leather-covered fist into his palm. "And how long do you think such a treaty line would hold this time?"

"As long as we can hold them. It is in my mind that the bear is somewhat stronger than the fox was, and that the bear can be stronger than the wolf if the bear defends his territory properly and the wolf is well-fed in his lair with his cubs."

"Fa! Do what you will, *Comes Britanniae*. I'll have none of it for my lands. And woe to the sea wolf who looks to set foot in Dumnonia!" Cador stamped from the room, his heavy cloak swinging out behind him. He flung the door to in what would have been a heavy slam if it had any longer hung straight on its hinges.

Even without the hoped-for bang, Cador's departure left a gaping hole in the council circle, which others drew into to fill. An uneasy discussion followed until Dubricius, much taken with the "spears into plowshares" argument, took the lead. "My friends, let us look to the holy Scriptures for an example. Abigail came to King David and, beseeching mercy, did obtain mercy. Shall we Christians, therefore, be worse than the Jewish king and deny mercy unto these? Mercy is what they beseech, mercy let them have! Broad is this island of Britain, and in many places void of inhabitants. Let us therefore make covenant with them that they may dwell in the treaty lands of their fathers, but be vassal unto us."

In the end the chieftains and princelings admitted the impracticability of attempting to do more than free their lands in a line that ran roughly from Lindum to the Vectis Water and from the western borders to just past Londinium. The Romans' Saxon Shore, built as a defense against the Saxon, would be by law, as it had long been by force, truly the Saxons' Shore.

It was a hard bannock to swallow, but once it was down and the lines were drawn, men squared their shoulders and adjusted their cloaks. The thing would be done as the Count of the Britains said it should.

Much time was spent in going over the details with Aelle and Cheldric. When it was time to slap hands on the striking of the bargain, Balduf brought forward a bag from a dark corner and passed around a great curved bull's horn of vilely sour fermented mare's milk. Many in the British circle made a face at the unspeakable smell and even worse taste of the Saxon treaty drink. But men who would keep faith with each other must drink from the same cup.

When the cup had completed the circle and the last of its foamy contents emptied, Aelle spoke. "There remains one thing more. The offering of hostages."

"We have struck hands. We have drunk the treaty cup. The taking and giving of hostages is not our way," Arthurius said.

"And yet it is our way. If the treaty is to have meaning beyond a cup of mare's milk in the eyes of any of my lesser chieftains who may choose to look to a British steading for new lands, there must be a hostage."

"I give no hostage," Arthurius repeated. His heart sank. Would all their efforts go for nothing at this late hour? And yet he would not begin the bargain on the enemy's terms. If the day's work was to mean anything, he must abide by his beliefs. "The rule of British law is enough. We will stand true to our word."

"It may be, Arthurius Pendragon, that you have the strength to hold all your chiefs." Aelle paused with a meaningful look at the place where Cador had sat earlier. "Although I am not so certain of that." Again he paused. "However that may be, Arthurius Pendragon, I am willing to bow to your way for your side of the bargain. For my side, I must abide by the way of our people. For us, lines on a map are not sufficient. You must accept a hostage."

Arthurius leaned forward to hear these unusual terms, but said nothing.

"As Bretwalda war king, it is my place to offer myself hostage. And yet I do not do so. The treaty needs my rule among my people—you need my rule among my people. I have sworn to this. My chieftains beyond this room have not, and they are many, and they are mighty. I who have sworn and whom they will obey must keep their steadings and their seax within the boundary."

Arthurius nodded. He agreed to the sense of this.

"That is why I offer you another." Arthurius drew his breath. He did not want Cheldric living at his court. "I offer you one of great value to our people not for today, but for the future to which we look and to which our treaty speaks. I have no cub of my own, as you have not, Arthurius Pendragon. It is in my mind that we have both been too long upon the war trail for cub-getting." Arthurius forced himself to respond to Aelle's harsh laughter with a smile. "So I offer you instead the pride of our pack. It has been in your mind perhaps to wonder why one so young as the son of Cheldric sat at our council fires today? For the faith-keeping of our treaty, we offer you in pledge Medraut Cheldricson."

The thin-faced boy rose quietly and came to stand before the leaders, his narrow shoulders squared, his mouth held firm in a set line. It was in Arthurius's mind to send the boy back to his mother, and yet he knew that would be an unspeakable insult to people he was trying to make into peaceful neighbors. At a nudge from Dubricius at his side, Arthurius knew what to say. "You have made a most generous offer, Aelle Bretwalda. We will withdraw once more. The discussion of the council is the British way."

The little side room seemed colder than before as Artos faced his Cambrogi once again. Dubricius spoke first. "Do not do it, Lord Artos. He will be an Achan in the camp, one who would bite you at your first back-turning. That is probably why his father would have him come to you—for biting in the back."

Arthurius was quiet for a space, looking deep into the Merlinus's eyes. "And if I bid him go—is this the valor so prized by my mother's people the Cymrikind—to refuse hearth space to a kinsman because I have aught against his grandsire? Or is it the justice of the law which my father's people the Romankind so prized—to cast him out for no actions of his own? I do not forget that it was for doubts about my own blood, not for any misdeeds of my own, that many would have denied me my place of leadership."

"Think, Artos. Will you let him run with the noble cubs of Caer Cam—the sons of all your chiefs who will come to you for training? Will you train a royal Saxon cub in your own warskill—that he may use it against you one day?"

"It is in my mind that sword-skill he already has. I will train him in the ways of order, justice, and law. If ever there is to be lasting peace between our peoples—as there must be if the dark is to be conquered—these are the things the sea wolves must learn. They are a new people—not ancient like our Celtic forebears that go back to the dawn of the world, far far before the Romankind. The Saxons are to live in a world of civilized men—and if that world is to survive with the Saxons in it, they must be taught like the wolf cub one takes from the wild and teaches the ways of a hound."

Dubricius stamped his staff on the floor as if he would stamp his words into Arthurius's mind. "Think, think, my Lord Count. Think hard and recall the lessons of history. It is bad enough that this one is the great grandson of Vortigern the Fox who mingled his marriage blood with the royal line of Constantus. On the dam's side the cub is also of the line of Hengist who on St. Bartholomew's day invited three hundred of Vortigern's nobles to a peace feast and then gave the signal for each Saxon to seize the Britain next to him at the table and slay him with the weapon concealed beneath his wolf skin cloak. Think, Arthurius."

"I have thought. It is to my thinking that it is to prevent more such massacres that we must train the royal Saxon cub to British ways." He strode from the room with his companions following behind. Back on the dais he faced Aelle.

"So. We will take Medraut."

6

he long shadows of evening crept over the land in the light of a watery sunset after rain, but even so late the Saxons departed to gather their sword brothers who waited, licking their wounds, to return to whatever fate should decree for them. The Cambrogi, however, built up the fire in the drafty treaty hall and gathered around for the night. Arthurius had bidden Medraut to say farewell to his father, and the boy had obeyed in a wooden, stoical fashion. Then Arthurius presented him to Bors. "It is in my mind that Balin, your armorbearer, is ready to take his place among the warriors. Let you train Modredus to his duties."

A growl from deep in the boy's throat cut short Bors's quick agreement. "My name is Medraut."

"Sa, sa. We know your name well enough, although it is seeming you do not know your manners. If you are to take your place in a court where Roman law and Roman ways are remembered, it is no bad thing to have a Roman name. But if the cub will come only to the calling of his old name, so be it, Medraut."

Each man opened his food pouch and drew to the fire. Medraut, watching other armorbearers who had come in from the old Roman stabling place, attempted to do his job with a cold efficiency, filling Bors's cup from the cow's stomach beer bag whenever it was empty. Arthurius looked around the circle. "It has been a good day's work, my brothers. We need now only the song of a harper to make it complete." And he left unspoken his missing of Baudwin.

"Will my harpsong serve, my Lord Arthurius?" a gentle voice at Arthurius's side asked.

He turned in surprise and looked into Blaise's bright blue eyes fringed with long golden lashes. "And is my new armorbearer also a harper, and I not knowing it?"

"I am learning my skill, my lord. I have studied with Ulfius, my Lord Dubricius's harper."

Now Arthurius turned to his other side. "Ah, Myrddin Emrys, and is this why you recommended Blaise to me?"

"It is a fortunate thing to find two servants for one mouth to fill, is it not, Lord Artos?"

Though the song of the victory of Mount Badonicus which Baudwin had promised must wait, they sat long around the fire listening to the sweet light voice of Blaise singing of victories of long ago Cymric heroes. More than one man, when he rolled in his cloak with his head pillowed on his pack, wondered if in years to come, so would the bards sing of their victory of the past days.

It was not the sweet strains of a harpsong that wakened them the next morning, however, but a screeching, wailing, rising-and-falling sound such as none had heard before. With sleep-glazed eyes Arthurius sprang to the corner where all the weapons had lain since the gathering of the treaty circle. So soon were the Saxons turned upon them? How could they have been so carelessly overconfident as to set no pickets last night?

Every man was fighting to untangle himself from his own cloak and force a sleep-and-drink-fuddled mind into battle readiness. The bawling and howling drew closer as in the weapons corner each grabbed for his sword and swore as sheath straps tangled and blades scratched against each other. Armorbearers rushing forward to help their eques with discarded mail shirts only added to the hopeless uproar.

"Stand aside!" Arthurius ordered. "There will be no need for treaty breakers to turn on us if we trample each other and push one another upon our own swords in confusion. That doesn't sound like any Saxon war horn I've ever heard." In spite of Gwalchmai's restraining hand, he strode to the door and flung it open to look out.

Then he stepped back in surprise, making those in the room behind him draw their swords. "My friend, The Ancelot, what is that terrible caterwauling?"

All with raised swords lowered them sheepishly as The Ancelot, red and saffron cloak and long blond hair billowing behind him, strode into the room. "Ah, and have you ever heard a grander sound? Dineidyn is the finest piper in all Caledonia, and I bring him to you to pipe for your coronation."

Dineidyn stepped into the room with something resembling a dead animal under his arm, holding one of the legs in his mouth. "Piper?" Arthurius shouted as the last dying notes made him raise his hands to his ears. He was well acquainted with the panpipes played sometimes in the feast hall and often by shepherds on the hillside. But never had he heard any such sound from a reed pipe.

Dineidyn held out the bag fashioned from the forequarters of a goatskin with cow horns protruding from the leg poles. He seemed about to demonstrate its working, but The Ancelot shooed him out the door. "Enough of that for now. We'll enjoy more later." Then he turned to Arthurius. "Did I not tell you I would return for your king-making?"

"I know of no king-making."

"Then you are the last to know. All men talk of it. Is it not so, Lord Dubricius?"

"I doubt that any could deny it him now, nor that any would try when we come again to Caerleon," the archbishop replied.

"Sa. That is as I thought." The Caledonian laird looked satisfied. "But we shall make extra sure—for the marriage lord of a queen of the blood has a kingship which no man may nay say."

Arthurius, who had stood to one side observing this exchange, suddenly felt every nerve in his body come alert as one on guard duty who sees the creeping of a shadow. "What mean you—marriage lord of a queen?"

The Ancelot flung his arm out toward the door in a grand gesture. "I bring you my daughter Gwenhumara, royal daughter of the Caledonians in which the noble line lives, as in her mother who passed it to her and her grandmother before her and back in time for as far as the bards may sing of."

The doorway of the forum hall stood open, morning sunlight streaming into the dark room. And suddenly, as Arthurius's gaze followed The Ancelot's pointing arm, the doorway framed the most beautiful woman he had ever seen, surrounded by golden light.

The four summers of his manhood had been spent in incessant campaigning—moving from battle to battle as quickly as his men could lick their wounds and relocate the enemy that melted into forest and glen after each battle, only to resurface, stronger than before, to be beaten again by the grace of God and the valor of the Pendragon and his men. And the four winters of his manhood had gone to quartering men and animals, to negotiating with local chieftains for men and supplies, to building and planning. There had been no time to give thought to women, no opportunity to look for one particular woman.

But if he had spent those four years devoting the same effort to finding a woman that had gone into those victories, Arthurius, who had always been a quick and acute judge of people, knew that he could have found no better than the one who stood before him now. Tall and serene she was in her blue and scarlet checkered gown with golden balls braided in her tawny hair and a level look of tranquility in her gull-gray eyes.

Arthurius stood in awe before the greatest stillness he had ever met in any human being. Even Dubricius, who was able to go away inside himself for hours—even days at a time, was not so calm at the very core of his being when around others. This woman had within her the reserves of the regal women of her people from time beyond time. Although a true Celtic royal woman through which the life of the tribe passed and who could confer royalty on the man of her choice, she was no wild-eyed, battle-frenzied warrior like Boudicca or Cartimandua or many of their kind who had led their tribes on the war trail. Gwenhumara's strength was the greater for its quiet and its depth.

Arthurius knew then that he would far rather cross swords with a battle-frenzied Boudicca than to try to move against the enormous strength of Gwenhumara's calm.

Blaise put a guest cup into his hand, and he held it out to her. "Welcome, Gwenhumara, daughter royal of Berwick of Caledonia."

As she drank, Arthurius noticed that she wore an exquisite amber and carved ivory necklace, strung so the chains of beads interchanged in an intricate pattern, the bottom row hanging loose in a fringe, each with a tiny golden bell at the end. She saw his eyes on it and smiled. When she spoke, her voice sounded like the chiming of gold bells to him. "It has been in my family long and long. I think it is not possible to get such ivory now that the traders come so seldom for fear of the sea wolves. But always this necklace has been worn by our queens and passed to the daughters royal."

The Ancelot stepped forward, between his daughter and Arthurius. "And now, my Lord Pendragon. You have made treaty with the Saxons. Will you also make treaty with the royal house of Caledonia? High King-to-be Arthurius, I offer you my daughter of the blood royal of Caledonia to be High Queen of Britain and hearth queen of your heart. Our lands to the north and the south of the wall have never been united. To my mind it will be a good thing."

Arthurius, the man of battle, the man of action, never a man of courting or a man of speech-making, stood silent. Never in his farthest-flung imaginings had he thought . . . and yet . . .

"Is it good?" The Ancelot boomed with a note of challenge in his voice. He was not a man accustomed to being kept waiting, even by his own battle lord.

"It is seeming very good," Arthurius said softly. Then he turned to Gwenhumara. "And how is the seeming to you? Do you willingly leave your land to follow the sword of Britain?"

Her shining stillness seemed to reach out and engulf the two of them in a quiet place of their own, even as all the Cambrogi looked on. "It is seeming good, my lord."

The guest cup was still in her hands. She held it out to Arthurius who put his hands over hers. He drank first, then held the cup to her lips. They might have stood so for the rest of the morning, looking into one another's eyes in the stream of golden sunlight with birds singing in the trees beyond, but The Ancelot stepped forward with a mighty slap to Arthurius's shoulder that sent the last of the heather beer sloshing out of the cup. "And so shall we stand ever buckler to buckler, my brother. May your sword arm never grow weak." He turned to the door. "Dineidyn, where are those hounds? My daughter brings a betrothal gift."

The piper, who had stayed just beyond the door, now entered with a matched pair of the finest red hounds Arthurius had ever seen. Even tall as he was, their heads came to his waist, their coats shone with health, and their eyes with intelligence. At the slightest signal from Gwenhumara, they sat at her feet.

"This is Brucea, my lord, and this Cabal." She rested a hand gently on each head. "We shall have good hunting, shall we not?"

"We shall have excellent hunting." And suddenly the realization of the momentous change the past hour had brought to his life struck Arthurius fully, and he flung out his arms and threw back his head with a bellow of his famous laughter.

It was not until late that afternoon, after they had ridden back to the camp at Mount Badonicus and were preparing to move the wounded who were able to travel to Caer Cam or to their own steadings and those in need of longer nursing to a house of holy brothers nearby, that Dubricius drew Arthurius aside. "I would speak plainly with you, Artos."

"So speak, my Emrys."

"You would make a marriage treaty with The Ancelot? Be yoked with a nonbeliever?"

Arthurius gave a roar of laughter. He could not believe his ears. "My Lord Archbishop! We have made treaty with the Saxons—are you now to say we should not make treaty with one of our own Cambrogi, eques-made by the shoulder-tapping of Caliburnus?"

"A battle treaty is not a marriage."

"So." And because he could not believe this conversation to be serious, Arthurius added, "And one would be hoping that a marriage is not a battle treaty." But he could see from the lack of humor in Dubricius's eyes that the archbishop was serious. "And by what do you know that the Caledonian is an unbeliever—that it would be an 'unequal yoking'?"

"He is unrepentant."

"By 'unrepentant' you are meaning unshriven by the church? But he attended the Christ Mass."

"So did many. But he made no confession."

Now Arthurius became serious. He clapped a hand on Dubricius's shoulder. "Merlinus, my Lord Archbishop, it is in my mind that those beyond the reach of the church may show how they treat the Christ by how they show compassion to those of His children around them."

"Artos! You would argue for salvation outside the church? Salvation without faith?"

"I would argue for salvation by loving for those who do not know of salvation by faith."

Dubricius was struck silent by such daring apostasy from one he regarded as closer than a son.

Arthurius gave another shout of infectious laughter which made men in the camp below them turn their heads and smile. "Then by all means, my holy Father, you must lead the way in this treaty that The Ancelot and his daughter may come under the teaching of Mother Church. Such a good man must not go from life unshriven when his time comes."

Dubricius bowed his head. "So. Make your treaty. And God help you. I will leave in the morning for Caerleon. If it is your wish, I shall speak to The Ancelot that the lady travel with me. Come to me there when you may. All shall be ready."

As he watched the tall, thin figure of the archbishop walk down the hillside leaning on his staff, Arthurius shrugged off Dubricius's words of warning, but they brought to memory the bitter aftertaste of the heather beer in the betrothal cup.

The trees were in full leaf; the apple blossoms had fallen, and in their place small green pips hung on the trees; fledgling willow wrens had left the nest, and the spring's lambs were no longer wobbly on their legs when at last the court and all the high-born of Britain, including the still-scowling Cador and dark-visaged Maelgwyn, turned their thoughts to the gathering call of the archbishop at Caerleon.

Arthurius had seen neither Gwenhumara nor Dubricius in all that time, as he had been as busy organizing the land for peace as before he had organized it for war. Groups of watch-guards were set at intervals along the treaty lines, much as the Romans had set mile castles along the wall—only farther apart. Many warriors departed, their pouches bulging with battle booty, to see to the planting in their own garths. But the Cambrogi, the circle of eques closest to Arthurius, remained at Caer Cam training horses in the fields beyond the hill-fort to replace those lost in battle, hunting in the rich runs of the Summer Country woods, and building Caer Cam to a fineness there had been no time for before. They designed a chamber for their queen with softest furs for the bedplace, finest weavings for wall hangings, and glass and pottery vessels from Gaul as well as bronze mirrors and carved bone combs from their own merchants.

Finally the day arrived in high summer when Arthurius threw on his finest scarlet cloak with his best gold brooch and torque and rode to Caerleon with the Cambrogi.

More than half a year had passed since last he strode across the snow-covered courtyard around the archbishop's enclosure. Now the rough stone flags were warm under his feet, and bright red and yellow flowers grew among the bushes around the old buildings.

Amidst the birdsong he heard the tinkling of tiny bells, a light golden sound that rang joy in his memory, although he could not think why. He turned in the direction of the sound. Gwenhumara stood, as he had first seen her, surrounded by golden sunshine, this time framed by two dark green yew trees, the gift hounds at her feet. Cabal, who recognized Arthurius, sprang forward with a bark and licked his hand, but Brucea stayed by her mistress.

Gwenhumara wore a green and saffron plaid tunic, the golden bells of her necklace shining, the sun making a halo of her braided hair. She waited for Arthurius to come to her. But just as he reached her, she stretched her hands out to him. He clasped them in his and looked at her deeply. How could it be that she was even more beautiful and more tranquil than he remembered her? He had been almost afraid to see her again after this long time apart, fearing he should find that those memories of that first brief time they had had together were the imaginings of a bardsong and that she was in truth quite ordinary. But now he knew that for all time, *ordinary* was the one word that could never be applied to this woman.

"Gwenhumara, you have changed."

"I have. Is my lord not pleased?"

"I think I am pleased. What has happened?"

She led the way to a small bench where they could sit in the shade of an apple tree. "I have only just returned to Caerleon with the brothers who have come for the mass. Dubricius took me many weeks ago to your holy island of Avalon. He said that the High Queen must worship the same God as the King, and so I must learn of Him and be baptized."

"And so you did?"

"And so I did. I lived at the house of the holy women with the Lady Nimue of the Lake, and the brothers taught me of the Christ. My Lord Artos, your holy one has been explaining to me the difference in the gods—how it is that Lugh and the old kind demand man come to them with sacrifices, but how it is that the Christ reaches to man by making His own sacrifice. That is seeming to me something only the highest God of all could do. I have taken Him for my God. And I had much time for reading of their holy books." Suddenly she turned to him with a great bubbling joy he had never seen in her before. "Oh, Arthurius, I had done little reading before and never of such books—such wonderful stories! I felt I could spend my life there reading and praying." She caught her breath as if she realized what she had said. "Were I not to be your marriage queen, that is. But one, Brother Gildas, a strange, angry-seeming brother who is writing a great history, told me of a kinswoman of yours of whom the bards sing. Eurgain, she was, and back and back in time, before the coming of the eagles, she was a princess, and it was her desire to establish a druid cors for such study of the Christian God. Brother Gildas said he did not know if ever she did so, for soon the Romans came, and she was carried prisoner. Arthurius, I would establish a holy house in her name."

Arthurius smiled and agreed readily to the plan, and they talked long in the dappled shade of the apple tree. But her words struck a small note of worry in his mind. Was he taking for himself one who would be better wed to Christ in the church? Surely, her great beauty and royal blood were meant for the high throne. And yet, would she ever find the joy at his hearth that she had found on the holy island? In taking Gwenhumara for wife and queen, was he robbing God?

One of the great blessings of being a man of action rather than a philosopher, however, was being able to throw off such misgivings by taking action, and the bronze bell of the church of St. Julius and St. Aaron was signaling to all who had come for the double king-making and bride-making. Arthurius stood and offered his hand to Gwenhumara to lead her to the church.

And so Arthurius and Gwenhumara came to their marriage and coronation. Dubricius led them to the altar, followed by those who would attend them—Baudwin, Gwalchmai, and Caius for Arthurius; and Elayne, Morgana, and Elidor from among Gwenhumara's attendants. As on that Christ Mass which Arthurius had attended, a seeming lifetime ago, the brothers from Ynis Witrin chanted psalms in plainsong:

May the Lord bless you this holy day.
May the Lord send you help from His holy place.
From Zion may He watch over you.
May the Lord bless you.
May He grant you your heart's desire.
May He lend His aid to all your plans.
The Lord bless you.

The royal couple walked slowly up the aisle of the crowded church and knelt at the altar before the archbishop and Abbot Indract who was assisting him. As the chant ended, Dubricius spread his elevated arms wide, and his voice rang out to pronounce the invitatory: "Come, let us worship the Lord, the King who was and is and yet will come. Glory to the great God on high, and peace to us, His people on earth. Lord God, Heavenly King, Almighty God and Father, we worship You, we give You thanks, we praise You for Your glory. May we, Your children here, find peace on earth through Your presence in our hearts and through the leading of this king You have given us to rule over us as our earthly king, even as You are our Heavenly King."

He turned and took the golden grail from under its white linen cover on the altar. Arthurius and Gwenhumara drank from the cup, and Dubricius replaced it on the altar. Then the archbishop placed his hands on the bowed heads of the couple before him and addressed them. "By the sacrament of marriage you signify and share in the mystery of the unity that exists between Christ and His Church. Each partner freely bestows an irrevocable covenant on the other that they enter into this intimate union in total fidelity and unbreakable oneness."

Then he stretched his arms wide above them in prayer: "God our Father, You have made the bond of marriage a holy mystery, a symbol of Christ's love for His Church. Hear our prayers for Arthurius and Gwenhumara this day. . . . May they ever rule this land You have given them for Your glory. . . . We pray that this High King may bear Your anointing and prepare the world again for the coming of Your Son. May all men live in peace that the Prince of Peace may reign in their hearts."

The church was filled with a strong, sweet smell of spices as Dubricius poured the precious imported oil over Arthurius's head and face. His voice rang to the farthest corners of the church. "Arthurius of Britain, you have been endowed from your birth with princely gifts. Arthurius of the ancient Celtic line, of royal stock that ruled these islands long before wild Latin herdsmen on the continent pitched their tents among seven hills by a river and called it Rome; Arthurius, in whose veins runs the blood of ancient valor and majesty, I anoint you High King of Britain in the name of the Father, and of the Son, and of the Holy Spirit. World without end, amen."

Dubricius placed the scepter of Britain with Maximus's gleaming amethyst set in its handle in Arthurius's hands.

Gwenhumara, born a queen without dispute, needed no anointing, but only the placing of a slimmer version of Arthurius's golden circlet around her forehead and the archbishop's hands laid on her head in blessing.

Then Arthurius stood, with his queen beside him, his face shining in the light of a hundred candles from the shimmer of the anointing oil and from a radiance deep within. All were silent, as if holding their breath. Not a man to whom speech-making came naturally, Arthurius knew what he would say. "My friends, my people, I declare to you that this is Logres—the true Britain—the land of truth to which God led Joseph of Arimathea with the light of truth, the land which God's Holy Spirit had prepared to receive His Word in the fullness of His time.

"But the dark is rising against this light as it has countless times before and will countless times after us. And as in every age men will be called on to repel this darkness in the name of the God of Light, so are we called for our age. We have been given a space of time to build in peace. So must we build well so that our space can be filled with His light that will radiate beyond our own time. Long and long have I dreamed of a land of peace where the weak are protected from the strong, where the good are triumphant over the evil. With your help, I shall go forward from here to make this dream into truth."

The brothers began a concluding chant, but before the first line was completed, a wild wailing and shrieking cut through their song. Every head turned to the back of the church, and many a hand flew to an empty sword sheath. A smile spread over Arthurius's face as the raucous cacophony advanced, ever growing in volume, up the aisle in the person of Dineidyn and his bag of pipes.

When the piper reached the altar and the last wailing note was squeezed from the goatskins under his arm, The Ancelot jumped from his seat on the front benches with a shout. "Aye, and did I not tell you he would play for your king-making? Let us go now to the marriage feast, for I'm hungry!"

Arthurius's laughter joined the cheers of the crowd, and hand-in-hand he and Gwenhumara led the way into the warm evening.

7

Then followed a time of peace and rebuilding in the kingdom, of planting and reaping in the garth and birthing in the byre and at the hearth. And there was a decade and more of joy at Caer Cam—a joy that radiated to all the kingdom. The Saxons behind the treaty line remained quiet save for occasional cattle raids.

All was as it should be—all save one heavy sadness for the High King and his queen. On a soft day in late May when the hawthorn blossoms were just fading from the trees, Arthurius found Gwenhumara in the small courtyard behind her chambers. She sat on a bench with Brucea's twin pups in her lap, gently stroking their soft ears and singing a light little melody to them. At the sound of his step she looked up. Her smile of greeting was immediate. Almost. But not quite before he could read the look of hollow longing in her eyes. Two strides brought him to her, and he knelt, his arms encircling her lap. "My Gwenhumara. I am so sorry." There was no more to say.

Her hand was warm from the puppies when she placed it on his head. "I know, my dearling. I, too, am sorry."

They sat long thus close to each other as the bees visited the yellow and purple flowers by the timber wall. Through the years Gwenhumara had lost none of her composed tranquility—if anything, it had deepened. What at first had been a natural stillness had grown with her love of God to become true peace. But it seemed to Arthurius, loving her as he did, that with the coming of each month's course, announcing that Artos the bear would have no cub of his own, her shining radiance dimmed a little.

Brucea, now slow in her own maturity, padded forward and stuck her nose in Gwenhumara's lap with the pups. The queen set them on the ground by their mother, brushing the fine red hairs from her skirt. She picked up a book from beside her on the bench. "Ah, I would sit here and read all day—this book

Dubricius brought me from the holy brothers is most absorbing—but always there is the guilt pushing at my mind that I should be seeing to the beer-making and the weaving."

Arthurius moved a little to lean his back against the bench. "And how is all on the women's side?"

"The new cloak I am weaving for you is almost finished, my lord. You shall have it in time to wear for these battle games you will hold. But I much fear you shall be outdone for the fineness of the weaving Elayne is making for Olwin. It is in my mind that soon we shall be celebrating the bride-taking of your eques, and I shall be without my best serving lady."

"Ah, so." The crinkles at the corners of his eyes had deepened with the passing seasons, and the clear May-time sun revealed a few lightened hairs among the red-gold highlights of his dark locks, but the boyishness of his grin was unfaded. "And that is why our Olwin has missed his spear thrust at the practice post three times this week." Brucea lifted her languid head at his laughter. "It is well. We shall make a feast for them that my eques may get his aim straight again. And your other ladies, they are well?"

Gwenhumara hesitated. "They are well. But Morgana . . ."

"Yes?"

"I cannot say. It may be nothing, and yet she seems to have withdrawn from me in a kind of secrecy."

"All reports are that her father Urien holds true to his treaty with your father. Perhaps she, too, has her mind filled with thoughts of one of my eques."

"Perhaps. But that usually does not cause slyness in a maiden—rather a desire to talk and talk."

Again Arthurius laughed. "If that is so, I think I should be thankful for the withdrawing. I have ever been thankful that the daughter of The Ancelot was not given to magpie chatter."

At the sound of a footstep in the courtyard they turned. Arthurius jumped to his feet and strode forward. "Ah, my Lord Dubricius. Well come. It is an honor that you should join our council meeting this afternoon."

The queen signaled a servant to fetch a guest cup and turned to greet the archbishop. "My lord, we do not see you often enough at Caer Cam. What news do you bring us of the world?"

The archbishop's beard had increased considerably in length and volume in the past seasons, while the rest of him seemed frailer than ever as he leaned more and more heavily on his staff. But the keen insight of his dark intelligent eyes was undimmed. "Ah, news of comings and goings, of much doing and making and grasping and bickering—in short, people continue very much as people always have. But of greater import, my lady, I have brought you two books. The sermons of John Chrysostom the golden-tongued, and the wisdom writings of Augustine of Hippo. Brother Indract was much loath to let them leave his house, even in my care, until I told him they were for you. But I promised to take St. Augustine with me when I return, as Brother Gildas has not finished with it yet, and all are fearful of his tongue when he is unhappy."

Gwenhumara laughed, and the golden bells of her necklace tinkled. "I will go straightaway to my reading. I would not have our archbishop chastised by a holy brother for my sake."

Arthurius and Merlinus turned toward the council meeting in the Great Hall. The High King's hall stood much improved from the first hastily rebuilt structure the men had thrown up to shelter themselves from the cold in that winter of frantic preparations before the battle of Mount Badonicus. Now the timbered walls were thickly sealed with a heavy clay daub and lime-washed a glistening white. Bright weavings, many from the loom of the queen herself, and rich animal skins from the hunting successes of the king and his eques adorned the walls and added warmth. Hide-covered shields, intricately adorned with highly polished bronze bosses, also hung around the walls. At the far end of the room was a raised dais with three carved and painted wooden chairs where the High King sat with the queen and archbishop on either side. But today Arthurius and Dubricius strode across the rush-covered floor, strewn with fresh herbs for the council meeting, and took seats, not on the dais, but at a large round table. It had come from Arthurius's long tradition of using the Roman officer's field cloth for drawing battle maps on the eve before combat. For the first council meeting at Caer Cam, the king had ordered the building of a series of curved tables which could be moved closer together or farther apart, depending on the number of Cambrogi present—leaving an open space in the middle for the fire needed in all but the warmest of high summer days.

Several of the Cambrogi were already seated around the table in their unbleached woolen council robes. These loose-fitting coats, that could be flung on even over battle armor should the need arise, had sprung from the Roman tradition of wearing special togas in the Senate.

However, the archbishop, when he addressed the council on his occasional visits to Caer Cam, liked to refer to their robes in symbolic terms of even older traditions—the special garments provided by the host for banquet guests in ancient Judea—symbolic of the robes of righteousness to be worn in the new Kingdom. But few at the council table would make any claims of special righteousness, or even of possessing the wisdom so needful in governing the country.

Dubricius, as Father of the Council, opened the meeting with the Eucharist as always. He looked around the circle. "Today we are twelve at table, which is most appropriate at the table round, symbolizing that all are equal in the eyes of God . . ."

He spoke on, his voice frequently wavering with age but his vision for this golden age of Britain clearly undimmed. Arthurius, however, found his mind wandering as his gaze circled the table. On his right, just past the standing Dubricius, sat Baudwin, his right hand grown double-strong in the service of Britain since the loss of his left; then Bors, his body and face rounded with evidence of his avid appetite and his thong-held hair sticking out like a horse's tail; Olwin and Eleden both with eyes courteously on the archbishop, but minds obviously elsewhere. One section of the table had been pushed back to the far wall since many, such as The Ancelot, Teliau, and Doldavius, were away tending to their own lands.

Then Arthurius's gaze came to the younger eques, those who had not known the early battles against the dark, but had trained in the sunlight of peace and freedom—Balin and Blaise, long graduated from their armorbearer roles. Blaise's harp over his shoulder signified that he would always be a harper first and a warrior second. Next to him sat Galaad, son of The Ancelot. The more boisterous knights teased this newest member, accusing him of being best suited for a monk's cell on Ynis Witrin when he declined to join them in visits to the village girls. And indeed, Arthurius often thought Dubricius looked at the youngest eques with a certain possessiveness, as if he would claim him for the church. Next, in sharp contrast to the soft-looking Galaad, sat a sharp-eyed, sharp-featured Medraut who long ago had accepted Christian baptism and claimed a right to a council seat as kinsman to the king. In recent times he had been drawing some of the younger eques under his sphere of influence with his incisive remarks and biting humor.

Arthurius's brow clouded as his gaze held on Medraut, then cleared as it moved on to the two seats to his own immediate left. They were occupied by the still-brash and outspoken Caius, looking more and more like his father, but as yet with little of his father's wise patience; and the small, quiet, but ever-reliable Gwalchmai on whose latest undertaking so much of Arthurius's hopes for the future rested.

The archbishop's words cut through Arthurius's musings. "This is the Lamb of God. Happy are those who are called to His table." The king turned to drink from the grail the archbishop held out to him.

The ceremony continued around the table. Then the meeting turned to secular affairs of state. Arthurius, as was his custom, remained seated to speak. "Gwalchmai ap Gwyar, it is springtime and harvest to our eyes to see you again seated at our council table. Of all things we are most anxious to hear how our shipbuilding progresses."

Gwalchmai had for more than a year now been overseeing the building of ships in a secluded harbor on the River Ebona half a day's ride west and slightly north of Aqua Sulis. He shook his head before he raised his dark eyes with the surprising long lashes and spoke. "The builders are gathered and housed; we have drawn plans from not entirely rotted Roman galleys and captured Saxon ships, and we now have five vessels under construction, but progress is halted for lack of supplies. Men who would be master shipbuilders are forced to fell and rough-cut their own trees because the chieftains refuse to pay their duties." He paused at the angry exclamation this news brought from the High King, then continued, "They say why should they pay for an army—let alone the building of a navy—when all is at peace?"

Arthurius struck the table and jumped to his feet, knocking over his stool in his agitation. Cabal, under the table, growled. "Fools! Cannot they understand? Why are we at peace? Because we were strong enough to overcome our enemies and have continued strong enough to enforce the treaty—a treaty which we were able to negotiate only because we were strong. Weakness will never win nor keep peace. Cannot they see that?"

He paused and the anger went from him, leaving a determined fortitude that made his prominent cheekbones and square jaw stand out more than ever. "The bards among us," he looked at Baudwin and Blaise, "would remind us most rightly that three things are inviolate in the house of any Briton—the harp, the book, and the sword. The harp and the book because in the time of peace, music and poetry are the best occupation of an honest man and the gracious accompaniment of hospitality, but the sword is needed to defend these treasures of the hearth. These weak-minded chieftains will lose harp, book, and hearth if they forget their swords.

"That is why we have our battle fetes such as you now prepare for. If my eques grow slack in their battle skills and their sword arms weaken, so weakens the sword arm of Britain. But war games to keep cavalry and foot warrior skills sharp are not enough."

The High King paused and surveyed every man in the room. He hoped they would understand, because Britain must be solid at its core if they were to persuade the chieftains and kinglets at its farthest fringes. "With the new threats from sea raids, even on our western shores, we cannot maintain our superior strength unless we can keep the enemy from landing. With only the cavalry, we have to wait until the enemy is entrenched on the land before we strike, or we will only drive them back into their ships to strike at another shore village or steading. We are an island nation. We must have a navy. Even the sea-hating Romans understood that. Why cannot our native chieftains?" Again he struck the table, this time for emphasis, not in anger.

Arthurius took a deep breath and announced his resolution. "After next week's battle contest, I shall go to my chieftains myself. If my words cannot make sense to them, perhaps Caliburnus may. Gwalchmai, Baudwin, Caius, and Bors—you will accompany me." Because he was looking for confirmation from the chosen Cambrogi, the king did not see the look that passed between Medraut and Eleden.

Arthurius sat down to close the council. But Dubricius rose and held out his hands in his manner of quiet command. "The High King has rightly spoken. To be strong, Britain must be strong at the core. You are her core. We must maintain strong military might, but even more important, we must maintain strong spiritual might. Each man who sits in this council must be as strong for God as he is strong for Britain.

"You have all taken of the cup of the Last Supper. You have partaken of the body and blood of Christ. You must now go forward and live as He lives in you. Live strong for God and strong for Britain." The archbishop's call produced a variety of expressions on the faces of the men seated around the table, but the glow on Galaad's face was riveting.

The next week passed quickly in gay preparation at Caer Cam. The field below the hillfort, usually used for rough cavalry and sword practice, was now made festive for the accommodation of the ladies and visiting chieftains who would attend the fete. Daily the guards at the top of the entrance called out the arrival of a distant chieftain and his entourage or of a Cambrogi who had been long from court. The greatest joy and tumult accompanied the arrival of The Ancelot and his soek piper Dineidyn, and the greatest surprise came at the arrival of King Maelgwyn of Arfon, who had not been seen in Arthurius's court since the anointing in Caerleon where he and his followers had remained stoically silent and aloof. But Dubricius proclaimed himself too old for such hubbub and departed for the quiet of Avalon.

On the appointed day the broad green field was alive at earliest light with flying spear pennants identifying each contestant, armorbearers rushing to and fro seeing to their eques' needs, the pounding of horses' hooves as contestants took practice runs at the targets on the field, and the ring of metal on metal as the knights readied their sword-skill.

Gwenhumara and her ladies took seats next to the king on raised benches set up at one side of the field. The composed, regal High Queen, as always Gwenhumara Regina, today wore a graceful tunic of blue and saffron plaid belted with braided golden cords, and her amber and ivory necklace glowed in the bright morning. Her style and manner were impeccable, quietly commanding attention and respect.

But today there seemed to be the slightest crack in her perfect calm as a narrow furrow creased her brow and a look of worry momentarily clouded her eyes. Yet not even the queen could determine why she felt uneasy. It was a perfect day, free of the rainy weather many had feared. And many more chieftains from far-flung holdings had come to Caer Cam than had been expected. This alone was cause for rejoicing, for now Arthurius could ask them to pay their assessments for the navy without having to travel to them. So why, she asked herself, should she feel this heaviness in her chest? Surely it was the departure of her old friend Dubricius and somewhat perhaps her dislike of noisy crowds—

although today the sense of celebration in the throng more than made up for these.

When the ladies were seated, Arthurius nodded, and the first event began. This was the stave combat where contestants on foot faced each other across a knee-high wooden barrier, thrusting and countering blows with heavy poles. They wore their bucklers on their shoulders in order to be able to whirl away from an enemy and deflect a blow to the back. Many of the younger eques entered this battle of brute strength, but as each contestant was challenged by a stronger, the championship quickly devolved upon the two broadest, heaviest of the Cambrogi, Caius, and Bors.

For long they exchanged heavy blows to one another's staves, always deflected by a two-handed parry or a direct lunge. At last Caius jumped the barrier and flung forward with a blow that surely would have broken Bors's oaken rod had not the older man whirled to take the blow on his buckler-protected shoulder. Bors completed his spin to the front and thrust a blow at Caius's stave that knocked it from his hand and the contestant from his feet.

To the accompaniment of much cheering and applause, Bors helped Caius to his feet, and they walked across the field to present their arms to their king. Elidor, the youngest of the queen's ladies, was the first to present the trophies. With her characteristic air of shy gracefulness, she stepped forward and conferred the prized armlets on the winners—copper for Caius and silver for Bors.

The contest of the foot warriors' spear-skill was next. Unlike the stave competition, which had matched one set of challengers at a time, the field was now covered with battling pairs thrusting their spears at opponent after opponent, parrying and counterthrusting with shields in reply. As soon as one man's spear broke on another's shield, or he was nicked and bloodied, he withdrew to the side, and the one who had bettered him turned to another. At first the scene was a sea of sunlight glinting off flashing spears, shield bosses, and chain mail shirts. The thud of iron spear tips on hide-covered wooden shields mingled with the contestants' grunts of focused energy.

At last, however, the field began to thin as more and more chagrined eques took their places next to their standard-carrying armorbearers at the edge of the field. As the heat of the contest grew, more often now the field was deserted by those whose shields had been splintered by an expertly ferocious spear thrust, or who had been bloodied by a thrust that got past their shields. A glad cry broke from Elayne as she spotted Olwin still victorious on the field. "Oh, my lady, he's still there—see—" She directed Gwenhumara's look toward the melee in the center of the field where an eques battled bravely, in his shoulder brooch a scrap of green fabric that matched Elayne's apple-green tunic. "Is he not fine-looking?"

"Very fine, indeed, Elayne. May the sun and moon ever shine on the joy of your hearthside," the queen replied. The last act the archbishop had performed before leaving Caer Cam the day before had been blessing the marriage vows of these two.

"Oh, it is Doldavius. He has bested Doldavius!" Elayne bounced up and down on the bench as she clapped her hands. Her tension and excitement communicated to all on the observation benches.

But as the sun drew higher in the sky and heat added to the stress of combat, the spear contest began to seem interminable. At last there were only three left in the center of the field. Olwin, green pennant fluttering on his shoulder, fought valiantly with well-timed thrusts and counter-thrusts against Balin whose superior strength and experience made him an equal match for Olwin's speed and excellent rhythm. And then, as Teliau left the field with a small red trickle running from his right wrist, the pair was engaged by a third challenger. Medraut of the sharp eyes thrust at Balin with his black buckler as he attacked Olwin with his spear.

Elayne's cry was the first to focus their attention on what none had seen before in the confusion of massed contestants. Medraut fought with a double-headed spear. "I've never seen anything like it!" she cried. None of them had—a spear with an iron point at each end so that a well-positioned wielder was as deadly on the withdraw as on the thrust.

With whirlwind speed Medraut jumped between his two opponents, thrust at one, and with a mere glance over his shoulder, thrust at the other on the return. It was over in the space of two spear thrusts—Balin with a nasty gash on his cheek and Olwin with a bloody scratch on his neck.

"Is that allowed, my lord?" Gwenhumara turned to Arthurius.

"There is no rule made against something no one thought to forbid. He is clever that one."

"Will you have your eques use such a weapon in battle?"

"Na, na. It is in my mind that such a one could be as deadly to one's companions on the battlefield as to the enemy." The king left it uncertain as to whether he referred to the innovative weapon or the one who wielded it.

Elayne walked to the edge of the field to present the king's awards, silver armlet to Medraut and matching copper bands to Balin and Olwin. There was no mistaking the far louder cheering for the awarding of the copper.

A cart loaded with kegs of barley beer made its lumbering way down from the caer, and there was a pause in the festivities while everyone refreshed themselves with foaming cups of the pale yellow drink and opened their pouches of cold roast meat, cheese, and barley cakes. Gwenhumara took a few drinks from her cup, but was too hot to feel like eating. "My lord, I would walk in the shade of the trees by the river. Would you join me?"

Arthurius started to agree, but then Gwalchmai called him to attend to some matter, so Gwenhumara asked Elidor to walk with her. Once in the cool shade both ladies breathed a sigh of relief and walked more slowly, their tunics barely brushing the undergrowth as they walked along the soft riverbank. For a time the swishing of the river cut off the distant noises of the fete, and Gwenhumara focused on the chorus from the bird-filled trees overhead. Then the peace of the scene was broken by a moaning sound and a sharp cry. At first the queen thought an animal had been hurt; then she realized the sound was human. She turned in the direction of the cry and hurried through the brush. But a few steps brought her to an abrupt stop.

For a moment she thought the girl who lay with leaf-tangled hair in lovers' embrace was one of the village girls from the small settlement on the other side of the fort. But as she looked again from the scowling countenance of the eques lying on the grass beside the woman back to her face, the queen gasped, "Morgana. I will not have my ladies behave as the cattle of the field. Get you to your chambers and wash yourself. I shall speak to you of this later." Her waiting lady shot a malevolent look at the queen as she left. There was nothing the queen could say to Eleden of Gwynedd, so she turned furiously away.

The sword combat was well underway by the time Gwenhumara returned to her place beside the king. Although three pairs of swordsmen contested in different parts of the field at once, the contest seemed to go on forever. Gwenhumara wanted to speak to Arthurius about Morgana, but he was fully engaged in watching the skills of his Cambrogi. With a sigh she forced her attention to the contest field, even though the stress of the scene with Morgana, the heat of the day, and the incessant noise was giving her a ringing headache. Always she preferred the quiet of her courtyard and the words of one of the monk's books to the raucous shouts of the crowds.

But then her wandering attention was caught by Maelgwyn, who stood not far from the royal benches cheering loudly for his favorite. At first she thought it must be one of the black-haired warriors who had accompanied him from Arfon. She searched the now-thinning field to see which of the northwestern Cymri was besting his opponent with the wooden practice sword that Arthurius had decreed must be used in the field—over the protests of warriors who would rather have slashed at one another with battle-sharp weapons. At last she found the man Maelgwyn cheered—Eleden of Gwynedd, grass from his tryst still clinging to the long hair hanging beneath his iron battle helm. Why should Maelgwyn the renegade cheer so for one who had sworn fealty to Arthurius from the first? Of course Arfon and Gwynedd were neighboring regions, separated only by a long valley in the Cymri mountains, but surely that could mean nothing sinister. Surely Maelgwyn only cheered out of sportsmanship for one bred near him. The answer was so innocent Gwenhumara could not understand why it caused a cold tingling low in her spine.

Then the entire field of spectators erupted in cheers as the final champions faced each other. Eleden had defeated a warrior who had come south from

Caledonia with The Ancelot and now turned to face the only other eques left on the field.

Baudwin of the one hand, with his buckler strapped to his left forearm and his flashing sword employed skillfully in his strong right hand, rained swift, well-aimed thrusts on the Cymri eques, forcing him ever backward, allowing no time for Eleden to get in a spear thrust of his own. It was over before the second round of cheers could be raised. Eleden miscalculated the timing of a thrust and was pushed backward by Baudwin's skillful buckler-shove and sprawled to the ground. In classic fashion, Baudwin held his sword tip to his opponent's neck, with one foot resting lightly on his chest. "Do you yield, Eleden of Gwynedd?"

The anger in the fallen warrior's voice was unmistakable as he growled, "I yield me."

Gwenhumara started to signal to Elidor that she must present the trophies for this event, as Morgana who was scheduled to do so was absent. But even as her hand was raised in a half-gesture, Gwenhumara stopped. Morgana, clothed in her best scarlet tunic with a wealth of glass beads around her neck, her black hair freshly combed and braided high on her head, her back straight and her shoulders stiff, walked onto the field, purposely avoiding looking in the queen's direction. Morgana took the trophy bracelets from the king and walked forward to present the silver to Baudwin and the copper to Eleden. Gwenhumara was probably the only person in the cheering throng who noted the long, intense look that passed between Morgana and Eleden. But even she could not discern its meaning.

The queen's attention was then fully claimed by the final event of the day, the one that would determine the champion eques among them. The prize for the cavalry event was the most coveted and most hotly contested. Each competitor was to run his horse at full speed across the field to the target laid in the center—a large circle of stones with a smaller circle inside that, a clay water pot in the very center. As the warrior galloped by the target, it took perfect timing and aim for him to hit the clay pot dead center so as to shatter it and darken the smaller ring of stones equally with splashed water.

Horses thundered across the field, pennants fluttered in the late afternoon breeze, and the crowd cheered with each fierce spear thrust of a competitor. Few knights found their aim so unpracticed as to miss the outer circle of stones, and most landed their weapons inside the smaller circle. Gwalchmai was the first to crack the water pot. The water poured from its side, wetting several stones on the side away from his horse. It would take skillful work, indeed, to better that.

With grim determination reddening his face, Caius thrust his horse at the target, the mighty creature's hooves striking the earth with such force that the ground trembled under the spectators. But in his intensity, he overshot slightly, merely tipping the pot over and pouring the contents on the ground.

Bors matched Gwalchmai's performance, and it appeared for some time that Arthurius must part with two golden bands for the championship. But then Baudwin, who controlled his horse with his knees in order to leave his right hand free for his weapon, bested Gwalchmai's thrust by wetting half the inner circle.

Only two competitors left. Maelgwyn of Arfon had stood aside from all events until now, merely observing the performance of others and occasionally cheering one of his own warriors. But now the Cymri kinglet thundered across the field, his black horse half a hand taller than any around it and a green and white pennant fluttering from the end of his spear. An astonished cheer rose from the crowd following the loud crack of the water pot. Every stone had been wetted.

The High King stood, holding the wide golden champion's arm band high to catch the rays of the afternoon sun, but he was almost physically pushed back into his seat by a piercing wail from Dineidyn's pipe, announcing that the contest was not yet over. The Ancelot of Caledonia had yet to throw his spear, and he would do so as long ago generations of his kind had marched into battle—to the accompaniment of the shrill skirl of the pipes. When the last drone of the bass note had died away, none could believe their eyes. The Ancelot had wetted not only the stones of the inner circle, but also those of the outer ring.

Shining with pride and delight, Gwenhumara Regina stepped to the front of the field to present the golden band of the champion eques of all Britain to her own father.

Only after the second place silver had been awarded to Maelgwyn and third place copper to Baudwin did her pleasure dim as she saw the oddly disturbing sight of Maelgwyn and Medraut walking away shoulder to shoulder.

8

That night all feasted in the great round hall of Caer Cam in honor of the winners of the fete and of the marriage couple. The round table had been removed from the hall and stored in one of the outbuildings. Long tables now filled the massive room where nobility and champions dined while their armorbearers and the younger warriors were served in the courtyard outside. The hall was sweet with the scent of fresh herbs strewn on the floor and tossed into the central fire, which was only lightly fueled as it had been a warm day. Flaming torches in iron brackets on every beam provided ample light.

Arthurius's court dined Roman-style, which allowed the women to be seated as they wished among the men, rather than Celtic-style, which required the women to serve the men and then eat at a table to one side. Servants in short tunics scurried like ants between the caer kitchens and the hall, supplying the long tables with trenchers of roasted meats and sweet cakes that the cooks had been preparing for weeks and bringing tall pots of the best-brewed beer as well as a few rare imported amphorae of wine from Gaul.

Blaise was allowed only a few mouthfuls of his favorite roasted swan before an eager banging of dagger hilts on the tables relayed the company's impatience for a bardsong to accompany their meal. At a signal from the king, the harper took his seat on a high stool near the hearth and ran his fingers lovingly over the strings. As the evening's celebration was to honor a bride-making, a song of marrying was called for. The bard's eyes suddenly sparkled with delighted humor, and his fingers plucked playfully at the strings. "My friends, I give you a song that bears moral advice for the groom. And as 'twas told to me, it happened to our own eques Gwalchmai." Another mirthful trill. "But this was long and long before my coming to court, so perhaps I mistook, or perhaps the teller misspoke—the song of Gwalchmai and the Loathsome Lady."

A shout of laughter and a reverberation of hilts and fists pounding the table filled the hall. Those in the courtyard drew near the open door or unshuttered windows to hear. "And in the early days of the kingdom, Arthurius and his bold eques sat feasting when a maiden came into their midst. Graceful and lithe was she, and young and fair was her voice, and richly robed and jeweled was she. And heavily veiled was she." A note of warning sprang from the harp.

"But young and fair was her voice as she knelt before the high seat of Arthurius the true and the brave. 'Oh, my noble lord, hear my plea,' cried she. 'A boon I ask, a boon.' And every bold warrior 'round the hearth felt his heart leap within him, and every good man would gladly have pledged his sword and his honor for this maid.

"'You have but to ask,' quoth Arthurius Boldheart, 'up to half my kingdom, and it shall be yours.'

"'Oh, my noble lords,' quoth she, 'I ask not for your kingdom, but for my father's. An evil witch hath imprisoned my princeling brother and noble father and rules our kingdom for evil.'

"And every eques, for his honor's sake, drew his sword ready to ride forth to free the maiden's land. But Arthurius of the calm mind and steady hand stayed them and asked instead, 'Sweet maiden, how may this spell be broken?'

"'Naught by sword nor by might of arms,' she cried. 'But only by an eques of Arthurius's companionship taking me to bride.'

"And a great cheer rose from the lips of the Cambrogi, and many raised their cups in praise to the maiden and swore their willingness to be the king's man to fulfill the promised boon. For happy must a man be to wed so graceful a lady with such a fine robe and so pleasing a voice."

The harpstrings sang, and at a nod from the harper all in the hall raised cups to the bridal couple in whose honor the song was made. But then a somber, discordant melody struck warning to the hearts of the listeners. "And then the lady unveiled before the company. A great gasp rose from their lips, for the lady was loathsome beyond measure—her eyes squinty, her skin pock-marked and warty, her nose hooked and crooked, her mouth misshapen and teeth jagged." A discordant plucking followed each statement.

"Noble Arthurius, all color drained from his face, stepped to her and took her hand, and now all could see that under her long sleeve, the hand was a claw, rough and twisted. Arthurius held the unfortunate hand and spoke the more gently. 'Maiden, I have sworn. You shall have your boon.'

"For the sake of his king, Gwalchmai stepped forward wavering not. 'I will wed her, my lord.'"

All in the great hall laughed at the bard's gentle jest, for valiant Gwalchmai, always quiet and intent on his work for his king, had little time for women and was one of the few unwed eques in the hall, save the younger ones.

Then the bard's skill brought them back to the story. "A priest was called forth, and Gwalchmai and the loathsome lady placed their hands on the sacred Book and drank of the sacred wine and plighted their troth. And Gwalchmai, his head held high, but looking not at the face of his bride, led her forth to the bedplace. Slow he was in unbelting his sword. And slow he was in removing his tunic. And slow he was in lighting the bedside candle." Snickers and bawdy jests ran through the crowd.

A brave glissando recalled them to the tale. "And at last Gwalchmai looked upon his lady. His eyes would not believe the seeing, for she was fair indeed—fairer than any lady in the land. That was before the coming of the Lady Gwenhumara. And her golden hair hung shimmering to her waist, and her skin was softer than a newborn cub, and her eyes brighter than the sea at midday. The heart of Gwalchmai rejoiced. 'Is this the truth I see?' he cried. 'Are you my wife?'

"'Thus may I be your wife,' she replied. 'And thus may I be yours every night. But you must choose, my lord. For such is the evil spell laid upon me that I may be fair by day when all the world may look upon me, and foul by night when I come to my marriage lord. Or I must be foul for the world by day and fair for my marriage lord. The choice is yours.'

"Gwalchmai turned from his fairest of brides with a great groan, and a sob stole from his lips. He paced the floor to and fro. And still he could not decide. Her shame before the world and his pleasure at night? Or her glory before the world and his abhorrence at night? The pity of all and the delight of one? Or the praise of all and the repugnance of one?

"The night wore on as Gwalchmai paced and turned and strove in his mind. At last he fell on his knees before his lady, the waning moonlight falling across her fairest of faces. 'My lady, I cannot choose. It is you who must face the world; it is you who must come at night to your marriage chamber. Choose you the form in which you would live. Do as you will. The decision is yours.'

"At those words a joyous cry broke from her lips, and with a rapturous sob she threw herself into his arms. 'Oh, my lord, my most noble and most gracious of lords! At last the spell is truly broken, and I am free. For in giving me the freedom to choose, you have given me freedom in all. The witchery is defeated. I may be fair for the world and fair for you. But truly, I shall ever strive to be fairest of all for you.'"

The joyous ending notes of the harpsong were lost in the tumultuous cheering and banging for the bard and his song and the marriage couple. All threw their meat scraps to the hounds sitting under the tables and called for fresh platters.

Gwenhumara laughed and voiced praise with the others, yet the vague unease she had felt all day had not left her. All evening she had watched Morgana sitting with downcast eye far across the room from Eleden. But in moments when others were occupied, her lady sought him out with her dark glance. Eleden was seated at the shadowed end of a long table far from Maelgwyn, and yet it seemed that many times in the drinking the two men raised their cups to one another. Though in the crush of the crowd and wavering torchlight, one could not be certain. And Medraut, whom one could never wholly trust and yet could never put into words the reason for it, sat remote by the curve of the wall watching all. What did those sharp, fox-like eyes see that none else in the festive hall saw?

Next, Baudwin took his harp from its doeskin bag and sat in the bard's seat vacated by Blaise. Steadying the instrument with his left forearm, he began the song that no feast in Arthurius's court could be complete without: "The Victory of Mount Badonicus."

Although Gwenhumara knew the story as well as the singer, she never grew tired of the hearing, nor did any in the room. But tonight, albeit the familiar words were soothing, she could not force her tired, troubled mind into it. ". . . And the motley barbarians from many kingdoms did come together to make the final slaying of Arthurius Pendragon and the kingdom of Britain, for fain would they extinguish the light of Logres . . ." Was that a messenger approaching Maelgwyn, carrying a message from Medraut, or merely a servant filling the beer cups?

". . . And the brave British troops assembled on bold Badonicus's side and called on the God of all for His help in that day of dire need. Then they thundered forth to battle. Archers and footmen and horsemen bold—they thundered forth to battle the barbarian enemies of God and of man. And the blood ran deep in the valley. And the arrows flew and the swords clashed and many and many a warrior—valiant, brave, and bold—fell that day. Yet the sea wolves raged and howled and their bite was terrible indeed.

"And the blood welled forth. Arthurius saw his habergeon and shield all red therewithal, and his wrath waxed yet more burning hot. With the battle cry loud on his lips and the faith of God strong in his heart, he raised mighty Caliburnus aloft. The sword of cut steel he wielded with all his force . . ."

Morgana had left the hall. Was she merely tired with the strain of the day, or had she arranged a tryst? The torch along the far wall had guttered and darkened. The shadows were too deep at the end of the table to reveal the whereabouts of Eleden. Gwenhumara shuddered with a wave of sickness in her stomach. She did not relish the necessity of punishing her waiting lady, the daughter of a king—however disloyal Urien may have been at times.

"And firm in Arthurius's hand, Caliburnus struck with sure and deadly aim and missed not once in all the day. Rising against nine hundred of the enemy, Arthurius dashed them to the ground with an incredible slaughter of wolves. Arthurius slew nine hundred, and by his own hand did they fall, and Caliburnus was triumphant. Badonicus was won, and Britain stood secure. Praise be to God."

Although Gwenhumara sought his face, none in the room could see the response of Medraut to this song of the defeat of his half-brothers.

Heavy with drink and feasting and the activity of the battle fete, Caer Cam slept late the next morning and then erupted in a sudden urgent bustle of those who would depart to their own holdings and those who would speed the king and his chosen eques on their way for the assessment collecting. Caught in the busy scurrying, the queen forgot her misgivings of the day before. Indeed, it was the morning of the following day before all was at last quiet from the many departures. The Ancelot, who was to guard the caer in the king's absence, had taken a group of horsemen hunting to replenish the larders, and Gwenhumara found a moment to relax in her walled garden. She would have a time of meditation before she sent for Morgana.

But her solitude did not last long, for she was only on her second page of reading when the disgraced lady came quietly into the courtyard unbidden and knelt at her feet with bowed head. "My lady, I have come to seek your forgiveness and your help. I have been most evil in my behavior and most miserable in your displeasure. May I speak?"

Gwenhumara laid her book aside with a suppressed sigh. She could not postpone the moment any longer. "Speak, Morgana."

"I ask your forgiveness, my queen. I know I did wrong to lie with Eleden. But my love for him is so great—indeed our love for each other is so great—"

"I will forgive you, Morgana, but it is a higher One than I that you must beg forgiveness of. You must seek a priest and be forgiven of this mortal sin. Our Lord is wounded by your impurity."

"Yes, my lady. That is why I have come. The burden of my sin is heavy upon my soul. I would be shriven by our archbishop."

"Yes. That would be a fine thing for your soul, Morgana. But he has gone away to his hermitage on the holy island. I do not know when he will return. But Brother Logor or one of the priests from the island will come to us on Sunday for all who will partake of the holy Eucharist. You may make confession to him and be shriven then."

Morgana clasped a hand to her heart and raised stricken eyes to her queen. "Oh, my lady. Do not say that I must live yet so many days with this sin on my soul. What if I should die before he comes?" Her voice rose in hysteria. "My soul would be cast into eternal burning. Oh, my lady, do not say so. Do not make me wait so long in mortal fear of my eternal soul. Oh, my queen, take me now to the holy island that I may be shriven . . ." She collapsed in sobs at Gwenhumara's feet.

"Very well, Morgana, I shall call a boatman." Then after observing the girl's distraught condition, she added, "Perhaps it would be well for you to pack a few belongings and stay some days at the house of holy sisters on the island."

Morgana darted away with barely audible gratitude.

A short time later, Gwenhumara ascended the ramparts of Caer Cam, for in her husband's and father's absences she would instruct the guards herself. "The Ancelot will return by nightfall. See that you guard the caer well. Tell him that I have gone to Avalon."

The guard saluted palm to forehead. Gwenhumara looked from the ramparts to the northwest, and because it was a clear afternoon, she could see the hazy outline of the Tor rising above the marshland and waterways that separated them. "I shall return in two days' time."

Again the guard saluted, and Gwenhumara, with her waiting lady and two servants, left the caer.

That was the last anyone saw of them.

The Ancelot and his hunters returned with full bounty that night, and he received the news of the queen's departure. When she did not return in two days, he worried little. His daughter had always known her own mind and set her own course, as had her mother.

But Brother Logor arrived from the hermitage to say mass on Sunday and informed them that the queen was not there. Panic swept the court.

The queen was always composed, always confident. One could always seek her advice in time of trouble. She was unshakeable. Trouble could not come to her. As Logres was the shining at the heart of Britain, so Gwenhumara was the shining at the heart of Caer Cam. The shining could not disappear. It was unthinkable.

9

rother Gildas laid down his stylus, rubbed his forehead to ease the perennial ache, and then moved his candle closer to read what he had just written. Although it was midday, his room was dim and his eyes weak, causing him to squint at his work. "Thus did our ancestors send their piteous appeals to Rome. And so did the Saxon blaze spread until it licked the western ocean with its fierce red tongue. Thus some of the Britons caught in the mountains were slaughtered in large numbers. Others, weakened by hunger, came forward and surrendered to their enemies to be slaves forever—if they were not immediately cut to pieces, which was the greatest kindness that remained to them . . ."

What was that disturbance outside? How dare anyone disturb the peace of this holy island—especially on the Lord's Day? With a heavy sigh, Gildas pushed his sheets of parchment aside and crossed to the small window of his cell. Some rowdy travelers seeking shelter for the night, no doubt. Let the brothers see to it. The fact that Brother Indract had left the hermitage in his care while the abbot was about business in Caerleon with the archbishop did not mean that he must fly to the side of every rabble of visitors who chanced to cross the waterways to their island—as happened all too often to his mind. What good was it being a hermit if the world beat a path to your door?

He turned again to his manuscript. ". . . Then, some time intervening, Ambrosius Aurelianus, a moderate man, who alone of the Roman nation had survived in the shock of so great a calamity, gained strength and challenged the conquerors to battle. By God's favor the victory fell to them . . ." Again he scowled. Would that hubbub never cease? He blew out his candle with an angry puff and left his cell, banging the door behind him.

His eyes momentarily blinded by the bright daylight, he crashed soundly into young Brother Breden who was hurrying to fetch him. "What is the matter with you? Cannot you watch where you are going?"

"Forgive me, brother. They said I was to bring you. It's The Ancelot from Caer Cam. He seeks the queen."

"Well, can none tell him as well as I that she isn't here? Why must I do everything? I am a historian, not the Pope. I do not wish to be disturbed."

"I am sorry, brother. But the abbot said—"

"Yes, yes, I know. Never mind. I'll deal with it." Still scowling he hurried down the path toward the disruptive visitors from court. "The queen is not here. We have not seen her since she made pilgrimage with the archbishop at Eastertide," he announced without preamble or greeting.

The Ancelot took no offense at the monk's abrupt manner, but seemed instead to appreciate so direct an approach. "She left the caer four days ago with her servants, saying she was coming here and would return in two days. No one has seen her."

"Well, our twelve hides are not the whole of the island. Ask you at the holy house of St. Bridget. Perhaps she has made retreat there with the Lady of the Lake. I cannot help you more." He started to turn away, then added almost as an afterthought, "But we shall say prayers for her."

"Aye. And see that you make them fervent." The laird and his men were already started down the path toward the convent on Wirral Hill. But the Lady Nimue knew no more of the queen's whereabouts than did the monks.

The Ancelot's fierce blue eyes snapped above his flowing yellow moustache. "All right, men. I want every cranny of this island searched from the top of the Tor to the water's edge." He pointed his men in separate directions, then started eastward himself toward Windsome Hill. The hill was not really a part of Ynis Witrin, but more an island itself, separated from the larger series of hills by a marshy swamp which could be crossed on foot only in the dry season.

In the end it was Brucea who showed them the way. The faithful hound bitch had been so mournful at her mistress's absence that The Ancelot brought her with him, and the nursing pups, too. The hound stood with her feet planted on the ground at the shore's edge, her nose in the long grasses, and refused to move, tiny whimpering noises coming from deep within her throat. "And what is it now, ye troublesome dog? I've not time for such foolishness. It won't hurt you to get yer feet wet in the bog. Urbgen here knows the way." A young lad who helped in the hermit's kitchen in return for a warm place to sleep and stew in his stomach had offered to serve as guide.

But still Brucea would not move, and The Ancelot started with an impatient gesture to grasp the leather band around her neck. Then the breeze blew the grass, and he saw what held the hound. One of the tiny golden bells from Gwenhumara's necklace lay on the bank. "So. And now we know she's here." He held the bell up to examine it carefully and then slipped it into the pouch he carried inside his tunic. "Urbgen, fetch my men. We'll storm the island." The Ancelot's hand was already on his sword, but then he thought better.

"Ah, no, lad. If she's held against her will, they might do her harm before we can reach her. Get you instead to the hermitage and bring that monk in charge—Gildas, is that his name?"

Such urgent errands had never been entrusted to the scullery brat before, and he hurried away full of importance. In spite of the boy's speed, however, it was long before the scowling, brown-robed figure of Brother Gildas, huddling under his goat-hide cloak, answered The Ancelot's summons. He nodded when The Ancelot showed him the bell, but shook his head firmly at the suggestion that they cross to the thickly wooded hill that evening. "Too dangerous. This time of day mists come up in moments. Besides, it'll be dark by the time we get there, and you couldn't find anything in the dark—solid tree-cover there. The hangdog scoundrels will be there in the morning. We'll go at first light. Unless there's a mist."

The Ancelot ordered a guard set in case a flare of torches should show itself across the swamp and give them a clue to Gwenhumara's whereabouts. Then he submitted to the locum abbot's pronouncement.

There was a mist next morning—thick, wet, and gray—making travel impossible and forcing the teeth-gritting Ancelot to sit through early morning prayers and midmorning prayers as well. At last the fog lifted. The guard had seen no sign of fires on Windsome, although little could have shown through the shrouding mists. This helped confirm The Ancelot's suspicion that the party they sought would be on the far side of the hill.

Once more the Caledonian had to stifle his impulse to rush the island hill with armed men. Far better to yield to Brother Gildas's suggestion that he, too, go robed as one of the holy brothers, even though that meant leaving his sword behind and carrying only the small, sharp dirk he wore strapped to the side of his leg. Thus they could approach the island openly in coracles in the guise of monks fishing to fill their midday stewpots.

The coracles had barely touched the reed-bound eastern bank of Windsome Hill when Brucea lifted her head, sniffed the air, and sprang forward. She led them straight to the camp, halfway up the hill where several hide tents were pitched in a thicket of trees. But without the hound, they would surely, albeit more slowly, have found the way—for it was marked by five more tiny golden bells. The queen herself had made preparation for her rescue.

Maelgwyn, his feet planted wide, his arms folded across his chest, stood waiting their approach before the nearest of the tents. The Ancelot, longing for his sword, threw back the cowl Gildas had insisted he pull over his head and faced the Cymri king. "I've come for my daughter, the High Queen, you dog. And if Arthurius grants you your life after what you've done in holding her here, it's more than you deserve."

Maelgwyn spread his arms wide, and an ingratiating smile interrupted his rough face. "Ah. You mistake the matter, my lord, The Ancelot. And why should the High King be displeased with me for lending assistance to his lady when her boatmen wrecked her coracle on these shores and her waiting lady fell ill of a fever?"

The Ancelot took another menacing step forward. "You lie, you wretch! If you've harmed Gwenhumara, I'll not wait for Arthurius to separate your lying head from your shoulders."

"The Lady Gwenhumara is well, and her waiting maid Morgana is nearly recovered sufficiently to continue the pilgrimage to Avalon."

The Ancelot growled so fiercely Maelgwyn was forced to take a step backward and wipe the smirk from his face. "I'll not believe a word of it. I'll be taking the queen back to Caer Cam now." He pressed forward.

But this time his way was barred by two warriors with drawn swords standing on either side of Maelgwyn. "Before we bother the ladies, it is in my mind that we might discuss my reward for rescuing the queen." The smile had returned to Maelgwyn's thick lips.

"I'll see you burn first! I'll pay no ransom." The Ancelot flung himself at Maelgwyn. His thrust was blocked, however, not by one of the warriors, but rather by Brother Gildas.

"Perhaps the church might be of assistance. If we could negotiate this in peace without bloodshed . . ."

Such soft words from one who was ever wont to growl and complain stilled The Ancelot more than the monk's physical imposition between the two chiefs. The antagonists stood silent while Brother Gildas spoke. "We would have the queen unharmed now. We have come in peace to take her with us. If you have been her protector, as you claim, I'm sure she will see that you are adequately rewarded." After a significant pause he added, "I'm sure she will see that you are appropriately rewarded whatever your role has been. What do you ask?"

At that moment the door-flap lifted on a nearby tent, and a mail-shirted figure approached. "I believe I have some concern at this bargaining also."

"The High King's men do not bargain with outlaws." The Ancelot shook his fist in Maelgwyn's face.

But the Arfon chief seemed relieved at the younger man's approach. "Eleden, I would have you beside me." He turned to the two brown-robed figures. "Eleden of Gwynedd, which marches with my own Arfon, has of late done me considerable service. I have named him my heir. We would ask of the High King the holding of Powys as well." He paused as the audacious demand brought an outcry from The Ancelot, then continued, "Without payment of tribute, that is."

"Dog!" The Ancelot jerked his dirk from under his robe and flung at Maelgwyn. A thin red line appeared on the Cymri's cheek before the Caledonian was pulled off.

"My brother, I will not be able to bring this to a happy conclusion pleasing to God and the High King if you continue to interrupt." Again the soft answer turned away wrath.

Maelgwyn dabbed at his cheek with a cloth as Gildas continued. "If you and Eleden here agree to combine your holdings, that is your matter. I have no thinking that Arthurius will have need of his services any longer—not after your 'service' in luring the queen here. The suggestion that the king grant you the land of Powys is beyond laughing at. Even in our secluded sanctuary here we know those lands are held by Rhavader."

"Aye, Rhavader the constant, who swore fealty to Arthurius long and long ago!" The Ancelot growled.

"Your payment of tribute is a matter for you and the High King to settle," Gildas continued. "But hear me, Maelgwyn. The wolves howl ever nearer our coasts. If you pay no tribute, you'll get no protection. Think you well on it. And think you on something else. If you do not choose to release the queen to us now, think you that you can stand against Arthurius and all his Cambrogi when word reaches him? Think you he'll believe this abduction was a 'helping' of the queen?"

Suddenly Brucea, who had waited quietly under Urbgen's hand, sprang forward with a wild bark. The flap of the farthest tent lifted, and Gwenhumara, as calmly as if she crossed her own courtyard, stepped out. "My father. Brother Gildas. I grew weary of waiting for you to come. Let us go now."

"My daughter, are you unharmed?"

"Of course I am unharmed. Had he lain one hand on me, I would have killed him—or myself. Maelgwyn of Arfon," she said, leveling a cold stare at the cowed kinglet, "you will no longer be welcome at Caer Cam." She turned slightly. "Nor you, Eleden of Gwynedd. If you will have my lady Morgana after you used her to ensnare me, take her with you. If not, I will take her to the house of holy sisters. I would not turn her out to starve."

"Take her then," he spat. "She's nothing to me."

The party made ready to return to Ynis Witrin, and Gildas was already shepherding them down the path to the waiting coracles when he turned once more to Maelgwyn standing with slumped shoulders. "It is in my mind that you reckoned rightly in one matter—the queen was Arthurius's only vulnerability. But you reckoned without her strength."

At the hermitage, they found that Dubricius and Indract had returned from their duties in Caerleon. But the greatest surprise was the arrival a short time later of Arthurius himself and the four Cambrogi. They had been in Dumnonia, forcing a hard bargain for supplies from Cador when a messenger had arrived from Caer Cam with the dire news of Gwenhumara's disappearance. "We rode the sun out of the sky and the moon beyond the mountains to get here. I will make short work of that cur Maelgwyn." The king's hand was on Caliburnus.

But Gwenhumara's hand was on his arm. As always her deep calm steadied him. "Brother Gildas has seen to all. Let there be no bloodshed, my husband. It is my thinking that you will have no more trouble from Maelgwyn."

Slowly the king lowered his hand from his sword and extended it to clasp Brother Gildas's arm. "Truly are you called Gildas the Wise. The matter might have ended with much unhappiness for Britain and for myself had you not intervened."

He turned to the four Cambrogi standing below him on the path. "Let it be voiced far and beyond what this brother has done this day in service to his king and country." Then he turned back to the stooped, brown-robed figure. "In your honor, Gildas the Wise, I shall grant my personal holdings at Brent Knoll on the Sabrina to the hermitage in your name, that its rich lands may provide well for generations of holy brothers, whom we pray will be as wise as you. And, Baudwin, let you make a harpsong of the abduction of Queen Gwenhumara and of her rescue by The Ancelot and the intermediation of the good Gildas. And let peace reign forever on this land."

Gildas knew he should return a pleasant speech of gracious acceptance, but his head ached abominably. All his being was engulfed in a desire to return quietly to his cell and take up again the stylus hastily laid aside two days ago. Apparently Brother Indract saw his need, for the abbot stepped forward to reply to the king, dismissing Gildas in doing so.

The brother's feet found the familiar grooved path across the green space to his cell without the aid of his eyes. He kept them almost shut to rest them from the strain and focus more clearly on the words pushing from his mind to be placed on paper.

The pale light of evening filtering through his single window would suffice. He wouldn't light a candle until forced to by absolute darkness. The only sound in the room was the scratching of the stylus. "Our foes drove us to the sea, and the sea threw us back on our foes. We would die either by the sword or by the sea. Then came the mighty Battle of Mount Badonicus, the last slaughter wrought by us on the Saxon. The slaughter of sea wolves was nine hundred and more in that one day by Arthurius's own hand. And no fairer king than he ruled the land."

Dark shadows came suddenly to his east-facing window, forcing Gildas to lay aside his writing. Beyond his dark room, he could see the Tor glowing red and gold in the sunset. Rubbing his tonsured forehead, he walked to the window. The king and queen were passing by with the archbishop.

"You do well to choose the way of peace, Lord Artos. It is that I would speak to you of," said Dubricius.

"Speak, my Emrys."

"I would speak in the chapel of our St. Patricius." He looked to the top of the Tor where the small stone oratory was gilded in the flames of lowering sun and then led off with long strides, his staff striking the ground ahead of him as he ascended. But his pace slowed, and his breathing came harder as the way grew steeper.

He faltered, then caught himself on his staff. Gwenhumara moved quickly to one side and Arthurius to the other. So supported, Merlinus Ambrosius Dubricius made his way to the top of the Tor. Once there he stood outside the chapel, facing west, and closed his eyes in the sun so that all was golden inside and out, as indeed, in recent years, he had come to find the gold inside the truer one. When he spread his arms toward the sun and spoke, it was not to his two companions, but to the One he knew closest of all.

"Great God, You have given such riches, such goodness, such beauty—let Your people, those of Your name and Your pasture, ever honor You for Your greatness and Your mercy. For if ever they lose the summer vision of light and glory—if ever they turn away from Your great gifts, the enemy will return, and the glory will depart. Let there always be those who keep Your vision alive. And if ever the flame weakens, if extinction of the vision threatens—let Arthurius Your king and Your servant return to remind the people of Logres of the work of Your hand in their land and of the honor they owe You." He was quiet for long and long, the red and gold rays blazing on him as if he would be consumed. At last he lowered his arms. "Amen."

The sun sank into the western sea, and a chill breeze swept the Tor. "Arthurius?" Gwenhumara's whisper held a note of fear.

Arthurius put his right hand to the old man's thin chest, supporting him with his other arm. "His heart beats. But barely. He has gone away from us. We will take him to his cell."

And so the High King bore the one who had been father, teacher, and king-maker to him to a secluded cell on the holy island and placed him on a bed-place heaped high with thickest furs. Gwenhumara lit a rushlight held in a deep glass bowl. And when it was set on a low table in the center of the room, it turned the round whitewashed walls into a crystal cave.

10

t was three years before Arthurius's navy was fully operational. And in those three years the sons of Caw, led by Hueil, the eldest and roughest, renewed their ties with the Picts that had been broken many years earlier at the battle of Cat Coit Caledon. Raids in the Sabrina and along the north and west of Arthurius's lands grew fiercer.

Laughter rang less often now through the courts of Caer Cam, and the infectious grin of the High King shone less often. But even though the battles inside and out did not lessen, his graying hair was thick and his energy and determination undimmed.

One day Arthurius returned at midday to Gwenhumara's chamber ashen-faced and tight-lipped without the sparkle in his eyes that so lightened her heart. Even Cabal, as ever at his master's heels, drooped his head. "My lord, what is it?"

"Long I have known that the time must come, but today it was upon me that I must turn my sword arm upon one who always bore me to victory in battle."

"Magnus?"

"Sa, sa. It has been long and long since I rode him in battle practice, and many are the fine foals he has fathered in the garth. My herders have long called him the father of the horse-runs. But he could no longer eat. His time was come."

"It was right that you should do it." Gently the queen fondled the ears of Brucea whose gray muzzle told the weight of the years that she too carried. "Such it is for all of God's creatures." She took the king's hand. "So shall it be for us one day, too, my Artos."

He leaned heavily against the piled furs. "Perhaps it would have been easier to think of had our bedplace been granted fruit."

"My dear . . ."

He put a finger to her lips to stop her. "No, it is as it is. And Cador's Constantine will make a fitting heir. But I must not let the naming wait too late as Ambrosius did. Of course, in Constantine's case there is no clouding of the lineage, so there should be little dispute anyway."

Arthurius leaned deeper yet into the furs and closed his eyes as if resting.

Gently so as not to disturb him, the queen returned to the bright yarns of her embroidery. But inside Arthurius was anything but at peace. So as not to hurt Gwenhumara, he had ever kept a brave front over his lack of a son. And his words as to Constantine's qualifications were true. But inwardly he often raged at God. Why must he, of all men, go childless when the whole nation was so in need of one to succeed him? Was all he had worked for his whole life to come to naught in the end because he was denied the simple fulfillment that God granted to his horse and his hound as well as to any beast of the field?

In the folds of the soft skins he clenched his fists. He wondered who was angrier—himself at God, or God at him?

The respectful approach of a messenger prevented his further attempt to answer the unanswerable. "My Lord Arthurius, the Cambrogi are assembled around the council table, and the brothers are arrived from Avalon."

Arthurius grimaced. The taking of the Eucharist was the last thing he wanted to do. But the council must meet. The realm must be seen to.

Indeed, as the messenger reported, a full complement of Cambrogi sat in their council robes at the Round Table, with none of the sections pushed against the wall to shorten the circle. In the seat next to his own, in that place so long occupied by the sorely-missed Merlinus Dubricius, sat a familiar scowling brown-robed figure. "We welcome you to Caer Cam, Brother Gildas." Arthurius made his greeting sound as cordial as possible. Although he honored the monk for his wisdom, he could feel no warmth for him.

Gildas returned the king's greeting abruptly and presented another brown-robed, tonsured brother who had accompanied him. "Brother Columba, who has made pilgrimage from his holy house in Donegal to visit the grave of St. Patricius on Avalon."

Although dressed and tonsured alike, no two figures could have presented a greater contrast. Round-faced and full-bellied Brother Columba bustled across the hall, grinning broadly, to bend his knee before the High King and laughed aloud when he tripped on the hem of his robe in the process. Arthurius warmed to him instantly. "Welcome, Brother Columba. We hope the sun has shone on your journey."

"Oh, indeed, indeed. Although it has rained almost every day, I am never without the blessing of the Son." And he chuckled at his little joke which remained obscure to most in the room. "I have come by way of the monastery of Tintagel in Dumnonia. A fine house. A fine house, indeed. None finer in all of Eire, I should say, save at Armagh, the seat of our St. Patricius himself." From there he went on to describe the holy house at Tintagel perched on one of the steepest seal-cliffs in all Dumnonia—the fineness of the guesthouse, the richness of the library and scriptorium with their many heavy presses full of books and scrolls, the many huts devoted to writing, with entire ends of the rooms left open for light, and the fine new cors built just higher up the cliff above the sea-crashed rocky coast.

At last Arthurius cut into his rhapsody. "That is fine hearing, indeed. You must tell us more later, brother."

At the front of the room Gildas stood frowning his impatience to begin the service. Obediently, Arthurius and Columba took their seats, and Gildas began the homily. "Our Lord has promised to be present where two or more are gathered in His name. So are we gathered here. He is among us." And yet this was not a joyful pronouncement. One could feel the impending judgment of God as if the words came from the lips of an Old Testament prophet.

And then the scowl deepened. "But the Scripture warns us of partaking unworthily of the Lord's Supper. Many of you have come to His table unworthily because you do not seek Him. Through the prophet Jeremiah God has promised, 'When you seek me, you shall find me. If you search with all your heart, I will let you find me, says the Lord.'"

The monk stretched forth an accusing finger and slowly circled it around the table. "'Let the wicked abandon their ways and evil men their thoughts.'" And then he turned and faced fully the high seat of the king. "Arthurius of Britain, you have brought us peace, law, order—these are good things, things for men's bodies, but what have you done for the souls of your people? What do you, King Arthurius, do for that part of your people that will live beyond this life and beyond this land?

"Oh, I hear you saying, 'I've kept the churches from being plundered and the priests from being slaughtered; do you count that as naught?'

"And I say to you, High King, it is a start. But what of inspiration? What of a vision for the people? The prophet tells us that without a vision the people perish. Look to the grail, look to the blood of our Savior, and lead your people to so look. Become not just Arthurius of Britain but Arthurius of Logres."

And then the sweeping, penetrating gaze returned to all in the room. "He who would take the blessing of the grail must also take the burden of the rood. As our Savior said, 'Let him take up his cross and follow me.' Who among you, whom He willed to make new by His death and resurrection, is willing to suffer pain and to travail for Jesus Christ? Who among you, good eques, valiant and true, would so journey forth for your Savior?

"Our land is a dry and thirsty desert, panting for the rain of God's blessing. Our enemy is not the sea wolves to the east nor the raiders to the west. Our enemy is those among us who do not seek God. And until He is found, the drought will continue. But when He is found, His promise stands: He will hear from heaven and heal our land.

"You who put your faith in swords, in treaties, and in navies must put your faith in the One who is above these. You must cry with the psalmist, 'O God, you are my God, I long for you. I seek you with a thirsty heart. Like a dry and thirsty land that has no water, with such longing I seek your strength and your glory.'"

The scolding voice stopped, and the room was silent. Some faces showed open shock that a priest would dare to chastise the High King and his Cambrogi; some faces reflected scorn for such ideas. But as Gildas turned from his preparation of the gifts and held the golden grail high for all to look on, one face in the room shone with rapture. Galaad of Caledon reflected an ecstasy that could come only from his heart's hearing and responding to a call it had long awaited. Forgetting that the king and priest were to be served first, Galaad rose and walked to the center of the room. He knelt before Gildas, but did not bow his head. His eyes never left the elevated grail which, indeed, appeared to all in the room to take on a glow of its own.

"My Lord High King, I have sworn fealty to you, and I would not leave your service. But I ask your permission to follow a yet higher King. I would go from Caer Cam to seek God."

Before the king could reply, Gildas served the communion elements to Galaad. Then returning the chalice and salver to the table, he placed his hands on the head of the kneeling eques in a benediction. "Who shall climb the mountain of the Lord? Who shall stand in His holy place—the holy place of the Most High? The man with clean hands and pure heart, the man who desires not worthless things, the man who has sworn no falsehood. He shall receive blessings from the Lord and reward from God his Savior. Rise, Galaad the pure, rise and go in the grace and peace of our Lord and Savior Jesus Christ."

Galaad, glowing in dedication, returned to his seat, and Gildas continued the Eucharist as if nothing unusual had happened. But Arthurius knew nothing would be the same again. Galaad's search for God would divide the Cambrogi as no squabble over taxes or defection of a rebel kinglet had ever done. Arthurius now knew a new fear. Not only would the Cambrogi never be the same, but neither would the High King. For Galaad's quest would go beyond anything ever attempted before in Logres.

Communion over, the council now looked to the high seat of the king. Arthurius looked at Gwalchmai. The report the captain of his navy had brought him the night before was to have been the first order of business. Hueil's increasingly frequent and violent raids called for more men and arms to protect the western shores. Today's council meeting had been called to establish these battle lines and to commit the resources of Britain to such a battle. But suddenly this was no longer a war council.

The silence grew. Then it was broken from an unexpected quarter. Brother Columba stood to his feet as an oak growing before them. "My Lord Arthurius, if it is in your mind to grant your eques leave to seek God's higher calling, may I suggest that he might accompany me on my mission?"

"Mission? We have heard of no mission, Brother Columba, only of a pilgrimage."

"Ah, yes. But my pilgrimage is accomplished. Now I set forth to begin my work."

"Which is?" It was strange that one so forceful as Brother Columba seemed to need prodding.

"Just as our sacred Brother Patricius took the gospel of Christ to his enemies, the heathen raiders of Eire, so would I take the light of the gospel to the Picti and Scoti."

Mingled gasps and shocked laughter met this outrageous suggestion. But the High King knew this was no laughing matter. Anger rose in him, burning away the doubts and fears he had felt earlier. Now the issue was focused. He slammed his fist against the table with such force that all in the room started. "Columba of Donegal, you would come before the council of all Britain to insult the High King? You come here to announce that you would go from here to preach to our enemies? To the very men who pillage our shores? Men who rape and steal and burn—you would take to them the love of God?"

"That is precisely what I would do. Our Lord spent His whole life on earth demonstrating that love is the highest good. We must follow His example."

"You would have us love the Picts and the Scoti, those who would burn our land and slaughter our women and children? What do they know of love?"

Columba's voice was so gently quiet in the wake of Arthurius's blast that for the space of a heartbeat no one realized he was speaking. "They know nothing of love. That is why they must be told. I would introduce them to the love of God—let Him love them—or more accurately, let them know He loves them already—and let the knowledge of that love transform their lives."

The monk's audacity left Arthurius speechless, and the quiet of his voice soothed the king's anger. At last Arthurius shook his head. "It is in my mind that long and long ago I said something like that to Dubricius in my more foolish, youthful days. It is seeming I quoted to him about beating swords into plowshares. But in all the years since, in spite of our well-hammered treaty, we have never been able to do without our swords."

Caius, seated as always to Arthurius's left, grew dangerously purple as if he would explode. He hit the table with both fists and jumped to his feet. "Love *transform* the Scoti! Beat our swords into plowshares! Does this monk have stirabout for brains? The Saxon and the Scoti and all vile animals of their kind are the spawn of the devil. God doesn't love them any better than I do, and there is only one way to deal with them. I know blessed little of the Scriptures, but I do know that God directed the Children of Israel to annihilate the godless ones in the Promised Land. Britain is our promised land, and I'm here to annihilate my share of heathen!"

Columba turned an open-faced smile on the angry eques. "Ah, my energetic friend, you remind me most sharply of what the Apostle Peter must have been like, and you are right." Even Caius could not stand against such a reply. He sank to his seat. "We are indeed to annihilate the godless; that is our mission. But there is more than one method for the accomplishing of this great task. For when they have the love of God in their hearts, they will no longer be godless."

All eyes now returned to the king. In all the years since they had laid Merlinus Emrys in his crystal cave, never had Arthurius missed his wise counsel so severely. He had begun the day sore at heart over the loss of his beloved Magnus and had looked again at the old ache of having no son, and then had suddenly been thrust from what should have been the simple council of war that he understood so well into the deep waters of searching for God and loving your enemies—doctrines to which he had given lip service all his life, but had not expected to have to rule on in the council chamber.

What of his own actions? Always he had striven to serve the right. But had he done so? Had he been the true servant of God he thought himself? If he had been, would God have withheld His blessing on the line of Arthurius?

But if he had not been wielding his sword for God, could he have been so successful? Was it possible to accomplish all he had against so great odds without God's help? Surely his victories had been far more moral victories than victories of sheer strength.

Victories for Britain, yes. But what of the heart of the king?

After a yet longer pause, he spoke. "Each man must do what he finds right in his own heart." He looked long at Galaad and Columba. "But the king must speak for Britain. From the time Joseph of Arimathea brought the light of the Logos to King Arviragus, and that flame was relit by my ancestor King Lucius, the king must speak for all Britain.

"Let each of you search your own heart. So will I search. I will go now to the holy island and pray at the Old Church built by St. Joseph. When I have an answer, I will return." Arthurius strode from the room, sending a messenger scurrying ahead of him for his boatman.

Two days later he returned.

The guard blew the aurochs' horn, and the council assembled quickly. Arthurius sent a messenger to the queen's chambers to request that she join the council and then put on his council robe and took his place on the high seat. In a few moments he heard the tiny tinkling of golden bells and looked up to see his queen walking toward him, a smile of greeting in her eyes that had no need to make display on her lips.

The room filled and was quiet. Arthurius remained seated to speak. "Brother Indract sends you his greetings and God's. He bade me bring you a message in the words of St. Matthew, 'Set your mind on seeking God's Kingdom and His justice before everything else, and all the rest will come to you as well. Do not be anxious about tomorrow; tomorrow will look after itself.'

"I thought long on those words as I kept vigil in the Old Church. Hear my decision. We shall seek God's Kingdom and God's justice. Those who would join Brother Columba and our Cambroga Galaad in their quest go with the blessing of the High King. Those who choose to stay by the sword of Britain will join me in fighting for justice."

None was surprised when Caius was the first to shout, "Aye, my sword for justice!"

But few would have foreseen The Ancelot's reply. "The sons of Caw with their treatied Scoti shields and their foul-friended Pictikind have long and long harried my borders. The sword, even the sword triumphant at Cat Coit Caledon, has not controlled them. I will go with my son Galaad to seek God's Kingdom."

Bors and Baudwin rose together from their places at the table to kneel before Arthurius with their swords at his feet, as on that long ago day when they first pledged him their fealty. "Our Lord Artos, our swords are yours to command. But with your leave, we would join the search for truth before we return to the use of our swords."

"So be it."

And so each man again lay his sword at Arthurius's feet, but none other requested leave to journey forth. Arthurius had watched the struggle in gentle Gwalchmai's face. The king would grant his captain freedom with the rest, but he was sorely needed with the navy, and Gwalchmai recognized that loyalty. He chose it as the higher.

When all had spoken, Arthurius turned to Columba, who had remained quiet throughout the proceeding. "Always I have been the man of war, my brother. Always I have worked for a stronger cavalry, for more mail shirts, for sharper swords and heavier ships. And yet always I knew war could not be the ultimate answer. The end of war must not be just killing and more killing until there is no one left to kill. This I knew, but my mind did not have an answer for the why of all that I knew in my heart.

"Now I have the answer. We must have our cavalry, and we must have our navy because there are those in the world who will listen to nothing else. But the end of the use of ships and swords must be to keep men quiet long enough to listen to the higher way. I am a man of the sword; that was given to me. You, Columba, have had the higher way given to you. I will use my cavalry and my navy to hold men quiet that they may listen to your way.

"And may your way win."

When all had filed from the room, Arthurius turned to Gwenhumara still sitting quietly beside him. She was first to speak. "Galaad and the others can venture off on their search. The king has the harder role. He must stay and search in his own heart. It has been long in my heart to ask God why we have no child, as I know it is in yours too, my king, although you will not speak it—for fear of hurting me, I am thinking. But while you were at Avalon I, too, sought God."

"And did you find an answer, my queen?"

"I did, but it is not an easy one. Especially it will not be an easy answer, I think, for a great king who has always fought for his goals and won—save in this one thing."

"And that answer?"

"That we must accept the ways of God. Can you do that, my dearling?"

Arthurius looked long at her, and again the smile that had no need for lips warmed his heart. "I can accept."

11

nd with acceptance the sparkle returned to Arthurius's eyes. Five more summer seasons passed in the kingdom of Britain. The corn grew and ripened in the garths, and the harvest was good as the cattle grew fat in the pen, and apples grew red and sweet in the orchard. The flame burned brightly in Logres.

But not all was peace, and the keeping of the peace was a constant vigilance for Arthurius and his Cambrogi. For although the Saxon treaty line held, there were rumors of Cheldric gathering a war band, so that the guard posts along the line must be strengthened, and to the north the Scoti whitened their war shields, and the Picti drums beat as they had not been heard since before Mount Badonicus. Word reached Caer Cam that while Hueil ruled in Strathcluta and gathered Scoti warriors to him, the three other sons of Caw—Turach, Carruth, and Wemys—had gone to the courts of Gwynedd and Arfon to make treaties.

And so came the sea raiders, not from the enemy outside, but from within the borders of Britain and Caledonia. For always the enemy is active, and always there are those who will take what is not theirs and destroy what is beautiful to another. Always there are the takers, the destroyers, the smashers.

In a day of golden autumn sunshine while harvesters were gathering the ripe corn, a messenger arrived at Caer Cam from Gwalchmai: "The strength of

Hueil grows; the burning and plundering increase daily. The raiders' ships outnumber ours, and we can no longer prevent their raiding our shores at will."

Arthurius knew that the time had come when he must take the field himself. Never had he more sorely missed Bors, Baudwin, and The Ancelot, still off on their soul-quests, than he did now. But he called his remaining captains—Caius, Teliau, Olwin, and Doldavius—and once again the table round bore the field map, and the council table of Logres became the battle table of Britain. As it was impossible to know where the raiders would strike, the entire shore of the Sabrina must be guarded the best they could with archers and spearmen posted on both its eastern and western banks and with cavalry units to patrol the thirty-three Roman miles on each side.

Not since the time of Mount Badonicus had the hosting call gone out to every chieftain. Supply wagons were loaded with armor, weapons, and food and sent lumbering down the steep, curved entryway of Caer Cam.

Arthurius sought out Gwenhumara. "My queen, I would that The Ancelot were here to help you."

"Na, na. Am I not a queen born and queen crowned? Cannot Arthurius's queen hold the caer while her lord sees to the peace-keeping?"

She could see that, while his mind was not entirely at rest over the matter, her words had soothed his leave-taking. "The God of peace and might go with you, my king, and may you return with His speed."

Arthurius mounted Valere, grandson of the noble Magnus, well-trained in the practice field, but never before battle-tested. With a flourish from his trumpeter and a waving of the Pendragon pennant carried by his armorbearer, the High King led forth into battle.

Gwenhumara climbed the stairway to the guardhouse over the gate that she might watch as long as she had sight of the equitata and foot warriors marching to the northwest. When she could no longer see the glimmer of midmorning sun off their battle helms and bucklers, she turned her gaze to the always welcome, more peaceful sight of Ynis Witrin, floating like a green jewel in the misty distance. Then she turned with a sharp order to a nearby servant to move her things from her quiet courtyard to the Great Hall of Caer Cam from whence she would rule.

On the second day after Arthurius's departure, the quiet of the hillfort was shattered by the trumpeted arrival of a messenger. Gwenhumara's heart leaped to her throat. It was too early to receive word of Arthurius. Surely there could have been no decisive battle yet. *Dear God, let it not be that; his troops have not had time to gather to his hosting call.* But with perfect outward calm, she sent Elidor for the guest cup and took her place on the high seat to receive the messenger.

"My lady, is it true as I hear that the High King is gone from Caer Cam?" The dusty, sweating rider dipped briefly to one knee before the queen.

"It is true. He has gone two days hence to deal with the raiders in the Sabrina. I will hear your message."

The scout looked doubtful, but after he had refreshed himself with the cup of barley beer Elidor presented him, he sat on a stool before her and delivered his message. "Long we have heard rumors that Cheldric of the fox-red horse-tail gathers troops in far greater number than his need for keeping his own people in order and builds ships beyond his need for fishing. But as he stayed well behind the treaty lines and made no trouble, there was nothing we could do but watch. Now our scouts report that the gathered men practice with well-sharpened swords and that the ships are armored with bull-hide as Arthurius armors his battle horses."

"And do your scouts give a reason for this change?"

"None can be sure. But there are rumors that the white-haired Aelle Bretwalda, whom many now call Aelle the Treaty-keeper, lies on his deathbed."

The queen received the news without change of expression. "Very well. We thank you for your report, Menw of the sharp eye. We will call together those of the council that remain at Caer Cam that they may hear your report."

Only two sections of the Round Table were needed as only Cambrogi of too great an age or for some other reason unfit for the battlefield remained behind. Gwenhumara, wearing Arthurius's council robe over her yew-green tunic, had just turned to Menw that he might speak to the council when a clatter of horses' hooves in the courtyard announced another arrival.

A gasp of surprise was felt rather than heard in the council chamber when the newcomer strode across the hall and dropped to one knee before the queen. Medraut, his dark red hair in uncharacteristic disarray from his long ride, turned with a gleam of excitement in his bright eyes and a flush on his normally pale cheeks. With barely a glance at Menw and without the queen's permission, he addressed the council, "It is well you are assembled, fellow Cambrogi. I see that you have received report of the sea wolves. You may be thankful indeed that the lameness of my mount caused my late return from my errand of spreading the hosting call among the Dumnoni."

Gwenhumara blinked at his audacity. Had no one noticed earlier that Medraut was not among Arthurius's captains? Or had they merely assumed that he would join them at the hosting with the Dumnoni warriors, which would have been the reasonable course of action? And were they now to believe this smooth story of a lame mount? As if there were no fresh horses to be had in all the horse-runs of Cador's holdings. How dare he stride into the Great Hall and usurp charge of the council in the presence of the High Queen?

With no outward show of anger, Gwenhumara rose and took two steps toward the interloper. With practiced smoothness Medraut again dipped to one knee before her. "My lady, forgive my rashness. In my concern for the kingdom I am afraid I forgot the common courtesies. I have come in such haste merely to offer my services to you, knowing full well that my, ah, unique qualifications might be of service in dealing with Cheldric.

"In the absence of the High King I am here to put myself entirely at the service of the council. Not to take anything away from your queenship over the purely, er, domestic affairs of the kingdom, my lady. But rather to relieve you of the matter of war strategies and treaty holdings."

With studied smoothness he turned to the council and said almost humbly, "With your leave, Cheldric will listen to me. I know his mind."

Gwenhumara stood her ground. "It shall not be so. I know Arthurius's mind. I am his queen and High Queen of Britain."

But this was a treaty matter, and such matters of policy were open to council debate. Menw completed his report, adding fuel to the fire Medraut had sparked, and the discussion went around the table. Gwenhumara heard again, as if echoing from the roof beams, *I know his mind.* That was exactly what she feared. Medraut, who had come to them as a hostage, had studied so well the ways of his kinsman Arthurius and had become so thoroughly British that only those with longest memories recalled his Saxon beginnings. And yet in the close-on thirty years since Mount Badonicus and the treaty-making, Medraut had demonstrated no disloyalty—none that could be proven in the light of day.

And the council meant no disloyalty to Gwenhumara when it yielded to Medraut's persuasion and allowed him power to hold the treaty line. All but Ulfius, Dubricius's former bard, voiced their "aye." And so it was decided. Menw was sent back to the lines with word that they would soon receive orders from Arthurius's captain, Medraut. Medraut ap Cheldric, but never did he style himself so.

Gwenhumara, feeling a virtual prisoner in her own caer, retired to her chambers with Elidor and Elayne, her most trusted ladies. After dark in the night-quiet of the caer, Elidor followed her lady's bidding and slipped like a shadow to summon Ulfius. He was nursing a broken arm from a horse kick or he would have been away with the war host.

"You would have me take word to Arthurius, my lady?"

"No. I will not have Arthurius disturbed before he has finished with Hueil. One enemy at a time is enough and more. If the army is divided now, we could well lose on both fronts and be caught in the middle like an apple in the cider press."

Ulfius nodded his agreement.

"Does your arm permit you to ride, Ulfius?"

"I can ride, my lady. I was excluded from battle duty because my sword arm is broken, but my horse will know no difference from reins held in my left hand."

"Sa, sa. I would have you ride to the border guards with my signet and bid them to obey no orders given without the express seal of Arthurius. For a time it will be enough if they post double pickets against Cheldric. All scouts are to report directly to me."

But at second thought of Medraut's control over Menw, she amended that. "No, have them report to the Lady of the Lake at the holy house of St. Bridget. Even Medraut will not attempt to prevent the queen from attending prayers with the holy abbess, and I may freely receive messages there."

Ulfius agreed.

"Go now then, and the prayers of all Britain speed your way. I fear our times are doubly perilous." She snuffed her candle before Ulfius departed so that no spy of Medraut's might see a light in the queen's chamber.

Although no longer his land, since his gifting of it to the brothers at Ynis Witrin, Arthurius had named Brent Knoll on the southeastern bank of the Sabrina as the hosting place. All to whom he had sent summons had answered, save Cador of Dumnonia. Arthurius had not expected the aging Cador himself, but had expected the battle-ready Constantine to arrive with a full contingent of warriors. It was not likely that Medraut would fail to get through or that the Dumnonian realm would fail to respond, prime target that it was for raiders. It was possible, however, that their warriors were engaged in their own battles with raiders along any side of Dumnonia's long, exposed coastline. Yet Arthurius's scouts on land and Gwalchmai's on sea had reported no skirmishes.

Raiders and pirates presented a new challenge for Arthurius. Always before he had commanded some choice of the battleground or time of attack. And always he had known he would meet an army. Five hundred and upward British swordsmen had answered his hosting call. But now he could not know until the marauders arrived whether they were to face three boat loads of adventurous pirates or twenty ships full of battle-ready warriors. He hoped for the battle of warriors. It was not befitting for the High King to send out hosting calls to stamp out sparks among the whin bushes.

Long Arthurius and his captains sat around the battle map drawing contingent plans according to the raiders' most likely points of attack. In the flickering light of the torches with the horses stamping in the garth below and the gentle flickering of campfires, it was as if they were young men again and the world was new and all the years since Mount Badonicus had not happened. Then Arthurius drew yet another plan.

"Gwalchmai and his ships will lie hidden in his harbor until we receive word that the ships of Hueil are in the Sabrina. Then Gwalchmai will close in behind, so." A black line closed the mouth of the water. "They will drive the raiders landward, so." A black X marked the shoreline. "And when they are well ashore, we will attack while Gwalchmai fires their ships."

While the search for the best battle plan went on by day, Arthurius's soul-searching that had been begun many seasons ago by the sharp-tongued Gildas and the strong-visioned Columba, continued within the king at quiet moments. Galaad and the others sought God on their quest, but Arthurius could search only in his soul. And now, missing Merlinus Dubricius more than ever, without a priest to guide him, he searched alone.

Lying rolled in a bearskin rug by a low-burning campfire, awaiting the enemy's arrival, Arthurius groped in the dark. *Where are You, Great One?* his soul cried. Where was the beauty, the joy, the sense of right he had formerly known? Where was the benediction and awareness of God's presence he had once taken for granted?

I would have You help me. But no help came. Instead, his mind swirled with ugly visions of broken, bloody bodies; crying, fatherless children; charred, flame-devoured steadings . . . The weight of the horror descended on him, and he didn't know where to turn. His mind sought for comfort, but no comforting words came. He sought for a sense of peace, but none came. What did God want of him? Was God withdrawn that He no longer answered? Withdrawn from the king? Withdrawn from Britain?

Arthurius recalled his words of vision to the council when they made him Pendragon; he recalled his words to his Cambrogi at the time of the treaty-making; he recalled his words to the nation at his king-making. And more than his words, his sense of assured rightness—where was it gone?

Then long-ago words of Merlinus's came to him—came as clearly as if the Emrys stood before him. *The enemy's greatest weapon is fear. Always the dark brings fear. This is not the way of the Christos. Our Christ conquered fear when He conquered Satan.* The image faded and all was silent.

Again the pictures assaulted his mind—blood . . . crying . . . flames . . . But this time they could not penetrate. The peace came slowly as the dark receded with its swirling images, leaving Arthurius exhausted, but victorious.

Arthurius faced the worst the enemy had to fling at him. He had faced fear and emerged with faith. The light had flickered, the flame dimmed, but it still burned. The darkness was conquered. And now Arthurius would be stronger for the next assault—as it surely would come—would always come—but could always be beaten by those of faith.

At last he understood why the heavens had so long been silent. His vision had been given to him long ago at the beginning of it all—a vision and a promise. They were his beacon, his calling. No matter how much Gildas or any other accused or questioned him, he was to hold to his vision for all time and not be continually hounding God for a fresh sign as if He were a messenger boy.

This was Arthurius's faith. He was to cling to it and live by it as long as it was given to him to live.

It was yet another two days of waiting before the scouts spotted the long, low raiding ships gliding through the rough seas of the western shore. Arthurius had no more than received word when the late afternoon clouds boiled into a black mass and opened with a drenching rain. Arthurius, missing the prayers of Dubricius that had always before sped him into battle, sighed heavily. Rain that would barely slow the raiding party could quickly make the already-soft land thoroughly impassable for a cavalry. He could only hope that Gwalchmai could drive the raiders ashore before the entire battle had to be fought on foot. At least the whipping wind that made the rain so uncomfortable kept the mists from gathering. Otherwise the entire raiding party could land, pillage a steading, and depart under a cloud cover that would make all the High King's guards useless.

From his hidden position on a sea cliff, Arthurius strained his eyes until at last he could just make out the ships. With the rising and tossing of the water, it was impossible to count, but this appeared to be the full-scale battle contingent he had hoped for. Without the scout's warning, however, he would have thought them nothing more than logs tossed in the stormy sea. He hoped Gwalchmai had received the scout's report and could spot the enemy from his cove. Gwalchmai's men were good sailors, recruited from the native fishers whose people had lived along these shores from time out of mind, and the British ships were the best they could build, yet a battle on this stormy sea would be a severe test.

At last the waiting was over. Gwalchmai's ships appeared in a sturdy line, driving the raiders forward like hounds driving the prey in a hunting-run. The wind and the rain made the plan of firing the enemy ships with flaming arrows impossible, but the cold iron spears launched at the raiders whenever a British ship drew within range effectively drove them forward.

At last the storm that had so hampered Arthurius's plans turned to help him. Built lower than the British ships, the raiding vessels were easier to swamp, and a particularly heavy storm-tossed wave sent three vessels high in the air and brought them down again, spilling all aboard into the churning black waters. Gwalchmai followed this with a barrage of arrows that stilled many an oar in the rear ships, and the remaining vessels made for shore.

With the wind blowing fiercely inland, Arthurius could use trumpet signals without fear of being heard by the enemy, and so his men were readied. They would indeed have to abandon the cavalry charge onto the soggy beach, but an entire contingent of archers already lay hidden behind rocks near the shore with foot warriors ready to march behind them from every position.

Arthurius waited until all the enemy ships were well-beached and their men scrambling to cross the shore before he signaled the attack. If the sky had not already been dark with clouds, it now would have been dark with arrows. In spite of the archers' difficulty of aiming into the wind, many raiders fell, slowing the progress of those behind them.

And then all was a melee of sword-clash and spear-thrust as Arthurius threw his warriors into battle. He chose his own quarry, the captain of the nearest ship, marked as a son of Caw by the raven crest on his helm. Long had it been since Caliburnus had rung in battle, but the sharp blade did not fail its king now. With one slash Arthurius splintered the white battle shield and with a second knocked the sword from his opponent's hand and cut a red streak in his sword arm on the return. Caliburnus flew to the rebel's neck, and a single plunge would have ended the contest. But Arthurius stayed his hand. Something in his opponent's squinting eyes rang a chord within the king. "Falin!" he shouted to his armorbearer. "Take you my prisoner."

A sudden flare of light at the water's edge told Arthurius that Gwalchmai and his men had cut through the churning sea to board and fire the raiders' boats, soaking them with barrels of pitch loaded in their own holds for that very purpose. Arthurius cut his way deeper into the battle, his old skill and rhythm of thrust and slash unslowed by the passing of peaceful years. In the darkness of cloud and rain the light from the burning ships helped Arthurius find his prey. He had spotted him when the first ship put to shore. These were not merely Hueil's men. King Hueil of Strathcluta himself was leading the raid. Arthurius claimed him for his own.

Taller than most men, yet oddly stoop-shouldered for a warrior king, Hueil fought in the center of the fray, rainwater and blood turning the rocky beach into a slippery mess under his feet. But Hueil kept his feet as more than one British warrior fell under his sword.

In the end Hueil fell under the sword of Arthurius of Britain. With the collapse of their leader, the spirit went out of the raiders, and man after man went down to a triumphant British cry. "Burn their bodies in their ships," Arthurius ordered. "They'll raid our shores no more."

By the light of the burning ships Arthurius's men worked late into the night clearing the beach of bodies and burying their own men. Brothers were summoned from a holy house nearby to aid in nursing the wounded and saying prayers over the dead. As their house would surely have been one of the first to be raided of its meager possessions, they set about their tasks with industry born of gratitude.

Arthurius sat on the cliff above the beach, watching the ring of death fires flicker along the shoreline and reflect in the white-capped waves. The rain had long ceased, but the wind continued, blowing sparks from the burning ships heavenward to replace the cloud-covered stars. Falin, still carrying the Pendragon banner, dropped to one knee beside his king. "Your prisoner, Turach, son of Caw, had his wound bound by the holy brothers and waits under guard."

Arthurius nodded. "Are there other prisoners?"

Falin shook his head. "None, my lord." Arthurius knew what that meant. The wounded had been dispatched with quick sword thrusts as was always his order in the old days. It was the humane thing to do, but now the slaughter bothered him.

"And the other sons of Caw?"

"There has been no sure report, my lord, save of Hueil himself, as you know. But others among the dead wore raven-crested helms. It may be we have rid the earth of them all."

Arthurius nodded his acceptance of the report and dismissal of the reporter. He had done what he came to do. There would be an end to the raiding parties of Hueil of Strathcluta and the sons of Caw. The western shores would be at peace for a time.

But he felt no elation; rather, a strange foreboding. His men had proved battle-worthy and his own sword arm unweakened. But there was no pleasure in the victory. Pleasure in the peace that would follow, yes, but not in the war. Yet his unease was more than that. He had called forth five hundred and more warriors to overcome the enemies' two hundred and less. The victory had been easy and the victors' losses light. But the very ease bore its own seeds of trouble. How many chieftains would ride from here, how many captains return to report that their response to the High King's call had been unnecessary? How many men had left their crops at harvest time to answer what they would see as an unneeded call? How many would refuse another time should the call come at an inconvenient season such as seedtime or harvest?

Arthurius had never before left a field of victory with a heavy heart and sense of foreboding. He could think of only one place where he might find peace. Tomorrow, if all was well among his captains and his wounded so that he might depart, he would take his closest eques and make pilgrimage to Avalon.

It was not until the morning of the day following, however, after he had seen to ordering repairs to his damaged ships and the distribution of spoils among departing chieftains, that Arthurius, his four captains, their armorbearers, and their sole prisoner were able to make the fifteen-mile ride to Ynis Witrin. In spite of the heavy rains of the day before, it had been a dry Lugnasad. Falin, who knew the area from childhood, was able to guide them to the island on foot, although several times it was necessary to dismount and lead their horses through the soft places.

The weight of foreboding in Arthurius's breast had not lifted with the ride in spite of his captains' happy talk of the success of freeing the land from the raiders. If it had not been discourtesy to fail to greet the abbot first, Arthurius would have gone straight to the Old Church to seek solace for his soul. For the first time in the two years since their departure, he had thought to envy Galaad and the others who had set out to seek spiritual peace with Brother Columba.

Arthurius and the Cambrogi had made little way through the cider-smelling apple garth that lay between the island shore and the hermitage before they were approached by two familiar brown-robed figures. Brothers Indract and Gildas hurried forward to greet their guests. Indract smiled an open-armed welcome, and Gildas squinted against the afternoon sun.

"Ah, well come, well come, indeed. We are honored by your presence, our king. I trust you bring us reason to rejoice from your venture," Indract cried.

Arthurius, who was still leading Valere, handed his reins to Falin and stepped forward to answer. Before he could any more than return the abbot's greeting, a clutter of voices and footfall from up the path took his attention. Enormous joy took Arthurius's heart, such as he had feared not to feel again, when the leaves parted, and he saw that the first of the figures was his own Gwenhumara. "My lady, what joy is this?" He started forward, then stopped; the joy dimmed. Her smile of greeting was on her lips, but not in her eyes.

Then he looked beyond the queen and her ladies and recognized Baudwin, Bors, and The Ancelot. "And so you are returned, my eques?"

Abbot Indract spread his arms to encompass the company. "Sa, sa. You can see that we have had a day of great arrivals, although our lady queen has been here for many days at the house of St. Bridget. But come, come, you are weary. Let us not stand talking in the middle of the garth. Let us make way to my table for refreshment."

The entire company turned to follow the abbot, but one figure stood rooted where he was. Gildas, his stooped shoulders clad in his familiar goat-hair cloak and his frowning countenance fixed firmly on the prisoner led by Falin, growled, "Turach. Why has the High King brought Turach, son of Caw, here?"

Arthurius started to explain, but as he turned his gaze from the monk to the stoop-shouldered, squint-eyed warrior, Arthurius, who had long practiced powers of understanding men and situations, felt as one who has been led suddenly into a lighted room. "Is it possible—Turach, son of Caw, and Gildas the Wise . . ."

"Aye, aye," Gildas snarled at the king. "Caw had a fifth son. This hang-dog pirate is my brother. Had it not been for the accident of ship's spar falling on my head and my nursing by these holy brothers where I stayed on to study, I too should have followed such a life. I will see to his wounds."

He started toward the figure, who in spite of the rougher clothing and lack of tonsure was a mirror image of himself, but stopped when Turach addressed him in a harsh northern dialect the others did not understand. Arthurius caught little of their conversation besides the name Hueil. White-faced and shaking with anger, Gildas raised his hand and whirled toward Arthurius. "Is this the truth? He says you have slain Hueil by your own sword, Arthurius of Britain. He says you outnumbered them three to one and waited in ambush. He says you could easily have taken them prisoner or demanded surrender, but that you attacked from the blackness of a storm and the shelter of rocks. You killed Hueil our brother by your own hand. And the other sons of Caw may have fallen and their bodies burned as heathen. Is this truth?" The gravelly voice was shouting by the time he finished his tirade.

Arthurius inclined his head. "It is truth. Hueil and the raiding sons of Caw made treaty with Britain's enemies and made war on Britain. I have slain the enemy of our people and have brought peace to our land."

"Arthurius of Britain, you have slain the brothers of Gildas and have brought war between us. There can never be peace between me and the man who killed my brothers. Hueil died unshriven. His soul burns in Hell, as may the others, and it is on your head." Gildas whirled and stomped up the path.

Arthurius turned to Falin. "Take Turach his brother to him, but see you he remains under guard."

As shaken as if they had fought another skirmish, the Cambrogi followed the abbot to his hall. Arthurius and Gwenhumara followed slowly behind the others. "I see trouble in your eyes, my queen."

"My Artos, do not bid me speak; I would not lay more burdens on you now."

For the first time in days Arthurius smiled. "And think you my shoulders not broad enough or that I am unused to harsh tidings? Speak, for my mind will imagine far worse than you can tell if you do not."

And so she told him of Menw, of Medraut's seizing power from the council, of her dispatching Ulfius to warn the border guards, and of her seeking refuge on Avalon to await word.

"And have you received word yet?"

"None. Until today all has been as peaceful here as becomes a holy house. Except on the day after my arrival when the Abbess Nimue had to expel my former Lady Morgana. She had been leading some of the younger sisters astray in offering prayers and sacrifices to the old gods."

They walked on up the green-gold, apple-strewn path. Much needed to be said, but to Arthurius the peace of the moment was far more needful.

The brothers were serving the Cambrogi heather beer and barley cakes with cheese when Arthurius and Gwenhumara arrived to take their places at the head of the table.

Arthurius turned to his long-absent eques. "Baudwin, Bors, my friend, The Ancelot, it is sun and moon to my eyes to look on you again. You have been sorely missed. Did you find that which you sought?"

The Ancelot shook his gray beard. "We found much, but we found ourselves no closer to God than in doing His work anywhere else, I think. Except for Galaad, of course. But he always was the holiest of the lot of us. He will tell you himself, I'm thinking."

Arthurius's heavy eyebrows shot up in surprise. "He is returned also then? When I did not see him, I thought him still with Columba."

"Aye, he is returned. For a space. He is about his prayers now in the Old Church."

Time passed for the taking of no more than three bites of barley cake when Galaad entered the hall through the western door, the golden sunlight surrounding him like a nimbus, his face glowing as if he knew a truth too shining for words.

Arthurius rose and went to him. "Walk apart with us, Galaad. We would hear of your quest." He signaled Gwenhumara to join them.

In the quiet of the setting sun with the chant of the brothers' evening prayers following them, they made their way to the chapel atop the Tor. When at last they were seated on the single stone bench, Arthurius said, "Now, tell us, Galaad."

Galaad was quiet for a long time, as if gathering his thoughts. "I believe, my king, that the search for God is not an earthly quest although I learned much in following the saintly Columba. God is within us. I enter His presence by applying my spirit to Him, by reaching to Him in quiet confidence.

"I have learned that communion with God is held in the very depth of the soul, not in any distant land. In the center of the soul one speaks heart to heart to God in peace and joy."

"I think you have been greatly blessed in your quest, Galaad," the battle-weary king said. "And what will you now do?"

"With your leave, I will return to Brother Columba to tell others. We would found a monastery for a center of learning such as St. Patricius founded in Eire and as Brother Columba visited at Tintagel."

"Sa, sa. And have you chosen your place for this great work?"

Galaad shook his head. "We wait for God to direct."

Arthurius turned on the bench and looked out the stone archway toward Caer Cam, although in the evening mists the hillfort was invisible. Then as his gaze shortened, he saw a small dark coracle darting swiftly through the marsh. Was this Gwenhumara's messenger? He stood up with a sigh. Apparently their moment of quiet peace was over. He placed a broad, battle-scarred hand on Galaad's slim shoulder.

"We will wait for God to direct, my eques. We all wait. But some would choose to have the waiting be longer."

Gwenhumara, who had listened quietly the entire time, now spoke. "I think I know of a place for your monastery, Galaad, my brother—a place much in need of the peace of God—for it is on the very coast of Strathcluta long ruled by the warlike Caw and his sons. Yet as Caledonian land, it is in the gifting of the royal queens. Have you thought of the Isle of Ioua?"

At her very suggestion Galaad's face shone as if he had had another vision. "It would be perfect, my lady sister. You will give me a charter for Brother Columba? I can take it to him immediately?"

Gwenhumara laughed, and her tiny golden bells tinkled. "Perhaps it would be best to wait until morning, my zealous brother."

They made their way down the Tor with lightened step to face whatever news awaited them. Back in the abbot's hall Arthurius met not the newcomer he dreaded, but the sourly familiar figure of Gildas standing at the end of the long table with a stack of parchment sheets in front of him. Arthurius strode to the other side of the table and waited for the monk to speak.

"Hueil, my brother, lies dead by your hand. Turach, my brother, lies sick of the wound-fever by your hand. Carruth and Wemys, my brothers, lie we know not where, but lost by your rash doing, Arthurius High King. All unshriven. You must do penance before God to cleanse your soul of the foul deeds of your hand and the weight of their souls.

"But first I repent of the deeds of my hand. Before you is the history of this land of Britain written by my hand. Pages I have inscribed in praise of the deeds of the High King Arthurius. I repent of this praise. With my own hand I destroy the works of my hand." He grabbed the top sheets and ripped the heavy parchment into shreds; then he flung them into the central fire where they curled in the flame, crackled, turned black, and fell to ashes. Three times he repeated the act until all the pages were gone. "Arthurius of Britain, I have expunged your name and your deeds from the history of this land. May all that you have done sink into oblivion as your body will sink into the grave. May none live to sing the praises of the king who slew the brothers of Gildas."

With a final crackle of flaming parchment, he flung from the room.

12

The messenger Arthurius had glimpsed from the Tor had indeed been Ulfius, but his message was good news. He had sent Gwenhumara's command to all the border guards where it was received without question, but with some surprise at the urgency of its tone, for the borders were not threatened, and their scouts had reported no sign of recent movements by Cheldric. For the moment the kingdom knew its most complete peace for many seasons.

And all was peaceful when they reached Caer Cam. Medraut half-dipped a knee to his king and repeated what Ulfius had reported, that Cheldric was making no threatening moves. Nevertheless, by the inflections given certain words, Medraut conveyed that the victory was somehow due to his skillful handling of the situation.

No sooner died the feast fires and no sooner faded the last notes of the bards' songs of the victory of Mor Hafren—as Blaise preferred the old Celtic name for the Sabrina—than trouble came to Caer Cam from another source. Arthurius was seated in the high place in the Great Hall listening to the accounts of his councilors when a dark-haired woman strode into the chamber and knelt before the king in a manner that implied anything but humility. None in the room had seen her for many years, but in spite of the gray streaks in her raven hair, her brazen beauty was unmistakable. "Why have you come to us, Morgana?" Arthurius's eyes and voice were cold.

"I have come to prove my love and loyalty to you, Arthurius of Britain. Although I have been treated unfairly at your hand in the past, I have borne nothing but love for you in my heart. Now I will prove it."

"The Lady of the Lake told us you were sent from her for desecrating her holy house with blasphemous prayers to evil spirits. Why should we give you hearing in Caer Cam?"

A bright gleam snapped in Morgana's dark eyes, and spots of high color appeared on her cheeks. "There are powers the Lady Nimue knows nothing of, but I do not come here to speak of such, rather to report to the High King matters of all too human action."

The stiffness remained in Arthurius's voice. The very presence of this woman filled him with foreboding. It was as if a spirit of darkness emanated from her. Yet he would deny no one in his kingdom the right to speak. "We will hear you, Morgana."

At a slight wave of Morgana's hand a slim figure moved forward from the back of the room. Clad in the dark green tunic of a Caer Cam kitchen servant, a middle-aged woman with scarlet hair springing from the leather cords that would bind it back stood beside Morgana. "This is Tarna, my lord. A loyal servant of your household. She will swear to seeing with her own eyes what I tell you."

"Speak it out!" Never a patient man, Arthurius's irritation made all in the room start.

Her head high, her voice clear, Morgana spoke. "Much as it wounds me to tell you, my lord, I know no one else will tell you the truth. So I will speak. In your absence your queen, the Lady Gwenhumara, has been unfaithful to you with your kinsman Medraut."

The words were too stunning even to elicit a gasp. Absolute silence filled the hall. After the space of five heartbeats the king rose slowly to his full height and took three threatening strides toward Morgana. His voice was low and terrible. "You lie."

Morgana stood her ground. "If I alone knew of this great treason, it might be dealt with quietly without undermining your power in the kingdom. But I have here one who will swear to what she has seen with her own eyes. The corruption must not go untreated, or it will spread like wound-fever until the whole body is black."

"You and your lies are the only corruption here." But by the raising of his voice, Arthurius revealed that he was shaken.

"Will you hear Tarna, sir?"

"I will not. Not I alone. Send for the High Queen."

In a few minutes she came to him with swift, smooth steps, her shining lighting the shadows of the hall. Arthurius calmed inwardly. Such peace as the queen's could not be feigned. At a gesture from the king, Gwenhumara sat on the skin-piled seat next to his. "My queen, I would have you hear the charge these women bring."

Tarna's voice barely reached above a whisper, but in the breath-held stillness of the room every word was audible. "On the night of Medraut's return from Dumnonia, after the king and all had departed for the hosting by the Sabrina, I was bidden to take red wine and cold meats to the eques Medraut's private chamber."

"Who bade you do so?" the king asked.

"The queen bade me. To welcome home her lord's loyal Cambroga, she said. I heard voices as I approached—a man and a woman. But when I lifted the leather flap to enter his door, Medraut was alone in his chamber."

"So? What evidence is this?"

"I saw no one, my lord, but I saw a lady's slipper behind the wall draperies, and I heard the tinkle of the queen's bells."

Arthurius slammed the arm of his seat. "This is wild imaginings."

"But then I waited outside the door-flap. When they thought me gone, I clearly heard the queen's voice. And I heard their words."

"Go on. Spill all your lies that they may be denounced at once."

"I will not repeat the words of love." Her mouth drew into a prim line. "My maidenhood would not be so soiled. But I will speak of the words of treason to Britain." It was all Arthurius could do to remain seated. Under any other circumstances he would have flung himself at the accuser and silenced such lies with his hands around the speaker's neck. He gripped the arms of his seat. "They agreed that he should take control of the council. Then if the king were killed in battle, Medraut would hold the power that might otherwise go to Constantine. She wanted to remain here with him, but he said it was too dangerous and that she must go to Avalon so that they wouldn't be discovered." Tarna paused, then spoke hurriedly before her story could be interrupted. "I listened for other words, but heard only sighs and moans."

Gwenhumara's face was drained of all color, but her voice was level. "Medraut arrived at the time of the council meeting. Not the night before."

Tarna had her answer ready. "So you conspired to make it appear, my lady."

The queen turned to the king. "My lord, you will find no other servant in Caer Cam that will credit these lies, unless they are in the conspiracy also. My ladies will tell you I was never unaccompanied—and the council will tell you I opposed Medraut's seizing of the power."

"But that is what they would say, isn't it, my lord?" Morgana's voice was honey-sweet, as if she whispered in his ear.

Gwenhumara continued. "Tarna, I recall you from long ago. You were serving maid to Morgana when she was in my service." She turned to the other woman. "So have you now come with the aid of a servant who still bears you loyalty to take your revenge for my dismissing you, Morgana?"

"That is unfair, my lady. I long and long ago repented of any misdeeds of loves a girlish heart may have led me into. And I dwelt long at the house of St. Bridget, until the abbess grew jealous of my prayers which knew greater powers than hers. I ask no reward for what I do today. I speak for the good of Britain and her king whom you would undermine."

"The queen is not the only one accused here today." Arthurius's voice was still unnaturally loud. "Send for Medraut. We will hear what he has to say to this."

In a time so short as to suggest he was listening outside the hall, Medraut entered and knelt before the king in his most obsequious manner. "I have heard the charge, my lord. You know that what small power I held, I held for you and for Britain. I have already told you of that. And as to the other—if the queen has been unfaithful to you, my lord, I can only assure you it has not been with me—never would I touch the fair body of one who is as a sacred goddess to me." Then he added hastily, as if in afterthought, "And sure I am that none in the kingdom would commit so foul an act against your royalty. I heard reports of Ulfius visiting her chamber in the darkest hours of the night. But I would make no accusations." But as in all that Medraut did, his manner managed to convey the opposite of his words, and the evidence was less clear than if he had not spoken.

The Ancelot jumped forward and hotly defended his daughter's honor, calling witness after witness to swear to her purity. The first to speak was Caius, who amazed all his hearers when, in the midst of an angry denunciation of any who would sully the name of so pure a lady, his voice shook and broke in a sob. "I would as soon hear the Virgin Mother herself vilified as this pure lady slandered," he cried. "And my answer to any who would do either is the same." He drew a knife from his belt and flung himself at Tarna.

Only the quick work of Bors and The Ancelot halted the blade inches from the servant's throat. Soon the speeches continued. None of the Cambrogi would be satisfied until he had defended his queen and denounced her accusers.

In his heart Arthurius never wavered. He knew his queen; he knew Morgana and Medraut—although he could not see what Morgana hoped to gain by involving Medraut in her scheme for revenge. But the damage had been done. Arthurius was High King, sworn to uphold all the laws of Britain, laws made by his own decree. Justice demanded a full clearing of the queen's name, and justice must come not from the hand of the king who loved her better than he loved himself. It must come from an ecclesiastical court.

"Noble Ancelot." Arthurius's voice cut into the laird's challenge for witnesses to come forward. "I accept all you say to the queen's defense. She stands innocent in my eyes and in my heart. But I would have her so held by all people. Therefore I will have you ride to Caerleon and appeal to Archbishop Dyfed to convene a court of the church."

None in the room could have known what this decision cost Arthurius better than the queen herself. Perhaps from jealousy over the fact that he could never fill the place Dubricius had held, the new prince of the church had remained aloof from the court and from personal ties with the king. "I would have all see her innocence by having her declared so by an impartial court," Arthurius repeated, lest any misunderstand his motives.

"It is good, my lord." Gwenhumara paused and looked long at him that he might know that she understood. "And that the kingdom may be weakened by no further charges of treachery, I will bide at the house of St. Bridget while awaiting my trial."

Arthurius started to protest. Christ Mass could be the soonest possible for the ecclesiastical court to convene. And if the archbishop chose to spend the winter season in Menevia, then the waiting could last until Eastertide.

"I would have you with me. . ." *my dear one.* His eyes concluded what his tongue could not say in the crowded room.

"And I would be with you. But this will be best. My prayers will be with you, and my love will be with you. It must be enough for a space." She looked at him long, then turned to The Ancelot. "My lady Elidor will accompany me. We will be ready to depart in one hour, Father." Gwenhumara walked from the hall without looking back.

So the waiting began. The storm at the battle of the Sabrina proved to be a harbinger of early winter. As the kingdom had been blasted by enemies from without and by treacheries from within, the weather now blasted it with wind and snow piling ever deeper and choking the roads until they were impassable.

Even if Archbishop Dyfed had been minded to convene his court at Christ Mass, he could not have done so.

At Caer Cam hearth fires blazed, joints sizzled on roasting spits, and bards sang the old songs, but there was no joy. For with the going of the queen all joy had left the king, and all joy had left the people. As Medraut and Morgana remained at court awaiting the trial with heads held high and bold words on their lips, it seemed that the chill of doubt crept into more and more hearts. The High King had protected his kingdom and his people from the enemy without, but he could not protect them from the evil within. Only they could do that for themselves.

Finally, a quick thaw came on a warm wind suddenly in mid-February, the first relief in a long, unremittingly gray winter. As the snows melted and ran in rivulets down the sides of the hillfort to swell the marsh waters between Caer Cam and Ynis Witrin, Arthurius climbed to the guardhouse and looked across the water. Just being able to make out the dim shape of the Tor made him feel closer to Gwenhumara in her holy house on the far side of the stark white hill. While he was gazing, he spotted the small dark shape of a coracle making its way across the water. Hope leapt in Arthurius's chest. Had Gwenhumara changed her mind? He ran down the rampart and ordered the gate opened long before the boat had time to reach the hillfort.

But when it at last arrived, its passenger was not the queen, but the stooped, frowning figure of Brother Gildas.

"I had not thought to see you at Caer Cam after our last parting, brother." Arthurius tried to keep any note of unwelcome from his voice. He did not want to worsen his relations with the monk.

"Arthurius, my king, I have spent much time in prayer and in soul-searching this winter, and I have been led by the hand of God to write many epistles on the subject of the value of moderation, never my most likely topic. I saw that I must bring you the kiss of peace. I have come at the first thaw to do so." He clasped the king by the shoulders and kissed him on each cheek. "Peace be unto you."

"And peace to you," Arthurius replied in the words of the ritual, too surprised to examine his heart as to whether or not there was any peace there to offer.

"And I have brought the sacred elements with me if you would take holy communion at my hand in the sealing of our peace-making."

"Yes. And all my household." It had been long since they had gathered at the Round Table for any purpose, and longer still since any had been shriven. Arthurius realized now that they had entered the Lenten season when such duties should be seen to regularly in preparation for celebrating their Lord's passion in the coming Eastertide. Gildas set up his cell in a small chamber off the

Great Hall for all who would make confession, beginning with the High King himself.

It was late that evening before all had been shriven and the table prepared for the mass of the Eucharist. While all of the caer who chose to found a seat in the hall, Arthurius and his Cambrogi gathered at the Round Table: Caius and Baudwin, Gwalchmai and The Ancelot, always on his right and left, then Teliau, Doldavius, Olwin, Ulfius, and Blaise, then two of the younger eques, and finally Medraut completing the circle.

Gildas, with arms thrust forward, led in prayer and the familiar ritual. Arthurius partook of the bread and wine, and the cup was served to each around the table. He saw Gildas pause before he served Medraut, waiting in an attitude of holy submission at the far side of the circle. Arthurius started at the clarity of the words he heard in his head at the moment, *One of you shall betray me*. The ringing of the words was so strong that when the priest moved on, Arthurius looked across at Medraut, and their eyes held. The king said in a quiet, but clear voice, "What you do, do quickly."

The next day many were amazed at Medraut's disappearance from court. But Arthurius was not. From that time, through the gentling days of spring, Arthurius and his Cambrogi once again began the weary process of preparing for war. Although the treaty borders held and no scout reported enemy movement to the east, there was an uneasiness in the wind, and all knew they must prepare.

Now the roads were passable, but still Dyfed did not return to Caerleon. Arthurius wished with all his heart for an end to that matter and repented that he had asked for a judgment by the church. Why had he placed so much importance on upholding the law? Why didn't he just declare the queen innocent and banish Morgana? Medraut was gone now, so how could there be a trial without one of the key witnesses? But also Arthurius worried that Gwenhumara might think that he, in some small part of him, believed the charge and that she would find it hard to forgive him. He longed to send The Ancelot to Ynis Witrin to bring her from her cloister and declare all forgotten—even if such a declaring would not bring about the forgetting, he would declare it anyway.

On a day of warm spring sunshine Morgana and her flame-haired conspirator, who had been held under an unofficial house arrest all winter, went for a walk along the River Cam, slipped from the sight of their escort, and were gone. So with no one left to accuse the queen, she could return to court with no cloud of censure. The heart of Arthurius rejoiced. He would not send The Ancelot. He would go himself the next day.

But the next day brought its own evil. Word came, word which must have reached the traitors by other means days or perhaps weeks earlier, that Aelle the Treaty-keeper was dead. There was now no one in all the South Seax nor in all of the old Canti lands to hold honor with Arthurius of Britain.

Fast on that word arrived even more fearful news. Cheldric, with Medraut riding by his side, had arrived with Saxon war hosts on British soil—not along the treaty lines to the east as had always been expected, but from the south. The long black war boats had sailed under cover of night up the Vectis Water, and after only a single day's march—unimpeded save for the burning of a few steadings—they conquered Sorviodunum. Once one of Vortigern the Fox's favorite lairs, it was now the seat of the valiant Caius. If the scout's message was to be believed, there had been little resistance to the overpowering strength of those who marched under the red fox tails. Cheldric had proclaimed himself Dux Gewissi, the title Vortigern had inherited from his British wife before he put her away for the tempting Saxon Rowena.

Then a third scout, following fast on the heels of the second, reported that a small band of warriors led by Medraut himself had swept on five miles north of Sorviodunum and destroyed the holy house of Amesdunum. Ambrosius Aurelianus himself had consecrated this house of brothers, where a perpetual choir ever sang the praises of God. All voices of praise were silent there now.

That left Cheldric the revived Fox and Medraut the traitor in control of all the lands to the southeast and just over a two days' march from Caer Cam. Arthurius had yet issued no hosting call. Aware of the sour wine taste with which many had left the Sabrina last autumn, the High King had been loath to call the troops earlier than he must. He had hoped he could wait until after garth-seeding time when men would be less reluctant to leave.

And, truth to tell, his mind had been much occupied of late by matters closer to home. Now at least he was glad the queen was safe on Avalon. He would send her a message, but he would bid her stay there until she could come to Caer Cam in peace.

Now the most urgent hosting call ever issued by Arthurius of Britain went out to every chieftain and kinglet of the kingdom: Stand against the foe now, or Britain will live forever with a Saxon thrall-ring around its neck.

But Arthurius held little hope that even the fastest troops would reach Caer Cam in time. Cheldric would not long delay his march, and even if he did, Medraut would not be restrained from the triumph he saw within his grasp. Arthurius's rage flared at the thought of Medraut's betrayal. All his years of being one of the inner circle of Cambrogi had done nothing to teach him the way of right as Arthurius had hoped. Nothing could overcome the jealousy and ambition that ruled the great grandson of the Fox.

Always the dark strove to betray the light. Now the power of the dark was growing strong. The lights of Sorviodunum had been extinguished, and the lights of Amesdunum. Across the kingdom the lights were going out. Who would rekindle them if he and his handful of warriors failed? But with God's help, they would not fail. The dark had not conquered until Caliburnus was stilled. He had won many times against great odds. He would fight again.

13

he next morning all were wakened by the aurochs' horn. Every man in the caer and within reach of the horn call would be armed and readied for battle, every sword sharpened, and every horse armored. There was no hope of The Ancelot's warriors from Caledonia reaching them in time, so he must command men from the nearby steadings. And there was little hope of Gwalchmai's men arriving so soon from the ancient Brigante runs. But Baudwin's warriors from the Silurian lands they could hope for and those who remained alive from Sorviodunum, if any had escaped. The call had gone to Cador the day before. Constantine and his father's troops could well arrive within two days' time. They would still have only hundreds to fight Cheldric's thousands, but they would fight.

With the familiar acts of preparing for battle, hope and energy returned to Caer Cam. Each man, woman, and child bent to the task. Arthurius chose the long ridge known as Camel Hill just beyond Caer Cam as the high point from which he would direct his troops. The Cam, the winding stream below the hill, would serve as the battle line for his men to hold and to push beyond.

They were granted twice the time they might have had. It was four days before a scout rode into Caer Cam after dark and shouted to the guards to open the gate. He reported that Cheldric and the sea wolves advanced from the south. Medraut and a pack of his own traitor-kind approached from the east. All that they had expected—except for one piece of news. Cheldric had delayed for his marriage feast. His Saxon wife had died long ago, and the chief had never bothered with a new bride-making. But this bride was not of the Saxonkind. The woman who rode beside Cheldric of the Canti lands was not a pale-haired Saxon, but a raven-tressed Briton. Morgana, daughter of the traitorous Urien of Lothian, had joined her line with that of the Saxon. Now it was clear why Cheldric had taken a title, Dux Gewissi, that could be granted only by a British wife of royal blood. And it was also clear why Morgana had plotted to destroy Gwenhumara. Morgana would be High Queen in the Saxon kingdom to come.

Those of Caius's warriors who had escaped the sacking of Sorviodunum arrived, tattered and weary, but to much rejoicing, as every additional sword arm answered a great need. Then, to even greater cheers, an entire war host that nearly doubled their numbers arrived from Baudwin's lands to the west. But no more had the shouts of their welcome died away than a Cymri scout followed with dire report. The warriors of the rebels Maelgwyn and Eleden were a half-day's march behind.

Arthurius arranged his troops on Camel Hill—Baudwin facing to the west, his valorous warriors to oppose the enemy from beyond their own green hills; Caius with his weary but bold warriors facing southeast toward the oppressor of Sorviodunum; and Arthurius himself with his own handful of loyal Cambrogi including Gwalchmai, Bors, and The Ancelot, as well as those who had answered the call from nearby steadings, facing the approach of Medraut from the east. Arthurius rolled up his field map for what he felt within him would be the last time and bade his captains a good night. Although they were within five arrow-flights of Caer Cam, they would camp the night on Camel Hill, ready at the first light of dawn for the enemy approach.

As on any night before battle, Arthurius slept but lightly and was up and armored well before first light. He sent Falin to see to Valere and climbed to the top of Camel Hill. He felt a strong desire within himself to see the sunrise, as if it might be the last he would see. Arthurius sat with a chill predawn breeze ruffling the long tufts of spring grass around him and watched while the eastern sky reddened and the golden streaks heralding the rising sun itself broke beyond the edge of the world. He recalled the sunset he had watched on the Tor before setting out to prepare for the battle of Mount Badonicus. If this day ended in dark, would there be a sunrise to follow? Was the sunrise a sign of promise as God gave Noah the rainbow? Curious, he thought, that a long-ago sunset should have signaled the beginning of his reign, and he now felt within him the sunrise was a symbol of its end. It should be the other way around. Were all beginnings really endings and all endings really beginnings?

His reverie was interrupted by the arrival of a guard. "A coracle approaches from Ynis Witrin." He gave the sketch of a salute.

Arthurius nodded and stood with a slight smile. "Ah, that is good. We have much need of upholding in prayer this day, as the good Merlinus Dubricius was always wont to do in the old days. Bring the holy brother to me when he arrives."

The scout scurried off. With a last long look at the red-gold sky, Arthurius Pendragon turned to war.

The guard returned with a brown-robed monk, and Arthurius was surprised, but not displeased to recognize Brother Gildas bundled under his goatskin cloak. The king hurried forward to greet the monk, then stopped at the sight of another long-robed figure behind him. Only slightly muffled by the borrowed gray cloak of a sister of St. Bridget came a tinkle of tiny golden bells. With a flick of her hand the headpiece fell back, and Gwenhumara's golden hair was aureoled by the rising sun. "I bade you stay in safety." He had not meant the words to sound unwelcoming.

But the queen did not flinch. "I would not displease you, my lord, but perhaps my prayers can follow you more closely this day if my eyes can follow you as well."

He stepped forward and took both her hands in his. "My dearest heart, you are very sun and moon to my eyes. So shall I fight better for your presence and your prayers. So shall we all."

He would have said more. He would have spoken of their first meeting and of their coming together in Caerleon after the long separation before their marriage. He would have spoken of the joys and sorrows of their shared years and of the years he would share with her yet if there were time. He would have spoken of his great loneliness for her this past winter and his heart-rejoicing at seeing her now. But there was no time. So they stood on the hilltop in the morning sunlight with birdsong melodious around them. And he drew strength from her calm. And it was enough.

Then the press of duty was upon him, and he turned from her.

Long and long afterward the bards sang of that day, sang in company great and small, sang around hearth fires and in the chill of rain, sang in springtime gentleness and autumn melancholy. But always it was a song of lament, always a cry of anguish for the passing of the great ones of the land, always a mournful song for Arthurius and his Cambrogi.

Maelgwyn and Eleden were first to attack. With a great shout and full blaring of horns, Baudwin led his warriors into battle with a force that drove the enemy backward the length of a spear throw and another and another.

But then the enemy regrouped and pressed forward once more. Little by little they pressed again over the land they had abandoned. With a shout of his ancient war cry, "*Yr Widdfa!*" Baudwin countered. And a third time the land was soaked in blood beneath the ring of clashing sword.

But not for long could the sword-clash and battle cry from the western slopes of Camel Hill be distinguished from the clash of arms to the south as Caius threw his forces, hot for revenge, against those who had so recently ravaged their homeland.

And to the east Arthurius waited, but not long. For with a tramping of feet that shook the ground and a beating of sword on shield that jolted the air, Medraut led his warriors forward in open challenge. Arthurius answered challenge for challenge and sword thrust for sword thrust.

The bards, singing their songs of lament, chronicle the fall of the great ones that day. First was the faithful Gwalchmai ap Gwyar, who by his own sword arm stilled the seax of twoscore and upwards of the enemy before his own sword was stilled forever. Arthurius, seeing the fall of his captain, flung himself from the back of Valere and bore the bleeding Gwalchmai to a spot where his wounds could be tended by the brother from Avalon, but to no avail.

Back into the fray rode Arthurius, Caliburnus slashing and thrusting in double duty now, one thrust for Arthurius and one thrust for Gwalchmai. Then was Caliburnus called on for triple thrusting, as Bors was taken in the back of the neck by a Saxon axe. The true red blood flowed into the waters of the River Cam.

Well past the high time of the sun and on into its westering fought the forces of Britain. For every man that fell they carried ten of the enemy with them. Then Arthurius heard the ever-rousing, screeching din of Dineidyn and his soek pipe and knew that The Ancelot yet stood. All weariness left his sword arm, and all thought of defeat left his heart. He looked to the waving red and saffron plaid banners up the river from the flying of his own red dragons. Medraut's traitors and treaty-breakers were driven back and back again. But then the clamor of the pipes became a wail and a keening and a weeping, and Arthurius knew in his heart, although he could not see the sad sight, that his most noble and valiant friend, the beloved father of his queen, had fallen. And he knew that high on her overlooking hill, Gwenhumara mingled her tears with the sobs of the pipes.

Yet he fought on.

To the south of Camel Hill, Caius the untiring fought also. Time and time again he cut a path nearly to Cheldric archfoe, but never could he cross swords with him. All around, Caius's men fought bravely—bravely to the death. The wolves pressed closer and howled louder, their swords biting deeper and deeper into Caius's brave troops. The Saxon pressed forward. Caius, with his small band battling valiantly still, backed across the Cam Water, running red and foul, and the enemy closed over them.

And then the miracle happened. Constantine of Dumnonia, Pendragon-designate, thundered upon the Saxon with a hundred fresh troops, and two hundred, and three. With flashing of swords and horses' hooves Cheldric fell back.

With a great shout of triumph the weary band who had battled since early dawn's light saw the foe turn and flee before the strong sword arm of Constantine. They knew that Cheldric would not stop his flight, nor would Constantine still his sword until Cheldric had crawled to the ground in Sorviodunum or beyond.

But when they turned from their cheering for Constantine, the shouts died on their lips, for valiant Caius lay slain at the foot of the hill of the Camel. Hearts heavy and sword arms aching but unslowed, they went on to fight beside their High King, for yet the Pendragon banners flew over Cam Water. From the other side of the hill rode the word of victory—but a sad and lonely victory. Maelgwyn, traitor of Arfon, was slain, and Eleden, traitor of Gwynedd, mingled his blood in the same pool. And all their men were slain or fled. But of the noble Cymri who fought that day, one alone returned to report to Arthurius.

And yet he was the greatest of all—Baudwin of the strong right hand took his place now beside the High King. His coming cheered the Cambrogi who fought on, and Baudwin led them forward, pressing the foe back and back toward the east from which they had come.

But Medraut alone would not be pushed. He stood, astride his black steed by the side of the twisting River Cam. As the battle surged away from them, Arthurius on Valere rode to meet him. Blow for blow they clashed and thrust and slashed and parried, until at last Caliburnus struck Medraut's shield from him, and with the blow Medraut was unhorsed.

Arthurius flung himself from the back of Valere and fell upon Medraut, blow upon ringing blow. Arthurius thrust his buckler from him that he might use both hands on Caliburnus, for this foe must be defeated. Medraut, the dark-bringer, must not live out this day.

And Medraut did not live. A final, mighty sword thrust pierced Medraut Iscariot through the heart. Yet the bardsong knows no rejoicing. For with one last effort, while Arthurius pulled Caliburnus from the disloyal breast, Medraut raised his sword in both hands and brought it down with a great crashing blow on the side of Arthurius's head. The royal battle helm dented under the force and bit deep into the head that in happier days wore the golden crown of the realm. Arthurius staggered and fell. A great darkness and a heavy sleep came upon him.

Baudwin two times in that day had the sad triumph of being the only survivor of all his battle forces. Medraut's warriors lay slain with their leader, but also slain were the forces of Britain. Save only Baudwin who knelt by the scarcely breathing body of his king and with great effort and yet great gentleness pulled the crushed helm from the broken skull.

Gwenhumara and the holy Gildas, who had watched all with unflagging prayers from the top of Camel Hill, ran to Baudwin's aid and knelt by the side of the king.

"He breathes yet." Gwenhumara spoke. "We must get him to Avalon for nursing by the holy brothers."

"Aye. We will nurse him," said Gildas the Wise, "but it is in my mind that our prayers will have more avail."

Tenderly Gildas and Baudwin bore the body of their king to the far side of the hill where the waterways to Avalon washed its feet, and Gwenhumara walked at the royal side carrying Caliburnus. But when they reached the coracle, they saw that the prone body of the High King would not fit into so small a craft.

"In happier times these shores are fished by many a local boy," Baudwin said. "Surely we can find a hollowed log among the reeds."

Gwenhumara sat by the still body of her lord while Gildas and Baudwin searched the banks. She shivered in the cool of the rising evening damp, but she did not notice it, for her thoughts were all for her beloved. As Baudwin had forecast, a local fisherboy had hidden his log canoe among the rushes. Gwenhumara sat in one end of the log, for it was a mighty oak that had been well-hollowed, and there was room for two. Baudwin and Gildas lay Arthurius in the boat with his broken head in Gwenhumara's lap and, towing the canoe behind them, they set out in the coracle for the Isle of Avalon.

Mist rose across the marsh, and the setting sun turned all a gentle pink-tinged gray. Curlew and kestrel sang them on their way. When they reached the island, the sun had set, and no pink remained in the misted world; the Tor was shrouded from sight, and no more birdsong could be heard, but the chant of the monks at evening prayers bade them welcome.

Arthurius was laid on a pile of softest furs in the best of the guest huts with a flickering candle to keep vigil. Through the night the holy brothers sang prayers for the High King in the Old Church, and Baudwin and Gwenhumara sat by his side.

The night was long, and yet not long enough for Gwenhumara sitting by the side of her husband-king who was there and yet was not there. Through the open window of the cell the night bird's call and the scent of earliest apple blossoms kept company with the prayers of those who watched. Gwenhumara's heart-prayer and soul-cry would not be stilled. Again and again her longing approached the throne of Heaven. She called upon her God to grant this, her one last request. When at last through the small square opening the queen saw the Tor, gold-etched with the sun rising behind it, she knew her day had come.

Even so the end was not yet. For with the dawn the king opened his eyes as if from natural sleep and spoke in a voice weak, but clear, "Gwenhumara, my heart's light, bide you with me."

"I will, lord of my heart; always I will." She shifted closer to his cot and held his hand.

Then he turned his gaze from Gwenhumara to Caliburnus lying close beside him as it ever had since first it was given to him on that same misted island. "Baudwin, worthy one, Caliburnus of the cut steel has felled her last foe for Britain from my hand. Take her now and make return to the Lady of the Lake for the great prize with which she gifted me. And bid her pray for the soul of Arthurius."

"My lord . . ." Baudwin choked on his words.

"Na, na, my eques. By God's grace we have done what we set ourselves to do. And the doing was good. We have kept alive for a space the last glimmering flames of the old order. And it has been good. Perhaps on the other side of the dark that now closes over us, perhaps when men build a new order, the stories told of us will help them. And that will be good."

Baudwin protested, "But why must it be so? Why must the dark come?"

"We must go down into the dark just as the year does every twelve-month cycle at Samain. Every year the winter dark descends, but the spring lightness follows. So will it be for Britain. It grows cold; our wintertime approaches, but the spring of new birth will follow, and after that the bright glory of summer."

None in the room could make answer, for fullness of heart. Baudwin stood uneasily, clasping Caliburnus to his chest. Arthurius spoke with a ring of his old command in his voice, "Take the sword now, Baudwin, but tell no one when I am dead. Such knowledge would be a weapon for Cheldric. Say rather that I have gone away for healing, and that I will return when Britain has need of me."

Baudwin left the room, and a few minutes later his place at Arthurius's side was taken by Brother Gildas. "I will hear him confess if he will." The look that followed the words clearly suggested that Gwenhumara leave them alone.

"I will stay by his side."

In the end, it didn't matter, for although Arthurius still breathed, he had spoken his last. The priest leaned down and placed the tiniest crumb of the bread of Christ's body on the king's tongue. "Whoever eats this bread will live forever."

"Lord, have mercy," the queen responded in a whisper.

The priest followed with a single drop of the wine of Christ's blood. "Our crucified and risen Lord has redeemed us, alleluia."

"Christ, have mercy." The response was little more than a deep breath.

Gildas then pulled the stopper from a small vial of sweet-smelling oil and poured it over the king's head. "As Christ was anointed Priest, Prophet, and King, so may you live always as a member of His body, sharing the life everlasting in this world and the next. In the name of the Father, and of the Son, and of the Holy Ghost, may the Lord who has freed you from sin bring you safely to His kingdom in Heaven. Glory to Him forever and ever." The priest departed before the queen's response.

"Into Your hands, Lord, I commend my spirit."

When Baudwin returned, Arthurius breathed no more. But as the eques turned to comfort the queen, he saw that she too had breathed her last. The smallest of gentle smiles was still on her lips that her prayer had been granted. "Bide with me," Arthurius had said. Faithful ever, she meant her "I will."

So the great hollowed oak that had borne Arthurius and Gwenhumara to Avalon became their coffin, like the ancient royalty of the Celtic people who at their death had been put in ships to sail to the land of Avallach.

But even in death the royal pair was not without controversy. The ever-frowning Gildas held up his hand when the body of Gwenhumara would be placed beside that of her king. "It will not do. She was accused of adultery. One so branded cannot be buried in holy ground."

Abbot Indract stepped forward. "Accused she was, but never proved."

Gildas held his position. "Sa, sa. But we cannot take such a risk. If we bury her unworthily, we will dishonor all who lie in this hallowed soil. And the shame will be on our heads."

"So let it be on my head." Indract was firm. "I will not bear the shame of having the queen torn from the king's side in death. Let God who knows all hearts judge."

Gildas gave a curt nod that was more a jerk. "So. Let her share the coffin. But let her lie at his feet, as a dishonored wife."

Indract dipped his head in assent. "So be it. And if we are wrong, God forgive us." He crossed himself that his words might have the force of prayer.

"The grave must be deep and deep. It must not be discovered by the enemies of the Britain that Arthurius lived ever to protect." Baudwin directed Brothers Logor and Breden who were turning the sod beside the old church with sharp spades.

At a depth of five feet they stopped. But Baudwin would not declare it deep enough and took the spade from a weary Logor to dig on. It was late that evening when Baudwin and Wencreth, who had taken the spade from Brother Breden, had doubled the depth of the grave and Baudwin declared it was well. The oaken coffin had been sealed and lowered with ropes and most of the shovelfuls of earth returned to their resting when Brother Benegius joined the small circle, followed by two serving boys bearing a large flat stone on which he had labored all day. The stone bore a leaden cross inscribed painstakingly by the monk's own hand, "HIC JACET SEPULTUS INCLYTUS REX ARTHURIUS IN INSULA AVALONIA."

"Here lies buried the renowned King Arthurius in the Isle of Avalonia," Indract read by the light of the wavering taper in the fading day. "It is well, my brother . . ."

"No." Baudwin spoke sharply, then recalled himself. "Forgive me, holy Father, but the High King's orders were clear. His grave is to be unmarked."

"So it shall be." Indract nodded. "We will bury the memorial stone with him." So the stone, leaden cross facing the buried coffin, was placed in the grave and all covered with the fresh brown earth.

With the last shovelful Indract raised his hands over the grave. "If we believe that our Lord Jesus Christ died and rose again, God will bring forth with Him from the dead those also who have fallen asleep believing in Him at the last day, at the sound of the trumpet, when all shall rise."

And the brothers responded, "I will praise You, Lord, for You have rescued me. I will praise You, for You have turned my sorrow into joy."

"Glory be to the Father, and to the Son, and to the Holy Ghost, as it was in the beginning, is now, and ever shall be, world without end, amen."

As the monks turned to go, Brother Breden, youngest of their number and yet not so young anymore, said, "We are so few. Are we all that is left of Logres? Does the flame flicker so dimly?"

Gildas stopped still and, for once unfrowning, turned to his brothers. "I would speak to you in comfort the words of our long gone-away Archbishop Merlinus Ambrosius Dubricius who said, 'The light was before the dark, righteousness before evil, grace before sin. God the Creator existed before Satan the destroyer. So will light outlive dark, so is righteousness stronger than evil, so will grace overcome sin.' The darkness closes over us, my brothers, but the light will shine again. And this light—the shining of Logres—will be remembered on the other side of the dark."

The brothers made their silent, brown-shadowed way up the path to the chanting of their nighttime prayers in the Old Church, leaving Baudwin alone by the grave of Arthurius High King and Gwenhumara High Queen. He sat on the evening dew-damp grass and brought from the soft golden doeskin bag on his shoulder the harp he had carried with him from Camel Hill. A night thrush sang from the overhanging branch of a flowering apple tree, and he waited until her song was finished, for the bard would not stifle his sister. Then his fingers moved across the strings. "The Summer Kingdom has gone. It could not last upon this earth. It was but a vision, a foretaste of what is to come for those who love—for those who love Him who is the King above all High Kings. His Kingdom of Summer, of peace, and of love will come for all time."

The words came out in a strange chanting to a random plucking of strings, not at all the flowing bardsong Baudwin was wont to make. Yet the words rang with conviction. They were the words he found in his heart, and he knew they were true.

"But even so the end is not yet. The evil will not triumph forever. All that you did, my Arthurius, all that you lived for, my king, will rise again. It will live for generation unto generation. It will come again and again to each age with its own truth. Truth, like light, cannot die.

"It is given unto man—even such a man as you, my Arthurius—for you were but a man—once to die. In the end, all must die. But what you lived for, lives beyond and beyond.

"The triumph will be ours."

BOOK IV

The Raising of the Stone

ANGLO-SAXON ENGLAND

Just as the flame of faith flickered low after the time of Joseph of Arimathea, so it faltered after the passing of Arthur. Now came the time of shadows, the time we call the Dark Ages. The heathen English marched over the land, swallowing up whole kingdoms and establishing their often-weak kings who could not hold off northern raiders. It was, in truth, a time for men who loved darkness rather than light because their deeds were evil.

But even then Christianity was still a flame of light and hope in this land, though often only a weak flicker. Perhaps an old story tells it best.

Late on a dark night, a holy brother spoke the Word of Life to the king and his nobles, to their unlighted hearts. As he spoke, a sparrow, tiny and brown, which had flown in through a window, darted out of the gloom and into the firelight. For a fleeting second everyone saw it—radiant with golden reflection. Then it vanished into the shadows. "Brother John, I see," cried one of the nobles. "If the Christian truth you proclaim can shed just such a beam of light on the darkness from which we have come and the even greater darkness into which we go after life, I accept it." Truly, Arthur had held onto the light long enough for the tinder of its rekindling to dry. There would not be long to wait.

But what of Glastonbury and the light planted by Joseph of Arimathea? What, my perpetual question rises, of the grail? Was it lost forever in these murky times? Perhaps carried off by a viking raider? Or did it remain still in a place of safety, waiting to shed its light on the land? Why did Arthur's knights fail to find the holy object? Or did they fail? Perhaps the quest of the grail should be seen as a search for union with God—not to be completely fulfilled in this life. Is that why the knights failed—because they relied on their own strength rather than on God's?

Oh, my God, Holiest of Holy, that it might be given to this, Thy humblest of servants, to understand this great mystery. Aid my faltering jour-

ney. Help me to know what I should seek. I seek salvation—I seek to know and to do Thy will—I seek Thy guidance—I seek Heaven. Will I never find fulfillment until I am at home with Thee?

PART ONE

1

Smoke curled from the three hearths down the center of King Aethelberht's mead hall and rose to the smudge-darkened rooftrees, obscuring the great branched antlers that hung over the high place. The bright, rich colors of the shields and war trophies that hung along the walls glowed in the flickering light of pine-knot torches. The king, sitting halfway up the hall on a massive carved and painted chair covered with a black bearskin, signaled for Queen Berthe and her ladies to refill the mead horns.

Berthe, her thick, hip-length braids as full and luxurious as when her father gave her to King Aethelberht thirty years ago, although now glimmering more silver than gold in the firelight, smiled at her lord and instantly did his bidding. All her ladies followed her example. The carles and thanes of Aethelbert's court held out their empty horns, and the thick pottery mead jars the women carried quickly emptied of their pale amber liquid.

After serving the king, Berthe moved in her regal, yet unobtrusive way to fill the cup of Gyrth the scop. Unlike the others who drank from horns which must be held until empty, the king's glee-man used a beaker with a flat bottom, in order to free both hands for his silver-stringed harp. He took a quick drink that fitted perfectly into the timing of the broken line of his tale:

Then out from the moor / and the mist-laden slopes
Grendel came gliding, / great anger he bare.
The worker of ill / thought within the high hall
to take one in his toils / of the race of mannes-kind.

As the light glimmered on the fine silk and gold embroidery of her amber kirtle and on the royal gold work around her forehead, Berthe moved down the hall from the king's highest house carles to the lesser thanes, and on to those at the end of the trestle tables. Her mind easily followed the familiar words of Gyrth's song as he chanted, striking a chord on each accented syllable of the poem:

Waded he under the welkin / till he the wine-house,
the gold-hall of men / might get well in sight.

Far from the first / of his frenzied assaults
was Grendel's attack / on Hrothgar's fair hall.

At the end of the hall, where a small slave boy still turned what remained of an ox carcass over the hearth and a huddle of hounds slavered over their bones, Berthe stood quietly, head erect, awaiting the king's signal. When it came, she returned the gesture with a smile and led her ladies to the women's bower behind the embroidered hangings at the far end of the hall. Behind them the scop's silvery notes glided on. Soon the great wooden trenchers before the feasters would be emptied of their joints of ox and boar meat, the last of the juices sopped up with crusts of barley loaves and flung to the hounds waiting on the rush-strewn floor. Later yet, the trestle tables would be stacked against the wall to make room for those who, in the style of Hrothgar's warriors of an older time, would sleep on wolfskin rugs on the benches or on straw-filled bolsters on the floor. The mead-drinking and scop-singing would continue many hours yet. But Berthe and her women had higher duties to attend to.

Wrapped in warm woolen cloaks with hoods pulled well over their heads to keep off the fine rain and their skirts held above the damp fringe of the grass, Berthe and her twelve waiting ladies left the warmth and light of the hall. They hurried past the various barns, byres, and workshops of the royal enclosure and out the gate of the old Roman wall with a small wave to the guards.

In spite of the moonless sky, the women needed no torches to light their way on the familiar path that led across an open barley garth and up a pine-covered hill. Indeed, Queen Berthe gave no thought at all to finding the way as she chatted with the two women closest to her. She could have done it with her eyes closed or in a thick fog. For she had made this journey three times a day, every day of her life, for the past thirty years—save for the three times she had remained in her bower after childbirth. Even when the rains fell for days on end and turned the yellow dust of the path into porridge-like mud that splashed up to her knees and made her long for the sun-blessed land of her birth, she never failed in her commitment.

Three of her ladies—Beadohild, Maethild, and Hygd—had made the journey with her with the same unflagging faithfulness. For these three, now bowed with age, had come with Berthe from the kingdom of the Franks. At the age of twelve, she had been given in marriage to King Aethelberht of the Canti according to the treaty agreed to by her father, King Charibert of Paris, and her mother who had lived retired in a nunnery near Tours in order to bring up the Princess Berthe as a Christian. So the young girl had come to the royal tun of Cantwaraburg to be queen of the ancient Canti lands in the country men were now calling Angleland or England.

No one but Maethild, the closest of her serving women, had known how frightened the young Frankish girl was when she sailed along those great white chalk cliffs and took port in this wet, green land to become the wife of a fierce-looking barbarian. But Berthe had ever held her head up and her small shoulders erect. Her steady blue gaze never wavered, even when it first fell on the giant Saxon with his long yellow hair and beard and piercing eyes. And when his harsh features broke in a great smile revealing white teeth under his flowing moustache, her smile quickly leaped to meet his.

She had ever been a good wife, attending to the smooth running of the hall—the weaving, brewing, and ordering of the ladies' bower as well as the cutting and adorning of the king's tunics and cloaks. And most important, she had provided Aethelberht with three healthy heirs—Eadbald, Ethelberga, and Edwin.

Aethelberht, too, had kept his part of the bargain. He was ever kind to her, kept the ladies' bower well supplied with gold thread, embroidery silks, and all they requested, and, whenever his eyes strayed, did not embarrass her by flaunting his leman in the hearth-hall.

But most important, King Aethelberht had never interfered with Queen Berthe's Christian faith. Her priest, Father Luithard, was housed and fed as well as any royal thane, and she was allowed unhindered use of the ruined Roman chapel atop the hill. At her request Father Luithard had done what he could to restore the tumbled Roman tile walls with salmon-colored plaster formed out of pounded brick dust mixed with mortar. Then he consecrated the building to St. Martin of Tours, the greatest of the Gallo-Roman saints, to whom Berthe's great-grandfather Clovis had given thanks after his victory over the Visigoths. King Aethelberht had never taken part in worship of his wife's "White Christiani God," no matter how she might entreat him on special days such as Christmas and Easter. But he saw no harm in keeping the ladies' bower happy by such innocent practices, and he coldly overlooked the smirks they at first evoked from his house carles and thanes.

"And have you and your ladies worshiped thus for so many years, my lady?" Frytha, the youngest of Berthe's serving-maids was out of breath from the rapid climb up the steep hill.

"Without fail, Frytha. It is my greatest burden and my greatest joy to pray without ceasing for the conversion of England and its people."

The women entered the whitewashed stone chapel and pulled their hoods back, spraying silver drops of water around the room. Father Luithard, who was kneeling on the stone floor at the altar, rose stiffly. In the wavering candlelight he gave his queen the sign of peace. "The grace and peace of God our Father and the Lord Jesus Christ be with you."

"Blessed be God, the Father of our Lord Jesus Christ," the ladies replied, crossing themselves.

The priest then placed a small bowl of water on the altar and held his hands over it. "May this water ever remind us of our baptism and of those for whose baptism we unceasingly pray. We ask God our Heavenly Father and Jesus Christ His Son to bless this water and to keep us faithful to the Spirit He has given us that we might not falter in the high calling, through Christ our Lord."

All in the little room made golden by candlelight said, "Amen."

The priest sprinkled himself with a few drops of the holy water. Then he lightly showered the queen's bowed head, a few shining drops clinging to the golden circlet of her crown. Then he sprinkled the other women.

Next the Eucharistic elements were elevated and placed on the altar, and again Father Luithard spread forth his hands. "We come to You, Father Almighty, with praise and thanksgiving through Jesus Christ Your Son, and ask You to accept and bless these gifts we offer. We offer them for Your holy Catholic Church, asking You to watch over it and guide it in these perilous times, as You have for almost six hundred years. We offer our prayers and these gifts for our Holy Father, Pope Gregory.

"Remember, Lord, Your people, especially, as we pray for our King Aethelberht, that he might have his mind enlightened to receive Your holy faith and so lead his people into Christian baptism and to become followers of Your holy way."

Berthe's lips moved as she followed the priest's prayer. "Through Him, with Him, in Him, in the unity of the Holy Spirit, all glory and honor is Yours, Almighty Father, forever and ever. Amen." She crossed herself and raised a shining face to receive the grace of Christ through His body and blood.

The beautiful service never failed to delight her heart, but on her way back down the path, with silver stars twinkling through the black branches of the pine trees—for the rain had ceased and the sky cleared while they were in the church—Berthe found herself beset with unaccustomed doubts.

Perhaps it had been the note of incredulity in Frytha's question earlier—the implication that praying for something for thirty years and continuing to pray for, who could say, perhaps another thirty years was unthinkable. Thirty years was indeed a long, long time. Almost her whole life. Practically the only thing she could now remember of her girlhood home in the kingdom of Francia, which stretched from the English Channel to Italy and from the western Gothic Kingdom of Hispania on the south to the Slavic lands on the north, was the brightness of the sunshine, the intensity of the sky—a shade of blue she had not seen in thirty years except in memory—and the brilliance of the flowers. Lovely, jewel-like memories, but she would not exchange them for the gentle, moist hues of this island that had become her home, had become the land for whose salvation her soul cried out daily, if not hourly.

She could no longer remember her father's face. At times it seemed as if she saw him in her dreams, but when she awoke, she would realize that it was not the face of the King of Paris but the chiseled features and flowing yellow hair of King Aethelberht. Sometimes stern and off-handed, her husband had been ever kind and good-humored to her for these many years. But he had never once shown the slightest softening toward her God.

Could she keep on asking God? Was it right to so besiege the throne of Heaven, to so importune the Blessed Virgin and all the saints? Was this a test of her own faith and determination? She was ever faithful to keep the fast days of the church—should she do more? Could she do penance for the king's sins? For all of England's?

Without so much as bidding her ladies a peaceful night, Berthe removed her golden jewelry and richly embroidered kirtle and lay folded in the soft furs of her cushioned sleeping bench. She had found no answers for the questions that flooded her mind, but her heart needed no answers to follow its own course. As it had since the day of her marriage, her heart cried out: *Move Aethelberht to accept Your holy faith. Let England become a Christian land.*

Much later word reached Cantwaraburg that in King Raedwald's East Anglian kingdom to the northeast, raiders from the far north-over-sea had struck at Saxon steadings and carried Anglish herd boys off into slavery.

2

elfric stood in the Roman slave market, the sun beating on his head. Dust from the dirt-filled spaces in the broken tiles of the forum clogged his eyes. The stench of animal droppings and unwashed, unhealthy bodies in the crowds of strange, idle people, who eyed him suspiciously, clogged his nose. A cacophony of cackling chickens, bleating goats, and babbling voices murmuring, arguing, and shouting in strange languages clogged his ears. Aelfric and Wulfnoth, who had been kidnapped from the sheepfold of an English steading on a horror-filled night many weeks ago, stood at the end of a long row of ragged slaves. Almost equally ragged bidders haggled over the row for hours.

The only word Aelfric had heard in his native English tongue all morning was from Tullus, the trader who knew enough languages to dicker with all who came to Rome—whether slave or free. "Stand straight!" "Show your teeth!" "Hold out your hands!" he would shout at his wares whenever a prospective buyer strolled by. This was the third day of such indignities, but Aelfric was coming to understand that he must cooperate if he hoped to be purchased in Rome rather than being jammed into yet another slave galley and sent to the markets of Constantinople. Although that might be the better fate, assuming he escaped dying of fever on the voyage. His eyes had filled in for him the story that Tullus's limited vocabulary had conveyed only in broad outlines: Rome was a city long abandoned by the emperor, its former glory faded and crumbled like the broken tiles, pillars, and statues of the forum around him; its near-starving population was overtaxed, disease-ridden, and living in constant fear of attack from their enemies. The barbarian Lombards already possessed most of Italy, both north and south of Rome. The Eternal City had become a huddle of hills covered with scraggly vineyards, massive ruins, and tiny, miserable human dwellings interspersed with larger but no more wealthy churches and monasteries—all looking down on their muddy, stinking river.

The only hope for the city and its inhabitants lay in the newly proclaimed Pope Gregory Anicius. Member of a noble Roman family, he had turned down high political office to live the life of a monk, but could not refuse the unanimous acclamation of the people that he be their Sanctissime Pater, Holy Father.

Aelfric shook his head. Whatever a Pope was—something like a king, he supposed—it looked like an impossible task. No wonder the slave trade was so slow—starving men could not afford slaves. And it seemed unlikely that anyone would choose a nineteen-year-old slave who did not know the Roman tongue, when so many mature native peasants born to the local language, soil, and customs flocked to the market to sell themselves as slaves. Tullus had explained the competition to his wares the night before. Thinking it better to live in slavery for a time than starve on their own soil, farmers from territories taken over by the Lombards offered themselves for sale, leaving their purchase price in trust in a monastery to guarantee that they could buy back their freedom when happier times came.

"Back straight!" "Eyes open!" Tullus's sharp prod announced the approach of a possible buyer.

Aelfric jerked to attention with a surge of hope that this ordeal might at last be ending. Even slaving for a harsh master seemed preferable to endless hours standing chained to this spot. Then he looked at the figures before him, and his heart sank. Not a farmer, miller, or merchant—but two emaciated-looking, black-robed monks. Why had Tullus bothered to prod him up for them?

The older man with the thin, aesthetic-looking face surveyed Aelfric and Wulfnoth. Aelfric returned his look levelly, noting the well-trimmed pale brown beard and the tanned skin of his tonsure, indicating that he must spend a lot of time outdoors in this blazing Roman sun, although he leaned heavily on his walking stick.

The monk said something to Tullus, and Aelfric heard Tullus reply, "Angli."

The older monk's reply brought laughter from Tullus and the younger monk as if he had told a joke. Aelfric frowned. He could not imagine anything about this circumstance that could be a laughing matter.

Tullus stood respectfully aside, more deferentially than Aelfric had ever seen him behave before, while the monks conferred. Then he stepped over to Aelfric and Wulfnoth. "Look as intelligent as you can, you worthless curs. Ye have the honor to be observed by His Holiness, Pope Gregory."

"It seems he found us amusing."

"Ah, the Domine asked the race of such tall, fair-haired, blue-eyed men. I told him you were Angles.

"'Surely, you do not mean Angles, but angels,' he said." Tullus clearly showed that his amusement had been a sign of respect for the eminent man, not agreement with the sentiment. "He asked whether ye be heathen or Christian. I told him as heathen as any I'd met—worse than those barbarian Lombards with their Arian heresy."

Aelfric looked surprised, and Tullus gave him a sharp slap on the arm. "Ha, didn't think I heard ye prayin' to that savage Woden of yers, did ye? Try that again in my Christian slave shed, and ye'll feel the rod on yer backs even if it does reduce yer value a few shekels."

The monks moved on, and dreary hopelessness returned to the slave market. Long blue shadows striped the once-white marble of the forum, and the reek of boiled onions and cabbages from evening cookpots filled the air. Tullus unlocked their chains for them to return to the slave shed when Wulfnoth elbowed Aelfric and pointed to a black-robed figure rapidly approaching. It was the monk.

Aelfric could not follow his conversation with Tullus, but there was no mistaking the meaning of the clinking of brass coins into the slave trader's outstretched hand.

"I can't imagine what the Holy Father wants with the likes of you, but I'll not quarrel with his brass." Tullus clinked the coins in his hand. "Brother Damien here is to be takin' ye to St. Andrew's monastery—which the Sanctissime Pater established in his ancestral villa." Tullus waved an arm in the general direction of the Caelian Hill. "It seems Prior Augustine there is to have the task of makin' ye heathen into Christians and teachin' ye civilized Latin." Tullus threw back his head with a bellow of laughter. "And good luck to him, I says!" With a twist of Tullus's rusty key, the chains fell from their wrists and landed with a clunk on the marble-tiled court. "And see that ye behave yerselves. I'll not have ye be givin' my future wares a bad name now."

"Peace, brothers." Aelfric did not understand Brother Damien's Latin greeting, but there was no mistaking the serene look on his face.

The five years at St. Andrew's Monastery were the most peaceful of Aelfric's life. Turbulence raged outside the walls of Rome and sometimes knocked even at the walls of St. Andrew's as Lombard armies threatened and plague and famine raged. But inside the monastery, run on strict Benedictine rules by Prior Augustine's firm hand, there was ever something to eat, if only a small wheat roll and cup of chicken broth. The days ran in orderly precision from Matins to Compline with the offices of the day punctuating the schedule of work and study.

Aelfric and Wulfnoth were much occupied with learning their new language. Aelfric took quickly to speaking Latin, but found writing much harder, since he had never before written in any language. Wulfnoth rebelled at having a foreign tongue thrust upon him and spoke it unwillingly, never making a serious attempt at the written language. For Wulfnoth it was enough to be back with animals, tending the monastery's tiny flock of scrawny sheep and goats whose cheese and milk was doled out daily to the poor who thronged St. Andrew's gates. Aelfric, on the other hand, found Roman sheep no more appealing than English sheep and quickly decided that goats were quite as stupid as his father's swine. But the monastery barns boasted one prize that made all the difference—Leander, the sole survivor of the once-superb stable of chariot horses maintained by the Anicius family. Every morning after Prime, Aelfric walked as quickly to the barn as Father Augustine's narrowed eye would approve—once he had broken into a run and been severely reprimanded—to brush the stallion's rich bay coat and take him whatever fresh feed could be found.

But supreme of all to Aelfric, who tolerated the language study and sheep herding, an even greater thrill than caring for a fine-blooded horse, was learning of the Christian God. Although he had prayed to Woden since childhood and gave respectful lip-service to the other gods, they were never an important part of his life. But learning of the Christos who had lived on earth as a man and now ruled in Heaven with the Father and Spirit while at the same time living in His believer's hearts, Aelfric discovered what he had been seeking all his life without knowing it. The peace this new God brought to his heart gave him more freedom than had the manumission papers Pope Gregory gave him after his release from the slave market. He readily accepted Christian baptism when Father Augustine suggested it, and Wulfnoth shrugged his shoulders and followed suit.

The brothers' initial veiled hints that Aelfric should take vows and become one of them soon changed to overt urgings. Aelfric just gave them his slow smile and excused himself to the stables whenever their pressing became too much. Indeed, he would not be adverse to becoming a monk, except that it would mean he could never own a horse like Leander. Private property did not exist in a monastery. Even so, he might have eventually given in to their urgings out of a simple lack of anything better to do. But one day Prior Augustine was called to the Pope's residence in the Lateran Palace and returned with startling news.

After many years of wars and rumors of wars, Pope Gregory had at last negotiated peace with the Lombards. Italy, though largely still occupied, was no longer under siege. The threat to Rome had been averted. As if that weren't good news enough, now the Holy Father deemed it time to launch one of his longest-held, most dearly-cherished dreams: He would send a mission to England. The former Christian nation that had been lost to the faith when Rome abandoned it to barbarian hordes could now be reclaimed for God and the church.

To the brothers and students gathered in the Chapter House after the evening meal, Augustine laid out in detail Gregory's plans. "We go to a divided land. The Holy Father's desire is that under the banner of Christ we shall make one people of them both—English and Britain—once the boundary of religion is down; for to a Christian there can be no other boundary. From the ruins of the past a new and better world will arise. Such is the vision of the Sanctissime Pater."

From the far corner of the room Aelfric leaned forward on his bench. He wasn't sure what those fine words meant, for he knew little of England save what he could remember of herding sheep and swine on his father's steading. But it was his land, his family was still there, and just to hear its name made his heart leap.

"So, my brothers, in three months' time I shall set out from here to carry out the will of His Holiness. I am to take forty of the brethren with me—if so many will answer God's call to face danger and hardship for the sake of spreading His blessed word."

The bell for Compline interrupted the murmuring among the brothers, and there was no chance for Aelfric to ask the question bursting inside him. Surely Augustine would take him and Wulfnoth—he would need their language skills and knowledge of the country—but the prior had said "brethren," and they were not brothers.

The rule of silence after Compline was strictly observed at St. Andrew's, so it was not until after Lauds the next morning that Aelfric was able to speak to Father Augustine. It ever afterward amazed Aelfric that something on which his whole life hung could be treated so brusquely by the abbot, but at least he had his answer. "Certainly. You are to go." Augustine had not even bothered to nod his tonsured head.

3

hroughout the days of preparation, in the tumult of deciding which brothers would go, how many supplies should be taken and how they would be carried, which books, which vestments and precious relics, and the conflict of opinions over whether it would be better to set out now, in midsummer (which would put the sea crossing to England in winter), or wait for better weather, it seemed to Aelfric that the more the upheaval around him, the greater the peace grew inside him.

At first he felt merely excitement to be returning to the land of his birth, to escape the choking heat and dust of an arid land made drier still by years of war and disease—the excitement of seeing his family again. His sister Bruni would be of marriageable age by now—had their father given her to Cenred who had smiled on her many years ago? And his cubbling brothers Ulf and Scaef—they must be grown now to do a man's work in the fields rather than roll with Garm's puppies around the door where their mother stood by her loom. His mother—the thought suddenly took him—had she had another child since he had gone? His father—had the pains in his legs grown worse so that he found working the barley garth more difficult? Had his flaxen beard grown gray, as Aelfric's grandfather's had before he died?

Thoughts long, long suppressed because they would be too painful when he feared never to see his family again now filled his mind through every waking hour. Was his whole family there in the timber and thatch steading so familiar in his mind, carrying on the life he had always known, or had disaster overtaken them?

But slowly, as the days wore on, filled with preparations and plans layered between the persistent offices of the days, Aelfric discovered a gradual change in his feelings. Now his feelings of urgency were not for his family only, but for his country. It began when he thought of how his own life had changed through the teachings of the monks—how his mind had been opened to the light of learning through reading, how his habits had changed with the emphasis on cleanliness and gentleness, but most of all, how the great light had begun to shine in his soul with the knowledge of the true God.

It was as if he saw himself striding through a thick forest where the sun never shone, carrying a blazing torch with which he would light the hearthplace of his home, and all would shine with an inner light. This light would spread throughout all of Canti and East Angli and all of England—although he had only dim ideas of the extent of the land. Indeed, the rough maps Pope Gregory had procured from the few seamen who visited England's isolated shores were the first he had seen of his own country. But his imagination needed no map to see a great rolling back of dark and squalor and ignorance to be replaced by shining cleanness and knowledge and faith. In his mind, the new England to which he would help give birth was akin to the new heavens and new earth the Apostle John saw in Revelation. An England without war, without greed, without squalor—a place of green serenity and beauty filled with God's love and peace.

Then Wulfnoth would come in grumbling about having to take orders from Father Laurentius and Brother Peter, Prior Augustine's assistants in organizing the mission, and Aelfric would return to reality. He was to care for the cattle they were taking along for provisions—and for Leander whom Prior Augustine would ride—and teach the English tongue to the brothers as they had taught him Latin. Then the mundane replaced his dreams. He would light no fires, build no new heavens. If anyone struck any sparks at all, it would be Augustine with the help of the brothers—and that only if raiding barbarians, disease, or the hazards of land and sea travel didn't overtake them first; if this King Aethelberht would allow them to live and preach in his land. Yet several times a day in the midst of a mundane task, flashes of the vision would return.

It was midsummer of the year 597 when their Frankish boatmen set the forty monks and lay brethren ashore on the Isle of Thanet. To that very piece of land Aelfric's forebears had first come when Hengist answered Vortigern's invitation for an auxiliary army to protect him from the invading Scoti about a hundred and fifty years earlier. Augustine's orders were clear. The party would set up a camp with the tents and equipment they carried; they would attempt to establish friendly relations with the inhabitants of the island—farmers who lived in separate steadings and a small clutch of villagers who had built timber and thatch dwellings against the walls of the old Roman fort of Rutupiae. But under no circumstances were they to begin preaching or converting the people until they had leave from King Aethelberht.

Augustine would remain with the missioners while Father Laurentius and Brother Peter, with Aelfric to interpret, would follow the trail along the River Stour. According to a native farmer's directions, the path should bring them directly to the royal tun in half a day's walk. If Queen Berthe and Bishop Luithard had received the letters Queen Berthe's Aunt Brunhild, Queen of the Franks, had sent, all might be prepared for their arrival. If not, it would be the emissaries' task to explain their presence to the king and beg an audience for Augustine.

With the first touch of his feet to his native soil, Aelfric's heart felt at home. But the thick, dark woods through which they traveled seemed to fulfill his vision of a land waiting in darkness. And the fear on the dull faces of the peasants they met was proof of the darkness of their hearts and minds, especially as Aelfric repeatedly saw them make a furtive sign against evil when the tonsured, black-robed monks passed.

The forest began to give way to cleared land, dwellings, and serfs watching cattle. The travelers were nearing Cantwaraburg when Father Laurentius stopped suddenly beneath a giant ash tree. A look of horror filled his face. He backed up several paces and crossed himself with a trembling hand.

"God preserve us. Christ preserve us. Saint Michael preserve us. Holy Mary, Mother of God . . ." His voice faltered as he continued to cross himself.

Three human bodies in varying stages of decay, one being plucked by a large black crow perched on a branch beside it, hung in the high branches of the ash. Brother Peter fell to his knees, clutching the cross he wore around his neck and muttering prayers. Had the court received Brunhild's letters? Was this, then, a warning to foreigners who would bring their God to this land?

Aelfric stood for a moment, swallowing hard and trying not to breathe the stench emanating from the tree. Then he remembered. "Quickly, move back, Father, Brother. This is Yggdrasill, the tree of the gods. I had forgotten—I did not pay much heed to such things when I lived here. But Woden, the great god; Tiev, the dark god; Frigga, goddess of the home—there are many others—this is their tree. It is believed that they planted it, and many others of its kind. The tree draws strength from the human bodies left there to bleed to death."

"Whom do they sacrifice? Criminals? Virgins? Foreigners?" Father Laurentius continued backing up until he was well away from Yggdrasill.

"Usually the widows of important men. The chieftains have many wives . . ." Aelfric turned away. He could say no more. His visions of heathen darkness were nothing compared to the reality. "Come. We must see the king. We must light the torch." The monks had no idea what he was talking about, but they quickly turned away from the tree.

The door thralls standing guard at the gate of the royal palisade did not question Aelfric's story, but they did not admit the party either. Instead they sent a runner to the women's bower where Bishop Luithard attended the queen and her ladies. "They dress as Father Luithard," the guard said pointing to the monks, "and shave the head."

In a few minutes an elderly priest, followed by the queen herself and several of her brightly-gowned, chattering ladies, arrived at the gate and ushered the visitors into the royal hall. King Aethelberht and his house carles were away on a hunt. No, they had received no letters informing them of the mission, but the queen was not surprised. She had for the past year felt a new urgency in her long prayer vigil. She had for many months felt that an answer was near.

As soon as the travelers had refreshed themselves with food and drink served by thralls with iron slave rings around their necks, the queen and her guests walked in the soft evening light across a field strewn with small blue and white flowers and up the hill to St. Martin's Church. Bishop Luithard invited Father Laurentius to lead the evening prayers and lent him his own stole for the service. The prayers for King Aethelberht and for the conversion of all England had never been more fervent nor more hopeful than they were that night, nor had the candles flickered with more golden promise, or the incense smelled more blessed.

But by the next morning the king had not returned, and there was no message of when the hunt was expected to end. The queen suggested that the missionaries return to their party. She would inform the king of their arrival and do her best to prepare the way. She would send messengers to them as soon as possible.

Two weeks of anxious waiting followed. Aelfric, seemingly endued with the missionary spirit far more than those ordained to the task, would have enthusiastically shared the good news with all on the tiny island where they camped. But Augustine's command was clear, and his grip was firm. And so they waited.

Early in the third week the brothers had finished their noon meal and were just beginning Nones when the chanting of the Second Psalm was disrupted by a trumpet blast, followed by pounding hooves and shouting. It seemed that the monks were the last to know their fate. Surely all the Island of Thanet had received word of their king's arrival and had gathered to shout their welcome. Even though their steadings lay only a few miles from Cantwaraburg, few of the people had ever seen a nobleman before, and certainly not King Aethelberht himself. Dogs barked, children cried, royal banners whipped in the wind of their passing. The monks themselves surely would have rushed to join the tumultuous throng had not Augustine controlled his brethren with stern eyes. The prayers continued unbroken to the end of the chant. Augustine held his hands out over his small flock, as though they were alone on earth. "He has rescued us from the power of darkness and has brought us into the Kingdom of His Son, alleluia! Help us to pass from our old life of sin to the new life of grace. We ask this through our Lord Jesus Christ, Your Son, who lives and reigns with You and the Holy Spirit, one God, forever and ever."

And all the brethren said, "Amen."

Augustine then signaled his crossbearer to follow him, and he walked sedately forward, as though the bishop were to receive the king, rather than the other way around.

Aelfric was too far back to hear, but he could tell he would not be called on to translate, as the king obviously spoke fluent Latin. Later when the king and his carles were welcomed into the monks' camp, Aelfric, Wulfnoth, and the young brothers scurried to and fro bringing wine for the noblemen's refreshment and stools for their comfort. At last Aelfric could slip away for a closer look at what interested him far more than the king or his carles. Beyond the circle of tents the new arrivals had staked their horses in a clearing.

These were longer-legged than the ponies in Italy, which had been mostly the property of conquering Lombards. Even Leander, the descendant of a noble Roman line, looked small and underfed in comparison. And the gloss on the English horses told Aelfric that these animals were not the product of a famine-plagued land. He held his hand out and stroked a sleek brown neck, murmuring gentle words to the spirited animal.

"Well, I never. Most strangers he'd take their hand off if they got familiar with him."

Aelfric jumped back at the sound of the English voice just behind him.

"Oh, no fear. If High-strider has no complaints, I don't give mind." Aelfric turned to the speaker, a young man about his own age or younger, with straight flaxen hair cut bowl-shape around his head and the beginnings of a moustache on his upper lip. His blue, belted tunic hung to his knees, and the usual cross-gartered leggings encased his legs, but the fine fabric and sturdy leather boots marked him for more than a villein.

"Greetings. I'm Aelfric, servant to the missioners."

"Wiglaf. Churl to three of the king's house carles. You have the English tongue?"

And before he knew it, Aelfric was telling Wiglaf about his capture, the slave market, his time in the monastery, and their mission.

"And is your Christ-god then a son of Woden?"

Aelfric was well into his answer, explaining all that his years at St. Andrew's had taught him of the person of Christ and the triune God when he realized he was disobeying Augustine's strictest orders. He faltered in his monologue, then concluded, "I will tell you more if the king permits."

Wiglaf nodded a careless consent and turned the conversation to the horses.

Perhaps an hour later a signal from Aethelberht's trumpeter called Wiglaf and the other churls to ready the horses, and the court departed with as much noise and confusion as with which they arrived. Aelfric hurried forward. Were they to be welcomed as Pope Gregory envisioned, or would his few words spoken out of turn to Wiglaf be the extent of his preaching in England?

But he was not to learn the answer yet. The sun was nearing the horizon; if Vespers were to be said before dark, there was no time for delay. Augustine turned to lead the office as calmly as if they were within the enclosure of St. Andrew's Monastery. Aelfric couldn't help wondering if the others felt as impatient and gave as little thought to their prayers as he did.

But at last they said the final "amen," and Augustine made his announcement. "King Aethelberht bids us welcome. He is not prepared to turn aside from his gods, but we are free to tell his people of our Christ if they wish to listen."

At last the bishop's feelings broke through his austerity. "Praise be to God! His Holy Spirit will empower our speaking."

But before the brothers could express their joy, Augustine continued in his strict voice. "We are to be given a parcel of ground between the royal enclosure and the foot of the hill of the queen's chapel. When the barley is harvested next month, which I assured the king we would help with, we may then build accommodations there.

"Brothers, you must eat quickly if you are not to break the injunction against taking food after dark. Compline tonight will be a special praise service for the Lord's blessing on the beginning of our mission. In the morning I will write a letter informing His Holiness, Pope Gregory, of our success."

4

Augustine first undertook to rebuild Queen Berthe's church. He directed the brothers and workers lent by the king to carry load after load of brick from fallen Roman buildings up the steep hill to repair the crumbling walls and then fitted St. Martin's with a fine square tower in the style of a Roman church. With God's house intact, they turned to the building of their own quarters.

Many hands took up the work of cutting the timbers and fitting them in snug upright rows to form walls. These they plastered over with daub of the yellow clay from Cantwaraburg's fields and coated them with a white lime wash, leaving the sturdy little buildings a pale amber color beneath the thick straw-colored thatch—which ever looked to Aelfric like one of the native villeins in need of a haircut.

In the course of the work Aelfric found opportunities to continue the story he had begun telling Wiglaf. Many of the other churls gathered to hear Aelfric, for he was a good storyteller—having entertained himself telling stories in his head on long lonely vigils watching his father's cattle. And the villeins—freemen from the tun—and thralls in their iron slave-rings gathered to the sound of his soft English voice, unhampered by the formal Latin the monks used. Many nodded agreement to the truths he told, and many prayed to the White Christiani God. Including Wiglaf.

But none was baptized. So although there were many believers, none could be counted as converts. Many gathered to hear the monks' prayers, but none took communion. They awaited the decision of their king. For as the king went, so went the kingdom. And King Aethelberht, as all Saxon kings, was descended from Woden himself. Abandoning the old gods would also mean abandoning his own ancestors. Therefore, although Abbot Augustine, Father Laurentius, and Brother Peter spent many long hours in the royal hall explaining Christianity to Aethelberht, he made no decision.

By the beginning of Advent the workers had completed the cluster of square timber and rough-thatch buildings. All the countryside referred to it as the steading of the White Christiani, but Augustine dedicated it as the Monastery of St. Peter and St. Paul. A letter came from Pope Gregory appointing Augustine the abbot.

Now that the monastery was complete and the preaching of the missioners seemed to have reached a stalemate, Aelfric thought that this would be a good time to seek permission to visit his family. Wulfnoth had been urging the idea for months; indeed, he would have slipped from their camp the first night on the Isle of Thanet if Aelfric would have gone with him. Both men had been making inquiries and had garnered a fair idea of the way. Following the remains of an old Roman road into the land of the East Angli should take them to their former homes in three days.

Now Aelfric must examine the strange hesitancy he felt within. Since Gregory had given him his freedom at the time the Pope turned him over to the monastery, Aelfric theoretically could have returned home any time in the past five years. But although he had often thought of his family, he had never seriously considered returning to his old life. Now he looked at what a return home might mean.

The monks had opened the world of reading to him. Could he return to a life of swine herding? He had become a Christian. Could he go back to living where no one knew or loved the God he served? Or was this exactly what God would have him do—was this the fulfillment of his vision of spreading the light in a dark land? But if he were meant to bring the faith of Christ to his people in East Anglia, shouldn't he first take the cowl and go as a monk? Why should something that sounded so reasonable to his head feel so heavy to his heart?

Then suddenly news spread through the monastery that drove all self-examination and travel plans completely out of mind. The king had received the faith. After thirty-five years of Queen Berthe's faithful prayers and many months of Augustine's careful teaching, King Aethelberht of the Kingdom of Canti was to be baptized as a Christian.

Christmas Day was selected for the momentous event. Word spread rapidly to the farthest, most isolated steadings of the kingdom and beyond. Several days before the appointed time people poured into Cantwaraburg, filling the guest lodgings of the royal tun and of the monastery and establishing a whole new stead of tents and hastily assembled huts.

On Christmas Day hundreds, if not thousands, of his own people from the East Angli and the South Folk came to witness the baptism of King Aethelberht. Word went out from the royal hall that the ceremony would take place at midday on the banks of the River Stour just beyond the royal enclosure.

Right after breaking fast Aelfric and Wulfnoth set out in hopes of getting a good place to watch the proceedings. But already they were late arrivals, as many had camped along the river the night before. Unfortunately the flat land didn't provide convenient overlooks, so those to the rear would know what was taking place only by word of mouth. Aelfric's enthusiasm overcame his manners, and he elbowed a few steps closer.

"Ow! This is my place!" A tall young woman with long blond braids hanging beneath the hood of her mantle turned to him with snapping eyes. "Mind your manners!"

Aelfric took a step backward and opened his mouth to apologize, but before he could get a word out, the girl's brindled wolfhound sprang at him. The dog landed with its forepaws on Aelfric's shoulders and sent him sprawling backward, knocking him into Wulfnoth before he hit the ground. All Aelfric could see was the beast's yellow eyes and pointed muzzle a few inches from his nose. He flung up his arm to protect his face and closed his eyes. The next thing he felt was the warm, rough wetness of being licked all over his face by the animal's long, slavering tongue.

"Garm! Stop that! Come you here!" the girl's voice commanded.

With a final lick the dog obeyed his mistress. Aelfric sat up and shook his head. He looked up at the girl, frowning. Was it possible? Garm was a common enough name for a dog—but would any other react so to him? The creature was standing obediently by his mistress, but looking back at Aelfric, wagging his long-haired tail.

"Garm?" Aelfric spoke to the dog and held out his hand.

With a small yelp, the dog was beside him in one leap, nuzzling his hand. Aelfric excitedly scratched the animal behind the ears with both hands. "Garm! Garm! It is you! Good girl! I was so afraid the raiders had killed you."

Slowly Aelfric rose to his feet to regard the girl standing just behind the dog. "Bruni? Is it possible? Are you then my sister Bruni?"

The girl took one long look at his face and with a small cry threw herself into his arms. "Aelfric! We thought you dead! I would never have recognized you if Garm hadn't!" She burst into tears that might have gone unchecked for some time had not Aelfric pulled her braids in a cow-milking fashion, just as he had done when she was small. And just as it always did, the gesture made her laugh. "No one has done that these five years." She choked, caught between laughing and crying.

Aelfric put his hands on her shoulders to steady her. "And now, little-sister-grown-big, you must tell me all that has happened these five years. Modor? Faeder? Ulf? Scaef? The steading?"

She nestled her head on his shoulder for support, but spoke more calmly now. "Oh, Aelfric, Modor and Faeder were killed by the raiders. I had taken the boys with me to drive the geese to a new field. When we returned at dusk, the houseplace still smoldered. Faeder lay in the rye garth, his axe bloody in his hand. Modor was in the houseplace when they fired it . . ."

Aelfric put his arms around her and held her until her shoulders relaxed and she could continue. "It was long ago—but I still have dreams. Uncle farms our land strips with Ulf and Scaef. I went to live with Wulfnoth's family—perhaps I made up to them a little for the loss of their son. They have brought me here today—Oh!" The final outcry came when Wulfnoth stepped forward. "Oh! You are both returned to us from the dead! Oh!" She left her brother to embrace her long-lost friend.

And then trumpets sounded from the royal tun, announcing that the procession was about to begin. A guard of mounted house carles came first, carrying the king's white horse banner on long spear-poles. Their progress was slow as they cut a path through the waiting throng. Behind them walked the forty monks of the monastery, all wearing silver crosses on the breasts of their black robes, with their cowls pushed back and the pale winter sun shining coldly on the round tonsures of their bare heads. Brother Severus came first with a massive bronze cross on a long pole, and Brother Peter and Father Laurentius brought up the rear.

For weeks the brothers had been at choir practice, polishing every hymn and psalm they would sing that day. It began low, a barely perceived murmuring as the procession made its slow way across the crowd-thronged field. Then, as they drew closer, the chant grew in strength and clarity and Aelfric could make out the familiar words:

Cry out with joy to the Lord, all the earth.
Serve the Lord with gladness.
Come before Him, singing for joy.
Sing forever, how good is the Lord,
Eternal His merciful love.
He is faithful from age to age.

Several of the brothers carried censers emitting clouds of incense with every rhythmic swing until the crisp winter air was full of a wonderful spicy scent.

Queen Berthe, radiant in a white mantle that covered her head, fit snugly under her chin, and fell to her toes, came next with three of her closest waiting ladies and Bishop Luithard. Aelfric could not begin to imagine what this day must mean to the woman who had faithfully prayed for it for so many years.

The Lord is faithful to those who call on Him.
The Lord has come to His people and set them free.

Last of all, with his bare head bowed, his hands folded in front of him, wearing a simple white belted tunic that came to his knees and his feet bare, walked the king accompanied by Bishop Augustine. Unlike Aethelberht, who approached the moment in humility and repentance, Augustine had never walked taller with his shoulders squarer or his head more erect. His commanding brown eyes with which he could control an entire community of monks today radiated joy and triumph.

The procession came to the river. At a spot where the riverbank sloped down to a little beach, the monks formed a semicircle. The queen and her party halted behind the black-robed wall, and only the king and Augustine went on to the water's edge. Augustine raised his hands over the water. "*Exorciso te, creature aque, in nomine Dei Patris omnipotentis . . .*" He blessed and sanctified the water.

Holding the abbot's hand for support, the king stepped knee-deep into the icy, flowing river. Augustine raised his hands over Aethelberht's bowed head and prayed, "Our Father Almighty, . . . in Your mercy forgive the sins of this one who comes to You through the waters of the new birth, and give him life in Jesus Christ our Lord . . ."

Aelfric wished that the people standing on both banks of the river could understand Latin—especially those who hung back, crossing their fingers against evil in fear of this new God.

". . . Increase the faith and understanding of this one who comes before You for holy baptism. . . . and make him a member of Your chosen family. We ask this through Christ our Lord."

All the monks and the queen's party responded, "Amen," and Aelfric joined them in making the sign of the cross.

Augustine stooped and, with his two hands cupped together, scooped up the water and poured it over the king's bowed head. "In the name of the Father." He poured a second scoop of water over the king as he said, "and of the Son," and a third scoop, "and of the Holy Spirit."

In a chant that sounded more like a cheer, those on the tiny beach proclaimed, "Blessed be God who chose you in Christ!"

Augustine led the king from the water, and Father Laurentius stepped forward with a vial of chrism. As the anointing oil flowed over the royal head, the monks chanted in a great tumult of triumph, "Alleluia, alleluia!"

One of the queen's ladies wrapped a heavy fur-lined mantle around the king's shoulders as he shivered in the December breeze, but Augustine, although dripping wet from the waist, stood as if impervious to the chill. The message he had brought from Pope Gregory in anticipation of such an event was in Latin and addressed to the king, but he chose to proclaim it in the native tongue and in a ringing voice that reached out over the crowd.

"'King Aethelberht, *Rex Anglorum,* you have been brought to the office of ruler in order that you might give to your fellow-subjects the blessings of the Christian faith that have now been bestowed upon you. In the strength of God our Father, may you ever be heedful in keeping the grace given to you by God and eager in spreading the Christian faith among your subjects. As your guide in the holy faith, I direct you to be zealous for the conversion of your people, to attack the worshiping of idols, and to overthrow all heathen temples in order to turn your people to the worship of the true God. . . . I have spoken these things now, my illustrious son, to the end that the Christian faith shall increase in your kingdom to the glory of God and His Kingdom.'"

For the first time that afternoon Aethelberht raised his head. He was no longer the penitent sinner. He was now a glorious son of the true God and the spiritual as well as temporal ruler of the Kingdom of Canti. He spoke in a commanding voice to all his subjects gathered there, and the echo that followed each sentence told those standing near the king that his message was being picked up by those on the edge of hearing and shouted back in relay to those standing beyond.

"My people, my subjects, my children. I, your king, have found the true God and have accepted His true faith. From this day hence the Kingdom of Canti shall be a Christian kingdom. In token that there shall be no more sacrifices to the old gods, Yggdrasill shall be cut down at my order. My own hand shall strike the first blow. Temples dedicated to Woden and the gods of the old way shall be cleansed and the Christian brethren made free to celebrate holy communion in them. And you, my beloved people, will please me by following my example and accepting holy baptism."

The monks began chanting the closing psalm, and Brother Severus raised the cross aloft to lead the procession to the church for the planned communion service. But they got no more than three steps before they were pressed backward almost into the river by the crush of people moving forward. Almost everyone within hearing was coming for baptism. When the brothers understood what was happening, a great "Alleluia!" rose from them. They plunged into the water, some wading well out past their waists to assist.

But with the best effort in the world and the fastest possible scooping of water, there was no way conceivable for each one to be individually poured. In the end, Augustine climbed to the highest spot the riverbank afforded and did all he could do. With his crossbearer behind him and with his arms stretched over the crowd-choked water, he blessed the mass baptism. The brothers did what they could, but many of the new converts scooped the water over their own heads or anointed the heads of their neighbors, while others simply bent down and stuck their heads in the frigid flow.

Although there was no way an accurate count could be taken of the new communicants, Augustine later wrote to Pope Gregory that he that day baptized ten thousand Englishmen. His more immediate concern was the Eucharist that was to come next at St. Martin's Church. Elements of bread and wine had been prepared for the king, the queen and her party, and the brothers. Now the Eucharistic meal must become another miraculous feeding of the ten thousand. At a hurried word from Augustine, runners slipped through the crowd and ran to the royal hall to gather all the bread and wine they could find and take it up the hill to the little church. Such unorthodoxy bothered the scrupulous Augustine, but Gregory had ordered him to do whatever seemed best in the awkward situations he was sure to encounter in foreign lands, and this certainly qualified.

It was long after dark before the crowd that had covered the hillside of St. Martin's Church and spread into the garth below had all partaken of the communion elements and so received the grace of God through the body of His Son Jesus Christ. Augustine, under the pressure of need, was willing to accept a mass baptism, but holy Eucharist was not to be slighted.

At last, in the slowly thinning crowd, Aelfric, Bruni, and Wulfnoth walked down the hill. They had managed to stay together after Bruni's baptism, for which Aelfric had scooped the water over his sister's head. Although he was not ordained, he reasoned that he was more qualified to administer the rite than one of those who only moments earlier had been a heathen. She gave a small gurgle of laughter. "Even Garm is a Christiani, for he went into the water with me."

Aelfric was wondering whether he should attempt a theological explanation to her remark when she gave a small shout, "Modor! Faeder!"

Aelfric jerked his head in the direction she was pointing. Then the couple turned to her voice, and he understood. It was Wulfnoth's mother and father. But Aelfric saw a thing that surprised him even more. As Wulfnoth sprang forward to greet his parents with huggings and back-poundings and exclamations, he did not once let go of Bruni's hand, save to put his arm around her shoulders.

And so this was to be the way of it—Wulfnoth and Bruni to marry and farm his steading after his parents, Ulf and Scaef to farm their family steading with Uncle until they should become men and take wives. And where was there a place in all of this for him? He had returned to his home. Yet it was not his home. There was no place for him.

5

he days from cockcrow to owl-hoot spun into seasons from bud-bursting to geese-flighting four times while Aelfric remained tending cattle for the monastery, saying prayers with the brothers, and spending his leisure hours in the horse pens with Wiglaf. Father Laurentius and Brother Peter journeyed back to Rome to report on the mission to Pope Gregory and returned bringing for Augustine a white woolen pallium with pendants in front and back to wear as symbol of his full episcopal authority upon his investiture as Archbishop of Cantwaraburg. Gregory instructed the new archbishop to assume authority over all the weak, primitive Christian churches the surprised missionaries had discovered still clinging to the faith established from the time of Constantine in out-of-the-way places.

Soon after Augustine took up his new office, Aethelberht's nephew, Saberht, king of Essex, accepted the faith. On the highest ground in his nephew's capital city of Lunden, Aethelberht built a church and dedicated it to St. Paul.

Then a mission ventured into East Anglia, and Aelfric went along to see his old home and to greet Bruni and Wulfnoth's new cubbling. It was a good visit. But when Raedwald, king of East Anglia, was successfully converted and baptized, Aelfric drank a parting cup of mead with his family, gave a small silver cross to his namesake, the infant Aelfric, and bade them farewell, for there was nothing in that place to hold him.

When the mission returned to Cantwaraburg, they found the monastery astir with news. There was to be a great council. Taking to heart the Pope's injunction to exercise authority over all bishops in England, both Roman and British, Archbishop Augustine had sent out messengers to all parts of the land to seek out churches and bid their heads attend a council. He wished to see the British churches for himself and to remove reasons for their leaders, especially those reputedly stubborn Waelisc from the western mountains, to refuse his summons. So he set the site for the meeting at a village called Aust on the Sabrina River.

Preparations for the council were tremendous. This was the biggest undertaking since the mission had journeyed to England from Rome, and the territory and peoples were as foreign. The Holy Father envisioned making all peoples one under the cross of Christ. This could only be accomplished by bringing all on the island, whether English or British, into the church. Therefore the brothers packed baskets and leather satchels full of sacred vessels, ornaments, vestments, relics, and books. British Christianity was sure to be primitive and error-riddled, if not containing outright heathen aspects. They must have all their equipment to fight Satan. And they packed one large casket full of specially prepared copies of Gregory's *Book of Rules for Pastors*. The Pope had directed that this spiritual and practical guide be placed in every church in the land.

Aelfric rejoiced in his assignment—he was to take charge of the five monastery horses that would provide transportation. Then, as an added joy, Wiglaf was put in charge of the six horses Aethelberht loaned from the royal garth. Aelfric brushed every coat to a high gloss, curried every mane and tail until it hung like silk, and trimmed and re-shod every hoof in his care. But he lavished his greatest devotion on Leander. The bay stallion was getting old. A few gray hairs appeared in his muzzle, and he romped in the garth with less speed, but the fire was not gone from his intelligent eyes, and his limbs and wind were as sound as ever. When Aelfric brushed his rust-red coat until it looked as if it had been sprinkled with gold dust and the black mane and tail shone like jet, none would believe the horse's age.

Aelfric's care proved its value two months later when Augustine, sitting proudly on the tall bay horse, led his delegation through the collection of wattle and daub huts that constituted the village of Aust. Leander stepped as proudly as the archbishop rode. But Augustine was the only one who managed to keep his head up and dismay off his face. Ragged children peered at them from behind shabby buildings, and scruffy dogs raced along a muddy road, nipping at the horses' hooves. What could Augustine have been thinking of to call a council in such a place? Aelfric wondered. Certainly they had ridden through some of the most verdant countryside with some of the most prosperous farmsteads they had seen, and the Sabrina offered easy access by boat, but the village itself . . .

They halted before the largest building, which, although round and made of thatched wattle and daub like the others huddling around it, must surely be the chief's hall. Augustine seemed unsure whether or not to dismount. Aelfric smiled. Uncertainty in the archbishop was rare.

But the moment passed quickly as a tall, golden-haired man wearing a blue cloak and a shining gold torque thrust aside the leather door apron and strode forward. The stream of words he uttered was undecipherable, but his broad smile and outstretched arms gave welcome. Still Augustine did not dismount. He apparently had not considered that these British would not speak the English tongue which he had mastered.

"Ave Domine." Heads turned in amazement as it seemed that the strange man had suddenly greeted the archbishop in Latin. Then the mystery was solved as the door hanging fluttered again and two brown-robed monks stepped out. They spoke to Augustine and his party in fluent but strangely accented Latin. "Indeed you are expected, and accommodations have been made for your comfort in the guest lodge—although we did not foresee quite so a large delegation—so some may wish to pitch tents in the oak circle on the hill. We are the first to arrive, but many more will be coming. This is Brother Amulf," said the taller monk, placing his hand on his comrade's shoulder, "and I am Ogmar. We are from St. Patrick's Monastery in Armagh in Eire, but we now serve in the monastery on Ynis Witrin—which you undoubtedly know of as it was founded by St. Joseph of Arimathea himself. Therefore, it is fitting that our Abbot Wogret, who will arrive on the morrow, should receive the emissary from His Holiness, the Pope, and we are certain . . ."

"Wait! Stop!" Augustine held up his hand as if to halt the spate of curious-sounding Latin. He did not want to admit that he had heard of none of these traditions. No matter what claims to precedence the monks made, Aelfric quickly gathered from the murmurs of the brothers around him that the most glaring obstacle to communication was not the Celts' strange accent but their hair.

A short time later, after declining hospitality in the guest lodge and retreating to the oak trees, the Roman delegation expressed their shock and disgust at such barbarian tonsuring. The late-May sunshine made dappled patterns through the oak leaves on the smoothly-shaved domes of their proper Roman heads as the righteous indignation poured forth.

"Our circular tonsure that leaves only a fringe of hair around the head is ever a symbol of the Lord's crown of thorns—to reject this is to reject identity with His suffering. What could a tonsure that shaves the head in a crescent shape across the top from ear to ear possibly signify? A half-moon—in honor of some pagan moon goddess? A crown—in honor of some heathen king?"

"The true tonsure is a mark of humility and submission to God. How can we fellowship with those who would desecrate such a symbol?"

"The tonsure is one of the most important parts of the ceremony admitting a man to monastic life. If this is not done correctly, can the rest of the ceremony be valid? Is not error in this to be taken as a warning of error in other, even deeper matters?"

It was indeed fortunate that Pope Gregory had given all authority in such matters to Archbishop Augustine, for there could be no wavering on such a vital issue.

Aelfric smiled as he went off to join Wiglaf in the field with the horses. For perhaps the ten hundredth time he was glad he had not yielded to pressure to become a monk. He ran the ivory curry comb through his own blond locks and laughed with a great sense of freedom.

As he laughed, Aelfric realized how fresh and invigorating the scented air was, how clear his head felt, how the joy bubbled in his heart. What was it about this west country that seemed so much freer, so much lighter—as if the sun shone more directly on this land—than the rest of the island? He recalled his vision in Rome of England being a land of darkness through which they would travel under tunnels of trees, beset by pagan spirits. Such had not been the case, yet the vision persisted. And now it was as if he had emerged at the end of the tunnel into daylight. But he was not even in England now; he was in Britain. This was not the land of his birth. He could not even speak the native tongue. Why should he feel so at home here?

He found Wiglaf deep in conversation with Brother Ogmar, who had apparently come out to care for the Ynis Witrin horses. Aelfric smiled to note that neither the monk's awkward Latin nor his improper tonsure hindered communication with the churl. "And to my seeming it is strange that the conference should not have been at Ynis Witrin. Surely your Holy Father would wish to be worshiping at the church which our Lord Himself built with His own hands. And the thorn—are you not knowing that we have a tree growing from the very same plant that the crown of thorns came from—the very same which pierced His sacred brow . . ."

Aelfric moved beyond hearing as he examined each of his charges, running his hand down each satiny neck and calling each horse by name. But when he turned toward Leander, Aelfric caught his breath in dismay. Leander limped. Speaking calmly and reassuringly to his beloved animal, Aelfric ran his hand down the slim shank, detecting no weakness.

When his fingers spread out to run over the hoof, however, he stopped, raised his hand, and felt again. Certainly, there was a slight swelling just at the top of the hoof. "Come on, boy, let me look." He yanked at the fetlock and raised the hoof. He could see nothing amiss.

"Wiglaf! Have you your knife with you?" he called across the field.

Wiglaf and Ogmar both hurried to his side. With a few deft slashes, Aelfric cut away the dead tissue on the pad of the foot. A small trickle of blood directly beneath the swollen area told the story. "He has something imbedded in there. But I can't see. He is an old horse . . ." Aelfric could say no more, but there was no need.

"I will bring a torch. Also Amulf's tools and healing salves. Our herbalist he is, and a fine one. His remedies ever serve for man and beast." Ogmar had already turned toward the chieftain's hall.

"Find a short length of rope and a small stick," Aelfric directed Wiglaf. "We will need a twitch if I am to cut into his hoof." Aelfric set the hoof gently back on the ground and began soothing Leander—as much for his own reassurance as for the horse's.

Within minutes Ogmar strode back across the garth, the pine-knot torch he carried leaving black curls of resin-scented smoke in the breeze. Two paces behind him Amulf, his brown robe kilted to his knees to give more freedom to his short legs, trotted along carrying a rush basket of pots, herbs, and surgery tools.

The healer of man and beast examined the hoof. "Aye. He's picked up something in there, that's a certainty. If it hasn't pierced the bone he should mend—but there's no knowing yet. Shall you be doing the cutting yourself, or shall I?"

"I will." Aelfric took a firmer grip on the hoof and rested Leander's foreleg against his own knee. "Wiglaf, ready with the twitch?"

Wiglaf had placed a small circle of rope around Leander's lower lip and inserted a small stick which he could twist to tighten the rope if necessary. The mild pain in the lip would keep Leander's mind off the pain of the cutting on his hoof so he wouldn't jerk the leg.

"I'm thinking you'll not be needing that twitch," Ogmar said. "I'll talk to the beast. It is in my mind that all God's creatures speak the same tongue, and our Eirran horses were ever content when I recounted tales of their Creator in their ears. I'll tell him the story of our Lord riding a donkey into Jerusalem." He paused for a minute. "Unless you think he'd rather be hearing about Balaam's ass? Does he have a sense of humor, do you think?"

Aelfric had never considered the matter. "The triumphal entry will be fine."

"Aye, that's my thinking, too. It'll remind him of your fine procession into Aust today. And if the mount wasn't thinking himself our Lord's ass, there was no saying the archbishop's mind was so very far removed."

Ogmar took his place by Leander's ear and murmured to him in a lilting, rhythmic tongue akin to singing while Aelfric began. Amulf assisted, handing him tools as needed and once dabbing away a trickle of blood with a square of white linen. Throughout the operation the enrapturing chant continued, and Wiglaf never once had to twist the twig in the twitch.

At last Aelfric gave a pull with the iron tweezers. "Ah, there's the offender." He held a shard of rusty metal about two inches long that had perhaps broken from a plow or sickle and lain in a muddy road for months before Leander chanced to step on it.

Amulf held the torch closer and bent over the hoof. "I fear it went right into the bone. But we must hope for the best." With Aelfric still supporting the hoof, Amulf opened first one pot and then another, applying their contents to the hoof. First he dusted it with an astringent-smelling white powder; then he smeared it thickly with a greasy black salve wafting the odor of tar. At last he bound the entire hoof with fresh, sweet-scented, green herbs. "We must change the dressing three times each day." He took the last vessel from his basket, a small clay jar with a wooden stopper and sprinkled what looked like plain water on Leander's hoof and head.

"What was that?" Aelfric asked.

"Holy water. Father Wogret ever blesses two portions for me—one sanctified to my human patients and one for the creatures—for it's a sure thing the Lord God loves them all."

Wiglaf removed the unused rope and stick from Leander's lip, but Ogmar still stood with his hand on the black mane just behind the horse's ear, continuing with his lyrical chant. It was several minutes before he concluded with a final stroke and pat to the red-rust neck. He looked at the others and smiled, as if startled that they were still there. "Sorry I am to be making you wait. But you see, I wasn't through with my story."

Three days later when the rest of the bishops and delegates had all assembled for the council, Leander's hoof had been tended regularly with the best skills of both British and English. He seemed to be in no great distress, yet the hoof showed no signs of healing. If anything, the swelling was worse. "Aye, but he did enjoy the story of Balaam's ass. I've told it to him three times in the last three days." And Ogmar's brown eyes twinkled with a pleasure that did seem to be reflected by Leander's.

But preparations for the council were not going well. Augustine had determined to be lenient on unimportant matters—although the tonsure could under no circumstances be deemed unimportant. But then he received word that the British insisted on baptism by immersion and did not consider pouring sufficient.

Abbot Wogret arrived the morning after the Roman delegation and tried to explain the matter to the archbishop in preliminary meetings. "It was the method undergone by our Lord when He Himself was baptized by John the Baptist. It was the method prescribed for Naaman the leper to achieve a complete cleansing. It is the method by which the first Christian in this island, Bran the Blessed, was taken into the faith by St. Joseph of Arimathea." Augustine looked as if he would explode if he had Joseph of Arimathea thrown in his teeth one more time, but Wogret continued. "And how can anything but complete immersion symbolize death to the old life and the resurrection. Unless the waters close completely over the head . . ."

Augustine gripped the arms of the chief's chair. "Do you mean to say that you British make a claim to greater spirituality than Rome? Do you actually claim greater inerrancy than His Holiness, the Pope, who is descended in authority from St. Peter himself?"

"St. Joseph of Arimathea . . ." Wogret began, but Augustine rose to his feet and strode majestically from the tribal hall.

Augustine issued his order. He would not go to the British. He had traversed the width of the island, but the British bishops would come to him. The council would be held in the circle of oaks under which the Roman delegation camped.

Aelfric was sitting around the central fire in the chief's hall, eating midday stew with Amulf and Ogmar when the raised voices of the British prelates interrupted their conversation. The monks took turns translating for Aelfric.

"Oh, aye. We've come this far—all the way from Gwynedd myself. I'll not be going home without having a look at him. But if this foreigner thinks he has any authority over me—"

"Our house in Tintagel was founded by the blessed St. Patrick himself. We'll not be giving in to any Roman ways," insisted a gray-robed brother.

"It is in my mind that his Pope Gregory could be no nearer the heart and mind of God than St. Columba who laid down our regulations in Iona. Now if he thinks we're going to sit under an oak tree with him and agree to celebrate Easter on the wrong day . . ."

And the rest of the company hotly took up the explosive issue of the proper method for calculating when Easter should be celebrated.

Finally the gray-robed bishop from Gwynedd spoke again. "Oh, aye, it's serious matters you are raising, and I'm quite agreeing with your sentiments. But to my mind the most serious matter is the Italian's manner. Disrespectful of our practice of our faith, he is. It is to my seeming that he's entirely unaware of the great things our churches have done without benefit of Roman support."

"Aye, there's no reason for us to be giving over to him and his foreign ways."

Again a babble of excited voices filled the hall—not one word of which Aelfric could understand, but with the emotion entirely clear. At last the Bishop of Gwynedd, who seemed to have assumed chairmanship of the gathering because he had traveled the farthest, put a proposal before his brothers. "Since the major barrier to fellowship is the Italian's attitude, I suggest that we put his willingness to cooperate to the test. We will go to his meeting at the appointed hour. If he rises to greet us, we will stay and consider his proposals. If he does not extend us the courtesy of a proper greeting, we will leave."

Aelfric's eyebrows rose when the plan was explained to him in Latin. A small smile curled his lips. "I think I should wait by the oak circle— in case any of the brothers are in need of my service," he said. He licked the last of the venison stew from his wooden spoon and hurried with Ogmar just behind him along the narrow village street, scaring chickens out of his way.

They didn't have long to wait. Augustine was already seated in an elaborately carved chair that must have been borrowed from the chief. His cross-bearer stood behind him, and two Cantwaraburg monks sat on lower stools on each side. A richly robed layman whom Aelfric had seen earlier with Abbot Wogret had apparently been granted an audience with the archbishop, for he stood before him discussing something in earnest detail. The man's green and rust plaid cloak was held at his shoulder with a great ring brooch, and sun filtering through the oak leaves glittered on the gold torque at his neck and on his golden arm bands. The fact that his green breeks were not cross-gartered told Aelfric as quickly as the man's red hair that he was British, not English. The man drew a wooden tablet spread with wax from the folds of his cloak and handed it to Augustine with a metal stylus. The archbishop began drawing on the tablet, but Aelfric could not see what he drew.

Amulf had remained in the hall to accompany his abbot to the council, but Ogmar, whose main duty was to tend the horses, stood just behind Aelfric. Aelfric turned to the British monk with a questioning look on his face, indicating the man with Augustine.

"That is Bleddyn. He owns the most prosperous steading in all the land from here to Ynis Witrin. He was ever a devout man, but has become increasingly so in the three years since his wife's death. It is his desire to build a chapel in her memory for our monastery. He has heard rumors of Roman churches built in stone, and he has come with his daughter and Abbot Wogret to inquire how such is done." Ogmar raised his eyebrows in question. "Is such hearing correct? Do they build churches of cut stone in Italy?"

Aelfric nodded. "Certainly. Great buildings many times the size of a chief's hall, with glass windows."

Ogmar nodded. "Many churches are built of the stones of the field in Eire, and many have stood these two hundred and fifty years since St. Patrick directed their raising. But sea traders have told us of Italian churches built in the shape of a cross with each stone carved from a mountain."

Aelfric would have said more, but a noise from the direction of the village told them that the bishops were approaching. Bleddyn replaced the writing tablet in the folds of his cloak and withdrew. By now those within the oak ring had heard the approaching murmur. The monks surrounding Augustine craned their necks to see, but Augustine sat rigidly straight, looking ahead as if his eyes beheld nothing but his own vision. The monks shifted their positions on their stools, but they did not rise. Only the crossbearer standing firmly behind the archbishop was on his feet.

The line of delegates, led by the Bishop of Gwynedd, reached the oak circle. The procession of black-, gray-, and brown-robed monks, all wearing the British half-moon tonsure, stopped. The Bishop of Gwynedd walked on alone. Two paces, three paces, four . . . Aelfric, leaning against an oak tree, counted the bishop's deliberate steps, each one measured to give Augustine ample time to rise to greet him.

Aelfric wondered whether it was only his imagination that the archbishop's fingers grasping the carved posts of his chair were white with the effort of holding firm. But there was no question as to the result.

Augustine sat.

Six more paces into the circle the bishop halted. The procession of British bishops filed into the clearing and stood in a semicircle behind the prelate.

Augustine sat.

"In the name of St. David who brought the faith to the Cymri and in the name of St. Patrick of Eire and in the name of St. Columba of Iona, and St. Fagan, St. Dyfan, St. Benignus, St. Indract, and St. Bridget, and in the hallowed name of St. Joseph of Arimathea, we of the British church choose to continue in the practice of our faith as revealed to us through the chosen servants of God in the name of His Son Jesus Christ under the guidance of the Holy Spirit." The Bishop of Gwynedd turned and walked from the oak ring, all the British bishops following.

Augustine sat.

Amazed, frightened, yet strangely inspired by what he had witnessed, Aelfric turned from the gathering. He must find Wiglaf. Surely the keeper of the king's horses would know more of the gossip, would understand better what had taken place. Not really looking where he was going, Aelfric sped down the path.

"Oh! Have a care, barbarian!"

Aelfric did not understand the British words, but their meaning was clear as he looked into the flashing green eyes of the young woman he had almost knocked into the mud in his haste. Her fine green and purple cloak and gold ornaments told him she must be the daughter of the man Ogmar had told him about earlier. "*Sarig!* I'm sorry. *Forgif!* Forgive me." Unthinkingly he babbled at her in English.

"Heathen English!" She all but spit at him. Tossing her mane of hair in the breeze she walked proudly past him.

Aelfric stood in the middle of the path, blinking. All thought of the council fled from his mind. That girl—her hair was the color of Leander's rust-red coat. And he felt as if Leander had just kicked him.

6

rders went around the Cantwaraburg camp. They were to be ready to leave by midmorning on the morrow. Aelfric was shattered. For the first time since he had been abducted from home ten years ago, he had found a place where it seemed to him that he could put down roots—a place where he could begin a real life of his own, not merely fill in time as he had been doing for so many years.

But now he must be ready to leave in a few hours. With dragging steps he made his way to the horse garth. Leander, with his head bowed even lower than Aelfric's, limped over to him. And then the most horrible truth of all struck him. Leander could not make the journey. The fine old stallion could still do good service in the breeding pen, but he could not make a journey the width of England. So Aelfric must also leave his best friend behind.

Aelfric turned at the sound of a soft footstep. Ogmar had come to see to his horses. "It is said you must be leaving in the morning."

Aelfric did not answer. There was nothing to say.

"And it is in my mind that you must be leaving this fine one also."

Again Aelfric could not answer.

"Would you like me to be taking care of him for you? There is ample room in our byres on Ynis Witrin, and I am thinking he would like to have the hearing of more of my stories."

A moment ago Aelfric had thought nothing could bring a smile to his lips again, but the British monk's kindness did.

"Please. I will tell the archbishop the horse is too old and lame for the journey. He will think nothing of leaving him behind."

Ogmar nodded. "What will Augustine do now?"

Aelfric thought for a moment. "He grows old. Even all the stiffness inside him will not last forever. He has done a good work, Ogmar, even a mighty work in much of the land. Augustine will return to Cantwaraburg, and when it is his time, he will be buried where his successes were great."

"And what of yourself?"

Aelfric blinked at the question.

"What of yourself?" Ogmar repeated. "Would not you like the hearing of more of my stories? There is room also for another with your skill with animals in the byres of Ynis Witrin."

Aelfric's first thought was that the suggestion was so overwhelming he must give it careful consideration. His second thought was that it was too overwhelming to think about. He would simply act. "I will tell Wiglaf he must care for the monastery's horses as well as the king's. He will do it for me."

And so it was done. With an off-handed nod from Augustine that Leander must be left behind and an equally off-handed nod from Wogret that Aelfric would come to them, it was done.

It was a day's journey on the road along the Sabrina down to Brent Knoll, the rich farm steading which Amulf told Aelfric had been given to the monastery by a great British king named Artos near to a hundred years before. The lame horse made the journey slower, but none complained. Ogmar walked most of the way beside Aelfric, murmuring a steady flow of strange Celtic words that seemed to keep Leander's pace steady.

After noon prayers the next day, the group turned away from the Sabrina and headed southeast. Aelfric noticed how the land gradually flattened, and much of the area seemed covered by marsh reeds. Their path was constantly crisscrossed by little streams, and when a gentle rain began to fall, it hardly made any difference, for his cross-gartered leggings were already soaked to the knees.

An alder-fringed stream ran to the right of the path, and nesting birds sang incognito from the green branches. The warm scent of bog myrtle blended with a saltier tang when the breeze blew from the west, and wisps of thick marsh fog blew in with the more silvery rain-mist. "We must walk single file here now," Ogmar said. "Only one as well-versed in the ways of the marsh as Father Wogret can travel on foot to our island. Take care not to step too far to either side."

Aelfric's care increased as the rain and fog did, and he began to wonder what strange place he had pledged himself to. Then, with what proved to be a farewell tug at his cloak, the wind blew on, driving the rain and fog before it, and the landscape cleared. The clouds thinned, and a pale, watery sun shone on the tangle of wood and marshland. Aelfric raised his eyes to the Tor. With the sun gleaming on the dark wet rock of the small chapel it wore like a crown, the green hill rose from the watery marsh surrounding it. "Ynis Witrin—the Glass Isle," Ogmar announced.

A pealing bell welcomed the returning abbot and his party. Aelfric, shivering wet himself, could think of nothing but the need to get Leander to dry straw, to get clean bindings on his hoof, and to rub down his dripping coat, but he looked with misgiving at the back of Wogret's head leading their party toward the continuing bronze peal. Augustine would have declared that prayers must have priority. After Vespers there would be ample time to see to the creatures; the Creator must be worshiped first.

As if Ogmar had read his mind, the monk touched Aelfric's arm when they cleared the side of a long, low hill. A cluster of buildings came into view between them and the great green Tor Aelfric had hardly ceased looking at since it had come into view. "There be the horse byres." Ogmar pointed to a group of small, thatched sheds along a wooden palisade to the right of the buildings from which the sound of the bell came. "The Father will lead prayers, but he will want God's creatures cared for before we pray for our own souls. Does not the holy Scripture say, 'A righteous man regardeth the life of his beast'?"

As the days passed and Aelfric fitted his life into that of the monastery, he thought many times on Ogmar's words and realized how that gentle regard for all life seemed a part of the place. He especially loved the sight of the white ewes and their growing lambs grazing on the steep sides of the Tor. And he enjoyed taking Leander and the monastery horses around to the lush pasture on Ynis Witrin by three ancient oak trees on the far side of the Tor. Ogmar told him they had once been part of a worship place for the druid religion that ruled in Britain before the time of Christ.

Ogmar's introduction to the monastery had also included a thorough telling of the story of St. Joseph of Arimathea—and how Joseph carried a staff made from the very same tree from which the crown of thorns was cut. And when followers of the old religion confronted Joseph with threats while he tried to preach to them on the side of Wirral Hill, Joseph stuck his staff into the ground, and it miraculously burst forth into flower—just as it still did every year at the season of Christ's nativity as well as in the springtime. And here was the most sacred tomb of the blessed St. Patrick himself, in whose footsteps Eirran monks had never ceased serving at Ynis Witrin since it was hallowed by the blessed Patrick himself.

Then Brother Ogmar led the way to the cluster of monastery buildings themselves. He stopped and crossed himself with bowed head as he stood before a small wattle and daub building standing under the cover of a stronger timber roof supported by four heavy beams that stood well beyond the corners of the church. "Aye, and this is the Old Church, built by the hand of our Lord Himself and dedicated to the honor of His Holy Mother."

Aelfric frowned. "But is this true? How could you know such a thing?"

"Aye, and well you are to be asking. None knew it to be so, for much knowledge has been lost in these long years since our Lord came here as a wee lad with his uncle. But it was revealed to St. David in a vision of the Lord. For when the blessed Bishop of Menevia came to us from Wales and learned of the antiquity and sanctity of our Old Church—but not of its true origins, all memory of such having been lost—he determined to dedicate it to St. Patrick, whom he greatly venerated.

"But the night before the dedication service, Bishop David went to sleep and saw the Lord standing by his bed. The blessed Savior gently inquired why David had come to this place, and David told him of his intention. Then our Lord spoke to him. 'The church has long ago been dedicated by My own hand in honor of My blessed Mother Mary. It is not seemly that it should be rededicated by human hands.' Our Lord then pierced the palm of David's hand with His finger, saying, 'Let this be a sign to you that you might not repeat what I Myself have done beforehand.'

"On the following morning when the bishop was celebrating the mass, he recited the words, 'Through Him, with Him, in Him,' and the full strength of salvation flowed back into him, and the holy David knew what he was to do." Ogmar suddenly stopped and looked around as if, so caught up was he in his tale, he had forgotten Aelfric. "Come, I will show you what the sainted David built under the inspiration of our Lord."

He led Aelfric around the Old Church a few feet to the east where he stopped before another chapel. Still small and poor-looking to Aelfric, who had become accustomed to the great stone churches of Rome, it was larger and newer than the Old Church. "This is the fine new chapel St. David built here fifty years ago and dedicated to Mary, Mother of God, when he was directed not to rededicate the Old Church."

Walking around the east end of the chapel, Ogmar pointed northward to a fine stone pillar reaching skyward well above the head of the monk and almost higher than the church. "It was in Bishop David's mind that the site or size of the Old Church might be forgotten, even as our Lord's dedication of it had been—especially should others build additions such as his own and they become muddled in people's minds. So David had this pillar erected." He pointed to chiseled markings on the stone and translated their meaning for Aelfric. "See, here are inscribed the exact location of the Old Church, measuring from this pillar, and the measurements of the length and breadth of the sacred building so that none may forget."

Aelfric would have gazed long at these wonders. Indeed, it was too much to take in at one swoop—that the Christ Himself had stood on this very spot—that His sacred feet had hallowed this ground—that the church before him had been built by the Carpenter of Galilee with His own hands—all far overshadowing the fact that the sainted Joseph of Arimathea had performed miracles on this very place as well. Surely outside of the Holy Land itself this was the holiest place on earth. Except Rome, he quickly amended. Then he wondered—was it possible that this ground was more holy than Rome? And he smiled at the outrage such heresy would trigger in Augustine.

A few paces more brought them suddenly to a small hubbub of activity, in sharp contrast to the peace that reigned over the rest of the island. The same Briton Aelfric had seen discussing church building with Augustine at Aust stood now in the center of the activity, the wax tablet bearing the archbishop's sketch in his hand. Bleddyn had assigned twelve builders, selected on the advice of the Bishop of Iona, to build the chapel. Bleddyn came to Ynis Witrin every few days to oversee the progress of the work, as he had today. His red hair and moustache matched the russet cloak that billowed over one shoulder as he paced the side of the foundations. Seeing Ogmar and Aelfric approach, he hailed them. "Aye, and is it not a fine sight! It is in my mind that we'll have the dedication before the apple buds burst next spring."

Ogmar nodded and answered him in the British tongue, a few words of which Aelfric was beginning to understand. "And a fine bunch of builders you've hired here. They go on apace from sun rising to setting. They mason the stones more quickly than the boatmen can bring rock from the crumbled Roman buildings across the Sabrina. And have you yet decided whom you shall be dedicating your fine stone chapel to?"

"Aye, I'll be dedicating it to St. Stephen the Martyr, for like him was my

Eurgana martyred. Like him she cared for widows and orphans, and like him she stood against evil and forgave those who took her life."

Ogmar nodded again. "It is so. You could not have chosen better. So shall she ever be remembered as one who did good in God's name and loved even her enemies."

Bleddyn returned to his work, and Aelfric and Ogmar walked on. "You said his wife died," Aelfric said. "I am thinking there is more to the story. It is not like you to hold back on the telling of a story, Ogmar, who might have been a scop."

Ogmar looked at him for a moment, then seemed to turn inward, to be watching the events in the story. "Aye, and it is a sad telling. The men of a servant family died of the fever, leaving a sickly wife and a boy and girl of eight and nine, or thereabouts. Bleddyn could as like as not have turned them out to beg, as most would have, but Eurgana wanted the children to have a Christian upbringing. As God had granted her just one child—the daughter Olwena—Eurgana said these needy ones were a gift of God."

Ogmar paused, and Aelfric thought that if they were in a mead hall, the scop would surely have played an interlude on his harp. But after a moment Ogmar continued. "Bleddyn and Olwena were away when the raiders came, but one old servant who lived long enough to tell the story said Eurgana fought like Boudicca that the little ones might not live with a Saxon thrall ring around their necks . . ."

"Saxon?" Aelfric interrupted. "The raiders were English?"

Ogmar held him with the level look of his eye for several heartbeats. "Aye." When Aelfric made no reply, Ogmar continued.

"The holy Scriptures tell us it is right to defend the poor and fatherless—and so Eurgana did, and so she died, and so she shall be honored. For, like St. Stephen, at death she prayed for the souls of the Saxon raiders as well."

They stood in silence. Then they slowly turned their steps toward the horse byres, for Aelfric had not yet taken the horses out to pasture that day. But they did not progress far, for coming up the path from Wirral Hill, her yellow tunic shining like the sun, was Bleddyn's daughter. Her hair blew free in the breeze without the long palla with which women in Italy covered their heads or the kerchief women of his own kind wore. She smiled at Ogmar, who was ahead of Aelfric on the narrow path, and held up a small red and green apple from the basket she bore on her arm. "Look, brother. I've just been in-gathering the first of the season. Will they not be sweet for your evening meal?"

Ogmar took the fruit she held out to him. "Ah, it is indeed a fine *aval*—for such sweetness is our island often called the Isle of Avalon." He handed the apple to Aelfric standing just behind him.

Aelfric polished the colorful skin on his rough brown tunic and held the gleaming fruit to catch the glow of the sun. "*Glaesting,*" he said. "So in our tongue this would be *Glaestingaburg.*" And then he sorely regretted his rash reference to his origins as he felt the air suddenly chill.

"May this holy place never be spoken of in the heathen English tongue." Olwena plucked the apple from his hand as she brushed past him and continued on up the path, her back straight and her hair flying like Leander's mane.

At the garth attached to the horse byre Aelfric took comfort that Leander did not turn his back on him, but came readily to his call. The horse no longer limped perceptibly, but the hoof would never again be strong enough to support a rider. Yet he well paid for his keeping. Come next apple-blossoming time at least three of the stallion's foals should be romping in the abbey's horse-runs. In his mind Aelfric could already see the wobbly-legged creatures with their red-gold coats gleaming in the sun as they tottered after their mothers, nuzzling them for milk.

Then his daydream was interrupted by a warm nuzzle on his hand, and he turned to see a small, milk-white mare. "Where did this fine lady come from, Ogmar?" He stroked her neck.

"From the steading of Bleddyn. It is his daughter's. She calls her White One. His is the black yonder." Ogmar pointed to the far side of the garth.

But Aelfric did not look at the other horse—he was busy about the mare. "Well, my pretty one, it seems that you have no objection to having your neck stroked by a heathen English." He was careful, however, to use as many Celtic words to her as he could, just in case.

"Heathen English," mused Aelfric ruefully. He was a Christian, taught by the Pope's direct orders. The English weren't heathen—wasn't he himself present at the baptism of King Aethelberht of Canti and of King Raedwald of his own East Angli?

The northern raiders who killed his parents and carried him into slavery were the enemy. In Rome the Lombards were the enemy. But here in these ancient British lands, the Angles and Saxons were the enemy. They had killed Eurgana. He was an Angle. He was the enemy.

Pope Gregory had had a vision of English and British coming together and forging a better world from the ruins of the past. Was that possible? Even if the barriers of religion came down, was it truly possible to love an ancient enemy as God had commanded?

In the coming weeks Aelfric, too, had cause to worry about the heathen English. These, indeed, were heathen, for the men of Wessex under their King Coelwulf were true followers of Woden in his warlike spirit. As high summer turned into the tangy days of autumn, almost daily reports reached the abbey of Coelwulf's troops advancing ever nearer the marshy land of Somerset.

One afternoon, while Aelfric helped Amulf with his autumn ingathering of healing herbs, the monk told Aelfric of the Kingdom of Wessex that had grown from the stronghold of Cerdric the Saxon around the old town of Sarum. Amulf tactfully forbore using the adjective *heathen* although Aelfric had become so accustomed to its hearing that he had begun using it in his own mind. "There was a great battle somewhere—no one remembers just where. But the tellers of old tales say that the greatest British king that ever was fell with all his men, and so many of the enemy were slain that there has been no new threat to our lands until now."

He pulled a clump of dark green leaves from a small low-growing bush, then straightened up with a hand on his back. "Aye, until now—but what is to be holding them back now only the Lord God Himself is knowing. For we have no great war-leading king. What can farmers and monks be doing against the strong hand of the Wessex war band?"

Aelfric added a small white mushroom to the gathering basket he carried. "I have thought long on this. All along the eastern shores of this land the heathen kings have accepted Christian baptism, and their people followed them. Could not this happen here also? If Coelwulf were a baptized Christian, it's not likely he'd be ravaging Christian farms and churches."

Amulf nodded with a wistful smile. "Aye, and that's a pretty thought. Others have asked the bishops to be sending missionaries to our pagan neighbors. But I fear the truth of the matter is twofold. Most would be too fearful of their lives to walk into Coelwulf's camp and preach against Woden, and the rest would as soon the barbarians take their just reward and burn in Hell—far prefer it, I'd say. But whatever their motives, if half the reports we hear are true, I fear it's too late for any such Christian effort now." He returned to his herb-gathering.

The truth of his words became clear when they returned to Ynis Witrin for the evening meal and prayers. A messenger had arrived that afternoon with the news that the Wessex men had taken over Wincanton. This was grave news indeed, following as it did on the heels of the word they received less than a week ago that Westburg had fallen. Could the army be moving that fast?

The following week news arrived with Bleddyn who came to admire his now shoulder-high walls. "Aye, Somertun it is now, as they call it. I'm thinking we'll soon have no need of messengers. We'll soon be able to sit in the chapel atop the Tor and watch the black smoke of their heathen ravagings."

No matter how he tried to avoid Olwena's gaze, Aelfric couldn't resist stealing a glance at her. Then he regretted it as the look from her flashing green eyes again left him feeling as if he'd had the breath kicked from him.

But next week after a sharp October frost, the news improved. Wessex had taken Gillingham, a village considerably to the east of Somertun. Wessex was withdrawing from Somerset. The dire prediction of seeing battle fires from atop the Tor had not come to pass. At least not yet. And not likely to for this winter at least.

Aelfric hurried to the horse byre. He held an apple on the palm of his hand for Leander, then produced a second for White One. "Ah, and the news is good tonight, Leander. Would you like a cheerful hearing?" And because his heart was light, he dared to speak the mare's name in English, "Hwiting." Then his smile increased, for she did not kick him.

7

ure enough, the winter passed peacefully. When a white blanket of snow covered the Tor, Aelfric quit taking his horses around to the oak grove and instead fed them hay brought in from outlying abbey steadings. Frozen ground on the marshes made travel to the island easier, but cold weather kept most travelers at home. So the gentle days filled with prayers and caring for animals were seldom interrupted. Bleddyn, occasionally accompanied by his daughter, still made the trip as often as possible. The timbered roof had been raised just before the first big snowfall, and now work was progressing on the chapel furnishings—an engraved stone altar and cross, carved wooden benches, and a brass-fitted kist where valuable vessels and holy relics could be kept. Bleddyn often spoke of the fine altar cloth Olwena was embroidering with her own hands and the wall hangings she planned to weave. Aelfric would have liked to hear her speak of it herself, but Hwiting was the only member of their household who responded to his attentions.

As often as his duties would allow, Aelfric liked to slip into the nearly finished chapel and watch the master woodcarver at work. On his high ladder he carved the words into the dedicatory beam by the light of a smoking torch. White oak chips fell to the timbered floor, and when the kitchen boy did not get over to sweep them up for a few days, the older ones yellowed and curled in the waiting. Then another ladder was set up for the painter with his pots of bright scarlet, blue, and ochre to fill in the carefully chiseled letters.

For Aelfric the whole process held a fascination he could not understand, but each day he looked forward to seeing the new words. At last it was finished: "Let All Who Worship Here Imitate the Goodness of St. Stephen and So Shine with Love for Our Enemies."

The dedication of the chapel was set for Easter with the Bishop of Caerleon to preside. Whenever the coming event was mentioned, the brothers would nod and agree that the holy day was indeed an appropriate time. And none said, although the look in their eyes told what they were thinking, that it was well it was early in the spring before the Saxons would be likely to attack. For in spite of the peace of the snow-blanketed Isle of Avalon, rumors continued to reach them of Wessex war plans to spread their golden dragon banner over all the west lands. These were followed by rumors of plans for British resistance. Cadwallon, king of the Cymri, had sent out a hosting call for the British to meet in Aqua Sulis after the first spring thaw . . . na, na, the hosting was not to be in the village the greedy Saxons called Bathum; it was to be in Glevum . . . no, no, in Viroconium and the hosting was to be after the second thaw, not the first, for the first thaw was ever a false beginning to be followed by fierce March storms . . .

And so the rumors continued. The latter must have been correct, for the first thaw brought no sign of warriors. Surely they would not be so foolish as to wait until after spring planting, for that would be to plant for a Saxon reaping.

But then lambing time was full upon them, and a lamb wanting to be born knew nothing of daylight or dark or times for prayers or eating. And so the days spun on with a snatched bowl of stew here and a half-hour's sleep there, until it seemed that all there was in the world was the smell of birthing waters and wet wool and warm milk and the bleating of lambs combined with a morning lark song or an evening curlew call.

Then one morning Aelfric found a clump of bright yellow flowers blooming in a sheltered corner of the horse garth, and around on the south side of the oldest of the oak trees, which Brother Amulf called Gog, and its fellow Magog, pale blue and white snowdrops greeted him. That morning Hwiting was among his charges, for Bleddyn and Olwena had arrived the night before to make sure all was in readiness for the dedication service. It seemed impossible to Aelfric that Easter was just over a week away, although he had certainly noted for many weeks now the absence of meat from the monastery kitchens when he took his Lenten meals with the other lay workers.

He rubbed White One's back and belly absently as she grazed the tender, bright green spring grass. Then he paused and ran his hand more slowly the length of her belly. He leaned his ear to her side and listened carefully. Then he walked to the other side and, pushing Leander away to make more room, repeated the procedure. The mare was carrying her foal too low if the birth was indeed to occur in May as Ogmar had told him. He pressed his ear harder against the round white belly. Then he jumped away. He hadn't been able to hear a heartbeat—or the two heartbeats he suspected—but there was no doubting the sharp little hoof that kicked inside its mother.

"Easy, my little white mother. That must have been sharper to you than to me." He stroked the milky neck, but the mare continued her placid grazing, undisturbed by the activity inside her.

The following week even the rumor that the Kingdom of Mercia to the north had combined with Wessex for a mass assault on Somerset was overwhelmed by the glory of celebrating Holy Week. Passion Sunday began with a joyful peal of the monastery bell at sunrise calling all within its hearing to Lauds. All those on Ynis Witrin, lay and religious, and those from the tiny marsh villages came to worship the Lord's entry into Jerusalem. Father Wogret served mass to the religious community in the Old Church, and the lay worshipers took the sacrament from the prior, Father Connal, in St. David's Chapel, with many waiting their turn on the green grass outside.

Father Connal, who led the brothers in choir, had composed a hymn to Eurgana's honor, and for days St. David's Chapel rang with the chant as the brothers practiced for the dedication.

Bishop Eulogius of Caerleon arrived on Holy Thursday and said a mass especially for the monastery members to renew their commitment to Christ. As the bishop and his party arrived by boat, there were no new additions to the horse byres until Good Friday when Bleddyn and his party arrived just after midday prayers. The guest huts were now full. Later arrivals who would come in to celebrate Easter at Avalon would be directed to pitch tents around the well that bubbled from the small hillside lying low to the west of the Tor. When Leander nickered a soft welcome to White One, Aelfric also felt his byre was complete. For always when Hwiting—and her mistress—were absent from the island, Aelfric felt a strange uneasiness, as if in the old days of sheepherding he had counted his fold at night and found some missing.

But that night Hwiting did not seem herself. She moved restlessly around the garth, took small sips of water, but refused even the handfuls of tender spring grass Aelfric offered her.

Aelfric watched the mare closely all the next day, but could find no reason for the vague restlessness they both felt. By sunset Saturday she seemed more settled, so he decided to leave the horse byre in charge of Morvidd, a lad from the monastery school who had not worked out as a kitchen helper, but who seemed to find his place working with the animals.

In spite of the chill in the air, Aelfric slipped away to the river for a thorough washing and rubbed his body with an aromatic musk herb before donning his best blue tunic. After a careful combing of his shoulder-length, glossy yellow hair, he picked up the small piece of pumice stone he had brought with him from Rome. If a trader didn't find his way westward soon, Aelfric would have to adopt the style of some of the brothers and wear a beard, or learn to shave with his eating knife as he had observed the British doing. But for now he rubbed his chin smooth with the porous gray stone.

He stooped to wrap his garters around his legs. Then he stopped. With a small smile he took his knife from his belt and cut the long leather thongs from his shoes. He would wear his leggings ungartered—British style.

The last red streaks faded from the western sky as Aelfric arrived at the site the brothers had prepared for the Easter vigil. Ogmar and Amulf had been among those who had spent several hours that day clearing dead wood from the apple garth and piling it in the open space in front of the Old Church. Now all was dark. Not a candle or cook fire flickered anywhere on the island or across the marsh. Even in his unbleached sheep's wool robe, the bishop showed as only a pale form walking at the head of a procession of chanting monks who moved like shadows in their dark robes.

When he came to the congregation waiting beyond the piled wood, Bishop Eulogius held out his hands in a blessing. "My children, who have gathered here in the name of our Savior on this most holy night, we wait in the dark in the memory of His death. Then as we light the Easter fire in the memory of His resurrection, let you be certain that so shall we share His victory over death and darkness."

At a signal from the bishop, Prior Connal knelt at the foot of the wood pile and struck the flint. The first two strikes failed, but on the third a spark caught a dry leaf. In moments the orange and gold tongues were licking heavenward, sending up sharp crackling noises and showers of sparks. Bishop Eulogius threw a handful of incense grains on the flames, and a sweet spicy aroma mingled with the clean scent of burning applewood.

The smoke carried their prayers upward, as the bishop stood with his hands spread toward the fire. "Father in Heaven, we ask Your blessing on this fire. We share in the light of Your glory through Your Son, the Light of the World. Inflame us with new hope. Purify us by this Easter celebration and bring us one day to Your feast of eternal light. We ask through Jesus Christ our Lord, in Your holy name."

All crossed themselves and said, "Amen." Then, while the brothers chanted a hymn, all passed by the Easter fire, lighting their own tarred sticks and passing on to light the hearth in their own huts or the campfire before their tents. Their hymn swelled over the whole island:

Rejoice, voices of heaven! Sing, choir of angels!
Exult, all creation round the Great White Throne,
Christ our King is risen!
Christ has conquered darkness!
Glory reigns forever!
Dark is ever vanquished!
Let this place resound with joy,
Rejoice, O earth in shining splendor!

Around the island tiny fires sprang to life. And up the side of the Tor, a winding zigzag of flickering torches signaled the progress of monks taking the good news of the resurrection light to the mountaintop. Their chanting voices echoed down to the valley, accompanied by the call of night birds. At last the procession reached the top, and in a few moments a great beacon of flame flared across the marshes. *If Coelwulf sees that from his strongplace, he will know the worshipers of the White Christiani are not cowed by his threats,* Aelfric thought with satisfaction.

He had barely turned toward the byre when Morvidd reached him, panting. "Aelfric, Aelfric. Come. Quick. It is the white mare. She is down. Something is wrong."

Aelfric held the lad by the shoulder and made him repeat his jumble of words, more to gain time to think than for failure of understanding—he had understood all too well. His first thought was Ogmar. He sorely needed his help, but the black shadows that were the brothers were still atop the Tor. Precious time would be wasted waiting for him. "Is it the foal?"

Morvidd threw out his hands. "I cannot tell. I have never seen a foal come. I—I know not. If the mare dies . . ."

Aelfric shook him to stop the whimpering. "You must go calmly. It is Olwena's horse. She must be told. But I'll not have you frightening her with your blubbering. Go to the guest hut—" Then he thought better of his idea. "No. I'll go myself. You gather the rope and sticks—we'll need two sturdy sticks—this long." He measured three feet with his hands. "And a fresh pot of goose grease. Have it ready and plenty of torches lit when I get there."

Nodding vigorously, Morvidd scampered off, and Aelfric strode to the guest hut. On the way he found a lad to send scurrying up the Tor for Ogmar. He had no time to worry about Olwena's reception, but he was glad he could speak to her in British now, if only to save time in communicating.

At Aelfric's news Olwena sent a servant with a message to her father and turned immediately to match her step to Aelfric's. "I think it is the foal," he said.

"But it can't be. Her time isn't for six weeks yet."

"I know. But she is heavy—I noticed before."

"Can you help her? And the babe?"

"I shall try. I don't know yet. It may not be that—"

But even before they saw the white mare, her deep-throated, abrupt nickering told them she was in distress. "Help me raise her. She'll do better on her feet if we can get her up." Aelfric's directions came out in a strange blend of English, British, and Latin, but Olwena understood. She went to her mare's head and murmured soothing encouragement while Aelfric pushed from the far side.

By the time Morvidd arrived with a pot of goose grease and the rope and sticks, White One was standing, shifting restlessly in the pen. "Clean straw," Aelfric ordered Morvidd as he pulled his tunic off over his head and slathered his right arm with goose grease to the elbow. "Can you hold her hoof to keep her still?"

Olwena didn't break her flow of talk to the mare, but bent and lifted a foreleg in reply.

Holding the silky white tail aside, Aelfric inserted his greased arm in the mare's rectum. He had to cease his exploring for several seconds as a strong contraction gripped the mare's uterus. Then he nodded. "As I expected. Twins."

Olwena's first reaction was delight. "Ah, that's a fine thing!" But she quickly caught Aelfric's look of concern. "Something's amiss?"

Again Aelfric nodded, and then explored a bit further, this time up the very birth canal. "The first one's stuck. A big one. And it's the wrong way round."

"I've heard of turning a bairn."

"Not with two of them in there, you haven't."

And then it was quiet in the byre save for White One's little throaty sounds and Olwena's whispers, which had changed from murmurs to her horse to prayers to her God.

Just then Morvidd returned with an armful of fresh straw which he dumped behind Aelfric. "The rope." Morvidd scrambled to do Aelfric's bidding. Aelfric tied a slip knot in the looped middle of the rope, covered it with goose grease, and took it with his arm inside the mare. In a few minutes he had secured the loop around the foal's hind feet, and Morvidd, following his directions, tied the sturdy sticks like handles to the ends of the rope.

"When I say—pull!" Aelfric waited until the contraction started. "Pull!" and they pulled, working with the mare's own body. The foal moved a few inches, but seemed to slip back when the contraction ended. "Harder next time."

The night air was chill, but the sweat poured off Aelfric's forehead and ran into his eyes. Soon his neck and shoulders were wet as well. And his arms ached. He lost all track of time in his intense concentration on the rhythmic pull and rest of the mare's body. At last a pair of tiny hooves appeared. Then the legs extended to the knees. The fetlocks were black; then above the knees grew red-gold hair.

It was three more contractions before the tail and rump were out; then the entire foal slid out on the next contraction. Aelfric lay it in the clean straw and checked nose and mouth to be sure the breathing passages were clear. Morvidd had already begun rubbing the tiny wet creature with handfuls of clean straw. Aelfric smiled at Olwena. "It's a colt."

"Aye, I'm thinking he'll be as fine as his father one day."

And then Aelfric realized. How silly of him not to have thought sooner. "You mean—Leander?"

"Yes, yes. My fine British mare bred to an English stallion."

Aelfric's laughter filled the byre. "Na, na. Leander belonged to the

Archbishop of Cantwaraburg—you'll not be saying he's heathen. If ever there was a Christian horse, it must be Leander, who came from the very stables of Pope Gregory."

Olwena's laughter joined his. Briefly, though, for White One's contractions started again. This time Aelfric and Olwena simply sat on the straw as observers, for before they could turn from the colt, Ogmar hurried into the byre with his robe kilted above his knees, evidence that he had made haste once the messenger had located him. And then the little white filly slipped from her mother with no need of assistance since her lumbering big brother was out of her way. Again Olwena shared Aelfric's joyful laughter as they rubbed the little girl-foal dry and set both newborns sucking for their breakfast.

Sunrise was breaking over the Tor when they finally emerged from the byre—a glorious golden Easter sunrise—signaling the new life Christ brought to the world and celebrating the new life they had helped into the world. Olwena hurried away to wash. She could not miss the dedication of her mother's chapel.

But Aelfric turned toward his bed in the hut beyond the horse byre. He wanted to rest his aching muscles, but he knew he would not sleep. The last hours spun and flickered in his mind as the flaming Easter fire had branched into the sputtering torches, turning everything golden. The flames whirled and danced in his head like frolicking foals, and he heard over and over again his voice coming as from afar and Olwena's voice bright and clear. His voice was telling her the Greek legend for which Leander was named, as it had been told him by an educated brother in Rome. And she was clapping her hands with delight. "And then I shall be naming these two Hero and Leander, for the night of lovers guided by a beacon on a hill!"

And whatever her dizzy-tired meaning might have been for that—it's unlikely she knew herself—there was no mistaking the smile she gave him after she thoroughly congratulated her mare on the fine offspring and called her "Hwiting."

8

The Monday after Easter, Bleddyn and his daughter left Ynis Witrin to see to the spring planting on their steading, but Hwiting and the newborn foals remained there in Aelfric's care. "I will miss your companionship—you who are so dear to me. But I will carry you next to my heart, and I will return as soon as I may. We shall have many good times together, you and I. See now that you take good care of the little ones." Olwena's soft loving words were spoken to Hwiting, but Aelfric, standing quietly in a corner of the byre, could not help hoping that a little of their tenderness might be for himself as well.

Then followed a time of great activity on Ynis Witrin, for seedtime and harvest were ever the busiest of the year. The planting of crops could mean the difference between starvation and survival should the rumored hostings of warriors cut off supplies from outside sources, or should, God forbid, their blessed island be overrun. Throughout four hundred years of Roman occupation, Avalon had remained sacred. Throughout periods of repeated attacks by fierce Eirran and Scoti raiders, Avalon had remained sacred. Throughout the succeeding two hundred years of repeated threats from Angles, Saxons, Jutes, and assorted barbarians, Avalon had remained sacred. Was it now to be violated? Now, after six hundred years as the cradle of British Christianity, was Avalon to fall to Coelwulf and his English hoard?

None could tell, for only God knew the future, but every person, male or female, religious or lay, gave only the briefest time possible to eating and sleeping, and the rest was divided between fervent prayers and tending the fields. Brother Amulf worked all sunlight hours, even gaining Abbot Wogret's permission to miss prayers on occasion, to fill his store-shed with herbs, roots, and berries of medicinal nature. He then worked into the long dark hours extracting elixirs and pounding salves to fill all his bottles and pots. Ogmar, Aelfric, and Morvidd took their turns as well at the seed planting. And all fell on their cots at night as if they had been doing battle with the English, who were in fact miles away but never far from mind.

But never a day passed, no matter how long or tiring, that Aelfric did not find time for White One and her Hero and Leander, as well as for the other horses.

Yet with all the attention of the monastery focused on bringing new life into the world, with all of nature sending spring sunshine and sweet rains to foster green growth, with the garths and trees flowering white apple blossoms and green leaves and the nests of new-hatched birds, there was no escaping the pall of death and destruction that hung over them. The rumors would not cease. Once one had heard them, it was impossible to put them entirely out of mind. Coelwulf and the men of Wessex marching under their golden dragon banners had joined with a handful of middle Anglian lords and their warriors and were marching westward, pillaging and burning as they went. The reports and rumors varied in the degree of destruction they had to recount, and the route and rate of progress of the enemy was told differently by every refugee who passed across Ynis Witrin. But the end was the same. A wave of darkness was rolling toward them. No matter what its speed or fury, it rolled inexorably onward, and they would be engulfed.

Cadwallon, High King of the Cymri, had sent out his hosting call, and the British farmers were gathering with his warriors at Glevum. But none needed to add what all knew—that they would be a pitiful handful against the numberless English forces.

Aelfric spent considerable concern on the safety of his animals, but the main of his waking hours were given to worry over Olwena and Bleddyn. The finest steading north of the marshes, nestling in its green hills, was an open invitation to both armies. It would doubtless be stripped by the British men making their way to Glevum, and then when the English rolled over them . . . he could allow his mind to go no further. At times he thought of going there himself and offering his service as a guard—poor though such service would be. At other times he thought of asking Abbot Wogret to send servants to fetch Olwena to the island for safety—but Wogret would remind him that such was her father's responsibility.

So Aelfric worried. And increased his prayers. For once the crops were planted and the animals tended and the herbs gathered, all human preparations were done. There would be no gathering of sticks and pitchforks for the monks of Ynis Witrin. There would be no building of barricades of turf and timber. The weapons they would stockpile and the palisades they would erect would be spiritual.

From the first of the threat even when the load of work was heaviest, Abbot Wogret announced a rota of monks to pray day and night in the Old Church. Not one moment of the twenty-four hours would be without prayer. As the reports of the enemy's approach increased, Wogret increased the prayer vigil. First two monks were to be praying at all times. Then three. And after the evening meal all on the island, whether cowled or not, were to pray in one of the chapels for as long as their strength would uphold them.

Aelfric chose always to pray in St. Stephen's Chapel, for it made him feel closer to Olwena. Always when he entered, he read the words he had watched being carved on the rooftree so many months ago: "Let All Who Worship Here Imitate the Goodness of St. Stephen and So Shine with Love for Our Enemies." And always he felt the same confusion. The Angli who marched upon them were his people in blood, but they marched upon those who were his people in spirit. He knew that that should have given added fervor to his prayers. He should have prayed mightily for the deliverance of the British and the salvation of the souls of the English. But after his first confusion of thoughts and rote mouthing of memorized prayers, the cry of his heart always emerged, *Keep Olwena safe.* More than that he could not focus on.

Late in May when Aelfric was on his way to such a vigil, he met Olwena and Bleddyn coming up the path from the boat place followed by an old servant. They went on past him in search of the abbot. Wogret, who had received word of their approach, emerged from the Old Church. "Welcome, my children. You have come to us in this time of danger. It is good. The guest hut is ever yours."

But Bleddyn shook his head. "I bring you Olwena and the old Elni that they may bide under your care. I will spend the night praying in Eurgana's chapel that her courage may be with me. I go to join the Cymri men."

"You have abandoned the steading?"

"A few servants remain with the cattle. They will drive them into the woods when Coelwulf comes. A few may survive. God forgive me. It is all I can do."

"You have done well, my son." Wogret placed his hand on Bleddyn's shoulder and walked with him into the new chapel.

In the morning Bleddyn departed. And just five days later they heard the news. A lad who couldn't have been more than fourteen years, black to the waist with mud, his left arm red to the shoulder with blood, and his face and belly shrunken from starvation, was dumped at the infirmary by a fisherman who had pulled him half-drowned from the marsh.

Aelfric hurried to offer assistance. But Amulf had all under control. By the time Aelfric arrived, the monk had sent a boy running for the abbot and had the lad's leather tunic cut off so he could tend the wound. He sent Aelfric to the kitchen for a bowl of broth. "The strongest they have—made with red meat. And tell Brother Uthdra to add a dose of red wine. This one has lost blood enough; we must be filling his veins with something else."

For the rest of that day and night and into the next, Amulf fought the fever that raged in the frail body. After midday prayers the next afternoon, the boy's forehead cooled, and he slept without tossing and moaning. "Tell Wogret he may have speech with him when he wakes, in an hour or two, I am thinking," Amulf, who had never once left his patient's side, ordered Aelfric.

And so it was at the evening meal that Abbot Wogret gave voice to the news that all had known in their hearts for days. "The battle is over. It is lost." He made the sign of the cross over himself and then over his beloved community, for he knew not how many more times he would be able to do so.

"The armies met at Aqua Sulis. The British fought bravely. Cadwallon and his war chiefs all fell. Brothers, let us go to prayer."

All in the room bowed, and Wogret prayed, "O God, the heathen are come into Your inheritance; they have laid Jerusalem on heaps. The heathen rage, O Lord. You have promised Your people the heathen for an inheritance—grant it, we ask. Let the heathen be judged in Your sight. Declare Your glory among the heathen. Say among the heathen that the Lord reigns. Save us, O Lord, our God, and gather us from among the heathen, to give thanks unto Your holy name and to triumph in Your praise. Amen."

The monks filed from the hall in absolute silence, every head bowed beneath its cowl, every hand folded in prayer. But Aelfric could not so easily abandon earthly thoughts and go inward to find strength. Instead he turned from the cluster of chapels, huts, and byres that had become home to him. He walked away—away and upward, as if by climbing to the highest peak around, he could rise above the hopeless turmoil of the earth. Perhaps he had some dim instinct of climbing upward to God, but his clearer instinct was that he longed to escape from the darkness and despair. He wanted to climb the Tor where such a short time ago on Easter Eve the beacon of light had blazed forth declaring that the Light of the World lived.

But there was no beacon of light tonight. All the lights burned north of the marsh. The campfires of the Saxons lashed red in the darkness. *O God, the heathen are come into Your inheritance.* And he turned to the east. And the south. All around the red dots flickered. *The heathen rage, O Lord.* Ynis Witrin was surrounded on every side save the west.

That was it! Aelfric ran headlong down the steep hill, sometimes sliding, sometimes rolling, ignoring sharp stones and sticks. He must tell the abbot. The west was open. They could flee to the mountains of the Cymri. Even tonight, their boatmen would know the river channels. No, at first light. All must go. Drive the cattle as far as they could, take what crosses and relics they could and bury the rest. Tomorrow, or the next day at the latest, it would all be over. The enemy was at the door. The heathen raged. He had seen. He had all but smelled them.

Suddenly he realized that he was yelling all this to Wogret who had come to the doorway of the Old Church to meet this one who would rush in on their prayers. Aelfric stopped. He did not know how much of his frenzied thought he had voiced, or if he had made sense. Had Wogret understood?

The abbot nodded solemnly. "Yes, my son. I understand. The Saxons surround us. The only way of escape is to the west. Certainly you may go. And all who would go with you. All are free to take what they can carry and go to the Cymri."

He stepped forward into the night. "I will go now and tell the boatmen to prepare all they can, for many may wish to go."

"But what of you, Father? Will not you go?"

"No. Not I. My place is here. I will stay, and all who wish may stay with me. We will stay on this holy island and build a shield wall of prayer around it. God has promised His people the heathen for an inheritance. It may be that our shield wall will hold, or it may not. It is in God's hands. Perhaps He will gather us from among the heathen. Perhaps not. But we are men of prayer. It is what we do best. So we will pray."

The next morning the boatmen were ready at first light. But none left. Aelfric had known from the moment he heard Wogret's words that he would not leave either—unless Olwena should go and wish him to accompany her. He was not a man of prayer like the monks, but this was his home. All that he cared about was here. The fate of Ynis Witrin would be his fate.

A few smoke curls from campfires showed in the morning light when Aelfric climbed the Tor to see if he could learn anything new. In his imagination he thought he could see the sunlight glinting off sharpened swords and boar-crested war helms, and he thought he could hear the hollow booming of the great round war horns.

Wogret had given complete freedom for every monk and lay member of the community to decide—whether to go or to stay, whether to work or to pray, whether to eat or to fast. Many went about their usual tasks as quietly and as efficiently as they could, then hurried back into one of the chapels to pray, or simply knelt before one of the wooden crosses on the grounds, or paused in their labors in the fields to bow their heads. But Abbot Wogret and a cluster of the older monks never left the Old Church. They had vowed a perpetual vigil. Wogret urged old Brother Bramwel, the most ancient of the community whose joints ached continually even in the best of times, to rest one hour out of six. But Bramwel replied that he did not choose for God to take a break in His watchcare over them, so he'd not ask less of himself.

All that day the shield wall held. And that night all gathered to thank God. Amulf even brought Ossian, his patient from the infirmary, still frail and bloodless, but able to walk the distance on his own legs. Olwena came, carrying a pillow for old Elni to kneel on, but refusing one for herself. All sang praises to God that the wall of prayer had shielded them for that day and asked that it might continue. "Grant, our God, that we may abide evermore under the shadow of the Almighty. Be our refuge and our fortress—You, our God, in whom we trust. . . . Under Your wings let us abide. Your truth shall be our shield and buckler. Let us not be afraid for the terror by night; nor for the arrow that flies by day; nor for the pestilence that walks in darkness; nor for the destruction that wastes at noonday. A thousand shall fall at Your side and ten thousand at Your right hand, but it shall not come nigh."

Aelfric crept from the chapel. Tonight he moved calmly up the Tor. And the view that greeted him did not strike terror to his heart. The ring of Saxon fires blazed as bright as before. Perhaps brighter. But they blazed no closer. The enemy was near, but no nearer.

And so on the next night.

And so the next.

The Saxon fires burned at the edge of the marsh. They stayed as if held off by the monks' shield wall of prayer.

When Aelfric turned to descend the hill, he was startled by a small rustling within the chapel that stood with open archways looking out each direction from the top of the Tor. He looked in and saw a dark figure on the stone bench. "Olwena? And is that you?"

"It is I. The shield wall holds."

"Sa. It holds."

"But what think you of the other side of the Saxon fire ring? What is it like beyond?"

He had a pretty good idea what the answer was. Empty villages. Burned-out steadings. Lifeless bodies. But that was her home. The home of her family for generations past and before that. He could not speak what he feared. "I do not know. I suppose we shall receive more reports when the fire ring recedes."

"And think you that is what will happen? That the Saxons will go away?"

"They have not advanced against our shield wall, yet there is nothing stopping them. Nothing human, that is. They will not sit forever by their campfires. They will return to their own steadings."

"Or to the steadings they have stolen from the British." Her voice bore the old scorn. Then it changed. "Na, na. Forgive me. I have been thinking much as you say, and I would ask you a favor."

"Ask anything."

"When the fire ring recedes, I will return to our steading. I would have you accompany White One as the foals are yet so young."

"Olwena . . ." He stopped and shook his head.

"Na, na. Do not say it. I know much will be destroyed—perhaps all. But perhaps not. The servants and cattle may indeed have escaped into the woods as my father said. And in any case, that is where I shall meet my father again. I would not make him come to the island to fetch me when there will be so much to do."

He knew the insane hopelessness of her plan. And yet he heard the determination in her voice. If he did not go, she would go alone. "I will go."

In the dark he felt her hand grope for his and then clasp it with a sudden warm sureness. "Hwiting would have no other."

The next night Aelfric and Olwena climbed the Tor together. The fire ring was thinner. Fewer tongues of red lashed at the peace of the horizon. Coelwulf's war host was departing. They must think they had conquered everything to the Cymri border. Save Dumnonia below that. Did they not know Ynis Witrin was there? Or did they not think it worth bothering about? Or had God hidden it from them with angels' wings? At that moment the why didn't matter. It was enough that they were departing. Olwena flung her arms around Aelfric in great joy. And in greater joy, Aelfric returned the embrace. Then they turned and hand-in-hand sped down the Tor to spread the good news.

Abbot Wogret gathered his community. In remarkably short time Father Connal had his choir of monks assembled in the Old Church expressing their praise and gratitude by chanting a *gloria*:

Glory to God in the highest and peace to His people on earth.
Lord God, Heavenly King, Almighty God and Father, Ruler over all,
We worship you,
We thank you,
We praise you.
You alone are powerful;
You alone are worthy;
You alone are the Holy One;
You alone are the Lord;
You alone are the Most High.
Glory to God in the highest.

The next morning Aelfric attended the horses with the words of the *gloria* on his lips and in his heart. The island was saved. The enemy was departing. Olwena had turned to him.

Suddenly he saw all as possible, all he had dreamed but never dared admit even to himself. He and Olwena and their horses in a fine houseplace of sturdy timber and thick thatch, well-built byres within the enclosure, and lush green garths of corn and barley beyond. He and Olwena . . . And he gave Hwiting an extra measure of grain that should have been saved for winter feed.

But before even he had slipped a rope through Leander's halter—Leander the father, that is—to lead him to the thick grass beneath the oak trees, the world stopped.

It was old Elni—Olwena's stooped and wrinkled servant who had spent all her time on Avalon seeking a sunny spot to sit in—whose wail he heard rising from Brother Amulf's herb patch. And the sound was a rising and falling lament that spoke of the utter despair of the end of all things. And he knew that for him all things had ended.

He made his way to St. Stephen's Chapel where he was surest of finding Olwena. And she was there. Not keening for her dead like Elni, but standing stiff and dry-eyed before the altar cross. She turned at the sound of his entrance. "My mother was killed by heathen English raiders. My father was killed by heathen English warriors. I have no more that can be taken from me."

She did not give them voice, but the words hung vibrating in the air between them as if she had, *Nothing more that can be taken by you who are also English, Aelfric of the East Angli.*

9

The resurrection of Christ is the hope of the faithful." Abbot Wogret stood before the altar in St. Stephen's Chapel. Incense, symbolic of the soul rising to its Maker, filled the air.

A double row of dark-robed monks on either side of the altar responded, "Why are you cast down, my soul? Why groan you within me? I will hope in God. I will praise Him still—my Savior and my God."

And the tiny congregation with Olwena on the front row responded, "The resurrection of Christ is the hope of the faithful."

A shaft of morning sunlight fell through the tall eastern window and lit the gold cross on the altar as Wogret continued. "I am the resurrection and the life; whoever believes in me, though he should die, will come to life; and whoever is alive and believes in me will never die."

And again the responsory, "The resurrection of Christ is the hope of the faithful."

Wogret dipped his hand into a bronze basin and sprinkled holy water in front of the altar where the body of Bleddyn would have lain had it been possible to recover it. Then he crossed himself and prayed, "God of mercy, Lord of love and light, hear our prayers and be merciful to Your son, Bleddyn, whom You have called from this life. Welcome him into the company of Your saints in the kingdom of light and peace. We ask this, as all things, through Christ our Lord."

And all responded, "Amen."

The service was ended. Aelfric, sitting just inside the door, had intended to duck out quickly so as not to distress Olwena with his presence. They had come so close, the two of them, that night on the Tor—so close to overcoming the animosities that had existed between their peoples for hundreds of years. But they had been torn apart by the clash of armies.

Aelfric though was slow in turning and so did not escape Olwena's eyes. He fled. His pace did not slacken until he reached the horse garth where acceptance and solace ever awaited him.

It was not until he stopped that he realized he was not alone. Olwena had followed. "Will tomorrow be too soon? There is nothing more for me here."

"Tomorrow? Too soon for what?"

"And did you not promise to accompany me to our—my, it is now—steading?"

He blinked at her words. Did he understand aright? "You . . . you would still have my company?" It was not necessary to add "my English company."

"White One will have you." And it was true, for even now the mare was nudging his shoulder.

But they did not leave on the morrow, nor yet on the next day. Each night Aelfric climbed the Tor to check the Saxon fire ring. And every night fewer red eyes blinked back at him. Yet he would wait until there were fewer.

It was many weeks after the saying of the office for Bleddyn's soul before the lights to the north were so few as to be thought only the campfires of native herdsmen. In that time the monastery had received a few travelers who told tales of destruction, but not of danger. The apples on Wirral Hill were streaked with red and the barley in the field a harvest-silver when at last Aelfric gave in to Olwena's urging that if they didn't go soon, it would be too late to save anything.

Late summer dryness made travel by foot across the marshes easier. The colts, now sturdy-legged, frolicked beside their mother who bore the faithful Elni. Ossian, now recovered from his battle wounds, bore a heavy pack of food supplies and sleeping rugs, for they could not be sure of finding enough to live on for even a few days. Although Coelwulf's army had withdrawn, Aelfric insisted they avoid the old Roman road once they crossed the marshes and instead keep to the woods. At the very least the area might be full of cattle raiders, *as likely British as English,* he thought, but he did not say so.

And so the trip that should have been an easy day took two.

Yet Aelfric would have had it take longer, for he so dreaded what Olwena would find. He was not far from wrong. Even before they came in sight of the houseplace, while the green hills were still merely a backdrop, a blackened field that should have been golden spelt wheat warned them of worse to come.

They went slowly over a small rise, and Olwena in the lead stopped. She stood long, her head up, her back straight, her red-gold hair blowing loose in the evening breeze. She did not weep nor cry out. She merely stood in great quietness.

But Elni showed no such restraint. Her wailing keen for the destroyed steading was like that for its slain master, rising and falling across the blackened, lifeless buildings like the sound of a wounded animal. Aelfric started to move to quiet her, for if anyone were about, this would surely give notice of their own presence. But the deadness of the scene before them spoke of such emptiness that caution seemed unnecessary.

It was Olwena who silenced her. "Quiet, Elni. This is not a death, but a rebirth. This is my homecoming."

Elni snuffled to a hiccuping silence. "But, my lady, lamb of my heart, it is all gone—all—it is . . ."

And for a moment it seemed as if she would launch again into her mourning, but Olwena silenced her. "No. It is not all gone. One wall of the houseplace remains. We shall make a camp by that." She looked at Aelfric as if demanding his approval.

"Sa. There is grass for the horses. It will do."

In truth, more than one wall of the houseplace remained. An entire semicircle of the outer wall stood, the flames that blackened the clay of its daub having baked it hard as stone. And half of the thatched roof, fallen from its central support pole, formed a sheltering lean-to on the other side. "It must have rained shortly before they fired it," Aelfric said, looking at the unburned straw.

"Or started to rain before the flames reached this side," Olwena suggested.

Aelfric pushed back a clump of hanging thatch as if making his way through a heavily grown wood and stepped into the dimness of the ruin. A sudden scurrying movement in the darkest corner told him rats had found the shelter ahead of them.

Then he stopped. The huddled form was too large for a rat.

Olwena, a footstep behind, bumped into him. "What is it?"

"There is someone here. A child, I think."

Aelfric would have stopped her, but Olwena darted in front of him, her arms outstretched. "Child? Don't be afraid. Is this your home? Are you a servant's child? Don't you know me? I am your mistress."

By that time she had reached the corner where the little thing crouched, whimpering. She reached out to take it by the arm, but drew back with a cry, "Ow! It scratched me! Don't you understand? I will help you."

Aelfric took Olwena by the shoulders and pulled her back. "I think I understand. *Angli?*" he asked the child in his native tongue.

"*Gese.*"

"*Boi oththe gurle?*"

"*Gurle.*" The reply was almost lost in the whimpering sobs that seemed to engulf the small bit of humanity.

Aelfric nodded. "As I thought, the child of a soldier probably. Her mother was most likely a camp follower. Her parents are lost or dead. Amazing she's been able to stay alive."

He felt Olwena go rigid beside him. "Out! Get that thing out of my house."

The wailing increased at her harsh tone.

"Olwena, it's only a child. Not yet six years, I'd guess."

"An English child! Vermin!"

Aelfric felt his eating knife slip from the sheath at his waist and looked down to see it in Olwena's grip. "Her father or one of his kind killed my father. I shall even the score."

Aelfric stepped in front of the child. "Even the score on me, Olwena, for I too am English."

She raised her arm. The blade caught a glint of light through the broken thatch. The open doorway behind her silhouetted the proud Celtic warrior—as her mother had once been—Boudicca defending her people.

For the space of a heartbeat Aelfric thought she would strike. He stood to receive the blow. And then the knife clattered to the broken floor boards, and Olwena fell sobbing into his arms.

It was the first time she had cried—cried for her father, for her home, for her country. And all the cries of the bereaved daughter, of the desolate homeless, of the defeated people tore from her as if they would break her apart. Aelfric held her steady in his arms while all the storm raged. And it increased in fury as if there would be no abatement. Then at last the sobs decreased, and she was quiet, save for small, tearing cries in her throat. Still her shoulders shook, and she trembled as if all her earthly supports were gone. She would have fallen had not Aelfric held her, but his hold was sure.

Finally it was over. But she did not leave Aelfric's hold as he moved her through the open doorway to the golden sky of an autumn sunset. He led her to sit on a soft mound of grass and lean against him. Long they sat so, for Aelfric would not speak first, and she was too drained.

Then she pulled apart a bit and looked at him. "I would have killed her. I would have killed a child, orphaned like myself. I who am a Christian. The daughter of Eurgana who ever loved the fatherless and prayed for her enemies."

He paused before asking, for his whole life hung on her answer, and he wasn't sure this was the right time—but he must know. Soon or late, he must know. "And you, Olwena. Can you love your enemy?"

She shook her head. "You were never my enemy. I do not know how it is. You were ever English, but never an enemy."

He held her close again. That was enough answer for now. Then even in the circle of his arms she shivered in the evening air.

He released her and stood up. "I will build a fire. Shall you both warm by it? You and the child?"

Her nod was barely perceptible.

They returned to Ynis Witrin to be wed by Abbot Wogret. The monastery gave them a wedding gift—a milch cow for now and in the spring two ewes that would come heavy with lamb from Avalon's best tup. Enough had escaped unburned in garden and garth to feed them and their three servants through the winter. Elni had taken Ossian and the little English girl Gytha under her wing immediately and had no trouble communicating her orders to the child, whose fear vanished once she was warm and her stomach filled.

With Morvidd and others sent from the monastery to help him, Aelfric had a fine new houseplace built before the first heavy frosts. Although he did not tell Olwena that the strange style he built in was English, she knew, but she did not protest. She did, though, ask many questions. Why did he dig out a hollow space for the flooring to lay over? And when he explained that the air space kept the floor boards from rotting and provided a handy place to store items, she nodded and was quiet. Quiet, that is, until she thought to ask why the timber walls had to be rectangular. Did not the corners hold the cold? He replied that he would lay a rectangular hearth in the middle to warm the corners as well. And what was the use of that strange platform suspended between floor and roof trees at the far end? His eyes twinkled and his smile softened as he explained that it was to be the sleeping loft, their own bedplace that would remain private when they had cubblings sleeping on the hearth benches. They would pile the loft with softest fur rugs, and Olwena would hang the walls with her finest embroidery, and no queen would have a finer bower.

But on the morning when he carried a small hammer and awl up the ladder leaning against the support beam running the length of the room, he refused to answer all her questions. So she turned to her weaving, sitting this day in the sunshine beyond the doorway, for it was a golden late autumn day—perhaps the last for that year.

When she returned to the hearth to stir the noontime stewpot, she was too amazed at first to ask a question. Aelfric came down from the ladder, and she simply shook her head and looked at him with admiration. "I did not know my husband could write."

"But did I not tell you I was taught by the monks in Rome?"

"Yes, yes. So you said. To mouth a few prayers and sign your name, I supposed. But this—whatever it is—" She waved her hand toward the beam that bore the beginnings of a text much as the one the builders had carved in the support beams of her mother's chapel. Yet the letters looked different. She frowned. "I think that is not Latin as the monks use."

Aelfric nodded, but he would only tell her to wait and see. The needs of the steading interrupted Aelfric many times, and it was many days, even weeks, before the work was finished. After the first snowfall, when he had long since moved Olwena's loom inside so she could weave by the fire, he climbed down from the ladder that had inched its way the length of the west side of the room and back up the east. Both beams were now covered with neatly carved letters painted in glowing red, blue, and saffron that made the room look as bright as a robe with embroidered bands.

He carried the ladder out to store it in a hastily erected bothie, which would need to be rebuilt more sturdily when there was time, and returned to sit on a bench by the hearth. Pointing at each group of letters he read, "'One generation passes unto another; but the earth abides forever, and the sun also rises.'"

She nodded. "It is beautiful. It is a promise."

"Yes. A promise for the future. I shall teach our children to read from those words." And he smiled at the thought, for he had not carved in the monk's Latin, but in the good solid English which even Olwena was beginning to use a bit.

But Olwena did not seem to be thinking of words as she smiled and nodded. "Yes, you will." And she patted her newly rounding tummy.

PART TWO

10

hat do the letters mean, Ealdmodor?"

Aelfgud sighed and shook her head as she smoothed her dark green kirtle over her knees. "I have told you before. Many times. What is the good of telling again? You do not listen."

"Please, Ealdmodor. We listen. We like to hear the story." That was Ulnoth the eldest, with the winning smile.

Then Elfwyn, Wilfra, and Beada joined in. "Yes, a story." "Please a story." "We love stories, Ealdmodor."

Again Aelfgud sighed and shook her gray head, but secretly she was pleased. For she loved the stories, and she loved passing them on to her children's children. She felt that was something of what the words on the brightly painted roof beams meant, although she could not have explained it. Besides, it would keep her mind from her own worries. "All right. But you must listen carefully." They drew closer to her skirt, Beada leaning her shining red head against the green kirtle and Wilfra of the sea-green eyes fondling the three kittens in her lap. "It was carved by my ealdfaeder's faeder's faeder, almost one hundred years ago when first our people came to the west country. Not many of our people were Christians then, so he carved words from the Bible that we should not forget God's goodness to us."

"Not Christians?" Elfwyn interrupted her. For no matter how many times he heard the story, the idea was unthinkable. "So were they heathen?"

"Did they worship the devil? The one with horns? And did they burn forever and ever in Hell?" Beada's eyes were round and blue as the cornflowers that danced in the meadow.

"They worshiped old gods because they didn't know any better. But when the king turned to the true God, the people too became Christians."

"I remember!" Wilfra jumped so suddenly she startled the kittens in her lap into leaping out and scratching her. "Ooo, but I've forgotten his name." She sank back, sucking her scratched finger.

"Cenwalh—you mean Cenwalh; can't you remember anything, Wilfra?" Her brother Elfwyn gave her a jab which made her cry out more sharply than at the kitten's scratch. "Cenwalh was the first Christian king of Wessex, wasn't he, Ealdmodor?"

"But the story, aren't you going to tell us the story?" Beada, ever the quiet listener, pleaded.

"Ulnoth, go see if there is any sign of your faeder. If not, we may as well await him telling stories." She watched him cross the hall—Ulnoth the firstborn, the pride of her old eyes, on whom she and all relied when his father was gone.

Wilfra's high-pitched voice gave words to the question that bore heavily on the gray-haired woman. "But where is Faeder? Why is he so long? I thought he was to return yesterday."

Aelfgud would not let the children see her concern. "Your faeder is about his duties. A king's reeve has much to do. I am certain King Ine set him a task, and he will return when it is done."

"But the king left his hunting lodge yesterday. We heard the horns when he passed through the woods." Beada was ever the practical, logical one.

Aelfgud was spared making an answer by Ulnoth's return. "No sign of him. Nithhad was swilling the swine. He said he'd seen no one pass all evening, but he'll bring us word if he does."

"So. Then we will have a story before you go to your sleeping benches." The four shining heads drew closer to the old gray one, and Aelfgud's voice took on a dreamy faraway sound. "In the days when my ealdfaeder's faeder's ealdfaeder built the stone church at Glastingaburg, this part of the land was not English, but British, and hereabouts only the British were Christian, for the true faith came to them by the Christ Child Himself, who came here with His Uncle Joseph of Arimathea. It was a good land of flowering apple trees and singing birds and running brooks full of silver fish. The Christ Child loved it so much that He built a church at Glastingaburg, which in those days men called the Isle of Avalon. He built it with His own hands and dedicated it to His blessed Mother Mary.

"And then our Lord left this land He loved and returned to His own country to do the work for which the Faeder had sent Him to earth. But ever Glastingaburg was blessed—ever a place where holy men worshiped the true God and kings and martyrs and saints were buried. And so did my ealdfaeder's faeder's ealdfaeder build the chapel of St. Stephen in honor of his beloved wife who died like the first martyr with the love of God on her face and prayers for her enemies on her lips.

"But then came the King of Wessex who was but a heathen and knew not the true God. Yet Christ in Heaven protected the spot He loved so dearly. All the other houses of worship in Wessex fell to the strong Wessex men, but no heathen foot put its print on the holy island.

"And then in the day of your ealdfaeder's faeder, King Cynegils of Wessex became a Christian. But his son Cenwalh hardened his heart against God. So, as God must always deal strongly with those who refuse His light, when Cenwalh became King of Wessex, God sent the heathen Mercian King Penda with a great army to drive Cenwalh out of Wessex. And Cenwalh fled to King Anna of the East Angles—a fine Christian king. You see God had all things in His hand."

Here Aelfgud's narrative was interrupted by Beada of the shining eyes clapping her hands. "Oooh, I love this part."

"And so must all who love light and the right." Aelfgud nodded with satisfaction. "For King Anna persuaded the hard-hearted Cenwalh to became a Christian."

"Then God let him have the throne of Wessex back!" cried Elfwyn, who could have told the story as well as Aelfgud.

Aelfgud nodded. "And God let him have Glastingaburg, for at last the English were no longer heathen, and they were worthy of having so holy a place in their kingdom. And Cenwalh made Glastingaburg a bridge between the British and English. The British abbot took English monks into the brotherhood. And English and British worshiped there together in the love of God—as they still do today."

Beada raised her head from Aelfgud's knee and stared at the letters on the carved beam above her head. The firelight flickered on them, for it had now become quite dark. But Beada was too young to read her letters, although, as a reeve's daughter, she would soon be taught. However, tonight it was enough that she had memorized the words. "Is that what it means, 'One generation passes unto another'?"

"Yes, I think that's something of what it means." Aelfgud stood slowly with one hand to her back, for she had become stiff sitting so long in one position. "Now, Ulnoth, Elfwyn, unstack the benches from the wall. Wilfra, put the kittens down and help your sister bring the sleeping rugs." She smoored the fire for the night with blocks of peat and turned to climb the ladder to the loft, the bower that had been her own place since she was a bride, where her seven bairns had been born. Five little stone crosses stood in the meadow beyond the steading—all she had left of them except the youngest Theodric, who had taken the cowl at Glastingaburg, and Ulfric, reeve for all the king's lands in their shire. He was an important man, and she was glad for it, even if it did leave much of the running of the steading in her old hands. Since the death of his wife last year when the milch fever carried her and the new-bairn away, Aelfgud had had to look after the children, too.

Yes, she was glad for his reeveship, and yet she was not glad. The burdens for herself she would gladly bear, but it was hard on the children. The girls missed their father, but it was worse for the boys. They should be at school at the monastery, but were forced to stay home and care for the fields like serf's sons. Elfwyn she did not worry about, for he showed no desire for learning and books, but Ulnoth, the eldest and brightest, held her heart. She saw how he chafed when with each new season he must stay at Ulfstead for another round of planting and harvesting. Perhaps this winter . . . Aelfgud promised herself she would do what she could for the boy.

Aelfgud was almost to the top of the ladder when an insistent banging on the door made her stop. *Ulfric has returned!* Her heart lightened. Then she realized it was not Ulfric; he would not knock at his own hall. "No, Ulnoth. Do not answer it." She stopped him just in time. It was too late at night for careless unbarring of the door, especially when the master was away and the male servants slept in huts beyond the hall.

She descended the ladder and crossed to the door. "What is your business?"

"It is Eda, serving maid from the king's hunting lodge." The voice came muffled through the heavy door. "It is an emergency."

Aelfgud felt her hands and forehead grow cold. She had known it all day. Always she could sense when something was amiss with one of her family. Nothing but the direst necessity would bring a maid scurrying through woods and fields at this time of the night. She unbarred the door.

If her son was sick or injured or worse, she would not hear it through a barred door. She looked at the girl, still gasping to catch her breath. "What is it, girl?"

"Your son Ulfric has sent us." The maid indicated two serving lads behind her, and Aelfgud relaxed. At least her son wasn't dead if he was sending the message. "He needs your sow. He has sent us to fetch it."

"My sow?" She couldn't have heard right. "Ulfric needs my sow? In the middle of the night?"

But the girl insisted. "Your son, the reeve, has sent us—on the queen's orders. Queen Aethelburga has need of your sow."

11

The girl held out a wax tablet on which Ulfric had pressed the stamp of his signet ring. There was no doubting it. Ulfric wanted Hamma, their great pink and black-spotted sow, the oldest, largest, and rudest in the shire, to be taken to King Ine's hunting lodge in the middle of the night.

"But I have plenty of pork put by. Let me send you a side of bacon and all the hams you can carry from the smokehouse. If the king and his court have eaten you out of supplies, that will do much better than an old sow. What can my son be thinking of?"

But the girl was insistent. "It is not for the eating. It is the queen. The queen ordered a sow."

Aelfgud sighed. There was no help for it. She turned to cover her hair with her white head-rail and take a heavy, hooded, woolen cloak from the peg by the door. It was a cold night, as ever June nights were—cold and damp and not a time for old bones to be about. But she had raised Hamma from a piglet, and the cranky old sow would obey no other.

In the end it required Nithhad, roused from his sleeping place beside the swine byre, armed with a heavy staff walking behind, and Ulnoth holding a wooden bucket of corn mash in front of her snout to make Hamma obey the tug of the rope. Elfwyn, Wilfra, and Beada each carried two squirming, squealing suckling piglets that could not be left behind.

They made a strange procession through the woods with the lads from the lodge lighting their way with smoking torches. Eda sniveled that this was not according to the reeve's order, and Her Majesty had clearly said a sow and did not require piglets, and what was to become of her when she was turned out of her job?

"Quiet, girl, or I'll turn you out myself!" In her irritation Aelfgud yanked on the rope, which made Hamma retaliate by plunking her full three hundred pounds down in a particularly sloppy mudhole by the side of the path. The piglets, seeing their mother on her side with a row of teats exposed, wriggled from the children's arms with squeals of delight and began rooting noisily.

By the time the mud-bathed piglets were back in their carriers' arms and Hamma had been pried from her comfortable spa, all the party was as mire-caked as the pigs. Tempers were not improved by Hamma's attempt to dash off into the woods when she sniffed an acorn tree or by the drizzling rain that began falling when they were just over halfway there. It was not enough to wash off the mud, only enough to make track and pigs slippery by the time the party arrived at the king's lodge.

And what a sight met them. And a stench. Hamma slipped free of her lead rope and dashed forward with grunts of delight, her piglets squealing after her. All the others pulled back in dismay. "Ugh! It stinks!" Wilfra clapped her hands over her nose, then thrust them away. She had forgotten she was covered with mud.

"Oh, it's awful!" Beada burst into tears and buried her face in her ealdmodor's cape, not caring how wet and muddy it was.

But Aelfgud had no time for such sniveling and complaining. She strode forward, planting her feet firmly so as not to slip on the excrement and refuse that covered the floor of the king's Great Hall. The only thing undisturbed by the chaos were the antlers hanging so high in the rooftrees as to be out of the reach of vandalism. "Ulfric! Where is my son? What is the meaning of this? Have you taken leave of your senses?"

At the sound of his mother's voice, a frazzled-looking Ulfric appeared on the landing in front of the royal bed chamber at the top of the hall. "Modor, I am sorry you were disturbed. I need Hamma up here. Can you get her up the stairs, do you think?"

"Up there? You want my sow in the royal bed chamber?" At last she lost her composure. "My son, my son. He has run mad! It is brain fever! We will all die for this!" She threw her arms in the air and wailed. "We will be executed. The king will have our heads."

Ulfric clattered down the narrow staircase and across the littered floor to his mother. "No, no! Listen to me! We haven't much time left. It is the queen's orders. She wants the sow put in their bed. Now hurry! They will be here soon. Queen Aethelburga said they would travel all night—that she would make an excuse to turn back, and they would arrive before morning. Now help me with Hamma—the piglets, too. I suppose we must have them as well. It must be ready, or the effect will be lost."

That was all the explanation Aelfgud was to receive, and she could see it was no use arguing with her son. So with Aelfgud pulling and Ulfric pushing and the children again carrying the piglets under their arms, Hamma and her young ones were deposited in the royal bed. Then all in the lodge settled down to await the arrival of their king and queen.

Aelfgud sat beneath the bed chamber loft on the one bench that had not been overturned in the madness that had seized the lodge and its servants, wrapped her smelly, sodden cloak around her, and leaned against the wall to doze. If they were all to lose their heads in the morning, she might as well meet her Maker well-rested . . .

She startled awake at the sound of a hunting horn. Then she heard the gallop of horses' hooves. The king and his party approached. Silver streaks of light showed through the eastern windows, and the thrushes and wood wrens had begun their dawn chorus. The door of the lodge flung open.

King Ine strode in three steps and then stopped. "What is the meaning of this?" he howled. His thanes and house carles fell back, but Queen Aethelburga stepped forward and took his arm with a gentle smile. "Come, my lord, there is more." She led him up to the bed chamber.

Aelfgud heard the door open and the king's outraged cry. "A pig! There is a pig in my bed! Get the filthy thing out!" There was a sharp whack, followed by a squealing oink. "Out! Out!" Aelfgud hoped he had not hurt Hamma, surely the most innocent of all.

Then Queen Aethelburga's voice carried clearly from the landing. "Have I not done well, my lord? Do you not see my lesson clearly?"

The king's reply was indistinguishable, but he had quit raging.

"Take heed, my lord," the queen continued. "For so passes away all worldly pleasures. So are all of man's works dust, dross, and dung before his Maker. Only that which is done for God will last."

There was a long silence.

All in the lodge held their breath. Would the king have Queen Aethelburga's head off along with their own?

Then from the royal chamber thundered a voice that echoed from one end of the hall to the other. "Indeed, my queen, you have done well!"

King Ine bounded down the stairs three at a time and jumped on an upended table in the middle of the hall. He flung his arms out and cried with the exuberant energy with which he did everything, "Is not my queen a wonder! Does not she care mightily for the soul of her king? I see so clearly what I never saw before. Others warned me. Priests, monks, and bishops warned me. And I said yes, yes, and went my way. I did not truly hear. Now I hear. Now I see. Only what is done for God will last. So I will do all for God. And my earthly works will not go to the judgment like the dung that covers this floor. And I will not appear before my Maker as a swine who has no understanding. My queen, I thank you. My servants, I thank you. But most of all, my God, I thank You that I could receive this lesson before it was too late!"

The king's eyes seemed to look at something no one else could see. His was the word of one whose sight is clear and whose hearing is perfect for the things of God—one who has had a vision from the Almighty.

"The land has long been dry—as in the days before Samuel when the Word of the Lord was seldom heard and no vision was granted. We have been too long without a vision, my people—and without a vision the people perish.

"But we shall not perish. The time of spiritual dryness is over. Now shall come the promised time when our old men will dream dreams and our young men shall see visions and the King of Glory shall come in. The Lord High and Mighty, He is the King of Kings."

And with a great shout of laughter, he jumped from the table, grabbed Queen Aethelburga around the waist and whirled her off her feet while Aelfgud and all the others laughed and clapped their hands.

12

lfric stood in the shadow of the Tor, Abbot Hemgisl on his right, Brothers Beorhwald and Etfrith on his left, and his own brother Theodric behind him. They waited with folded hands and bowed heads and with a patience that only one trained in contemplation could achieve. Yet Ulfric could sense their concern waiting on his answer. It would not be easy. King Ine's instructions to his reeve were clear. Glastingaburg would be the earthly site of a great base for eternity. Warfare and government no longer contented the soul of the king. He would build a magnificent church to the glory of God. And he chose Ulfric to carry this out. The king's chief administrative officer for the shire was a natural choice, but King Ine was doubly happy when he learned that an ancestor of Ulfric's had built the small stone chapel dedicated to St. Stephen that stood solitary and weathering among the cluster of sad thatched daub huts that comprised the monastery.

Ulfric shook his head. Of course, the situation looked worse than it might on a better day. The cold, late February mist partly shrouded the buildings, but it did not cover their tattered construction, nor did it enhance the brown grass and weeds at their doors or the bare tree branches scraping the walls. And the rain that drizzled from gray clouds did not brighten the mood of the one assigned to make this sorry site shine forth as a symbolic foretaste of heavenly glory.

"The building is to glorify God and express the zeal of the royal builder," said Abbot Hemgisl peering out from under his cowl.

"Like a prayer." Prior Beorhwald kept his head bowed.

Ulfric nodded, shaking drops of rain off his head. He didn't need to be reminded. His eyes traced the irregular circle of the shallow ditch that enclosed the cluster of buildings.

"Perhaps a fine wall of turf and timber, with stone corner pillars and carved gate," Ulfric suggested hesitantly. Of course, the plans for the church would come from the king himself. But it would take far more than one new building to transform the scene before him into a reflection of divine grace.

"Well . . ." He felt Abbot Hemgisl's hesitancy. "The king will endow the church, of course . . ."

Ulfric nodded again, then wished he hadn't when he felt the rain on his nose. The problem was always the same—money. The abbey treasury was small. And always there were dues to be paid. "Yes, King Ine will pay for the raising of the stone. But that is merely the beginning if we are to fulfill his vision. And Bishop Aldhelm will have his share."

Etfrith, the youngest brother, looked up. "Aldhelm? But I thought the Bishop of Sherborne was the very one who convinced King Ine that Glastingaburg should receive the royal endowments."

Ulfric gave a wry laugh. Were the brothers really so innocent of the ways of the world? If so, all the more needful to build a solid enclosure for them. "Of course, Aldhelm wants the king's endowments to fall within his bishopric—how else can he collect his share?"

Abbot Hemgisl, his words softened by his Gaelic heritage, said, "We can but be doing our best. It is for God's glory; God must give the means." And he led the way to the Ealdchurch where he rang the bell for the singing of Vespers.

Beorhwald and Etfrith went with their abbot, but Theodric stayed behind. "I would have words with you, Ulfric."

Ulfric gave a wry smile at his brother's sharp tone. "Go easy now, little brother. I am the elder, do not forget."

"Aye. And the one with all the responsibilities and burdens, I don't forget. But your bairns are like to my own, as I'll not be having any, so I'll speak. I would remind you that the boy's place is here at the monastery, more than yours. Unless I've lost count, Ulnoth will be fourteen this birthday, and he's had no schooling except the learning of his letters from our modor. Boys half his age fill the benches of our school and are writing Latin. It is not right, Ulfric of Ulfstead."

Ulfric's hood slipped back, and he submitted to the cold rain on his head like a penance. "Aye. I know. But there are not thralls enough to run the steading without more help, and there is not enough money to buy more thralls."

"And without your hand at the plow there will like to never be enough money . . . I do understand, Ulfric, my brother." Theodric went on to his prayers, but Ulfric did not. He stood yet in the rain thinking about Theodric's words.

He knew his mother was too old to be left with the running of the steading, and his sons too young. He had the most excellent thralls possible, many of them born right on that land for many generations back, and Nithhad, his chief villein, was as well-trained and responsible as any sprung from sturdy peasant stock. But the land needed the master's foot in the field—and his was far across the marsh, likely for many days yet. It seemed hopeless.

He had appropriated all the stone from fallen Roman buildings for as far away as Bathum. If the frost held the marshland firm another fortnight, it could all be brought to Glastingaburg by cart, which would be much quicker than having to send it down the Saefern (once called Sabrina) and then up the Brue by boat. But even if God granted such favors, that was only the beginning. Then they must wait for the thaw so that deep footings could be dug for the foundations. At least that would be under the direction of the Frankish builder King Ine was having sent to them. Only continental builders understood the mysteries of building in stone, and King Ine would not have his church constructed by natives whose experience consisted of raising cattle byres from field rubble.

No, he dare not leave yet. Aelfgud would have to cope the best she could. He would ask Abbot Hemgisl to light a candle for her, for surely her efforts were as much a part of the building of King Ine's church as those of the serfs and thralls who loaded stone and cut timber.

In the following months it seemed that God did honor the many candles lit with prayers that King Ine's church might go forward speedily. The master builder Serenus arrived from Paris, carrying the plans for the church stamped with the royal approval. Although he quickly demonstrated that his temper in no way matched the calm his name indicated, he as quickly showed that he knew his job.

Finally the assessed stone arrived, most of it by cart, but the last two loads by boat. Then Serenus hired a full crew of churls to aid the trained craftsmen he had brought with him—stonemasons who would build the walls, carpenters to build the scaffolding and wooden formers, blacksmiths to make tools for masons and carpenters.

When at last the deep, solid foundations were laid, Ulfric felt that he could return to his farm for more than a few hours at a time. With luck he would stay until after harvest, and when he returned to the island, he would find the walls rising apace. Already there was talk among masons of the glassworkers who would be needed by next year. The crowning glory of King Ine's church was to be stained-glass windows—the like of which had never been seen in this part of England. So with the clear image of the glory of glass and stone rising at Glastingaburg, Ulfric left.

At the end of the day's journey he stood on a small green rise and smiled. Spread before him was the sight in all the world dearest to his heart—a snug steading nestled in a fold of the Mendips, level garths and a winding stream in front, the sheltering hills to the back, with woods and orchards curving half around on the left. A high wooden stockade surrounded his ancestral manor—the long thatched roof of the timbered hall standing high in the center of chapel, byres, and work sheds. Scattered steep-roofed serfs' huts dotted nearby fields.

But if Ulfric had expected a peaceful homecoming, he was disappointed. "And so you come home as a stranger to your own hearth—Ulfric of Ulfstead. If I weren't your own mother, I'd not be knowing you, and it's not so sure I am now. Like as not if I set your own dogs on you, they'd attack, for they'll not be knowing you any better than I am."

And little Beada hung shyly on her grandmother's skirts, peering at her father with alarmed blue eyes while Aelfgud continued. "This steading has the finest horse-runs in all Wessex from your ealdfaeder's ealdfaeder's time until now—and yet your brood mares go uncovered."

Then Wilfra, in a saffron kirtle that matched her ripe-wheat hair, showed him a full-grown hound from a litter he had not even known had whelped.

Ulfric turned to Ulnoth. "My son, tomorrow we will inspect the steading from one side to the other and consider what we can do to better it."

His announcement was greeted with an unenthusiastic, "Yes, Faeder."

"Ulnoth of Ulfstead! What ails you? You will need to know such things, for someday this steading will be yours."

"Yes, Faeder."

Ulfric wondered why Ulnoth had treated his reminder more like a threat than a promise. Always that had been the way of it. The steading had belonged to his father and to his father's father and to his father's father's father, back until their people had first come to this shire. Yet it seemed that Elfwyn had more true love for the land and its ways. Ulfric shook his head. Ah, well, there was no need fretting over Elfwyn, for he could find his way—move afield and intake more land for a steading of his own, or serve the church like Theodric, or as the son of a reeve, go into service of the king. He would have to choose, but Ulnoth's future was assured.

The next day he and Ulnoth reviewed the whole of his lands with Nithhad and saw that, although he might have made more of them, they were good lands indeed. They stood before a moon-silver garth of knee-high barley blowing in the breeze. Ulfric snapped off a head and ground it between his fingers. "It will be ripe to harvest next week, think you?"

The villein nodded. "Aye, if the weather holds. It should yield a fine crop." And so they continued to the horse-runs, apple garth, and sheep folds.

The weather did hold hot and dry for the next week, so that the first streaks of sunlight on reaping day found all hands on the steading out in the garth, from Ulfric to the newest thrall and from Aelfgud to the serfs' toddlers. A full half the garth was cut and shocked by sundown in spite of the oppressive heat, unrelieved by any breeze, as if the sky pressed down upon them. "Aye, it's a fine harvest. We'll have round bellies at Ulfstead all winter." Ulfric sat long at his trestle by the hearth that night with his sons. "One more cup of mead," he called to his serving thrall, "then we'll a-bed. Ah, but it's been a fine day. It seems as good a thing to cut barley for men's stomachs as to raise stone for their souls—but I'd not let Abbot Hemgisl hear me say so."

It was late when he and Ulnoth stacked the trestles against the wall and smoored the fire for the night. It was later yet when he was shaken from sleep by a thunder roll so close over his head he thought for sure it would tumble Aelfgud out of her bower. Through the window in his chamber he saw jagged lines of white lightning leap from the sky toward the earth. Each one lit the room for an instant, then left it in total darkness while the thunder resonated off the walls. Then silence, until the next white streak cut through the night and the thunder boomed on its tail.

Suddenly his chamber door flew open, and the room seemed full of small girls and dogs, all howling to match the thunder. He clutched the older girl by the shoulders and ordered, "Beada, get your sister into my bedplace." He strode to the door opening. "Ulnoth, Elfwyn, get you from your sleeping benches and help me with these hounds!" By then Aelfgud had descended from her bower to see what the commotion was.

A sudden bolt of lightning lit the room as if it were on fire, and the simultaneous thunder made the girls muffle their screams under the bed rugs. It was several seconds before Ulfric realized that the light from the bolt had not faded. Indeed, it was growing lighter—lighter with an ominous, flickering brightness.

"Fire!" Ulfric was the first to yell. "Ulnoth, rouse the thralls!" He was already halfway out the door. "Elfwyn, bring the buckets!"

They battled through the night. It was already too late to save the barley and the byres nearest the garth, but if they could wet the thatch thoroughly enough, there was a chance of saving the hall. While Nithhad and several of the thralls saw to the animals, driving them to the woods beyond the enclosure, Ulfric and Ulnoth climbed the ladder to the roof and began dousing the dry straw with buckets of water handed up to them in a human chain from the stream.

"Here! Faeder!" Ulnoth shouted his attention to a spark that had caught and was blazing right behind him. Ulfric flung the contents of his bucket on it, then handed the leather pail down the ladder, and took a full clay pot in his other hand.

"Ulnoth!" With horror Ulfric saw that his son's hair had caught a spark. He flung the contents of the pot. In the next second the lad was sputtering and shaking his head, flinging drops of water in every direction.

And so they battled the raging monster of heat, light, and wind. It seemed that surely it should have consumed all they had to offer hours ago, yet it ravaged on. With arms and backs that ached and throats parched, all were covered with black ash and smelled of singed hair and eyebrows. All knew they couldn't go on another moment, and yet they continued another hour. Still the monster was winning. The timber palisade surrounding the buildings flamed a solid row of torches. The thatch over Aelfgud's bower fell in, a shower of black ash and straw covering the chamber and sending sparks onto embroidered hangings that had graced the bower for a hundred years.

In a moment the greedy devourer would reach them.

"Go down!" Ulfric commanded Ulnoth. He could build a new hall. His son he could not replace. Ulnoth continued dumping. "Down!"

Then a sharp shift in the wind flung a wall of flame at their very feet, cutting them off from the ladder. "The other side!" Ulfric grabbed his son's hand and pulled him up the roof, away from the pursuing flame. "Can you jump?" The roof was high above the ground, but there was no choice. In the end, it was not a decision at all, for Ulnoth slipped on the wet thatch.

Ulfric was never certain whether the cry that brought everyone to that side of the hall was from his own lips or Ulnoth's, for all seemed to go blank as he watched his son plummet to the ground. He would surely have followed had not Elfwyn flung himself around the hall with the ladder for his father's rescue.

"He breathes still." Aelfgud raised her ear from her grandson's chest.

Ulfric began feeling the strong-muscled young arms and legs, laying them straight, feeling for breaks. But there was no need feeling the left leg that was twisted so crazily beneath the boy. Even in the dim dawn light, the gleam of jagged white bone showed through the skin.

It was not until, at Aelfgud's careful direction, the leg had been straightened on a board and bound tight with strips of cloth that Ulfric realized the miracle that had happened. It was raining.

They carried Ulnoth inside the broken, smoldering hall and laid him where no rain dripped through the thatch. Ulfric sat by the still-unconscious boy, blaming himself for the disaster that had befallen Ulfstead and yet not seeing where he could have done differently. Sometimes it was necessary even for a God-fearing Christian to believe in wyrd. Such was as it was.

But what for the future? Of course, he must stay at the steading now. There would be little enough to eat this winter, but they must salvage what they could—bring in all the nuts from the woods and dry berries from the bramble hedges. Cattle that would have been better grown for another season they must slaughter now before lack of winter feed made them gaunt. And the hall must be re-roofed and new byres built. But where they would get straw for the thatch now that all was burned?

He must have dozed by the hearth, for the next he knew Aelfgud was stirring the pot of wheat meal over the fire, and a watery sun shone in through the holes in the roof. Ulfric looked at the destruction around him. Charred beams and patches of blackened thatch littered the floor, the acrid tang of smoke filled his nose and stung his eyes, and beyond the open doorway stretched the black waste of the barley garth that yesterday had lain in ripples of silver.

A small brown bird flew in through the largest gap in the roof and perched on a rooftree. Ulfric's gaze followed it. And then he saw what he hadn't really noticed for years—the words his ancestor had carved there: "One generation passes unto another; but the earth abides forever, and the sun also rises." It was true. Even after such a night of horrors, the sun, a weak watery one, but sun nonetheless, had risen. Life did go on. He looked at the still form on the pallet beside him, then blinked to see Ulnoth looking at him. "You are awake, my son?"

Ulnoth managed a weak smile, a mere shadow of his usually brilliant one. "We saved the hall, Faeder."

"Yes, we saved it." And inwardly he vowed to rebuild it better than before—somehow. Perhaps with a timbered roof. There were trees in the woods if there was no straw in the garth. He would begin making plans after he had eaten.

But he had reckoned without King Ine. Before he had finished his bowl of morning porridge, a clatter of horses' hooves sounded on the path beside the burned enclosure. Aetherius, Serenus's first assistant, and Cunor, a Waelisc stone worker, bore urgent messages from Serenus and Abbot Hemgisl. Ulfric must come to Glastingaburg. Now. Only the king's word could save the work. And only he could give the king's word.

13

By midafternoon Ulfric was back at the monastery, painfully aware that he reeked of smoke and mentally engaged with the problems of Ulfstead. But his attention swung sharply to the present when he came upon an entirely quiet island. At first he thought it was deserted. Then a faint murmur from the Ealdchurch told him that monks were at prayer. He walked to the partially raised stone walls and wooden scaffoldings of King Ine's church and saw that it was not abandoned either. The workers were merely still. It was as if an anthill had been caught in a sudden frost, and all were frozen in place. A bee flying around a nearby clump of yellow flowers made the only noise he heard.

And then he heard a louder buzzing. Through the half-raised wall-pillars he saw three figures approaching in a buzz of argument. The shorter, older, dark-robed figure was a familiar one—Abbot Hemgisl. Next to him in a winered tunic and green leggings, his uncovered dark hair blowing in the breeze, strode Serenus. The third figure, in a long blue robe of finest wool trimmed with wide bands of gold embroidery, was the less familiar but exceedingly imposing figure of Bishop Aldhelm.

"But if I pay all you ask, our treasury will be empty. We will be obliged to quit work on the church. It is the king's orders . . ." The few overheard words from Abbot Hemgisl made all clear to Ulfric.

Bishop Aldhelm's voice carried clearly across the building site. "And would you rob God? The tithe must be paid into the storehouse. The commandment is clear."

"But also the worker is worthy of his pay—is that not also Holy Writ, my Lord Bishop? My workers will not work without pay. I will not work without pay, and the king desires that I work—do you defy your king?" Few would dare so raise his voice to a bishop.

"If my earthly king must be disobeyed in order to honor my Heavenly King, then so be it. But it is not I who defy King Ine by stopping work—indeed, I am about *my* work."

The argument stopped when Ulfric approached. Hemgisl was the first to speak. "The bishop demands a tithe of all the king has paid into our treasury. It is all we have left to pay the workers for this wage period."

"My men will not work without pay!"

"Nor should you ask God to go unpaid. The church asks no more than her right."

The king—the church—the men—the arguments buzzed around Ulfric. It was not unheard of for king's agents to solve such problems by opening their own coffers. But this was not possible now. If it hadn't been for the fire, at least he could have offered to feed the workers through the winter, but now he could not even feed his own family. Ulfric would have liked to cover his ears, but he held his hands up, palms flat out, for silence. And the buzzing ceased.

"There is only one way. All sides must be content. The bishop must accept half his dues; the workers must accept half their pay; the king must accept slower work. I shall put the matter before King Ine when next he holds Witan here. Until then we must make do with what we have."

The outrage was unanimous. The three warring sides now united against Ulfric. But he held strong in his decision. Of course, it pleased no one. It did not please him either. But because there was no other way, he won—at least partly. Bishop Aldhelm departed with two boat loads of their winter's grain from the tithe byre and a leather pouch of gold. Serenus ordered his men back to work. But the sight of their winter rations sailing down the Brue was not an energizing one. Before the week was out, several of the workers likewise sailed down the Brue, including Serenus's first assistant Aetherius and four of the Frankish craftsmen, who carried their tools with them.

"And how am I to build for your king with no food, no workmen, not even a first assistant?" Serenus threw his own hammer and chisel in the dust and stamped a foot beside them for emphasis.

"At least their departure leaves more food for the workers who remain." Ulfric looked at the bare framework that he was supposed to turn into King

Ine's vision of heavenly glory. The unfinished walls reminded him of the gaping roof in his own hall with his family sheltering in one corner and his oldest son—who knew yet how badly hurt? But the king's command was the king's command. And Ulfric was ever loyal to his duty. It seemed he had fought overlong to do his divided duty to his family and to his king. An Englishman always did his duty. But it was hopeless. He had lost nearly all at home, and he had lost nearly all here. Why did he try? What was the use? He turned and walked away, his shoulders drooping.

But he got no more than ten paces before he heard his name called. "Ulfric! My brother Ulfric! I have heard the news of Ulfstead. I am so sorry. But do not lose heart. I have a message for you."

Ulfric looked up in amazement. Surely Theodric was the only radiant person in Glastingaburg. "A message?"

"A message from God. In the scriptorium today I began supervising the copying of a new volume of 2 Samuel, and the words leapt out at me. Then I heard of Ulfstead, and I knew why. Come you."

Ulfric followed his brother to the hut that bore the grand name scriptorium. Several monks sat hunched over tables covered with great books of bound parchment, copying words from one into the other. These books were Theodric's life-love—the words of holy Scripture, the lives of the saints, the history of the land. Theodric saw to their care more tenderly than any mother her children. "Here—" Theodric thrust a beautifully illuminated volume before Ulfric, its ornate letters glowing with rich color. "Here, read. And insert your own name for that of King David. See you, it is God's Word."

Ulfric read with growing excitement, "'What am I, Lord God, and what is my family, that You have made good Your Word; it was a small thing in Your sight to have planned for Your servant's house in days long past. But such, O Lord God, is the lot of a man embarked on a high career. And now what more can I say, for well You know Your servant Ulfric, O Lord God. You have made good Your Word. Great indeed are You, O Lord God; no one is like unto You . . .

"'Now, Lord God, perform what You have promised for Your servant Ulfric and his house, and for all time. . . . You, O Lord God, are God; You have made these noble promises to Your servant Ulfric, and Your promises come true. Be pleased now to bless Your servant's house that it may continue always before You, as You, O Lord God, have promised.'"

He pushed the volume toward Theodric and stood up as if in a dream. Yes, he could see now. King Ine had said, "Without a vision the people perish." Ulfric had, indeed, been perishing without a vision. But the miracle was that God's promises still stood. Without really seeing where he was going, Ulfric made his way to the Ealdchurch.

Inside the tiny wattle structure he fell to his knees at the altar. For too long he had relied on the prayers of the abbot and of his brother Theodric. Now Ulfric would seek God on his own. He must have his own vision. "Give me a vision," he prayed, then waited long.

His answer came with an inner certainty, and he walked from the church to Serenus.

"Serenus, I will remain as your first assistant. And I will send to King Ine for permission to gather more taxes to feed those who remain—although he is needing all he can gather for his Devonian war. But you must grant me one thing. My own hall is without a roof and my family without shelter. Send you three of your best builders to build my steading as well."

Winter months always passed more slowly than others, and for men with half-full bellies the time could seem endless. Ulfric joined the community in prayer. But unlike times past, he no longer sat with bowed head and let the monks do the praying. He prayed his own words. "O God, You are my God. I seek You with a heart that thirsts for You and a body as wasted with longing for You as the people are with hunger. So longing, I come before You in the sanctuary to look upon Your power and glory. Feed our bodies, we ask, Lord, but more, renew our vision of Your glory. For ever we remember, Lord, that without a vision the people perish, and Lord, we perish."

Then just two weeks before Christmas, when the cellarer feared he must cut rations again, a load of wheat arrived from King Ine. In truth, it was only half of what had been asked for, but if God granted an early thaw, it was just possible it would suffice. Ulfric asked for his portion in a bundle—a pitifully small bundle, it was—and took it home to his family on the day before Christmas. It was the first he had seen the roof Cunor of Porugs and the others had raised over the hall. He was satisfied with the sturdy job they had made of it, however odd a half-timbered, half-thatched roof might look. And inside the hall, with lack of time and supplies to rebuild byres, a row of stalls had been constructed down each side where the most valuable of the steading's animals were stabled. It made a warm, if somewhat noisy and smelly atmosphere.

Ulfric slaughtered the last of the pigs, save what must be kept for breeding stock, and they feasted on roast pork Christmas day. Wilfra, ever the animal-lover, kept all their spirits up with her childish delight over having the animals in hall with them—just like the Christ Child's manger. And when the serving thrall brought round cups of mead, they all sang out a hearty, "*Wass heil!*"

All except Ulnoth. The son who had been the pride of the hall in his tall, fair manliness, the son who had ever lit the darkest day with his smile and merry heart, now sat glumly by the fire and, when necessary, hobbled forth on a crutch, for the leg had not mended straight. Although the cold made it ache like a wolf bite, he did not complain, but his face grew whiter and the lines around his mouth deeper and the few words he spoke fewer and yet fewer.

Ulfric did not know what to say to him. He felt Ulnoth draw back whenever he approached, so he respected his son's silence. He would ask Abbot Hemgisl that the brothers say special prayers for this one. He could think of nothing else to do. Perhaps Theodric . . . he would ask Theodric for advice. There had always been a special bond between Ulnoth and his uncle.

So leaving his small bundle of wheat behind for his family's survival, Ulfric returned to Glastingaburg and the weary work of forming a living building from cold stone. Except on days when it was too wet and chill to work—when the moisture in the mortar would turn to ice and cause it to crumble when the thaws came—the work went on. Seeing the walls rise helped the men forget their half-empty stomachs.

And spring would bring warmth and new growth—and the Witan. Hemgisl, Serenus, and Ulfric would lay their case before the king in person. Surely King Ine would give more to raise his vision to the glory of God. Then there would be gold in the treasury and corn in the tithe byre—even if it did mean that the bishop would collect more.

But then, on a day when all had gone well, when Ulfric had heard a lark sing that morning and had spotted the first purple blossom in a sheltered spot near the Ealdchurch, and the scaffold had been raised to a new height, came another disaster.

The plan for the church called for two low sections connected in the middle by a tall square tower more than twice the height of the two sections. The lower sections had risen quickly, but the tower, which was decorated with three levels of arched stone strip-work, was a slower process. They were now well up the second level of strips, however, with work progressing inside and out from scaffoldings on both sides of the walls.

Ulfric was on the outer scaffolding against the highest level of the north wall when he saw a fishing coracle approach over the spring-swollen marsh waters. It seemed to come in a straight line from Ulfstead. Fear clamped his heart. Something was amiss at home.

He started to turn and descend without being called, but the mason he was assisting yelled at him not to move. Although Ulfric was Serenus's first assistant, he was no trained builder, and so he assisted any mason wherever an extra hand was needed. "It must be steadied until it's set; then we can take the former away." The mason indicated the key stone Ulfric was holding over the wooden support which held the stone arches together during construction. So he stood with his shoulder bracing a great chunk of gold Bathum stone while Elfwyn, who had come up from the coracle, stood beneath the scaffolding, shouting up at him.

"It's the cows, Faeder."

"Sows?" he shouted down.

"No. Cows. Dark-Eye. It was her time to calve, but I suppose she was frightened—it being her first—and she . . ."

"Elfwyn!" Ulfric's exasperation was growing by the moment. "I cannot come down. You must come up."

So Elfwyn scrambled up the scaffolding as if it were his favorite beech tree in Eaker Wood. "Dark-Eye—she ran off into the wood to drop her calf. We missed her at sheep-folding time, so we all went into the woods to look for her—Wilfra, Beada, Nithhad, and three serfs. We searched until dark and long past, but found no trace. When we came back to the steading, all returned but Wilfra. So we took fresh lanterns with extra candles and went again. This morning all three are lost."

"Three?"

"Wilfra, Dark-Eye, and Ulnoth."

"Ulnoth?"

"My brother did not hunt for the cow, but went later to look for his sister. He took with him Docga, best of the hounds, for there are wolves aplenty in the woods."

"But you found none of them? No trace?"

"None, Faeder. Have I not said so this many times?"

Ulfric turned from his son and shouted down the scaffolding, "Cunor! Send Cunor to me! Now!"

The Waelisc mason appeared beneath Ulfric. "Come up, take my place. I am needed at my steading." And without waiting for Cunor to ascend the scaffolding, Ulfric turned to go.

The shouts of the men and the cracking, scraping, and crashing of stone and timber blended into one tumult of horror in Ulfric's mind, with his own voice shouting at Cunor to move.

But there was no time. Cunor had come the quickest way—stepping into the open archway, and so was trapped by the double scaffolding on either side. He twisted aside and managed to thrust his head under the scaffold platform, but that was all. When the dust settled, Cunor lay buried under a pile of rough-cut blocks of stone.

Frozen with horror at what he had done, Ulfric never remembered descending the scaffolding or giving orders for workmen to clear the rubble and for a boy to run for the infirmarer. All he remembered was his brother Theodric's steadying hand on his arm, guiding him to a waiting boat. Theodric promised to say prayers for the family and all his troubles and requested in parting, "Bring you the boy when you return."

It was long after dark when Ulfric and Elfwyn arrived at Ulfstead. Aelfgud pushed them onto benches before the hearth and thrust bowls of steaming barley broth into their hands. "Drink you. The foolishness of this family is beyond imagining. Whoever heard of crossing the marsh in the middle of the night?"

Ignoring her rebuke, Ulfric asked, "Wilfra, Ulnoth?"

"And thought you to help them by getting lost yourself in the marshes?"

She flung out her long bony arms. "Aie—what use? No one listens to an old woman anyway. Nithhad and the thralls still search. Like as not they'll be eaten by the wolves as well, and then I'll be left to run the steading completely alone. As well I might have been these many months and more than a year past, for all you care, Ulfric of Ulfstead. Was it not enough that my son Theodric must leave the land for the church; must you also?"

Although Ulfric knew his mother was scolding to cover her fear, he acquiesced to her request that he sleep before searching Eaker Wood.

It was many hours later that his mother's voice penetrated his clouded consciousness. "And where have you been keeping these past days? Thought you to set the whole steading on its ears while you romp in the woods?"

Ulfric sprang to his feet, and Wilfra ran into her father's arms with Docga bounding at her heels. But his eyes were all for his firstborn son who limped toward him. Ulnoth carried his white ashwood crutch, but he did not lean on it, and his eyes sparkled as they had not since the fire so many months ago. Then he saw the blood on the crutch.

"Aye, and there is a story to tell here, worthy of a scop, I am thinking."

Ulnoth settled himself by the hearth and took a bowl of porridge from his grandmother. "Wilfra will tell you. It is her story."

"Dark-Eye calved, Faeder. And I was alone with her in the woods. And I helped her. It was beautiful—the silver moon shone on the calfling while Dark-Eye licked her and I rubbed her with grass, and everything was shiny." Ulfric could see that what might have been a terrifying experience for most six-year-olds had been a moment of pure joy for his daughter. "I named her Wilfra, because I am like to her ealdmodor."

Ulfric laughed and tousled the matted red locks. "Aye, my daughter. And may you always set so fine an example for your namesake."

"Aye, she was grand, our little sister. I found her sleeping so with the calfling and Dark-Eye standing over them as if she'd birthed twins." Ulnoth continued the story from his end of the trestle table. "But the calf was slow traveling, and even Docga got many times lost in the bramble tangle, and so we did not get home that day. And that night the wolf came."

Wilfra looked up with fear shining from her round blue eyes for the first time. "A very large wolf, Faeder. Bigger than Docga—although our Docga wasn't afraid. And it had green eyes and great yellow teeth." She buried her head in her father's tunic.

"So. It is as she says." Ulnoth nodded and set his porridge bowl down empty. "Docga the Valiant proved her name, and I had the learning that a heavy ashwood crutch is none so bad a weapon." At long last, after many months of eclipse, Ulnoth's smile shone forth.

So now Ulfric could have returned to Glastingaburg, but so also could he stay home in peace and quiet. It was time to prepare the soil for spring planting, and the buds were swelling in the apple garth. It was time for a man to be about his own steading, even when he had orders to the contrary from his king.

After many a day in his fields with his thralls and his sons, Ulfric would return to his hearth to admire the progress his daughters had made on the fine new striped cloak they were weaving for him under Aelfgud's supervision. He gave barely a thought to the cloud that hung over him.

The king and his court were in Gleawanceaster, the old Roman town of Glevum, for Eastertide. When the Lenten fasting was ended and the Triddum prayers said and the Holy Easter Mass sung, then Ulfric must report all his bad news to the king. But no matter how often the two great duties of an Englishman—to his family and to his king—seemed to clash in Ulfric's life, he knew now that somehow he would balance them without being disloyal to either.

Far worse than facing King Ine was the prospect of standing before the Witan. For every man in the land had his man-price. There were men of twelve hundred value, men of six hundred, and men of two hundred. The value of the British was only about half of that of the English. If Cunor died from the pile of stone and timber that Ulfric caused to rain down on him, Ulfric must pay. Since Cunor was Waelisc and a laborer, his wergild would be one hundred twenty. Where Ulfric was to lay his hands on one hundred twenty silver Ina pennings, he could not imagine. What troubled him more, Cunor was a good man and a good worker. That Ulfric might cause any man's death was a sore burden to him.

14

But Ulfric did not have to face the Witan that year. When he went back to the monastery, he found that Cunor lived. His left hand was smashed and useless, but all other wounds seemed likely to heal. The hand he bore in a heavy bandage and could yet lose to the amputator's saw if it turned black inside the wrappings.

King Ine had not been displeased with the progress of his church. He searched his royal treasury, and whatever the cost to the war grinding on in Devon against the ancient Dumnonian kingdom, another chest of gold came to the monastery. And though Bishop Aldhelm's eyes lit with a greedy glint, Ulfric reckoned that there would be enough for the carved wooden choir stalls, the carved stone figures of the Lord and of Peter and Paul, and the gold altar cross. Most important, they could continue with plans for the central glory of the church—three small stained-glass windows. Serenus had already hired Flemish glaziers who were teaching the stonecutters how to shape their traceries.

By late summer word came that Ine had driven the Dumnonian king back to his own lands. Wessex was secure. And, great happiness to Ulfric's heart, it seemed that at long last, Ulnoth the restless had found peace. For Ulfric had not forgotten Theodric's words. When he returned to the holy island, his eldest son had come too. Immediately Ulnoth had settled into the routine of the school, and though he was older than the other boys, so sharp was his mind and so diligent his study that he soon surpassed those who had studied for many years. Without it being spoken, it seemed likely that when he was fully trained, he would become Theodric's assistant in the scriptorium. Already he was showing the fine hand of a copyist, though he lacked enthusiasm for the work.

By apple-harvesting time, Ulfric could climb to the chapel atop the Tor with a heart full of praise. The dedication service was to be next Eastertide, and all should be ready then. He gazed down on the carpenters in their orange, rust, and brown tunics looking like autumn leaves on the sturdy rooftrees they were erecting. The well-hewn timbers should be snugly fit over those before the Christmas snows, and they would be able to concentrate on the interior decoration. Of course, the work of painting colorful wall decorations and weaving hangings would go on for years, generations perhaps, as the Lord gave His people ever more reasons to express their gratitude to Him. But by spring they would be near enough finished that mass could be said, and King Ine's vision of glory could grow from there.

Only one matter ran behind schedule. The stonemasons, with wonderful skill and careful direction from the Flemish masters, had fashioned a small arched window in the east end of the church and two smaller ones in the tower. Patterns had long ago been sent to a Flemish glass-making center where by now all the small pieces of glass to fill the spaces between stones with jeweled radiance should have been cut and painted and shipped in well-packed rush baskets to Glastingaburg. But although Serenus had sent workers down the Brue to await the trading ships at the Saefern, there was no sign of them.

The windows were to be Ine's jewels, chief symbol of heavenly radiance on his holy island. They could not have the dedication service without these in place. Ulfric sighed.

Again the treasury was nearly empty. The monastery lands beyond the island promised a good harvest, so the workers could be fed, but there was no gold to buy more glass, should this have been set on by raiders.

And Bishop Aldhelm could be counted on to be prompt in demanding his harvest tithes. With a shake of his head, Ulfric descended the hill. He had done his best. But if the glass did not arrive soon, his best would not be enough, for autumn storms would soon close the trading routes.

It was a fortnight and more before Ulfric learned that, indeed, his best was not enough. He was again atop the Tor when he saw the black dots of boats making slow progress against the current up the Brue, and he hurried down to meet them. It was, as he hoped, the workers Serenus had stationed at the Saefern. But they brought no glass—only word of disaster—a great wind—three weeks ago and more.

"We felt little of it here—perhaps that spell of rainy days we had—but in the northern waters many ships were lost."

"Among them the ship carrying the king's windows."

Ulfric left Serenus to question his workers further. He would face this new blow alone. He made his way to the Ealdchurch. Its tiny eastern window let in the afternoon sun and air unrestricted—a bitter reminder of his failure with King Ine's windows. The glory, the radiance, the vision had been smashed on a rocky coast of Northumberland. All was dark. The king had ordered—and his reeve had failed . . .

Ulfric fell on his knees at the ancient altar, but no words of prayer came. He knelt there in silence for some time before he realized that he was not alone. He turned to view the bowed golden head at his right and realized it was Ulnoth. Perhaps sensing eyes on him, Ulnoth looked up at the same time.

"You, too, are burdened, my son?"

Ulnoth sighed. "I must decide, Faeder. Uncle Theodric would have me take holy orders and work forever in the scriptorium."

"And you?"

"And I am uncertain. I am content here on the Glass Isle." His smile told how content he was. "But I would not choose to spend my life copying books. Surely there is more to a vocation than contentment . . ." His voice trailed off. "But you, Faeder, why come you here?"

Ulfric told him of the disaster with the stained glass.

"All is lost?" Ulnoth asked. "There is no chance the boat will yet be found blown into a safe harbor?"

Ulfric shook his head. "They found pieces of the packing baskets battered on the rocks."

Ulnoth nodded. "And there is neither time nor money to repeat the order?"

"Neither."

"What of the Flemish glassworkers already here?"

"They came to guide the stonemasons in following the design. Such has been done. But without the glass they cannot finish."

Ulnoth nodded. He had seen the carefully cut pieces of stone lying, like a woman's embroidery, in a delicate pattern on the floor of the church before the workers had put each piece into place in the wall. It had been a sight of great wonder. He had heard of such things in Rome and Gaul, but never in England. And now perhaps none ever would be.

"Do these Flems know the art of making glass? Or only of fitting in the made pieces?" Ulnoth asked after a long silence, his wide forehead knit in furrows of deep thought.

Ulfric shrugged. "I do not know. What difference does it make?"

Ulnoth shrugged likewise. "Perhaps none. But it was to my thinking that if they know the art and if we have the ingredients here . . . This has ever been called the Glass Isle . . ."

Ulfric fought against the hope that suddenly sprang within him. He did not want to be disappointed again. He had no idea what was needed for glass-making, but at least he could ask. "Come with me, Ulnoth, my son; we will seek out these Flems."

They sat around the hearth in Serenus's hut and talked late into the night. When the brothers had ended the singing of Lauds at daybreak, Ulnoth sought out Abbot Hemgisl to join them. They would need his permission for new uses of abbey lands and resources.

The abbot listened carefully, nodding his head. "Yes, sand, lime, and potash are all readily available here, as is clay for the making of furnaces. Perhaps this would be pleasing to God. Let me put it to the brotherhood at Chapter, for the bringing in of workers from across the marsh would change the isolation of our island, and we have ever held our solitude dear." Then he gave a wry smile, for the past years of building and conflict could hardly be called solitude, though the brothers had remained as aloof as possible and kept to their work and prayers except in rare emergencies.

The glass-making operation did not begin until after Bishop Aldhelm had visited Glastingaburg for his harvest dues, lest he forbid their scheme. *Perhaps it is God's will that the bishop not be bothered with such details,* thought Ulfric. Shortly after the bishop's departure a fine beehive-shaped clay furnace was erected far down the island beneath Wirral Hill where there was plenty of good applewood. A full company of boys was employed to run constantly around the furnace for arm loads of wood to stoke the furnace white-hot.

Ulfric watched in fascination when the first clay pot was pulled from the oven, its contents of sand, lime, and potash now transformed into molten glass. The Flemish worker dipped the end of a metal blowpipe into the clear liquid. He blew the glass blob into a bubble, then swung the pipe to form a long cylinder. On a table set up near the furnace the second master craftsman cut the cylinder with a hot iron, then put it back into the furnace where it was softened just enough to make a flat sheet. Ulfric felt he could have watched all day. Seeing the formless blob of sand transformed into a sheet of shining glass was a magic he could not have imagined. With this sight, the vision returned to Ulfric in all its radiance. He saw God's glory shed on all His people—people who would honor Him before all else in their lives.

But it was in a work shed nearer the church that Ulnoth found his fascination. Under the supervision of the third Flemish master, the sheets of glass were cut with a grazing iron into pieces to fit the window patterns and then painted the jewel colors that would bring King Ine's vision to life. When a section of glass was ready, it was placed in a metal tray and the paint melted into the glass in a small furnace at the end of the shed—in a fire carefully kept from becoming hot enough to melt the glass itself. Once cooled, the glass pieces were banded together with strips of lead.

Ulnoth managed to restrain himself through the first day, but then he felt he must have a hand in the work or he himself would shatter like a piece of glass dropped on the stone floor by a careless worker.

So throughout the winter, with only a short break for Christmastide, the work moved ahead. There were days when cold and sickness slowed the work; there were accidents when too hot or too cool a furnace spoiled many hours or days of work, but always they moved forward. And none happier than Ulnoth cutting, painting, and leading the tiny sections of glass to form pictures of St. Peter and St. Paul. This he could spend his life on without the old restlessness returning and without caring a fig for his twisted leg.

Then spring returned to the land with birdsong and bursting bud. Only the shadow of the Witan still hung over Ulfric. As feared, Cunor's hand swelled and the fingers blackened. Clamping his teeth on an oak twig so that he might not bite his tongue, the workman submitted to the saw. With liberal application of the infirmarer's salves the stump healed clean, and Cunor learned to complete his tasks one-handed, but compensation must be paid. It was the law—forty silver for the hand of an Englishman, twenty for a Britain. It was little enough for Cunor's family, for whom he would ever earn lower wages, but it was impossible for Ulfric whose steading had not yet recovered the losses of the fire.

Aelfgud, who had come with her grandchildren to Glastingaburg for the dedication of the church, could see no sense in the predicament. "Tell Cunor that he must wait his payment. You will pay, and he is sure to need the money more later—such is the way of things."

But Ulfric shook his head. "Cunor might well agree, but it is the law. It must be paid before the next Witan, or I will be subject to harsher penalties."

"Harsher penalties! This is harsh enough. And you carrying out the king's orders when it happened. Let the king pay."

Theodric's advice was similar to his mother's. "The law clearly states that if its requirements are too heavy, one may appeal to the king. You are his officer, and he pays you a pittance. Let you appeal to him."

And that is what Ulfric would have done, could he have spoken with the king in private. But although the reeve was often in the king's company, they were never out of earshot of Bishop Aldhelm, to whom Ulfric would not reveal his troubles—especially when Aldhelm cornered Abbot Hemgisl about paying dues on the glassworks.

So it was with a great rejoicing for the completed church, but with a burden of worry that Ulfric joined his family at the dedication of the Church of Our Savior and Saints Peter and Paul, which Ulfric rightly thought would ever after be known as King Ine's Church.

15

lfric led his family to a place of honor on the front bench before the quire. Many of the benches in the back were yet to be carved and painted, but this one was adorned with rows of saints intertwined with leaves and animals—the saints' robes glowing blue, red, and saffron among the green leaves. All stood for the procession as two boys from the monastery school entered swinging golden censers emitting spicy clouds of incense.

King Ine and Queen Aethelburga walked behind the crossbearer, the purple and scarlet of their robes catching shafts of light falling from the eastern window, their gold crowns turning to aureoles in the morning radiance. Bishop Aldhelm walked behind them in a robe of white and gold, his tall, golden miter repeating the pointed arch of the windows.

In sharp contrast to this splendor, Abbot Hemgisl led his community of dark-robed monks, each wearing a plain wooden cross on his habit. They carried wooden reading tablets, for not all had memorized the chants letter-perfect, long though they had practiced.

The chant began at the back of the church, then swelled as the brothers moved slowly forward under the great three-story tower glowing with colors from the high stained-glass windows.

Blessed be the Lord God, the God of Israel, who alone does marvelous things;
Blessed be His glorious name forever, and may His glory fill all the earth.
Rejoice in the glory of His majesty.
Let all people see His glory.

Then they came into the east end, their voices sounding louder under its lower roof. The sounds no longer echoed off bare stone, as the benches were filled with worshipers from villages on every side of the marsh and with the workers who had raised every stone, every timber, every piece of glass in the whole glorious building.

May the glory of the Lord stand forever, and may He rejoice in
His words!
Let them sing of the Lord's ways, for great is the glory
of the Lord.
Rejoice in the glory of His majesty.

Before the altar the brothers divided right and left into the carved and painted quire stalls lining the walls and there concluded their chant. King Ine and Queen Aethelburga sat on thrones to the right of the altar, Aldhelm on his Bishop's Seat to the left. Then Aldhelm stood and walked to the altar. Facing the people, he held his arms out wide in a blessing. "My house will be called a house of prayer."

The monks and people, led by Hemgisl, replied, "Alleluia!"

"Blessed are You, O Lord, in Your holy temple," the bishop proclaimed.

"Alleluia!"

"Praise the Lord in the assembly of His holy people."

Ulfric responded "Alleluia!" with the others, but he would have been more fervent had he not felt the bishop's rejoicing was partly due to the richness of the church which he could tax.

Abbot Hemgisl stood with bowed head before the altar to lead in intercessions. "O Lord, our God, we are the living stones, laid upon the Cornerstone that is Christ, Your Son. We pray to You, our all-powerful Father, for Your Son's beloved church. This is the house of God and the gate of Heaven."

In the fervency of the moment Hemgisl's voice wavered, and Ulfric looked up sharply; engulfed with his own concerns, he had not realized the abbot had aged so sharply during these years of building. He looked as if he had poured his own life-strength into the walls as his prayers supported their raising. "Wise Builder, sanctify Your home and Your family. Let our worship always be sincere, and help us to find Your saving love in this church. Grant this through our Lord Jesus Christ, Your Son, who lives and reigns with You and the Holy Spirit, one God, forever and ever."

All made the sign of the cross and replied, "Amen."

Bishop Aldhelm stood before a basin of water and blessed it. Then, using a golden salver, he sprinkled the altar, quire, and front benches with holy water before he pronounced the dedicatory prayers.

As the bishop returned to his throne, King Ine left his, for the king himself was to offer a special dedicatory prayer for the eastern window. Ulfric could not help thinking that the king approached his office with more humility than did the bishop, as he stood with the royal head bowed so low that only the top of the crown on his flaxen hair was visible to the audience. "To Him who loves us and freed us from our sins with His life's blood, who made of us a royal house, to serve as the priests of His God and Father—to Him be glory and dominion forever and ever!"

King Ine raised his head, and the light of the window fell on his closed eyes, thin cheeks, and yellow beard. "You are worthy, O Lord our God, to receive glory and honor and power, because You did create all things; by Your holy will they have their being. Honor and glory and praise be unto You. In the temple of the Lord let all peoples say glory to You forever and ever, amen."

Then he moved to the reading table where a great illuminated volume, prepared by the brothers from Theodric's scriptorium, stood open to the Revelation of St. John. Pools of azure, emerald, and ruby fell on the stone floor beside him as he read. "'And I saw the holy city of Jerusalem coming down out of heaven from God. It shone with the glory of God; it had the radiance of some priceless jewel, like a jasper, clear as crystal. And the city had no need of sun or moon to shine upon it, for the glory of God gave it light, and its lamp was the Lamb. By its light shall the nations walk, and the kings of the earth shall bring into it all their splendor. . . . but nothing unclean shall enter, nor anyone whose ways are false or foul, but only those who are inscribed in the Lamb's roll of the living. . . . and they shall reign forevermore.'"

As Ine moved away from the reading table and Queen Aethelburga came to stand beside him, Bishop Aldhelm stood to follow the recessional from the church. The monks began the closing chant.

But Ine did not follow the crossbearer and censers down the aisle. Instead he stood in the open area before the quire and held up his hand to silence the chant. Ulfric, catching the tension of a strange happening, sat up straighter. He saw a gleam of anticipation and something that could only be described as mischievous pleasure in the king's eyes. At another gesture from the king the monks resumed their seats, and Aldhelm returned to his throne. It was good that the bishop was sitting, for when the thrust of King Ine's words became clear, the prelate would certainly have stumbled.

Queen Aethelburga drew a roll of parchment from the long, loose sleeve of her scarlet gown and handed it to her husband. He unrolled it and read, "In the name of our Lord Jesus Christ, I, Ine, King of Wessex, do grant to Glastingaburg out of those places which I possess by paternal inheritance . . ." And so continued the royal charter, richly endowing the monastery from the royal lands nearby, so that never again would monks or workers have to go hungry as they did God's work on earth. With each new item on the list Bishop

Aldhelm's eyes glinted brighter, and his smile widened, as he thought of the dues he could charge.

Then the smile faded as the king continued. ". . . I appoint and establish that all lands, places, and possessions of Glastingaburg be free from all taxes and dues, both royal and ecclesiastical. And that no bishop, on any account, may presume to take his episcopal seat, or celebrate divine service, or ordain, or do anything whatever, either in the church itself or on its lands unless he be specially invited by the abbot or brethren of that place. On this day and by my own hand I so ascribe and declare, Ine, King of Wessex."

Not even a chirping of birds or rustling of wind could be heard as all took in the overwhelming meaning of the king's words. The only movement seemed to be the color draining from Bishop Aldhelm's face and his shoulders sagging. Finally there was a small rustle in the quire, and Abbot Hemgisl stood. "In the temple of the Lord all peoples will say glory to You." It was unclear whether the pronoun referred to the King of Wessex or of Heaven.

"Alleluia," responded the monks.

Then Ine took the royal purse from his belt and, opening it, drew out several leather pouches. Now it was Ulfric's turn to blanch, but for the opposite reason. His name was the first to be called, and he walked forward to receive a purse of coins from King Ine in appreciation for his work. He dipped a bow and received the heavy bag in numb fingers. Back in his seat he was barely aware of Serenus, the glass workers, master stonemasons, and others being singled out for royal honor. At first he thought he would explode with joy at the lifting of a great weight—he could pay the wergild. He was free. Ulfstead was free. He could rebuild the hall to its former fineness; he could erect sturdy byres; he could rebuild his herds with the best stock. The horse-runs of Ulfstead would again be famous . . .

But then his joy turned to dismay. Free? What did he mean, free? Certainly, he could pay his debts; but never had he been less free. For with such a bestowal of royal favor, he now could never resign from Ine's service. Always it had been at the back of his mind—when the church was finished, then he would quit his office. This one last task for Ine and for God; then he would retire, and all his efforts could go to his own land. His mother was ancient; his eldest son was established at Glastingaburg; his second son was just finding his place on the land he loved and needed guidance; his daughters were growing up fatherless. All needed his leadership at Ulfstead, and they should have it. But now, now Ine had bought him as surely as if he had been a thrall in the slave market. He would never be free.

However, Ulfric had reckoned too soon. King Ine was not finished. He called a page from behind the royal throne and handed him the empty purse. But that was not all, for as the page stood with outstretched arms, the king unfastened the great jeweled brooch which held his purple cloak in place and laid it in his servant's hands. Next followed the long saffron tunic with its wide bands of intricate gold embroidery intertwined with fantastic animals.

Likewise, Queen Aethelburga beside him was removing her splendid royal robes and jewels and handing them to a page, until both king and queen stood before their people clad only in long white tunics of undyed lambs' wool. With a deliberate gesture, King Ine bowed his head and removed the gold circle from his brow, as did the queen. And the king said, "I, King Ine of the Kingdom of Wessex and Queen Aethelburga, do tell you, our people here assembled, as we will tell our carles, thanes, and witans, that we do hereby renounce all worldly thrones, principalities, and powers. With our eyes firmly fixed on the only true and abiding Kingdom of glory, that of our Lord Jesus Christ, we leave our kingdom in the hands of our cousin Athelheard, of equal royal descent from Cerdic of royal Saxon lineage, and will make holy pilgrimage to Rome, there to live the life of humble hermits, worshiping our Heavenly King until such time as He chooses to take us into that greater glory around the great white throne. In the name of the Father, and the Son, and the Holy Spirit, we declare this to be our full and most righteous intent." King and queen crossed themselves and then, turning toward the cross on the altar, knelt on the cold stone floor in the radiance of the window above them.

With a day of so many wonders, it was some time after the monks had finally finished their interrupted recessional and all had departed from the church that Ulfric, sitting still on his front bench with his family around him, fully realized what had happened. He was free. The king no longer needed his service. Now he could return to the land of his ealdfaeder's faeder's ealdfaeder without divided loyalty. Now he could build Ulfstead secure for his generation to pass to another in the rising of the sun.

Then, as if he had spoken his thoughts aloud, Theodric, who had returned to his family group after marching out with the brothers, clasped the cross hanging around his neck and raised it as if in blessing over his family. Standing in a pool of colored light from the window Ulnoth had helped create, Theodric said, "This, says the Lord, is My covenant which I make: My Spirit which rests on you and My words which I have put into your mouth shall never fail you from generation to generation of your descendants from now onward forever."

Ulfric held his brother's gaze and returned his smile. "Such are the words of the Lord," he said. Then he turned to the rest of his family. "Thus may we live in His glory."

PART THREE

16

he moor mist rose gray and damp. Wisps and feathers of pale vapor floated over the dark waters, and a breath of dank air stirred the marsh grasses. Under a tangle of winter-bare branches the company huddled deeper into their cloaks and drew closer to the fire. King Alfred ran his long, agile fingers over the strings of the alderwood harp, and it seemed that every chord sent the mist a little farther back into the night. The infant princess Aelfthryth at last slept in her mother's arms, and her six-year-old sister Ethelgifu nodded on the shoulder of the queen's serving lady. The two older royal children, ten-year-old Princess Aethelflaeda and eight-year-old Eadweard the Aetheling, sat farther back among the house carles who had fled with their king into the marshes of the west country, the last outpost of the Kingdom of Wessex.

Since the vikings had routed them from their outpost at Chippenham on Twelfth Night three months ago, the tiny island of Athelney in the marshes was the last spark of official Christianity in England. Adrift in the fog, surrounded by ravaging heathen, Athelney was England's hope for salvation.

Alfred's fingers continued to make music on the harp strings, but the roving mind beneath the great head of russet hair seemed to have leapt far ahead. Perhaps he laid war plans against Guthrum's great viking army which held them virtual prisoners in their own kingdom. Or perhaps his thoughts turned to history, literature, or religion—for the king was equally at home in battle, church, or the councils of government. Tonight, though, it seemed his mind was on recent history, for his fingers struck a final chord, and he thrust the harp at Deor his scop. "Glee-man, open your word-hoard; we would have a song."

"Assuredly. What would please my lord?"

"I was thinking on the "Battle of Ashdown." Give us a song of victory, for we are in sore need of happy remembrance tonight."

For a hundred years since King Ine, the seasons of mists and sun had come to the marshlands. And Wessex had grown to be the greatest kingdom in all England. It was a golden time as learning and art and faith increased in the land. Then far to the north on the rocky seashore off Northumberland, a dragon-prowed ship had appeared out of the sea spray to massacre the monks in a lonely monastery called Lindisfarne. The age of the viking had descended on England.

For nearly another hundred years of mist and sunshine, Egbert and Ethelwulf and Ethelbald and Ethelbert and Ethelred—all of Alfred's ancestors—had continued to increase the power and prosperity of Wessex. But always they had to fight the evil plague of vikings.

First the Danes came as simple raiders—striking and pillaging, then departing. But then came the great army sweeping ever southward under the black raven banner of Halfdene, swallowing up Northumbria and Mercia and East Anglia, until Wessex alone had remained free English soil. Then the rich country around Chippenham was the only district of Wessex not ravaged, but now the Danes were wasting a wide circle of land around their base camp.

Last night Alfred's scouts had brought even darker tidings. Sigurd Smoke-Eye, brother of Halfdene, son of Ragnar, had descended on the coast of Devon. This would complete the conquest. Not just plundering and departing, as England had suffered for a hundred years, but permanent settlement of all the land.

Somehow they must fight on. Alfred did not know how they could, but he knew raising their spirits was a first step.

Deor caught his king's determination. "Aye, a hero-lay for the king and for all good Englishmen true." The scop took Gleewood, the king's own harp and struck a cadence of minor chords.

And then was the sorrow-time / with fiend-fury sped,
the viking spearheads flew / tearing blood-rents in the land.
War-troops of Danes ravaged the realm / long demon-head ships
  savaged the sail-road,
and doom overhung the land / doom as a hail cloud,
  destruction-heavy.
The devil-prows sailed, / accursed of God in the mist,
up rivers gentle-smooth; / and jumped from the doom-ships
barbarian battlers, bloody bent, / peaceful peasants to dispossess.
Seized from their beds, / humble herdsmen were heaven-sent
by blood-spilling butchers, / fire-dragging their victims for sport.
The wave of ruin west-rolled / a satanic void, virtue-vacant.
The sky hung dark all-while, / and death descended
  from heathendom.

The scop's fingers hovered over the strings like the clouds of doom hanging over the marsh island, but the next chord they struck sounded a new note of tenuous hope.

Then hurried the horde to Wessex, / hurling havoc and massacring many.
And Ethelred-King / rode forth to face the foe.
There fought Dane and English / with slaughter great on every hand.
The tumult of spears rang ear-sharp; / the clash of standard tore eye-anguish.
And Aethelwulf-Ealdorman fell slain, / and the Danes had power in the place of slaughter.
For four days were the Danes supreme, / and destruction death-dark reigned over all
Then Alfred, king's brother, / rode valiant to Ashdown.
The sword-slaughter held long; / the air hovered low, blood-flecked.
But Alfred held sway over Danish defeat, / and the land was peace-preserved.
Short though was the grace-favor. / And Ethelred-King died at Easter.
So Alfred, new-made king, / Alfred of shining countenance,
rode forth in the grace of God, / and glory attended the crown.
But short was the God-gift of peace, / for the Danes marched on slaughter-bent.
Alfred meted mighty opposition, / and the welkin rang with sword-clash,
and long was the victory his, / but the Danes held power in the place of slaughter.
Yet on marched the Danish-destruction. / So followed Alfred, hero-bold and unflinching.
He put them to sword-flight, / but the Danes held power in the place of slaughter.

And then, as if in defiance of the dismal surroundings of the royal camp and the disheartening words of the song, the notes of the harp sang a tune of golden victory.

And the heathen horde stole out in midwinter / while Christians at Twelfth Night feasted
and overrode all Wessex-land; / so desolation lay snow-blanketed.
And barbarians sat down in the land / and left the people homeless.
But Alfred mighty-heart / refused defeat's dishonor.
Alfred strong-will / would not be enemy-bent.
So into the woods and moor-fastness / his little band we came.

And forth shall march / with victory-rings valiant-voiced.
From Athelney's solitude / shall Alfred's battle-bellow ring
With the victory-voice of God / Heaven's triumph He will send.

The king sighed. Did he still have the courage the scop sang of? The courage to lead forth into yet another battle against the great army of Guthrum? His small band against the seemingly numberless viking horde?

Baby Aelfthryth whimpered in her mother's arms. That the queen and royal children should be in an army camp with him! But there was no place else. This was all that remained of Wessex—the only God-fearing, law-abiding kingdom in all England. He had no choice. Guthrum must be faced. Guthrum must be defeated. The task was his.

The greatest enemy was not Guthrum, but war-weariness. No matter how many battles they won, it seemed that the Danes were winning the war. The thanes and their men had been kept away from their farms and families for the better part of two years, and they had nothing to show for it. To expect them to turn out for yet another campaign in the coldest part of the year could well be too much. They knew it would mean nights spent sleeping in the open on frozen ground, as the court itself now was.

And what would be the end of it? What but another futile peace, with the Danes taking another geld and giving in return another of their worthless oaths—which they would break as soon as it suited them. Was a man to blame for thinking that his first duty was to defend his own hearth? No, there was little likelihood of a great rallying to Alfred's summons, should he send out the hosting call. And he questioned whether he himself possessed the will to send it.

Also he wondered about his decision to take refuge in Athelney. He could have gone east to more secure—and less damp—refuge. But it was important to keep the Welsh princes loyal to his cause, which would be easier if he were only a few miles from their border. And the swamps of Somerset not only offered security for his small band, but also provided a base from which they could harry Guthrum's wandering bands of plunderers. One more thing, so vague he hardly reckoned it as a factor and yet it remained in his mind, was his memory of the few golden days spent at the monastery at Glastingaburi just twelve swamp-miles north of Athelney.

In the days before he had taken on the burden of kingship, Alfred had visited his half-brother Neot in his hermitage on the Glass Island. No two brothers, even accounting for their different mothers, could have been less alike than Alfred and Neot. Alfred, commandingly tall, bursting with energy in spite of frequent attacks of pain, lived constantly in the whirlwind center of the royal court. Neot, so short he had to stand on an iron stool to be seen when he said mass, always went about his quiet duties with soft voice and bowed head, living the life of a hermit on a marsh-surrounded island. Yet there was a true bonding of spirit between the two.

Alfred appreciated his brother's gentle wisdom, and Neot's devout spirit appreciated another heart in tune with God. Neot showed Alfred around the island telling him all the wonderful stories of how Joseph of Arimathea had brought the Christ Child there and later returned as a missionary, about how St. Patrick of the Irish had so loved the holy place he had spent his last years organizing the brotherhood and was now buried there, and how King Ine had honored the isle . . . The days had been an island of peace in a sea of turmoil.

What had cemented Alfred's relationship with his brother and with Glastingaburi was the night Alfred had a severe attack of incapacitating pain in his bowels. Leaning so heavily on the little Neot he feared crushing him, Alfred had gone to the Ealdchurch where he fell at the altar in agony. Neot anointed Alfred's forehead with holy chrism and, kneeling beside him, prayed through the night for healing. In the morning the pain was gone. Nor was he left weak and melancholy as usual after such attacks. Most wonderful of all, the pain had never returned. Alfred still sometimes suffered from near-to-blinding headaches, but never again from the pain in his bowels that had formerly kept him on his cot for days at a time.

Although Neot had moved from Glastingaburi to a more remote hermitage in Cornwall a number of years ago, and then gone on to his heavenly reward, the isle remained special to Alfred for another reason. At Glastingaburi the answer had come, not only for his ailment, but the answer to his search for the meaning of his life. For at their parting, Neot had quoted Psalm 85 to his brother, and the words became God's special promise to Alfred:

Deliverance is near to those who worship Him, that glory may
dwell in our land.
Justice and peace join hands.
Fidelity springs up from the earth, and justice looks down
from heaven.
The Lord will add prosperity, and our land shall yield its harvest.
Justice shall go in front of him, and the path before his feet shall
be peace.

Alfred heard in those sacred words God's purpose and promise for him, a purpose that Alfred should fulfill for God and for England. He didn't know what it was, but he knew that it was there and that God was there, and that was enough. Usually.

But tonight the mists drew in ever closer and darker, so close they seemed to touch his soul. The song of his scop had failed to shake the gloom from his heart. The memory of his sainted brother Neot had failed to dispel the sense of doom. Perhaps his priest . . . "Father Grimbald," Alfred called from the little group around the fire. "Come with me to my tent. What words of comfort have you for your king?"

Alfred lifted the flap on his deer-hide tent, and the priest went before him to light a small lantern with the burning stick he carried from the campfire. Alfred pulled over him a heavy fur rug from his cot, and the priest sat on a cushion on the floor.

"I can give you no better than the words of another king who waited on God when his enemies surrounded him. Would you hear from King David, my lord?"

Alfred gestured for Father Grimbald to proceed, then pressed his hand to his aching temple. The walls of the tent and the thickness of the rugs kept some of the damp chill at bay as the flickering of the single lantern pushed back a few rags of the dark. The priest's words filled all the space in the tent:

My heart waits silently for God;
my deliverance comes from Him.
In truth He is my rock of deliverance,
my tower of strength, so that I stand unshaken.
Men plan to topple me from the height and stamp on the fallen stones . . .
My deliverance and my honor depend upon God—
God who is my rock of refuge and my shelter . . .
All power belongs to Him.

17

It was noon the next day when Alfred learned why the sense of doom had been so strong the night before. The guard he had set at the north side of the island pushed through the thick tangle of brush, prodding a small gray-brown creature before him at spear point. But what at first appeared to be an animal straightened itself and suddenly became a boy of about sixteen clad in a wolfskin cloak.

The boy gave something like a military salute, then dropped to his knees before the king. "The vikings, my lord!" He paused to gasp for breath, and Alfred could judge from the mire clinging to his leggings and spattered above his waist that the lad must have crossed the frozen marshes on foot and slipped often into partially thawed bogs. "The vikings! They attack Glastingaburi!"

Instantly Alfred's armorbearer was off after his lord's sword and shield, and from the first shout of *viking*, the house carles were arming themselves. But Alfred, in his thorough manner, questioned the lad. "And who are you?"

"Coelfrid of Ulfstead, my lord. My aunt Athelis is waiting lady to your queen."

Alfred gave a sharp nod. "So. And that is how you knew our whereabouts. And why were you chosen messenger?"

"My Uncle Tumbert, brother to Athelis, is sacristan for the monastery. Sometimes I help him polish the vessels. I was there when word came that horn-helmed ravens marched down the Fosse."

Again Alfred gave his jerky nod, even as his armorbearer pulled the chain mail sark over his head and settled the straps of his sword sheath and dirk scabbard around his waist. "So. If Guthrum is at Chippenham as our spies say, that is how they would come. Know you if the ravens have turned off the Roman way yet?"

Coelfrid shook his head. Alfred had a pretty good idea of the panic and confusion that such a warning must have spread among the monks. It was possible Guthrum's raiding band would pass on by the monastery, but it was unlikely. If the Danes had crossed the Mendip Hills, there was little else to raid save a few scattered steadings. Most likely the boy was right. And if he was, there was little Alfred and his men could do, for the burning and pillaging would be done before they could reach the holy island. Yet they must try. "Get you to your Aunt Athelis for a washing and some food."

"No!" Then Coelfrid remembered himself. "I mean, if it please my king, I will lead you back through the swamp. I know the way well."

Alfred raised an eyebrow at the boy's mud-caked condition. "Do you think you could find a drier route than that you came by?"

But in spite of Coelfrid's assurances, they were overtaken by dark and forced to camp the night in the Poldern Hills south of Glastingaburi. It was noon the next day that they arrived at the monastery.

They could tell from the thin streams of black smoke in the air that were too straight to be fog and too dark to be hearth fires that they were too late. Brother Tumbert, who had been keeping watch for his nephew, met them at the edge of the marsh on the south side of the Tor. "I knew you would come. I thank God you have arrived safely, even though it is too late. The destruction has fallen."

His words were simple, spoken without emotion, but Alfred knew far more lay behind them. The monk's raised face still bore an expression of unspeakable horror. And his eyes held the hollowness of a man who had looked into

Hell. Alfred gripped his shoulder. "Tell me what it is." This could be no simple case of burning and looting.

But Brother Tumbert merely shook his head as if he knew no words to express what he had seen. He turned, and they followed the fat, brown-robed monk around the foot of the hill to the monastery. Many of the round wattle cells lay in a heap of ashes, no longer even smoking they had burned so fast. Smoke still rose, however, from the remains of the rectangular, thatched dining hall and the timbered roof of a small stone church. Tumbert waved an arm that direction. "St. Stephen's Chapel, built by an ancestor of mine. I do not see why they felt they must burn it—they had nothing to gain once they had stripped it of its golden cross and vessels. But fortunately they didn't think it worth bothering to fire the Ealdchurch—such do heathen know about true value. My ancestor's roof we can rebuild, and the vessels can be replaced. The Ealdchurch could never be replaced."

The destruction was bad enough, but as Brother Tumbert said, they could rebuild. The burned buildings could not account for the devastation in the monk's face. "The brothers. Injured? Killed?" the king prodded.

"Three killed." Tumbert paused so long Alfred thought he would say no more. Then a shudder passed through the long-robed body. "Abbot Elmund bade us take all the books we could carry to the top of the Tor and pray. There we could hope to be out of the way of the raiders. All but five did so." Again he paused, his head bowed so low that his cowl completely obscured his face.

Then he raised his head with a jerk. "Brothers Waldun and Guthlac had been here only a short time. They lost their heads with fear and ran into the swamp. Both now bide in a corner of the burned-out infirmary with grippe on their chests."

They stood before the largest structure of the cluster of buildings, a stone church with a tall square tower in the center. Charred debris lay on the winter-brown grass, apparently a hurried attempt by the monks to clean out the church for the service under way now. A low, mournful dirge came from the building.

Alfred took Brother Tumbert out of the hearing of the others. "You must tell me about the other three. I am the king. I must know."

Again the cowl slipped over the bowed head, obscuring Tumbert's voice, but Alfred could hear. "Eanfrid, the eldest of our community, much loved and revered for his gentleness and his wisdom; Prior Wigthane, ever a man of powerful prayer, certain to be our abbot someday; and Plegmund, one of our youngest, but so devout his face fairly shone with love of God, even when he came to office in the middle of a winter night—never did he complain, all he did was for his Savior—even to staying to pray in Ine's church. Those three, they did not want to go even so far away as the top of the Tor, you see . . ."

For a time he could say no more. Alfred waited. Then, "All that would burn of Ine's church was the wall hangings, the wooden furnishings—and our brothers. We found their burned bodies lashed to the quire stalls where they had knelt to pray. Their robes had been torn off them and . . ."

Even without hearing the rest, Alfred now understood. They stood there for a long time, the only sound the requiem from inside the church. At last they turned slowly and entered the smoke-blackened doorway. The church had been swept clean, but it still reeked of charred wood and a stronger smell one would rather not identify. Three plain wooden coffins stood on the bare stone floor in a pool of colored light beneath the window of St. Peter and St. Paul.

Abbot Elmund read from a Bible held for him by a young monk because no reading stands remained. "Oh God, see how the heathen rage. From a far land the heathen have set foot in Your domain, defiled Your temple, and laid Jerusalem in ruins. They have spilled the blood of Your royal servants like water. . . . Let Your vengeance for the bloody slaughter of Your servants fall on these heathen before our very eyes. . . ."

The mass continued, but Alfred heard nothing else. The words rang in his mind as if emblazoned in fire: *Let Your vengeance for the bloody slaughter of Your servants fall on these heathen.* Alfred would wreak God's vengeance on Guthrum's animals—no, no, not animals. These were far worse than animals. For no animal would do such to his own kind as they had done to these holy, gentle men. Would even a devil do so?

The king turned and left the church. But he had as well have stayed. There was no solace anywhere. The whole land had become to him a barren desert. The peace and beauty he had found on Avalon when he was there with Neot was no more. The isle of the blessed had been raped and disfigured by the hand of evil. Alfred was dismayed at his sense of personal loss. Something untouchably holy and precious had been torn out of the world by Guthrum's monsters.

Now, more than ever before, after years of battle, Alfred truly saw what he fought against. Not mere men, but the raw force of evil. "It must be stopped!" he cried aloud and shook his fist at the sky. He fell to his knees on the frozen ground. "God, give me Guthrum. Let me avenge these holy brothers."

It was spoken as a request, but in his heart it was a vow. He would kill Guthrum. Wiping this heathen menace from the earth was now Alfred's single goal, brought into focus more sharply by the brutal savaging of these three monks than by the deaths of thousands of his people before.

Alfred sat long considering plans for reaching this goal—questioning veterans of other battles, visiting victims of devastation, sending spies closer to the enemy camp . . . nothing seemed adequate.

Two days later, when the small party from Athelney that had followed the warriors more slowly arrived in Glastingaburi, a plan had begun to form in Alfred's mind. He had set his soldiers to helping the monks throw up shelters for the community to eat and sleep in. After a long day the king's men sat around a campfire apart from the religious community, who observed silence after sundown. Deor drew his harp from the leather bag he carried slung over his shoulder and gently fingered the strings. This was not Gleewood, the king's own harp, but an older, plainer instrument darkened and mellowed by age as it had been carried by generations of harpers before Deor. He looked to his lord for direction.

"I would hear 'The Wanderer,'" Alfred replied. A lover of the old tales of heroism and adventure of his people, tonight he felt at one with the poet of old who, alone in exile, brooded on the passing of earth's joys. Deor's harpstrings and voice sang at the king's bidding:

Often the lonely one / longs for mercy;
for the grace of God, / though he, heart-weary
far from his home / must long wait.
So speaks the wanderer, / mindful of woe,
of cruel slayings, / his kinsmen's cold death.
The mead-halls are crumbled / the monarchs thrown down,
The proud warriors fallen / lie low by the wall, war-ravaged.
Where are the horses?
Where fled the heroes?
Where the high giver of treasures?

Deor, in the small circle of light that fell around the fire, sang of the lonely poet, lost and homeless, forced to flee the darkness that had fallen on the earth when disaster struck the lord he served. Then with hopeful notes, he sang of the new knowledge the wanderer acquired when he saw the wastelike end of worldly wealth and found solace in spiritual gain.

Alas, the bright cup!
Alas, the brave deed!
Alas, the bountiful gift!
Here treasure is fleeting; / here true friends are fleeting.
All the face of the earth / stands idle and empty.
So says the sage in his heart, / he sits and secretly ponders.
So must man stand true / nor speak the woe of his heart
But lean all on the soul-cure / to show forth stirring succor.
Glory be to God on high / who grants us heaven's grace.

The final chord vibrated on the night air, and all sat silent in the firelight, looking to the king for direction. At last Alfred knew what he would do. He had found his direction not in the words of the song, but in the very act of singing. In all the world one man was welcome at every fireside—High King's hall or base peasant's hut, Christian or heathen. No one would refuse a wandering minstrel space at the hearth for as many days as his song would last.

Alfred looked at each man around the fire. His words were to all and yet to each individual. "I would have you continue here until the brothers' shelters are built; then return to the queen at Athelney. Wait there, and after a few days I will join you."

All those sitting around the fire plied the king with questions, but he would tell them no more. Except to Deor, to whom he said, "I will have need of your harp. Keep you Gleewood singing for me until I return to Athelney."

But it seemed that one in his company understood at least part of what was in his mind, for later young Coelfrid approached him. "If my lord is going alone through the marsh, he will need a guide again."

Alfred smiled for the first time since Coelfrid had broken in on them with his news. "Ah. It is the colt of Ulfstead. Think you to be my guide?"

"Yes." Then thinking better of his abrupt answer, he quickly added, "If it please my lord."

Alfred's smile broadened. "It pleases me."

18

Hold, my brave guide," Alfred called to Coelfrid a good twenty paces ahead. "You race like a horse returning to his stable."

Coelfrid turned, looking shame-faced. "Well, my lord will need a place to stay for the night, so I thought . . ."

"So. I was not far wrong in my analogy, Coelfrid of Ulfstead. The colt heads to home pasture. That is well. But you must not call me your lord. I am a simple scop, a wandering minstrel, lord of no one and nothing."

"What shall I call you then?"

Alfred thought for a moment. Then his eyes lit with pleasure. "I shall take the name of a poet I much admire in hope that I bring honor, not shame, to his name. Call me Cynewulf."

Coelfrid grinned. "Cynewulf. So I shall." Then his smile faded. "There is just one thing, my l—, er, Cynewulf. I am worried about returning home . . ."

Alfred nodded. "Yes. The vikings. We must hope your steading is far enough off the Roman way to be Dane-safe."

Coelfrid nodded and turned to lead them on with quickened pace. But even with his hurrying, the shadows were long before they reached the sheltered spot at the foot of the Mendips that had been home to Coelfrid's family for three hundred years as best anyone could reckon. As they crested the last gentle rise, Coelfrid gave a small shout of relief. It stood unharmed—the hall built of sturdy walls of upright logs, its row of tall, narrow windows, each just one log wide under the steep, timbered roof, with smoke from the central hearth curling out of the smoke-hole of the roof; the little square stone chapel where his family, those of neighboring steadings, and serfs from all the fields heard mass whenever a traveling priest came near; and all the thickly thatched wattle and daub outbuildings of barns, workshops, and storeplaces—all enclosed in the sturdy turf and timber palisade that separated it from the fields, pastures, and serfs' huts beyond.

Even though it was near to evening meal time, Wulfstan, Coelfrid's father, was still in the field guiding the curved handles of a heavy wooden plow that ran on two wide wooden wheels behind yoked oxen. A serf in a brown tunic and cloth cap walked beside the oxen with a stick over his shoulder. The sturdy team veered from their line, wandering to the left. The serf gave the near ox a sharp prod with his stick, and with a soft lowing, the animals returned to a straight plow line. Farther on, a young boy in a short green tunic with cross-gartered leggings watched over a flock of honking geese near a pond in one corner of the yard, and two serfs chopped firewood beyond a small shed. From one of the workshops came the ring of hammer on anvil, and the horse tethered at the door stamped as if bored with waiting for his new shoes. Two girls in bright kirtles and white head-rails walked from the dairy shed carrying wooden buckets of milk. Alfred paused to breathe the scent of newly turned earth, wood smoke, and seed-time freshness. Yes, this was what he was fighting for—the peaceful home and hearth of good Englishmen.

Coelfrid ran forward with a shout. When Wulfstan saw his son, he turned the plow over to the serf and walked to meet the newcomers. "Father, this is—" Coelfrid began with a sweep of his arm.

But Wulfstan did not need to be told. He pulled his leather cap from his head and went down on one knee. "Welcome to Ulfstead, my lord."

Alfred immediately reached out to raise him to his feet. "Nay, nay. You mistake. I am Cynewulf. A wandering minstrel come to beg a meal and a pallet of straw at your hearthside for the price of a song."

Wulfstan considered for a moment. "So that's the way of it, is it? Then let you put off your king's cloak for a homespun tunic. And welcome to the hearth of Wulfstan, in whatever guise you come."

Later, they sat at the trestle table, finishing the last bites of barley cakes and meat roasted on the turnspit. Alfred looked down at the coarse-woven blue tunic he wore over the long-sleeved, hooded undersark Wulfstan had given him. "Think you I look like a homeless harper now?"

Wulfhere, the youngster they had earlier seen herding the geese, bobbed his head up and down. "Oh, yes. And will you give us a song?"

Alfred smiled and pulled Deor's harp from its leather pouch. "What say you to a riddle?"

The boy and his little sister sitting at the women's end of the table clapped their hands as Alfred struck a chord. Then they leaned closer to catch every word.

A moth ate words, / a strange-seeming thing it was
that a worm should swallow / the song of a man,
a thief in the dark / ate his wondrous sayings
yet was none the wiser / for swallowing words of great wisdom.

With a final flourish, Alfred ended the tune with an upward scale that left a question mark in the air.

Wulfhere clapped his hands. "Oh, I know that one! It's a moth—a book moth!"

Alfred laughed. "Right! Let us hope the answer came so readily from your wit and my skill in singing, not from my choice of an overworked subject." He passed the harp to his host. "Your turn now, Wulfstan."

Though the man was less skillful in harping, a clear, simple tune sprang from his fingers. After a moment's thought, he sang:

My beak is turned earthward; / I burrow low
and break the ground. / I go as I'm guided
by my master and lord / who guards me behind.
And green and earth-brown / is the path of my going.

The blond girl in the apple-green kirtle laughed. "Oh, Faeder, it's a plow! But I knew it would be. You ever make riddles to match what you did that day."

"And am I so predictable, Bryna, my daughter?"

Again she laughed. "Predictable, Faeder. But a skillful riddle, nonetheless."

The harp went around the table, and again Alfred was filled with the sense that this, the home-hearth of a peaceful steading, was the heart of England. For this he would continue to fight. Then his gaze went upward to the carved painted beams that supported the hall. At first he thought the carvings were just a design. Then he saw that they were crude letters. The words were erratically spelled, partially obscured by the smoke and dust of the years, but he could make them out. "'One generation passes unto another; but the earth abides forever, and the sun also rises,'" he read aloud.

"Aye," Wulfstan said. "My ancestor who first built this hall carved that—or so my family has always said. It's a fine saying, whatever the truth of it. Of course, the hall has been rebuilt many times, but the rooftrees have stood strong."

Alfred nodded. "Yes, your family has built well—and so they should with such a verse to guide them. Your ancestor was a man of great vision that he should have carved in English. That was a day when the tongue was little regarded."

Wulfstan shrugged. "I never thought of it."

"It was so. But I am determined to change that—if this endless war will give me leisure." Suddenly, Alfred leaned forward, his eyes alight with the excitement of his vision. "It is my dream for England to be a land of book-strength—a land with people strong in mind and soul. For that we must have people who can read in our own tongue—and books for them to read. I would have—" He paused as if to correct himself. "With God's help, if we have peace, I would have all the youth of free men be bound to learning so that they should all know how to read English. I would have the most valuable books translated into our own tongue—and then I would set the whole nation to school with those textbooks." And he swept on with his dream, as if seeing those very scenes before him, rather than the family around a trestle table at Ulfstead. "And I would build monasteries—rebuild all those that have been emptied of their books and treasures by the heathen horde—I would make them places where lovers of beauty could live at peace."

Then, with a small shake of his head, Alfred's mind returned to his present surroundings. "Ah, but we are encumbered with world-troubles. I love the arts of peace better than the arts of war, but we must have the war until it makes way for the peace. Then I would lay down my sword for the pen. In the meantime you must keep the peace here, Wulfstan of Ulfstead, in the place the Lord helped your ancestors to build, for the Lord has promised, 'My Spirit which rests on you and My words which I have put into your mouth shall never fail you from generation to generation of your descendants from now onward forever.'"

Having pronounced the invocation, Alfred stood up abruptly. "So. Tomorrow I set out as a roving singer to learn what I can to put us closer to such dreams. I thank you for your hospitality, Wulfstan. It may be that I shall pass this way again. And when my summons comes, will you leave your land to fight for England?"

Wulfstan's gaze went to the wall where hung the sword and shield that had been his father's and his father's father's for as far back as anyone knew. "I will come and all my serfs. For ever it is a tradition of Ulfstead that one should serve the hearth stead, the church, and the king."

Then Coelfrid, who had long sat quiet, spoke. "And while you bide at the hearth stead, Faeder, I will serve the king."

Wulfstan turned to his son. "What mean you?"

"Why, that I shall go with King Alfred—er, Cynewulf here—as apprentice glee-man."

The king threw back his head and laughed. "And when did a wandering scop ever take a learner with him?"

"Whenever one wanted to learn his skill, I should think," Coelfrid answered in perfect seriousness.

"And can you juggle? Dance on your hands? Eat fire?" Alfred asked.

"If I could, I would not need to apprentice—I should be a minstrel on my own. For now it is enough that I am learning—and that I know my way through the woods hereabouts."

To Alfred's surprise, there was no protest from Wulfstan or his quiet wife over such a dangerous errand. "So. We shall put it to the test," Alfred agreed. "Tomorrow you shall go with me. We will find a steading in a distant clearing and try our disguise on the family of some swineherd or sheep-tender. If we succeed, you may lead me to Chippenham; if we are suspect, we shall both abandon this madness."

"Yes, Cynewulf—so be it." And Coelfrid carefully slid his master's harp into its bag.

They were nearing Froom the next day when they heard the sound of an axe in the wood. A few more yards down the dirt road, they came upon a partially plowed field waiting till danger of spring frosts passed for the farmer to sow his seeds. At the far end of the field was an A-shaped wooden hut, the eaves of its steep, thatched roof reaching to the ground on both sides. A woman sat at a loom in the doorway, two small children pulling at her skirts. Alfred paused. He was uncertain how to address the woman. The age of the children would suggest she was a young mother, but her deeply wrinkled skin and the dull wisps of hair escaping from her head-rail suggested a grandmother.

The question was quickly satisfied, however, when the youngest child began to whimper, and she sat him on her lap, opened the front of her kirtle, and began nursing him. As soon as the infant was guzzling happily, she looked up at the newcomers. "Goodwyfe," Alfred greeted her. "I am Cynewulf the scop, and this is my boy Coelfrid. Would you have a song for a cake at your fire?" Even as he spoke, he could smell the buns baking on the hearth behind her.

She looked him up and down twice before she spoke. "Aye. My man would be glad enough of a song with his ale and cake tonight. But you must do more than sing for it. Bid your boy to mind the cubblings here, and you watch the cakes while I bring in the swine from the woods."

Alfred agreed readily and pulled a three-legged stool close to the fire. Through the open door he could see Coelfrid holding the infant while chasing after the toddler who was romping with a shaggy gray puppy. The king/scop looked at the wheat cakes baking on a flat stone by the glowing coals. They smelled wonderfully of warm yeast. He judged they would need turning in about ten minutes—for all he knew of baking. As a boy, he had spent considerable time loitering in the royal cookplace when similar cakes were due to emerge, golden and crusty from the large clay ovens. If he closed his eyes and just concentrated on the smell, he could imagine himself back there . . .

Then his thoughts went from the past to the future. Once Guthrum was defeated, the real work would begin—that of holding the kingdom secure. He went over again the plan he had been forming in his mind for some time—a system of defensive burks with strong earthwork walls—something like the Roman system of forts. He would plan them so that no settlement would be more than twenty miles—a day's march—from one of these fortified towns. And for the seacoast—he must defend against a return of the dragon ships. The plundering by pirate raids must be stopped. He would build ships twice as long as the vikings'—with sixty oars and more. They would be swifter and more stable than the enemy ships—an entirely new design. He picked up a straw from the floor reeds and began sketching designs in the hearth ash . . .

Suddenly Alfred was jerked out of his reverie by a harsh cry. "What are you about? You worthless cur!" At the same moment the smell of charred wheat cakes penetrated his senses, and he felt the stinging smack of the woman's hand on the side of his head. "Are you so good-for-nothing that you cannot watch my cakes for the time it takes to bring in the swine?" A second blow would have fallen on his other ear, but he ducked just in time.

The irate woman held a cake up to him, black on one side, doughy white on the other. "Here, take you all of them, and may they rot in your stomach! For now my man who has worked hard in the field all day and not sat dreaming at the fire must eat nothing but stirred porridge with his evening stew. A fine meal for a hard-working man!"

Alfred ducked to avoid a third blow that took him just on the top of the head. Coelfrid, who had apparently done a creditable job of child-tending, stood in the doorway, torn between amusement and horror at seeing his king so boxed about. "Quickly, Coelfrid, open your sack. The goodwyfe bids us take the batch and be gone." Alfred pulled the pointed cloth cap from his head and made her a sweeping bow. "I thank you for your kindness, good mother."

By the time they were out of sight of the hut, both Alfred and Coelfrid were shaking so hard with laughter they had to sit on the ground. "It seems we have no need to doubt our disguise," Coelfrid gasped.

"Not unless the virago was in Guthrum's pay." Alfred gingerly rubbed his tender ear.

Night was drawing on quickly, so they went only a little further into the woods before Coelfrid built a campfire to sleep by. They cut the charred sides from the cakes, tossing the blackened bits into the forest for the birds and baked the still-doughy parts by their own coals, this time, with Coelfrid's help, managing not to burn them.

Then Alfred took out his harp and sang the song that had been his favorite since boyhood, of the mighty Beowulf and the heathen monster Grendel. Even as he sang, he was thinking of himself in the role of Beowulf, as he ever had when he heard the story in his father's hall, and now cast Guthrum as Grendel. Suddenly Coelfrid jerked to a sitting position, and his hand flew to the knife at his belt.

Alfred quit singing and quietened his harpsong to a soft strumming. They heard nothing more. Coelfrid's hand relaxed from his knife handle, and Alfred struck a new chord to go on with his song. Then the sound came again. Unmistakable now. A snapping of twigs in the forest blackness just beyond the reach of their firelight. Alfred carefully lay the harp down and curled his fingers around the pommel of his knife, but he did not raise it. "Be you man or animal?" he called. "If man of good intent, welcome to our fire and song, although we've little food but charred cake. If animal, get you into the forest. We've no desire of hunting tonight."

The thrashing of underbrush grew louder from every side, and suddenly they were surrounded by a ring of giant, ring-mailed, horn-helmed Danes with flowing yellow beards.

19

lfred let his knife fall back into the grass. It would be useless against so many, nor would it be a scop's instincts to fight. "Care you for a song?" he asked in English, holding his harp high. Alfred spoke the Danish tongue, which was not so far different after all from Old Saxon, but if his spying was to be successful, they must not know that.

The Danes did not move. Alfred struck a chord on the harp and then gestured to the warrior in a purple, scarlet, and gold cloak who appeared to be the leader. Still they did not move, so Alfred went on with his song. Gradually the men's weapons lowered, and they drew near to the fire. By the time Grendel's mother was ready to make her appearance, the northmen were sitting within the circle of firelight, and several had opened their packs to munch on slabs of black bread and a dark orange cheese. When he judged them to be sufficiently relaxed, Alfred drew a long, floating chord, let his fingers rest, and nodded to the leader who was now seated near him.

"I am Hakon Seal-slayer," the Dane replied.

Alfred ducked his head in acknowledgment of the name-giving, much relieved that the man spoke a halting English. That would make matters much simpler. "Cynewulf of the harp and Coelfrid who would learn," Alfred offered.

Hakon grunted like a great animal and gestured with the back of his hand for Alfred to continue with his song. By the time the battle with Grendel's mother was fought to its bloody conclusion, the Danes had finished eating and were sprawled before the fire, most with their helmets laid aside, sharing wine-skins.

That night Alfred slept with one eye open as he was wont to do the night before a battle. To keep himself awake, Alfred repeated to himself the words of a psalm:

Show thyself, O God, high above the heavens,
let Your glory shine over all the earth.
Men have prepared a net to catch me as I walk,
but I bow my head to escape from it.
My heart is steadfast, O God,
my heart is steadfast.
I will sing and raise a psalm;
awake, my spirit; awake, lute and harp.
I will awake at dawn of day,
I will confess You, O Lord, among the peoples,
among the heathen I will raise a psalm to You.

In the morning Hakon invited Cynewulf and his boy to sing for the great army encamped at Chippenham. He even produced transport in the form of a horse cart that had been left deeper in the woods with the warrior's mounts the night before. As Alfred hoisted himself on the back of the wooden wagon, he wondered how much English plunder had ridden in the same cart and if some of it came from Glastingaburi. He did not look too closely for fear of betraying himself, but the thought was enough to fire anew his hatred of Guthrum and his determination to exterminate the Dane and all of his kind.

It had been only months since Alfred had been driven from his camp at Chippenham, but already it was hardly recognizable. Litter and animal refuse clogged the muddy streets. Buildings that had been burnt through accident or intent showed no signs of repair, and the small stone church where Alfred and his men had worshiped stood scarred with broken cross and windows, an obvious target of Danish weapons practice. Alfred's Great Hall, however, where last the English had feasted, stood strong behind newly fortified earthworks, the Danes' favorite war defense. Alfred made note of the difficulties he would find were he to launch a return attack on Chippenham. *Better to draw Guthrum out than to attempt a surprise here,* he thought.

The jarls and chief warriors were gathering for the evening feasting.

Halfway up the hall, in Alfred's great carved black oak chair, Guthrum sat on a sealskin rug. His long moustache flowed from beneath a broad, flat nose and fell to his chest with the golden curls of his beard. He wore heavy gold armlets from wrist to elbow on each brawny arm and great chunks of amber, jasper, and blue glass beads clanked together on his rust and purple tunic. The bellowing energy and vibrant color of the scene impressed Alfred. He could not help thinking that Guthrum would find the more soberly dressed English warriors dull-looking. *Until he meets us on the battlefield,* he added with an internal smile.

Alfred and Coelfrid stood at the bottom of the room while Hakon and two other jarls approached Guthrum to report on their raiding successes. Apparently the report pleased the viking lord, for he slammed his drinking horn on the table and bellowed for ale for Hakon and his party. Alfred stepped back into the shadows. The longer he could stand there forgotten while the lesser warriors around him consumed tongue-loosening ale, the better his chances of learning something useful. But although he stood long in a hive of chatter, he heard nothing but rough boasts, idle talk, and lewd jests.

Slaves, most of them taken from the local English population, hurried from cooking hearth to table with great wooden trenchers piled high with slabs of oxen and boar from the roasting spits. Alfred and Coelfrid loosened their eating knifes from their belts and speared their share of the meat. They ate sitting in floor reeds, which Alfred judged had not been changed since Twelfth Night.

At last Hakon remembered him, for Alfred was called forth with a jab on his shoulder so sharp it sloshed his ale down his front. He signaled Coelfrid to remain by the door while he took his scop's seat by the fire. In the days long past before Guthrum's army had gobbled up England, an Icelandic scop had visited at the court of Ethelwulf, Alfred's father. From the visitor Alfred had learned several sagas of the north people. So now, although he sang in the English tongue which few understood, Alfred peopled his tale with names his audience recognized: Sigurd who fought a fire-breathing dragon and Brunhild who rode valiantly through the fire. At each name a great roar went up in the hall, so that Alfred knew his audience was following his story, probably filling in words of their own where they didn't understand his. When it was finished, they clamored for more. Alfred thought wryly that he could have had a successful career as a scop—perhaps more successful than he was having as king. His store of north-land sagas exhausted, he turned once more to the perennial pleaser, *Beowulf*. Whether the Danes were drunk enough to enjoy anything, or whether they knew some of the story, they remained enthusiastic listeners.

So it was not until long into the night when the feasting, drinking, and singing were ended that Alfred could sit quietly in a corner and listen. Drunken boasting broke forth somewhere down the room from him. "Ja. Ja. The raven flutters bravely as always."

"And why should Halfdene's banner droop in the land of Devon?"

Alfred closed his eyes and turned his head into his cloak, but his ears strained for every word. He had heard of the atrocities committed in Wales by the younger brothers of Halfdene, the sons of Ragnar Lodbrok. They marched under the legendary black raven banner sewn by the daughters of Ragnar. It fluttered on its own when victory was to come in battle, but hung limp if the vikings were to face defeat. Apparently the raven had swept with spread wings across Wales and now swooped upon Devon. The only dispute seemed to be over whether Inquar Vikinglord and Sigurd Snake-Eye commanded eighteen, twenty-three, or twenty-nine ships and how far upwards of a thousand men his warriors numbered. But either way, the boasters were certain that victory over the fortress of Cynwit would be an accomplished fact by now. They only waited for news of the wing-fast raven's victory flight to reach their ears.

Alfred grew cold inside. His fortress on Exmoor had been his one hope of holding Dumnonia for England. It was an excellent location unapproachable except through a narrow valley from which the attackers could be bombarded with spears. But he knew too well its one great weakness—there was no water supply inside its rocky fastness. And doubtless so had the enemy known. The vikings were ever fond of digging in behind sturdy defenses themselves and so skilled in siege warfare. Sick at heart, Alfred thought of the starvation and suffering his men must have undergone, only to die with a viking axe in their necks.

So died his hopes for support from the south. Reinforcements would not arrive for England, but for Guthrum, as Ragnar Lodbrok's black raven banner would lead the dragon-prows up the Saefern and march overland to close in behind Alfred's already outnumbered troops. His only hope now would be to strike before they could arrive, flushed with victory, the smell of blood fresh in their nostrils to add to their battle-frenzy. Perhaps he and Coelfrid could sneak away tonight, and he could send out his desperate battle summons by the light of the moon.

For an insane moment, Alfred even thought of throwing himself on Guthrum as the viking now sprawled surrounded by his sated jarls. Alfred would get in only one blow, but his would be the first. And he would die with the satisfaction of having accomplished his one great goal—killing Guthrum.

But the madness passed. Even killing Guthrum was not worth sacrificing England. While there remained the slimmest hope, he must continue. He slipped quietly to his feet to locate Coelfrid. If the lad had remained, obedient to his orders, by the door, there was a chance for their escape. But if he lay somewhere mingled among this drunken, snoring throng, Alfred might search till morning before finding him.

A slight movement at the bottom of the hall caught Alfred's eye, and he saw that he needn't have worried. Coelfrid, from generations of a family trained "one for the hearth, one for the church, and one for the king," had not taken his eyes off Alfred all evening. As soon as the king stood, Coelfrid slipped to his feet and started down the hall toward him. The lad picked his way through sleeping warriors and hounds, sometimes slipping on the remains of greasy food, sometimes tripping over a sleeping form. He had reached the center of the hall where the fire burned low in the hearth, but the coals would still glow red in the morning for the porridge pots, when a warrior stumbled to his feet, probably to answer the call of nature.

His sleepy, ale-clogged vision fell on the youth, probably thinking him an English slave, in his path. He flung out both arms with a growl of rage and shoved Coelfrid into the red-glowing fire. Alfred jumped forward with a shout louder than Coelfrid's anguished cry.

Suddenly the hall was alive with fuddled warriors thinking they were set upon by the enemy. They slashed at one another with their eating knives and knocked each other to the floor in a tangle of howling dogs. Somehow Alfred managed to reach Coelfrid through the mayhem and smother the smoldering sparks on his tunic and hair. The harm might have been much worse than it was had the boy not sprung from the fire so quickly. But his left hand and arm, which he had thrust into the fiery ash to break his fall, suffered severe burns.

Alfred barked an unscoplike order for a doctor, and someone scurried from the hall. A hand gripped Coelfrid's unburnt right arm, and one of Guthrum's youngest jarls led the dazed victim toward the door.

Morning light was breaking over Chippenham when Alfred, sitting by Coelfrid, at last salved, bandaged, and asleep in a Danish-style box bed, realized that his hurried escape from Guthrum had failed. Snorri, the doctor, had enough Latin to inform him that his patient must not be moved for at least three days, and Alfred, well-versed in the danger of infections to severe wounds, agreed. Grimly he calculated how far north the black raven could sweep while he sat helpless in the enemy camp.

20

A man of action, Alfred had never spent three more difficult days in his life than those of waiting by Coelfrid's box bed in Chippenham while the enemy advanced on his rear. But he played his part perfectly, singing every night in Guthrum's hall.

Inwardly, however, Alfred fought with God. *Why am I so hindered? Why do You hold me here? Why let such information fall into my hands and then prevent my using it? Why? Why? Why?* Alfred's mind went round and round while his fingers mechanically strummed his harp.

On the evening of the third day Alfred got his answer. He was sitting at Guthrum's feet when the exhausted, tattered messenger arrived. Within a few minutes the news spread all over Chippenham. Inquar was slain, and more than a thousand Danish warriors with him. The black raven banner hung limp and lifeless. Superstitious as all their pagan kind, the Danes lamented the ill omen. Odin was displeased. Long had it been since the raven's wings had been so clipped. Could the banner, once defeated, soar again?

The next morning, Alfred and Coelfrid, with his hand and arm freshly swabbed by Snorri, slipped from Chippenham. Alfred's summons went out to all the thanes of Somerset, Wiltshire, and Hampshire to meet at Edgbert's Stone in the Selwood where the three shires met. Never had a more triumphant rallying issued from a king, for Alfred had seen the fear on enemy faces.

All the warriors caught Alfred's spirit and rallied to his call. Many had thought never to receive such a summons, for rumors had swept the shires that the king was sick and defeated . . . hiding for his life . . . fled to Rome . . . dead . . . The news that Alfred was alive and ready to lead his troops to battle beneath the golden dragon banner of Wessex swept a joyous wildfire through the land. All the warriors who had fled in terror on Twelfth Night sharpened their swords, polished their shields, and galloped their horses to Edgbert's Stone.

But even with such momentum, Alfred knew the battle would not be easy. He knew how far outnumbered his troops were. He knew how well-supplied the Danes were—he had seen their plunder. And he knew that he must strike fast, before his men lost their enthusiasm. They must march immediately and with such show of arms and rallying cries that Guthrum would be drawn into battle on the open field, rather than being allowed to dig in deeper behind his fortifications, as the Danes were ever wont to do.

The last great victory his men had tasted had been seven summers ago in Ashdown, beneath a white horse carved in the chalk of the South Saxon downs. Alfred would choose again a battle site beneath a white horse on the chalk uplands near Ethandune. The horse was not a superstitious omen like the raven banner, but a visible reminder of God's faithfulness in days past. The white horse had been a symbol of victory to the Saxons, even from their pagan days when the sacred white horse was sacrificed to the god Frey. Now Alfred would march his troops toward Chippenham, and they would call on God to remember His people as He had in times past.

After a day's northward march, a scout met them with the news that Guthrum had indeed answered Alfred's challenge. The vikings were gathered under their blood-banner with the black raven. The English troops knelt on a green hillside with the white horse before them. Alfred, on his knees at the head of his men, held aloft his sword with the symbol of the four evangelists inlaid in silver on the upper guard. It caught the setting sun and glowed as a cross on an altar surrounded by candles. In that great green cathedral all in the camp heard mass and partook of the sacraments that night, that none who might die in battle should be unshriven to meet his Maker.

Father Grimbald led them in a prayer for victory, that every man might go into battle with the words of the Lord ringing in his heart. "O Lord, our God, You command Your children to be still and know that You are God, and so we do. You have promised that You will be exalted among the heathen, that You will be exalted in the earth. Let the time be now, we pray."

All signed themselves with the cross and responded, "Praise be to You, Lord Jesus Christ."

And then while the rest of the field remained kneeling, Alfred stood before the priest with bowed head, his arms crossed over his chest while Grimbald read the blessing on the king from the Psalms:

With your sword ready at your side, warrior king,
your limbs resplendent in their royal armor,
ride on to execute true sentence and just judgment.
. . . You have loved right and hated wrong;
so God, your God, has anointed you.
You shall have sons, O king, in the place of your forefathers
and you will make them rulers over all the land.
I will declare Your fame to all generations;
therefore the nations will praise You forever and ever.

And a great shout went up from the men of England.

That shout still rang in their ears and in their hearts as they rode forward to the field of battle the next day. At the king's command they dismounted, sent their horses to the rear of the lines, and formed the tight shield wall behind which they would march. Across the way they caught the glint of the morning sun on the forest of Danish spears. Alfred, commanding the advance guard, strained his eyes for sight of Guthrum's banner. The golden dragon of Wessex curled over his own head from the standard Tica, his armorbearer, bore so proudly, but what of the black raven? Surely the Danes would not take the field without their banner, but it seemed so.

Then a flutter of breeze brought a ruffle of red to his sight. Ah! The raven did not soar. God had sent a windless day. This was not Ragnar Lodbrok's banner of oracular power, but the limp-hanging reminder of their recent defeat. Alfred raised his spear with a shout of triumph and began beating his shield loudly as he marched his men forward.

All the English took up their king's cry, and the field below the white horse rang with the clashing of spear on shield and the shout of voices assured of victory. As the armies closed, the hum of bows and the swish of arrows joined the sounds. Then a great clashing and ringing of metal as sword fell on sword and shield smashed against shield. War horns cried, calling forth wave after wave of fresh shield walls, and the tumult rang from hillside to hillside.

Then the English horns changed tunes, no more calling to fight, but ringing with victory. And a greater shout than any yet went up from Alfred's men as before them the Danes broke and fled. The listless raven fell in the blood-mixed mud, and the English pursued through the wood, following the trail of abandoned weapons the Danes threw behind them in their frenzy to escape.

Alfred and his men pursued the fleeing enemy to the very gates of Chippenham, and there the Danes went to earth behind their battlements like a fox to its hole. So Alfred besieged the camp where so recently he had sung at the hearth. Coelfrid served as one-handed armorbearer to Wulfstan, his father, who had answered the hosting call as promised.

The siege lasted two weeks. In that time Alfred saw to it that no viking left the camp to bring in fresh food, for he had a close idea of the size of Guthrum's stores at the end of winter camp. And he knew the aching of empty viking stomachs would put more pressure on their leader than English spears. Nightly he ordered his archers to assail the camp with flaming arrows so that soon they should be burnt out of shelter and firewood and valuable water stores would be used up in dowsing the flames. On the night that the blue of the flames told Alfred that the desperate Danes were dowsing the fire with ale, he knew that surrender would come in the morning.

That night Alfred went to the fur-piled cot in his tent in fevered elation. At last he was to have his vengeance. Guthrum would pay tomorrow for every drop of English blood he had spilled. He would pay for the ravaged land. He would pay for the massacred cattle. He would pay for the burned and pillaged farmsteads, towns, and monasteries. When Guthrum surrendered, Alfred would set his troops to put every viking to the sword, but Guthrum's blood would be his. By sundown tomorrow there would be no more heathen rulers in England.

He fell asleep with visions of flames, banners, and blood mingling their redness, twisting and running across a green vale to the sea. And the sea turned blood-red, and the steam boiled up, and a red mist covered all . . . With a cry Alfred jerked upright in his bed. Was this vision of Armageddon what he wanted for England?

Shaking, he pulled a heavy bearskin rug to his chin and lay down. His shout must not have been loud, for Tica still slept on his pallet by the door. Or had he shouted at all? What had he heard? What had he seen? Fighting to make sense of the confused images in his mind, Alfred lay still, his eyes focused on the black tent roof. Then the walls of the tent lightened, as if it were daybreak, although that was hours away yet. Slowly the diffused light focused, and his half-brother Neot stood before Alfred.

Little Neot, whom Alfred had not seen these many years, stood before him as alive and laughing as he had been when last they walked together on the sacred Isle of Avalon. Then Neot spoke—his words would remain with Alfred without fading for the rest of his life. "Your appointed task, my kingly brother, is not to kill the heathen, but to turn them to good. Kill one barbarian, and ten more will spring up in his place, for their hordes are without number. But turn one barbarian to Christ, and hundreds will follow.

"You have been a mighty war leader. And it was good. But that is not the end of things. Armies are necessary to hold off the heathen long enough for men of God to do their work. That is the end of things—God's work. In the end armies are useless to change people's hearts. Only the Christ can do that. His work is the end of things. Your task is not to slaughter the heathen, but to preach the Son of God among them. So fulfill you His commandments."

The light faded, and Alfred slept peacefully until morning.

The first golden rays of morning had barely called forth the wood-ringing dawn chorus of birdsong when guards brought the news that Guthrum and six of his jarls approached bearing the green willow branch. The time had come. Alfred must choose. So long he had borne his hope of vengeance. He had fed on his vision of requiring blood for blood. Could he now abandon it?

Then, mingled with the birdsong, more clearly spoken than merely remembered, Neot's words returned. "Your task is not to slaughter the heathen, but to preach the Son of God among them . . ."

"It is good," said Alfred. "Bid them wait in peace, and send me Father Grimbald. I will have his blessing on me before I go out."

As if he had been awaiting the summons, the priest appeared almost immediately. Alfred and his closest house carles knelt in the dew-wet grass before the king's tent. Grimbald kissed the silver cross which he carried and then held it above the king as he praised God for the great victory, welcomed a new day of justice and peace, and asked for the salvation of the Danes.

That prayer confirmed Neot's words in the king's heart. Alfred broke a green bough from a tree. "Let Guthrum be brought to me."

If the Danish king recognized his former scop, he made no sign. But the burly jarl behind him, who carried his sword arm in a bloodied sling, gave a grunt that made Alfred regard Hakon with a half-smile. Alfred accepted Guthrum's branch of peace and extended his own. "Guthrum, for too long have our people been at war. For too long has Dane spilled English blood, and English spilled Danish. I would have this peace be a lasting one. I would have us draw borders for the Danelaw to rule on one side and the English on the other. I would have Danish children grow up in peace on green and prosperous farmland as I would have English children. But as things stand this cannot be.

"As oil and water will not mix, so Christian and heathen will not mix. My God is a great and jealous God. He will have no other in His land. And hear me, Guthrum, it is His land on which you stand. If you will have your people live in peace beside my people, you must learn of my God. Guthrum of Odin worship, will you and your jarls submit to the teaching of my priests that you may learn of the great One-God and serve Him and live in His peace?"

Guthrum turned to his jarls in confusion. A sword-point conversion was not unusual—indeed, there was one old warrior among Guthrum's household who had boasted of undergoing Christian baptism twenty times—although he thought the garments he was supplied with the last time were very substandard. But this was different. Alfred was not holding him at sword point. Alfred had exchanged peace boughs and was asking him to learn of his God, not demanding that he undergo a mindless ceremony.

"Ja. It is good. I will study. I and thirty of my jarls. And if we like what we learn, we will worship your God, for we have seen that He is mighty in battle and that His followers are not like the barbarians."

As word spread through the ranks, there was murmuring behind both kings. Guthrum's men had expected to undergo the strange Christian dunking that routinely followed defeat in battle. They had not expected to be told by their leader that they would study conversion—a conversion they were to hold to for the rest of their lives, not merely until they were next battle-ready. And Alfred's men, many of whom had lost steadings and kinsmen to viking torches, and all of whom had for years had their eyes and minds filled with scenes and stories of viking atrocities, longed to put this remnant of the defeated enemy to the sword.

So Alfred, holding Guthrum's green willow bough aloft, spoke to his men what Neot had said to him the night before. "Our task, thanes of England, is not to kill the heathen, but to turn them to good. Kill one barbarian, and ten more will spring up in his place; turn one barbarian to Christ, and hundreds will follow . . ."

Alfred's men heard the wisdom in his words. They considered, and at last they saluted him with a single voice of acceptance.

So the vikings came once more to Glastingaburi—this time not to rape and burn and pillage, but to be taught of Christ and His way of peace and love. For three weeks Father Grimbald worked with Abbot Elmund, Brother Tumbert, and the others to convey the essence of the faith and its mysteries to Guthrum and his heathen warriors. Priests who spoke no Danish toiled through halting translators to convey an understanding of the Trinity to men who spoke little English and less Latin. In the end only the kindness of the monks to their former enemies and perhaps the spirit of awesome reverence in their dim, quiet churches penetrated the warriors' understanding. But whatever it was, it was enough.

On the appointed day Abbot Elmund and Father Grimbald led the strangest group who ever graduated from the monastery school to Aller, a tiny village near Athelney. Clad in white linen robes, these long-haired warrior-chiefs who usually strode across the countryside in leather, metal-studded mail with colorful cloaks and horned or winged helms looked to be new men, indeed. The church was large enough only for the the king, priests, and converts inside, but the fields for far around were filled with those who came to witness the great occasion.

The converts walked in single file behind their white-robed king, each carrying a lighted taper. Inside the church they watched in awed, if confused, silence as consecrated oil was poured on Guthrum's head and a linen filet bound over it in the shape of a cross while Latin prayers were chanted. Alfred, as godfather to Guthrum, raised him from the baptismal font and pronounced the Christian name being bestowed upon him as a sign of his new personhood in Christ. "As Guthrum, you were my enemy. As Aethelstan, a name you share with my father's brother, you shall be my foster brother." Alfred gave him the kiss of peace.

Guthrum/Aethelstan and his men were to remain at Alfred's court for twelve days of feasting and gift-giving. But Alfred knew that, whatever gold bracelets and jeweled filets might be exchanged, the two leaders could give each other and their people nothing more precious than the peace they now shared. Alfred knew again the rightness of the message Neot had brought him in his night-vision. Had he carried out his vengeance, he might have brought a blood feud upon the land. But by showing love to his enemies and forming bonds of Christian brotherhood, he had converted them into friends.

Now at last, he would be free to practice the arts of peace for which he yearned. He could create the book-strong England of his vision. Long after the last prayer at the baptismal service and after the songs of the scops at the first of the twelve feasts with the new Danish brothers, Alfred sat by a flickering candle in his room, a plain woolen cloak over his nightsark and his royal goldwear locked in a chest against the wall. He wrote in his handbook, the little volume into which he copied favorite extracts from his reading or wrote his inmost thoughts. On the eve of the day that had been the turning point for England, Alfred wrote to God:

> Lord, Almighty God, Worker and Wielder of all things shaped, I beg Thee by Thy great mild-heartedness . . . that Thou guide me to do better than I have done to Thee; and guide me to Thy will and to my soul's need better than I know myself how to do; and make stable my heart to Thy Will and to my soul's need, and strengthen me against the devil's temptings; and put far from me foul uncleanness; and shield me against my foes; seen and unseen; and teach me to work Thy Will; that I may love Thee inwardly

> before all things; with clean thought and with clean body. For Thou art my Shaper and my Deliverer, my Help, my Comfort, my Trueness and my Hope. To Thee be praise and glory, now and for ever, ever, world without end. Amen.

Alfred sprinkled sand over the vellum page to dry the ink, then closed the book. With God's help he would accomplish all God had for him and for England.

PART FOUR

21

unstan fought the onrush of darkness. As harsh voices pounded his eardrums, fists and booted feet pummeled his body.

"And that's how we treat sorcerers!"

"Spend all your time reading—books of the devil!" A note of hysteria mingled with the hatred.

"You'll think twice before you bring your black arts to King Athelstan's court again!"

Dunstan struggled against the rough hands dragging him to the edge of the bog. He tried to answer the accusations they were shouting at him—those voices that rang above the clawing hands. But even if he could have caught enough breath to speak, they would not have listened. The horror of it was that they were all familiar hands, familiar voices. Liofa, Heorrenda, Waerferth—fellows he had hunted with, joked with around the king's table, slept with in the hall. Fellows just like himself. Almost.

"Use your black arts to win favor with the king, will you!"

"Now we'll see what the fair Godrith thinks of you, Bogman!"

With one last jarring shove that he thought would dislocate his shoulder, he was flung face downward into the swamp.

For a terrible moment Dunstan thought he had reached his end. He could not breathe, and his flailing arms could find no handhold. Even lightly built as he was, his straining efforts served only to dig him deeper into the mire. There was nothing to pull against to raise his head from the mud that clogged his eyes, nose, and mouth. Twenty-six years made too short a lifetime, and he had accomplished nothing yet.

With great force of gathered will Dunstan flung himself over in the mire. His first gasp of breath took in as much mud as air, making him cough and sputter. He managed to spit globs of muck from his mouth, but attempts to rub the slime away from his nose and eyes only coated them more heavily. In the distance he could hear the jeering laughter of his companions fade as they returned to the court.

Dunstan's watering eyes stung as mud clouded his vision. But in the fading light and through half-opened eyes, he managed to spot a clump of marsh grass and reeds he could slither toward. Finally he pulled himself up on the matted island of rushes and crow-foot. A gray wagtail sang its funny song, and Dunstan's chin rose. He was not alone.

He had for a long time been aware of dislike and jealousy from the young sports at court—ever since his uncle, the Archbishop of Canterbury, took him to King Athelstan nine years ago. They did not understand his bookish ways nor his interests. He would rather design a metalwork ornament or compose a tune for the flute than roar through the woods hunting the hind with them. But he knew that what had brought it to a head was not that the king smiled on him, but that Godrith of the golden hair and sea-blue eyes smiled on him. They could not stomach seeing the fairest maiden in the land favor any but one of them—even though Dunstan had made no offer for her hand. He wasn't entirely certain he wanted to marry at all . . . however, if he did . . . even bruised, mud-caked, and shivering in the March wind as he was, he smiled at the thought of the candlelight on Godrith's golden hair.

But his enemies were clever, indeed. They raised the one effective charge against things people didn't understand, the one all feared most—sorcery. It would do no good for Dunstan to protest that the books he studied were holy Scripture and the history and philosophy of the ages, such as King Alfred had directed all Englishmen to know. For what did the ignorant care of such things? They could yell witchcraft, and all the fools within hearing would make the sign against evil. Even if he showed them his books, there were none to prove him right, for even the priests at court could read no Latin and little English, in spite of King Alfred's great efforts with a past generation.

No, it wasn't worth fighting them, especially as Dunstan wasn't certain that a place at court was what he truly wanted for his life. But what should he do? Another blast of icy wind that drove the chill through his soaking cloak brought the question more sharply into focus. Where could he go? He would not return to the court at Cheddar. The monastery at Glastingbury was close, but not close enough for crawling through the swamp on a wind-tossed night—nor was his own home at Balsbury. Again the wagtail sang, and the wind, though cold, pleasantly rustled the alder and birch trees behind him.

As his mind relaxed at the calming sound, he thought of Alphage, a distant uncle who was Bishop of Winchester. He had received word that Alphage was come to Ulfstead, their ancestral home that Dunstan's mother had known well as a child. But Dunstan had not yet called on the bishop. Dunstan was in no condition to make such a call, but he could think of nowhere else to go. He squelched his way through knee-deep swamp water to the grass-covered bank. There he rolled in the long, tough blades to remove as much of the filth as possible. What a way for a member of Athelstan's court to make his long overdue appearance at the family steading to present himself to Bishop Alphage.

The sheep and cattle were long folded and the gate barred by the time Dunstan found his way to the ancient steading at the foot of the Mendip Hills.

The hounds in the yard set up a fearful howl, and Dunstan thought he might well end the night with the final ignominy of being set upon by dogs.

But a commanding voice silenced them, and in a few minutes, after he had shouted his identity, the master of Ulfstead welcomed him in. "I fear I come at an awkward hour and in an—er—unexpected condition, Cynefrith, my mother's kinsman," Dunstan told the large, brown-bearded man who met him.

Cynefrith's laugh was as hearty as his welcoming slap on the shoulder, which fortunately struck a spot not already bruised. "Never awkward, Dunstan, son of Heorstan. But your condition I would call catastrophic rather than unexpected. Here, wash you in the trough." And Cynefrith shouted for a theow to bring linen towels and a clean tunic and leggings. With a fresh cake of lye soap Dunstan soon had the shine back in his light brown hair with its silver-blond streaks. He looked more himself, enough to greet his Uncle Alphage, whose smile of welcome spread above his close-trimmed pale beard shot with red luster. But even wrapped in Cynefrith's thickest woolen cloak, Dunstan felt he could not draw close enough to the hearth nor drink enough of the heated ale that Eanfled, Cynefrith's wife, served him.

"Ebert, get you to your bed." Eanfled turned to a tousled, yellow-haired boy of about six or seven years, whose face was repeatedly stretching itself into great, gaping holes of noisy yawns.

But even in his drowsy state, the youngster's eyes snapped with stubborn resistance. "I'm not tired."

Eanfled gave her son a firm shove toward the bower at the far end of the hall. She was surprisingly agile for one in such a late stage of pregnancy. "Get you up the stairs."

His foot on the first step, Ebert turned back. "I won't miss anything. I'm sure Faeder was going to tell that boring old story of how his ealdfaeder won his scars in the Dane-fire when he sneaked into their camp with King Alfred." He turned with a sullen look and stomped on up the stairs.

Cynefrith, however, was not talking about the old king and his Dane wars, but rather about the gift ship with purple sail and golden prow overlaid with gilded shields that the Norse King Harold had given Athelstan.

As soon as Ebert was out of earshot, however, the conversation changed. Cynefrith sighed. "You see how it is, Alphage, my kinsman. So young and already he would defy his faeder. He takes no interest in the steading that will someday come to him. Is it to end now? After all our generations of serving God, king and hearth, will my son amount to nothing?"

"But as you say, Cynefrith, he is young . . ." The Bishop of Winchester faltered.

"Coming eight his birthday, although small for his age. At as many years I readily worked by my faeder's side in the garth when I was not at my lessons with the monks." Cynefrith shook his head. "But I am a poor host to keep you from your beds, and our kinsman Dunstan is much in need of his. We will talk of Ebert tomorrow. You have all you need for tonight?"

The guests assured him they did, and indeed the thick straw-filled bolsters and soft sleeping rugs beside the half-smoored fire couldn't have looked more comfortable to the beaten and near-drowned Dunstan.

The bishop laid aside his finely embroidered outer robes and curled into his bed. "I can see there is much you would talk of, Dunstan, my sister's son, but words were never made the worse for following a night of sleep."

Dunstan was too tired to do more than murmur agreement. As he pulled the sleeping rug to his chin, he wondered at the strange carvings that flickered on the rooftrees. But his eyes were closed before he could look again.

And so it was late the next day, when the rest of the household were about their tasks, before Dunstan could tell his Uncle Alphage of all that had happened to him—the jealousies, conflicts, and hateful charges that had abruptly ended his life at court. Alphage, sitting in Cynefrith's large, carved chair in the center of the hall, listened quietly to his nephew's melodious voice, so surprisingly deep for one of his slight build. At times the bishop would raise his head and nod in an understanding way. At last Dunstan ran long slim fingers through his hair and fell silent.

Alphage nodded. "Yes. And so was Joseph cast into the pit by his own brothers. And so did he later say, 'You meant it to me for evil, but God meant it for good.' God means it for your good, my son, if you will let Him use it so."

"With all my heart!" Dunstan sat forward on his stool, his intelligent gray eyes shining. "I want God's good. But I do not know what He would have me do to obtain it."

"Will you be guided by me?"

"That is why I crawled here, mud-caked from the marsh, for hope of your guidance." Dunstan's thin, eloquent face broke in a smile.

Again Alphage nodded, then leaned back in his chair. Dunstan saw that his eyes were on the carved beams above their heads. And now he could make out the words, "One generation passes unto another . . ." And as if the bishop followed his reading, he said, "And so it is written, 'One generation shall praise His works to another and shall declare His mighty acts . . . Tell your children of it and let your children tell their children and their children another generation.' But such have we failed to do, and such is the great spiritual morass that has come upon our land.

"Glastingbury, where you were taught by a handful of faithful brothers, is the best of the land, but the flames of learning and devotion flicker low even there. Will you now return there and praise His works to the children of this generation? Even to such rebellious younglings as Ebert that he in his time might pass the light to another generation—a stronger light of faith and learning because of what I believe you, Dunstan, can build at Glastingbury? Will you, with your own courage and mind for the right, reestablish the rule of St. Benedict that the holy houses of this land have so far abandoned?"

Dunstan shook his head. "You'd need a saint for that job. I'm far too impatient."

"Oh, maybe God would have things to teach you as well as your teaching others."

Dunstan sprang to his feet and began pacing. It was an exciting possibility. He had been given the best education in the land—although that was little enough to say—and with his own love of learning he had continued to read and think, until it could be said that he possessed one of the most scholarly minds in England. Perhaps that was what he should do—pass this on to future generations. Certainly he had failed miserably to shed any light in the political world; perhaps he could in the spiritual.

Yet he might be as hated for his bookish ways in the small community of a monastery as he had been in the small community around the king. Perhaps more so. At court he had been merely different; he had challenged no one's skill with horse, sword, or hunting bow. But at the monastery, he would be challenging them in the skills they claimed, no matter how far that might be from the actual truth.

Dunstan's pacing had carried him to the end of the hall where the stairs rose to the women's bower. He turned and started back toward Alphage. The timbered floor, though newly relaid, creaked under his tread, for even when pacing, his stride was strong, his step purposeful. This handsome young man with silver-shot hair was not one who could do anything in a meandering way. He must be convinced of what he did; then he would run straight at it, and nothing could stop him. But he was not convinced of this step.

"With all the strife around us and all the activity in the great world, you would have me withdraw to a little monastery kept from ancient times? An isolated island that is no longer a house of monks, but merely a school maintained by clerks? Is this what you ask, Uncle?"

Alphage smiled at Dunstan's description. Then he struck the arm rest of his chair and fairly shouted his answer, for the Bishop of Winchester was also a man who ran straight at what he wanted. "Yes! That is precisely what I ask. A challenge even for one of your energetic abilities! In the midst of turmoil you can turn the holy island into a strong fortress of peace. Relight the lamp of learning. Tend culture as a lamp that, if trimmed and kept filled with oil, will shine forth a golden glow of learning such as has not been in this land for two centuries.

"Now is the time. Now we have the peace of Alfred kept strong by his grandson Athelstan, and we have the books of Alfred—those writ by his own hand and those he encouraged others to write—all in our own English tongue. Put them to work, Dunstan."

Alphage rose and gripped Dunstan by the shoulders. "It can be done. And you are the man to do it."

They stood silent for a time, as if listening to the rafters echo the bishop's challenge.

"Let me think on it, Uncle."

Dunstan walked from the hall, across the grassy yard populated with dogs, chickens, and serfs' children, and out the sturdy palisade to seek a sheltered spot in the hills beyond the apple garth. Already there were a few early-born lambs sheltering against their mothers. In a month the fields would be dotted white with them, to be followed soon after by the white-flowering of the apple trees. But for now the land slept in that uneasy time between seasons. Could he help usher in a springtime revival of arts and learning? Could he lay a basis for the return to the monastic traditions of the past as laid down by St. Benedict, St. Martin of Tours, and St. Patrick? Could he build the New Jerusalem in this dry and thirsty land?

And even if he could, did he want to? In spite of the unhappy ending to his days at court, they had held many happy times. Could he, under cowl and tonsure, turn his back forever on the stimulating discussions of politics and of art . . . the meetings with leaders from France, from Germany, from Flanders . . . the society of pleasant and attractive women—for a moment Godrith's laughing blue eyes danced before his vision.

Then he thought of what he would be turning to. As a schoolboy, he had loved the monastery and the stories of its past—the most hallowed ground in England—the very land as full of mystery as the clouds that hung over the Tor—the ancient British people in the lake village practicing arts in bronze, clay, and iron long before the Romans came—and there, before Cenwalh, the first Christian king of Wessex, captured the land, some said even long before St. Patrick, some said even when our Lord Himself was on this earth, was raised the Old Church.

But more personal was the vision he had had as a child no older than Ebert, a vision of being led by a shining, white-robed figure through the cloisters and chapels of a new abbey, far nobler than the cluster of small buildings standing there now. And in the morning the sacristan had found him curled between the supporting arches of Ine's church, sound asleep.

Now as he recalled those still-vivid images, the pictures grew soft as if fading into a morning mist . . . then they sharpened again and brightened, an illumination of the vision of St. John the Divine. He saw the holy city of Jerusalem shining with the glory of God—the radiance of a priceless jewel like jasper—clear as crystal—with a great high wall—a wall built of jasper—the city itself of pure gold—bright as clear glass . . .

The mist rose before his eyes, the vision faded, and he was once again sitting on a clump of winter brown grass just showing tender green shoots in a sun-facing curve of a low hill. He stood and walked beneath bare-branched apple trees lining the horse-runs back to the hall.

There he found Alphage talking to the young Ebert. "Uncle, I will go to Glastingbury," Dunstan said.

Ebert regarded him with a suspicious look that seemed old beyond his years. "So you're to be sent to the monks, too? Have you also been disrespectful of your elders?"

Dunstan smiled at him. "Perhaps I have, although I didn't mean it so." His smile widened; he suddenly felt more confident in his decision. "Yes, Ebert, we shall go to Glastingbury together. You will learn your letters and your mathematics, and you will say your catechism with your school fellows. And I will learn the life of a Benedictine monk, and I will say the Divine Office with as many of the abbey's brethren as are awake or can be awakened to the same call. And together we will learn obedience."

So Dunstan received the tonsure from the hand of Bishop Alphage, his kinsman. A decent round tonsure as all good sons of Rome wore to mark their submission to the will of God, just as Christ had worn the crown of thorns in submission. For such matters as tonsure style had been settled long ago at a council in Whitby in the year 664, and now all churches were Roman. The cowled robe Dunstan put on when he laid off his fine-woven, silk-embroidered cloaks and tunics, which had blended with the clothing of the nobles at Athelstan's court, was the somber black of the strictest Benedictine order. For Dunstan was determined to begin by setting the right example.

The decision was a good one, for the six years Dunstan spent as a monk at Glastingbury were the happiest he had known since his school days there. The sheltering, though crumbled, walls of the monastery kept out the worries, jealousies, and frenzy of life at court. And many of the problems he had worried about encountering did not occur, for the brothers were too apathetic to be resentful or jealous. Dunstan found a peace to pursue his skill in the arts and crafts that he loved most. Now he had the chance to develop his drawings and limn portraits, as well as to pore over poetry—both Latin and English—and to delight anew in the songs, legends, and history of his ancestors. His skill grew in the music that seemed to come as naturally to him as to the birds. Skills he had formerly used to amuse others at court, he now practiced solely before God. And he felt God's pleasure.

The school, which others were happy enough to leave to his care, produced students along with Ebert who could read, write, and do mathematics—once he broke through their initial resistance. But in the spiritual development of the community Dunstan could see no progress. Although he strictly followed the offices set out by St. Benedict, he and three Irish monks, who had come to Glasting in reverence for St. Patrick, most often found themselves alone in King Ine's Church, even at such easy-to-attend hours as Sext at noon and Vespers just before sunset. They never had company at the Nocturnes or Terce vigils in the dark hours of the morning. And although Dunstan and the three devout Irishmen kept silence after Compline following the evening meal, that was when their fellows became the loudest, telling bawdy jokes on bellies full of ale.

As Dunstan had no authority over the others, he could do nothing but set the right example and see that his students followed the best order he could muster. But he knew his achievements fell far short of what Bishop Alphage had hoped for him. Yet even as far as it had fallen, Glastingbury was one of the most religious houses in the land. Many a night after the three A.M. vigil when he found he couldn't get back to sleep, Dunstan was haunted by his boyhood vision. Night after night the tall, gray-bearded man with the sad eyes and kind smile who had led the awe-stricken boy through a magnificent abbey of great stone pillars, soaring arches, and stained glass came to his mind again. It seemed impossible that the worldly, self-centered people living on this beautiful island could ever be inspired to build such a structure for the glory of God.

Yet Dunstan knew that if he did not bring this vision to pass, he would have failed himself and God. In despair, Dunstan prayed with the psalmist, "I will teach transgressors the ways that lead to You, and sinners shall return to You again. Let it be Your pleasure to do good to Zion, to build anew the walls of Jerusalem."

But he did not see how it could be.

22

Then the likelihood of fulfilling the vision seemed less than ever, for Athelstan died at Gloucester and was buried with great pomp and procession in Malmesbury Abbey. Edmund, Athelstan's younger brother, likewise a grandson of King Alfred, ascended the throne. And Edmund called Dunstan back to court.

The new monarch, a rash eighteen-year-old bursting with vigorous enthusiasm for everything around him, had known Dunstan at Athelstan's court and admired him with whole-hearted affection. "I, Edmund, hereby revoke the banishment on our beloved Dunstan and would have his attendance in our court whether at Winchester or at Cheddar."

Thus Dunstan's life changed with one sentence. He rolled the single sheet of vellum and placed it on the table beside the stool that comprised the only furniture in his cell besides the narrow bed. Now he must decide anew. This was not a decision of action. The king had called. Dunstan would obey. But it was a decision of will. It was important to Dunstan to know how he felt about this abrupt change, this sudden jerking from his quiet, focused life back into the hurly-burly of the court. If he had been given a choice in the matter, what would it be?

He loved the past six years lived under Glastingbury's green Tor. He had developed in every area of the arts he so loved, and he had grown spiritually. Practicing the disciplines of the Rule had brought him ever closer into the presence of God. But what had he accomplished?

Ebert, now thirteen, had, after a time of kicking against the pricks, settled into his studies. It was dear to Cynefrith's heart that his eldest son return to Ulfstead prepared to become one of the king's chief thanes. Dunstan thought that the lad had been crammed with his familial responsibilities at far too early an age, and it had taken careful handling by Uncle Dunstan to bring him this far. What would become of his problem child if left to his own devices or to those of Brother Oswy, the lax Master of Boys and Novices?

And what of Ethelwold who had the finest mind any teacher could ever hope to inspire? The young man's studies were almost complete, and he stood on that critical threshold of deciding whether or not to take the cowl. Dunstan felt he had never met one more suited to be a monk. Ethelwold possessed the vigor and devotion so desperately needed in these days. If he failed to follow the religious life because his mentor was gone, who could say what would be the loss to learning and religion in England?

And what of the lesser students and the very school itself if it were to sink to its former ways, as surely it would?

Dunstan shook his head as he walked to the single window of his tiny cell and looked over the green expanse to the clutch of cells, workshops, and chapels that comprised the monastery. Brother Ogram, the oldest of the Irish monks, had died last year. That left only Lurgan and Nenagh who kept the full office of hours. They would continue without him. And Abbot Eanwulf, aged even when Dunstan had been there as a student, was a good man, but never a forceful man, and now he was a dying man. All real leadership in the abbey would pass to Sigebehrt, who opposed all regulation of offices and scoffed at vows of chastity, poverty, and obedience. Little wonder, as his wife Aude was constantly stirring up the female companions of the other clerics to demand a larger portion of the tithes and rents from the abbey farms for their personal use.

Now all the religious life of Glastingbury would be in the hands of Lurgan and Nenagh who, though devout, were not strong leaders. Dunstan turned away from his window sick at heart. He had accomplished so little of permanence there. No, if he were given his choice, he would not go. But the choice was not his.

Dunstan turned to his packing. A very small satchel could contain all his personal belongings. Just how little he really needed, or even wanted, never failed to amaze Dunstan, who had once owned chests of fine clothing and possessions. It would take him longer, however, to pack the large trunk standing open on his cot. For he must have his books. After all, King Edmund wanted his counsel. Perhaps Dunstan could accomplish more at court. Edmund was young and impressionable. Yes, maybe this was Dunstan's rightful place—guiding his monarch.

Then he paused, a handful of papers in midair. There was a new king, but the court would be the same. His old enemies would be there: Liofa, Heorrenda, Waerferth . . . and his old friends—for a moment Godrith's smiling image was so alive before his eyes that he caught his breath.

Three days later Dunstan, riding the monastery's only donkey, arrived at Cheddar. Godrith's shining countenance was the first to welcome him back to court.

"And so you have come back to us. Although you are much changed on the outside." She paused to observe his black robe and tonsure. "I have no doubt you still possess the same lively mind inside. I know the court will be much the brighter for your presence." And she took him by the hand to lead him forward. But a broad, flame-haired man with narrowed green eyes blocked the entrance to Edmund's hall. "Ah," Godrith continued, "and Waerferth is my husband now."

Before Dunstan could reply, Waerferth spoke in a low voice that sounded as if it would have been harsh had he not just oiled it. "Aye, it's plain to see he remembers *you,* my wife. And he'll be remembering me, I'm sure, for we had a memorable parting."

He eyed Dunstan's black robe. "I hope this means you've mended your ways. But if all one hears of those that wear the cowl is true, or even the half-part of it, it'll be to the other direction you'll have mended." Then with a bellow of a laugh he ushered them through the doorway with a deep bow. But Dunstan could feel the narrow green eyes following them as they crossed the hall.

Life at court was not unpleasant, although even after removing the tapestries and golden candlesticks from his room, Dunstan still felt uncomfortable in his lavish surroundings. He slipped easily into the routine of his new life, managing to keep a rough approximation of his former schedule of prayers in the little-used stone chapel. When he was not actually counseling Edmund, he spent much time alone with books and pen.

And such was the source of the trouble. For again after Dunstan had been but a few months at court, the whisperings arose. One could not be sure that Waerferth or his cousin Liofa was the source. But whatever their wellspring, the whisperings grew to a murmur, and the murmur to a talking, and the talking to a shouting.

"Dunstan the sorcerer!"

"Black arts practiced in a black monk's robe!"

"Chants of evil in the king's chapel in the dark of night!"

At first Edmund did not hear. Then he did not believe. But then came the night when he, his brain thick with ale from the feast for the ambassadors of King Otto of Germany, and some of his courtiers passed the open door of the chapel.

The notes of a chanted psalm rose strange-sounding from a lone dark figure at the altar. The king would have passed on by, but Heorrenda plucked at his tunic sleeve. "How long will Your Majesty suffer such behavior?"

Liofa made the sign against evil. "Worship of the dark one in your own chapel, my king."

Edmund shook his head and would have walked on, but Waerferth turned him again toward the chapel with its single flicker of candlelight. "If God is to give you victory over Olaf Guthfrithson in Northumberland, your court must be cleansed of evildoers."

"Nay, think not of the encroaching Danish king," Eormanric said. "Think of your own thanes. They believe you weak, Your Grace."

"Under the spell of the black monk, they say." Liofa pressed closer.

Yet for all their pressing, the moment might have passed had Dunstan not at that moment finished his prayers and walked from the chapel into their path. Liofa would not let it go. He seized the monk by the cowl and spun him around. "And will you now run from us, sorcerer? We saw you make the sign of the cross backwards!"

Dunstan was speechless. The old charges again. They could have seen nothing in the dark, no matter how properly he had made the blessing.

Weary of the wrangling and longing for his bed, Edmund turned to Dunstan. "Enough! I will hear no argument! Dunstan, it will be best if you seek your friends away from my court. Tomorrow I hunt. Be you gone when I return."

Even in the dim light of the smoking torch Heorrenda carried, Dunstan could see Liofa's smile of triumph. The king and his attendants walked off, leaving Dunstan alone in the dark.

It was too much. Twice he had been taken from monastic life where he was happy, even if his successes were limited. Twice he had had charges of sorcery and evildoing hurled at him by ignorant, jealous men. Twice he had been banished from court by English kings whom he had tried to serve. It was too much.

He would see that it did not happen again. He would put himself beyond the reach of such men.

He had heard of the great monastic houses on the continent where learning flourished, the arts flowered, and worship flowed to God. He would abandon his struggle in England and go where his abilities would be appreciated by like-minded men.

In spite of the hour, he made his way to the guest lodgings of Gunnar and Hogni from the court of King Otto. Just a few hours earlier he had spent a delightful afternoon with them discussing the heroic Teutonic tales of the Volsungs and Nibelungs. He had found them kindred spirits in matters of faith and of learning. Now he poured out his heart to them. "I am in disgrace. Disaster has fallen on me. Perhaps God would have me serve him in a more receptive climate. Would I be welcome, do you think, in Germany?"

Gunner cried, "You would be welcomed by Otto as was Sigurd at the court of the Rhineland king!"

"Tomorrow we hunt with Edmund and depart the next day, for Otto is anxious that we return with your king's reply to the treaty Otto proposes. Can you be ready to travel by then?" Hogni asked.

"I must be ready sooner than that," Dunstan replied. "The king said I am to be gone when the hunt returns. I will meet you at Saefern harbor on the day of your sailing."

It was agreed. Dunstan returned to his room to write letters of farewell to his parents and brother Wulfric at home in Balsbury, to his Uncle Alphage at Winchester, and to Ebert and Ethelwold. Each letter brought a new wrench to his thoughts of leaving. He knew they all relied on him, but his work here was ended—if not completed. They must carry on the best they could.

23

Even before the hunting horn sounded the next morning, Edmund was having second thoughts. He had never believed the charges of sorcery against Dunstan, and he had, in the short time the monk had been at court, found his counsel of great worth. "Loet!" He shouted for a servant. He would send word to Dunstan. They would discuss the matter when he returned from the day's hunt.

But it was not the small, ever-eager serving boy who entered the chamber at Edmund's shout. Rather it was Liofa, clad in leather breeches and green tunic, a quiver of hunting arrows on his shoulder. "How may I serve you, my lord?" He bent his knee deeply.

Though half the age of the man before him, Edmund must not forget that he was king. And he must not look foolish in his decisions, or in his change of decisions. The matter must wait. "Ah, well come, Liofa. I would but send to inquire if the party is ready."

"All await Your Grace." Liofa bowed deeply for Edmund to pass and led the way to the courtyard.

Edmund swung to the saddle of his great white horse Frey, and with a ringing of hunting horses and belling of hounds, the hunt swept from the royal enclosure. The morning freshness was on the earth, the mist not yet lifted; and dew falling from the trees like rain was golden as amber beads from the kiss of the morning sun. Edmund began to feel exhilaration. Today's hunt would be supreme.

Although they started on the edge of the moor, the hounds, sharing their sovereign's exultation, sniffed more surely, barked more sharply, and ran faster than ever before—until the entire pack worked as one dog, flying arrow-straight after the sharp, clear scent. When they reached the edge of the forest, a stag burst into view. A magnificent eight-point buck with a spread of massive antlers that must have reached three feet. Never, in a lifetime of hunting had Edmund seen such a creature. It must be his. Only a king's arrow would be worthy of such a kill.

Edmund had only one clear view of the golden brown animal with eyes as bright as jet before it turned and bounded into the forest. The hounds flew after it, their belling changing from a frenzied, searching bark to a focused call as sure and melodic as any musician's. And Frey heard it as clearly as did Edmund. Every nerve and muscle in the great white steed strained after the hounds and their quarry. Frey sensed the importance of this chase to his master, and the hunt-fervor caused his hooves to strike the ground ever harder, faster, his flying stride to stretch ever longer.

To Edmund there was nothing in the world but the buck, the hounds, and Frey pounding beneath him. The wind of their going whipped through his hair and cloak. Patches of light and dark flashed before his eyes at ever greater speed as they flew through the forest.

Suddenly they broke into the clear. There was the stag in full view before him—no trees, no bushes, no ground, just the stag in a perfect, still pose against the blue sky, his antlers reaching to the sun, his legs spread in a powerful leap.

And then he was gone.

Now Edmund realized where they were. In the madness of the chase the stag had raced straight to the edge of Cheddar Gorge. And plunged over. Even now Edmund heard the anguished cry as the magnificent creature plummeted hundreds of feet down a sheer granite cliff and smashed on the rocks below.

A cry tore from him too late. His hounds disappeared over the edge with screams of terror.

And Frey, completely out of control, lunged forward a few yards from the brink. Then, as if time stood still, a clear vision of Dunstan flashed before the king's eyes. The precipice toward which he was plunging was not Cheddar Gorge, but the catastrophe of losing Dunstan. "God, spare my life, and I will make amends!" Edmund shouted to the universe.

Frey, his front feet already into the void, spun on his hind legs and set down on firm ground. Frey was quivering violently. Against all possibility of human or animal effort, God had reached from Heaven and set them on solid rock—because Edmund had sworn to restore Dunstan.

Without pausing even to catch his breath, Edmund spurred Frey back toward Cheddar. He had ordered Dunstan to be gone from court before his return. But it was still early in the day. He glanced skyward. The sun was no more than straight overhead. Surely it would take even a monk some time to pack his possessions. How could he have been such a fool as to listen to the wagging tongues of jealous and foolish men? Even with the ale doing his thinking for him last night, Edmund knew the charges were false. Now he must tell the world that the accusations were false. By making amends with Dunstan, he would make amends with God.

Frey was nearly foundered when Edmund flung his reins to a stable slave and strode toward the smallest guest house in the quietest corner of the royal enclosure. The door stood open. Edmund's heart leaped with hope. He wasn't too late.

"Dunstan! Dunstan, forgive your foolish king. I will—"

The figure in the dark corner turned, and Edmund gasped. It was not Dunstan, but the red-bearded Liofa doubled back early from the hunt. "How can I serve Your Grace?" The smooth voice came with a deftly performed bow.

"By taking yourself from court! You are banished from my sight!" Edmund barked as he turned and flung from the room. At the doorway he turned. "Do not return on pain of death."

The king gathered himself with a firm grip of will and began a calm, orderly questioning of hall servants, stable theows, and field serfs until he had a clear picture of a black-robed monk walking beside a donkey laden with a small satchel and a large trunk shortly after the departure of the hunt, heading toward the mouth of Saefern.

The formerly golden sunshine had long been drowned in a cold drizzle of rain, and the bay horse, which Edmund had taken as the best left in a horse garth thoroughly depleted by the hunt, pulled each hoof slowly from the sucking mud. They finally reached the cluster of fishing boats that clogged the quay where the Axe flowed into Saefern. And there he met success, for a black-robed monk had sought a night's lodging among the villagers.

"Make haste!" the king shouted, barely inside the door of the tiny wattle and thatch hut where Dunstan had found a guest cot.

Only Dunstan's startled reply, "My Lord King!" told the churls sitting before their hearth who it was that had burst in upon them at this late hour. They fell to their knees before their king, but Edmund barely noticed as he strode to Dunstan. "Make haste! Abandon your journey, for you go with me on one of our own."

The wife of the cottage collected herself to offer a cup of their best ale to the royal intruder. As soon as Dunstan understood the king's intent, he persuaded Edmund with a few calm words that, especially since the land between there and Glastingbury was all marsh, they could well do with a night's sleep first.

By morning a cluster of royal attendants arrived from Cheddar with fresh mounts. Their stomachs full of the goodwyfe's warm oat cakes and goat cheese, the small party picked their way through the marshes to Glastingbury.

When they arrived, Edmund ordered his attendants to remain behind, and he and Dunstan went on alone. At King Ine's Church the king took Dunstan by the hand and led him to the abbot's seat. "Sit you there, Dunstan, for the aged Eanwulf has gone to a seat in his Maker's house. Yours shall be this seat and yours its power and yours the abbacy."

With a firm but gentle shove from Edmund, Dunstan sat, and the king continued. "And this is my pledge to you. Whatever you find lacking, whatever you need to increase holy worship or to further the holy Rule, that will I supply in abundance." And King Edmund went on one knee before Abbot Dunstan.

Still in a state of shock from the turn-around of events, Dunstan felt the carved surface of the arms of the chair. He smelled the faintly stale scent of incense and candle wax, and he raised his eyes to the radiant colors of sunlight falling through stained glass and warming the cold stone.

To be set at the head of the place he loved best in the world was a challenge worthy of all his energies, for it was crumbling morally and physically before his eyes. Yet the excitement and challenge themselves were the problem, for Dunstan was first of all a scholar and an artist. He would rather live in a secluded cell in the farthest corner of the abbey and be allowed to read and draw and compose, ruled over by a wise and kindly abbot.

His sigh drew a sharp look from King Edmund who waited patiently for his reply. There was only one possible answer. Because there was no wise and kindly abbot, there could be no secluded cell in a quiet corner. Although Dunstan disliked the prospect of managing abbey business affairs and doubted he would ever be able to keep the account books in order—his mathematics were woefully weak—the alternative of serving under Prior Sigebehrt was unthinkable.

Surely the king's doing was in truth God's doing. Dunstan spoke, his melodious voice intense as if making a vow to God, although he faced Edmund. "I do not know what I may accomplish; I can only promise this—to attempt manfully and strongly to carry out the task of God."

24

unstan's first challenge now that he had authority to lead was to inspire the brotherhood. With a small smile he mused that perhaps it was not such a bad thing that the silver-blond streaks in his tonsured brown hair made him look older than his thirty-two years. He needed all the appearance of power he could muster.

Glastingbury was crumbling into the marsh. The once-fine churches needed repair; the crumbled wall could no longer be called an enclosure, and although Dunstan believed the monks should live in simplicity, that did not mean leaking roofs, broken shutters, and rotting floors in their cells. A major building program was long overdue.

Even the industry of the island and its small secular population outside the monastery walls had drifted into lethargy. Those who supported their families at all were obliged to row through the waterways daily to working farmsteads or to nearby villages that maintained small industries such as cider-making, pottery-making, or fishing.

Dunstan sat at the small square table that served him as a desk. For weeks—or had it become months now?—Dunstan had wrestled futilely with the problem. He feared that if he didn't find a way to break through the stagnation soon, he would sink into the slough of sloth himself. In front of him were the three largest wax tablets he could unearth from the dusty corners of Abbot Eanwulf's little-used study. One tablet he headed "Problems," another "Goals," and the third "Action." The list of problems was long: lack of discipline, lack of faith, lack of moral fiber, lack of money . . . The goals reflected those problems: to establish the Rule, to build the intellectual excellence of the school, to get the monastery and village on a firm economic footing . . . He could fill dozens of tablets with problems and things that should be accomplished. The third tablet, sitting blank in front of him, was the difficulty. What steps could he take to accomplish this impossible task?

Material arguments would speak loudest to this secular brotherhood, he decided. He would start there. But what could he do to build the economy of the whole area? King Edmund had promised help, and Dunstan was certain the king would add to the depleted treasury. But that was a short-term solution. Dunstan wanted the abbey to become self-supporting. And in so doing, he would be establishing one of the tenets of the Rule, for St. Benedict believed in the sanctity of work, and his monks were to spend part of each day working for their daily bread. But what could they do? The third tablet remained blank.

"It wasn't my fault! I didn't do it! Uncle Dunstan!" Ebert's frantic shout so startled Dunstan that his stylus gouged the soft surface of the tablet.

"Young man! That is no way to address His Reverence!" Brother Oswy, Master of Boys, the gray fringe around his tonsure blown askew, his black robe kilted above his knees, and sweat pouring down his red face, puffed in behind Ebert.

Ebert bent one knee in a sketch of a reverence to his uncle, but did not drop the volume of his voice. "It was the jackdaw! She steals things! She does—I saw her pecking at Father Lurgan's silver chain with the cross on it—the one he hangs on St. Patrick's grave. I only threw the rock to scare her away! Honest! I swear it on all our Savior's wounds and on the blessed Virgin Mary, and on St. Peter, and . . ." The boy ran out of breath to declare more saints, but continued crossing himself.

"That will do, Ebert!" Dunstan rose to stand between Ebert and the angry Oswy who looked as if he would lay violent hands on his young charge. "Brother Oswy, will you kindly tell me what is going on?"

It was several seconds before Oswy was in control of himself enough to talk. "It is the window. King Ine's window. This young wolf put a stone through it."

Dunstan felt as if he had been hit by the stone. He groped his way backward to his stool. King Ine's window, the one uncrumbled glory remaining to Glastingbury, smashed by his own nephew.

"I didn't mean to, Uncle. I was only trying to scare the jackdaw out of the apple tree. I threw too hard. Honest! I swear it by St. Peter and St. Paul and St.—"

"Yes, yes. That's enough."

Eventually Dunstan got the story. A pair of thieving crows had set up housekeeping in the monastery's orchards. Widrith, the ancient brother who tended the fruit trees, had done nothing about it because they did not harm his trees. But Ebert had seen one of the birds attempting to rob St. Patrick's grave.

With a sigh Dunstan pushed himself to his feet. "Let us go view the damage." Ebert, his head held defiantly high, followed his uncle, with Oswy close behind, taking swats at the youngster whenever he came within arm's length.

Inside the church they all stood and stared. In the lower corner of the window through the russet-colored rock symbolic of St. Peter, a jagged shaft of harsh light shone beside the muted jeweled tones of the rest of the window. On the stone floor beside the altar lay shards of glass—and a heavy black stone.

Dunstan's shoulders drooped. Just when he sought to launch his program to bring order and beauty to the abbey. "You may begin your penance by cleaning up the broken glass, Ebert. You will find a basket for collecting the bits in the garden shed. And see that you don't cut yourself. When you bring me the basket, I will assign you prayers."

"Yes, Uncle Dunstan, Your Reverence. I am sorry, even if I didn't mean to. Honest. I swear—"

"Stop! No more of that." Dunstan held up his hand. "Brother Oswy, you may return to your charges. I will deal with this matter." The monk's face clearly said there was little he would like less than returning to the schoolroom, but he obeyed.

A short time later Dunstan sat in his quiet room studying the basket of colored glass his nephew had presented to him. Ebert sat before him on a small stool. Dunstan couldn't help admiring the boy. He had been genuinely shaken by his misadventure—the abbot had never seen him so penitent—and yet his spirit was not broken. He would declare what he knew to be right.

"Ebert, I believe that this was an accident. But the spirit of rebellion, the attitude of taking matters into your own hands when they should be left to your elders or to God, was at the heart of the situation. You are to do one hour of prayer-penance every day for a week kneeling on the spot your ill-thrown stone landed. I would have you look to the mending of your soul while I see to the mending of the window."

"I will, Father."

Dunstan watched the boy leave. If only Cynefrith could see his son now. The miracle he had hoped for was happening. But much as Dunstan might believe in divine miracles, some human action would be necessary to repair Ine's window. The question was, what could he do? Where would he send to have new glass made or to find workmen to install it?

Of course, the easiest answer would be simply to appeal to King Edmund to send to the continent for Flemish workers to come and bring glass with them, but Dunstan still preferred a long-range answer. He gave thought to stories he had heard in his own family of a glassworks right here on the Glass Island. If the stories were to be believed, the very fragments of the window now collected on his table were made in ovens on monastery lands.

Dunstan jumped to his feet so quickly he almost upset the basket of glass. Yes. That was what he would do. He would ask King Edmund to secure master workmen for him, and he would reestablish the glass-making industry on this island. He began pacing the floor of his tiny square room, excitement bubbling within him.

The silhouette of a dark figure appeared in Dunstan's doorway, causing him to break the stride of his pacing. It took him just a moment to recognize the robed, but uncowled, untonsured figure. "Ethelwold! My dear fellow! It is time and past that you called on your old teacher! I hoped you had not forgotten me in my brief time at court." He had seen Ethelwold daily since his return, but they had not talked at length.

Ethelwold made a quick bow to his new abbot. "Never, Father Dunstan. How could I forget the man who taught me all I know?"

"Ah, but I see you have not acted on it yet." Dunstan nodded to Ethelwold's uncowled robe.

"I would talk to you, Father, if you have time."

Dunstan glanced at the sun hanging midway in the August sky. "A good hour till Vespers, I should judge. Come, climb the Tor with me. It will provide an admirable vantage for us to view the land and all that stands in need of doing."

They walked out past Ethelwold's herb garden. "I see you've kept up your work admirably in my absence."

"I do love gardening." Ethelwold spoke with enthusiasm. "That is what makes me wonder . . . I mean, the Lord seems to have given me a talent for making things grow. Perhaps I could serve Him best on the land."

Dunstan didn't answer for several paces as they now began their ascent of the hill, and the steep path took all one's breath. When they came to a smoother place in the trail, he turned his startling gray eyes on the novice. "And how is it that you could serve our Lord better on secular land than on sacred? Is there not a wide enough variety of plants to grow here?"

"Oh, aye, of course there are—"

"And what of growing believers in the faith? Would you not have that be part of your work, too?" Dunstan could tell by the look on Ethelwold's face that he had hit on the heart of the matter.

"Yes, yes. Truly. If only one could, but it seems so hopeless. I ask myself whether God has abandoned us, or we have abandoned God, and I can find no answer. But either way it comes to the same thing—there is no active faith to be found."

"None?"

"Well, there's yours. And mine. And Brothers Lurgan and Nenagh . . . but that's so little."

"And what did God tell Abraham when he asked God to spare Sodom and Gomorrah if fifty believers could be found?"

"God said He would."

"And forty believers?"

"God would spare them."

"And twenty?"

"Yes."

"And ten?"

"Even so. But I do not believe there are ten righteous in Glastingbury."

"Ah, the impatience of youth. Ethelwold, you are our gardener. But before you can harvest your fine crop of herbs to be dried and ground and brewed into healing concoctions, what must you do?"

"Tend them carefully."

"Aye. And before there are sprouts to tend?"

"I plant the seeds."

They were now to the top of the path, and Dunstan led the way to a stone bench before the chapel. "So. You have answered rightly. And so would God have us sow and water the seeds of righteousness. But it will take time."

Ethelwold shook his head. "Perhaps. I will think on it."

"Good." Dunstan clapped a long-fingered hand on the young man's shoulder and pointed with his other. "Now, I want to tell you of the plans I've been making—of the seeds I would sow of a great monastery." First he told Ethelwold of his plans for renewing Glastingbury's long-dead glassworking industry. "But that is only the beginning. I would repair Ine's window, but we must not stop there." Again he pointed, his finger tracing a pattern around the cluster of little churches where what worship that went on occurred in a haphazard manner. "It is no wonder we have so little order to our days and to our offices. I will direct the building of these scattered chapels into one magnificent abbey of stone and glass and carved wood that will bring symmetry to our activities."

Even as his resonant voice rose and his pointing finger moved along the green landscape, the vision took form before their eyes. "I will add side aisles along King Ine's Church, with a fine, high tower at the end, and extend the building farther east. It will be a great basilica like those one hears about on the continent, with such space that no one can claim he or she avoided divine service because there was no room."

Then Dunstan stood, and his eyes were open, but he did not see the scene spread before him. "Hear me, Ethelwold. Long ago when I was a student here, I dreamed a dream—a dream of great power and beauty that I always felt was more prophecy than dream. An old man in shining raiment led me through a great church with stone pillars and sweeping arches and the worship of God rang from those stone walls.

"Many times in later years I have thought the vision lost, the dream dashed to pieces, but now I see it is to be a reality. Now I see—" His voice flowed into a mellow chant, and Ethelwold voiced with him the words of Psalm 22:

Now we stand within your gates, O Jerusalem;
Jerusalem that is built to be a city where people come together in unity . . .

Abruptly his vision cleared, and Dunstan turned to Ethelwold with bright eyes. "Ah, but vision is not enough. We must raise solid stone walls, hand-mortared, with stone-slabbed pavements. We must build stout furnaces for the glass. We must drain the swamps so there will be more land to farm, and the people will prosper with the land."

The two men stared at each other, aware of the boldness of Dunstan's words. Then Dunstan threw back his head and gave a shout of laughter that must have reached to the monastery. "Yes! That is what we shall do! With easier access to the rest of the land it will be easier to journey forth and do good and easier for those in need to come to us. And with productive land around us every serf will have all he can farm for his own family and abundant over for his tithe. All will benefit."

Already Dunstan was headed down the hill at such a pace Ethelwold, though longer-legged, had to hurry to keep up. "Come!" Dunstan called over his shoulder. "It will not do for the abbot to be late for Vespers. We must set a good example for those who stir themselves to attend. And then I will call a Chapter meeting and announce our new program. This will inspire them to action—if not to godliness."

There was just time before Vespers to inform Prior Sigebehrt of his plans. "Ethelwold, send the prior to me, if you would be so good."

At the mention of the monk just below Dunstan in the monastic hierarchy, Ethelwold froze. He opened his mouth as if to protest, then closed it. At last he bowed, "I will, my Lord Abbot."

Alone in the abbot's lodging, Dunstan pondered Ethelwold's reaction. Of course he expected a certain amount of resistance from the man he had replaced. Until Dunstan came, Sigebehrt had held complete control of the house since the death of Abbot Eanwulf. And certainly Sigebehrt had long enjoyed the lax, secular life into which the monastery had fallen, including his taking of a wealthy, aristocratic wife—even if she did have a face like a horse.

Sigebehrt stood before the abbot's desk, tall and commanding, his silver tonsure shining like a halo around his head, his long thin face set in a rigid look of autocratic saintliness. Dunstan wondered how anyone who looked the epitome of a sainted church father could act so in league with the devil. "I do not think this plan will succeed, my Lord Abbot." His voice, soft and silvery as his hair, carried its meaning as straight as an oaken arrow shaft. "The brothers will not care to undertake such labors as glass-making and marsh-draining. It would be unseemly work."

"Nonsense! Was it unseemly for our Lord to work as a carpenter, or St. Peter as a fisherman, or St. Paul as a tent-maker? It is precisely their example Benedict would have us follow in giving part of each day to labor." Dunstan sighed inwardly. "Brother Sigebehrt, like St. Benedict, I do not wish to lay down something harsh and burdensome. Remember, Benedict called his work 'a little rule for beginners,' so let us begin. The monastery is to be viewed as a 'school for the Lord's service' where monks learn to serve the Lord in obedience to their abbot." Dunstan paused. He felt he had said enough, although he would have liked to pound the table and say, *And I mean to be obeyed in this.*

But apparently Sigebehrt did not take his meaning—or perhaps he took it too well. For in a voice even softer and more controlled than Dunstan's he said, "It will not do. The Rule will not be workable here—not any part of it."

Holding strict control of his emotions, Dunstan stood. "Thank you for providing me with your opinion, Prior Sigebehrt. I will see you in Chapter after Vespers."

Dunstan found concentration on the psalms he sang at Vespers impossible. The implied threat in Sigebehrt's cool rebellion worried him more than he would admit.

But no sign of this care showed on the abbot's face when he met the assembled brotherhood in the dining hall for Chapter. Before announcing his plans, he read to them Benedict's chapter on daily manual labor. "'Idleness is the enemy of the soul. Therefore, the brothers should have specified periods for manual labor as well as for prayerful reading . . .'"

Before he could go on to announce his grand design, Sigebehrt stood. "Abbot Dunstan, we would not have this Rule to govern us. We do not care for regulated labor and prayers." He paused for emphasis. "And we will *not* live celibate."

Ah, so that was the crux of the issue—their wives and female companions. Dunstan let out his breath in relief. Now that he understood the issue, he could deal with it. Land reclamation and glass manufacturing had nothing to say to the point. The monks of Glastingbury would not live without ready satisfaction of the lusts of the flesh.

Secular clergy could marry if they wished, but not those who had taken vows of celibacy when they chose the monastic life. Dunstan knew that he must deal with this sore issue when the time was right, but the time was not yet.

Dunstan smiled, his relief clear. "Brothers, celibacy is indeed a subject we must address, as we must consider bringing our lives into order in every area in which we can better please the Lord. But that is not the subject of this Chapter—"

Sigebehrt cut him off. "Your mistake, Abbot Dunstan. It is precisely the heart of the matter. You will abandon this plan of forced labor," again one of his significant pauses, "or King Edmund and His Holiness Pope Stephen will hear of your, shall we say, indiscretions with the Lady Aethelwynn and with the Lady Aethelflaed."

The room, which a moment before had been astir with whispers, was deathly silent. Sigebehrt waited for the full impact of the charge to hit home. Then he continued, "Do not think that I would be so rash as to make this charge without proof, Lord Abbot. My wife is a clever woman of many means. For some time she has been my aide in gathering evidence. And now it shall all come to light."

He took a stride toward Dunstan and towered over the shorter man with a sneer of equal parts delight and malice. "Accept defeat. The charges that twice before cost you your positions in royal favor are well known. Do not think you bear any immunity this time. Accept defeat, deceiver."

25

unstan stared. The audacity. The outrage. The sheer ridiculousness of the charge. The ladies named were his friends of longstanding. The Lady Aethelflaed was a wealthy widow with a strong religious bent who had taken residence in Glastingbury shortly after her husband's death. She was related to the royal family and to Dunstan. When King Athelstan was living, he had often called at his niece's cottage and enjoyed her hospitality, as had Dunstan. She was far more regular at prayers than most of the monks. But Dunstan now saw how her very devoutness could be used against him.

Aethelwynn, also of noble birth, took a great interest in Dunstan's artistic work, encouraging him and delighting in the songs and designs he managed to produce despite his busy schedule. Sometimes he carried his harp to her house and spent a few quiet moments singing while she plied her needle.

And that was the extent of it. But Dunstan saw the insidiousness of the charge. How did one prove a negative? If the ladies' servants could be bribed to lie—what could he do?

His steely gray eyes ran the length of the table, looking at the black-robed monks gathered around it: Brothers Lurgan and Nenagh, the faithful Irish; Brother Oswy, the ineffective Master of Novices; Brother Widrith, who even now had his mind on his orchards; Brother Maethild, the subprior, a mouse of a man; Brother Hrethric, the cellarer with a red nose and a laugh as round as his belly . . . Dunstan's gaze continued on . . . How many of them would stand with him?

Dunstan took a stride toward Sigebehrt. Although shorter, the abbot seemed to grow in stature until he regarded his subordinate with a level gaze, which he held for the space of several heartbeats. Then he drew a deep breath. "Speak you then. I shall go ahead with my projects, as I will continue with my prayers. And what brothers will shall join me."

The bell pealed for Compline, as if calling the brotherhood to a vote. But the evening office was not to be a division of the house, for Sigebehrt, aristocratic head erect, long Roman nose in the air, outdistanced Dunstan and arrived first for prayers. Indeed, it had been many years since there had been such a complement of brothers in a service at Glastingbury.

After the service they filed out of King Ine's Church. In spite of his usually careful observance of silence after Compline, Dunstan waited outside and took Ethelwold by the elbow. "I need your help." His voice was just above a whisper as he led the way to his lodgings.

He briefly explained what had taken place in Chapter and then asked the novice to wait while he wrote a letter. It was a long wait with the song of an evening thrush and the scratching of Dunstan's sharpened reed on a large sheet of vellum the only sounds in the little room. Ethelwold sat with his chin on his chest. At last Dunstan sprinkled sand over the sheet, rolled it, and sealed it with a blob of wax from his candle, marking it with his ring.

"A good job that you've had a doze, young man." At Dunstan's words Ethelwold jerked awake. Then he gave his abbot a sheepish grin.

"Sorry."

"Not a bit—don't apologize. You shall need your rest, for I want you to ride through the night. I have laid all before King Edmund and shall abide by his decision in the belief that our highest authority on earth will be guided by the Highest Authority of all." He slipped the vellum scroll into a soft leather pouch and handed it to Ethelwold. "Unfortunately the court left Cheddar some weeks ago. It will be a longer journey for you to Winchester. But at least only the first part will needs be on foot." He pulled a small gold ring off his little finger. "You know the path to Balsbury. It should be dry enough now in late August. Give this to my brother Wulfric at the steading of Heorstan. He will give you the best horse in my father's stable when you tell him your errand."

He hurried Ethelwold off into the night with a bag full of bread, cheese, and cold meats from the larder, for Brother Hrethric, no matter how lax in his prayers, could be counted on to keep ample provisions. It was not until he had seen Ethelwold out the gate that second thoughts attacked Dunstan. Twice before, rumors had lost him favor with kings and cost him his place. Would it be so again?

In the following days, which rolled into weeks of waiting, there was no knowing what action Sigebehrt had taken or planned to take. But Dunstan forged ahead as if there had been no controversy. The dry season would last no more than six to eight weeks, so his swamp-drainage program must be started immediately. He would begin with the low-lying country westward toward the sea. Construction of an embankment to confine the River Brue and a sea wall around the lake at Meare would create a several-mile-wide area to be crisscrossed with drainage ditches and made fit for farming. If they worked quickly and the rains held off, it was just possible that next summer—or more likely the one after—could see the first crop. Dunstan smiled at his thoughts—he was ever impatient—wanting every good thing implemented immediately, but he had a feeling this project would teach him patience.

Dunstan spent the next several days walking over every foot of passable ground, sketching lines for embankments and drainage ditches on a map. Then he was ready to put out the call for workers. In theory he could command the monks—the question was whether or not they would obey his call. The village he had no authority over, but they responded to his call for a fole-gemot, or town meeting. He laid his plan before them, explaining the benefits for the village, its inhabitants, and all the countryside. He asked that all who would help in the project bring their shovels and meet at the foot of Wirral Hill on the morrow. The monks he excused from all daytime offices while working on the reclamation—not that such permission would make any difference in the schedules of most of them anyway.

The villagers listened respectfully, but it was impossible to know how many would respond, even when they had been promised pay and a share in the benefits. Dunstan was even less certain about the response from the monks. Lurgan and Nenagh he could count on. Widrith seemed to agree with him in spirit, but would be hard to pry away from the orchards he considered his sole duty. All of the others had obeyed Sigebehrt for so many years it was unlikely they would switch sides now. Dunstan wondered long into the night whether he and the two Irish monks working with a handful of villeins could accomplish anything on his grand design.

In the morning when Dunstan made his way to Wirral Hill with the faithful Lurgan and Nenagh, he saw that he had been none too pessimistic. Six churls from the village stood in a sad little huddle at the base of the hill. Dunstan looked at the weather-beaten thorn tree standing its lonely sentinel against the morning sky. He felt as alone and exposed as it was, and he wondered whether he could stand up to the storms as patiently. Many said it was hundreds of years old, but no one seemed to know where it had come from.

He turned to his little group of laborers. He would instruct them, bless them, and lead them forth to channel the meandering waters of the Brue, but it seemed as hopeless as trying to stem the tide of Saefern itself.

After hours of working knee-deep in mud with aching backs and blistered hands, they had progressed only a few feet. Try as he might, Dunstan could not keep himself from thinking of the length of the Brue from Glastingbury to Saefern and calculating how long it would take them to reach those broad waters at their present rate. Although outwardly calm, Dunstan seethed inside.

Time was passing. So much had been squandered in squabbles and procrastination. If twenty other duties hadn't claimed him, he would have seized a shovel and spent the day digging. He felt he should be able to press them forward by the sheer force of his own mental energy, but in truth, all he accomplished was to give himself a splitting headache.

Well, the Scriptures said that "tribulation works patience," and patience was ever the virtue he most lacked. But while it seemed he had never lacked for tribulation, he was still not patient. "So must You complete Your work in me, Lord, as I would complete my work here. And let me not be as difficult to work with as these around me."

He was rolling his shoulders backwards and forwards to ease the tension when a strange noise reached him. It sounded like a particularly shrill singing, unlike anything that could be expected of villagers or monks. His first thought was that Edmund had decided against him and had sent a troop of house carles for his removal.

But then his worried frown curled up into a broad smile. The midmorning sun shone on a forest of shovels carried by twenty or more small boys, some wearing the short black tunic of the monastery school, others in a variety of tattered homespun garments with cross-gartered leggings. At the head of the group marched Ebert, fairly shouting an old Saxon warrior's song that he must have learned from a scop at his father's hearth.

"Sorry we're late, Uncle Dunstan." He started to do a reverence in the mud, but the abbot stopped him. He would be mire-caked soon enough. "It took longer than we thought to beg shovels from Widrith and to raise these lazy louts from the village. The Lady Aethelflaed sent all her theows, and Aethelwynn says you may have hers tomorrow, for they were already in the pease fields today."

Dunstan stood speechless for a moment, looking at the shining faces of strong-armed, willing workers.

"Don't you have work for us, Uncle?" Ebert sounded crestfallen.

Dunstan threw out his arms. "Indeed I do! Welcome, boys!"

By the end of the week many workers had joined them, and a lengthy strip of the Brue flowed between well-defined banks, leaving a space of dry ground on either side of it. Dunstan found exceptional workers in two churls from the village, and with careful instruction he delegated much directing to Pybba and Aswulf. Now Dunstan could divide his time between supervising the ditching and dyking and making plans for his glassworks, which he would initiate when the weather ended their drainage work for the season. With such work the island could be prosperous the year around. If Dunstan were allowed to stay.

Widrith joined the workers when the leaves were fallen and the bare trees needed no more attending. Subprior Maethild skittered out to dig with them whenever the prior's attention seemed to be turned another direction.

All was quiet at the monastery, but the tension grew. Dunstan had received little word from Ethelwold, only that the king had heard his case. And Sigebehrt had made no disclosure of his plans. Had he also sent an appeal to the king? Or did he await the sitting of the Christmas Witan at Cheddar where he would make a public scandal of the matter? Dunstan worried more for the reputation of the ladies than for his own fate.

As the year turned, Dunstan continued quietly but inexorably with his work. Sometimes he thought he was winning—winning over his own impatience at least. Though it was clear that what he thought could be accomplished in months would in fact take years, and the glassworks he had envisioned starting this year could not be hoped for for another year, yet his inward seething lessened. And he seemed to be winning over the indolences in the monastery, for each week more black-robed figures appeared at the offices, and more heads turned in attention to his reading of the Chapter of the Rule of St. Benedict at each evening meal. The question was—would he be allowed to continue on to complete victory?

Then came the day Dunstan had been waiting for. The spring thaws would soon bring seedtime and plowing upon them and the interminable ditch-digging. But for today Dunstan could take himself to his long-abandoned metal-working shop. The past months of controversy and labor had left little leisure for artistic endeavors. But today, as he stoked his forge to a white heat, his head swam with the design for a chalice he would make for Ine's altar—medallions of three-flamed sunswirls on four sides of the cup, linked by trailing leaves and vines. He would make the chalice of silver, the suns of gold, and the vines of bronze. Working the bellows to raise the fire, he was contemplating setting the center of each sun with polished amber when he heard a pounding of horse's hooves.

Could this be Ethelwold or a king's officer? Good news or bad? Dunstan removed the heavy leather apron he wore to protect his robe, straightened his cowl, and walked to the door. Ethelwold was walking toward him in the early spring rain. There was no need to ask what news. Ethelwold's smile told all.

Indeed, Sigebehrt had laid his charges before the king. They arrived by the hand of Aude's brother soon after Ethelwold had presented Dunstan's letter. Although the prior's brother-in-law cut a dashing figure at court, and his story was eagerly latched onto by Dunstan's old enemies, his testimony to the king bore less weight than that of the somber novice. The former rumors and their disastrous results, rather than counting against Dunstan, simply worked to make King Edmund more careful in his decision-making. But such careful sifting of evidence among the other claims of a busy court had taken these many months. Ethelwold had not been privy to all the proceedings, but he knew that Godrith's sworn testimony of Dunstan's ever-respectful behavior to her, even in his days as a carefree young courtier, had carried much weight, as did the written statements of the Ladies Aethelflaed and Aethelwynn. So now Dunstan had full royal authority to enforce any measures he saw fit—including requiring attendance at all offices and assigning penance for those who refused.

Again Dunstan's enemies had meant a thing for evil, but God meant it for good. Sigebehrt's charges had strengthened the abbot's authority tenfold. Dunstan hugged Ethelwold with exuberant thanks and sent the young man off to the kitchen to see what Hrethric could find for him to eat. Now Dunstan must decide what to do about Sigebehrt. He sat on the stool beside his forge and tried to think, but it seemed that no plan would come clear in his mind.

Suddenly Sigebehrt himself burst in upon him in a frenzy. Dunstan was so startled he clasped the iron tongs near to hand as if to defend himself. "This is an outrage! You have lied to the king! Sorcery! I've heard rumors—don't think I haven't—" The prior shook his fist in Dunstan's face, inches from his nose. "You worked black arts on King Edmund to cover your vile actions! You think you've won! But you haven't! I'm still here! I'll never submit to your ways! I'll—"

With every new outburst Sigebehrt's voice rose higher, and his face grew redder. The prior was exuding more heat than the forge. Dunstan became alarmed that he might be taken by a fit of apoplexy any moment. The abbot looked at the trough of cold water where he plunged red-hot metals from the forge to cool them. Then he looked back at the scarlet face of the rage-fired monk. Dunstan reached out with the tongs he still held in his hand and grasped Sigebehrt's prominent nose, forced the much taller man two steps to the left, and plunged him face-downward into the tank of water.

He held him under for only a few seconds. Sigebehrt arose, fuming, sputtering, and flinging water from his silver hair, but indeed, much cooler. Dunstan's bright gray eyes sparkled as he watched the prior's retreating figure across the green lawn, but he did not give way to the urge to laugh.

Sigebehrt was a powerful man, and he would not bear this insult lightly. If Dunstan had been a man to give in to fear, now would have been the moment. It would not have surprised him if Sigebehrt should carry his grievance to Pope Stephen. Had his own rashness plunged his victory into defeat? Now Dunstan must hold out an olive branch to the prior if anything was to be salvaged from this.

He thought of the prime moving force behind Sigebehrt—his wife—and of the fear that must be moving her should the abbot force her husband to choose between wife and position. And he thought of the other monks who had chosen to live like secular clergy. For a moment, a face he had not seen for two years and more—perhaps three years—filled his mind so sharply it was as if she stood before him again—Godrith of the golden hair and laughing sea-blue eyes, as she had been when he first came to King Athelstan's court. He could understand the feelings of the married brothers.

Then the vision faded, and with it Dunstan's turmoil. It was as if Godrith had brought him the answer to a problem that had plagued his abbacy from the first. Now was the time to deal with it.

As Dunstan expected, Sigebehrt was absent from the dining room that night, but the abbot knew Brother Maethild would scurry to him with all the news. Without any reference to Edmund's decree—there would be time enough for rejoicing later—Dunstan went about his routine schedule of reading a chapter from the Rule. "Tonight chapter 1, 'The Kinds of Monks. There are clearly four kinds of monks. First, there are the cenobites, that is to say, those who belong to a monastery where they serve under a rule and an abbot . . .'"

Dunstan folded the wooden covers of his little book and placed it on the table before him. "Brothers, this is what I wish for us at Glastingbury, this ancient holy house, the most ancient and most holy in the land—I wish us to become strong cenobites." In his clear, sonorous voice he announced the enforcement of Benedict's rules for attendance at offices and pattern of life divided between prayer, work, and study.

He then picked up the book again and opened it to the first page. "Hear the words of St. Benedict, as the words of your own abbot. 'This is advice from a father who loves you; welcome it, and faithfully put it into practice. The labor of obedience will bring you back to Him from whom you had drifted through the sloth of disobedience. This message of mine is for you, then, if you are ready to give up your own will, once and for all, and armed with the strong and noble weapons of obedience to do battle for the true King, Christ the Lord.'" Again he closed the book.

"There is now one more matter I would lay before you. That is the question of celibacy. It is clearly right that all monks and those with religious vocations separate from the secular clergy should live solely unto God, clinging only to Him. So hear my decision on this matter over which our house has become lax. I will take no married monks into this house. Nor will I countenance the marriage or fornicating of any now living here." The faces of the community before him were a study in color. Some blanched white, some grew red. Brother Hrethric, whose wife even now awaited him in the kitchen with a pan of freshly mulled spiced wine, turned something of a violet-blue under his puffy cheeks. Dunstan hurried on before the inevitable outburst. "But in keen awareness of the sanctity God places on the marriage bond, those who are now living in this house already married will not be required to leave, nor should they put away their wives."

He sat down. That was as far, in conscience before God, as he could go. But it was his olive branch to Sigebehrt. He would not make the prior leave Glastingbury for sake of his wife.

The next morning a clear, sunny sky greeted them, a perfect day for dyking. So with shouts of joy at release from the classroom, Ebert and the other boys led the way to the marshes just behind Pybba and Aswulf with their workers from the village. Dunstan waited until after Terce at nine o'clock in case Sigebehrt should seek audience with him, but then he mounted his little gray donkey from the stable and rode out to see the progress. Three miles down the sturdy embankment of the Brue he encountered the work crew. When he spotted Pybba, he reined in his donkey and inquired about the work.

"Eh, fine! Fine, Your Reverence. There's aught but one thing bothering some of the lads."

"And what's that?"

"They're saying that when all this ditching and draining's done, the blessed Isle of Avalon'll no longer be an isle."

Dunstan felt the sun warm on his tonsure as he smiled at the workers' sentiment. "Aye. But it's in my mind that it'll always be blest."

The sense of benediction remained with Dunstan until he arrived back at the monastery. Three heavily-loaded wagons met him at the gate. With a sinking heart he read their meaning. Brother Maethild scampered forward and his mouse-gray tonsure bowed. "Prior Sigebehrt begs to inform Your Reverence that he is departing, as is Brother Oswy, and Brother Hrethric, and . . ." The list went on, ending with Maethild's own name. Dunstan was surprised that Hrethric would leave the ready supply of his cellar. Widrith was not among them—he would not leave his trees—but the length of the list was disheartening. Dunstan would be left brothers Lurgan, Nenagh, and maybe five other loyal brothers to run the entire monastery. And just when he was ready to launch vigorous new programs. True, they had needed a ruthless weeding out, but where was he to find workers to labor in the Lord's vineyard? By the simple tactic of virtually emptying the monastery of monks, had Sigebehrt won after all?

26

The following day was so dark and rainy Dunstan was obliged to burn a candle in his study at midday. Perhaps because he was depressed anyway, he turned to the task he hated most—his account books. He had to give accurate account of all the monastery's resources, so he was a careful record keeper—but when he attempted to transfer all his bills and notes to the neat columns of his account books, the numbers never made sense, and the books were ever out of balance.

He shook his head and determined to try again. He dipped his reed pen in the pot of newly mixed ink on his table. Then when a blob of the black liquid fell from the tip onto the one set of figures that tallied, he growled in irritation. At that moment his door opened for a welcome interruption from Brother Lurgan. But Dunstan's relief was short-lived. The monk wore a frown.

"It's the ale, my lord. They are quarreling over it again."

"Who is quarreling?"

"All who came for the midday meal." Dunstan had chosen to work through the mealtime; perhaps his absence had prompted a voicing of long-quiet resentments. "Baldric, Eowa, Eanfrith . . . Hrethric kept no count. All could have as much ale as they desired. I tried to enforce your order that each was to have one tankard at a meal. They are saying it is unfair because the tankards differ in size."

Dunstan sighed and walked to the window to view the dreary rain. "Tell them we will fix pegs inside each tankard to mark equal limits."

Lurgan's face brightened immediately. "I will, Lord Abbot. Excellent!"

"And Lurgan—"

"Yes, my lord?"

"Remind them that I will ever attempt to be fair, but I will be obeyed."

The monk left, but Dunstan did not return to his accounts. If only all of his problems could be solved as easily. Seedtime would soon be upon them, and summer and harvest would follow as rapidly. He must not let another year go by without beginning the glassworks. But the Flemish masters King Edmund had promised to send had not arrived yet. And without them, the furnace-building and laying-in of supplies could not even begin. Soon another whole season—if not year—would be lost.

The study door opened again, and this time Ethelwold entered. His face was dark, and his young shoulders looked bowed as if under a heavy weight. If he had come to say he was leaving for a secular life, this was not the moment, so Dunstan spoke swiftly. "Ethelwold, my soul is heavy. Would you walk with me, even in the rain?"

Ethelwold pulled his cloak over his head, but Dunstan did not put up his cowl, letting the rain fall on his tonsure.

The abbot led the way to Ine's church, but did not go in. Instead they walked along the outside of the stone walls with Dunstan repeating much of the conversation they had had long ago on the Tor, sketching his dream for the abbey. Now their feet trod the very earth where the stones would stand—but it was still just a dream. With impatient stride Dunstan led first down the north side. "This aisle chapel I would dedicate to St. John the Baptist; and its twin on the south to St. Andrew . . ." He took them east of the existing church, stopped abruptly, and flung out his arm. "Here I will build a large chancel with a crypt below." He paced forward. "It will extend to here." The cross-headed staff which he had taken to carrying with him wherever he walked he now thunked into the ground like a builder's stake. "Look back, Ethelwold." Obediently, Ethelwold peered westward through the rain. From where he stood he could just see St. Stephen's Chapel, the chapel of St. David, and the ancient Church of St. Mary, appearing dim in the dusky light.

"Just think, Ethelwold, when we are finished with connecting doors and passageways, a monk could walk dry-shod from one end of the great abbey to the other through all these scattered chapels. Now look up." Ignoring the rain that fell on his eyes and nose, Ethelwold obeyed. "Picture our great tower here, far taller than King Ine's. We will place a bell in it that will sound to every steading across the marshes. When it rings, all will come to mass."

Ethelwold started to make a polite answer, but Dunstan strode ahead of him, leading the way to the sanctuary of the Old Church. He sat on a bench before the bare altar. "Ethelwold, you needn't speak. You needn't tell me it is a fine vision, but an impossible one. I would raise the stone with my bare hands if I could. But I fear it will never be." He interrupted his words with a sigh. "Glastingbury has ever been a temple of reconciliation for our people—between English and British in the days of Cenwalh, between English and Danish in the days of Alfred, and I would have it be between religious and secular in our day . . . I would build the New Jerusalem."

He sat silent. The rain splashed loud on the wooden cover that protected the ancient thatch of the church. "But it will not be. We won the battle with Sigebehrt, but we have lost the war. There are not enough secular to build, nor enough religious to pray. The temple of reconciliation in the New Jerusalem will ever be only a haunting vision in my own mind."

"Not only in your mind, Lord Abbot. But in mine also. I have come to tell you that I share your vision. And in order that I might better work for its reality, I am ready to take the cowl."

Dunstan jumped to his feet. "Blessed be God!" Gripping Ethelwold's shoulders, the abbot exulted, "Praise to our God!"

Although everyone attended Ethelwold's dedicatory service the next morning, what was left of the brotherhood fit easily in the Old Church. "Blessed be God! He has chosen us to live in love, holy and without blemish in his sight." Dunstan's melodious voice filled the room as he read from Romans. And after he served the sacred elements, the abbot closed with prayer. "Lord God, You have inspired our brother Ethelwold to follow faithfully Christ's pattern of poverty and humility as You inspired St. Benedict. May our brother's prayers help us to live in fidelity to our calling and bring us to the perfection you have shown us in your Son, who lives and reigns with You and the Holy Spirit, one God, forever and ever."

With a final reverence before the altar, the monks filed from the church. But Dunstan remained. A fervent prayer of his heart had been answered. Their numbers had increased by one. His heart rejoiced. Yet his mind worried. Would the addition of one, even so fine a one, make any difference? Dunstan slipped to his knees before the altar, but no words, either of praise or of supplication, came to his lips. He bowed there in silence at the feet of Jesus.

As he bowed deep in meditation, in his mind formed an image of a great green tree with sturdy branches and lush foliage. But instead of fruit, the branches bore monks' cowls. At the top a larger cowl overspread all the others. It was Ethelwold's.

Dunstan rose from his meditation with renewed courage. Yes, one more could be enough, when he was such a one as Ethelwold, for he could bring many more into the Lord's vineyard. That brought Dunstan to another answer. He marveled that he had not thought of it sooner. The monastery needed more monks, so they would seek for them from the lands to the west that had stood firm in the faith. He would send Ethelwold into Wales and Ireland to gather those who would respond to the call, both lay and religious. But they must hurry now to be returned before next winter's storms made travel impossible in the western mountains and across the Irish Sea.

Dunstan had not had breakfast yet, but, as always, once he saw his way clear, he would not hesitate. He hurried to his lodgings and pulled from under his narrow bed an old carved wooden chest he had found there when first he moved in. The box was covered with dust, its hinges corroded. There was no telling how long it had been there or even how it came to be. He pulled a scroll of cracking parchment from the chest. There was no way to know whether or not it was authentic, but doubtless the story of Patrick, purported to be told in his own words, would inspire Irish religious to serve in a land sacred to their patron saint.

He took the scroll to his table and brushed aside the muddled books that had lain untouched since yesterday. Drawing a fresh sheet of vellum from his cupboard, Dunstan began copying, for Ethelwold must be armed with all the weapons they could muster. "Charter of Patrick," he wrote in bold script at the head and then in a flowing hand, "By the guidance of God, who is the Life and the Way, I chanced upon the isle of Ynis Witrin, wherein I found a place holy and ancient, chosen and sanctified by God in honor of Mary the pure Virgin, the Mother of God: and there I found certain brethren imbued with the rudiments of the Catholic faith . . ."

Dunstan paused to re-dip his pen, and Ebert, who had taken to stopping by the abbot's lodging to do small jobs for his uncle, looked in through the unshuttered window. "Ah, Ebert, the very lad I need. Bring our new-made brother Ethelwold to me." Ebert scampered off, and Dunstan returned to his copying. ". . . and when I found them meek and gentle, I chose to be in low estate with them, rather than to dwell in kings' palaces. And, since we were all of one heart and one mind, we chose to dwell together, and eat and drink in common, and sleep in the same house. And so they set me, though unwilling, at their head . . ."

Before he was finished, Ethelwold arrived. Dunstan told him first of the vision he had had of the monastic tree, headed by Ethelwold's cowl. "If it is for me to interpret, I would say that you will be spiritual father to many monks. And I would have you set out now on a venture for spiritual harvest, as you have long delighted in the harvest of your herb garden." And Dunstan explained the task upon which he would set him.

The newest and youngest of the brothers was overwhelmed. "My Lord Abbot, it is too great. I am so young. There are others far more worthy. Brothers Lurgan and Nenagh would delight to return to the land of their birth . . ."

Dunstan held up a hand to silence him. "Indeed, I have thought of that. I cannot spare Brother Lurgan, but Nenagh I shall send with you." Here he was interrupted by a still form inside the door who had followed Ethelwold back.

"Let me go also, Uncle—er, my Lord Abbot." Dunstan hesitated. It would be an enormous undertaking. Was the once-wayward Ebert ready for such a responsible position? Dunstan thought of how in the past months Ebert had proved his worth. It now appeared that the unruly stubbornness that had made the boy rebel against the wishes of his father and all family tradition had been channeled into a healthy firmness that would serve him well in such a venture.

"Yes, Ebert, I believe this will be the very thing for you. I would have you go as servant to these two brothers."

Dunstan did not miss the flash of fire that told him being a servant was not what Ebert had in mind. "Remember, Ebert, he who would be master of all, must first be servant of all, as our Lord showed us."

Ebert bowed his head obediently—the first truly submissive gesture Dunstan had witnessed from the strong-willed boy. Then he turned again to Ethelwold. "And so, Nenagh will accompany you, and Ebert will attend you both. But you must be head. Do not worry about your age. As Paul told Timothy, 'Let no man despise your youth,' and in the words of St. Benedict, ever our guide, 'Absolutely nowhere shall age automatically determine rank. Remember that Samuel and Daniel were still boys when they judged their elders.'" So Ethelwold also bowed to the challenge.

A few days later the small party set out with glad hearts, Nenagh bearing St. Patrick's charter in a leather pouch. But once they were off, the numbers remaining at the monastery were even less. As the burden of spring work grew into the labor of summer and prayers were shortened as work lengthened, spirits fell. Then, just when Dunstan despaired of the rightness of his action, the very thing they needed most happened.

Two Flemish master glass-makers arrived from a job they had just completed on the minster at Winchester. Immediately the whole island was astir. Though now the building of ovens and the drawing of plans and the constructing of workshops and ingathering of materials was added to their other labors, the vision of progress heartened everyone, and the gladness of their hearts sped their hands. The greatest joy to Dunstan was that, once the project was in motion, Edmund's craftsmen took competent charge, leaving him free for other duties.

In the flush of such successful delegation, Dunstan's mind turned to his own brother Wulfric—the one with good business sense, to whom book-balancing and accounting came easily. As readily as if he'd been waiting to be asked, Wulfric accepted a lay position at the monastery.

Dunstan then launched another innovation that had long been on his heart. Their numbers at worship had grown steadily, for when the villagers saw the monks themselves worshiping regularly and behaving themselves in a seemly manner, they began to mend their own ways. But it worried Dunstan that so little of what occurred at mass was comprehensible to his flock. Since even the brothers had little Latin, although they knew the prayers and psalms by heart, it was unlikely that anyone could follow his homilies. So Dunstan began preaching in English.

Rather than spring it on the brothers unawares, he warned them in Chapter on a cold autumn Saturday night with the wind howling around the dining hall and sending sudden gusts down the smoke hole to scatter ashes from the hearth. His announcement caused shock, so he hurried on. "People must be taught from the pulpit in strong and straight language—their own language." There was no arguing.

The results could not have been more gratifying. By the time the year turned the corner and men were looking for the first bud-swellings on the willow branches and the soon-return of those who had journeyed westward, all the benches in King Ine's Church were filled at every public service. Now Dunstan renewed his determination to begin building in the spring, for it was a practical necessity to offer more room to worshipers. He would realize his vision yet. He would raise the stone.

Then a new disaster struck.

27

t first it seemed like the usual end-of-winter fever suffered by boys in the schoolroom. Dunstan ordered Lurgan to dose his charges on sulphur and fish oil. But then old Brother Widrith took to his bed with aching, swollen joints, followed by Baldric and Eowa, the most vigorous of the brotherhood. And soon reports came from the village. First Dunstan noted a falling away of numbers at mass. Then Brother Eanfrith, who put what herbal skills he possessed to use in the infirmary, came to Dunstan to report that the call on their store of medicines was so great he could no longer meet the need.

Dunstan himself took a hand in the workshop beside the herb garden rolling pills, grinding poultices, and brewing draughts. And many a night the abbot himself missed Matins because a special elixir could not be left unattended while it boiled. Dunstan longed for Ethelwold and his God-given herbalist skill.

But their best efforts were not enough. For every one that recovered to sit with pale, blotched skin, shading dark-circled eyes, in a sun-warmed corner of the garden, two died. Three youngsters from the school were no more sealed in their small wooden boxes than Brother Widrith joined them. Dunstan's one consolation was that the gentle monk would be glad of a coffin cut from one of the trees he had tended so lovingly. Then Dunstan met his greatest sorrow.

It was barely five of the morning. He was making his sandal-shod way across the dewy grass to Lauds when the porter came for him. A young serving maid from the Lady Aethelwynn awaited him in great agitation. "It's my lady. The doctor said to run, and so I did. But I fear we may be too late."

Dunstan kilted his robe to his knees that he might move faster and returned to his room only to gather the needed items. God was gracious, for they were not too late. When Dunstan was done administering the last rites to the gentle friend who had been an encouragement in many of his darkest hours, she opened her eyes full on him and smiled. Then the lady Aethelwynn breathed her last.

Dunstan returned to his cell to be alone. He knew no words or prayers to console his aching heart. He sat mute at his desk, a pen in his hand, thinking of the lady's love of art and joy in his designs. The pen moved as if at its own volition. And when he struck a flint and lit the candle on his table, Dunstan saw that he had sketched a picture of himself—a sorrowing cowled figure, kneeling at the cross of his Lord. Comfort spread like a balm over his soul.

The solace came none too soon, for there were new problems to face. Brother Eowa, still none too steady on his feet, but sufficiently recovered to lend a hand with the laying-out and burying, knocked at the abbot's door. "There is no more room in the cemetery, Lord Abbot. Everywhere the lads set their spades they turn up bones."

Dunstan rose and took up his staff. Odd, how that had come to be a source of comfort. He had been carrying it for some time when he realized that the ancient man who had led him through the yet unbuilt aisles and chapels of the great abbey in his youthful vision had carried such a staff, although in Dunstan's memory that one was of simple wood without the cruciform top his own bore. Somehow, grasping his staff as he strode forth to do battle with yet another problem gave him a sense of continuity with generation after generation of devout men who had worshiped here.

Eowa led the way to the cemetery on the south side of the cluster of chapels. The schoolboys, who had been pressed into service as grave diggers, were still there leaning on their shovels, looks of fascinated horror on their faces. With ghoulish enthusiasm they described the bones they had exhumed.

"Would you like to see, Lord Abbot?" The shorter, freckled-faced one thrust his shovel into the soft earth.

Dunstan held up his hand. "Certainly not. They have been disturbed once. That is more than enough. You may return to Brother Lurgan."

The boys departed, dragging their shovels behind them. Dunstan surveyed the field. "And we dug there," Eowa said pointing, "and there, and there."

"All occupied?" Dunstan asked.

"All, my lord."

"Well . . ." Dunstan paused to consider. "We could perhaps consecrate more ground." He thought about how all the land inside the enclosure was used and then shook his head. "No, that would not leave room for our building plans."

He extended his gaze to beyond the turf and timber wall that enclosed the monastery. Most of the twelve hides of land the monastery owned lay beyond the wall. Legally they could expand at will. But the village occupied the land to the north; a row of monastery guest houses stood across the road to the west; to the east the land rose steeply up to the well that provided their water, and behind that stood the Tor. The only possibility would be to move the wall southward into the monastery's cultivated fields of pulse. Pease, beans, and lentils would flower there in a few months. No, the crops were needed, and that would be such a long ways away from the other graves.

Dunstan walked the length of the cemetery, thinking. When he came to the western-most end, he paused before a rough, nameless memorial stone. "It would seem that this marks a grave of some importance—odd that it bears no name. Do you know whose it is?"

Brother Eowa had no idea, nor did anyone else Dunstan asked. Nor did there appear to be any indication in the records he consulted in his study and in the library attached to the scriptorium. Dunstan shook his head over the smell of stale ink and mold upon opening the book room door. When there was time, he would renew the copying of manuscripts. When there was time . . . Engrossed in reading manuscripts he hadn't seen since his school days, Dunstan missed the call to Nones, and would likely have missed Vespers had not the setting sun taken away the light. The room contained no candle and flint—a sign of disuse.

But it would no longer remain disused—at least by the abbot, for Dunstan had found great inspiration in his reading. The church fathers were always a great comfort and inspiration, next to the holy Scripture itself. But today the work Dunstan had found most gripping was by a Glastingbury monk of days long past who recounted in bitter, stinging words the coming of Dunstan's own Saxon people to this land. Yes, Dunstan would indeed spend more time reading Gildas. And so would he study an authentic-looking document bearing the signature of King Ine. Although Dunstan himself had been appointed by King Edmund, as was usual, it appeared that Glastingbury possessed special status, had anyone known or cared to invoke it. Dunstan shook his head over the weight of matters to be organized.

But for now he must attend to more pressing matters. After Vespers he stopped Brother Eowa. "I have decided. I have found nothing in the ancient records of this house to indicate that such action should be in error, so tomorrow we will begin building a new cemetery."

"To the south—the pease field, Lord Abbot?"

"No indeed. In our already consecrated ground. Only we will give these recently departed a boost on their journey to paradise. We will add another layer of dirt to the cemetery."

Brother Eowa considered a moment, blinking at the revolutionary idea. Then his round face broke in a smile. "Yes! That will do."

Dunstan nodded. "You may use the services of the schoolboys; they are ever ready for a day from Brother Lurgan's schoolroom. And, brother—" He paused as if still considering.

"Yes?"

"That unnamed grave. It seems that it must be of some importance to be marked out when so few are. Perhaps a great saint lies there. I would have you erect a marker over the spot—a pair of pyramids. Perhaps someday we will learn who it is, and I would not have it lost."

All was done according to Dunstan's orders. At last the fever burned itself out so that grass could be sown over the new graves that covered the old, and all could rest content in mother earth. Dunstan returned to his long-interrupted reading of Gildas's history. But this evening after Vespers he felt he could not be confined in a reading room. It was coming spring, and the thrushes sang, and all across the marsh the hawthorn flowered.

So Dunstan took his staff and walked out the east gate to sit in the garden that surrounded Glastingbury's ever-flowing well. This spot had always held a particular peace for Dunstan. This evening, with birds singing in the ancient yew trees circling the well and tiny purple and yellow flowers growing in the grass, it seemed as near to heaven as possible on earth. Dunstan sat on a lichen-covered stone bench. Strange, but in this spot more than any other, he felt close to the gray-bearded man of his childhood vision, closer even than on the site of the church the man had shown him he would build.

Tonight Dunstan felt closer to his vision than ever before, for today the builders had shown him Ine's fully repaired chapel and the master plans for the great new church. With but four weeks to Pentecost, what could be more perfect? They would celebrate a great mass to rededicate King Ine's Church and to launch at last the building of Dunstan's grand design.

Slowly the pictures in his head faded, and Dunstan came back to the present with a frown. What was that disturbance at the monastery? Something must be alarmingly amiss for the hubbub to reach him in this solitary sanctuary. With a sigh of resignation he picked up his staff and turned to do battle with whatever new obstacle he must face.

28

But it was no obstacle this time, rather a great answer to prayer. Ethelwold, Nenagh, and Ebert had returned. And with them a host of companions—perhaps twelve dark-robed monks and novices, and a slightly lesser number of cross-gartered laymen, all attesting in heavily accented Welsh and Gaelic voices their desire to serve God in Glastingbury.

It took Dunstan some time to sort the matter out, order Eanfrith to find what he could in the kitchen to feed so many, and assign sleeping quarters. A new dorter to replace the scattered cells now in use was part of his plan, but he had had no idea they would need it so suddenly. A triumphant Ethelwold led his new recruits to the dining hall, but Ebert remained behind, holding tightly to the edge of the green and gold plaid cloak of one of the new-come laymen. "Uncle Dunstan, you must meet Gwyndoc. I found him."

The young man's blue eyes flashed a smile under his thick black eyebrows and curling dark hair with red highlights. "Aye, and he's a persuasive lad. But I'm thinking I'll like it here very much. If you have need of a harper, that is."

Dunstan had already noted the embroidered leather bag the man wore slung over his shoulder. "He calls himself a bard, Uncle. But I think he could do very well as a scop—although his stories are different. He doesn't even know *Beowulf*."

Dunstan smiled. "Well, bard or scop, we can use all the help God sends us for our music. Since my nephew seems so fond of you, perhaps you'll start in the school. Brother Lurgan is in much need of help with the younglings."

That seemed to be one of Dunstan's happiest assignments, although sometimes he wondered about Gwyndoc. Dunstan heard snatches of strange tales the dark-visaged bard sang to the boys in their hour of recreation between dinner and Compline—stories of fierce battles and a mighty war leader named Artos who had never died, but only slept . . . Dunstan wondered if he should speak to Gwyndoc, but then shrugged. Such tales could do no more harm than ones of Beowulf battling his monsters. And it seemed that Gwyndoc's Artos put his reliance on God rather than on Beowulf's wyrd—so perhaps they were an improvement.

Dunstan returned to the anthem he was composing for the great Pentecost celebration. It must be finished tonight so the brothers could practice it in his absence. Tomorrow he would journey to Pucklechurch beyond Cheddar where King Edmund was hosting a feast on the Saint's Day of Augustine of Canterbury. Dunstan smiled as he thought of it. He had not seen the king for four years—since Edmund had brought Dunstan to Glastingbury and set him in the abbot's seat. Now the abbot could extend his invitation to the celebration mass in person to King Edmund. That would put the crowning touch on all their accomplishments and on all their efforts yet to come—to have their king in attendance.

Dunstan was still smiling the next morning as he journeyed across the green Mendip Hills. In his mind the songs of thrush and tit blended into the anthem he was still rehearsing. He turned to Ethelwold accompanying him to be his servitor at the feast, for every guest must have his own server. "If I may say so without losing all humility, Ethelwold, I do believe this is the finest I've ever composed. I see it as doing double honor—to our Heavenly King and to our earthly, for I'm certain Edmund will not refuse our invitation. It will be a great thing for our abbey to have such a mark of royal approval on our building."

The two-day journey could not have gone smoother. The weather held clear, and Wulfric's horses, which they rode instead of the monastery's donkeys, made quick going on the old Roman road that was still passable for much of the way.

They arrived just in time to wash and change into clean robes before the feast began. As always when he returned to the secular world, Dunstan was amazed at the bustle and noise and the glare of fine furnishings and clothing. He bowed before the king and received a warm greeting, and then he was shown to a seat at the high table. Ethelwold stood behind his abbot's chair, quick to see to the refilling of his glass and the serving of meats. The heaped platters of fowl, venison, and mutton fairly made Dunstan's head swim after the abbey's meager rations. He had not realized he had become so accustomed to the life of the Rule, nor that he so preferred it to any other. Wavering torchlight cast shadows across his long hands, and Dunstan reached up to brush the fringe around his tonsure. His struggles had not turned him prematurely gray at his thirty-six years, but he knew the pale blond streaks in his hair were more silvery than when last he sat at the king's table. Oh, but the effort was worth all, for they stood on the threshold of success.

"Have you spoken to the king yet?" Ethelwold asked as he bent forward to refill Dunstan's glass.

"Not yet. But there will be plenty of time. The night is young."

Ethelwold started to reply when the king's voice stopped all conversation. All heads at the high table and others nearby turned toward King Edmund. He stood and pointed halfway down the hall. "Who is the redbeard that sits with Ealdorman Edrith of my own special inviting?" The rich gold embroidery on Edmund's scarlet tunic glimmered in the torchlight as did the gold circlet on his forehead and the gold hilt of the dagger at his belt.

Waerferth, seated at the end of the high table, answered and his voice held the ring of a challenge. "That is Liofa whom you banished for seditious conniving in the first year of your reign, my Lord King."

"As I thought!" Edmund pulled his dagger from his belt and leaped across the table. "I'll have no outlaws at my feast!" The king sprang at Liofa's throat.

The hall was in immediate uproar. Platters of meat tumbled to the floor to be pounced upon by the hounds. Jugs of wine splashed the length of the tables as guests jumped on the trestles and leaped over benches to see what was happening. Dunstan sat quietly, praying. He had seen the gleam in Waerferth's eye, and he felt that King Edmund's rashness had led him into a carefully laid trap.

In seconds the tide turned. All those who had surged forward now fell backward, horror and confusion on their faces. The silence rang as loudly as the former tumult. The king lay dead. A dark red stain spread over the brightness of his tunic.

Then the tide flowed again, this time toward the single door in the side of the hall. None wanted to be accused of playing a part in so dreadful a scene. And none wanted to be detained by the sheriff for questioning.

The only still figures in the hall were the motionless king and the black-robed monk sitting at the high table with his tonsured head bent in prayer. Or seeming prayer. For in truth the words would not come to Dunstan. Instead he was thinking of the ruin that had come to all their plans on the very eve of success. He knew he should be praying for the soul of the king, but all he could think of were his visions of Glastingbury's glory that now lay as dead as their fallen monarch.

At last he forced himself to his feet and picked up an unspilled cup of wine. He knelt beside a mourning figure at the king's side—Edred, Edmund's brother, who was certain to follow him to the throne. Edred, a sickly boy who had grown into a none-too-vigorous man, looked paler than the corpse. "It was that Waerferth's doing. I'll see him dealt with."

Dunstan agreed, but he had a more immediate duty. With gentle fingers he closed the staring eyes that looked out in such an expression of blank surprise. Then he moistened the stilled tongue with a drop of wine. "In this moment of sorrow the Lord is in our midst . . ."

When the rites were concluded, Dunstan stood to see the room filling again as witnesses were ushered in under the strong command of Gloucestershire's Sheriff Beornwulf. Dunstan approached to ask if there was more he could do. "Get you some sleep tonight, my Lord Abbot. You'll have duties enough tomorrow. My men and I can take care of what's needful now."

"Did the outlaw escape?"

"Aye. For the moment. But never fear. My men will bring him in. Edmund was much loved. His murder won't go unavenged."

Dunstan and Ethelwold went to their assigned guest lodge. Even though the bed was far more comfortable than his narrow monk's cot, Dunstan could not sleep. Over and over he prayed for forgiveness for his earlier elation over his own success and then for his thinking first of the crushing blow to his own hopes rather than of Edmund's soul. But the doors of Heaven seemed closed. He could find no relief. Just when he thought he had learned patience and submission to God's ways, he had failed again. He knew nothing to do but continue praying.

Night's blackness was turning a soft gray when Dunstan heard a gentle tapping at his door. He opened it to admit a still ghostly pale Edred. "My Lord Abbot, I've come to ask a favor—two favors."

Dunstan ushered the future king into his room and wished for some wine to steady his royal guest's nerves. "Ethelwold." He shook his companion who still slept deeply. "Run to the kitchen for some wine. Edred the Aetheling is our guest, and I would not have him slighted."

Dunstan tucked a heavy rug around the frail young man. In spite of his fragile looks, however, there was strength and purpose in his voice. "Sheriff Beornwulf assures me that my brother's murderers will be brought to justice.

But he believes, as do I, that this was a conspiracy far more than the simple slashing of an outlaw. Until all traitors are dealt with, he feels that the royal treasury should be moved to a safer place. Will you take care of this, Lord Abbot? I feel you are the one man in the kingdom I can completely rely on."

Dunstan was stunned. The royal treasury—a vast collection of jewels, golden vessels, silver plate, and chests of coins. What would he do with them? "Surely, you need armed men to guard such riches. What can a mere monk do?"

"But don't you see, that is just the point. An armed man is all the more dangerous if he's on the traitor's side. And at this moment I don't know which of my brother's house carles I can trust. I would send two wagon loads of 'hay' to your monastery. What of such fodder your cows don't care to eat you can keep for me in the crypt."

Dunstan nodded, amazed at the clear, clever thinking of one who appeared to be an ineffectual boy. If Edmund's murderers had thought to replace the king with a puppet that they might have their own way, they would find it otherwise. "I would be happy so to serve my king and my country."

Edred smiled as if a great burden had been lifted. "And now to my second matter. I have decided that Pucklechurch Hall shall be set apart as a chapel of intercession for my brother's soul, but I know of the great love he bore for Glastingbury. It was ever the joy of his heart, and he delighted in the reports of your progress. I have heard him say more than once that Glastingbury was where he would be buried when his work was done. Will you make the arrangements?"

If Dunstan had been amazed over the royal treasury, he was completely speechless at this news. By so honoring their house in his death, Edmund had graced it as he never could have in life. For now Glastingbury would ever stand as a royal house to which other kings would grant favors and to which royalty from all Christian lands would make pilgrimage. Dunstan bowed in silent gratitude before Edred.

The king's body was carried in full state to Glastingbury. So did Edmund attend the great service on Pentecost. His body lay on a purple and gold draped bier in a pool of colored light before King Ine's altar, the spicy aroma of incense filling the air. But instead of the triumphant *gloria* Dunstan's rich tenor voice would have sung for his king, they now sang the somber *Requiem aeternam dona eis, Domine,* "Rest eternal grant, O Lord."

The royal body would rest in state for many days with candles burning at the head and feet, always with no fewer than three monks kneeling at the altar praying for the king's soul. From far and wide, men and women of every station, from highest thane to lowest theow, would file by, bend the knee, cross themselves, and murmur prayers. Until at last Edmund's remains would be moved in full state to rest until the Judgment Day before the high altar of the new church.

So the procession of a mournful nation began—headed by Edred, who would be crowned at Westminster the next week, and the royal family, then the house carles, ealdormen, and thanes.

Cynefrith of Ulfstead came in his turn. As the line of mourners moved slowly, he spoke in a soft voice to the son he had seen so little of these past years. "And so, Ebert, your time has been good here. Will you stay now with the monks, or do you return to Ulfstead?"

Ebert looked surprised at his father's question. "The kingship will pass to Edred now—as it says on our rooftrees—'one generation passes to another'?"

Cynefrith nodded. "So it will."

"And I would have it be the same at Ulfstead. I will return that the sun may continue to rise on our family."

Again Cynefrith nodded. "It is good." Then they were before the bier. Father and son knelt together.

Dunstan, observing them, felt moved to step forward and place his hand on the bowed head of the youth. "'I have been reminded of the sincere faith which lived before you in your grandmother and in your mother, and I am persuaded now lives in you also. For this reason I remind you to fan into flame the gift of God which is in you.' Amen."

Together father and son left the church.

The solemnities of the day ended at last, and the monks filed with bowed heads and folded hands to the dining hall. Dunstan remained long, kneeling by the king's body, but at length he stood and walked to the door leaving brothers Baldric, Eowa, and Nenagh to maintain the first vigil. Outside the door he saw Gwyndoc leaning against the stone wall, apparently waiting for him. "Will you walk to the meal with me?" Dunstan invited.

Gwyndoc straightened the harp on his shoulder. "Gladly. I waited to ask you a question."

Dunstan nodded. "You may ask."

"I know this is a day of great solemnity. But among my people, it is not thought so sad a thing to have one's soul sped to God. It was in my mind to ask if I might claim a bard's privilege to sing your hymn after the meal, my Lord Abbot."

Dunstan considered. The singing of a hymn as a form of the prayer after meat was not unheard of, and whatever else this day had held, Pentecost was a feast day for the church. "Yes. I believe that would be appropriate. We need to be reminded of our blessings right now. And, indeed, I believe they are many. Glastingbury has been the final home of many saints, but today we have laid to rest our first king. I do not believe that Edmund will be our last. I think many more will be buried here in Avalon."

Dunstan spoke lightly, as if giving voice to thoughts he was just forming in his mind, but they had a surprising impact on Gwyndoc. He stopped still in the middle of the path. "My Lord Abbot! Do you not know? Is it possible that you could be uninformed—?"

"I am never surprised at my own ignorance." Dunstan's gray eyes lit with a gentle smile. "Tell me what it is that I do not know."

"Yes, assuredly there will be many more kings for Glastingbury, but Edmund is not the first. It is often spoken of among my people in the green hills where the bards still sing—how could you not know what my people know so well?" Again he paused, and Dunstan's wide gray eyes encouraged him to go on. "This is, as you say, the blessed Isle of Avalon—blessed because the great King Artos sleeps here."

More than his words, it was the fervency with which Gwyndoc spoke them that touched something deep within Dunstan. What could that ancient Celtic king have to do with the old man who led him in his own vision? And yet they seemed somehow linked. After the serving loets had removed the last wooden trencher from the table and Gwyndoc had uncovered his harp, the words of his own hymn blended with the singing of the harpstrings. But Dunstan's mind pictured not the gates of the New Jerusalem which he had written about, but a tall, russet-haired warrior in a flaring cloak wafting a golden-hilted sword beneath a red-dragoned banner. In some strange way he felt that the two visions were not so dissimilar as they seemed.

"I will teach you to build anew the walls of Jerusalem," Gwyndoc sang.

> *Command kings to bring gifts for the honor of Your temple.*
> *So shall the Lord's name be on men's lips*
> *and His praise shall be told in Jerusalem.*
> *O praise the Lord.*

Then, perhaps because he had so recently celebrated mass, the king in Dunstan's vision placed his sword before a crude wooden altar, much like the one in the Old Church, and partook of the Eucharist from a golden grail. As Dunstan looked again, it was not a cup of gold, but one of simple carved olive-wood. And Gwyndoc sang on:

> *As the hills enfold Jerusalem,*
> *mighty is our Lord and great His power.*
> *Sing to the Lord a song of thanksgiving.*
> *Sing to the Lord, Jerusalem. O praise the Lord.*

BOOK V

The Flowering of the Legend

Norman England

My God, is all vanity? Are all our struggles useless in Thy sight? In a thousand years of Christianity in this land, in a thousand victories, in the raising of a thousand stones to build a great house of God, was nothing permanent?

Is there an end to the quest? It is long past the time that Lauds should have been sung. Indeed, the dawn broke outside my window this hour past—but all the voices in the land that would praise Thee are silenced. Yet Thy Word declares that if man would not worship Thee, the very stones would cry out. O Lord, let them cry. Let the stones of Glastonbury Abbey cry unto Thee, for the mouths of Thy poor servants are hushed.

But to my story. The end is not yet—and when it comes, it may be void of meaning—but still I must journey on.

In 1066 William of Normandy landed at Hastings. In a brief battle his army defeated the English, and William claimed the throne promised him by Edward the Confessor. Norman prelates quickly succeeded to all the high church offices in Britain, and thus it was that we Glastonbury monks fought our own "Battle of Hastings" with a Norman.

The Norman Archbishop of Canterbury appointed Thurston as Abbot of Glastonbury to succeed our beloved Abbot Ailnoth, who had followed the sainted Dunstan. This new abbot had the unhappy idea that we should substitute the Dijon method of chanting for our time-honored Gregorian chants. The monks disagreed. There arose a furious quarrel in the Chapter House, and Abbot Thurston summoned men-at-arms. The monks fled into Dunstan's church and barricaded themselves inside, collecting benches and candlesticks as weapons. The soldiers burst into the gallery and shot arrows at the monks near the altar, hitting the crucifix. Other soldiers, armed with spears, forced an entry into the choir. Two monks were killed, twelve wounded.

It was an outrage. But we were more fortunate than Harold. Our

Battle of Hastings drove off the invader, and we returned to our traditional ways.

In 1085 William ordered the compilation of the Domesday Book *where our original grant of the twelve hides was officially recorded. Oh, my heart aches for the lost books, but with the Lord's help I struggle to recall the words, "The Domus Dei, in the great monastery of Glastonbury, called The Secret of Our Lord. This Glastonbury Church possesses in its own ville XII hides of land which have never paid tax."*

And then was another great making of books. The upstart Norman lords, wanting to appear the rightful rulers of England, cast about for a great British hero to make their own. So they harkened to bards from the green mountains of the west land, and they discovered King Arthur—Arthur whose great foe had been the English Saxonkind. So there was a great renewal of the stories of Arthur and also of the martyred George. For these were the times of crusading, and there in the Holy Land was rediscovered the patron saint of England, the waving of whose banner helped the Norman rulers sit more firmly on their thrones.

There must remain yet in this sorrowful land copies of such books—Henry can't have destroyed everything—so perhaps my reader can correct any failure in my memory. I must have faith that life will go on—faith that the end of Glastonbury Abbey is not the end of all for us.

Perhaps that is the meaning for which I search. Perhaps the grail is renewal of faith—a new touch of light—the light of understanding—the light of truth and love—truth found only in the heart.

Yes, my heart leaps. It is true—these gropings of an old man sick at heart are reaching the truth. And yet my heart tells me there is more. I must search on, although my niece rags at me constantly that I burn too many candles.

PART ONE

1

he dream came again. Bors stood on the threshold of a vast, high-ceilinged room, filled from floor to rafters with precious jewels. They winked at him and beckoned with their red, blue, and green radiance. In that room was every rich thing he could desire for this world or the next. And yet even in his dream, Bors knew that the jewels were only symbolic. For it was not earthly riches that he longed to achieve, but the following and fulfilling of a vision. But what was the vision? What was he to follow? If he could only cross the threshold, he would find the answer in the treasure room. But he did not know how to cross. The door stood open. Unguarded. Yet he could not cross.

Always when he awoke, he gave them the name he could not form in his sleep. Surely the jewels were the knighthood he longed for—so far beyond his reach—and surely the barrier had been raised by his brother Nyall, who had shut off all possibility of honors to him. And as always the answers satisfied his need for a motivating anger, although they seemed forced.

Still more dreaming than awake, Bors gritted his teeth, the frustration spurring him to action—even if the action was only to see to the sheep. Tending sheep for a monastery when he would be serving as squire—or at least varlet—on the manor to which he had been born.

Bors rolled onto his side and flung out an arm. With the motion he came wide awake. "Garth?" He reached out for the shaggy coat of the black and white sheepdog who ever slept curled next to his pallet. The dog was gone.

Still rubbing his eyes, Bors sprang to his feet. "Garth!" If there had been danger to the sheep peacefully sleeping in the fold behind him, the dog would have wakened him. All was quiet in the byre.

Bors left the doorway of the fold and rounded the corner of the building. Then he stopped. How long had he slept? How could the sky be so light already? Surely this was the blackest hour when the brothers at the abbey across the fens should have been saying their first prayers. But a strange glow came from the direction of the abbey.

His dreams mingled with reality, and Bors wondered if this golden radiance could be from the room in his dream. But then Garth ran to him, jumping up with his muddy paws, an insistent whimpering in his throat, as if he would lead Bors to a lamb caught in a bramble. Bors shook his head to clear it.

No mere dream or endangered lamb filled the night with such strangeness. Garth's yapping cut through the last wisps of sleep-fog, and Bors knew. "Fire! Fire! The abbey's on fire!" Even in his alarm Bors made certain the sheepfold door was barred before he ran toward the grange. "Brother Gellert! Brother Gellert! Brother Arald!"

Bors ran faster, for even as he ran, he could see the sky growing redder, as if the firmament had suddenly chosen to defy its Creator's laws and decided to spread forth a blazing sunrise at two o' the morning.

"Brothers! Brothers! Wake up!" Bors sobbed as he beat on the door of the grange while Garth's earlier whines and throat-throttled growls burst into impatient barks. It was now as if they could smell the smoke, although surely that wasn't possible at a distance of almost a mile.

Then Bors's flailing fists hammered on empty air, as Brother Arald, gray and insubstantial as the smoke that even now must billow over the marshes, opened the door.

"The abbey's on fire!" But as he heard his own words, Bors's mind argued. Impossible. Great chunks of solid stone couldn't burn. Perhaps some of the barns and outbuildings, perhaps a few of the older chapels built of wattle and daub, but not St. Dunstan's church—the largest and holiest church in England. Impossible. Yet no mere burning of outbuildings could so set the sky on fire.

The iron-bound door creaked open wider, and Brother Gellert burst into the night. He took one look to the northeast. "Run, lad. Run to the abbey. Bring us word as quickly as you can. I'll bide with the sheep." His shove propelled Bors forward.

He ran, Garth sometimes leading, sometimes yapping at his heels. Every stride carried them farther under the infernal canopy of flaring red and billowing smoke. Even before his eyes were stinging from the smoke, Bors could hear the roar of the devouring flame.

He sped across the newly sprouted pease field, then flung himself, gasping for breath, against the stone wall of the enclosure. His whole body shook. Sweat poured down his body, both from the exertion of the run and from the heat of the inferno roaring on the other side of the wall. Even here gusts of wind brought sparks and ash down upon him.

"Here, lad. To the well." A man with black singe-holes peppering his short homespun tunic thrust a wooden bucket into Bors's hands.

He hadn't caught his breath yet, but Bors turned toward the spring that had never failed the abbey. The brigade began at the foot of the hill where the brook from the well tumbled in a little waterfall that made bucket-filling a matter of seconds. The field gate that the brothers used as the quickest way to tend their crops stood open, and from his place in the line handing along filled buckets,

Bors could see similar lines of figures, silhouetted darkly against the redness beyond, passing buckets of water from the abbot's fish pond. But their best effort could only be as a gentle falling of dew on hundreds of glass-making furnaces.

As he strained his eyes against the heat and smoke, Bors could see that, impossible as it seemed, St. Dunstan's great church was ablaze. It could only be the timbered roof, the wooden rafters supporting the vaulted aisles, and the woven tapestries on the walls that burned, yet it looked as if the very stones blazed. The bucket brigades did not even extend to pouring their poor drops of water on so great a conflagration, but focused instead on saving the scriptorium, from which even through the confusion, Bors could see dark-robed figures running with armfuls of precious books and scrolls. And they tried to save their newest building, the elegant residence built by their beloved departed abbot, Henry of Blois. There was no attempt to save the barns, storehouses, and shops from the rain of sparks, but everywhere Bors could see figures, dark robes flapping in frenzy, struggling to save the affrighted animals.

Then Bors saw the miracle. The Old Church standing at the far west end of Dunstan's church under its lead cover (in which some said St. Patrick and some said St. David had encased it) stood unscathed. Always, since first Bors had been given to the abbey at the age of five, he had loved the Old Church. In recent years when his dreams came to him with greater frequency and sometimes the sense of expectancy swelled within his chest to the bursting, he had felt that somehow the Old Church was part of whatever it was that God wanted him to do. Perhaps this was it.

Perhaps this was the great mission for which he, a penniless, uneducated, orphaned sheep-herder, had been chosen by God—to protect the ancient church, which the hand of Christ Himself had built to honor His blessed virgin mother. With a shout Bors bounded from the bucket line, bringing a hail of shouts on his departing back as he caused the woman to his right to drop her bucket and the man on the left to slosh his half empty. But Bors could think only of one thing. The Old Church must be saved. He must save it.

As he ran, his desperation increased, for he could see smoke rising from blackened patches on the sacred wattled walls and the lead-covered roof sagging as the soft metal bent in the heat. Dark figures thronged around this, the most sacred building in the land, doing all humanly possible to save it. Bors sought desperately for water and a vessel to carry it in. Why had he not brought a bucket with him? His eye lighted on a half-filled watering trough in front of the smoldering remains of a cow shed against the wall. In his confused frenzy he thought of trying to carry the water in his cupped hands. But then he remembered the sacred vessels inside the church. Had anyone thought to carry them out?

Dimly aware of someone shouting a warning to him, he darted inside the smoke-filled chapel. Coughing and choking, his watering eyes could barely see by the red glow through the east window. But he was right. The brothers had been so intent on saving their most precious building that they had not thought to carry out its sacred relics. Bors lunged across the room and with one hand grasped the golden grail from the altar and with the other snatched at a loaf-sized stone carved in the shape of a fish. He had often wondered why such a crude object was kept there among the gold and silver vessels, but now his grasp was instinctive.

He turned toward the door. The grail would serve. He would fill it with water and so fight for the life of the building with all his might. But he never made it to the door. Overcome by smoke, he staggered against a bench and dropped the stone fish. He thought of leaving it. Then without conscious decision, he dropped to his knees to search for it under the bench.

The bench saved his life. For barely were his head and shoulders under the heavy oak form when the thatch of the roof parted just inside the door, and molten lead poured down through the hole, flinging burning thatch into the room.

When Bors woke late that afternoon in an infirmary set up in the abbey guest houses, they told him how, in answer to Garth's frantic insistence, Brothers Jerome and Ambrose had pulled him from the burning chapel only seconds before all four of the wattle walls fell at once, as if God Himself had abandoned the building. Far sicker from the news of the destroyed building than from the searing fire in his burned legs, Bors turned his head. On a small table beside his improvised bed he saw them—the stone fish and the grail.

The harried infirmarer's assistant smeared his goose grease unguent on the last of Bors's burns, slapped a clean rag on it none too gently, and hurried to his next patient. The tallest of the monks, long-faced Brother Ambrose, with a fringe around his tonsure that looked more like straw than hair, stepped forward, his singed robe reeking of smoke. "Ah, you've spotted them then, lad. That was a very foolish thing you did. Foolish, but brave." A tired smile lit the pale blue eyes and made his thin shoulders seem less stooped. "Abbot Peter will be glad to hear of their saving amid so much loss." He stooped and looked more closely at the small figure on the pallet. "Unless my eyes are fading before my years, I believe you to be Bors, the orphan who served at the Beckery grange."

Bors nodded. "Aye. But how did you know?"

"I was assistant to the Master of Novices—was it six years ago now?—when your brother brought you to the abbey with a dower of six sheep because he could not support his younger brothers and sister on the land strips that devolved on him at your father's death. I was much struck by his plight to provide for you all and, praise God, was able to put forth a small urging to Abbot Peter that room and useful work could be found for you when your dowry ran out, for six sheep made but short provision for you."

Bors shifted restlessly on his pallet, then winced as searing pain shot up his leg. Before he could reply, the harried assistant scurried over from the end of the row of pallets that lined the long room and thrust a cup of evil-smelling black liquid at Bors's mouth. "What is it, Brother Eluid?" Ambrose asked.

Eluid blinked nearsightedly and sniffed at the concoction. "Mint, borage, and poppy, mulled in red wine, I should think. Brother Jerome said 'tis soothing."

"Ah, if it's one of Jerome's, it will serve." Ambrose took the cup from Eluid. "I'll see that your patient drinks it."

Eluid looked relieved and hurried to the next pallet. Brother Ambrose put a hand under Bors's head to raise it and held the cup to his lips. When Bors had taken a sip, the monk talked to him again in order to take his mind off the pain. "And what of the brother a few years older than yourself? He must be near fifteen now? Did he also find a place?"

Bors took another sip of the foul-tasting medicine and dropped his head back to the straw mat. "Sir d'Emercy took Ivo to serve as a varlet on the manor. I have heard he is to be made squire to my lord's youngest son at his knighting next Eastertide." Bors tried to keep the envy out of his voice. Yet it was so unfair.

Almost the only thing he could remember of his mother was her long yellow braids hanging below her wimple and her telling him how he was named for an old English knight that once served a great king long and long before the coming of William of Normandy. She must have known such things, for although Bors's father's ancestor had come over with the Conqueror—alas, only as second squire to a landless junior knight—his mother's people had been yeoman farmers on these lands from ancient times. Even with his five-year-old mind, Bors had grasped the implication—he was named for a great knight that he might grow up to become a knight. But when the fever had carried off his parents, Bors was made sheep-herder at the abbey while Ivo served the knights and trained with the squires on his lord's manor. But what galled him most and filled him with aching confusion was the cold loathing from his oldest brother Nyall. He turned his face toward the chalice and fish, but his eyes were closed.

Brother Ambrose laid a cool hand on his forehead. "Ah, Brother Jerome's potion is working. The fever lessens. Sleep now, lad. When Abbot Peter has time for such, he will reward your bravery in saving these precious items."

In his half-conscious state Bors wasn't sure whether Ambrose actually asked him what he would want his reward to be and whether he answered, or whether he only dreamed that he had spoken aloud his desire to learn to read. Really read. Read books such as he had seen the monks carrying from the scriptorium in defiance of the devouring flames.

The poppy juice dulled the pain, and he stood again on the threshold of his treasure house. Were the great jewels letters? No, no, knighthood . . . Then he saw the jeweled hilt of a sword and would have reached into the room for it if he had known how. Yes! Knighthood was the great shining that he saw. Yet, even in his poppy-sleep he knew that knighthood was impossible—no matter how he longed for it. For to be a landless knight meant to be at the beck and call of any lord who would hire a sword to pay a debt of homage to his overlord. The jewels beckoned, and he felt the great swelling of expectancy in his chest—and the frustration of not knowing what it meant or how to reach it.

He tossed his head back and forth on the mat, and the golden chalice of the Old Church floated into the treasure room. It grew to fill the doorway, and its shining overpowered all the jewels in the room. Bors stepped backward and fell to his knees before it. The dream faded, and he slept.

By the next morning, with all the quickly recovered vigor of an eleven-year-old, Bors wanted two things—food and activity. A serving lad brought him a small wheat loaf and mug of ale to break his fast. Sometime later when Eluid, who looked as if he hadn't slept for days, came to check his impatient patient, he shook his head. "Nay, and if you be getting up now, you'll tear the healing from your burns, and God and I'll have it all to do over again. Bide you on your pallet." He replaced the dressing on the most severe burns on Bors's left calf and ankle and hurried on to the next mat. Bors tangled his fingers in the singed coat of the faithful Garth who hadn't left his side all night and determined to wait.

May turned to June, and Bors knew that in the sheep pastures of Beckery the primroses would long have faded, and tiny yellow and white daisies would be dotting the green fields. But when Brother Ambrose escorted him from the infirmary, still propped on a crutch on his left side, there was little of flowers and greenness to be seen in the enclave.

He stood for a long time amid the charred rubble where once had stood the elegant gatehouse of Abbot Henry de Blois, he who was brother to King Stephen. "But it's all gone." The words were spoken in amazement and mourning. Piles of charred rubble and broken stone filled the enclosure from wall to wall. Only two structures remained—a small chamber and chapel built by Abbot Robert, where Ambrose told him the monks were now living, and the fine bell tower—one of Abbot Henry's last achievements before he became Bishop of Winchester.

The great Church of St. Dunstan with its round arches, supporting buttresses, and stalwart pillars that proclaimed the glory of God with such assurance; the new Chapter House where monks carried out the business of running the monastery; the new cloister with its symmetrical rows of arches and pillars on all four sides of an Italian garden; the new infirmary, dormitory, and the reredorter with its finely engineered system for washing and waste disposal—all were gone. Now the fine drains and flushing waterways were clogged with ash and fallen stone, and if Bors had not had a keen memory born of a voracious curiosity to understand everything around him, he would have no idea what the blackened mounds had once been.

And who could list what had been inside those buildings? Tapestries and silks, vestments of brocade and gold embroidery, carved and ivory-inlaid altar furniture, jeweled vessels of silver and gold . . . Brother Ambrose followed Bors's gaze to the spot where the library and scriptorium had once stood. "Aye. We rescued what we could—but the rest are all gone. The works of Origen, Jerome, and Augustine . . ." Ambrose's voice caught, and he stood silent, shaking his head.

All across the enclave black-robed brothers bent over the piles of rubble, some on their knees sifting ashes, others heaving heavy stones aside that nothing that could be recovered from the desolation would be missed. But it was little indeed. The rapacious flames had been thorough.

"An ancestor of mine—oh, far back in Saxon times—served in the scriptorium here. I was delighted to find an exquisite volume signed by Ulnoth of Ulfstead. He had a particularly fine hand with colors—like in the making of stained glass. It seemed to me that his reds outshone all others, and he had a special way of laying the gold beside it so that his capitals looked like fine jewelry that one could lift from the page and offer to a king to wear on his cloak . . ." His voice faded.

"Was it—?"

Ambrose shook his head. "All gone with the rest. There was a book—a very small book of Saxon poetry—two or three hundred years old. I recall one poem I loved for its aching sense of loss:

> *Splendid is this masonry; the fates destroyed it.*
> *The strong buildings crashed; the work of giants molder away.*

Again he was silent.

"Giants?" Bors blinked at this very unmonkish idea.

"Aye, child. Giants of the faith. Men gigantic in vision and faith and endurance." He paused. "But we can praise God that when Brother William came from Malmesbury to work and write here, he quoted from many of our books in his history, so the words will live on in another form."

Bors nodded. Then his eyes fell on the charred remains of the Old Church. He moved toward it at a jerking pace because his youthful energy would run and leap, but his awkwardness with his crutch and the pain of the still-unhealed burn held him back, as did the clutter in his way. He stopped before the pitifully small mound of ashes. They looked much like the remains of a reed basket brother Gellert had once let get too near the fire. After several moments, he looked up, his dark eyes snapping fiercely. "How could our Lord let such happen to something built by His own hand?"

Brother Ambrose shook his head. "Bors, lad, is not the whole earth His handiwork? And do not storms, fires, and, yes, the hand of man ravage it? Is not man himself created by God and even made in His image—yet do not sickness, hunger, and wars ravage him—to say nothing of the wages of sin?"

Bors looked at his own bandaged leg beneath his short brown tunic. Brother Jerome had assured him it would be sound in time, but severely scarred and prone to pain in winter chills. Yes, all on earth was perishable.

If the great monastery and its treasures could go so quickly, nothing could be permanent. And then he thought of the treasure house of his dreaming. Was this what he had been dreaming of and now could never reach because it was destroyed? Or was the dream a warning that if he ever reached it, whatever his treasures signified would be lost as quickly as this?

Brother Ambrose smiled down at him from his six-foot height, and his pale blue Saxon eyes twinkled. "And not quite all is lost. I saved the greatest of the chronicles. Geoffrey of Monmouth is still with us."

The bell tolled from Abbot Henry's tower, calling the brotherhood to High Mass. It was ten of the morning and, catastrophic fire or no, the Rule continued, the need for prayer continued, God's grace continued. From every corner of the grounds monks with their hands and faces as black as their robes picked their way around charred piles to the small chapel that was all that remained to them. Still they gathered in order, hands folded, heads bowed, moving forward in a line, chanting a psalm of praise.

Bors felt inside his tunic and brought out the little packet he wore hung on a thong around his neck. He drew out the string of smooth, round wooden beads Brother Arald had given him when first he went to work at the grange. When the great bell of Glastonbury sounded the hours across the marshes, he would join the brothers in their prayers wherever he happened to be in the field. At least he could join them in the spirit of prayer, as he did now, though he lacked the Latin to recite the actual psalms.

He assured Brother Ambrose he could get back to the infirmary on his own and then hobbled to a tumbled stone beside the crumbled gatehouse. There, with the sun of a June morning warming his dark curls and the chants of the monks echoing across the monastery grounds, Bors crossed himself and ran the beads through his fingers as Brother Arald had taught him. At the end of the chain Bors felt comforted and more in tune with God's world than he had since the fire-filled night that now seemed long ago.

"Come on, Garth. Brother Eluid will be serving dinner. Mayhap he'll have a bone for you." The infirmary was allowed meat every day for those who needed it to speed their recovery.

He lifted his eyes to the east beyond the wall where the Tor rose clean and green above the destruction. He watched the white specks of sheep grazing peacefully on the steep slopes. A smile that had been too long dampened crossed his face. There was something of God's creation that was indestructible. The Tor stood eternal watch over all, the ancient chapel on its brow untouched by smoke or spark. The brothers were right to continue their worship, for surely God had given them a symbol of His abiding presence. But one must lift his eyes above the debris to see it.

Though Bors made his way slowly, he still arrived before dinner was ready. He was sitting on a bench by the doorway when he saw a familiar broad-shouldered figure striding toward him with a smile on his ruddy face, his robe kilted above his knees that he might move faster. "Gellert!" Bors cried. Garth saw him at the same moment and sprang forward with a yip of excitement.

Gellert stood before them, his feet spread wide, hands on his hips, his thick eyebrows drawn together in a scowl. "And is this the way ye obey my orders? Did not I tell you to run quickly and bring us word? Not to take up residence here that ye might spend your days sitting in the sun."

Bors started to answer, but Brother Gellert couldn't hold his pose and threw back his head in a bellow of laughter. "Aye, never fear, lad. They told us of your bravery in saving the sacred grail and the stone fish carved by the hand of St. Peter the Big Fisherman himself."

"Oh—!" Bors was speechless. No one had told him the history of the little rock carving.

Then Gellert looked at the crutch leaning against the wall, and his eyes went soft. "And how are ye, lad?" He sat down beside Bors.

"Oh, I'm fine. That is, I will be. Brother Jerome says I must hobble on a stick for several weeks yet so I won't pull the healing apart. But it doesn't hurt—much." He had been going to say at all, but he had been trained to strict honesty. "I'll be back to help with the sheep before autumn."

"Nay, lad. Did not they tell you? I've just been speaking with Abbot Peter. You're to be given schooling as a reward for your bravery. The Old Church chalice is the only one saved from the fire—I doubt not that the brothers are using it at their mass right now." He paused to clear his throat. "You'll like that, won't you? I always thought you had a liking for thoughtful things." When Bors didn't reply, he hurried on. "But if it doesn't suit you, Brother Arald and the sheep and I'll take you back in a minute." He smiled.

"No—I—I'll like it fine—I think. But what about Garth? Will they let me keep him here?"

Brother Gellert's big freckled hand rested on Bors's knee. "Nay, lad. We can make do without ye, but not without our best sheepdog."

Bors reached out by instinct and tangled his fingers in the shaggy coat. The hair that he kept well-brushed was alive and springy under his fingers. Garth leaned toward him and rested his head in Bors's lap. Bors nodded—more to shake down the lump in his throat than to agree to Garth's leaving.

The tinkle of a bell inside the infirmary told him dinner was ready. He pushed Garth's head off his lap. "Off with you then. Look what you've done—shedding hair on my tunic so I'll be scolded by Brother Jerome." He turned to Brother Gellert. "We must wash before *and after* every meal here."

Gellert laughed and shoved himself to his feet. "Aye, lad, but a gentleman must have fine manners. They'll make one of ye that could serve at King Henry's court."

Bors watched them leave. Gellert's rusty hair was as shaggy as the black and white sheepdog that trotted beside him—the two best friends he'd ever had. He sat long, unmoving. Then, when the bend in the road took them out of sight, he grasped his crutch and thrust himself up on his good foot to claim his share of the roast mutton he smelled behind him.

2

By the time the grapes in the vineyard on the south side of Wearyall Hill were bursting with purple ripeness and the apples in the orchard were sweet to fermenting for perfect cider-making, Bors had long abandoned his crutch and was studying under the guidance of Brother Ambrose, now Master of Boys and Novices. Bors prayed all the hours, crowded into the tiny chapel with seventy-some other souls, but he still slept on the improvised pallet in the infirmary, for there was no other place. When the coming winter should make study out of doors impractical, they did not know where they would continue, for no progress had been made toward rebuilding. Abbot Peter had died a month ago, and Prior Edmund's worried brow and nervous fluttering told how little hope he held for a quick replacement.

Brother Ambrose gathered the seven abbey schoolboys around his tall form and, with the heavy volume balanced on his thin knees, bent his straw-thatch tonsured head over the words and read. No boy sat with more rapt attention than Bors as their teacher read to them from the chronicle of Geoffrey of Monmouth:

> After the death of Uther Pendragon, the barons of Britain did come together from the divers provinces and did bear on hand Dubric, Archbishop of

> Caerleon, that he should crown as king, Arthur, the late king's son. For sore need was upon them; seeing that when the Saxons heard of Uther's death, they had invited their fellow-countrymen from Germany and were bent upon exterminating the Britons . . .

So Bors reveled in his daily lessons. But as the autumn gold of the leaves deepened and the scurry of animals preparing for winter increased, so did the activity of the brothers, who knew that this winter after the fire must be a hard one. There was less and less time for studies as Brother Eluid worked to increase his store of herbs and medicines and the cellarer required much help and long hours to press the yellow curds from cows' and sheep's milk into thick, round cheeses. Then came the day when all other labors must be put aside. As soon as the boys had attended Prime and eaten their usual breakfast of bread and ale, they were sent out into the orchard where all from the monastery, and the village as well, were gathering for cider-making. The abbey's large stone cider press stood in the middle of the fruit-heavy trees. Harnessed to its pole, the abbey's best ox plodded in a circle as basket after basket of fruit was dumped into the wooden hopper feeding into the press, and a sweet, amber stream ran into buckets below. The brother in charge gave Bors and the other schoolboys willow baskets and set them to gathering fruit from branches and ground.

All day it went on, as all from the village and the abbey's outlying farms, as well as the boys, tipped basket after basket of fruit into the press. The vats of juice were drawn off in rambling carts to the brew-house.

It was the heady scent of the half-fermented apples more than anything else that stirred memories for Bors. These were his only clear memories of life on d'Emercy's manor, save brief ones of his mother. There the cider-making had been the same as here and was always his favorite time. He and Nyall and Ivo had taken the apples from the trees in their toft to their lord's press. Their lord's steward had extracted his share for use of the mill, and then the three boys trudged home with buckets of heavy, sweet-smelling liquid for their mother to brew. She liked to brew her own rather than send it to the manor brew-house as most chose to do.

Those were the days before Nyall came to hate him, when the return of the handsome eldest son to the cottage of Martin Bachiler was a great event for the Bachiler family—especially to young Bors who idolized his big brother.

Neither of the elder Bachiler men were much at home. Martin, as the most prosperous freeman on the manor—having behind him many generations of ancestors who had their own assarts—served as d'Emercy's bailiff. He left much of the overseeing of their own landstrips to his wife Elswith, whose family had been yeomen farmers also for generations. But that meant that Martin spent much of his time at the hall in the service of Sir Heribert d'Emercy. And Nyall, varlet to Herlwin d'Emercy, who would someday succeed his father as lord of the manor, was much away following his squire. But they were jolly times when father and eldest son returned to their own hearth. Bors liked best hearing Nyall's stories of life at the castle of d'Emercy's overlord, Baron Walter de Clifford, where Herlwin was serving his squirehood, learning the manners and skills of a great knight. It seemed, in his memory, the return had most often coincided with cider-making time and increased its joy.

Until the year their parents died and Nyall turned against Bors as sharply as if their parents' deaths had been of his doing—and his fault as well that Nyall must resign his service to Herlwin and see to the Bachiler landstrips. In desperate seeking for reasons, the small Bors had even wondered if the resentment could have sprung from the fact that he alone bore the dark curly hair shot with streaks of red from their Norman ancestry while the others of the Bachiler cottage were Saxon-fair from their mother.

"Bors! Catch!" A boy not much older than himself who had climbed the tree to gather the fruit on the top branches (excepting that which should be left for the birds who would need food this winter) tossed down a rust-and-green-striped sphere. Bors caught it and added it to the basket.

Here on the west side of the hill out of view of the blackened buildings, here where all was sweet-scented and sticky with God's abundance, amid the happy voices of villagers and crowding serfs, it was possible to forget the hopeless situation within the monastery enclosure.

But when the cold weather set in, and unfortunately that year of our Lord 1184 the snows came early and deep, it was impossible to forget the lack of shelter. Never had the brothers spent a less joyful Advent season than that one huddled in their tiny chamber. The only joy was that the snow covered the blackened rubble and broken buildings. Their enforced closeness provided some warmth as the boys huddled around a single candle to hear Brother Ambrose's reading of his beloved chronicles of Geoffrey of Monmouth. And then for the boys came a joyful surprise. Brother Ambrose suggested to Prior Edmund that all boys who had family within traveling distance should be sent home for the whole twelve days of Christmastide.

Great joy for all but Bors, who must face the dislike of his brother, now head of the family. But that was the only position held by the elder Bachiler, for in the six years since Bors had been gone, Nyall had failed to rise to the position of trust on the manor that his father had held. It was a serious comedown for one who had been varlet to Herlwin d'Emercy and in the normal course of things would have become squire when Herlwin won his knighthood. Bors supposed Nyall would somehow manage to blame his lack of fortune on him. But there would also be Ivo, four years his senior, and Aline, two years younger than Bors. What memories he had of them were happy. So perhaps it would not be so bad. Perhaps he could make his peace with Nyall, or at least keep out of his way, and renew acquaintance with his brother and sister. And Christmas on the manor was certain to be a much merrier affair than at the monastery. To Bors's mind double time spent in prayers did not constitute merrymaking.

The manor lay a full day's travel to the northwest where on a clear day one could look across Severn into Wales. It was recorded in the *Domesday Book* in the time of Sir Heribert's ancestor who had served William of Normandy: "Of the land of the manor of d'Emercy, Gilbert holds 9½ hides, land for 9 plows. Now in lordship 2 plows. 20 villagers with 3 smallholders have 7 plows. Meadow, 200 acres less 20; pasture, 80 acres."

Alan Bachiler had been one of those smallholders in the year of our Lord 1086, farming his own freely held fields to supplement his income as servant to Sir Gilbert. And so the pattern remained.

The manor house stood at the top of the road, a little apart from the village next to the stone church with its square Norman tower. Beyond the manor house lay the level, well-drained fields of the lord's demesne with gentle wooded slopes beyond. Inside the wooden fence of the manor were the stable, bakehouse, fish pond, and dovecote. At the bottom of the street past the smithy, alehouse, well, and marketplace were the cottages of the freeholders and tenant farmers with their field strips beyond their enclosed tofts. Bors rode into town in the soft straw bed of a farmer's cart, having had the great good fortune to catch a ride for the better part of his journey, thus freeing the young brother who had accompanied him. Black and white speckled chickens fluttered every which way to the side of the dirt road before the cart, but the two red cows being driven to the common pasture made no hurry to unblock the road. At the first cottage, Bors jumped off the back of the wagon and waved his thanks to the farmer, who continued on his way.

The Bachiler cottage was a sturdy wattle and daub house, well whitewashed with its oak half-timbers blackened with pitch to prevent weathering. The thick thatch of the roof hung low over the eaves. Although the air bore a late December chill, a pale sun shone intermittently, and the slatted windows were unshuttered.

A nine-year-old girl appeared in the doorway, the skirts of her long yellow kirtle tucked into its armholes and the hem of her green undershirt pinned up for ease of movement. Pale hair fell loose down her back from under the smooth white coif banded under her chin. She had the front of her kirtle gathered into a pouch to hold bread crumbs and wheat. "Here, chick, chick. Here—" She stopped mid-cast as the chickens scurried to her call. "If you seek my brother, he is at the alehouse." She stared with frank curiosity at Bors.

"Aline?" he asked. She gave a startled nod at hearing her name on the lips of a stranger. "Of course you don't remember me." He broke into his ready, winning smile. "You were only three years old when I was sent to the monks, but I am your brother."

The girl dropped her kirtle, dumping the chicken feed in a single mound for the hens to fight over, and fled into the darkness of the cottage. "Ancret!" she shouted.

Bors heard a scuttling and scraping within the cottage. A sharp-featured old woman with wrinkled skin and bright eyes poked her white-coifed head out the door.

"Who comes here claiming right to this house? Get you up to the hall. Sir Heribert's cooks will find scraps enough if ye're in need of food."

Bors stood his ground, the smile still on his lips. "Aye. Dear old Ancret. And have you forgotten me? You who were a better nurse to me than my own mother when I fell from the apple tree and broke my arm."

The gnarled hands reached out to clasp his and draw him near for closer scrutiny before Ancret gave a gap-toothed grin. "Saints be praised! It is my Bors who was like to my own son when your dear mother Elswith was needin' my help. And you so long gone to the monks these old eyes thought never to see you again. Come in, come in, I've a warm bannock for ye—same as you loved when you were no more than four years old." She turned into the house. "Don't fret, Aline, it's your brother, true enough."

So Bors was welcomed home. Into the dreamlike familiarity of the blue-washed walls, trestle table and stools, storage chests and benches, with hams and sausages hanging from the rafters to cure over the smoking fire. He looked around for the rest of the family. He was unlikely to see Ivo unless at church or at the Christmas feast Sir Heribert would give for all on his manor, for Ivo slept in the Great Hall of the manor with the other varlets and servants. But Nyall he would see soon enough, for he heard a stomping of heavy boots and a tall, broad-shouldered form filled the doorway. "See who has come!" Aline dropped the wool she was carding for Ancret's spindle and ran to the newcomer.

Nyall pulled his thick wool capuchon off his head with a yank at its pointed end, tossed his shock of straight yellow hair out of his eyes, and stood, feet planted squarely in the middle of the room, scowling at the interloper. "What do ye here? The brothers did not put you out?"

"No. It's just a Christmas visit. There was a fire at the monastery—" He would have offered his smile to show that he came in hope of peace, but Nyall cut him off.

"Ah! Then they'll take ye back as quick."

"No, Nyall—you can't mean it!" Aline gripped his arm with both hands. "He's only just come—a brother I'd forgotten I had."

Ancret looked out through the open doorway. "You'll not be sending one out tonight. I smell a north wind rising. There'll be snow before morning."

"Aye. There's straw in the byre. We've no extra brychans." Nyall turned to pour himself a mug of ale from the tankard on the trestle. And that was as close to a welcome as Bors was to receive.

But there was little enough time to worry about his welcome, for it was the eve of Christmas. Already the dark was gathering in, and soon it would be time for Bors and Aline to join the other village children in leading a cow, a sheep, and a donkey into the village church that the animals might warm the Holy Babe with their breath.

With brightly colored capuchons pulled tight over their ears and woolen cloaks wrapped around their shoulders, for the first white flakes Ancret predicted had already begun to fall, the sixty-some children of the village led, prodded, and pushed the lowing, bleating, braying animals up the muddy road. Wooden torches, sputtering as the snowfall increased, lighted their way. Even inside the sacred building the babble was little subdued, for the joy of Christmas was on all, and smiling Father Cenred, round of face and belly, was never harsh with those who came to celebrate.

The animals were led to the altar, but Bors held back, struck anew with wonder at the paintings on the walls. In the six years of his absence they had neither faded nor shrunk, as so many things will with the passage of time, but glowed with seeming life and motion in the wavering candlelight—from Creation to the Last Judgment, the whole story was here. Tonight the Babe in the manger held him for a special time, but he hurried on past the Calling of the Twelve and the Sermon on the Mount and the Crucifixion and the Resurrection, to his favorites—the Baptism of Bran the Blessed, the first Christian Briton; St. Patrick floating over from Ireland on his own altar; and St. Augustine baptizing King Aethelberht.

An elbow in his ribs made him step forward to make room for latecomers, and Bors's gaze swept quickly past the Last Judgment with its angels, demons, and scarlet flames of Hell. Then Father Cenred called his flock to worship. "Let us pray that Christmas morning will find us at peace." As Bors prayed for peace within his family, his mind wandered, trying to understand his own shortcomings that caused Nyall's dislike. He was brought back to the service by the responsorial psalm.

"Sing to the Lord, all you lands. Sing to the Lord; bless His name," Father Cenred chanted.

"Today is born our Savior, Christ the Lord," the people answered.

"Announce His salvation day after day. Tell His glory among the nations."

"Today is born our Savior, Christ the Lord."

"They shall exult before the Lord, for He comes; He comes to rule the earth. He shall rule the world with justice."

"Today is born our Savior, Christ the Lord."

Bors knelt with Aline and Ancret at the altar and received the grace of Christ's broken body from Brother Cenred. But he did not see Nyall at the service.

The next day fresh white snow lay piled against the doors and shutters of the cottages and barns when Bors awoke to the joyful chiming of the church bell. A sharp wind gusted in icy blasts, but no blizzard could have deterred the villagers from making their way at midday to Sir Heribert's annual Christmas feast.

By now Aline had taken her newfound brother to her heart, and all the way up the village street she called to her friends to see him—"new-come from the black monks in Glastonbury." Then they made their way through the gatehouse of the manor, past the gentle cooings from the dovecote that provided fresh meat for their lord's table all winter. Up the outside stairs they climbed to the Great Hall decorated with branches of fir, yew, holly, ivy, and mistletoe that gave a fresh, spicy scent to mingle with that of the dried herbs strewn in the floor rushes. The fire in the central hearth blazed high, and the smoke swirled round the garlanded rafters before making its way out the hole in the roof. Torches in iron brackets on the side beams gave additional light, for it was a gray day, and the windows, recessed deep in the thick walls, admitted little light.

On a raised platform at the far end of the hall Heribert d'Emercy and Lady Athelais sat in the center of a long table. Bors recognized Father Cenred at the end of the table, but none of the others. "That is Herlwin, he whom Nyall says broke our family fortunes." Aline pointed to a darkly handsome young man in his late twenties. "The lady in the blue dress is Alys. She was eighteen at Michaelmas. Everyone says she's soon to be betrothed. I do hope the groom is handsome, for I think her most beautiful—" Aline paused to enjoy a dreamy sigh before she continued, "In the green and scarlet coat with a peacock feather in his cap—that's Rychart, he who our Ivo is varlet to— Oh! There he is now!" And she bolted forward to greet her brother who stood at the elbow of the youngest d'Emercy, waiting to do him service.

Bors was reluctant to follow, but was unable to shake off the firm grip she had on his sleeve. "Ivo, Ivo—can you guess who I have?" She paused long enough to be sure she had her brother's attention, but not long enough for him to answer. "Bors! Our brother Bors who has been with the monks these many years! I had not known him. Would you?"

Ivo shook his head as if to make sense of the words and looked at the youth in front of him who was his equal, if not superior in height, even though four years his junior. Ivo rubbed his temple with the palm of his hand, and as if that brought it all into focus, bounded forward with a jerk and clasped Bors by the shoulder. "Bors! Have you come back? Will you stay?"

Bors smiled and bobbed his head in time to Ivo shaking his shoulders as if his head were loose, which made them all laugh and averted any need to answer awkward questions. "I'm just here for Christmas," he said at last. "Then I'll return to the black brothers."

Ivo turned to his master and presented Bors to Rychart. The youngest d'Emercy was a friendly, easygoing lad of sixteen who found amusement in all life had to offer and welcomed all who came. "You must let my father greet you, for he'll remember the son of his former bailiff—even if I don't." He grinned and gave Bors a slap on the back that nearly landed him at Lord Heribert's feet.

Then it was time to take their places at the long trestle tables that filled the room, for the musicians began a merry tune on pipe, drums, and trumpet, and the steward entered the hall bearing to the high table a boar's head on a great platter. An army of servants followed, carrying first trays piled high with flat loaves of bread to be used as trenchers, and then platters of ham, bacon, and cheese, great bowls of meat stew, jug after jug of ale, and that wonderful annual treat for the village children—sweetmeats.

At first Bors, who had for years known nothing but the plain fare of the abbey and even plainer, though plentiful, food of the Beckery grange, found such abundance overwhelming. Since the fire, although all had continued to be fed regularly, and Brother Almoner even managed to continue his usual doles to the poor, the food had been plainer than ever. So Bors, with the appetite of a growing boy, attacked everything with both hands in his enthusiasm, forgetting to reserve his little finger free of grease for sprinkling salt, and not bothering to cut his meat into smaller portions with the knife he wore in his belt. Something in the back of his mind reminded him that Brother Ambrose would be appalled, but Brother Ambrose was not here, and everyone around him, thus far down the room to be out of sight of the nobility, was eating with the same gusto.

But at last Bors found he could hold not another bite—not even the leg of the excellent roast capon he held in his hand. Reluctantly, he flung it to the brown hound enjoying his Christmas feast under the table. When all in the hall were equally sated, servants cleared pitchers, platters, and salt cellars from the lower tables, and the trestle boards were stacked against the wall to make more room for the entertainment. Corviere, Lord d'Emercy's minstrel, was first, skipping into the room in a gold and scarlet belted knee-length tunic, moving in time to the bells on the pointed toes of his shoes and on the point of his capuchon. Tonight Corviere would direct the entertainment as the Lord of Misrule. Accompanying himself on a pear-shaped rebec, whose three strings he sometimes bowed and sometimes plucked, he began the festivities with a carol in honor of the drink Sir Heribert had supplied in such abundance:

To English ale, and Gascon wine,
doth Christmas much incline
May all such joys from God above
freely flow to all who Christmas love.
Lords, by Christmas and our host,
listen now to hear my toast—
Let Christmas reign
with all misrule,
and so I bid you all, Wassail!

The toast was greeted with a hearty "Drink hail!" from all in the room, for that was one Saxon custom not even William the Conqueror and all his Norman overlords had been able to abolish.

A traveling jongleur in a much-patched tunic that had once been a bright red and blue came next, catapulting to the center of the hall with a series of handsprings that brought cries of delight from his audience. Then he amazed them with feats of skill—juggling balls, plates, and rings in rapid succession, some tossed so high it seemed surely they would tangle in the yew-boughs hanging from the rafters. Then came the finale—juggling flaming torches with his feet—the excitement enhanced by the element of danger should he falter and drop a torch to set the floor rushes alight—even though servants stood in a ready ring with pitchers of water. At the end none cheered louder nor clapped harder than the youngster who for six years had celebrated the birth of the Christ Child with a solemn mass and a rare addition of meat to the dinner menu.

Daring to sit on Lord Heribert's high table itself—for nothing was forbidden the Lord of Misrule on this night—Corviere entertained with another carol and had begun a jig to the tune of his own bells when a louder ringing of bells and clapping of sticks turned every head to the entrance. "The mummers! The mummers!" The cry rose, and Corviere sprang off the table in a great leap, turned a series of somersaults that took him to the door, and welcomed the troupe of players with a sweeping bow. They crowded through the opening, stamping the snow from their rough boots, their masks and headdresses picking up the light of torches and roaring fire. "The mummers!" the cry continued. "Make way!" All pushed against the walls that the players might have ample room.

Corviere, shaking a stick tied with ribbons and bells, capered to the head of the hall and swept another bow before the high table and the assembled villagers. "With joy, with joy, come strike a light, draw near and see our merry act tonight. We've dreadful scenes enough in store, so faint not, ladies, at our antics. A fearsome dragon you shall see, foul fiend of Hell; the innocent maid he would devour. And lusty Turk, the devil's man, with curved scimitar to rule the Holy Land. But have no fear, for all will right. God has a champion to win the day, for we here present—St. George's play!"

With a great jingling of bells the minstrel sprang back to sit on a corner of the dais below the high table while the audience clapped and called, "Come in! Come in, St. George! England's knight! Come in, brave George!" For ever since the return of the first Crusaders near to a hundred years ago with their tales of the martyred soldier who had been raised to sainthood by Emperor Constantine, St. George had become the champion knight of Christendom.

In answer to their cries the tallest player strode to the center of the room, clad in white tunic with a glowing red cross on his breast, brandishing a wooden sword. But the cheers that greeted him turned to boos and snarls as his antagonist followed in his wake—a black-clad, black-bearded heathen Turk, brandishing an evilly curved scimitar.

But both hero and villain were overshadowed by the next entrance. Roaring and snorting, jagged bits of red-silk flame fluttering from his saw-toothed snout, the dragon swept around the room, sending small children tumbling backward with delighted shrieks. "Fire-eater, I of tooth and claw, I must have meat for me to eat!" The dragon made another sweep around the hall, whipping at his proposed victims with his tail and flailing his sharp claws, until his eye lighted on the youngest mummer lad, clad in a blue tunic with a gold circlet around his long black wig. "Ah, the King of Egypt's daughter—she'll be meat for my delight." Fire-eater flung at the Egyptian princess who ran shrieking around the room.

"St. George! St. George! Save me, save me, St. George!"

Into the fire-lit circle strode St. George, no less glorious for what he might lack in Christian humility. "Here come I, St. George the brave. Here come I, St. George the noble. Here come I, St. George, to rescue you, fair maid." After several more bows to the audience, he finally turned to engage the dragon.

"Who is this that seeks my dragon blood? Who mocks my strength with words so loud?" Fire-eater clacked his great evil teeth at St. George.

"It is I, St. George of England! To fight for right and truth and ever for the God of might. 'Tis I who've come to do you battle, and I who'll kill you till you're dead. With one blow I'll lop off your head." The hall rang with cheers.

"My head is iron, my body steel, my arms and legs are beaten brass. No man can draw my blood or bring my strength to heel."

The ensuing battle was fierce and bloody, fought first on one side of the hall, then on the other, with both characters pausing to sneak bows to the audience after a particularly good foray. But at last came the climax, locked combat of sword, tooth, and claw, right before the high table, the noise of battle drowned in the children's shrieks and the adults' shouts. Until at last, both Christian hero and evil villain lay on the scrambled floor rushes, the firelight suggesting blood flowing out in pools.

A tiny girl in front of Bors flung her hands to her face and sobbed. Another ran to her mother's arms. "St. George, he's dead!" Even those who had seen the play many times held their breath. Would this be the year the miracle didn't happen? Was St. George truly slain this year?

Then with a single leap, George bounded to his feet, grasped his dropped sword, and capered around the hall to the relieved shouts of his audience. "I am St. George of England's pride, God's man of courage bold! With sword and buckler by my side, and Christ's cross upon my breast, I won a crown of gold! I fought the fiery dragon to the slaughter and saved the King of Egypt's daughter!"

The princess danced around the circle with curtsies while Corviere dragged the dragon off by one foot.

Bors had dim memories of the scene that would come next when St. George would fight the heathen Turk—a battle that would end in his own martyrdom for the faith. Bors didn't want to miss a single moment of the action, but he had drunk as much ale and cider at one meal as he would normally in several days, and he simply must go outside. "I'll be right back," he whispered to Aline, and hurried across the crowded room to the door.

The gray afternoon had deepened to the black of a midwinter night, although the white snow gave lambent light for Bors to make his way quickly across the courtyard and around the corner of the stable. He was just heading back to the hall when he caught sight of the tall figure he had looked for all day. Nyall opened the door of the croft under the stairs that led up to the Great Hall and entered the storage room there. *Probably to fetch another cask of ale for Sir Heribert's steward,* Bors thought, and on impulse followed his brother.

The storeroom door stood open, and Bors crossed quietly on the soft snow. An angry voice came from within. "What is the meaning of this?" The voice that was not Nyall's continued, "What trick would you try to bleed me by now?"

Nyall's voice muttered an answer Bors couldn't distinguish.

"I'm warning you, Bachiler, just you try, and I'll tell all. Little difference it would make now anyway with the lady in her grave."

Again Bors could not hear the reply. He strained forward, then flung himself back into the shadows as two dark figures emerged from the storeroom and stamped up the stairs. Bors just dared to stick his head out as he heard the door creak open, and he saw the leading figure in the light of the open doorway, fleetingly, but it was enough. Why was Herlwin d'Emercy making threats about a dead lady to his brother? What lady? The only lady Bors knew that was in her grave was his mother. But what could the death of Elswith Bachiler mean to d'Emercy?

Bors determined to ask Ancret. If anyone would know she would. She had lived on this manor since Sir Heribert's father was a boy.

But Bors did not have the opportunity to ask, for all the cottage slept late the next morning in honor of the first day of Christmas and rose to see a bright sun shining on snow-free roads. Nyall grasped onto the sudden thaw as an excuse to hustle Bors off the manor. "We'll to Glastonbury today. It may be our only chance to return ye to the monks, for who knows how long the thaw will last."

He shoved bread, cheese, and cold meat into a saddlebag over the protests of Ancret and Aline. "You can't be taking him now." "Not today, with the Twelve Days just begun!" "He was to stay for the whole time. The trained bear hasn't come yet. Just one more day, Nyall?"

But the pleas went unheard, and Bors had no more than time to hug Ancret and Aline farewell before he was hoisted up pillion behind his brother and found the d'Emercy manor at his back. All across the silent, muddy miles, Bors wondered whether this was an act of kindness that Nyall should take him to the abbey himself, as he had the first time six years ago, or whether it was simply his best assurance that the task was done promptly and surely.

3

ut Bors did not return to the somber place he had left behind. The entire village and monastic enclosure vibrated with energy and excitement and a muddle of activity, for word had come that King Henry was holding his usual Christmas court at Windsor. Then he would ride to Salisbury where his queen, Eleanor of Aquitaine, had been kept as his virtual prisoner these past ten years—she who had dared urge their sons to rebellion against their father. Then the royal party would continue to Gloucester Castle—with a stop at Glastonbury.

The king never traveled with fewer than one hundred courtiers and attendants. Where in all the village and burned-out monastery were so many beds to be found? Even if the royal courtiers would deign to lie on the monks' improvised straw pallets, there would not be enough. And what of provisions? One meal for the court, and a scanty one at that, would exhaust their fire-ravaged stores.

There was no choice. The largest of the guest houses would be prepared the best possible for the king, while Prior Edmund and the brothers staying there crowded with the other monks, novices, and schoolboys into a crudely restored corner of the old dormitory. The others of the entourage must simply fend the best they could. At least they had been spared some treasures. *Our Lady of Glastonbury,* a fine painting of the virgin from the days of St. Dunstan or beyond, and many said painted by the very hand of St. Dunstan himself, had been miraculously spared the flames in King Ine's Church and had been the brothers' great solace in their mourning for all else that was lost. They would place *Our Lady* in the king's chamber that she might bless his visit. And they had the golden grail to serve him at High Mass. There would be no new hangings of blue and scarlet in the king's chamber, no succulently roasted capons and suckling pigs to grace the royal table, nor fine Gascon wines for the king's palate, but such as they had they would give.

And one other treasure remained, untouched by the fire because it stood outside the enclosure. Fire or no fire, the Glastonbury thorn had made its glorious annual Christmas blooming—perhaps more glorious and more a promise this year because of the greater need. If only the blooming would stay fresh, unspoiled by frost or winter wind, branches of it should adorn the king's chamber.

Bors joined into the frenzy with the others, continuing to haul off carts of rubble that King Henry's progress might be as little impeded as possible when he walked around the enclosure to view their sorry devastation. For surely that was why he was coming. Why else would the king choose now to favor them with a royal visit after so many years of passing by without a pause, even when Henry of Blois, the king's own kinsman, was abbot? Or perhaps he came to pay homage to the martyred Saxon King Edmund, whose grave rightly should have been visited long before, especially when King Henry went through a period of public mourning and pilgrimage-making to atone for his part in the martyrdom of Archbishop Thomas á Becket at Canterbury fifteen years ago . . . But now, when they had so little to offer, when mere survival was so difficult, when they hadn't even an abbot, but merely a prior, and a nervous flutter of a prior at that, to do the honors, now King Henry must visit.

For all their effort, however, when the day came for Henry's arrival three weeks later, there was little accomplished to show. But at least one small branch of the sacred thorn with white blossom, red berries, and green leaves of miraculous blooming stood in a water pitcher on a table beside the bed prepared for the king. It was a clear day, the ground frozen hard to make traveling firm under foot and the sun sparkling hard and cold on frosted rocks and branches. Bors and the other boys, freed from Brother Ambrose for the day, scrambled to the top of the Tor to see who should catch first glimpse of the great procession. It was cold, and there was no protection save their cloaks and capuchons, but they hadn't long to wait.

On the clear winter air they heard the notes of a trumpet before their eyes caught sight of sun glinting on metal trappings. "I see!" shouted Bors, but his shout was drowned by similar cries from at least two other boys, and so the matter was never settled as to who was first. Within moments the little cluster on the hill were all shouting and pointing, for all could see the red and blue quartered gonfalon of Henry Plantagenet. From that distance they couldn't make out the gold lions of England and fleur-de-lis of France that decorated the banner, but they knew they were there. And soon they could distinguish individual figures making their way toward them on the old Roman road. There could be no mistaking the figure riding the rangy roan horse behind the heralds. The tall, broad frame of King Henry was royally garbed in purple and scarlet with touches of gold and miniver. But it wasn't just the fine apparel. Surely none but king of the empire stretching from Wales to Italy could ride so proudly, attended so closely by knights and squires of such magnificence. In stark contrast to the bright colors, the king's chaplains came next, all three on white horses to better exhibit their dark attire. But none made a finer show than the ladies, some riding pillion behind knights, some astride their own mounts with their long skirts trailing over the horse's rumps, many with falcons on their wrists.

"You'd think their arms would get tired holding them out for the birds to perch like that," Bors said.

Another boy laughed. "But what lady would want to forego the royal honor of being allowed to fly a falcon?"

Sleek, brown deerhounds bounded at the horses' heels, their keepers walking on the verge. Then a large wagon, its cylinder-shaped red and gold cover providing protection for the ladies inside lumbered by, pulled by four horses.

"Do you suppose Queen Eleanor's in there?" Gildon, the youngest of the boys, asked.

Roger, the oldest, scowled at Gildon from his superior height of knowledge. "Don't be stupid. The king hasn't let her out of guard at Salisbury for ten years. He won't be about to now."

"How do you know?" Gildon held his ground.

"Because everybody who knows anything knows that. He's afraid of her and her sons."

Bors spoke up. "Even since Prince Henry died last year?"

Roger, who never failed to make clear that he was at the monastery to learn Latin and mathematics in order to take his place in the great world and not for any taking of priest's orders, gave a supercilious smile with his answer. "More to the point, why does he bother to keep her prisoner so long after the death of Rosamund the Fair, she that he acknowledged his mistress as soon as Queen Eleanor was safely locked away?"

But Bors's attention was back on the great procession passing below them. The brightly clad knights, ladies, and squires had passed out of view beneath the Tor, and now came the household servants, mostly afoot, leading the pack horses and carts of provisions.

Bors had spent three long days helping weave wattle fences for the confining of the horses—but surely they had greatly underestimated the space they would need. Even in the best of times, how could they or any monastery entertain such an entourage fresh from holding high revels at Windsor Castle?

"Look! They're riding on!" shouted Roger.

Gildon's shout held a note of desperate disappointment. "He's not stopping. The king's not stopping!"

Bors drew aside for a clearer view. "No. Look again. The king stopped. It's the courtiers and servants that are going on!" He yanked his capuchon from his head and flung it into the air in elation. They were saved! He looked closer at the departing cavalcade. The king, his closest knot of perhaps five knights and nine squires, and one of the priests had turned aside. The others were going on to Gloucester where there would be accommodation and supply in abundance. And may they make merry of it! The abbey was to be granted the honor of a royal visit, yet spared the humiliation of offering inadequate provision.

As the boys ran pell-mell down the Tor—risky enough at any time, but doubly treacherous with frost underfoot—Bors noted that King Henry's forethought had extended to making his own provision as well, for a cart and three pack horses also entered the abbey.

King Henry II was to be hosted by Prior Edmund and some of the senior brothers such as Ambrose and Jerome. The rest were to keep the offices. But bodily attendance had little to say to mental attention, and Bors was not the only boy, not to mention monk, who spent more time looking out the unshuttered windows for a glimpse of the royal personage than he spent looking at the cross or with eyes devoutly closed in prayer.

However, it was not until the next day after High Mass, where Bors saw King Henry served from the very grail he had saved from the flames and wondered whether the royal vision might light on the stone fish on the altar, that the assembled company saw their king full-face in his royal splendor. The red hair and well-trimmed beard glowed in the light of the altar candles, and the powerful, broad form showed the full magnificence of the royal robes. But more than any outward adorning, it was the sheer energy of the man that filled the tiny chapel and commanded attention. And his voice—a voice that just in speaking rang from the highest rafters and, Bors was sure, must have carried to the top of the Tor. Frightening to think what such a voice might do if raised in anger from this king who was reported to have chewed bedposts when in a rage.

But now the voice rang with excitement, not anger, for Henry was recounting for his audience the story that had brought him to Glastonbury. Bors was glad of his education, incomplete as it was, for Henry spoke not a word in English but told his story in a combination of French and Latin. "My forebear, William of Normandy, as the troubadours never tire of singing, rode into this land at Hastings' shore behind his brave minstrel-knight Taillefer, who sang 'The Song of Roland' until an arrow silenced the golden glee-man's voice forever. But long have I found inspiration, not in the deeds of Roland or Charlemagne, but in those of one who sprang from this very English soil—I speak of none less than Arthur of Britain."

A murmur of voices and nodding of cowled heads spoke appreciation. Henry continued, "The words of William of Malmesbury, some written at this very house and dedicated to my kinsman and your abbot, Henry of Blois, and the words of that great chronicler of the *History of the Kings of Britain,* Geoffrey of Monmouth, have inspired the one whom God has chosen to sit upon the throne once occupied by Arthur.

"And long I have grieved that no monument exists to this great king outside the words and songs of chroniclers and minstrels. But one could not know where to build such a monument, for we have no relics, no record of his remains. So great is this loss that in the shires west of here I have heard it declared, yea, even sworn to by sober men that Arthur lives still and will yet return.

"But I have had great fortune, for in His Almighty providence, God has willed that I should discover the burial place of this Arthur. While making royal progress through Wales last summer, there came into our presence a Celtic bard of great and ancient learning. He informed us, with all particulars and evidences, that the burial place of Arthur—the Avalon where Geoffrey of Monmouth tells us he went mortally wounded after his last battle—is none other than our own Glastonbury."

Clamors of questions, cries of excitement, and gasps of amazement blended into a confused hosannah until Brother Othbert, the music master, led forth in a chant of praise, "Clap your hands, all ye nations! Shout to God with cries of joy. How awesome is the Lord Most High, the great King over all the earth."

Other voices joined in a great paean of praise. "Praise be to the Lord God of Israel, who alone does marvelous deeds. He has made known to us His great and mighty works."

Henry stood, feet apart, hands on hips, beaming. He was pleased at the response. But there was one in the chapel to whom the announcement brought terror. Prior Edmund stood fluttering his long, white, nervous hands, his thin, thought-worn features and sunken cheeks more shadowed than ever. For he alone saw the awesome responsibility, indeed the terrible burden, this placed on the monastery of Glastonbury, and most squarely on the shoulders of its prior. How could they locate this lost burial of near to seven hundred years before? How could such wonderful remains be adequately venerated, lacking all facilities as they did? And the pilgrims such a shrine would bring—how could they be cared for? What was he to do? He turned desperate eyes on King Henry.

Henry Plantagenet raised his hand in signal, and a nobleman from his retinue stepped forward. Even from the back of the crowded chapel Bors could see the strong bones and square jaw line of the man's face and his clear dark eyes under level brows. Even next to Henry's overwhelming energy, this man stood in calm assurance. His long over-tunic was of a fine blue wool trimmed with sleek, dark fur. His belt was of gold and his cloak secured at his shoulder with a massively jeweled ring brooch. Henry beamed with pride in the plans he had laid. "Having discovered the great significance of this place, and having compassion at the great calamity that has befallen this house of Glastonbury, I hereby commit this abbey and its lands for repair to my chamberlain, Radulphus FitzStephen, on the condition that he shall henceforth, until its completion, spend all incomes and rents of the abbey lands on the repair of the buildings and the construction of the church."

Henry then held out a jeweled hand into which the chamberlain placed a rolled parchment sheet. "I have also prepared this charter which I grant forthwith." He unrolled the document and, holding it in both hands, he read, taking obvious pride in the words, "Henry, by the grace of God, King of England, Duke of Normandy and Aquitaine and Count of Angiers . . . to all his faithful French and English subjects in all of England. . . . I have decided to lay a foundation for the church of Glastonbury, which was consumed by fire and receded into ashes while it lay in my hands, and to repair it more magnificently as a work to be finished by me or my heirs. I have ordered a diligent search, presentation before me, and reading of the charters and privileges of my predecessors . . . and of the ancients—St. Edgar, Edmund, Alfred, Ine, Cenwalh, and the glorious Arthur. Whatever has been confirmed in these documents to the aforesaid church . . . I also concede, to the honor of God . . . the often-mentioned church, therefore, shall hold and possess in peace and quiet, freely and without interference, all its possessions and lands . . . but especially, the village of Glastonbury, in which the Old Church of the mother of God is located (for that church is held with certainty as the fount and origin of all religion in England) . . . I desire it to remain forever unshakeably settled, and I command it to be strictly observed by all."

Henry returned the charter to the hand of Radulphus FitzStephen.

From that moment Radulphus reigned at Glastonbury. He attacked all with the fullest powers of Norman energy and organization and as one who bore the full stamp of approval of his king. In one sweep the precious, pitiful remains of the Old Church were cleared away that a new chapel of St. Mary might replace it.

Everywhere across the enclosure the sound of hammer and chisel rang, and again there was a great raising of stone into soaring arches. St. Mary's church grew magnificently on the spot where the Old Church had originally stood. Using squared stones and the best workmanship, Radulphus FitzStephen spared nothing in its ornamentation. At the same time, builders worked on a cloister, dorter, Chapter House, and outbuildings. And so it would be that less than three years after the work was begun Reginald, Bishop of Bath, would dedicate the completed chapel.

Meanwhile, priests, brothers, novices, laypeople, and schoolboys, as well as those without the enclosure in the village, went about in the benediction of God and their king as beauty and order rose from the chaos around them. Prayers and hymns rose with the regularity of the hours from Matins at midnight through Compline at sunset, and all knew that truly no place on earth was more blessed than Glastonbury, which they now knew to be Avalon of the Blest as well.

Living in the glow that seemed to have fallen from Heaven and touched all in that place, Bors continued in his studies more intently. Seldom did he think of his family at d'Emercy, but when he did he thought of Aline's affection, Ancret's caring, and Ivo's enthusiasm. He could spare little worry for Nyall's spurning of him—placing him as it did in this sanctuary.

And seldom anymore did he have his dream. When he did, he would wake to a belief that the learning and life at Glastonbury were the jewels in the treasure room. And sometimes he wondered if taking the cowl was the entry key across the threshold.

But then sudden despair descended on the monastery again. For King Henry was dead, taken by one of those quick fevers which men said ran in the family of William the Conqueror. Henry's son Richard, whom some were calling Heart-of-the-Lion, was crowned at Winchester. Then Richard immediately departed for his lands in France directing his interest to matters of war and diverting his interest from the building of Glastonbury.

No sooner was England deprived of its monarch than Glastonbury was bereft of its leader, for Radulphus FitzStephen died also. There was no one to replace him in vigor or vision or royal validation.

Only St. Mary's Chapel was completed. The rest of the work ceased.

4

hen there was another death. It was strange that among the passing of the high and powerful, in the end it was the death of the lowliest brother that brought the greatest impact on the fortunes of Glastonbury. Brother Athanasius had, in the near to eighty years he spent at Glastonbury, been notable for two things—quiet and humility. He could rush along the hollowest of stone cloisters without an echo. He could sing all the offices with a fervent glow on his face, yet the words would be inaudible to the brother in the nearest stall. With the best of humor, he could take his stool in the warming room for the half-hour before Compline when levity was allowed and never disturb a current of air with his own noise. He was greatly loved, but he passed all affection directly on to his Lord. Young brothers soon learned the inestimable value of seeking a soft word from him whenever they needed advice or comfort, and they never left his presence without finding what they had come for. It was always sometime later that the supplicant would realize with amazement that Brother Athanasius had spoken not a word of his own, but had quoted those of the Lord or of the holy prophets or church fathers.

No one had received Brother Athanasius's wisdom and comfort more readily than had Bors in his twelve years at Glastonbury. In the year of our Lord 1190, when Bors marked his seventeenth birthday, outwardly he had grown to manhood—tall and broad-shouldered, with thick black curls ever a tumble on his forehead. But inwardly he had found no peace. For with the deaths of King Henry and Radulphus FitzStephen two years ago, the dream had returned frequently, leaving its longing and its questions imprinted more strongly than ever on his consciousness. He had spent increasing time in Brother Athanasius's tiny bare cell at the far end of the dorter.

When first the dream had returned with force, Bors had told it in all detail to Athanasius, who sat listening with head bowed so low that only the round, smooth skin of his tonsure showed above his folded hands. At last he raised his head and sat quietly for so long Bors thought he was not going to speak. Then he heard the words, almost without realizing the monk was saying them. "My son, if you will receive My words and hide My commandments with you; so that you incline your ear to wisdom and apply your heart to understanding; yes, if you cry after knowledge and lift up your voice for understanding; if you seek her as silver and search for her as for hid treasures; then shall you understand the fear of the Lord, and find the knowledge of God. For the Lord gives wisdom; out of His mouth comes knowledge and understanding."

The words ceased and hung gently in the room like the warm presence of a dearly loved one who has slipped into another chamber. Bors hated to break the spell, but he had much to ask. "So the treasure I have long dreamed of is the wisdom of God? Yes, I see how that could be. And yet it explains so little. What am I to understand of my past, and what am I to do for my future? I must leave the monastery school this Eastertide."

"The ox knows his owner, and the ass his master's crib. A wise child knows his father." How was he to know his father—he that was long dead? Bors wondered, but did not speak, waiting for Brother Athanasius to go on. "A wise son makes his father glad, but a foolish son is the heaviness of his mother." Bors carried tender, fleeting memories of his mother in his heart. He hoped he had not been a heaviness to her. But the monk's words continued to raise more questions and offer no answers. "The king's favor is toward a wise servant, but his wrath is against him that causes shame."

In the coming days the phrase "a wise son knows his own father" was much in Bors's mind. His desire grew to know more of his own father. The talk with Ancret that he had been denied when he returned home those six years ago now became a loss he mourned daily.

But then he knew a fresh mourning, for Brother Athanasius departed this life as quietly as he had lived it. When he was in his place for neither Matins nor Lauds and was still absent at Prime, Abbot Henry de Soilly, whom King Richard had offhandedly thought to recommend to them from Bermondsey, asked Brother Jerome to check on him. Bors was in the storeroom when the request came, and he accompanied the infirmarer, bearing a basket of tonics likely to be needed.

But one glimpse at the serenely smiling form on the cot told them that Brother Athanasius had gone beyond the need of such poor medicines. And that final tranquility, more than anything else, determined Bors to deal with his own long-standing restlessness. Athanasius had encouraged him to seek the truth, and so he would, as a sort of pilgrimage in honor of this holy brother's life. If Abbot Henry would permit.

"How long would you be gone?" Abbot Henry's chiseled features, proud bearing, and straightforward dealings left no doubt to the fact that he sprang from royal stock.

"Two days' travel—one each there and back, and two days on the manor, if it please my Lord Abbot."

Abbot Henry rose and walked to the window of his fine lodge—one of the last buildings completed before the death of Radulphus. "Four days would be acceptable. No more. We should have laid our departed brother to rest on the third day, except a strange matter has come to light. Strange it is that the most unassuming and least demanding of all our brotherhood should leave such a request behind him, but perhaps that is all the more reason to grant it."

Henry pointed out the window with a long, beringed finger to the far northeast corner of St. Mary's Chapel where Bors could just see a pair of tall pillars. "Brother Jerome informs me that, apparently in anticipation of his death, Brother Athanasius expressed a desire to be buried between those two pillars. Because of the great example of his life of holiness, we should like to honor that request, even though it will take an extra day to prepare the ground there, located as it is in the oldest part of our yard."

Henry sighed at the inconvenience and gave Bors a nod of dismissal. "You may fill your scrip with provisions from the kitchen."

With a full scrip and a full heart Bors set out after Prime the next morning on the most perfect of spring days. Willow-wren, thrush, and robin chorused together from the rowan, crack-willow, and wild fruit trees. Then a gentle breeze arose, shaking the catkins hanging from the hazel trees, and a shower of gold fell on him, mingled with drops of dew shining with the rays of early morning sun-gold. Tonight he would be at d'Emercy, and, hindrances or no, he would find the truth he sought.

When he reached the village, Bors could have thought that no time had passed in the six years since his Christmas visit. Surely those weren't the same speckled chickens clacking on the muddy verge nor the same red and brown cows blocking the road. But when he came again to the half-timbered, thatched cottage at the top of the street near the marketplace and saw a graceful girl of fifteen years with long blond plaits hanging beneath her wimple, he knew that, in truth, time had passed. "Aline, and is that you, or do I mistake?"

The years between them made no difference, for she recognized him immediately and flew into his arms in greeting. "Bors! Bors! Oh, I had hoped you would come at Christmas this year. And I was disappointed. But now it's no matter, for here you are."

"Why so this Christmas? Was there an especially fine trained bear?"

She laughed, a particularly pleasing sound in the long gold light of a spring evening. "So you remember how I wanted to show you the trained bear? Yes, as a matter of fact, this year's bear danced the best I've ever seen. But St. George was a sad disappointment. His sword broke across the dragon's nose."

"Ah, and then did the dragon eat the King of Egypt's daughter?"

"Oh, never mind this nonsense." She tugged him toward the door of the cottage. "Come, you must greet Ancret." She lowered her voice. "I fear you'll find her much changed. She lost her sight two winters ago, but she still spins a fine thread."

"What are you muttering about out there?" the familiar old voice called through the open doorway. "I may be blind, but I'm not deaf. Who's come?"

In a few long strides Bors stood by her stool. He knelt and took her hand. "And don't you remember the bairn you nursed like your own these seventeen summers ago?"

She tossed distaff and spindle aside without tangling her wool. "And so you've come back at last, have ye? Well, if you thought to come for my burying you're too early."

Bors kissed her leathery cheek and then sat on the floor with a laugh. "Take your time. I've four days leave, and only one spent. Then I must be back to bury a dear old brother. That will be enough of sending souls to Heaven for me."

Aline brought him a jug of ale to wash the dust of the road from his throat, and Ancret picked up her spindle and distaff to continue her sightless spinning. Aline seated herself at the small loom just beyond Ancret and began work on the length of green fabric she was weaving while the three of them talked in rhythm to the spindle and loom.

"And Ivo?" Bors asked.

"We see near to as little of him as we do of you. Rychart d'Emercy won his knight's spurs five years ago, and Ivo was raised to squire. They're off at Clifford Castle in Herefordshire paying knight's fee this month and next. Then there'll be a grand tournament in Nottingham or Winchester or somewhere for them to ride off to."

"Tournaments!" Ancret growled. "As much use as a mummer's play."

"Oh, no, Ancret," Aline said. "Ivo explained it to me. It keeps the knights in fighting form so that whenever King Richard has need of them, they'll be ready."

But her answer didn't placate Ancret. "Richard, bah! What good is it to England to have a king who lives in France and speaks not one word of the English tongue? As well to be ruled by the King of France, I say."

Aline started to argue with her, but Bors's mind was following another track. "Clifford Castle? Yes, I remember, Clifford is d'Emercy's overlord—the same baron that Herlwin d'Emercy served when Nyall was squire to him."

At last he had the conversation where he wanted it. "Ancret, you were here then. You'll remember. Why did Nyall not continue in Herlwin's service?"

The old cheeks hollowed deeper as she sucked them in thought, her wrinkled lips pursed. Then she shrugged. "Your father died. It was for his oldest son to take his place." She shut her lips firmly.

But Bors would not be put off. "No. That won't do. I was five years old; I remember a bit. Nyall came home in disgrace before our parents died. Young as I was, I remember my mother's tears."

The clacking of the loom stopped, and Aline turned, shuttle in her hand. "Yes, why didn't I ever think of that. No—" she added hastily when Bors looked at her in surprise. "No, I don't remember. I was too young, but it's just sense. If Nyall had come to fill our father's place, he would have been given a place on the manor—not bailiff, of course, but a chance to work up to it. There have been no favors from the manor such as should have devolved on the family of a bailiff, save the taking of Ivo as varlet. It is odd."

"There were the additional landstrips given at Bors's birth," Ancret said, then stopped suddenly.

Bors set his empty mug aside and slipped to his knees beside Ancret again, grasping her arms. "Ancret, please tell me. You're the only one I can ask. There's a mystery somewhere, I know it. It haunts me, and I can't get any understanding. This is what Abbot Henry gave me leave to search out so that my soul may be peaceful as Brother Athanasius whom we lay to rest soon."

Ancret shook his hands off and continued her spinning. The only indication that she heard him was a little shake of her head.

Bors leaned back with a sigh. "Where's Nyall?"

Aline's voice was small. "He should be in the south field plowing. I helped him yoke Rosie this morning. But I don't know—I'm afraid—"

Now Bors turned to his sister. "Aline! What is it? What else do I not know about my family?"

Aline shrugged and kept weaving. "It's nothing new. It's just that Nyall prefers the alehouse to attending our field strips . . ."

"See!" Bors turned back to Ancret. "Nyall is unhappy too. Unhappy over something he blames me for. That's why he sent me to the monastery. Something he lost his position with Herlwin d'Emercy over, and somehow it's my fault. It has something to do with a dead lady, that much I know."

The spindle hung still, swaying from its thread of ivory wool. "And how do you know that?"

"I heard them fighting—Herlwin and Nyall—when I came for Christmas. But that's all I know."

It was silent in the cottage. Ancret still would not speak. "Who is the lady Herlwin spoke of, Ancret? Is she my mother? Was Herlwin d'Emercy in love with my mother? Did Nyall challenge him for her honor?"

Ancret gave a cackle of a laugh. "What! A fine Norman lordling in love with the Saxon wife of a common freeman? Albeit she was fair enough to have taken any eye." Ancret seemed lost in her own thoughts for a time. Then she said with a nod, "Yes, it may be that it was your mother Herlwin referred to as the dead lady. But not to Elswith Bachiler."

Bors and Aline both blinked and leaned nearer the old woman. "I don't understand," Bors said. "Was not Elswith Bachiler my mother—she whom I remember with the fair plaits and kind smile?"

"She you remember was wife ever faithful and loving to Martin Bachiler and mother to his six children."

"Yes, six children, two died with my parents, so—"

"But the third son was a sickly babe and weak. He had not the strength to cry when he entered the world, although he drew breath for a few days. The tiniest, reddest bairn that ever I midwifed into this world, and before he drew his last breath, Nyall came home, riding hard at night clear from the castle, he said. And the bundle in his arms was the same age as that pitiful rag that lay by my Elswith, but twice his size and triple his lustiness. And at last a babe's cry was heard as it should have been in the bailiff's cottage."

"And that was me?" Bors's voice was so quiet it was more as if he breathed than spoke.

Ancret nodded.

"And my brother—er, rather—he whose changeling I am?"

Ancret shook her head. "Nyall said he was dead before he made the change. And well he may have been, for the thread of life was spider's web thin. It could have snapped at any moment."

"Could have?" Bors pushed to his feet, his hands over his eyes. "And yet you don't know. Nyall could have killed to give me a place? Me—whoever I was—that had no rightful place here? Me—I—I who am no one?"

He paced for a while, his long strides making circles around the small cottage. "Then where did I come from? Who is my father? Did Nyall get me on some dairymaid? Is that why he hates me? Is he my own father?"

Ancret shook her head. "Who knows? God and the bairn's father—the mother did know, but like as not she's in her grave. Aye, Nyall may be your father, but you're nothing alike—you with your dark curls and broad build, and he like a rail wearing a hay thatch. But then I've known it to happen. Not all bear their father's stamp."

It was too much for Bors. He had come looking for answers that would put his mind at rest and help him find guidance for the future. Instead he found all uprooted. Where there had been one question, now there were twenty. And none likely to be answered.

He flung out the door. Blinded with emotion and rage, he turned down the road. It was not until he slowed his steps on entering the next village that he realized night was on him. At the edge of a field he spotted a barn with some of last winter's hay still piled in one corner. That would serve for a bed for the night, and his scrip was still more than half-full of bread and cheese. He drank at a little stream and slept without dreaming. Whatever the meaning of Ancret's revelations, his sleep was the most peaceful in weeks.

There seemed to be no reason to return to d'Emercy, so the next morning he continued on toward Glastonbury. If he walked quickly, he would arrive in time for Vespers. So he was a nameless orphan—he whose mind had been filled with dearly hoarded family memories. Now he knew they were all lies. He increased his pace until he was almost running—although he knew he could never outrun the truth. As his own confusion grew, though, the order and peace of the monastery enclosure beckoned ever more strongly.

But when he arrived, all was not peaceful as he had expected. The bell was just ringing for Vespers, and the brotherhood was filing two by two in orderly procession to St. Mary's Chapel, chanting the psalm of the evening. But beside the chapel where he had thought to find a neat pile of sod and a small brown mound between the stone pillars where Brother Athanasius would be laid in two days' time, he found a large area roped off by a heavy cord which he nearly stumbled over in the twilight. Beyond that was a huge pile of dirt, enough to have filled several graves, but the area of digging itself was obscured by a hastily erected tent, for already the ill-cut poles were leaning and the curtain sagging.

Bors took his place in the procession into the chapel, but he could not get his mind off the strange rigging outside. Had another died while he was gone that they must dig many graves? Perhaps one of the pillars had fallen on a careless worker—or the ground caved in under the grave diggers? None seemed to be very good explanations, but it helped to have a new, less personal puzzle to work on.

After Vespers he caught Brother Ambrose to ask the meaning of the strange structure beside the chapel.

"Seeming a great wonder has been revealed, for early yesterday on the second day of grave digging, when we thought to have the task completed, Brother Eluid's shovel struck a stone."

Bors shrugged. Was that all? Surely there were many stones in the soil here. "So?"

"I don't mean a crude rock of the field; I mean the diggers uncovered at a depth of some seven feet, a burial stone as would mark a grave."

"At seven feet?"

Ambrose nodded. "It is said that when the sainted Dunstan ruled as abbot here, he ordered a new layer of soil placed on the old cemetery—perhaps it was even he who raised the pillars."

"And this gravestone—was it inscribed?"

"Smoothed and shaped with great care, but unmarked by name or date."

"So? Surely there were many graves so covered when new soil was added."

"Ah, yes, but under the stone—" Ambrose's long, somber face suddenly lit with an excitement he could not contain, and he gripped Bors's shoulder. "Oh, it is too wonderful to tell—that such should be granted in my lifetime. I know now in at least a small part how the holy Simeon felt when the Christ Child was presented to him."

Bors was growing impatient over the muddled tale he was hearing. "But tell me what it means!" he demanded.

"On the underside, as if the stone sheltered too great a secret for the eyes of man, was a leaden cross with the inscription: 'HIC JACET SEPULTUS INCLYTUS REX ARTHURIUS IN INSULA AVALONIA.'" He repeated the words as the holiest of prayers, and his face took on a radiance.

Bors nodded slowly. "'Here lies buried the renowned King Arthur in the Isle of Avalon.' Yes, I remember when King Henry came to Glastonbury and told us he had heard of some such from a Welsh bard—but there was never any search made for the grave. It is strange that at last it should be stumbled over . . ."

"No, no! Do not you see?" Ambrose's grip tightened on Bors's shoulder, and he trembled so with excitement that he nearly shook the boy. "It is divine revelation. It is God's great gift to so favor us at this time. His special blessing visited on us—we who are so undeserving. It is a parable of all His grace—His great love and mercy given freely to sinners like as we. I cannot praise Him enough for His goodness . . ."

In the presence of such ecstasy Bors could but devoutly cross himself. The same excitement vibrated through all the brotherhood in the silence of the evening meal and the singing of the night offices. It was doubtful that anyone slept much in the intervening hours between Lauds and Prime. Surely, it was only the iron control of Abbot Henry that kept his charges from rushing off with shovels, spades, and spoons before breakfast to learn what the grave would reveal. But the Rule was supreme over their lives, the offices would be kept no matter what. So it was not until after morning mass that the entire community, and many from the village who had heard rumors, crowded against the roped-off area on the north side of the church. But as always, Henry de Soilly was firm. They would maintain order. "Brother Petrus and Brother Aelfric, it is your turn to dig this morning. Gildon and Noger, you will assist with hauling back the soil."

Those that hoped for an early answer to the secret of the grave were disappointed. When it was time to stop for High Mass, the diggers had found nothing. And no matter how willingly many would have foregone their dinner to return to the task, Abbot Henry would not hear of it. But in the afternoon came the long hours normally given to study, work, and personal devotions when they could dig at the grave site. By now word had spread, and seeming the entire population of Glastonbury village filled the space between church and wall, including several ragamuffins who sat perched on top of the wall—until Abbot Henry caught sight of them.

"Brother Jerome and Brother Ambrose, it is your turn to dig." Henry consulted his rota table which Prior Edmund held for him. "Bevis and—" The abbot paused to mark a change with the stylus. "Bors, since you are returned early from your pilgrimage, you will assist."

Nearly nine feet beneath the site of the stone and leaden cross, Brother Ambrose's shovel struck something hard. He thrust again. It was unmistakable—the firm, hollow thud against a wooden surface. The brothers in the pit fell to their knees and began digging with their hands in a frenzy to fill their buckets with the concealing dirt. Bors and Bevis hauled on the ropes, dumped full buckets, and lowered empty ones with such eagerness that Bors's hands soon burned with blisters from the rough rope. But he did not slacken his pace.

All the time Abbot Henry stood at the head of the excavation, Prior Edmund a nervous flutter beside him. None dared cross the rope barricade Henry had ordered. Anything done in his domain would be done in order. At last Ambrose turned from his digging. "My Lord Abbot—it is so. Surely this is a coffin."

Ambrose nearly shouted, and even from the sixteen-foot depth of the pit, his voice reached those beyond the curtained area.

But Henry held steady. "That is as expected. Boys, lower your ropes," he directed Bors and Bevis. "Thomas, Cerdric." He summoned two novices. "Assist on this side."

Still the wait was long and breathless as those in the excavated trench struggled to attach ropes to the boat-shaped object that on its uncovering was seen to be a hollowed log—from an oak tree of colossal size.

At last the brothers nodded and tossed the ends of the ropes to the hands waiting above. Jerome and Ambrose scrambled up the ladders and lent their strength to the hauling. Prior Edmund darted forward as if he too would help, but he was called back by a quelling look from his superior. "Petrus, Aelfric, Othbert, Eluid." Four more brothers were summoned inside the tent to bend their muscles to the effort. The oak coffin raised a few inches. Bors gripped firmer and strained until his blisters broke and bled on the rope, but he was barely aware of anything except the need to bring the great log and its secret to the surface.

Once a brother stumbled and the entire weight fell to its depth. Bors feared the ropes might break under such strain. But at length, with a great heave, the coffin rose to ground level. Two of the brothers grasped the ends and guided it to a place beside the grave, and at last the ropes could be released. Bors saw the blood on his hands and stuck them in the sleeves of his tunic before he could be ordered to the infirmary for salving.

At a nod from Henry, Petrus and Aelfric took up axe and crowbar and wrenched the lid open. At the sound of splintering wood, the brothers waiting outside the curtained holy of holies would not be denied, no matter what the cost.

For once Abbot Henry forgot discipline and knelt himself beside the opened coffin. It was no wonder such an enormous tree trunk had been used for this most unusual burial, for the bones it contained were of gigantic proportions. "Brother Ambrose." Henry commanded the tallest of the brothers to his side. "Kilt your robe."

Ambrose pulled his robe above his knees, and Henry pulled a shin bone from the coffin. Measuring it against Ambrose's leg, his pale skin as white as the bleached bone next to it, all who could see gasped in amazement. No ordinary man had been buried here. The shin bone projected above their brother's knee by the breadth of three fingers and more.

Henry carefully replaced the leg bone, and Ambrose lowered his robe. Then Henry drew an even greater wonder from the coffin. A horrified, fascinated gasp went through the circle of observers as their abbot held up an equally colossal human skull. But it was not the seeming grin or sightless leer common to all skulls, or even the magnificent size of this once-living head that drew such a response, but the marks of the desperate damage done to it. There were signs of repeated blows, some apparently received earlier in the man's life, according to Brother Jerome, who knew much about the human body. He pointed to marks in the skull there, and there, and there where injuries had healed—mere bone-scrapes they had been—probably delivered by a heavy object such as a broadsword or battle-axe. But the great, gaping hole with shattered bone above the left ear—without doubt that had been the death blow.

The bottom end of the log lay covered yet. At a nod from Henry, Petrus stepped forward and inserted his crowbar between coffin and lid. As he threw all his weight against the bar, the ancient seal broke to reveal new wonders—

more bones, those of a much smaller figure, lay crumpled at the feet of the mighty warrior.

Not only bare, bleached bones remained, but also golden strands of hair, like a web of spun sunlight around the skull. With a sob Brother Ambrose, he who had long studied and taught his schoolboys the words of Geoffrey of Monmouth, fell to his knees. "It is true. This proves all—it is Arthur of the Britons and his lady Guinevere. Here is proof undeniable—she who was buried as an unfaithful wife."

Without thinking, he reached into the coffin and grasped the golden tresses. But even before he could lift them, as if truly they had been spun of light and air, they disintegrated on his fingers. Ambrose stared at his empty hands in shocked horror. Such desecration was beyond penance or punishment.

But Abbot Henry was not to be an avenging angel. Such events were beyond the disposal of men. "Let the curtain come down," he ordered. "Those who have waited may make their reverence that they may praise God the better for His grace and mercies. Tonight we shall keep vigil by this sacred tomb. Tomorrow the remains will be laid anew in carved chests and sepulchered in the church where for all generations penitents may come to pray."

Brother Othbert, ever quick to know his duty, hastily assembled his choir, and Prior Edmund, for once taking his own initiative, scurried into the church to return with their newly acquired silver gilt cross containing the relics of St. George for Abbot Henry to hold above the coffin. Ambrose, as one in deep prayer, never moved from his kneeling vigil. But Bors, at the sight of Prior Edmund's initiative, thought to offer his own homage.

It was only a few steps to the north door of St. Mary's Chapel. Barely taking time to genuflect before the altar, he darted forward. In almost the exact location where he had years ago pulled the same vessel from a burning altar, he seized the holy chalice. Back down the aisle he paused to fill the chalice from the basin of holy water. Lacking an aspergillum, he darted back outside the chapel and broke a small branch from a yew tree.

Even in the few moments he had been gone, the evening had deepened, and several had brought torches to stand in a semicircle around the open coffin. Othbert's choir had begun its song:

I have set my King upon my holy hill of Zion,
Sing praises to God, sing praises;
Sing praises unto our King, sing praises.
For God is the King of all the earth,
Sing ye praises with understanding.

As the chant echoed against the new-built stone walls that stood over the ancient sacred site of the Old Church and the torchlight flickered and flared in the dusk, streaming into golden, dragon-shaped banners when the breeze took the flame, Bors dipped his green branch into the chalice of holy water and sprinkled the whitened, long-buried bones. Then he stood aside, holding the chalice, and passed the branch to the next votary in line. Each in turn passed by, dipping the green into the holy water and anointing the king. For each was convinced in his own heart that in truth it was a king who lay before them.

5

s Abbot Henry had decreed, the bones were sealed in new chests and interred in the church. But from the beginning it was evident that things would never be the same at Glastonbury. Word ran like wildfire that Arthur, he of whom minstrels had sung and chroniclers had written, whom Queen Eleanor had honored above all at her court, truly lay in his legendary Isle of Avalon. Now it was no mere legend, rather solid wood and bone and earth. And Glastonbury was that Avalon.

Ambrose gathered his boys and novices and read to them in ringing tones the words of Geoffrey of Monmouth as if he saw in them prediction for the future as well as chronicle of the past:

> At that time was Britain exalted unto so high a pitch of dignity as that it did surpass all other kingdoms in plenty of riches, in luxury of adornment, and in the courteous wit of them that dwelt therein. Whatsoever knight in the land was of renown for his prowess did wear his clothes and his arms all of one same color. And the dames, no less witty, would apparel them in like manner in a single color, nor would they deign have the love of none save he had thrice approved him in the wars. Wherefore at that time did dames wax chaste and knights the noble for their love.

Pilgrims came from far and wide, noble and common, to the tomb before the high altar to do homage at the carved sepulcher containing the casks of precious bones. With loving care Brother Petrus, who was much skilled in rock-carving, inscribed upon the tomb: "Here lies Arthur, the flower of kingship, the kingdom's glory, whom his morals and virtue commend with eternal praise. Arthur's fortunate wife lies buried here, who merited heaven through the happy consequences of her virtues."

One who came, Gerald of Wales, was part pilgrim, part chronicler, and part royal messenger. Abbot Henry called Brother Ambrose that the Welsh prelate and historian might judge for himself the height and veracity of the monk against whose leg Arthur's shin bone had been measured and whose hands had touched the golden tresses of Guinevere. Gerald must have been impressed by the look of reverence in the monk's eyes and the note of awe in his voice. Then Henry took Gerald Cambrensis into his own chamber and showed him the lead cross that had lain hidden under its rock for more than six hundred years, holding its secret of the one lying beneath it. Gerald carefully sketched the cross and noted its inscription, explaining to the abbot that he would like to include it in the *Itinerarium Cambriae* he was writing.

When the pilgrim had offered his prayers and concluded his historical research, Gerald turned to the final item on his agenda. He mounted the steps of the marketcross just beyond the abbey gatehouse, extended his arms wide over the heads of the assembled brothers and villagers, and proclaimed in ringing tones, "The call of God is upon us! The will of God is before us! Jerusalem the fair, Jerusalem our treasure, is once more imperiled by heathen Turks. The land wherein the Most High God became man for our redemption and therein chose to pass his earthly life, Palestine our inheritance, the cradle of our salvation, is no longer esteemed sacred by those who occupy it.

"How can we live and not put an end to such an evil? How can we call on the name of God and not respond to His call? Hear me, brave men and true, Jerusalem—won from the infidels at such great price by brave men's blood on the First Crusade—has been overrun."

And here there was great consternation, for those who lived quietly and close to the earth, far from wars and rumor of wars, did not know that the Christian king of Jerusalem had been captured by the Turkish leader Saladin and that every member of those orders of Christian knights, the Templars and the Hospitalers in Jerusalem, had been executed. At this news a great moan went up from the crowd, and women began to weep.

Gerald flung out his arms again, wider this time. "Hear me! Jerusalem, the very heart of Christendom, has fallen. And it is only a matter of time before our forces still holding Tyre, Tripoli, and Antioch will be likewise expelled. This must not happen. We cannot stand idly by and let it happen. God in Heaven will not allow it! King Richard, he with the bravery of a lion in his heart, has taken the cross and called all true Christians to follow him on a new Crusade."

He held out a piece of red material cut in the shape of a cross. "Here it is—symbol of the cross of our Lord—soaked in His own red blood that is the cross of every Crusader—as it was the cross of our Lord's first Christian knight, St. George. Who will be the first to claim this cross for himself, and by so doing win immediate forgiveness of all past sins and the promise of a place in Heaven?"

Man after man from village and farm stepped forward and accepted a cross from the Welsh priest. Two black-robed, but uncowled novices from the monastery went forward. Watching from the back of the crowd, Bors longed to join them. Though fully awake, he saw his dream as if through sleeping eyes. Would taking the cross and going on Crusade be the crossing of his threshold? But no matter how openly his heart responded, the realities of life remained, for every man must furnish his own sword and helm. And Bors had none. Perhaps in the past, before he knew the part-truth about his birth, perhaps he would have appealed to Nyall or to d'Emercy, but now he knew that he had no rights. For though he felt allegiance in his heart to Sir Heribert, he had no proof that he was of the d'Emercy manor born. And he felt more truly alone than at any time in his life.

Three days after the departure of Gerald Cambrensis, Bors sat alone at his studies when Brother Aelfric on porter duty at the gatehouse came in search of him. "Your brothers have come to see you. They wait at the gate."

It seemed a cruel joke—like the twisting of the knife after mortal wound—that some should come declaring themselves to be his brothers when he was so deeply feeling his want of family. He pulled back, pain on his face. Aelfric, seeing it, hurried on. "It is no joke. They have named themselves—Nyall and Ivo. And they ride fine horses, and the younger is accoutered as a noble squire . . ." Bors hesitated, still with hard eyes and firmly set mouth. "I assure you—you have nothing to be ashamed of in such brothers."

There was no way to explain. Bors lay aside the fine-tipped brush and followed the porter. Though his steps dragged, Bors could not keep his heart from lifting at the sight of Ivo. His under-tunic was of fine linen, much finer than that woven at home by Aline, and his short, sleeveless over-tunic was a bright saffron banded with green and belted with soft leather. He wore his capuchon with a fashionable twist high on his head, and a well-wrought sword hung at his side. Nyall was dressed more soberly, but he sat well in his saddle with a straight back that told Bors that for this day, at least, he had not visited the alehouse.

Familiarity overcame Bors's hurt. "Leave your horses in the guest stables," he said indicating the low building to the west, "and come walk in the garden with me." He started to ask about Aline and Ancret, then stopped, a sudden thought making his throat tight. "Ancret—is she—?"

"She is well, as is our sister." Ivo swung easily from the saddle and tossed his reins to a stable lad. "Aline was much hurt that you broke off your visit so abruptly last spring."

Bors blinked at the strangeness of Ivo's words and then realized Ivo likely knew nothing of what had taken place. He still thought he was addressing his brother. But Nyall knew. "And you have come all this way to tell me that?" Bors strode quickly ahead of his guests. There was a bench by the fish pond where they could talk without being overheard—even should Bors raise his voice—as he felt in danger of doing. By the time they had passed chapel, cloister, reredorter, and herb garden and reached the fish pond, Ivo was laughing. "Whoa, my brother. I have come to talk to you, not to run a footrace. And I would not choose to be so out of breath that I cannot talk."

Bors sat on one end of the wooden bench. "Talk then."

Ivo sat on the other end. Nyall stood by the side of the fish pond with its floating thatched nest covers for the ducks and geese who shared living space with perch and carp. Ivo spoke. "I have come—that is, we have come—for it is my news, and Nyall has borne me company on the journey—to tell you of my extraordinary fortune and to ask you to join me in it." Though he was Bors's senior, he bounced with excitement like a boy at Christmas. "I am made knight!" He nearly burst with the news.

Bors sat very still, battling the unchristian urge to Jealousy. Gerald's visit had awakened his old desires for knighthood and adventure. "And how is this come about?"

"My Lord Clifford is to go on Crusade and has called all his underlords to pay increased knight's fees. For the honor of d'Emercy, my Lord Heribert must supply six knights with squires. I, who had thought never to rise above squire, am to be the sixth knight. And I have come to ask you, my brother, to be my squire."

Bors gasped and for a moment could not find words to form the questions flooding his mind. "How—? What—? Why me?" And before Ivo could answer, he flung the facts at him with voice pushed high by his emotions. "I am not trained for squirehood. And I am not your brother."

Nyall, strolling with assumed nonchalance, whirled sharply on his heel. "What did you say?"

Bors sprang to his feet. On the gently upward-sloping pond bank Bors looked Nyall level in the eyes. "You heard me. I know all. Tell him—you owe that much to your blood brother."

Nyall ignored Ivo's demands for an explanation and glared at Bors. "What do you mean you know all? How could you? Only I and one other living person know. Have you been listening to idle gossip?"

"Not idle, and not gossip. Ancret, for all her blindness, sees more sharply than many a marksman. She told me of your midnight visit to the cottage of Martin Bachiler with babe in arms near to eighteen years ago."

Nyall visibly relaxed. With an easy smile he shrugged and turned to Ivo. "He speaks true. The babe born to our parents sickened and died. On the same night I brought to our mother a babe born out of wedlock. She was happy enough to accept a healthy son. So our brother Bors is brother in name only, not in blood."

"Brother!" And now Bors was shouting at Nyall. "I'm no brother to you. Less than half a truth is no truth at all. I've had enough of your lies. Tell the truth for once in your life— your mother was not my mother, and your father was not my father. Who was my father, Nyall? Are you my father? Am I your son?" The last word came out on a strangled sob. He turned his back on Nyall, and only then did he see Abbot Henry standing quietly beside a well-fruited apple tree.

Bors now rushed to him in appeal. "My Lord Abbot! This one you see here who has for many years masqueraded as my brother is no brother to me—more like he is my father and I his ill-gotten offspring." And now he swung back to Nyall that he might see the full impact of his final accusation. "And I well believe him to be the murderer of the lawful son of the house where I was changeling."

"These are serious charges you level, my son." The abbot's voice flowed like oil on the troubled waters.

"Serious indeed," Bors agreed. "That is why I lay them before you here in your jurisdiction, my lord."

"It is true that my writ runs to all that occurs within the twelve hides," Abbot Henry replied. "But surely, these accusations are not of acts that occurred here."

"But does not the fact that I have been falsely sheltered here these many years as a result of Nyall Bachiler's crimes bring my affairs under your authority?"

The abbot considered. "It may well be. I will hear what you have to say. Then I will decide." He turned to Nyall. "What say you to this?"

Nyall bowed to the abbot with an easy grace that Bors hated. "My Lord Abbot, he speaks true on one point only. He is foster brother only to myself and my brother Ivo here. All else is sheer fantasy. I am not his father, and I certainly did not murder my infant brother. The babe was already dead."

"If you are not the father, then I would have you name the parents and explain your role in this affair." Generations of Norman nobility born to command spoke with Henry de Soilly. Refusal was impossible.

Nyall looked around. "May we speak in private, Lord Abbot?"

"If by 'we' you include these two here, we may go into my quarters."

Nyall bowed his yellow-thatched head in obedience, and they followed the abbot across the lawn to his apartment. Henry sat on the one chair in the room, high-backed, heavily carved and brightly painted, with a tapestry-cushioned seat. Ivo and Bors sat on a bench against the far wall. Nyall stood in the center of the rush-covered floor.

"Who was my father? Who was my mother? What happened to the babe? Why—?" In his agitation Bors started to his feet. Even in these exclusive quarters his voice rose.

"We have agreed this is my writ." It took only a gesture of Henry's hand to make Bors back quietly to his bench. "I will ask the questions. Now, Nyall Bachiler. Grave charges have been leveled at you. You will tell the truth. What of this boy's parentage?"

Nyall took a deep breath and shifted his weight from one foot to the other. In the dim light from the small, round-topped windows of the chamber his faded blue eyes and pale skin looked ghostly above his dark tunic. "Herlwin d'Emercy, son of my overlord, he whom I served as squire, is father."

Bors was stunned. His mind fought desperately for memory of Sir Heribert's heir. Christmas six years ago . . . a handsome young man with dark curling hair—not unlike his own, he realized . . . laughing eyes . . . easy grace . . . and his voice from the dark undercroft arguing with Nyall . . . what had the words been? . . . "the lady is dead" . . . "bleed me more."

"And the mother?"

Nyall looked about desperately, and Bors thought he might run from the abbot's presence. Nyall stood quivering like a hunted hart. Then he drew a deep, sobbing breath and suddenly surrendered, as visibly as if he had fallen to his knees. "The mother was Rosamund Clifford, daughter of Walter de Clifford, baron under whom Herlwin won his knighthood." The pent-up words tumbled from his lips. "Yes, yes, Rosamund the Fair, the Rose of Clifford, the adored mistress of King Henry for whom he locked away Queen Eleanor. Yes, it was she—she was the mother." He spoke so rapidly that his hearers had to lean forward to catch his words.

"My squire, to whom I was varlet, during King Henry's long absence in France courted and won Rosamund. The courtly admiration which all knights are to pay to their ladies went beyond its bounds. They loved without reason and without fear. Until they learned their love-making was to bear fruit, and Henry had been gone too long for the child to be of his getting."

Every mind in the room filled with images of the power of the king famous for his mattress-chewing rages. His broad, bearlike hands could easily have ripped his unfaithful mistress and her lover limb from limb. "The lady feigned a lingering malaise—brought on many said by the king's prolonged absence—and kept to her chamber for the final months so that none knew but her faithful serving lady. Her servant and the servant of Herlwin d'Emercy—myself."

The tumbling words halted abruptly and the narrator paced the floor, kicking dried rushes far askew. "And then word came that Henry had landed at Dover and was making progress to Herefordshire. Perhaps it was that news that brought the lady to bed, for if the babe could not be gotten rid of before the king's arrival, she would surely have killed herself. But the babe arrived before the king. The serving lady, in a panic to clear away all evidence—for there was word that Henry had reached Oxford—thrust the newborn into its father's arms."

A shadow of a smile played around Nyall's face. "The amazement and consternation on Herlwin's face when the old woman fled and left him standing alone with a crying babe in his arms was something to see. In her panic the maid had not even thought to bring milk. Like as not, she would have been glad had it starved to death. And it might have, but that I had had experience of the sheep pens. I had seen old shepherds fill gloves with milk and pierce a hole in one finger to get milk into a lamb whose mother had died. And so I did.

"But it would not do that the babe remain at Clifford castle. The danger to all was too great. Herlwin could not leave without his lord's permission, but I could. I knew my mother was with child. It was mere fortune that the two babes were so near in birth time, for I did not know she had been delivered, but I could think of nothing else to do, and someone must act, for Herlwin was like one struck dumb."

Nyall paused to draw a deep breath. "And the rest you know. I have spoken true, my Lord Abbot."

There was a deep silence in the room as each hearer thought of what he had heard. Rosamund the Fair had long, golden hair like candlelight and a broad white brow above a mouth that, whether laughing or pouting, was surely the most delectable God ever made. Henry was no longer there, and Rosamund was bored. Herlwin, who had been sent to Walter de Clifford to earn his spurs of knighthood, *was there* with his laughing eyes and sweet song. And their playful game of courtly love got out of hand, as such things are wont to do. So Rosamund, in fear for her life, and Herlwin, in fear for his knighthood, hid the babe away.

"I have spoken true," Nyall repeated.

Henry nodded his aristocratic head. "I believe you have."

Suddenly Bors wrenched himself from his awestruck silence. "No. It is yet but a part-truth. The rest I do not know. Why have you hated me these many years? Why have you kept me hidden away at this monastery as if I am vile to your sight? Why did not Herlwin reward you for such service rather than dismissing you?"

The result this produced was more amazing than the story that had preceded it. Nyall flung himself across the room at Bors as if he would throttle him. "Vile! Yes. What did your presence ever produce in reward but a few landstrips added to our holdings? I did all for Herlwin d'Emercy, and did he reward me? Did he offer me for knighthood? Was there gold in my coffers? I bided my time. When our father dies, I thought, then he'll make me bailiff. In time steward, perhaps. But there was nothing. No reward. No advancement.

"So when my father lay on his deathbed of fever, I spoke my mind. I told Herlwin, whom I still served faithfully as squire, that I would have my reward.

I would have money and advancement, or I would see that King Henry heard of his exploits.

"And he laughed. Herlwin d'Emercy laughed. I must prove myself worthy of advancement by more than ability to carry tales, he said. I had been rewarded for my good deed. I must prove my loyalty by work and skill. Bah! I had had enough of fetching and carrying for Herlwin d'Emercy. Our family was as Norman as his. We had as much right to position and manors. Ever since Giles Bachiler was squire to Gilbert d'Emercy at the Battle of Hastings, clear until now—near to a hundred and twenty years later—the Bachilers are still serving the d'Emercys. I burned to change that. And here was the first rung in the ladder—an inconvenient squalling brat." He glared at Bors as if he would spit at him, then began to rave again.

"And then when our parents died of fever within a week of each other and I was left to provide for the family, I judged it was time to let Herlwin know that at least *one* had not forgotten the service rendered five years before. And he laughed, I tell you. Herlwin d'Emercy laughed in my face. 'And who would believe your tales? The word of a disgruntled underling against the word of the son of one of King Henry's most loyal knights and the word of the king's favorite lady, she who was acknowledged by Henry in court—think you they would believe your tales?'

"I had played my hand and lost. I must keep my head low and voice quiet if I didn't want to lose what was already mine. And so I got the inconvenient brat out of everyone's sight in hopes that the whole mess would be forgotten by the time Lord Heribert should die and Herlwin become lord of the manor to rule the Bachiler fortunes. But never was there any reward."

Nyall's voice had become hysterical. "And I did all for him—all—and he would not reward me—all I did—"

"All you did, *all*?" Bors would not be held back by the abbot. "What is all? I would know what happened to the babe I supplanted!"

"He died. I have said. He died." Nyall's voice was now as spent as his drooping body. "He died. I buried him with my own hands."

"What?" For the first time Abbot Henry raised his voice. "You buried him? Without aid of priest to administer rites? You buried him in unconsecrated ground?"

Nyall spread his hands in appeal. "What else could I do? I could not tell the priest what had happened. No one could know that the babe Elswith Bachiler nursed that morning was not the one she had nursed the evening before. What else could I do?"

"That is a question you must ask your Creator on the day of judgment, Nyall Bachiler. For I tremble to think what answer you will receive."

But still Bors was unsatisfied. "But the babe—he died, yes. But *how* did he die? Did he die by your hand, Nyall?"

There was no answer.

"Speak," Henry commanded.

"N-no. No! Not by my hand. He was born weak. He was dead when I arrived home. How else would my mother have taken a changeling to her breast? I did not do it. I did not. No!"

"I have heard you." Abbot Henry's voice flowed calmly across the room. "And Heaven has heard you. Nyall Bachiler, you stand accused of a crime you deny. There is no proof this side of Heaven that could be presented to any court. Let us therefore appeal to Heaven. Nyall Bachiler, will you submit to trial by ordeal of communion?"

And as if by prearranged plan, the bell calling to mass rang from the bell tower.

Nyall jerked his head from side to side, looking around like a trapped animal. The bell chimed with more insistence.

"I submit," he said.

The black-robed Benedictine brothers were all in their places in the choir when the abbot, wearing fresh vestments, led the way down the center aisle followed by Bors, Ivo, and Nyall with his pale eyes fixed firmly on the stone floor.

The order of the mass seemed interminable. Surely Brother Othbert was leading the choir at half pace through all the sections. During the *Sanctus* Bors thought of Nyall as the monks chanted, "Holy, holy, holy." Was the very holiness of God striking terror in Nyall's heart? Would a holy God look away from him and cause his throat to close on the sacred elements, declaring him guilty of murder before all men? Would the broken body of Christ bring eternal damnation to one who was to partake today?

And then with seeming studied slowness, Abbot Henry washed his hands and broke the host over the silver paten on the altar. He picked up a small piece of the element and placed it in the wine-and-water-filled chalice. The abbot genuflected, then held the host elevated over the paten, that all could remember that so was Christ raised on a cross for their sins. "This is the Lamb of God who takes away the sins of the world."

Though none in the church except the abbot and the three sitting on the first row beneath the choir knew of the trial that was to come, it seemed to Bors that the tension mounted steadily in the chapel as the brothers filed forward and each in his turn partook of the sacred elements.

At last Bors rose and led the way down the short aisle that seemed to lengthen under his feet. His feet grew heavy as if the very stones of the floor would suck him in. It was not Nyall's guilt he was worried about, but his own—he was the vile sinner for whom the precious blood of Christ had been spilled. He had these many years hated his brother as surely as he felt Nyall had hated him. And now, it was his accusation that was bringing Nyall to judgment. His condemnation. That was not his place. He was to love his brother—all in the brotherhood of man. What if Nyall's throat closed and he choked to death on the body of Christ? Would not Bors be equal in guilt for bringing one to his death? The weight of his sins made it all but impossible for him to walk. When at last he reached the altar, he fell to his knees rather than turning to the priest for the elements.

The words of the mass echoed in his mind and heart as a desperate cry to Heaven. *Lord have mercy. Christ have mercy. Lord have mercy.* "My Lord, I am not worthy to receive You. But speak the word, and I shall be healed." And suddenly his heart lightened. God had heard. God understood—understood the desperation of his longing for knowledge, understood the desperation of his desire for forgiveness, understood the desperation of love for his brother that had twisted into hatred. God understood and God forgave. He turned to Abbot Henry with his lips apart, his tongue extended.

"The body of Christ."

The element rested on his tongue with a sweet burning.

"Amen."

And then he stood apart, for each man must come to his own encounter with God, his own judgment, and Nyall had come to his.

Nyall knelt before the abbot. Henry paused with the elements raised like a descending dove or an executioner's sword. And he prayed, "God of truth, O holy One, Revealer of all, hear us now. You are our Father who knows the hearts of all men, before whom nothing is hidden. We come to You with faith in Your love and mercy and in Your justice. As this one now eats Your body, let it not bring condemnation unjustly, but speak forth the truth of Heaven in Your omniscience."

Then many of the monks, realizing what was taking place before them, crossed themselves, and responded, "Amen."

Abbot Henry lowered the bread to Nyall.

But Nyall did not open his mouth.

Henry waited.

Silence.

Suddenly Nyall sprang to his feet and bolted down the aisle and out the door. Two monks made as if they would follow him, but Abbot Henry raised his hand. "Let him depart. If not in peace, at least not hindered by us. He cannot outrun God or his own conscience." And then he returned to the order of the service. "The mass is ended. Go in peace to love and serve the Lord."

The abbot invited Bors and Ivo to take dinner with him. Sitting in the quiet of the abbot's hall, the foster brothers were silent for a long time with the uneasy silence of strangers forced to share an emotional experience. The excellent baked perch served with fennel sauce by the lay brother who attended at the abbot's kitchen took all their attention until at last Ivo spoke. "You have had answers to many questions today, Bors. But you have not answered mine."

Bors placed a morsel of the cheese for which Glastonbury Abbey was becoming famous back on his trencher and looked at Ivo. "Question?"

"I asked if you would take the cross with me."

Bors shook his head in amazement that such a proposal could have gone completely forgotten. Could so much have happened in so short a space? He had had no time to think what Nyall's revelations would mean to him. Would he claim his sonship to Herlwin d'Emercy? At the moment it was too overwhelming to consider. But one thing did seem clear—as grandson to Sir Heribert d'Emercy, he owed him fealty, even if the old lord did not know of the relationship. And d'Emercy's knights would march under the Clifford banner—that of his other grandfather—although not above five people in the world would know it. Bors knew, and that was enough. "I will. I will squire you, foster brother, but you must teach me all my duty. Brother Ambrose has taught me letters and numbers, and I read and write a good hand in Latin, French, and English, but I have never polished a sword or helped a knight into his helm."

Ivo raised his ale glass and beamed. "But at least you know that will be part of your duty. I think we might go forward from there."

Bors smiled and drank with him.

Then Ivo turned to the abbot who sat quietly observing from his end of the long planked table. "My Lord Abbot, I would lay one more request before you."

Abbot Henry inclined his head.

"I kept vigil on the eve of my knighting in the d'Emercy chapel where I have prayed since birth, and the others of d'Emercy's knights will likewise keep vigil there before setting out on Crusade, but with your permission, I would keep my Crusade vigil at the ancient Chapel of St. Bridget."

The abbot nodded his head. "And so, I understand, did many brave knights keep vigil there before the glorious First Crusade. May your endeavors be as blessed as theirs were in winning Jerusalem from the infidel. When would you keep your vigil?"

"Tonight, if it please Your Lordship. For tomorrow we meet Clifford's troops making for Winchester."

"I will instruct Brother Aelfric to have candles lighted in the chapel for you. It is little used except by pilgrims from Ireland who would pray in the chapel of one of their favorite saints before visiting the tomb of St. Patrick—although we have little enough to show them since the fire." He selected an apple from the wooden bowl in the center of the table and polished it thoughtfully on his napkin. "It will be a long night. Bors, you can find him a spare cot in the boys' end of the dorter where he may sleep first. Then I'm sure you will have much to do before leaving us."

Bors nodded sharply. He had not yet thought of the farewells he would have to make from this place that had been home to him for thirteen years. He must run to Beckery where Gellert still minded the sheep—although old Brother Arald had long ago gone to the arms of the Good Shepherd. And old Garth was gone, but pups of his pups still greeted Bors on his infrequent visits . . . and here, Brother Ambrose and Brother Jerome and Brother Eluid . . . now that he was to leave it, he realized how much he truly loved the place and what a great favor Nyall had done him in bringing him here . . . And the Tor—he must make a final pilgrimage to the top of the green sentinel that had guarded his time here through all the days that he had seen it gold at sunrise and red at sunset . . .

"Will you say Compline with us or keep the office by yourself?" Abbot Henry was asking Ivo.

"Compline to Prime I will keep vigil. The offices I will say with you." And then he broke into the boyish smile that won friends so readily. "I fear, Father, I do not know them well enough, except to follow the brothers."

Later, with the last notes of the monks' chant following them and the last ray of reflected sunset extinguished on the Tor behind them, Bors and Ivo walked out the gatehouse and along the path to the tiny, ancient white wattle chapel that had once stood on the edge of a lake before St. Dunstan drained the marshes.

Both boys had eaten a light supper with the brothers, and then, in his first squire's duty, Bors had helped dress Ivo for his vigil. Now he looked in amazement at Ivo walking so easily in the hauberk that Bors could scarcely lift. He could still feel the dead weight of the interlinking iron mesh garment he had held above Ivo's head as Ivo, wearing a padded tunic, stooped under and crawled into it—like a turtle into his shell. The coif of the hauberk was loose around Ivo's neck, and the flat-topped iron helm, that many called a pot helm because of its likeness to a cooking pot, lay still on the cot, for a knight must go bare-headed to vigil.

Next he had belted on the sword—the sword that their great, great grandfather had carried at Hastings and that had hung on the wall of their cottage for as long as anyone could remember.

Then Bors held the mail-covered war mittens for Ivo to slide his hands into and handed him his shield. Of leather-covered wood, curved at the top and pointed at the bottom, the shield was five feet long so that it would cover a mounted knight from head to foot. But unlike the brightly painted shields of most knights, this was merely a virgescue—a plain white shield carried by a new-made knight who had not yet earned a distinguishing device.

Beside the fully attired Ivo, Bors walked clad merely in the short, dark tunic of an abbey schoolboy. He would be given a squire's hauberk to protect him before they set out on Crusade. He wondered if he would receive his chain-mail coat from the hand of Herlwin who was to lead the d'Emercy troops in the place of his aging father, but he wasn't sure it mattered much. There was so much else to think of as he set out on this new life that until a few hours ago had been an impossible dream.

The mail strips on Ivo's legs clinked as they walked, and the white linen surcoat over his hauberk flapped around his knees and shone bright in the pale light. Bors's heart was too full for speech. So they came silently to the lime-washed chapel set in its green circle of apple trees where the beloved Irish saint had once established a monastery after her own pilgrimage to St. Patrick's tomb. Bors was glad Ivo had chosen this chapel for his vigil because St. Bridget had been a favorite of his.

The door stood ajar, and in the deepening dark a warm light welcomed them. Four lighted beeswax candles stood on the altar at the east end of the tiny room, filling it with the sweet, warm scent of honey. Inside the door Bors drew apart and melted into the shadows. A knight must keep vigil alone with God. Bors watched while Ivo went forward, his mailed feet ringing on the bare wooden floor planks. At the altar he stopped, held out his white shield as if in offering, and placed it on the table beside the most precious relic in the room—St. Bridget's tiny bell that she had used to summon her flock to worship.

Then he drew his sword and knelt before the altar, holding the sword aloft by its blade so that hilt and hand-guard formed a cross. The flickering candle-light played on the sword, links of mail, and on Ivo's golden hair, making an aureole around the kneeling knight. All was silent within the church save for the soft whisper of Ivo's barely moving lips.

Holding his breath, lest he desecrate the holy scene, Bors backed out of the chapel. It would be a long night. The floorboards and white-washed walls would grow cold. The mail of his leggings would bite cruelly into Ivo's knees before he could rest them with movement. Bors turned his back on the chapel. But his feet did not return him to the comparative warmth and comfort of his cell. Rather, he climbed Wearyall Hill and knelt by the holy thorn. Here he would keep his own vigil, praying for his own soul, for sustenance for his knight, and most of all for Nyall, the foster brother whose hatred he no longer returned.

The golden plover was crying over the marshes even before the bell for Prime signaled the end of the vigil. Bors pulled himself slowly to his feet—cramped, cold and weary—but with a heart lightened and strengthened. Just as he had kept faith through the long night, so would God keep faith with him on the long road he now determined to travel.

He made his way to the chapel at the foot of the hill. The candles had burned low and guttered, but that had been the only movement in the room, for Ivo knelt just as Bors had left him, his sword raised in a cross above his bowed head. Bors walked forward. Only when he shook Ivo's shoulder did the kneeling figure move. He looked up at Bors and blinked, as if struggling to recall who he was and what he was doing there. Then Ivo broke into a radiant smile and accepted his squire's hand to rise.

After Prime they broke their fast with the ritual quarter-pound loaf of bread and one-third pint of ale. Then they rode forth to meet Clifford's men, Bors on a small sturdy pony that Ivo had purchased from the abbot.

About noon on the fourth day of their journey they rode over a green swell in the downs and into the ancient city of Winchester, the sun glinting on armor, trappings, and colorful banners. Their way took them past the massive gray stone cathedral where Alfred the Great lay buried and on to William the Conqueror's castle where he and all the kings since his time—William II, Henry I, Stephen (when he wasn't imprisoned by his cousin the Empress Matilda), Henry II, and now King Richard—assembled their barons when they wanted laws passed or taxes levied.

Frequently on the way when Bors neared Herlwin d'Emercy riding under the green and gold banner carried by his first squire, Bors would wonder if Herlwin ever gave thought to the babe he had fathered and disposed of in such desperation eighteen years ago and whether he would ever have courage to reveal himself to his father—or what the reaction would be if he did. Of course Herlwin knew who Bors was, but he did not know that Bors knew. And perhaps it was best left at that for the time.

All the barons in the land had responded in one form or another to Richard's call—although some preferred to pay their fee by sending money rather than men. The town and castle overflowed with knights, squires, horses, and camp followers of every description. Clogging the narrow streets, knots of revelers gathered around minstrels, jongleurs, trained animal acts, and sellers of roast nuts, gingerbread, and honey cakes. Passage even up the High Street was next to impossible for the clutter of small ragged boys and scruffy dogs. As Clifford's men were late arrivals, no space could be found for them inside the castle walls. They were allotted the first field beyond the moat. Within a few hours the meadow bloomed with round, pointed-top tents of brightly striped and patterned fabrics. The tents, which would be used in the Holy Land as well, were made of sewn linen strips soaked in linseed oil to make them waterproof. The tents of barons and lords were draped inside with fine fabrics to keep out insects. Ivo's tent was small, dull green, and much patched, but to the new-made knight and squire the whole affair was the stuff of minstrel's song.

On the morrow was to be the great assembly of barons in the castle hall. Bors slept outside the door of his knight's tent, and the two were up at the break of dawn to prepare for the ceremonies. Ivo would not go in mail, but he would wear his white surcoat over a plain tunic and breeches, and today for the first time he wore the red Crusader cross sewn on his breast. Bors wore a tunic of d'Emercy green and gold with his cross, smaller than Ivo's, sewn on his shoulder.

The castle hall was the largest Bors had ever seen. Its stone walls and timber rafters reached as high as any cathedral, and it was so far from one end to the other that, full of knights and squires as it was even at this early hour, he had to squint to see to the far end. Morning sunlight streaked through the round-topped eastern windows recessed deep in the six-foot thick stone walls. In the center the roof was supported by a great, rounded stone arch. At the far end of the room was a fireplace built into the outside wall, nearly as tall as the narrow, arched window recesses on either side of it. But that was all Bors could see above the crush of people, and he despaired of being able to see the ceremony and King Richard.

Then a movement above him drew his eyes to the arched gallery running around the upper level of the hall. A lady and her servant leaned over the rail, rapt on the proceedings below. Bors grabbed Ivo's arm. "Look, the gallery is nearly deserted. We can see all from there. How do we get up?"

Ivo craned his neck this way and that, considering the room. "A staircase in the angle turret, I should judge. It's worth a try."

They hurried up the narrow stone stairway corkscrewing toward the sky, Ivo's spurs jingling on each step. Along the gallery an archway opened out full-view over the hall below, and they had it all to themselves. Now they could see in the center of the room a great round table formed from a slab of solid oak eighteen feet in diameter, supported on twelve study legs. "It is said Arthur of old assembled his valiant knights around just such a table," Ivo said.

"No, around this very table." Bors and Ivo swung around at the sound of a musical female voice. It was the young woman Bors had observed in the gallery earlier. Monastery-raised Bors stood speechless before the beauty with her long plaits the color of moonlight on snow peeking beneath a round veil held in place by a metal circlet. Her round blue eyes, reflecting the gentian color of her linen under-tunic, smiled at him with amusement. A little brown dog peeked out beneath her primrose yellow over-tunic—the sleeveless, low-cut garment which fitted her slender form tight to the waist, then flowed out freely from rounded hips. Her jeweled belt, knotted loosely in front, accentuated her tiny waist. "I am Marie," she said in the most beautiful French Bors had ever heard spoken, "waiting lady to Queen Eleanor." Her little dog tugged at her skirt, and she stooped to pick him up with a chime of laughter that rang like a silver bell.

Ivo, schooled in the knightly courtesies, introduced himself and his squire. He was just attempting to point out their lord somewhere in the mass on the floor below when two red-and-scarlet-clad trumpeters appeared at the arch in the gallery on the opposite side of the hall and signaled the approach of King Richard Coeur-de-Lion. All those on the crowded floor and in the gallery bowed at the entrance of their king. Even without the trumpet fanfare, however, Richard would have attracted the attention of all. Well over six feet tall, his red hair and beard gleamed beneath his golden crown. He wore a crimson surcoat with three gold lions emblazoned on the chest, and he carried the two-handed sword with which he had earned such fame.

Behind him followed the twenty-four mightiest barons of the land. "Which is Walter de Clifford?" Bors asked.

Ivo pointed out a gray-haired man in an ankle-length, fur-trimmed purple and blue tunic. Bors followed the pointing finger. He said nothing, but it was long before he shifted his gaze. Somehow it was more wonderful to him to see his grandfather than Herlwin d'Emercy, his own father.

The barons took their places on stools tightly packed around the table with Richard seated at the side nearest the fireplace. The king made a speech to his barons, little of which was audible to those leaning over the rail above. Bors caught only enough to understand that Richard was delivering his kingdom into the keeping of his chamberlain, William Longchamps.

After some discussion, questioning, and voting by the barons on a matter which Bors couldn't make out, Richard rose from his high carved chair and spoke in a voice that carried to every person in the hall and probably also to any in the courtyard beneath the open windows. "My noble barons, in order to distinguish my valiant knights from all other Crusaders who will gather for this great venture, those from Germany and France, from Italy and Austria, I hereby institute a device for the knights of England." He spoke in French, for everyone knew and complained that the King of England spoke no English.

King Richard signaled a page who came forward and knelt before him, holding out a strip of bright blue leather on a silver salver. Richard took the thong and held it aloft for all to see. "I hereby instruct all my barons and knights to fasten to their legs a blue thong as their king does." And so saying, he drew up his scarlet surcoat, planted his long leg on a stool, and signaled his page to fasten the garter just below the royal knee. "Therefore," the task completed, he continued, "being so marked and identified in brotherhood, may we ever stand in readiness. And minded of future glory, let us go forth to acquit ourselves valiantly." Richard drew his sword and held it aloft while the hall rang with cheers. Dozens of royal pages circulated the best they could through the crowd, distributing blue garters.

"St. George for England!" The cry rose.

"May God give the victory!" King Richard the Lionhearted responded.

6

he shining glory of that moment remained even through the long voyage in the fleet of two hundred ships. Even when word reached them that King Frederick Barbarossa of Germany had been drowned crossing a river, and his troops had turned back. Even when winter storms in the Mediterranean forced them to make winter camp on the island of Sicily, far from their goal.

But the brightness faded when fever swept the crowded camp. And it faded more when their hot-tempered king quarreled with Tancred, King of Sicily, and the local people quit bringing food and other much-needed supplies to their camp. The final flicker of glory faded when word went round that King Tancred had received a letter from Philip of France accusing the English king of treacherous motives. The Germans were gone. King Richard was isolated from the French and Italian leaders. Could the English conquer the Holy Land alone with perhaps a handful of Austrians?

But Richard was quick to make amends where it suited him, and he never missed a chance to inspire his men and to keep before them the visions of glory that drove him. He made peace with Tancred. And Tancred, to make amends for offending the most powerful king in Europe, paid Richard 20,000 ounces of gold. Richard, in his turn, announced a great assembly for the placing of a lasting seal on the friendship.

In response to the royal decree, Richard's barons and knights assembled in full armor on the field beyond the wooden castle which Richard had erected as his winter quarters. A red carpet ran across the green field up to a gold-and-crimson-draped canopy where two massive carved thrones stood on a raised dais. Six banner-bearers stood on each side of the dais holding aloft Richard's scarlet banner with its three gold lions. Below the banners trumpeters lining both sides of the red carpet played a fanfare. The clear winter sun shone on armor and flapping banners as far as one could see while the two kings strode toward their thrones.

A small gilt table stood at the front of the dais, bearing a golden sword on a crimson, gold-fringed cushion. Richard stood before the table and signaled his trumpeters for a final flourish to ensure that he commanded all eyes and ears. "Barons and knights of England! Servants of God and St. George! I announce to you today a great victory for England and a great victory for all Christendom! Tancred, true and lawful King of Sicily—" Richard swung around, his right arm extended full-length to focus every eye on the Italian ruler "—has restored to us the person of our royal sister Joan, who was wife and queen to the late King of Sicily. And he has restored to us the dowry of that same sister Joan who shall now accompany us on our Crusade."

A great cheer went up from the assembled troops, for indeed, winning the release of Joan and her dowry was a great victory for King Richard. He enjoyed the cheers of his men for a space, then continued. "And further, I, Richard, King of England, Duke of Aquitaine and of Gascony, do declare that my nephew, Arthur of Britany, shall be my true and lawful heir and that this same Arthur shall marry King Tancred's daughter."

By their cheering response, it was clear that Richard would have no difficulty in securing his barons' agreement to the treaty. Richard signaled for another fanfare, this even louder and more elegant than before. And as if all the elements obeyed Richard's cue as well, the sun, which had gone behind a cloud, reappeared in dazzling glory, and a light breeze blew across the field to ripple the silken banners.

"And now," Richard, having drunk his full pleasure of the display before him, continued, "to seal this treaty, in emblem of faith, and as mark of the friendship between England and Sicily, I present to Tancred one of England's greatest treasures." Richard reached out both hands to lift the golden, jewel-encrusted sword from the scarlet silk pillow before him.

Bors, who had been edging forward in hopes of obtaining a better view, at that moment moved into the front ranks and saw the sun gleaming on the engraving of the jeweled hilt. "This you see before you," Richard said, his voice ringing to the farthest corners of the field, "is none other than Excalibur, sword of that other Arthur who was King of Britain in ancient times. It has recently been recovered from the tomb of King Arthur in the western parts of our kingdom, and we brought it on Crusade that the same spirit that endued Arthur to fight and overcome the heathen Saxons might fill us to fight the heathen Turks. And now," he said turning to Tancred who rose to meet him, "we give it into the hands of Tancred of Sicily in token that Arthur of Britany, the future King Arthur, and the daughter of Tancred, who will be his Queen Guinevere, may rule in equal glory and service to God."

Tancred accepted the sword into his outstretched hands and bowed deeply to Richard the Lionhearted. All around him banners waved, trumpets blared, and men cheered, but Bors stood blinking, his face narrowed into a frown. In all this great throng he was the only one who had actually been present at the opening of Arthur's tomb. And he alone knew that no sword had been discovered. But surely others there had read the account of Geoffrey of Monmouth. Surely many—including Richard himself—knew that Arthur's great sword

Excalibur had been thrown into the lake by his faithful knight Bedivere and reclaimed by the white samite-draped arm of the Lady of the Lake. But no one made objection. Nor did Bors object, but neither did he cheer.

Then the Crusaders continued their journey eastward. In June they reached the city of Acre, already under siege by the troops of Leopold, Duke of Austria. The arrival of the English and French troops carried the day, and a month later the city of Acre was in Christian hands.

Then Richard turned his face to Jerusalem.

Ever after, Bors's memories of that long march in mailed hauberk across burning desert sands would make his mouth parch and his throat rasp as if filled with dust. The constant attacks by Saladin's savage warriors, the gnawing hunger when Richard's daring raids failed to produce food, even the piercing screams of knights being eaten alive by crocodiles when they camped too close to a riverbank, were as nothing in his mind compared to the incessant scorching of the sun. Heat rose in waves that pounded inside his skull in a headache that would not end. At night he would close his eyes and find, not blessed darkness, but glaring, white-hot light that burned on the inside of his eyelids.

And then they came to Arsuf.

Sunstroke had claimed many victims among the Crusaders—almost as many as the Turkish arrows had claimed on their daily forays against the hundred thousand Crusaders marching to Jerusalem. But it was clear even to the lowliest squire that such harassment would never bring victory to Saladin. If the Turkish leader wanted to stop the Crusaders, he must risk committing the mass of his troops, not just marauding bands.

On the sixth morning of September Bors woke before the trumpet call. There was a current in the air, like that he remembered from his long-ago days sheep-herding that would tell him wolves were on the prowl. He went to the river to get a basin of water for Ivo's washing. And by the time he was back the air was already hot and dry, the morning coolness burned away with the first rays of the sun. But Bors still felt the air tingle, and he spent extra effort dressing and serving Ivo.

When they had broken camp and assembled for march, it seemed clear to Bors that Richard also scented wolf in the air, for it had been long since he had taken such care in organizing his line of march. In the van he placed the Templars, next Bretons and Angevins, then the Poitevins with their King George. In the forth division came the Norman and English troops, each grouped around the standards of their barons. During the long march southward Bors had given little thought to being close to his father or grandfather, but today, with Muslim wolves prowling just out of sight, Bors found himself edging ever closer to the green and gold banner and the dark-haired lord on the great gray charger.

Bors was vaguely aware that behind them marched the French contingents and that Richard had placed the Hospitalers in the rear guard—the position of greatest danger. When he came over a slight rise, Bors could see their troops in both directions. The order was perfect. Files three-men thick of infantry marched on the inland side to protect their valuable cavalry from attack, and to the right, where the sun glinted off the sea, bobbed the dark forms of their navy. In spite of the possible refuge the ships offered to wounded or exhausted men, today the action would be on the hot, dry sands where Bors rode behind his knight and blinked against the glare. Ten times ten, and ten times that the September sun glinted on metal helms and mailed coifs—a solid wall of iron, moving as one great war machine, for Richard had his men packed so tightly together he could not have thrown an apple into the ranks without hitting either man or horse.

Still there was no sign of the Turks brandishing their curved scimitars. Yet the air vibrated. Richard, with a retinue of hand-picked knights, rode up and down the line of march, checking and re-checking their formation and urging the men forward with shouts of encouragement.

For all of Richard's urgings, the pace slackened as they neared the wood of Arsuf. A rumor ran through the ranks of marching men that the Turks would wait until they were in the midst of it and then set the trees and September-dry underbrush ablaze. But Ivo was not unnerved—or at least he covered it. "Oh well." He shrugged. "It can scarcely be any hotter than marching across the desert."

In spite of their fears, the line kept going. The comparatively cool greenness engulfed them, shafts of sunlight piercing through the pale olive green leaves and the darker pine needles. The quivering air tingled with the sharp scent of pine, and the oily pollen of the olive made man after man sneeze, the hollow explosions filtering back through the ranks. And then something else filtered back from the Templars in front, through the three divisions of French troops to the English in the middle. The news reached the d'Emercy men in the middle of the march that the Templars were through the forest. Not a spark. Not a single arrow. Not so much as a false owl hoot. The forest was not ambushed. Spirits soared as men straightened their shoulders and clucked to their mounts or lengthened their stride. The line swept forward out of the tree cover toward the blazing desert sun that for once did not seem like a blast from the mouth of Hell.

Only when they were clear into the light and their eyes adjusted to its brightness, did Bors, riding close behind Ivo, see what others farther forward had long seen. They had marched into a great mass of Turkish troops.

Bedouin and Nubian auxiliaries rained a nuisance of arrows on the advancing flanks, charging in, then wheeling round and charging again, pressing ever closer and closer. As the fury increased, so did the rain of arrows, and still Richard advanced. On their left, partly sheltered by the edge of the forest, waited the elite cavalry, the savage Mamelukes. Their richly colored pennons streamed in numberless blazes of red, gold, saffron, and emerald. The equally colorful silk scarves fluttered from thousands of pointed iron helmets.

It was as if at any minute the entire wall of Saracens would crash down upon them. Bors thought fleetingly of how the children of Israel must have felt crossing the Red Sea with its waters standing up in walls on either side. But as the Red Sea held, so held the wall of Saracens. Only the rain of arrows on Richard's main battle line continued, until the thickly padded arrow-proof jackets of the infantry were stuck so full that the men looked like porcupines.

The tension up and down the ranks now made as nothing the earlier unrest in the Wood of Arsuf. For here in full view were Saladin's hosts waiting to pounce on them. Now instead of sending a few harrying bands that loosed a rain of arrows and a few fierce slashes of scimitars and then withdrew across the desert as if riding the hot wind itself, Saladin had committed his full force.

Yet the Crusaders did not engage. By the sheer force of his own personality, Richard kept his men in line, and archers of the infantry returned shots while marching ever forward as human shields to the precious horses of the cavalry. Then the rear guard, the Hospitalers, broke from the woods. All of Richard's army was now in the open.

The Mamelukes attacked. With a blare of trumpets and a clash of drums and tabors, the first lines of Muslim cavalry spurred forward focusing their attack on Richard's rear guard in an obvious attempt to cut them off and take Richard from the back. Yet Richard held. He would force Saladin to bring all his troops into battle by remaining on the defensive.

Twice a desperate request came from the Master of Hospital begging Richard for permission to attack. And yet through the heat and dust, the clash and clamor and shrieks of battle, Richard held. He had waited too long for this chance to throw it away on a premature charge.

In their own corner of the field Sir Ivo Bachiler and his squire fought to hold their defense line with the others of Clifford's men. Occasionally the line of foot soldiers wielding spears, pikes, axes, and short bows would weaken, and the mounted knights with their long swords would ride forward to close the ranks. Yet Richard held.

"Will he not strike?" Bors wiped the dust-clogged sweat from his brow.

Ivo shouted back, "Not until the Mamelukes are too close to retreat—and their horses tire. We'll engage them all when the cowards can't run!" Ivo brandished his sword, which was still unbloodied since Bors's polishing of the night before.

Suddenly from the rear, where the Hospitalers held the thick of a desperate battle, a trumpet sounded followed by the cry of, "St. George! Forward!" "Upon them, St. George!"

Bors spun around in his saddle. Could that be right? The charge had sounded from the Master of the Hospital, not from Richard. Where was the Lionheart?

Then Bors saw him astride his great white charger as he raised his broadsword in signal, and the air was split with the signal for the general charge—six clear trumpet blasts. As if the whole earth gave a great heaving shudder, the troops surged forward. "Upon them, St. George!" "For God and St. George!" The cavalry squadrons rode through the protecting infantry and charged all along the line.

Then all was drowned in the clashing of swords and cries of men and animals, with always the incessant beat of the Turkish drums throbbing on the hot, choking air.

Bors, like other squires, carried only a short dagger for his own protection. It was his job to look to his knight's safety. If his weapon was lost, Bors would grab one from a slain knight. If his shield, helm, or hauberk failed, Bors would mend or replace it as best possible. If Ivo's horse was wounded or slain, Bors would give him his own or seize that of a fallen warrior. And, saints forbid, if Ivo was wounded, Bors would tend him.

Bors held his breath, his teeth gritted and his hand clamped on the hilt of his dagger as Ivo traded sword blows with a dark-skinned, black-bearded Saracen. The Turk was twice Ivo's size and age, but Ivo had the greater speed and skill. For pass after pass they exchanged strokes in hollow clangs of sword on scimitar. Bors feared Ivo would tire, his sword arm weaken, but he held. And finally, with a perfectly timed blow, he lunged with all his weight behind a thrust that left the Muslim's dappled white horse riderless.

Bors, who had followed every blow with unblinking intensity, heaved a sigh and looked up, suddenly aware that there were hundreds, nay, thousands of such clashes all around them. His attention followed the riderless Turkish horse plunging into the thickest part of the fray. And he saw ahead of him King Richard more than a head higher than any man on the field, wielding his great broadsword, slashing first on one side, then the other, spinning his horse so that his blows fell on all sides, carving a lane of dead as he pressed forward.

Then Bors looked back to Ivo. A Turk with a blue silk scarf streaming down his back lunged forward, the sun glinting off his curved scimitar. He was afoot and approaching head-on so Ivo could not see him in the swirl of dust, men, and horses. "Ivo!" Bors shouted, but the warning was swallowed by the roar of battle.

Bors started to shout again, but the word strangled in his throat as the scimitar carved a blood-red path across the red-gold coat of Ivo's horse. The valiant animal staggered and lunged forward on his front knees, sending Ivo forward over his head. The Turk's blood-reddened blade rose high over Ivo's head, but Bors flung himself off his horse and lunged toward the blade.

His lunge had caused the Turk to check his first motion, but it took only a second to regain his footing. Bors saw the flash of light as the scimitar curved toward him.

And then he saw a flutter of blue silk as the Turk fell at his feet, the battle-axe of a foot soldier in his neck.

Before Bors could shout his gratitude, the infantryman spun away. But too late. The spear-sharp boss of a Saracen shield dug deep into his padded coif as a Mameluke whirled into battle on a small gray horse, then swept on in the surge of battle.

Suddenly Bors and Ivo were alone with the wounded foot soldier, the battle raging some distance to their left. For the first time Bors looked at the man who had saved both Ivo and himself. The straw-thatch hair that had been uncovered by the Turkish shield turned sticky red with the flow from the deep gouge. The soldier staggered to his knees.

Bors rushed forward, grasping him in both arms. He lay the limp form on the ground. "Nyall. You saved my life. And Ivo's."

The blue-gray eyes were dimming as the sand under his head stained a brighter red. "Mayhap that evens the score." His rasping voice faded to a whisper. "I don't know. I think the bairn was dead. I don't know. Now I go to learn the truth." A shudder went through his body, and he lay still.

Bors lay his foster brother in the sand of the Holy Land, closed his eyes, folded his arms over his chest, and made the sign of the cross over him. Bors and Ivo stood in silence for several moments beside the body.

Then suddenly a new throb in the air made Bors look up. The sound of the battle had changed. The drums beat a different rhythm. The Turkish trumpets sounded a wail of defeat. All across the field, as far as they could see, Saracens fled for their lives, and Crusaders pursued. At the edge of the forest Bors could see Mamelukes spring from their saddles and climb the trees to escape the terrible pursuing swords and slashing axes.

But Richard's trumpeters called the lines sternly back into formation. At the battle of Acre so many months ago, the Crusaders had similarly routed the Turks and scattered in hot pursuit, hoping to finish the enemy. Then Saladin had turned his fleeing army, and the Crusaders had been cut to ribbons in the rally. Richard would not be caught in such a trap a second time. His trumpets insistently reformed the lines. Calvary, many of them, like Ivo, remounted on horses of fallen fellows, stood ready for the next charge—an orderly charge which could be repeated as many times as necessary until Richard had the complete victory.

They didn't have long to wait. The Turks were as determined as the Crusaders that this would be a decisive victory. This time the line held, without a preemptory rush by the Hospitalers, until Richard could choose his moment. Once again, to the shout of trumpets and men, Bors spurred his sturdy Welsh pony forward into battle behind Ivo under the green and gold silk banner of d'Emercy. And this time it was as if the earlier charge had been merely a practice charge at a tournament for the contesting knights to size each other up and choose whom they would challenge. Now the earlier frenzy had died, replaced with a deadlier grimness.

The green pennon whirled and whipped in the afternoon wind, held bravely aloft by Herlwin d'Emercy's squire who ever followed his lord into the thickest of battle where the lightning-stroke of his sword was most needful. As Bors followed Ivo in the surge of battle, this time Bors came closer to the green-flying banner where with a choke of pride he watched his father in battle. Herlwin had never owned him, had never spoken to him as son, had hardly given him a nod of recognition, and yet Bors's heart swelled at the knowledge that he was of the blood of one so valiant. If he could choose from any on the field, Herlwin d'Emercy he would choose for father.

But then the desperate thing happened. Herlwin's ferocious fighting had led them deeper into the battle, fighting Turks on every side, without thought to their own safety. Wherever the green banner had gone, Ivo and the other d'Emercy knights had followed with their squires. Herlwin gave a great back-handed slash with his sword that more shoved his opponent from his mount than wounded him, and the sword-sharp hooves of his gray charger finished the job. In the moment's respite Herlwin raised his head and looked around him. Bors saw the look of triumph fade and his eyes widen. Their peril was writ clear on Herlwin d'Emercy's face. In his rash bravery, Herlwin had charged too far forward. They were now cut off from the ranks. Their little band was entirely surrounded by a whirl of Saracens.

At the worst of all moments, a Saracen arrow shot at close range pierced the hauberk of Herlwin's squire. The green and gold pennon hurled toward the ground.

Miraculously, the way was clear. Bors lunged forward. With a great straining of muscles, he swooped downward and forward. His fingers just closed over the fluttering end of silk. In a flash he hauled the pennon to its full height and spun his pony around where he could see Richard battling on the edge of the Crusaders' line.

"St. George! Forward!" Bors shouted and bolted forward, impervious to the slash of a scimitar that missed his cheek by the thickness of a silk banner. This small, instinctive act of bravery was enough. "For God and St. George!" Herlwin took up his cry, and the d'Emercy band was at his back as one man, slashing their way to the comparative safety of Richard's lines.

The sun was near to setting in eerie long golden streaks over the desert—so unlike anything Bors had known in England—when Richard signaled for the battle's end. Saladin and the tattered remains of his troops retired into the forest of Arsuf. The Crusaders stood in silent lines watching the enemy limp away. When the dark branches closed over the last of them, a great cry went up from Richard's men.

After months of looking for a sign of God's pleasure, at last He had smiled on them. The enemy had suffered severely while their own losses were light. But more, they had achieved a moral victory. Saladin had lost Acre because his men would not charge. Now they had charged and been soundly beaten. They would not charge again. Through the summer of hit-and-run attacks, Saladin had developed an aura of invincibility with his own men. That aura was shattered.

It was late that evening, after Bors had seen to their horses and all of his knight's needs, before he could pull off his own hauberk and sink to the still-warm ground for a rest.

"Bors! Why didn't you tell me you'd been wounded?" Ivo dropped to his knees beside him.

Bors turned in surprise to regard his right shoulder which Ivo now gripped firmly. "I didn't know. It can't be much. Only a scratch or I'd have known."

"Scratches don't bleed that much." Ivo pulled the blood-encrusted sleeve of the tunic away from the wound, causing Bors to wince.

"I don't know. I ache all over. Everything hurts. I didn't notice one spot in particular. Must have been when I rushed by that Turk when I was carrying the banner."

Ivo shook his head and grinned. "More courage than sense. Get you to the Hospitalers and have that bound up." He helped Bors to his feet.

Putting his bone-weary muscles into motion again caused old injuries to protest. He never thought of the scars on his legs unless they ached and itched in cold weather, but now they made their presence known. Bors gave a weak grin. "I haven't been in an infirmary since I was a youngling. I seem to remember one of the brothers saying something about more enthusiasm than sense then, too. But it was worth it."

7

y the wee hours of the next morning, however, the fire in Bors's shoulder was even sharper. He lay still, for movement increased the pain. In the stillness he thought of his old life—the cool greenness, the serene peace, the awareness of God's presence in the secure world of the monastery under the sheltering Tor. Was life still unchanged there? Was there still an island of peace and beauty in the world where men worshiped God unhindered by war, unchoked by dust?

He slid into an uneasy sleep, pictures whirling in his mind—of knights and Saracens thundering with clashing swords across the abbey enclosure and then flying off to the top of the Tor. And he struggled with slow, weighted feet to climb the Tor, but for every step upward he slid back two, until he tumbled and came to rest beside the Chalice Well. He plunged his burning arm into its clear-flowing waters, up to the shoulder. When he withdrew, the wound no longer burned, and in his hand he grasped a simple olivewood cup. As he started to drink of the water in the cup, it turned to blood, and a voice said, "This is My blood of the new covenant; drink ye all of it." As he drank, his closed eyes saw the jeweled cavern he had ever longed to enter, and he knew the cavern lay inside the well—or, the dream flowed . . . was it in the Tor—or . . .

A sharp trumpet blast sounded reveille. Bors sat up with a groan. The miraculous healing of his wound had been only a dream. Today, he knew they must spend the day helping the Hospitalers and Templars comb the field for dead and wounded. It would be a solemn day of binding and burying, needful tasks, although not ones he anticipated. But with the few skills he had acquired from Brothers Jerome and Eluid he could feel most useful. Bors had no more than washed down the last of his corn cake with the sour wine all—from King Richard to the lowliest camp-follower—drank, when Herlwin announced that the order of the day had been changed. They were to march the short distance to the city of Lydda. King Richard would lead his troops in worship and thanksgiving to God before they returned to the grimmer realities of the aftermath of battle. However, a small contingent would remain to tend the wounded.

The ancient city, visited in Bible times by St. Peter, stood on the southeast corner of the Plain of Sharon, the length of which the Crusaders had marched through so many weary days. Today, however, it was not the memory of the agony of that trek that Bors carried with him, but rather the greenness and peace of his dream. The setting toward which they rode was as conducive to such a dream as perhaps any in the Holy Land. After the endless sand and dust of their journey, Lydda was embowered in green. Olive groves circled the tiny town and stretched far beyond over the surrounding plain, their dull gray-green interspersed with the brighter foliage of apricot and mulberry trees. After the few villages of huddled mud huts on the way from Acre, the town itself bore a sense of unreality with its sugarloaf white houses and garden walls covered with creeping vines and bright blossoms.

The village sheltered on the lower slopes of a gentle hill, but Richard the Lionhearted rode with red and gold banners flying to higher ground. For here were the ruins of an ancient church first built by Constantine the Great. And here lay buried that noblest and most gallant of all soldier saints. Perhaps next in importance to the Holy Sepulcher in Jerusalem was the sepulcher of St. George.

The church of Constantine's building had been destroyed by the Persians and rebuilt by the Emperor Justinian in the sixth century. Justinian's great edifice had been destroyed by the Saracens during the First Crusade. Only two delicate towers and one of the smaller white domes remained intact. But now hundreds of soldiers, most still wearing tattered and blood-stained white surcoats with the red cross of St. George on their breasts, followed their king in solemn procession up the olive-tree-covered hillside to their patron saint's tomb. Templars and Hospitalers—the soldier/monks—went first. Then came Richard's barons and knights, wearing the blue thong of the Order of the Garter, then others of the Franks and King Guy's men. Most squires remained with their knights' horses, but Ivo bade Bors accompany him. Bors smiled, and his feet fell into the familiar rhythm of his monastery days as the Templars at the front of the procession began a hymn of praise.

At the church the singers formed rows higher up the hill, replacing the ruined stones of the church with a human wall. And with the broken remains of the high altar at his feet, Richard stood before the tomb of St. George. Sun poured through the roofless opening, turning Richard's hair as bright a red as the cross on his breast. Although a knight would not normally carry his sword into church, Richard now unsheathed his and signaled for all his knights to follow. In this desecrated church no crosses remained; they must furnish their own. And so each man, following his king, knelt and turned his sword hilt-upward to form a cross.

"Lord, our God, hear the prayers of those who praise Your mighty power, God King most high, may we now our voices raise in thanks, in worship and in praise . . ." Richard began. "As St. George was ready to follow Christ in suffering and death, and as he was willing in time past to help those who fought for Your holy name, as in glorified body he led Your troops to victory at the first taking of Antioch and Jerusalem, so with his spirit of humility and praise we thank You today for this fresh victory over the heathen, and ask that we may soon see Your holy tomb . . ."

The prayer continued, but Bors's mind wandered to the stories of St. George he had heard knights tell and retell as they sat over their evening wine cups . . . "Aye, my great, great-grandfather was there at the taking of Antioch. My grandfather would tell the story in his ancestor's words: 'We were right near to victory, and then the Sultan of Nicaea ordered flaming flax thrown into the dried grass and bushes. The wind billowed smoke and sparks into our faces. In the thick cloud our knights broke rank. All that remained was for the Sultan to rush in and snatch our standard. Then suddenly, the wind shifted. The smoke cleared. And we saw them. On a hill high above our wavering ranks they stood gleaming on white horses wearing snow-white mail and holding white-bannered lances. I saw them. With my own eyes, I saw. I saw, but I did not know until another cried out, "St. George! It is St. George, the great martyr! He and his fellows have come to lead us to victory! It is the will of God!" And then we all took up the battle cry, "It is the will of God! The will of God! It is His will!" The words echoed off the mountain and rolled over the Turks as their evil smoke had rolled over us earlier. The Turks had heard that battle signal before. It struck terror to their hearts. The heathen infidels fled before St. George and the will of God.

"'And so we took Antioch. And it was the will of God, for there we found the holy lance that had pierced the precious side of our bleeding Lord as He hung on the cross. But that was not all—no, not all—for St. George appeared again at the siege of Jerusalem and led us to the greatest victory of all. . . .'"

The memory faded, and Bors realized that Richard's priest was concluding the celebration of the Eucharist. And he realized that his shoulder ached abominably. But Bors had no time to think of his wound, for the ceremony was not at an end.

Richard, who had remained kneeling throughout the service, stood now, his sword/cross thrust forward and upward in straight arms. "Before Almighty God and in the name of His most precious Son, our Lord Jesus Christ, and His holy mother, Mary ever-virgin, and the glorious St. George, I here swear that in gratitude for the great victory He has vouchsafed us, I shall rebuild this church over the precious tomb of the sainted George." The king bent his elbows and lowered his sword to his lips. He kissed the cross, then dropped to his knees before the tomb while his priest sprinkled king and grave site of martyred saint with holy water.

At the conclusion of mass word went around to the d'Emercy men that their lord would have words with them outside the church. This assemblage was surely called just for the knights, but Bors followed at Ivo's heels as he had been trained to do. In the shade of a cluster of walnut trees with green vines twining their trunks, under the green and gold pennon now carried by Herlwin's second squire, they assembled. Five knights and four squires (fresh-called to their master's sides) were all that remained of those who had ridden out from Winchester. Herlwin, though thin with the exertion and lean rations of battle, seemed to stand taller than ever. His black curls tumbled in a mass to his shoulders, and in his face, tanned Saracen-brown from the desert sun, his bright gray-blue eyes and white teeth gleamed brighter than ever. "Men of d'Emercy," he began, "you have deported yourselves with great valor as becomes knights and squires of England. I am proud of you. My father shall be proud of you when he hears. Our overlord Baron Clifford is pleased with you. King Richard is pleased. God is pleased."

He paused and looked around, the bright eyes searching the somber faces before him until they found and held a pair that were the mirror image of his own. "But for one here, this might not have been the case. So hear me. For nigh to twenty years I have carried the secret of a youthful folly of passion which I committed when I was the age of the one I now name."

Bors felt a shock go through him. Then he felt nothing. It was as if his heart had stopped, his breathing stopped, as if he were stone. Herlwin d'Emercy looked at him, spoke of him. "For many years now, I have known the son of my getting bore the stamp of my likeness, but until yesterday I did not know that he also bore my rash bravery. Yesterday my rashness led us into danger. The bravery of my son Bors led us to safety. I hereby claim him son which is his by birth and declare him knight which is his by right of valor." Herlwin drew his sword and pointed to the grass in front of him where Bors was to kneel.

Bors did not move. His mind told him to, but he could not believe his mind. It had just told him things incredible. Things too wonderful to be believed. His mind said that Herlwin d'Emercy had claimed him son. His mind said that Herlwin d'Emercy waited to make him knight. But this could not be. Bors, the orphan sheep-herder from the grange at Beckery, could not rise to such heights.

And then Ivo gave him a shove forward. "Go. We're all waiting!" Bors moved forward and dropped to his knees at the tip of the pointing sword. He bowed his head before Herlwin d'Emercy, his lord and his father. He hardly felt the blow of the broad side of the sword between his neck and his shoulder. "Rise, Sir Bors d'Emercy." He heard the sword slip into its sheath. But he did not move.

Two long-boned brown hands reached down to him. But he did not grasp them; instead he folded his own and slipped them between d'Emercy's. "Here, my lord, I become liege man of yours for life and limb and earthly regard, and I will keep faith and loyalty to you for life and death, God helping me." Now, with the vassal's oath still sweet on his lips, he blundered to his feet.

He did not think it odd that his head swam and that his body felt shot with arrows of fire and ice. His knees were weak, and the world seemed to be slipping from him, but such it should be at the apotheosis of the world. All things had passed away, all things had been made new.

He did not feel the ground when he fell to it. Nor was he aware of Ivo and Herlwin lifting him with careful hands and bearing him, not back to camp outside the woods of Arsuf, but on westward to Jaffa where Richard's navy lay in port.

Three days later when the fever broke and Bors became aware of the gentle rocking of the ship beneath him, the attendant seaman told Bors that he was on a French vessel in the middle of the Mediterranean Sea bearing a load of wounded Crusaders homeward to better nursing at King Richard's orders. But the seaman could tell him nothing of what had taken place before he was brought on board. So through all the long days of the journey as Bors slipped in and out of consciousness, sometimes aware of pain and weakness, but often not feeling anything, he wondered if all that had taken place had been real, or if it had been an extension of the visions he had always reached for. Although he could not answer the question, he knew that if, in the end, all had been a dream, the pain would be much worse than that in his shoulder.

8

ors groaned, rolled over on his narrow cot, and opened his eyes. Clear, steady sunlight streamed in through a small window above him. He blinked, then realized what was different. The room did not rock. The rolling waves that had borne him for weeks past lay quiet. Then he blinked again. He was not aboard a ship. He lay long, reveling in the stillness, hearing gentle, muted sounds from outside his tiny room, trying to figure out where he was. A bell rang, an insistent calling to duty, and he heard soft footsteps swish past his door and down the hallway. Shortly after, a sound of light, melodious chanting wafted through his window. His first thought was to wonder if he'd been brought back to Glastonbury. Then he realized that no monk could sing in such a fair soprano as that now enchanting his ears. Choirboys, perhaps? A monastery with a fine lot of boys in their school? A convent of nuns? Why would they bring him to a house of holy sisters? His next thought left him hot with excitement and cold with fear—could those wondrous voices be angelic? Was that why he remembered so little of

the past days? Was he dead? But did angels sing in purgatory? Brother Ambrose had taught him so little of what to expect in the next life . . .

The next moment he was sure he was in the presence of angelic beings, for the door opened and a fair creature, swathed in white from head to toe, glided in and stood in the pool of sunlight beside his bed. A few wisps of silvery-pale hair curled around the opalescent face framed in a white linen wimple. She reached out a slim, white hand and touched his forehead. Her hand was light and cool. Surely no human being could have such a soft touch.

"Your fever has cooled. You are better." The words were so simple, the voice divine. And yet it somehow had a familiar ring. It was not possible he could have heard it before, and yet . . .

"Who are you, my lady?"

"I am Marie."

"Mary. Oh, my Lady!" He struggled to rise from his cot to kneel at her feet. How was it possible that he should be so honored to be visited by the Queen of Heaven. "Holy Mary, mother of God . . ." He fell back on his pillow too weak to rise and had to make do with crossing himself. "Forgive me, I . . ."

Her laughter was like the chime of silver bells filling the room. Not even the tiny bell of St. Bridget had such a sweet ring. "No, no, you mistake. You have been long ill, but you have not died. I am neither saint nor vision. I am simply Marie. At the court of Queen Eleanor I was called Marie de France. But now I have withdrawn to this holy house that I may devote myself to the study, meditation, and writing for which there was never time at court."

Bors struggled to grasp the thread of memory. "Marie. The court of Queen Eleanor . . . And were you in Winchester when King Richard distributed the blue garters to his knights and they set forth on Crusade?"

"I was."

"Watching from the gallery? With a little brown dog under your skirts?"

Again the chime of laughter. "My little Leda. She is with me still. I live in a guest house provided by the good sisters."

"Where?"

"Ah, *mon pauvre*, of course you do not know. You were unconscious when they brought you in—so many brave knights—so many wounds. Mother of God." She crossed herself. "The sisters are skilled in nursing and in praying, but I think it is the prayers that will avail most."

"Yes, but where are we?"

"Oh, *oui*. This is la Ville de Bretagne."

Bors frowned. "The village of Britain? We are in Brittany?"

"But, yes, in Lesser Britain. You were on a ship of France. You expected it to take you to Great Britain?"

At the moment he couldn't have cared less why he was here. He was just glad he was. "And you are not a nun?"

"But I have said not. I have come here to study the romances of Brittany—my people are Breton. But there was such a great load of wounded men to be seen to that I have laid my books aside to help the nursing sisters. Especially now when they are at mass, I can help because I am not required to attend."

She picked up a spoon from the small table beside his bed, drew the cork from a vial, and poured some of its thick brown contents into the spoon. She held it out to him. He frowned, but opened his mouth obediently. It was surprisingly sweet. He smiled.

"You sleep now." Marie re-stoppered the bottle and straightened his coverlet. "I have many to see to." She crossed to the door, then turned back with a smile. "But none of the others can I claim as old friends."

At noon a timid young novice in a black wimple that emphasized her pallor crept into his room, spoon-fed him a thick gruel, and departed without saying so much as a single word. That evening the elixir beside his bed was administered by a large, hearty sister who followed the medicine with a mug of strong wine and a wedge of sharp cheese. The dose made Bors sleep again. When he awoke the next morning to the sound of the bells tolling Prime, he wondered whether he had dreamt the exquisite Marie.

After his breakfast of bread and wine, a sturdy village lad in a short brown homespun tunic who introduced himself as "Roget, the-lad-who-helps-the-sisters," came in to help him to his feet. Bors could not believe the weakness of his legs as Roget half-dragged, half-carried him to the infirmary's lavatorium. But back in his cell, although exhausted, he was amazed at how good that wash had felt—and how little his shoulder hurt. Now that he thought about it, he realized the wound had not bothered him for days. He stretched wide the neck of his tunic and pulled at his bandages. The sight was reassuring. The wound was healing to a clean red line with no sign of putrefaction. He must not have had the wound-fever, but common camp fever, probably made more severe from his loss of blood and exhaustion. Bors lay back on his pillow with a satisfied sigh. All he need do was gain his strength, and he would be fit again. *Fit to— Hmm.* He paused. *Fit for—what will I do now?*

Through the fog that filled his mind like a wash of muddy water, he brought back the memory of Herlwin d'Emercy claiming him before all the d'Emercy men and knighting him. That's right—he was now Sir Bors d'Emercy. And the first thing he had done at his knighting was to faint. Not an auspicious beginning to his career. Then he realized that the question of what he would do or where he would go were not his to worry about. He had sworn fealty to his lord. He would serve in the Holy Land or on the manor or at the Barony of Clifford as his lord saw fit. It was a comforting thought.

But he did not really want to return to the heat and dust of the Holy Land. He wondered if Richard had taken Jerusalem by now. Had Ivo and Herlwin and the others heard mass the at Holy Sepulcher? Were they now on their way home? Home. And was d'Emercy now his home once again? What of Glastonbury? He wondered if he would ever see his green Avalon again. Yes, it was good to be a knight with a lord, but he would ever be a knight without lands. Ivo had once spoken of the awkward position of a landless knight. Yet now, with Nyall dead, Ivo would inherit the small Bachiler holdings. But Bors was illegitimate, and nothing could change the Norman law that such a one could not inherit.

The bell for High Mass interrupted his thoughts. He closed his eyes and gave himself to the softness of his pillow. A few moments later a gentle stirring of the air made him open his eyes. And she stood before him again, as vision-like as ever. But this time she bore a leather-bound manuscript in her left arm. "Roget said you are much recovered. I thought perhaps you would like some reading to help the time pass—" She stopped suddenly and clasped her free hand over her mouth. "Oh, I am sorry. I did not think. Perhaps it is that you do not—er, that is—not care for reading?"

Bors smiled at her tact. "No, no, do not worry. I am monastery-educated. I care much for reading—in French, English, or Latin."

Marie's smile was radiant. "*Bon!*" She placed the volume on the cot beside him. "It is Chretien de Troyes, whom I came to study. It is such a pity that he died two years ago, or I might have learned from his own mouth rather than from the works of his hand."

Bors lifted the cover and read the title in French, *The Lancelot*, and beneath it an explanation:

> Since my lady of Champagne wishes me to undertake to write a romance, I shall very gladly do so, being so devoted to her service as to do anything in the world for her, without any intention of flattery. But if one were to introduce any flattery upon such an occasion, he might say, and I would subscribe to it, that this lady surpasses all others who are alive, just as the south wind which blows in May or April is more lovely than any other wind. But upon my word, I am not one to wish to flatter my lady. I will simply say the countess is worth as many queens as a gem is worth pearls and sards.

He put the book down. "He writes a very pretty tongue." And then with a rush that left him breathless because he had never spoken so before, he added, "But I think Marie of Champagne could not have been half so fair as another of her name."

Marie of France, raised at the court of Queen Eleanor as had been Marie of Champagne, was no less comfortable with courtly manners and praise. She smiled. "Thank you, sir knight. You speak most becomingly."

Bors had no idea how to continue the game, so he hastily raised the book.

"Shall we see how he goes on?" He read until he was fairly certain his blush had receded, and then he raised his head. "Shall I read more?"

Marie had settled herself comfortably on the foot of his cot, her head leaning against the wall. "I fear it may tire you. Here." She held her hands out for the book. "Let me read to you." His arms relaxed; the weight of even such a slim volume had begun to pull. He closed his eyes to concentrate better on her silvery voice and to picture the scenes of the story in his mind:

> "Upon a certain Ascension Day King Arthur had come from Caerleon and had held a very magnificent court at Camelot as was fitting on such a day. After the feast the King did not quit his noble companions, of whom there were many in the hall. The Queen was present, too, and with her many a courteous lady able to converse in French. And Kay—"

"Wait." Bors opened his eyes. "Forgive my interruption, your reading is beautiful. But surely that's not right. Brother Ambrose at the monastery read much to us from the old chronicles. Surely your writer means they spoke in Celtic—or perhaps the Latin tongue?"

Raised within the monastery enclosure, Bors had thought he would never hear a sweeter sound than the ringing of their bells, but now he knew that the silvery laughter of Marie de France was sweeter far. And it pealed freely at his objection. "What! Would you insult Marie, countess of Champagne, daughter of Queen Eleanor and King Louis VII of France? My lady speaks French, so must her heroine."

Bors smiled at this most practical of answers and relaxed again to the musical tones of Marie's voice reading the story of the abduction of Guinevere by Meleagant. Lancelot, her lover, rode in an executioner's cart to rescue her after his horse was slain. But then Bors's frown returned. He could not so easily be weaned from Brother Ambrose's careful teaching of the histories. "A fine tale, I heartily agree. But Brother Ambrose would never hold with Lancelot as a Breton, no matter how thoroughly Celtic they may have been. Surely Arthur's truest and bravest knight was a Briton?" Bors took so much pleasure in Marie's laugh he was beginning to question his motives—did he ask provoking questions just to hear it?

"Briton-Breton, what difference is it? Should Lancelot come from Berwick in Britain or from Benwick in Brittany? It is a matter of a single stroke of the pen. And so convenient for our overlords that the Matter of Britain should spring from soil long under Norman domination. It makes it much easier for a population sprung from the barbaric Saxons to accept their overlordship."

The memory of gentle Elswith Bachiler, whom once he called mother, sprang to Bors's memory, and Brother Ambrose, of long Saxon lineage. "And were they truly, do you believe, such savage animals?"

Now Marie was not laughing as the light of her own noble Norman lineage snapped in her eyes. "But of course! Why else would they have need of our brave Norman lords to give them governance?"

Whether it was wisdom or fatigue that stilled Bors's tongue, he did not answer. The entrance of the shy, cobweb-colored novice with the dinner tray ended the reading session. Bors watched Marie leave the room, but it was long before he turned to the steaming bowl of chicken and vegetable broth, even though today the sister infirmarer had deemed him well enough to have chunks of tender chicken meat in his broth. In the almost two years that he had been in the world following Richard the Lionheart, he had seen many women. Mostly the smooth, olive-skinned beauties of the East smelling of heavy, sweet musk, with their flowing dark curls and ready smiles. In listening to the camp talk and in looking around him he had learned much that the brothers had not taught him. Although he would not have minded a closer acquaintance with some, whenever he thought of women, the picture that came to his mind was of Aline—she who was no longer his sister. Aline in her soft green kirtle with long fair plaits hanging beneath her coif, flinging her arms out in welcome to him.

Until now. Here was a woman far beyond any experience—a rare jewel of a woman with a mind as brilliant and many-faceted as a diamond, yet with a beauty and a spirit as soft and alluring as a pearl. All that with a solid underpinning of common sense. Now he could understand the idea of courtly love of which the troubadours sang. Here was a lady of such noble character that a lover might truly attain more worth by doing her bidding.

That afternoon the broad-built infirmarer, Sister Patrice, strode into Bors's cell and gave him a thorough going-over with her strong capable hands and pronounced him sound enough to begin moving about. "Try to walk the length of the south cloister every morning and every afternoon. When that is easily accomplished, you may walk the entire square around the garden. Roget will assist you." She spoke in rapid French with a voice that brooked no argument. "And lots of red wine and meat—I'll tell Sister Celia." Bors had no intention of arguing with such orders.

So the next morning, after two cups of red wine and a slab of creamy cheese with his roll, Bors was able to walk the length of the south cloister with Roget bearing only a little of his weight. At the far end of the walk they sat down on a smooth stone bench against the wall, and Bors viewed his surroundings. The stonework of the French convent was far more elegant than any he had seen in England, although the religious house was similar in plan. The three silvery gray towers of the abbey showing above the east walk of the cloister rose in graceful spires surrounded with carved ornamentation that looked more like lace than stone. And, closer to them, beyond the traceried arches of the cloister, itself fan-vaulted like the ceiling of the finest cathedral, was a garden of sweet-smelling red, blue, and golden flowers blooming in an intensity of color seldom seen in his green island. Even in the summer, English flowers bloomed with more gentleness, and certainly as it was now November, they would not be blooming at all.

Roget noted the direction of his gaze. "Would you like to sit in the garden? Sister Patrice is a firm believer in the healing powers of the sun."

Bors grinned. "Anything to please Sister Patrice."

When Bors was sitting in the warmest corner of the garden he turned to Roget. "One last request, if I might, before you return to your other duties?"

"Just say."

"On the table by my cot. There's a book."

"Yes." Roget bounded across the garden and through the cloister with a burst of energy.

So it was that Bors was sitting amid the flowers with only the sound of bees accompanying his thoughts when Marie found him later. She wore a soft blue gown that fitted snugly around her slim waist and then fell from her golden girdle to the floor in the graceful lines of a lily.

"And how is our favored patient progressing?"

He laid the book aside and blinked at her radiance. "My Lady Marie. I do very well. So well that soon Sister Patrice shall send me on my way, I'm sure."

"But not before you've finished your reading?"

As he was nearing the end, there was little danger of that.

"Shall I read to you?" she asked.

"No!" Then Bors blushed at his rudeness. "That is, I mean—er, no thank you, my lady."

Then the silver-bell tinkle of Marie's laughter rang. "*Oui*. I understand. You are at the passage where Lancelot, his fingers dripping blood from injuries received tearing apart the bars on Guinevere's window, takes himself to her bed, are you not?"

Bors dropped his head in acquiescence. "How can it be, my lady, that he writes so of the noble queen of such a great king as Arthur of the Britons? Does it not demean his subject and the patroness for whom he writes? Must not Marie of Champagne blush to have such a tale of adultery dedicated to her?"

Marie's laughter now was so gentle it was more as if the bell had been forged of glass than of silver. "My most innocent knight. You told me you were monastery-educated, but do you know nothing of the world? It appears to be precisely at the behest of the lady that he wrote the story so, for he made it clear in his introduction that he was writing at her orders, as if to disclaim responsibility. And see—" She took the book from his lap and turned a page. "Here." Her slim white finger pointed to the passage. "He refuses to tell more. And so the countess, sitting in her bower doing fine embroidery with her ladies around her and her musicians playing their lutes softly in the corner, who from one month to the next has the male attentions of only her minstrel and her priest while her lord is off on Crusade, can dream of such tales to fire her imagination and make interesting conversation with her women through many long hours of needlework."

Bors shook his head. "I know nothing of such things. Perhaps you are right. But I do know of history, for Brother Ambrose was very particular. King Arthur ruled near to seven hundred years ago. Surely such fine coats of mail as the writer describes, such elegant tournaments, and acts of Norman courtliness . . ."

Marie shrugged. "Events set so long ago . . . who knows or cares? The lady whose silver paid for its writing will like reading of such finery. She can picture the deeds more clearly in her mind if the settings seem familiar."

"And what do you dream of, my lady, when you sit at needlework in your bower?" Bors gasped at the rashness of his own words. He had given voice to his thoughts before he considered.

But Marie was not offended. Rather, she seemed pleased by his interest. "The guest house of the convent sisters has no bower, merely a small solar where I read and write. I despise needlework—never have I managed to perform it without pricking my fingers. I was the despair of poor Sister Theresa in the convent where I was educated." She held out her delicately tapered fingers. Her thumb bore a telltale ink smudge.

"But I fear you will be no more pleased with my efforts than you are with that of Chretien. I am striving to compose a group of Breton lays—fairy tales, you might call them—set in Arthur's court, but they are the romance of today—not the history you demand."

"But, my lady, that is most wonderful!" And Bors, ever rash of action, but never before now so rash of speech, clasped her hands in his. "You must come to England with me—when I am fully recovered, that is—but it cannot be long. You must come to Avalon; you must see Arthur's grave. Write fairy tales if you will, but see first the true land of King Arthur's ruling."

And though Bors was too optimistic as to how soon the journey could be made—due more to treacherous seas in the channel from midwinter storms than to delays in his recovery—at last the day came. In late February Bors bid Roget and Sister Patrice, the infirmarer, and little Celia, the novice who had at length learned to raise her head and speak to him, a fond farewell full of gratitude. He escorted Marie, her little dog Leda, and her maid Diota to the quay of Morlaix, which most men called Ville de Bretagne. A small trading vessel bound for the west coast of England rocked gently in the waters of the estuary, waiting to sail with the tide.

"Aye, with fair winds we will round the coast of Cornwall tomorrow and put in at Bristol the next day," the captain said, pocketing the fares Bors paid him. "The ladies I'll give my cabin to, but ye'll be obliged to sleep on the deck."

Bors, who recalled with distaste the dark, stuffy quarters below deck in sea-tossed vessels, was more than happy to sleep on deck rolled in a heavy, home-spun brychan. In spite of the fresh air and the relatively gentle rocking of the boat, however, Bors did not sleep well. So it was that shortly after the hour for Lauds (for the rhythms of the monastery stay with one even long after their departure, and Bors's upbringing had been reinforced in the convent of nursing sisters), Bors found himself wide awake. He saw a slim figure swathed in a heavy cloak slip from the captain's cabin and walk the deck. This time Bors knew firmly that he was seeing flesh and blood and not the angelic visitation the scene appeared to be.

"My lady cannot sleep either?" He spoke softly when she was close to him.

"I hoped you would be awake." She drew from the sheltering folds of her cape a small flickering lantern and set it between them as Bors smoothed a place on his brychan for her to sit. "I have been writing long, and now I cannot get the ideas from my mind that I may sleep. Would you like to hear?" She unrolled the sheet of parchment she held in her left hand.

"Yes, please, my lady. I should like it above all."

"We shall see how well you like it. I fear it has many of the elements you dislike in the work of Chretien de Troyes, but we shall see. It is *The Lay of Sir Launfal,* a favorite tale of the minstrels of the Bretons." He nodded at her encouragingly across the flickering lantern, and she leaned forward that the light might shine more brightly on her parchment:

> King Arthur—that fearless knight and courteous lord—removed to Wales and lodged at Caerleon-on-Usk, since the Picts and Scots did much mischief in the land. For it was the wont of the wild people of the north to enter the realm of Logres and burn and damage at their will. At the time of Pentecost, the king cried a great feast. Thereat he gave many rich gifts to his counts and barons, and to the knights of the Round Table. Never were such worship and bounty shown before at any feast, for Arthur bestowed honors and lands on all his servants—save only on one. This lord, who was forgotten and misliked of the king, was named Launfal. He was beloved by many of the court, because of his beauty and prowess, for he was a worthy knight, open of heart and heavy of hand. These lords, to whom their comrade was dear, felt little joy to see so stout a knight misprized . . .

Bors thought to wonder why King Arthur should misprize so goodly a knight, but he would not for the world have interrupted his lady. The beauty of her voice on the crisp night air accompanied by the gentle wash of the waves against the boat and the beauty of her face in the flickering light, enhanced now and again by silvery moonlight, were sound and vision that he would carry in his heart to the end of time. And if he could have spoken, it would not have been to argue the rightness of historical detail, but rather would he speak of his love. For surely this was the love of which all the troubadours sang; this was the love which the lords and ladies experienced in the romances of Arthur's court; this was the meaning of his vision. Love was the great treasury of his dreams. Marie herself was the key. Now he understood—he could not cross the threshold before because he had not known Marie. And for the moment all the problems, the height of her station of birth, his own lack of property, his illegitimate birth—all were forgotten in the beauty of the moment. He reached out across the rough woven mat and sought her hand.

The slim, soft fingers, white even in this dim light, entwined themselves in his, and the voice, light and melodious as if the words were sung rather than spoken, continued, telling of the fortunes of Sir Launfal who went from court and was directed to the silken pavilion of a fair maiden. As the story recounted the love of Launfal and the maiden, Bors could see every picture clear in his mind, with Marie and himself in the roles of the lovers. Surely for her, he, too, would renounce all family claims and serve only her and do only her bidding. How fitting that he to whom Avalon had been home for so many years, he who had touched the very bones of the true King Arthur and his queen, that he should ride forth in quests of valor and right for the sake of the fairest lady in the land.

But then even in the fairy story the demands of daily life bore in upon the lovers, and their perfect idyll was torn apart. Marie stopped and laid the parchment aside. "And so does it end? With Launfal stripped of riches, scorned by the queen, and separated from his maiden?" Bors asked.

"*Mais non,* no, no." Marie clapped her right hand over his that was holding her left. "The maiden will return, riding on the whitest of milk-colored palfreys, clad in a shift of spotless linen, and above her showy kirtle a mantle of royal purple. And all the barons will declare her more fair than the queen, and the maiden and Launfal will be rapt away to the fair island of Avalon." As Bors made no answer, after the space of three wave-slaps on the hull of the boat, she said, "I suppose you think it very silly, this matter of May-time and kisses."

He looked at her through eyes widened with love. "I could never speak disrespectfully of love, my lady. If I were but worthy a little to adore, I could be forever happy. Although its very hopelessness may ennoble my love. For the minstrels say that through adoration comes peace. And I shall be blest that I may offer service to take my lady to Avalon."

The lady did not speak, but she did not remove her hands from his.

9

rue to the captain's words, on the evening of the second day, with sea gulls circling overhead and a pink-tinted western sky running into the sea, they arrived at the busy seaport of Bristol. And the next morning, after a night's lodging at an inn, Bors secured horses for himself and Marie and a cart for Diota and the baggage. They set out through the thickly wooded landscape on the day that crossed the line between winter and spring. It seemed that the land before them lay in winter with frost on the bare tree branches and gray in the sky, but when the enchanted lovers passed through, the frost melted, the trees budded, birds sang in the branches, and tiny snow-drops blossomed around their feet. As they drew nearer to Avalon, the air seemed to lighten and grow sweeter.

On midmorning of their second day no sooner had they left the bubbling spring and the half-finished, scaffolding-supported walls of the Cathedral of Wells behind them than the hillocky road began to rise and fall. It reminded Bors of the sand dunes in the Holy Land. But now he felt he was approaching land almost as holy and a great deal more pleasant. They had traveled for perhaps an hour or two when, at the top of one hill, Marie raised her head and gave a cry of delight. "Oh! Oh, *oui!* It is as if *le bon Dieu* has prepared a beacon to light our way."

Bors looked and saw the midday sun shining on St. Patrick's Chapel atop the Tor. As they rode nearer, Bors told Marie the story of St. Patrick, the first abbot of Glastonbury. "Next to King Arthur himself, surely his are the most precious bones, the holiest relics of our house." And Bors did not realize he had said "our house," for he thought he had put his monastery days behind him.

Marie was fascinated. "Oh, yes, yes. I shall write a lay of St. Patrick. Oh, Bors, my dear one, you have done well. It is right that you should bring me here. I shall write and study in Avalon far better than I could in Brittany."

The rebuilding of the abbey had not resumed, so the enclosure was filled with half-constructed stone walls and graceful pointed arches pointing to nothing but an open sky. But the grass grew green and lush to the base of the walls, and the bushes and hedges bore a green frosting of soon-to-burst leaf buds, all speaking of the life-force of the land watered by the crystal brook tumbling from the Chalice Well and ever guarded on one side by the Tor and on the other by the gentler Wearyall Hill. Marie was thrilled on the next day as Bors, from atop the Tor, pointed to the dim, distant shape of the hillfort to the southeast and gave it the magic name—Camelot.

"Yes, yes. I shall write my lays here atop this mystical, ancient hill with the true Camelot in my view and Avalon spread at my feet." And in her joy, Marie kissed the knight who had borne her to this enchanted spot.

Bors knew, when he gave it strictest consideration, that he should make his way to d'Emercy with speed and present himself and his sword to Sir Heribert, who may not yet know that he had a grandson in the service of his honor. Or perhaps Herlwin and the others had also returned from the Holy Land, and his lord awaited word of his strayed knight. Bors did not know, but he knew that his true duty lay at the manor of the lord to whom he had sworn fealty. Yet he could not leave. Brother Ambrose, much withered and stooped since Bors had last seen him, had the abbot's permission to give Bors his old room in the dorter. Marie and her household found lodging in the smaller guest house across Magdalen Street from the enclosure.

Many days Bors spent sitting in the shelter of the south cloister with Brother Ambrose, now retired from his work as Master of Boys and Novices. The brother divided his time between prayers and the study he loved. More dear than ever to him were the chronicles he had so diligently taught the boys. Over and over again, when his eyes dimmed, he would ask Bors to read to him the words of Geoffrey of Monmouth. He could as well have told them from memory, but the voice of his former student delighted him. "Read to me of Arthur's glorious victory over evil. I have fought lifelong with weapons of a different forging to overcome the Evil One, but it seems always that victories of the spirit are harder to define . . ." It seemed that he would say more, but the old eyes closed, and the thin blue lips relaxed into a gentle, half-dreaming smile as he waited with his thin, blue-veined hands folded in his lap, listening for Bors's voice to begin:

> When the high festival of Whitsuntide began to draw nigh, Arthur, filled with exceeding great joy at having achieved so great success, was fain to hold high court, and to set the crown of the kingdom upon his head, and he made choice of Caerleon wherein to fulfil his design. . . . When all at last were assembled in the city on the high day of the festival, the archbishops were conducted unto the palace to crown the King with the royal diadem. Dubric, therefore, upon whom the charge fell, for that the court was held within his diocese, was ready to celebrate the service. As soon as the King had been invested with the ensigns of kingship, he was led in right comely wise to the church. . . .

The bells ringing for Vespers and the chanting of the monks as they entered the chapel were so attuned to the setting of the story that both Bors and

Ambrose were several minutes coming back to the present. At last, though, Bors helped his companion to his feet, and they went to prayers with full hearts.

In the mornings when Ambrose was occupied with the duty of the hours, Bors sought a favorite place in the corner study carrel of the north cloister where he could read the chronicles of his youthful study and some newer volumes the brothers had added to their collection. Even with the lack of funds under King Richard's administration, the brothers were diligently restocking their library. Bors asked the custodian of the scriptorium if he might help with the copying of a volume recently loaned them for such purpose by a sister Benedictine house in France.

Bors had offered simply as a courtesy to his beloved mentor and to the brothers who housed and fed him, but then he looked at the volume the librarian brought to him, and his eyes lit up. Surely God had intended this. It was *Perceval, le Conte del Graal,* by the very writer Marie so admired—Chretien de Troyes. As he bent over his tiny writing desk, ink staining his fingers, the beauty and rhythm of the octosyllabic French couplets gripped him until finally he lay down his brush and gave himself to reading.

So Marie found him when the bell rang for High Mass. "My lady, it is wonderful!" He pointed to the book. "In the beginning, the poor country lad does not even know what knights and churches are, but once he learns of knighthood, Perceval sets his heart on achieving it. He has just come to Castle Carbunek in the middle of a wasted land and found his host the fisherking gravely wounded." He opened the heavy, leather-bound cover. "Here, I will read to you, shall I?"

Then the bell pealed more insistently, and he closed the book with a sigh. "*S'il vous plaît,* you must read to me. But after we pray." And Marie preceded him into St. Mary's Chapel, as radiant as the Queen of Heaven for whom she was named.

But afterwards, when the brothers were at their dinner, Marie and Bors returned to the cloistered carrel and bent their heads over the flickering light of the single candle as they read together of Perceval, new and uneasy in his knighthood, sitting beside the suffering king on his couch. At each course of the feast Perceval's amazement grows at the magnificence of the procession that emerges from a chamber at one end of the hall, passes before the table, and disappears into another chamber. Finally a beautiful and comely maiden enters, holding a grail worked with fine gold and adorned with many precious stones, the finest and most costly in the world. But this magnificent serving vessel contained only a single morsel—a lone mass wafer, which sustains the life of the king. Marie's sudden, exasperated cry interrupted the flow of Bors's mellow voice. "Oh, but it would have been so simple—why will Perceval not *ask* the meaning?"

Bors considered. "I do not know. Mayhap he lacked the spiritual insight to seek deeper meaning?"

Marie then read in her light, musical voice the episode set on Good Friday where Perceval spoke with a holy hermit and heard the explanation of the grail castle and his own failings. "Oh, *le pouvre.*" She looked up. "It would have been so simple. The king could have been healed, the land fertile again. It is so sad."

Bors nodded thoughtfully. "Yes, Perceval's pain must have been great, indeed, and yet he rediscovered God, so it was not wasted."

In spite of the joy Bors experienced sharing the story of the grail with Marie, the delight of hearing her exclaim over the beauty of Chretien's grail procession and the suffering of the fisherking—or perhaps because of the poignancy of these moments—Bors became restless. In the following days spring awoke the earth and he knew that in d'Emercy the field strips would soon be yielding to the plow. He should return to his manor.

On his last night, he and Marie climbed the Tor after Vespers to watch the sun sink red and gold into the west. They sat long, watching the newborn lambs tottering behind their mothers on the steep sides of the hill. At last Marie asked, "Have you ever thought, *mon cherie,* that even so might Arthur and Guinevere have sat here?"

Bors took her hand. "I wonder what they would have talked of—of love or of war?"

"Surely not of war in this holy place. Here they would talk only of love and peace."

"I wonder if they had any idea that near to seven hundred years later two others would sit here looking at the same view they must have looked at and talk of them?"

She laughed, and Bors realized that it had been long since he had heard her silver bell laughter. "And do you think that seven hundred years from now others will sit here still and talk of Arthur and Guinevere—or of us?"

As inviting as her question was, Bors did not explore it, for another one suddenly troubled him. Why had he not heard Marie's laughter of late? She was happy with her place, happy with her work—what could so trouble her? He caught his breath at the thought that it might be his going. But he did not think that the answer, for now he realized that the laughter had been silent some days before he announced his decision to return to d'Emercy. It had been, as best he could recall, since they had read the story of the grail together.

As if she had followed his thoughts, she asked, "And when will you return from your manor? Will I see my bold knight again?"

"I hope you will ever see me in your heart, my lady. For I believe you know that I leave part of mine with you. But as to when you will see me in body, that is for my Lord Herlwin or his father Sir Heribert to say, for I am their man."

"And is it so far, this d'Emercy of yours?"

"But a day's ride to the northwest."

"So we will not be far parted."

"Not unless I am sent to serve knight's fee to Clifford, my lord's overlord. That is a goodly ride farther." He stopped with that—he did not want to suggest the possibility that he could be sent back to the Holy Land. But if King Richard demanded, his barons would obey, and so would their knights. Suddenly Bors was filled with a great desire to hear fresh news of the Crusade and of Herlwin and of Ivo and of Jerusalem itself. Was it now free from the infidels?

"If your lord will allow, come to me in the summer. I will know then." Her face was soft, her eyes faraway, focused beyond the distant Camelot, seeing a land of their own.

"You will know what?"

"I will know." She sat in silence for some time. "Come when the honeysuckle is sweet on the air—when it hangs heavy at the Vesper hour. I am writing of Tristan and Iseult—Tristan and the queen are the honeysuckle and the hazel tree, so entwined that one cannot live without the other. Come. By then I will know if it is true."

The ringing of the bell and the melodious rising and falling of the plainsong told them that Compline had begun. Bors rose and held out his hand. She placed hers in his, and so, hand in hand, they descended the green, sheep-dotted Tor as the last red streaks faded in the west.

In the morning even before the brothers began Prime, Bors bade the porter farewell and rode up High Street of Glastonbury village to Wells Road on the horse he had borrowed from the abbot. Brother Ambrose had been the only other one he had taken leave of, for he had set his face to his new life, and it was important that he not give in to too much looking back.

10

ust as old Father Cenred rang the tiny village church bell for Vespers, Bors started up the familiar dirt road that led past the lengthening shadows of the cottar's huts and freemen's farms. He passed the alehouse, marketplace, smithy, carpenter's sheds, and well to the white-washed, thatched-roofed cottage at the top of the road. No matter how much he told himself that this was not his home, he could not help dismounting before the door and hoping that a lithe girl with golden braids in

a green kirtle would come out, perhaps to feed the chickens that still pecked around the door, and call him brother.

But instead a mature woman with solemn blue-gray eyes looking at him beneath a snowy wimple that framed her face and covered her shoulders met him on the threshold. The aroma of fresh-baked bread issued from the open door. They regarded each other levelly for a full minute before she spoke. "And is it Bors whom once I called brother?"

"Aline! It is you. And do you no longer welcome only a foster brother to the home of Ivo Bachiler?"

"I have heard it said that you were made knight and claimed son by Herlwin d'Emercy. The son of my lord's son is always welcome at our poor cottage. But I would not presume to call him brother."

"Aline!" He was struck with anger. He would have liked to take her by the shoulders and shake her. "If you will be so distant, there is one within who will welcome me. Where is Ancret?"

Aline pointed toward the gray stone church at the end of the street. "For a year and a half she has lain in the churchyard."

Ancret dead? He should have thought. But always in his memory nothing changed here. He might roam the world on Crusade, but manor, village, and Aline should remain the same. "And Ivo is still on Crusade? Who runs the farm—sees to the field strips?"

"I do. I hire villeins to do the heavy work. For now."

"For now? Until Ivo returns, you mean?"

"I have begged Sir Heribert to allow me so long. He has been most patient, but it must be done in June whether or not Ivo has returned."

Bors was growing more irritated by this cold, stiff reception from one who had always greeted him with open arms. He realized now that he had looked forward to such a greeting during the slow hours of his journey. But now—Ancret dead and Aline distant and unwelcoming—was he to receive such a welcome at the manor also? What would Sir Heribert say to receiving his illegitimate grandson? "What is to take place in June?" He asked it harshly, angry that he had to drag every word from her.

"I am to be given in marriage to Ket Osgodbi."

Bors blinked, trying to remember. "His father has the farm beyond the village?"

"*He* has the farm. There is no son. Or rather, his sons are all married."

"What!" Just the news that Aline was to be married was strangely painful, but this enraged him. "That cannot be! Surely he must be as old as Ancret was!"

"Not quite as old. But fully as wrinkled."

"Aline! This must not be. Surely you do not wish it?"

"Wish it! What do my wishes matter? My lord says I am to marry. It is good for the manor. Ket Osgodbi has asked for me. The manor cattle are bred in the spring. So must the women be."

"No! I won't have it! You must refuse!" Bors reached out blindly for her, then reeled backward, almost into his horse, when her hand landed sharply across his cheek.

"And who are you to come here and demand that I defy my lord? What am I to do? Would you refuse d'Emercy orders? Perhaps you could do so as you are of his family."

And the door of the cottage slammed in his face.

Annion, the d'Emercy seneschal, ordered meat for Bors and pointed to a spot on the north wall of the hall where he could spread his pallet. Such matter-of-fact acceptance at the manor told Bors that word of his knighting at least had preceded him. As he sat at the end of the table in the busy hall, with Sir Heribert and Lady Athelais at the far end, he recalled that Aline had spoken of his parentage. So all was known. And yet, other than acknowledging his presence and agreeing to the seneschal's arrangements, Sir Heribert had said nothing. Was he to overrule his son's actions? Could a knighthood be revoked? But after weeks of monastery rations, the meat, rich and filling in its thick gravy, and the wine, the best he'd tasted since he left France, required his attention.

After the meal, Corviere entered. The sight of the minstrel whom he had not seen since that long-ago Christmas brought back memories: Aline's delight in the mummers and in his company—would he ever see her eyes shine so again? . . . Nyall, he who should have been a respected knight and bailiff after his father, but chose instead to seek shortcuts to advancement—now dead under the sands of Arsuf . . . Ancret, she who had been like a grandmother to him (he could think of Sir Heribert as his grandfather, but never could he think of Lady Athelais as grandmother) now at rest in the old Saxon churchyard . . .

Corviere strummed his lute and sang "The Lay of the Oriflamme," a tale of the love of the troubadour Huon for the fair Lady Blanche. "New wine for new love, old wine for memories!" sang Corviere, and his lute called more sweetly than the birds in the flowering boughs over the lovers' heads.

This sweet pain I bear in your presence, my lady,
teaches me things undreamed of.
Your beauty, lady, is more than fame,
a glance of your eyes, worthier than all wealth.

As the minstrel sang, Bors's mind filled with newer memories: Of his lady Marie who was fairer far than the Lady Blanche of the lay, of reading *The Lancelot* with Marie in France and reveling in his own vision of serving his fair love faithfully with no thought of his own welfare, as Lancelot served Guinevere. Yet subtle contradictions remained—contradictions between the code of love and the code of knight's chivalry. In serving his lady above all, he could not always be true to his sworn fealty to his lord and therefore to his king. And did not God his Maker have prior claim on his service and his love? He thought of his old dream of crossing into a treasure house. What was the key to crossing the threshold? Would he ever find it? His questions muddled further when Corviere's song continued:

This love shall not endure, this passion of springtime and roses.
I tell you, no. It is wine soon poured. What then remains?
In some, who have neither bravery nor honor—nothing.
So choose you well those things which are true,
those loves which remain when springtime and roses fade.

And with a strum of the lute, the song faded.

After the night sleeping among the rushes on the hall floor, Bors still felt unsettled. He waited for the seneschal to bring him orders from Sir Heribert. Having a job to do would settle him into his new life. But no orders came that day. Or the next. On the third morning as Sir Heribert still had no orders for him, he decided he would ride around the manor. After a breakfast of ale and porridge he saddled the abbot's horse for one last ride before he returned it to the abbey with a groom.

It was a fair mid-April morning, and the gently rolling field strips were alive with teams of yoked oxen pulling heavy wooden plows guided by villeins and freemen in their short tunics and long, pointed capuchons. The lord's demesne fields were first to be plowed. Then the manor's oxen could be used by cottars and freemen for their own fields.

Bors stopped on a gentle rise beneath a budding oak tree and watched the scene before him. To his left on the new field, where wheat and rye had been harvested the previous autumn, a team of eight oxen plodded along the furlong. The village of d'Emercy possessed sixty-two oxen—twenty-eight belonging to Sir Heribert and thirty-four belonging to the various freemen including Ivo Bachiler, Ket Osgodbi, and Father Cenred. As it took one day to plow each strip and each man had about thirty strips, every fine day from March to May must be spent plowing.

Near to Bors a woman with a white wimple and yellow apron over her darker tunic paused to lean on her hoe and observe the birds flocking around the new-turned earth, pecking for worms, while her man broke the clods of clay with a long-handled mallet. The two drivers of the eight-oxen team, one at the front, one behind the plow, called to their cattle with rhythmic, melodic encouragements. They wielded their prods in time to their chant, never actually hitting the patient creatures, but more emphasizing the rhythm of the march.

It was the rhythm of it all that most struck Bors. The rhythms of monastery life had been unvarying throughout the year from Matins to Compline, the hours for Vespers and Compline adjusted just one hour to account for earlier winter sunsets. But here the meter and melody were directed by a higher Power than even the Rule, for the whole creation hummed to the melody of the Creator's season.

Bors sat long, watching the iron share cutting through the old brown stubble, leaving a trail of rich, black earth. His eye followed the direction of the furrow toward the village where there was a hub of activity around the well, and he looked on down the muddy road, across a rising field to the cluster of trees that marked the Osgodbi farmstead. He felt a jolt to the gentle flow of the day. Would Aline soon be living there with the sourly wrinkled Ket as husband? He could remember seeing him only once in the long-ago days when he lived here, but that time had been memorable, for the young Bors had painfully skinned his knee when he darted away from the surly farmer, his heart racing from fear of being kicked. It was no wonder he had found Aline much changed.

But there was nothing he could do for Aline. He turned his attention again to the pattern of life before him and tried to see a place for himself. Sir Heribert had nothing for him to do today. Would he ever? Or would the door of the manor be slammed in his face as firmly as that of the Bachiler cottage? It seemed there was no place for him in cottage or manor. He was now more of an outcast orphan than before Herlwin claimed him. Was there a place elsewhere for him? He had been happy in the monastery and yet, save for Marie's presence, he knew there was nothing for him there either. He had no vocation for the religious life. What of the storehouse of treasures he had dreamt of? Could he never cross the threshold because all doors were closed to him?

Then suddenly, there was no more time for morose soul-searching. At noon the next day the entire manor was thrown into a flurry with the arrival of Herlwin and his knights, fresh from the Holy Land.

Ivo, Herlwin, and the others greeted him with raucous bonhomie. Although Herlwin showed genuine pleasure in seeing the son who had saved his life, it was Ivo who most warmly greeted him, having expected more the notice of his death than the encounter with this robustly healthy person.

While the servants rushed helter-skelter through the hall preparing for the homecoming feast, Bors and Ivo sought a quiet corner in the manor courtyard. "What of the Crusade? Did you take Jerusalem? It must have been glorious! I have long thought of riding into the Holy City behind King Richard with pennons flying and trumpets blaring. All the misery and horror of the long march from Acre must have seemed worth it then."

But Ivo shook his head. "We reoccupied Jaffa. Richard would not march to Jerusalem without strong fortifications at his back. But when the forts at Jaffa and Ascalon were finished, Richard knew he could not take Jerusalem—not take it and hold it as a stable part of the kingdom. So these many months we have kicked our heels in the desert sands while Richard and Saladin and Saladin's brother al'Adil made peace proposals and counter-proposals, including Richard offering a marriage alliance between his sister Joan and al'Adil."

"What? Richard would give his sister to an infidel?" It was farther away, but the proposal seemed as abhorrent as Sir Heribert giving Aline to Ket Osgodbi.

"I think part of the negotiations was that he should become a Christian." Ivo shrugged. "Then Richard cleverly stalled for time by applying to Pope Celestine for sanction. It will not happen." He grinned and shook his head. "No one ever faulted Richard for his strategy. Well, we've secured the coast from Acre to Jaffa for Christianity, and pilgrims will be allowed to visit the Holy Sepulcher, so I suppose it wasn't all a waste, though most people will see it so since we failed to capture Jerusalem."

"And is Richard returned to England?"

"Not yet. There will be a treaty of peace before he sails. It may last a few years. Rumor is that Richard may have as little luck wresting the throne of England from his brother John as he did prying Saladin from Jerusalem. They say John is over-fond of the power of collecting taxes."

"And Arthur who will be king after Richard, has he married the daughter of Tancred yet?"

"What? Have you been in England longer than we and not heard?"

"There is little news in our quiet monastery."

Ivo shrugged again. "It must be so. I said John is fond of his power. He would not have his brother's son rule after Richard. Some say Arthur is his prisoner, some say his murderer's victim. Either way I think we have heard the last of Prince Arthur."

The next day the entire manor was bid to the feast. The servants had worked through the night roasting and boiling meats, baking breads, and stewing sauces from the remains of last year's apples and raisins. Bors thought several times of approaching Ivo with the matter of Aline's marriage.

But it seemed so useless. What could he say—that Ket was too old for her? Obvious. That Aline had no caring for him? That spoke loudly enough in Aline's face. That the whole idea was an affront? Obedience to one's overlord was the way of the system. There was nothing to be done. Ivo could no more refuse Sir Heribert in this than Sir Heribert could refuse Baron Clifford, or Clifford could refuse King Richard. It was the order of things.

That afternoon they sat at the long trestle tables filling the hall, replete with meat and ale and even the honeyed sweetmeats that normally would be served only at Christmas. Corviere followed his juggling act with a merry dance tune on the rebec which he dedicated to the couple soon to be wed. But then, as if to emphasize the wretchedness of the situation, the minstrel bade the couple to lead in the dancing at the end of the hall where the servants had hastily stacked the tables away.

"And have you agreed to this?" Bors growled at Ivo.

"What choice had I? She must be married. Ket is a valued tenant on the manor. There are no other suitors."

Ivo was right. It was all reasonable. No! It was absurd. The thought of how Aline had carried on alone, running the Bachiler holding with only a little hired help filled him with admiration. The thought of her beauty and sweetness going to Ket Osgodbi filled him with desperate rage. He jumped to his feet as if he would rush to Sir Heribert at the high table. Then he turned with a jerk as if he would fling himself between the dancing couple who had now been joined by many others. For an instant he surveyed his bench as if he would jump upon it and shout. Shout what? Shout that the proceeding was immoral? Shout that he did not give permission for his one-time sister to be so married? Shout that he would marry her himself?

The thought jolted him. What if he should do such an audacious thing? What if the unheard of should happen and she were to be given to him? What would they live on? He was that most hopeless of all figures—a landless knight. Far better for her to marry the ancient Ket and have a roof over her head and meat in the pot than to share his penniless state. For illegitimate sons, even those who were acknowledged, could not inherit land in England, and he had no prospects of winning any. His shoulders slumped, and he walked from the hall.

It was the following day when the groom who had taken the abbot's horse to Glastonbury returned and sought out Bors. "The old monk sent word to you. If you would see him in this world, it must be soon. But if you are not free to come, he'll see you in the next."

"Brother Ambrose? Was it he? He is dying?"

"Most like that was the name. They all look alike—except this one grayer and more stooped than most."

Bors nodded and turned without stopping to thank the messenger. He would go to Herlwin, who had been off-handedly pleasant to his acknowledged son—much as one would be to a not-favored, but accepted hound dog. At least Herlwin noted his presence, which Sir Heribert barely did, although it was unlikely that either would deny his request to return to Glastonbury, for no one seemed to have need of him here.

So though it was late in the day, Bors set out on yet another borrowed horse. It was bad enough to be a landless knight, but a horseless one was unheard of. He rode hard, stopping to sleep only during the darkest hours in a barn, and so arrived at Glastonbury by noon the following day. He went straight to Brother Ambrose's cell. As his steps silenced on the long wooden hall of the dorter and he opened the heavy plank door, he froze. The cell was as empty as death.

The small cubicle smelled of lye soap; the cot was stripped of its covers, its brychan folded at the foot of the straw-filled mattress. An unburnt candle stood cold in the clay holder on the small table, and the square wooden chest which had held Brother Ambrose's few worldly belongings was gone. Too late. Why must he always be too late? Was his life ever to be filled with almosts and might-have-beens? Why had God chosen that his unwanted person should have been born at all? He turned without the least idea of where he would go.

And he bumped squarely into Brother Jerome. "There you are, Bors. The porter sent me after you. I'll take you to Ambrose."

"Take me to him? You mean he's—"

"He's still with us. Just barely. We moved him into the infirmary several days ago. I think he waits for you. He has asked several times."

Bors hardly recognized the wraith that lay propped on a white pillow. But the humor in the shaky voice was unmistakable. "So you've come, have you? You were ever dependable. I regret shirking my duty. A trust is a trust, but a Higher Authority overrules."

Bors suppressed a sob as he clasped the frail hand held out to him. Brother Ambrose was obviously wandering in his mind. But then perhaps that was a mercy. "Is he in pain?" he asked Brother Jerome.

"Not much. Mostly just weakness. He refuses our medicines. He could sleep with Brother Eluid's poppy juice, but he wanted to be awake when you came. His duty, he says. Seems set on it. Best not to argue with him. I'll leave you now."

The door closed behind the swish of the infirmarer's black robe. Brother Ambrose's long, bony fingers plucked at the blanket as if he would rise. "What can I get for you?" Bors asked, placing his hand over the restless ones.

"In my chest. A parchment leaf rolled in leather."

Bors knelt at the foot of the bed, opened the wooden lid of the chest, and drew out the long, thin leather case. "Read," Ambrose directed.

The parchment cracked brittlely as Bors unrolled the leaf, but it did not break. Bors skimmed the contents of the page, then lowered it slowly. "I—I don't understand. I am to inherit a manor in Wales? How can that be? The law is very clear. One born out of wedlock cannot inherit. What is this?"

Ambrose struggled as if he would sit up, and Bors put his arm under the pillow to raise it. "You read the instructions. You were not to know until you were twenty-five, but the bearer didn't calculate how old that would make his trustee. I could have passed the responsibility on to the abbot, of course, but as I'd seen to your care all these years, I wanted to finish the job." He stopped with a gasping cough, but then his voice gained strength. "You were ever the best of the boys—the readiest to learn—the most willing to help—the most impetuous and troublesome, too—like the day of the fire when we almost lost you. But that was a blessing in disguise, for then you could be set to your books. Ah, and didn't we have a grand time reading—" Again the cough interrupted his reminiscence.

"But the parchment? Where did it come from? What does it mean?" Bors prompted.

"It came with a messenger when you were seven years old—"

Bors held up a hand for Ambrose to wait and frowned as he calculated the dates, trying to remember. "1176? The year Rosamund, my mother, died. So my father had not forgotten me or left me abandoned. He merely awaited the right time." A broad smile broke across his face. He had not been acknowledged out of simple battlefield excitement and the act perhaps regretted later. Always Herlwin d'Emercy had planned for his future. "Yes, I see," he said slowly. "But is it legal?"

"Quite legal. The manor is in Wales. Welsh law is not Norman. A son may inherit—whether his parents were married or no. Did you note the terms? You may live there when you will, and it will pass to you on the death of your father. Not great riches, but a goodly holding—well worth passing on to your own son in God's time."

Bors was in shock. His mind flooded with questions, but he could give words to none. He sat still and quiet, supporting Brother Ambrose's head. The next coughing fit brought Brother Jerome who could not have been far away.

"Father Abbot wants to be called. You will stay with him?" Bors nodded.

It was only a few minutes until the hurried tread of sandals on the wooden floor told Bors that the abbot must have run the distance from his house. Bors started to move, but Abbot Savary signaled for him to sit still and made the sign of the cross over the dying man. Then the abbot leaned close to his mouth to hear his whispered confession. "The grace and peace of God our Father and the Lord Jesus Christ be with you."

"And also with you," Bors answered.

"May Almighty God have mercy on us, forgive us our sins, and bring us to everlasting life."

"Amen."

The priest then placed a morsel of bread dipped in wine on Ambrose's tongue. "The body of Christ. The blood of Christ."

Ambrose made his own response. "Amen."

The abbot prayed. "God of peace, You offer eternal healing to those who believe in You. You have refreshed Your servant with food and drink from Heaven. Lead him safely into the kingdom of light. We ask this through Christ our Lord."

Ambrose's "Amen" was surprisingly strong, and then he opened his eyes and held the abbot in a searching gaze. "Father, will I go to Heaven?"

Abbot Savary regarded his spiritual son levelly for several moments. "The blood of Christ paid for your sins long ago. You belong to Him. He will not turn you away."

Ambrose closed his eyes with a smile and sank back on his pillow, freeing Bors's arm. When the abbot had gone Bors asked, "Shall I read to you?"

"Yes. Read Geoffrey."

Bors looked around and found the heavy, leather-bound parchment pages on a table in the corner. He turned to the last section and read the account he and Ambrose had loved to share since Bors was ten years old. No matter how often he read it, he was gripped with the words.

> Even the renowned King Arthur himself was wounded deadly, and was borne thence unto the Isle of Avalon for the healing of his wounds, where he gave up the crown of Britain unto his kinsman, Constantine, son of Cador, Duke of Cornwall, in the year of the Incarnation of our Lord five hundred and forty-two.

Bors paused, thinking his patient asleep, but as soon as the rhythm of his voice faltered, the transparent-seeming eyelids flickered. He understood the signal to read on. He picked up the book of Revelation and turned to the vision of the greater King and His greater Kingdom.

> Then I saw a new heaven and a new earth, for the first heaven and the first earth had vanished, and there was no longer any sea. I saw the holy city, new Jerusalem, coming down out of heaven from God, made ready like a bride adorned for her husband. I heard a loud voice proclaiming from the throne: 'Now at last God has his dwelling among men! He will dwell among them and they shall be his people, and God himself will be with them. He will wipe every tear from their eyes; there shall be an end to death, and to mourning and crying and pain; for the old order has passed away!'
>
> Then he who sat on the throne said, 'Behold! I am making all things new!' . . . A draught from the water-springs of life will be my free gift to the thirsty. All this is the victor's heritage; and I will be his God and he shall be my son.

Bors closed the book and lay it aside. But there was no need to do more, for the unearthly radiance of Brother Ambrose's smile told all.

11

n the two days of preparation before they buried Brother Ambrose, Bors did little but watch by the body. This was not a vigil, but merely the companionship of friends. On the second night he dozed in the quiet of the chapel and the flickering of the candles set at the head and foot of the resting body. His dream returned—a vast and beautiful room walled with richly carved wood and windows of the finest stained glass, filled with every jewel and treasure of the world. The door stood open, yet he could not cross the threshold.

He woke long before the bell for Prime and sat in the warm silence thinking. He had recalled the dream often, but it had been years since he had experienced it—the unearthly beauty of the jewels, the desperation of not being able to enter. In the meantime, he had experienced it all—monastery life, the life of a religious and a scholar; knighthood, traveling to the Holy Land and sharing a momentous victory with Richard the Lionhearted; love—a great, elevated love for a fair and pure lady. And yet none provided his answer. Was there an answer in this life? Was the treasure house Heaven? Was death the crossing of the threshold? Was that why he dreamt it now? Had Brother Ambrose crossed into the room that was barred to him?

Or did the leather pouch containing the precious parchment of his inheritance bring back his dream? He had not felt at home at the manor of d'Emercy, but there was a place of his own over the border in Welsh Monmouth—near to where Geoffrey had been born. He would go there when Ambrose was laid to rest. Would he go alone? For now he was not a landless knight. Now he would not be required to ride a borrowed horse. Lands and horses would be his.

Marie. He could speak to Marie. He could give words to the great and shining love he cherished for her. Marie—his highest inspiration, his lady, his love.

Even as his mind filled with exultation, he wondered if this could be right. Was it right for another to be the highest good in one's life—even such a one as Marie? Should not that place be filled only by his Redeemer? Yet did not earthly love come from Him? The radiance and purity of such love as he bore for Marie, it was that which inspired great art, music, and literature. It occupied the lives of young men and women in all the courts of Europe. All the troubadours sang of it as the highest good. And yet, was it so? Did it provide a basis for man and woman to build a lifetime together? What of his own mother and father? Was it high and shining admiration for a lady that led Herlwin d'Emercy into disgrace? Could the highest good cause such hardship to so many from that one act of love? Or was it simply lust?

The next day, after the sacred sod of Avalon blanketed Brother Ambrose, Bors made his way to Marie's guest lodgings. Diota answered the door. "My lady awaits you in her solar. She did not wish to interrupt your time of mourning."

Diota ushered him into the solar, and Bors stood transfixed in the presence of his lady. She was fairer, more radiant, purer than ever he remembered. "How can this be? How do I find you so changed, my lady? How is it possible?"

Now her smiling voice held the quality of silver bells which before he had heard only in her laughter. It was as if she spoke from such a great well of joy that the words were borne from her on wings. "Yes. I have found what I sought." She paused, and he felt blinded by her smile. "Or rather I am finding it. I know my quest."

Marie, who was never farther than an arm's length from a book, picked up a volume bound in precious red vellum embossed with gold letters. The beauty of the illuminated pages was such that Bors thought it must be holy Scripture or a Book of Hours. "It is Robert de Boron." Her voice held a hush of reverence. "He has made it all clear. It is what Chretien de Troyes hinted at in his *Perceval*, but now it is clear. It is the grail."

Bors nodded encouragement rather than understanding.

"The *Joseph d'Arimathie*, the story of the grail—not a grail, as in *Perceval*, but *the* grail—the cup of our Lord's Last Supper." She held out her book. "De Boron makes it all clear—how the vessel of the Last Supper was given by Pilate to Christ's disciple, Joseph of Arimathea, who used it to collect the blood of our crucified Lord when He was taken down from the cross. And Joseph came to the vale of Avalon with the holy grail."

Still clutching the book, she sat on a cushioned chair near the window and motioned Bors to sit on the stool near her feet. "Oh, that is but a pale sketch of the story. It is magnificent. A vision of universal history centered on our Lord's grail and those who choose to follow His vision and live for Him. The grail is the bridge between sacred history and worldly history—the plan of God from before the foundation of the world to redeem that world and the story of King Arthur."

"Yes." Bors nodded. "I see—at least a glimpse of what you say. But is it true? A magnificent story, truly. But did all that we are told about Arthur really happen?"

Marie's voice now turned from ecstatic and bell-like to a mellow harmony flowing from depths of peace, words spoken with the assurance of one who has seen a vision. "Who knows?" she said. "What does it matter? The truth is there—the truth that is above mere daily events. The truth is not in what happened, but in what it means—the value of law over force and might, of good over evil; the importance of living for truth, justice, and honor; the truth of following God and His Christ—these are what Arthur means. That I've always seen. But now with the grail it is complete. The quest of the grail is a search for mystical union with God. It is the highest of all. Just think, that God should even want to be one with those He has created. And I have found it. I have found my quest."

"You will write?" Bors's voice was barely a whisper. He felt he was in the presence of great holiness.

"But do you still not see? I've done that. I have studied. I have written. I have understood. We each have only one quest in life. But once it is accomplished, we are freed for service. This is the whole purpose of achieving the grail—for me, oneness with God—not for that union itself, but for the service that flows out of it.

"The grail could only be approached by the world's holiest knight—so it is for us. Does not our Lord say, 'Be ye perfect as I am perfect'?"

Bors sat in silent awe before her rapture. At last he spoke. "And this service of which you speak?"

"I shall enter a convent and take vows of perpetual obedience. Shaftesbury, I think, for it is renowned as a house of exceeding holiness."

"A nun? You? You will deny all? Shut yourself up forever?" He wanted to add, *What of my love? Is it nothing?* but he dared not be so profane, for he knew her vision was much higher.

"Deny all? No, no. I deny nothing. I embrace all. If I were to deny my Lord, that were to deny all. In accepting Him, I accept all."

"But—" Bors groped, "But, is there no other way? Must it be a convent?"

Marie rose, and the light from the window fell on her face and on the rings of golden hair hanging beneath her coif. "Each must find his own answer. This is my way." She held her hands out as if in supplication. "I said, 'What shall I render to the Lord for all His benefits toward me?' I cried out in prayer, and He answered with a vision of the grail. And I said, 'I will take the cup of salvation and call upon the name of the Lord. I will pay my vows to the Lord now in the presence of all His people.'"

She raised her eyes, and Bors knew she was not looking at him. She held her hands upward toward heaven. "O Lord, truly I am Your handmaid. You have loosed my bonds. You have given me life. You *are* my life, my very life. Jesus, You are the Lover of my soul, the Lord of my heart. Your love is deeper than my deepest longing. In seeking what You want, I find all that I want. I will offer to You all that I am and have. . . ."

Bors turned and quietly left the room, the light of Marie's apotheosis blinding him and enlightening him at the same time. His steps took him across Magdalen Street and through the gate of the enclosure, past the new-turned sod of Brother Ambrose's grave, to the simple mound between two pillars where Arthur of Britain and his Guinevere lay in the vale of Avalon. He knelt, and as he crossed himself, his hand brushed the leather pouch around his neck. Then at last he knew. The key to crossing the threshold was so simple. He had looked all his life, and in the end it was so uncomplicated. The key was obedience. Obedience to one's own quest—as given by God. And God called everyone into oneness with Himself. Some were to seek it by coming apart from the world, and some were to find God with them as they filled their place in the world. When the door opened, simply follow. The words of Scripture came to him like a voice, "I know your works. Behold, I have set before you an open door and no man shall shut it; for you have a little strength and have not denied my name."

His door was before him, the open door to his service. He would be the best lord of a manor in all of Monmouth—in all of Wales. And he would have the best lady. For he would ask Sir Heribert for the hand of Aline. And perhaps his lord would say yes. But if he said no, Bors would be patient, for Ket Osgodbi was an old man, and Bors and Aline were young. They could wait if need be—for he would speak to her, and they would have the vision of life's great treasures before them. If his quest were to wait, he would obey.

But in the end he did not have to wait, for two days later Bors rode into d'Emercy to the pealing of bells from the old Saxon church tower. At first his heart froze, for he thought the bells rang for Aline's wedding, but then he listened more carefully. They told of the burial of one of the manor. And Ket Osgodbi, whose old heart had simply quit during the night, was laid with his fathers. Three weeks later when the bells pealed in truth for the marriage of Aline Bachiler, it was Bors d'Emercy who stood with her before Father Cenred, surrounded by all from the manor and the clouds of witnesses—saints and apostles painted on the walls, including Joseph of Arimathea baptizing Bran the Blessed.

PART TWO

12

ow—with my son lost in the Welsh wars and my daughter disappeared on the eve of her betrothing? King Edward would have me attend him for Eastertide at Glastonbury *now?*" Reynald d'Emercy thrust the parchment bearing the royal seal back at the messenger. "Far better that I attend to the planting of my crops to pay Edward's taxes for the subduing of my neighbors than to follow him, fawning on his fur-trimmed robes at Easter court. Does the king not know we are a bereaved house?"

The messenger could not look Reynald in the eye, and yet he blurted out the truth. "Perhaps it is that His Majesty knows which side your son died fighting for that he would be assured of your loyalty by your attendance."

Reynald slammed a fist into his other hand. He was a dark, slim-built man, tough as whipcord and far stronger than many twice his size. His grandfather, Bors d'Emercy, had been the first of their line to make Penallt Manor his favored residence, some said because Bors was born out of wedlock and such details made little difference on this side of the border. Reynald's own father had married Roscelinda from a fine Norman/English family. She brought the manor of Rosecranly as her dower, and as a youth Reynald had spent equal time on both sides of the border. He never questioned, however, but that his heart remained to the west—a fact which could not have been more significantly displayed than when he chose for wife Angharad, the daughter of a Welsh lord. Angharad brought a small, but well-run manor into the family fortunes and bore him a fine pair of twins—a son, Janyn, who looked like his father, and a daughter, Joscelena, who favored her mother.

But that was eighteen years ago, and now the times were sorely changed. The messenger was not the proper person to bear the brunt of Reynald's anger, but he was handy. "And have I ever given King Edward the least reason to doubt my loyalty? Did I not pay knight's fee in solid currency for him to war against my wife's own people? And is it any wonder if the daughter of Elis ap Cynan should breed a son who has no tolerance for his mother's people being labeled 'debris of the devil'? We hear aplenty the tales told by Edward's followers—tales of Welsh sexual promiscuity, of theft, of rapine, and of sloth. I ask you, if it were true—as the rumor mongers put out—that these people are so depraved that only a few have learned to till the soil—how is it then that the land flourishes with green abundance, excepting where Edward's armies have trampled the crops and spilled red blood over the green land?"

The messenger stood erect as he had been trained, but his eyes flew first to the right, then to the left, then remained staunchly staring at the fashionably pointed toe of his riding shoe. Fortunately, Reynald's question was merely rhetorical and required no answer. "I know, I know! I speak of lost wars. Llywelyn ap Gruffudd has acknowledged defeat. And as a loyal liegeman of King Edward, I should be happy. But there is no victory for d'Emercy. My son does not return from the war. And now my daughter, pledged to Ninian Herbeaard, has disappeared."

His rantings had carried him to the end of the hall in long strides. He turned in time to see the gently plump form of Lady Angharad, silver-streaked dark curls peeking under her flat-topped white wimple, appear from her solar. Reynald sighed. "Very well. We shall attend." He turned to his wife. "My dear, see that King Edward's messenger has meat and wine before he continues his journey. Then inform Lewin we shall depart on Monday next. Our presence is required at Easter court at Glastonbury."

Lady Angharad was still regarding the messenger. "Is there word? Janyn? Joscelena?"

Reynald gripped the edge of the table to keep from flinging his anger at his wife. Of course there was no news of Janyn. Could she not accept that not even his body could be recovered? Why must she persist in this idea that he would return—like that long-dead King Arthur who, the Welsh minstrels sang, would come forth and lead his people in their hour of greatest need. And Joscelena—who knew where Janyn's headstrong twin had gone? If she spurned marrying Ninian, let her say so—there were young lords aplenty. Although Ninian would come into some very fine manors one day, the d'Emercys had no need to marry for wealth. Angharad had some notions their daughter had run off to take the veil. With Janyn gone, that would be a bitter herb indeed, for then who should inherit the estates but some distant cousin from the manor of d'Emercy. But even so, he would not refuse her—had he ever been able to refuse his daughter anything?

"No!" he growled at his wife who stood with her hands folded patiently, waiting for his answer. "There is no news, save that at this most inconvenient time of all we are to make a journey. Go prepare for it." As Reynald spun on his heel to march from the hall, he heard Angharad calling servants to care for the messenger.

So late in the day on the Wednesday before Easter, the small party from Penallt rode dutifully down Glastonbury High Street. Though accustomed to seeing processions of the high and mighty from all the countries of Europe in their narrow, muddy streets, the villagers welcomed with delight the visitors, who enriched the coffers of village and abbey alike.

Since the main structure of the abbey had been completed some thirty years before, pilgrims had streamed to the shrines of King Arthur, St. Patrick, and King Edmund. And now the regular Benedictine life went on under the firm hand of Abbot John of Taunton and the ever-inviolable Rule. True prayer of heart and mind lifting before God continued without cessation, as did the education, charity, and hospitality that defined the brothers' calling. Yet Glastonbury was more than an exemplary holy house. It was the preeminent shrine of knighthood, the sacred sanctuary of the monarchy, and the wellspring of the British church.

Though they were lesser nobility, the d'Emercys were given a room in a comfortable village home and their horses were well-stabled. They took bread that night at the abbot's table, the meal sent from his own kitchen conveniently near the fish ponds that provided tender-fleshed fish during Lent. After supper the abbot called in a group of lay brothers to act as hosts for a tour around the famous abbey and grounds.

Reynald would have refused, but Angharad was most eager to see the sights. For the first time, it struck Reynald that his wife was not so distressed over the disappearance of their daughter as he would have expected. As he thought back, he realized that only for the first day of Joscelena's disappearance ten days ago had Angharad taken to her bed to be nursed by her ladies. He regarded his complacent wife with narrowed eyes. Indeed, considering that no good news had reached Penallt in the intervening days, his wife's recovery was remarkable.

Then a black-robed, but untonsured young man was before them, offering to be their guide, and Reynald rose from the table to follow in his wake. Brother Matthew explained that the "brother" was but honorary since he had not yet taken vows. He led them first to the cloister. In the dorter he showed them the results of King Henry III's vigorous building program—rooms with glazed windows and wainscotted walls for protection against the chilling cold and damp; oaken bedsteads in the sleeping rooms and built-in fireplaces in the Chapter House and larger work rooms; above the cloister a range of studies with paneled carrels, each with a comfortable reading desk. Then they crossed the sheltered garden surrounded by cloistered walls where spring flowers bloomed in the sunnier recesses.

"The passage here leads into the church," Matthew said, "but if my lord and lady will permit, I will take you to see St. Mary's Chapel first, for it is our oldest and holiest place."

Inside the chapel Matthew bade them pray at the holiest shrine in Glastonbury and told them of its history as the site of the Old Church where men had worshiped God since the days of the apostles.

And Reynald did pray. For his son, fallen in battle defending what he saw as a just cause. And for Joscelena that her rashness had not led her into danger, that she would be restored to her father, that she should be a good and dutiful wife to Ninian Herbeaard.

They left the chapel and crossed the lawn to the north porch, used for entrance by villagers and visitors who would join the brothers in their prayers. Under the door they paused, and Matthew pointed upward to the clock. This mechanical clock, which told time by means of moving parts wound once a week by the sacristan using a large brass key, was one of the delights of Glastonbury. One might say its pride, except that the brothers had foresworn such worldly emotion.

Then they were within the great church. The pale evening light slanting through the tall traceried windows from the west fell in pools of varying blue and gold. On either side of them eight great stone pillars rose to a high vaulted ceiling whose carved fans looked like nothing so much as intertwined angels' wings spread in sheltering holiness over those who worshiped below. As they walked toward the transept, Reynald looked around at the cobalt-painted walls of the outer aisles beyond the march of pillars. Here bright-robed saints lived a life beyond the hand of the artist who had painted them to sing in an eternal choir to the God of all the universe.

Past the sarcophagi of lords and kings, their effigies lying in eternal serenity on their carved stone coffins, the visitors walked over red, scarlet, and saffron mosaic tiles to the presbytery and stood before the high altar. On either side were the brothers' choir stalls, richly-carved and brilliantly painted, even to gold inlays. Heavy, elaborate canopies overhead protected the brothers from icy downdrafts from the celestial reaches of the roof. An ornate gold cross stood beneath the jeweled eastern window, and candles burned on the brocaded altar cloth with its heavy embroidery and fringe of spun gold.

But for all the magnificence, that night as they lay beneath the heavy hangings of their bedstead, Reynald could not help but berate his wife for her pleasure in their visit. Her sturdy placidity had been one of the things he had loved most about her thirty-five years ago when he had taken her from her father's manor. And through the ups and downs of life her double portion of serenity had more than made up for his lack and had borne them both through many a storm. But this time it was too much. "Care you not, wife, that our daughter is gone from us, we know not where? It is bad enough that our son—eldest and only son of the manor—lies fallen with Llywelyn ap Gruffudd's men, but at least we know where he is and why. Of Joscelena we know nothing, except that she left willingly, for her room showed no signs of struggle and her maid is with her. What is it with you, woman? Are you so unmotherly that both your chicks can be taken from you and you not utter a word of protest?"

"When I am sure they are gone, there will be plenty of time for lamenting. Our son has not returned from war. The Prince of Wales's army was defeated.

That is true. It does not follow that Janyn is slain. I refuse to mourn without cause."

"Yes, and Joscelena? What hope do you hold for her? Not dead—I'll grant you hope of that—but run off with another lover who cannot possibly be so fine a man as Ninian? Or taken the veil in some rash act of worldly denial? And all so lost to us that not even the servants I sent in search could bring us hopeful word. Do you not mourn such prospects, woman?"

"The girl is safe. I know it." And that was all he could get from her.

The next morning at the abbot's table Reynald was feeling no happier, but he was obliged to give polite attention to King Edward's questions to Abbot John. "And is it true, as rumor would have it, that the actual bones of King Arthur and Queen Guinevere were discovered buried here? I have read the account of Gerald of Wales—but surely the good clerk exaggerated?"

"I have not seen them myself, Your Majesty. But I have every reason to believe the accounts of Gerald of Wales and others are essentially correct. It was little less than a hundred years ago that the discovery was made just beyond St. Mary's Chapel, and the remains have lain undisturbed since then."

Edward slammed his napkin on the table with such force that his goblet bounced, and a few red drops of wine spilled over. The page standing at attention behind him hurried to wipe up the spill and refill the royal cup. "We would see these wonders! Let the caskets be opened! In the presence of King Edward and Queen Eleanor. Then no man can doubt!" He took a deep drink from his refilled cup. "A great gash on the side of the head, they say? From which no man could have recovered? Truly dead and buried these eight hundred years and more? Ha! So much for these accursed Welsh scoundrels who look for the return of their ancient king to save them! Let the coffins be opened! We shall show the world!"

Abbot John kept a careful countenance before his king, but it appeared to cost him great effort. "As you wish, Your Majesty. But as we have the Chrism Mass and all the celebrations of Maundy Thursday today, may I suggest the undertaking be after Easter Sunday?" King Edward's brow darkened, so the abbot hurriedly added, "That way, nothing will detract from the importance of the undertaking. And might I further suggest that the bishops and abbots throughout Wales be sent a directive stressing that their hope be placed in the return of our Savior Jesus Christ, and not in any earthly king, as was the error of the Jews."

Edward's drooping left eyelid closed even further, but he nodded assent. Sitting to his left in the simplicity of her pearl-gray cotta and folded white wimple, Queen Eleanor smiled.

So, as ordained by God, all hearts and minds turned to the worship of His Son through Maundy Thursday and Good Friday. At midnight on Holy Saturday all from the royal court, from the enclosed brotherhood, and from the villages and other holy houses far afield gathered outside the great abbey for the tolling of the bells that ushered in the Easter vigil. All was dark; not a candle flickered; not a star shone; not a beam from the moon, as all the world waited in darkness. All light lay buried with the crucified Christ.

Then as the final peal of the bells echoed off the Tor and drifted into silence, Prior Mark struck a flint and touched it to the dry tinder of the Easter fire prepared beyond the north porch. The choir brothers began the plainchant. "Alleluia, the Lord is risen as He promised. Alleluia, He is risen. Lord Jesus, light shining in the darkness, You lead Your people into life and give our mortal nature the gift of holiness. May we spend this day in praise of Your glory. . . ."

The Easter candle was lighted from the fire, and the procession began as the brothers took up another chant. "May the light of Christ, rising in glory, dispel the darkness of our hearts and minds. The Lord be in your heart and on your lips, that you may worthily proclaim His Easter praise . . ."

First king and queen, then members of the brotherhood, then all in attendance stepped to the candle and lighted the small taper each held. Then they proceeded into the church and down the long nave, holding the golden, flickering lights high, until the entire abbey was filled with a golden radiance like that of the heavenly host around the Great White Throne.

Through the long wait of the vigil, as the world waited for the dawn of Easter morning and the return of light to the world, Reynald was gradually swept into praise and worship with the others. His heart, for so long burdened with woes, moved upward to God. When the congregation made the stones and arches of the hallowed building ring with the Easter proclamation, Reynald joined them fervently:

Rejoice, heavenly powers! Sing choirs of angels!
Exalt, all creation around God's throne!
Jesus Christ, our King is risen!
Sound the trumpet of salvation!
Rejoice, O earth, in shining splendor,
Radiant in the brightness of your King!
Christ has conquered! Glory fills you!
Darkness vanishes forever!

As they left with the last alleluias ringing in their hearts, Reynald caught a glimpse of a clutch of Benedictine sisters ahead of him. He drew in his breath at the familiar grace with which one of them carried herself. But before he could summon Angharad's attention, the sisters moved on and were lost to him. It was useless to inquire of the Brother Hospitaler, for there were far too many guests for even that efficient brother to know every member.

Most returned to their beds to sleep until time to prepare for High Easter Mass at ten o'clock, but Reynald was unable to sleep. Every time he closed his eyes he saw the little nun, so graceful in her small, soft roundness like Joscelena. If only he could have seen her eyes. No wimple or veil, no matter how securely it might hide her thick black tresses, could have obscured her wide, blue eyes that shone from infinite depths. And her face—the beguiling softness that belied her headstrong rashness . . . but he had not seen. And so he was tormented with maybes and whys. At last, creeping softly so as not to bother the peacefully sleeping Angharad, he slipped from under the bed draperies, put on his fur-lined surcoat and capuchon, and left the house.

It was barely an hour till dawn, and the sky, turning from gray to pink, silhouetted the dark shape of the Tor beyond the abbey. Picking his way carefully around the outside of the enclosure and across a plowed pease field, Reynald strode toward the sentinel. The exercise of a vigorous climb would do him good.

It was perhaps half an hour later that he arrived, panting heavily, at the small stone chapel, still dark in shadows. He threw himself onto a stone bench to catch his breath, then bolted up with such a start that he nearly fell into the stone wall on the other side. He was not alone.

"Forgive me." A gentle female voice came from the dark form on the bench.

And that sound startled him even more. "Joscelena! Can it be?"

The dark form moved to stand in the open eastward door of the chapel where the pink sky silhouetted her familiar form. "Father, forgive me. You must have been so worried. But I knew you would prevent my going, and I had to, you see."

Reynald sank onto the bench. "And so it is true, you ran from your home to take the veil. It is as I feared. But why? There was no need for stealth. It's true, I'm heartsick at your choice. I would have seen you bride of Ninian Herbeaard. But I would not have prevented you. Have I been so cruel and unreasonable a father?"

Her rich, mellow voice filled the tiny chapel. "No father. Never cruel, and seldom unreasonable. Always kind and protective—too protective—that was the problem. I knew I must go. It was as if I could hear my twin calling me, and I knew you would prevent it. So, taking Iveta, I went to Ninian for help. But he said my maid was not sufficient to lend me countenance in his company. He would have sent me home and searched himself, but I would none of it. So the first night he took me to a house of sisters. They gave me shelter and novice habit and Sister Magdalena to bear me company on my quest. For I told the holy mother I had taken a vow that I would not rest until I had found my brother dead or alive."

Reynald had been shaking his head in disbelief throughout her speech, but now he drew his breath with a jolt. "You are returned—you found—"

Joscelena nodded. "Yes. I—we—found him."

"And he is dead."

"No. I trust he is not, if God hears and grants prayers and gives healing to Sister Magdalena's medicines. But he was sorely wounded and would be long dead now if I had not followed my voice."

"Voice?"

"I told you, Father, although I did not expect you to believe me. I heard Janyn call me. Sister Magdalena says she has known it so before with twins. That is why she offered to go with me."

Now Reynald crossed the small space of the chapel and grasped his daughter. "Yes, yes, girl. So you found your brother. Not dead, you say! And where is he?"

"Taken and held in Abergavenny Castle."

"But how is this?"

"When we found Janyn fallen on the field, Sister Magdalena bound his wounds, and we thought to bring him home or perhaps to the sisters' house for nursing. Ninian made a litter, and by easy stages of travel, I am sure we could have accomplished it. But, alas, we did not think to watch for patrols. Gwent was such a peripheral part of the conflict, and Llywelyn had called for peace."

Her throat closed, and she dropped her head into her hands.

"So he was recognized for one of Llywelyn's men and taken?"

She nodded, then lifted her head, her hands clenched beneath her chin. "And Ninian—although he swore he bore no arms in the conflict—and if he had it would have been most likely on the king's side. But they would not believe him, so both are imprisoned." Suddenly her tight control slipped, and she flung herself into her father's arms. "Oh, Father, I thought to help—to save my brother and do good. Instead I have lost them both. Sister Magdalena slipped Ninian some herbs for treating Janyn's wounds, but I doubt not they've confiscated them. Oh, Father, I've made such a mess. Things are now double worse than before, and I don't know what to do."

Reynald held her for some time until her sobs quieted. "Not worse—at least you are restored to me. How is it, daughter, that they let you go?"

"The habit—Sister Magdalena said I should wear it for protection—and they honored it. They said King Edward wanted no trouble with Pope Nicholas, so he'd touch no one of the church. They took the horses, but left us Sister's donkey, which we took turns riding."

"And you came here seeking me?"

She looked up at him, eyes wide in astonishment. "No. I had no notion you were here. It was all I could do at the Easter vigil to keep from flinging myself into Mother's arms, but I had such bad news to tell you—I didn't want you to know of my failure. And now I must tell Ninian's father also, although he had leave to go."

"Then why are you here?"

"When we got back to Sister Magdalena's convent, they were making ready to come to the service, and I—I . . . Oh, Father, don't laugh at me or forbid me—please—it's our only hope. Please let me try."

"Try what, daughter?"

"To seek the mercy of the king for the release of Janyn and Ninian. They say he's not an unreasonable man. Sister Magdalena and Mother Superior could see nothing else to be done. And all the sisters have vowed perpetual prayers for all of Holy Week that our petition will be successful. And if it's not . . ."

"Yes?"

"If I fail, I can return to the convent with them."

Reynald nodded. He would not oppose her. He understood. Over Joscelena's shoulder the full glory of morning was now filling the sky with gold and red, and from below, the abbey bells chimed in exultation. It was Easter morning. Christ was risen, bringing hope to the world. Reynald prayed that he could find that hope to carry on.

Throughout the rest of the Easter Sunday, joyously celebrated by all—except by the father and daughter—and through the next day, Reynald contemplated what he should do.

On Tuesday he awoke with the bells, convinced that he must be the one to approach his sovereign. No matter if his son's Welsh loyalties and his own wife's birth, to say nothing of the location of his best manors, brought his allegiances into question and therefore might expose him to Edward's wrath. What did it matter now if he wound up in Abergavenny Castle with his son and would-be son-in-law? He must try.

But the king was not to be approached, for this was the day he had awaited with scarcely concealed impatience. After High Mass and dinner five black-robed brothers were dispatched with shovels in the presence of the king, queen, and abbot to exhume the bones. All the court and brotherhood gathered, standing back a respectful distance. Although the carved chests were buried this time at no great depth, all must be done with order and circumspection, the unearthed caskets swept clean of all soil and polished, prayers said, and candles lighted. And so it was twilight when at last the tomb was opened to full view.

All leaned forward for a better view as the librarian held the heavy volume for Abbot John, and he read the words of Gerald of Wales. He described the long legs, longer than Edward's, who was himself a tall man, the dented skull with the jagged death-wound over the left ear . . . The smaller, but equally beautifully carved casket containing the more delicate bones of a woman—surely the queen herself.

Edward studied the contents of the chests long and silently, his left eyelid drooping almost closed in concentration. At last he turned. "Let it be heard clearly and carried henceforth that this casket before me contains the true and hallowed bones of King Arthur. Let all who come here do him reverence. And let the word go into Wales that their *Rex Futurus* will not avenge them.

"Let no man mistake the matter. By royal decree I order that the skulls of Arthur and Guinevere be set on posts by the gate of Glastonbury Abbey for a period of twenty-four hours for all men to see. At the hour of Vespers tomorrow the caskets shall be reclosed, and Queen Eleanor and I shall bear them to the high altar. Let it be done."

The next day when Edward held court in the abbot's hall, Reynald knew what he must do. He had discussed it with Angharad, and they were agreed. They would give all their manors to the royal coffers if need be. They would pay any ransom necessary.

The hall was crowded with lords and courtiers as well as with common men who had matters to lay before their sovereign. The king sat in the abbot's high seat at the far end of the hall, his marshall on one side, his chaplain on the other, and a row of clerks busily writing at tables at his feet. The d'Emercys waited three hours until at last Sir Reynald's name was called. Although inwardly his knees trembled, he walked straight to the king and made a deep bow. Except for the drumming of ringed fingers on the arm of the chair, Edward seemed to listen attentively as Reynald explained how his son was wounded in battle—fighting on Llywelyn's side out of loyalty to his mother's people, although Angharad herself swore loyalty to His Majesty, and how their daughter had found him and begun his nursing, only to have him and his friend snatched by the patrol.

Edward scowled. "We *will* be master in Wales. We do not countenance rebels from the manors of our nobility. It much displeases me that you should so excuse your son."

Reynald bowed, fighting desperately to find words that might soften his sovereign. But nothing came. He stood in silence.

Edward's sharp eyes scanned the room. "Let the sister speak."

Numbly Reynald stepped aside. Joscelena's habit made a soft swish on the floor as she bowed deeply. "My king," she said simply.

"You are of the Benedictine order, my daughter?" Edward asked in a far kinder tone than he had used on the father.

"Not yet, my lord. But I have vowed to take the veil if my brother and betrothed are not returned by your gracious mercy."

"And why should we do so? Would you have us turn all traitors to England loose to plague the king's peace?"

"My brother is condemned to die. But so are we all. I would have his death be in God's time and not Your Majesty's. For my brother and my betrothed, I do ask, as we must all, for mercy. It is our only plea. What will you do, Your Majesty, when you stand before your Judge, but ask for mercy? Let your own example to my brother and his friend count to you for God's mercy on your own soul." She stood quietly, her head bowed as if in prayer, her hands clasped still and white before her.

The room was silent, save for the drumming of the king's hand on the chair. At last he turned again to Reynald. "I wonder if your son is of so fine a spirit as his sister. It would be a pity, indeed, to snuff such a flame. And you say both young men are knight-trained and will swear fealty to their king?"

"They will, my lord."

Again Edward considered. Joscelena's lips moved in silent prayer. At last the king spoke. "It is my plan to secure my Welsh victories by a program of castle building. We shall ring Gwynedd from Anglesey to Harlech with the strongest castles ever built in this land. We are not so flush in manpower and gold that we can afford to have our knights languishing in prison when they might be raising fortifications. You may take your son home for nursing. When he is fully recovered, I order that he and his companion report to my steward at Caernarfon to build for the peace between England and Wales—fully supplied with stone, timber, and mortar from your manors' purse."

A clerk, who had been writing in such haste that his stylus scratches could be heard halfway down the hall, dusted his parchment with sand, blew it off, and held the document before King Edward. The king gave it a cursory reading and nodded. The clerk poured a blob of red wax on the bottom of the page and King Edward affixed his seal from the great signet ring he wore on his right hand.

Reynald, clutching his precious parchment, bowed his way from the hall, trembling so with relief he thought he would fall. Outside, his wife and daughter enfolded him in their praises. "Oh, well done, my husband!"

"Forgive me, Father. I was wrong to take matters into my own hands. Now all will be well. I will never behave in such a foolish, headstrong manner again."

Reynald regarded his daughter. "That I doubt. Nor do I think it wise to take vows one is incapable of fulfilling. Your speech before the king more than made amends, but next time, daughter, let your mother or me know what you are doing."

There was a sudden silence. Then he understood. Her mother had known. "Angharad?" he bellowed.

"Shhhh, dear. Not here, outside the abbot's hall with the king inside. You may berate me to your heart's content when we are safely at Penallt with Janyn and Ninian, but not now, dear."

The reference to the young men did the trick. "Yes, let us be off. Order our horses saddled."

Angharad laid a plump white hand on his arm. "My dear, don't be too harsh on our daughter's rashness. We know where she gets it. It is but an hour to Vespers. Wouldn't it be best to set out fresh in the morning? We could send word to Sir Herbeaard. I'm sure he would wish to join us at Abergavenny. And Sister Magdalena as well, with a full scrip of ointments and salves."

Reynald agreed. So it was that Reynald d'Emercy, grandson of that Bors who had been in attendance when the bones of King Arthur and Queen Guinevere were first discovered, Bors who had seen the leaden cross dug from the earth, the oaken lid pried off the hollowed log, the long leg bone measured to Brother Ambrose, and the golden tresses of Queen Guinevere disintegrate into nothing at human touch—the descendant of that same young boy who had so rashly saved the golden chalice and carved stone from the Old Church—had a seat in the front of the nave when King Edward wrapped King Arthur's bones in a pall of the costliest linen, as Queen Eleanor did the same for Queen Guinevere and enclosed them in their carved chests. Edward read the inscription for Arthur's casket aloud to the assembled congregation before sealing it in the tomb: "These are the bones of the most noble King Arthur, which were placed here on 19 April in the year of the Lord's Incarnation 1278 by the illustrious Lord Edward, King of England, in the presence of the most serene Eleanor, wife of the Lord King and daughter of Lord Fernando, King of Spain. . . ."

The scroll was placed in the casket, the lid closed, and the king's seal set upon it. Then, at a signal from the choir master, the chant began. The abbot, bearing a staff with a golden cross, walked behind two brothers swinging censers as the procession made its way down the north aisle, then turned again toward the high altar. The sweet fragrance of the incense mingled with that of the hundreds of spiced candles lining the long nave.

Queen Eleanor came first bearing Guinevere's reliquary in quiet dignity. Next came the king, bearing the chest of King Arthur's bones. Around his head the gold circlet of kingship caught the light of the candles and glowed like a halo. But his face bore the brightest radiance of all. Edward might, indeed, have begun this exercise to prove to his enemies that their once and future king was dead. But in the process, perhaps through his touching the royal relics and thinking on the noble life of the one who had so valiantly saved England from her enemies, the ceremony had been transformed to a moment of great personal significance to Edward. It was written clear on the king's face that he would strive to be great, like the leader whose bones he now carried to the high altar of Glastonbury Abbey.

Arthur's casket was placed to the right of the altar and Guinevere's to the left. Edward and Eleanor knelt before the caskets. The abbot made the sign of the cross and then sprinkled both caskets and the kneeling king and queen with holy water.

Abbot John's voice rang to the farthest reaches of the great church. "The whole earth is the tomb of heroic people. But the memory of these heroes lives not only graven on the stones over their clay, but abides ever more woven into the stuff of others' lives. It is in serving God that people become heroes, royal and common alike. Heroes are made through living by the words, 'Your will be done.' Let us take our cross and follow Jesus—this is the only true heroism."

After the choir monks sang the anthem, "I have set my King upon my holy hill of Zion," the abbot stood at the high altar and blessed all the congregation.

On the morrow the d'Emercys went on their way, knowing they had seen wonders.

BOOK VI

THE TESTING OF THE FAITH

TUDOR ENGLAND

The end of my study nears. But am I any nearer the ultimate answer than when I began? Will I ever find the answer to that great mystery? The sacred cup was not buried with Arthur—which must mean that the knights of the Round Table never found it—if indeed they looked at all. If the grail eluded such valiant men as they, there is little hope for a humble monk.

Or did they fail because their questing was of the works of men? Is it that the grail may not be achieved by works because no one is good enough apart from Christ? I ponder long over the tales of the pure and holy Galaad. Not even he was good enough, not even when he forsook the maiden Blanchfleur when he realized that the meaning of the grail was not earthly love.

Yet the deeper mystery remains. Not where is the grail, but what is the grail? I have spent much time pondering Chretien de Troyes's idea of the grail as a dish of plenty, a life-giving vessel that brings healing to the parched land. And I see much merit in that. Our Lord promises that if His people will turn from their wicked ways and seek Him, He will hear from Heaven and heal their land. Did ever our poor land need healing more than now? Our promised land, the New Jerusalem, was to be a land flowing with milk and honey—but we are a land torn by poverty and riots, by wars and rumors of war.

Or was the grail not, as we always supposed, the cup Christ used at the Last Supper? Some would say it was instead a cruet in which Joseph of Arimathea caught Christ's blood as it flowed from the cross.

My mind falters at the thought of the existence of such an object. But surely, it cannot be—for frail men as we are, we would then venerate the object rather than the sacrifice of our Lord. Of such idolatry did the German monk Luther warn us—but I am no Lutheran.

So the answers remain good answers, but only partial answers, and I hunger for greater fulfillment.

Yesterday I came upon a pamphlet issued by the royal printer for visitors to our abbey called "The Lyfe of Joseph of Armathia." My eyes grow misty at the description of happier days here:

> *The hawthorns also that groweth in Werall*
> *As fresh as other in May when the nightingale*
> *Wrests out her notes musical as pure as glass . . .*

And with an ache in my heart that I struggle to keep from turning to bitterness, I think again on the year 1509—the year I took my holy vows—when a new monarch was crowned at Westminster. It still seems impossible—the king was young, brilliant, educated, a model Catholic. He had even studied for holy orders. We were filled with optimism for the good times ahead for our abbey and for the faith. I can still hear my own voice ringing with those of monks, peasants, and noblemen:

"God save the king! Long live King Henry the Eighth!"

1

bbot Richard Whiting sat at an inlaid oak table in a small parlor in Glastonbury Monastery staring at the strangely worded document in his hand. When he looked up at the messenger standing patiently on the other side of the table, the frown lines in his broad forehead deepened. "Master Lacey, you must give me time to consider."

The young man bowed, and his flashing black eyes held no displeasure as he replied, "As you wish, my Lord Abbot. You will note, however, that twenty-one other abbots have signed." He took a step backward toward the door.

The blood-red garnet in Abbot Whiting's signet ring flashed as he waved the messenger out. "Yes, yes. In spite of my seventy years I can still see quite well without eyeglasses, although I am told such is not the case with our sovereign."

He looked again at the document before him. "It is not the words I need to consider, but their meaning. Brother Gildas our hospitaler will find you and your servant accommodation in the George and Pilgrim Inn across the street. I can assure you of your comfort while you wait."

"My Lord Abbot, I have no worry about my comfort; it is His Majesty's comfort . . ."

"Yes, yes." Whiting stood to usher Master Lacey out. "King Henry has been seeking to put aside his marriage to Queen Catherine for three years now. I have no doubt that his royal impatience can survive a few more days."

The messenger, repeating his bow with a flourish of his blue velvet plumed cap, went off to the inn the monastery maintained for travelers. Whiting resumed his seat and rang a small bell to summon the abbey schoolboy who was his page that day. "Mark, I would have you summon Brother William . . ." He paused. William Benet, the abbey's expert on matters of canon law, was an obvious choice. Who else would he take counsel with? Not too many, just those brothers whose judgment he most valued—Brother Arthur, the subprior, and Brother Austin, the librarian. Mark scurried off.

In a matter of only a few minutes the black-robed monks stood before him. Brother William, clear-eyed, strong-featured, only three years in Glastonbury, had earned his doctorate at Cardinal College in Oxford. Brother Arthur, the tall, energetic, red-haired subprior, was just one of several brothers whose names proclaimed the blessed heritage of their house (along with Brothers Gildas, Arimathea, Joseph, and Dunstan). Slightly behind the others, his gentle eyes screwed into their perennial scholarly squint, stood Brother Austin Ringwode.

"Sit down, brothers." With a sweep of his hand Whiting indicated the stools they should draw to the table. "I have a matter of grave importance to put before you. Ultimately it is for my conscience alone, so I would not take it to Chapter, but I would have your counsel."

He pulled the parchment document from the leather pouch. "The letter I hold is addressed to His Holiness, Pope Clement VII. I know not which hand at court has drawn the thing up—but I can say with certainty that it is not from the Lord Chancellor, for never would Thomas More take such a position. Nor if he did, would he express it in such perplexing language. At any rate, this letter to His Holiness which purports to come from the Lords Spiritual and the Lords Temporal of all England urges the Pope to dissolve Henry's marriage to Queen Catherine and threatens dire, although unspecified consequences should the petition fail to be granted."

Brother William, with his precise lawyer's mind, was the first to speak. "And who has signed this document, Your Grace?"

Whiting glanced over the accompanying pages of signatures. "It would appear that all the lords in Parliament and my fellow abbots from the larger houses. Also Wolsey has signed as Archbishop of York—apparently he is anxious not to lose the one title left him . . ." He unrolled a second page and scanned the signatures. "All the peers and bishops appear to be here . . ." He looked back over the list one time more. "Hmm, I find it interesting to note that the Lord Chancellor's signature is missing."

Brother William nodded. "Perhaps the king meant it when he promised to give Sir Thomas full rein of his own conscience if he would accept the office."

"Did you say the document implies threats against His Holiness?" Brother Arthur, also still known by his secular name—John Thorne, asked.

Whiting nodded. "The petitioners warn the Pope that if he refuses to grant Henry a divorce, great calamities might befall the realm, and they might be forced to take action on their own to prevent this. Just what such calamities might be and what action might prevent them is left to the imagination."

A thoughtful silence prevailed in the room until Whiting spoke again. "I wonder at the Lord Chancellor's absence from the list, for I was present at Westminster last year when More addressed the House to the effect that there are some who say that the king is pursuing a divorce out of love for some lady and not out of conscience. 'But this is not true,' More said. And he read out the opinions of twelve foreign universities and showed a hundred books drawn up by doctors, all agreeing that the king's marriage was unlawful. And then the Lord Chancellor said, as best I recall his words, 'Now you of this Commons house may report in your counties what you have seen and heard, and then all men shall openly perceive that the king hath not attempted this matter of will or pleasure, as some strangers report, but only for the discharge of his conscience and surety of the succession of his realm.'"

The furrows deepened in Brother Austin's round forehead. "Sir Thomas More said that? And yet when Pope Julius issued the decree that Henry could marry his brother's widow, he based it firmly on Deuteronomy 25:5, 'If brethren dwell together, and one of them die, and have no child . . . her husband's brother shall go in unto her, and take her to him to wife . . . ' How can anything so clear now be set aside?" Brother Austin rubbed his shiny round tonsured head with a plump hand. "I would that this house should pleasure King Henry, but how can we in the face of the words of the Pope and of God?"

Brother Arthur, his broad shoulders shifting under his black robe, moved forward on his stool as if he would spring to his feet. "Ah, yes, Deuteronomy is well enough, but the king's conscience has been slain by Leviticus. In 20:21 God decrees that if a man takes his brother's wife, it is unclean; they will be childless. And the truth seems evident, for the king is childless."

"There is the Princess Mary," Abbot Whiting suggested almost apologetically.

Brother William returned to the fray. "Princess Mary is but a girl—all the king's sons were born dead or died within a few days. King Henry would not have this realm plunged into the civil war that tore our land when last we were ruled by a woman—we all know of the chaos under the Empress Matilda . . ."

Brother Arthur rose and restlessly paced the small parlor. "I doubt not that the king's conscience has been pinched. Certainly it pinches, but by what? God's law or desire for woman? Has the king's conscience been slain by God or by the Boleyn wench?"

Brother William also stood to answer. "Ah, now we come to the crux. All perhaps are honest factors—but which came first? Did the king first desire God's pleasure, the kingdom's good, or Anne Boleyn?"

Abbot Whiting rapped on his table. "Brothers! This is to no avail. It is not the king's conscience I have asked you to advise, but my own. The rightness of God's law is not settled by the king's conscience—or even by the Pope's decree. God's law is God's law, and so we must rightly discern, for sin is sin, even if committed unconsciously. Has the king sinned unknowingly in taking his brother's wife? Or do I sin in supporting his petition to put her away?"

The abbot sat for a moment with his head in his hands. "I thank you for your counsel, brothers. The time for Vespers draws nigh, and I would not keep you from your prayers." He rang the brass bell on his table, and ten-year-old Mark bounded into the room, hastily stuffing a small, furry creature into the pocket of his black tunic. "Mark, please tell Brother Gildas to make certain of our guests' comfort. I shall require a day or two to meditate on this matter. It is not an easy thing I have been asked to decide."

The page gave an obedient bob and turned to fly with his message, but he halted when he saw the portly figure sitting to the side. "Oh, Uncle Austin, my mother said I am to ask, can you get leave to take supper with us one evening next week?"

Brother Austin looked at the abbot and received a kindly nod. "I believe that can be arranged, young Mark. Our Lord Abbot is finished with my poor services; I will accompany you on your errand."

Outside the abbot's lodging the late afternoon sun made them blink. Mark slipped his hand into his uncle's and led him until they reached the speckled shade of the apple trees lining the path. "And who is your new friend?" Austin grinned at his nephew. "Would it not be polite to introduce us?"

Mark put a grubby hand into his pocket and drew out a small, golden mouse with tiny, bright eyes. "This is Squeakers." He ran one finger over the soft, furry head.

"And what does the Master of Boys say to having such guests in his dorter?"

Mark grinned. "Oh, Brother Joseph doesn't take any notice. He says we're too noisy. He leaves us to Brother Roger James. Brother Roger loves Squeakers. He says he had a pet snake named Godric until he took his final vows last year. Then he let Godric go because it didn't seem fitting—the brothers aren't supposed to have any personal property."

Brother Austin grinned. "Yes, I know."

"Oh. Yes. You always seem more like an uncle than a monk, so I forget."

Brother Austin ran his fingers along Squeakers's sleek tail. "Be off with you now. Mind you deliver the abbot's message properly. And tell your mother I will come to her on Tuesday next."

Mark bounded off, his slim legs flashing beneath his short black tunic. Brother Austin leaned back and looked at the ripening fruit on the bough above his head. He could almost smell its sweetness. He closed his eyes and felt the rough bark of the trunk through his robe. A robin began his evening song in a high branch. How was it possible that the world beyond could be in such turmoil when all was so peaceful here?

Twenty-one years he, Austin Ringwode, had been a brother at Glastonbury, serving in the kitchen, the school, the infirmary, until he finally came to rest in the library. He, like all of his order, spent several hours a day in manual labor as well. And for all he loved his books, he also well-loved the pease fields—sweet with white bloom in the spring, green vines heavy with succulent pods now, soon to be raked into mounds and harvested. But such beauty and peace, such harmony with the natural rhythms of life, were not to be found beyond these enclosed walls if one could believe but a portion of the reports that reached them: the English court divided and astir over the king's Great Matter, Emperor Charles of the Holy Roman Empire and King Francis I of France threatening war on the continent, the German church and universities torn apart by the teachings of the monk Luther . . .

The bell tolled for Vespers.

Brother Austin rolled to his feet and with bowed head and folded hands walked toward the great abbey church. Yes, the world might be in turmoil, but here the worship of God would continue in quietness and beauty.

A few miles to the north in Wells, however, the turmoil at Bucklesbury, the home of Robert Burgess, was of quite a different nature. Although all the world thought Robert Burgess a prosperous man, he was not a happy one, beset on every side as he was by recalcitrant females and decaying buildings.

He sat in the hall of his two-hundred-year-old medieval home and surveyed the smoke-blackened beams above his head. Although his wife Margery insisted that the floor rushes be changed weekly—despite the grumbling of servants that in most homes this was a twice-yearly process—the room smelled of age and decay. He pounded the heavy trestle table where he sat at the top of the room.

No matter how he tired of hearing his wife's nagging that they should rebuild, she was right. He must rebuild, remodel, refurbish—house, barns, mills, dairy, fences—all must be torn down and done anew in a style befitting the new age of King Henry.

Robert screwed up his broad, weathered face. His was a prosperous farm—but not that prosperous. Sheep, corn, dairy, wool mills—all flourished—and yet the costs flourished as well. Where would the money for such an extensive project come from—especially since Margery would insist that no corners be cut and only the finest of everything be used?

And if his wife's niece Cecily remained obstinate in the matter of marrying his ward Hugh Davington, there would be little hope of enriching his coffers in that direction. The prospective groom and he had an understanding regarding Cecily's dowry, but if she married elsewhere, he would lose control of her fortune. Of course, he could simply force the matter, but the girl's legal wardship was in the hands of Abbot Whiting, and he was ever wont to give Cecily her head. All this was quite aside from the fact that Margery would not take kindly to the use of force. He flinched from crossing Margery.

Even now he heard her voice sharply instructing the servants in the larder. "This cake is underbaked in the middle! The cheese is not properly cured! The perry is too weak! What if my uncle, the Abbot of Glastonbury, should call and I be forced to serve him fallen cake, rubbery cheese, and weak perry? It must all be done again . . ."

She moved away from the door and Robert was spared any more of her shrill voice. But the words remained—"my uncle, the Abbot of Glastonbury." Always she held that up in conversation, for she would have no one forget that she was from one of the best-established families of the West Country. *Her uncle, the abbot,* Robert mused, running a work-hardened hand through his thick hair. Richard Whiting was not only head of the largest monastery in England, he was also head of his old and respected family. Gentleman that he was, he took both jobs seriously. Richard Whiting would not want his niece to continue living in an uncomfortable, unsuitable manner. He could be appealed to for funds—if it were properly done.

Robert's broad features broke in to a smile. Yes, with a little subtlety the new buildings could be built. Whiting was reasonably warm toward Margery, and he positively doted on the fair Cecily, his grandniece. Robert would send them to Glastonbury. Margery could take a gift to the abbey, something showy, but not too costly—gilt candlesticks perhaps—but only overlaid, not solid gold. And Cecily could ask the abbot for spiritual advice on something, anything. Young maids were ever in turmoil of conscience over impractical matters, and especially Cecily since the abbot had so unwisely, to Robert's mind, taught her to read.

"Wife! Cecily!" Robert accompanied his bellows with repeated thuds on the table. Wyatt, the usher who had been drowsing in the corner awaiting his master's pleasure, sprang to his feet and bounded off to seek the women.

It did not take Cecily long to grasp the meaning of her uncle's orders. "But I have no crisis of conscience about which I need advice," she protested.

Ends of brown hair turning a mouse-gray straggled beneath Margery's kerchief, and her blue eyes snapped. "Nor have I any desire to make him a present of my best pair of candlesticks, my girl. But I have less desire to continue living in this unfashionable, uncomfortable manner. What my husband suggests is sound. Whiting likes you better than he does me—even if I am the only surviving child of his dearest sister." Her sharp voice broke into a whine. "You must go with me and smile at his table, or we'll be living in this ramshackle house until the stones fall down around our heads." Then she narrowed her eyes for a shrewd parting shot. "Unless you'd prefer to remain here and be betrothed to Hugh."

Cecily sighed and ran her hands over the skirt of her soft blue gown. "Yes, Aunt."

So by noon the next day Cecily was sitting between her aunt and an aging London merchant at the well-laid table in the abbot's hall. She took small bites of rabbit stew in a rich sauce served on little pancakes, accompanied by wild berry jelly, and listened to the conversation around her. She couldn't help feeling sorry for the abbot. It seemed that everyone at the table wanted something from him. The merchant could never let his conversation veer far from how excellent the fine fabrics he imported were for vestments and altar cloths. Dame Margery was none too subtle as she described, in what she apparently supposed to be an amusing manner, the embarrassing conditions at Bucklesbury. "But, of course, we tell no one of our connection with the Abbot of Glastonbury, for we wouldn't want our ramshackle condition to bring shame on the splendor of this house." She forced a bright laugh and took another bite of white manchet bread dipped in spiced lentil soup.

Then the guest sitting across the table from Cecily, apparently a court messenger, referred to some matter of conscience which he wanted her uncle to decide to coincide with his own conscience—or more likely the king's pleasure, Cecily thought. She doubted if the fashionable young man in the blue velvet coat had much cause to call on his own conscience—should he possess such an inconvenient organ.

Cecily added a pinch of cloves to her stew and studied him. His slick court manners and facile tongue were just what one would expect from a London courtier. Yet in quiet moments when he wasn't working to impress someone—the abbot, members of his own delegation, or even himself—there was a certain sweetness to his smile, a directness to the gaze of his snapping black eyes that hinted he had not been wholly corrupted by the world in which he lived. Once when the subprior made a particularly telling reply to one of his points, she even thought she saw a twinkle in his eye that bespoke a certain detachment—an ability to laugh at himself and the absurd games he must play to keep his place and climb ever higher. But then the abbot asked a question, and he returned to his role of perfect courtier, perfect gentleman, *perfect trained monkey,* she thought.

A bowl of purple and gold plums, fresh from the abbey orchards, passed three times around the table before the abbot dismissed his guests with a promise to see them on the morrow and have answers for them all. Brothers William, Arthur, and Austin filed out to their afternoon duties. Cecily could see that her aunt was torn between further direct application or attempting a less obvious ploy. But when Dame Margery announced in her shrill voice that she would spend the afternoon in the Lady Chapel praying for all their needs, Cecily blushed.

The others moved out of the hall ahead of her, and Cecily thought herself alone as she walked into the sun-warmed afternoon and turned her steps toward the fish pond. She had nearly reached the bench on the willow-shaded bank of the pond when she detected a footstep behind her. She turned sharply. "Am I followed?"

The courtier with the snapping eyes and silky manner swept his feathered cap off his curly black hair and made a graceful bow. "Forgive me, mistress, but as we just sat at meat together, I did not think it presumptuous to seek your acquaintance. Especially since the abbot apparently means to keep us here another day, and I would fill the time as pleasantly as possible."

Cecily couldn't resist a mischievous smile. "Ah, I believe it is Brother Austin you must apply to."

The young man looked confused. "Brother Austin?"

"That is the name of the librarian. Surely you could ask for no more useful or pleasant way to spend an afternoon than reading. I understand the Glastonbury library is world famous." She picked up the pomander that hung on a ribbon from her waistband and sniffed at it as if its clove and orange scent claimed all her attention.

"Yes. An excellent suggestion! And would you care to join me? Surely what is pleasure alone could be doubled by two."

Cecily tossed her waist-length blond hair, worn loose under a heart-shaped cap, and laughed. "I shouldn't be so surprised at the readiness of your tongue, Master Courtier. But if you think to turn the tables now by having me refuse on grounds that I don't read, you're quite out. Although I fear I have little Latin, so my claims to scholarship aren't great."

"Beauty and learning in one package—and both far surpassing anything one is likely to encounter in London. May I present myself, mistress? I am Giles Lacey."

"Courtier to His Majesty Henry the Eighth?" Cecily laughed again and held her yellow skirt wide as she sank in a deep, playful curtsey.

"You mock me, mistress. I am but a glorified messenger boy. But I flatter myself that I am a trusted messenger, for the matter I carry to all the Lords Spiritual of the realm is close to the king's heart. As I am but a third son, I must do my job well, for it is up to me to make my own way in the world."

"And you have chosen to make your way at court?" She made little effort to keep the distaste from her voice.

"As my eldest brother will get the estate, and my second brother has entered the church with the preferment my father purchased for him and a position at Oxford, there seemed little left for me to do. As you so obviously think the court no honest profession, let me say in my defense that I would advance by doing a good job and not as a toady." Even as he spoke, he wondered why it was so important to him to defend himself to this girl with whom he had only thought to pass a pleasant hour.

"Ah, so you would have me toady for you and urge my uncle to lend his signature to your endeavor?"

"Your uncle? Forgive me, mistress—I knew not—" For once the fluent courtier was unsure of his footing.

"I thought you knew. I assumed that was why you pursued me. I am Cecily Whiting."

"Oh, you are—er—" and Master Lacey blushed to the roots of his hair. "Forgive me, I—ah—"

Suddenly the source of his discomfort became clear to her, and her laughter caused a swan on the fish pond to flutter his wing. "No, no. You are quite wrong. The Abbot of Glastonbury is all that the world does not understand—

an honest and chaste man. I am his niece—*truly* his niece. Well, a grandniece or something—my Aunt Margery is his true niece—daughter of his sister." And without pausing to wonder why she did so, she went on to explain to him. "We are a numerous family here in the West Country. Another Richard Whiting was chamberlain of the Monastery of Bath in the 1450s—as my uncle was chamberlain of Glastonbury before he became abbot, and my Aunt Jane is a nun at Shaftesbury, and I have two cousins ready to make their novitiate."

Now his embarrassment seemed to change to disappointment. "Oh." He paused and swallowed. "And you—you would take vows also?"

Cecily's golden laughter mingled with the gold of her hair and the sunshine. "Alas, no. I have no vocation." She noted that Giles's smile revealed perfect white teeth, and some of the antagonism left her voice.

So it was that three hours later when the bells tolled for Vespers, two heads—one of short black curls and one of long golden tresses startled in total amazement that the time could have so sped.

2

On the next morning Abbot Whiting added his signature to the petition asking Pope Clement VII to declare that Henry's marriage to Catherine of Aragon was no true marriage.

With the successful completion of his mission Giles Lacey and his servant turned toward London. They rode under branches heavy with summer greenness, caroled on their way by tiny red-headed finches who, unlike many birds who sing only at morning and evening, continue to praise their Maker throughout the day. All the way the beauty of the song and the golden pools of sunshine on the path reminded Giles of the songlike laughter and golden hair of Cecily Whiting.

But as Dame Margery's petition had also met with success, and she and Cecily had returned to Wells immediately after mass, Giles had had no further opportunity to speak to her. Nor did he know if he ever would, for the London he returned to was an all-consuming world—a world of conspiracies, rumors, and counterrumors. No sooner was an issue raised than there were decrees and proclamations on all sides, and it was increasingly difficult to find the facts of a situation or the quiet to sort them out in order to find one's own conscience on any matter. Indeed, it was no wonder that the Lord Chancellor retired as often as possible to his quiet manor house on the banks of the Thames where he could read his own books and say his own prayers. Often Giles, in his small clerk's office, longed for such a retreat.

In the weeks and months that followed it became increasingly difficult—nay, impossible—to maintain a secure position at court by walking the narrow line between papist and Lutheran. In May Henry issued a proclamation against the writings and disciples of Luther. On taking office, every official had to swear an oath to help the bishops exterminate the heresy of Lutheranism. As Giles held no office, he was not required to take the oath, but he asked himself what his answer would be if he were.

The proclamation had also contained a list of books banned as heretical. Anyone who brought them into the country, or who failed to hand in to the authorities any copy which came into his hands, was to be brought before the king's council and punished. The books included Tyndale's *New Testament* and those ridiculing the clergy which had received such enthusiastic reading at court. When a public burning of the English *New Testament* took place at Paul's Cross, Giles did not attend.

And still there was no response from the Pope as to the king's Great Matter. Queen Catherine remained at court. The king, while riding and talking openly with Anne, left Catherine in charge of his personal wardrobe—so that when Henry needed new linen shirts he applied to Catherine. The matter was on everybody's minds and on most lips, but nothing was done, in spite of the emissaries and letters that traveled back and forth between London and Rome.

That winter Wolsey died. When word reached Giles, he left his chamber at Hampton Palace where the court was sitting and walked long in the winter-sleeping gardens. Wolsey had been the most powerful man in the realm, many said more powerful than the king himself. Wolsey, whose wealth and many offices were almost beyond reckoning, the most powerful commoner in England, had died in a north country abbey under arrest for treason. No wonder Cecily had been so disdainful of the courtier's life. Giles felt as never before the impermanence of wealth and position in such a world. Yet what was solid? Faith—ever a bulwark against fear and uncertainty for this life and the next? What security was there to be found between Lutheran heresy and papal abuses?

Giles threw a pebble into a smooth brown flower bed that next spring would be a blaze of red and gold tulips. Ahead of him he heard the thud of balls and the ring of laughter from Henry's indoor tennis courts—a sport of which the agile king never tired.

So in this strange, waiting manner did the months pass. Henry played tennis and hawked and hunted with the Lady Anne Boleyn while Queen Catherine appealed for help to the Pope and to her nephew, Charles, the Holy Roman Emperor. Fifteen months passed with no judgment from Rome. Giles was walking by the same flower bed, now ablaze with late summer marigolds and chrysanthemums, when a lanky form leaping a low hedge behind him startled three robins from a bush.

"Humphrey!" Giles turned with a surprised grin. "Didn't I warn you that those wild north country manners will get you into trouble?"

Humphrey returned a rueful look and bobbed his straw-thatched head. "It appears you were right, for I've torn my hose on this bramble." He extended a long, thin leg clad in scarlet hose with a gaping hole in it. "But I've wonderful news! No more shooting at butts for us—we are offered real sport. The king takes Mistress Boleyn—or she takes him, depending on whose gossip you hear—ahunting. And we are to attend. The New Forest is reported full of game—of all kinds, if reports of the foresters' daughters are to be believed."

"You'll get in worse trouble than tearing your hose!" Giles protested, but matched his step to Humphrey's as they went off to prepare for the hunt.

This would be a rare treat for Giles, who spent most of his time at court pushing a scratchy quill pen. It had been maneuvered, no doubt, by Humphrey, who, as the elder son of an important Yorkshire family, stood much higher in court circles than Giles. Almost as high as that sparkling young circle of courtiers from England's best houses whom Giles envied and strove to emulate. Giles would be one of them, but his star did not rise so high.

For the next few days, even into the second week, Giles thought he would never tire of riding through the fresh greenness of the New Forest, feeling Brigante's hooves striking the rich earth beneath them. They watched as goshawks and peregrines flown by the king and his nobles circled high in the sky until they were mere black specks and then swooped so suddenly for the kill that not even the pigeon or rabbit saw the shadow of its attacker. Giles joked with Humphrey as they rode to the rear of the party or sat at the end of the table in the evenings in the king's hunting lodge, laughing at the antics of Will Somers, the Master of Revels, and observing the Dukes of Norfolk and Suffolk who were never far from the king's elbows.

Supper went long into the evening. Beef basted with a sauce of chopped roots of wild succory and water arrowhead was followed with large platters of savory pies and tiny, crisp pickles so tart they made the mouth pucker. The minstrels entered the gallery above the serving screens and began playing the lilting tune of the king's newest composition—the "Ballad of My Lady Greensleeves."

"Greensleeves was all my love, Greensleeves was my delight." Humphrey sang the words sotto voce and looked at the green lining of the long flowing sleeves of the Lady Anne's yellow gown. He took a sip of the thin Greek wine that replaced the heady English ale, wiped his knife clean on his napkin, and carefully returned it to the sheath at his belt. Then he draped a long, thin arm across Giles's shoulder. "What say you to some sport of our own tomorrow?

There is a tidy freehold farm on the edge of the forest, so I am told by friends, and the farmer's daughters are as tidy as his fields and pens. We'll never be missed."

Giles grinned. "And if the ladies are so tidy, what will they have to do with the likes of you?"

Humphrey patted his forest green doublet, and for the first time Giles realized that more than once on the hunt when the wind blew Humphrey's coat back, he had seen a rectangle of lumpy padding on his friend's chest. "I bear gifts the maidens will not refuse."

"And all this time I thought your tailor iniquitously overpaid—or that your lanky frame was finally putting on some padding, albeit in odd places."

"So what say you to my plan?"

Giles hesitated. "I bear no lumpy gifts on my breast or anywhere else." He looked at the gold and amethyst ring on his little finger. "Of course, I suppose I could make do—but I'm not sure your sport is to my taste."

Humphrey raised his pale eyebrows until they disappeared under his straw fringe. "I believe you wear a hair shirt beneath your linen one. Would you become a monk? It's well known that you have no wench at court, and any waiting for you in—where is it, Oxfordshire?—can hardly expect you to do without sport."

Giles smiled less broadly. The minstrels had begun a new ballad, and soon the king was sure to call for the tables to be stacked against the wall and the dancing to begin. Already Giles was longing for his bed, but it would be hours before the king left, and none might leave before him.

In spite of his lack of enthusiasm, however, the next morning Giles found himself holding back on Brigante's bridle until he and Humphrey were quite alone in the forest. Humphrey stopped and looked around him to take his bearings. "Two miles northeast of the lodge should bring us to the path we desire. I judge we've ridden half a mile south this morning, so—" He pointed a long finger like an arrow from the quiver on his back. "—that way."

When they were certain to be out of hearing of the rest of the hunt, for not even the yapping of the hounds reached them any longer, Humphrey broke into a merry song to the rhythm of his horse's trotting hooves. Two hours later the shadows thinned, and the autumn sun shone more brightly as they rode through the edge of the forest. Farmer Leigh's holding was, indeed, as tidy as Humphrey had foretold with its long, low house, stables, and barns all newly thatched and not a sagging slat in the pasture fences.

Humphrey and Giles had no more than crested the rolling hill than two female figures approached them from a nearby field. The older and taller reached them first, her dark green kirtle blowing in the breeze and wisps of blond hair tossing from beneath her white kerchief. Her arms were full of sweet-smelling herbs. "This is Allie—Mistress Alice," Humphrey introduced her. Then she was joined by her little sister. "And this, Posey."

Giles struggled to maintain his composure. Were these the maidens Humphrey had led him to frolic with? Allie was undoubtedly marked for Humphrey, for she greeted him with the warmest of smiles, but Posey for himself? The girl bobbed a curtsey in her gentian blue frock, not yet cut below her ankles. She couldn't be above twelve years old—probably not above ten. What could Humphrey be thinking of? "We interrupt your herb-gathering, mistress?" he asked.

Posey's curls danced when she bobbed her head, and she held up handfuls of freshly gathered plants for him to smell. "Lavender, basil, and red mint to strew with the floor rushes and rosemary to use in boiling candles."

"Come, Father awaits you most anxiously." Allie turned and led the way toward the farmhouse. "Michael received word you would come if you could."

Stranger and stranger, thought Giles. *Perhaps Humphrey means to bespeak his wench—for surely no respectable farmer would admit him into his daughter's company on lesser terms.* This was not court where such matters were laughed at behind bedroom screens. The yeoman of England were staunch in their morals—which explained much of why Anne Boleyn had been so soundly rejected by them.

A lad took their horses and led them toward the stable while Giles followed the others into the house. A clean smell of herbs and spices greeted him in the dim coolness. In many poor houses the rushes lay on the floors unchanged for twenty years, breeding the vermin and disease so abhorred by European visitors. But in this house, though humble, there was none of that.

Farmer Leigh greeted them as warmly as his daughters, and his wife served tankards of cool, home-brewed ale. It seemed that they were all waiting for something as Humphrey asked about the year's harvest and inquired of Goodwyfe Leigh as to the success of her dairy. Smiling broadly, she led them down a narrow, well-scrubbed passage to the buttery, still smelling of fresh milk, and showed her guests the abundance of fat, round cheeses hanging there.

They were making their way back when they heard another horse arrive. "Aye, that'll be Michael." Allie darted forward. No matter how warmly she had greeted Humphrey, there could be no doubt as to where her affections lay when she and the young man in brown hose and doublet entered the room.

Humphrey drew Giles aside. "Perhaps I should have explained sooner—but I wanted you to *see*, not just judge by my words alone. Now I realize that I may have endangered all these good people should I have judged wrongly." He turned to look Giles straight in the eye, and Giles had never seen his carefree friend so serious before. "I trust you, Giles. You'll not let me down?"

Giles clasped a firm hand on his friend's shoulder. "I've never known you to be a bad judge of men."

Humphrey turned back to the group, unbuttoned his doublet, and pulled a leather pouch from beneath his linen shirt. Holding it carefully in both hands, he presented it to Thomas Leigh. With sun-browned hands Leigh gently opened the pouch and drew out the small book inside it. "God be praised. I never dared hope to hold His Word in my own hands." He offered it back to Humphrey. "Will you be the first to read to us? I have only enough of my letters to cast my accounts, and Master Michael here can read well enough for country folk, but it would be a rare treat to hear it first from a real scholar."

Humphrey blushed. In spite of his Cambridge training, "scholar" was not an adjective often applied to himself. He took the volume and opened it. But before he began reading, Allie caught her father's eye with a little motion. "Aye, daughter. It is fitting that we sing first." To Giles's amazement, the little cottage suddenly rang with the heartfelt words of a tune he had never heard before—something about God being a great stronghold.

At the end of the song they all sat with folded hands and waited for Humphrey to read. He cleared his throat and began. As he listened, Giles wondered at the beauty of it. Never before had he heard the holy Scripture read so—in English by a layman—and not even in a church. Was it possible that anything so filled with beauty could be the sin many declared it to be? He had been taught that it was unnecessary for salvation to read the Bible because people were saved by the seven sacraments and by obeying the church. Many argued that the Bible should not be translated into English with heresy so prevalent, for if people read the Bible for themselves, they would discuss its meaning, and heretical doctrines would result.

Henry had let it be known that this was a matter for the king. Perhaps at some time in the future, when heresy was less prevalent, the king might order that the Bible be translated into English—not by heretics such as William Tyndale, but by learned bishops and scholars chosen by the king.

So for now, reading the Bible in the English translation of that Lutheran, Tyndale, was a burning matter. Giles looked at the serious, sincere faces of those sitting around him. Were these people heretics? Should they be burned for listening to Humphrey read the Bible to them? Did his own presence here make *him* a heretic? Until that moment Giles had given the matter no consideration. He prayed as the church told him to pray; he believed as the church told him to believe. But with the turmoil in Europe and in the very court of King Henry, the time when a man could take such comfortable ease was drawing to a close. He must think for himself.

Giles was quiet on the return trip. By good fortune they arrived with the last of the hunt servants. But Henry had more fascinating things on his mind than the whereabouts of two minor courtiers. Indeed, Anne Boleyn appeared at supper that evening in a dress of heavy peach satin slashed with cloth of silver, its wide-cut square neckline showing her long, creamy neck, its graceful, wide-pointed sleeves lined with white fur to accent her tiny waist, and the silver-frilled cap lined with pearls to enhance her luxurious black hair. Few in the room had eyes or thought for much else, and few could blame Henry for his passion, even those who bore in their hearts sympathy for the serious-minded, plain-faced good Queen Catherine.

Day after day, Henry's laughter continued to ring through the New Forest by day and the hunting lodge by night. No one in his entourage was surprised that the hunting trip extended to many weeks. At length, Giles sorted his thoughts to form questions he would ask of Humphrey. One day when the hunt moved forward and left them in a quiet thicket by themselves, he said, "I would ask you if you are a Lutheran, but the answer would do me little good, for I have discovered that I know little of what the word means. What is the great uproar this man caused in Germany that seems to roll on and on across the continent slaying men's minds and consciences?"

Humphrey grinned.

"My carefree, unscholarly manner is no guise—I am woefully unaccustomed to serious thought or discourse, so that I hardly know whether or not I am a Lutheran. But in my time at Cambridge I spent many evenings listening to the discourses in the White Horse Inn and found that the networks of those who believe passionately reach far across the land, as you witnessed at Farmer Leigh's."

Giles nodded and patted Brigante who was growing restive. "From university scholar to yeoman farmer, it appears. But what does this Luther believe?"

Humphrey's mount shook his reins and stamped the soft earth, but remained obediently in place. "I have read, with much cudgeling of my poor brains to try to understand, a work explaining the Ninety-Five Theses Luther attached to his church door, starting all this. Let me see if I can recall the crux of the matter."

Not wanting to get entirely separated from the hunt, they moved forward, following the Lady Anne's hawk which circled wide above a meadow clearing. All around the green glade the trees were turning the gold, orange, and auburn of King Henry's hair and his wide, puffed-sleeved, rust velvet coat. With his gloved hand shading his eyes against the sun, Humphrey watched the hawk circle for several moments before he continued. "Luther contends that indulgences are unnecessary and the selling of them a great fraud on the people. He argues that the Pope cannot remit any penalties except those he himself has imposed—not any imposed by God. And all Christians who are truly contrite have already full remission of their sins through the work of Jesus Christ on the cross and need no indulgence from the Pope."

Brigante lowered his head and began grazing in the thick meadow grass as

Giles let his reins go slack. "For one unused to scholarly ideas, it seems you do well enough. Is there more you remember?"

Humphrey removed his violet velvet cap and scratched his pale hair, as if to stimulate activity beneath it. "I haven't the words exact, but Luther said something about how Christians ought to be taught that it is better to give alms to the poor than to use the money to buy an indulgence."

"And so you believe, and so you are a Lutheran?"

Humphrey shrugged. "Sometimes I think I believe it enough to stake my earthly neck and my immortal soul on such propositions. At other times I think I am only excited by the adventure of smuggling Bibles. Either way I am like to lose my neck, but if it comes to it, I hope I know for what I stand or fall."

The hunt moved on after fresh quarry, and Giles and Humphrey moved with them. It was a full week later when the party finally returned to court. When they did, Queen Catherine was not there. The court was full of the news. The messengers had come a week ago while Catherine and the Princess Mary were at mass. Under orders of King Henry the lackeys announced that His Grace the king did not wish to see the queen—ever again. She was commanded to retire instantly to Wolsey's former palace at Moor in Hertfordshire.

In spite of the valiant efforts of Henry's favorite fool, Will Somers, the Christmas court that year was the quietest, tensest of anyone's memory. Catherine and Mary had many loyal supporters there who withdrew themselves from Anne Boleyn's lavish entertainments in which she and her brother George often acted roles portraying delight over the real or imagined downfall of their enemies such as the Pope. Anyone who did not actively support Anne was styled as her enemy.

Not wanting to be among the downfallen, Giles put away thoughts of English Bibles and Lutheran monks and bade a relieved farewell to Humphrey who went home for Christmas. Giles spent every free moment cultivating his acquaintance with Anne Boleyn's favorite courtiers—especially Henry Norris whose kindness to all made friendship easy. It seemed that Giles had chosen well, for not only were his new friends of the glittering set, but the master clerk who had given so many orders to Giles in the past was on the rise as well.

For the leading figure at court that season was the once-shadowy figure who had been secretary to Wolsey and had so quietly and efficiently performed so many functions for Henry in the background. Thomas Cromwell now came to the fore and sat in state with the king's chief councilors. In contrast to the Christmas finery around them, his plain black doublet and brown hose seemed in perfect keeping with his square build and the broad, flat nose that overpowered all other features on his wide face. Cromwell was said to be the son of a blacksmith, but unlike Wolsey, the son of a butcher who tried to overcome his humble origin with lavish display, Cromwell seemed pleased with the plain manner that marked him as a practical man.

"And so, Your Majesty," Cromwell said nodding to his sovereign in the first session of the councilors held after the Twelve Days of Christmas. "Let us consider how we may best approach the Pope's inaction to your Great Matter. Never have I seen a man so vacillating and yet so stubborn inside the same hide."

Serving that day as a glorified page in the absence of Cromwell's secretary Richard Rich, Giles looked around the king's Presence Room at Greenwich Palace. The linen-fold paneling glowed softly in the reflected light of the fireplace. Yet there was a damp chill in the air. The council sat on stools around a long black oak table. The king, looking more than ever the Tudor lion now that he had elected to grow a red-gold beard, wore blue velvet slashed with cloth of gold and heavily furred sleeves. He sat in the one chair in the room at the head of the table. Sir Thomas More, wearing his perennial black robe trimmed with brown fur, the heavy gold chain of his chancellorship around his shoulders, sat to Henry's right. In robes as plain as More's but not as elegant, Cromwell sat to the left. Norfolk, Anne Boleyn's uncle, sat further down the table across from Suffolk, the king's boyhood friend and brother-in-law. Giles waited on a stool in the corner. He shivered in spite of the leaping fire and drew his coat around his shoulders. All this cold winter he had longed for furred sleeves. Perhaps his brother, Peter, could be applied to for a Lenten gift.

Cromwell's words brought Giles's attention back to the council table. "Your Majesty and my lords." Cromwell indicated a thick stack of papers piled on the table in front of him. "The full responses are now in from the university debates on the legality of the king's first marriage—or supposed marriage."

Everyone in the room leaned forward. This scheme had been Cromwell's masterstroke, the idea that moved an obscure lawyer and businessman from his clerk's post to a seat on the king's council. When Pope Clement refused to state a position on the king's marriage, Cromwell suggested that the matter be submitted instead to the great universities, both in England and abroad, for debate by their most learned scholars and theologians. The European universities, especially the German ones, had replied quickly, overwhelmingly in favor of Henry's position. But in the English universities opposition arose. The king's supporters regrouped and handpicked a number of university doctors known to support the king's case. Opposition at Oxford had been strongest, but Cromwell's broad smile was evidence of his final success.

"Gentlemen, by vote of twenty-seven to twenty-two, the governing body of Oxford University has declared that the king's marriage was against God's law."

A satisfying rumble of thumps on the table greeted this news. "Well done, Master Cromwell!" Henry sprang to his feet and embraced his councilor.

Giles noticed that Sir Thomas More was the only one not joining in the jubilation.

"Now, Your Majesty," Cromwell continued when the room quieted, "it is time to consolidate our victories in Parliament."

Cromwell then drew a long sheet of parchment from another stack and began reading a list of items. First, Parliament should threaten to abolish the skimming of the cream of annual church incomes that went directly into the Pope's coffers.

The king bellowed with pleasure and thumped the table. "Marvelous, Cromwell! Before we are through, we shall disconnect the church in England from its foreign ties in Rome. We'll have no foreign Pope ruling on English soil! And Parliament shall do it! What else is on that list of yours?"

"Second should be an act forbidding appeals to Rome on the ground that the king is the highest authority and supreme in his own land . . ."

"Yes! It shall be!"

Cromwell dipped his head. "And then, I think, we should seek a measure prohibiting Convocation to meet or legislate without royal assent, and allowing the king to appoint a royal commission to reform the canon law."

Henry thumped on the table with both hands. "Better and better! The people will like it! They have long fumed against canonical courts outside the regular law of the land and from which there is no appeal. We shall have equitable law in England!"

The list continued, followed by discussion by the councilors. Giles could think of it only as discussion, not debate, for after such wild enthusiasm from Henry, there could be little ground for opposing the measures. It appeared to Giles that More was the only one not genuinely enthusiastic.

In the next few months the matters were presented to Parliament one by one, and passed by Parliament one by one. When Parliament had done its work, Rome had little power left in England. Henry VIII was the supreme head of the Church of England.

Giles and Humphrey were sitting together in a corner window at the Palace of Whitehall when news came that this momentous act had passed.

Humphrey looked thoughtful.

"And are you not pleased?" Giles asked. "I should think one with your Lutheran leanings would be overjoyed."

"I cannot say what I feel. It is overwhelming. It has been ten centuries since St. Augustine came to these shores bringing the gospel of Christ and the rule of the Pope. And now it is all at an end. Is it possible to wipe out ten centuries of Christian history with the stroke of a pen?"

3

ummer came. And with summer, heat. And with heat, the sweating sickness. In the narrow, mud-choked streets of London where waste ran in the open gutters down the streets, many a passerby was overtaken with a sudden weakness while shopping or hurrying to pay a visit and fell to the ground, face and neck wet with sweat while the body chilled and felt as if there were tiny grains of millet under the skin. All night long one could hear the bells of the death carts ringing in the streets.

The court moved from Greenwich to Windsor to Hampton, ever farther into the countryside in hope of escaping. The sickness swept all of Europe, but it was so much worse in England that it was known as the "English disease."

No one was exempt—young or old, wealthy or poor, vigorous or sedentary. All ages and stations fell down in the streets and died there unless they could be roused from the coma they lay in. Giles thought with longing of his family on their estate in the green Oxfordshire countryside. Surely, if anywhere on earth was safe, it would be there with fresh, gentle breezes to sweeten the air. And yet deaths were reported at the university—fine young men, near to taking their degrees. Their stools in lectures and in hall were suddenly empty.

Suddenly the world seemed a more frighteningly insecure place than ever before. Giles became more attentive at mass, more careful in his prayers, and more regular in burning candles for his family. It seemed his sister Megotty and sister-in-law Ellen were most often on his mind, and it frightened him that it should be so—as if he had been visited by a premonition.

He longed to visit them, to take time from the stifling air of court and escape on Brigante back into his own world. And he missed Humphrey, for several weeks ago his friend had been granted leave to go to Yorkshire. Giles missed his companionship at tennis and shooting at butts and their quiet talks. But Humphrey remained in Yorkshire, and Giles could not get leave to go from court. Not even the king would leave court, although he long ago should have begun visiting his subjects around the countryside.

For their work was not yet finished, and King Henry was never a man to abandon a project amidship. One step remained—to make the clergy agree to the royal supremacy. Henry presented the matter to Convocation, the ruling assembly of bishops and representative clergy. And they resisted.

Yet the heat did not abate. In France the sweating sickness ran itself out, and the people breathed freer. But in England children and aged alike continued to be stricken. The commons muttered that it was the judgment of God on Henry for putting away good Queen Catherine and taking the "Bullen Witch" to his bed. For did not all the world know that she had a sixth finger on her left hand—for the hiding of which she had designed the long, flowing sleeves she always wore? Was that not a certain mark of a witch?

Henry stifled his impatience and anger and returned to Convocation. This time he went in person. Here was the greatest struggle in English law since Magna Carta; only this time it was the sovereign imposing his will on the people, not the reverse. Could the bishops be persuaded to disavow the oaths they had sworn to the Pope at their consecrations? Would there be a rebellion? Would the Pope at last take action? Would the emperor, Queen Catherine's nephew, invade England?

The court held its breath. Parliament watched. Convocation submitted. The king returned jubilant.

At last the bishops and clergy pledged never to make any new laws without the king's permission and agreed that the whole body of church law should be reformed by a commission which the king would name. The whole life of the church was now in the hands of the king.

That evening Humphrey returned. He looked taller and thinner than ever, but his pale blue eyes blazed with a new light. "Come, walk with me in the garden—no, the river, let's take a boat—we can be sure of privacy. I've much I would tell you."

They walked down the stairs where the gold and crimson royal barge awaited the king's pleasure and the flaming torches of several watermen reflected in the river as they waited to ferry people from the busy court to London. But Giles waved their services aside—they would row themselves.

The surface of the Thames flowed a liquid rose and gold of reflected sunset, broken only by the dipping of Humphrey's oars as he rowed upstream beside banks of long water grasses sheltering nesting waterfowl. Then he shipped his oars and let the boat drift while the sky and water softened to lavender and blue-gray. "You asked me once if I were a Lutheran. I didn't know how to answer you. Now I know."

"Humphrey, no. Henry will have no heretics at court—you'll lose your post or worse."

"Better than losing my soul—for now I know." The boat drifted toward the long rushes at the edge of the river, startling three long-necked birds from their nests and sending them, great, swooping silhouettes against the sky, over the boaters' heads. Humphrey took the oars and moved farther into the current before he continued. "I did not stay long in Yorkshire. I have been instead in Cambridge where Latimer is preaching again."

"Latimer! That convicted heretic?"

"He was accused of such, but freed by Cromwell's efforts."

"And what does the man preach that held you so long?"

"He spoke much of Luther and Erasmus and the New Learning. I was most taken with Erasmus's call for men to see Christ in the Gospels rather than in gilded images. And so I listened and thought, but most important, I read the Scriptures that I had formerly smuggled as a kind of game. Now I understand the crux of Luther's message and can say, 'Here I stand, I can do no else, so help me, God.'"

"That's a very stirring speech, Humphrey, but what do you mean? You haven't told me what you believe."

"I have come to see that grace is the true gift of God which Christ brought into the world on the cross—the true gift which no man may refuse for his soul's sake. Luther said it, and this time I do have it by heart—'Man without grace is a tree that can bring forth no good fruit. Without the faith that works through charity, even the works which appear good are sins. Man, doing the best he can, sins nevertheless, for he is unable by his own powers, either to will or to think rightly. Without grace the will necessarily only chooses what is bad.' Grace alone is good. We cannot earn our salvation by good works. So the Scriptures say, and so I believe."

The tide turned, taking the boat back downstream toward Hampton, and the full dark of night descended. Luckily there was a full moon, for neither young man had thought to bring a torch. Later that night, with the curtains of his bed pulled tightly around him in spite of the warmth of the night, Giles thought long. There was no denying Humphrey's assurance—or his joy. Was it possible that he, Giles, could also be so sure of his belief—of his salvation even?

Giles was still asking himself that the next morning as he washed in the ewer of rosewater his servant Luke brought him, as he dressed in his best blue coat, and as he breakfasted on meat, bread, and ale. Later he stood beside Humphrey at the back of the privy chamber and saw Sir Thomas More enter the room.

Then he understood the new light in Humphrey's eyes. It was still there this morning in spite of the shortness of their night's sleep. The same light burned steady and sure in the Lord Chancellor's eyes—a man who knew himself and knew his God and was on good terms with both. Yet how was that possible? Humphrey had just become a Lutheran; More was the staunchest Catholic in the realm. Was it possible that both could be right? And if so, what of the king's Church of England—must it then be wrong? Or could there be three avenues to God? The prospects were daunting, for if three were possible, what of four or five? How many ways could God be approached and found? Or was there a common thread to all ways that Giles could not see? What of love? Or grace?

Could they be found in the heart if the outward forms differed? There was so much he would talk to Humphrey about.

But not now. The councilors and courtiers parted for More, as the Red Sea for Moses, and he walked to Henry sitting in state at the head of the room. More knelt before the king, lifted the heavy gold chain of the highest office of the land from his shoulders, and presented it to his sovereign. A gasp went through the room.

Henry's dark eyes flashed, and his small mouth was drawn firm above his square beard. He held up his hand, refusing to take the chain. "No, Thomas. This matter of church business has nothing to do with the chancellorship. I would have your services. You are my most valued advisor, my most valued friend."

More shook his graying head and continued to hold out the chain. "Your Majesty, I am your chief minister. If I cannot give you my wholehearted support, what good am I to you?"

"You are of the highest good to me. You are respected. The people respect you; Parliament respects you; all over Europe you are respected."

More gave in to a little chuckle, the laugh lines crinkling at the corners of his kind eyes. "In other words, my king, you do not need me, but my respectability. You would have me for a figurehead. Your Grace, I love you well, but even for you I cannot sacrifice my conscience. All else I have is at your disposal, including my respectability, could I give it you without sacrificing conscience. But my conscience is my only gem, as you well know, for I leave office a poorer man than I entered it."

All in the room were straining forward so intently to see the king's hand open to receive More's chain of office that it was several minutes before Giles realized Humphrey no longer stood at his shoulder. He looked around sharply. Humphrey was slumped on the floor.

In a cold chill of fear Giles clasped his friend's hand—the sweaty skin felt as if it covered a poppet stuffed with grains of sand. He summoned servants to carry Humphrey to his room, and even on the way through the interminable tangle of rooms opening directly onto each other, he continued to shake Humphrey's shoulder and slap his cheeks. He must be roused from his coma, or he would never rouse. Once Humphrey was in his high four-poster bed, Giles instructed a servant, "Fetch Dr. Butts if you can!" Nothing but the royal physician would do for Humphrey.

In the end, Dr. Butts was unavailable, but he sent Wilcox, his first assistant, who wrapped the already sweat-drenched body in woolen blankets, ordered the fire built up, and placed hot bricks at Humphrey's feet. Yet the patient continued to sweat and shake with chill at the same time, and he resisted Giles's roughest efforts to rouse him.

The physician drew a green glass flask from his bag and placed it on the table in the middle of the room. "I would give him my elixir of philosopher's egg, but all I had prepared has been used up, and the new eggs I am preparing are still baking in the embers. We shall instead medicine him with my posset of marigold, endive, sow thistle, and nightshade. Have no fear—I steeped a full three handfuls to the quart of water, so it is full strength. It will now be your job to get it down his throat." Wilcox held out a wooden spoon. "A few drops at a time can be placed under the tongue without fear of choking him. If he rouses, you may give him a glassful to drink." The doctor snapped his bag shut and left.

Humphrey's servant paced around the room, scattering the floor rushes, folding and refolding Humphrey's clothes and dropping more objects than he managed to put away. At last Giles could stand no more. "Ned! That will do. I'll see to his needs. Why don't you try to get some sleep in case I need help tonight?"

Ned retired to his closet off Humphrey's room, and Giles was alone. Through all the dragging afternoon he repeatedly dropped Dr. Wilcox's posset into Humphrey's mouth, bathed his faced with cool, vinegar-soaked rags, and shook and pummeled him mercilessly. But Humphrey did not waken. It seemed to Giles that the coma deepened, and yet he would not abandon hope.

Toward evening, Ned emerged from his cot rubbing his eyes and stretching. "You'll be needing candles soon. Shall I fetch you a bowl of stew from the kitchen?"

Nothing appealed less to Giles, but he supposed he would need its strength to continue his nursing through the night, and the servant obviously needed something to do. "Take your own supper first. I'm in no hurry."

When Ned returned some time later with a steaming pewter platter of venison stew, bread, and ale, Giles knew what to do with him. "Ned, do you know the whereabouts of Humphrey's home in Yorkshire?"

"Aye, sir. I was just there with him."

"They must be told. Will you ride?"

"Aye, sir. But what shall I tell them? When I arrive, I'll not know whether or no he lives."

Giles nodded at the sense of that. And yet it seemed intolerable that his family should not know. "Right. Well, go to the stables and make sure Humphrey's horse is ready. Perhaps we shall know what message you shall take in the morning." It was the best he could do. He reached for the green flask and poured three drops into a spoon.

Toward midnight Giles, sitting on a bench along the wall of the room, let his head fall back and his eyelids droop. A few minutes later he startled awake. Something had moved in the room. He looked toward the door. No, Ned had not returned.

Then Giles turned to the bed. Humphrey's eyes were open. With an excited cry Giles sprang forward and grasped his friend's shoulder. "Humphrey! Thank God—I feared the worst!" With one hand he dipped a rag in vinegar-water, while pouring a glassful of posset with the other. "Here, drink this. It smells foul, but Dr. Wilcox says you must down it." He supported Humphrey's shoulders and held the glass to his lips. Humphrey forced a few swallows down.

"That's enough." His voice was weak and raspy, as if the grainy substance under his skin filled his throat, too. "I haven't long. I would rather talk."

"Humphrey, no! You're awake, you've had your medicine. You'll live." Giles continued rubbing his patient's hands and face with the vinegar-soaked cloth.

"This corruption must put on incorruption, this mortal put on immortality." Giles pulled back in dismay, but Humphrey was not wandering in his mind. His eyes were fever-bright, but clear. "Take no thought for any but the riches that are in Christ Jesus, for those are the riches that moth and rust do not corrupt. The trumpet shall sound, and we shall be raised. Giles, are you here?"

Giles clasped his friend's shoulders, and Humphrey's feeble voice continued urgently. "Giles, it is true. It is."

Humphrey raised his hand as if in a farewell salute, then lay still on his bolster. Giles reached for the slim, long-fingered hand. He held it long until even his most stubbornly hopeful insistence could no longer deny that a change had come over it. The sweat dried, and the fever cooled, but the temperature kept dropping. Giles felt as if he were holding a bundle of sticks in his hand, not a living creation.

He laid the lifeless hand on the blanket, but he did not move. He wanted a few more moments alone before he must call other hands to prepare the body for burial. Still he could not believe it. Not Humphrey. He had worried about his family in Oxfordshire; he had given a thought to those around him at court; he had even thought briefly of the golden-haired Cecily whom he still remembered vividly—vividly enough that he thought to light a candle for her at the height of the sweating sickness. But never once had he thought that his dearest friend, the lively and ebullient Humphrey, could succumb.

How could life have any meaning when all could be wiped out so quickly? And what good was Humphrey's new faith now that he could no longer live it? Or was that the point?

4

he handsome young courtier stood again before the inlaid oak table in the parlor of the abbot's lodging to present Whiting a document from the king. All was just as it had been three years earlier. All was the same, and yet nothing was the same. Nowhere was the different sameness more apparent than in England's oldest religious foundation. The daily round of prayers was the same, the mass was the same, the sacraments the same, and yet it was a different church, with different earthly authority, and a different feeling in the air. In this western remoteness they were not much troubled by the New Learning sweeping the continent, and yet even here the winds of change blew.

Whiting took the royal order from Giles and read it without comment. He let it roll up and come to rest on his desk while he sat with hands folded, thinking. "Know you what this contains?"

"My Lord Abbot, I do." Giles dipped his head.

"So it is official at last. Anne is queen and is to be proclaimed so by all the clergy of the land at Easter Mass." He unrolled the paper and read again the line from the prescribed prayer: "'And so rule the heart of Thy chosen servant, Anne, our Queen.'"

Again Giles nodded.

"We get little news here. I am to take it then that this is an accomplished fact and that the king has indeed wed the lady?"

Giles shuffled his feet uneasily. "We at court know little more than you. Perhaps less, because any truth we hear is so muddled by rumor and counter-rumor. But Thomas Cranmer, our new Archbishop of Canterbury, has tried the divorce matter and given judgment that Henry's marriage to Catherine is, and always has been, void because it was prohibited by God's law and that no papal dispensation could change."

"Thereby making our Henry officially a bachelor and free to wed his lady love," Whiting finished with a twinkle in his eye that put Giles at ease after struggling to explain the precise legality of the situation. Throughout the entire tangled matter, the king had been nothing if not a legalist. Even if he had to bludgeon new laws through Parliament so that he might have the laws he wished to obey, he did govern by law.

Giles nodded. "And so they were married. No one knows exactly when or where, but that the ceremony took place is certain, and that the queen is to give His Majesty an heir is equally certain."

Whiting indicated the document in front of him. "And we are to play our part by announcing the same to the commons on Easter morning, every priest in the land praying for Queen Anne simultaneously. So be it." He spent several moments reading the prescribed liturgy before him. "A rare man, this Thomas Cranmer. An obscure secular scholar he may have been, but he has a better feel for the beauty of words than any poet in the land." Whiting pushed his chair back and stood up. "And now that you have discharged your office, you must take dinner with me. Do you stay the night here, or must you ride on?"

"I have twin documents to yours for Bath, Wells, and Gloucester, so I must ride on."

"Good! I go to Wells after dinner and would be most grateful for your company. My niece and her husband there have undertaken some rather extensive improvements to their property, and I have agreed to advise, so I must needs view the workmen's progress. Had I realized the full extent of the project I might have been less blithe to encourage it, but now I must see it through." Whiting gave his guest a rueful smile. "Perhaps you remember my niece Dame Margery. I seem to recall she was here when last you called upon the king's business."

Giles smiled. Indeed, he retained a shadowy memory of the abbot's niece, but it was the niece's niece that glowed far more clearly in his memory. In truth, this was not the first time it had crossed his mind that duty and pleasure might be mixed in his assignment to carry the king's message to Wells.

As it fell out, Giles's business with the Bishop of Wells was so swiftly concluded that he was able to accept Dame Margery's invitation for the night's lodging. For in Wells, as everywhere else, the message had been received calmly. The established spiritual authority had raised skeptical eyebrows, evidencing their doubts as to the wisdom of so sudden and blunt an announcement to the people, but none demurred. It would be as King Henry, supreme head of the Church of England, decreed. And Giles was glad of the easy compliance, for now that his duty was discharged, he could enjoy the gentle spring green countryside with its white frosting of apple blossoms and baby lambs.

The yeoman farmer stock of which Robert Burgess sprang evidenced itself in careful husbandry at Bucklesbury, and Margery's insistence on ever sturdier fences and finer buildings showed in the new barn nearing completion. Giles stood in the center of the lofty stone structure and looked at the open sky through the intricate pattern of beams as Burgess explained the work process to Abbot Whiting. "It's a fine system they've devised, these two-tier cruck beams. It's no small matter to support a stone roof of this magnitude. Of course, it's not so fine as your tithe barn at the abbey . . ."

It seemed obvious to Giles that the denial was specifically to point out to the visitors that the barn was precisely as fine as the one where the abbey stored the corn, wood, fish, honey, and wine from its estates scattered throughout six counties. Giles looked at the crucks—the naturally curved main timbers—a pattern of Gothic arches against the sky. He wondered equally at the workmen's skill and the abbot's generosity in financing such a project. Apparently he felt the same responsibility to care for his large family as he felt to see to the needs of his fifty-some monks and three hundred schoolboys at Glastonbury. Giles's respect increased for the robed and tonsured man beside him. Abbot Whiting was perhaps not so great a scholar or saint as some of his predecessors, but he was a great gentleman. And far beyond the walls of the abbey, all the county felt his good works, for besides refurbishing the Edgar Chapel on his own land, Abbot Whiting had undertaken a vigorous program of public works to keep the Somerset sea wall in repair and to continue the drainage of marshlands St. Dunstan had begun six centuries ago.

Giles observed Whiting's attention to detail that showed his own knowledge of the building process and his care for the welfare of the workmen. Giles nodded to himself and repeated his assessment of the Abbot of Glastonbury—a great gentlemen. It was a pity that duties in the West Country so often kept him from his seat in Parliament. Though Thomas More represented the abbey's interests well with his proxy vote, men such as Whiting were all too much needed in Parliament and in too short supply.

"Uncle Whiting, my aunt would know if you are ready to take supper?"

Giles turned at the sound of the golden-toned voice. She stood in the open doorway, shafts of late afternoon sunlight slanting through the unfinished roof to shine on her hair and primrose gown. Their eyes held for a moment; then Cecily dropped her long-lashed lids. "She bids me welcome all our guests."

Inside, the hall of Bucklesbury was as old-fashioned as ever. The refurbishing had started, as was fitting, with the barns and outbuildings, for did not the Scripture admonish a man to build his business before he built his house? But that had not stopped Dame Margery from taking advantage of her uncle's generosity to improve the hall furnishings. The large room was lighted only by a few candles and the great fire that burned upon the hearth. The lower end was in shadow. But even in the dim light the arras hangings that decorated both sides of the room with scenes from the tales of King Arthur glowed from gold thread woven in the woof. The trestle table in the center of the room was the same sturdy slab of oak that had served this branch of the Whiting family for hundreds of years, but the usual stools had been replaced with chairs—and no plain oak chairs, but padded leather—a great luxury.

Everywhere Dame Margery's industry was in evidence. Hams, sides of bacon, strings of onions and leeks, sacks of herbs, and clusters of herrings hung from the hall rafters. Underfoot among the herb-scented rushes lay a long, pale green, tufted grass that Giles had never seen before. "Quaking-grass." Cecily identified it for him. "It keeps the mice away. Aunt prefers it to keeping cats in the hall."

Giles would have engaged her in conversation, but in her quicksilver way she was off to the kitchen at the end of the hall to see to their serving. As it was Lent the main dish was deep-dish eel and onion pie, rich in a sauce of butter, raisins, and milk. Slete soup, thick and flavorful with leeks, and a dish of boiled garlic accompanied the pie. Giles spread the soft garlic on his bread like butter and used it to sop up the savory eel sauce. No dessert would be served during the Lenten season, so Giles ate his fill of the tasty dishes before him. He was pleased not to be dining in a monastery where the best to be expected would have been pea soup, fish snacks, and fritters.

The next morning Giles was in no hurry, for he had only to ride to Gloucester to complete his mission. So rather than mounting Brigante right after his breakfast, he asked his host's permission to walk in his orchard. In the dew-fresh morning he at last found Cecily alone and unoccupied. For several minutes he walked quietly beside her while the spikes of white narcissus stars at their feet added their heavy sweet scent to the fresh green smell, and light-scented apple blossoms fell like snow on their heads. At length he spoke. "Do I show myself much conceited if I ask why my lady avoids my company? Or is it that she doesn't care enough to bother avoiding me?" For although he had expected some restraint after his long absence, he had hoped that by his second day they would have resumed some of the easy friendship they found that day in the abbey garden.

Cecily's smile was like the sun rising in full splendor in the midst of Bucklesbury's apple orchard. "It is not you I would avoid, but all that the court stands for."

"Heaven forbid that I should bring spiritual contamination upon my lady, but surely a short converse could be shriven."

Cecily smiled, but did not laugh at his speech as he had hoped. Instead she sighed and shook her head. "Nay, not contamination, but confusion. What think you, for example, of Thomas Cranmer?"

"Oh, I see the news reaches you here."

"Oh, aye, we know of King Henry's choice for our spiritual father. And my opinion matters naught in the great course of things. Yet I wonder what St. Augustine, who first held that title, must think of an Archbishop of Canterbury beholden to the king of England rather than to the Pope?"

"But if my lady is so well informed, she must know that papal bulls for Cranmer's appointment came in the ordinary way from Rome. The appointment is from the Pope—er, that is from the Bishop of Rome—as truly as was St. Augustine's."

"And would you suggest that Cranmer will convert Henry to the church of Rome as Augustine did Aethelberht?"

Giles removed his blue velvet feathered cap and swept a wide-arched bow which knocked a fresh shower of petals from the tree above them. "Forsooth, my lady has won her point. For our king and our archbishop are of one mind, and it is likely there will be little converting on either side."

But still his light-hearted attitude did not reach her. "And what of Queen Catherine with whom the king lived for twenty-some years? What is to become of this virtuous lady?"

"The Princess Dowager, you mean—for so Henry insists she is to be styled."

"Yes, yes. But what of her argument that she was never truly wife to Arthur—that he was too sick when they married to ever make her true wife. Haven't all your scholars, clerics, and archbishops forgotten that?"

"Nay, Cromwell has taken volumes of evidence on that question. The truth is—there is no provable truth on either side. We must trust God to bring good of it all."

"And the queen—er, Princess Dowager?"

"She is housed most comfortably and fully attended. But far enough from court that she can foment no uprising."

"Comfortable and sensible, yes, I have no doubt." Cecily stooped to pick a stalk of hyacinth and began plucking each star-blossom from the oval cluster, releasing its sweet scent into the air. "Yes, and very efficient. But is it *right?* That is what I would know, what is *right?*"

"But, Cecily—" She had not granted him the right to use her given name, and yet she did not protest. Perchance, if silence gave consent, he had won a point. He would have repeated it, but dared not call attention to his liberty. "You will be asked to swear no oath or sign no pledge. Why should it trouble you?"

"Oh, yes." And now she laughed, but not with the golden sound that Giles so prized. "I do very well with my woman's work—I help the housekeeper in the still room, I sit over my embroidery, I play the virginals, and on occasion I ride out hunting with my uncle. Woman's work should require no moral decisions, for we are too-fragile creatures to bear such weighty matters. But none considers that a woman might face a dilemma as well."

Giles stopped and turned to her full-face. "My lady, forgive me. I thought we were talking in the abstract. Have you a decision? Might I be so honored as to hear it? Perchance to advise?"

She shook her head, and Giles thought she would not speak, but then she did, more to herself than to him. "My Uncle Burgess would have me wed Hugh Davington for very sound business reasons, and I can offer no reasons except my aversion to the match. My uncle is very patient—much to avoid displeasing my Uncle Whiting who would not have me forced, I expect—but I cannot dillydally forever. Nor would I. I do not wish to live forever in Dame Margery's shadow, and Bucklesbury has no need of two housekeepers. So I have thought more of late of taking vows. I guess I am talking to you about this because you were the first who suggested such a course to me."

Giles was astounded. "I did?" He was flattered that Cecily remembered their conversation so many months ago, but surely he suggested nothing of the kind. "I put such an idea into your head?"

Cecily nodded. "You asked if I would follow my cousins who are preparing to take their vows."

"Oh. Yes, I do remember. And you replied that you had no vocation. Am I to understand that you have since discovered a call to the religious life?"

Cecily shrugged. "It seems better to be married to Christ without desire than to be married to Hugh Davington without desire. And when the world is so topsy-turvy, and the Pope's dispensations can be without meaning, and the king's marriages without meaning, and then the queen is not the queen, and the Pope is not the Pope, and an obscure cleric is suddenly Archbishop of Canterbury because he writes a treatise on the king's Great Matter—is it not better to turn away from all the world? Are not the holy houses the one true shelter left against the high tides of change that ravage our land? Well you may say a woman should not think. How can any person think with any solid basis these days?"

Giles did not answer. He knew all too well many of the same things Cecily was feeling. Especially did he feel so since Humphrey had died. All was fleeting. Nothing was sure. There was no solid rock. But Humphrey had found a solid rock. Humphrey, against all royal and religious orders, had read the Scriptures for himself and found the solid way. Should he tell Cecily? Dare he tell a member of the abbot's family that he had Lutheran leanings?

"And besides, to be seventeen and unmarried is a disgrace not to be spoken of." Cecily's murmur was no louder than the breeze in the apple branches so that Giles could not be certain he had heard her right.

Three weeks later Giles was still not certain of her words, or of what reply he might have made had Dame Margery not interrupted them then. But now as he gathered in the Great Hall at Westminster to go into Easter Eve mass with the rest of the court, Giles thought of the certainty King Henry had seemed to display for all the world throughout all of Holy Week. Never had there been a more pious king, a king more ready to uphold all the old traditions. On Palm Sunday Henry himself had personally assisted the younger Westminster priests in giving out hundreds of willow branches, and upon leaving the abbey after mass, Henry himself waved the longest of the palmlike branches as if he were indeed welcoming his Lord.

And on Spy Wednesday—the day Judas spied on Jesus so he could report His plans to the High Priest—Henry led forth in the chanting of the Tenebrae in mass commemorating the sufferings and death of Christ. "A man of suffering, accustomed to grief . . . and we held Him in no esteem, yet it was our infirmities that He bore—our sufferings He carried . . ." Down the great length of Westminster Abbey each candle was extinguished one by one. The darkness crept forward, each extinguished light reenacting Jesus' abandonment by each person around Him. And the dirgelike chant continued, "But He was pierced for our offenses, crushed for our sins. Chastisement for our sins was upon Him, by His stripes we were healed." The mood of gloom crept down the aisles with the dark. Despair. The despair of the tomb. Within the abbey not a single light. The dark supreme.

As the week progressed, none could say that King Henry in abandoning Rome had abandoned one jot or tittle of the faith. Maundy Thursday brought the foot-washing ceremony. As all the kings of England had done before him—King Edgar, Alfred the Great, perhaps as far back as King Arthur—all had washed the feet of beggars on this day, one for every year of the king's life. And this year Henry was forty-one. So Giles watched with all the court as Henry gird a towel around his waist in the Chapter House of Westminster Abbey and washed the feet of forty-one beggars in a ewer of rose-scented water and dried them with the whitest of linen towels.

Then Good Friday and the Veneration of the Cross. All day the court fasted, each alone in his room, no one speaking, wearing nothing but black. Church bells rang a dull, muffled clang as their metal clappers had been replaced by wooden ones—for no peal of joy could be heard on this day. On the table in the king's hall a single piece of meat was set out to grow worm-eaten and maggoty—a reminder of the end that awaits all mortal flesh.

At last the hour arrived. Three o'clock, the hour of Satan's triumph. Giles, feeling miserable over the loss of Humphrey, over his inability to help Cecily, over his own sins, joined the others in the silent blackness of the abbey. First came two priests of the new persuasion wearing their plain white collars rather than the rich vestments of the Roman faith, carrying lighted candles. Right behind them Cranmer carried a veiled cross to the altar. The archbishop lifted the veil from the top of the cross. "This is the wood of the cross on which hung the Salvation of the world."

"Come, let us worship," the congregation responded. Then all knelt and venerated the cross in silence while Cranmer held it high.

Accompanied by the candle-bearing priests, the archbishop carried the cross the full length of the great nave and placed it on the cold stone surface of the sanctuary entrance, flanked by the two candles.

No heads turned, but every eye looked sideways to see what King Henry would do next. For all the court had heard the rumor that Anne had laughed at the traditional procession of creeping to the cross on one's knees. But Henry had not laughed. The priests began the antiphon. "We worship Thee. Lord, we venerate Thy cross. We praise Thy resurrection. Through the cross Thou hast brought joy to the world."

Henry, wearing only a pair of thin black hose over the royal knees, led forth up the long nave on his knees, his eyes never wavering from the cross. So Henry had missed nothing. And Giles had missed nothing. Giles could only hope that his sovereign felt more fulfilled in his spiritual certainty than Giles did when he gathered with the rest of the court in the Great Hall of Westminster to walk to the abbey together for the great Easter Eve mass. Gone now was the somber black clothing of Good Friday. Now all members of the court were appareled in their newest and best. The king wore a red velvet coat bordered in gold braid and an ermine collar, his red velvet hat embroidered in gold and all adorned with heavy, brilliant-cut rubies and emeralds set in gleaming gold to sparkle and reflect in the light of torches and candles. Anne beside him was in cloth of silver, a moth spun of moonbeams to flutter around the red and gold of his candle flame.

They entered the dark, silent abbey, cold and still as the tomb. It was a slow, painful process for all to grope their way forward to their places. But at last the scraping and shuffling stilled. Now all held their breath. The moment for which the world lay in wait had come. The archbishop struck a spark on flint, and a moment later the paschal candle flamed alive. "Alleluia!" Cranmer proclaimed.

"Alleluia!" all responded.

"He is risen!" Trumpets blared the triumph, and across the abbey candles blazed into light.

"Let us sing to the Lord; He has covered Himself in glory." And so began the traditional Mass of the Resurrection with its procession of newly baptized Christians in their white robes, the sacred mysteries of the Canon, the Offering, the Consecration, the Communion. And yet for all the rejoicing, as the service progressed, a tension seemed to gather in the air. Perhaps it came from the king himself, or from the archbishop. Certainly Giles, privy to the instructions delivered to every priest in the land, felt the heightening. It was as if those in charge were listening, not to their own service, but straining their ears to hear the words of three million Englishmen across the land acknowledging and proclaiming Anne their new queen.

Then Cranmer's voice rang loud and clear. "That it may please Thee to keep and strengthen in the true worshiping of Thee, in righteousness and holiness of life, Thy servant Anne, our most gracious queen . . ." The archbishop went on, but his words were drowned in a shuffle of feet on stone. Could it be true? Giles turned to see. Yes, people were leaving.

The commons would not pray for Queen Anne. They would risk royal displeasure. They would insult Henry and Anne. But they would not pray as they were bidden. Those members of the court around Giles gave the murmured response, "We beseech Thee to hear us, good Lord," but it was barely audible over the sound of retreating footsteps.

Giles saw the rage on Henry's face. The blaze from the fierce eyes, the set of the strong jaw said that Henry would not be defied. One way or another, Henry would win.

5

n September 7, 1533, Queen Anne gave King Henry his long-desired heir. Only it was not the son Anne had so blithely promised. It was a girl, and they named her Elizabeth. Immediately scribes were set to work rewriting the endless stacks of oaths that had been prepared before the birth of the babe. Each sheet of parchment must be carefully scraped with a small knife to remove the name Prince Edward and insert Princess Elizabeth in its space. For prince or princess, Henry was determined that the succession should be insured through Anne, not the Princess Dowager Catherine who still plagued his life from her confinement at Buckden Manor, sending her pleading letters and protestations of love by her irritating foreign ministers.

The oath, carefully framed by Thomas Cromwell, was simple and straightforward. Commissioners would go to every town and village throughout the realm where all people would swear, by kissing a Bible or other holy relic, that they recognized Henry's marriage to Anne and Elizabeth as his sole heir. Giles recalled his words to Cecily that she would not be required to swear an oath and was amazed—for women as well as men were required to swear.

Secretly Giles wondered if it would all be as simple as the king's privy councilors declared, but he held his tongue. Before the oath could be administered to the commons, however, it must be passed by Parliament, for England was ruled by no tyrant. It was a kingdom under God and the law, then under the king—a king who sent his carefully worded laws to Parliament.

So it was that Giles, with all the other minor court members, crowded into the packed public gallery at Westminster Palace to see the king open Parliament. The Thames was frozen, so Henry could not be rowed to Westminster in his favorite royal barge, but he must walk along the Strand under a royal canopy, attended by retainers and advisors. When he reached the palace, the king was robed and crowned before entering the Lesser Hall where both houses of Parliament were assembled. Giles strained his neck when the clear call of trumpets and the voice of the royal crier announced the entrance of Henry of England. The king strode in magnificence down the long room, a blaze of gold, scarlet, and ermine. Jewels shone in the crown of state, in the mace of England, and on his royal person as he crossed the green and white tiles and passed between the four enormous tasseled woolsacks that symbolized the foundation of England's economic greatness—the wool trade.

Henry took his place on the throne on the blue and gold draped dais at the front of the room under a white silk canopy embroidered in gold Tudor roses and fleurs-de-lis. When firmly seated Henry looked out over the assembled body—the House of Lords, one hundred seven Lords Spiritual and Lords Temporal, seated on benches around the room, and the Commons, three hundred elected knights and burgesses from all the realm, standing at the back behind their speaker. The king took his time and seemingly directed his level gaze to each man present, fixing his attention and assuring his support. Giles knew then that the outcome of the matter before them was not in doubt.

Henry's argument was as clever as it was well-reasoned. He carefully assured Parliament that this oath was for the protection of the realm and their own persons. Had such an oath of succession been sworn to in earlier days, the bloody, costly dynastic wars could have been avoided. (No one mentioned that Henry's father had come to the throne through just such a bloody dynastic war.) And had an oath of loyalty been on record, many who lost position or life through the false accusation of enemies could have been been spared, for now treason would be carefully defined and each man's loyalty a matter of sworn record. Once a person had sworn that the king's marriage to the Princess Dowager was contrary to God's law and not subject to any earthly dispensation and that Succession passed to the king's issue through Queen Anne, there could be no mistake about that man's loyalty, and his protection was assured. Giles noted that Abbot Whiting was not among the Lord's Spiritual. It would not have made any difference if he had been, for the statutes were enacted by unanimous vote.

Perhaps the new method of voting the king instituted that day had some effect upon the outcome, for Henry announced that Parliament would vote by division of the House. Members would not merely raise the hand or voice, but rather those in favor of the king's measure walked to the right side of the room, and those opposed were to stand on the left. No one chose to stand on the left.

In March Parliament and the heads of all the London guilds took the oath. Then Giles was dispatched along with dozens of other commissioners to every village square, to every town guildhall or marketplace, and to every monastery.

Having developed a certain reputation for success in the West Country, Giles was assigned again to Somerset. This time, as evidence that he was moving up in importance, he had two assistants besides his servant Luke. So he ordered a thing he had long coveted—a coat with slashed sleeves, maroon with ivory lining.

His progress to Glastonbury was slow, but not unpleasant, for all along the way the taking of the oath brought a holiday atmosphere with it. In smaller hamlets and villages tucked away in hollows off the main road, the sight of royal commissioners riding fine horses and wearing feathered caps and slashed velvet coats was not an everyday event. The statute required that all people, male and female, rich and poor, educated and illiterate, take the oath. It was a great excuse for those who normally toiled from sunup to sundown in fields and sculleries to spend a morning on the village green drinking ale and gossiping with their neighbors—and incidentally swearing to whatever it was that those grandly dressed London men asked of them. Since their priests and the lord of the nearest manor took it all as a matter of course, it could be nothing for the common man or woman to bother his or her head about, especially as the sun had chosen to shine that day and the field could be as well planted tomorrow.

As chairman of his group of three commissioners, Giles arranged to leave Glastonbury until last. Perhaps he would send the sworn oaths back to London with George and Thomas and extend his own stay or make his way back to London through Oxfordshire to visit his family. He carefully did not admit to himself the pull he felt to Wells.

But the next morning after a comfortable night at The George and Pilgrim, Giles entered the public door of the abbey, and all his ideas changed. There, just two rows ahead of him, her hands folded and head bowed in devout prayer, her slim body encased in a plain black gown, Cecily knelt with the newest of the novitiates. She had spoken of taking vows, but he had not taken her seriously. He had not spoken to dissuade her. Could he have? Or would it have been wrong? Had she found the happiness she sought? Mass began, and Giles stood, knelt, and sat with the others. He crossed himself and gave the appropriate responses at the appropriate moments, but he had no realization of what he did.

Yet he argued. Could his perception be right? Glastonbury was not a double order, housing both monks and nuns. Could she be vowed here? Would her uncle's position give her special status that she could perhaps study here before going to a house of sisters such as Shaftesbury? How long had he been away—more than a twelvemonth? Was that time enough for her to have taken vows of perpetual obedience?

Until that moment when he saw her in somber clothing, shut into her own world of prayer, he had no idea how much he had relied on her being here. Someday, when he had won his security at court and had something to offer . . . if he had not been born a portionless younger son . . . but that was a fruitless line of thought. At least this state of affairs was better than discovering her wed to Hugh Davington, but he felt little comfort.

Dinner in the abbot's hall followed mass. In the seat of honor to Whiting's right, Giles carried the brunt of explaining the commission to the monks who dined with them. Although fiercely flying rumors had reached them, the brothers were anxious for a clear understanding of the situation. As always when a matter of law was under discussion, Brother William Benet sat at the abbot's left. Next to him was George, the Cambridge-educated commissioner new to court, then Brother Austin Ringwode, looking even plumper and more angelic than Giles remembered, then John Thorne, Brother Arthur the subprior, Prior Robert Clerke, the young Brother Roger James, Assistant Master of Boys, and then Thomas, an aged courtier unused to carrying out tasks away from London, who frowned and slumped forward on his stool.

William Benet took the lead in questioning Giles. "And so I understand our Convocation has finally agreed to Cranmer's decision on the king's marriage?"

Giles placed a bite of well-roasted duckling back on his plate. This was a question he had answered many times on this commission. He could quote exactly, "The marriage between Henry and Anne is 'undoubtful, true, sincere, and perfect,' according to Cranmer's just judgment. The grounds of the decision, as well as the marriage itself, are declared to be 'good and consonant to the law of Almighty God, without error or default.'"

"And should one disagree with this decision?" Red-haired Brother Arthur asked his question softly, but with a determined glint in his eye that said he was prepared to think for himself.

Again Giles was ready. "That would be considered high treason."

Whiting nodded. "And so was the Holy Maid of Kent burned at the stake with her five priests for prophesying against His Majesty's pleasure."

Giles spoke quickly, and truly as he believed, "She was a fraud, Your Grace. Her visitations were not from God. She was given fair trial."

No one argued. "And what will we be asked to swear?" Whiting asked.

"The usual oath sworn by all the population, agreeing to the succession of the Princess Elizabeth," Giles said. "And with all other religious, you will in addition be asked to sign a joint declaration repudiating the traditional faith."

Brother Austin rubbed his forehead beneath his gray-streaked tonsure. "And which is the traditional faith? In this day of comings and goings I find it hard to keep track."

Here George answered with supercilious precision. "You will swear that the Bishop of Rome has not, in Scripture, any greater jurisdiction in this kingdom of England than any other foreign bishop."

"And have all the prelates and all religious orders of the land so sworn?" Whiting asked.

Giles nodded. "All, Your Grace. With but three exceptions—the Franciscan Observants, the Carthusians, and the Bridgittine Order at Syon."

"And they will be—" Brother Roger did not finish his sentence.

"They will be silenced," Thomas looked up from his meat to growl.

The discussion continued around the table, but when Giles looked at Whiting in some concern for the time, the abbot brought it to a close, for the commissioners must spend the afternoon sitting under the marketcross collecting the signatures of all the people in Glastonbury and the nearby farms. The next day they would move their long table to the cloister for the swearing of all within the enclosure.

With Giles in the center, the three commissioners sat behind high stacks of the oaths, witnessing the signatures of all who came to swear upon their eternal souls that they recognized the marriage of Henry and Anne as true and Elizabeth as the king's sole heir—for the time being. Beside each stack of oaths a parchment scroll lay close to hand where the commissioners could inscribe, in the presence of witnesses, the name of any who refused to sign. The scrolls were blank so far, as Giles hoped they would remain.

The next morning, however, before the table could be set up under the bell tower in the cloister, before even the brothers could file in orderly fashion from mass, and before Giles could manage a word with Cecily, the entire community was interrupted by the porter scurrying among them seeking Brother Austin, Brother Dunstan the infirmarer, and Brother Robert the prior.

"What is the meaning of this, Brother Arimathea?" The unflappable prior stood a lofty presence before the flurried porter.

"It's Mistress Croft. Her young Mark's most drowned, and Master Horner says he'll none of it, although she says it's his fault, and whoever's the fault, Brother Dunstan must come a'quick for the lad's gone blue."

A muffled cry tore from Brother Austin as he shoved his bulky form through the assemblage. "It's his nephew that's fallen in the river," the porter explained and then took off at a trot, followed by the prior.

When they reached the lawn just inside the gatehouse a crowd had already gathered around the limp form of a small boy and his hysterical mother. "Help my boy! Someone, please! Why won't someone do something? This will be on your soul, John Horner. It was an evil thing you did, closing that footbridge. I told you . . ."

Horner's reply was lost in Brother Dunstan's barked orders as the infirmarer arrived to take charge. "Get back. All of you!" He rolled the small body over on its stomach, straightened the limbs, cleared the mouth, and began pressing rhythmically on the thin back.

Brother Austin knelt and picked up the limp, white wrist. After a moment or two of probing he stood and put a comforting arm around his niece. "God be praised, Avys, his heart is beating. If it's the Lord's will, he'll recover."

Avys Croft buried her head in her uncle's well-padded shoulder and sobbed harder than before, as if his good news was more than she could take. A few minutes later Brother Dunstan's ministrations brought a gurgle of water out of the lad's mouth and after a spell of coughing and sputtering, he began breathing on his own. Brother Dunstan picked the boy up and carried him to the infirmary, but Avys resisted Austin's attempts to lead her after him. "No! I'll not go until this man is properly charged." She pointed an accusing finger at John Horner who stood with his muddy boots firmly planted and his arms folded defiantly.

"It is my property, and I'll close what I like. I built that bridge with my own hands from timber grown on my own farm and not even the king of England can tell me, a free Englishman, what I can do with my own land."

"It is *not* your land, Jack Horner. It's abbey land as it's been time out of mind. And just because your grandfather made a sharp deal to rent that manor from Abbot Bere, you have no right to claim it for your own or to close off the only footbridge over the Brue for a quarter of a mile either direction." She looked around, flushed and bright-eyed. "Where is Abbot Whiting? I wish to make a formal charge. The river's barely safe for a grown man to ford this time of year, and our children are being forced into it." She turned back to Horner. "If my Mark dies, you're a murderer!"

She was still protesting loudly as Brother Austin led her away to the abbot's house to lodge her complaint. Giles shook his head to his fellow commissioners. It was plain that there would be no oaths sworn to that day—at least none dealing with the king's marriage. And he hoped that the case before the abbot would be merely a question of enclosure, with no death to bring a charge of murder. George and Thomas chose to return to their rooms in the inn, but Giles turned his steps toward the infirmary.

The small, still form made barely a bump under the covers of the bed in the quiet room. Brother Dunstan moved around his patient with steady, sure movements, cleansing the wound on Mark's head where he had struck a rock on the river bank. In the dimness of the room Giles did not notice the dark figure sitting quietly in the corner until Brother Dunstan directed his instructions that way. "Sleep is the best medicine. If he does not go into convulsions or fever, he will be quite recovered by tomorrow. When he wakens, give him this posset of camomile and wormwood to soothe him." The infirmarer started toward the door. "And call if you need anything at all. I'll be near."

Then they were alone, and Giles did not know what to say. "Cecily," he began. "Or should I call you Sister Cecily?"

Much to his surprise, the laughter he had failed to elicit before now came forth freely. "No, no. Not yet—perhaps later—or not. But I had to make sure, so I have come on an extended retreat. Mostly I help Prior Robert with the ten poor widows who live in the almshouses and also sometimes lend a hand in the infirmary, as you see."

"And have you found any answers yet?"

Cecily placed her hand lightly on her patient's forehead to make certain he was not feverish, then turned back to Giles. "Do you ever wish you had been born beforetimes when all was simpler, when there was but one religion, one spiritual authority, one way to believe?"

Giles made a noncommittal answer, for he was not yet certain what he believed. He was beginning to suspect that when he decided, it would not be for the old ways.

"It always seemed such a great treasure to me that Uncle Whiting taught me to read, but now I'm not so certain. Perhaps those who say a woman's mind is not fashioned for such are right, for the more I study, the more confused I get."

"Such as?"

Cecily hesitated. "You'll not betray me?" But she did not wait for his answer. "No. I know you won't. I have been reading the works of Tyndale and others condemned by the king as corrupt doctrine. If I am to accept the king's religion, must I not agree in my heart that such are heresy? And yet I am not certain."

Suddenly a great fear seized Giles. He gripped Cecily's arm far harder than he meant to. "Cecily, whatever you believe about the king as supreme head of the church, you do realize that that has nothing to do with your signing of the oath I carry?" In his intensity he shook her. "Cecily, you must sign. This is only about the king's marriage and the succession of the Princess Elizabeth. It has nothing to do with the faith. You must sign. The king will put to death any who refuse."

He released her, and she rubbed her arm with her other hand. "Gently, my friend. I am not the Holy Maid of Kent to defy His Majesty in the market-square. The king must see to his own conscience, and I'll not interfere. It is my own conscience I cannot clear."

Giles sighed. Her answer was inconclusive, but he would not press her. "And these corrupt doctrines that trouble you?"

Mark stirred, and Cecily straightened his covers, then turned back to Giles. "There are three that seem most troublesome—no, four—well, I'm not sure, but, for example—faith only justifies us; saints in heaven cannot help us thither; every man is a priest; purgatory is of the Pope's invention; we owe nothing to any man saving only love . . ."

And for Giles it was as if he were again in that small rocking boat at sunset on the Thames, listening to Humphrey expound on the exciting truths he had found. "I am no theologian. I have read little Scripture and can quote you none, but I had a friend who could, and he found such faith to be true unto death." It was the only comfort he had to offer.

A murmur from the bed told them Mark had wakened. Cecily turned to spoon Brother Dunstan's posset into her patient's mouth. For Giles it was all too like the sick room he had attended at Humphrey's death. He fled to the inn.

Two hours later he was preparing to take supper with his fellow commissioners when an abbey schoolboy arrived with a message for him. "My Lord Abbot bids you sup with him. The new music master and organist for the abbey has arrived and will sing for your enjoyment tonight."

Giles was about to dismiss the lad with a farthing when he paused. "Do you have news of your near-drowned school fellow?"

"Brother Dunstan says he'll do to go home tomorrow. But his mother won't leave until she's lodged charges against Master Horner. I don't think Abbot Whiting is blithe to give judgment against so powerful a landlord—"

"Yes, yes, that will do." Giles cut off the boy's flow of gossip with a penny.

The surly Thomas declined the abbot's invitation, but George donned his best green doublet to join Giles at the table that evening. The abbey fish house at Mere had supplied bass, now served with a spiced currant sauce, and flaky pink salmon, which came from the kitchen steaming in a pastry crust. The eggs were served in such a rich pool of butter that no matter how carefully Giles dipped his fingers into the serving bowl, he could not but drip golden blobs on the linen tablecloth. Although Cecily was seated too far from him for conversation, Giles knew that her presence meant that her patient was out of danger. He could at least smile at her down the length of the table, but his smile faded when he saw how thoroughly George engaged her attention.

As soon as the servants had cleared the dishes, everyone turned to the front of the room where Abbot Whiting introduced Renynger, his new musician. The music master's wide range of instruments and songs was astonishing. He sang first songs of earthly love from past ages, accompanying himself on a small, bowed rebec. Next came a merry dance tune on a small bagpipe. Giles thought of how gaily the court ladies would have danced to that, and for a moment he was again in the hunting lodge in New Forest where the minstrels sang so merrily of "My Lady Greensleeves," and the world had seemed a simpler place.

Then Renynger moved to a small portable organ set on a side table and motioned for Brother Joseph to work the hand bellows for him. "I will sing for you now the most popular song in all Europe, 'Ein feste Burg ist unser Gott.'" The round notes of the organ filled the hall as Brother Joseph pumped and Renynger pressed the keys. "A mighty fortress is our God," he sang in English, "A bulwark never failing . . ."

Giles jerked to attention. He had heard that before. Then he remembered—the Lutheran farmer Humphrey had smuggled a Bible to. So was the abbot's new musician a Lutheran? Did Whiting know the source of this new song? Giles looked at the abbot, who was smiling his approval—whether of his musician or the choice of music, Giles couldn't be certain, but there was no doubt that the performance had been a success.

However, as Giles followed the others out of the hall for Compline, he noticed that Cecily looked troubled. And that troubled him. But tomorrow all would be settled. They could be on their way, with all his friends here securely sworn loyal subjects of King Henry VIII with nothing to fear.

But on the morrow Giles's complacence faded when he realized that Prior Robert was presiding at mass. Abbot Whiting was not there. Could yet another emergency have claimed his attention? Could he have been called away on abbey business? Or could he be avoiding the signing of the oath? Giles tried to imagine himself inscribing the name of Abbot Richard Whiting on the scroll of traitors before witnesses, and he could not. Surely Whiting was a reasonable man. He had signed the petition to the Pope requesting the decree of divorce. He had prayed for Queen Anne in the Easter Mass. But where was the abbot? And where was Cecily? She was not in her usual pew.

With a troubled mind Giles, with George and Thomas, proceeded to set up their table in the cloister, placed neat stacks of parchment oaths in front of their stools, and waited. But no one came. Prior Robert and Subprior Arthur were as surprised as Giles. They were ready to follow their abbot's lead and take the oath, but it would not be fitting for them to take the lead, and so all waited.

At last the mystery was solved when the shrill voice of Dame Margery carried across the courtyard of the cloister. "And I will not be cheated. I am of no importance, but when the workmen cheat me, they are cheating you, Uncle, for you are to pay them, and you must receive good value for your money. And so I told Master Fulke."

Whiting looked both embarrassed and bored, as if he had heard her litany at least six times before. "I am sure you are quite right, my dear. I will investigate the matter at the earliest possibility. But you must understand—"

"And what's to investigate? Do you doubt my word? I tell you, nothing but lime, cheese, and spring water will do to glue the wainscotting on my new dining hall—no other glue sticks as well and so Fulke knows. And I found him using flour paste. It will not do. The Abbot of Glastonbury cannot hold with shoddy work. I'll see Fulke in court!"

"Now, Margery—"

"I'll have you take my deposition now, and you can send men to arrest him. There's nothing to be gained by dillydallying."

"No, no. That won't do. My writ doesn't extend to Wells."

"It extends to all your workmen. Don't think you can soften your duty."

It was the gentleness of Whiting's voice that finally got Dame Margery's attention. "I will investigate. But it must await a sitting of the court for formal charges to be brought. In the meantime I will speak to Master Fulke. Be satisfied, niece."

Then he turned as if seeing for the first time the commissioners and their unsigned oaths awaiting his attention. Giles handed him a sheet of parchment from the top of the stack. Whiting read the document carefully. The king had made it clear. He would not be opposed on this matter.

Whiting glanced at the traitor's scroll lying silently on the table. Then he picked up a quill, dipped it in the open ink pot, and signed the oath. In rapid succession fifty-one Glastonbury monks signed after him.

That afternoon the commissioners left for London with their signed oaths and blank scroll. In all the land, only one scroll bore the names of two individuals who had refused to sign: John Fisher, the aged and saintly Bishop of Rochester, and Sir Thomas More.

6

bbot Whiting knelt at the high altar of the abbey. All was silent in the great nave. Shafts of colored light fell on the bright mosaic floor, moats of dust dancing in the beams. But Whiting's closed eyes saw nothing. Instead his internal vision focused on the carved, gold-covered cross above the tomb of King Arthur, and his mind and heart groped toward God. It had been only four months since the signing of the oath, and yet in so short a time such darkness had fallen.

Word of the greatest crime yet had just reached Whiting. His ears heard, and yet he could not believe. Three days ago Sir Thomas More had been beheaded at the Tower of London. "O Lord, our God, what must Thou think of a country that puts its best man to death?"

His eyes still closed, his heart still at prayer, Whiting reached out and ran his fingers over the smooth carvings of King Arthur's casket. God had blessed this land under godly leaders. When the kings turned to God in repentance, so turned the people. But of late there had been no repentance.

"O, Lord," prayed Whiting as he lay face down before the cross, "we have grown wicked and worse than wicked—we have become proud of our wickedness. Lead us to repentance. Have mercy on us, O God, according to Thy unfailing love; according to Thy great compassion blot out all our transgressions. Wash our iniquity; cleanse us from sin.

"Cleanse our land. Let us again hear joy and gladness. Our sin has stopped the music of life. Restore us to the joy and assurance of a right relationship with Thee. Make Zion prosper. Build up the walls of Jerusalem. Let there be righteousness to delight Thee."

Whiting lay long prostrated before the cross, unaware of the cold and stiffness seeping into his body from the stone floor, unaware of the passing of time that would soon bring the community for Vespers. He was aware only of the strange peace that had overtaken him. He knew with a knowledge above all human certainty that God had heard his prayer. He did not know what God would do for the land he had prayed for so desperately. He did not know what God would do for him. But he did know that God was in control.

He needed that assurance to hold to, for the next day in Chapter, Prior Robert announced the news that he had just received from London. "There is to be a new suppression of monasteries. I have news that the king went in person to the House of Lords to request the suppression of all monasteries which contain fewer than twelve monks."

Tonsured heads nodded, and general discussion followed.

". . . been done before."

". . . so during the Hundred Years War did the Crown seize French monastic holdings in England."

"Wolsey suppressed several small houses to finance his college at Oxford . . ."

"As the king suppressed twenty-some years ago when his privy purse was empty."

"But this will make more impact. There are nearly four hundred houses to be suppressed by this act."

"Many houses have fallen into decline. It will be more efficient for the orders to maintain larger houses."

"But what is to happen to the brothers?"

"All will be transferred to large houses or pensioned off, at their own choice." Prior Robert's informant had been complete.

"There will be inconvenience, but it is perhaps a needed pruning."

Whiting listened to the discussion. Pruning. Gardening. This analogy had been used before. Henry had used it on the reforms he required in church government—a mere pruning, refining, purifying—before he changed everything. England was in need of a master gardener—a gardener to weed her, root out unhealthy growth, make her bloom.

It was true. It was sensible. And yet it struck fear to Whiting's heart. How many vigorous green plants would be pulled out with the weeds? How many healthy bushes killed from too-severe pruning?

"But even the small houses do good—charity to the poor, shelter for travelers, the saying of prayers."

And so the arguments went back and forth. Whiting knew of abuses, of houses living in sin, of houses living in luxury, of houses living in sloth. But he knew far more who lived in peace behind their honey-stoned enclosures, tilling the soil, raising sheep, studying and copying manuscripts, praying the offices—whether their numbers were twelve or multiples of twelve—there were many healthy plants among the weeds. This, Whiting feared, was not to be a weeding as Henry styled it, but a broad-bladed plowing.

Of course, it would not touch Glastonbury, for Glastonbury's brotherhood numbered above four times that required by the act. And surely several Benedictine brothers from houses to be suppressed would ask shelter in Glastonbury, so their numbers would be increased even more.

Prior Robert's next announcement was even more alarming. "We can expect the royal visitors within two weeks."

"Here?"

"They would inspect Glastonbury?"

"Why?"

The only answer to the questions was the sound of rain on the stained glass windows. It had begun again, as it had fallen intermittently for weeks now.

And through the coming days, no matter how often the question was asked, there was no answer to the why. No answer except one from Brother William, who had a greater understanding of laws and the reasons behind them than the other brothers. "It is really quite simple. The royal treasury is almost empty."

"Yes." Whiting was well aware of the condition of the king's purse. "For such did Parliament pass the law that one-tenth of all church incomes would go to the king instead of to Rome. We have just paid this year's portion. His Majesty's purse has done well by us."

Brother William nodded. "And so he knows there is more to be garnered. More from church pockets than any other in the land with the bad harvests this year." He paused, and they could hear the rain dripping incessantly against the Chapter House windows. There was much talk of famine this winter.

Brother Arthur nodded. "And so are the increased pilgrimages to our holy shrines bringing more revenue to tempt those who would look to others' purses to line their own."

Prior Robert nodded. "We only know that the king has ordered a *Valor Ecclesiasticus* to compile the records of the assets and holdings of all the clergy in England, and we can expect the visitors any day."

They arrived ten days later with mud-spattered cloaks and boots showing that the crop-rotting rains had not abated. Not just any commissioner had been sent to Glastonbury, but Richard Layton. The inspector with the toughest reputation for thoroughness—or harshness, depending on whether the description was from his admirers or his enemies—was to take charge of the Glastonbury inspection. It required no great imagination to guess Layton's motivation for such careful work. For had not Cromwell, like Wolsey before him, climbed from the humblest of origins to be the most powerful commoner in the realm? If they could do it, so could Layton, who believed himself to be even smarter. And he was to be aided in this inspection by one who knew the area well—Giles Lacey.

Although this time he was mere clerk rather than head of the commission, Giles felt his arrival at Glastonbury a homecoming. And he made no secret of his desire to see Cecily. Was she still there? He took the liberty of asking the porter and received a small smile with his affirmative answer, although smiles for the royal visitors were in short supply.

After dinner when the rain eased momentarily, Giles found Cecily in the cool of the honeysuckle arbor. Her smiles were in shortest supply of all. "Leech. You have come to suck our blood for the king's pleasure. And when we are dry, who will provide medicine for the poor farmers' cows and horses hereabouts—to say nothing of their children?"

"Cecily—"

"Who will provide shrouds for poor men's funerals, and candles, and graves? When stores from a poor harvest are exhausted and the winter frosts are long on the ground, who will distribute beans and bread to the poor?"

"Cecily—"

"You will milk us that the king may buy another jewel for the Great Whore who has taken the place of good Queen Catherine, but in the end it is the poor who will suffer."

"Cecily, please listen! Cecily, it is merely a report. We take nothing away but copies of accounts."

"So that Henry will know where to send his robbers when he has spent his income from the lesser houses and turns his gaze on the greater?"

Giles could not resist the urge to look over his shoulder to be sure Layton was not within hearing. Nothing would put an end to Giles's rise at court more quickly than having this kind of conversation reported. But Layton's cat-like, black-bearded face was nowhere to be seen. Giles turned back to Cecily. "That will not happen—not to Glastonbury. There has always been a Glastonbury, there always *will* be. We are merely keeping records."

Cecily turned away, her swift movement wafting the sweet honeysuckle scent on the September air. Giles put out his hand to stay her and frightened a hummingbird just coming to feed on the nectar-filled flowers. "How does your patient?" he called after her.

She stopped and turned, concern for the child showing in her face. "Oh, Mark! He does well. Praise to our Lord. But the bridge remains enclosed. The boy's family seeks legal redress, but Master Horner is a powerful man and Mark's father a mere blacksmith. They will have little chance when the matter comes to court." She tossed her head, trails of golden hair falling loose beneath her dark kerchief. "But then you know all about the uses of power." Again she turned away.

"Wait." Giles longed to ask her of her spiritual quest, to talk of important matters, but he could not breach the wall she had erected between them. Desperately he sought for a chink. "Your aunt. How goes her building?"

"It does not. Now she accuses Master Fulke of stealing from her—it all awaits the sitting of the court."

Then, because he could think of nothing more to ask, she was gone. He stood long, vaguely aware of the whirr of hummingbirds' wings and the perfumed air. Then slowly he sat on a small wooden bench at the back of the arbor. Life at court allowed so little time for introspection. He began to sort through the unformed feelings that had been teasing him. Gradually he was realizing a change in himself. Always he had been so determined to get on in the world—to do what was necessary to succeed at court. And then someday to retire to a manor in Oxfordshire—a man of substance. And somewhere along the way to marry a beautiful, biddable girl who would give him sons.

Certainly finding spiritual truth had figured nowhere in his plans. Nor would he have risked advancement for such. But now—when had it started? With Humphrey's death? Or earlier? With his first commission to Glastonbury perhaps? He wasn't sure, but now he seldom asked himself what would be most likely to win approval from his superiors at court. He found himself asking more and more what was *right*, as Cecily had once demanded to know. That was a question ever harder to answer as his two worlds, London and Glastonbury, seemed on a collision course.

And what of the beauty he would have to be chatelaine of his dreamed-of Oxfordshire manor? When he thought of the laughing, silk-robed court beauties, none would stay in his thoughts, but only Cecily Whiting in her black gown. Cecily, the least biddable female he had ever met.

The next morning when he sat in the abbot's office poring over his account books, the conflict in his mind was greater than ever. Layton had not even allowed time to attend mass, but had insisted they begin immediately. The columns of neat figures in the great ledger books appeared to be complete and accurate, but Giles worried. Richard Layton had a reputation for creative muckraking. His steely gray eyes never wavered in their cold calculations of how much value the abbey treasures could add to Henry's treasury. What if he should find something suspicious—or imagine he had?

Giles bent his head over the books. He wanted to make sure he summarized all the facts and figures so fairly that not even the most determined could find fault with Whiting's accounts. The main source of abbey revenue was the rent paid by tenant farmers. These were many, indeed, encompassing land throughout Somerset and in other counties as well. But the records were clear. The inflation the entire country suffered under had taken a deep toll here—most especially in the rents, which had been firmly fixed a century ago and could not be adjusted. On top of this was the monks' duty to cut the rent for the widows of deceased tenants and to provide free quarters for tenants too elderly to work.

Another section of the ledger showed attempts to bring in more income with new business ventures such as the fulling mill at Brent Knoll. But the next pages showed alarming expenses—repairs—replacement of broken glass in the chapel windows, water conduits overhauled, paving-stones laid, mending and laundering of priests' vestments . . . and then the regular supplies for mass—three hundred pounds of altar breads, eleven hundred pounds of wax candles, six hundred hogsheads of wine and spiced oil . . . and the gifts required of the abbot's position, including gratuities to undergraduates at Oxford . . .

Giles flexed his ink-stained fingers and leaned back on his stool to stretch his cramped back before he attacked the list of regular operating expenses. In a year the community and its dependents consumed 176 oxen, 634 sheep, 2183 shellfish, 8532 herrings, and 27,000 bundles of firewood . . . it was possible to imagine that the scale of living might be cut somewhat, especially as to the matter of such commodities as wine, butter, and geese, but it was impossible to imagine that there could be any more careful record keeper anywhere in the land than Abbot Whiting. Those who charged sloth and carelessness in the monasteries of the land should see these record books with every herring, every stick of firewood carefully accounted for.

With his mind a blur of figures, Giles thankfully put his work away, washed his hands, donned his short, full, slashed velvet coat, and went to the abbot's hall for dinner. When a joint of roast ox in a spicy juniper berry sauce was set before him, his first thought was to wonder which entry in the ledger this animal had been. He turned his attention to the gallery where Renynger was playing a small Welsh harp. Giles smiled at the sound. King Henry's fool, Will Somers, had recently acquired such an instrument, and its lilting sound was a great favorite at court. At the end of the song Renynger bowed and handed the instrument to a poorly clad figure who had earlier been almost invisible sitting on a low stool behind the music master. "This gentle instrument was most kindly loaned me by William Moore, a wandering minstrel of the old style, who today will entertain us for his night's meal and lodging," Renynger said.

The abbot's guests thumped the table politely to welcome Moore, and it was only as Renynger carefully placed the small wooden harp in Moore's hands and guided him forward that Giles saw that the man was blind. But his internal vision was not, for his rich melodies were full of color and bright images. The listeners forgot his ragged clothes and clouded eyes in the beauty of his songs. Giles could have spent the rest of the afternoon and evening listening to Moore, especially if Cecily would have acknowledged his presence, but Richard Layton was single-minded.

The chief visitor allowed himself one richly spiced warden's pie as a sweetmeat, then bowed curtly to their host, and, calling Giles forth with a severe look, strode ahead to see to the king's business. Giles was left alone again with the accounts, but Layton commandeered the labors of others throughout the monastery to work for him—Brother Austin to make a copy of the catalog of all the library manuscripts, the cooks to list all their stores, the sacristan to list in detail all holy relics with notes as to their jewel adornment and gilt plating, the chamberlain to list all vestments noting especially those embroidered with gold thread. . . . And the lists continued, each overseen in closest detail by the sharp, black eyes of Richard Layton.

It was two days later when Layton, his brow furrowed in a deep frown, called Giles into the abbot's office. "Choose your sharpest quill. I will dictate the report I shall carry to London." Obediently Giles dipped his best quill in the ink pot and drew out a fresh square of parchment. "To Master Thomas Cromwell of His Majesty's Privy Council . . ." Giles's pen made small scratching noises as it moved across the sheet. Layton succinctly summarized their work and gave the final tallies of row after row of figures. Then Layton paused and paced the width of the room several times.

Giles's mind raced. What would he do if the resulting recommendations were unfavorable to Glastonbury? He knew there would be little to be gained in throwing down his pen and refusing to write what Layton dictated. Layton would simply hire another clerk or write the letter himself, and Giles would be reported to Cromwell as a traitor. Yet he knew he could not live with himself if his hand brought about the downfall of Glastonbury. At last Layton turned abruptly and with rapid, clipped words completed his dictation.

It was nearing time for Vespers when Giles at last found Cecily. The rain clouds that had earlier darkened the sky had blown on across the Severn and over Wales, leaving a watery brightness behind. The Tor shone with a pale green-gold of reflected sunset when Giles turned to the honeysuckle arbor and found Cecily reading there. She looked at him in startled confusion. "What? You here? I had thought you must be nearing Trowbridge at least by now, for I saw Master Weasle depart hours ago."

"As you see, I did not accompany, er—Master Weasel." His uneasy countenance broke into a smile. "He does put one in mind of a weasel."

"And so has he gone to rob the eggs of another nest?"

"If so, he must do it without me, for I requested leave to visit my family, and his readiness to grant my absence was none too flattering."

"And are you not anxious to rejoin your friends at court?"

"My only friend at court died two years ago and more."

Cecily caught her breath sharply at the pain in his voice. "Giles, I had no idea." She held out her hand to him, but he did not see it.

"If it were not for the necessity of making my way in the world, I would never go back."

"But why must you? Any merchant in the land would be delighted to employ a clerk with your skills."

And would you be delighted to live on the salary of such a clerk? The thought was so loud in Giles's mind that for a moment he thought he had spoken. In consternation he turned sharply from her. "But I did not come to talk of myself." He pulled a scrap of parchment from his doublet. "I would tell you what I've already told your uncle. I took careful pains to memorize the exact words that I might write them down and report to you what Layton carries to London."

The color drained from Cecily's face, and she became very still. "It is final then?"

He nodded. "It is final."

"So. Let me hear it."

Giles smoothed out the parchment and cleared his throat. "At Glastonbury there is nothing notable. The brethren be so strait-kept that they cannot offend—"

A small cry broke from Cecily. "But that is good!"

Giles smiled. "Aye. It is good indeed." He continued reading, "—but fain they would if they might, as they confess, and so the fault is not with them. Much might be said in favor of Abbot Whiting who rules with a firm and fair hand all within his keeping."

It was a moment before Cecily responded, as it took time for the full impact of the words to strike her. And then with a shout of joy she flung herself off the bench and straight into Giles's arms.

7

The pall of fear that hung over all the abbey passed, and that night supper in the abbot's hall was a joyous occasion. Cecily put off her nun's dress and donned a wide-skirted gown of green brocade shot with gold threads over an amber petticoat with her golden hair loose under a small green cap embroidered with gold beads. They sat late listening to William Moore singing Welsh ballads of King Arthur and his mighty knights, of Lancelot and the fair Elaine, of Tristan and his Isolde.

"And have you decided?" Giles spoke in a soft voice so no other could hear him. "Is your putting off of black for good?"

Cecily nodded. "I have known for some time. But I thought if Glastonbury were to suffer disgrace, I would choose to be numbered with her. But now she is free, and so am I." Moore finished a ballad, and Cecily applauded with the others. Then she turned back to Giles. "Do you leave tomorrow?"

"Yes. May I be of some service to you?"

"I would return to Bucklesbury. Would it be too far out of your way to escort me?"

Giles had mixed emotions. There was nothing he would rather do than ride through the green and gold autumn countryside with Cecily. But was he taking her straight into the arms of Robert Burgess's ward? He felt again the brief delight of holding her in his arms in the arbor. Would such delight forever belong to Hugh Davington now?

"I will escort you with pleasure," he said, unconvincingly.

Cecily looked confused at his answer, but accepted it. "Good. And I will ask our blind musician to accompany us also. I heard him say he would be leaving in the morning, and I know Dame Margery would be happy for his entertainment."

When Cecily invited him to join them, however, the musician bowed deeply and replied, "I thank you, Madam-of-the-kind voice. But I am for Exeter."

"Seems a long way to go," Cecily remarked later to Giles.

He shrugged. "Perhaps he has a desire to learn Cornish ballads."

The next morning there was rejoicing in every field they passed, for though the harvest was poor, at least the rains had stopped so they could bring in what was there. The whole countryside smelled of new-mown hay and ripe wheat. Everywhere, uphill and down, were parties of harvesters—scything, binding, and stacking sheaths, or in fields earlier cut, piling the corn onto wagons. In one party working near the roadside Giles saw the landowner and caught his breath, for the man looked startlingly like his brother Peter, who undoubtedly was doing that very same thing on Layford, the Lacey estate. Giles simply urged Brigante to a faster pace. He never allowed himself to indulge in jealousy.

At the village of Coxley they stopped at the inn for lunch. Morris dancers were performing on the green, their bells tinkling on the harvest-scented air and their ribbons fluttering in the sun. Cecily laughed and grasped Giles's hand. "Come." She pulled him to the edge of the group where several youngsters capered in imitation of the dancers and matched her step to the rhythm of the tabor, tambourine, and pipe. With far greater joy than he had ever entered a court dance, Giles joined in.

At the end of the dance they made their way, laughing, to a table under the trees in the inn yard and ate their bread, cheese, and ale. "Cecily, you would never have made a nun. You were mad to consider it."

"I know that now. But I had to make sure. I couldn't spend the rest of my life wondering whether I'd made the right choice."

It was for Giles as if the sun had gone behind a cloud, although it continued to shine as brightly as ever on Cecily's Tudor green gown. "And is Hugh Davington the right choice for you?"

"I did not say that," was all the reply she would make.

Scarcely more than an hour later Dame Margery was welcoming them into her half-finished parlor. "That thief Fulke will leave me in this mess, and Master Burgess is too busy with his fields to take a hand in the matter, so it all falls on my shoulders."

She barely paused in her narrative to give Cecily a welcoming kiss. "But at least he finished my bower. Come see."

Giles saw that Wyatt the usher was attending to their bags, for his mistress had no thought for anything but her fine, new-style house. She pointed out the solid oak newel post on the stairs and the fact that they had windows of glass both upstairs and down—no mere sheets of oiled parchment for the house of Robert Burgess. The bower was painted in the new fashion with trailing vines, blue bachelor buttons, and scarlet poppies trailing around the walls. The bed was hung with curtains of sea-green damask, and a long mirror of polished steel dominated one end of the room.

But they barely had time to look before they were whisked off to see the kitchen with its stone-flagged floor. Since all the servants were giving a hand with the harvest, Margery directed Giles to help her move the table in the center of the room. "See!" She stood back with her arms planted on each side of her ample hips. "Is it not grand?"

Giles had never seen the like—a well in the center of the kitchen floor. "It must be a great convenience."

"Indeed, it is. Every morning we draw water for the day's washing and household needs, and all is at hand without any carrying or slopping."

Giles could only admire the skill that had planned and executed so fine a building program. And he wondered at the size of Abbot Whiting's bill for the project. The more he saw, the more hopeless he felt. The greater Robert Burgess's holdings, the less likelihood of his giving Cecily's hand to a third son who had yet to make his way in the world as a sometimes courtier and sometimes clerk. Giles would have ridden on for Layford yet that evening, for he did not relish the idea of seeing Cecily in Hugh's company, but Dame Margery would not be denied the pleasure of hearing all the latest court gossip.

Giles obliged. "Henry would have Princess Mary—or that is, the Lady Mary—with him, but she will not come to court, and Henry will not let her go to her mother, the Princess Dowager. The king keeps Catherine a virtual prisoner in Buckden, for it is said he fears a rebellion in her cause. Reginald Pole and those of the Catholic party abroad have many supporters."

"And what of the Bullen Witch?"

Giles looked around uncomfortably. "Queen Anne—"

But Margery would not be repressed. "Nay, I'll have none of your Queen Anne—for all the country knows she's naught but a whore that bewitched our king and replaced our good queen."

"She is with child again." Giles intended to stop with that, but then added the heart of court gossip. "But it is said the king spends little time with her. His Majesty seems to prefer his jousting and hunting and leaves the queen to be entertained by her brother and his friends."

Giles had not thought it possible that he would welcome the entrance of Hugh Davington, but when the stamp of heavy boots sounded at the back of the parlor, he breathed a sigh of relief to abandon such tittle-tattle. Although when Cecily turned from kissing her Uncle Burgess to greet a young man who was such a copy of Robert Burgess that one would have thought him his son rather than his ward, Giles would gladly have returned to gossip.

The next day, however, as the road wound through the gentle, wooded Cotswold Hills, Giles found it easier to put his worries behind him. He felt Brigante's pace quicken as the animal sensed the approach of home pasture, and even the usually inarticulate Luke voiced pleasure in seeing again the hills his family had lived among for as long as their Lacey masters.

It was midday two days later when they finally rode into Layford Manor. A dark-haired young girl with eyes as flashing as his own flung herself into Giles's arms with cries of joy. "Giles, Giles! Is it truly you? We had thought never to see you again with you so busy at court. Cannot King Henry run this country without my favorite brother?" Megotty kissed him soundly once again before relaxing her hug.

He held her at arms' length, smiling. "Margaret, Meg, Megotta, Megotty; she'll steal your heart and drive you potty." He repeated the childhood rhyme with which he had always teased her. "It's so good to be home!"

He grasped her by the waist and lifted her off her feet as if he would toss her into the air. She landed lightly with a squeal of delight. "Why did you not let me know? I would have ordered the best arras hung in the hall."

She pulled him into the comfortable house. It had none of the new-style conveniences of Bucklesbury, but even with the arras pegs bare and the floor rushes unchanged, Giles would not have altered one chip of its mellow homeliness. Peter's wife, Ellen, was just greeting her brother-in-law when Megotty looked out the open doorway and spotted dark clouds drawing near. "Oh, no! The feathers!" And they were all off at a run to gather in the trays of plucked goose feathers drying in the sun for the winter's featherbeds.

They had just lugged the last of the trays into the kitchen when a shower came down so heavy that it drove Peter and the workmen in from the fields. The women handed around mugs of ale and loaves of bread. "Are there not servants to see to the harvesters' needs?" Giles asked, taking a hand in the serving over Megotty's protest that he was guest of honor.

"Peter sent them to reap the high field. They'll not be back for two days yet, so Ellen and I make do."

So in the undefined position between brother, guest of honor, and servant-helper, the days of Giles's homecoming sped by. He was so glad to be free from cares of court and cloister that it was several days before he noticed the frequent frown on his eldest brother's brow. Whenever he asked a probing question, Peter put him off with vague answers about the poor harvest or general unrest in the country. Giles was far too content in being at home to worry. It was a blessing that Layton had been so off-handed in granting his leave that he failed to specify his return. On the fine days Giles entered fully into the harvest, and when the rain fell and the wind blew, he sat by the hearth and renewed his childhood companionships or rode into Oxford to talk to his second brother Edward who was Master at University College.

How long this idyll might have continued, Giles did not know, but into his third week there he received a message from Abbot Whiting carried by Avery Croft, the Glastonbury blacksmith. The message was ambiguous as to the nature of the abbot's problem, but he sought Giles's help. "My brother will give you lodging for the night, and we will leave in the morning," Giles told Avery.

In spite of interruptions from rain and mud, the harvest was full in, the cider and perry made, the pigs slaughtered, and sausages ground, and all prepared for the harvest feast. Now the best arras hung over the stone walls of the hall, and fresh, herb-strewn rushes covered the floor. New-dipped candles filled every iron bracket on the walls. A whole ox was roasted to crispness for all attached to Layford—servants, tenants, and master's family—who gathered in the hall and at tables set in the courtyard. Giles took full advantage of his last night there to enjoy the company of his family and old friends.

He was gently teasing Megotty about which of the young neighboring squires she would have Peter make her marriage arrangements with when a familiar tune caught his attention. He listened for a moment, straining to see more clearly the small, tattered figure sitting over a Welsh harp at the front of the hall. William Moore? Was it possible that the blind minstrel who had gone to Exeter to learn Cornish songs could now be making his way across Oxfordshire? There was no doubt. It was the same singer. Giles shrugged. There was no understanding the ways of a wandering musician. And Peter seemed pleased with the entertainment.

Early the next morning the lilting memory of Welsh ballads sang them on their way as Giles, Luke, and Avery Croft set out. "It's a pity to take you from your bed, Master Giles, but the Lord Abbot will be most pleased of our earliest arrival. It's weighty matters he must be dealing with."

"Do you know more than that?" Giles was mystified to think how he could be of service to Abbot Whiting.

Avery shook his head. "It's not for the likes of a simple blacksmith to know the ways of great ones—and glad I am, too. Horses and a good piece of iron I understand. Give me a red-hot fire and a solid anvil, and I can shoe any horse in the king's stable, but deal with those that ride the horses—I'd rather not." Giles admired the openness of Avery's unlined face and the clearness of his blue eyes. He knew that he had an honest man for companion.

Abbot Whiting, however, presented anything but an unlined face and untroubled eyes to Giles when they arrived at Glastonbury at noon of the next day. Whiting paced the floor of his small parlor. "It is intolerable. I do not know what to do." He waved a hand at a document bearing the royal seal.

Giles picked it up and read. Cromwell, having dissolved all the lesser monasteries in the land, was now instituting a series of reforms in the greater houses. The regulations were laid out in detail in this document. The stringent regulation of every aspect of daily life of the abbey was bad enough, but by far the worst part was the rule declaring that anybody who cared to inform about a breach of discipline, real or imaginary, could report it to the king at the abbot's expense. "But this is terrible. Anyone who desires a free trip to London could invent a piece of scandal. And you would be obliged to pay for your own false accusing."

Whiting nodded. "I knew you would see the heart of the matter. Read on to the end, and then tell me what you make of it."

A few moments later Giles gasped and flung the document on the table. "But this is blackmail. Cromwell demands gifts in return for making your life unbearable!"

As if in defeat, Whiting quit pacing and sank into his chair. "Yes. And I can see nothing to be done but to submit. I have already made over the documents to give Cromwell the advowson of Monkton Church." He pointed to the paper; then a glimmer of a smile played around his mouth. "And I thought it would please Master Cromwell to be given the honor of voting for us in Parliament since Sir Thomas More is—er, unavailable to vote."

Giles smiled. "As a warning that if one so high could fall, let others look to their necks?"

Whiting shrugged. "Let him make of it what he will. Would you be my ambassador to bear these gifts to London?"

Giles bowed his head. "If you wish it, my Lord Abbot."

Whiting stood up with decision. "Good. Then let us go into the abbey and choose something to sweeten the pot." He led the way across the green lawn now strewn with fallen leaves, with only the hardiest of Michaelmas daisies still blooming in corners. They went first to the Lady Chapel and stood long surveying the treasures and precious relics lining the altar. "This is the oldest part of the abbey. As such it houses our most ancient relics." Whiting picked up a small stone, roughly carved into the shape of a fish. It just filled his left hand, and he stroked its surface with a finger. "Many say this is the very oldest treasure of all. Some say it was carved by St. David, some say St. Patrick, others say it is from the hand of Joseph of Arimathea himself. Of course, there's no knowing the truth, but it's quite certain that it's from before the fire. It must have lain on the altar in St. Dunstan's church and perhaps even in the Old Church which our Lord Himself built here."

Giles put out a hesitant finger to touch an item of such antiquity. "You'll not send this to Cromwell?"

Whiting's laugh held a note of bitterness. "I do not think our king's First Minister would be impressed by an old rock." He reverently placed the fish back on the altar and picked up a cross. It was of the old style, surely Saxon workmanship, and set with oddly cut stones that more glowed than glittered in the light of the candles burning on the altar. "This also was saved from the great fire." He sighed. "Nothing else. I often wonder, were the abbey to burn now, what would I save? Everything here has a sacred history. It would be impossible to choose."

"Perhaps the manuscripts?" Giles suggested.

"Yes. Manuscripts without a doubt. And the tombs of Arthur and Patrick, and the Lady Chapel, and . . ." He threw up his hands. "You see my problem. There is no stopping. I would save it all. Therefore, I must give some." He turned for the door. "Come, let us choose something heavier with gold and shinier with jewels for Master Cromwell."

They were just turning from the high altar, the abbot bearing an intricately designed gold and silver chalice, its bowl encrusted with diamonds and emeralds, when the porter hurried toward them up the nave. "My Lord Abbot, it is the sheriff of Somerset. He says he must have audience with you."

With a look of resignation Whiting went to meet the officer. The sheriff was courteous, but straight to the point. "I am obliged to serve you with this summons, my Lord Abbot." He held out a document.

Whiting took the sheet and frowned. "What nonsense is this? Am I summoned to attend my own court? Who fears that I will abandon my writ over the Twelve Hides? The court sits in Glastonbury at the end of this month as ever it has."

He looked at the document and then handed it to Giles with a sigh. "What nonsense. Fulke has lodged a counterclaim against my niece's complaint. He says the bill is in arrears and demands payment. I'll have no more of such absurdity! What better surety could he have than the promise of the Abbot of Glastonbury? Have I ever failed to pay my bills? And yet this Fulke—a mere carpenter would demand my gold! You may tell your complainant that I'll gladly see him in court, but I am not accustomed to paying for unfinished work, and I understand Robert Burgess's house is not finished."

When the sheriff was gone, Giles pointed out, "The affidavit acknowledges the house is unfinished. Fulke is suing for payment for the barn and completed outbuildings, my Lord Abbot."

Whiting shook his head. "And Cromwell demands bribes, and harvest on the abbey farms is as thin as the rest of the country. What will be next?"

Whiting's question was answered the next morning before Giles had set out for London. The unaccustomed noise of an angry crowd in the monastery courtyard interrupted their breakfast. Giles followed the abbot out to investigate. Brothers Austin and Arthur hurried from their dining hall at the same time, and Giles fell into step with them. "Who are these people?" he asked, surveying the angry crowd dressed in country attire and muddy boots and leggings. Some carried shepherds' staffs, others pitchforks and shovels.

"Most are abbey tenants," Brother Arthur said. "Some are small landowners from the county as well."

"And a few from the village. I see my nephew Avery," Brother Austin added.

Before the abbot could ask their grievance, several hands shoved one member forward. "Well, Tom?" Whiting waited.

The uneasy Tom grabbed his fustian cap from his head and pulled at his forelock. "Saving Your Grace, my Lord Abbot, but it's that grasping thief, Horner."

"What? Has someone else drowned?"

"No. Water's low enough now. No, it's worse. He's gone and enclosed the common—"

Before Tom could finish, another voice called out, "Aye, we small farmers 've always had use of that for our cattle—and our fathers afore us, and their fathers afore them."

"Thas' right! And now where'll I graze that fine new cow I've scrimped and saved to buy?" Another yelled and brandished a pitchfork for emphasis.

Angry voices joined these from all over the courtyard, and Giles was beginning to fear they would turn on the abbot or march out to attack John Horner. Suddenly the crowd fell silent and the way parted from the back for a fine, prancing horse and a rider wearing a gold Tudor rose blazoned over his green coat. "Make way for the king's messenger!" he shouted. And they made way.

With the most perfunctory of bows the messenger presented a document to the abbot. Whiting asked Prior Robert to take the man to the hall for refreshment.

Realizing that they had been thoroughly upstaged, the mob in some confusion turned to go. "Tom," Abbot Whiting called. "Tell them I have heard their grievance. The matter shall come to court."

Tom's weather-beaten face broke in a grin that showed three missing teeth. "Thank you, my Lord Abbot. We thank you." He tugged vigorously at his forelock and backed himself halfway across the courtyard before he turned to catch up with his fellows.

Giles, Brother Austin, and Brother Arthur were alone with Abbot Whiting in the quiet courtyard when he broke the wax seal and read the document. Even Whiting's carefully controlled features now registered shock. "My brothers, by royal decree I have been relieved of jurisdiction over Glastonbury town. The court is to be closed. All cases are to be held pending. What is to be done? I cannot function. I cannot perform my duties."

Brother Austin shook his head. "It is not possible. Jurisdiction over the Twelve Hides descends directly to you from Joseph of Arimathea. The charter has been renewed by every king since Roman times. This cannot be."

8

Some people described Thomas Cromwell as pig-faced, and certainly Giles could see a resemblance as he looked at the broad face with its beady eyes and round nose. But the image that came most readily to him was that of a pudding—a brown, lumpy suet pudding with raisins for the eyes. Master politician that he was, Cromwell carefully controlled any outward signs of avarice as he accepted Whiting's gifts. "How kind of the good abbot. Most thoughtful. Please convey my appreciation to him."

Giles nodded. "He'll be most gratified to receive it. But could we perhaps discuss one matter striking most closely all His Majesty's subjects in Glastonbury?"

Cromwell did not give consent, but he was listening, so Giles continued, "As First Minister and one who must almost constantly be dealing with matters of a legal nature, I am sure you'll appreciate the importance of a smoothly functioning court system. Perhaps you did not realize that your latest stringency on the abbot has made impossible the sitting of the court in Glastonbury. Cases are waiting that need to be decided. His Majesty's subjects need justice. I'm sure that you, sir, of all people will appreciate this—"

Cromwell raised a thick hand. "I am merely a gardener. Glastonbury is a fine house, perhaps the finest in the land. But even such may need pruning. The finest roses in the land—perhaps in the world—grow in our gardens in Chelsea, and yet they are pruned regularly."

Giles bowed curtly and spun on his heel. He had heard it all before. He would win no justice from Cromwell, and there was only one higher power in the land. He would go to the king. Before he had time to let fear block his action, he strode down to the watergate and hailed a boat to take him to Greenwich.

The river between Westminster and Greenwich was choked with traffic. Lining the wharves were the great Flemish trading vessels that accounted for so much of England's wealth—especially now that trade with Spain had almost ceased in protest against Henry's treatment of Catherine of Aragon. A cold wind whipped the water, and seabirds cried the coming of winter. It had been a golden autumn after the rain-sogged summer, but the chill in the air promised brisk December storms and a cold winter. Ice-choked rivers would not help England's merchant trade, but would grow heavier coats on her sheep, so there would be thick bales of wool when spring shearing came.

But for now Giles drew his woolen cape around him and huddled deeper into the boat. Memories of being on the river with Humphrey always came to him whenever he took a boat. They came without the joy of the happy times, but with the sense of emptiness and loss that matched the weather and his mood after his interview with Cromwell.

So it was with great pleasure that he met Henry Norris just getting off a boat at the Greenwich watergate. "Giles! You've been gone from us a deuce of a time." He held up a basket of golden oranges. "Been out all day, I trow; these cost the worth of the jewels on Becket's tomb, but the queen would have them—nothing would do but fresh oranges for King Henry's son in her belly."

Giles forced a smile when Norris threw an arm around his shoulder and drew him up the path toward the palace. He had been away too long. It would take him time to fit again into court manners.

Yet it did not take as long as he thought, for the next night he was invited to an entertainment in the queen's chambers. In the midst of the free-flowing wine and jokes he warmed and relaxed and slipped into companionship with those whose easy manners he had once admired only from a distance. Thomas Wyatt, the premier poet in the land, had brought a new poem. Mark Smeaton played the trill of an introduction on his lute, and Anne, sitting on a well-cushioned chair, clapped her hands in delight. "Yes, Thomas, let us hear your latest work. Is it a sonnet to my beauty?"

Wyatt, in deep blue velvet slashed with lemon satin, made a deep bow. "It is a dream of love, my lady. The lover having dreamed of enjoying his love, complaineth that the dream is neither long enough nor true enough."

"Ah, but perhaps it is the lover himself that should be truer." Anne gave a brittle laugh. "For so the world goes that no lovers are true."

The edge on the queen's voice dropped an uneasy silence into the room. Smeaton, quick to his lady's service, strummed another trill to fill in where there should have been laughter. Giles wondered—he had been back at court for barely twenty-four hours, and yet he had heard rumors. Henry seldom came to the queen's chambers. He often danced with Anne's waiting lady, Jane Seymour. Anne's father, Thomas Boleyn, seldom sat on councils now, and Lord Seymour's sons were more and more in the ranks of power. And where was His Majesty tonight? Was it true that he was at Wolf Hall, the Seymour estate? Did that account for Anne's forced brightness and brittle humor?

"So, Thomas, let us hear your lover's complaint." Anne's pale blue and silver gown set off the moonlight whiteness of her skin and the midnight blackness of her waist-length hair. Except for a slight swelling under the front panel of her dress, her figure was as slim as ever. Wyatt bowed again and stood beside the musician to read:

Unstable dream, according to the place,
Be steadfast once, or else at least be true.
By tasted sweetness make me not to rue
The sudden loss of thy false feigned grace. . . .

The words of the poet were suddenly drowned by a buzzing whisper and sharp laughter from Anne and her brother George. Wyatt looked unsure of what to do, but Anne waved a white, bejeweled hand, "Pray, continue, sir poet."

Wyatt cleared his throat and looked again for his place:

The body dead, the spirit had his desire . . .
Why then, alas! did it not keep it right . . .
Such mocks of dreams do turn to deadly pain!

As the best poet of Henry's court, Wyatt was accustomed to much praise for his efforts, but tonight he did not receive his due. Instead of applauding, Anne turned to her brother. "I am stiff with sitting. Dance with me, George. Mark, give us a lively tune. No more of dirges with dead bodies and deadly pain."

Norris and Weston went to find partners among the waiting ladies sitting in the back of the room, but Giles did not enter in. When he first came to court, he could have imagined no greater success than being included in this glittering circle of the best-dressed, wittiest, most sought-after people in the English court. But now that he was here, it seemed empty. Even if climbing such a ladder could lead to his own manor—and he was less sure of that all the time—was it worth it?

Whatever Giles thought of court pleasures, it became daily more obvious that he would be stuck here for some time. He was determined to speak to the king on Abbot Whiting's behalf, and the king seemed equally determined to absent himself from Greenwich.

Then on New Year's Day, 1536, the king returned, but not to the festivities in Anne's chambers. Instead, he closeted himself with Chapuys—a partisan of the Princess Dowager, several of Cromwell's most-trusted assistants, and the royal doctor. By evening all Greenwich knew—Catherine was dying. The messenger from Kimbolton, where she had most recently been imprisoned on the edge of the Cambridgeshire fens, had read out the list: Unable to eat, heartbeat irregular, too weak to rise from her bed . . . Henry dispatched a delegation to her that night.

At two in the afternoon on January 8, Catherine of Aragon, once queen of England, was freed at last from her imprisonment. Those at court were first to hear the announcement. Then it was proclaimed throughout the land. Henry saw to all the arrangements personally, appointing chief mourners and arranging for the body to lie in state at Kimbolton, then be taken in cortege to Peterborough Abbey to be buried according to Catherine's wishes in a convent. He even sent black cloth for the mourning apparel. After all those years of ignoring her, who would have thought Henry would be so attentive? And he ordered solemn obsequies for her at court and commanded all to attend.

Giles walked alone to the chapel, picking his way carefully over the icy path. Inside, it was equally cold, though candles burned through the gloom at the altar. Archbishop Cranmer read the prayers from his new liturgy soon to be distributed throughout the land as *The Book of Common Prayer*. Staunch Catholic that Catherine was to the end, it would give her no comfort to know that she had been laid to rest with prayers from Henry's reformed church.

Giles looked to the front seats and saw that Henry sat alone. The queen's chair was empty.

The next morning the chambers of Greenwich Palace buzzed with the news. Henry had gone to Anne's chamber to upbraid her for failing to attend Catherine's obsequies and found her holding a revel. The king chided her for exulting in the death of a good woman, reproached her for endangering his son by dancing, and told her he would speak to her after the birth of the child. Whatever the truth of the reports, it was a fact that Henry was gone from Greenwich by noon. And so must Giles wait longer to put his case before the king. Perhaps months, for it was said that the babe was not due until spring. And so he waited.

At last, wearied with inaction, Giles decided to put his case before the king in writing. After several failed attempts he composed a letter that he felt set out the difficulties of Whiting's conditions clearly and fairly. He sanded the sheet carefully, then folded it and sealed it firmly with wax. It would not do for the letter to come to the hands of the wrong advisor. It must go to the king himself.

Giles placed the letter under a stack of books and documents on his table to await the proper courier. Then he turned to comb his tangled black curls into a semblance of order and straighten the collar of his embroidered French shirt beneath his bolstered doublet, before making his way to the Great Hall. Already he could hear the musicians entertaining those who had gathered for dinner and could smell the platters of roasted meats being carried forth by the seeming endless procession of servers from the kitchens below.

He was about to slip quietly into his place at the table when he stopped. The tall, thin form in front of him in the saffron coat and wine hose—surely no other man in the kingdom had possessed such lanky legs and such straw-thatched hair. It could not be, and yet the name flew from his mouth. "Humphrey!"

No more had he pronounced it than he was mortified by his own foolishness. He had helped prepare his friend's body for burial with his own hands. Yet when the young man turned with his pale blue eyes smiling and the freckles dancing across his nose, Giles could almost have sworn . . .

"You remember my brother! I was hoping I would find someone who did, for I knew he had good friends at court, but I did not know their names."

Giles gave the newcomer the most welcoming of hugs. "Is it Diccon? I seem to remember Humphrey talking of a pesky little brother by that name."

"Not so little now, but just as pesky, I fear."

"And have you come all the way from Yorkshire in this weather?" Before Diccon could answer, Giles moved closer to his ear that none could hear. "You've chosen an ill moment to come to court. The king is absent and the queen out of sorts." And Diccon opened his mouth, but again Giles rushed on. "But that's no reason to stand about without our meat. Come, there's plenty of room here."

Diccon, famished after his long journey over early February roads, did full justice to the meal. They talked little until later in Giles's room where Diccon stretched his great length out full on Giles's bed. In spite of his relaxed position, however, his voice rang with intensity. "You say the king is not here? So I must travel on? That is ill news, indeed."

"What business is so pressing that it requires travel in this weather?" Giles looked at the sleeting snow driving against the small glass panes of his window. He drew closer to the fire.

"It is His Majesty's business, if only he knew it. Many of us do not believe the king's ministers inform him well, for surely he would not allow his realm to be governed so if he knew. At least, that's the hope on which I've made this journey."

A knock sounded at the door, and a servant entered. "They told me you was 'ere, Master Diccon. I brought you a nice hot posset."

The servant set a steaming mug on the table in the center of the room.

"Ned!" Giles cried. He had not given a thought to Humphrey's servant since he sent him north to inform the family of their son's death. "And so you serve Diccon now!"

Ned pulled at his forelock. "That's right, but I never thought it'd bring me back London way again."

"Pull up a stool, Ned," Diccon directed. "I am just beginning to tell Giles of our business here, and as it's as much yours as mine, I'd have you stay." Ned obeyed. "You see," Diccon said leaving his prone position and moving closer to Giles, "the unrest is mostly among the commons—farmers, shopkeepers, servants like Ned here. Master Robert Aske, the lawyer who has always served our family's affairs, is the one who has talked to me most—convinced me of the wrongs, I should say."

"What wrongs?" Giles asked.

"Some the same as across the land—taxes too high, harvest too poor, land being enclosed so the poor man has no place to graze his cattle, but most of all is this matter of suppressing the monasteries. Here in the south you've inns and manors and other places for a traveler to spend a safe night. In the north we've naught. And the charities of the brothers and sisters—again, here you've got many great families whose kitchens will give leftovers to the poor. In all our great spaces of Yorkshire we've only a handful of such. Our poor are starving."

"That's right, tell 'im about the poor woman we found at the bridge," Ned encouraged.

Diccon took a drink of the hot cider his servant had brought him. "Snowing terrible, it was, when we came to cross the Ouse. We almost didn't see her, but the infant cried. A poor woman sheltering under the bridge with a babe in her arms. The woman was frozen, but we tried to get the babe into Selby." He shook his head. "We were too late."

"And dropping the sacraments," Ned prompted his master.

Giles nodded. The Ten Articles of Faith to Establish Christian Quietness, a document drawn up by Church of England bishops to clarify Christian belief and establish quietness in the land, had badly misfired even in the south. And he understood something of how much more slowly change was accepted in the north. "And you think there will be trouble?"

"I think the king needs to know that if he allows his ministers to proceed with closing our monasteries and turning our monks and nuns out on the countryside and changing our way of life, there will be much trouble. He needs to be warned."

Giles thought of the similar warning he had penned only a few hours earlier. Did Henry know what his policies—or Cromwell's policies—were doing to the country? Or was he too busy with his own marital problems and worrying about war with France or Spain to take any notice?

The roads continued impassable for several weeks, and so Giles could enjoy Diccon's company. To his surprise, Diccon was not a Lutheran but a staunch holder to the Old Faith, as it seemed were Robert Aske and most of the outspoken men of the north. They desired abolition of the heresy laws against Catholics and restoration of papal supremacy, but Giles persuaded Diccon to admit this to no one and to frame his message to the king in such a way that it could not be guessed at.

At last March brought lasting thaws and sharp winds to dry the roads, and the ice left the Thames so Diccon could continue his way by boat. He gladly added Giles's letter to his pouch and set off in full assurance of accomplishing his mission and returning with good news in a fortnight.

But the fortnight passed and almost another before the news that all the court awaited came—Henry was back. The king and his closest councilors—which meant the dukes of Norfolk and Suffolk and the Seymour brothers—were back at Greenwich, and Henry would hold a royal tournament. Jousting was one of his favorite pastimes, one in which he had excelled as a young man. It was rumored that he had done less of it of late because of a running sore on his leg that pained him greatly when sitting on a horse. Indeed, Giles had seen the king limp a few times, but such rumors were unsubstantiated. Henry, now anxious to appear youthful before the sweet young Jane, had ordered a new, larger suit of armor and would joust in his own tournament.

The meadow beyond Greenwich Palace was prepared, and the day dawned warm and sunny. Giles, making his way to the field with the rest of the court, looked about him continually. Surely now Diccon would return. Not a day passed but that he wondered about his friend. But there had been no word.

The efforts to make this a brilliant tournament, however, had been a great success. All across the field scarlet banners embroidered with gold Tudor roses caught the sun. At the side where the ladies' gallery had been erected, the stands filled with laughing courtiers wearing their lighter fabrics and brighter colors for the spring. Crocus bloomed in the meadow, and green buds swelled on the trees.

There had already been a couple of passes of armored knights to warm the crowd up by the time Giles took a seat. He found himself next to Henry Norris and Will Brereton. They greeted him pleasantly enough, but staunchly showed their loyalty to Anne by refusing to look at the lovely Jane Seymour whose blond hair and apple green gown formed the centerpiece of the front row. "When our Anne gives the king his prince, that plain Seymour girl will regret her impertinence," Norris said.

But Giles was spared replying, for just then the heralds blew a stirring fanfare, and a new pair of knights took the field. Though both had their visors closed, providing some anonymity, there was no mistaking the magnificent figure on the powerful dappled charger. Only Henry of England could sit a horse such. And there was no secret of the fact that the other rider was Jane's brother, Sir Thomas Seymour, who had accepted the king's challenge. The knights rode to the center of the field, one on each side of the barrier and then dipped their lances in salute to each other. Henry, none too subtly, turned toward the reviewing stand and dipped his lance, tipped with an apple-green scarf, to Jane Seymour.

Again the trumpets blared. The riders took their places opposite each other on the field. They charged, running full-tilt at each other. Henry's lance gave a sharp smack on Seymour's, and a great roar went up from the stands. But the pass was indecisive, so the knights accepted new lances from their squires and moved into position.

No one was ever sure what happened. Perhaps his horse shied at a fluttering banner, or perhaps it balked at the unaccustomed weight of the king's new armor, but suddenly Henry's horse reared high on his back legs and twisted. Horse and rider crashed to the earth with a thud that shook the gallery. And the king was underneath.

The horse struggled to its feet. But Henry's impressive, prostrate form did not stir inside his gleaming armor.

"He's dead! The king is dead!" a woman screamed.

The entire reviewing stand rushed onto the field in confusion. At last someone got Henry's helmet off, and the word went around that the king breathed—but just barely. His unconscious form was rolled onto a stretcher, and he was borne off to the palace to be attended by his physicians. Norris grabbed Giles's arm. "She mustn't know! Anne must not hear of this!" And he was off at a run.

For hours the court waited while rumors and counterrumors flew so fast that Giles sometimes heard the denial of a report before he heard the report itself. It was hard to make sense of anything, but of a certain, King Henry lived, although he lay like one dead. The fistula on his leg had broken open, and he had like to bled to death. But he lived.

Then the next rumor was the report that the prince was born. No, not born, but miscarried. It was said that, hearing of Henry's accident and that hope for his life had been abandoned, Anne had fallen in a swoon and miscarried. Apparently Norris's attempts to shield her had been unsuccessful. It was said that her uncle, the Duke of Norfolk, had been the one who pushed his way into her chambers to tell her. And Giles thought that in this case, at least, a mere courtier had shown better sense than one of the great dukes of the realm. But the harm was done.

The gossips said that the babe was a mere sixteen weeks old. Giles frowned and counted the months back. But that meant Anne had only been pregnant since December, and yet last fall all had been told of the coming of a prince. Had Anne known her place in Henry's affections insecure, and so she invented the story in hopes of being able to fulfill her own prophecy? If so, her desperate measure had almost succeeded.

Greater amazements yet followed. For a few weeks later more news eclipsed all former events. Queen Anne was arrested. The charge—treason—committing adultery against the king.

9

For Giles, however, it was not the conviction and execution of Anne Boleyn that was most shattering. Her fall from favor had been apparent for many months. But Giles was more shocked by the execution of those accused of being involved in her adultery: Henry Norris, who had early befriended Giles at court; Mark Smeaton, Anne's lovelorn lute player; Sir William Brereton; Sir Francis Weston; and finally George Boleyn—for the queen was convicted of committing adultery with her own brother. Those gifted, attractive young men Giles had so admired and sought to imitate on his climb to success were all beheaded in the space between breakfast and dinner on a mid-May morning.

Giles stood listening to the firing of the guns of ships on the Thames. How easily he could have been among them. Were they really Anne's lovers, or were they simply young and gay and thoughtless? When one considered Anne's drive for power and her instinct for survival, it seemed unlikely that she would have done anything so stupid as to cuckold the King of England.

Giles had escaped—because he had had to earn his place at court. Because he had had to work as a messenger and a clerk, he had found Glastonbury and Cecily. They had saved his life. No—Glastonbury, Cecily, and Humphrey. He still missed his friend, and now he missed Diccon, and he wondered again what had become of his mission to the king.

But it was to be many weeks, months even, before Giles heard. In the meantime Henry married his Jane Seymour. Henry was happy; therefore, the court was happy, and the commons were happy—about the marriage at least. For at last they had a truly English queen. Catherine, as much as they had loved her, had been Spanish, and Anne, although English-born, had been educated in

France and preferred French ways. But Jane was a sweet, simple country girl in spite of her noble birth. That summer the sun shone, and the crops grew green and lush. And Giles received another commission to travel to the West Country.

With warring emotions, Giles approached the chamber of Cromwell's clerk to whom he had been ordered to report. There was no place he would rather go than into Somerset, but he trembled at the thought of what his commission might be. Was he to collect yet more bribes for Cromwell? Had yet another stringency been ordered for the remaining monasteries? And what would he find when he visited Bucklesbury? For no matter how he dreaded the answer, he would visit there when his way lay near. Was Cecily now betrothed to her uncle's ward?

Giles stood before the clerk and noted the great stack of books on the table behind him. "Name?" the clerk demanded.

"Giles Lacey."

The clerk checked his list. "Ah, yes. Twenty copies. To be exhibited openly in every church where all people may come and read freely. Is that understood? It must be clear to every priest, for that is Parliament's order."

Giles looked confused. "What is it I am to deliver?" he asked, fearing the worst. Yet another set of rules? Perhaps another copy of the Ten Articles of Faith which had so confused and upset the people? An order for more taxes?

"Don't you know anything?" The harried clerk indicated the great stack of books behind him. "Bibles, man!" And then Giles understood. Yes, he had heard of the Bible put out by Miles Cloverdale—the first complete printed English Bible. It was said that Cloverdale had only slightly revised Tyndale's suppressed version of the New Testament and then completed the part of the Old Testament which Tyndale had been unable to finish before being put to death. And this was the Bible Henry would give to his people.

"It must remain freely open at all times for whomever wishes to read it," the clerk repeated. "Is that clear? It is your duty to explain that most emphatically to the priests, for Parliament is aware of the feelings of many that people should not read the Scriptures for themselves."

Giles smiled. If only Humphrey could have seen this come about. His friend had argued as they sat late over a tankard of ale that people must be free from false ideas about religion. The only way to accomplish this was through the Scriptures. The Bible in English must be available to all, Humphrey had said. And now Giles was to be allowed the great privilege of having a hand in it.

The clerk drummed impatiently on the table in front of him.

"Yes, yes." Giles snapped to attention. "All quite clear." He picked up a quill and signed for the Bibles.

No one could have been happier than Giles, riding Brigante across the summer countryside, with Luke leading a packhorse laden with Bibles. For once he had a commission that would bring joy to the people. It came as a great shock when the first priest he called on in Taunton gave a fierce frown and ordered Giles to put the Bible in a dark corner of the church. "That will not do. The orders are specific—it must be set up in a convenient place for reading."

The priest's frown was underscored with a growl, but he shrugged and led them to a tiny chapel on the north side of the nave. Again Giles protested. "Nay, this will not do. You are ordered by act of Parliament not to discourage anyone from reading this Bible or from listening to others read it. This chapel is too small to provide for a convenient public reading. You well know the large number of your parishioners who cannot read for themselves. They are not to be denied the hearing of the Word."

"I'll not be responsible. It'll cause unrest, confusion, and irreligion." The priest pointed a wrinkled, gnarled finger at Giles. "The Scriptures are given to the priests, just as the Word of God was given to the prophets of old. And it's our job to explain it to the people, just as it was the prophets' job." His shaky voice cracked with fervor. "Common people reading the Bible for themselves. I've never heard of such heresy. You'll have chaos. You'll have every man thinking he's his own priest—thinking he can approach God Almighty by himself without the church." He jabbed Giles in the chest with his bony finger. "Young man, the souls that go to Hell from reading this Bible will be on your head—not on mine!" And he spun around and left in a flurry of flapping robes.

But he did not try to prevent Giles from his task. With Luke's assistance Giles placed the heavy sacred volume on a reading table before the high altar, ran a chain through the space between cover and spine, and chained it securely to the table leg. Now no man in Taunton parish could be denied access to "the very lively word of God," as the act of Parliament called it.

At Othery, Bridgewater, and Street Giles and his commission were greeted with varying degrees of gladness and indifference, but no more hostility. When Giles rode beneath the smooth green Tor that had been beckoning him ever since he first caught sight of it several miles back, the familiar sense of peace and homecoming flooded his soul.

The porter told him Abbot Whiting was in the Chalice Well garden, so Giles left their precious baggage to Luke's care and walked past the great arches and towers of the abbey. Inside monks were at choir practice. The harmonies of the organ and their voices floated upward in praise. Whiting sat on a bench backed by a circle of ancient yew trees beside the gently bubbling waters flowing out of Chalice Well.

He welcomed his visitor with a smile, and Giles sat beside him on the bench. In all Glastonbury, perhaps in all the land, there was no more peaceful spot. A bird singing in a tree behind them was the only voice, for they were too far from the abbey for the sounds of the choir to reach them and too far from the pease field to hear the voices of the brothers working there. Then the tinkle of a bell and a gentle baaing reached them from the sheep grazing out of sight on the Tor behind them.

At last Whiting spoke. "Here it is possible to forget the turmoil, at least for a space."

"How is it since I left you?"

"It is as if it is Cromwell's intention that my life be made unbearable. He continues to demand gifts. He sends more and more demands to control every aspect of our daily life. I still have no power in the town. The court cannot sit."

"My Lord Abbot, I'm sorry I asked. I did not mean to bring your troubles before you in your place of quiet. I had hoped to cheer you. I bring good news—" Then he paused. He thought it to be good, but after the reaction of other priests, he couldn't be sure. "That is, I hope you find it good. I bring an English Bible for your parishioners to read as they will."

Whiting sighed and shook his head. "Who is to say? There is such unrest. The words of Scripture should bring them comfort. But will the people understand it right? I can only pray that they will. I can only pray that God will bring His will out of all of this—for I can see my way only as in a dark tunnel. Nay, I'm not even sure it's a tunnel. Perhaps I am just going deeper and deeper into a cave." He shook his white head again and then sat quietly with hands folded in his lap until Giles thought the priest had forgotten his presence.

The birdsong behind them and the bubbling water at their feet seemed to fill the small green space, circled as they were by trees and hillside. Then, when Giles was wondering if he should simply creep quietly away, Whiting spoke again, pointing to the red clay lining the pool at their feet. "It is said that this well turned to blood and stained the rocks red when Joseph of Arimathea dipped the Holy Grail into it. And it is said that our Lord Himself came here as a boy and trod this holy ground with His sacred feet. Surely so hallowed a spot as this should be kept safe from the graspings of such a one as Cromwell. Surely God would keep it so. But I do not know."

Then the bell rang for Vespers, and together they walked down the slope to pray in the most sacred church in England.

The next day Giles installed a Bible beneath the perpendicular tower of the parish church of St. John's in Glastonbury town where Father Thurgood welcomed him. "It'll be a fine thing for the people. Mayhap it'll take their minds off their troubles for a space. Goodness knows we've enough hereabouts."

Then Giles rode on to Wells, much in need of something to take his mind off his own troubles. Would he find Cecily betrothed to Hugh? Or worse, wed to him? Or would he find her with a new suitor? Would she welcome him? Or after the friendliness of their last parting, would she expect him to speak for himself and then be angry or hurt when he did not because he could not?

It was not a happy sight that greeted him two hours later when he rode into Bucklesbury. The new manor house with its brick bottom story and black-timbered upper floor that should have been the showpiece of all Wells, next to its great cathedral and buildings of the close, stood half-finished. The absence of workmen showed that the matter had not been settled yet.

But far grimmer to Giles was the sight of Cecily with her lime green worsted kirtle tucked above her ankles into the band of her apron, holding a wide wicker basket beneath a fruit-laden pear tree and looking up at Hugh Davington, who was tossing pears into her basket. "Be careful, Hugh, you'll bruise them!" she cried, but the chime of her laughter bespoke a carefreeness Giles had long wished she would display in *his* company. Whatever it meant, it was obvious that the barrier she had always kept between herself and Hugh was down. Giles handed Brigante's reins to Luke and went to make his presence known to Dame Margery.

Her greeting was generous, but her commission dismayed him. "Go find Mistress Cecily—she's gathering pears in the orchard, I think—and bid her come in to me."

Margery turned to instruct her servants about the cheese-making, so Giles had no choice but to obey. He arrived just as Hugh leaped from the tree limb and landed solidly at Cecily's feet. He grasped her by the waist and swung her around, above her laughing protests. "Cousin, behave yourself. You'll spill the pears."

To Giles's amazement, Hugh set her down abruptly and stalked off, his work boots leaving dark bent places in the thick grass. With a laugh Cecily stooped to pick up the pears that had tumbled from the basket. She didn't look up at the sound of Giles's approach. "There's no good being angry, Hugh. It's settled. Of course, if you want to take it to court whenever Cromwell—" She looked up and greeted Giles with a glad shout. "You! I thought you had abandoned us for good this time."

Giles had the impression she would have flung her arms around his neck as Megotty would, had she not been laden with the pear basket. "And would it have been for good if I had abandoned you?"

"Not good, but very evil, for I have much to tell you." Giles winced, for he was not sure he wanted to hear what she would tell him, but she rushed on. "But first, you must tell me of our new Queen Jane. Is it true she is as unspoiled as people say? Did she in truth reject a purse of gold the king sent her because she would not be bought?" She plunked the basket of pears into Giles's hands and turned toward the house.

Giles lengthened his stride to keep up with her. "And what is this great rush? And your sudden interest in court matters? I thought you loathed all at court."

She turned and gave him a saucy look—so alarmingly light-hearted. What had caused this sudden lightness in one who had always been so solemn? He found the change delightful, but feared its cause.

"Not *all* at court." She laughed and then became quite serious. "Besides, I've learned that the ways of the court can be exceeding useful for commoners as well."

They had reached the wall of the courtyard beside the house. Giles put the fruit basket down on a stone bench and stood his ground. "Cecily, what are you talking about? Tell me, what has come over you?"

"Is happiness so strange? Perhaps it is in this worried land, but they say the king is happy at last, so might I be."

Every word she spoke wounded him more, but he would hear it. He must know the worst. "Cecily, I will hear what you mean."

"I have found the perfect answer and confounded all of them—my aunt and uncle, Hugh, even Abbot Whiting, although he would not push me, so all the more I owed him an answer."

"You have answered Hugh?"

"I have rid myself of him in a way they cannot protest, and yet we remain friends."

"Rid yourself of Hugh? And how have you done this?"

"By following King Henry's lead. Hugh Davington is Uncle Burgess's nephew. I am his niece. We may not marry. It is forbidden to marry relatives." She flung out her arms and laughed.

"You cannot be serious. It is not even a blood relationship, only by marriage."

"Catherine was related to Henry only by marriage."

"By marriage to his brother. It is a far different thing."

Cecily raised her eyebrows in a pert manner. "Sobeit. I'll withdraw my objection if you wish it."

"No!" Giles grabbed her hand. "No! I don't wish it! Most heartily I do not. But I cannot see how you've made them accept it."

"They have no choice. Even if Uncle Burgess would take the question to court, there can be no sitting until Cromwell lifts his strictures. And Uncle Whiting is in the least of positions to argue an issue which would appear to run counter to the king's."

Giles shook his head. "I still don't understand. There are courts at Wells. It's only the abbot's court that has been restrained."

"Yes, but I am the abbot's niece, and I plead an issue of canon law. Besides, Uncle Burgess is in far too much legal wrangle over his buildings. He'll not take on more."

"And so you are free again, as once before you were free of taking the veil."

"Now I am free to marry whom I will." She stood straight and still, and her clear blue eyes looked levelly at Giles.

A gusting breeze caught a long strand of her golden hair and twined it with Giles's dark curls, and yet he could not answer. At last he turned away. "Cecily, it is my dearest wish. But I have no fortune. When I have won a secure place at court—"

"As Henry Norris and Francis Weston and the others won secure places at court?"

He could not answer.

"Giles, leave court. Leave now before you are caught in a tangle such as those once-innocent men. Leave before you are forced to do something so against your conscience you'll be forever corrupted."

The same fear had been plaguing Giles. He argued more with himself than with Cecily. "But what can I do? A clerk's salary—"

"Is a pittance. I know. But my dowry isn't."

His laughter was bitter. "You'd have me be a kept man? I might as well remain at court."

That silenced even Cecily. But not for long. "Cannot you go to your brother? Seek a place on your family's lands?"

"It is not a large estate. And Peter hopes for sons."

"But has none yet?"

"No."

"Nor daughters to dower?"

"None yet." And then he laughed at her intensity. "Cecily, Cecily. You should have been a lawyer. You could give the likes of Master Cromwell his comeuppance."

Though he thought the chances unlikely, Giles was so buoyed by her determination—and by their declared desire to marry each other—as if only determination and desire were necessary—that he set out the next morning for Layford.

The Lacey fields looked sweetest and greenest in all the land to him, and Megotty greeted him with open delight. Peter was away in Reading, so Giles must wait. It was evening of the second day before Peter returned. He greeted Giles in an off-hand manner and closeted himself in his room with his traveling companion until suppertime.

At supper the sound of a familiar ballad made Giles look up sharply. How odd that the blind minstrel, William Moore, seemed to have become an intimate of his family. But the pleasure of listening to Moore's songs soon lulled any questions from Giles's mind—except the one all-important question he had come to ask. The next morning after breakfast Moore set out toward the east, guided by a Lacey servant. Someone mentioned Colchester, but Giles didn't pay much attention, as he spotted his opportunity to talk to Peter alone. He laid his whole situation before his brother—his dislike of court life, his doubts about ever truly making a place for himself there, his reciprocated love for Cecily.

Peter's eyes seemed to light up for a moment when Giles told him that her dowry was sizeable, but in the end Peter was noncommittal. "It would be pleasant to have you here, Giles. But having an ear at court may prove to be useful. And you know our coffers have never been over-large. Besides, I must dower our sister."

"What, is Megotty thinking of marriage?"

"All girls think of marriage. And so do their families if they are careful of their duty."

"Yes, yes. But is there someone she cares for?"

"What has that to do with it? There are eligible men enough in the land when I have time to see to the matter. For now, I have much weightier concerns. Return you to court, and keep your ears open."

Peter did not say what Giles was to keep his ears open for. But when Giles returned to the court, now at Hampton Palace, every tongue buzzed, although he doubted the matter would have interested Peter. It had, however, supreme interest for Giles, for it finally answered the question he had been asking for eight months. And the answer was not good.

Apparently Diccon Marston had met with no more success in his attempt to quell the unrest in the north than Giles's letter had in his efforts to help Abbot Whiting. The north boiled with rebellion. An unruly mob had rioted in Lincolnshire, demanding lower taxes and the reopening of the dissolved monasteries. The insurrection had been quickly put down, but the government was alarmed. Cromwell's spies sent word of a much larger, better-organized uprising in Yorkshire, and Giles recognized the name Robert Aske in the reports.

Cromwell prepared for the worst. He drafted letters to all the major landholders in England, both lay and ecclesiastical, ordering them to raise an army among their tenants. England kept no standing army, but every able-bodied man was required by law to keep regular archery practice so he would be ready for just such an emergency. All the clerks and couriers at court were summoned to duty to dispatch the letters.

Giles looked at the document in his hand. "Sir, it's unreasonable—" The overworked clerk had already called the next messenger to present him his orders. Even now the rabble in the north might be on the move. This was a state of war.

Giles walked out into the hall and found a quiet alcove in a bay window where he could think. What was he to do? So recently had Cecily warned that he would be required to do something against his conscience. Was this it?

He was to demand of the Abbot of Glastonbury one hundred men, by far the largest contingent required of any monastery.

10

he next morning Giles could stall no longer, so he sent Luke to saddle Brigante. He had decided that, as the order would be sent, it was best that it arrive from a sympathetic hand. He had a vague uneasy feeling that he had used that justification before on something and that Cecily had rejected it as a meaningless sop. But he had argued firmly with himself that if need be, he could help Whiting gather his troops or even volunteer to join the force. So with a conscience somewhat soothed, he set out at a dragging pace along the road west.

At noon of the second day he was just in sight of Newbury when a clatter of horse's hooves and a shout of his own name made him turn and pull up his horse.

"Diccon!"

"Well met! I was told I might overtake you if I rode like the devil."

"I'm glad you did, but what's the emergency?"

"You are recalled."

"Recalled?"

"Yes. No sooner had you left than Cromwell countermanded the orders. It seems that those bringing news from the north, er—, persuaded him that the danger was exaggerated."

"What do you mean? Are you in Cromwell's service?"

Diccon looked around as if to be sure there were no spies behind the trees. "I serve the cause of the true faith."

Their mounts were so close Giles could clasp his friend on the shoulder. "And I'll not ask which faith that is. But take care, my friend, it is dangerous. The safe line between Lutheran and papist is a narrow one. I'd not gladly part with another of your family."

Diccon smiled. "It's less dangerous now that the order to raise the militia has been countermanded. Will you ride north with me?"

Giles considered. Was this the time when he should leave court? Should he fight for the rights of men he didn't know? For a cause he wasn't sure he agreed with? "Perhaps we could do more good at court," he suggested halfheartedly.

Diccon shook his head. "The nobility of the north don't rebel, only the poor people. Master Aske is little above the common variety of quill-scratchers; he needs every good man. I've done all I can do here."

Giles knew this was not his struggle, but he feared for his friend. "Be careful. And send me word how you fare."

Diccon had half turned his horse when Giles called after him, "Wait! You'll need a place to stay tonight. With so many monasteries closed that's not easy to find. You've just about time to make Layford by nightfall, and it's little off your way. Here." He gave quick directions and pulled a monogrammed handkerchief from his pocket. "Megotty will recognize you for a friend when she sees this—she embroidered it for me for a New Year's gift."

Giles watched until Diccon was out of sight. What dangers did his friend ride off to?

Within a month the whole world knew. The court, Giles among them, was still at Hampton Palace. He had not gone hawking with them that mellow October day, but he was walking by the river when the king and queen returned with their party, filling the air with their laughter. Giles turned his steps toward the courtyard where they were dismounting. He was within hearing when the messenger, who had been waiting by the gatehouse for several hours, rushed to the king. "There's an uprising, Your Majesty. They've taken Hull and Pontefract."

Henry swore. "The devil take those northerners. Lawless, clannish, uncivilized—they've ever been. They fear change like the ignorant beasts they are. Well, what of the Percys and the Nevilles? They keep peace for the Crown in that God-forsaken wasteland. You'll not tell me they've joined the rebels?"

"No, sir. They've done naught."

"What! They sit on their hands while the riffraff ravage the country and defy their king?"

The messenger tugged at his forelock and held out a pouch with reports. Henry snatched it and pulled out the contents, letting the leather bag fall on the ground. "Twenty thousand commoners wearing white uniforms with red patches for Christ's five wounds! . . . they march under the banner of St. Cuthbert with Christ and the cross on one side and a chalice and wafer on the other! . . . they call themselves pilgrims! . . ."

Henry sputtered between each outburst, growing increasingly redder in the face. He made as if he would tear the next sheet of parchment from top to bottom; then he stopped and bellowed out its contents in a voice that startled ducks on the Thames into flight. "The 'Oath of Honorable Men' they call it! Honorable! HONORABLE! This jumped-up lawyer would defy me with a pilgrim's oath—listen to this: 'Ye shall not enter into this our Pilgrimage of Grace for the Commonwealth, but only for the love that you do bear unto Almighty God, His faith, and to the Holy Church militant and the maintenance thereof, to the preservation of the king's person and his issue—' Well!" Henry paused and looked up. "At least they got that right." Then he returned to his reading at a slightly reduced volume. "'—to the purifying of the nobility, and to expel all villein blood and evil councilors against the Commonwealth from his Grace and his Privy Council of the same—' What, would this rabble choose my Privy Councilors for me?" Again he read, "'—to keep afore me the Cross of Christ, in my heart His faith, the restitution of the Church, the suppression of these heretics and their opinions.'"

Giles held his breath. Henry looked as if he would personally lead a charge of the king's guard against the rebels.

It was Queen Jane who saved the day. She urged her white palfry a few steps forward until she had barely to lean in her saddle to rest a delicate hand on Henry's shoulder. "But, my lord, they are but humble men. And they did speak dutifully of Your Grace. Is not the closing of the monasteries a much greater hardship on them than on others? Should not you be gentle with your more backward children?"

Henry had always seen himself as the great father-figure of his people. He was mollified. Besides, it was far pleasanter to remain here with Jane and make the heir that the country—or the Tudor dynasty—so desperately needed, than to go rushing off to the uncivilized north. Henry looked around at his court and councilors. His eye lit on Thomas Howard, the Duke of Norfolk, newly returned from self-imposed political exile since the fall of his niece—the Bullen Witch. "Thomas, see to this for us. Take who you will from court." Henry's small, bright eyes ranged over the faces before him. "Take him, and him, and him." Giles knew that the king didn't even know his name. Most likely the bright yellow feather in his cap had caught Henry's eye, and so Giles was to go to Yorkshire.

It was two and a half weeks later that Norfolk, with a small armed and well-mounted band at his back, arrived in Yorkshire. All the way north they had received reports. Aske had taken York. Archbishop Lee of York had joined with the rebels, and Lord Darcy, Baron of Templehurst, also. By now the rebel numbers were thirty thousand. And Giles knew that one among those thirty thousand was Diccon Marston whom he loved like a brother. He felt the smooth wood of the bow he wore slung over his shoulder. Could he fire into the rebel mob if he were ordered, knowing that it might be his arrow that pierced his friend? Far better if Diccon's shaft reached him instead.

They met at Pontefract Bridge, Henry's hundreds facing the rebel thousands. Norfolk rode forth alone and drew rein in the middle of the bridge. Aske, after what appeared to be a controversy with Lord Darcy, which the lawyer must have won, rode onto the bridge to meet Norfolk. "What is this? Why do you good folk rise against your loving king?" Norfolk spoke in a voice that addressed not only Aske but also the troops, close-packed along the north bank of the river.

Aske, likewise, answered in a voice that would send his message to more ears than Norfolk's. "We do not rise against the king's grace. We are but a band of pilgrims making our way to petition the king."

"And what would you ask of your king?"

"That His Grace would shed his evil, heretical advisors and ease a return to the better days when it was merry in England." The troops behind Aske cheered. Giles carefully scanned Aske's mounted men and thought he made out a tall, thin form that might be Diccon, but he wasn't sure.

"Fellow subjects, wise men and true to your good King Henry, hear me," Norfolk shouted to the rebels. "Your king has no desire to fight you. Lay down your arms. Go to your homes where your wives and daughters await you with open arms and warmed ale. Your king will give ear to your desires." He gestured to the pilgrim leader in his white tunic with its red gash in the side representing the soldier's sword-cut into Christ's side on the cross. "Let Master Aske here choose two hundred of his finest men. Treat with me at Pontefract Castle. We will hear you. Henry of England will hear you."

Aske turned to his banner-bearer and nearest men. In a few minutes he was back to Norfolk. "We will treat." The banner of St. Cuthbert dipped in a signal of dispersal to the troops, and a great shout went up from both sides of the bridge.

Giles and the others followed Norfolk on across the bridge and up the path toward Pontefract where the royal emissaries would spend the night in the castle formerly held by the rebels. They had ridden about halfway through the dispersing pilgrims when Giles sighted the one person among those thousands he longed to see. Now he needed an excuse to leave Norfolk. Thinking fast, he remembered Humphrey's ruse that had once lured him far from court. "My Lord Norfolk, may I beg your indulgence for leave?"

Norfolk frowned at him suspiciously. His look asked why anyone would want to go among these rebels.

"I have a long-time acquaintance with, er—, a fair friend who lives in this neighborhood."

Norfolk threw his head back and laughed. "Ah! And if she has fair sisters, send you them to Pontefract, for the night grows cold!"

Giles returned Norfolk's leer and rode off quickly before the duke could change his mind. After all, Diccon had the fairest hair he had ever seen. It took Giles some time before he could find Diccon again because his friend had ridden a distance toward the village with the band he commanded. After exchanging warm greetings both men looked around uncertainly. The night, as Norfolk had said, was indeed coming on cold. They did not relish sleeping in a haystack, and the meager village inn would long ago have been filled to the rafters.

"We could go to St. Swithin's Monastery," Diccon suggested. "It's a pity the Marston lands are too far north. I would fain return the welcome your family gave me at Layford, but the ride to Swithin's is far enough."

Indeed, the brothers had finished Compline when they arrived, but the porter took them swiftly to the hospitaler. He apologized that he could give them no more than cold meat, bread, and ale at that hour, but was happy to say that the sheets had been aired that day, so he could offer them a dry bed. When the white-robed figure had gone, Giles threw himself on the bench before the small fire the monk had built for them. "Lucky for us this house hasn't been suppressed."

Diccon laughed. "But, my friend, it has."

Giles looked around him at the mellow wainscotted walls, the fresh rushes on the floor, the fur pillows on the guest bed. He took a sip of the hearty ale he had been served. "It doesn't appear to be much dissolved."

Diccon explained, "When the people decided to protest the closing of our monasteries, many of the dispersed brothers banded together again and returned to their houses. This is one such. Did I endanger your position by bringing you here?"

Giles laughed. "My position is not worth a thought, but if it were, I'm in no danger. I have leave." He told Diccon about Humphrey's excuse for meeting with the Lutheran farmer and how he had just used a similar tack.

Diccon grew serious. "But I do not see how my brother could have been a Lutheran. I suppose it is as well he died of the sweat; it spared his burning at the stake. But what of his soul now? What of the soul of any who die without the true faith?"

Giles shook his head and chewed slowly on a thick crust of bread. "Who's to say which faith is true now? But I cannot think that beheadings and burnings in the name of faith can be pleasing to the One who said 'Blessed are the peacemakers.' Perhaps we have hope in Queen Jane, though. She is a Lutheran, and yet she would have stayed the king's hand against your papist rebels out there. Perhaps if the queen sets a pattern of love and charity, the country may follow."

It was a hopeful sentiment to hold to through the cold days that followed, as the wind whipped snow across the Yorkshire moors and all awaited the outcome of Norfolk's council. But on a gray December day when the northmen set their final demands before the king's men, Giles knew he had been too hopeful. The demands of the pilgrims touched every phase of national life, and all ran counter to the king's policy. They asked for punishment of the heretical bishops—beginning with Cranmer. They asked for punishment of the wicked ministers of the king—beginning with Cromwell. They asked for the suppression of the heretical books—beginning with the English Bible. They asked for the preservation and reopening of the suppressed monasteries as centers of religious life and for their social value. They asked for the repeal of the Act of Supremacy. And they asked for much more.

Norfolk made a show of accepting all. "My good people, I will take this to His Majesty." Giles could not join in the northerners' rejoicing, for he knew that Norfolk's instructions from the king had been to let the pilgrims talk themselves into a false security.

In the new year all knew how false the security had been, for the executions began. It was well known that the queen had argued clemency for the pilgrims, and the king would deny her nothing—for she was with child. Nothing, that is, except clemency for the rebels. As the somber months of 1537 progressed, so did the tally of those put to death—more than one hundred fifty lords and knights (including old Lord Darcy), half a dozen abbots, thirty-eight monks, and sixteen parish priests. And, last of all, Robert Aske was hanged at York on July 12, bringing the total to two hundred sixteen.

Giles worried constantly over whether Diccon's name was on that grisly roll. But he dared not inquire too closely for fear of bringing danger to his friend, and he could get no leave to travel north himself.

But then began the next series of executions, calling for long hours and ink-stained fingers from every available clerk. Giles was kept so busy he had little time for worry save over the present disasters. Henry, undoubtedly at Cromwell's urging, was not satisfied with demolishing the pilgrims. He would also demolish their religious houses. All of them. Not merely the lesser houses whose closure was required by Parliament, but the large houses as well: Jervaulx, the great Cistercian house in the North Riding, Whalley in Lancashire, then Kirkstead and Barlings in Lincolnshire, and Bridlington on its rocky ledge over the North Sea. This time the matter was more ominous, more final, for there was no question of moving the brothers to other houses of their choice. They were given a tiny pension approaching five pounds a year and turned out. The valuables in the houses were carted to London, the lead stripped from their roofs and melted down for cannon, and the property sold to the highest bidder, usually a neighboring farmer who wished to add rich land to his estate and use the stones of the roofless walls to build new barns.

Giles, with many of the clerks and court officials, knew that the rebellion was only an excuse for the forfeiture. In some cases, such as Jervaulx, the order to dispose of abbey properties had been given even before their abbot came to trial for his treasonous sympathy with the pilgrims.

As in all times, money was the root of evil behavior. Henry's coffers were virtually empty, and gaining possession of the lands of the dissolved monasteries switched the balance of economic power from the miter to the Crown. The stones of many an ancient abbey and cloister could be used to build fortifications along the channel.

With aching fingers and burning eyes, Giles lighted a new candle from his guttering one before beginning a new ledger page. Then he listed the items in the latest cart load of church plate to be added to the royal treasury. And he wondered how long it would be until greed drove those in power to look further south to far richer houses.

11

ut then all such gloomy questions were whisked away in a blaze of rejoicing, for at long last Henry had a son, a healthy, living son. Two days later, Giles squeezed into the king's gallery of the Chapel Royal at Hampton Court and looked down on the colorful panoply of lords and ladies gathered for the christening. The nobles' gold chains glimmered over their slashed velvet coats in the blazing candlelight, and their ladies shimmered in pearled caps and wide-skirted gowns of sumptuous damask.

The organ pealed from its loft above the choir, and the procession entered. The tiny, newborn infant in a christening gown that dragged the floor was carried in the arms of Lady Exeter. Next came his godparents and half-sisters—the soberly dressed Mary and the barely four-year-old Princess Elizabeth, her red hair bobbing in the glowing light as she was carried by the queen's younger brother, Thomas Seymour. Then, striding with great pride, Henry of England, eighth of that name, clad in richest scarlet and cloth of gold, barely restrained himself from waving in triumph to his loyal subjects. Beside the king, carried on a pallet from her childbirth bed, was Queen Jane, looking even paler than her pearl-white gown and cap. The crimson slashes of her ermine-trimmed sleeves provided the only color about her.

The king and queen took their seats in the royal pew, and the infant and his godparents proceeded to the high altar where Archbishop Cranmer waited in white vestments and gold miter. The archbishop prayed that the child might be baptized with water and the Holy Ghost and received into Christ's holy church.

Giles noted that Mary, staunch and faithful daughter of the church of Rome, looked straight ahead and did not acknowledge this new prayer of Cranmer's. Little Elizabeth, with a dignity beyond her years, sat on the hard bench, barely kicking her feet. But while Henry seemed to grow larger and brighter as the lengthy ceremony proceeded, the queen seemed to sink more and more deeply into the cushions of her chair, until it was almost impossible to distinguish her from the white fur pillows. Cranmer continued, "We receive this child, Edward, into the congregation of Christ's flock and do sign him with the sign of the cross." The archbishop made a cross on the child's forehead. "In token that hereafter he shall not be ashamed to confess the faith of Christ crucified and manfully to fight under His banner against sin, the world, and the devil and to continue Christ's faithful soldier and servant unto his life's end. Amen."

The organ pealed again, to be joined by a great ringing of bells, and the sleeping infant and his exhausted mother could be carried from the chapel, followed by the grand assemblage.

The child flourished. But within the week Jane was dead.

Henry mourned.

Always one to do things to the extreme, Henry took his grief out on everyone and everything around him. He swung from periods of absolute isolation where not even Cromwell or his closest ministers could reach him, to craving mad revels and lavish entertainments where he would laugh louder, sing longer, dance faster (in spite of the sore on his leg), and eat more (as many as six capons at a sitting) than anyone else at court. Then he would go from this frenzy of revels to bouts of black anger where he would rage at councilors, at courtiers, and at God. It seemed that no matter which of his moods prevailed, over all there was a desire to smash things as Henry felt his world had been smashed. Never had there been a more propitious time for Cromwell to move forward with his own agenda to wipe every trace of the church of Rome from English soil, including the remaining monasteries.

An important new precedent had been set since the fall of the great houses of Jervaulx, Whalley, Kirkstead, Barlings, and Bridlington. The abbot of the Cistercian Abbey of Furness in Cumbria knew that there were no grounds on which a charge of treason could be brought against him, but he realized that such legal niceties would be no barrier to Cromwell. The abbot simply agreed to execute a deed voluntarily transferring all abbey properties to the king. This had been the first voluntary surrender of a monastery, but Cromwell was determined that it not be the last. He had no carte blanche from Parliament to close the larger monasteries, but if he could simply force them to surrender, Parliament could be bypassed and all the power and money placed directly in Henry's hands.

And the common people learned quickly. Leaving the drudgery of their fields to help the royal commissioners strip the great buildings and throw relics on the great blazing bonfires could be better fun than any holiday. As soon as the commissioners had carted off all they wanted from the dissolved monasteries, the deserted buildings were free picking for looters. Soon the people were outstripping the commissioners.

As more and more surrenders took place, it became increasingly difficult for the remaining houses to stand against Cromwell. Yet Glastonbury held. With each passing day of that ice-drizzling winter, Giles dreaded the order that would take him to Glastonbury. He sometimes had nightmares of a great bonfire licking the golden stones of the Lady Chapel while frenzied villagers danced about like ancient savages, destroying, trampling, killing . . . and he would wake in a sweat and pray that the order would not come that day.

And his prayers were granted until a blustery day in March of 1538.

Whiting welcomed the dark-haired messenger who had always shown himself to be a friend of Glastonbury. But the abbot's hand trembled as he took Cromwell's letter. The wording was reassuring enough on the surface, but the hidden message was clear. The letter stressed the free and voluntary nature of such surrenders as had taken place and disclaimed any intention of forcing anyone to act. Between the lines, Whiting read, "The other abbots surrendered without undue fuss. Why don't you behave as a loyal subject and surrender your house?"

With a wordless nod Whiting dismissed Giles and sat alone at his table. Vespers had been sung. Prior Robert would have to act as host at the abbot's table for their supper guests. Whiting needed to be alone.

How much longer could he hold out? At times he could close his eyes and think how easy it would be—just write a short letter. Perhaps two words would do: *Glastonbury surrenders*. The messenger was here. The document could be in London within the week. Then the struggle would be over. The financial struggle—just the weight of bills to meet their daily needs in this time of rising inflation and falling incomes would be excuse enough, not to mention the pressure for "gifts" to be sent to London. Why not just make a gift of the whole abbey and be done with it? And the political struggle—the commissioners, inspections, directives that made his life ever more impossible, the fear of the next act of Parliament, the next royal decree. Whiting had celebrated his eightieth birthday. Was it not honorable for a man to lay aside his burdens by such an age?

But worst of all was the spiritual struggle—if he had been right in signing the Act of Supremacy and recognizing the king as his spiritual head, was he right to stand out against the royal will by retaining his office and his monastery? Or, if he had been wrong, as his careful conscience sometimes fretted him, was he right then to continue in a position in which he himself was giving false guidance to his flock?

He would have prayed, but no words would come. So he crossed himself and sat in the dimming light of his small parlor without bothering to light a candle. The darkness that filled the room seemed to reflect the darkness that covered the whole nation. Corruption in government was a terrible thing, but there was a thing far worse. When the priests whose job it was to correct the king became corrupt, there was no hope for the land. This was a fatal disease—a disease from which a land could not be cured. Only mourning remained. Had England reached such a state?

What of himself? He thought of the words of Jeremiah mourning over Israel, "Behold, I will feed them with wormwood and make them drink the water of gall; for from the prophets of Jerusalem is profaneness gone forth into all the land." If he took the easy way of surrender, would he become part of the corruption?

Whiting walked from his lodgings and slowly, thoughtfully made his way up the steep green slopes of the Tor. It was lighter here than it had been in his room, and the last rays of a red and gold sunset reflected on the western side of the hill. Ewes heavy with lambs tottered along the winding path, grazing a few mouthfuls of spring grass. At the little stone chapel on top Whiting sat and rubbed his stiff, aching knees through his robe. This was not a climb he made often anymore.

Bells rang for Compline, and from cloister and monk's hall, all across the enclosed grounds, dark-robed figures moved in obedient order toward the abbey. It was all so peaceful. It was all just as it had been for hundreds of years, many said since the time of St. Patrick.

This peace, this order, this continuation of the heritage of the past—this was England. And this was worth holding on for. This he would not surrender.

The chanted Latin words of the evening prayer reached Whiting, who knew it well enough to pray with them, "Lighten our darkness, we beseech Thee, O Lord; and by Thy great mercy defend us from all perils and dangers of this night; for the love of Thy only son, our Savior, Jesus Christ. Amen."

As if of their own volition, Whiting's feet carried him toward the abbey and the brotherhood of prayer.

"O God, make speed to save us."

"O Lord, make haste to help us."

Whiting's heart cried out for the help he knew he would need in the coming days. Tired as he was, he increased his pace. *The Sacrament,* he thought. *Christ Himself will be there in the Sacrament.* Whiting needed Christ—needed to see Him, needed to be with Him.

The next morning, carrying the circular letter addressed to all abbots to Wells, Giles set out early that he might dispose of his commission and be free to visit Cecily. She came to meet him, hands outstretched, welcoming smile lighting her face. And all seemed better on the estate of Robert Burgess, for the men were back at work, finishing up his fine, expensive new buildings. "The credit of the Abbot of Glastonbury was finally decided to be good enough, even for the likes of Master Fulke—although he grumbles enough." Cecily laughed and drew Giles forward.

But Giles had little time to bask in the warmth of Cecily's welcome and of Dame Margery's hospitality. Margery had just ordered a barrel of fresh oysters opened and a peck of last autumn's apples to be taken from their tray of sand, when they were interrupted by the clatter of a new-arrived horseman. Giles's green-doubleted servant was shown into the parlor.

"Luke! Did not I leave you work enough in London but that you must traipse across half the country after me?" Giles barely hid his agitation.

"It is a letter from Layford, Master Giles. I thought you should have it apace." Luke held out the folded sheet of heavy paper sealed with Peter's seal, but not inscribed by Peter's hand.

"Use my solar if you would read it in peace," Dame Margery offered. But Giles had no secrets from those he would have for family. When he had broken the seal, he saw there was little need for privacy, but great need for enlightenment. Megotty's spidery handwriting simply implored him, "Please come."

He showed it to Cecily, his disappointment at being torn from her so soon too great for words. Her large blue eyes clouded with a kindred disappointment. "And so you must go," she said.

He went. On the afternoon of the second day Giles and Luke rode into the familiar gates of Layford. At first flush all seemed the same—buildings, fields, servants, animals. It was not until Giles entered the warm, old-fashioned hall and Megotty greeted him gravely that he realized much was amiss. The air hung heavy as with whispered words. The servants' smiles seemed forced and uncertain. Giles had the uneasy feeling he was being watched, as if spies lurked behind the arras. When he inquired as to the whereabouts of their brother, Meg gave an evasive answer. Then he noticed her uneasy glance at his servant standing respectfully by the door.

"Luke, see to the horses. It may be that my brother's grooms would be glad of a hand." Luke left, and Giles turned to Megotty. "Odds, heartling, you cannot suspect Luke of treachery? What's amiss that you sent me such a summons?"

Now Megotty threw herself into Giles's arms like old times, but without the light-hearted joy. "Giles, Giles. I don't know whom to trust. I said nothing in the letter because I didn't know what would be safe to put in writing, and I knew you would come if I needed you."

"Of course." He drew her to a bench by the fireplace, for her hands were cold. "I would always come. But I could be of more help if I understood why."

Again she hesitated. Giles turned at the sound of a footstep behind him.

"Diccon!" He sprang to his feet and clasped his friend in an enormous hug. "I feared you were dead!"

"And so I would have been if Margaret hadn't hidden me these many months from Cromwell's spies."

"You've been here since the Pilgrimage?"

Diccon nodded. "I did not intend to impose so on your hospitality, but Cromwell has seized our lands, and I didn't know where else to go . . . besides," a slight flush added to the sparkle in his eyes as he said, "your Megotty has made me as welcome as you said she would."

Giles turned to his sister and saw a tender look in her face as she gazed at Diccon. "So, that is how it is! But what do you mean Cromwell has your lands? On what grounds? You've not been tried?"

"Cromwell claims Praemunire—that our aged father is not a loyal subject because he has taken in two monks from the suppressed monasteries. They had no place else to go." He gave a bitter laugh. "At least it would not be so unfair if it were on grounds of the son of the house being a rebel, but that fact mercifully seems to have escaped Cromwell's spies—as has the son. But it leaves us in a doubly awkward position."

Giles frowned his lack of understanding, but Megotty soon made it clear. "We would have you bless us—that is, I would have it. Diccon will not ask because he has no property, but he cannot stop my asking."

Giles threw back his head and laughed. "What has happened to the modesty of English women?" But having so recently argued the other side for himself and so gladly lost, he clasped their hands together. "With all my heart I give you my blessing. Or, at least, I would if it were my place to give it. Do you forget that I am but your third brother, Megotty?"

The sudden silence reminded Giles of the secretive atmosphere of the house, and he knew that Diccon's presence and the betrothal question were not all that hung in the air. "There is more you have not told me."

Diccon excused himself and left the room. Although they were alone in the hall, Megotty leaned forward and spoke softly. "Peter and Edward are abroad. Ellen and I care for Layford, although, in truth, Diccon has done most."

"Abroad?" Giles waited for an explanation.

"In Italy with Cardinal Pole," Megotty whispered. "There is much you must know. I know little enough myself, and Diccon nothing, for I will not let him—he has risked enough and lost enough already."

"Do you know enough to tell me what is going on?" Giles asked his sister.

"No, but you are not our only guest. Let him explain." When the tall, brown-bearded man in the rich olive coat strode forward, Giles knew why he had felt the walls had ears. Giles pursed his lips, trying to identify the man. He knew he had seen him at court in earlier days. A powerful lord that he somehow identified with the west, but he could not recall the name.

"Henry Courtenay," the newcomer introduced himself and held out a large, strong hand to Giles. Then Giles remembered—the Marquis of Exeter, the most influential nobleman in the West Country—the only courtier allowed to enter Henry's chamber without being summoned, for they had been brought up together. And he was cousin to Reginald Pole, that brilliant and much-admired scion of the house of Plantagenet. Much admired by many and much feared by those who, like Henry himself, saw the Plantagenet line as a threat to the Tudor dynasty. Henry's father had wrested the crown from a Plantagenet.

"Your brothers are in Italy with my cousin." He paused and looked Giles straight in the eyes as if to give special import to his next words. "I like well the proceedings of the Cardinal Pole."

Giles did not know what to answer. Was he being invited to join the secret papist sympathizers at court? He often disagreed with Henry; he almost always despised Cromwell; he was again and again invited to join those who would work against them . . . and he was tempted. But he would not. He would not work against his sovereign, no matter how despicable his advisors, and he would not work against the Reformed faith, no matter how much he admired those who held to the old ways. For he saw too much good in the new ways—if they were not drowned in the excesses of fanatics who would go too far too fast.

Exeter saw his hesitancy. "I see you are not ready. But I know the heads of your brothers and others of our party are in safekeeping with you. Let me ask another question. Would you help the Abbot of Glastonbury?"

Here there was no hesitation. "With all my heart!" Then Giles paused. "Is he of your party?"

"No." Exeter shook his head. "But we would protect him and others like him. So now I ask a hard thing of you. Knaves rule about the king. Go you back to court. Be ears for your friend Whiting. Use your position."

This was not the first time such had been asked of him. Was it Humphrey who first asked it? It seemed that he had been of little enough use then. Was the whole country full of nothing but spies? Cromwell's spy network was famous for its efficiency. Diccon had spied for the northerners. His brothers spied for Pole and Exeter. Now he too was to spy. But he would do it for Glastonbury.

Yet when the conspiracy came to a head, though Giles was in the vortex of it, there was little he could do but watch events unfold.

It was late when Giles put away his pen. He had spent all day in a small room in Whitehall making copies of Cromwell's correspondence with the House of Cleves, whence Cromwell was prospecting for another bride for Henry. Since Duke William of Cleves was the leader of the Protestants of western Germany, Cromwell considered the duke's sister Anne a most appropriate bride for his king. Henry himself showed little interest and did not bother to get angry when he heard that Francis I would not allow the ladies of his family to be lined up like brood mares for inspection by Henry's councilors. And he did not bother replying when it reached his ears that the Duchess of Milan had remarked that if only she had two necks, she would gladly put one of them at the disposal of the King of England. Wondering what would become of Cromwell's latest ambitions, Giles went out into the corridor just in time to see a handsome, aristocratic man being marched at double time down the torch-lit hall.

In the morning the news was all over court. Sir Geoffrey, younger brother to Reginald Pole, had been arrested. Little persuasion was needed to make him turn traitor. "A conspiracy on the lines of the Pilgrimage of Grace," was the alarm passed from one eagerly listening courtier to the next.

"Cardinal Pole had been touring the courts of Europe's Catholic monarchs for Pope Paul III to form an alliance against Henry."

"Lord Montagu, Sir Edward Neville, Lord Delawarr, Lady Salisbury . . ." The list of named conspirators went on and on. Giles held his breath and listened. Nowhere did he hear the Lacey name. But there were others he knew. Lady Exeter, who had once been Queen Catherine's faithful serving lady, had apparently been supplying the Spanish ambassador with lively reports that evidenced acute powers of observation. And Lord Exeter, whom Giles had come within a hair's breadth of joining, was already in the Tower. The charge was that he and others had been in contact with Reginald Pole, who took the side of the king's enemy, the Bishop of Rome.

But the fear that gripped the court far outstripped any mere papist leanings or correspondence with those at foreign courts. In a sort of frenzy nobles and servants alike pictured the courts of Europe arming in a crusade against England under the banner of the Holy Roman Empire. Visions of shiploads of armored men sailing the channel like something unseen since the Roman days filled even the less imaginative minds. It was not enough that the conspirators be locked in the Tower and executed. England must prepare for war. Fortifications all along her coastlines must be strengthened. More war ships must be built. And Henry needed money.

When he became king, Henry had hoped—even vowed—never to call a Parliament to ask for money. He refused to stand before the peers of his realm with cap in hand as he had had to beg from his parsimonious father when he was a child. No, he had determined, he would find other sources of income.

But it had not worked out like that. In the course of his many years he had had to go to Parliament for money—primarily to supply his troops for threatened war with France in the past. He had humbled himself and asked. But Henry disliked humbling himself. He did not want to ask again.

So Cromwell sent agents to forage for the royal treasury. Giles, thankfully spared from being sent on this mission, was only required to copy the orders for the agents. They were to see to all the bigger churches and gather "superfluous plate."

He entered into the ledger books many of the results of their diligence, including "a super altar garnished with silver gilt and part gold, called the Great Sapphire of Glastonbury." But even that was not enough. Sir Brian Tuke, Treasurer of the Chamber, told Cromwell in strictest confidence—which became general knowledge before Tuke had left Cromwell's chamber—that the treasury was virtually empty.

Amid the alarms of war and the fears of national bankruptcy, the trials of the Exeter conspirators went on. It was often asked how the conspirators with homes in different parts of the land had kept in touch. Certainly correspondence would have been far too dangerous for the usual channels. At last the turncoat Sir Geoffrey told. Their letters had been carried by a blind wandering minstrel.

Giles recalled the long-ago day when William Moore, harp slung over his shoulder in a leather bag, had said he was going to Exeter. Giles had thought he meant the town. And where else had Moore gone? With a cold tingle down his spine, Giles remembered. He had first met Moore at Glastonbury, and there had been casual reference to the minstrel singing at other monasteries. The names of Reading and Colchester came to Giles's mind. Was it possible that their abbots, desiring a return to the ways of the Old Faith, had been sympathetic to the conspirators? Exeter had clearly stated that Whiting was not involved, and Giles believed that with all his heart. Whiting was not a man for political conspiracy. The abbots of Reading and Colchester he knew little about except their reputations for being godly men who ran well-ordered houses. But would Cromwell believe that?

With a cloud of anxiety darkening over his head, Giles recalled Cromwell's skepticism a few weeks earlier when Whiting had written to the Vicar-General begging his pardon that ill health prevented the abbot's attending the House of Lords. If Cromwell had been unconvinced of the validity of Whiting's excuse then, what would he now think about the loyalties of the Abbot of Glastonbury?

It was not long until Giles knew. A routine matter took him into Cromwell's room. Later he could not even recall what message he had been carrying when, finding the room empty, he placed the document on Cromwell's table and saw the open memorandum book, the black ink glaring at him from its white pages: "Proceed against the abbots of Reading, Glaston, and the others, in their own counties."

12

hat evening Giles's orders arrived from Cromwell. He didn't even have to open them. He knew. He was to go to Glastonbury with Layton. "Someday you will be asked to do something that will spell death to your conscience. What will you do then?" Cecily's words were as fresh in his memory as if she had just spoken.

His first impulse was to tear the order from top to bottom and resign his post. Or would it be better simply to leave? Send Luke to the stable to saddle Brigante and ride away into clean, sunlit air from this labyrinth of conspiracy? No, he would simply be dragged back and probably tried on some charge or other himself. Should he make an excuse and beg permission to leave? Illness—his own or someone in his family? Any excuse he could think of sounded dangerously flimsy.

Then he heard again the Duke of Exeter's words, "Would you help the Abbot of Glastonbury? . . . Go back to court . . . Use your position . . ." Giles knew what he must do. He could not see how he could help Whiting. He could not see how anyone could help the abbot now that Cromwell's decision had been made. But Giles was determined to try.

The clock of Glastonbury Abbey had just struck ten of the morning, and the last vibrations had faded from the bell pealing for High Mass when Giles followed Layton and his fellow-inspectors Pollard and Moyle into the monastery. It had rained lightly all morning, and now a crystal bead clung to the tip of each September-gold leaf on every tree. Clung momentarily, then fell to the ground to become part of the never-ending chain of replenishing the earth.

The porter informed them that Whiting had gone to one of the monastery's granges two miles away. Layton did not even ride on into the enclosure, but spun his heavy black horse and rode off for Beckery. Giles desperately searched his mind for an idea. Layton's fierce, dark looks and harshly set jaw left little doubt as to his purpose in pursuing Whiting so relentlessly. If only Giles could think of some excuse to leave and ride ahead to warn Whiting. Perhaps he could plead a stone in his horse's shoe and then ride fast another route to the grange. But even if he knew the way, the ground was flat and open, and Layton would see him. Besides, Layton was traveling at a pace that would be hard to beat.

Outside the ancient stone and timber building, Layton banged with resounding thuds on the heavy wooden gate. He was admitted by an aged lay brother in a dusty black robe. "See to our horses," Layton commanded and strode up the stairs to the hall, across the oak-planked floor, and to the gallery at the end where the abbot's private rooms were sure to be. Layton flung the chamber door open without knocking.

At first Giles sighed with relief. The room was empty. Then they saw the still, white figure kneeling at the prie-dieu in the corner. A shaft of dim light fell through the oiled parchment window and made a halo of the white tonsure. Whiting, wearing the simple white robe he would have worn had he been celebrating mass at the abbey, stood at the noise of their interruption, leaning heavily on the prayer rail to ease his rheumatic knees. "You have need of me?"

His unflinching eyes registered his recognition of Layton. There was no surprise on his face. Giles would have cried out an apology when their eyes met, but the old gray-blue eyes held him in check. Anything he could say would only increase the danger to both of them.

Before Layton could bark his orders, Whiting asked, "May I finish my prayers?"

"Prayers to a papist God will do you no good."

Whiting was allowed to pack a small bag with Layton watching his every move. Giles hoped, prayed even, that he would be allowed to escort Whiting—perhaps here was the service he could do him—give him an opportunity to escape. But it was not to be. Layton turned with all speed, and they were off again before Giles could utter a single word of comfort. The hardest part to bear was the feeling that Whiting understood, understood and forgave all.

The first step of his commission accomplished, Layton led the way back to Glastonbury with no slacking of pace. It was as if, embarrassed by the good report he had given Glastonbury four years earlier, he was now bent on expunging all such ideas from the record. There would be nothing laudatory reported from Glastonbury this time.

It took less than four hours. Whiting sat silent in the small chair from his table pushed into a corner. He remained with hands folded still in his lap, a look of calm on his face. Giles stood at uncomfortable attention, holding quill and notebook, ready to write at Layton's orders. There was little to be thankful for in this situation, but at least he could be grateful that he was not the one required to search through Whiting's personal papers and turn out all the chests and baskets containing his belongings. But if Giles had been the one to do it, he would have done it with more respect and less disorder. He flinched as he saw Whiting's neat stacks of papers spread across the room in disarray and valuable books tumbled in a pile.

Pollard found the first piece of incriminating evidence. He handed it to Layton with a grin. Layton looked over the document and then approached

Whiting with glittering eyes. "What's this, my Lord Abbot? You dare to harbor treasonous material which speaks against His Majesty's conscience?"

Whiting obviously had no idea what the dusty parchment sheet contained. He reached out to read it, but Layton snatched it beyond his grasp. "Arguments against the royal divorce. Have you forgotten? No doubt, or you would have destroyed so dangerous a document. No loyal subject would own such a thing." He leaned over Whiting until the abbot could surely feel his breath. "No loyal subject would have such in his possession. So why do you, Richard Whiting?"

Whiting was silent.

Layton himself found the final piece of evidence. "Ah, this will do nicely."

Giles could not stop himself before he asked, "Do what?"

"Convict Whiting."

Fortunately Layton was too involved in his own triumph to hear Giles's anguished cry, "No!"

"A printed life of Thomas à Becket!" Layton exulted. "An archbishop who placed serving the Pope above serving his king. Do you do likewise, Master Whiting? Would you serve the Bishop of Rome rather than King Henry? Let us see if following Becket's example will not lead to a similar end."

And with no more evidence than that, Whiting was dispatched to London to be questioned by Cromwell. Moyle and two of Layton's servants gave little pretense that they served as escort rather than arresting officers.

And through the coming days Giles sat at the abbot's own desk, forced to record similar signs of Whiting's treason. "Write to my Lord Cromwell," Layton dictated, "that Glastonbury is the finest house we have ever seen, meet only for the king. No loyal subject could hold such against his king's grace. All occupants here are unworthy. They are men meanly learned. There is not a single monk with a Doctorate and only three Bachelors." He paused to growl at Giles. "Why do you stop? Write what I say!"

"But, Master Layton, that is not correct. Richard Whiting himself has a Doctorate." Giles pointed to the Latin-inscribed parchment made from highest quality sheepskin on the wall near Whiting's table. "See there, 'Richard Whiting, Doctor of Theology, 1505, Cambridge University,'" he translated.

"I know what that says. Do you not think I read Latin? But Whiting is no longer an occupant here. By now he is an occupant of the Tower unless Moyle has dawdled."

The search went on. They left no cellar sealed; they stripped loose wainscotting from walls, dismounted embroidered arras hangings from their pegs, and turned out every chest in the monastery.

With mounting gloom, Giles recorded their findings—a gold chalice, a gem-studded cross, a pair of silver candlesticks . . . "Hidden, no doubt, to thwart the king's collectors of superfluous plate! Well done, Pollard. This would be evidence enough if we had no other."

"But," Giles protested again, "there is no evidence the abbot did it. They were not hidden in his lodging. Would it not more likely be the work of the treasurer or sacristan responsible for keeping such objects?"

For a moment Layton's face clouded, and Giles thought that at last he had scored. But the frown was replaced with an even broader smile. "Not in the least! Pollard—check with these good brothers in case others may think as Master Lacey here. But I am sure they will deny all knowledge of hidden plate. I can tell you the real meaning of what we have found. No brother in this house will have knowledge of it, I assure you. Whiting hid it away with his own hand to rob his own church!"

The search went on beyond the walls of the enclosure to all the Twelve Hides. At night the commissioners arrived back at their rooms in the George and Pilgrim excited by what they had seen. They charged Giles with writing all their impressions. Layton dictated late into the night so that a servant might ride in the morning to carry the good news to London. And Giles, feeling more and more a Judas with every word he penned, could find no service he could do Whiting, could find no justification for the actions thrust upon him.

When he had been at Glastonbury one week, Giles received a visitor. Her cheeks flushed, her eyes blazing, Cecily stormed into Layton's private dining room at the inn where Giles sat at the table copying out a letter. "What is going on? They tell me my uncle is taken to London! And we are not notified?"

Giles would have rushed to take her in his arms and comfort her, but the blaze of her fury kept him at bay. "Indeed, I longed to come to you, but I had hoped to wait until I had better news."

"Better news? And think you that the news will get better?" For a moment the anger flickered with hope.

"I had hoped to tell you in a few days that your uncle was returned, rather than that he had been taken."

"And you are gathering here evidence for his defense?" It was a taunt. She knew the truth.

"Cecily, I would give anything I possess if I could tell you that were true. But they twist everything—no matter how I try."

"And how do you try? Do you defend my uncle? Or do you record matters that will send him to the block?"

"Cecily—I want to help him—"

"Do you deny that is Cromwell's purpose?"

"Cromwell's purpose is not my purpose. I—"

"A man cannot serve two masters." She turned to the door, a heavy sadness replacing the fire of her former fury. She turned once more. "Choose you this day whom you would serve." And then she was gone.

Her words haunted Giles for days. "Choose you . . . choose you." But that was the problem. There was no choice. If it were only a matter of making up his mind, that he had done long ago. The question was—how could he serve Whiting? How could he find a way of peace and truth? Was there any path of tolerance open in the land?

And as he wrestled with these questions, his orders from Layton became yet more distasteful. "The brothers are to be turned out."

"Turned out? You are evicting the monks while their abbot is in London? Do you have that power?"

"My Lord Cromwell has that power. I represent him here."

But what if Whiting is found innocent? Giles wanted to ask. Yet he knew the futility of that idea, so instead he asked, "But what will become of them?"

Layton smiled magnanimously. "Our policy is not a harsh one. They will be given a pension. Many from other houses have been happy enough for their freedom."

"Freedom?"

"Certainly. Many monks have married likewise freed nuns and settled down to happy country lives."

Yes, Giles had heard that was the case. And for the ones who were happy, that was fine. But what of the rest? There was now no option of being moved to another house, for the ruse of pruning a rose garden had long ago been abandoned.

So the next morning Giles, feeling more and more helpless, took part in dismissing the abbey servants and moving the monks from their cells. They had little enough to pack. It took little time. Giles tried to stay busy in the dorter so as to avoid the haunted, lost look in the monks' eyes. The first to finish was William Benet. With his Oxford degree and clear knowledge of the law, he would have little trouble finding a position in a lawyer's office in London. Apparently that was what he had in mind as he asked, "Who is going to walk to London? I would be happy of good companionship."

Giles was amazed at how calmly the dispersion took place. Of course, they had been sworn to obedience and trained in it by years of practicing the Rule. And this could not be a total surprise. They knew what had happened all over the land. Perhaps some had even made arrangements for the eventuality. Giles hoped so.

Brother Dunstan, with a rush basket filled to the brim with possets and salves from his beloved infirmary, accepted Brother William's offer. "Perhaps a hospital in London will be in need of my services. There is much talk of turning some suppressed monasteries into hospitals. Should that happen—" He did not bother finishing, for all knew how forlorn the hope was.

But Brother Joseph clutched at it all the same. "Yes, and schools, they say. I have many years of experience as Master of Boys. Perhaps I too could find a place."

Brother Gildas said nothing about using his experience as hospitaler in an inn, but he picked up his belongings rolled inside his blanket and turned to go with them. They were nearly across the cloister when Brother Arimathea, his sandals shuffling like autumn leaves on the stones, hurried to join them.

Giles turned to the last two remaining in the hall. "And you, have you shelter for the night?"

John Thorne, Brother Arthur, shook his tonsured head and drew his black-robed figure to its full height. "I am subprior. My abbot is in London, my prior sent away. It is my duty to remain. I will go when my Lord Abbot gives me orders. Not before." He went back into his cell and closed the door softly.

Giles turned to the remaining dark figure. "And you, Roger James?" he addressed the one monk younger than himself. He recalled that Brother Roger had come new-professed when Giles brought his first commission to Glastonbury.

"Our boys have not been seen to. Has Layton thought to see to their transportation home—or to any care for them? Would he turn three hundred schoolboys out on the roads to make their own way with autumn storms coming on?"

Giles had no answer for that. Had Layton thought at all about the school?

"I will see to my duty. They will need help with packing and sending messages to their homes."

When Brother Roger left for the other side of the cloister reserved for the schoolboys, Giles found the quiet of the empty dorter almost deafening. For how long had this spot been home to a brotherhood of monks? If the accounts of Joseph of Arimathea were accurate, it would be fifteen hundred years that this place had been a special shrine of prayer. Who would pray now? Who would toll the bells? Who light the candles? Who kneel in the dim-lighted church and chapels where ever the people of this island had approached God?

And what would happen to a land whose government so treated men and women of prayer? There was an inevitable consequence for wrongdoing. Ultimately, the judgment of God would come for this act and for so many like it across the land. If only Whiting were there. If only he could talk to someone who could help him find answers. He thought of knocking on Brother Arthur's closed door, but held back.

Then he heard a strange shuffling in the north cloister and hurried down the night stairs to see what new problem had arisen. He found the rotund Brother Austin attempting to shove a stack of chests, surely several times his own ample weight, across the courtyard toward the gate. He was making little progress. Giles hurried forward to help him, but Layton reached him first. "What is the meaning of this? Would you steal at the peril of your soul?"

"Oh, no! No, no—you mistake the matter. I take nothing for myself. It is against our vows to hold personal property."

"Then what is in here?" Layton kicked a chest.

"Books, sir. Books from the library. But I do not steal. I do not take them for myself. It is my work. I only borrow them to read and make notes. I will return them—"

"And what heresy do you write?"

"None. No heresy, I assure you. I merely record. I am but a simple scribe. I study the stories of old to find meaning in the thoughts and actions of past ages. Abbot Whiting gave me leave—"

"Abbot Whiting is no longer master here. I give you no leave."

"But, but—my work . . ."

"The books are abbey property. They may not be taken hence except by my order. Their value must be protected." He placed a black-booted foot on the nearest trunk. "Now go." He pointed toward the gate.

"Surely his own notes would be of little value. Could he not take those?" Giles suggested.

Layton frowned and started to repeat his order when Pollard approached him with a ledger. "I make it 71 ounces of gold and jewels, 7214 ounces of gilt plate, and 6387 ounces of silver, Master Layton."

Layton's eyes glinted at those figures, as Giles had seen some men's eyes light up at the figure of a beautiful woman. With a wave of his hand Layton left the matter of Brother Austin and his paltry books for Giles to deal with. When the commissioners had disappeared, Giles lifted the lid on the nearest trunk. "He did not say you could not take your own writings." He began filling Brother Austin's arms with heavy volumes.

"But that volume is not my work," he protested as Giles drew out one with particularly fine gold-edged papers.

"Did you not copy it with your own hand?"

"I and my students."

Giles picked up several more volumes. "Such will qualify as your work." They were several steps away from the half-empty trunks when Giles turned back. "And writing materials. You have pens, ink, a good penknife?"

"In that trunk." Austin pointed with his head.

They were well past the gatehouse before Giles paused. "Where do we take these—and yourself?"

Austin Ringwode puffed to a stop. Glastonbury High Street was a sharp incline for one of Brother Austin's girth, heavily laden as he was. "My niece Alys," he said when he had caught his breath. "Her husband has the blacksmith's shop in Silver Street. They have a small unoccupied garret. I think they will take me in."

Giles nodded and walked on at a more sedate pace. He remembered Avery Croft who had once served as his own guide. That sounded like an excellent solution for Brother Austin. And a short time later when he had deposited his companion and his books in the tiny room up the steep, winding steps, he wondered at the strange sense he had of an accomplished mission, as if that simple act of kindness had been a thing he was sent to do in Glastonbury.

But Layton had more that he would accomplish in Glastonbury. Now they must interview as many residents of the county as possible and take down all evidence they could find against Whiting. "Take down every statement about the abbot's treasonous opinions you can garner from local informers," Layton instructed Pollard. And they set forth to prepare the last document Cromwell would need to bring this matter to a satisfactory conclusion.

Giles claimed a sick stomach, and Layton dismissed him with a shrug. He and Pollard could do very well on their own. Three days later when Giles looked over the sworn statements, his heart grew far sicker than his stomach had been. Chief among those listed were John Horner and Master Fulke.

Strange, Giles thought, *that Fulke should testify against the man who owes him so much money.* Unless, of course, Layton had made him a better offer. Horner, he remembered, had conflicted with Whiting over the issue of enclosure, although that seemed flimsy enough reason for condemning a man for treason.

It was not long, however, before the whole county knew why Horner had been so helpful to the king's inquisitors. John Horner had been appointed auditor of the abbey lands. And that would put him in charge of the abbey title deeds from which he was sure to emerge as lord of the manor, thus boosting him to new fame. Just how great his fame would become Giles could only guess at the next evening as he walked up High Street and passed a group of former abbey schoolboys. In the center he recognized Mark Croft singing at the top of his voice:

Little Jack Horner sat in a corner
Eating his Christmas pie;
He put in his thumb and pulled out a plum,
And said, "What a good boy am I."

The boys laughed uproariously and began dancing about, singing it again. Giles smiled and walked on up the street toward the Tor. Tomorrow Layton would go back to London to lay his case against Whiting before Cromwell, and Giles must decide what he would do. The old questions went round and round in his mind as he followed the curving path. Where could he do the most good? Could he do anything either place? What was *right?* Always it came to that.

But once he reached the summit and looked out across the red and gold landscape blurred at the distant edges by a gentle haze, it was not his own turmoil he focused on, but the turmoil in the land. How did God view the closing of houses of prayer—houses that had stood for Him for hundreds of years?

Suddenly Giles realized he was not alone. Brother Austin sat in Saint Patrick's Chapel. "What think you, brother?" Giles asked.

Still in his monk's robe, although no longer a monk, Brother Austin remained silent so long that Giles thought he would make no answer. Then at last he spoke. "It seems that since the holy Scriptures speak of a judgment of the nations, and since nations cannot be punished or rewarded in the next life, surely their rewards or punishment will be on earth." Again he sat long, as if listening to his own voice inside his head. When he spoke this time, it was not to Giles. "O Lord, in Thy mercy, spare England. Lead us to repent. Let us turn from our wicked ways. We cry to Thee to hear from heaven and heal our land. We cry to Thee, Lord."

Brother Austin paused to watch the sun hang on the western horizon, a fiery red ball through the haze. When he spoke again, it was in part to Giles and in part to England, but all in the melodious chant of one who had spent every day of his adult life singing to God at the hour of sunset. "The day will come—it will come, soon or late, when every nation of the earth is gathered before Him, the great Judge whom none escape, and He will judge the nations as the shepherd separates the sheep from the goats. Oh, my England, how will He judge you then?

"Because you were six-times blessed, because you were capable of greater good than any nation on earth, will you then be six-times damned? Oh, England, my soul bleeds for you."

Giles stood quietly and slipped away down the back side of the Tor. He walked for some time in the deepening twilight until he came to the ancient oak trees that had once been a circle, but so long ago that many sturdy oaks had died and left now an imperfect ring. He felt as he did in so many places in the Twelve Hides, that here too men had long worshiped and sought the way to please God.

Then in the quiet of that place Giles knew. He did not know what he could do for Whiting. He did not know what he could do for Glastonbury. He did not know if Cecily would speak to him again. He did not know what he would do with the rest of his life. But one thing was certain. He would not go back to London. He was through with court life.

13

he trial of Richard Whiting was set for November 1. As a member of the House of Lords, he would be tried by that body—the only legally constituted body of his peers. But Parliament was delayed. Henry's new bride, Anne of Cleves, waited off the coast of Calais, held there by storms. Henry would meet her in Rochester. So the king was not there to open Parliament.

But Cromwell would not wait. Giles was still at the George and Pilgrim awaiting Luke's arrival from London with his belongings when his servant brought news that changed all his plans.

"It's all over court. Tired they are of speculating about this maid from Flanders who is to be our new queen, so they were happy enough for a new tid-bit."

"What is it, man? Get on with it."

But Luke was not one to be hurried. "They say Cromwell's personal memorandum was seen plain as day—careless of 'im, I say, for such a clever man to leave things lying about. But 'e's so sure of 'is power he don't have to be careful. Anyway, he writ, 'The Abbot of Glaston to be tried at Glaston and also executed there with his 'complices.'"

Giles sprang to his feet. "What! Cromwell is judge and jury? Cromwell has convicted and sentenced Whiting by himself? Is Cromwell indeed the supreme law of the land?"

"'Pears even Cromwell needs to look legal though. 'E's sending Whiting to Wells for a trial. That muckraker Pollard's bringing 'im."

Wells. Giles had fought long in his own mind whether or not he should go to Wells. Would his presence only further distress Cecily? Would Dame Margery receive one whose work, no matter how unwilling, had helped convict her uncle? But if Whiting was to be tried in Wells, he would go. Perhaps, at last, he could still do something for the abbot.

The confusion in Giles's mind, however, was nothing compared to the disorder at Bucklesbury when they arrived late that afternoon. At first Giles thought Fulke was continuing his work full pace with even more workers than before. Then he realized that the materials were not going in the gate, but out. Dame Margery, dark skirts flapping like an enraged crow, followed a workman across the courtyard. "I knew you used inferior glue! If that paneling had been put up with cheese and lime like I said, you'd not be robbing me of it now!" But the workman continued out the gate.

"Oh, it's you, is it?" Margery regarded Giles with arms akimbo. "Well, you might as well come in." She turned and went into the house without waiting for a reply.

Giles followed. Inside, the scene was no better. Robert Burgess sat at the table in the center of the parlor circled by carpenters, stonemasons, and lawyers—all waving bills and summonses. News of Whiting's fall had spread fast. Cecily, an apron over her dress of dark blue worsted and her hair bound back in a kerchief, was attempting to clean up the mess the workman had made in stripping the beautiful linen-fold paneling from the walls. Like her aunt, she barely acknowledged Giles's presence so, seeing nothing better to do, he picked up a broom and set to work with her.

They worked in silence for some time until, at last, that side of the room looked in order. "There, Violet," she said turning to a red-haired maid, "you may hang an arras over that. At least it will keep out the draughts."

Without a word to Giles she led the way to the kitchen. The stone pitcher was empty, so Giles helped her move the trestle table and draw a bucket of cold water from the new, unpaid-for well. Cecily sat on a stool, holding her cup in both hands. "When my uncle has rid himself of those vultures in there who now know they won't be having their bills paid by the Abbot of Glastonbury, he will settle the matter of my marriage." She looked straight ahead and spoke in an even voice. "Uncle Whiting is now no protection against my being forced. And with the certainty of bankruptcy staring him in the face, nothing will stop Uncle Burgess from forcing me to marry his ward so he can have my dowry."

"So it is all over?"

Cecily did not cry or rage. She simply sat there with all the light inside her extinguished. "It is all over. And in the end there was little enough choice between a country bumpkin and . . ." She looked at Giles with the first flicker of fire he had seen in her eyes. "Between a clodpate," she repeated, "and a Judas."

"Cecily, I have left court."

For a moment a hint of gladness crossed her face. Then her stony look returned. "After you had done all the harm you could do."

"After I was convinced I could do no good. Now I have no position at all to offer you—even if your uncle would listen to my offer—or if you would have me."

She stood with an air of finality. "And where do you go now?"

Suddenly he realized she did not know. "I—I thought you had heard—but perchance you have not . . ."

She did not flinch. "Is there more disaster come upon us?"

"Your uncle arrives tonight. Under guard. The trial is to be tomorrow. In Wells."

Cecily's hands flew to untie her apron and pull off her kerchief. "Can you take me to him? Will they let me see him?"

Giles weighed his light purse in the palm of his hand. "With luck I will have enough to bribe the keeper. Two angels should be sufficient."

But in the end the jailer demanded all three of Giles's golden angels to admit the pair into his prison. Whiting stood feebly at their coming. Cecily flew into her uncle's arms. Then she tenderly helped him back to his stool. "We have brought you bread and a fresh-baked pie." She removed the linen napkin from the basket she carried.

"Ah, none in all England makes such good pies as Margery."

Giles pulled the cork from the small bottle of wine also in the basket and poured a cup for Whiting. They were silent while he enjoyed three bites of his pie. Then Cecily could take it no longer. She flung herself at her uncle's feet and hugged his knees. "Uncle, surrender. Others have and survived. It is too late for the monastery, but your death will add nothing. Surrender and come live with me."

Then remembering how the uproar at Bucklesbury would seem to this man who had spent all his life in a quiet monastery, she quickly added, "No, no—far better—we'll go away together. You and I. Surrender and get out of this filthy prison with its rats and bugs, and let me take you abroad." Cecily warmed to her topic. "Think, Uncle, fresh air, books, gardens—"

He held up a hand to silence her. "Far better, my dear, that you bid me think on Heaven. For that is the only sure reward of those who serve Him. I am old. What could I hope to gain by surrender—one year? Two? Far better to die now upholding the truth."

"Is there nothing we can do for you?" Cecily let loose of his legs, but remained on her knees.

"Yes. Two things you can do to assure my going from this life with an easy mind. Both of you." At that invitation, Giles fell to his knees beside Cecily. The abbot placed a hand on each of their heads. Its warmth suffused through Giles, and for a moment it was as he had always dreamed—of kneeling beside Cecily before a priest on their wedding day. But this was not their wedding.

Whiting charged him, "Care for my niece. She is very dear to me. Stand by her as you stood by me in all these persecutions."

Cecily gave a gasp of joy. "You mean he was not traitor, Uncle?"

"There was little enough he could do. But he was always there. 'Watch with me,' was all Christ asked of His disciples. It is all we can ask of one another. Giles watched with me, and watches yet."

"Oh. Yes!" And her yes was all-encompassing.

Whiting raised them to their feet and clasped their hands together. Before

Giles or Cecily realized what was happening, and without asking any further questions, Whiting proceeded. "Giles Lacey, wilt thou have this woman to thy wedded wife, to live together after God's ordinance in the holy state of matrimony? Wilt thou love her, comfort her, honor and keep her in sickness and in health, and forsaking all others, keep thee only unto her, so long as ye both shall live?"

As if in a dream, in the coming together of all his dreams in a great Epiphany, Giles answered, "I will."

Cecily's answer to the same question was even more fervent.

Whiting pulled a plain gold ring off his finger. It had been so simple and small that his jailers had not bothered to rob him of it. He placed it in Giles's hand, and Giles found himself repeating the familiar words as he slipped it onto Cecily's finger, "With this ring I thee wed, with my body I thee worship, and with all my worldly goods I thee endow. In the name of the Father and of the Son and of the Holy Ghost." In the rapture of the moment he forgot that he had no worldly goods with which to endow her.

"Those whom God hath joined together let no man put asunder," Whiting said. Giles kissed his bride as joyously as if they had been wed in the finest cathedral in the land.

"You have given me joy, my children." Whiting embraced them.

"Uncle, you said there were two things," Cecily said after kissing her uncle's thin, wrinkled cheek.

He turned to the basket they brought. "I would have you celebrate holy Communion with me this one last time."

Again Cecily and Giles knelt in the filthy straw over the cold stone floor. Whiting broke the crusty loaf of fresh-baked bread. "This is the body of our Lord in whom we live and move and have our being. For the grace of God has dawned upon the world with healing for all mankind. Let us call upon Him in our hour of need that His grace may abound more and more."

And then he took the cup. "And all did drink the same spiritual drink; for they drank of that spiritual Rock that followed them; and that Rock was Christ. The cup of blessing which we bless, is it not the communion of the blood of Christ?"

When they had all partaken, Whiting slipped to his knees. He seemed to forget their presence as he entered fully into the presence of his Lord praying, "O God, my gracious Father, the contradiction of the cross proclaims Thy infinite wisdom. Help us to see that the glory of Thy Son is revealed in the suffering He freely accepted. Give us faith to claim as our only glory the cross of our Lord Jesus Christ.

"And help this Thy servant take on as gladly the suffering ordained for me. May glory arise to the Father from my groanings. May glory arise to the Son from my cries. May glory arise to the Spirit from my tears. Help me to remember Thee, my Lord, now in the hour of my testing."

The jailer rattled the door, and Giles and Cecily left.

The following day as Giles and Cecily sat in the packed Town Hall with the bulk of Dame Margery and the post-like form of Hugh Davington between them, Giles could not but feel a slight amusement at the thought of their great secret.

The town's silver-gilt mace and moot horn had been hastily arranged in the front of the room as symbols of law and justice to remind the people that this was a court of the king's law. But from the behavior of the crowd, it was apparent these were having little effect. Women moved among the people selling marzipan, gingerbread, and comfits from trays slung on straps around their necks. The porter tried futilely to do his duty, imploring people to keep silence that all might witness the event. Several small dogs trotted among the feet of the onlookers, licking up gingerbread crumbs.

At last a guard thumped his halberd butt upon the floor, and the clerk gave a mellow call on the moot horn that brought the crowd to order. "Oyez! Oyez! This court of special sessions in the town of Wells in the county of Somerset in the month of November, the year of our Lord 1539, under the guidance of God and our blessed King Henry VIII, does here begin!"

Lord Russell, one of Henry's new-made nobles, sat as judge in a richly furred robe, and the twenty-four principal freemen of the city of Wells who were to serve as jury stood, raised their right hands, and repeated the oath.

As the court system in Somerset had long been in disarray, there were many cases to come before Lord Russell that day. There were several common felons to be tried for rape, burglary, and contract-breaking. And disputes needed to be settled between neighbors arguing over such as a boundary marker or the ownership of a fine brown cow. Lord Russell sniffed a nosegay of herbs to dull the stink of the unwashed crowd in the rapidly warming room.

At last the dreaded moment came. "Richard Whiting, Abbot of Glastonbury, come into court," the clerk ordered. Whiting stood as the clerk read the indictment. "Conspiracy to deprive the king of his government and attempting to rob the church of valuable plate. Richard Whiting, do you plead guilty or not guilty to the charges?"

"Not guilty." Although he spoke quietly, not a soul in that packed room failed to hear him.

The town steward stepped forward and presented the judge with a parchment scroll setting forth all the evidence. Pollard, conducting the prosecution, told in great detail the case against the abbot, making a long story of the Exeter conspiracy.

At last Giles could stand it no longer. He jumped to his feet. "Your Honor, I have evidence. The accused had no part—" The guard's halberd thumped the floor.

The judge lowered his nosegay. "No defense." Giles sat down, stunned. No defense? No one was to be allowed to speak for Whiting? He was to be condemned without rebuttal of all those false testimonies? Russell turned to Whiting standing silent before him. "Prisoner, what say you to this evidence?"

"I have had no part in any such plot nor any knowledge of it."

All heads turned at a clatter at the rear of the hall. Two couriers, mud-spattered and stinking of horse, pushed their way past the guards, almost dragging two bewildered monks behind them. Pollard nodded and turned to the judge. "Your Honor, these two were found lurking in the closed monastery which is now Crown property. They are charged with trespass and being co-conspirators with Whiting."

Brother Arthur and Brother Roger likewise pleaded not guilty. As with their abbot, they were allowed no defense.

The jury was not even asked to retire for a verdict. "Prisoners at the bar," the judge said, running his fingers over the fur bands on his robe, "you have been convicted on the evidence of this court of seeking to deprive the king of the property willed to him by the high estates of the realm, in trust for the nation.

"The duty remaining to me is to pronounce upon you the awful sentence the law provides against this crime—that you be taken hence to the prison and from thence to be drawn on the morrow upon a hurdle to the summit of Glastonbury Tor, that all men far and wide may witness the royal justice. There you are to be hanged by the neck, but not until you are dead. For while you are still living, your bodies are to be taken down, your bowels torn out and burst before your faces. Your heads are then to be cut off, and your bodies divided, each into four quarters, to be at the king's disposal. And may God have mercy upon your souls."

Giles did not hear Cecily cry out. He did not even see her slump, but somehow he knew, and he caught her swooning figure before she fell to the floor. Whiting, his eyes raised to Heaven, did not change expression.

14

That night in his cell, with Brother Arthur and Brother Roger incarcerated in the next room, Whiting kept a prayer vigil. The poundings of the workmen erecting the three gibbets for their execution atop the Tor reminded him of a lonely hill with three crosses on it. *My Lord, when the foundations are being destroyed, what can the righteous do?* his soul cried.

And the answer returned to him, *The Lord is in His holy temple. The Lord is on His heavenly throne.*

In the darkest hours, even in this dark hour now, as it had been throughout history, God was still in charge—even in that darkest of all hours when His own Son died on a lonely hill.

And then the hill Whiting saw in his mind was not Golgotha, but his own dear, familiar Tor. In his vision, he no longer saw it muddy brown against the gray mid-November sky, but in fair spring green with the morning sun shining on it and baby lambs and small flowers dotting its slopes, as Whiting loved it best. And beyond that he saw woods and rivers and rich fields, gentle villages folded in hillocks, and then cities and palaces of beauty. There were books, music, art, the plumpest fresh fruit, the aching tenderness of spring mornings, the warmth of summer afternoons, the gold of autumn evenings, and the comfort of a winter's night by a hearty fire. There was a world of great, great beauty—a world God had made so by His own hand.

Those men who listened to the trickery of the Deceiver had done their best to spoil and foul it all, to diminish and soil the Creator's handiwork. And sometimes it seemed that those of the Destroyer were far greater than those of the Creator. Sometimes it seemed that the original sin brought into the world by the Evil One was greater than the original righteousness built into the world from the beginning by the Creator.

But he knew it was not so. Not ultimately. Good would triumph. The work of the Creator would outlast and shine far, far beyond the worst attacks of the Destroyer. England, this England, and the world beyond it would one day be washed clean of sin and strife and squalor. It would become part of God's new heaven and His new earth. For the Word declares that the world—the world to which the man of God was not to be conformed—would pass away. The hallelujah that rose in his heart all but broke from his lips.

In the morning Whiting was tied to the hurdle, and the bell began tolling the death knell—the slow, measured toll for each sixth step as they moved forward. And Abbot Richard Whiting began his last ascent of the Tor, dragged upside down, his head and shoulders scraping and lurching over every rock and mound, just as Christ's cross must have bumped and scraped over the rocky path up Golgotha. Even as a jagged stone gouged his head and he felt a warm trickle of blood flow onto the waiting earth, Whiting knew that this apparent victory of evil was only the Deceiver's hollow sham. The victory was Christ's. The Lamb was slain and the sacrifice made for the atonement of the world.

Whiting felt the hands unbind him from the hurdle. He felt the roughness of the thick rope around his neck, but he could not hear the harsh voices around him, for he heard as it were the voice of a great multitude crying, "Hallelujah! For the Lord our God the Almighty reigneth. Let us rejoice and be exceeding glad, for the marriage of the Lamb is come."

There was a tightness in his throat, a choking and a roaring in his head as his feet left the solidness of earth. And then it was as if he were part of a great multitude standing before the Great White Throne. In his heart he lifted his voice with theirs and cried, *Salvation to our God who sits upon the throne and to the Lamb!*

And all the angels stood around the throne, and all the other beings fell on their faces before the throne and worshiped God, saying, *Amen. Blessing and glory and wisdom and thanksgiving and honor and power and might be unto our God for ever and ever. Amen!*

Giles had seen enough. He had vowed to remain steadfast to the end, and although he was sure Whiting had had no awareness of his presence, he had fulfilled his vow. As he turned his steps from the Tor, he was amazed to find that it was not the blood and horror of the scene that stayed in his mind or even the determined courage with which Brother Arthur and Brother Roger had died on either side of their abbot, but it was the remarkable peace on Whiting's face. No, not peace—that was too placid a word. It was joy. Radiance. A brightness that was not of this world.

Giles rode slowly to Bucklesbury where his wife awaited him. Now he could acknowledge her as wife, for last night Cecily had told the Burgesses what had occurred in Whiting's cell. They had raged and stormed far into the night. But there was nothing they could do, for the fact was accomplished. Giles must now make a home for his wife.

When he stabled Brigante, Giles recognized the two horses in the next boxes. "Megotty! Diccon!" He hurried into the house to embrace his sister and her betrothed. "Have you brought news of our brothers? Are they returned?"

Megotty kissed him a second time on his cheek. "We thought to bring you pleasing news, but now we find that we have brought you a wedding present."

Giles held out his hand, and Cecily slipped hers into it. "It gives me great joy to give you a sister, my sister."

Megotty embraced Cecily. "Oh, yes—sister! And we shall grow as fond of one another as sisters born, for we shall be living close together—oh!" She clapped a hand over her mouth and turned to her brother. "That is, if you allow us."

Giles had always had trouble following his sister's flighty conversations, but now he was completely lost. "What have I to say to where you live?"

"It is what we have come to tell you—Layford is yours. Edward joins Cardinal Pole's staff in Italy, and Peter has sent for Ellen with word that he is most profitably employed by a Flemish merchant. They did not put into writing that one of the Old Faith is more like to keep his head on his shoulders abroad."

Before Giles could respond to the amazing news that he was suddenly lord of Layford, Megotty jumped to a new topic. "But I can't help but wonder how profitable his business will remain since the Flanders marriage has failed."

"What?" Giles and Cecily asked together. They had so focused on events close at hand that they had lost track of the wider world.

"Know you nothing since you left court that your news must come by way of Oxfordshire?" Diccon laughed.

"It's true," Meg rushed on. "Henry dislikes Anne of Cleves. A most violent dislike, it is said. He calls her the Flanders Mare." She clapped her hands and then looked around to be sure there were no servants listening. "And 'tis said he blames Cromwell for the fiasco. In London they are laying bets whether the Vicar-General can keep his head for another six-month."

As quickly as she had dropped her amazing news, Megotty's conversation veered again to talk of weddings and estates and family matters. "And I would have the hall at Layford refurbished—with your permission, brother. What do you say to linen-fold paneling? I am told that if it is applied with a glue made of fresh cheese, it is wondrously sturdy."

No matter how many times they explained to her afterwards, Megotty never could understand why Giles and Cecily both jumped to their feet and shouted, "No!" at the same time.

But the next day Giles could not remain in the joyful company of his family. He must return again to the abbey. What he would do there he was uncertain, but he knew that he must make his farewell to that sacred spot.

He was yet some distance away when he saw a billow of black smoke and the harsh glow of hungry flames. Already the destroyers were at work. A roaring fire had been kindled from the abbey's great roofing timbers to fuel a pit furnace dug where such a short time ago Brother Dunstan's healing herbs had grown. Here all the base metal in the abbey would be melted down for easier shipment to London. The bells that for so long had called men to prayer would be recast as cannon, and the lead roof made into shot for Henry's war against the French. Not yet was the day when men would beat their swords into plowshares.

Giles walked unnoticed among the crowd of villagers to the mouth of the conflagration. At first he didn't even notice when his foot struck the stone. It was such a small matter among all the heap of rubble, and yet there was somehow a special warmth to its feel through his soft, broad-toed shoe. He knelt to pick it up. And then he saw. It was the carved fish Abbot Whiting had pointed out to him when he had come to collect Cromwell's bribe. Carved by the hand that first brought the gospel to this land, Whiting had said. Giles rubbed the age-smoothed surface and thought, *Is it all worth it? All that men have struggled for through the ages—to come to this? Will God yet bring good of it? And if so, does it require so much blood and suffering to bring it about—like a woman's birth pains? Or is this merely the best that poor, fallen man can do in following God's will?*

The heat of the fire and the intensity of his questions drove Giles to seek a cooler spot. He turned his steps toward the cloister. He passed Jack Horner, directing his servants to cart off stones—stones that for generations had housed holy men of prayer would now be used to house Master Horner's cows and pigs.

"Master Lacey, is that you?" A familiar fat figure emerged from the shadows of the broken cloister where once one of the finest libraries in the land had been kept.

"Brother Austin." It was good to see a calm, friendly face.

"Give me your advice, Master Lacey." Austin was obviously not anxious to leave the shelter of the shadowing arches, so Giles went to him. From under the cowl of his robe Austin Ringwode pulled a small cross worked with gold and gems. "The looters dropped this." He clasped it to his bosom as a mother might a baby. "It is Joseph of Arimathea's. Not the cross itself, but, see—" He held it out again and pushed a little spring lock to reveal a wooden peg-nail. "It is one of the nails with which our Savior was fastened to the cross. Joseph brought it to this land. It was much revered by all the brothers. But tell me—I do not know what to do with it now."

Giles considered. Urging him to keep it would probably be to counsel a form of treason or robbery—it seemed that everything was labeled such these days. Yet what a sacrilege to send it to London to be melted down for its ounce or two of gold. Giles pulled the small carved fish from his purse and folded it in Austin's hand. "Keep them together, brother. Something of the old times should remain in Glastonbury."

Austin nodded and, with glowing face, tucked them into the folds of his robe. "It is good. I have been thinking—about my work—the materials you helped me salvage—"

"Yes?" Giles felt the need to encourage Brother Austin, for he seemed to be held by a reticence.

"It is great presumption in me, I know—but I have been thinking—of all this house has stood for throughout the ages—and even when Cromwell and his vandals do their worst, faith cannot be abolished—"

"Yes?"

"I would record it all—all the history—if God grants me strength."

"Yes, yes. I will pray for your strength, Brother Austin, for that is indeed a high calling."

The monk seemed pleased by Giles's words, but not yet satisfied. "Today I stood in the courtyard, for I would see what Henry's men did with our most sacred relic—the remains of King Arthur."

"And did you see?"

Austin hung his head. "I saw them carry the casket from the abbey, and my heart leaped for joy, for it was draped with the scarlet and gold altar cloth, and I thought they would show respect to this one treasure at least. But then the smoke blew in my eyes, and I must turn away. When I looked back, they had emptied the casket of its precious contents and were prying off the gold."

Giles sought for something to hearten his friend. "It is said that Arthur will return when England needs him. Perhaps he does. Perhaps he comes to each generation in the stories of his faith and courage. Perhaps your work, Brother Austin, will bring him back. Maybe it will be given to you to rally England to a new sense of national purpose."

"Yes!" Brother Austin clasped Giles's hands. "To a vision of Logres—to a sense of spiritual Britain . . . Oh, here—" Again he fumbled in the voluminous folds of his robe. "Here—this scrap I found in the library. It was torn from a book and the looters did not find it to fuel their fires."

Giles took the fragment and read:

Ancient ruins shall be rebuilt and sites long desolate restored;
they shall repair the ruined cities and restore what has long lain desolate.
And everlasting joy shall be theirs.
And I will grant them a sure reward and make an everlasting covenant with them;
their posterity will be renowned among the nations and their offspring among the peoples;
all who see them will acknowledge in them a race whom the Lord has blessed.

For, as the earth puts forth her blossom and thorns in the garden
burst into flower,
so shall the Lord God make righteousness and praise blossom
before all the nations.
This is the word of the Lord.

Giles handed the paper back to Brother Austin. "Yes, go and write your book. Perhaps that is part of how God will bring good of it all."

As Giles rode slowly from Glastonbury, he turned once in his saddle to look back. He would not look at the Tor where the three empty gibbets stood silhouetted against the sky, but instead he turned his gaze toward Wearyall Hill. And there he saw it—the ancient thorn tree, not yet in full flower, for it was yet several weeks to Christmastide, but showing a hint of white. A promise for the future.

I, Austin Ringwode, am the most blest of men. Today our Lord granted me a great blessing of which I am not worthy.

I have seen the grail.

I went, as is my custom, to the Lady Chapel to celebrate holy Eucharist, for I will not let His worship die out of this spot from which the light of Christianity spread to every part of our island. As long as Austin Ringwode lives, our Lord will be worshiped at Glastonbury. I carried with me a vial of holy wine and a morsel of bread, and in the Lady Chapel our Lord performed the great miracle of changing them to His blood and His blessed broken body as I partook in memory of Him. Blessed be His name forever and ever, amen.

And while I was kneeling, as His body was yet on my tongue, a great light descended from heaven, a great shaft of shimmering golden light coming through the broken ceiling of the chapel and falling on the altar before me. In the shaft of light was the holy grail—a cup of smoothest, purest olivewood, yet shimmering and glowing as surely was never carved by human hand.

The light grew until it filled the whole room and engulfed my body. And it sang, as if the beams of light were harp strings plucked by heavenly hands.

I fell to the floor sobbing, "Holy, holy, holy. Worthy is the Lamb that taketh away the sin of the world. None is holy but Thee."

And then I fell into a deep sleep. When I awoke, all was dark. The grail was gone. Yet it remains with me.

Never before have I seen so clearly my own unworthiness and His worthiness. I am the vilest of creatures, and yet He, in his love and mercy and grace, has visited me with this vision—this revelation of Himself.

I see now that it has been His power through all the ages—the direct hand of God working His will for good. So must I continue to believe that He still works. Even when one can see only evil on every side—He still works.

This poor, sick land could be cured if every day every soul would wait before God. That's all, no vows, no heroics—just turn humbly to God. The Promised Land could be here on earth. We wouldn't have to wait for Heaven for mankind to see what God intends for His children. It could be here. It could be now. This one spot of earth—this island—could be a holy place.

And at last I know. The grail for which I have so long sought is God's grace. It is His love freely poured out on all mankind in a stream of mercy we can never deserve, but for which we can cry, "Abba, Father! I adore You."

Now at the end of my journey, I understand. The quest is all—the journey—the process. The great secret of life is that it is a journey to Heaven—a questing for His presence, made possible by His grace.

So the grail—grace is the key. It is the food of eternal life that sustains us on this earthly pilgrimage toward Heaven. Grace is the ark of the new covenant that leads us on the journey, as the first ark led the children of Israel. And most blessed of all, the grail—grace—is the ultimate mystery. It is not found in seeking, but in accepting. Therefore, no quest will succeed, no purity be great enough, no effort strong enough—only faith will win. Faith and a grateful heart.

So often I have stumbled on my way, but the grail of grace was always there to set my feet aright. And now I shall see Him, the only begotten of the Father, full of grace and truth. From Him have we received grace for grace.

Blessing and honor, glory and power be unto Him who sits upon the throne forever and ever, world without end, amen.

AFTERWORD

hen we drive into Glastonbury, have the Kleenex handy." I smiled at Carole, my traveling companion. For us this was the trip of a lifetime—a pleasure trip long-dreamed of, a research trip for books we were each working on, and a religious pilgrimage.

Carole smiled and fished under the seat, behind the well-worn Ordnance Survey map by which she had navigated our journey over the maze of English roads, and finally pulled out the box of tissue.

As it happened, however, by the time I had maneuvered the little car around three more of the terrifying roundabouts at the high speed of English motorists, muddled through the rush of even heavier-than-usual closing-time traffic, and found that greatest of rarities—a parking spot in the vicinity of The George and Pilgrim Inn, my tears were from frustration, not religious ecstasy.

The next morning, though, rested by a night of sleep in the same Inn that had been accommodating pilgrims for five hundred years, we gathered umbrellas and raincoats and set out with renewed spirits.

Before leaving the Inn, we paused before the room marked Henry VIII. "The legend is that Henry sat in this room and watched the monastery burn—like Nero fiddling over the flames of Rome." I ran my finger over the white letters carved in the ancient dark brown door.

"Any truth to it?" Carole asked. I was supposed to be the historian.

"Only in the larger sense of spiritual metaphor. He was probably romping through the maze at Hampton Court with wife number five. Actually, I think the monastery more just crumbled into ruin after the dissolution. But it comes to the same thing, and it's a great image." I used my umbrella as a bow to pantomime Nero fiddling.

Carole smiled. "Well, you're the fiction writer."

In a mist too gentle to bother raising our umbrellas, we crossed the street and entered the ancient walls around Glastonbury Abbey. We stood by the modern oak cross given to the abbey by Queen Elizabeth II and read the inscription: "This symbol of our faith marks a Christian sanctuary so ancient that only legend can describe its origins."

Then we switched on the recording we had rented for a self-guided tour: "... Glastonbury was not a public church. It was only for the monks' worship—built for the glory of God. Here men of God kept alive the flame of faith through the Dark Ages and provided centers of learning.

"The unusual position of the Lady Chapel at the west of the great church was dictated by the fact that it replaced the Old Church, the most venerable of all the destroyed shrines, believed by some to have been built by Joseph of Arimathea when he came to Britain after the crucifixion of Christ . . ."

It was when we were at the sixth station that the tall, elderly gentleman we had noticed earlier approached us and removed his hat from his a balding head. "Are you enjoying that tape?"

"Oh, yes. Very much!"

The man's eyes twinkled. "And what do you think of that fellow's voice? Rather good tones, wouldn't you say?"

Carole caught on first. "Oh, it's you—on the tape!"

The twinkle changed to a full-fledged grin, and the Prebendary of Bath and Wells introduced himself. "Retired now, served in the Cathedral at Wells for many years. But I still come here every week for the communion service. Every Tuesday of the year without fail."

I was overwhelmed anew at the holiness of the ground we stood on. "So it's really true—what they say about Christian worship having continued here unbroken for two thousand years?"

"It certainly is. I had the opportunity to speak to the Archbishop of Canterbury once, and I told him that compared to Glastonbury, they were newcomers over there." He led us to a white stone altar of modern construction that held a bouquet of fresh flowers. "This is where we have the service. It's the crypt of the Lady Chapel. We worship here because it's the only place out of the weather." He looked up with a grin at the misty clouds hanging above the great broken arches of the abbey. "But they couldn't have chosen a better place—most people believe this is where the altar of St. Joseph stood."

Soon our guide left us, and we continued our tour to the end of the tape. "As you've gone around the abbey, you've been reminded of the history of the Christian church in England from its beginning to the present day. That history has included advance and retreat, building and decay, glory and shame, unity and division, conflict and peace. The abbey is a ruin and must remain so. But it is at least now treated with reverence and love as the most ancient Christian sanctuary in England and as a place of pilgrimage. It is our hope that it will have a place in the future of the Christian church, perhaps as a center of unity."

Reluctantly we turned away from the abbey enclosure. As we approached the massive Gothic gateway, a rather ragged street musician began a new tune on his violin:

And did those feet in ancient times,
Walk on England's mountains green . . .

Now I needed those Kleenex, and they were locked in the car two blocks away.

It was the next morning as we were driving toward Salisbury that Carole read aloud from a pamphlet she had picked up at a bookstall: "'Did our Lord ever come to Glastonbury as a lad? The story lingers not only here, but elsewhere as well. Briefly, the tradition is that our Lord, entrusted to the care of his Uncle Joseph of Arimathea by his mother Mary, daughter of Joseph's elder brother, accompanied Joseph on one of his expeditions to Britain to seek metals for his flourishing trading company.'"

I gave a shout of laughter. "What? That's crazy!"

But Carole kept on. "No, wait, this is interesting. It says, 'Perhaps there is some truth in the tradition which still lingers in Somerset that St. Joseph of Arimathea came to Britain first as a metal merchant seeking tin from the Scilly Isles and Cornwall, and lead, copper, and other metals from the hills of Somerset, and that our Lord Himself came with him as a boy. The tradition is so startling that the first impulse is to reject it summarily as ridiculous.'"

"It sure is," I said, but Carole kept on.

"'Amongst the old tin-workers, who always observed a certain mystery in their rites, there was regularly a moment when they interrupted their work to sing a quaint song beginning, "Joseph was in the tin trade."

"'If this is so, it is quite natural to believe that after the crucifixion, when the church was dispersing under persecution and in answer to the Great Commission, Joseph and his party, which included his son Josephes, would come to this land with which Joseph was already acquainted.

"'Among the cherished possessions the little band brought with them was the cup used at the Last Supper in Joseph of Arimathea's Jerusalem residence, an ordinary cup in everyday use in his house, now become a sacred treasure, since with this cup of olivewood our Lord had inaugurated the new covenant.'"

My imagination was now so thoroughly engaged I traveled the roundabout three times, and I wasn't laughing at all.

GLOSSARY

Advowson The right of presenting a nominee to a vacant ecclesiastical benefice
Aetheling Crown prince
Ala Cavalry regiment
Amphora Jar with large oval body, narrow cylindrical neck and two handles
Angel An English gold coin valued at about six or seven shillings
Angli Angles
Annates First fruits of an ecclesiastical benefice paid to the one presenting the benefice
Annona Levy of grain that supplied the army
Aqua Sulis Bath
Arfon Region of Wales
Arras Tapestry wall hangings
Aspergillum Short-handled brush used for sprinkling holy water
Assart Piece of land cleared of trees and made arable
Atrium Central hall of a Roman house
Aurochs' horn Ox horn
Bailiff Estate manager
Bannock Flat loaf of barley or oat bread
Baudwin Bedivere
Bee-skep Beehive
Bothie Celtic hut or stable
Branfad Celtic game similar to chess
Breeks Breeches, trousers that ended just below the knee; basic clothing, with a tunic and cloak, for Celtic man.
Bretwalda Supreme king or war leader (Saxon)
Britannia Prima Western Britain: Somerset, Wales, Cornwall
Britannia Secunda Northern Britain: York to Hadrian's Wall
Broch Oven
Brychan Heavy blanket or pad
Byre Barn
Caledonia Scotland
Caliga Military shoe or boot
Cambrensis Of Wales
Cambrogi Celtic for brotherhood or fellowship
Canonical hours:

Saxon

Terce Third hour

Sext About noon
None or **Matins** 3 P. M.
Vespers Before sunset
Compline Before bed
Nocturnes Midnight

Norman

Matins Midnight
Lauds 1:00 A.M.
Prime 7:00 (and early mass for servants)
Mass 9:00
High Mass 10:00
Vespers 5:00 winter, 6:00 summer
Compline 7:00 winter, 8:00 summer

Canti lands Kent
Cantref County or district
Cantwaraburg Canterbury
Capuchon Cap with a long point hanging down back
Carle, ceorl or **churl** Common, freemen who owed service in the militia
Carnyx Battle horn
Cena Main meal of the day
Cess Bad luck
Chalybeate Mineral water containing salts of iron
Civitas Civilian district ruled by native council
Codex A bound book manuscript
Cohort Military unit, 500 or 1,000 men
Coif Cap covering the head like a small hood
Coppice Trees cut back to produce shoots from old trunks
Corn Generic British term for grain—not to be confused with American corn
Corrody An allowance of provisions for maintenance
Cors Druid learning center; school or college
Crom Cruach Irish stone idol
Cubit Measure of length, a foot and a half
Curlew Brownish, long-legged bird with long, slender down-curved bill.
Currach, Coracle Small boat
Cymric Welsh or Celtic language, also called Brythonic
Cymri Welsh
Decurio Cavalry officer
Demesne All the lord's land except that held by freehold military service
Deon Druid religious leader; a dean
Dinas Emrys Ambrosius's Fort, Welsh name for hillfort on southern border of Snowdonia
Dorter Dormitory
Dumnonia Cornwall
Dumnoni Celtic tribe living in Cornwall
Dun Camulus Trinovante capital, Roman name Camulodunum, modern Colchester, on southeastern coast of England.
Dun Indicates a royal settlement

Dux Duke
Ealdfaeder Old father, grandfather
Ealdmodor Old mother, grandmother
Ebercanum York
Ebona River Avon
Eirran Irish
Epona Celtic moon goddess, also Iceni horse goddess
Equitata 500 cavalry men
Faeder Father
Fasces Bundle of rods, including an axe, borne before Roman magistrate as a symbol of office.
Father of Rivers Thames
Flatha King's guard (Irish)
Foederati Saxon federation, the foe
Fosse Way Major Roman road running from southwest to northeast Britain.
Fretum Gallicum Great Water, English Channel
Froom Frome
Furlong One-eighth of a mile
Fustian Cheap fabric
Fyrd National militia, Ireland
Garth Celtic for field or orchard
Gladius Short, broad Roman sword
Gleawanceaster, Glevum Gloucester
Gonfalon Standard of a medieval prince, hangs from a crosspiece
Gorsedd Yearly national assembly of druids
Groma Surveying instrument
Gustatio Appetizer
Gwalchmei Gawain
Habergeon, hauberk Mail jacket
Hibernian Irish
Hypocaust Heating system
Icthas Trading port, location uncertain: Isles of Scilly, Cornwall, or along the Severn River
Ioua Iona
Isca Silurum Caerleon
Jarl Danish chief
Jentaculum First meal of the day
Jongleur Itinerant minstrel who sang for hire
Kirtle A long gown
Kist Celtic for cupboard
Knight's fee The imposed obligation of knight's service
Legate Legionary commander
Lias stone Blue limestone
Lindum Lincoln
Liquamen Fermented fish sauce, Romans' favorite condiment
Locum Substitute
Loet Unfree men, but above slaves

Lough Irish lake
Lunden London
Maggot Strange notion, whim
Magus Mithras priest
Manchet bread Wheat bread of highest quality
Mansio Inn or guest house
Mare Aegaeum Aegean Sea
Maxima Caesariensis Southeastern Britain
Mensae secundae Sweet course, dessert
Modor Mother
Monstrance A vessel in which the consecrated host is exposed to receive the adoration of the faithful
Mon Celtic for Anglesey
Moot horn A horn blown before public debate of freemen
Mor Hafren, Saefern, Sabrina Severn River
Nobilis Decurio Lesser Roman official, something like city council member
Northfolk Norfolk
Noviomagus Chichester
Optio The man beneath the centurion, his understudy
Palla Woman's long mantle
Pallium Circular band of white wool conferred by Pope on archbishops as symbol of office
Peristyle Courtyard in the center of a Roman home, surrounded by columns.
Pillion To ride behind
Pilum Roman spear, heavy javelin
Pittancer Monk whose job it was to distribute an allowance of food, wine, etc. to the community
Poppet Doll
Praemunire The offense of procuring bulls or benefits from the Pope against the king
Praetorium Commanding officer's house
Primae Mensae Main course at dinner
Principia Headquarters
Quadrans A very small coin, one-fourth of an as; the plural is **quadrantes**
Quire Choir
Rath Irish fortress
Rebec Pear-shaped, three-stringed musical instrument played with a bow
Reed Unit of measure, about eleven feet
Reeve King's chief administrative agent for a region
Reredorter Bathroom
Roceaster Rochester
Sa, sa Yes, yes
Sacristan Monk whose job it was to care for vessels used in worship
Sark Shirt
Sarum, Searoburg, Sorviodunum Salisbury
Screpall Small silver coin, Irish
Scrip Knapsack

Sea Wolves Saxon invaders
Seax Small, sharp sword or knife
Shire County
Silurians Celtic tribe in western Britain
Slemish Place of Patrick's slavery, scholars unsure of exact location.
Smoor Damp a fire down for the night
Soek Sack or bag
Southfolk Suffolk
Spatha Long sword, usually used by cavalry
Stola Roman matron's long, draped gown
Summer Country Somerset.
Tantus Isle of Thanet
Tenebrae Church service during the final part of Holy Week usually commemorating the Stations of the Cross
Testudo Literally, turtle; Roman fighting position
Thane One holding lands from the king
Thrall, theow Slave
Toft Smallholder's private garden
Toga Dress of male Roman citizen, always white, perhaps with colored bands denoting high position
Triniculum Dining room in Roman villa
Trinovantes Celtic tribe along the Thames
Triumph Ceremony attending entry of Rome by a general who had won a decisive victory over a foreign enemy
Truath Celtic word meaning tribe
Tun Enclosure, later a town
Turma Cavalry unit of thirty horsemen
Tyrrhenum Roman word for arm of the Mediterranean Sea on the west side of Italy
Vallum Earthen wall
Varlet Menial servant
Venta Belgarum, Wincantun Winchester
Venta Silurum Caerwent
Vercovicium Fort on Hadrian's Wall, now Housesteads
Verulamium St. Albans
Vicus Settlement of civilians outside a fort
Villeins In Norman times people who owed service to a lord, serfs
Virginals A small rectangular spinet with no legs
Waelisc Welsh
Wattle and daub Framework of woven reeds, plastered with clay
Welkin The vault of heaven
Wergild Man price
Witan Meeting of highest council of kings, nobles, bishops
Wyrd Fate
Ynis Witrin The Glass Island, Glastonbury

Celtic Calendar

Samain November 1 to January 31. Samain marked beginning of the New Year.
Imbolc February 1 to April 30. Its festivals were fertility rites.
Beltine May 1 to July 31. Its festival was a symbol of optimism.
Lugnasad August 1 to October 31, named for Celtic high god Lugh

Roman Calendar

Kalends First day of a month in Roman calender
Nones Nine days before Ides
Ides Fifteenth day of March, May, July, October; thirteenth day of other months

Celtic Pronunciation

The differences in Celtic and English pronunciations are many and subtle, but remembering just four simple rules should help the reader:

G is always hard, as in go.
C is always hard, as in cat. (Therefore, the Kelts are an ancient British people; the Seltics are an American basketball team.)
CH is always hard, as in the Scottish loch (lock).
DD is pronounced as th.

SOURCES AND REFERENCES

Throughout the book, particularly in the matter of selecting which source to rely on or which legend to believe, my goal has been to tell the story in the most historically accurate way possible. Where the history is unknown or seriously disputed by experts, I have told it as it could have happened based on what is known about that time. This has led to spiritualizing such legends as Joseph of Arimathea taking Christ to England as a child and St. George fighting the dragon.

My goal in the Arthurian section was to tell the story in keeping with historical conditions of the time. The use of magic and shining armor, Norman inventions, come in legend form in a later section. Likewise, where it would not be too confusing, I have used name forms consistent with the time period. Hence, places and people have Celtic names, then Roman, then Saxon, and so on, reflecting changes in the language through history.

I couldn't possibly give all the references used in the writing of this book. I am grateful for all who have gone before me and paved the way. I have tried to list the major sources and would like to highlight three of my favorites for general background. *King Arthur's Avalon: The Story of Glastonbury* by Geoffrey Ashe is a superb summary of the history of Glastonbury, especially dealing with archeological evidence. Rosemary Sutcliffe's *The Sword at Sunset* is my favorite telling of the story of Arthur because it is so absolutely believable historically. And all of Ellis Peters's Brother Cadfael mysteries are a delightful entree into a Benedictine monastery in the medieval world.

DFC

Prayers, hymns, and meditations throughout adapted from *Christian Prayer: The Liturgy of the Hours,* translated by the International Commission on English in the Liturgy, Catholic Book Publishing, New York, (1976).

Book I

"Jerusalem" from *The Poems of William Blake* edited by W. B. Yeats, Lawrence and Bullen, London, (1893).

Story line for bardsongs and Celtic poem based on ideas in *The Celts* by Nora Chadwick, Penguin Books, Middlesex, England, (1979).

Hebrew Prayers based on traditional prayers as given in *Siddur Tehillat Hashem Nusach Ha-Ari Zal,* according to the text of Rabbi Shneur Zalman of Liadi, New Amended Hebrew Edition with an English Translation by Rabbi Nissen Mangel, Merkos l'Inyone, Chinuch, New York, (1978).

Book II

Mithra worship from *The Mysteries of Mithra* by Franz Cumont, translated from the second revised French edition by Thomas J. McCormack, Dover Publications, New York, (1956).

Book III

Anglo-Saxon riddles and poetry and King Alfred's prayer adapted from *Word-Hoard* by Margaret Williams, Sheed & Ward, New York, (1940, 1968).

Book IV

Dunstan's quotation of the Rule from *The Rule of St. Benedict in English* edited by Timothy Fry, O.S.B., The Liturgical Press, Collegeville, MN, (1982).

Book V

Corviere's carol based on the earliest known Anglo-Norman carol. *Christmas in the Olden Time*, James Pattie, London, (1839).

Quotations of Chretien de Troyes based on *Arthurian Romances* translated by W.W. Comfort, "Lancelot," Everyman's Library, Dent, London, (1984) and *The Arthurian Encyclopedia* edited by Norris J. Lacy, Garland Publishing, New York, (1986).

Quotations from "The Lay of Sir Launfal" by Marie de France, based on *The Arthurian Legends: An Illustrated Anthology* translated by Eugene Mason, selected and introduced by Richard Barber, Dorset Press, New York, 1979.

Quotations from Geoffrey of Monmouth, *Historia Regum Britanniae,* (c. 1136), from *History of the Kings of Britain*, translated by Sebastian Evans, revised by Charles W. Dunn, Dutton, New York, (1958).

Prayers from *The Book of Common Prayer, and Administration of the Sacraments*, The Church of England, Eyre and Spottiswoode, London, (1968).

Book VI

Abbey statistics, quotations from Layton's letters and Cromwell's memoranda from *King Arthur's Avalon: The Story of Glastonbury,* by Geoffrey Ashe, William Collins Sons, Great Britain, (1957).

Other References Consulted

English Literature and Its Backgrounds, volume 1, by B.D. Grebanier, et al., Holt, Rinehart and Winston, New York, (1962).

St. George: A Christmas Mummer's Play by Katherine Miller, Houghton Mifflin, Boston, (1967).

Saint Justin Martyr by Thomas B. Falls, The Catholic University of America Press, Washington, DC, (1948).

"St. Justin Martyr," "The Letters of Clement," "The Acts of Thomas," and the "Ode of Solomon" in *The Apocryphal New Testament* translated by Montague Rhodes James, Clarendon Press, Oxford, (1924).

The Chronicle of Glastonbury Abbey, an edition, translation and study of John of Glastonbury's *Cronica Sive Antiquitates Glastoniensis Ecclesie* by James P. Carley, The Boydell Press, Doven, NH, (1985).

The Early Christians After the Death of the Apostles by Eberhard Arnold, Plough Publishing House, Rifton, NY, (ND).

The Token by Sam Shellabarger, Little, Brown, Boston, (1955).